# THE GREEK MYTHS

Robert Graves was born in 1895 in Wimbledon, son of Alfred Percival Graves, the Irish writer, and Amalia Von Ranke. He went from school to the First World War, where he became a captain in the Royal Welch Fusiliers. His principal calling was poetry, and his *Selected Poems* have been published in the Penguin Poets series. Apart from a year as Professor of English Literature at Cairo University in 1926 he earned his living by writing, mostly historical novels which include: *I, Claudius*; *Claudius the God*; *Sergeant Lamb of the Ninth*; *Count Belisarius*; *Wife to Mr Milton* (all published as Penguins); *Proceed, Sergeant Lamb*; *The Golden Fleece*; *They Hanged My Saintly Billy*; and *The Isles of Unwisdom*. He wrote his autobiography, *Goodbye to All That*, in 1929 and it rapidly established itself as a modern classic. *The Times Literary Supplement* acclaimed it as 'one of the most candid self-portraits of a poet, warts and all, ever painted', as well as being of exceptional value as a war document. His two most discussed non-fiction books are *The White Goddess*, which presents a new view of the poetic impulse, and *The Nazarine Gospel Restored* (with Joshua Podro), a re-examination of primitive Christianity. He translated Apuleius, Lucan and Suetonius for the Penguin Classics, and compiled the first modern dictionary of Greek mythology, *The Greek Myths*. His translation of *The Rubáiyát of Omar Khayyám* (with Omar Ali-Shah) is also published in Penguins. He was elected Professor of Poetry at Oxford in 1961, and made an Honorary Fellow of St John's College, Oxford, in 1971.

Robert Graves died on 7 December 1985 in Majorca, his home since 1929. On his death *The Times* wrote of him, 'He will be remembered for his achievements as a prose stylist, historical novelist and memorist, but above all as the great paradigm of the dedicated poet, "the greatest love poet in English since Donne".'

PENGUIN BOOKS

ROBERT GRAVES

# THE GREEK MYTHS

COMBINED EDITION

PENGUIN BOOKS

**PENGUIN BOOKS**

Published by the Penguin Group
Penguin Books Ltd, 27 Wrights Lane, London w8 5tz, England
Penguin Books USA Inc., 375 Hudson Street, New York, New York 10014, USA
Penguin Books Australia Ltd, Ringwood, Victoria, Australia
Penguin Books Canada Ltd, 10 Alcorn Avenue, Toronto, Ontario, Canada m4v 3b2
Penguin Books (NZ) Ltd, 182–190 Wairau Road, Auckland 10, New Zealand

Penguin Books Ltd, Registered Offices: Harmondsworth, Middlesex, England

First published in two volumes in Pelican Books 1955
Both volumes reprinted with amendments 1957
Revised editions of both volumes 1960
This combined edition published in Penguin Books 1992
5 7 9 10 8 6

Printed in England by Clays Ltd, St Ives plc
Set in Monotype Bembo

# CONTENTS

# CONTENTS

# CONTENTS

# CONTENTS

# CONTENTS 7

The death of the Old Bull of the Year apparently poleaxed, and the birth of the New Year's Bull-Calf from a date cluster; under the supervision of a Cretan priestess, who identifies herself with the palm-tree. From a Middle-Minoan bead-seal in the author's collection (diameter enlarged 1½ times). About 1900 B.C.

# FOREWORD

SINCE revising *The Greek Myths* in 1958, I have had second thoughts about the drunken god Dionysus, about the Centaurs with their contradictory reputation for wisdom and misdemeanour, and about the nature of divine ambrosia and nectar. These subjects are closely related, because the Centaurs worshipped Dionysus, whose wild autumnal feast was called 'the Ambrosia'. I no longer believe that when his Maenads ran raging around the countryside, tearing animals or children in pieces (see 27. *f*) and boasted afterwards of travelling to India and back (see 27. *c*), they had intoxicated themselves solely on wine or ivy-ale (see 27. *3*). The evidence, summarized in my *What Food the Centaurs Ate* (Steps: Cassell & Co., 1958, pp. 319-343), suggests that Satyrs (goat-totem tribesmen), Centaurs (horse-totem tribesmen), and their Maenad womenfolk, used these brews to wash down mouthfuls of a far stronger drug: namely a raw mushroom, *amanita muscaria*, which induces hallucinations, senseless rioting, prophetic sight, erotic energy, and remarkable muscular strength. Some hours of this ecstasy are followed by complete inertia; a phenomenon that would account for the story of how Lycurgus, armed only with an ox-goad, routed Dionysus's drunken army of Maenads and Satyrs after its victorious return from India (see 27. *e*).

On an Etruscan mirror the *amanita muscaria* is engraved at Ixion's feet; he was a Thessalian hero who feasted on ambrosia among the gods (see 63. *b*). Several myths (see 102, 126, etc.) are consistent with my theory that his descendants, the Centaurs, ate this mushroom; and, according to some historians, it was later employed by the Norse 'berserks' to give them reckless power in battle. I now believe that 'ambrosia' and 'nectar' were intoxicant mushrooms: certainly the *amanita muscaria*; but perhaps others, too, especially a small, slender dung-mushroom named *panaeolus papilionaceus*, which induces harmless and most enjoyable hallucinations. A mushroom not unlike it appears on an Attic vase between the hooves of Nessus the Centaur. The 'gods' for whom, in the myths, ambrosia and nectar were reserved, will have been sacred queens and kings of the pre-Classical era. King Tantalus's crime (see 108. *c*) was that he broke the taboo by inviting commoners to share his ambrosia.

Sacred queenships and kingships lapsed in Greece; ambrosia then became, it seems, the secret element of the Eleusinian, Orphic and other Mysteries associated with Dionysus. At all events, the participants swore to keep silence about what they ate or drank, saw unforgettable visions, and were promised immortality. The 'ambrosia' awarded to winners of the Olympic footrace when victory no longer conferred the sacred kingship on them was clearly a substitute: a mixture of foods the initial letters of which, as I show in *What Food the Centaurs Ate*, spelled out the Greek word 'mushroom'. Recipes quoted by Classical authors for nectar, and for *cecyon*, the mint-flavoured drink taken by Demeter at Eleusis, likewise spell out 'mushroom'.

I have myself eaten the hallucigenic mushroom, *psilocybe*, a divine ambrosia in immemorial use among the Masatec Indians of Oaxaca Province, Mexico; heard the priestess invoke Tlaloc, the Mushroom-god, and seen transcendental visions. Thus I wholeheartedly agree with R. Gordon Wasson, the American discoverer of this ancient rite, that European ideas of heaven and hell may well have derived from similar mysteries. Tlaloc was engendered by lightning; so was Dionysus (see 14. *c*); and in Greek folklore, as in Masatec, so are all mushrooms – proverbially called 'food of the gods' in both languages. Tlaloc wore a serpent-crown; so did Dionysus (see 27. *a*). Tlaloc had an underwater retreat; so had Dionysus (see 27. *e*). The Maenads' savage custom of tearing off their victims' heads (see 27. *f* and 28. *d*) may refer allegorically to tearing off the sacred mushroom's head – since in Mexico its stalk is never eaten. We read that Perseus, a sacred King of Argos, converted to Dionysus worship (see 27. *i*), named Mycenae after a toadstool which he found growing on the site, and which gave forth a stream of water (see 73. *r*). Tlaloc's emblem was a toad; so was that of Argos; and from the mouth of Tlaloc's toad in the Tepentitla fresco issues a stream of water. Yet at what epoch were the European and Central American cultures in contact?

These theories call for further research, and I have therefore not incorporated my findings in the text of the present edition. Any expert help in solving the problem would be greatly appreciated.

R. G.

Deyá, Majorca,
    Spain, 1960.

# INTRODUCTION

THE medieval emissaries of the Catholic Church brought to Great Britain, in addition to the whole corpus of sacred history, a Continental university system based on the Greek and Latin Classics. Such native legends as those of King Arthur, Guy of Warwick, Robin Hood, the Blue Hag of Leicester, and King Lear were considered suitable enough for the masses, yet by early Tudor times the clergy and the educated classes were referring far more frequently to the myths in Ovid, Virgil, and the grammar school summaries of the Trojan War. Though official English literature of the sixteenth to the nineteenth centuries cannot, therefore, be properly understood except in the light of Greek mythology, the Classics have lately lost so much ground in schools and universities that an educated person is now no longer expected to know (for instance) who Deucalion, Pelops, Daedalus, Oenone, Laocoön, or Antigone may have been. Current knowledge of these myths is mostly derived from such fairy-story versions as Kingsley's *Heroes* and Hawthorne's *Tanglewood Tales*; and at first sight this does not seem to matter much, because for the last two thousand years it has been the fashion to dismiss the myths as bizarre and chimerical fancies, a charming legacy from the childhood of the Greek intelligence, which the Church naturally depreciates in order to emphasize the greater spiritual importance of the Bible. Yet it is difficult to overestimate their value in the study of early European history, religion, and sociology.

'Chimerical' is an adjectival form of the noun *chimaera*, meaning 'she-goat'. Four thousand years ago the Chimaera can have seemed no more bizarre than any religious, heraldic, or commercial emblem does today. She was a formal composite beast with (as Homer records) a lion's head, a goat's body, and a serpent's tail. A Chimaera has been found carved on the walls of a Hittite temple at Carchemish and, like such other composite beasts as the Sphinx and the Unicorn, will originally have been a calendar symbol: each component represented a season of the Queen of Heaven's sacred year – as, according to Diodorus Siculus, the three strings of her tortoise-shell lyre also did. This ancient three-season year is discussed by Nilsson in his *Primitive Time Reckoning* (1920).

Only a small part, however, of the huge, disorganized corpus of Greek mythology, which contains importations from Crete, Egypt,

Palestine, Phrygia, Babylonia, and elsewhere, can properly be classified with the Chimaera as true myth. True myth may be defined as the reduction to narrative shorthand of ritual mime performed on public festivals, and in many cases recorded pictorially on temple walls, vases, seals, bowls, mirrors, chests, shields, tapestries, and the like. The Chimaera and her fellow calendar-beasts must have figured prominently in these dramatic performances which, with their iconographic and oral records, became the prime authority, or charter, for the religious institutions of each tribe, clan, or city. Their subjects were archaic magic-makings that promoted the fertility or stability of a sacred queendom, or kingdom – queendoms having, it seems, preceded kingdoms throughout the Greek-speaking area – and amendments to these, introduced as circumstances required. Lucian's essay *On the Dance* lists an imposing number of ritual mimes still performed in the second century A.D.; and Pausanias's description of the temple paintings at Delphi and the carvings on Cypselus's Chest, suggests that an immense amount of miscellaneous mythological records, of which no trace now remains, survived into the same period.

True myth must be distinguished from:

(1) Philosophical allegory, as in Hesiod's cosmogony.
(2) 'Aetiological' explanation of myths no longer understood, as in Admetus's yoking of a lion and a boar to his chariot.
(3) Satire or parody, as in Silenus's account of Atlantis.
(4) Sentimental fable, as in the story of Narcissus and Echo.
(5) Embroidered history, as in Arion's adventure with the dolphin.
(6) Minstrel romance, as in the story of Cephalus and Procris.
(7) Political propaganda, as in Theseus's Federalization of Attica.
(8) Moral legend, as in the story of Eriphyle's necklace.
(9) Humorous anecdote, as in the bedroom farce of Heracles, Omphale, and Pan.
(10) Theatrical melodrama, as in the story of Thestor and his daughters.
(11) Heroic saga, as in the main argument of the *Iliad*.
(12) Realistic fiction, as in Odysseus's visit to the Phaeacians.[1]

Yet genuine mythic elements may be found embedded in the least promising stories, and the fullest or most illuminating version of a

1. See 4; 69; 83; 84; 87; 89; 99; 106; 136; 161; 162–5; 170.

given myth is seldom supplied by any one author; nor, when searching for its original form, should one assume that the more ancient the written source, the more authoritative it must be. Often, for instance, the playful Alexandrian Callimachus, or the frivolous Augustan Ovid, or the dry-as-dust late-Byzantine Tzetzes, gives an obviously earlier version of a myth than do Hesiod or the Greek tragedians; and the thirteenth-century *Excidium Troiae* is, in parts, mythically sounder than the *Iliad*. When making prose sense of a mythological or pseudo-mythological narrative, one should always pay careful attention to the names, tribal origin, and fates of the characters concerned; and then restore it to the form of dramatic ritual, whereupon its incidental elements will sometimes suggest an analogy with another myth which has been given a wholly different anecdotal twist, and shed light on both.

A study of Greek mythology should begin with a consideration of what political and religious systems existed in Europe before the arrival of Aryan invaders from the distant North and East. The whole of neolithic Europe, to judge from surviving artifacts and myths, had a remarkably homogeneous system of religious ideas, based on worship of the many-titled Mother-goddess, who was also known in Syria and Libya.

Ancient Europe had no gods. The Great Goddess was regarded as immortal, changeless, and omnipotent; and the concept of fatherhood had not been introduced into religious thought. She took lovers, but for pleasure, not to provide her children with a father. Men feared, adored, and obeyed the matriarch; the hearth which she tended in a cave or hut being their earliest social centre, and motherhood their prime mystery. Thus the first victim of a Greek public sacrifice was always offered to Hestia of the Hearth. The goddess's white aniconic image, perhaps her most widespread emblem, which appears at Delphi as the *omphalos*, or navel-boss, may originally have represented the raised white mound of tightly-packed ash, enclosing live charcoal, which is the easiest means of preserving fire without smoke. Later, it became pictorially identified with the lime-whitened mound under which the harvest corn-doll was hidden, to be removed sprouting in the spring; and with the mound of sea-shells, or quartz, or white marble, underneath which dead kings were buried. Not only the moon, but (to judge from Hemera of Greece and Grainne of Ireland) the sun, were the goddess's celestial symbols. In earlier Greek myth, however, the sun yields precedence to the moon – which inspires the greater superstitious fear, does not grow dimmer as the year wanes, and is credited with the power to grant or deny water to the fields.

The moon's three phases of new, full, and old recalled the matriarch's three phases of maiden, nymph (nubile woman), and crone. Then, since the sun's annual course similarly recalled the rise and decline of her physical powers – spring a maiden, summer a nymph, winter a crone – the goddess became identified with seasonal changes in animal and plant life; and thus with Mother Earth who, at the beginning of the vegetative year, produces only leaves and buds, then flowers and fruits, and at last ceases to bear. She could later be conceived as yet another triad: the maiden of the upper air, the nymph of the earth or sea, the crone of the underworld – typified respectively by Selene, Aphrodite, and Hecate. These mystical analogues fostered the sacredness of the number three, and the Moon-goddess became enlarged to nine when each of the three persons – maiden, nymph, and crone – appeared in triad to demonstrate her divinity. Her devotees never quite forgot that there were not three goddesses, but one goddess; though, by Classical times, Arcadian Stymphalus was one of the few remaining shrines where they all bore the same name: Hera.

Once the relevance of coition to child-bearing had been officially admitted – an account of this turning-point in religion appears in the Hittite myth of simple-minded Appu (H. G. Güterbock: *Kumarbi*, 1946) – man's religious status gradually improved, and winds or rivers were no longer given credit for impregnating women. The tribal Nymph, it seems, chose an annual lover from her entourage of young men, a king to be sacrificed when the year ended; making him a symbol of fertility, rather than the object of her erotic pleasure. His sprinkled blood served to fructify trees, crops, and flocks, and his flesh was torn and eaten raw by the Queen's fellow-nymphs – priestesses wearing the masks of bitches, mares, or sows. Next, in amendment to this practice, the king died as soon as the power of the sun, with which he was identified, began to decline in the summer; and another young man, his twin, or supposed twin – a convenient ancient Irish term is 'tanist' – then became the Queen's lover, to be duly sacrificed at midwinter and, as a reward, reincarnated in an oracular serpent. These consorts acquired executive power only when permitted to deputize for the Queen by wearing her magical robes. Thus kingship developed, and though the Sun became a symbol of male fertility once the king's life had been identified with its seasonal course, it still remained under the

Moon's tutelage; as the king remained under the Queen's tutelage, in theory at least, long after the matriarchal phase had been outgrown. Thus the witches of Thessaly, a conservative region, would threaten the Sun, in the Moon's name, with being engulfed by perpetual night.

There is, however, no evidence that, even when women were sovereign in religious matters, men were denied fields in which they might act without female supervision, though it may well be that they adopted many of the 'weaker-sex' characteristics hitherto thought functionally peculiar to man. They could be trusted to hunt, fish, gather certain foods, mind flocks and herds, and help defend the tribal territory against intruders, so long as they did not transgress matriarchal law. Leaders of totem clans were chosen and certain powers awarded them, especially in times of migration or war. Rules for determining who should act as male commander-in-chief varied, it appears, in different matriarchies: usually the queen's maternal uncle, or her brother, or the son of her maternal aunt was chosen. The most primitive tribal commander-in-chief also had authority to act as judge in personal disputes between men, in so far as the queen's religious authority was not thereby impaired. The most primitive matrilineal society surviving today is that of the Nayars of Southern India, where the princesses, though married to child-husbands whom they immediately divorce, bear children to lovers of no particular rank; and the princesses of several matrilineal tribes of West Africa marry foreigners or commoners. The royal women of pre-Hellenic Greece also thought nothing of taking lovers from among their serfs, if the Hundred Houses of Locris and Epizephyrian Locri were not exceptional.

Time was first reckoned by lunations, and every important ceremony took place at a certain phase of the moon; the solstices and equinoxes not being exactly determined but approximated to the nearest new or full moon. The number seven acquired peculiar sanctity, because the king died at the seventh full moon after the shortest day. Even when, after careful astronomical observation, the solar year proved to have 364 days, with a few hours left over, it had to be divided into months – that is, moon-cycles – rather than into fractions of the solar cycle. These months later became what the English-speaking world still calls 'common-law months', each of twenty-eight days; which was a sacred number, in the sense that the moon could be worshipped as a woman, whose menstrual cycle is normally twenty-eight days, and that this is also the true period of the moon's revolutions in terms of the sun. The seven-day week was a unit of the common-law month, the character of each day being deduced, it seems, from the quality attributed to the corresponding month of the sacred king's life. This system led to a still closer identification of woman with moon and, since the 364-day year is exactly divisible by twenty-eight, the annual sequence of popular festivals could be geared to these common-law months. As a religious tradition, the thirteen-month years survived among European peasants for more than a millennium after the adoption of the Julian Calendar; thus Robin Hood, who lived at the time of Edward II, could exclaim in a ballad celebrating the May Day festival:

> *How many merry months be in the year?*
> *There are thirteen, I say . . .*

which a Tudor editor has altered to '. . . There are but twelve, I say . . .' Thirteen, the number of the sun's death-month, has never lost its evil reputation among the superstitious. The days of the week lay under the charge of Titans: the genii of sun, moon, and the five hitherto discovered planets, who were responsible for them to the goddess as Creatrix. This system had probably been evolved in matriarchal Sumeria.

Thus the sun passed through thirteen monthly stages, beginning at the winter solstice when the days lengthen again after their long autumnal decline. The extra day of the sidereal year, gained from the solar year by the earth's revolution around the sun's orbit, was intercalated between the thirteenth and the first month, and became the most important day of the 365, the occasion on which the tribal Nymph chose the sacred king, usually the winner of a race, a wrestling match, or an archery contest. But this primitive calendar underwent modifications: in some regions the extra day seems to have been intercalated, not at the winter solstice, but at some other New Year – at the Candlemas cross-quarter day, when the first signs of spring are apparent; or at the spring equinox, when the sun is regarded as coming to maturity; or at midsummer; or at the rising of the Dog Star, when the Nile floods; or at the autumnal equinox, when the first rains fall.

Early Greek mythology is concerned, above all else, with the changing relations between the queen and her lovers, which begin with their yearly, or twice-yearly sacrifices; and end, at the time when the *Iliad*, was composed and kings boasted: 'We are far better than our fathers!', with her eclipse by an unlimited male monarchy. Numerous African analogues illustrate the progessive stages of this change.

A large part of Greek myth is politico-religious history. Bellerophon masters winged Pegasus and kills the Chimaera. Perseus, in a variant of the same legend, flies through the air and beheads Pegasus's mother, the Gorgon Medusa; much as Marduk, a Babylonian hero, kills the she-monster Tiamat, Goddess of the Sea. Perseus's name should properly be spelled *Pterseus*, 'the destroyer'; and he was not, as Professor Kerenyi has suggested, an archetypal Death-figure but, probably, represented the patriarchal Hellenes who invaded Greece and Asia Minor early in the second millennium B.C., and challenged the power of the Triple-goddess. Pegasus had been sacred to her because the horse with its moon-shaped hooves figured in the rain-making ceremonies and the instalment of sacred kings; his wings were symbolical of a celestial nature, rather than speed. Jane Harrison has pointed out (*Prolegomena to the Study of Greek Religion*, chapter v) that Medusa was once the goddess herself, hiding behind a prophylactic Gorgon mask: a hideous face intended to warn the profane against trespassing on her Mysteries. Perseus beheads Medusa: that is, the Hellenes overran the goddess's chief shrines, stripped her priestesses of their Gorgon masks, and took possession of the sacred horses – an early representation of the goddess with a Gorgon's head and a mare's body has been found in Boeotia. Bellerophon, Perseus's double, kills the Lycian Chimaera: that is, the Hellenes annulled the ancient Medusan calendar, and replaced it with another.

Again, Apollo's destruction of the Python at Delphi seems to record the Achaeans' capture of the Cretan Earth-goddess's shrine; so does his attempted rape of Daphne, whom Hera thereupon metamorphosed into a laurel. This myth has been quoted by Freudian psychologists as symbolizing a girl's instinctive horror of the sexual act; yet Daphne was anything but a frightened virgin. Her name is a contraction of *Daphoene*, 'the bloody one', the goddess in orgiastic mood, whose priestesses, the Maenads, chewed laurel-leaves as an intoxicant and periodically rushed out at the full moon, assaulted unwary travellers, and tore children or young animals in pieces; laurel contains cyanide of potassium. These Maenad colleges were suppressed by the Hellenes, and only the laurel grove testified to Daphoene's former occupancy of the shrines: the chewing of laurel by anyone except the prophetic Pythian Priestess, whom Apollo retained in his service at Delphi, was tabooed in Greece until Roman times.

The Hellenic invasions of the early second millennium B.C., usually called the Aeolian and Ionian, seem to have been less destructive than the Achaean and Dorian ones, which they preceded. Small armed bands of herdsmen, worshipping the Aryan trinity of gods – Indra, Mitra, and Varuna – crossed the natural barrier of Mount Othrys, and attached themselves peacefully enough to the pre-Hellenic settlements in Thessaly and Central Greece. They were accepted as children of the local goddess, and provided her with sacred kings. Thus a male military aristocracy became reconciled to female theocracy, not only in Greece, but in Crete, where the Hellenes also gained a foothold and exported Cretan civilization to Athens and the Peloponnese. Greek was eventually spoken throughout the Aegean and, by the time of Herodotus, one oracle alone spoke a pre-Hellenic language (Herodotus: viii. 134–5). The king acted as the representative of Zeus, or Poseidon, or Apollo, and called himself by one or other of their names, though even Zeus was for centuries a mere demi-god, not an immortal Olympian deity. All early myths about the gods' seduction of nymphs refer apparently to marriages between Hellenic chieftains and local Moon-priestesses; bitterly opposed by Hera, which means by conservative religious feeling.

When the shortness of the king's reign proved irksome, it was agreed to prolong the thirteen-month year to a Great Year of one hundred lunations, in the last of which occurs a near-coincidence of solar and lunar time. But since the fields and crops still needed to be fructified, the king agreed to suffer an annual mock death and yield his sovereignty for one day – the intercalated one, lying outside the sacred sidereal year – to the surrogate boy-king, or *interrex*, who died at its close, and whose blood was used for the sprinkling ceremony. Now the sacred king either reigned for the entire period of a Great Year, with a tanist as his lieutenant; or the two reigned for alternate years; or the Queen let them divide the queendom into halves and reign concurrently. The king deputized for the Queen at many sacred functions, dressed in her robes, wore false breasts, borrowed her lunar axe as a symbol of power, and even took over from her the magical art of rain-making. His ritual death varied greatly in circumstance; he might be torn in pieces by wild women, transfixed with a sting-ray spear, felled with an axe, pricked in the heel with a poisoned arrow, flung over a cliff, burned to death on a pyre, drowned in a pool, or killed in a pre-arranged chariot crash. But die he must. A new stage was reached when animals came to be substituted for boys at the sacrificial altar, and the king refused death after his lengthened reign ended. Dividing the realm into three parts, and awarding one part to each of his successors, he would reign for another term; his excuse being that a closer approximation of solar and lunar time had now been found, namely nineteen years, or 325 lunations. The Great Year had become a Greater Year.

Throughout these successive stages, reflected in numerous myths, the sacred king continued to hold his position only by right of marriage to the tribal Nymph, who was chosen either as a result of a foot race between her companions of the royal house or by ultimogeniture – that is to say, by being the youngest nubile daughter of the junior branch. The throne remained matrilineal, as it theoretically did even in Egypt, and the sacred king and his tanist were therefore always chosen from outside the royal female house; until some daring king at last decided to commit incest with the heiress, who ranked as his daughter, and thus gain a new title to the throne when his reign needed renewal.

Achaean invasions of the thirteenth century B.C. seriously weakened the matrilineal tradition. It seems that the king now contrived to reign for the term of his natural life; and when the Dorians arrived, towards the close of the second millennium, patrilineal succession became the rule. A prince no longer left his father's house and married a foreign princess; she came to him, as Odysseus persuaded Penelope to do. Genealogy became patrilineal, though a Samian incident mentioned in the Pseudo-Herodotus's Life of Homer shows that for some time after the Apatoria, or Festival of Male Kinship, had replaced that of Female Kinship, the rites still consisted of sacrifices to the Mother Goddess which men were not eligible to attend.

The familiar Olympian system was then agreed upon as a compromise between Hellenic and pre-Hellenic views: a divine family of six gods and six goddesses, headed by the co-sovereigns Zeus and Hera and forming a Council of Gods in Babylonian style. But after a rebellion of the pre-Hellenic population, described in the Iliad as a conspiracy against Zeus, Hera became subservient to him. Athene avowed herself 'all for the Father' and, in the end, Dionysus assured male preponderance in the Council by displacing Hestia. Yet the goddesses, though left in a minority, were never altogether ousted – as they were at Jerusalem – because the revered poets Homer and Hesiod had 'given the deities their titles and distinguished their several provinces and special powers' (Herodotus: ii. 53), which could not be easily expropriated. Moreover, though the system of gathering all the women of royal blood together under the king's control, and thus discouraging outsiders from attempts on a matrilineal throne, was adopted at Rome when the Vestal College was founded, and in Palestine when King David formed his royal harem, it never reached Greece. Patrilineal descent, succession, and inheritance discourage further myth-making; historical legend then begins and fades into the light of common history.

The lives of such characters as Heracles, Daedalus, Teiresias, and Phineus span several generations, because these are titles rather than names of particular heroes. Yet myths, though difficult to reconcile with chronology, are always practical: they insist on some point of tradition, however distorted the meaning may have become in the telling. Take, for instance, the confused story of Aeacus's dream, where ants, falling from an oracular oak, turn into men and colonize the island of Aegina after Hera has depopulated it. Here the main points of interest are: that the oak had grown from a Dodonian acorn; that the ants were Thessalian ants; and that Aeacus was a grandson of the River Asopus. These elements combined to give a concise account of immigrations into Aegina towards the end of the second millennium B.C.

Despite a sameness of pattern in Greek myths, all detailed interpretations of particular legends are open to question until archaeologists can provide a more exact tabulation of tribal movements in Greece, and their dates. Yet the historical and anthropological approach is the only reasonable one: the theory that Chimaera, Sphinx, Gorgon, Centaurs, Satyrs and the like are blind uprushes of the Jungian collective unconscious, to which no precise meaning had ever, or could ever, have been attached, is demonstrably unsound. The Bronze and early Iron Ages in Greece were not the childhood of mankind, as Dr Jung suggests. That Zeus swallowed Metis, for instance, and subsequently gave birth to Athene, through an orifice in his head, is not an irrepressible fancy, but an ingenious theological dogma which embodies at least three conflicting views:

(1) Athene was the parthenogenous daughter of Metis; i.e. the youngest person of the Triad headed by Metis, Goddess of Wisdom.

(2) Zeus swallowed Metis; i.e. the Achaeans suppressed her cult and arrogated all wisdom to Zeus as their patriarchal god.

(3) Athene was the daughter of Zeus; i.e. the Zeus-worshipping Achaeans spared Athene's temples on condition that her votaries accepted his paramount sovereignty.

Zeus's swallowing of Metis, with its sequel, will have been represented graphically on the walls of a temple; and as the erotic Dionysus – once a parthenogenous son of Semele – was reborn from his thigh, so the intellectual Athene was reborn from his head.

If some myths are baffling at first sight, this is often because the mythographer has accidentally or deliberately misinterpreted a sacred picture or dramatic rite. I have called such a process 'iconotropy', and examples of it can be found in every body of sacred literature which sets the seal upon a radical reform of ancient beliefs. Greek myth teems with iconotropic instances. Hephaestus's three-legged workshop tables, for example, which ran by themselves to assemblies of the gods, and back again (*Iliad* xviii. 368 ff.), are not, as Dr Charles Seltman archly suggests in his *Twelve Olympian Gods,* anticipations of automobiles; but golden Sun-disks with three legs apiece (like the emblem of the Isle of Man), apparently representing the number of three-season years for which a 'son of Hephaestus' was permitted to reign in the island of Lemnos. Again, the so-called 'Judgement of Paris', where a hero is called upon to decide between the rival charms of three goddesses and awards his apple to the fairest, records an ancient ritual situation, outgrown by the time of Homer and Hesiod. These three goddesses are one goddess in triad: Athene the maiden, Aphrodite the nymph, and Hera the crone – and Aphrodite is presenting Paris with the apple, rather than receiving it from him. This apple, symbolizing her love bought at the price of his life, will be Paris's passport to the Elysian Fields, the apple orchards of the west, to which only the souls of heroes are admitted. A similar gift is frequently made in Irish and Welsh myth; as well as by the Three Hesperides, to Heracles; and by Eve, 'the Mother of All Living', to Adam. Thus Nemesis, goddess of the sacred grove who, in late myth, became a symbol of divine vengeance on proud kings, carries an apple-hung branch, her gift to heroes. All neolithic and Bronze Age paradises were orchard-islands; *paradise* itself means 'orchard'.

A true science of myth should begin with a study of archaeology, history, and comparative religion, not in the psycho-therapist's consulting-room. Though the Jungians hold that 'myths are original revelations of the pre-conscious psyche, involuntary statements about unconscious psychic happenings', Greek mythology was no more mysterious in content than are modern election cartoons, and for the most part formulated in territories which maintained close political relations with Minoan Crete – a country sophisticated enough to have written archives, four-storey buildings with hygienic plumbing, doors with modern-looking locks, registered trademarks, chess, a central system of weights and measures, and a calendar based on patient astronomic observation.

My method has been to assemble in harmonious narrative all the scattered elements of each myth, supported by little-known variants which may help to determine the meaning, and to answer all questions that arise, as best I can, in anthropological or historical terms. This is, I am well aware, much too ambitious a task for any single mythologist to undertake, however long or hard he works. Errors must creep in. Let me emphasize that any statement here made about Mediterranean religion or ritual before the appearance of written records is conjectural. Nevertheless, I have been heartened, since this book first appeared in 1955, by the close analogues which E. Meyrowitz's *Akan Cosmological Drama* (Faber & Faber) offers to the religious and social changes here presumed. The Akan people result from an ancient southward emigration of Libyo-Berbers – cousins to the pre-Hellenic population of Greece – from the Sahara desert oases (see 3. 3) and their intermarriage at Timbuctoo with Niger River negroes. In the eleventh century A.D. they moved still farther south to what is now Ghana. Four different cult-types persist among them. In the most primitive, the Moon is worshipped as the supreme Triple-goddess Ngame, clearly identical with the Libyan Neith, the Carthaginian Tanit, the Canaanite Anatha, and the early Greek Athene (see 8. 1). Ngame is said to have brought forth the heavenly bodies by her own efforts (see 1. 1), and then to have vitalized men and animals by shooting magical arrows from her new-moon bow into their inert bodies. She also, it is said, takes life in her killer aspect; as did her counterpart, the Moon-goddess Artemis (see 22. 1). A princess of royal line is judged capable, in unsettled times, of being overcome by Ngame's lunar magic and bearing a tribal deity which takes up its residence in a shrine and leads a group of emigrants to some new region. This woman becomes queen-mother, war-leader, judge, and priestess of the settlement she founds. The deity has meanwhile revealed itself as a totem animal which is protected by a close *tabu*, apart from the yearly chase and sacrifice of a single specimen; this throws light on the yearly owl-hunt made by the Pelasgians at Athens (see 97. *4*). States, consisting of tribal federations, are then formed, the most powerful tribal deity becoming the State-god.

The second cult-type marks Akan coalescence with Sudanese worshippers of a Father-god, Odomankoma, who claimed to have made the universe single-handedly (see 4. *c*); they were, it seems, led by elected male chieftains, and had adopted the Sumerian seven-day week. As a compromise myth, Ngame is now said to have vitalized Odomankoma's lifeless creation; and each tribal deity becomes one of the seven planetary powers. These planetary powers – as I have presumed also happened in Greece when Titan-worship came in from the East (see 11. *3*) – form male-and-female pairs. The queen-mother of the state, as Ngame's representative, performs an annual sacred marriage with Odomankoma's representative: namely her chosen lover whom, at the close of the year, the priests murder, skin, and flay. The same practice seems to have obtained among the Greeks (see 9. *a* and 21. *5*).

In the third cult-type, the queen-mother's lover becomes a king, and is venerated as the male aspect of the Moon, corresponding with the Phoenician god Baal Haman; and a boy dies vicariously for him every year as a mock-king (see 30. *1*). The queen-mother now delegates the chief executive powers to a vizier, and concentrates on her ritual fertilizing functions.

In the fourth cult-type, the king, having gained the homage of several petty kings, abrogates his Moon-god aspect and proclaims himself Sun-king in Egyptian style (see 67. *1* and *2*). Though continuing to celebrate the annual sacred marriage, he frees himself from dependence on the Moon. At this stage, patrilocal supersedes matrilocal marriage, and the tribes are supplied with heroic male ancestors to worship, as happened in Greece – though sun-worship there never displaced thunder-god worship.

Among the Akan, every change in court-ritual is marked by an addition to the accepted myth of events in Heaven. Thus, if the king has appointed a royal porter and given his office lustre by marrying him to a princess, a divine porter in Heaven is announced to have done the same. It is likely that Heracles's marriage to the Goddess Hebe and his appointment as porter to Zeus (see 145. *i* and *j*) reflected a similar event at the Mycenaean Court; and that the divine feastings on Olympus reflected similar celebrations at Olympia under the joint presidency of the Zeus-like High King of Mycenae and Hera's Chief Priestess from Argos.

I am deeply grateful to Janet Seymour-Smith and Kenneth Gay for helping me to get this book into shape, to Peter and Lalage Green for proof-reading the first few chapters, to Frank Seymour-Smith for sending scarce Latin and Greek texts from London, and to the many friends who have helped me to amend the first edition.

R. G.

Deyá, Majorca,
    Spain.

## NOTE

Each myth is first recounted as a narrative, the paragraphs being identified by italic letters (*a, b, c, . . .*). Next follows a list of sources, numbered in accordance with the references in the text. Then comes an explanatory comment, divided into paragraphs identified by italic numbers (*1, 2, 3, . . .*). Cross-references from one explanatory section to another are made by giving the myth number and paragraph number, thus: (43. *4*) directs the reader to par. 4 of the third (explanatory) section of myth 43.

# THE GREEK MYTHS

## VOLUME ONE

# I

## THE PELASGIAN CREATION MYTH

In the beginning, Eurynome, the Goddess of All Things, rose naked from Chaos, but found nothing substantial for her feet to rest upon, and therefore divided the sea from the sky, dancing lonely upon its waves. She danced towards the south, and the wind set in motion behind her seemed something new and apart with which to begin a work of creation. Wheeling about, she caught hold of this north wind, rubbed it between her hands, and behold! the great serpent Ophion. Eurynome danced to warm herself, wildly and more wildly, until Ophion, grown lustful, coiled about those divine limbs and was moved to couple with her. Now, the North Wind, who is also called Boreas, fertilizes; which is why mares often turn their hind-quarters to the wind and breed foals without aid of a stallion.[1] So Eurynome was likewise got with child.

*b.* Next, she assumed the form of a dove, brooding on the waves and, in due process of time, laid the Universal Egg. At her bidding, Ophion coiled seven times about this egg, until it hatched and split in two. Out tumbled all things that exist, her children: sun, moon, planets, stars, the earth with its mountains and rivers, its trees, herbs, and living creatures.

*c.* Eurynome and Ophion made their home upon Mount Olympus, where he vexed her by claiming to be the author of the Universe. Forthwith she bruised his head with her heel, kicked out his teeth, and banished him to the dark caves below the earth.[2]

*d.* Next, the goddess created the seven planetary powers, setting a Titaness and a Titan over each. Theia and Hyperion for the Sun; Phoebe and Atlas for the Moon; Dione and Crius for the planet Mars; Metis and Coeus for the planet Mercury; Themis and Eurymedon for the planet Jupiter; Tethys and Oceanus for Venus; Rhea and Cronus for the planet Saturn.[3] But the first man was Pelasgus, ancestor of the Pelasgians; he sprang from the soil of Arcadia, followed by certain others, whom he taught to make huts and feed upon acorns, and sew pig-skin tunics such as poor folk still wear in Euboea and Phocis.[4]

1. Pliny: *Natural History* iv. 35 and viii. 67; Homer: *Iliad* xx, 223.
2. Only tantalizing fragments of this pre-Hellenic myth survive in Greek literature, the largest being Apollonius Rhodius's *Argo-*

*nautica* i. 496–505 and Tzetzes: *On Lycophron* 1191; but it is implicit in the Orphic Mysteries, and can be restored, as above, from
the *Berossian Fragment* and the Phoenician cosmognies quoted by
Philo Byblius and Damascius; from the Canaanitish elements in
the Hebrew Creation story; from Hyginus (*Fabula* 197 – see
62. *a*); from the Boeotian legend of the dragon's teeth (see 58. 5);
and from early ritual art. That all Pelasgians were born from
Ophion is suggested by their common sacrifice, the Peloria
(Athenaeus: xiv. 45. 639–40), Ophion having been a *Pelor*, or
'prodigious serpent'.

3. Homer: *Iliad* v. 898; Apollonius Rhodius: ii. 1232; Apollodorus:
   i. 1. 3; Hesiod: *Theogony* 113; Stephanus of Byzantium *sub* Adana;
   Aristophanes: *Birds* 692 ff.; Clement of Rome: *Homilies* vi. 4. 72;
   Proclus on Plato's *Timaeus* ii. p. 307.

4. Pausanias: viii. 1. 2.

\*

1. In this archaic religious system there were, as yet, neither gods nor
priests, but only a universal goddess and her priestesses, women being
the dominant sex and man her frightened victim. Fatherhood was not
honoured, conception being attributed to the wind, the eating of beans,
or the accidental swallowing of an insect; inheritance was matrilineal and
snakes were regarded as incarnations of the dead. Eurynome ('wide
wandering') was the goddess's title as the visible moon; her Sumerian
name was Iahu ('exalted dove'), a title which later passed to Jehovah as
the Creator. It was as a dove that Marduk symbolically sliced her in two
at the Babylonian Spring Festival, when he inaugurated the new world
order.

2. Ophion, or Boreas, is the serpent demiurge of Hebrew and Egyptian
myth – in early Mediterranean art, the Goddess is constantly shown in his
company. The earth-born Pelasgians, whose claim seems to have been
that they sprang from Ophion's teeth, were originally perhaps the neolithic 'Painted Ware' people; they reached the mainland of Greece from
Palestine about 3500 B.C., and the early Hellads – immigrants from Asia
Minor by way of the Cyclades – found them in occupation of the Peloponnese seven hundred years later. But 'Pelasgians' became loosely
applied to all pre-Hellenic inhabitants of Greece. Thus Euripides (quoted
by Strabo v. 2. 4) records that the Pelasgians adopted the name 'Danaans'
on the coming to Argos of Danaus and his fifty daughters (see 60. *f*).
Strictures on their licentious conduct (Herodotus: vi. 137) refer probably
to the pre-Hellenic custom of erotic orgies. Strabo says in the same
passage that those who lived near Athens were known as Pelargi ('storks');
perhaps this was their totem bird.

3. The Titans ('lords') and Titanesses had their counterparts in early

Babylonian and Palestinian astrology, where they were deities ruling the seven days of the sacred planetary week; and may have been introduced by the Canaanite, or Hittite, colony which settled the Isthmus of Corinth early in the second millennium B.C. (see 67. 2), or even by the Early Hellads. But when the Titan cult was abolished in Greece, and the seven-day week ceased to figure in the official calender, their number was quoted as twelve by some authors, probably to make them correspond with the signs of the Zodiac. Hesiod, Apollodorus, Stephanus of Byzantium, Pausanias, and others give inconsistent lists of their names. In Babylonian myth the planetary rulers of the week, namely Samas, Sin, Nergal, Bel, Beltis, and Ninib, were all male, except Beltis, the Love-goddess; but in the Germanic week, which the Celts had borrowed from the Eastern Mediterranean, Sunday, Tuesday, and Friday were ruled by Titanesses, as opposed to Titans. To judge from the divine status of Aeolus's paired-off daughters and sons (see 43. 4), and the myth of Niobe (see 77. 1), it was decided, when the system first reached pre-Hellenic Greece from Palestine, to pair a Titaness with each Titan, as a means of safeguarding the goddess's interests. But before long the fourteen were reduced to a mixed company of seven. The planetary powers were as follows: Sun for illumination; Moon for enchantment; Mars for growth; Mercury for wisdom; Jupiter for law; Venus for love; Saturn for peace. Classical Greek astrologers conformed with the Babylonians, and awarded the planets to Helius, Selene, Ares, Hermes (or Apollo), Zeus, Aphrodite, Cronus – whose Latin equivalents, given above, still name the French, Italian, and Spanish weeks.

4. In the end, mythically speaking, Zeus swallowed the Titans, including his earlier self – since the Jews of Jerusalem worshipped a transcendent God, composed of all the planetary powers of the week: a theory symbolized in the seven-branched candlestick, and in the Seven Pillars of Wisdom. The seven planetary pillars set up near the Horse's Tomb at Sparta were said by Pausanias (ii. 20. 9) to be adorned in ancient fashion, and may have been connected with the Egyptian rites introduced by the Pelasgians (Herodotus: ii. 57). Whether the Jews borrowed the theory from the Egyptians, or contrariwise, is uncertain; but the so-called Heliopolitan Zeus, whom A. B. Cook discusses in his Zeus (i. 570–76), was Egyptian in character, and bore busts of the seven planetary powers as frontal ornaments on his body sheath; usually, also, busts of the remaining Olympians as rear ornaments. One bronze statuette of this god was found at Tortosa in Spain, another at Byblos in Phoenicia; and a marble stele from Marseilles displays six planetary busts and one full-length figure of Hermes – who is also given greatest prominence in the statuettes – presumably as the inventor of astronomy. At Rome, Jupiter was similarly claimed to be a transcendent god by Quintis Valerius Soranus,

though the week was not observed there, as it was at Marseilles, Byblos, and (probably) Tortosa. But planetary powers were never allowed to influence the official Olympian cult, being regarded as un-Greek (Herodotus: i. 131), and therefore unpatriotic: Aristophanes (*Peace* 403 ff.) makes Trygalus say that the Moon and 'that old villain the Sun' are hatching a plot to betray Greece into the hands of the Persian barbarians.

5. Pausanias's statement that Pelasgus was the first of men records the continuance of a neolithic culture in Arcadia until Classical times.

# 2

## THE HOMERIC AND ORPHIC CREATION MYTHS

SOME say that all gods and all living creatures originated in the stream of Oceanus which girdles the world, and that Tethys was the mother of all his children.[1]

*b.* But the Orphics say that black-winged Night, a goddess of whom even Zeus stands in awe,[2] was courted by the Wind and laid a silver egg in the womb of Darkness; and that Eros, whom some call Phanes, was hatched from this egg and set the Universe in motion. Eros was double-sexed and golden-winged and, having four heads, sometimes roared like a bull or a lion, sometimes hissed like a serpent or bleated like a ram. Night, who named him Ericepaius and Protogenus Phaëthon,[3] lived in a cave with him, displaying herself in triad: Night, Order, and Justice. Before this cave sat the inescapable mother Rhea, playing on a brazen drum, and compelling man's attention to the oracles of the goddess. Phanes created earth, sky, sun, and moon, but the triple-goddess ruled the universe, until her sceptre passed to Uranus.[4]

1. Homer: *Iliad* xvi. 201.
2. *Ibid.*: xiv. 261.
3. *Orphic Fragments* 60, 61, and 70.
4. *Ibid.*: 86.

*

1. Homer's myth is a version of the Pelasgian creation story (see 1. 2), since Tethys reigned over the sea like Eurynome, and Oceanus girdled the Universe like Ophion.

2. The Orphic myth is another version, but influenced by a late mystical doctrine of love (*Eros*) and theories about the proper relations

of the sexes. Night's silver egg means the moon, silver being the lunar metal. As Ericepaius ('feeder upon heather'), the love-god Phanes ('revealer'), is a loudly-buzzing celestial bee, son of the Great Goddess (see 18. 4). The beehive was studied as an ideal republic, and confirmed the myth of the Golden Age, when honey dropped from the trees (see 5. b). Rhea's brazen drum was beaten to prevent bees from swarming in the wrong place, and to ward off evil influences, like the bull-roarers used in the Mysteries. As Phaëthon Protogenus ('first-born shiner'), Phanes is the Sun, which the Orphics made a symbol of illumination (see 28. d), and his four heads correspond with the symbolic beasts of the four seasons. According to Macrobius, the Oracle of Colophon identified this Phanes with the transcendent god Iao: Zeus (ram), Spring; Helius (lion), Summer; Hades (snake), Winter; Dionysus (bull), New Year. Night's sceptre passed to Uranus with the advent of patriarchalism.

# 3

## THE OLYMPIAN CREATION MYTH

AT the beginning of all things Mother Earth emerged from Chaos and bore her son Uranus as she slept. Gazing down fondly at her from the mountains, he showered fertile rain upon her secret clefts, and she bore grass, flowers, and trees, with the beasts and birds proper to each. This same rain made the rivers flow and filled the hollow places with water, so that lakes and seas came into being.

b. Her first children of semi-human form were the hundred-handed giants Briareus, Gyges, and Cottus. Next appeared the three wild, one-eyed Cyclopes, builders of gigantic walls and master-smiths, formerly of Thrace, afterwards of Crete and Lycia,[1] whose sons Odysseus encountered in Sicily.[2] Their names were Brontes, Steropes, and Arges, and their ghosts have dwelt in the caverns of the volcano Aetna since Apollo killed them in revenge for the death of Asclepius.

c. The Libyans, however, claim that Garamas was born before the Hundred-handed Ones and that, when he rose from the plain, he offered Mother Earth a sacrifice of the sweet acorn.[3]

1. Apollodorus: i. 1–2; Euripides: *Chrysippus*, quoted by Sextus Empiricus, p. 751; Lucretius: i. 250 and ii. 991 ff.

2. Homer: *Odyssey* ix. 106–566; Apollodorus: iii. 10. 4.

3. Apollonius Rhodius: iv. 1493 ff.; Pindar: *Fragment* 84, ed. Bergk.

*

1. This patriarchal myth of Uranus gained official acceptance under the Olympian religious system. Uranus, whose name came to mean 'the sky', seems to have won his position as First Father by being identified with the pastoral god Varuna, one of the Aryan male trinity; but his Greek name is a masculine form of *Ur-ana* ('queen of the mountains', 'queen of summer', 'queen of the winds', or 'queen of wild oxen') – the goddess in her orgiastic midsummer aspect. Uranus's marriage to Mother Earth records an early Hellenic invasion of Northern Greece, which allowed Varuna's people to claim that he had fathered the native tribes he found there, though acknowledging him to be Mother Earth's son. An emendation to the myth, recorded by Apollodorus, is that Earth and Sky parted in deadly strife and were then reunited in love: this is mentioned by Euripides (*Melanippe the Wise*, fragment 484, ed. Nauck) and Apollonius Rhodius (*Argonautica* i. 494). The deadly strife must refer to the clash between the patriarchal and matriarchal principles which the Hellenic invasions caused. Gyges ('earth-born') has another form, *gigas* ('giant'), and giants are associated in myth with the mountains of Northern Greece. Briareus ('strong') was also called Aegaeon (*Iliad* i. 403), and his people may therefore be the Libyo-Thracians, whose Goat-goddess Aegis (see 8. 1) gave her name to the Aegean Sea. Cottus was the eponymous (name-giving) ancestor of the Cottians who worshipped the orgiastic Cotytto, and spread her worship from Thrace throughout North-western Europe. These tribes are described as 'hundred-handed', perhaps because their priestesses were organized in colleges of fifty, like the Danaids and Nereids; perhaps because the men were organized in war-bands of one hundred, like the early Romans.

2. The Cyclopes seem to have been a guild of Early Helladic bronze-smiths. *Cyclops* means 'ring-eyed', and they are likely to have been tattooed with concentric rings on the forehead, in honour of the sun, the source of their furnace fires; the Thracians continued to tattoo themselves until Classical times (see 28. 2). Concentric circles are part of the mystery of smith-craft: in order to beat out bowls, helmets, or ritual masks, the smith would guide himself with such circles, described by compass around the centre of the flat disk on which he was working. The Cyclopes were one-eyed also in the sense that smiths often shade one eye with a patch against flying sparks. Later, their identity was forgotten, and the mythographers fancifully placed their ghosts in the caverns of Aetna, to explain the fire and smoke issuing from its crater (see 35. 1). A close cultural connexion existed between Thrace, Crete, and Lycia; the

Cyclopes will have been at home in all these countries. Early Helladic culture also spread to Sicily; but it may well be (as Samuel Butler first suggested) that the Sicilian composition of the *Odyssey* explains the Cyclopes' presence there (see 170. *b*). The names Brontes, Steropes, and Arges ('thunder,' 'lightning', and 'brightness') are late inventions.

3. Garamas is the eponymous ancestor of the Libyan Garamantians who occupied the Oasis of Djado, south of the Fezzan, and were conquered by the Roman General Balbus in 19 B.C. They are said to have been of Cushite-Berber stock, and in the second century A.D. were subdued by the matrilineal Lemta Berbers. Later they fused with the Negro aboriginals on the south bank of the Upper Niger, and adopted their language. They survive today in a single village under the name of Koromantse. *Garamante* is derived from the words *gara*, *man*, and *te*, meaning, 'Gara's state people'. Gara seems to be the Goddess Ker, or Q're, or Car (see 82. 6 and 86. 2), who gave her name to the Carians, among other people, and was associated with apiculture. Esculent acorns, a staple food of the ancient world before the introduction of corn, grew in Libya; and the Garamantian settlement of Ammon was joined with the Northern Greek settlement of Dodona in a religious league which, according to Sir Flinders Petrie, may have originated as early as the third millennium B.C. Both places had an ancient oak-oracle (see 51. *a*). Herodotus describes the Garamantians as a peaceable but very powerful people, who cultivate the date-palm, grow corn, and herd cattle (iv.174 and 183).

# 4

## TWO PHILOSOPHICAL CREATION MYTHS

SOME say that Darkness was first, and from Darkness sprang Chaos. From a union between Darkness and Chaos sprang Night, Day, Erebus, and the Air.

From a union between Night and Erebus sprang Doom, Old Age, Death, Murder, Continence, Sleep, Dreams, Discord, Misery, Vexation, Nemesis, Joy, Friendship, Pity, the Three Fates, and the Three Hesperides.

From a union between Air and Day sprang Mother Earth, Sky, and Sea.

From a union between Air and Mother Earth sprang Terror, Craft, Anger, Strife, Lies, Oaths, Vengeance, Intemperance, Altercation, Treaty, Oblivion, Fear, Pride, Battle; also Oceanus, Metis, and the other Titans, Tartarus, and the Three Erinnyes, or Furies.

From a union between Earth and Tartarus sprang the Giants.

*b.* From a union between the Sea and its Rivers sprang the Nereids. But, as yet, there were no mortal men until, with the consent of the goddess Athene, Prometheus, son of Iapetus, formed them in the likeness of gods. He used clay and water of Panopeus in Phocis, and Athene breathed life into them.[1]

*

*c.* Others say that the God of All Things – whoever he may have been, for some call him Nature – appearing suddenly in Chaos, separated earth from the heavens, the water from the earth, and the upper air from the lower. Having unravelled the elements, he set them in due order, as they are now found. He divided the earth into zones, some very hot, some very cold, others temperate; moulded it into plains and mountains; and clothed it with grass and trees. Above it he set the rolling firmament, spangling it with stars, and assigned stations to the four winds. He also peopled the waters with fish, the earth with beasts, and the sky with the sun, the moon, and the five planets. Lastly, he made man – who, alone of all beasts, raises his face to heaven and observes the sun, the moon, and the stars – unless it be indeed true that Prometheus, son of Iapetus, made man's body from water and clay, and that his soul was supplied by certain wandering divine elements, which had survived from the First Creation.[2]

1. Hesiod: *Theogony* 211–32; Hyginus: *Fabulae, Proem*; Apollodorus: i. 7. 1; Lucian: *Prometheus on Caucasus* 13; Pausanias: x. 4. 3.
2. Ovid: *Metamorphoses* i–ii.

*

1. In Hesiod's *Theogony* – on which the first of these philosophical myths is based –the list of abstractions is confused by the Nereids, the Titans and the Giants, whom he feels bound to include. Both the Three Fates and the Three Hesperides are the Triple Moon-goddess in her death aspect.

2. The second myth, found only in Ovid, was borrowed by the later Greeks from the Babylonian Gilgamesh epic, the introduction to which records the goddess Aruru's particular creation of the first man, Eabini, from a piece of clay; but although Zeus had been the Universal Lord for many centuries, the mythographers were forced to admit that the Creator of all things might possibly have been a Creatrix. The Jews, as inheritors

of the 'Pelasgian', or Canaanitish, creation myth, had felt the same
embarrassment; in the *Genesis* account, a female 'Spirit of the Lord'
broods on the face of the waters, though she does not lay the world egg;
and Eve, 'the Mother of All Living', is ordered to bruise the Serpent's
head, though he is not destined to go down to the Pit until the end of the
world.

3. Similarly, in the Talmudic version of the Creation, the archangel
Michael – Prometheus's counterpart – forms Adam from dust at the
order, not of the Mother of All Living, but of Jehovah. Jehovah then
breathes life into him and gives him Eve who, like Pandora, brings mischief on mankind (see 39. *j*).

4. Greek philosophers distinguished Promethean man from the imper-
fect earth-born creation, part of which was destroyed by Zeus, and the
rest washed away in the Deucalionian Flood (see 38. *c*). Much the same
distinction is found in *Genesis* vi. 2–4 between the 'sons of God' and the
'daughters of men', whom they married.

5. The Gilgamesh tablets are late and equivocal; there the 'Bright
Mother of the Hollow' is credited with having formed everything –
'Aruru' is only one of this goddess's many titles – and the principal
theme is a revolt against her matriarchal order, described as one of utter
confusion, by the gods of the new patriarchal order. Marduk, the Babylonian city-god, eventually defeats the goddess in the person of Tiamat
the Sea-serpent; and it is then brazenly announced that he, not anyone
else, created herbs, lands, rivers, beasts, birds, and mankind. This Marduk
was an upstart godling whose claim to have defeated Tiamat and created
the world had previously been made by the god Bel – Bel being a
masculine form of Belili, the Sumerian Mother-goddess. The transition
from matriarchy to patriarchy seems to have come about in Mesopo-
tamia, as elsewhere, through the revolt of the Queen's consort to whom
she had deputed executive power by allowing him to adopt her name,
robes, and sacred instruments (see 136. *4*).


# 5

## THE FIVE AGES OF MAN

SOME deny that Prometheus created men, or that any man sprang
from a serpent's teeth. They say that Earth bore them spontaneously,
as the best of her fruits, especially in the soil of Attica,[1] and that Alalcomeneus was the first man to appear, by Lake Copais in Boeotia, before

even the Moon was. He acted as Zeus's counsellor on the occasion of his quarrel with Hera, and as tutor to Athene while she was still a girl.[2]

b. These men were the so-called golden race, subjects of Cronus, who lived without cares or labour, eating only acorns, wild fruit, and honey that dripped from the trees, drinking the milk of sheep and goats, never growing old, dancing, and laughing much; death, to them, was no more terrible than sleep. They are all gone now, but their spirits survive as genii of happy music retreats, givers of good fortune, and upholders of justice.

c. Next came a silver race, eaters of bread, likewise divinely created. The men were utterly subject to their mothers and dared not disobey them, although they might live to be a hundred years old. They were quarrelsome and ignorant, and never sacrificed to the gods but, at least, did not make war on one another. Zeus destroyed them all.

d. Next came a brazen race, who fell like fruits from the ash-trees, and were armed with brazen weapons. They ate flesh as well as bread, and delighted in war, being insolent and pitiless men. Black Death has seized them all.

e. The fourth race of man was brazen too, but nobler and more generous, being begotten by the gods on mortal mothers. They fought gloriously in the siege of Thebes, the expedition of the Argonauts, and the Trojan War. These became heroes, and dwell in the Elysian Fields.

f. The fifth race is the present race of iron, unworthy descendants of the fourth. They are degenerate, cruel, unjust, malicious, libidinous, unfilial, treacherous.[3]

1. Plato: Menexenus 6–7.
2. Hippolytus: Refutation of All Heresies v. 6. 3; Eusebius: Preparation for the Gospel iii. 1. 3.
3. Hesiod: Works and Days 109–201, with scholiast.

*

1. Though the myth of the Golden Age derives eventually from a tradition of tribal subservience to the Bee-goddess, the savagery of her reign in pre-agricultural times had been forgotten by Hesiod's day, and all that remained was an idealistic conviction that men had once lived in harmony together like bees (see 2. 2). Hesiod was a small farmer, and the hard life he lived made him morose and pessimistic. The myth of the silver race also records matriarchal conditions – such as those surviving in Classical times among the Picts, the Moesynoechians of the Black Sea

(see 151. *e*), and some tribes in the Baleares, Galicia, and the Gulf of Sirté – under which men were still the despised sex, though agriculture had been introduced and wars were infrequent. Silver is the metal of the Moon-goddess. The third race were the earliest Hellenic invaders: Bronze Age herdsmen, who adopted the ash-tree cult of the Goddess and her son Poseidon (see 6. 4 and 57. 1). The fourth race were the warrior-kings of the Mycenaean Age. The fifth were the Dorians of the twelfth century B.C., who used iron weapons and destroyed the Mycenaean civilization.

Alalcomeneus ('guardian') is a fictitious character, a masculine form of Alalcomeneïs, Athene's title (*Iliad* iv. 8) as the guardian of Boeotia. He serves the patriarchal dogma that no woman, even a goddess, can be wise without male instruction, and that the Moon-goddess and the Moon itself were late creations of Zeus.

# 6

## THE CASTRATION OF URANUS

URANUS fathered the Titans upon Mother Earth, after he had thrown his rebellious sons, the Cyclopes, into Tartarus, a gloomy place in the Underworld, which lies as far distant from the earth as the earth does from the sky; it would take a falling anvil nine days to reach its bottom. In revenge, Mother Earth persuaded the Titans to attack their father; and they did so, led by Cronus, the youngest of the seven, whom she armed with a flint sickle. They surprised Uranus as he slept, and it was with the flint sickle that the merciless Cronus castrated him, grasping his genitals with the left hand (which has ever since been the hand of ill-omen) and afterwards throwing them, and the sickle too, into the sea by Cape Drepanum. But drops of blood flowing from the wound fell upon Mother Earth, and she bore the Three Erinnyes, furies who avenge crimes of parricide and perjury – by name Alecto, Tisiphone, and Megaera. The nymphs of the ash-tree, called the Meliae, also sprang from that blood.

*b*. The Titans then released the Cyclopes from Tartarus, and awarded the sovereignty of the earth to Cronus.

However, no sooner did Cronus find himself in supreme command than he confined the Cyclopes to Tartarus again together with the

Hundred-handed Ones and, taking his sister Rhea to wife, ruled in Elis.[1]

> 1. Hesiod: *Theogony* 133–87 and 616–23; Apollodorus: i. 1. 4–5; Servius on Virgil's *Aeneid* v. 801.

*

1. Hesiod, who records this myth, was a Cadmeian, and the Cadmeians came from Asia Minor (see 59. 5), probably on the collapse of the Hittite Empire, bringing with them the story of Uranus's castration. It is known, however, that the myth was not of Hittite composition, since an earlier Hurrian (Horite) version has been discovered. Hesiod's version may reflect an alliance between the various pre-Hellenic settlers in Southern and Central Greece, whose dominant tribes favoured the Titan cult, against the early Hellenic invaders from the north. Their war was successful, but they thereupon claimed suzerainty over the northern natives, whom they had freed. The castration of Uranus is not necessarily metaphorical if some of the victors had originated in East Africa where, to this day, Galla warriors carry a miniature sickle into battle to castrate their enemies; there are close affinities between East African religious rites and those of early Greece.

2. The later Greeks read 'Cronus' as *Chronos*, 'Father Time' with his relentless sickle. But he is pictured in the company of a crow, like Apollo, Asclepius, Saturn, and the early British god Bran; and *cronos* probably means 'crow', like the Latin *cornix* and the Greek *coróne*. The crow was an oracular bird, supposed to house the soul of a sacred king after his sacrifice (see 25. 5 and 50. 1).

3. Here the three Erinnyes, or Furies, who sprang from the drops of Uranus's blood, are the Triple-goddess herself; that is to say, during the king's sacrifice, designed to fructify the cornfields and orchards, her priestesses will have worn menacing Gorgon masks to frighten away profane visitors. His genitals seem to have been thrown into the sea, to encourage fish to breed. The vengeful Erinnyes are understood by the mythographer as warning Zeus not to emasculate Cronus with the same sickle; but it was their original function to avenge injuries inflicted only on a mother, or a suppliant who claimed the protection of the Hearth-goddess (see 105. k, 107. d, and 113. a), not on a father.

4. The ash-nymphs are the Three Furies in more gracious mood: the sacred king was dedicated to the ash-tree, originally used in rain-making ceremonies (see 57. 1). In Scandinavia it became the tree of universal magic; the Three Norns, or Fates, dispensed justice under an ash which Odin, on claiming the fatherhood of mankind, made his magical steed. Women must have been the first rain-makers in Greece as in Libya.

5. Neolithic sickles of bone, toothed with flint or obsidian, seem to

have continued in ritual use long after their supersession as agricultural instruments by sickles of bronze and iron.

6. The Hittites make Kumarbi (Cronus) bite off the genitals of the Sky-god Anu (Uranus), swallow some of the seed, and spit out the rest on Mount Kansura where it grows into a goddess; the God of Love thus conceived by him is cut from his side by Anu's brother Ea. These two births have been combined by the Greeks into a tale of how Aphrodite rose from a sea impregnated by Uranus's severed genitals (see 10. *b*). Kumarbi is subsequently delivered of another child drawn from his thigh – as Dionysus was reborn from Zeus (see 27. *b*) – who rides a storm-chariot drawn by a bull, and comes to Anu's help. The 'knife that separated the the earth from the sky' occurs in the same story, as the weapon with which Kumarbi's son, the earth-born giant Ullikummi, is destroyed (see 35. 4).

# 7

## THE DETHRONEMENT OF CRONUS

CRONUS married his sister Rhea, to whom the oak is sacred.[1] But it was prophesied by Mother Earth, and by his dying father Uranus, that one of his own sons would dethrone him. Every year, therefore, he swallowed the children whom Rhea bore him: first Hestia, then Demeter and Hera, then Hades, then Poseidon.[2]

*b.* Rhea was enraged. She bore Zeus, her third son, at dead of night on Mount Lycaeum in Arcadia, where no creature casts a shadow[3] and, having bathed him in the River Neda, gave him to Mother Earth; by whom he was carried to Lyctos in Crete, and hidden in the cave of Dicte on the Aegean Hill. Mother Earth left him there to be nursed by the Ash-nymph Adrasteia and her sister Io, both daughters of Melisseus, and by the Goat-nymph Amaltheia. His food was honey, and he drank Amaltheia's milk, with Goat-Pan, his foster-brother. Zeus was grateful to these three nymphs for their kindness and, when he became Lord of the Universe, set Amaltheia's image among the stars, as Capricorn.[4] He also borrowed one of her horns, which resembled a cow's, and gave it to the daughters of Melisseus; it became the famous Cornucopia, or horn of plenty, which is always filled with whatever food or drink its owner may desire. But some say that Zeus was suckled by a sow, and rode on her back, and that he lost his navel-string at Omphalion near Cnossus.[5]

*c.* Around the infant Zeus's golden cradle, which was hung upon a tree (so that Cronus might find him neither in heaven, not on earth, nor in the sea) stood the armed Curetes, Rhea's sons. They clashed their spears against their shields, and shouted to drown the noise of his wailing, lest Cronus might hear it from far off. For Rhea had wrapped a stone in swaddling clothes, which she gave to Cronus on Mount Thaumasium in Arcadia; he swallowed it, believing that he was swallowing the infant Zeus. Nevertheless, Cronus got wind of what had happened and pursued Zeus, who transformed himself into a serpent and his nurses into bears: hence the constellations of the Serpent and the Bears.[6]

*d.* Zeus grew to manhood among the shepherds of Ida, occupying another cave; then sought out Metis the Titaness, who lived beside the Ocean stream. On her advice he visited his mother Rhea, and asked to be made Cronus's cup-bearer. Rhea readily assisted him in his task of vengeance; she provided the emetic potion, which Metis had told him to mix with Cronus's honeyed drink. Cronus, having drunk deep, vomited up first the stone, and then Zeus's elder brothers and sisters. They sprang out unhurt and, in gratitude, asked him to lead them in a war against the Titans, who chose the gigantic Atlas as their leader; for Cronus was now past his prime.[7]

*e.* The war lasted ten years but, at last, Mother Earth prophesied victory to her grandson Zeus, if he took as allies those whom Cronus had confined in Tartarus; so he came secretly to Campe, the old gaoleress of Tartarus, killed her, took her keys and, having released the Cyclopes and the Hundred-handed Ones, strengthened them with divine food and drink. The Cyclopes thereupon gave Zeus the thunderbolt as a weapon of offence; and Hades, a helmet of darkness; and Poseidon, a trident. After the three brothers had held a counsel of war, Hades entered unseen into Cronus's presence, to steal his weapons; and, while Poseidon threatened him with the trident and thus diverted his attention, Zeus struck him down with the thunderbolt. The three Hundred-handed Ones now took up rocks and pelted the remaining Titans, and a sudden shout from Goat-Pan put them to flight. The gods rushed in pursuit. Cronus, and all the defeated Titans, except Atlas, were banished to a British island in the farthest west (or, some say, confined in Tartarus), and guarded there by the Hundred-handed Ones; they never troubled Hellas again. Atlas, as their war-leader, was awarded an exemplary punishment, being ordered to carry the sky on his shoulders; but the Titanesses were spared, for the sake of Metis and Rhea.[8]

*f.* Zeus himself set up at Delphi the stone which Cronus had disgorged. It is still there, constantly anointed with oil, and strands of unwoven wool are offered upon it.[9]

*g.* Some say that Poseidon was neither eaten nor disgorged, but that Rhea gave Cronus a foal to eat in his stead, and hid him among the horseherds.[10] And the Cretans, who are liars, relate that Zeus is born every year in the same cave with flashing fire and a stream of blood; and that every year he dies and is buried.[11]

1. Scholiast on Apollonius Rhodius: i. 1124.
2. Apollodorus: i. 1. 5; Hesiod: *Theogony* 453–67.
3. Polybius: xvi. 12. 6 ff.; Pausanias: viii. 38. 5.
4. Hyginus: *Poetic Astronomy* ii. 13; Aratus: *Phenomena* 163; Hesiod: *loc. cit.*
5. Philemon: *Pterygium Fragment* i.1 ff.; Apollodorus: i. 1. 6; Athenaeus: 375f. and 376a; Callimachus: *Hymn to Zeus* 42.
6. Hesiod: 485 ff.; Apollodorus: i. 1. 7; First Vatican Mythographer: 104; Callimachus: *Hymn to Zeus* 52 ff.; Lucretius: ii. 633–9; Scholiast on Aratus: v. 46; Hyginus: *Fabula* 139 .
7. Hyginus: *loc. cit.*; Apollodorus: *loc. cit.*; Hesiod: *loc. cit.*
8. Hesiod: *loc. cit.*; Hyginus: *Fabula* 118; Apollodorus: i. 1. 7 and i. 2. 1; Callimachus: *Hymn to Zeus* 52 ff.; Diodorus Siculus: v. 70; Eratosthenes: *Catasterismoi* 27; Pausanias: viii. 8. 2; Plutarch: *Why Oracles Are Silent* 16.
9. Pausanias: x. 24. 5.
10. *Ibid.*: viii. 8. 2.
11. Antoninus Liberalis: *Transformations* 19; Callimachus: *Hymn to Zeus* 8.

*

1. Rhea, paired with Cronus as Titaness of the seventh day, may be equated with Dione, Diana, the Triple-goddess of the Dove and Oak cult (see 11. 2). The bill-hook carried by Saturn, Cronus's Latin counterpart, was shaped like a crow's bill and apparently used in the seventh month of the sacred thirteen-month year to emasculate the oak by lopping off the mistletoe (see 50. 2), just as a ritual sickle was used to reap the first ear of corn. This gave the signal for the sacred Zeus-king's sacrifice; and at Athens, Cronus, who shared a temple with Rhea, was worshipped as the Barley-god Sabazius, annually cut down in the cornfield and bewailed like Osiris or Lityerses or Maneros (see 136. *e*). But, by the times to which these myths refer, kings had been permitted to prolong

their reigns to a Great Year of one hundred lunations, and offer annual boy victims in their stead; hence Cronus is pictured as eating his own sons to avoid dethronement. Porphyry (*On Abstinence* ii. 56) records that the Cretan Curetes used to offer child sacrifices to Cronus in ancient times.

2. In Crete a kid was early substituted for a human victim; in Thrace, a bull-calf; among the Aeolian worshippers of Poseidon, a foal; but in backward districts of Arcadia boys were still sacrificially eaten even in the Christian era. It is not clear whether the Elean ritual was cannibalistic or whether, Cronus being a Crow-Titan, sacred crows fed on the slaughtered victim.

3. Amaltheia's name, 'tender', shows her to have been a maidengoddess; Io was an orgiastic nymph-goddess (see 56. *1*); Adrasteia means 'the Inescapable One', the oracular Crone of autumn. Together they formed the usual Moon-triad. The later Greeks identified Adrasteia with the pastoral goddess Nemesis, of the rain-making ash-tree, who had become a goddess of vengeance (see 32. *2*). Io was pictured at Argos as a white cow in heat – some Cretan coins from Praesus show Zeus suckled by her – but Amaltheia, who lived on 'Goat Hill', was always a she-goat; and Melisseus ('honey-man'), Adrasteia and Io's reputed father, is really their mother – Melissa, the goddess as Queen-bee, who annually killed her male consort. Diodorus Siculus (v. 70) and Callimachus (*Hymn to Zeus* 49) both make bees feed the infant Zeus. But his foster-mother is sometimes also pictured as a sow, because that was one of the Cronegoddesses's, emblems (see 74. *4* and 96. *2*); and on Cydonian coins she is a bitch, like the one that suckled Neleus (see 68. *d*). The she-bears are Artemis's beasts (see 22. *4* and 80. *c*) – the Curetes attended her holocausts – and Zeus as serpent is Zeus Ctesius, protector of store-houses, because snakes got rid of mice.

4. The Curetes were the sacred king's armed companions, whose weapon-clashing was intended to drive off evil spirits during ritual performances (see 30. *a*). Their name, understood by the later Greeks as 'young men who have shaved their hair', probably meant 'devotees of Ker, or Car', a widespread title of the Triple-goddess (see 57. *2*). Heracles won his cornucopia from the Achelous bull (see 142. *d*), and the enormous size of the Cretan wild-goat's horns have led mythographers unacquainted with Crete to give Amaltheia an anomalous cow's horn.

5. Invading Hellenes seem to have offered friendship to the pre-Hellenic people of the Titan-cult, but gradually detached their subjectallies from them, and overrun the Peloponnese. Zeus's victory in alliance with the Hundred-handed Ones over the Titans of Thessaly is said by Thallus, the first-century historian, quoted by Tatian in his *Address to the Greeks*, to have taken place '322 years before the seige of Troy': that is to say 1505 B.C., a plausible date for an extension of Hellenic power in Thes-

saly. The bestowal of sovereignty on Zeus recalls a similar event in the Babylonian Creation Epic, when Marduk was empowered to fight Tiamat by his elders Lahmu and Lahamu.

6. The brotherhood of Hades, Poseidon, and Zeus recalls that of the Vedic male trinity – Mitra, Varuna, and Indra – (see 3. 1 and 132. 5) who appear in a Hittite treaty dated to about 1380 B.C. – but in this myth they seem to represent three successive Hellenic invasions, commonly known as Ionian, Aeolian, and Achaean. The pre-Hellenic worshippers of the Mother-goddess assimilated the Ionians, who became children of Io; tamed the Aeolians; but were overwhelmed by the Achaeans. Early Hellenic chieftains who became sacred kings of the oak and ash cults took the titles 'Zeus' and 'Poseidon', and were obliged to die at the end of their set reigns (see 45. 2). Both these trees tend to attract lightning, and therefore figure in popular rain-making and fire-making ceremonies throughout Europe.

7. The victory of the Achaeans ended the tradition of royal sacrifices. They ranked Zeus and Poseidon as immortals; picturing both as armed with the thunderbolt – a flint double-axe, once wielded by Rhea, and in the Minoan and Mycenaean religions withheld from male use (see 131. 6). Later, Poseidon's thunderbolt was converted into a three-pronged fish-spear, his chief devotees having turned seafarers; whereas Zeus retained his as a symbol of supreme sovereignty. Poseidon's name, which was sometimes spelt Potidan, may have been borrowed from that of his goddess-mother, after whom the city Potidaea was called: 'the water-goddess of Ida' – Ida meaning any wooded mountain. That the Hundred-handed Ones guarded the Titans in the Far West may mean that the Pelasgians, among whose remnants were the Centaurs of Magnesia – centaur is perhaps cognate with the Latin centuria, 'a war-band of one hundred' – did not abandon their Titan cult, and continued to believe in a Far Western Paradise, and in Atlas's support of the firmament.

8. Rhea's name is probably a variant of Era, 'earth'; her chief bird was the dove, her chief beast the mountain-lion. Demeter's name means 'Barley-mother'; Hestia (see 20. c) is the goddess of the domestic hearth. The stone at Delphi, used in rain-making ceremonies, seems to have been a large meteorite.

9. Dicte and Mount Lycaeum were ancient seats of Zeus worship. A fire sacrifice was probably offered on Mount Lycaeum, when no creature cast a shadow – that is to say, at noon on midsummer day; but Pausanias adds that though in Ethiopia while the sun is in Cancer men do not throw shadows, this is invariably the case on Mount Lycaeum. He may be quibbling: nobody who trespassed in this precinct was allowed to live (Aratus: Phenomena 91), and it was well known that the dead cast no shadows (Plutarch: Greek Questions 39). The cave of Psychro, usually

regarded as the Dictaean Cave, is wrongly sited to be the real one, which has not yet been discovered. Omphalion ('little navel') suggests the site of an oracle (see 20. 2).

*10.* Pan's sudden shout which terrified the Titans became proverbial and has given the word 'panic' to the English language (see 26. *c*).

# 8

## THE BIRTH OF ATHENE

ACCORDING to the Pelasgians, the goddess Athene was born beside Lake Tritonis in Libya, where she was found and nurtured by the three nymphs of Libya, who dress in goat-skins.[1] As a girl she killed her playmate, Pallas, by accident, while they were engaged in friendly combat with spear and shield and, in token of grief, set Pallas's name before her own. Coming to Greece by way of Crete, she lived first in the city of Athenae by the Boeotian River Triton.[2]

1. Apollonius Rhodius: iv. 1310.
2. Apollodorus: iii. 12. 3; Pausanias: ix. 33. 5.

*

1. Plato identified Athene, patroness of Athens, with the Libyan goddess Neith, who belonged to an epoch when fatherhood was not recognized (see 1. *1*). Neith had a temple at Saïs, where Solon was treated well merely because he was an Athenian (Plato: *Timaeus* 5). Virgin-priestesses of Neith engaged annually in armed combat (Herodotus: iv. 180), apparently for the position of High-priestess. Apollodorus's account (iii. 12. 3) of the fight between Athene and Pallas is a late patriarchal version: he says that Athene, born of Zeus and brought up by the River-god Triton, accidentally killed her foster-sister Pallas, the River Triton's daughter, because Zeus interposed his aegis when Pallas was about to strike Athene, and so distracted her attention. The aegis, however, a magical goat-skin bag containing a serpent and protected by a Gorgon mask, was Athene's long before Zeus claimed to be her father (see 9. *d*). Goat-skin aprons were the habitual costume of Libyan girls, and *Pallas* merely means 'maiden', or 'youth'. Herodotus writes (iv. 189): 'Athene's garments and aegis were borrowed by the Greeks from the Libyan women, who are dressed in exactly the same way, except that their leather garments are fringed with thongs, not serpents.' Ethiopian girls still wear this costume, which

is sometimes ornamented with cowries, a yonic symbol. Herodotus adds here that the loud cries of triumph, *olulu, ololu*, uttered in honour of Athene above (*Iliad* vi. 297-301) were of Libyan origin. *Tritone* means 'the third queen': that is, the eldest member of the triad – mother of the maiden who fought Pallas, and of the nymph into which she grew – just as Core-Persephone was Demeter's daughter (see 24. 3).

2. Pottery finds suggest a Libyan immigration into Crete as early as 4000 B.C.; and a large number of goddess-worshipping Libyan refugees from the Western Delta seem to have arrived there when Upper and Lower Egypt were forcibly united under the First Dynasty about the year 3000 B.C. The First Minoan Age began soon afterwards, and Cretan culture spread to Thrace and Early Helladic Greece.

3. Among other mythological personages named Pallas was the Titan who married the River Styx and fathered on her Zelus ('zeal'), Cratus ('strength'), Bia ('force'), and Nicë ('victory') (Hesiod: *Theogony* 376 and 383; Pausanias: vii. 26. 5; Apollodorus: 2. 2-4); he was perhaps an allegory of the Pelopian dolphin sacred to the Moon-goddess (see 108. 5). Homer calls another Pallas 'the father of the moon' (*Homeric Hymn to Hermes* 100). A third begot the fifty Pallantids, Theseus's enemies (see 97. g and 99. a), who seem to have been originally fighting priestesses of Athene. A fourth was described as Athene's father (see 9. a).

# 9

## ZEUS AND METIS

SOME Hellenes say that Athene had a father named Pallas, a winged goatish giant, who later attempted to outrage her, and whose name she added to her own after stripping him of his skin to make the aegis, and of his wings for her own shoulders;[1] if, indeed, the aegis was not the skin of Medusa the Gorgon, whom she flayed after Perseus had decapitated her.[2]

b. Others say that her father was one Itonus, a king of Iton in Phthiotis, whose daughter Iodama she killed by accidentally letting her see the Gorgon's head,[3] and so changing her into a block of stone, when she trespassed in the precinct at night.

c. Still others say that Poseidon was her father, but that she disowned him and begged to be adopted by Zeus, which he was glad to do.[4]

*d*. But Athene's own priests tell the following story of her birth. Zeus lusted after Metis the Titaness, who turned into many shapes to escape him until she was caught at last and got with child. An oracle of Mother Earth then declared that this would be a girl-child and that, if Metis conceived again, she would bear a son who was fated to depose Zeus, just as Zeus had deposed Cronus, and Cronus had deposed Uranus. Therefore, having coaxed Metis to a couch with honeyed words, Zeus suddenly opened his mouth and swallowed her, and that was the end of Metis, though he claimed afterwards that she gave him counsel from inside his belly. In due process of time, he was seized by a raging headache as he walked by the shores of Lake Triton, so that his skull seemed about to burst, and he howled for rage until the whole firmament echoed. Up ran Hermes, who at once divined the cause of Zeus's discomfort. He persuaded Hephaestus, or some say Prometheus, to fetch his wedge and beetle and make a breach in Zeus's skull, from which Athene sprang, fully armed, with a mighty shout.[5]

1. Tzetzes: *On Lycophron* 355.
2. Euripides: *Ion* 995.
3. Pausanias: ix. 34. 1.
4. Herodotus: iv. 180.
5. Hesiod: *Theogony* 886–900; Pindar: *Olympian Odes* vii. 34 ff.; Apollodorus: i. 3. 6.

\*

1. J. E. Harrison rightly described the story of Athene's birth from Zeus's head as 'a desperate theological expedient to rid her of her matriarchal conditions.' It is also a dogmatic insistence on wisdom as a male prerogative; hitherto the goddess alone had been wise. Hesiod has, in fact, managed to reconcile three conflicting views in his story:

1. Athene, the Athenians' city-goddess, was the parthenogenous daughter of the immortal Metis, Titaness of the fourth day and of the planet Mercury, who presided over all wisdom and knowledge.
2. Zeus swallowed Metis, but did not thereby lose wisdom (i.e. the Achaeans suppressed the Titan cult, and ascribed all wisdom to their god Zeus).
3. Athene was the daughter of Zeus (i.e. the Achaeans insisted that the Athenians must acknowledge Zeus's patriarchal overlordship).

He has borrowed the mechanism of his myth from analogous examples:

Zeus pursuing Nemesis (see 32. *b*); Cronus swallowing his sons and daughters (see 7. *a*); Dionysus's rebirth from Zeus's thigh (see 14. *c*); and the opening of Mother Earth's head by two men with axes, apparently in order to release Core (see 24. *3*) – as shown for instance, on a black-figured oil-jar in the Bibliothèque Nationale at Paris. Thereafter, Athene is Zeus's obedient mouthpiece, and deliberately suppresses her ante-cedents. She employs priests, not priestesses.

2. Pallas, meaning 'maiden', is an inappropriate name for the winged giant whose attempt on Athene's chastity is probably deduced from a picture of her ritual marriage, as Athene Laphria, to a goat-king (see 89. *4*) after an armed contest with her rival (see 8. *1*). This Libyan custom of goat-marriage spread to Northern Europe as part of the May Eve merry-makings. The Akan, a Libyan people, once flayed their kings.

3. Athene's repudiation of Poseidon's fatherhood concerns an early change in the overlordship of the city of Athens (see 16. *3*).

4. The myth of Itonus ('willow-man') represents a claim by the Itonians that they worshipped Athene even before the Athenians did; and his name shows that she had a willow cult in Phthiotis – like that of her counterpart, the goddess Anatha, at Jerusalem until Jehovah's priests ousted her and claimed the rain-making willow as his tree at the Feast of Tabernacles.

5. It will have been death for a man to remove an aegis – the goat-skin chastity-tunic worn by Libyan girls – without the owner's consent; hence the prophylactic Gorgon mask set above it, and the serpent con-cealed in the leather pouch, or bag. But since Athene's aegis is described as a shield, I suggest in *The White Goddess* (p. 279) that it was a bag-cover for a sacred disk, like the one which contained Palamedes's alphabetical secret, and which he is said to have invented (see 52. *a* and 162. *5*). Cyrian figurines holding disks of the same proportionate size as the famous Phaestos one, which is spirally marked with a sacred legend, are held by Professor Richter to anticipate Athene and her aegis. The heroic shields so carefully described by Homer and Hesiod seem to have borne pictographs engraved on a spiral band.

6. Iodama, probably meaning 'heifer calf of Io', will have been an antique stone image of the Moon-goddess (see 56. *1*), and the story of her petrification is a warning to inquisitive girls against violating the Mysteries (see 25. *d*).

7. It would be a mistake to think of Athene as solely or predominantly the goddess of Athens. Several ancient acropolises were sacred to her, including Argos (Pausanias: ii. 24. 3), Sparta (*ibid*.: 3. 17. 1), Troy (*Iliad* vi. 88), Smyrna (Strabo: iv. 1. 4), Epidaurus (Pausanias: ii. 32. 5), Troezen (Pausanias: iii. 23. 10), and Pheneus (Pausanias: x. 38. 5). All these are pre-Hellenic sites.

# 10

## THE FATES

THERE are three conjoined Fates, robed in white, whom Erebus begot on Night: by name Clotho, Lachesis, and Atropos. Of these, Atropos is the smallest in stature, but the most terrible.[1]

b. Zeus, who weighs the lives of men and informs the Fates of his decisions can, it is said, change his mind and intervene to save whom he pleases, when the thread of life, spun on Clotho's spindle, and measured by the rod of Lachesis, is about to be snipped by Atropos's shears. Indeed, men claim that they themselves can, to some degree, control their own fates by avoiding unnecessary dangers. The younger gods, therefore, laugh at the Fates, and some say that Apollo once mischievously made them drunk in order to save his friend Admetus from death.[2]

c. Others hold, on the contrary, that Zeus himself is subject to the Fates, as the Pythian priestess once confessed in an oracle; because they are not his children, but parthenogenous daughters of the Great Goddess Necessity, against whom not even the gods contend, and who is called 'The Strong Fate'.[3]

d. At Delphi only two Fates are worshipped, those of Birth and Death; and at Athens Aphrodite Urania is called the eldest of the three.[4]

1. Homer: *Iliad* xxiv. 49; *Orphic Hymn* xxxiii; Hesiod: *Theogony* 217 ff. and 904, *Shield of Heracles* 259.
2. Homer: *Iliad* viii. 69 and xxii. 209; xvi. 434 and 441-3; Virgil: *Aeneid* x. 814; Homer: *Odyssey* i. 34; *Iliad* ix. 411.
3. Aeschylus: *Prometheus* 511 and 515; Herodotus: i. 91; Plato: *Republic* x. 14-16; Simonides: viii. 20.
4. Pausanias: x. 24. 4 and i. 19. 2.

*

1. This myth seems to be based on the custom of weaving family and clan marks into a newly-born child's swaddling bands, and so allotting him his place in society (see 60. 2); but the Moerae, or Three Fates, are the Triple Moon-goddess – hence their white robes, and the linen thread which is sacred to her as Isis. Clotho is the 'spinner', Lachesis the 'measurer', Atropos is 'she who cannot be turned, or avoided'. *Moera* means

'a share' or 'a phase', and the moon has three phases and three persons: the new, the Maiden-goddess of the spring, the first period of the year; the full moon, the Nymph-goddess of the summer, the second period; and the old moon, the Crone-goddess of autumn, the last period (see 60. *2*).

2. Zeus called himself 'The Leader of the Fates' when he assumed supreme sovereignty and the prerogative of measuring man's life; hence, probably, the disappearance of Lachesis, 'the measurer', at Delphi. But his claim to be their father was not taken seriously by Aeschylus, Herodotus, or Plato.

3. The Athenians called Aphrodite Urania 'the eldest of the Fates' because she was the Nymph-goddess, to whom the sacred king had, in ancient times, been sacrificed at the summer solstice. 'Urania' means 'queen of the mountains' (see 19. *3*).

# II

## THE BIRTH OF APHRODITE

APHRODITE, Goddess of Desire, rose naked from the foam of the sea and, riding on a scallop shell, stepped ashore first on the island of Cythera; but finding this only a small island, passed on to the Peloponnese, and eventually took up residence at Paphos, in Cyprus, still the principal seat of her worship. Grass and flowers sprang from the soil wherever she trod. At Paphos, the Seasons, daughters of Themis, hastened to clothe and adorn her.

b. Some hold that she sprang from the foam which gathered about the genitals of Uranus, when Cronus threw them into the sea; others, that Zeus begot her on Dione, daughter either of Oceanus and Tethys the sea-nymph, or of Air and Earth. But all agree that she takes the air accompanied by doves and sparrows.[1]

> 1. Hesiod: *Theogony* 188–200 and 353; Festus Grammaticus: iii. 2; *Homeric Hymn to Aphrodite* ii. 5; Apollodorus: i. 1. 3.

*

1. Aphrodite ('foam-born') is the same wide-ruling goddess who rose from Chaos and danced on the sea, and who was worshipped in Syria and Palestine as Ishtar, or Ashtaroth (see 1. *1*). Her most famous centre of

worship was Paphos, where the original white aniconic image of the
goddess is still shown in the ruins of a grandiose Roman temple; there
every spring her priestess bathed in the sea, and rose again renewed.

2. She is called daughter of Dione, because Dione was the goddess of
the oak-tree, in which the amorous dove nested (see 51. *a*). Zeus claimed
to be her father after seizing Dione's oracle at Dodona, and Dione therefore became her mother. 'Tethys' and 'Thetis' are names of the goddess
as Creatrix (formed, like 'Themis' and 'Theseus', from *tithenai*, 'to
dispose' or 'to order'), and as Sea-goddess, since life began in the sea
(see 2. *a*). Doves and sparrows were noted for their lechery; and sea food
is still regarded as aphrodisiac throughout the Mediterranean.

3. Cythera was an important centre of Cretan trade with the Peloponnese, and it will have been from here that her worship first entered
Greece. The Cretan goddess had close associations with the sea. Shells
carpeted the floor of her palace sanctuary at Cnossus; she is shown on a
gem from the Idean Cave blowing a triton-shell, with a sea-anemone
lying beside her altar; the sea-urchin and cuttle-fish (see 81. *1*) were sacred
to her. A triton-shell was found in her early sanctuary at Phaestus, and
many more in late Minoan tombs, some of these being terracotta
replicas.

# 12

## HERA AND HER CHILDREN

HERA, daughter of Cronus and Rhea, having been born on the island
of Samos or, some say, at Argos, was brought up in Arcadia by
Temenus, son of Pelasgus. The Seasons were her nurses.[1] After banish-
ing their father Cronus, Hera's twin-brother Zeus sought her out at
Cnossus in Crete or, some say, on Mount Thornax (now called Cuckoo
Mountain) in Argolis, where he courted her, at first unsuccessfully.
She took pity on him only when he adopted the disguise of a bedraggled
cuckoo, and tenderly warmed him in her bosom. There he at once
resumed his true shape and ravished her, so that she was shamed into
marrying him.[2]

b. All the gods brought gifts to the wedding; notably Mother Earth
gave Hera a tree with golden apples, which was later guarded by the
Hesperides in Hera's orchard on Mount Atlas. She and Zeus spent their
wedding night on Samos, and it lasted three hundred years. Hera

bathes regularly in the spring of Canathus, near Argos, and thus renews her virginity.[3]

c. To Hera and Zeus were born the deities Ares, Hephaestus, and Hebe, though some say that Ares and his twin-sister Eris were conceived when Hera touched a certain flower, and Hebe when she touched a lettuce,[4] and that Hephaestus also was her parthenogenous child – a wonder which he would not believe until he had imprisoned her in a mechanical chair with arms that folded about the sitter, thus forcing her to swear by the River Styx that she did not lie. Others say that Hephaestus was her son by Talos, the nephew of Daedalus.[5]

1. Pausanias: vii. 4. 4 and viii. 22. 2; Strabo: ix. 2. 36; Olen, quoted by Pausanias: ii. 13. 3.
2. Diodorus Siculus: v. 72; Pausanias ii. 36. 2 and 17. 4.
3. Scholiast on Homer's *Iliad* i. 609; Pausanias: ii. 38. 2.
4. Homer: *Iliad* iv. 441; Ovid: *Fasti* v. 255; First Vatican Mythographer: 204.
5. Servius on Virgil's *Eclogues* iv. 62; Cinaethon, quoted by Pausanias: viii. 53. 2.

*

1. Hera's name, usually taken to be a Greek word for 'lady', may represent an original Herwā ('Protectress'). She is the pre-Hellenic Great Goddess. Samos and Argos were the chief seats of her worship in Greece, but the Arcadians claimed that their cult was the earliest, and made it contemporary with their earth-born ancestor Pelasgus ('ancient'). Hera's forced marriage to Zeus commemorates conquests of Crete and Mycenaean – that is to say Cretanized – Greece, and the overthrow of her supremacy in both countries. He probably came to her disguised as a bedraggled cuckoo, in the sense that certain Hellenes who came to Crete as fugitives accepted employment in the royal guard, made a palace conspiracy and seized the kingdom. Cnossus was twice sacked, apparently by Hellenes; about 1700 B.C., and about 1400 B.C.; and Mycenae fell to the Achaeans a century later. The God Indra in the Ramayana had similarly wooed a nymph in cuckoo disguise; and Zeus now borrowed Hera's sceptre, which was surmounted with the cuckoo. Gold-leaf figurines of a naked Argive goddess holding cuckoos have been found at Mycenae; and cuckoos perch on a gold-leaf model temple from the same site. In the well-known Cretan sarcophagus from Hagia Triada a cuckoo perches on a double-axe.

2. Hebe, the goddess as child, was made cup-bearer to the gods in the Olympian cult. She eventually married Heracles (see 145. *i* and *5*), after Ganymedes had usurped her office (see 29. *c*). 'Hephaestus' seems to have

been a title of the sacred king as solar demi-god; 'Ares', a title of his war-chief, or tanist, whose emblem was the wild boar. Both became divine names when the Olympian cult was established and they were chosen to fill the roles, respectively, of War-god and Smith-god. The 'certain flower' is likely to have been the may-blossom: Ovid makes the goddess Flora – with whose worship the may-blossom was associated – point it out to Hera. The may, or whitethorn, is connected with miraculous conception in popular European myth: in Celtic literature its 'sister' is the blackthorn, a symbol of Strife – Ares's twin, Eris.

3. Talos, the smith, was a Cretan hero born to Daedalus's sister Perdix ('partridge'), with whom the mythographer is identifying Hera. Partridges, sacred to the Great Goddess, figured in the spring equinox orgies of the Eastern Mediterranean, when a hobbling dance was performed in imitation of cock-partridges. The hens were said by Aristotle, Pliny, and Aelian to conceive merely by hearing the cock's voice. Hobbling Hephaestus and Talos seem to be the same parthenogenous character; and both were cast down from a height by angry rivals (see 23. *b* and 92. *b*) – originally in honour of their goddess-mother.

4. In Argos, Hera's famous statue was seated on a throne of gold and ivory; the story of her imprisonment in a chair may have arisen from the Greek custom of chaining divine statues to their thrones 'to prevent escape'. By losing an ancient statue of its god or goddess, a city might forfeit divine protection, and the Romans, therefore, made a practice of what was politely called 'enticing' gods to Rome – which by Imperial times had become a jackdaw's nest of stolen images. 'The Seasons were her nurses' is one way of saying that Hera was a goddess of the calendar year. Hence the spring cuckoo on her sceptre, and the ripe pomegranate of late autumn, which she carried in her left hand to symbolize the death of the year.

5. A hero, as the word indicates, was a sacred king who had been sacrificed to Hera, whose body was safely under the earth, and whose soul had gone to enjoy her paradise at the back of the North Wind. His golden apples, in Greek and Celtic myth, were passports to this paradise (see 53. 7, 133. 4, and 159. 3).

6. The annual bath with which Hera renewed her virginity was also taken by Aphrodite at Paphos; it seems to have been the purification ceremony prescribed to a Moon-priestess after the murder of her lover, the sacred king (see 22. *1* and 150. *1*). Hera, being the goddess of the vegetative year, spring, summer and autumn (also symbolized by the new, full, and old moon) was worshipped at Stymphalus as Child, Bride, and Widow (Pausanias: vii. 22. 2 – see 128. *d*).

7. The wedding-night on Samos lasted for three hundred years: perhaps became the Samian sacred year, like the Etruscan one, consisted of

ten thirty-day months only: with January and February omitted (Macrobius: i. 13). Each day was lengthened to a year. But the mythographer may here be hinting that it took the Hellenes three hundred years before they forced monogamy on Hera's people.

# 13

## ZEUS AND HERA

ONLY Zeus, the Father of Heaven, might wield the thunderbolt; and it was with the threat of its fatal flash that he controlled his quarrelsome and rebellious family of Mount Olympus. He also ordered the heavenly bodies, made laws, enforced oaths, and pronounced oracles. When his mother Rhea, foreseeing what trouble his lust would cause, forbade him to marry, he angrily threatened to violate her. Though she at once turned into a menacing serpent, this did not daunt Zeus, who became a male serpent and, twining about her in an indissoluble knot, made good his threat.[1] It was then that he began his long series of adventures in love. He fathered the Seasons and the Three Fates on Themis; the Charites on Eurynome; the Three Muses on Mnemosyne, with whom he lay for nine nights; and, some say, Persephone, the Queen of the Underworld, whom his brother Hades forcibly married, on the nymph Styx.[2] Thus he lacked no power either above or below earth; and his wife Hera was equal to him in one thing alone: that she could still bestow the gift of prophecy on any man or beast she pleased.[3]

*b.* Zeus and Hera bickered constantly. Vexed by his infidelities, she often humiliated him by her scheming ways. Though he would confide his secrets to her, and sometimes accept her advice, he never fully trusted Hera, and she knew that if offended beyond a certain point he would flog or even hurl a thunderbolt at her. She therefore resorted to ruthless intrigue, as in the matter of Heracles's birth; and sometimes borrowed Aphrodite's girdle, to excite his passion and thus weaken his will. He now claimed to be Cronus's first-born son.[4]

*c.* A time came when Zeus's pride and petulance became so intolerable that Hera, Poseidon, Apollo, and all the other Olympians, except Hestia, surrounded him suddenly as he lay asleep on his couch and bound him with rawhide thongs, knotted into a hundred knots, so that he could not move. He threatened them with instant death, but they had placed his thunderbolt out of reach and laughed insultingly at him. While they were celebrating their victory, and jealously discussing who was to be his successor, Thetis the Nereid, foreseeing a civil war on Olympus, hurried in search of the hundred-handed Briareus, who swiftly untied the thongs, using every hand at once, and released his master. Because it was Hera who had led the conspiracy against him, Zeus hung her up from the sky with a golden bracelet about either wrist and an anvil fastened to either ankle. The other deities were vexed beyond words, but dared attempt no rescue for all her piteous cries. In the end Zeus undertook to free her if they swore never more to rebel against him; and this each in turn grudgingly did. Zeus punished Poseidon and Apollo by sending them as bond-servants to King Laomedon, for whom they built the city of Troy; but he pardoned the others as having acted under duress.[5]

1. *Orphic Fragment* 58; Hesiod: *Theogony* 56.
2. Apollodorus: i. 3. 1–2.
3. Homer: *Iliad* xix. 407.
4. *Ibid.*: i. 547; xvi. 458; viii. 407–8; xv. 17; viii. 397–404; xiv. 197–223; xv. 166.
5. Scholiast on Homer's *Iliad* xxi. 444; Tzetzes: *On Lycophron* 34; Homer: *Iliad* i. 399 ff. and xv. 18–22.

*

1. The marital relations of Zeus and Hera reflect those of the barbarous Dorian Age, when women had been deprived of all their magical power, except that of prophecy, and come to be regarded as chattels. It is possible that the occasion on which the power of Zeus was saved only by Thetis and Briareus, after the other Olympians had conspired against him, was a palace revolution by vassal princes of the Hellenic High King, who nearly succeeded in dethroning him; and that help came from a company of loyal non-Hellenic household troops, recruited in Macedonia, Briareus's home, and from a detachment of Magnesians, Thetis's people. If so, the conspiracy will have been instigated by the High-priestess of Hera, whom the High King subsequently humiliated, as the myth describes.

2. Zeus's violation of the Earth-goddess Rhea implies that the Zeus-worshipping Hellenes took over all agricultural and funerary ceremonies. She had forbidden him to marry, in the sense that hitherto monogamy had been unknown; women took whatever lovers they pleased. His fatherhood of the Seasons, on Themis, means that the Hellenes also assumed control of the calendar: Themis ('order') was the Great Goddess who ordered the year of thirteen months, divided by the summer and winter solstices into two seasons. At Athens these seasons were personified

as Thallo and Carpo (originally 'Carpho'), which mean respectively 'sprouting' and 'withering', and their temple contained an altar to the phallic Dionysus (see 27. 5). They appear in a rock-carving at Hattusas, or Pteria, where they are twin aspects of the Lion-goddess Hepta, borne on the wings of a double-headed Sun-eagle.

3. Charis ('grace') had been the Goddess in the disarming aspect she presented when the High-priestess chose the sacred king as her lover. Homer mentions two Charites – Pasithea and Cale, which seems to be a forced separation of three words: *Pasi thea cale*, 'the Goddess who is beautiful to all men'. The two Charites, Auxo ('increase') and Hegemone ('mastery'), whom the Athenians honoured, corresponded with the two Seasons. Later, the Charites were worshipped as a triad, to match the Three Fates – the Triple-goddess in her most unbending mood (see 106. 3). That they were Zeus's children, born to Eurynome the Creatrix, implies that the Hellenic overlord had power to dispose of all marriageable young women.

4. The Muses ('mountain goddesses'), originally a triad (Pausanias: ix. 19. 2), are the Triple-goddess in her orgiastic aspect. Zeus's claim to be their father is a late one; Hesiod calls them daughters of Mother Earth and Air.

# 14

## BIRTHS OF HERMES, APOLLO, ARTEMIS, AND DIONYSUS

AMOROUS Zeus lay with numerous nymphs descended from the Titans or the gods and, after the creation of man, with mortal women too; no less than four great Olympian deities were born to him out of wedlock. First, he begat Hermes on Maia, daughter of Atlas, who bore him in a cave on Mount Cyllene in Arcadia. Next, he begat Apollo and Artemis on Leto, daughter of the Titans Coeus and Phoebe, transforming himself and her into quails when they coupled;[1] but jealous Hera sent the serpent Python to pursue Leto all over the world, and decreed that she should not be delivered in any place where the sun shone. Carried on the wings of the South Wind, Leto at last came to Ortygia, close to Delos, where she bore Artemis, who was no sooner born than she helped her mother across the narrow straits, and there, between an olive-tree and a date-palm growing on the north side of Delian Mount

Cynthus, delivered her of Apollo on the ninth day of labour. Delos,
hitherto a floating island, became immovably fixed in the sea and, by
decree, no one is now allowed either to be born or to die there: sick
folk and pregnant women are ferried over to Ortygia instead.[2]

*b.* The mother of Zeus's son Dionysus is variously named: some say
that she was Demeter, or Io;[3] some name her Dione; some, Persephone,
with whom Zeus coupled in the likeness of a serpent; and some, Lethe.[4]

*c.* But the common story runs as follows. Zeus, disguised as a mortal,
had a secret love affair with Semele ('moon'), daughter of King Cadmus of Thebes, and jealous Hera, disguising herself as an old neighbour,
advised Semele, then already six months with child, to make her mysterious lover a request: that he would no longer deceive her, but reveal
himself in his true nature and form. How, otherwise, could she know
that he was not a monster? Semele followed this advice and, when
Zeus refused her plea, denied him further access to her bed. Then, in
anger, he appeared as thunder and lightning, and she was consumed.
But Hermes saved her six-months son; sewed him up inside Zeus's
thigh, to mature there for three months longer; and, in due course of
time, delivered him. Thus Dionysus is called 'twice-born', or 'the
child of the double door'.[5]

1. Hesiod: *Theogony* 918; Apollodorus: i. 4. 1; Aristophanes: *Birds*
   870; Servius on Virgil's *Aeneid* iii. 72.
2. *Homeric Hymn to Apollo* 14 ff.; Hyginus: *Fabula* 140; Aelian:
   *Varia Historia* v. 4; Thucydides: iii. 104; Strabo: x. 5.5.
3. Diodorus Siculus: iii. 67 and 74; iv. 4.
4. Scholiast on Pindar's *Pythian Odes* iii. 177; *Orphic Fragment* 59;
   Plutarch: *Symposiacs* vii. 5.
5. Apollodorus: iii. 4. 3; Apollonius Rhodius: iv. 1137.

*

1. Zeus's rapes apparently refer to Hellenic conquests of the goddess's
ancient shrines, such as that on Mount Cyllene; his marriages, to an
ancient custom of giving the title 'Zeus' to the sacred king of the oak cult.
Hermes, his son by the rape of Maia – a title of the Earth-goddess as
Crone – was originally not a god, but the totemistic virtue of a phallic
pillar, or cairn. Such pillars were the centre of an orgiastic dance in the
goddess's honour.

2. One component in Apollo's godhead seems to have been an oracular
mouse – Apollo Smintheus ('Mouse-Apollo') is among his earliest titles
(see 158. 2) – consulted in a shrine of the Great Goddess, which perhaps

explains why he was born where the sun never shone, namely underground. Mice were associated with disease and its cure, and the Hellenes therefore worshipped Apollo as a god of medicine and prophecy; afterwards saying that he was born under an olive-tree and a date-palm on the north side of a mountain. They called him a twin-brother of Artemis Goddess of Childbirth, and made his mother Leto – the daughter of the Titans Phoebe ('moon') and Coeus ('intelligence') – who was known in Egypt and Palestine as Lat, fertility-goddess of the date-palm and olive: hence her conveyance to Greece by a South Wind. In Italy she became Latona ('Queen Lat'). Her quarrel with Hera suggests a conflict between early immigrants from Palestine and native tribes who worshipped a different Earth-goddess; the mouse cult, which she seems to have brought with her, was well established in Palestine (1 *Samuel* vi. 4 and *Isaiah* lxvi. 17). Python's pursuit of Apollo recalls the use of snakes in Greek and Roman houses to keep down mice. But Apollo was also the ghost of the sacred king who had eaten the apple – the word *Apollo* may be derived from the root *abol*, 'apple', rather than from *apollunai*, 'destroy', which is the usual view.

3. Artemis, originally an orgiastic goddess, had the lascivious quail as her sacred bird. Flocks of quail will have made Ortygia a resting-place on their way north during the spring migration. The story that Delos, Apollo's birthplace, had hitherto been a floating island (see 43. 4) may be a misunderstanding of a record that his birthplace was now officially fixed: since in Homer (*Iliad* iv. 101) he is called Lycegenes, 'born in Lycia'; and the Ephesians boasted that he was born at Ortygia near Ephesus (Tacitus: *Annals* iii. 61). Both the Boeotian Tegyrans and the Attic Zosterans also claimed him as a native son (Stephanus of Byzantium *sub* Tegyra).

4. Dionysus began, probably, as a type of sacred king whom the goddess ritually killed with a thunderbolt in the seventh month from the winter solstice, and whom her priestesses devoured (see 27. 3). This explains his mothers: Dione, the Oak-goddess; Io and Demeter, Corngoddesses; and Persephone, Death-goddess. Plutarch, when calling him 'Dionysus, a son of Lethe ("forgetfulness")', refers to his later aspect as God of the Vine.

5. The story of Semele, daughter of Cadmus, seems to record the summary action taken by Hellenese of Boeotia in ending the tradition of royal sacrifice: Olympian Zeus asserts his power, takes the doomed king under his own protection, and destroys the goddess with her own thunderbolt. Dionysus thus becomes an immortal, after rebirth from his immortal father. Semele was worshipped at Athens during the *Lenaea*, the Festival of the Wild Women, when a yearly bull, representing Dionysus, was cut into nine pieces and sacrificed to her: one piece being burned, the

remainder eaten raw by the worshippers. *Semele* is usually explained as a form of Selene ('moon'), and nine was the traditional number of orgiastic moon-priestesses who took part in such feasts – nine such are shown dancing around the sacred king in a cave painting at Cogul, and nine more killed and devoured St Samson of Dol's acolyte in medieval times.

# 15

## THE BIRTH OF EROS

SOME argue that Eros, hatched from the world-egg, was the first of the gods since, without him, none of the rest could have been born; they make him coeval with Mother Earth and Tartarus, and deny that he had any father or mother, unless it were Eileithyia, Goddess of Childbirth.[1]

*b.* Others hold that he was Aphrodite's son by Hermes, or by Ares, or by her own father, Zeus; or the son of Iris by the West Wind. He was a wild boy, who showed no respect for age or station but flew about on golden wings, shooting barbed arrows at random or wantonly setting hearts on fire with his dreadful torches.[2]

1. *Orphic Hymn* v; Aristotle: *Metaphysics* i. 4; Hesiod: *Theogony* 120; Meleager: *Epigrams* 50; Olen, quoted by Pausanias: ix. 27. 2.
2. Cicero: *On the Nature of the Gods* iii. 23; Virgil: *Ciris* 134; Alcaeus, quoted by Plutarch: *Amatorius* 20.

*

1. Eros ('sexual passion') was a mere abstraction to Hesiod. The early Greeks pictured him as a *Ker*, or winged 'Spite', like Old Age, or Plague, in the sense that uncontrolled sexual passion could be disturbing to ordered society. Later poets, however, took a perverse pleasure in his antics and, by the time of Praxiteles, he had become sentimentalized as a beautiful youth. His most famous shrine was at Thespiae, where the Boeotians worshipped him as a simple phallic pillar – the pastoral Hermes, or Priapus, under a different name (see 150. *a*). The various accounts of his parentage are self-explanatory. Hermes was a phallic god; and Ares, as a god of war, increased desire in the warrior's womenfolk. That Aphrodite was Eros's mother and Zeus his father is a hint that sexual passion does not stop short at incest; his birth from the Rainbow and the West Wind is a lyrical fancy. Eileithyia, 'she who comes to the aid of women in

childbed', was a title of Artemis; the meaning being that there is no love so strong as mother-love.

2. Eros was never considered a sufficiently responsible god to figure among the ruling Olympian family of Twelve.

# 16

## POSEIDON'S NATURE AND DEEDS

WHEN Zeus, Poseidon, and Hades, after deposing their father Cronus, shook lots in a helmet for the lordship of the sky, sea, and murky underworld, leaving the earth common to all, Zeus won the sky, Hades the underworld, and Poseidon the sea. Poseidon, who is equal to his brother Zeus in dignity, though not in power, and of a surly, quarrelsome nature, at once set about building his under-water palace off Aegae in Euboea. In its spacious stables he keeps white chariot horses with brazen hooves and golden manes, and a golden chariot at the approach of which storms instantly cease and sea-monsters rise, frisking, around it.[1]

b. Needing a wife who would be at home in the sea-depths, he courted Thetis the Nereid; but when it was prophesied by Themis that any son born to Thetis would be greater than his father, he desisted, and allowed her to marry a mortal named Peleus. Amphitrite, another Nereid, whom he next approached, viewed his advances with repugnance, and fled to the Atlas Mountains to escape him; but he sent messengers after her, among them one Delphinus, who pleaded Poseidon's cause so winningly that she yielded, and asked him to arrange the marriage. Gratefully, Poseidon set Delphinus's image among the stars as a constellation, the Dolphin.[2]

Amphitrite bore Poseidon three children: Triton, Rhode, and Benthesicyme; but he caused her almost as much jealousy as Zeus did Hera by his love affairs with goddesses, nymphs, and mortals. Especially she loathed his infatuation with Scylla, daughter of Phorcys, whom she changed into a barking monster with six heads and twelve feet by throwing magical herbs into her bathing pool.[3]

c. Poseidon is greedy of earthly kingdoms, and once claimed possession of Attica by thrusting his trident into the acropolis at Athens, where a well of sea-water immediately gushed out and is still to be seen; when the South Wind blows you may hear the sound of the surf far below. Later, during the reign of Cecrops, Athene came and took possession in a gentler manner, by planting the first olive-tree beside the well. Poseidon, in a fury, challenged her to single combat, and Athene would have accepted had not Zeus interposed and ordered them to submit the dispute to arbitration. Presently, then, they appeared before a divine court, consisting of their supernal fellow-deities, who called on Cecrops to give evidence. Zeus himself expressed no opinion, but while all the other gods supported Poseidon, all the goddesses supported Athene. Thus, by a majority of one, the court ruled that Athene had the better right to the land, because she had given it the better gift.

*d.* Greatly vexed, Poseidon sent huge waves to flood the Thriasian Plain, where Athene's city of Athenae stood, whereupon she took up her abode in Athens instead, and called that too after herself. However, to appease Poseidon's wrath, the women of Athens were deprived of their vote, and the men forbidden to bear their mothers' names as hitherto.[4]

*e.* Poseidon also disputed Troezen with Athene; and on this occasion Zeus issued an order for the city to be shared equally between them – an arrangement disagreeable to both. Next, he tried unsuccessfully to claim Aegina from Zeus, and Naxos from Dionysus; and in a claim for Corinth with Helius received the Isthmus only, while Helius was awarded the Acropolis. In fury, he tried to seize Argolis from Hera, and was again ready to fight, refusing to appear before his Olympian peers who, he said, were prejudiced against him. Zeus, therefore, referred the matter to the River-gods Inachus, Cephissus, and Asterion, who judged in Hera's favour. Since he had been forbidden to revenge himself with a flood as before, he did exactly the opposite: he dried up his judges' streams so that they now never flow in summer. However, for the sake of Amymone, one of the Danaids who were distressed by this drought, he caused the Argive river of Lerna to flow perpetually.[5]

*f.* He boasts of having created the horse, though some say that, when he was newly born, Rhea gave one to Cronus to eat; and of having invented the bridle, though Athene had done so before him; but his claim to have instituted horse-racing is not disputed. Certainly, horses are sacred to him, perhaps because of his amorous pursuit of Demeter, when she was tearfully seeking her daughter Persephone. It is said that

Demeter, wearied and disheartened by her search, and disinclined for passionate dalliance with any god or Titan, transformed herself into a mare, and began to graze with the herd of one Oncus, a son of Apollo's who reigned in Arcadian Onceium. She did not, however, deceive Poseidon, who transformed himself into a stallion and covered her, from which outrageous union sprang the nymph Despoena and the wild horse Arion. Demeter's anger was so hot that she is still worshipped locally as 'Demeter the Fury'.[6]

1. Homer: *Iliad* xv. 187–93; viii. 210–11; xiii. 21–30; *Odyssey* v. 381; Apollonius Rhodius: iii. 1240.
2. Apollonius: iii. 13. 5; Hyginus: *Poetic Astronomy* ii. 17.
3. Tzetzes: *On Lycophron* 45 and 50.
4. Herodotus: viii. 55; Apollodorus: iii. 14. 1; Pausanias: 24. 3; Augustine: *On the City of God* xviii. 9; Hyginus: *Fabula* 164.
5. Pausanias: ii. 30. 6; Plutarch: *Symposiacs* ix. 6; Pausanias: ii. 1. 6; ii. 15.5; ii. 22. 5.
6. Pindar: *Pythian Odes* vi. 50; Pausanias: viii. 25. 3–5; Apollodorus: iii. 6. 8.

\*

1. Thetis, Amphitrite, and Nereis were different local titles of the Triple Moon-goddess as ruler of the sea; and since Poseidon was the Father-god of the Aeolians, who had taken to the sea, he claimed to be her husband wherever she found worshippers. Peleus married Thetis on Mount Pelion (see 81. *l*). Nereis means 'the wet one', and Amphitrite's name refers to the 'third element', the sea, which is cast about earth, the first element, and above which rises the second element, air. In the Homeric poems Amphitrite means simply 'the sea'; she is not personified as Poseidon's wife. Her reluctance to marry Poseidon matches Hera's reluctance to marry Zeus, and Persephone's to marry Hades; the marriage involved the interference of male priests with female control of the fishing industry. The fable of Delphinus is sentimental allegory: dolphins appear when the sea grows calm. Amphitrite's children were herself in triad: Triton, lucky new moon; Rhode, full harvest-moon; and Benthesicyme, dangerous old moon. But Triton has since become masculinized. Aegae stood on the sheltered Boeotian side of Euboea and served as a port for Orchomenus; and it was hereabouts that the naval expedition mustered against Troy.

2. The story of Amphitrite's vengeance on Scylla is paralleled in that of Pasiphaë's vengeance on another Scylla (see 91. *2*). Scylla ('she who rends' or 'puppy') is merely a disagreeable aspect of herself: the dog-headed Death-goddess Hecate (see 31. *f*), who was at home both on land and in the waves. A seal impression from Cnossus shows her threatening

a man in a boat, as she threatened Odysseus in the Straits of Messina (see 170. *t*). The account quoted by Tzetzes seems to have been mistakenly deduced from an ancient vase-painting in which Amphitrite stands beside a pool occupied by a dog-headed monster; on the other side of the vase is a drowned hero caught between two dog-headed triads of goddesses at the entrance to the Underworld (see 31. *a* and 134. *1*).

3. Poseidon's attempts to take possession of certain cities are political myths. His dispute over Athens suggests an unsuccessful attempt to make him the city's tutelary deity in place of Athene. Yet her victory was impaired by a concession to patriarchy: the Athenians abandoned the Cretan custom which prevailed in Caria until Classical times (Herodotus: i. 173) when they ceased to take their mother's names. Varro, who gives this detail, represents the trial as a plebiscite of all the men and women of Athens.

It is plain that the Ionian Pelasgians of Athens were defeated by the Aeolians, and that Athene regained her sovereignty only by alliance with Zeus's Achaeans, who later made her disown Poseidon's paternity and admit herself reborn from Zeus's head.

4. The cultivated olive was originally imported from Libya, which supports the myth of Athene's Libyan origin; but what she brought will have been only a cutting – the cultivated olive does not breed true, but must always be grafted on the oleaster, or wild olive. Her tree was still shown at Athens during the second century A.D. The flooding of the Thriasian Plain is likely to be a historical event, but cannot be dated. It is possible that early in the fourteenth century B.C., which meteorologists reckon to have been a period of maximum rainfall, the rivers of Arcadia never ran dry, and that their subsequent shrinking was attributed to the vengeance of Poseidon. Pre-Hellenic Sun-worship at Corinth is well established (Pausanias: ii. 4. 7 – see 67. 2).

5. The myth of Demeter and Poseidon records a Hellenic invasion of Arcadia. Demeter was pictured at Phigalia as the mare-headed patroness of the pre-Hellenic horse cult. Horses were sacred to the moon, because their hooves make a moon-shaped mark, and the moon was regarded as the source of all water; hence the association of Pegasus with springs of water (see 75. *b*). The early Hellenes introduced a larger breed of horse into Greece from Trans-Caspia, the native variety having been about the size of a Shetland pony and unsuitable for chariotry. They seem to have seized the centres of the horse cult, where their warrior-kings forcibly married the local priestesses and thus won a title to the land; incidentally suppressing the wild-mare orgies (see 72. 4). The sacred horses Arion and Despoena (this being a title of Demeter herself) were then claimed as Poseidon's children. Amymone may have been a name for the goddess at Lerna, the centre of the Danaid water cult (see 60. *g* and 4).

6. Demeter as Fury, like Nemesis as Fury (see 32. 3), was the goddess in her annual mood of murder; and the story also told of Poseidon and Demeter at Thelpusia (Pausanias; viii. 42), and of Poseidon and an un-named Fury at the fountain of Tilphusa in Boeotia (Scholiast on Homer's *Iliad* xxiii. 346) was already old when the Hellenes came. It appears in early Indian sacred literature, where Saranyu turns herself into a mare, Vivaswat becomes a stallion and covers her; and the fruit of this union are the two heroic Asvins. 'Demeter Erinnys' may, in fact, have stood not for 'Demeter the Fury', but for 'Demeter Saranyu' – an attempted reconciliation of the two warring cultures; but to the resentful Pelasgians Demeter was, and remained, outraged.

# 17

## HERMES'S NATURE AND DEEDS

WHEN Hermes was born on Mount Cyllene his mother Maia laid him in swaddling bands on a winnowing fan, but he grew with astonishing quickness into a little boy, and as soon as her back was turned, slipped off and went looking for adventure. Arrived at Pieria, where Apollo was tending a fine herd of cows, he decided to steal them. But, fearing to be betrayed by their tracks, he quickly made a number of shoes from the bark of a fallen oak and tied them with plaited grass to the feet of the cows, which he then drove off by night along the road. Apollo dis-covered the loss, but Hermes's trick deceived him, and though he went as far as Pylus in his westward search, and to Onchestus in his eastern, he was forced, in the end, to offer a reward for the apprehension of the thief. Silenus and his satyrs, greedy of reward, spread out in different directions to track him down but, for a long while, without success. At last, as a party of them passed through Arcadia, they heard the muffled sound of music such as they had never heard before, and the nymph Cyllene, from the mouth of a cave, told them that a most gifted child had recently been born there, to whom she was acting as nurse: he had constructed an ingenious musical toy from the shell of a tortoise and some cow-gut, with which he had lulled his mother to sleep.

b. 'And from whom did he get the cow-gut?' asked the alert satyrs, noticing two hides stretched outside the cave. 'Do you charge the poor child with theft?' asked Cyllene. Harsh words were exchanged.

*c.* At that moment Apollo came up, having discovered the thief's identity by observing the suspicious behaviour of a long-winged bird. Entering the cave, he awakened Maia and told her severely that Hermes must restore the stolen cows. Maia pointed to the child, still wrapped in his swaddling bands and feigning sleep. 'What an absurd charge!' she cried. But Apollo had already recognized the hides. He picked up Hermes, carried him to Olympus, and there formally accused him of theft, offering the hides as evidence. Zeus, loth to believe that his own new-born son was a thief, encouraged him to plead not guilty, but Apollo would not be put off and Hermes, at last, weakened and confessed.

'Very well, come with me,' he said, 'and you may have your herd. I slaughtered only two, and those I cut up into twelve equal portions as a sacrifice to the twelve gods.'

'*Twelve* gods?' asked Apollo. 'Who is the twelfth?'

'Your servant, sir,' replied Hermes modestly. 'I ate no more than my share, though I was very hungry, and duly burned the rest.'

Now, this was the first flesh-sacrifice ever made.

*d.* The two gods returned to Mount Cyllene, where Hermes greeted his mother and retrieved something that he had hidden underneath a sheepskin.

'What have you there?' asked Apollo.

In answer, Hermes showed his newly-invented tortoise-shell lyre, and played such a ravishing tune on it with the plectrum he had also invented, at the same time singing in praise of Apollo's nobility, intelligence, and generosity, that he was forgiven at once. He led the surprised and delighted Apollo to Pylus, playing all the way, and there gave him the remainder of the cattle, which he had hidden in a cave.

'A bargain!' cried Apollo. 'You keep the cows, and I take the lyre.'

'Agreed,' said Hermes, and they shook hands on it.

*e.* While the hungry cows were grazing, Hermes cut reeds, made them into a shepherd's pipe, and played another tune. Apollo, again delighted, cried: 'A bargain! If you give me that pipe, I will give you this golden staff with which I herd my cattle; in future you shall be the god of all herdsmen and shepherds.'

'My pipe is worth more than your staff,' replied Hermes. 'But I will make the exchange, if you teach me augury too, because it seems to be a most useful art.'

'I cannot do that,' Apollo said, 'but if you go to my old nurses, the Thriae who live on Parnassus, they will teach you how to divine from pebbles.'

*f.* They again shook hands and Apollo, taking the child back to Olympus, told Zeus all that had happened. Zeus warned Hermes that henceforth he must respect the rights of property and refrain from telling downright lies; but he could not help being amused. 'You seem to be a very ingenious, eloquent, and persuasive godling,' he said.

'Then make me your herald, Father,' Hermes answered, 'and I will be responsible for the safety of all divine property, and never tell lies, though I cannot promise always to tell the whole truth.'

'That would not be expected of you,' said Zeus, with a smile. 'But your duties would include the making of treaties, the promotion of commerce, and the maintenance of free rights of way for travellers on any road in the world.' When Hermes agreed to these conditions, Zeus gave him a herald's staff with white ribbons, which everyone was ordered to respect; a round hat against the rain, and winged golden sandals which carried him about with the swiftness of wind. He was at once welcomed into the Olympian family, whom he taught the art of making fire by the rapid twirling of the fire-stick.

*g.* Afterwards, the Thriae showed Hermes how to foretell the future from the dance of pebbles in a basin of water; and he himself invented both the game of knuckle-bones and the art of divining by them. Hades also engaged him as his herald, to summon the dying gently and eloquently, by laying the golden staff upon their eyes.[1]

*h.* He then assisted the Three Fates in the composition of the Alphabet, invented astronomy, the musical scale, the arts of boxing and gymnastics, weights and measures (which some attribute to Palamedes), and the cultivation of the olive-tree.[2]

*i.* Some hold that the lyre invented by Hermes had seven strings; others, that it had three only, to correspond with the seasons, or four to correspond with the quarters of the year, and that Apollo brought the number up to seven.[3]

*j.* Hermes had numerous sons, including Echion the Argonauts' herald; Autolycus the thief; and Daphnis the inventor of bucolic poetry. This Daphnis was a beautiful Sicilian youth whom his mother, a nymph, exposed in a laurel grove on the Mountain of Hera; hence the name given him by the shepherds, his foster parents. Pan taught him to play the pipes; he was beloved by Apollo, and used to hunt with Artemis, who took pleasure in his music. He lavished great care on his many herds of cattle, which were of the same stock as Helius's. A nymph named Nomia made him swear never to be unfaithful to her, on pain of being blinded; but her rival, Chimaera, contrived to seduce him when he was drunk, and Nomia blinded him in fulfilment of her threat. Daphnis consoled himself for a while with sad lays about the loss of sight, but he did not live long. Hermes turned him into a stone, which is still shown at the city of Cephalenitanum; and caused a fountain called Daphnis to gush up at Syracuse, where annual sacrifices are offered.[4]

1. *Homeric Hymn to Hermes* 1–543; Sophocles: *Fragments of The Trackers*; Apollodorus: iii. 10. 2.
2. Diodorus Siculus: v. 75; Hyginus: *Fabula* 277; Plutarch: *Symposiacs* ix. 3.
3. *Homeric Hymn to Hermes* 51; Diodorus Siculus: i. 16; Macrobius: *Saturnaliorum Conviviorum* i. 19; Callimachus: *Hymn to Delos* 253.
4. Diodorus Siculus: iv. 84; Servius on Virgil's *Eclogues* v. 20; viii. 68; x. 26; Philargyrius on Virgil's *Eclogues* v. 20; Aelian: *Varia Historia* x. 18.

*

1. The myth of Hermes's childhood has been preserved in a late literary form only. A tradition of cattle raids made by the crafty Messenians on their neighbours (see 74. *g* and 171. *h*), and of a treaty by which these were discontinued, seems to have been mythologically combined with an account of how the barbarous Hellenes took over and exploited, in the name of their adopted god Apollo, the Creto-Helladic civilization which they found in Central and Southern Greece – boxing, gymnastics, weights and measures, music, astronomy, and olive culture were all pre-Hellenic (see 162. *6*) – and learned polite manners.

2. Hermes was evolved as a god from the stone phalli which were local centres of a pre-Hellenic fertility cult (see 15. *1*) – the account of his rapid growth may be Homer's playful obscenity – but also from the Divine Child of the pre-Hellenic Calendar (see 24. *6*, 44. *1*, 105. *1*, 171. *4*, etc.); from the Egyptian Thoth, God of Intelligence; and from Anubis, conductor of souls to the Underworld.

3. The heraldic white ribbons on Hermes's staff were later mistaken for serpents, because he was herald to Hades; hence Echion's name. The Thriae are the Triple-Muse ('mountain goddess') of Parnassus, their divination by means of dancing pebbles was also practised at Delphi

(Mythographi Graeci: *Appendix Narrationum* 67). Athene was first credited with the invention of divinatory dice made from knuckle-bones (Zenobius: *Proverbs* v. 75), and these came into popular use; but the art of augury remained an aristocratic prerogative both in Greece and at Rome. Apollo's 'long-winged bird' was probably Hermes's own sacred crane; for the Apollonian priesthood constantly trespassed on the territory of Hermes, an earlier patron of soothsaying, literature, and the arts; as did the Hermetic priesthood on that of Pan, the Muses, and Athene. The invention of fire-making was ascribed to Hermes, because the twirling of the male drill in the female stock suggested phallic magic.

4. Silenus and his sons, the satyrs,, were conventional comic characters in the Attic drama (see 83. 5); originally they had been primitive mountaineers of Northern Greece. He was called an autochthon, or a son of Pan by one of the nymphs (Nonnus; *Dionysiaca* xiv. 97; xxix. 262; Aelian: *Varia Historia* iii. 18).

5. The romantic story of Daphnis has been built around a phallic pillar at Cephalenitanum, and a fountain at Syracuse, each probably surrounded by a laurel grove, where songs were sung in honour of the sightless dead. Daphnis was said to be beloved by Apollo because he had taken the laurel from the orgiastic goddess of Tempe (see 21. 6).

# 18

## APHRODITE'S NATURE AND DEEDS

APHRODITE could seldom be persuaded to lend the other goddesses her magic girdle which made everyone fall in love with its wearer; for she was jealous of her position. Zeus had given her in marriage to Hephaestus, the lame Smith-god; but the true father of the three children with whom she presented him – Phobus, Deimus, and Harmonia – was Ares, the straight-limbed, impetuous, drunken, and quarrelsome God of War. Hephaestus knew nothing of the deception until, one night, the lovers stayed too long together in bed at Ares's Thracian palace; then Helius, as he rose, saw them at their sport and told tales to Hephaestus.

*b.* Hephaestus angrily retired to his forge, and hammered out a bronze hunting-net, as fine as gossamer but quite unbreakable, which he secretly attached to the posts and sides of his marriage-bed. He told Aphrodite who, returned from Thrace, all smiles, explaining that she

had been away on business at Corinth: 'Pray excuse me, dear wife, I
am taking a short holiday on Lemnos, my favourite island.' Aphrodite
did not offer to accompany him and, when he was out of sight, sent
hurriedly for Ares, who soon arrived. The two went merrily to bed
but, at dawn, found themselves entangled in the net, naked and unable
to escape. Hephaestus, turning back from his journey, surprised them
there, and summoned all the gods to witness his dishonour. He then
announced that he would not release his wife until the valuable
marriage-gifts which he had paid her adoptive father, Zeus, were
restored to him.

*c.* Up ran the gods, to watch Aphrodite's embarrassment; but the
goddesses, from a sense of delicacy, stayed in their houses. Apollo,
nudging Hermes, asked: 'You would not mind being in Ares's position,
would you, net and all?'

Hermes swore by his own head, that he would not, even if there were
three times as many nets, and all the goddesses were looking on with
disapproval. At this, both gods laughed uproariously, but Zeus was so
disgusted that he refused to hand back the marriage-gifts, or to interfere
in a vulgar dispute between a husband and wife, declaring that Hephaestus was a fool to have made the affair public. Poseidon who, at
sight of Aphrodite's naked body, had fallen in love with her, concealed
his jealousy of Ares, and pretended to sympathize with Hephaestus.
'Since Zeus refuses to help,' he said, 'I will undertake that Ares, as a fee
for his release, pays the equivalent of the marriage-gifts in question.'

'That is all very well,' Hephaestus replied gloomily. 'But if Ares
defaults, you will have to take his place under the net.'

'In Aphrodite's company?' Apollo asked, laughing.

'I cannot think that Ares will default,' Poseidon said nobly. 'But if he
should do so, I am ready to pay the debt and marry Aphrodite myself.'

So Ares was set at liberty, and returned to Thrace; and Aphrodite
went to Paphos, where she renewed her virginity in the sea.[1]

*d.* Flattered by Hermes's frank confession of his love for her, Aphrodite presently spent a night with him, the fruit of which was Hermaphroditus, a double-sexed being; and, equally pleased by Poseidon's
intervention on her behalf, she bore him two sons, Rhodus and Hero-
philus.[2] Needless to say, Ares defaulted, pleading that if Zeus would
not pay, why should he? In the end, nobody paid, because Hephaestus
was madly in love with Aphrodite and had no real intention of divor-
cing her.

*e.* Later, Aphrodite yielded to Dionysus, and bore him Priapus; an ugly child with enormous genitals – it was Hera who had given him this obscene appearance, in disapproval of Aphrodite's promiscuity. He is a gardener and carries a pruning-knife.[3]

*f.* Though Zeus never lay with his adopted daughter Aphrodite, as some say that he did, the magic of her girdle put him under constant temptation, and at last he decided to humiliate her by making her fall desperately in love with a mortal. This was the handsome Anchises, King of the Dardanians, a grandson of Ilus and, one night, when he was asleep in his herdsman's hut on Trojan Mount Ida, Aphrodite visited him in the guise of a Phrygian princess, clad in a dazzlingly red robe, and lay with him on a couch spread with the skins of bears and lions, while bees buzzed drowsily about them. When they parted at dawn, she revealed her identity, and made him promise not to tell anyone that she had slept with him. Anchises was horrified to learn that he had uncovered the nakedness of a goddess, and begged her to spare his life. She assured him that he had nothing to fear, and that their son would be famous.[4] Some days later, while Anchises was drinking with his companions, one of them asked: 'Would you not rather sleep with the daughter of So-and-so than with Aphrodite herself?' 'No,' he replied unguardedly. 'Having slept with both, I find the question inept.'

*g.* Zeus overheard this boast, and threw a thunderbolt at Anchises, which would have killed him outright, had not Aphrodite interposed her girdle, and thus diverted the bolt into the ground at his feet. Nevertheless, the shock so weakened Anchises that he could never stand upright again, and Aphrodite, after bearing his son Aeneas, soon lost her passion for him.[5]

*h.* One day, the wife of King Cinyras the Cyprian – but some call him King Phoenix of Byblus, and some King Theias the Assyrian – foolishly boasted that her daughter Smyrna was more beautiful even than Aphrodite. The goddess avenged this insult by making Smyrna fall in love with her father and climb into his bed one dark night, when her nurse had made him too drunk to realize what he was doing. Later, Cinyras discovered that he was both the father and grandfather of Smyrna's unborn child and, wild with wrath, seized a sword and chased her from the palace. He overtook her on the brow of a hill, but Aphrodite hurriedly changed Smyrna into a myrrh-tree, which the descending sword split in halves. Out tumbled the infant Adonis. Aphrodite, already repenting of the mischief that she had made, concealed Adonis in a chest, which she entrusted to Persephone, Queen of the Dead, asking her to stow it away in a dark place.

*i.* Persephone had the curiosity to open the chest, and found Adonis inside. He was so lovely that she lifted him out and brought him up in her own palace. The news reached Aphrodite, who at once visited Tartarus to claim Adonis; and when Persephone would not assent, having by now made him her lover, she appealed to Zeus. Zeus, well aware that Aphrodite also wanted to lie with Adonis, refused to judge so unsavoury a dispute; and transferred it to a lower court, presided over by the Muse Calliope. Calliope's verdict was that Persephone and Aphrodite had equal claims on Adonis – Aphrodite for arranging his birth, Persephone for rescuing him from the chest – but that he should be allowed a brief annual holiday from the amorous demands of both these insatiable goddesses. She therefore divided the year into three equal parts, of which he was to spend one with Persephone, one with Aphrodite, and the third by himself.

Aphrodite did not play fair: by wearing her magic girdle all the time, she persuaded Adonis to give her his own share of the year, grudge the share due to Persephone, and disobey the court-order.[6]

*j.* Persephone, justly aggrieved, went to Thrace, where she told her benefactor Ares that Aphrodite now preferred Adonis to himself. 'A mere mortal,' she cried, 'and effeminate at that!' Ares grew jealous and, disguised as a wild boar, rushed at Adonis who was out hunting on Mount Lebanon, and gored him to death before Aphrodite's eyes. Anemones sprang from his blood, and his soul descended to Tartarus. Aphrodite went tearfully to Zeus, and pleaded that Adonis should not have to spend more than the gloomier half of the year with Persephone, but might be her companion for the summer months. This Zeus magnanimously granted. But some say that Apollo was the boar, and revenged himself for an injury Aphrodite had done him.[7]

*k.* Once, to make Adonis jealous, Aphrodite spent several nights at Lilybaeum with Butes the Argonaut; and by him became the mother of Eryx, a king of Sicily. Her children by Adonis were one son, Golgos, founder of Cyprian Golgi, and a daughter, Beroë, founder of Beroea in Thrace; and some say that Adonis, not Dionysus, was the father of her son Priapus.[8]

*l.* The Fates assigned to Aphrodite one divine duty only, namely to make love; but one day, Athene catching her surreptitiously at work on a loom, complained that her own prerogatives had been infringed and threatened to abandon them altogether. Aphrodite apologized profusely, and has never done a hand's turn of work since.[9]

1. Homer: *Odyssey* viii. 266–367.
2. Diodorus Siculus: iv. 6; Scholiast on Pindar's *Pythian Odes* viii. 24.
3. Pausanias: ix. 31. 2; Scholiast on Apollonius Rhodius: i. 932.
4. *Homeric Hymn to Aphrodite* 45–200; Theocritus: *Idylls* i. 105–7; Hyginus: *Fabula* 94.
5. Servius on Virgil's *Aeneid* ii. 649.
6. Apollodorus: iii. 14. 3–4; Hyginus: *Poetic Astronomy* ii. 7 and *Fabulae* 58, 164, 251; Fulgentius: *Mythology* iii. 8.
7. Servius on Virgil's *Eclogues* x. 18; *Orphic Hymn* lv. 10; Ptolemy Hephaestionos: i. 306.
8. Apollonius Rhodius: iv. 914–19; Diodorus Siculus: iv. 83; Scholiast on Theocruitus's *Idylls* xv. 100; Tzetzes: *On Lycophron* 831.
9. Hesiod: *Theogony* 203–4; Nonnus: *Dionysiaca* xxiv. 274–81.

*

1. The later Hellenes belittled the Great Goddess of the Mediterranean who had long been supreme at Corinth, Sparta, Thespiae, and Athens, by placing her under male tutelage and regarding her solemn sex-orgies as adulterous indiscretions. The net in which Homer represents Aphrodite as caught by Hephaestus was, originally, her own as Goddess of the Sea (see 89. *2*), and her priestess seems to have worn it during the spring carnival; the priestess of the Norse Goddess Holle, or Gode, did the same on May Eve.

2. Priapus originated in the rude wooden phallic images which presided over Dionysian orgies. He is made a son of Adonis because of the miniature 'gardens' offered at his festivals. The pear-tree was sacred to Hera as prime goddess of the Peloponnese, which was therefore called Apia (see 64. *4* and 74. *6*).

3. Aphrodite Urania ('queen of the mountain') or Erycina ('of the heather') was the nymph-goddess of midsummer. She destroyed the sacred king, who mated with her on a mountain top, as a queen-bee destroys the drone: by tearing out his sexual organs. Hence the heather-loving bees and the red robe in her mountain-top affair with Anchises; hence also the worship of Cybele, the Phrygian Aphrodite of Mount Ida, as a queen-bee, and the ecstatic self-castration of her priests in memory of her lover Attis (see 79. *1*). Anchises was one of the many sacred kings who were struck with a ritual thunderbolt after consorting with the Death-in-Life Goddess (see 24. *a*). In the earliest version of the myth he was killed, but in later ones he escaped: to make good the story of how pious Aeneas, who brought the sacred Palladium to Rome, carried his father away from burning Troy (see 168. *c*). His name identifies Aphrodite with Isis, whose

husband Osiris, was castrated by Set disguised as a boar; 'Anchises' is, in fact, a synonym of Adonis. He had a shrine at Aegesta near Mount Eryx (Dionysius of Halicarnassus: i. 53) and was therefore said by Virgil to have died at Drepanum, a neighbouring town, and been buried on the mountain (*Aeneid* iii. 710, 759, etc.). Other shrines of Anchises were shown in Arcadia and the Troad. At Aphrodite's shrine on Mount Eryx a golden honeycomb was displayed, said to have been a votive offering presented by Daedalus when he fled to Sicily (see 92. *h*).

4. As Goddess of Death-in-Life, Aphrodite earned many titles which seem inconsistent with her beauty and complaisance. At Athens, she was called the Eldest of the Fates and sister of the Erinnyes: and elsewhere Melaenis ('black one'), a name ingeniously explained by Pausanias as meaning that most love-making takes place at night; Scotia ('dark one'); Androphonos ('man-slayer'); and even, according to Plutarch, Epi-tymbria ('of the tombs').

5. The myth of Cinyras and Smyrna evidently records a period in history when the sacred king in a matrilineal society decided to prolong his reign beyond the customary length. He did so by celebrating a marriage with the young priestess, nominally his daughter, who was to be queen for the next term, instead of letting another princeling marry her and take away his kingdom (see 65. *1*).

6. Adonis (Phoenician: *adon*, 'lord') is a Greek version of the Syrian demi-god Tammuz, the spirit of annual vegetation. In Syria, Asia Minor and Greece, the goddess's sacred year was at one time divided into three parts, ruled by the Lion, Goat, and Serpent (see 75. *2*). The Goat, emblem of the central part, was the Love-goddess Aphrodite's; the Serpent, emblem of the last part, was the Death-goddess Persephone's; the Lion, emblem of the first part, was sacred to the Birth-goddess, here named Smyrna, who had no claim on Adonis. In Greece, this calendar gave place to a two-season year, bisected either by the equinoxes in the Eastern style, as at Sparta and Delphi, or by the solstices in the Northern style, as at Athens and Thebes; which explains the difference between the respective verdicts of the Mountain-goddess Calliope and Zeus.

7. Tammuz was killed by a boar, like many similar mythical characters – Osiris, Cretan Zeus, Ancaeus of Arcadia (see 157. *e*), Carmanor of Lydia (see 136. *b*), and the Irish hero Diarmuid. This boar seems once to have been a sow with crescent-shaped tusks, the goddess herself as Persephone; but when the year was bisected, the bright half ruled by the sacred king, and the dark half ruled by his tanist, or rival, this rival came in wild-boar disguise – like Set when he killed Osiris, or Finn mac Cool when he killed Diarmuid. Tammuz's blood is allegorical of the anemones that redden the slopes of Mount Lebanon after the winter rains; the Adonia, a mourning festival in honour of Tammuz, was held at Byblus

every spring. Adonis's birth from a myrrh-tree – myrrh being a well-known aphrodisiac – shows the orgiastic character of his rites. The drops of gum which the myrrh-tree shed were supposed to be tears shed for him (Ovid: *Metamorphoses* x. 500 ff.). Hyginus makes Cinyras King of Assyria (*Fabula* 58), perhaps because Tammuz-worship seemed to have originated there.

8. Aphrodite's son Hermaphroditus was a youth with womanish breasts and long hair. Like the *androgyne*, or bearded woman, the hermaphrodite had, of course, its freakish physical counterpart, but as religious concepts both originated in the transition from matriarchy to patriarchy. Hermaphroditus is the sacred king deputizing for the Queen (see 136. *4*), and wearing artificial breasts. Androgyne is the mother of a pre-Hellenic clan which has avoided being patriarchalized; in order to keep her magistratal powers or to ennoble children born to her from a slave-father, she assumes a false beard, as was the custom at Argos. Bearded goddesses like the Cyprian Aphrodite, and womanish gods like Dionysus, correspond with these transitional social stages.

9. Harmonia, is, at first sight, a strange name for a daughter borne by Aphrodite to Ares; but, then as now, more than usual affection and harmony prevailed in a state which was at war.

# 19

## ARES'S NATURE AND DEEDS

THRACIAN Ares loves battle for its own sake, and his sister Eris is always stirring up occasions for war by the spread of rumour and the inculcation of jealousy. Like her, he never favours one city or party more than another, but fights on this side or that, as inclination prompts him, delighting in the slaughter of men and the sacking of towns. All his fellow-immortals hate him, from Zeus and Hera downwards, except Eris, and Aphrodite who nurses a perverse passion for him, and greedy Hades who welcomes the bold young fighting-men slain in cruel wars.

*b.* Ares has not been consistently victorious. Athene, a much more skilful fighter than he, has twice worsted him in battle; and once, the gigantic sons of Aloeus conquered and kept him imprisoned in a brazen vessel for thirteen months until, half dead, he was released by Hermes; and, on another occasion, Heracles sent him running in fear back to Olympus. He professes too deep a contempt for litigation ever to

appear in court as a plantiff, and has only once done so as a defendant:
that was when his fellow-deities charged him with the wilful murder of
Poseidon's son Halirrhothius. He pleaded justification, claiming to have
saved his daughter Alcippe, of the House of Cecrops, from being violated by the said Halirrhothius. Since no one had witnessed the incident,
except Ares himself, and Alcippe, who naturally confirmed her father's
evidence, the court acquitted him. This was the first judgement ever
pronounced in a murder trial; and the hill on which the proceedings
took place became known as the Areiopagus, a name it still bears.[1]

1. Apollodorus: iii. 14. 2; Pausanias: i. 21. 7.

*

1. The Athenians disliked war, except in defence of liberty, or for some
other equally cogent reason, and despised the Thracians as barbarous
because they made it a pastime.

2. In Pausanias's account of the murder, Halirrhothius had already
succeeded in violating Alcippe. But Halirrhothius can only be a synonym
for Poseidon; and Alcippe a synonym for the mare-headed goddess. The
myth, in fact, recalls Poseidon's rape of Demeter, and refers to a conquest
of Athens by Poseidon's people and the goddess's humiliation at their
hands (see 16. 3). But it has been altered for patriotic reasons, and combined with a legend of some early murder trial. 'Areiopagus' probably
means 'the hill of the propitiating Goddess', *areia* being one of Athene's
titles.

# 20

## HESTIA'S NATURE AND DEEDS

It is Hestia's glory that, alone of the great Olympians, she never takes
part in wars or disputes. Like Artemis and Athene, moreover, she has
always resisted every amorous invitation offered her by gods, Titans,
or others; for, after the dethronement of Cronus, when Poseidon and
Apollo came forward as rival suitors, she swore by Zeus's head to
remain a virgin for ever. At that, Zeus gratefully awarded her the first
victim of every public sacrifice,[1] because she had preserved the peace
of Olympus.

b. Drunken Priapus once tried to violate her at a rustic feast attended

by the gods, when everyone had fallen asleep from repletion; but an
ass brayed aloud, Hestia awoke, screamed to find Priapus about to
straddle her, and sent him running off in comic terror.²

*c.* She is the Goddess of the Hearth and in every private house and
city hall protects suppliants who flee to her for protection. Universal
reverence is paid Hestia, not only as the mildest, most upright and most
charitable of all the Olympians, but as having invented the art of building houses; and her fire is so sacred that, if ever a hearth goes cold, either
by accident or in token of mourning, it is kindled afresh with the aid
of a fire-wheel.³

1. *Homeric Hymn to Aphrodite* 21–30.
2. Ovid: *Fasti* vi. 319 ff.
3. Diodorus Siculus: v. 68.

\*

*1.* The centre of Greek life – even at Sparta, where the family had been
subordinated to the State – was the domestic hearth, also regarded as a
sacrificial altar; and Hestia, as its goddess, represented personal security
and happiness, and the sacred duty of hospitality. The story of her mar-
riage-offers from Poseidon and Apollo has perhaps been deduced from
the joint worship of these three deities at Delphi. Priapus's attempt to
violate her is an anecdotal warning against sacrilegious ill-treatment of
women-guests who have come under the protection of the domestic or
public hearth: even the ass, a symbol of lust (see 35. *4*), proclaims Priapus's
criminal folly.

*2.* The archaic white aniconic image of the Great Goddess, in use
throughout the Eastern Mediterranean, seems to have represented a heap
of glowing charcoal, kept alive by a covering of white ash, which was the
most cosy and economical means of heating in ancient times; it gave out
neither smoke nor flame, and formed the natural centre of family or clan
gatherings. At Delphi the charcoal-heap was translated into limestone
for out-of-doors use, and became the *omphalos*, or navel-boss, frequently
shown in Greek vase-paintings, which marked the supposed centre of the
world. This holy object, which has survived the ruin of the shrine, is
inscribed with the name of Mother Earth, stands 11¼ inches high, and
measures 15½ inches across; about the size and shape of a charcoal fire
needed to heat a large room. In Classical times the Pythoness had an
attendant priest who induced her trance by burning barley grains, hemp,
and laurel over an oil lamp in an enclosed space, and then interpreted
what she said. But it is likely that the hemp, laurel, and barley were once
laid on the hot ashes of the charcoal mound, which is a simpler and more
effective way of producing narcotic fumes (see 51. *b*). Numerous tri-

angular or leaf-shaped ladles in stone or clay have been found in Cretan and Mycenaean shrines – some of them showing signs of great heat – and seem to have been used for tending the sacred fire. The charcoal mound was sometimes built on a round, three-legged clay table, painted red, white, and black, which are the moon's colours (see 90. *3*); examples have been found in the Peloponnese, Crete, and Delos – one of them, from a chamber tomb at Zafer Papoura near Cnossus, had the charcoal still piled on it.


# 21

## APOLLO'S NATURE AND DEEDS

APOLLO, Zeus's son by Leto, was a seven-months' child, but gods grow up swiftly. Themis fed him on nectar and ambrosia, and when the fourth day dawned he called for bow and arrows, with which Hephaestus at once provided him. On leaving Delos he made straight for Mount Parnassus, where the serpent Python, his mother's enemy, was lurking; and wounded him severely with arrows. Python fled to the Oracle of Mother Earth at Delphi, a city so named in honour of the monster Delphyne, his mate; but Apollo dared follow him into the shrine, and there despatched him beside the sacred chasm.[1]

*b*. Mother Earth reported this outrage to Zeus, who not only ordered Apollo to visit Tempe for purification, but instituted the Pythian Games, in honour of Python, over which he was to preside penitentially. Quite unabashed, Apollo disregarded Zeus's command to visit Tempe. Instead, he went to Aigialaea for purification, accompanied by Artemis; and then, disliking the place, sailed to Tarrha in Crete, where King Carmanor performed the ceremony.[2]

*c*. On his return to Greece, Apollo sought out Pan, the disreputable old goat-legged Arcadian god and, having coaxed him to reveal the art of prophecy, seized the Delphic Oracle and retained its priestess, called the Pythoness, in his own service.

*d*. Leto, on hearing the news, came with Artemis to Delphi, where she turned aside to perform some private rite in a sacred grove. The giant Tityus interrupted her devotions, and was trying to violate her, when Apollo and Artemis, hearing screams, ran up and killed him with a volley of arrows – a vengeance which Zeus, Tityus's father, was pleased to consider a pious one. In Tartarus, Tityus was stretched out for torment, his arms and legs securely pegged to the ground; the area covered was no less than nine acres, and two vultures ate his liver.[3]

*e*. Next, Apollo killed the satyr Marsyas, a follower of the goddess Cybele. This was how it came about. One day, Athene made a double-flute from stag's bones, and played on it at a banquet of the gods. She could not understand, at first, why Hera and Aphrodite were laughing silently behind their hands, although her music seemed to delight the other deities; she therefore went away by herself into a Phrygian wood, took up the flute again beside a stream, and watched her image in the water, as she played. Realizing at once how ludicrous that bluish face and those swollen cheeks made her look, she threw down the flute, and laid a curse on anyone who picked it up.

*f*. Marsyas was the innocent victim of this curse. He stumbled upon the flute, which he had no sooner put to his lips than it played of itself, inspired by the memory of Athene's music; and he went about Phrygia in Cybele's train, delighting the ignorant peasants. They cried out that Apollo himself could not have made better music, even on his lyre, and Marsyas was foolish enough not to contradict them. This, of course, provoked the anger of Apollo, who invited him to a contest, the winner of which should inflict whatever punishment he pleased on the loser. Marsyas consented, and Apollo impanelled the Muses as a jury. The contest proved an equal one, the Muses being charmed by both instruments, until Apollo cried out to Marsyas: 'I challenge you to do with your instrument as much as I can do with mine. Turn it upside down, and both play and sing at the same time.'

*g*. This, with a flute, was manifestly impossible, and Marsyas failed to meet the challenge. But Apollo reversed his lyre, and sang such delightful hymns in honour of the Olympian gods that the Muses could not do less than give the verdict in his favour. Then, for all his pretended sweetness, Apollo took a most cruel revenge on Marsyas: flaying him alive and nailing his skin to a pine (or, some say, to a plane-tree), near the source of the river which now bears his name.[4]

*h*. Afterwards, Apollo won a second musical contest, at which King Midas presided; this time he beat Pan. Becoming the acknowledged god of Music, he has ever since played on his seven-stringed lyre while the gods banquet. Another of his duties was once to guard the herds and flocks which the gods kept in Pieria; but he later delegated this task to Hermes.[5]

*i*. Though Apollo refuses to bind himself in marriage, he has got many nymphs and mortal women with child; among them, Phthia, on whom he fathered Dorus and his brothers; and Thalia the Muse, on whom he fathered the Corybantes; and Coronis, on whom he fathered Asclepius; and Aria, on whom he fathered Miletus; and Cyrene, on whom he fathered Aristaeus.[6]

*j*. He also seduced the nymph Dryope, who was tending her father's flocks on Mount Oeta in the company of her friends, the Hamadryads. Apollo disguised himself as a tortoise, with which they all played and, when Dryope put him into her bosom, he turned into a hissing serpent, scared away the Hamadryads, and enjoyed her. She bore him Amphissus, who founded the city of Oeta and built a temple to his father; there Dryope served as priestess until, one day, the Hamadryads stole her away, and left a poplar in her place.[7]

*k*. Apollo was not invariably successful in love. On one occasion he tried to steal Marpessa from Idas, but she remained true to her husband. On another, he pursued Daphne, the mountain nymph, a priestess of Mother Earth, daughter of the river Peneius in Thessaly; but when he overtook her, she cried out to Mother Earth who, in the nick of time, spirited her away to Crete, where she bcame known as Pasiphaë. Mother Earth left a laurel-tree in her place, and from its leaves Apollo made a wreath to console himself.[8]

*l*. His attempt on Daphne, it must be added, was no sudden impulse. He had long been in love with her, and had brought about the death of his rival, Leucippus, son of Oenomaus, who disguised himself as a girl and joined Daphne's mountain revels. Apollo, knowing of this by divination, advised the mountain nymphs to bathe naked, and thus make sure that everyone in their company was a woman; Leucippus's imposture was at once discovered, and the nymphs tore him to pieces.[9]

*m*. There was also the case of the beautiful youth Hyacinthus, a Spartan prince, with whom not only the poet Thamyris fell in love – the first man who ever wooed one of his own sex – but Apollo himself, the first god to do so. Apollo did not find Thamyris a serious rival; having overheard his boast that he could surpass the Muses in song, he maliciously reported it to them, and they at once robbed Thamyris of his sight, his voice, and his memory for harping. But the West Wind had also taken a fancy to Hyacinthus, and became insanely jealous of Apollo, who was one day teaching the boy how to hurl a discus, when the West Wind caught it in mid-air, dashed it against Hyacinthus's skull, and killed him. From his blood sprang the hyacinth flower, on which his initial letters are still to be traced.[10]

*n.* Apollo earned Zeus's anger only once after the famous conspiracy to dethrone him. This was when his son Asclepius, the physician, had the temerity to resurrect a dead man, and thus rob Hades of a subject; Hades naturally lodged a complaint on Olympus, Zeus killed Asclepius with a thunderbolt, and Apollo in revenge killed the Cyclopes. Zeus was enraged at the loss of his armourers, and would have banished Apollo to Tartarus for ever, had not Leto pleaded for his forgiveness and undertaken that he would mend his ways. The sentence was reduced to one year's hard labour, which Apollo was to serve in the sheep-folds of King Admetus of Therae. Obeying Leto's advice, Apollo not only carried out the sentence humbly, but conferred great benefits on Admetus.[11]

*o.* Having learned his lesson, he thereafter preached moderation in all things: the phrases 'Know thyself!' and 'Nothing in excess!' were always on his lips. He brought the Muses down from their home on Mount Helicon to Delphi, tamed their wild frenzy, and led them in formal and decorous dances.[12]

1. Hyginus: *Fabula* 140; Apollodorus: i. 4. 1; *Homeric Hymn to Apollo* 300–306; Scholiast on Apollonius Rhodius: ii. 706.
2. Aelian: *Varia Historia* iii. 1; Plutarch: *Greek Questions* 12; *Why Oracles Are Silent* 15; Pausanias: ii. 7. 7; x. 16. 3.
3. Apollodorus: i. 4. 1; Pausanias: ii. 30.3 and x. 6. 5; Plutarch: *Greek Questions* 12; Hyginus: *Fabula* 55; Homer: *Odyssey* xi. 576 ff.; Pindar: *Pythian Odes* iv. 90 ff.
4. Diodorus Siculus: iii. 58–9; Hyginus: *Fabula* 165; Apollodorus: i. 4. 2; Second Vatican Mythographer: 115; Pliny: *Natural History* xvi. 89.
5. Hyginus: *Fabula* 191; Homer: *Iliad* i. 603.
6. Apollodorus: i. 7. 6; i. 3. 4; iii. 10. 3; iii. 1. 2; Pausanias: x. 17. 3.
7. Antoninus Liberalis: 32; Stephanus of Byzantium *sub* Dryope; Ovid: *Metamorphoses* ix. 325 ff.
8. Apollodorus: i. 7. 9; Plutarch: *Agis* 9.
9. Hyginus: *Fabula* 203; Pausanias: viii. 20. 2; x. 5. 3; Parthenius: *Erotica* 15; Tzetzes: *On Lycophron* 6.
10. Homer: *Iliad* ii. 595–600; Lucian: *Dialogues of the Gods* 14; Apollodorus: i. 3.3; Pausanias: iii. 1. 3.
11. Apollodorus: iii. 10. 4; Diodorus Siculus: iv. 71.
12. Homer: *Iliad* i. 603–4; Plutarch: *On the Pythian Oracles* 17.

1. Apollo's history is a confusing one. The Greeks made him the son of Leto, a goddess known as Lat in Southern Palestine (see 14. *2*), but he was also a god of the Hyperboreans ('beyond-the-North-Wind-men'), whom Hecataeus (Diodorus Siculus: ii. 47) clearly identified with the British, though Pindar (*Pythian Odes* x. 50–55) regarded them as Libyans. Delos was the centre of this Hyperborean cult which, it seems, extended south-eastward to Nabataea and Palestine, north-westward to Britain, and included Athens. Visits were constantly exchanged between the states united in this cult (Diodorus Siculus: *loc cit.*).

2. Apollo, among the Hyperboreans, sacrificed hetacombs of asses (Pindar: *loc. cit.*), which identifies him with the 'Child Horus', whose defeat of his enemy Set the Egyptians annually celebrated by driving wild asses over a precipice (Plutarch: *On Isis and Osiris* 30). Horus was avenging Set's murder of his father Osiris – the sacred king, beloved of the Triple Moon-goddess Isis, or Lat, whom his tanist sacrificed at midsummer and midwinter, and of whom Horus was himself the reincarnation. The myth of Leto's pursuit by Python corresponds with the myth of Isis's pursuit by Set (during the seventy-two hottest days of the year). Moreover, Python is identified with Typhon, the Greek Set (see 36. *1*), in the *Homeric Hymn to Apollo*, and by the scholiast on Apollonius Rhodius. The Hyperborean Apollo is, in fact, a Greek Horus.

3. But the myth has been given a political turn: Python is said to have been sent against Leto by Hera, who had borne him parthenogenetically to spite Zeus (*Homeric Hymn to Apollo* 305); and Apollo, after killing Python (and presumably also his mate Delphyne), seizes the oracular shrine of Mother Earth at Delphi – for Hera was Mother Earth, or Delphyne in her prophetic aspect. It seems that certain Northern Hellenes, allied with Thraco-Libyans, invaded Central Greece and the Peloponnese, where they were opposed by the pre-Hellenic worshippers of the Earth-goddess, but captured her chief oracular shrines. At Delphi, they destroyed the sacred oracular serpent – a similar serpent was kept in the Erechtheum at Athens (see 25. *2*) – and took over the oracle in the name of their god Apollo Smintheus. Smintheus ('mousy'), like Esmun the Canaanite god of healing, had a curative mouse for his emblem. The invaders agreed to identify him with Apollo, the Hyperborean Horus, worshipped by their allies. To placate local opinion at Delphi, regular funeral games were instituted in honour of the dead hero Python, and his priestess was retained in office.

4. The Moon-goddess Brizo ('soother') of Delos, indistinguishable from Leto, may be identified with the Hyperborean Triple-goddess Brigit, who became Christianized as St Brigit, or St Bride. Brigit was patroness of all the arts, and Apollo followed her example. The attempt

on Leto by the giant Tityus suggests an abortive rising by the mountaineers of Phocis against the invaders.

5. Apollo's victories over Marsyas and Pan commemorate the Hellenic conquests of Phrygia and Arcadia, and the consequent supersession in those regions of wind instruments by stringed ones, except among the peasantry. Masyas's punishment may refer to the ritual flaying of a sacred king – as Athene stripped Pallas of his magical aegis (see 9. *a*) – or the removal of the entire bark from an alder-shoot, to make a shepherd's pipe, the alder being personified as a god or demi-god (see 28. *1* and 57. *1*). Apollo was claimed as an ancestor of the Dorian Greeks, and of the Milesians, who paid him especial honours. The Corybantes, dancers at the Winter Solstice festival, were called his children by Thalia the Muse, because he was god of Music.

6. His pursuit of Daphne the Mountain-nymph, daughter of the river Peneius, and priestess of Mother Earth, refers apparently to the Hellenic capture of Tempe, where the goddess Daphoene ('bloody one') was worshipped by a college of orgiastic laurel-chewing Maenads (see 46. *2* and 51. *2*). After suppressing the college – Plutarch's account suggests that the priestesses fled to Crete, where the Moon-goddess was called Pasiphaë (see 88. *e*) – Apollo took over the laurel which, afterwards, only the Pythoness might chew. Daphoene will have been mareheaded at Tempe, as at Phigalia (see 16. *5*); Leucippus ('white horse') was the sacred king of the local horse cult, annually torn in pieces by the wild women, who bathed after his murder to purify themselves, not before (see 22. *1* and 150. *1*).

7. Apollo's seduction of Dryope on Oeta perhaps records the local supersession of an oak cult by a cult of Apollo, to whom the poplar was sacred (see 42. *d*); as does his seduction of Aria. His tortoise disguise is a reference to the lyre he had bought from Hermes (see 17. *d*). Phthia's name suggests that she was an autumnal aspect of the goddess. The unsuccessful attempt on Marpessa ('snatcher'), seems to record Apollo's failure to seize a Messenian shrine: that of the Grain-goddess as Sow (see 74. *4*). Apollo's servitude to Admetus of Pherae may recall a historical event: the humiliation of the Apollonian priesthood in punishment for their massacre of a pre-Hellenic smith-guild which had enjoyed Zeus's protection.

8. The myth of Hyacinthus, which seems at first sight no more than a sentimental fable told to explain the mark on the Greek hyacinth (see 165. *j* and *2*) concerns the Cretan Flower-hero Hyacinthus (see 159. *4*), also apparently called Narcissus (see 85. *2*), whose worship was introduced into Mycenaean Greece, and who named the later summer month of Hyacinthius in Crete, Rhodes, Cos, Thera, and at Sparta. Dorian Apollo usurped Hyacinthus's name at Tarentum, where he had a hero

tomb (Polybius: viii. 30); and at Amyclae, a Mycenaean city, another 'tomb of Hyacinthus' became the foundation of Apollo's throne. Apollo was an immortal by this time, Hyacinthus reigned only for a season: his death by a discus recalls that of his nephew Acrisius (see 73. *3*).

9. Coronis ('crow'), mother of Asclepius by Apollo, was probably a title of Athene's (see 25. *5*); but the Athenians always denied that she had children, and disguised the myth (see 50. *b*).

10. In Classical times, music, poetry, philosophy, astronomy, mathematics, medicine, and science came under Apollo's control. As the enemy of barbarism, he stood for moderation in all things, and the seven strings of his lute were connected with the seven vowels of the later Greek alphabet (see 52. *8*), given mystical significance, and used for therapeutic music. Finally, because of his identification with the Child Horus, a solar concept, he was worshipped as the sun, whose Corinthian cult had been taken over by Solar Zeus; and his sister Artemis was, rightly, identified with the moon.

11. Cicero, in his essay *On the Nature of the Gods* (iii. 23), makes Apollo son of Leto only the fourth of an ancient series: he distinguishes Apollo son of Hephaestus, Apollo the father of the Cretan Corybantes, and the Apollo who gave Arcadia its laws.

12. Apollo's killing of the Python is not, however, so simple a myth as at first appears, because the stone *omphalos* on which the Pythoness sat was traditionally the tomb of the hero incarnate in the serpent, whose oracles she delivered (Hesychius *sub* Archus's Mound; Varro: *On the Latin Languages* vii. 17). The Hellenic priest of Apollo usurped the functions of the sacred king who, legitimately and ceremonially, had always killed his predecessor, the hero. This is proved by the Stepteria rite recorded in Plutarch's *Why Oracles Are Silent* (15). Every ninth year a hut representing a king's dwelling was built on the threshing floor at Delphi and a night attack suddenly made on it by . . . [*here there is a gap in the account*] . . . The table of first-fruits was overturned, the hut set on fire, and the torchmen fled from the sanctuary without looking behind them. Afterwards the youth who had taken part in the deed went to Tempe for purification, whence he returned in triumph, crowned and carrying a laurel branch.

13. The sudden concerted assault on the inmate of the hut recalls the mysterious murder of Romulus by his companions. It also recalls the yearly Buphonia sacrifice at Athens when the priests who had killed the Zeus-ox with a double-axe, fled without looking behind them; then ate the flesh at a communal feast (see 53. *7*), staged a mimic resurrection of the ox, and brought up the axe for trial on a charge of sacrilege.

14. At Delphi, as at Cnossus, the sacred king must have reigned until the ninth year (see 88. *6*). The boy went to Tempe doubtless because the Apollo cult had originated there.

## ARTEMIS'S NATURE AND DEEDS

ARTEMIS, Apollo's sister, goes armed with bow and arrows and, like him, has the power both to send plagues or sudden death among mortals, and to heal them. She is the protectress of little children, and of all sucking animals, but she also loves the chase, especially that of stags.

b. One day, while she was still a three-year-old child, her father Zeus, on whose knees she was sitting, asked her what presents she would like. Artemis answered at once: 'Pray give me eternal virginity; as many names as my brother Apollo; a bow and arrows like his; the office of bringing light; a saffron hunting tunic with a red hem reaching to my knees; sixty young ocean nymphs, all of the same age, as my maids of honour; twenty river nymphs from Amnisus in Crete, to take care of my buskins and feed my hounds when I am not out shooting; all the mountains in the world; and, lastly, any city you care to choose for me, but one will be enough, because I intend to live on mountains most of the time. Unfortunately, women in labour will often be invoking me, since my mother Leto carried and bore me without pains, and the Fates have therefore made me patroness of childbirth.'[1]

c. She stretched up for Zeus's beard, and he smiled proudly, saying: 'With children like you, I need not fear Hera's jealous anger! You shall have all this, and more besides: not one, but thirty cities, and a share in many others, both on the mainland and in the archipelago; and I appoint you guardian of their roads and harbours.'[2]

d. Artemis thanked him, sprang from his knee, and went first to Mount Leucus in Crete, and next to the Ocean stream, where she chose numerous nine-year-old nymphs for her attendants; their mothers were delighted to let them go.[3] On Hephaestus's invitation, she then visited the Cyclopes on the Island of Lipara, and found them hammering away at a horse-trough for Poseidon. Brontes, who had been instructed to make whatever she wanted, took her on his knee; but, disliking his endearments, she tore a handful of hair from his chest, where a bald patch remained to the day of his death; anyone might have supposed that he had the mange. The nymphs were terrified at the wild appearance of the Cyclopes, and at the din of their smithy – well they might be, for whenever a little girl is disobedient her mother threatens her with Brontes, Arges, or Steropes. But Artemis boldly told them to abandon Poseidon's trough for a while, and make her a silver bow, with a quiverful of arrows, in return for which they should eat the first prey she brought down.[4] With these weapons she went to Arcadia, where Pan was engaged in cutting up a lynx to feed his bitches and their whelps. He gave her three lop-eared hounds, two parti-coloured and one spotted, together capable of dragging live lions back to their kennels; and seven swift hounds from Sparta.[5]

*e*. Having captured alive two couple of horned hinds, she harnessed them to a golden chariot with golden bits, and drove north over Thracian Mount Haemus. She cut her first pine torch on Mysian Olympus, and lit it at the cinders of a lightning-struck tree. She tried her silver bow four times: her first two targets were trees; her third, a wild beast; her fourth, a city of unjust men.[6]

*f*. Then she returned to Greece, where the Amnisian nymphs unyoked her hinds, rubbed them down, fed them on the same quick-growing trefoil, from Hera's pasture, which the steeds of Zeus eat, and watered them from golden troughs.[7]

*g*. Once the River-god Alpheius, son of Thetis, dared fall in love with Artemis and pursue her across Greece; but she came to Letrini in Elis (or, some say, as far as the island of Ortygia near Syracuse), where she daubed her face, and those of all her nymphs, with white mud, so that she became indistinguishable from the rest of the company. Alpheius was forced to retire, pursued by mocking laughter.[8]

*h*. Artemis requires the same perfect chastity from her companions as she practises herself. When Zeus had seduced one of them, Callisto, daughter of Lycaon, Artemis noticed that she was with child. Changing her into a bear, she shouted to the pack, and Callisto would have been hunted to death had she not been caught up to Heaven by Zeus who, later, set her image among the stars. But some say that Zeus himself changed Callisto into a bear, and that jealous Hera arranged for Artemis to chase her in error. Callisto's child, Arcas, was saved, and became the ancestor of the Arcadians.[9]

*i*. On another occasion, Actaeon, son of Aristaeus, stood leaning against a rock near Orchomenus when he happened to see Artemis bathing in a stream not far off, and stayed to watch. Lest he should afterwards dare boast to his companions that she had displayed herself naked in his presence, she changed him into a stag and, with his own pack of fifty hounds, tore him to pieces.[10]

1. Callimachus: *Hymn to Artemis* 1 ff.
2. *Ibid.*: 26 ff.
3. *Ibid.*: 40 ff.
4. *Ibid.*: 47 ff.
5. *Ibid.*: 69 ff.
6. *Ibid.*: 110 ff.
7. *Ibid.*: 162 ff.
8. Pausanias: vi. 22. 5; Scholiast on Pindar's *Pythian Odes* ii. 12.
9. Hyginus: *Poetic Astronomy* ii. 1; Apollodorus: iii. 8. 2.
10. Hyginus: *Fabula* 181; Pausanias: ix. 2. 3.

*

1. The Maiden of the Silver Bow, whom the Greeks enrolled in the Olympian family, was the youngest member of the Artemis Triad, 'Artemis' being one more title of the Triple Moon-goddess; and had a right therefore to feed her hinds on trefoil, a symbol of trinity. Her silver bow stood for the new moon. Yet the Olympian Artemis was more than a Maiden. Elsewhere, at Ephesus, for instance, she was worshipped in her second person, as Nymph, an orgiastic Aphrodite with a male consort, and the date-palm (see 14. *a*), stag, and bee (see 18. *3*) for her principal emblems. Her midwifery belongs, rather, to the Crone, as do her arrows of death; and the nine-year-old priestesses are a reminder that the moon's death number is three times three. She recalls the Cretan 'Lady of the Wild Things', apparently the supreme Nymph-goddess of archaic totem societies; and the ritual bath in which Actaeon surprised her, like the horned hinds of her chariot (see 125. *a*) and the quails of Ortygia (see 14. *3*), seems more appropriate to the Nymph than the Maiden. Actaeon was, it seems, a sacred king of the pre-Hellenic stag cult, torn to pieces at the end of his reign of fifty months, namely half a Great Year; his co-king, or tanist, reigning for the remainder. The Nymph properly took her bath after, not before, the murder. There are numerous parallels to this ritual custom in Irish and Welsh myth, and as late as the first century A.D. a man dressed in a stag's skin was periodically chased and killed on the Arcadian Mount Lycaeum (Plutarch: *Greek Questions* 39). The hounds will have been white with red ears, like the 'hounds of Hell' in Celtic mythology. There was a fifth horned hind which escaped Artemis (see 125. *a*).

2. The myth of her pursuit by Alpheius seems modelled on that of his hopeless pursuit of Arethusa which turned her into a spring and him into a river (Pausanias: v. 7. 2), and may have been invented to account for the gypsum, or white clay, with which the priestesses of

Artemis Alpheia at Letrini and Ortygia daubed their faces in honour of the White Goddess. *Alph* denotes both whiteness and cereal produce: *alphos* is leprosy; *alphe* is gain; *alphiton* is pearl barley; *Alphito* was the White Grain-goddess as Sow. Artemis's most famous statue at Athens was called 'the White-browed' (Pausanias: i. 26. 4). The meaning of *Artemis* is doubtful: it may be 'strong-limbed', from *artemes*; or 'she who cuts up', since the Spartans called her *Artamis*, from *artao*; or 'the lofty convener', from *airo* and *themis*; or the 'themis' syllable may mean 'water', because the moon was regarded as the source of all water.

3. Ortygia, 'Quail Island', near Delos, was also sacred to Artemis (see 14. *a*).

4. The myth of Callisto has been told to account for the two small girls, dressed as she-bears, who appeared in the Attic festival of Brauronian Artemis, and for the traditional connexion between Artemis and the Great Bear. But an earlier version of the myth may be presumed, in which Zeus seduced Artemis, although she first transformed herself into a bear and then daubed her face with gypsum, in an attempt to escape him. Artemis was, originally, the ruler of the stars, but lost them to Zeus.

5. Why Brontes had his hair plucked out is doubtful; Callimachus may be playfully referring to some well-known picture of the event, in which the paint had worn away from the Cyclops' chest.

6. As 'Lady of Wild Things', or patroness of all the totem clans, Artemis had been annually offered a living holocaust of totem beasts, birds, and plants, and this sacrifice survived in Classical time at Patrae, a Calydonian city (Pausanias: iv. 32. 6); she was there called Artemis Laphria. At Messene a similar burnt sacrifice was offered to her by the Curetes, as totem-clan representatives (iv. 32. 9); and another is recorded from Hierapolis, where the victims were hung to the trees of an artificial forest inside the goddess's temple (Lucian: *On the Syrian Goddess* 41).

7. The olive-tree was sacred to Athene, the date-palm to Isis and Lat. A Middle Minoan bead-seal in my possession shows the goddess standing beside a palm, dressed in a palm-leaf skirt, and with a small palm-tree held in her hand; she watches a New Year bull-calf being born from a date-cluster. On the other side of the tree is a dying bull, evidently the royal bull of the Old Year.

# 23

## HEPHAESTUS'S NATURE AND DEEDS

HEPHAESTUS, the Smith-god, was so weakly at birth that his disgusted mother, Hera, dropped him from the height of Olympus, to rid herself

of the embarrassment that his pitiful appearance caused her. He survived this misadventure, however, without bodily damage, because he
fell into the sea, where Thetis and Eurynome were at hand to rescue
him. These gentle goddesses kept him with them in an underwater
grotto, where he set up his first smithy and rewarded their kindness by
making them all sorts of ornamental and useful objects.[1]

One day, when nine years had passed, Hera met Thetis, who happened to be wearing a brooch of his workmanship, and asked: 'My
dear, where in the world did you find that wonderful jewel?'

Thetis hesitated before replying, but Hera forced the truth from her.
At once she fetched Hephaestus back to Olympus, where she set him
up in a much finer smithy, with twenty bellows working day and night,
made much of him, and arranged that he should marry Aphrodite.

*b.* Hephaestus became so far reconciled with Hera that he dared
reproach Zeus himself for hanging her by the wrists from Heaven
when she rebelled against him. But silence would have been wiser,
because angry Zeus only heaved him down from Olympus a second
time. He was a whole day falling. On striking the earth of the island of
Lemnos, he broke both legs and, though immortal, had little life left in
his body when the islanders found him. Afterwards pardoned and restored to Olympus, he could walk only with golden leg-supports.[2]

*c.* Hephaestus is ugly and ill-tempered, but has great power in his
arms and shoulders, and all his work is of matchless skill. He once made
a set of golden mechanical women to help him in his smithy; they can
even talk, and undertake the most difficult tasks he entrusts to them.
And he owns a set of three-legged tables with golden wheels, ranged
around his workshop, which can run by themselves to a meeting of the
gods, and back again.[3]

1. Homer: *Iliad* xviii. 394–409.
2. *Ibid.*: i. 586–94.
3. *Ibid.*: xviii. 368 ff.

*

*1.* Hephaestus and Athene shared temples at Athens, and his name
may be a worn-down form of *hemero-phaistos*, 'he who shines by day'
(i.e. the sun), whereas Athene was the moon-goddess, 'she who shines by
night', patroness of smithcraft and of all mechanical arts. It is not generally
recognized that every Bronze Age tool, weapon, or utensil had magical
properties, and that the smith was something of a sorcerer. Thus, of the

three persons of the Brigit Moon-triad (see 21. 4), one presided over poets, another over smiths, the third over physicians. When the goddess has been dethroned the smith is elevated to godhead. That the Smith-god hobbles is a tradition found in regions as far apart as West Africa and Scandinavia; in primitive times smiths may have been purposely lamed to prevent them from running off and joining enemy tribes. But a hobbling partridge-dance was also performed in erotic orgies connected with the mysteries of smithcraft (see 92. 2) and, since Hephaestus had married Aphrodite, he may have been hobbled only once a year: at the Spring Festival.

Metallurgy first reached Greece from the Aegean Islands. The importation of finely worked Helladic bronze and gold perhaps accounts for the myth that Hephaestus was guarded in a Lemnian grotto by Thetis and Eurynome, titles of the Sea-goddess who created the universe. The nine years which he spent in the grotto show his subservience to the moon. His fall, like that of Cephalus (see 89. j), Talos (see 92. b) Sciron (see 96. f), Iphitus (see 135. b), and others, was the common fate of the sacred king in many parts of Greece when their reigns ended. The golden leg-supports were perhaps designed to raise his sacred heel from the ground.

2. Hephaestus's twenty three-legged tables have, it seems, much the same origin as the Gasterocheires who built Tiryns (see 73. 3), being golden sun-disks with three legs, like the heraldic device of the Isle of Man doubtless bordering some early icon which showed Hephaestus being married to Aphrodite. They represent three-season years, and denote the length of his reign; he dies at the beginning of the twentieth year, when a close approximation of solar and lunar time occurs; this cycle was officially recognized at Athens only towards the close of the fifth century B.C., but had been discovered several hundred years before (*White Goddess*, pp. 284 and 291). Hephaestus was connected with Vulcan's forges in the volcanic Lipari islands because Lemnos, a seat of his worship, is volcanic and a jet of natural asphaltic gas which issued from the summit of Mount Moschylus had burned steadily for centuries (Tzetzes: *On Lycophron* 227; Heyschius *sub* Moschylus). A similar jet, described by Bishop Methodius in the fourth century A.D., burned on Mount Lemnos in Lycia and was still alight in 1801. Hephaestus had a shrine on both these mountains. Lemnos (probably from *leibein*, 'she who pours out') was the name of the Great Goddess of this matriarchal island (Hecataeus, quoted by Stephanus of Byzantium *sub* Lemnos – see 149. 1).

## DEMETER'S NATURE AND DEEDS

THOUGH the priestesses of Demeter, goddess of the cornfield, initiate brides and bridegrooms into the secrets of the couch, she has no husband of her own. While still young and gay, she bore Core and the lusty Iacchus to Zeus, her brother, out of wedlock.[1] She also bore Plutus to the Titan Iasius, or Iasion, with whom she fell in love at the wedding of Cadmus and Harmonia. Inflamed by the nectar which flowed like water at the feast, the lovers slipped out of the house and lay together openly in a thrice-ploughed field. On their return, Zeus guessing from their demeanour and the mud on their arms and legs what they had been at, and enraged that Iasius should have dared to touch Demeter, struck him dead with a thunderbolt. But some say that Iasius was killed by his brother Dardanus, or torn to pieces by his own horses.[2]

*b.* Demeter herself has a gentle soul, and Erysichthon, son of Tropias, was one of the few men with whom she ever dealt harshly. At the head of twenty companions, Erysichthon dared invade a grove which the Pelasgians had planted for her at Dotium, and began cutting down the sacred trees, to provide timber for his new banqueting hall. Demeter assumed the form of Nicippe, priestess of the grove, and mildly ordered Erysichthon to desist. It was only when he threatened her with his axe that she revealed herself in splendour and condemned him to suffer perpetual hunger, however much he might eat. Back he went to dinner, and gorged all day at his parents' expense, growing hungrier and thinner the more he ate, until they could no longer afford to keep him supplied with food, and he became a beggar in the streets, eating filth. Contrariwise, on Pandareus the Cretan, who stole Zeus's golden dog and thus avenged her for the killing of Iasius, Demeter bestowed the royal gift of never suffering from the belly-ache.[3]

*c.* Demeter lost her gaiety for ever when young Core, afterwards called Persephone, was taken from her. Hades fell in love with Core, and went to ask Zeus's leave to marry her. Zeus feared to offend his eldest brother by a downright refusal, but knew also that Demeter would not forgive him if Core were committed to Tartarus; he therefore answered politically that he could neither give nor withhold his consent. This emboldened Hades to abduct the girl, as she was picking flowers in a meadow – it may have been at Sicilian Enna; or at Attic Colonus; or at Hermione; or somewhere in Crete, or near Pisa, or near Lerna; or beside Arcadian Pheneus, or at Boeotian Nysa, or anywhere else in the widely separated regions which Demeter visited in her wandering search for Core. But her own priests say that it was at Eleusis. She sought Core without rest for nine days and nights, neither eating nor drinking, and calling fruitlessly all the while. The only news she could get came from old Hecate, who early one morning had heard Core crying 'A rape! A rape!' but, on hurrying to the rescue, found no sign of her.[4]

d. On the tenth day, after a disagreeable encounter with Poseidon among the herds of Oncus, Demeter came in disguise to Eleusis, where King Celeus and his wife Metaneira entertained her hospitably; and she was invited to remain as wet-nurse to Demophoön, the newly-born prince. Their lame daughter Iambe tried to console Demeter with comically lascivious verses, and the dry-nurse, old Baubo, persuaded her to drink barley-water by a jest: she groaned as if in travail and, unexpectedly, produced from beneath her skirt Demeter's own son Iacchus, who leaped into his mother's arms and kissed her.

e. 'Oh, how greedily you drink!' cried Abas, an elder son of Celeus's, as Demeter gulped the pitcherful of barley-water, which was flavoured with mint. Demeter threw him a grim look, and he was metamorphosed into a lizard. Somewhat ashamed of herself, Demeter now decided to do Celeus a service, by making Demophoön immortal. That night she held him over the fire, to burn away his mortality. Metaneira, who was the daughter of Amphictyon, happened to enter the hall before the process was complete, and broke the spell; so Demophoön died. 'Mine is an unlucky house!' Celeus complained, weeping at the fate of his two sons, and thereafter was called Dysaules. 'Dry your tears, Dysaules,' said Demeter. 'You still have three sons, including Triptolemus on whom I intend to confer such great gifts that you will forget your double loss.'

f. For Triptolemus, who herded his father's cattle, had recognized Demeter and given her the news she needed: ten days before this his brothers Eumolpus, a shepherd, and Eubuleus, a swineherd, had been out in the fields, feeding their beasts, when the earth suddenly gaped open, engulfing Eubuleus's swine before his very eyes; then, with a heavy thud of hooves, a chariot drawn by black horses appeared, and dashed down the chasm. The chariot-driver's face was invisible, but his right arm was tightly clasped around a shrieking girl. Eumolpus had been told of the event by Eubuleus, and made it the subject for a lament.

*g*. Armed with this evidence, Demeter summoned Hecate. Together they approached Helius, who sees everything, and forced him to admit that Hades had been the villain, doubtless with the connivance of his brother Zeus. Demeter was so angry that, instead of returning to Olympus, she continued to wander about the earth, forbidding the trees to yield fruit and the herbs to grow, until the race of men stood in danger of extinction. Zeus, ashamed to visit Demeter in person at Eleusis, sent her first a message by Iris (of which she took no notice), and then a deputation of the Olympian gods, with conciliatory gifts, begging her to be reconciled to his will. But she would not return to Olympus, and swore that the earth must remain barren until Core had been restored.

*h*. Only one course of action remained for Zeus. He sent Hermes with a message to Hades: 'If you do not restore Core, we are all un-done!' and with another to Demeter: 'You may have your daughter again, on the single condition that she has not yet tasted the food of the dead.'

*i*. Because Core had refused to eat so much as a crust of bread ever since her abduction, Hades was obliged to cloak his vexation, telling her mildly: 'My child, you seem to be unhappy here, and your mother weeps for you. I have therefore decided to send you home.'

*j*. Core's tears ceased to flow, and Hermes helped her to mount his chariot. But, just as she was setting off for Eleusis, one of Hades's gardeners, by name Ascalaphus, began to cry and hoot derisively. 'Having seen the Lady Core,' he said, 'pick a pomegranate from a tree in your orchard, and eat seven seeds, I am ready to bear witness that she has tasted the food of the dead!' Hades grinned, and told Ascalaphus to perch on the back of Hermes's chariot.

*k*. At Eleusis, Demeter joyfully embraced Core; but, on hearing about the pomegranate, grew more dejected than ever, and said again: 'I will neither return to Olympus, nor remove my curse from the land.' Zeus then persuaded Rhea, the mother of Hades, Demeter, and himself, to plead with her; and a compromise was at last reached. Core should spend three months of the year in Hades's company, as Queen of Tartarus, with the title of Persephone, and the remaining nine in Demeter's. Hecate offered to make sure that this arrangement was kept, and to keep constant watch on Core.

*l.* Demeter finally consented to return home. Before leaving Eleusis, she instructed Triptolemus, Eumolpus, and Celeus (together with Diocles, King of Pherae, who had been assiduously searching for Core all this while) in her worship and mysteries. But she punished Ascalaphus for his tale-bearing by pushing him down a hole and covering it with an enormous rock, from which he was finally released by Heracles; and then she changed him into a short-eared owl.[5] She also rewarded the Pheneations of Arcadia, in whose house she rested after Poseidon had outraged her, with all kinds of grain, but forbade them to sow beans. One Cyamites was the first who dared do so; he has a shrine by the river Cephissus.[6]

*m.* Triptolemus she supplied with seed-corn, a wooden plough, and a chariot drawn by serpents; and sent him all over the world to teach mankind the art of agriculture. But first she gave him lessons on the Rarian Plain, which is why some call him the son of King Rarus. And to Phytalus, who had treated her kindly on the banks of the Cephissus, she gave a fig-tree, the first ever seen in Attica, and taught him how to cultivate it.[7]

1. Aristophanes: *Frogs* 338; *Orphic Hymn* li.
2. Homer: *Odyssey* v. 125–8; Diodorus Siculus: v. 49; Hesiod: *Theogony* 969 ff.
3. Servius on Virgil's *Aeneid* iii. 167; Hyginus: *Fabula* 250; Callimachus: *Hymn to Demeter* 34 ff.; Antoninus Liberalis: *Transformations* 11,; Pausanias: x. 30. 1.
4. Hyginus: *Fabula* 146; Diodorus Siculus: v. 3; Scholiast on Sophocles's *Oedipus at Colonus* 1590; Apollodorus: i. 5. 1; Scholiast on Hesiod's *Theogony* 914; Pausanias: vi. 21. 1 and i. 38. 5; Conon: *Narrations* 15; *Homeric Hymn to Demeter* 17.
5. Apollodorus: i. 5. 1–3 and 12; *Homeric Hymn to Demeter* 398 ff. and 445 ff.
6. Pausanias: viii. 15. 1 and i. 37. 3.
7. *Homeric Hymn to Demeter* 231–74; Apollodorus: i. 5. 2; *Orphic Fragment* 50; Hyginus: *Fabula* 146; Ovid: *Metamorphoses* v. 450–563 and *Fasti* iv. 614; Nicander: *Theriaca*; Pausanias: i. 14. 2 and 37. 2.

\*

1. Core, Persephone, and Hecate were, clearly, the Goddess in Triad as Maiden, Nymph, and Crone, at a time when only women practised the mysteries of agriculture. Core stands for the green corn, Persephone for the ripe ear, and Hecate for the harvested corn – the 'carline wife' of the English countryside. But Demeter was the goddess's general title, and

Persephone's name has been given to Core, which confuses the story. The myth of Demeter's adventure in the thrice-ploughed fields points to a fertility rite, which survived until recently in the Balkans: the corn-priestess will have openly coupled with the sacred king at the autumn sowing in order to ensure a good harvest. In Attica the field was first ploughed in spring; then, after the summer harvest, cross-ploughed with a lighter share; finally, when sacrifices had been offered to the Tillage-gods, ploughed again in the original direction during the autumn month of Pyanepsion, as a preliminary to sowing (Hesiod: *Works and Days* 432–3, 460, 462; Plutarch: *On Isis and Osiris* 69; *Against Colotes* 22).

2. Persephone (from *phero* and *phonos*, 'she who brings destruction'), also called Persephatta at Athens (from *ptersis* and *ephapto*, 'she who fixes destruction') and Proserpina ('the fearful one') at Rome, was, it seems, a title of the Nymph when she sacrificed the sacred king. The title 'Hecate' ('one hundred') apparently refers to the hundred lunar months of his reign, and to the hundredfold harvest. The king's death by a thunderbolt, or by the teeth of horses, or at the hands of the tanist, was his common fate in primitive Greece.

3. Core's abduction by Hades forms part of the myth in which the Hellenic trinity of gods forcibly marry the pre-Hellenic Triple-goddess – Zeus, Hera; Zeus or Poseidon, Demeter; Hades, Core – as in Irish myth Brian, Iuchar, and Iucharba marry the Triple-goddess Eire, Fodhla, and Banbha (see 7. 6 and 16. 1). It refers to male usurpation of the female agricultural mysteries in primitive times. Thus the incident of Demeter's refusal to provide corn for mankind is only another version of Ino's conspiracy to destroy Athamas's harvest (see 70. c). Further, the Core myth accounts for the winter burial of a female corn-puppet, which was uncovered in the early spring and found to be sprouting; this pre-Hellenic custom survived in the countryside in Classical times, and is illustrated by vase-paintings of men freeing Core from a mound of earth with mattocks, or breaking open Mother Earth's head with axes.

4. The story of Erysichthon, son of Tropias, is moral anecdote: among the Greeks, as among the Latins and early Irish, the felling of a sacred grove carried the death penalty. But a desperate and useless hunger for food, which the Elizabethans called 'the wolf', would not be an appropriate punishment for tree-felling, and Erysichthon's name – also borne by a son of Cecrops the patriarchalist and introducer of barley-cakes (see 25. d) – means 'earth-tearer', which suggests that his real crime was daring to plough without Demeter's consent, like Athamas. Pandareus's stealing of the golden dog suggests Cretan intervention in Greece, when the Achaeans tried to reform agricultural ritual. This dog, taken from the Earth-goddess, seems to have been the visible proof of the Achaean High King's independence of her (see 124. 1).

5. The myths of Hylas ('of the woodland' – see 150. *1*), Adonis (see 18. *7*), Lityerses (see 136. *e*), and Linus (see 147. *1*) describes the annual mourning for the sacred king, or his boy-surrogate, sacrificed to placate the goddess of vegetation. This same surrogate appears in the legend of Triptolemus, who rode in a serpent-drawn chariot and carried sacks of corn, to symbolize that his death brought wealth. He was also Plutus ('wealthy'), begotten in the ploughed field, from whom Hades's euphemistic title 'Pluto' is borrowed. Triptolemus (*triptolmaios*, 'thrice daring') may be a title awarded the sacred king for having three times dared to plough the field and couple with the corn-priestess. Celeus, Diocles, and Eumolpus, whom Demeter taught the art of agriculture, represent priestly heads of the Amphictyonic League – Metaneira is described as Amphictyon's daughter – who honoured her at Eleusis.

6. It was at Eleusis ('advent'), a Mycenaean city, that the great Eleusinian Mysteries were celebrated, in the month called Boedromion ('running for help'). Demeter's ecstatic initiates symbolically consummated her love affair with Iasius, or Triptolemus, or Zeus, in an inner recess of the shrine, by working a phallic object up and down a woman's top-boot; hence Eleusis suggests a worn-down derivative of *Eilythuies*, '[the temple] of her who rages in a lurking place'. The mystagogues, dressed as shepherds, then entered with joyful shouts, and displayed a winnowing-fan, containing the child Brimus, son of Brimo ('angry one'), the immediate fruit of this ritual marriage. Brimo was a title of Demeter's, and Brimus a synonym for Plutus; but his celebrants knew him best as Iacchus – from the riotuous hymn, the *Iacchus*, which was sung on the sixth day of the Mysteries during a torchlight procession from Demeter's temple.

7. Eumolpus represents the singing shepherds who brought in the child; Triptolemus is a cowherd, in service to Io the Moon-goddess as cow (see 56. *1*), who watered the seed-corn; and Eubuleus a swineherd, in service to the goddess Marpessa (see 74. *4* and 96. *2*), Phorcis, Choere, or Cerdo, the Sow-goddess, who made the corn sprout. Eubuleus was the first to reveal Core's fate, because 'swineherd', in early European myth, means soothsayer, or magician. Thus Eumaeus ('searching well'), Odysseus's swineherd (see 171. *a*), is addressed as *dios* ('god-like'); and though, by Classical times, swineherds had long ceased to exercise their prophetic art, swine were still sacrificed to Demeter and Persephone by being thrown down natural chasms. Eubuleus is not said to have benefited from Demeter's instruction, probably because her cult as Sow-goddess had been suppressed at Eleusis.

8. 'Rarus', whether it means 'an abortive child', or 'a womb', is an inappropriate name for a king, and will have referred to the womb of the Corn-mother from which the corn sprang.

9. Iambe and Baubo personify the obscene songs, in iambic metre, which were sung to relieve emotional tension at the Eleusinian Mysteries; but Iambe, Demeter, and Baubo form the familiar triad of maiden, nymph, and crone. Old nurses in Greek myth nearly always stand for the goddess as Crone. Abas was turned into a lizard, because lizards are found in the hottest and driest places, and can live without water; this is a moral anecdote told to teach children respect for their elders and reverence for the gods.

10. The story of Demeter's attempt to make Demophoön immortal is paralleled in the myths of Medea (see 156. a) and Thetis (see 181. r). It refers, partly, to the widespread primitive custom of 'saining' children against evil spirits with sacred fire carried around them at birth, or with a hot griddle set under them; partly to the custom of burning boys to death, as a vicarious sacrifice for the sacred king (see 92. 7), and so conferring immortality on them. Celeus, the name of Demophoön's father, can mean 'burner' as well as 'woodpecker' or 'sorcerer'.

11. A primitive taboo rested on red-coloured food, which might be offered to the dead only (see 170. 5); and the pomegranate was supposed to have sprung – like the eight-petalled scarlet anemone – from the blood of Adonis, or Tammuz (see 18. 7). The seven pomegranate seeds represent, perhaps, the seven phases of the moon during which farmers wait for the green corn-shoots to appear. But Persephone eating the pomegranate is originally Sheol, the Goddess of Hell, devouring Tammuz; while Ishtar (Sheol herself in a different guise) weeps to placate his ghost. Hera, as a former Death-goddess, also held a pomegranate.

12. The ascalaphos, or short-eared owl, was a bird of evil omen; and the fable of his tale-bearing is told to account for the noisiness of owls in November, before the three winter months of Core's absence begin. Heracles released Ascalaphus (see 134. d).

13. Demeter's gift of the fig to Phytalus, whose family was a leading one in Attica (see 97. a), means no more than that the practice of fig-caprification – pollenizing the domestic tree with a branch of the wild one – ceased to be a female prerogative at the same time as agriculture. The taboo on the planting of beans by men seems to have survived later than that on grain, because of the close connexion between beans and ghosts. In Rome beans were thrown to ghosts at the All Souls' festival, and if a plant grew from one of these, and a woman ate its beans, she would be impregnated by a ghost. Hence the Pythagoreans abstained from beans lest they might deny an ancestor his chance of reincarnation.

14. Demeter is said to have reached Greece by way of Crete, landing at Thoricus in Attica (Hymn to Demeter 123). This is probable: the Cretans had established themselves in Attica, where they first worked the silver mines at Laureium. Moreover, Eleusis is a Mycenaean site, and Diodorus

Siculus (v. 77) says that rites akin to the Eleusinian were performed at Cnossus for all who cared to attend, and that (v. 79) according to the Cretans all rites of initiation were invented by their ancestors. But Demeter's origin is to be looked for in Libya.

15. The flowers which, according to Ovid, Core was picking were poppies. An image of a goddess with poppy-heads in her headdress was found at Gazi in Crete; another goddess on a mould from Palaiokastro holds poppies in her hand; and on the gold ring from the Acropolis Treasure at Mycenae a seated Demeter gives three poppy-heads to a standing Core. Poppy-seeds were used as a condiment on bread, and poppies are naturally associated with Demeter, since they grow in corn-fields; but Core picks or accepts poppies because of the soporific qualities, and because of their scarlet colour which promises resurrection after death (see 27. 12). She is about to retire for her annual sleep.

# 25

## ATHENE'S NATURE AND DEEDS

ATHENE invented the flute, the trumpet, the earthenware pot, the plough, the rake, the ox-yoke, the horse-bridle, the chariot, and the ship. She first taught the science of numbers, and all women's arts, such as cooking, weaving, and spinning. Although a goddess of war, she gets no pleasure from battle, as Ares and Eris do, but rather from settling disputes, and upholding the law by pacific means. She bears no arms in time of peace and, if ever she needs any, will usually borrow a set from Zeus. Her mercy is great: when the judges' votes are equal in a criminal trial at the Areiopagus, she always gives a casting vote to liberate the accused. Yet, once engaged in battle, she never loses the day, even against Ares himself, being better grounded in tactics and strategy than he; and wise captains always approach her for advice.[1]

b. Many gods, Titans, and giants would gladly have married Athene, but she has repulsed all advances. On one occasion, in the course of the Trojan War, not wishing to borrow arms from Zeus, who had declared himself neutral, she asked Hephaestus to make her a set of her own. Hephaestus refused payment, saying coyly that he would undertake the work for love; and when, missing the implication of these words, she entered the smithy to watch him beat out the red-hot metal, he suddenly turned about and tried to outrage her. Hephaestus, who does not often behave so grossly, was the victim of a malicious joke: Poseidon had just informed him that Athene was on her way to the smithy, with Zeus's consent, hopefully expecting to have violent love made to her. As she tore herself away, Hephaestus ejaculated against her thigh, a little above the knee. She wiped off the seed with a handful of wool, which she threw away in disgust; it fell to the ground near Athens, and accidentally fertilized Mother Earth, who was on a visit there. Revolted at the prospect of bearing a child which Hephaestus had tried to father on Athene, Mother Earth declared that she would accept no responsibility for its upbringing.

c. 'Very well,' said Athene, 'I will take care of it myself.' So she took charge of the infant as soon as he was born, called him Erichthonius and, not wishing Poseidon to laugh at the success of his practical joke, hid him in a sacred basket; this she gave to Aglauros, eldest daughter of the Athenian King Cecrops, with orders to guard it carefully.[2]

d. Cecrops, a son of Mother Earth and, like Erichthonius – whom some suppose to have been his father – part man, part serpent, was the first king to recognize paternity. He married a daughter of Actaeus, the earliest King of Attica. He also instituted monogamy, divided Attica into twelve communities, built temples to Athene, and abolished certain bloody sacrifices in favour of sober barley-cake offerings.[3] His wife was named Agraulos; and his three daughters, Aglauros, Herse, and Pandrosos, lived in a three-roomed house on the Acropolis. One evening, when the girls had returned from a festival, carrying Athene's sacred baskets on their heads, Hermes bribed Aglauros to give him access to Herse, the youngest of the three, with whom he had fallen violently in love. Aglauros kept Hermes's gold, but did nothing to earn it, because Athene had made her jealous of Herse's good fortune; so Hermes strode angrily into the house, turned Aglauros to stone, and had his will of Herse. After Herse had borne Hermes two sons, Cephalus, the beloved of Eos, and Ceryx, the first herald of the Eleusinian Mysteries, she and Pandrosos and their mother Agraulos were curious enough to peep beneath the lid of the basket which Aglauros had carried. Seeing a child with a serpent's tail for legs, they screamed in fear and, headed by Agraulos, leaped from the Acropolis.[4]

e. On learning of this fatality, Athene was so grieved that she let fall the enormous rock which she had been carrying to the Acropolis as an additional fortification, and it became Mount Lycabettus. As for the crow that had brought her the news, she changed its colour from white to black, and forbade all crows ever again to visit the Acropolis. Erich-

thonius then took refuge in Athene's aegis, where she reared him so
tenderly that some mistook her for his mother. Later, he became King
of Athens, where he instituted the worship of Athene, and taught his
fellow-citizens the use of silver. His image was set among the stars as
the constellation Auriga, since he had introduced the four-horse
chariot.[5]

*f.* Another, very different, account of Agraulos's death is current:
namely that once, when an assault was being launched against Athens,
she threw herself from the Acropolis, in obedience to an oracle, and so
saved the day. This version purports to explain why all young Athenians, on first taking up arms, visit the temple of Agraulos and there
dedicate their lives to the city.[6]

*g.* Athene, though as modest as Artemis, is far more generous.
When Teiresias, one day, accidentally surprised her in a bath, she laid
her hands over his eyes and blinded him, but gave him inward sight
by way of a compensation.[7]

*h.* She is not recorded to have shown petulant jealousy on more than
a single occasion. This is the story. Arachne, a princess of Lydian
Colophon – famed for its purple dye – was so skilled in the art of
weaving that Athene herself could not compete with her. Shown a
cloth into which Arachne had woven illustrations of Olympian love
affairs, the goddess searched closely to find a fault but, unable to do so,
tore it up in a cold, vengeful rage. When the terrified Arachne hanged
herself from a rafter, Athene turned her into a spider – the insect she
hates most – and the rope into a cobweb, up which Arachne climbed
to safety.[8]

1. Tzetzes: *On Lycophron* 520; Hesychius *sub* Hippia; Servius on
   Virgil's *Aeneid* iv. 402; Pindar: *Olympian Odes* xiii. 79; Livy: vii.
   3; Pausanias: i. 24. 3, etc.; Homer: *Iliad* i. 199 ff.; v. 736; v. 840–
   863; xxi. 391–422; Aeschylus: *Eumenides* 753.
2. Hyginus: *Poetic Astronomy* ii. 13; Apollodorus: iii. 14. 6; Hyginus:
   *Fabula* 166.
3. Pausanias: i. 5. 3; viii. 2. 1; Apollodorus: iii. 14. 1; Strabo: ix. 1.
   20; Aristophanes: *Plutus* 773; Athenaeus: p. 555c; Eustathius: *On
   Homer* p. 1156; Parian Marble: lines 2–4.
4. Apollodorus: iii. 14. 3 and 6; *Inscriptiones Graecae* xiv. 1389;
   Hyginus: *Fabula* 166.
5. Antigonus Carystius: 12; Callimachus: *Hecale* i. 2. 3; Philostratus: *Life of Apollonius of Tyana* vii. 24; Hyginus: *Poetic Astronomy* ii. 13; *Fabula* 274; Apollodorus: iii. 14. 1.
6. Suidas and Hesychius *sub* Agraulos; Plutarch: *Alcibiades* 15.

7. Callimachus: *The Bathing of Pallas.*
8. Ovid: *Metamorphoses* vi. 1–145; Virgil: *Georgics* iv. 246.

\*

1. The Athenians made their goddess's maidenhood symbolic of the city's invincibility; and therefore disguised early myths of her outrage by Poseidon (see 19. 2), and Boreas (see 48. 1); and denied that Erichthonius, Apollo, and Lychnus ('lamp') were her sons by Hephaestus. They derived 'Erichthonius' from either *erion*, 'wool', or *eris*, 'strife', and *chthonos*, 'earth', and invented the myth of his birth to explain the presence, in archaic pictures, of a serpent-child peeping from the goddess's aegis. Poseidon's part in the birth of Erichthonius may originally have been a simpler and more direct one; why else should Erichthonius introduce the Poseidonian four-horse chariot into Athens?

2. Athene had been the Triple-goddess, and when the central person, the Goddess as Nymph, was suppressed and myths relating to her transferred to Aphrodite, Oreithyia (see 48. *b*), or Alcippe (see 19. *b*), there remained the Maiden clad in goat-skins, who specialized in war (see 8. 1), and the Crone, who inspired oracles and presided over all the arts. *Erichthonius* is perhaps an expanded form of *Erechtheus* (see 47. 1), meaning 'from the land of heather' (see 18. 1) rather than 'much earth', as is usually said; the Athenians represented him as a serpent with a human head, because he was the hero, or ghost, of the sacrificed king who made the Crone's wishes known. In this Crone-aspect, Athene was attended by an owl and a crow. The ancient royal family of Athens claimed descent from Erichthonius and Erechtheus, and called themselves Erechtheids; they used to wear golden serpents as amulets and kept a sacred serpent in the Erechtheum. But Erichthonius was also a procreative wind from the heather-clad mountains, and Athene's aegis (or a replica) was taken to all newly married couples at Athens, to ensure their fertility (Suidas *sub* Aegis).

3. Some of the finest Cretan pots are known to have been made by women, and so originally, no doubt, were all the useful instruments invented by Athene; but in Classical Greece an artisan had to be a man. Silver was at first a more valuable metal than gold, since harder to refine, and sacred to the moon; Periclean Athens owed her pre-eminence largely to the rich silver mines at Laureium first worked by the Cretans, which allowed her to import food and buy allies.

4. The occasion on which Cecrops's daughters leaped from the Acropolis may have been a Hellenic capture of Athens, after which an attempt was made to force monogamy on Athene's priestesses, as in the myth of Halirrhothius (see 19. *b*). They preferred death to dishonour – hence the oath taken by the Athenian youths at Agraulos's shrine. The other story of Agraulos's death is merely a moral anecdote: a warning against

the violation of Athene's mysteries. 'Agraulos' was one more title of the Moon-goddess; *agraulos* and its transliteration *aglauros* mean much the same thing, *agraulos* being a Homeric epithet for shepherds, and *aglauros* (like *herse* and *pandrosos*) referring to the moon as the reputed source of the dew which refreshed the pastures. At Athens girls went out under the full moon at midsummer to gather dew – the same custom survived in England until the last century – for sacred purposes. The festival was called the Hersephoria, or 'dew-gathering'; Agraulos or Agraule was, in fact, a title of Athene herself, and Agraule is said to have been worshipped in Cyprus until late times (Porphyry: *On Vegetarianism* 30) with human sacrifices. A gold ring from Mycenae shows three priestesses advancing towards a temple; the two leaders scatter dew, the third (presumably Agraulos) has a branch tied to her elbow. The ceremony perhaps originated in Crete. Hermes's seduction of Herse, for which he paid Aglauros in gold, must refer to the ritual prostitution of priestesses before an image of the goddess – Aglauros turned to stone. The sacred baskets carried on such occasions will have contained phallic snakes and similar orgiastic objects. Ritual prostitution by devotees of the Moon-goddess was practised in Crete, Cyprus, Syria, Asia Minor, and Palestine.

5. Athene's expulsion of the crow is a mythic variant of Cronus's banishment – *Cronus* means 'crow' (see 6. 2) – the triumph, in fact, of Olympianism, with the introduction of which Cecrops, who is really Ophion-Boreas the Pelasgian demiurge (see 1. 1), has here been wrongly credited. The crow's change of colour recalls the name of Athene's Welsh counterpart: Branwen, 'white crow', sister to Bran (see 57. 1). Athene was, it seems, titled 'Coronis'.

6. Her vengeance on Arachne may be more than just a pretty fable, if it records an early commercial rivalry between the Athenians and the Lydio-Carian thalassocrats, or sea-rulers, who were of Cretan origin. Numerous seals with a spider emblem which have been found at Cretan Miletus – the mother city of Carian Miletus and the largest exporter of dyed woollens in the ancient world – suggest a public textile industry operated there at the beginning of the second millennium B.C. For a while the Milesians controlled the profitable Black Sea trade, and had an *entrepôt* at Naucratis in Egypt. Athene had good reason to be jealous of the spider.

7. An apparent contradiction occurs in Homer. According to the *Catalogue of the Ships* (*Iliad* ii. 547 ff.), Athene set Erechtheus down in her rich temple at Athens; but, according to the *Odyssey* (vii. 80), she goes to Athens and enters his strong house. The fact was that the sacred king had his own quarters in the Queen's palace where the goddess's image was kept. There were no temples in Crete or Mycenaean Greece, only domestic shrines or oracular caves.

## PAN'S NATURE AND DEEDS

SEVERAL powerful gods and goddesses of Greece have never been enrolled among the Olympian Twelve. Pan, for instance, a humble fellow, now dead, was content to live on earth in rural Arcadia; and Hades, Persephone, and Hecate know that their presence is unwelcome on Olympus; and Mother Earth is far too old and set in her ways to accommodate herself to the family life of her grandchildren and great-grandchildren.

*b.* Some say that Hermes fathered Pan on Dryope, daughter of Dryops; or on the nymph Oeneis; or on Penelope, wife of Odysseus, whom he visited in the form of a ram; or on Amaltheia the Goat.¹ He is said to have been so ugly at birth, with horns, beard, tail, and goat-legs, that his mother ran away from him in fear, and Hermes carried him up to Olympus for the gods' amusement. But Pan was Zeus's foster-brother, and therefore far older than Hermes, or than Penelope, on whom (others say) he was fathered by all the suitors who wooed her during Odysseus's absence. Still others make him the son of Cronus and Rhea; or of Zeus by Hybris, which is the least improbable account.²

*c.* He lived in Arcadia, where he guarded flocks, herds, and bee-hives, took part in the revels of the mountain-nymphs, and helped hunters to find their quarry. He was, on the whole, easy-going and lazy, loving nothing better than his afternoon sleep, and revenged himself on those who disturbed him with a sudden loud shout from a grove, or grotto, which made the hair bristle on their heads. Yet the Arcadians paid him so little respect that, if ever they returned empty-handed after a long day's hunting, they dared scourge him with squills.³

*d.* Pan seduced several nymphs, such as Echo, who bore him Iynx and came to an unlucky end for love of Narcissus; and Eupheme, nurse of the Muses, who bore him Crotus, the Bowman in the Zodiac. He also boasted that he had coupled with all Dionysus's drunken Maenads.⁴

*e.* Once he tried to violate the chaste Pitys, who escaped him only by being metamorphosed into a fir-tree, a branch of which he afterwards wore as a chaplet. On another occasion he pursued the chaste Syrinx from Mount Lycaeum to the River Ladon, where she became a reed; there, since he could not distinguish her from among all the rest, he cut

several reeds at random, and made them into a Pan-pipe. His greatest
success in love was the seduction of Selene, which he accomplished by
disguising his hairy black goatishness with well-washed white fleeces.
Not realizing who he was, Selene consented to ride on his back, and let
him do as he pleased with her.[5]

*f.* The Olympian gods, while despising Pan for his simplicity and
love of riot, exploited his powers. Apollo wheedled the art of prophecy
from him, and Hermes copied a pipe which he had let fall, claimed it as
his own invention, and sold it to Apollo.

*g.* Pan is the only god who has died in our time. The news of his
death came to one Thamus, a sailor in a ship bound for Italy by way of
the island of Paxi. A divine voice shouted across the sea: 'Thamus, are
you there? When you reach Palodes, take care to proclaim that the
great god Pan is dead!', which Thamus did; and the news was greeted
from the shore with groans and laments.[6]

1. *Homeric Hymn to Pan* 34 ff.; Scholiast on Theocritus's *Idylls* i. 3;
   Herodotus: ii. 145; Eratosthenes: *Catasterismoi* 27.
2. *Homeric Hymn to Pan: loc. cit.*; Servius on Virgil's *Georgics* i. 16;
   Duris, quoted by Tzetzes: *On Lycophron* 772; Apollodorus: 1. 4. 1;
   Scholiast on Aeschylus's *Rhesus* 30.
3. Theocritus: *Idylls* i. 16; Euripides: *Rhesus* 36; Hesychius *sub*
   Agreus Theocritus: *Idylls* vii. 107.
4. Ovid: *Metamorphoses* iii. 356–401; Hyginus: *Fabula* 224; *Poetic
   Astronomy* ii. 27.
5. Lucian: *Dialogues of the Gods* xxii. 4; Ovid: *Metamorphoses* i.
   694–712; Philargyrius on Virgil's *Georgics* iii. 392.
6. Plutarch: *Why Oracles Are Silent* 17.

*

1. Pan, whose name is usually derived from *paein*, 'to pasture', stands
for the 'devil', or 'upright man', of the Arcadian fertility cult, which
closely resembled the witch cult of North-western Europe. This man,
dressed in a goat-skin, was the chosen lover of the Maenads during their
drunken orgies on the high mountains, and sooner or later paid for his
privilege with death.

2. The accounts of Pan's birth vary greatly. Since Hermes was the
power resident in a phallic stone which formed the centre of these orgies
(see 14. 1), the shepherds described their god Pan as his son by a woodpecker, a bird whose tapping is held to portend the welcome summer
rain. The myth that he fathered Pan on Oeneis is self-explanatory, though
the original Maenads used other intoxicants than wine (see 27. 2); and

the name of his reputed mother, Penelope ('with a web over her face'), suggests that the Maenads wore some form of war paint for their orgies, recalling the stripes of the *penelope*, a variety of duck. Plutarch says (*On the Delays of Divine Punishment* 12) that the Maenads who killed Orpheus were tattooed by their husbands as a punishment (see 28. *f*); and a Maenad whose legs and arms are tattooed with a webbed pattern appears on a vase at the British Museum (Catalogue E. 301). Hermes's visit to Penelope in the form of a ram – the ram devil is as common in the North-western witch cult as the goat – her impregnation by all the suitors (see 171. *l*), and the claim that Pan had coupled with every one of the Maenads refers to the promiscuous nature of the revels in honour of the Fir-goddess Pitys or Elate (see 78. *1*). The Arcadian mountaineers were the most primitive in Greece (see 1. *5*), and their more civilized neighbours professed to despise them.

3. Pan's son, the wryneck, or snake-bird, was a spring migrant employed in erotic charms (see 56. *1* and 152. *2*). Squills contain an irritant poison – valuable against mice and rats – and were used as a purge and diuretic before taking part in a ritual act; thus squill came to symbolize the removal of evil influences (Pliny: *Natural History* xx. 39), and Pan's image was scourged with squill if game were scarce (see 108. *10*).

4. His seduction of Selene must refer to a moonlight May Eve orgy, in which the young Queen of the May rode upon her upright man's back before celebrating a greenwood marriage with him. By this time the ram cult had superseded the goat cult in Arcadia (see 27. *2*).

5. The Egyptian Thamus apparently misheard the ceremonial lament *Thamus Pan-megas Tethnēce* ('the all-great Tammuz is dead!') for the message: 'Thamus, Great Pan is dead!' At any rate, Plutarch, a priest at Delphi in the latter half of the first century A.D., believed and published it; yet when Pausanias made his tour of Greece, about a century later, he found Pan's shrines, altars, sacred caves, and sacred mountains still much frequented.

# 27

## DIONYSUS'S NATURE AND DEEDS

AT Hera's orders the Titans seized Zeus's newly-born son Dionysus, a horned child crowned with serpents and, despite his transformations, tore him into shreds. These they boiled in a cauldron, while a pomegranate-tree sprouted from the soil where his blood had fallen; but, rescued and reconstituted by his grandmother Rhea, he came to life again. Persephone, now entrusted with his charge by Zeus, brought him to King Athamas of Orchomenus and his wife Ino, whom she persuaded to rear the child in the women's quarters, disguised as a girl. But Hera could not be deceived, and punished the royal pair with madness, so that Athamas killed their son Learches, mistaking him for a stag.[1]

b. Then, on Zeus's instructions, Hermes temporarily transformed Dionysus into a kid or a ram, and presented him to the nymphs Macris, Nysa, Erato, Bromie, and Bacche, of Heliconian Mount Nysa. They tended Dionysus in a cave, cosseted him, and fed him on honey, for which service Zeus subsequently placed their images among the stars, naming them the Hyades. It was on Mount Nysa that Dionysus invented wine, for which he is chiefly celebrated.[2]

When he grew to manhood Hera recognized him as Zeus's son, despite the effeminacy to which his education had reduced him, and drove him mad also. He went wandering all over the world, accompanied by his tutor Silenus and a wild army of Satyrs and Maenads, whose weapons were the ivy-twined staff tipped with a pine-cone, called the *thyrsus*, and swords and serpents and fear-imposing bull-roarers. He sailed to Egypt, bringing the vine with him; and at Pharos King Proteus received him hospitably. Among the Libyans of the Nile Delta, opposite Pharos, were certain Amazon queens whom Dionysus invited to march with him against the Titans and restore King Ammon to the kingdom from which he had been expelled. Dionysus's defeat of the Titans and restoration of King Ammon was the earliest of his many military successes.[3]

c. He then turned east and made for India. Coming to the Euphrates, he was opposed by the King of Damascus, whom he flayed alive, but built a bridge across the river with ivy and vine; after which a tiger, sent by his father Zeus, helped him across the river Tigris. He reached India, having met with much opposition by the way, and conquered the whole country, which he taught the art of viniculture, also giving it laws and founding great cities.[4]

d. On his return he was opposed by the Amazons, a horde of whom he chased as far as Ephesus. A few took sanctury in the Temple of Artemis, where their descendants are still living; others fled to Samos and Dionysus followed them in boats, killing so many that the battle-field is called Panhaema. Near Phloeum some of the elephants which he had brought from India died, and their bones are still pointed out.[5]

*e.* Next, Dionysus returned to Europe by way of Phrygia, where his grandmother Rhea purified him of the many murders he had committed during his madness, and initiated him into her Mysteries. He then invaded Thrace; but no sooner had his people landed at the mouth of the river Strymon than Lycurgus, King of the Edonians, opposed them savagely with an ox-goad, and captured the entire army, except Dionysus himself, who plunged into the sea and took refuge in Thetis's grotto. Rhea, vexed by this reverse, helped the prisoners to escape, and drove Lycurgus mad: he struck his own son Dryas dead with an axe, in the belief that he was cutting down a vine. Before recovering his senses he had begun to prune the corpse of its nose and ears, fingers and toes; and the whole land of Thrace grew barren in horror of his crime. When Dionysus, returning from the sea, announced that this barrenness would continue unless Lycurgus were put to death, the Edonians led him to Mount Pangaeum, where wild horses pulled his body apart.[6]

*f.* Dionysus met with no further opposition in Thrace, but travelled on to his well-beloved Boeotia, where he visited Thebes, and invited the women to join his revels on Mount Cithaeron. Pentheus, King of Thebes, disliking Dionysus's dissolute appearance, arrested him, together with all his Maenads, but went mad and, instead of shackling Dionysus, shackled a bull. The Maenads escaped again, and went raging out upon the mountains, where they tore calves in pieces. Pentheus attempted to stop them; but, inflamed by wine and religious ecstasy, they rent him limb from limb. His mother Agave led the riot, and it was she who wrenched off his head.[7]

*g.* At Orchomenus the three daughters of Minyas, by name Alcithoë, Leucippe, and Arsippe, or Aristippe, or Arsinoë, refused to join in the revels, though Dionysus himself invited them, appearing in the form of a girl. He then changed his shape, becoming successively a lion, a bull, and a panther, and drove them insane. Leucippe offered her own son Hippasus as a sacrifice – he had been chosen by lot – and the three sisters, having torn him to pieces and devoured him, skimmed the mountains in a frenzy until at last Hermes changed them into birds, though some say that Dionysus changed them into bats.[8] The murder of Hippasus is annually atoned at Orchomenus, in a feast called Agrionia ('provocation to savagery'), when the women devotees pretend to seek Dionysus and then, having agreed that he must be away with the Muses, sit in a circle and ask riddles, until the priest of Dionysus rushes from his temple, with a sword, and kills the one whom he first catches.[9]

h. When all Boeotia had acknowledged Dionysus's divinity, he made a tour of the Aegean Islands, spreading joy and terror wherever he went. Arriving at Icaria, he found that his ship was unseaworthy, and hired another from certain Tyrrhenian sailors who claimed to be bound for Naxos. But they proved to be pirates and, unaware of his godhead, steered for Asia, intending to sell him there as a slave. Dionysus made a vine grow from the deck and enfold the mast, while ivy twined about the rigging; he also turned the oars into serpents, and became a lion himself, filling the vessel with phantom beasts and the sound of flutes, so that the terrified pirates leaped overboard and became dolphins.[10]

i. It was at Naxos that Dionysus met the lovely Ariadne whom Theseus had deserted, and married her without delay. She bore him Oenopion, Thoas, Staphylus, Latromis, Euanthes, and Tauropolus. Later, he placed her bridal chaplet among the stars.[11]

j. From Naxos he came to Argos and punished Perseus, who at first opposed him and killed many of his followers, by inflicting a madness on the Argive women: they began devouring their own infants raw. Perseus hastily admitted his error, and appeased Dionysus by building a temple in his honour.

k. Finally, having established his worship throughout the world, Dionysus ascended to Heaven, and now sits at the right hand of Zeus as one of the Twelve Great Ones. The self-effacing goddess Hestia resigned her seat at the high table in his favour; glad of any excuse to escape the jealous wranglings of her family, and knowing that she could always count on a quiet welcome in any Greek city which it might please her to visit. Dionysus then descended, by way of Lerna, to Tartarus where he bribed Persephone with a gift of myrtle to release his dead mother, Semele. She ascended with him into Artemis's temple at Troezen; but, lest other ghosts should be jealous and aggrieved, he changed her name and introduced her to his fellow-Olympians as Thyone. Zeus placed an apartment at her disposal, and Hera preserved an angry but resigned silence.[12]

1. Euripides: Bacchae 99–102; Onomacritus, quoted by Pausanias: viii. 37. 3; Diodorus Siculus: iii. 62; Orphic Hymn xlv. 6; Clement of Alexandria: Address to the Greeks ii. 16.

2. Apollodorus: iii. 4. 3; Hyginus: *Fabula* 182; Theon on Aratus's *Phenomena* 177; Diodorus Siculus: iii. 68–69; Apollonius Rhodius: iv. 1131; Servius on Virgil's *Eclogues* vi. 15.

3. Apollodorus: iii. 5. 1; Aeschylus: *The Edonians, a Fragment*; Diodorus Siculus: iii. 70–71.

4. Euripides: *Bacchae* 13; Theophilus, quoted by Plutarch: *On Rivers* 24; Pausanias: x. 29. 2; Diodorus Siculus: ii. 38; Strabo: xi. 5. 5; Philostratus: *Life of Apollonius of Tyana* ii. 8–9; Arrian: *Indica* 5.

5. Pausanias: vii. 2. 4–5; Plutarch: *Greek Questions* 56.

6. Apollodorus: iii. 5. 1; Homer: *Iliad* vi. 130–40.

7. Theocritus: *Idylls* xxvi.; Ovid: *Metamorphoses* iii. 714 ff.; Euripides: *Bacchae, passim*.

8. Ovid: *Metamorphosis* iv. 1–40; 390–415; Antoninus Liberalis: 10; Aelian: *Varia Historia* iii. 42; Plutarch: *Greek Questions* 38.

9. Plutarch: *loc. cit.*

10. *Homeric Hymn to Dionysus* 6 ff.; Apollodorus: iii. 5. 3; Ovid: *Metamorphoses* iii. 577–699.

11. Scholiast on Apollonius Rhodius: iii. 996; Hesiod: *Theogony* 947; Hyginus: *Poetic Astronomy* ii. 5.

12. Apollodorus: iii. 5. 3; Pausanias: ii. 31. 2.

\*

1. The main clue to Dionysus's mystic history is the spread of the vine cult over Europe, Asia and North Africa. Wine was not invented by the Greeks: it seems to have been first imported in jars from Crete. Grapes grew wild on the southern coast of the Black Sea, whence their cultivation spread to Mount Nysa in Libya, by way of Palestine, and so to Crete; to India, by way of Persia; and to Bronze Age Britain, by way of the Amber Route. The wine orgies of Asia Minor and Palestine – the Canaanite Feast of Tabernacles was, originally, a Bacchanal orgy – were marked by much the same ecstasies as the beer orgies of Thrace and Phrygia. Dionysus's triumph was that wine everywhere superseded other intoxicants (see 38. 3). According to Pherecydes (178) *Nysa* means 'tree'.

2. He had once been subservient to the Moon-goddess Semele (see 14. 5) – also called Thyone, or Cotytto (see 3. 1) – and the destined victim of her orgies. His being reared as a girl, as Achilles also was (see 160. 5), recalls the Cretan custom of keeping boys 'in darkness'(*scotioi*), that is to say, in the women's quarters, until puberty. One of his titles was *Dendrites*, 'tree-youth', and the Spring Festival, when the trees suddenly burst into leaf and the whole world is intoxicated with desire, celebrated his emancipation. He is described as a horned child in order not to particularize the horns, which were goat's, stag's, bull's, or ram's according to the place of his worship. When Apollodorus says that he was disguised as a kid to save him from the wrath of Hera – 'Eriphus' ('kid') was one of his titles

(Hesychius *sub* Eriphos) – this refers to the Cretan cult of Dionysus-Zagreus, the wild goat with the enormous horns. Virgil (*Georgics* ii. 380–84) wrongly explains that the goat was the animal most commonly sacrificed to Dionysus 'because goats injure the vine by gnawing it.' Dionysus as a stag is Learchus, whom Athamas killed when driven mad by Hera. In Thrace he was a white bull. But in Arcadia Hermes disguised him as a ram, because the Arcadians were shepherds, and the Sun was entering the Ram at their Spring Festival. The Hyades ('rain-makers') into whose charge he gave Dionysus, were renamed 'the tall', 'the lame', 'the passionate', 'the roaring', and 'the raging' Ones, to describe his ceremonies. Hesiod (quoted by Theon: *On Aratus* 171) records the Hyades' earlier names as Phaesyle (? 'filtered light'), Coronis ('crow'), Cleia ('famous'), Phaeo ('dim'), and Eudore ('generous'); and Hyginus's list (*Poetis Astronomy* ii. 21) is somewhat similar. *Nysus* means 'lame', and in these beer orgies on the mountain the sacred king seems to have hobbled like a partridge – as in the Canaanite Spring Festival called the *Pesach* ('hobbling' – see 23. *1*). But that Macris fed Dionysus on honey, and that the Maenads used ivy-twined fir-branches as thyrsi, records an earlier form of intoxicant: spruce-beer, laced with ivy, and sweetened with mead. Mead was 'nectar', brewed from fermented honey, which the gods continued to drink in the Homeric Olympus.

3. J. E. Harrison, who first pointed out (*Prolegomena* ch. viii) that Dionysus the Wine-god is a late superimposition on Dionysus the Beer-god also called Sabazius, suggests that *tragedy* may be derived not from *tragos*, 'a goat', as Virgil suggests (*loc. cit.*), but from *tragos*, 'spelt' – a grain used in Athens for beer-brewing. She adds that, in early vase-paintings, horse-men, not goat-men, are pictured as Dionysus's companions; and that his grape-basket is, at first, a winnowing fan. In fact, the Libyan or Cretan goat was associated with wine; the Helladic horse with beer and nectar. Thus Lycurgus, who opposes the later Dionysus, is torn to pieces by wild horses – priestesses of the Mare-headed goddess – which was the fate of the earlier Dionysus. Lycurgus's story has been confused by the irrelevant account of the curse that overtook his land after the murder of Dryas ('oak'); Dryas was the oak-king, annually killed. The trimming of his extremities served to keep his ghost at bay (see 153. *b* and 171. *i*), and the wanton felling of a sacred oak carried the death penalty. Cotytto was the name of the goddess in whose honour the Edonian Rites were performed (Strabo: x. 3. 16).

4. Dionysus had epiphanies as Lion, Bull, and Serpent, because these were Calendar emblems of the tripartite year (see 31. *7*; 75. *2*, and 123. *1*). He was born in winter as a serpent (hence his serpent crown); became a lion in the spring; and was killed and devoured as a bull, goat, or stag at midsummer. These were his transformations when the Titans set on him

(see 30. *a*). Among the Orchomenans a panther seems to have taken the serpent's place. His Mysteries resembled Osiris's; hence his visit to Egypt.

5. Hera's hatred of Dionysus and his wine-cup, like the hostility shown by Pentheus and Perseus, reflects conservative opposition to the ritual use of wine and to the extravagant Maenad fashion, which had spread from Thrace to Athens, Corinth, Sicyon, Delphi, and other civilized cities. Eventually, in the late seventh and early sixth centuries B.C., Periander, tyrant of Corinth, Cleisthenes, tyrant of Sicyon, and Peisistratus, tyrant of Athens, deciding to approve the cult, founded official Dionysiac feasts. Thereupon Dionysus and his vine were held to have been accepted in Heaven – he ousted Hestia from her position as one of the Twelve Olympians at the close of the fifth century B.C. – though some gods continued to exact 'sober sacrifices'. But, although one of the recently deciphered tablets from Nestor's palace at Pylus shows that he had divine status even in the thirteenth century B.C., Dionysus never really ceased to be a demi-god, and the tomb of his annual resurrection continued to be shown at Delphi (Plutarch: *On Isis and Osiris* 35), where the priests regarded Apollo as his immortal part (see 28. *3*). The story of his rebirth from Zeus's thigh, as the Hittite god of the Winds had been born from Kumabi's (see 6. *6*), repudiates his original matriarchal setting. Ritual rebirth from a man was a well-known Jewish adoption ceremony (*Ruth* iii. 9), a Hittite borrowing.

6. Dionysus voyaged in a new-moon boat, and the story of his conflict with the pirates seems to have been based on the same icon which gave rise to the legend of Noah and the beasts in the Ark: the lion, serpent, and other creatures are his seasonal epiphanies. Dionysus is, in fact, Deucalion (see 38. *3*). The Laconians of Brasiae preserved an uncanonical account of his birth: how Cadmus shut Semele and her child in an ark, which drifted to Brasiae, where Semele died and was buried, and how Ino reared Dionysus (Pausanias: iii. 24. 3).

7. Pharos, a small island off the Nile Delta, on the shore of which Proteus went through the same transformations as Dionysus (see 169. *a*), had the greatest harbour of Bronze Age Europe (see 39. *2* and 169. *6*). It was the depôt for traders from Crete, Asia Minor, the Aegean Islands, Greece, and Palestine. From here the vine cult will have spread in every direction. The account of Dionysus's campaign in Libya may record military aid sent to the Garamantians by their Greek allies (see 3. *3*); that of his Indian campaign has been taken for a fanciful history of Alexander's drunken progress to the Indus, but is earlier in date and records the eastward spread of the vine. Dionysus's visit to Phrygia, where Rhea initiated him, suggests that the Greek rites of Dionysus as Sabazius, or Bromius, were of Phrygian origin.

8. The Corona Borealis, Ariadne's bridal chaplet, was also called 'the

Cretan Crown'. She was the Cretan Moon-goddess, and her vinous children by Dionysus – Oenopion, Thoas, Staphylus, Tauropolus, Latromis, and Euanthes – were the eponymous ancestors of Helladic tribes living in Chios, Lemnos, the Thracian Chersonese, and beyond (see 98. *o*). Because the vine cult reached Greece and the Aegean by way of Crete – *oinos*, 'wine', is a Cretan word – Dionysus has been confused with Cretan Zagreus, who was similarly torn to pieces at birth (see 30. *a*).

9. Agave, mother of Pentheus, is the Moon-goddess who ruled the beer revels. The tearing to pieces of Hippasus by the three sisters, who are the Triple-goddess as Nymph, is paralleled in the Welsh tale of Pwyll Prince of Dyffed where, on May Eve, Rhiannon, a corruption of Rigantona ('great queen'), devours a foal who is really her son Pryderi ('anxiety'). Poseidon was also eaten in the form of a foal by his father Cronus; but probably in an earlier version by his mother Rhea (see 7. *g*). The meaning of the myth is that the ancient rite in which mare-headed Maenads tore the annual boy victim – Sabazius, Bromius, or whatever he was called – to pieces and ate him raw, was superseded by the more orderly Dionysian revels; the change being signalized by the killing of a foal instead of the usual boy.

10. The pomegranate which sprouted from Dionysus's blood was also the tree of Tammuz-Adonis-Rimmon; its ripe fruit splits open like a wound and shows the red seeds inside. It symbolizes death and the promise of resurrection when held in the hand of the goddess Hera or Persephone (see 24. *11*).

11. Dionysus's rescue of Semele, renamed Thyone ('raging queen'), has been deduced from pictures of a ceremonial held at Athens on the dancing floor dedicated to the Wild Women. There to the sound of singing, piping, and dancing, and with the scattering of flower petals from baskets, a priest summoned Semele to emerge from an *omphalos*, or artificial mound, and come attended by 'the spirit of Spring', the young Dionysus (Pindar: *Fragment* 75. 3). At Delphi a similar ascension ceremony conducted wholly by women was called the *Herois*, or 'feast of the heroine' (Plutarch: *Greek Questions* 12; Aristophanes: *Frogs* 373–96, with scholiast). Still another may be presumed in Artemis's temple at Troezen. The Moon-goddess, it must be remembered, had three different aspects – in the words of John Skelton:

> Diana in the leavës green;
> Luna who so bright doth sheen;
> Persephone in Hell.

Semele was, in fact, another name for Core, or Persephone, and the ascension scene is painted on many Greek vases, some of which show Satyrs assisting the heroine's emergence with mattocks; their presence indicates that this was a Pelasgian rite. What they disinterred was probably a corn-doll buried after the harvest and now found to be sprouting green. Core, of course, did not ascend to Heaven; she wandered about on earth with Demeter until the time came for her to return to the Underworld. But soon after the award of Olympic status to Dionysus the Assumption of his virgin-mother became dogmatic and, once a goddess, she was differentiated from Core, who continued heroine-like to ascend and descend.

12. The vine was the tenth tree of the sacral tree-year and its month corresponded with September, when the vintage feast took place. Ivy, the eleventh tree, corresponded with October, when the Maenads revelled and intoxicated themselves by chewing ivy leaves; and was important also because, like four other sacred trees – El's prickly oak on which the cochineal insects fed, Phoroneus's alder, and Dionysus's own vine and pomegranate – it provided a red dye (see 52. 3). Theophilus, the Byzantine monk (Rugerus: On Handicrafts, ch. 98), says that 'poets and artists loved ivy because of the secret powers it contained . . .one of which I will tell you. In March, when the sap rises, if you perforate the stems of ivy with an auger in a few places, a gummy liquid will exude which, when mixed with urine and boiled, turns a blood colour called "lake", useful for painting and illumination.' Red dye was used to colour the faces of male fertility images (Pausanias: ii. 2. 5), and of sacred kings (see 170. 11); at Rome this custom survived in the reddening of the triumphant general's face. The general represented the god Mars, who was a Spring-Dionysus before he specialized as the Roman God of War, and who gave his name to the month of March. English kings still have their faces slightly rouged on State occasions to make them look healthy and prosperous. Moreover, Greek ivy, like the vine and plane-tree, has a five-pointed leaf, representing the creative hand of the Earth-goddess Rhea (see 53. a). The myrtle was a death tree (see 109. 4).

# 28

## ORPHEUS

ORPHEUS, son of the Thracian King Oeagrus and the Muse Calliope, was the most famous poet and musician who ever lived. Apollo presented him with a lyre, and the Muses taught him its use, so that he not only enchanted wild beasts, but made the trees and rocks move from their places to follow the sound of his music. At Zone in Thrace a number of ancient mountain oaks are still standing in the pattern of one of his dances, just as he left them.[1]

*b.* After a visit to Egypt, Orpheus joined the Argonauts, with whom he sailed to Colchis, his music helping them to overcome many difficulties – and, on his return, married Eurydice, whom some called Agriope, and settled among the savage Cicones of Thrace.[2]

*c.* One day, near Tempe, in the valley of the river Peneius, Eurydice met Aristaeus, who tried to force her. She trod on a serpent as she fled, and died of its bite; but Orpheus boldly descended into Tartarus, hoping to fetch her back. He used the passage which opens at Aornum in Thesprotis and, on his arrival, not only charmed the ferryman Charon, the Dog Cerberus, and the three Judges of the Dead with his plaintive music, but temporarily suspended the tortures of the damned; and so far soothed the savage heart of Hades that he won leave to restore Eurydice to the upper world. Hades made a single condition: that Orpheus might not look behind him until she was safely back under the light of the sun. Eurydice followed Orpheus up through the dark passage, guided by the sounds of his lyre, and it was only when he reached the sunlight again that he turned to see whether she were still behind him, and so lost her for ever.[3]

*d.* When Dionysus invaded Thrace, Orpheus neglected to honour him, but taught other sacred mysteries and preached the evil of sacrificial murder to the men of Thrace, who listened reverently. Every morning he would rise to greet the dawn on the summit of Mount Pangaeum, preaching that Helius, whom he named Apollo, was the greatest of all gods. In vexation, Dionysus set the Maenads upon him at Deium in Macedonia. First waiting until their husbands had entered Apollo's temple, where Orpheus served as priest, they seized the weapons stacked outside, burst in, murdered their husbands, and tore Orpheus limb from limb. His head they threw into the river Hebrus, but it floated, still singing, down to the sea, and was carried to the island of Lesbos.[4]

*e.* Tearfully, the Muses collected his limbs and buried them at Leibethra, at the foot of Mount Olympus, where the nightingales now sing sweeter than anywhere else in the world. The Maenads had attempted to cleanse themselves of Orpheus's blood in the river Helicorn; but the River-god dived under the ground and disappeared for the space of nearly four miles, emerging with a different name, the Baphyra. Thus he avoided becoming an accessory to the murder.[5]

*f.* It is said that Orpheus had condemned the Maenads' promiscuity and preached homosexual love; Aphrodite was therefore no less angered than Dionysus. Her fellow-Olympians, however, could not agree that his murder had been justified, and Dionysus saved the Maenad's lives by turning them into oak-trees, which remained rooted to the ground. The Thracian men who had survived the massacre decided to tattoo their wives as a warning against the murder of priests; and the custom survives to this day.[6]

*g*. As for Orpheus's head: after being attacked by a jealous Lemnian serpent (which Apollo at once changed into a stone) it was laid to rest in a cave at Antissa, sacred to Dionysus. There it prophesied day and night until Apollo, finding that his oracles at Delphi, Gryneium, and Clarus were deserted, came and stood over the head, crying: 'Cease from interference in my business; I have borne long enough with you and your singing!' Thereupon the head fell silent.[7] Orpheus's lyre had likewise drifted to Lesbos and been laid up in a temple of Apollo, at whose intercession, and that of the Muses, the Lyre was placed in heaven as a Constellation.[8]

*h*. Some give a wholly different account of how Orpheus died: they say that Zeus killed him with a thunderbolt for divulging divine secrets. He had, indeed, instituted the Mysteries of Apollo in Thrace; those of Hecate in Aegina; and those of Subterrene Demeter at Sparta.[9]

1. Pindar: *Pythian Odes* iv. 176, with scholiast; Aeschylus: *Agamemnon* 1629–30; Euripides: *Bacchae* 561–4; Apollonius Rhodius: i. 28–31.
2. Diodorus Siculus: iv. 25; Hyginus: *Fabula* 164; Athenaeus: xiii. 7.
3. Hyginus: *loc. cit.*; Diodorus Siculus: *loc. cit.*; Pausanias: ix. 30. 3; Euripides: *Alcestis* 357, with scholiast.
4. Aristophanes: *Frogs* 1032; Ovid: *Metamorphoses* xi. 1–85; Conon: *Narrations* 45.
5. Aeschylus: *Bassarids*, quoted by Eratosthenes: *Catasterismoi* 24; Pausanias: ix. 30. 3–4.
6. Ovid: *loc. cit.*; Conon: *loc. cit.*; Plutarch: *On the Slowness of Divine Vengeance* 12.
7. Lucian: *Against the Unlearned* ii; Philostratus: *Heroica* v. 704; *Life of Apollonius of Tyana* iv. 14.
8. Lucian: *loc. cit.*; Eratosthenes: *Catasterismoi* 24; Hyginus: *Poetic Astronomy* ii. 7.
9. Pausanias: ix. 30. 3; ii. 30. 2; iii. 14. 5.

\*

*1*. Orpheus's singing head recalls that of the decapitated Alder-god Bran which, according to the *Mabinogion*, sang sweetly on the rock at Harlech in North Wales; a fable, perhaps, of funerary pipes made from alder-bark. Thus the name Orpheus, if it stands for *ophruoeis*, 'on the river bank', may be a title of Bran's Greek counterpart, Phoroneus (see 57. *1*), or Cronus, and refer to the alders 'growing on the banks of' the Peneius and other rivers. The name of Orpheus's father, Oeagrus ('of the wild sorb-apple'), points to the same cult, since the sorb-apple (French = *alisier*) and the alder (Spanish = *aliso*) both bear the name of the pre-Hellenic River-goddess Halys, or Alys, or Elis, queen of the Elysian Islands, where Phoroneus, Cronus, and Orpheus went after death. Aornum is Avernus, an Italic variant of the Celtic Avalon ('apple-tree island' – see 31. *2*).

*2.* Orpheus is said by Diodorus Siculus to have used the old thirteen-consonant alphabet; and the legend that he made the trees move and charmed wild beasts apparently refers to its sequence of seasonal trees and symbolic animals (see 52. *3*; 132. *3* and *5*). As sacred king he was struck by a thunderbolt – that is, killed with a double-axe – in an oak grove at the summer solstice, and then dismembered by the Maenads of the bull cult, like Zagreus (see 30. *a*); or of the stag cult, like Actaeon (see 22. *i*); the Maenads in fact, represented the Muses. In Classical Greece the practice of tattooing was confined to Thracians, and in a vase-painting of Orpheus's murder a Maenad has a small stag tattooed on her forearm. This Orpheus did not come in conflict with the cult of Dionysus; he *was* Dionysus, and he played the rude alder-pipe, not the civilized lyre. Thus Proclus (Commentary on Plato's *Politics*: p. 398) writes:

> Orpheus, because he was the principal in the Dionysian rites, is said to have suffered the same fate as the god.

and Apollodorus (i. 3. 2) credits him with having invented the Mysteries of Dionysus.

*3.* The novel worship of the Sun as All-father seems to have been brought to the Northern Aegean by the fugitive priesthood of the mono-theistic Akhenaton, in the fourteenth century B.C., and grafted upon the local cults; hence Orpheus's alleged visit to Egypt. Records of this faith are found in Sophocles (*Fragments* 523 and 1017), where the sun is referred to as 'the eldest flame, dear to the Thracian horsemen', and as 'the sire of the gods, and father of all things.' It seems to have been forcefully resisted by the more conservative Thracians, and bloodily suppressed in some parts of the country. But later Orphic priests, who wore Egyptian costume, called the demi-god whose raw bull's flesh they ate 'Dionysus', and reserved the name Apollo for the immortal Sun: distinguishing Dionysus, the god of the senses, from Apollo, the god of the intellect. This explains why the head of Orpheus was laid up in Dionysus's sanctuary, but the lyre in Apollo's. Head and lyre are both said to have drifted to Lesbos, which was the chief seat of lyric music; Terpander, the earliest historical musician, came from Antissa. The serpent's attack on Orpheus's head represents either the protest of an earlier oracular hero against Orpheus's intrusion at Antissa, or that of Pythian Apollo which Philostratus recorded in more direct language.

4. Eurydice's death by snake-bite and Orpheus's subsequent failure to bring her back into the sunlight, figure only in late myth. They seem to be mistakenly deduced from pictures which show Orpheus's welcome in Tartarus, where his music has charmed the Snake goddess Hecate, or Agriope ('savage face'), into giving special privileges to all ghosts initiated into the Orphic Mysteries, and from other pictures showing Dionysus, whose priest Orpheus was, descending to Tartarus in search of his mother Semele (see 27. k). Eurydice's victims died of snake-bite, not herself (see 33. 1).

5. The alder-month is the fourth of the sacral tree-sequence, and it precedes the willow-month, associated with the water magic of the goddess Helice ('willow' – see 44. 1); willows also gave their name to the river Helicon, which curves around Parnassus and is sacred to the Muses – the Triple Mountain-goddess of inspiration. Hence Orpheus was shown in a temple-painting at Delphi (Pausanias: x. 30. 3) leaning against a willow-tree and touching its branches. The Greek alder cult was suppressed in very early times, yet vestiges of it remain in Classical literature: alders enclose the death-island of the witch-goddess Circe (Homer: Odyssey v. 64 and 239) – she also had a willow-grove cemetery at Colchis (Apollonius Rhodius: iii. 220 – see 152. b) and, according to Virgil the sisters of Phaëthon were metamorphosed into an alder thicket (see 42. 3).

6. This is not to suggest that Orpheus's decapitation was never more than a metaphor applied to the lopped alder-bough. A sacred king necessarily suffered dismemberment, and the Thracians may well have had the same custom as the Iban Dayaks of modern Sarawak. When the men come home from a successful head-hunting expedition the Iban women use the trophy as a means of fertilizing the rice crop by invocation. The head is made to sing, mourn, and answer questions and nursed tenderly in every lap until it finally consents to enter an oracular shrine, where it gives advice on all important occasions and, like the heads of Eurystheus, Bran, and Adam, repels invasions (see 146. 2).

# 29

## GANYMEDES

GANYMEDES, the son of King Tros who gave his name to Troy, was the most beautiful youth alive and therefore chosen by the gods to be

Zeus's cup-bearer. It is said that Zeus, desiring Ganymedes also as his bedfellow, disguised himself in eagle's feathers and abducted him from the Trojan plain.[1]

b. Afterwards, on Zeus's behalf, Hermes presented Tros with a golden vine, the work of Hephaestus, and two fine horses, in compensation for his loss, assuring him at the same time that Ganymedes had become immortal, exempt from the miseries of old age, and was now smiling, golden bowl in hand, as he dispensed bright nectar to the Father of Heaven.[2]

c. Some say that Eos had first abducted Ganymedes to be her paramour, and that Zeus took him from her. Be that as it may, Hera certainly deplored the insult to herself, and to her daughter Hebe, until then the cup-bearer of the gods; but she succeeded only in vexing Zeus, who set Ganymedes's image among the stars as Aquarius, the water-carrier.[3]

1. Homer: *Iliad* xx. 231–5; Apollodorus: iii. 12. 2; Virgil: *Aeneid* v. 252 ff.; Ovid: *Metamorphoses* x. 155 ff.
2. Scholiast on Euripides's *Orestes* 1391; Homer: *Iliad* v. 266; *Homeric Hymn to Aphrodite* 202–17; Apollodorus: ii. 5. 9; Pausanias: v. 24. 1.
3. Scholiast on Apollonius Rhodius: iii. 115; Virgil: *Aeneid* i. 32, with scholiast; Hyginus: *Fabula* 224; Virgil: *Georgics* iii. 304.

*

1. Ganymedes's task as wine-pourer to all the gods – not merely Zeus in early accounts – and the two horses, given to King Tros as compensation for his death, suggest the misreading of an icon which showed the new king preparing for his sacred marriage. Ganymedes's bowl will have contained a libation, poured to the ghost of his royal predecessor; and the officiating priest in the picture, to whom he is making a token resistance, has apparently been misread as amorous Zeus. Similarly, the waiting bride has been misread as Eos by a mythographer who recalled Eos's abduction of Tithonus, son of Laomedon – because Laomedon is also said, by Euripides (*Trojan Women* 822), to have been Ganymedes's father. This icon would equally illustrate Peleus's marriage to Thetis, which the gods viewed from their twelve thrones; the two horses were ritual instruments of his rebirth as king, after a mock-death (see 81. 4). The eagle's alleged abduction of Ganymedes is explained by a Caeretan black-figured vase: an eagle darting at the thighs of a newly enthroned king named Zeus typifies the divine power conferred upon him – his *ka*, or other self – just as a solar hawk descended on the Pharoahs at their coronation. Yet the tradition of Ganymedes's youth suggests that the

king shown in the icon was the royal surrogate, or *interrex*, ruling only for a single day: like the Phaëthon (see 42. *2*), Zagreus (see 30. *1*), Chrysippus (see 105. *2*), and the rest. Zeus's eagle may therefore be said not only to have enroyalled him, but to have snatched him up to Olympus.

2. A royal ascent to Heaven on eagle-back, or in the form of an eagle, is a widespread religious fancy. Aristophanes caricatures it in *Peace* (1 ff.) by sending his hero up on the back of a dung-beetle. The soul of the Celtic hero Lugh – Llew Llaw in the *Mabinogion* – flew up to Heaven as an eagle when the tanist killed him at midsummer. Etana, the Babylonian hero, after his sacred marriage at Kish, rode on eagle-back towards Ishtar's heavenly courts, but fell into the sea and was drowned. Etana's death, by the way, was not the usual end-of-the-year sacrifice, as in the case of Icarus (see 92. *3*), but a punishment for the bad crops which had characterized his reign – he was flying to discover a magical herb of fertility. His story is woven into an account of the continuous struggle between Eagle and Serpent – waxing and waning year, King and Tanist – and as in the myth of Llew Llaw, the Eagle, reduced to his last gasp at the winter solstice, has its life and strength magically renewed. Thus we find in *Psalm* ciii. 5: 'Thy youth is renewed, as the eagle's.'

3. The Zeus-Ganymedes myth gained immense popularity in Greece and Rome because it afforded religious justification for grown man's passionate love of a boy. Hitherto, sodomy had been tolerated only as an extreme form of goddess-worship: Cybele's male devotees tried to achieve ecstatic unity with her by emasculating themselves and dressing like women. Thus a sodomistic priesthood was a recognized institution in the Great Goddess's temples at Tyre, Joppa, Hierapolis, and at Jerusalem (1 *Kings* xv. 12 and 2 *Kings* xxiii. 7) until just before the Exile. But this new passion, for the introduction of which Thamyris (see 21. *m*) has been given the credit by Apollodorus, emphasized the victory of patriarchy over matriarchy. It turned Greek philosophy into an intellectual game that men could play without the assistance of women, now that they had found a new field of homosexual romance. Plato exploited this to the full, and used the myth of Ganymedes to justify his own sentimental feelings towards his pupils (*Phaedrus* 79); though elsewhere (*Laws* i. 8) he denounced sodomy as against nature, and called the myth of Zeus's indulgence in it 'a wicked Cretan invention'. (Here he has the support of Stephanus of Byzantium [*sub* Harpagia], who says that King Minos of Crete carried off Ganymedes to be his bedfellow, 'having received the laws from Zeus'.) With the spread of Platonic philosophy the hitherto intellectually dominant Greek woman degenerated into an unpaid worker and breeder of children wherever Zeus and Apollo were the ruling gods.

4. Ganymedes's name refers, properly, to the joyful stirring of his own

desire at the prospect of marriage, not to that of Zeus when refreshed by nectar from his bedfellow's hand; but, becoming *catamitus* in Latin, it has given English the word 'catamite', meaning the passive object of male homosexual lust.

5. The constellation Aquarius, identified with Ganymedes, was originally the Egyptian god, presiding over the source of the Nile, who poured water, not wine, from a flagon (Pindar: *Fragment* 110); but the Greeks took little interest in the Nile.

6. Zeus's nectar, which the later mythographers described as a supernatural red wine, was, in fact, a primitive brown mead (see 27. 2); and ambrosia, the delectable food of the gods, seems to have been a porridge of barley, oil, and chopped fruit (see 98. 7), with which kings were pampered when their poorer subjects still subsisted on asphodel (see 31. 2), mallow, and acorns.

# 30

## ZAGREUS

ZEUS secretly begot his son Zagreus on Persephone, before she was taken to the Underworld by her uncle Hades. He set Rhea's sons, the Cretan Curetes or, some say, the Corybantes, to guard his cradle in the Idaean Cave, where they leaped about him, clashing their weapons, as they had leaped about Zeus himself at Dicte. But the Titans, Zeus's enemies, whitening themselves with gypsum until they were unrecognizable, waited until the Curetes slept. At midnight they lured Zagreus away, by offering him such childish toys as a cone, a bull-roarer, golden apples, a mirror, a knuckle-bone, and a tuft of wool. Zagreus showed courage when they murderously set upon him, and went through several transformations in an attempt to delude them: he became successively Zeus in a goat-skin coat, Cronus making rain, a lion, a horse, a horned serpent, a tiger, and a bull. At that point the Titans seized him firmly by the horns and feet, tore him apart with their teeth, and devoured his flesh raw.

b. Athene interrupted this grisly banquet shortly before its end and, rescuing Zagreus's heart, enclosed it in a gypsum figure, into which she breathed life; so that Zagreus became an immortal. His bones were collected and buried at Delphi, and Zeus struck the Titans dead with thunderbolts.[1]

1. Diodorus Siculus: v. 75. 4; Nonnus: *Dionysiaca* vi. 296 and xxvii. 228; Harpocration *sub* apomatton; Tzetzes: *On Lycophron* 355; Eustathius on Homer's *Iliad* ii. 735; Firmicus Maternus: *Concerning the Errors of Profane Religions* vi; Euripides: *The Cretans, Fragment* 475. Orphic Fragments (*Kern*, 34).

*

1. This myth concerns the annual sacrifice of a boy which took place in ancient Crete: a surrogate for Minos the Bull-king. He reigned for a single day, went through a dance illustrative of the five seasons – lion, goat, horse, serpent, and bull-calf – and was then eaten raw. All the toys with which the Titans lured him away were objects used by the philosophical Orphics, who inherited the tradition of this sacrifice but devoured a bull-calf raw, instead of a boy. The bull-roarer was a pierced stone or piece of pottery, which when whirled at the end of a cord made a noise like a rising gale; and the tuft of wool may have been used to daub the *Curetes* with the wet gypsum – these being youths who had cut and dedicated their first hair to the goddess Car (see 95. 5). They were also called *Corybantes*, or crested dancers. Zagreus's other gifts served to explain the nature of the ceremony by which the participants became one with the god: the cone was an ancient emblem of the goddess, in whose honour the Titans sacrificed him (see 20. 2); the mirror represented each initiate's other self, or ghost; the golden apples, his passport to Elysium after a mock-death; the knuckle-bone, his divinatory powers (see 17. 3).

2. A Cretan hymn discovered a few years ago at Palaiokastro, near the Dictaean Cave, is addressed to the Cronian One, greatest of youths, who comes dancing at the head of his demons and leaps to increase the fertility of soil and flocks, and for the success of the fishing fleet. Jane Harrison in *Themis* suggests that the shielded tutors there mentioned, who 'took thee, immortal child, from Rhea's side,' merely pretended to kill and eat the victim, an initiate into their secret society. But all such mock-deaths at initiation ceremonies, reported from many parts of the world, seem ultimately based on a tradition of actual human sacrifice; and Zagreus's calendar changes distinguish him from an ordinary member of a totemistic fraternity.

3. The uncanonical tiger in the last of Zagreus's transformations is explained by his identity with Dionysus (see 27. *c*), of whose death and resurrection the same story is told, although with cooked flesh instead of raw, and Rhea's name instead of Athene's. Dionysus, too, was a horned serpent – he had horns and serpent locks at birth (see 27. *a*) – and his

Orphic devotees ate him sacramentally in bull form. Zagreus became 'Zeus in a goat-skin coat', because Zeus or his child surrogate had ascended to Heaven wearing a coat made from the hide of the goat Amaltheia (see 7. b). 'Cronus making rain' is a reference to the use of the bull-roarer in rain-making ceremonies. In this context the Titans were *Titanoi*, 'white-chalk men', the Curetes themselves disguised so that the ghost of the victim would not recognize them. When human sacrifices went out of fashion, Zeus was represented as hurling his thunderbolt at the cannibals; and the *Titanes*, 'lords of the seven-day week', became confused with the *Titanoi*, 'the white-chalk men', because of their hostility to Zeus. No Orphic, who had once eaten the flesh of his god, ever again touched meat of any kind.

4. Zagreus-Dionysus was also known in Southern Palestine. According to the Ras Shamra tablets, Ashtar temporarily occupied the throne of Heaven while the god Baal languished in the Underworld, having eaten the food of the dead. Ashtar was only a child and when he sat on the throne, his feet did not reach the footstool; Baal presently returned and killed him with a club. The Mosaic Law prohibited initiation feasts in Ashtar's honour: 'Thou shalt not seethe a kid in his mother's milk' – an injunction three times repeated (*Exodus* xxiii. 19; xxxiv. 26; *Deuteronomy* xiv. 21).

# 31

## THE GODS OF THE UNDERWORLD

WHEN ghosts descend to Tartarus, the main entrance to which lies in a grove of black poplars beside the Ocean stream, each is supplied by pious relatives with a coin laid under the tongue of its corpse. They are thus able to pay Charon, the miser who ferries them in a crazy boat across the Styx. This hateful river bounds Tartarus on the western side,[1] and has for its tributaries Acheron, Phlegethon, Cocytus, Aornis, and Lethe. Penniless ghosts must wait for ever on the near bank; unless they have evaded Hermes, their conductor, and crept down by a back entrance, such as at Laconian Taenarus,[2] or Thesprotian Aornum. A three-headed or, some say, fifty-headed dog named Cerberus, guards the opposite shore of Styx, ready to devour living intruders or ghostly fugitives.[3]

b. The first region of Tartarus contains the cheerless Asphodel

Fields, where souls of heroes stay without purpose among the throngs of less distinguished dead that twitter like bats, and where only Orion still has the heart to hunt the ghostly deer.[4] None of them but would rather live in bondage to a landless peasant than rule over all Tartarus. Their one delight is in libations of blood poured to them by the living: when they drink they feel themselves almost men again. Beyond these meadows lie Erebus and the palace of Hades and Persephone. To the left of the palace, as one approaches it, a white cypress shades the pool of Lethe, where the common ghosts flock down to drink. Initiated souls avoid this water, choosing to drink instead from the pool of Memory, shaded by a white poplar [?], which gives them a certain advantage over their fellows.[5] Close by, newly arrived ghosts are daily judged by Minos, Rhadamanthys, and Aeacus at a place where three roads meet. Rhadamanthys tries Asiatics and Aeacus tries Europeans; but both refer the difficult cases to Minos. As each verdict is given the ghosts are directed along one of the three roads; that leading back to the Asphodel Meadows, if they are neither virtuous nor evil; that leading to the punishment-field of Tartarus, if they are evil; that leading to the orchards of Elysium, if they are virtuous.

*c.* Elysium, ruled over by Cronus, lies near Hades's dominions, its entrance close to the pool of Memory, but forms no part of them; it is a happy land of perpetual day, without cold or snow, where games, music, and revels never cease, and where the inhabitants may elect to be reborn on earth whenever they please. Near by are the Fortunate Islands, reserved for those who have been three times born, and three times attained Elysium.[6] But some say that there is another Fortunate Isle called Leuce in the Black Sea, opposite the mouths of the Danube, wooded and full of beasts, wild and tame, where the ghosts of Helen and Achilles hold high revelry and declaim Homer's verses to heroes who have taken part in the events celebrated by him.[7]

*d.* Hades, who is fierce and jealous of his rights, seldom visits the upper air, except on business or when he is overcome by sudden lust. Once he dazzled the Nymph Minthe with the splendour of his golden chariot and its four black horses, and would have seduced her without difficulty had not Queen Persephone made a timely appearance and metamorphosed Minthe into sweet-smelling mint. On another occasion Hades tried to violate the Nymph Leuce, who was similarly metamorphosed into the white poplar standing by the pool of Memory.[8] He willingly allows none of his subjects to escape, and few who visit

Tartarus return alive to describe it, which makes him the most hated of the gods.

*e.* Hades never knows what is happening in the world above, or in Olympus,[9] except for fragmentary information which comes to him when mortals strike their hands upon the earth and invoke him with oaths and curses. His most prized possession is the helmet of invisibility, given him as a mark of gratitude by the Cyclopes when he consented to release them at Zeus's order. All the riches of gems and precious metals hidden beneath the earth are his, but he owns no property above ground, except for certain gloomy temples in Greece and, possibly, a herd of cattle in the island of Erytheia which, some say, really belong to Helius.[10]

*f.* Queen Persephone, however, can be both gracious and merciful. She is faithful to Hades, but has had no children by him and prefers the company of Hecate, goddess of witches, to his.[11] Zeus himself honours Hecate so greatly that he never denies her the ancient power which she has always enjoyed: of bestowing on mortals, or withholding from them, any desired gift. She has three bodies and three heads – lion, dog, and mare.[12]

*g.* Tisiphone, Alecto, and Megaera, the Erinnyes or Furies, live in Erebus, and are older than Zeus or any of the other Olympians. Their task is to hear complaints brought by mortals against the insolence of the young to the aged, of children to parents, of hosts to guests, and of householders or city councils to suppliants – and to punish such crimes by hounding the culprits relentlessly, without rest or pause, from city to city and from country to country. These Erinnyes are crones, with snakes for hair, dogs' heads, coal-black bodies, bats' wings, and blood-shot eyes. In their hands they carry brass-studded scourges, and their victims die in torment.[13] It is unwise to mention them by name in conversation; hence they are usually styled the Eumenides, which means 'The Kindly Ones' – as Hades is styled Pluton, or Pluto, 'The Rich One'.

1. Pausanias: x. 28. 1.
2. Apollodorus: ii. 5. 2; Strabo: viii. 5. 1.
3. Homer: *Iliad* viii. 368; Hesiod: *Theogony* 311; Apollodorus: *loc. cit.*; Euripides: *Heracles* 24.
4. Homer: *Odyssey* xi. 539; xi. 572–5; xi. 487–91.
5. *Petelia Orphic Tablet.*
6. Plato: *Gorgias* 168; Pindar: *Olympian Odes* ii. 68–80; Hesiod: *Works and Days* 167 ff.

7. Pausanias: iii. 19. 11; Philostratus: *Heroica* x. 32–40.
8. Strabo: viii. 3. 14; Servius on Virgil's *Eclogue* vii. 61.
9. Homer: *Iliad* ix. 158–9; xx. 61.
10. Homer: *Iliad* ix. 567 ff.; Apollodorus: ii. 5. 10; Scholiast on Pindar's *Isthmian Odes* vi. 32.
11. Apollonius Rhodius: iii. 529; Ovid: *Metamorphoses* xiv. 405; Scholiast on Theocritus's *Idylls* ii. 12.
12. Hesiod: *Theogony* 411–52.
13. Apollodorus: i. 1. 4; Homer: *Iliad* ix. 453–7; xv. 204; xix. 259; *Odyssey* ii. 135 and xvii. 475; Aeschylus: *Eumenides* 835 and *Libation Bearers* 290 and 924; Euripides: *Orestes* 317 ff.; *Orphic Hymn* lxviii. 5.

\*

*1.* The mythographers made a bold effort to reconcile the conflicting views of the afterworld held by the primitive inhabitants of Greece. One view was that ghosts lived in their tombs, or underground caverns or fissures, where they might take the form of serpents, mice, or bats, but never be reincarnate as human beings. Another was that the souls of sacred kings walked visibly on the sepulchral islands where their bodies had been buried. A third was that ghosts could become men again by entering beans, nuts, or fish, and being eaten by their prospective mothers. A fourth was that they went to the Far North, where the sun never shines, and returned, if at all, only as fertilizing winds. A fifth was that they went to the Far West, where the sun sets in the ocean, and a spirit world much like the present. A sixth was that a ghost received punishment according to the life he had led. To this the Orphics finally added the theory of metempsychosis, the transmigration of souls: a process which could be to some degree controlled by the use of magical formulas.

*2.* Persephone and Hecate stood for the pre-Hellenic hope of regeneration; but Hades, a Hellenic concept for the ineluctability of death. Cronus, despite his bloody record, continued to enjoy the pleasures of Elysium, since that had always been the privilege of a sacred king, and Menelaus (*Odyssey* iv. 561) was promised the same enjoyment, not because he had been particularly virtuous or courageous but because he had married Helen, the priestess of the Spartan Moon-goddess (see 159. *1*). The Homeric adjective *asphodelos*, applied only to *leimōnes* ('meadows'), probably means 'in the valley of that which is not reduced to ashes' (from *a* = not, *spodos* = ash, *elos* = valley) – namely the hero's ghost after his body has been burned; and, except in acorn-eating Arcadia, asphodel roots and seeds, offered to such ghosts, made the staple Greek diet before the introduction of corn. Asphodel grows freely even on waterless islands and ghosts, like gods, are conservative in their diet. Elysium seems to mean 'apple-land' – *alisier* is a pre-Gallic word for sorb-apple – as do the Arthurian 'Avalon' and the Latin 'Avernus', or 'Avolnus', both formed from the Indo-European root *abol*, meaning apple.

3. Cerberus was the Greek counterpart of Anubis, the dog-headed son of the Libyan Death-goddess Nephthys, who conducted souls to the Underworld. In European folklore, which is partly of Libyan origin, the souls of the damned were hunted to the Northern Hell by a yelling pack of hounds – the hounds of Annwm, Herne, Arthur, or Gabriel – a myth derived from the noisy summer migration of wild geese to their breeding places in the Arctic circle. Cerberus was, at first, fifty-headed, like the spectral pack that destroyed Actaeon (see 22. *1*); but afterwards three-headed, like his mistress Hecate (see 134. *1*).

4. Styx ('hated'), a small stream in Arcadia, the waters of which were supposed to be deadly poison, was located in Tartarus only by late mythographers. Acheron ('stream of woe') and Cocytus ('wailing') are fanciful names to describe the misery of death. Aornis ('birdless') is a Greek mistranslation of the Italic 'Avernus'. Lethe means 'forgetfulness'; and Erebus 'covered'. Phlegethon ('burning') refers to the custom of cremation but also, perhaps, to the theory that sinners were burned in streams of lava. Tartarus seems to be a reduplication of the pre-Hellenic word *tar*, which occurs in the names of places lying to the West; its sense of infernality comes late.

5. Black poplars were sacred to the Death-goddess (see 51. 7 and 170. *l*); and white poplars, or aspens, either to Persephone as Goddess of Regeneration, or to Heracles because he harrowed Hell (see 134.*f*) – golden head-dresses of aspen leaves have been found in Mesopotamian burials of the fourth millennium B.C. The Orphic tablets do not name the tree by the pool of Memory; it is probably the white poplar into which Leuce was transformed, but possibly a nut-tree, the emblem of Wisdom (see 86. *1*). White-cypress wood, regarded as an anti-corruptive, was used for household chests and coffins.

6. Hades had a temple at the foot of Mount Menthe in Elis, and his rape of Minthe ('mint') is probably deduced from the use of mint in funerary rites, together with rosemary and myrtle, to offset the smell of decay. Demeter's barley-water drink at Eleusis was flavoured with mint (see 24. *e*). Though awarded the sun-cattle of Erytheia ('red land'), because that was where the Sun met his nightly death, Hades is more usually called Cronus, or Geryon, in this context (see 132. *4*).

7. Hesiod's account of Hecate shows her to have been the original Triple-goddess, supreme in Heaven, on earth, and in Tartarus; but the Hellenes emphasized her destructive powers at the expense of her creative ones until, at last, she was invoked only in clandestine rites of black magic, especially at places where three roads met. That Zeus did not deny her

the ancient power of granting every mortal his heart's desire is a tribute to the Thessalian witches, of whom everyone stood in dread. Lion, dog, and horse, her heads, evidently refer to the ancient tripartite year, the dog being the Dog-star Sirius; as do also Cerberus's heads.

8. Hecate's companions, the Erinnyes, were personified pangs of conscience after the breaking of a taboo – at first only the taboo of insult, disobedience, or violence to a mother (see 105. *k* and 114. *1*). Suppliants and guests came under the protection of Hestia, Goddess of the Hearth (see 20. *c*), and to ill-treat them would be to disobey and insult her.

9. Leuce, the largest island in the Black Sea, but very small at that, is now a treeless Rumanian penal colony (see 164. *3*).

# 32

## TYCHE AND NEMESIS

TYCHE is a daughter of Zeus, to whom he has given power to decide what the fortune of this or that mortal shall be. On some she heaps gifts from a horn of plenty, others she deprives of all that they have. Tyche is altogether irresponsible in her awards, and runs about juggling with a ball to exemplify the uncertainty of chance: sometimes up, sometimes down. But if it ever happens that a man, whom she has favoured, boasts of his abundant riches and neither sacrifices a part of them to the gods, nor alleviates the poverty of his fellow-citizens, then the ancient goddess Nemesis steps in to humiliate him.[1] Nemesis, whose home is at Attic Rhamnus, carries an apple-bough in one hand, and a wheel in the other, and wears a silver crown adorned with stags; the scourge hangs at her girdle. She is a daughter of Oceanus and has something of Aphrodite's beauty.

b. Some say that Zeus once fell in love with Nemesis, and pursued her over the earth and through the sea. Though she constantly changed her shape, he violated her at last by adopting the form of a swan, and from the egg she laid came Helen, the cause of the Trojan War.[2]

1. Pindar: *Olympian Odes* xii. 1–2; Herodotus: i. 34 and iii. 40; Apollonius Rhodius: iv. 1042–3; Sophocles: *Philoctetes* 518.
2. Pausanias: i. 33. 3; Homer's *Cypria*, quoted by Athenaeus p. 334b; Apollodorus: iii. 10. 7.

*

1. Tyche ('fortune'), like Dice and Aedos (personifications of Natural Law, or Justice, and Shame), was an artificial deity invented by the early

philosophers; whereas Nemesis ('due enactment') had been the Nymph-goddess of Death-in-Life (see 18. 3) whom they now redefined as a moral control on Tyche. That Nemesis's wheel was originally the solar year is suggested by the name of her Latin counterpart, Fortuna (from *vortumna*, 'she who turns the year about'). When the wheel had turned half circle, the sacred king, raised to the summit of his fortune, was fated to die – the Actaeon stags on her crown (see 22. *i*) announce this – but when it came full circle, he revenged himself on the rival who had supplanted him. Her scourge was formerly used for ritual flogging, to fructify the trees and crops, and the apple-bough was the king's passport to Elysium (see 53. 5; 80. 4; and 133. 4).

2. The Nemesis whom Zeus chased (see 62. *b*), is not the philosophical concept of divine vengeance on overweening mortals, but the original Nymph-goddess, whose usual name was Leda. In pre-Hellenic myth, the goddess chases the sacred king and, although he goes through his seasonal transformations (see 30. *1*), counters each of them in turn with her own, and devours him at the summer solstice. In Hellenic myth the parts are reversed: the goddess flees, changing shape, but the king pursues and finally violates her, as in the story of Zeus and Metis (see 9. *d*), or Peleus and Thetis (see 81. *k*). The required seasonal transformations will have been indicated on the spokes of Nemesis's wheel; but in Homer's *Cypria* only a fish and 'various beasts' are mentioned (see 89. 2). 'Leda' is another form of Leto, or Latona, whom the Python, not Zeus, chased (see 14. *a*). Swans were sacred to the goddess (Euripides: *Iphigeneia Among the Taurians* 1095 ff.), because of their white plumage, also because the V-formation of their flight was a female symbol, and because, at mid-summer, they flew north to unknown breeding grounds, supposedly taking the dead king's soul with them (see 33. 5 and 142. 2).

3. The philosophical Nemesis was worshipped at Rhamnus where, according to Pausanias (i. 33. 2–3), the Persian commander-in-chief, who had intended to set up a white marble trophy in celebration of his con-quest of Attica, was forced to retire by news of a naval defeat at Salamis; the marble was used instead for an image of the local Nymph-goddess Nemesis. It is supposed to have been from this event that Nemesis came to personify 'Divine vengeance', rather than the 'due enactment' of the annual death drama; since to Homer, at any rate, *nemesis* had been merely a warm human feeling that payment should be duly made, or a task duly performed. But Nemesis the Nymph-goddess bore the title Adrasteia ('inescapable' – Strabo: xiii. 1. 13), which was also the name of Zeus's foster-nurse, an ash-nymph (see 7. *b*); and since the ash-nymphs and the Erinnyes were sisters, born from the blood of Uranus, this may have been how Nemesis came to embody the idea of vengeance. The ash-tree was one of the goddess's seasonal disguises, and an important one to her

pastoral devotees, because of its association with thunderstorms and with the lambing month, the third of the sacral year (see 52. 3).

4. Nemesis is called a daughter of Oceanus, because as the Nymph-goddess with the apple-bough she was also the sea-born Aphrodite, sister of the Erynnyes (see 18. 4).

# 33

## THE CHILDREN OF THE SEA

THE fifty Nereids, gentle and beneficent attendants on the Sea-goddess Thetis, are mermaids, daughters of the nymph Doris by Nereus, a prophetic old man of the sea, who has the power of changing his shape.[1]

b. The Phorcids, their cousins, children of Ceto by Phorcys, another wise old man of the sea, are Ladon, Echidne, and the three Gorgons, dwellers in Libya; the three Graeae; and, some say, the three Hesperides. The Gorgons were named Stheino, Euryale, and Medusa, all once beautiful. But one night Medusa lay with Poseidon, and Athene, enraged that they had bedded in one of her own temples, changed her into a winged monster with glaring eyes, huge teeth, protruding tongue, brazen claws and serpent locks, whose gaze turned men to stone. When eventually Perseus decapitated Medusa, and Poseidon's children Chrysaor and Pegasus sprang from her dead body, Athene fastened the head to her aegis; but some say that the aegis was Medusa's own skin, flayed from her by Athene.[2]

c. The Graeae are fair-faced and swan-like, but with hair grey from birth, and only one eye and one tooth between the three of them. Their names are Enyo, Pemphredo, and Deino.[3]

d. The three Hesperides, by name Hespere, Aegle, and Erytheis, live in the far-western orchard which Mother Earth gave to Hera. Some call them daughters of Night, others of Atlas and of Hesperis, daughter of Hesperus; sweetly they sing.[4]

e. Half of Echidne was lovely woman, half was speckled serpent. She once lived in a deep cave among the Arimi, where she ate men raw, and raised a brood of frightful monsters to her husband Typhon; but hundred-eyed Argus killed her while she slept.[5]

f. Ladon was wholly serpent, though gifted with the power of human speech, and guarded the golden apples of the Hesperides until Heracles shot him dead.[6]

g. Nereus, Phorcys, Thaumas, Eurybia, and Ceto were all children born to Pontus by Mother Earth; thus the Phorcids and Nereids claim cousinhood with the Harpies. These are the fair-haired and swift-winged daughters of Thaumas by the Ocean-nymph Electra, who snatch up criminals for punishment by the Erinnyes, and live in a Cretan cave.[7]

1. Homer: *Iliad* xviii. 36 ff.; Apollodorus: i. 2. 7.
2. Hesiod: *Theogony* 270 ff. and 333 ff.; Apollodorus: ii. 4. 3; Ovid: *Metamorphoses* iv. 792–802; Scholiast on Apollonius Rhodius iv. 1399; Euripides: *Ion* 989 ff.
3. Hesiod: *Theogony* 270–4; Apollodorus: ii. 4. 2.
4. Hesiod: *Theogony* 215 and 518; Diodorus Siculus: iv. 27. 2; Euripides: *Heracles* 394.
5. Homer: *Iliad* ii, 783; Hesiod: *Theogony* 295 ff.; Apollodorus: ii. 1. 2.
6. Hesiod: *Theogony* 333–5; Apollonius Rhodius: iv. 1397; Apollodorus: ii. 5. 11.
7. Apollodorus: i. 2. 6; Hesiod: *Theogony* 265–9; Homer: *Odyssey* xx. 77–8; Apollonius Rhodius: ii. 298–9.

\*

1. It seems that the Moon-goddess's title Eurynome ('wide rule' or 'wide wandering') proclaimed her ruler of heaven and earth; Eurybia ('wide strength'), ruler of the sea; Eurydice ('wide justice') the serpent-grasping ruler of the Underworld. Male human sacrifices were offered to her as Eurydice, their death being apparently caused by viper's venom (see 28. 4; 154. *b* and 168. *e*). Echnidne's death at the hand of Argus probably refers to the suppression of the Serpent-goddess's Argive cult. Her brother Ladon is the oracular serpent who haunts every paradise, his coils embracing the apple-tree (see 133. 4).

2. Among Eurybia's other sea-titles were Thetis ('disposer'), or its variant Tethys; Ceto, as the sea-monster corresponding with the Hebrew Rahab, or the Babylonian Tiamat (see 73. 7); Nereis, as the goddess of the wet element. Electra as provider of amber, a sea product highly valued by the ancients (see 148. 11); Thaumas, as wonderful; and Doris, as bountiful. Nereus – *alias* Proteus ('first man') – the prophetic 'old man of the sea', who took his name from Nereis, not contrariwise, seems to have been an oracular sacred king, buried on a coastal island (see 133. *d*); he is pictured in an early vase-painting as fish-tailed, with a lion, a stag, and a viper emerging from his body. Proteus, in the *Odyssey*, similarly

changed shapes, to mark the seasons through which the sacred king moved from birth to death (see 30. 1).

3. The fifty Nereids seem to have been a college of fifty Moon-priestesses, whose magic rites ensured good fishing; and the Gorgons, representatives of the Triple-goddess, wearing prophylactic masks – with scowl, glaring eyes, and protruding tongue between bared teeth – to frighten strangers from her Mysteries (see 73. 9). The Sons of Homer knew only a single Gorgon, who was a shade in Tartarus (*Odyssey* xi. 633–5), and whose head, an object of terror to Odysseus (*Odyssey* xi. 634), Athene wore on her aegis, doubtless to warn people against examining the divine mysteries hidden behind it. Greek bakers used to paint Gorgon masks on their ovens, to discourage busybodies from opening the oven door, peeping in, and thus allowing a draught to spoil the bread. The Gorgons' names – Stheino ('strong'), Euryale ('wide roaming'), and Medusa ('cunning one') – are titles of the Moon-goddess; the Orphics called the moon's face 'the Gorgon's head'.

4. Poseidon's fathering of Pegasus on Medusa recalls his fathering of the horse Arion on Demeter, when she disguised herself as a mare, and her subsequent fury (see 16. *f*); both myths describe how Poseidon's Hellenes forcibly married the Moon-priestesses, disregarding their Gorgon masks, and took over the rain-making rites of the sacred horse cult. But a mask of Demeter was still kept in a stone chest at Pheneus, and the *priest* of Demeter assumed it when he performed the ceremony of beating the Infernal Spirits with rods (Pausanias: viii. 15. 1).

5. Chrysaor was Demeter's new-moon sign, the golden sickle, or falchion; her consorts carried it when they deputized for her. Athene, in this version, is Zeus's collaborator, reborn from his head, and a traitress to the old religion (see 9. 1). The three Harpies, regarded by Homer as personifications of the storm winds (*Odyssey* xx. 66–78), were the earlier Athene, the Triple-goddess, in her capacity of sudden destroyer. So were the Graeae, the Three Grey Ones, as their names Enyo ('warlike'), Pemphredo ('wasp'), and Deino ('terrible') show; their single eye and tooth are misreadings of a sacred picture (see 73. 9), and the swan is a death-bird in European mythology (see 32. 2).

6. Phorcys, a masculine form of Phorcis, the Goddess or Sow (see 74. 4 and 96. 2), who devours corpses, appears in Latin as *Orcus*, a title of Hades, and as *porcus*, hog. The Gorgons and Grey Ones were called Phorcides, because it was death to profane the Goddess's Mysteries; but Phorcys's prophetic wisdom must refer to a sow-oracle (see 24. 7).

7. The names of the Hesperides, described as children either of Ceto and Phorcys, or of Night, or of Atlas the Titan who holds up the heavens in the Far West (see 39. 1 and 133. *e*), refer to the sunset. Then the sky is green, yellow, and red, as if it were an apple-tree in full bearing; and the

Sun, cut by the horizon like a crimson half-apple, meets his death dramatically in the western waves. When the Sun has gone, Hesperus appears.
This star was sacred to the Love-goddess Aphrodite, and the apple was
the gift by which her priestess decoyed the king, the Sun's representative,
to his death with love-songs; if an apple is cut in two transversely, her
five-pointed star appears in the centre of each half.

# 34

## THE CHILDREN OF ECHIDNE

ECHIDNE bore a dreadful brood to Typhon: namely, Cerberus, the
three-headed Hound of Hell; the Hydra, a many-headed water-serpent
living at Lerna; the Chimaera, a fire-breathing goat with lion's head
and serpent's body; and Orthrus, the two-headed hound of Geryon,
who lay with his own mother and begot on her the Sphinx and the
Nemean Lion.[1]

1. Hesiod: *Theogony* 306 ff.

\*

*1.* Cerberus (see 31. *a* and 134. *e*), associated by the Dorians with the
dog-headed Egyptian god Anubis who conducted souls to the Underworld, seems to have originally been the Death-goddess Hecate, or
Hecabe (see 168. *1*); she was portrayed as a bitch because dogs eat corpse
flesh and howl at the moon.

*2.* The Chimaera was, apparently, a calendar-symbol of the tripartite
year (see 75. *2*), of which the seasonal emblems were lion, goat, and
serpent.

*3.* Orthrus (see 132. *d*), who fathered the Chimaera, the Sphinx (see
105. *e*), the Hydra (see 60. *h* and 124. *c*), and the Nemean Lion (see 123. *b*)
on Echidne was Sirius, the Dog-star, which inaugurated the Athenian
New Year. He had two heads, like Janus, because the reformed year at
Athens had two seasons, not three; Orthrus's son, the Lion, emblemizing
the first half, and his daughter, the Serpent, emblemizing the second.
When the Goat-emblem disappeared, the Chimaera gave place to the
Sphinx, with her winged lion's body and serpent's tail. Since the reformed
New Year began when the Sun was in Leo and the Dog Days had now
begun, Orthrus looked in two directions – forward to the New Year,
backward to the Old – like the Calendar-goddess Cardea, whom the
Romans named Postvorta and Antevorta on that account. Orthrus was
called 'early' presumably because he introduced the New Year.

# THE GIANTS' REVOLT

ENRAGED because Zeus had confined their brothers, the Titans, in Tartarus, certain tall and terrible giants, with long locks and beards, and serpent-tails for feet, plotted an assault on Heaven. They had been born from Mother Earth at Thracian Phlegra, twenty-four in number.[1]

b. Without warning, they seized rocks and fire-brands and hurled them upwards from their mountain tops, so that the Olympians were hard pressed. Hera prophesied gloomily that the giants could never be killed by any god, but only by a single, lion-skinned mortal; and that even he could do nothing unless the enemy were anticipated in their search for a certain herb of invulnerability, which grew in a secret place on earth. Zeus at once took counsel with Athene; sent her off to warn Heracles, the lion-skinned mortal to whom Hera was evidently referring, exactly how matters stood; and forbade Eros, Selene, and Helius to shine for a while. Under the feeble light of the stars, Zeus groped about on earth, in the region to which Athene directed him, found the herb, and brought it safely to Heaven.

c. The Olympians could now join battle with the giants. Heracles let loose his first arrow against Alcyoneus, the enemy's leader. He fell to the ground, but sprang up again revived, because this was his native soil of Phlegra. 'Quick, noble Heracles!' cried Athene. 'Drag him away to another country!' Heracles caught Alcyoneus up on his shoulders, and dragged him over the Thracian border, where he despatched him with a club.

d. Then Porphyrion leaped into Heaven from the great pyramid of rocks which the giants had piled up, and none of the gods stood his ground. Only Athene adopted a posture of defence. Rushing by her, Porphyrion made for Hera, whom he tried to strangle; but, wounded in the liver by a timely arrow from Eros's bow, he turned from anger to lust, and ripped off Hera's glorious robe. Zeus, seeing that his wife was about to be outraged, ran forward in jealous wrath, and felled Porphyrion with a thunderbolt. Up he sprang again, but Heracles, returning to Phlegra in the nick of time, mortally wounded him with an arrow. Meanwhile, Ephialtes had engaged Ares and beaten him to his knees; however, Apollo shot the wretch in the left eye and called to Heracles, who at once planted another arrow in the right. Thus died Ephialtes.

*e.* Now, wherever a god wounded a giant – as when Dionysus felled Eurytus with his thyrsus, or Hecate singed Clytius with her torches, or Hephaestus scalded Mimas with a ladle of red-hot metal, or Athene crushed the lustful Pallas with a stone, it was Heracles who had to deal the death blow. The peace-loving goddesses Hestia and Demeter took no part in the conflict, but stood dismayed, wringing their hands; the Fates, however, swung brazen pestles to good effect.[2]

*f.* Discouraged, the remaining giants fled back to earth, pursued by the Olympians. Athene threw a vast missile at Enceladus, which crushed him flat and became the island of Sicily. And Poseidon broke off part of Cos with his trident and threw it at Polybutes; this became the nearby islet of Nisyros, beneath which he lies buried.[3]

*g.* The remaining giants made a last stand at Bathos, near Arcadian Trapezus, where the ground still burns, and giants' bones are sometimes turned up by ploughmen. Hermes, borrowing Hades's helmet of invisibility, struck down Hippolytus, and Artemis pierced Gration with an arrow; while the Fates' pestles broke the heads of Agrius and Thoas. Ares, with his spear, and Zeus, with his thunderbolt, now accounted for the rest, though Heracles was called upon to despatch each giant as he fell. But some say that the battle took place on the Phlegraean Plain, near Cumae in Italy.[4]

*h.* Silenus the earth-born Satyr claims to have taken part in this battle at the side of his pupil Dionysus, killing Enceladus and spreading panic among the giants by the braying of his old pack-ass; but Silenus is usually drunken and cannot distinguish truth from falsehood.[5]

1. Apollodorus: i. 6. 1; Hyginus: *Fabulae, Proem.*
2. Apollodorus: i. 6. 2.
3. Apollodorus: *loc. cit.*; Strabo: x. 5. 16.
4. Pausanias: viii. 29. 1–2; Apollodorus: *loc. cit.*; Diodorus Siculus: iv. 21.
5. Euripides: *Cyclops* 5 ff.

*

1. This is a post-Homeric story, preserved in a degenerate version: Eros and Dionysus, who take part in the fighting, are late-comers to Olympus (see 15. *1–2* and 27. *5*), and Heracles is admitted there before his apotheosis on Mount Oeta (see 147. *h*). It purports to account for the finding of mammoth bones at Trapezus (where they are still shown in the

local museum); and for the volcanic fires at Bathos near by – also at Arcadian, or Thracian, Pallene, at Cumae, and in the islands of Sicily and Nisyros, beneath which Athene and Poseidon are said to have buried two of the giants.

2. The historical incident underlying the Giants' Revolt – and also the Aloeids' Revolt (see 37. b), of which it is usually regarded as a doublet – seems to be a concerted attempt by non-Hellenic mountaineers to storm certain Hellenic fortresses, and their repulse by the Hellenes' subject-allies. But the powerlessness and cowardice of the gods, contrasted with the invincibility of Heracles, and the farcical incidents of the battle, are more characteristic of popular fiction than of myth.

3. There is, however, a hidden religious element in the story. These giants are not flesh and blood, but earth-born spirits, as their serpent-tails prove, and can be thwarted only by the possession of a magical herb. No mythographer mentions the name of the herb, but it was probably the *ephialtion*, a specific against the nightmare. Ephialtes, the name of the giants' leader means literally 'he who leaps upon' (*incubus* in Latin); and the attempts of Porphyrion to strangle and rape Hera, and of Pallas to rape Athene, suggest that the story mainly concerns the wisdom of invoking Heracles the Saviour, when threatened by erotic nightmares at any hour of the twenty-four.

4. Alcyoneus ('mighty ass') is probably the spirit of the sirocco, 'the breath of the Wild Ass, or Typhon' (see 36. 1), which brings bad dreams, and murderous inclinations, and rapes; and this makes Silenus's claim to have routed the giants with the braying of his pack-ass still more ridiculous (see 20. b). Mimas ('mimicry') may refer to the delusive verisimilitude of dreams; and Hippolytus ('stampede of horses') recalls the ancient attribution of terror-dreams to the Mare-headed goddess. In the north, it was Odin whom sufferers from 'the Nightmare and her ninefold' invoked, until his place was taken by St Swithold.

5. What use Heracles made of the herb can be deduced from the Babylonian myth of the cosmic fight between the new gods and the old. There Marduck, Heracles's counterpart, holds a herb to his nostrils against the noxious smell of the goddess Tiamat; here Alcyoneus's breath has to be counteracted.

# 36

## TYPHON

IN revenge for the destruction of the giants, Mother Earth lay with Tartarus, and presently in the Corycian Cave of Cilicia brought forth her youngest child, Typhon: the largest monster ever born.[1] From the thighs downward he was nothing but coiled serpents, and his arms which, when he spread them out, reached a hundred leagues in either direction, had countless serpents' heads instead of hands. His brutish ass-head touched the stars, his vast wings darkened the sun, fire flashed from his eyes, and flaming rocks hurtled from his mouth. When he came rushing towards Olympus, the gods fled in terror to Egypt, where they disguised themselves as animals: Zeus becoming a ram; Apollo, a crow; Dionysus, a goat; Hera, a white cow; Artemis, a cat; Aphrodite, a fish; Ares, a boar; Hermes, an ibis, and so on.

b. Athene alone stood her ground, and taunted Zeus with cowardice until, resuming his true form, he let fly a thunderbolt at Typhon, and followed this up with a sweep of the same flint sickle that had served to castrate his grandfather Uranus. Wounded and shouting, Typhon fled to Mount Casius, which looms over Syria from the north, and there the two grappled. Typhon twined his myriad coils about Zeus, disarmed him of his sickle and, after severing the sinews of his hands and feet with it, dragged him into the Corycian Cave. Zeus is immortal, but now he could not move a finger, and Typhon had hidden the sinews in a bear-skin, over which Delphyne, a serpent-tailed sister-monster, stood guard.

c. The news of Zeus's defeat spread dismay among the gods, but Hermes and Pan went secretly to the cave, where Pan frightened Delphyne with a sudden horrible shout, while Hermes skilfully abstracted the sinews and replaced them on Zeus's limbs.[2]

d. But some say that it was Cadmus who wheedled the sinews from Delphyne, saying that he needed them for lyre-strings on which to play her delightful music; and Apollo who shot her dead.[3]

e. Zeus returned to Olympus and, mounted upon a chariot drawn by winged horses, once more pursued Typhon with thunderbolts. Typhon had gone to Mount Nysa, where the Three Fates offered him ephemeral fruits, pretending that these would restore his vigour though, in reality, they doomed him to certain death. He reached Mount Haemus in Thrace and, picking up whole mountains, hurled them at Zeus, who interposed his thunderbolts, so that they rebounded on the monster, wounding him frightfully. The streams of Typhon's blood gave Mount Haemus its name. He fled towards Sicily, where Zeus ended the running fight by hurling Mount Aetna upon him, and fire belches from its cone to this day.[4]

1. Hesiod: *Theogony* 819 ff.; Pindar: *Pythian Odes* i. 15 ff.; Hyginus: *Fabula* 152.
2. Apollodorus: i. 6. 3.
3. Nonnus: *Dionysiaca* i. 481 ff.; Apollonius Rhodius: ii. 706.
4. Apollodorus: *loc. cit.*; Pindar: *loc. cit.*

\*

1. 'Corycian', said to mean 'of the leather sack', may record the ancient custom of confining winds in bags, followed by Aeolus (see 170. *g*), and preserved by medieval witches. In the other Corycian Cave, at Delphi, Delphyne's serpent-mate was called Python, not Typhon. Python ('serpent') personified the destructive North Wind – winds were habitually depicted with serpent tails – which whirls down on Syria from Mount Casius, and on Greece from Mount Haemus (see 21. *2*). Typhon, on the other hand, means 'stupefying smoke', and his appearance describes a volcanic eruption; hence Zeus was said to have buried him at last under Mount Aetna. But the name Typhon also meant the burning Sirocco from the Southern Desert, a cause of havoc in Libya and Greece, which carries a volcanic smell and was pictured by the Egyptians as a desert ass (see 35. *4* and 83. *2*). The god Set, whose breath Typhon was said to be, maimed Osiris in much the same way as Python maimed Zeus, but both were finally overcome; and the parallel has confused Python with Typhon.

2. This divine flight into Egypt, as Lucian observes (*On Sacrifices* 14), was invented to account for the Egyptian worship of gods in animal form – Zeus-Ammon as ram (see 133. *j*), Hermes-Thoth as ibis or crane (see 52. *6*), Hera-Isis as cow (see 56. *2*), Artemis-Pasht as cat, and so on; but it may also refer historically to a frightened exodus of priests and priestesses from the Aegean Archipelago, when a volcanic eruption engulfed half of the large island of Thera, shortly before 2000 B.C. Cats were not domesticated in Classical Greece. A further source of this legend seems to be the Babylonian Creation Epic, the *Enuma Elish*, according to which, in Damascius's earlier version, the goddess Tiamat, her consort Apsu, and their son Mummi ('confusion'), let loose Kingu and a horde of other monsters against the newly-born trinity of gods: Ea, Anu, and Bel. A panic flight follows; but presently Bel rallies his brothers, takes command and defeats Tiamat's forces, crushing her skull with a club and slicing her in two 'like a flat-fish'.

3. The myth of Zeus, Delphyne, and the bear-skin records Zeus's humiliation at the hands of the Great Goddess, worshipped as a She-bear, whose chief oracle was at Delphi; the historical occasion is unknown, but the Cadmeians of Boeotia seem to have been concerned with preserving the Zeus cult. Typhon's 'ephemeral fruits', given him by the Three

Fates, appear to be the usual death-apples (see 18. 4; 32. 4; 33. 7, etc.).
In a proto-Hittite version of the myth the serpent Illyunka overcomes the
Storm-god and takes away his eyes and heart, which he recovers by a
stratagem. The Divine Council then call on the goddess Inara to exact
vengeance. Illyunka, invited by her to a feast, eats until gorged; whereupon she binds him with a cord and he is despatched by the Storm-god.

4. Mount Casius (now Jebel-el-Akra) is the Mount Hazzi which
figures in the Hittite story of Ullikummi the stone giant, who grew at an
enormous rate, and was ordered by his father Kumarbi to destroy the
seventy gods of Heaven. The Storm-god, the Sun-god, the Goddess of
Beauty and all their fellow-deities failed to kill Ullikummi, until Ea the
God of Wisdom, using the knife that originally severed Heaven from
Earth, cut off the monster's feet and sent it crashing into the sea. Elements
of this story occur in the myth of Typhon, and also in that of the Aloeids,
who grew at the same rate and used mountains as a ladder to Heaven
(see 37. b). The Cadmeians are likely to have brought these legends into
Greece from Asia Minor (see 6. 1).

# 37

## THE ALOEIDS

EPHIALTES and Otus were the bastard sons of Iphimedeia, a daughter
of Triops. She had fallen in love with Poseidon, and used to crouch on
the seashore, scooping up the waves in her hands and pouring them
into her lap; thus she got herself with child. Ephialtes and Otus were,
however, called the Aloeids because Iphimedeia subsequently married
Aloeus, who had been made king of Boeotian Asopia by his father,
Helius. The Aloeids grew one cubit in breadth and one fathom in
height every year and, when they were nine years old, being then nine
cubits broad and nine fathoms high, declared war on Olympus.
Ephialtes swore by the river Styx to outrage Hera, and Otus similarly
swore to outrage Artemis.[1]

b. Deciding that Ares the God of War must be their first capture,
they went to Thrace, disarmed him, bound him, and confined him in
a brazen vessel, which they hid in the house of their stepmother
Eriboea, Iphimedeia being now dead. Then their siege of Olympus
began: they made a mound for its assault by piling Mount Pelion on
Mount Ossa, and further threatened to cast mountains into the sea until

it became dry land, though the lowlands were swamped by the waves. Their confidence was unquenchable because it had been prophesied that no other men, nor any gods, could kill them.

*c.* On Apollo's advice, Artemis sent the Aloeids a message: if they raised their seige, she would meet them on the island of Naxos, and there submit to Otus's embraces. Otus was overjoyed, but Ephialtes, not having received a similar message from Hera, grew jealous and angry. A cruel quarrel broke out on Naxos, where they went together: Ephialtes insisting that the terms should be rejected unless, as the elder of the two, he were the first to enjoy Artemis. The argument had reached its height, when Artemis herself appeared in the form of a white doe, and each Aloeid, seizing his javelin, made ready to prove himself the better marksman by flinging it at her. As she darted between them, swift as the wind, they let fly and each pierced the other through and through. Thus both perished, and the prophecy that they could not be killed by other men, or by gods, was justified. Their bodies were carried back for interment in Boeotian Anthedon; but the Naxians still pay them heroic honours. They are remembered also as the founders of Boeotian Ascra; and as the first mortals to worship the Muses of Helicon.[2]

*d.* The siege of Olympus being thus raised, Hermes went in search of Ares, and forced Eriboea to release him, half-dead, from the brazen vessel. But the souls of the Aloeids descended to Tartarus, where they were securely tied to a pillar with knotted cords of living vipers. There they sit, back to back and the Nymph Styx perches grimly on the pillar-top, as a reminder of their unfulfilled oaths.[3]

1. Apollodorus: i. 7. 4; Pausanias: ii. 3. 8; Pindar: *Pythian Odes* iv. 88–92.
2. Homer: *Odyssey* xi. 305–20; *Iliad* v. 385–90; Pausanias: ix. 29. 1–2.
3. Apollodorus: i. 7. 4; Hyginus: *Fabula* 28.

\*

1. This is another popular version of the Giants' Revolt (see 35. *b*). The name Ephialtes, the assault on Olympus, the threat to Hera, and the prophecy of their invulnerability, occur in both version. Ephialtes and Otus, 'sons of the threshing-floor' by 'her who strengthens the genitals', grandsons of 'Three Face', namely Hecate, and worshippers of the wild Muses, personify the incubus, or orgiastic nightmare, which stifles and outrages sleeping women. Like the Nightmare in British legend, they are associated with the number nine. The myth is confused by a shadowy

historical episode reported by Diodorus Siculus (v. 50 ff.). He says that
Aloeus, a Thessalian, sent his sons to liberate their mother Iphimedeia and
their sister Pancratis ('all-strength') from the Thracians, who had carried
them off to Naxos; their expedition was successful, but they quarrelled
about the partition of the island and killed each other. However, though
Stephanus of Byzantium records that the city of Aloeium in Thessaly was
named after the Aloeids, early mythographers make them Boeotians.

2. The twins' mutual murder recalls the eternal rivalry for the love of
the White Goddess between the sacred king and his tanist, who alternately meet death at each other's hands. That they were called 'sons of the
threshing-floor' and escaped destruction by Zeus's lightning, connects
them with the corn cult, rather than the oak cult. Their punishment in
Tartarus, like that of Theseus and Peirithous (see 103. c), seems to be
deduced from an ancient calendar symbol showing the twins' heads
turned back to back, on either side of a column, as they sit on the Chair of
Forgetfulness. The column, on which the Death-in-Life Goddess perches,
marks the height of summer when the sacred king's reign ends and the
tanist's begins. In Italy, this same symbol became two-headed Janus; but
the Italian New Year was in January, not at the heliacal rising of two-
headed Sirius (see 34. 3).

3. Ares's imprisonment for thirteen months is an unrelated mythic
fragment of uncertain date, referring perhaps to an armistice of one whole
year – the Pelasgian year had thirteen months – agreed upon between
the Thessalo-Boeotians and Thracians, with war-like tokens of both
nations entrusted to a brazen vessel in a temple of Hera Eriboea. Pelion,
Ossa, and Olympus are all mountains to the east of Thessaly, with a
distant view of the Thracian Chersonese where the war terminated by
this armistice may have been fought.


# 38

## DEUCALION'S FLOOD

DEUCALION's Flood, so called to distinguish it from the Ogygian and
other floods, was caused by Zeus's anger against the impious sons of
Lycaon, the son of Pelasgus. Lycaon himself first civilized Arcadia and
instituted the worship of Zeus Lycaeus; but angered Zeus by sacrificing
a boy to him. He was therefore transformed into a wolf, and his house
struck by lightning. Lycaon's sons were, some say, twenty-two in
number; but others say fifty.[1]

*b*. News of the crimes committed by Lycaon's sons reached Olympus, and Zeus himself visited them, disguised as a poor traveller. They had the effrontery to set umble soup before him, mixing the guts of their brother Nyctimus with the umbles of sheep and goats that it contained. Zeus was undeceived and, thrusting away the table on which they had served the loathsome banquet – the place was afterwards known as Trapezus – changed all of them except Nyctimus, whom he restored to life, into wolves.[2]

*c*. On his return to Olympus, Zeus in disgust let loose a great flood on the earth, meaning to wipe out the whole race of man; but Deucalion, King of Phthia, warned by his father Prometheus the Titan, whom he had visited in the Caucasus, built an ark, victualled it, and went aboard with his wife Pyrrha, a daughter of Epimetheus. Then the South Wind blew, the rain fell, and the rivers roared down to the sea which, rising with astonishing speed, washed away every city of the coast and plain; until the entire world was flooded, but for a few mountain peaks, and all mortal creatures seemed to have been lost, except Deucalion and Pyrrha. The ark floated about for nine days until, at last, the waters subsided, and it came to rest on Mount Parnassus or, some tell, on Mount Aetna; or Mount Athos; or Mount Othrys in Thessaly. It is said that Deucalion was reassured by a dove which he had sent on an exploratory flight.[3]

*d*. Disembarking in safety, they offered a sacrifice to Father Zeus, the preserver of fugitives, and went down to pray at the shrine of Themis, beside the river Cephissus, where the roof was now draped with seaweed and the altar cold. They pleaded humbly that mankind should be renewed, and Zeus, hearing their voices from afar, sent Hermes to assure them that whatever request they might make would be granted forthwith. Themis appeared in person, saying: 'Shroud your heads, and throw the bones of your mother behind you!' Since Deucalion and Pyrrha had different mothers, both now deceased, they decided that the Titaness meant Mother Earth, whose bones were the rocks lying on the river bank. Therefore, stooping with shrouded heads, they picked up rocks and threw them over their shoulders; these became either men or women, according as Deucalion or Pyrrha had handled them. Thus mankind was renewed, and ever since a 'people' (*laos*) and 'a stone' (*laas*) have been much the same word in many languages.[4]

*e*. However, as it proved, Deucalion and Pyrrha were not the sole survivors of the Flood, for Megarus, a son of Zeus, had been roused from his couch by the scream of cranes that summoned him to the peak of Mount Gerania, which remained above water. Another who escaped was Cerambus of Pelion, whom the nymphs changed to a scarabaeus, and he flew to the summit of Parnassus.[5]

f. Similarly, the inhabitants of Parnassus – a city founded by Parnasus, Poseidon's son, who invented the art of augury – were awakened by the howling of wolves and followed them to the mountain top. They named their new city Lycorea, after the wolves.[6]

g. Thus the flood proved of little avail, for some of the Parnassians migrated to Arcadia, and revived Lycaon's abominations. To this day a boy is sacrificed to Lycaean Zeus, and his guts mixed with others in an umble soup, which is then served to a crowd of shepherds beside a stream. The shepherd who eats the boy's gut (assigned to him by lot), howls like a wolf, hangs his clothes upon an oak, swims across the stream, and becomes a werewolf. For eight years he herds with wolves, but if he abstains from eating men throughout that period, may return at the close, swim back across the stream and resume his clothes. Not long ago, a Parrhasian named Damarchus spent eight years with the wolves, regained his humanity and, in the tenth year, after hard practice in the gymnasium, won the boxing prize at the Olympic Games.[7]

h. This Deucalion was the brother of Cretan Ariadne and the father of Orestheus, King of the Ozolian Locrians, in whose time a white bitch littered a stick, which Orestheus planted, and which grew into a vine. Another of his sons, Amphictyon, entertained Dionysus, and was the first man to mix wine with water. But his eldest and most famous son was Hellen, father of all Greeks.[8]

1. Apollodorus: iii. 8. 1; Pausanias: viii. 2. 1; Scholiast on Caesar Germanicus's *Aratea* 89; Ovid: *Metamorphoses* i. 230 ff.
2. Apollodorus: *loc. cit.*; Tzetzes: *On Lycophron* 481; Pausanias: viii. 3. 1; Ovid: *Metamorphoses* i. 230 ff.
3. Ovid: *ibid.* i. 317; Scholiast on Euripides's *Orestes* 1095; Hyginus: *Fabula* 153; Servius on Virgil's *Eclogues* vi. 41; Scholiast on Pindar's *Olympian Odes* ix. 42; Plutarch: *Which Animals Are Craftier?* 13.
4. Apollodorus: i. 7. 2; Ovid: *Metamorphoses* i. 260–415.
5. Pausanias: i. 40. 1; Ovid: *Metamorphoses* vii. 352–6.
6. Pausanias x. 6. 1–2.
7. Pausanias: viii. 2. 3 and vi. 8. 2; Pliny: *Natural History* viii. 34; Plato: *Republic* viii. 16.

8. Pausanias: x. 38. 1; Eustathius on Homer: p. 1815; Apollodorus; i. 7. 2.                    *

1. The story of Zeus and the boy's guts is not so much a myth as a moral anecdote expressing the disgust felt in more civilized parts of Greece for the ancient cannibalistic practices of Arcadia, which were still performed in the name of Zeus, as 'barbarous and unnatural' (Plutarch: *Life of Pelopidas*). Lycaon's virtuous Athenian contemporary Cecrops (see 25. *d*) offered only barley-cakes, abstaining even from animal sacrifices. The Lycaonian rites, which the author denies that Zeus ever countenanced, were apparently intended to discourage the wolves from preying on flocks and herds, by sending them a human king. 'Lycaeus' means 'of the she-wolf', but also 'of the light', and the lightning in the Lycaon myth shows that Arcadian Zeus began as a rain-making sacred king – in service to the divine She-wolf, the Moon, to whom the wolf-pack howls.

2. A Great Year of one hundred months, or eight solar years, was divided equally between the sacred king and his tanist; and Lycaon's fifty sons – one for every month of the sacred king's reign – will have been the eaters of the umble soup. The figure twenty-two, unless it has been arrived at by a count of the families who claimed descent from Lycaon and had to participate in the umble-feast, probably refers to the twenty-two five-year *lustra* which composed a cycle – the 110-year cycle constituting the reign of a particular line of priestesses.

3. The myth of Deucalion's Flood, apparently brought from Asia by the Hellads, has the same origin as the Biblical legend of Noah. But though Noah's invention of wine is the subject of a Hebrew moral tale, incidentally justifying the enslavement of the Canaanites by their Kassite and Semitic conquerors, Deucalion's claim to the invention has been suppressed by the Greeks in favour of Dionysus. Deucalion is, however, described as the brother of Ariadne, who was the mother, by Dionysus, of various vine-cult tribes (see 27. 8), and has kept his name 'new-wine sailor' (from *deucos* and *halicus*). The Deucalion myth records a Mesopotamian flood of the third millenium B.C.; but also the autumnal New Year feast of Babylonia, Syria and Palestine. This feast celebrated Parnapishtim's outpouring of sweet new wine to the builders of the ark, in which (according to the Babylonian Gilgamesh Epic) he and his family survived the Deluge sent by the goddess Ishtar. The ark was a moon-ship (see 123. 5) and the feast was celebrated on the new moon nearest to the autumnal equinox, as a means of inducing the winter rains. Ishtar, in the Greek myth, is called Pyrrha – the name of the goddess-mother of the Puresati (Philistines), a Cretan people who came to Palestine by way of Cilicia about the year 1200 B.C.; in Greek, *pyrrha* means 'fiery red', and is an adjective applied to wine.

4. Xisuthros was the hero of the Sumerian Flood legend, recorded by Berossus, and his ark came to rest on Mount Ararat. All these arks were built of acacia-wood, a timber also used by Isis for building Osiris's death barge.

5. The myth of an angry god who decides to punish man's wickedness with a deluge seems to be a late Greek borrowing from the Phoenicians, or the Jews; but the number of different mountains, in Greece, Thrace, and Sicily, on which Deucalion is said to have landed, suggests that an ancient Flood myth has been superimposed on a later legend of a flood in Northern Greece. In the earliest Greek version of the myth, Themis renews the race of man without first obtaining Zeus's consent; it is therefore likely that she, not he, was credited with the Flood, as in Babylonia.

6. The transformation of stones into a people is, perhaps, another Helladic borrowing from the East; St John the Baptist referred to a similar legend, in a pun on the Hebrew words *banim* and *abanim*, declaring that God could raise up *children* to Abraham from the desert *stones* (*Matthew* iii. 3–9 and *Luke* iii. 8).

7. That a white bitch, the Moon-goddess Hecate, littered a vine-stock in the reign of Deucalion's son Orestheus is probably the earliest Greek wine myth. The name Ozolian is said to be derived from *ozoi*, 'vine shoots' (see 147. 7). One of the wicked sons of Lycaon was also named Orestheus, which may account for the forced connexion which the mythographers have made between the myth of the umble soup and the Deucalionian Flood.

8. Amphictyon, the name of another of Deucalion's sons, is a male form of Amphictyonis, the goddess in whose name the famous northern confederation, the Amphictyonic League, had been founded; according to Strabo, Callimachus, and the Scholiast on Euripides's *Orestes*, it was regularized by Acrisius of Argos (see 73. *a*). Civilized Greeks, unlike the dissolute Thracians, abstained from neat wine; and its tempering with water at the conference of the member states, which took place in the vintage season at Anthela near Thermopylae, will have been a precaution against murderous disputes.

9. Deucalion's son Hellen was the eponymous ancestor of the entire Hellenic race (see 43. *b*): his name shows that he was a royal deputy for the priestess of Helle, or Hellen, or Helen, or Selene, the Moon; and, according to Pausanias (iii. 20. 6), the first tribe to be called Hellenes came from Thessaly, where Helle was worshipped (see 70. 8).

10. Aristotle (*Meteorologica* i. 14) says that Deucalion's Flood took place 'in ancient Greece (Graecia), namely the district about Dodona and the Achelous River'. *Graeci* means 'worshippers of the Crone', presumably the Earth-goddess of Dodona, who appeared in triad as the Graeae (see 33. *c*); and it has been suggested that the Achaeans were forced to

invade the Peloponnese because unusually heavy rains had swamped
their grazing grounds. Helle's worship (see 62. *3*; 70. *8* and 159. *1*) seems
to have ousted that of the Graeae.

*11*. The scarabaeus beetle was an emblem of immortality in Lower
Egypt because it survived the flooding of the Nile – the Pharoah as
Osiris entered his sun-boat in the form of a scarabaeus – and its sacral
use spread to Palestine, the Aegean, Etruria, and the Balearic Islands.
Antoninus Liberalis also mentions the myth of Cerambus, or Terambus,
quoting Nicander.

# 39

## ATLAS AND PROMETHEUS

PROMETHEUS, the creator of mankind, whom some include among
the seven Titans, was the son either of the Titan Eurymedon, or of
Iapetus by the nymph Clymene; and his brothers were Epimetheus,
Atlas, and Menoetius.[1]

*b*. Gigantic Atlas, eldest of the brothers, knew all the depths of the
sea; he ruled over a kingdom with a precipitous coastline, larger than
Africa and Asia put together. This land of Atlantis lay beyond the
Pillars of Heracles, and a chain of fruit-bearing islands separated it from
a farther continent, unconnected with ours. Atlas's people canalized
and cultivated an enormous central plain, fed by water from the hills
which ringed it completely, except for a seaward gap. They also built
palaces, baths, race-courses, great harbour works, and temples; and
carried war not only westwards as far as the other continent, but eastward as far as Egypt and Italy. The Egyptians say that Atlas was the son
of Poseidon, whose five pairs of male twins all swore allegiance to
their brother by the blood of a bull sacrificed at the pillar-top; and that
at first they were extremely virtuous, bearing with fortitude the burden
of their great wealth in gold and silver. But one day greed and cruelty
overcame them and, with Zeus's permission, the Athenians defeated
them single-handed and destroyed their power. At the same time, the
gods sent a deluge which, in one day and one night, overwhelmed all
Atlantis, so that the harbour works and temples were buried beneath a
waste of mud and the sea became unnavigable.[2]

*c*. Atlas and Menoetius, who escaped, then joined Cronus and the

Titans in their unsuccessful war against the Olympian gods. Zeus killed Menoetius with a thunderbolt and sent him down to Tartarus, but spared Atlas, whom he condemned to support Heaven on his shoulders for all eternity.[3]

*d*. Atlas was the father of the Pleiades, the Hyades, and the Hesperides; and has held up the Heavens ever since, except on one occasion, when Heracles temporarily relieved him of the task. Some say that Perseus petrified Atlas into Mount Atlas by showing him the Gorgon's head; but they forget that Perseus was reputedly a distant ancestor of Heracles.[4]

*e*. Prometheus, being wiser than Atlas, foresaw the issue of the rebellion against Cronus, and therefore preferred to fight on Zeus's side, persuading Epimetheus to do the same. He was, indeed, the wisest of his race, and Athene, at whose birth from Zeus's head he had assisted, taught him architecture, astronomy, mathematics, navigation, medicine, metallurgy, and other useful arts, which he passed on to mankind. But Zeus, who had decided to extirpate the whole race of man, and spared them only at Prometheus's urgent plea, grew angry at their increasing powers and talents.[5]

*f*. One day, when a dispute took place at Sicyon, as to which portions of a sacrificial bull should be offered to the gods, and which should be reserved for men, Prometheus was invited to act as arbiter. He therefore flayed and jointed a bull, and sewed its hide to form two open-mouthed bags, filling these with what he had cut up. One bag contained all the flesh, but this he concealed beneath the stomach, which is the least tempting part of any animal; and the other contained the bones, hidden beneath a rich layer of fat. When he offered Zeus the choice of either, Zeus, easily deceived, chose the bag containing the bones and fat (which are still the divine portion); but punished Prometheus, who was laughing at him behind his back, by withholding fire from mankind. 'Let them eat their flesh raw!' he cried.[6]

*g*. Prometheus at once went to Athene, with a plea for a backstairs admittance to Olympus, and this she granted. On his arrival, he lighted a torch at the fiery chariot of the Sun and presently broke from it a fragment of glowing charcoal, which he thrust into the pithy hollow of a giant fennel-stalk. Then, extinguishing his torch, he stole away undiscovered, and gave fire to mankind.[7]

*h*. Zeus swore revenge. He ordered Hephaestus to make a clay woman, and the four Winds to breathe life into her, and all the goddesses of Olympus to adorn her. This woman, Pandora, the most beautiful ever created, Zeus sent as a gift to Epimetheus, under Hermes's escort. But Epimetheus, having been warned by his brother to accept no gift from Zeus, respectfully excused himself. Now even angrier than before, Zeus had Prometheus chained naked to a pillar in the Caucasian mountains, where a greedy vulture tore at his liver all day, year in, year out; and there was no end to the pain, because every night (during which Prometheus was exposed to cruel frost and cold) his liver grew whole again.

*i.* But Zeus, loth to confess that he had been vindictive, excused his savagery by circulating a falsehood: Athene, he said, had invited Prometheus to Olympus for a secret love affair.

*j.* Epimetheus, alarmed by his brother's fate, hastened to marry Pandora, whom Zeus had made as foolish, mischievous, and idle as she was beautiful – the first of a long line of such women. Presently she opened a jar, which Prometheus had warned Epimetheus to keep closed, and in which he had been at pains to imprison all the Spites that might plague mankind: such as Old Age, Labour, Sickness, Insanity, Vice, and Passion. Out these flew in a cloud, stung Epimetheus and Pandora in every part of their bodies, and then attacked the race of mortals. Delusive Hope, however, whom Prometheus had also shut in the jar, discouraged them by her lies from a general suicide.[8]

1. Eustathius: *On Homer* p. 987; Hesiod: *Theogony* 507 ff.; Apollodorus: i. 2. 3.
2. Plato: *Timaeus* 6 and *Critias* 9–10.
3. Homer: *Odyssey* i. 52–4; Hesiod: *loc. cit.*; Hyginus: *Fabula* 150.
4. Diodorus Siculus: iv. 27; Apollodorus: ii. 5. 11; Ovid: *Metamorphoses* iv. 630.
5. Aeschylus: *Prometheus Bound* 218, 252, 445 ff., 478 ff., and 228–36.
6. Hesiod: *Theogony* 521–64; Lucian: *Dialogues of the Gods* 1 and *Prometheus on Caucasus* 3.
7. Servius on Virgil's *Eclogues* vi. 42.
8. Hesiod: *Works and Days* 42–105 and *Theogony* 565–619; Scholiast on Apollonius Rhodius ii. 1249.

\*

1. Later mythographers understood Atlas as a simple personification of Mount Atlas, in North-western Africa, whose peak seemed to hold up the Heavens; but, for Homer, the columns on which he supported the firmament stood far out in the Atlantic Ocean, afterwards named in his honour by Herodotus. He began, perhaps, as the Titan of the Second Day

of the Week, who separated the waters of the firmament from the waters of the earth. Most rain comes to Greece from the Atlantic, especially at the heliacal rising of Atlas's star-daughters, the Hyades; which partly explains why his home was in the west. Heracles took the Heavens from his shoulders in two senses (see 133. 3–4 and 123. 4).

2. The Egyptian legend of Atlantis – also current in folk-tale along the Atlantic seaboard from Gibraltar to the Hebrides, and among the Yorubas in West Africa – is not to be dismissed as pure fancy, and seems to date from the third millennium B.C. But Plato's version, which he claims that Solon learned from his friends the Libyan priests of Saïs in the Delta, has apparently been grafted on a later tradition: how the Minoan Cretans, who had extended their influence to Egypt and Italy, were defeated by a Hellenic confederacy with Athens at its head (see 98. 1); and how, perhaps as the result of a submarine earthquake, the enormous harbour works built by the Keftiu ('sea-people', meaning the Cretans and their allies) on the island of Pharos (see 27. 7 and 169. 6), subsided under several fathoms of water – where they have lately been rediscovered by divers. These works consisted of an outer and an inner basin, together covering some two hundred and fifty acres (Gaston Jondet: *Les Ports submergés de l'ancienne île de Pharos*, 1916). Such an identification of Atlantis with Pharos would account for Atlas's being sometimes described as a son of Iapetus – the Japhet of *Genesis*, whom the Hebrews called Noah's son and made the ancestor of the Sea-people's confederacy – and sometimes as a son of Poseidon, patron of Greek seafarers. Noah is Deucalion (see 38. *c*) and, though in Greek myth Iapetus appears as Deucalion's grandfather, this need mean no more than that he was the eponymous ancestor of the Canaanite tribe which brought the Mesopotamian Flood legend, rather than the Atlantian, to Greece. Several details in Plato's account, such as the pillar-sacrifice of bulls and the hot-and-cold water systems in Atlas's palace, make it certain that the Cretans are being described, and no other nation. Like Atlas, the Cretans 'knew all the depths of the sea'. According to Diodorus (v. 3), when most of the inhabitants of Greece were destroyed by the great flood, the Athenians forgot that they had founded Saïs in Egypt. This seems to be a muddled way of saying that after the submergence of the Pharos harbour-works the Athenians forgot their religious ties with the city of Saïs, where the same Libyan goddess Neith, or Athene, or Tanit, was worshipped.

3. Plato's story is confused by his account of the vast numbers of elephants in Atlantis, which may refer to the heavy import of ivory into Greece by way of Pharos, but has perhaps been borrowed from the older legend. The whereabouts of the folk-tale Atlantis has been the subject of numerous theories, though Plato's influence has naturally concentrated popular attention on the Atlantic Ocean. Until recently, the Atlantic

Ridge (stretching from Iceland to the Azores and then bending south-eastward to Ascension Island and Tristan da Cunha) was supposed to be its remains; but oceanographic surveys show that apart from these peaks the entire ridge has been under water for at least sixty million years. Only one large inhabited island in the Atlantic is known to have disappeared: the plateau now called the Dogger Bank. But the bones and implements hauled up in cod-nets show that this disaster occurred in paleolithic times; and it is far less likely that the news of its disappearance reached Europe from survivors who drifted across the intervening waste of waters than that the memory of a different catastrophe was brought to the Atlantic seaboard by the highly civilized neolithic immigrants from Libya, usually known as the passage-grave builders.

4. These were farmers and arrived in Great Britain towards the close of the third millennium B.C.; but no explanation has been offered for their mass movement westwards by way of Tunis and Morocco to Southern Spain and then northward to Portugal and beyond. According to the Welsh Atlantis legend of the lost Cantrevs of Dyfed (impossibly located in Cardigan Bay), a heavy sea broke down the sea-walls and destroyed sixteen cities. The Irish Hy Brasil; the Breton City of Ys; the Cornish Land of Lyonesse (impossibly located between Cornwall and the Scilly Isles); the French Île Verte; the Portuguese Ilha Verde: all are variants of this legend. But if what the Egyptian priests really told Solon was that the disaster took place in the Far West, and that the survivors moved 'beyond the Pillars of Heracles', Atlantis can be easily identified.

5. It is the country of the Atlantians, mentioned by Diodorus Siculus (see 131. m) as a most civilized people living to the westward of Lake Tritonis, from whom the Libyan Amazons, meaning the matriarchal tribes later described by Herodotus, seized their city of Cerne. Diodorus's legend cannot be archaeologically dated, but he makes it precede a Libyan invasion of the Aegean Islands and Thrace, an event which cannot have taken place later than the third millennium B.C. If, then, Atlantis was Western Libya, the floods which caused it to disappear may have been due either to a phenomenal rainfall such as caused the famous Mesopotamian and Ogygian Floods (see 38. 3–5), or to a high tide with a strong north-westerly gale, such as washed away a large part of the Netherlands in the twelfth and thirteenth centuries and formed the Zuider Zee,* or to a subsidence of the coastal region. Atlantis may, in fact, have been swamped at the formation of Lake Tritonis (see 8. a), which apparently once covered several thousand square miles of the Libyan lowlands; and perhaps extended northward into the Western Gulf of Sirte, called by the geographer Scylax 'the Gulf of Tritonis', where the dangerous reefs

*Since this was written, history has repeated itself disastrously.

suggest a chain of islands of which only Jerba and the Kerkennahs survive.

6. The island left in the centre of the Lake mentioned by Diodorus (see 131. *l*) was perhaps the Chaamba Bou Rouba in the Sahara. Diodorus seems to be referring to such a catastrophe when he writes in his account of the Amazons and Atlantians (iii. 55): 'And it is said that, as a result of earthquakes, the parts of Libya towards the ocean engulfed Lake Tritonis, making it disappear.' Since Lake Tritonis still existed in his day, what he had probably been told was that 'as a result of earthquakes in the Western Mediterranean the sea engulfed part of Libya and formed Lake Tritonis.' The Zuider Zee and the Copaic Lake have now both been reclaimed; and Lake Tritonis, which, according to Scylax, still covered nine hundred square miles in Classical times, has shrunk to the salt-marshes of Chott Melghir and Chott el Jerid. If this was Atlantis, some of the dispossessed agriculturists were driven west to Morocco, others south across the Sahara, others east to Egypt and beyond, taking their story with them; a few remained by the lakeside. Plato's elephants may well have been found in this territory, though the mountainous coastline of Atlantis belongs to Crete, of which the sea-hating Egyptians knew only by hear-say.

7. The five pairs of Poseidon's twin sons who took the oath of allegiance to Atlas will have been representatives at Pharos of 'Keftiu' kingdoms allied to the Cretans. In the Mycenaean Age double-sovereignty was the rule: Sparta with Castor and Polydeuces, Messenia with Idas and Lynceus, Argos with Proetus and Acrisius, Tiryns with Heracles and Iphicles, Thebes with Eteocles and Polyneices. Greed and cruelty will have been displayed by the Sons of Poseidon only after the fall of Cnossus, when commercial integrity declined and the merchant turned pirate.

8. Prometheus's name, 'forethought', may originate in a Greek misunderstanding of the Sanskrit word *pramantha*, the swastika, or fire-drill, which he had supposedly invented, since Zeus Prometheus at Thurii was shown holding a fire-drill. Prometheus, the Indo-European folk-hero, became confused with the Carian hero Palamedes, the inventor or distributor of all civilized arts (under the goddess's inspiration); and with the Babylonian god Ea, who claimed to have created a splendid man from the blood of Kingu (a sort of Cronus), while the Mother-goddess Aruru created an inferior man from clay. The brothers Pramanthu and Manthu, who occur in the *Bhagavata Purāna*, a Sanskrit epic, may be prototypes of Prometheus and Epimetheus ('afterthought'); yet Hesiod's account of Prometheus, Epimetheus, and Pandora is not a genuine myth, but an anti-feminist fable, probably of his own invention, though based on the story of Demophon and Phyllis (see 169. *j*). Pandora ('all-giving') was the Earth-goddess Rhea, worshipped under that title at Athens and elsewhere (Aristophanes: *Birds* 971; Philostratus: *Life of Apollonius of Tyana* vi. 39), whom the pessimistic Hesiod blames for man's mortality and all the ills

which beset life, as well as for the frivolous and unseemly behaviour of wives. His story of the division of the bull is equally unmythical: a comic anecdote, invented to account for Prometheus's punishment, and for the anomaly of presenting the gods only with the thigh-bones and fat cut from the sacrificial beast. In *Genesis* the sanctity of the thigh-bones is explained by Jacob's lameness which an angel inflicted on him during a wrestling match. Pandora's jar (not box) originally contained winged souls.

*9.* Greek islanders still carry fire from one place to another in the pith of giant fennel, and Prometheus's enchainment on Mount Caucasus may be a legend picked up by the Hellenes as they migrated to Greece from the Caspian Sea: of a frost-giant, recumbent on the snow of the high peaks, and attended by a flock of vultures.

*10.* The Athenians were at pains to deny that their goddess took Prometheus as her lover, which suggests that he had been locally identified with Hephaestus, another fire-god and inventor, of whom the same story was told (see 25. *b*) because he shared a temple with Athene on the Acropolis.

*11.* Menoetius ('ruined strength') is a sacred king of the oak cult; the name refers perhaps to his ritual maiming (see 7. *1* and 50. *2*).

*12.* While the right-handed *swastika* is a symbol of the sun, the left-handed is a symbol of the moon. Among the Akan of West Africa, a people of Libyo-Berber ancestry (see *Introduction, end*), it represents the Triple-goddess Ngame.

# 40

## EOS

AT the close of every night, rosy-fingered, saffron-robed Eos, a daughter of the Titans Hyperion and Theia, rises from her couch in the east, mounts her chariot drawn by the horses Lampus and Phaëthon, and rides to Olympus, where she announces the approach of her brother Helius. When Helius appears, she becomes Hemera, and accompanies him on his travels until, as Hespera, she announces their safe arrival on the western shores of Ocean.[1]

*b.* Aphrodite was once vexed to find Ares in Eos's bed, and cursed her with a constant longing for young mortals, whom thereupon she secretly and shamefacedly began to seduce, one after the other. First, Orion; next, Cephalus; then Cleitus, a grandson of Melampus; though she was married to Astraeus, who came of Titan stock, and to whom she bore not only the North, West, and South Winds, but also Phosphorus and, some say, all the other stars of Heaven.[2]

*c.* Lastly, Eos carried off Ganymedes and Tithonus, sons of Tros or Ilus. When Zeus robbed her of Ganymedes she begged him to grant Tithonus immortality, and to this he assented. But she forgot to ask also for perpetual youth, a gift won by Selene for Endymion; and Tithonus became daily older, greyer, and more shrunken, his voice grew shrill, and, when Eos tired of nursing him, she locked him in her bedroom, where he turned into a cicada.[3]

1. Homer: *Odyssey* v. 1 and xxiii. 244–6; Theocritus: *Idylls* ii. 148.
2. Apollodorus: i. 4. 4; Homer *Odyssey* xv. 250; Hesiod: *Theogony* 378–82.
3. Scholiast on Apollonius Rhodius: iii. 115; *Homeric Hymn to Aphrodite* 218–38; Hesiod: *Theogony* 984; Apollodorus: iii. 12. 4; Horace: *Odes* iii. 20; Ovid: *Fasti* i. 461.

\*

1. The Dawn-maiden was a Hellenic fancy, grudgingly accepted by the mythographers as a Titaness of the second generation; her two-horse chariot and her announcement of the Sun's advent are allegories rather than myths.

2. Eos's constant love affairs with young mortals are also allegories: dawn brings midnight lovers a renewal of erotic passion, and is the most usual time for men to be carried off by fever. The allegory of her union with Astraeus is a simple one: the stars merge with dawn in the east and Astraeus, the dawn wind, rises as if it were their emanation. Then, because wind was held to be a fertilizing agent, Eos became the mother by Astraeus of the Morning Star left alone in the sky. (Astraeus was another name for Cephalus, also said to have fathered the Morning Star on her.) It followed philosophically that, since the Evening Star is identical with the Morning Star, and since Evening is Dawn's last appearance, all the stars must be born from Eos, and so must every wind but the dawn wind. This allegory, however, contradicted the myth of Boreas's creation by the Moon-goddess Eurynome (see 1. *1*).

3. In Greek art, Eos and Hemera are indistinguishable characters. Tithonus has been taken by the allegorist to mean 'a grant of a stretching-out' (from *teinō* and *ōnē*), a reference to the stretching-out of his life, at Eos's plea; but it is likely, rather, to have been a masculine form of Eos's own name, Titonë – from *titō*, 'day' (Tzetzes: *On Lycophron* 941) and *onë*, 'queen' – and to have meant 'partner of the Queen of Day'. Cicadas are active as soon as the day warms up, and the golden cicada was an emblem of Apollo as the Sun-god among the Greek colonists of Asia Minor.

# ORION

ORION, a hunter of Boeotian Hyria, and the handsomest man alive, was the son of Poseidon and Euryale. Coming one day to Hyria in Chios, he fell in love with Merope, daughter of Dionysus's son Oenopion. Oenopion had promised Merope to Orion in marriage, if he would free the island from the dangerous wild beasts that infested it; and this he set himself to do, bringing the pelts to Merope every evening. But when the task was at last accomplished, and he claimed her as his wife, Oenopion brought him rumours of lions, bears, and wolves still lurking in the hills, and refused to give her up, the fact being that he was in love with her himself.

*b.* One night Orion, in disgust, drank a skinful of Oenopion's wine, which so inflamed him that he broke into Merope's bedroom, and forced her to lie with him. When dawn came, Oenopion invoked his father, Dionysus, who sent satyrs to ply Orion with still more wine, until he fell fast asleep; whereupon Oenopion put out both his eyes and flung him on the seashore. An oracle announced that the blind man would regain his sight, if he travelled to the east and turned his eye-sockets towards Helius at the point where he first rises from Ocean. Orion at once rowed out to sea in a small boat and, following the sound of a Cyclops's hammer, reached Lemnos. There he entered the smithy of Hephaestus, snatched up an apprentice named Cedalion, and carried him off on his shoulders as a guide. Cedalion led Orion over land and sea, until he came at last to the farthest Ocean, where Eos fell in love with him, and her brother Helius duly restored his sight.

*c.* After visiting Delos in Eos's company, Orion returned to avenge himself on Oenopion, whom he could not, however, find anywhere in Chios, because he was hiding in an underground chamber made for him by Hephaestus. Sailing on to Crete, where he thought that Oenopion might have fled for protection to his grandfather Minos, Orion met Artemis, who shared his love of the chase. She soon persuaded him to forget his vengeance and, instead, come hunting with her.[1]

*d.* Now, Apollo was aware that Orion had not refused Eos's invitation to her couch in the holy island of Delos – Dawn still daily blushes to remember this indiscretion – and, further, boasted that he would rid the whole earth of wild beasts and monsters. Fearing, therefore, that his sister Artemis might prove as susceptible as Eos, Apollo went to Mother Earth and, mischievously repeating Orion's boast, arranged for a monstrous scorpion to pursue him. Orion attacked the scorpion, first with arrows, then with his sword, but, finding that its armour was proof against any mortal weapon, dived into the sea and swam away in the direction of Delos where, he hoped, Eos would protect him. Apollo then called to Artemis: 'Do you see that black object bobbing about in the sea, far away, close to Ortygia? It is the head of a villain called Candaon, who has just seduced Opos, one of your Hyperborean priestesses. I challenge you to transfix it with an arrow!' Now, Candaon was Orion's Boeotian nickname, though Artemis did not know this. She took careful aim, let fly, and, swimming out to retrieve her quarry, found that she had shot Orion through the head. In great grief she implored Apollo's son Asclepius to revive him, and he consented; but was destroyed by Zeus's thunderbolt before he could accomplish his task. Artemis then set Orion's image among the stars, eternally pursued by the Scorpion; his ghost had already descended to the Asphodel Fields.

*e.* Some, however, say that the scorpion stung Orion to death, and that Artemis was vexed with him for having amorously chased her virgin companions, the seven Pleiades, daughters of Atlas and Pleione. They fled across the meadows of Boeotia, until the gods, having changed them into doves, set their images among the stars. But this is a mistaken account, since the Pleiades were not virgins: three of them had lain with Zeus, two with Poseidon, one with Ares, and the seventh married Sisyphus of Corinth, and failed to be included in the constellation, because Sisyphus was a mere mortal.[2]

*f.* Others tell the following strange story of Orion's birth, to account for his name (which is sometimes written Urion) and for the tradition that he was a son of Mother Earth. Hyrieus, a poor bee-keeper and farmer, had vowed to have no children, and he grew old and impotent. When, one day, Zeus and Hermes visited him in disguise, and were hospitably entertained, they enquired what gift he most desired. Sighing deeply, Hyrieus replied that what he most wanted, namely to have a son, was now impossible. The gods, however, instructed him to sacrifice a bull, make water on its hide, and then bury it in his wife's grave. He did so and, nine months later, a child was born to him, whom he named Uroin – 'he who makes water' – and, indeed, both the rising and setting of the constellation Orion bring rain.[3]

1. Homer: *Odyssey* xi. 310; Apollodorus: i. 4. 3–4; Parthenius: *Love Stories* 20; Lucian: *On the Hall* 28; Theon: *On Aratus* 638; Hyginus: *Poetic Astronomy* ii. 34.
2. Apollodorus: *loc. cit.*
3. Servius on Virgil's *Aeneid* i. 539; Ovid: *Fasti* v. 537 ff.; Hyginus: *Poetic Astronomy* ii. 34.

*

1. Orion's story consists of three or four unrelated myths strung together. The first, confusedly told, is that of Oenopion. This concerns a sacred king's unwillingness to resign his throne, at the close of his term, even when the new candidate for kingship had been through his ritual combats and married the queen with the usual feasting. But the new king is only an *interrex* who, after reigning for one day, is duly murdered and devoured by Maenads (see 30. *1*); the old king, who has been shamming dead in a tomb, then remarries the queen and continues his reign (see 123. *4*).

2. The irrelevant detail of the Cyclop's hammer explains Orion's blindness: a mythological picture of Odysseus searing the drunken Cyclops's eye (see 170. *d*) has apparently been combined with a Hellenic allegory: how the Sun Titan is blinded every evening by his enemies, but restored to sight by the following Dawn. Orion ('the dweller on the mountain') and Hyperion ('the dweller on high') are, in fact, identified here. Orion's boast that he would exterminate the wild beasts not only refers to his ritual combats (see 123. *1*), but is a fable of the rising Sun, at whose appearance all wild beasts retire to their dens (compare *Psalm* civ. 22).

3. Plutarch's account of the scorpion sent by the god Set to kill the Child Horus, son of Isis and Osiris, in the hottest part of the summer, explains Orion's death by scorpion-bite and Artemis's appeal to Asclepius (Plutarch: *On Isis and Osiris* 19). Horus died, but Ra, the Sun-god, revived him, and later he avenged his father Osiris's death; in the original myth Orion, too, will have been revived. Orion is also, in part, Gilgamesh, the Babylonian Heracles, whom Scorpion-men attack in the Tenth Tablet of the Calendar epic – a myth which concerned the mortal wounding of the sacred king as the Sun rose in Scorpio. Exactly at what season the wounding took place depends on the antiquity of the myth; when the Zodiac originated, Scorpio was probably an August sign, but in Classical times the precession of the equinoxes had advanced it to October.

4. Another version of Orion's death is recorded on one of the Hittite Ras Shamra tablets. Anat, or Anatha, the Battle-goddess, fell in love with

a handsome hunter named Aqhat, and when he vexatiously refused to give her his bow, asked the murderous Yatpan to steal it from him. To her great grief the clumsy Yatpan not only killed Aqhat, but dropped the bow into the sea. The astronomical meaning of this myth is that Orion and the Bow – a part of the constellation, which the Greeks called 'The Hound' – sink below the southern horizon for two whole months every spring. In Greece this story seems to have been adapted to a legend of how the orgiastic priestesses of Artemis – Opis being a title of Artemis herself – killed an amorous visitor to their islet of Ortygia. And in Egypt, since the return of the constellation Orion introduces the summer heat, it was confusingly identified with Horus's enemy Set, the two bright stars above him being his ass's ears.

5. The myth of Orion's birth is perhaps more than a comic tale, modelled on that of Philemon and Baucis (Ovid: *Metamorphoses* viii. 670–724), and told to account for the first syllable of his ancient name, Urion – as though it were derived from *ourein*, 'to urinate', not from *ouros*, the Homeric form of *oros*, 'mountain', Yet a primitive African rain-producing charm, which consists in making water on a bull's hide, may have been known to the Greeks; and that Orion was a son of Poseidon, the water-god, is a clear allusion to his rain-making powers.

6. The name Pleiades, from the root *plei*, 'to sail', refers to their rising at the season when good weather for sailing approaches. But Pindar's form *Peleiades*, 'flock of doves', was perhaps the original form, since the *Hyades* are piglets. It appears that a seventh star in the group became extinct towards the end of the second millennium B.C. (see 67. *j*); since Hyginus (*Fabula* 192) says that Electra disappeared in grief for the destruction of the House of Dardanus. Orion's vain pursuit of the Pleiades, which occur in the Bull constellation, refers to their rising above the horizon just before the reappearance of Orion.

# 42

# HELIUS

HELIUS, whom the cow-eyed Euryphaessa, or Theia, bore to the Titan Hyperion, is a brother of Selene and Eos. Roused by the crowing of the cock, which is sacred to him, and heralded by Eos, he drives his four-horse chariot daily across the Heavens from a magnificent palace in the far east, near Colchis, to an equally magnificent far-western palace, where his unharnessed horses pasture in the Islands of the

Blessed.[1] He sails home along the Ocean stream, which flows around the world, embarking his chariot and team on a golden ferry-boat made for him by Hephaestus, and sleeps all night in a comfortable cabin.[2]

*b.* Helius can see everything that happens on earth, but is not particularly observant – once he even failed to notice the robbery of his sacred cattle by Odysseus's companions. He has several herds of such cattle, each consisting of three hundred and fifty head. Those in Sicily are tended by his daughters Phaetusa and Lampetia, but he keeps his finest herd in the Spanish island of Erytheia.[3] Rhodes is his freehold. It happened that, when Zeus was allotting islands and cities to the various gods, he forgot to include Helius among these, and 'Alas!' he said, 'now I shall have to begin all over again'.

'No, Sire,' replied Helius politely, 'today I noticed signs of a new island emerging from the sea, to the south of Asia Minor. I shall be well content with that.'

*c.* Zeus called the Fate Lachesis to witness that any such new island should belong to Helius;[4] and, when Rhodes had risen well above the waves, Helius claimed it and begot seven sons and a daughter there on the Nymph Rhode. Some say that Rhodes had existed before this time, and was re-emerging from the waves after having been overwhelmed by the great flood which Zeus sent. The Telchines were its aboriginal inhabitants and Poseidon fell in love with one of them, the nymph Halia, on whom he begot Rhode and six sons; which six sons insulted Aphrodite in her passage from Cythera to Paphos, and were struck mad by her; they ravished their mother and committed other outrages so foul that Poseidon sank them underground, and they became the Eastern Demons. But Halia threw herself into the sea and was deified as Leucothea – though the same story is told of Ino, mother of Corinthian Melicertes. The Telchines, foreseeing the flood, sailed away in all directions, especially to Lycia, and abandoned their claims on Rhodes. Rhode was thus left the sole heiress, and her seven sons by Helius ruled in the island after its re-emergence. They became famous astronomers, and had one sister named Electryo, who died a virgin and is now worshipped as a demi-goddess. One of them, by name Actis, was banished for fratricide, and fled to Egypt, where he founded the city of Heliopolis, and first taught the Egyptians astrology, inspired by his father Helius. The Rhodians have now built the Colossus, seventy cubits high, in his honour. Zeus also added to Helius's dominions the new island of Sicily, which had been a missile flung in the battle with the giants.

*d.* One morning Helius yielded to his son Phaëthon who had been constantly plaguing him for permission to drive the sun-chariot. Phaëthon wished to show his sisters Prote and Clymene what a fine fellow he was: and his fond mother Rhode (whose name is uncertain because she had been called by both her daughters' names and by that of Rhode) encouraged him. But, not being strong enough to check the career of the white horses, which his sisters had yoked for him, Phaëthon drove them first so high above the earth that everyone shivered, and then so near the earth that he scorched the fields. Zeus, in a fit of rage, killed him with a thunderbolt, and he fell into the river Po. His grieving sisters were changed into poplar-trees on its banks, which weep amber tears; or, some say, into alder-trees.[5]

1. *Homeric Hymn to Helius* 2 and 9–16; *Homeric Hymn to Athene* 13; Hesiod: *Theogony* 371–4; Pausanias: v. 25. 5; Nonnus: *Dionysiaca* xii. 1; Ovid: *Metamorphosis* ii. 1 ff. and 106 ff.; Hyginus: *Fabula* 183; Athenaeus: vii. 296.
2. Apollodorus: ii. 5. 10; Athenaeus: xi. 39.
3. Homer: *Odyssey* xii. 323 and 375; Apollodorus: i. 6. 1; Theocritus: *Idylls* xxv. 130.
4. Pindar: *Olympian Odes* vii. 54 ff.
5. Scholiast on Pindar's *Olympian Odes* vi. 78; Tzetzes: *Chiliads* iv. 137; Hyginus: *Fabulae* 52, 152 and 154; Euripides: *Hippolytus* 737; Apollonius Rhodius: iv. 598 ff.; Lucian: *Dialogues of the Gods* 25; Ovid: *Metamorphoses* i. 755 ff.; Virgil: *Eclogues* vi. 62; Diodorus Siculus v. 3; Apollodorus: i. 4. 5.

*

1. The Sun's subordination to the Moon, until Apollo usurped Helius's place and made an intellectual deity of him, is a remarkable feature of early Greek myth. Helius was not even an Olympian, but a mere Titan's son; and, although Zeus later borrowed certain solar characteristics from the Hittite and Corinthian god Tesup (see 67. 1) and other oriental sun-gods, these were unimportant compared with his command of thunder and lightning. The number of cattle in Helius's herds – the *Odyssey* makes him Hyperion (see 170. t) – is a reminder of his tutelage to the Great Goddess: being the number of days covered by twelve complete lunations, as in the Numan year (Censorinus: xx), less the five days sacred to Osiris, Isis, Set, Horus, and Nephthys. It is also a multiple of the Moon-numbers fifty and seven. Helius's so-called daughters are, in fact,

Moon-priestesses – cattle being lunar rather than solar animals in early European myth; and Helius's mother, the cow-eyed Euryphaessa, is the Moon-goddess herself. The allegory of a sun-chariot coursing across the sky is Hellenic in character; but Nilsson in his *Primitive Time Reckoning* (1920) has shown that the ancestral clan cults even of Classical Greece were regulated by the moon alone, as was the agricultural economy of Hesiod's Boeotia. A gold ring from Tiryns and another from the Acropolis at Mycenae prove that the goddess controlled both the moon and the sun, which are placed above her head.

2. In the story of Phaëthon, which is another name for Helius himself (Homer, *Iliad* xi. 735 and *Odyssey* v. 479), an instructive fable has been grafted on the chariot allegory, the moral being that fathers should not spoil their sons by listening to female advice. This fable, however, is not quite so simple as it seems: it has a mythic importance in its reference to the annual sacrifice of a royal prince, on the one day reckoned as belonging to the terrestrial, but not to the sidereal year, namely that which followed the shortest day. The sacred king pretended to die at sunset; the boy *interrex* was at once invested with his titles, dignities, and sacred implements, married to the queen, and killed twenty-four hours later: in Thrace, torn to pieces by women disguised as horses (see 27. *d* and 130. *1*), but at Corinth, and elsewhere, dragged at the tail of a sun-chariot drawn by maddened horses, until he was crushed to death. Thereupon the old king reappeared from the tomb where he had been hiding (see 41. *1*), as the boy's successor. The myths of Glaucus (see 71. *a*), Pelops (see 109. *j*), and Hippolytus ('stampede of horses' – see 101. *g*), refer to this custom, which seems to have been taken to Babylon by the Hittites.

3. Black poplars were sacred to Hecate, but the white gave promise of resurrection (see 31. *5* and 134. *f*); thus the transformation of Phaëthon's sisters into poplars points to a sepulchral island where a college of priestesses officiated at the oracle of a tribal king. That they were also said to have been turned into alders supports this view: since alders fringed Circe's Aeaea ('wailing'), a sepulchral island lying at the head of the Adriatic, not far from the mouth of the Po (Homer: *Odyssey* v. 64 and 239). Alders were sacred to Phoroneus, the oracular hero and inventor of fire (see 57. *1*). The Po valley was the southern terminus of the Bronze Age route down which amber, sacred to the sun, travelled to the Mediterranean from the Baltic (see 148. *9*).

4. Rhodes was the property of the Moon-goddess Danaë – called Cameira, Ialysa, and Linda (see 60. *2*) – until she was extruded by the Hittite Sun-god Tesup, worshipped as a bull (see 93. *1*). Danaë may be identified with Halia ('of the sea'), Leucothea ('white goddess'), and Electryo ('amber'). Poseidon's six sons and one daughter, and Helius's seven sons, point to a seven-day week ruled by planetary powers, or

Titans (see 1. 3). Actis did not found Heliopolis – Onn, or Aunis – one of the most ancient cities in Egypt; and the claim that he taught the Egyptians astrology is ridiculous. But after the Trojan War the Rhodians were for a while the only sea-traders recognized by the Pharaohs, and seem to have had ancient religious ties with Heliopolis, the centre of the Ra cult. The 'Heliopolitan Zeus', who bears busts of the seven planetary powers on his body sheath, may be of Rhodian inspiration; like similar statues found at Tortosa in Spain, and Byblos in Phoenicia (see 1. 4).

# 43

## THE SONS OF HELLEN

HELLEN, son of Deucalion, married Orseis, and settled in Thessaly, where his eldest son, Aeolus, succeeded him.[1]

*b.* Hellen's youngest son, Dorus, emigrated to Mount Parnassus, where he founded the first Dorian community. The second son, Xuthus, had already fled to Athens after being accused of theft by his brothers, and there married Creusa, daughter of Erechtheus, who bore him Ion and Achaeus. Thus the four most famous Hellenic nations, namely the Ionians, Aeolians, Achaeans, and Dorians, are all descended from Hellen. But Xuthus did not prosper at Athens: when chosen as arbitrator, upon Erechtheus's death, he pronounced his eldest brother-in-law, Cecrops the Second, to be the rightful heir to the throne. This decision proved unpopular, and Xuthus, banished from the city, died in Aegialus, now Achaia.[2]

*c.* Aeolus seduced Cheiron's daughter, the prophetess Thea, by some called Thetis, who was Artemis's companion of the chase. Thea feared that Cheiron would punish her severely when he knew of her condition, but dared not appeal to Artemis for assistance; however, Poseidon, wishing to do his friend Aeolus a favour, temporarily disguised her as a mare called Euippe. When she had dropped her foal, Melanippe, which he afterwards transformed into an infant girl, Poseidon set Thea's image among the stars; this is now called the constellation of the Horse. Aeolus took up Melanippe, renamed her Arne, and entrusted her to one Desmontes who, being childless, was glad to adopt her. Cheiron knew nothing of all this.

*d.* Poseidon seduced Arne, on whom he had been keeping an eye, so soon as she was of age; and Desmontes, discovering that she was with child, blinded her, shut her in an empty tomb, and supplied her with the very least amount of bread and water that would serve to sustain life. There she bore twin sons, whom Desmontes ordered his servants to expose on Mount Pelion, for the wild beasts to devour. But an Icarian herdsman found and rescued the twins, one of whom so closely resembled his maternal grandfather that he was named Aeolus; the other had to be content with the name Boeotus.

*e.* Meanwhile, Metapontus, King of Icaria, had threatened to divorce his barren wife Theano unless she bore him an heir within the year. While he was away on a visit to an oracle she appealed to the herdsman for help, and he brought her the foundlings whom, on Metapontus's return, she passed off as her own. Later, proving not to be barren after all, she bore him twin sons; but the foundlings, being of divine parentage, were far more beautiful than they. Since Metapontus had no reason to suspect that Aeolus and Boeotus were not his own children, they remained his favourites. Growing jealous, Theano waited until Metapontus left home again, this time for a sacrifice at the shrine of Artemis Metapontina. She then ordered his own sons to go hunting with their elder brothers, and murder them as if by accident. Theano's plot failed, however, because in the ensuing fight Poseidon came to the assistance of his sons. Aeolus and Boeotus were soon carrying their assailants' dead bodies back to the palace, and when Theano saw them approach she stabbed herself to death with a hunting knife.

*f.* At this, Aeolus and Boeotus fled to their foster-father, the herdsman, where Poseidon in person revealed the secret of their parentage. He ordered them to rescue their mother, who was still languishing in the tomb, and to kill Desmontes. They obeyed without hesitation; Poseidon then restored Arne's sight, and all three went back to Icaria. When Metapontus learned that Theano had deceived him he married Arne and formally adopted her sons as his heirs.[3]

*g.* All went well for some years, until Metapontus decided to discard Arne and marry again. Aeolus and Boeotus took their mother's side in the ensuing wrangle, and killed Autolyte, the new queen, but were obliged to forfeit their inheritance and flee. Boeotus, with Arne, took refuge in the palace of his grandfather Aeolus, who bequeathed him the southern part of his kingdom, and renamed it Arne; the inhabitants are still called Boeotians. Two Thessalian cities, one of which later became Chaeronaea, also adopted Arne's name.[4]

*h.* Aeolus, meanwhile, had set sail with a number of friends and, steering west, took possession of the seven Aeolian Islands in the Tyrrhenian Sea, where he became famous as the confidant of the gods and guardian of the winds. His home was on Lipara, a floating island of sheer cliff, within which the winds were confined. He had six sons and six daughters by his wife Enarete, all of whom lived together, well content with one another's company, in a palace surrounded by a brazen wall. It was a life of perpetual feasting, song, and merriment until, one day, Aeolus discovered that the youngest son, Macareus, had been sleeping with his sister Canache. In horror, he threw the fruit of their incestuous love to the dogs, and sent Canache a sword with which she dutifully killed herself. But he then learned that his other sons and daughters, having never been warned that incest among humans was displeasing to the gods, had also innocently paired off, and considered themselves as husbands and wives. Not wishing to offend Zeus, who regards incest as an Olympic prerogative, Aeolus broke up these unions, and ordered four of his remaining sons to emigrate. They visited Italy and Sicily, where each founded a famous kingdom, and rivalled his father in chastity and justice; only the fifth and eldest son stayed at home, as Aeolus's successor to the throne of Lipara. But some say that Macareus and Canache had a daughter, Amphissa, later beloved by Apollo.[5]

*i.* Zeus had confined the winds because he feared that, unless kept under control, they might one day sweep both earth and sea away into the air, and Aeolus took charge of them at Hera's desire. His task was to let them out, one by one, at his own discretion, or at the considered request of some Olympian deity. If a storm were needed he would plunge his spear into the cliff-side and the winds would stream out of the hole it had made, until he stopped it again. Aeolus was so discreet and capable that, when his death hour approached, Zeus did not commit him to Tartarus, but seated him on a throne within the Cave of the Winds, where he is still to be found. Hera insists that Aeolus's responsibilities entitle him to attend the feasts of the gods; but the other Olympians – especially Poseidon, who claims the sea, and the air above it, as his own property, and grudges anyone the right to raise storms – regard him as an interloper.[6]

1. Apollodorus: i. 7. 3.
2. Herodotus: i. 56; Pausanias: vii. 1. 2.
3. Hyginus: *Fabula* 186; *Poetic Astronomy* ii. 18.

4. Diodorus Siculus: iv. 67. 6; Pausanias: ix. 40. 3.
5. Ovid: *Heroides* xi; Homer: *Odyssey* x. 1 ff.; Hyginus: *Fabula* 238;
   Plutarch: *Parallel Stories* 28; Diodorus Siculus: v. 8; Pausanias:
   x. 38. 2.
6. Homer: *Odyssey loc. cit.*; Virgil: *Aeneid* i. 142–5.

*

1. The Ionians and Aeolians, the first two waves of patriarchal Hellenes
to invade Greece, were persuaded by the Hellads already there to worship the Triple-goddess and change their social customs accordingly,
becoming Greeks (*graikoi*, 'worshippers of the Grey Goddess, or Crone').
Later, the Achaeans and Dorians succeeded in establishing patriarchal
rule and patrilinear inheritance, and therefore described Achaeus and
Dorus as first-generation sons of a common ancestor, Hellen – a masculine form of the Moon-goddess Helle or Helen. The *Parian Chronicle*
records that this change from Greeks to Hellenes took place in 1521 B.C.,
which seems a reasonable enough date. Aeolus and Ion were then rele-
gated to the second generation, and called sons of the thievish Xuthus,
this being a way of denouncing the Aeolian and Ionian devotion to the
orgiastic Moon-goddess Aphrodite – whose sacred bird was the *xuthos*,
or sparrow, and whose priestesses cared nothing for the patriarchal view
that women were the property of their fathers and husbands. But Euripides, as a loyal Ionian of Athens, makes Ion elder brother to Dorus and
Achaeus, and the son of Apollo as well (see 44. *a*).

2. Poseidon's seduction of Melanippe, his seduction of the Mare-
headed Demeter (see 16. *f*), and Aeolus's seduction of Euippe, all refer
perhaps to the same event: the seizure of Aeolians of the pre-Hellenic
horse-cult centres. The myth of Arne's being blinded and imprisoned in
a tomb, where she bore the twins Aeolus and Boeotus, and of their subsequent exposure on the mountain among wild beasts, is apparently
deduced from the familiar icon that yielded the myths of Danaë (see
73. *4*), Antiope (see 76. *a*), and the rest. A priestess of Mother Earth's
is shown crouched in a *tholus* tomb, presenting the New Year twins to
the shepherds, for revelation at her Mysteries; *tholus* tombs have their
entrances always facing east, as if in promise of rebirth. These shepherds
are instructed to report that they found the infants abandoned on the
mountainside, being suckled by some sacred animal – cow, sow, she-goat,
bitch, or she-wolf. The wild beasts from whom the twins are supposed
to have been saved represent the seasonal transformations of the newly-
born sacred king (see 30. *1*).

3. Except for the matter of the imprisoned winds, and the family
incest on Lipara, the remainder of the myth concerns tribal migrations.
The mythographers are thoroughly confused between Aeolus the son of
Hellen; another Aeolus who, in order to make the Aeolians into third-

generation Greeks, is said to have been the son of Xuthus; and the third
Aeolus, grandson of the first.

4. Since the Homeric gods did not regard the incest of Aeolus's sons
and daughters as in the least reprehensible, it looks as if both he and
Enarete were not mortals and thus bound by the priestly tables of kindred
and affinity, but Titans; and that their sons and daughters were the
remaining six couples, in charge of the seven celestial bodies and the
seven days of the sacred week (see 1. *d*). This would explain their privileged and god-like existence, without problems of either food, drink, or
clothing, in an impregnable palace built on a floating island – like Delos
before the birth of Apollo (see 14. 3). 'Macareus' means 'happy', as only
gods were happy. It was left for Latin mythographers to humanize
Aeolus, and awaken him to a serious view of his family's conduct; their
amendment to the myth permitted them to account both for the foundation of Aeolian kingdoms in Italy and Sicily and – because 'Canache'
means 'barking' and her child was thrown to the dogs – for the Italian
custom of puppy sacrifice. Ovid apparently took this story from the
second book of Sostratus's Etruscan History (Plutarch: *Parallel Stories* 28).

5. The winds were originally the property of Hera, and the male gods
had no power over them; indeed, in Diodorus's account, Aeolus merely
teaches the islanders the use of sails in navigation and foretells, from signs
in the fire, what winds will rise. Control of the winds, regarded as the
spirits of the dead, is one of the privileges that the Death-goddess's representatives have been most loth to surrender; witches in England, Scotland,
and Brittany still claimed to control and sell winds to sailors as late as the
sixteenth and seventeenth centuries. But the Dorians had been thorough:
already by Homer's time they had advanced Aeolus, the eponymous
ancestor of the Aeolians, to the rank of godling, and given him charge of
his fellow-winds at Hera's expense – the Aeolian Islands, which bore his
name, being situated in a region notorious for the violence and diversity
of its winds (see 170. *g*). This compromise was apparently accepted with
bad grace by the priests of Zeus and Poseidon, who opposed the creation
of any new deities, and doubtless also by Hera's conservative devotees,
who regarded the winds as her inalienable property.

# 44

## ION

APOLLO lay secretly with Erechtheus's daughter Creusa, wife to
Xuthus, in a cave below the Athenian Propylaea. When her son was
born Apollo spirited him away to Delphi, where he became a temple

servant, and the priests named him Ion. Xuthus had no heir and, after many delays, went at last to ask the Delphic Oracle how he might procure one. To his surprise he was told that the first person to meet him as he left the sanctuary would be his son; this was Ion, and Xuthus concluded that he had begotten him on some Maenad in the promiscuous Dionysiac orgies at Delphi many years before. Ion could not contradict this, and acknowledged him as his father. But Creusa was vexed to find that Xuthus now had a son, while she had none, and tried to murder Ion by offering him a cup of poisoned wine. Ion, however, first poured a libation to the gods, and a dove flew down to taste the spilt wine. The dove died, and Creusa fled for sanctuary to Apollo's altar. When the vengeful Ion tried to drag her away, the priestess intervened, explaining that he was Creusa's son by Apollo, though Xuthus must not be undeceived in the belief that he had fathered him on a Maenad. Xuthus was then promised that he would beget Dorus and Achaeus on Creusa.

*b*. Afterwards, Ion married Helice, daughter of Selinus, King of Aegialus, whom he succeeded on the throne; and, at the death of Erechtheus, he was chosen King of Athens. The four occupational classes of Athenians – farmers, craftsmen, priests, and soldiers – are named after the sons borne to him by Helice.[1]

    1. Pausanias: vii. 1. 2; Euripides: *Ion*; Strabo: viii. 7. 1; Conon: *Narrations* 27.

*

    1. This theatrical myth is told to substantiate the Ionians' seniority over Dorians and Achaeans (see 43. *1*), and also to award them divine descent from Apollo. But Creusa in the cave is perhaps the goddess, presenting the New Year infant, or infants (see 43. *2*), to a shepherd – mistaken for Apollo in pastoral dress. Helice, the willow, was the tree of the fifth month, sacred to the Triple Muse, whose priestess used it in every kind of witchcraft and water-magic (see 28. *5*); the Ionians seem to have subordinated themselves willingly to her.

# 45

## ALCYONE AND CEYX

ALCYONE was the daughter of Aeolus, guardian of the winds, and Aegiale. She married Ceyx of Trachis, son of the Morning-star, and they were so happy in each other's company that she daringly called herself Hera, and him Zeus. This naturally vexed the Olympian Zeus and Hera, who let a thunderstorm break over the ship in which Ceyx was sailing to consult an oracle, and drowned him. His ghost appeared to Alcyone who, greatly against her will, had stayed behind in Trachis, whereupon distraught with grief, she leapt into the sea. Some pitying god transformed them both into kingfishers.

*b.* Now, every winter, the hen-kingfisher carries her dead mate with great wailing to his burial and then, building a closely compacted nest from the thorns of the sea-needle, launches it on the sea, lays her eggs in it, and hatches out her chicks. She does all this in the Halcyon Days – the seven which precede the winter solstice, and the seven which succeed it – while Aeolus forbids his winds to sweep across the waters.

*c.* But some say that Ceyx was turned into a seamew.[1]

> 1. Apollodorus: 1. 7. 3; Scholiast on Aristophanes's *Birds* 250; Scholiast and Eustathius on Homer's *Iliad* ix. 562; Pliny: *Natural History* x. 47; Hyginus: *Fabula* 65; Ovid: *Metamorphoses* xi. 410–748; Lucian: *Halcyon* i.; Plutarch: *Which Animals Are the Craftier?* 35.

*

1. The legend of the halcyon's, or kingfisher's, nest (which has no foundation in natural history, since the halycon does not build any kind of nest, but lays eggs in holes by the waterside) can refer only to the birth of the new sacred king at the winter solstice – after the queen who represents his mother, the Moon-goddess, has conveyed the old king's corpse to a sepulchral island. But because the winter solstice does not always coincide with the same phase of the moon, 'every year' must be understood, as 'every Great Year', of one hundred lunations, in the last of which solar and lunar time were roughly synchronized, and the sacred king's term ended.

2. Homer connects the halcyon with Alcyone (see 80. *d*), a title of Meleager's wife Cleopatra (*Iliad* ix. 562), and with a daughter of Aeolus, guardian of the winds (see 43. *h*). *Halcyon* cannot therefore mean *hal-cyon*, 'sea-hound', as is usually supposed, but must stand for *alcy-one*, 'the queen who wards off evil'. This derivation is confirmed by the myth of Alcyone and Ceyx, and the manner of their punishment by Zeus and Hera. The seamew part of the legend need not be pressed, although this bird, which has a plaintive cry, was sacred to the Sea-goddess Aphrodite, or Leucothea (see 170. *y*), like the halcyon of Cyprus (see 160. *g*). It seems that late in the second millennium B.C. the sea-faring Aeolians, who had

agreed to worship the pre-Hellenic Moon-goddess as their divine ancestress and protectress, became tributary to the Zeus-worshipping Achaeans, and were forced to accept the Olympian religion. 'Zeus', which
according to Johannes Tzetzes (*Antehomerica* 102 ff. and *Chiliades* i. 474)
had hitherto been a title borne by petty kings (see 68. *1*), was henceforth
reserved for the Father of Heaven alone. But in Crete, the ancient mystical tradition that Zeus was born and died annually lingered on into
Christian times, and tombs of Zeus were shown at Cnossus, on Mount
Ida, and on Mount Dicte, each a different cult-centre. Callimachus was
scandalized, and in his *Hymn to Zeus* wrote: 'The Cretans are always
liars. They have even built thy tomb, O Lord! But thou art not dead, for
thou livest for ever.' This is quoted in *Titus* i. 12 (see 7. *6*).

3. Pliny, who describes the halcyon's alleged nest in detail – apparently
the zoöphyte called *halcyoneum* by Linnaeus – reports that the halcyon is
rarely seen, and then only at the two solstices and at the setting of the
Pleiades. This proves her to have originally been a manifestation of the
Moon-goddess, who was alternately the Goddess of Life-in-Death at the
winter solstice, and of Death-in-Life at the summer solstice; and who,
every Great Year, early in November, when the Pleiades set, sent the
sacred king his death summons.

4. Still another Alcyone, daughter of Pleione ('sailing queen') by
Atlas, was the leader of the seven Pleiades (see 39. *d*). The Pleiades'
heliacal rising in May began the navigational year; their setting marked
its end, when (as Pliny notes in a passage about the halcyon) a remarkably
cold north wind blows. The circumstances of Ceyx's death show that the
Aeolians, who were famous sailors, worshipped the goddess as 'Alcyone'
because she protected them from rocks and rough weather: Zeus wrecked
Ceyx's ship, in defiance of her powers, by hurling a thunderbolt at it.
Yet the halcyon was still credited with the magical power of allaying
storms; and its body, when dried, was used as a talisman against Zeus's
lightning – presumably on the ground that where once it strikes it will
not strike again. The Mediterranean is inclined to be calm about the time
of the winter solstice.

# 46

## TEREUS

TEREUS, a son of Ares, ruled over the Thracians then occupying
Phocian Daulis – though some say that he was King of Pagae in
Megaris[1] – and, having acted as mediator in a boundary dispute for

Pandion, King of Athens and father of the twins Butes and Erechtheus, married their sister Procne, who bore him a son, Itys.

b. Unfortunately Tereus, enchanted by the voice of Procne's younger sister Philomela, had fallen in love with her; and, a year later, concealing Procne in a rustic cabin near his palace at Daulis, he reported her death to Pandion. Pandion, condoling with Tereus, generously offered him Philomela in Procne's place, and provided Athenian guards as her escort when she went to Daulis for the wedding. These guards Tereus murdered and, when Philomela reached the palace, he had already forced her to lie with him. Procne soon heard the news but, as a measure of precaution, Tereus cut out her tongue and confined her to the slaves' quarters, where she could communicate with Philomela only be weaving a secret message into the pattern of a bridal robe intended for her. This ran simply: 'Procne is among the slaves.'

c. Meanwhile, an oracle had warned Tereus that Itys would die by the hand of a blood relative and, suspecting his brother Dryas of a murderous plot to seize the throne, struck him down unexpectedly with an axe. The same day, Philomela read the message woven into the robe. She hurried to the slaves' quarters, found one of the rooms bolted, broke down the door, and released Procne, who was chattering unintelligibly and running around in circles.

'Oh, to be revenged on Tereus, who pretended that you were dead, and seduced me!' wailed Philomela, aghast.

Procne, being tongueless, could not reply, but flew out and, seizing her son Itys, killed him, gutted him, and then boiled him in a copper cauldron for Tereus to eat on his return.

d. When Tereus realized what flesh he had been tasting, he grasped the axe with which he had killed Dryas and pursued the sisters as they fled from the palace. He soon overtook them and was on the point of committing a double murder when the gods changed all three into birds; Procne became a swallow; Philomela, a nightingale; Tereus, a hoopoe. And the Phocians say that no swallow dares nest in Daulis or its environs, and no nightingale sings, for fear of Tereus. But the swallow, having no tongue, screams and flies around in circles; while the hoopoe flutters in pursuit of her, crying 'Pou? Pou?' (where? where?). Meanwhile, the nightingale retreats to Athens, where she mourns without cease for Itys, whose death she inadvertently caused, singing 'Itu! Itu!'[2]

e. But some say that Tereus was turned into a hawk.[3]

1. Apollodorus: iii. 14. 8; Thucydides: ii. 29; Strabo: ix. 3. 13; Pausanias: i. 41. 8

2. Apollodorus: iii. 14. 8; Nonnus: *Dionysiaca* iv. 320; Pausanias: i. 5. 4; i. 41. 8 and x. 4. 6; Hyginus: *Fabula* 45; Fragments of Sophocles's *Tereus*; Eustathius on Homer's *Odyssey* xix. 418; Ovid: *Metamorphoses* vi. 426–674; First Vatican Mythographer: 217.

3. Hyginus: *Fabula* 45.

\*

1. This extravagant romance seems to have been invented to account for a series of Thraco-Pelasgian wall-paintings, found by Phocian invaders in a temple at Daulis ('shaggy'), which illustrated different methods of prophecy in local use.

2. The cutting-out of Procne's tongue misrepresents a scene showing a prophetess in a trance, induced by the chewing of laurel-leaves; her face is contorted with ecstasy, not pain, and the tongue which seems to have been cut out is in fact a laurel-leaf, handed her by the priest who interprets her wild babblings. The weaving of the letters into the bridal robe misrepresents another scene: a priestess has cast a handful of oracular sticks on a white cloth, in the Celtic fashion described by Tacitus (*Germania* x), or the Scythian fashion described by Herodotus (iv. 67); they take the shape of letters, which she is about to read. In the so-called eating of Itys by Tereus, a willow-priestess is taking omens from the entrails of a child sacrificed for the benefit of a king. The scene of Tereus and the oracle probably showed him asleep on a sheep-skin in a temple, receiving a dream revelation (see 51. *g*); the Greeks would not have mistaken this. That of Dryas's murder probably showed an oak-tree and priests taking omens beneath it, in Druidic fashion, by the way a man fell when he died. Procne's transformation into a swallow will have been deduced from a scene that showed a priestess in a feathered robe, taking auguries from the flight of a swallow; Philomela's transformation into a nightingale, and Tereus's into a hoopoe, seem to result from similar misreadings. Tereus's name, which means 'watcher', suggests that a male augur figured in the hoopoe picture.

3. Two further scenes may be presumed: a serpent-tailed oracular hero, being offered blood-sacrifices; and a young man consulting a bee-oracle. These are, respectively, Erechtheus and Butes (see 47. *1*) who was the most famous bee-keeper of antiquity, the brothers of Procne and Philomela. Their mother was Zeuxippe, 'she who yokes horses', doubtless a Mare-headed Demeter.

4. All mythographers but Hyginus make Procne a nightingale, and Philomela a swallow. This must be a clumsy attempt to rectify a slip made by some earlier poet; that Tereus cut out Philomela's tongue, not

Procne's. The hoopoe is a royal bird, because it has a crest of feathers; and is particularly appropriate to the story of Tereus, because its nests are notorious for their stench. According to the Koran, the hoopoe told Solomon prophetic secrets.

5. Daulis, afterwards called Phocis, seems to have been the centre of a bird cult. Phocus, the eponymous founder of the new state, was called the son of Ornytion ('moon bird' – see 81. b), and a later king was named Xuthus ('sparrow' – see 43. 1). Hyginus reports that Tereus became a hawk, a royal bird of Egypt, Thrace, and North-western Europe.

# 47

## ERECHTHEUS AND EUMOLPUS

KING PANDION died prematurely of grief when he learned what had befallen Procne, Philomela, and Itys. His twin sons shared the inheritance: Erechtheus becoming King of Athens, while Butes served as priest both to Athene and Poseidon.[1]

b. By his wife Praxithea, Erechtheus had four sons, among them his successor, Cecrops; also seven daughters: namely Protogonia, Pandora, Procnis, wife of Cephalus, Creusa, Oreithyia, Chthonia, who married her uncle Butes, and Otionia, the youngest.[2]

c. Now, Poseidon secretly loved Chione, Oreithyia's daughter by Boreas. She bore him a son, Eumolpus, but threw him into the sea, lest Boreas should be angry. Poseidon watched over Eumolpus, and cast him up on the shores of Ethiopia, where he was reared in the house of Benthesicyme, his half-sister by the Sea-goddess Amphitrite. When Eumolpus came of age, Benthesycime married him to one of her daughters; but he fell in love with another of them, and she therefore banished him to Thrace, where he plotted against his protector, King Tegyrius, and was forced to seek refuge at Eleusis. Here he mended his ways, and became priest of the Mysteries of Demeter and Persephone, into which he subsequently initiated Heracles, at the same time teaching him to sing and play the lyre. With the lyre, Eumolpus had great skill; and was also victorious in the flute contest at Pelias's funeral games. His Eleusinian co-priestesses were the daughters of Celeus; and his well-known piety at last earned him the dying forgiveness of King Tegyrius, who bequeathed him the throne of Thrace.[3]

*d.* When war broke out between Athens and Eleusis, Eumolpus brought a large force of Thracians to the Eleusinians' assistance, claiming the throne of Attica himself in the name of his father Poseidon. The Athenians were greatly alarmed, and when Erechtheus consulted an oracle he was told to sacrifice his youngest daughter Otionia to Athene, if he hoped for victory. Otionia was willingly led to the altar, whereupon her two eldest sisters, Protogonia and Pandora, also killed themselves, having once vowed that if one of them should die by violence, they would die too.[4]

*e.* In the ensuing battle, Ion led the Athenians to victory; and Erechtheus struck down Eumolpus as he fled. Poseidon appealed for vengeance to his brother Zeus, who at once destroyed Erechtheus with a thunderbolt; but some say that Poseidon felled him with a trident blow at Macrae, where the earth opened to receive him.

*f.* By the terms of a peace then concluded, the Eleusinians became subject to the Athenians in everything, except the control of their Mysteries. Eumolpus was succeeded as priest by his younger son Ceryx, whose descendants still enjoy great hereditary privileges at Eleusis.[5]

*g.* Ion reigned after Erechtheus; and, because of his three daughters' self-sacrifice, wineless libations are still poured to them today.[6]

1. Ovid: *Metamorphoses* vi. 675 ff.; Apollodorus: ii. 15. 1.
2. Ovid: *loc. cit.*; Suidas *sub* Parthenoi; Apollodorus: *loc. cit.*; Hyginus: *Fabula* 46.
3. Plutarch: *On Exile* 17; Apollodorus: ii. 5. 12; Theocritus: *Idyll* xxiv. 110; Hyginus: *Fabula* 273; Pausanias: i. 38. 3.
4. Apollodorus: iii. 15. 4; Hyginus *Fabula* 46; Suidas: *loc. cit.*
5. Pausanias: vii. 1. 2 and i. 38. 3; Euripides: *Ion* 277 ff.
6. Scholiast on Sophocles's *Oedipus at Colonus* 100.

\*

1. The myth of Erechtheus and Eumolpus concerns the subjugation of Eleusis by Athens, and the Thraco-Libyan origin of the Eleusinian Mysteries. An Athenian cult of the orgiastic Bee-nymph of Midsummer also enters into the story, since Butes is associated in Greek myth with a bee cult on Mount Eryx (see 154. *d*); and his twin brother Erechtheus ('he who hastens over the heather', rather than 'shatterer') is the husband of the 'Active Goddess', the Queen-bee. The name of King Tegyrius of Thrace, whose kingdom Erechtheus's great-grandson inherited, makes a further association with bees: it means 'beehive coverer'. Athens was famous for its honey.

2. Erechtheus's three noble daughters, like the three daughters of his ancestor Cecrops, are the Pelasgian Triple-goddess, to whom libations were poured on solemn occasions: Otiona ('with the ear-flaps'), who is said to have been chosen as a sacrifice to Athene, being evidently the Owl-goddess Athene herself; Protogonia, the Creatrix Eurynome (see 1. 1); and Pandora, the Earth-goddess Rhea (see 39. 8). At the transition from matriarchy to patriarchy some of Athene's priestesses may have been sacrificed to Poseidon (see 121. 3).

3. Poseidon's trident and Zeus's thunderbolt were originally the same weapon, the sacred *labrys*, or double-axe, but distinguished from each other when Poseidon became god of the sea, and Zeus claimed the sole right to the thunderbolt (see 7. 7).

4. Butes, who was enrolled among the Argonauts (see 148. 1), did not really belong to the Erechtheid family; but his descendants, the Buteids of Athens, forced their way into Athenian society and, by the sixth century, held the priesthoods of Athene Polias and of Poseidon Erechtheus – but was a fusion of the Hellenic Poseidon with the old Pelasgian hero – as a family inheritance (Pausanias: i. 26. 6), and seem to have altered the myth accordingly, as they also altered the Theseus myth (see 95. 3). They combined the Attic Butes with their ancestor, the Thracian son of Boreas, who had colonized Naxos and in a raid on Thessaly violated Coronis (see 50. 5), the Lapith princess (Diodorus Siculus: v. 50).

# 48

## BOREAS

OREITHYIA, daughter of Erechtheus, King of Athens, and his wife Praxithea, was one day whirling in a dance beside the river Ilissus, when Boreas, son of Astraeus and Eos, and brother of the South and West Winds, carried her off to a rock near the river Ergines where, wrapped in a mantle of dark clouds, he ravished her.[1]

b. Boreas had long loved Oreithyia and repeatedly sued for her hand, but Erechtheus put him off with vain promises until at length, complaining that he had wasted too much time in words, he resorted to his natural violence. Some, however, say that Oreithyia was carrying a basket in the annual Thesmophorian procession that winds up the slope of the Acropolis to the temple of Athene Polias, when Boreas tucked her beneath his tawny wings and whirled her away, unseen by the surrounding crowd.

*c.* He took her to the city of the Thracian Cicones, where she became his wife, and bore him twin sons, Calais and Zetes, who grew wings when they reached manhood; also two daughters, namely Chione, who bore Eumolpus to Poseidon, and Cleopatra, who married King Phineus, the victim of the Harpies.[2]

*d.* Boreas has serpent-tails for feet, and inhabits a cave on Mount Haemus, in the seven recesses of which Ares stables his horses; but he is also at home beside the river Strymon.[3]

*e.* Once, disguising himself as a dark-maned stallion, he covered twelve of the three thousand mares belonging to Erichthonius, son of Dardanus, which used to graze in the water-meadows beside the river Scamander. Twelve fillies were born from this union; they could race over ripe ears of standing corn without bending them, or over the crests of waves.[4]

*f.* The Athenians regard Boreas as their brother-in-law and, having once successfully invoked him to destroy King Xerxes's fleet, they built him a fine temple on the banks of the river Ilissus.[5]

1. Apollodorus: iii. 15. 1–2; Apollonius Rhodius: i. 212 ff.
2. Ovid: *Metamorphoses* vi. 677 ff.; Scholiast on Homer's *Odyssey* xiv. 533; Apollodorus: iii. 15. 3.
3. Pausanias: v. 19. 1; Callimachus: *Hymn to Artemis* 114 and *Hymn to Delos* 26 and 63–5.
4. Homer: *Iliad* xx. 219 ff.
5. Herodotus: vii. 189.

\*

1. Serpent-tailed Boreas, the North Wind, was another name for the demiurge Ophion who danced with Eurynome, or Oreithyia, Goddess of Creation (see 1. *a*), and impregnated her. But, as Ophion was to Eurynome, or Boreas to Oreithyia, so was Erechtheus to the original Athene; and Athene Pōlias ('of the city'), for whom Oreithyia danced, may have been Athene Polias – Athene the Filly, goddess of the local horse cult, and beloved by Boreas-Erechtheus, who thus became the Athenians' brother-in-law. The Boreas cult seems to have originated in Libya. It should be remembered that Hermes, falling in love with Oreithyia's predecessor Herse while she was carrying a sacred basket in a similar procession, to the Acropolis, had ravished her without incurring Athene's displeasure. The Thesmophoria seems to have once been an orgiastic

festival in which priestesses publicly prostituted themselves as a means of fertilizing the cornfields (see 24. 1). These baskets contained phallic objects (see 25. 4).

2. A primitive theory that children were the reincarnations of dead ancestors, who entered into women's wombs as sudden gusts of wind, lingered in the erotic cult of the Mare-goddess; and Homer's authority was weighty enough to make educated Romans still believe, with Pliny, that Spanish mares could conceive by turning their hindquarters to the wind (Pliny: *Natural History* iv. 35 and viii. 67). Varro and Columella mention the same phenomenon, and Lactantius, in the late third century A.D., makes it an analogy of the Virgin's impregnation by the *Sanctus Spiritus*.

3. Boreas blows in winter from the Haemus range and the Strymon and, when Spring comes with its flowers, seems to have impregnated the whole land of Attica; but, since he cannot blow backwards, the myth of Oreithyia's rape apparently also records the spread of the North Wind cult from Athens to Thrace. From Thrace, or directly from Athens, it reached the Troad, where the owner of the three thousand mares was Erichthonius, a synonym of Erechtheus (see 158. g). The twelve fillies will have served to draw three four-horse chariots, one for each of the annual triad: Spring, Summer, and Autumn. Mount Haemus was a haunt of the monster Typhon (see 36. e).

4. Socrates, who had no understanding of myths, misses the point of Oreithyia's rape: he suggests that a princess of that name, playing on the cliffs near the Ilissus, or on the Hill of Ares, was accidentally blown over the edge and killed (Plato: *Phaedrus* vi. 229b). The cult of Boreas had recently been revived at Athens to commemorate his destruction of the Persian fleet (Herodotus: vii. 189). He also helped the Megalopolitans against the Spartans and earned annual sacrifices (Pausanias: viii. 36. 3).

# 49

## ALOPE

THE Arcadian King Cercyon, son of Hephaestus, had a beautiful daughter, Alope, who was seduced by Poseidon and, without her father's knowledge, bore a son whom she ordered a nurse to expose on a mountain. A shepherd found him being suckled by a mare, and took him to the sheep-cotes, where his rich robe attracted great interest. A fellow-shepherd volunteered to rear the boy, but insisted on taking the robe too, in proof of his noble birth. The two shepherds began to quarrel, and murder would have been done, had their companions not led them before King Cercyon. Cercyon called for the disputed robe and, when it was brought, recognized it as having been cut from a garment belonging to his daughter. The nurse now took fright, and confessed her part in the affair; whereupon Cercyon ordered Alope to be immured, and the child to be exposed again. He was once more suckled by the mare and, this time, found by the second shepherd who, now satisfied as to his royal parentage, carried him to his own cabin and called him Hippothous.[1]

*b.* When Theseus killed Cercyon, he set Hippothous on the throne of Arcadia; Alope had meanwhile died in prison, and was buried beside the road leading from Eleusis to Megara, near Cercyon's wrestling ground. But Poseidon transformed her body into a spring, named Alope.[2]

> 1. Hyginus: *Fabulae* 38 and 187.
> 2. Pausanias: i. 39. 3; Aristophanes: *Birds* 533; Hyginus: *Fabula* 187.

*

1. This myth is of familiar pattern (see 43. *c*: 68. *d*; 105. *a*, etc.), except that Hippothous is twice exposed and that, on the first occasion, the shepherds come to blows. The anomaly is perhaps due to a misreading of an icon-sequence, which showed royal twins being found by shpeherds, and these same twins coming to blows when grown to manhood – like Pelias and Neleus (see 68. *f*), Proetus and Acrisius (see 73. *a*) or Eteocles and Polyneices (see 106. *b*).

2. Alope is the Moon-goddess as vixen who gave her name to the Thessalian city of Alope (Pherecydes, quoted by Stephanus of Byzantium *sub* Alope); the vixen was also the emblem of Messenia (see 89. *8* and 146. *6*). The mythographer is probably mistaken in recording that the robe worn by Hippothous was cut from Alope's dress; it will have been the swaddling band into which his clan and family marks were woven (see 10. *1* and 60. *2*).

# 50
## ASCLEPIUS

CORONIS, daughter of Phlegyas, King of the Lapiths, Ixion's brother, lived on the shores of the Thessalian Lake Beobeis, in which she used to wash her feet.[1]

*b*. Apollo became her lover, and left a crow with snow-white feathers to guard her while he went to Delphi on business. But Coronis had long nursed a secret passion for Ischys, the Arcadian son of Elatus, and now admitted him to her couch, though already with child by Apollo. Even before the excited crow had set out for Delphi, to report the scandal and be praised for its vigilance, Apollo had divined Coronis's infidelity, and therefore cursed the crow for not having pecked out Ischys's eyes when he approached Coronis. The crow was turned black by this curse, and all its descendants have been black ever since.[2]

*c*. When Apollo complained to his sister Artemis of the insult done him, she avenged it by shooting a quiverful of arrows at Coronis. Afterwards, gazing at her corpse, Apollo was filled with sudden remorse, but could not now restore her to life. Her spirit had descended to Tartarus, her corpse had been laid on the funeral pyre, the last perfumes poured over it, and the fire already alight, before Apollo recovered his presence of mind; then he motioned to Hermes, who by the light of the flames cut the still living child from Coronis's womb.[3] It was a boy, whom Apollo named Asclepius, and carried off to the cave of Cheiron the Centaur, where he learned the arts of medicine and the chase. As for Ischys, also called Chylus: some say that he was killed by Zeus with a thunderbolt, others that Apollo himself shot him down.[4]

*d*. The Epidaurians, however, tell a very different story. They say that Coronis's father, Phlegyas, who founded the city of that name where he gathered together all the best warriors of Greece, and lived by raiding, came to Epidaurus to spy out the land and the strength of the people; and that his daughter Coronis who, unknown to him, was with child by Apollo, came too. In Apollo's shrine at Epidaurus, with the assistance of Artemis and the Fates, Coronis gave birth to a boy, whom she at once exposed on Mount Titthion, now famous for the medicinal virtues of its plants. There, Aresthanas, a goatherd, noticing that his bitch and one of his she-goats were no longer with him, went in search of them, and found them taking turns to suckle a child. He was about to lift the child up, when a bright light all about it deterred him. Loth to meddle with a divine mystery, he piously turned away, thus leaving Asclepius to the protection of his father Apollo.[5]

*e*. Asclepius, say the Epidaurians, learned the art of healing both from Apollo and from Cheiron. He became so skilled in surgery and the use of drugs that he is revered as the founder of medicine. Not only did he heal the sick, but Athene had given him two phials of the Gorgon

Medusa's blood; with what had been drawn from the veins of her left side, he could raise the dead; with what had been drawn from her right side, he could destroy instantly. Others say that Athene and Asclepius divided the blood between them: he used it to save life, but she to destroy life and instigate wars. Athene had previously given two drops of this same blood to Erichthonius, one to kill, the other to cure, and fastened the phials to his serpent body with golden bands.[6]

f. Among those whom Asclepius raised from the dead were Lycurgus, Capaneus, and Tyndareus. It is not known on which occasion Hades complained to Zeus that his subjects were being stolen from him – whether it was after the resurrection of Tyndareus, or of Glaucus, or of Hippolytus, or of Orion; it is certain only that Asclepius was accused of having been bribed with gold, and that both he and his patient were killed by Zeus's thunderbolt.[7]

g. However, Zeus later restored Asclepius to life; and so fulfilled an indiscreet prophecy made by Cheiron's daughter Euippe, who had declared that Asclepius would become a god, die, and resume godhead – thus twice renewing his destiny. Asclepius's image, holding a curative serpent, was set among the stars by Zeus.[8]

h. The Messenians claim that Asclepius was a native of Tricca in Messene; the Arcadians, that he was born at Thelpusa; and the Thessalians, that he was a native of Tricca in Thessaly. The Spartans call him, Agnitas, because they have carved his image from a willow-trunk; and the people of Sicyon honour him in the form of a serpent mounted on a mule-cart. At Sicyon the left hand of his image holds the cone of a pistachio-pine; but at Epidaurus it rests on a serpent's head; in both cases the right hand holds a sceptre.[9]

i. Asclepius was the father of Podaleirius and Machaon, the physicians who attended the Greeks during the siege of Troy; and of the radiant Hygieia. The Latins call him Aesculapius, and the Cretans say that he, not Polyeidus, restored Glaucus, son of Minos, to life; using a certain herb, shown him by a serpent in a tomb.[10]

1. Strabo: ix. 5. 21 and xiv. 1. 40.
2. Pausanias: ii. 26. 5; Pindar: *Pythian Odes* iii. 25 ff.; Apollodorus: iii. 10. 3.
3. Pindar: *Pythian Odes* iii. 8 ff.; Pausanias: *loc. cit.*; Hyginus: *Fabula* 202; Ovid: *Metamorphoses* ii. 612 ff.
4. Apollodorus: iii. 10. 3; Hyginus: *loc. cit.* and *Poetic Astronomy* ii. 40.
5. Pausanias: ix. 36. 1 and ii. 26. 4; *Inscriptiones Graecae* iv. 1. 28.

6. Diodorus Siculus: v. 74. 6; Apollodorus: iii. 10. 3; Tatian: *Address to the Greeks*; Euripides: *Ion* 999 ff.

7. Apollodorus: iii. 10. 3–4; Lucian: *On the Dance* 45; Hyginus: *Fabula* 49; Eratosthenes, quoted by Hyginus: *Poetic Astronomy* ii. 14; Pindar: *Pythian Odes* iii. 55 ff., with scholiast.

8. Germanicus Caesar: *On Aratus's Phenomena* 77 ff.; Ovid: *Metamorphoses* 642 ff.; Hyginus: *loc. cit.*

9. Pausanias: ii. 26. 6; viii. 25. 6; iii. 14. 7 and ii. 10. 3; Strabo: xiv. 1. 39.

10. Homer: *Iliad* ii. 732; Hyginus: *Poetic Astronomy* ii. 14.

*

1. This myth concerns ecclesiastical politics in Northern Greece, Attica, and the Peloponnese: the suppression, in Apollo's name, of a pre-Hellenic medical cult, presided over by Moon-priestesses at the oracular shrines of local heroes reincarnate as serpents, or crows, or ravens. Among their names were Phoroneus, identifiable with the Celtic Raven-god Bran, or Vron (see 57. *1*); Erichthonius the serpent-tailed (see 25. *2*); and Cronus (see 7. *1*), which is a form of Coronus ('crow' or 'raven'), the name of two other Lapith kings (see 78. *a*). 'Asclepius' ('unceasingly gentle') will have been a complimentary title given to all physician heroes, in the hope of winning their benevolence.

2. The goddess Athene, patroness of this cult, was not originally regarded as a maiden; the dead hero having been both her son and her lover. She received the title 'Coronis' because of the oracular crow, or raven, and 'Hygieia' because of the cures she brought about. Her all-heal was the mistletoe, *ixias*, a word with which the name Ischys ('strength') and Ixion ('strong native') are closely connected (see 63. *1*). The Eastern-European mistletoe, or loranthus, is a parasite of the oak and not, like the Western variety, of the poplar or the apple-tree; and 'Aesculapius', the Latin form of Asclepius – apparently meaning 'that which hangs from the esculent oak', i.e. the mistletoe – may well be the earlier title of the two. Mistletoe was regarded as the oak-tree's genitals, and when the Druids ritually lopped it with a golden sickle, they were performing a symbolic emasculation (see 7. *1*). The viscous juice of its berries passed for oak-sperm, a liquid of great regenerative virtue. Sir James Frazer has pointed out in his *Golden Bough* that Aeneas visited the Underworld with mistletoe in his hand, and thus held the power of returning at will to the upper air. The 'certain herb', which raised Glaucus from the tomb, is likely to have been the mistletoe also. Ischys, Asclepius, Ixion and Polyeidus are, in fact, the same mythic character: personifications of the curative power resident in the dismembered genitals of the sacrificed oak-hero. 'Chylus', Ischys's other name, means 'the juice of a plant, or berry'.

3. Athene's dispensation of Gorgon-blood to Asclepius and Erichthonius suggests that the curative rites used in this cult were a secret guarded by priestesses, which it was death to investigate – the Gorgon-head is a formal warning to pryers (see 73. 5). But the blood of the sacrificed oak-king, or of his child surrogate, is likely to have been dispensed on these occasions, as well as mistletoe-juice.

4. Apollo's mythographers have made his sister Artemis responsible for Ischys's murder; and, indeed, she was originally the same goddess as Athene, in whose honour the oak-king met his death. They have also made Zeus destroy both Ischys and Asclepius with thunderbolts; and, indeed, all oak-kings fell beneath the double-axe, later formalized as a thunderbolt, and their bodies were usually roasted in a bonfire.

5. Apollo cursed the crow, burned Coronis to death for her illegitimate love affair with Ischys, and claimed Asclepius as his own son; then Cheiron and he taught him the art of healing. In other words: Apollo's Hellenic priests were helped by their Magnesian allies the Centaurs, who were hereditary enemies of the Lapiths, to take over a Thessalian crow-oracle, hero and all, expelling the college of Moon-priestesses and suppressing the worship of the goddess. Apollo retained the stolen crow, or raven, as an emblem of divination, but his priests found dream-interpretation a simpler and more effective means of diagnosing their patients' ailments than the birds' enigmatic croaking. At the same time, the sacral use of mistletoe was discontinued in Arcadia, Messenia, Thessaly, and Athens; and Ischys became a son of the pine-tree (Elatus), not of the oak – hence the pistachio-cone in the hands of Asclepius's image at Sicyon. There was another Lapith princess named Coronis whom Butes, the ancestor of the Athenian Butadae, violated (see 47. 4).

6. Asclepius's serpent form, like that of Erichthonius – whom Athene also empowered to raise the dead with Gorgon-blood – shows that he was an oracular hero; but several tame serpents were kept in his temple at Epidaurus (Pausanias: ii. 28. 1) as a symbol of renovation: because serpents cast their slough every year (see 160. 11). The bitch who suckled Asclepius, when the goatherd hailed him as the new-born king, must be Hecate, or Hecabe (see 31. 3; 38. 7; 134. 1; 168. n and 1); and it is perhaps to account for this bitch, with whom he is always pictured, that Cheiron has been made to tutor him in hunting. His other foster-mother, the she-goat, must be the Goat-Athene, in whose aegis Erichthonius took refuge (see 25. 2); indeed, if Asclepius originally had a twin – as Pelias was suckled by a mare, and Neleus by a bitch (see 68. d) – this will have been Erichthonius.

7. Athene, when reborn as a loyal virgin-daughter of Olympian Zeus, had to follow Apollo's example and curse the crow, her former familiar (see 25. e).

8. The willow was a tree of powerful moon-magic (see 28. 5; 44. 1 and 116. 4); and the bitter drug prepared from its bark is still a specific against rheumatism – to which the Spartans in their damp valleys will have been much subject. But branches of the particular variety of willow with which the Spartan Asclepius was associated, namely the *agnus castus*, were strewn on the beds of matrons at the Athenian Thesmophoria, a fertility festival (see 48. 1), supposedly to keep off serpents (Arrian: *History of Animals* ix. 26), though really to encourage serpent-shaped ghosts; and Asclepius's priests may therefore have specialized in the cure of barrenness.

# 51

## THE ORACLES

THE Oracles of Greece and Greater Greece are many; but the eldest is that of Dodonian Zeus. In ages past, two black doves flew from Egyptian Thebes: one to Libyan Ammon, the other to Dodona, and each alighted on an oak-tree, which they proclaimed to be an oracle of Zeus. At Dodona, Zeus's priestesses listen to the cooing of doves, or to the rustling of oak-leaves, or to the clanking of brazen vessels suspended from the branches. Zeus has another famous oracle at Olympia, where his priests reply to questions after inspecting the entrails of sacrificial victims.[1]

b. The Delphic Oracle first belonged to Mother Earth, who appointed Daphnis as her prophetess; and Daphnis, seated on a tripod, drank in the fumes of prophecy, as the Pythian priestess still does. Some say that Mother Earth later resigned her rights to the Titaness Phoebe, or Themis; and that she ceded them to Apollo, who built himself a shrine of laurel-boughs brought from Tempe. But others say that Apollo robbed the oracle from Mother Earth, after killing Python, and that his Hyperborean priests Pagasus and Agyieus established his worship there.

c. At Delphi it is said that the first shrine was made of bees' wax and feathers; the second, of fern-stalks twisted together; the third, of laurel-boughs; that Hephaestus built the fourth of bronze, with golden song-birds perched on the roof, but one day the earth engulfed it; and that the fifth, built of dressed stone, burned down in the year of the fifty-eighth Olympiad [489 B.C.], and was replaced by the present shrine.[2]

*d.* Apollo owns numerous other oracular shines: such as those in the Lycaeum and on the Acropolis at Argos, both presided over by a priestess. But at Boeotian Ismenium, his oracles are given by priests, after the inspection of entrails; at Clarus, near Colophon, his seer drinks the water of a secret well and pronounces an oracle in verse; while at Telmessus and elsewhere, dreams are interpreted.[3]

*e.* Demeter's priestesses give oracles to the sick at Patrae, from a mirror lowered into her well by a rope. At Pharae, in return for a copper coin, the sick who consult Hermes are granted their oracular responses in the first chance words that they hear on leaving the market place.[4]

*f.* Hera has a venerable oracle near Pagae; and Mother Earth is still consulted at Aegeira in Achaea, which means 'The Place of Black Poplars', where her priestess drinks bull's blood, deadly poison to all other mortals.[5]

*g.* Besides these, there are many other oracles of heroes, the oracle of Heracles, at Achaean Bura, where the answer is given by a throw of four dice;[6] and numerous oracles of Asclepius, where the sick flock for consultation and for cure, and are told the remedy in their dreams after a fast.[7] The oracles of Theban Amphiaraus and Mallian Amphilochus – with Mopsus, the most infallible extant – follow the Asclepian procedure.[8]

*h.* Moreover, Pasiphaë has an oracle at Laconian Thalamae, patronized by the Kings of Sparta, where answers are also given in dreams.[9]

*i.* Some oracles are not so easily consulted as others. For instance, at Lebadeia there is an oracle of Trophonius, son of Erginus the Argonaut, where the suppliant must purify himself several days beforehand, and lodge in a building dedicated to Good Fortune and a certain Good Genius, bathing only in the river Hercyna and sacrificing to Trophonius, to his nurse Demeter Europe, and to other deities. There he feeds on sacred flesh, especially that of a ram which has been sacrificed to the shade of Agamedes, the brother of Trophonius, who helped him to build Apollo's temple at Delphi.

*j.* When fit to consult the oracle, the suppliant is led down to the river by two boys, thirteen years of age, and there bathed and anointed. Next, he drinks from a spring called the Water of Lethe, which will help him to forget his past; and also from another, close by, called the

Water of Memory, which will help him to remember what he has seen
and heard. Dressed in country boots and a linen tunic, and wearing
fillets like a sacrificial victim, he then approaches the oracular chasm.
This resembles a huge bread-baking pot eight yards deep, and after
descending by a ladder, he finds a narrow opening at the bottom
through which he thrusts his legs, holding in either hand a barley-cake
mixed with honey. A sudden tug at his ankles, and he is pulled through
as if by the swirl of a swift river, and in the darkness a blow falls on his
skull, so that he seems to die, and an invisible speaker then reveals the
future to him, besides many mysterious secrets. As soon as the voice
has finished, he loses all sense and understanding, and is presently
returned, feet foremost, to the bottom of the chasm, but without the
honey-cakes; after which he is enthroned on the so-called Chair of
Memory and asked to repeat what he has heard. Finally, still in a dazed
condition, he returns to the house of the Good Genius, where he
regains his senses and the power to laugh.

*k*. The invisible speaker is one of the Good Genii, belonging to the
Golden Age of Cronus, who have descended from the moon to take
charge of oracles and initiatory rites, and act as chasteners, watchers,
and saviours everywhere; he consults the ghost of Trophonius who is
in serpent form and gives the required oracle as payment for the suppliant's honey-cake.[10]

1. Herodotus: ii. 55 and viii. 134; Dionysius of Halicarnassus: i. 15;
   Homer: *Odyssey* xiv. 328; Aeschylus: *Prometheus Bound* 832;
   Suidas *sub* Dodona; Sophocles: *Oedipus Tyrannus* 900.
2. Aeschylus: *Eumenides* 1–19; Pausanias: x. 5. 3–5.
3. Pausanias: ii. 24. 1; Plutarch: *Pyrrhus* 31; Herodotus, viii. 134
   and i. 78; Tacitus: *Annals* ii. 54.
4. Pausanias: vii. 21. 5 and 22. 2.
5. Strabo: viii. 6. 22; Pliny: *Natural History* xxviii. 41; Apollodorus:
   i. 9. 27.
6. Pausanias: vii. 25. 6.
7. *Ibid.*: ii. 27. 2.
8. *Ibid.*: i. 34. 2; Herodotus: viii. 134.
9. Plutarch: *Cleomenes* 7; Pausanias: iii. 26. 1.
10. Pausanias: ix. 39. 1–5; Plutarch: *On Socrates's Demon* xxii. and
    *The Face on the Orb of the Moon* xxx.

*

*1*. All oracles were originally delivered by the Earth-goddess, whose
authority was so great that patriarchal invaders made a practice of seizing
her shrines and either appointing priests or retaining the priestesses in

their own service. Thus Zeus at Dodona, and Ammon in the Oasis of Siwwa, took over the cult of the oracular oak, sacred to Dia or Dione (see 7. 1) – as the Hebrew Jehovah did that of Ishtar's oracular acacia (1 *Chronicles* xiv. 15) – and Apollo captured the shrines of Delphi and Argos. At Argos, the prophetess was allowed full freedom; at Delphi, a priest intervened between prophetess and votary, translating her incoherent utterances into hexameters; at Dodona, both the Dove-priestesses and Zeus's male prophets deliver oracles.

2. Mother Earth's shrine at Delphi was founded by the Cretans, who left their sacred music, ritual, dances, and calendar as a legacy to the Hellenes. Her Cretan sceptre, the *labrys*, or double-axe, named the priestly corporation at Delphi, the Labryadae, which was still extant in Classical times. The temple made from bees' wax and feathers refers to the goddess as Bee (see 7.3; 18.3 and 47.1) and as Dove (see 1. *b* and 62.*a*); the temple of fern recalls the magical properties attributed to fern-seed at the summer and winter solstices (Sir James Frazer devotes several pages to the subject in his *Golden Bough*); the shrine of laurel recalls the laurel-leaf chewed by the prophetess and her companions in their orgies – Daphnis is a shortened form of Daphoenissa ('the bloody one'), as Daphne is of Daphoene (see 21. 6 and 46. 2). The shrine of bronze engulfed by the earth may merely mark the fourth stage of a Delphic song that, like 'London Bridge is Broken Down', told of the various unsuitable materials with which the shrine was successively built; but it may also refer to an underground *tholos*, the tomb of a hero who was incarnate in the python. The tholos, a beehive-shaped ghost-house, appears to be of African origin, and introduced into Greece by way of Palestine. The Witch of Endor presided at a similar shrine, and the ghost of Adam gave oracles at Hebron. Philostratus refers to the golden birds in his *Life of Apollonius of Tyana* vi. 11 and describes them as siren-like wrynecks; but Pindar calls them nightingales (*Fragment* quoted by Athenaeus 290e). Whether the birds represented oracular nightingales, or wrynecks used as love-charms (see 152. *a*) and rain-inducers (Marinus on Proclus 28), is disputable.

3. Inspection of entrails seems to have been an Indo-European mantic device. Divination by the throw of four knucklebone dice was perhaps alphabetical in origin: since 'signs', not numbers, were said to be marked on the only four sides of each bone which could turn up. Twelve consonants and four vowels (as in the divinatory Irish Ogham called 'O'Sullivan's') are the simplest form to which the Greek alphabet can be reduced. But, in Classical times, numbers only were marked – 1, 3, 4, and 6 on each knucklebone – and the meanings of all their possible combinations had been codified. Prophecy from dreams is a universal practice.

4. Apollo's priests exacted virginity from the Pythian priestesses at

Delphi, who were regarded as Apollo's brides; but when one of them was scandalously seduced by a votary, they had thereafter to be at least fifty years old on installation, though still dressing as brides. Bull's blood was thought to be highly poisonous, because of its magical potency (see 155. *a*): the blood of sacred bulls, sometimes used to consecrate a whole tribe, as in *Exodus* xxiv. 8, was mixed with great quantities of water before being sprinkled on the fields as a fertilizer. The priestess of Earth, however, could drink whatever Mother Earth herself drank.

5. Hera, Pasiphaë, and Ino were all titles of the Triple-goddess, the interdependence of whose persons was symbolized by the tripod on which her priestess sat.

6. The procedure at the oracle of Trophonius – which Pausanias himself visited – recalls Aeneas's descent, mistletoe in hand, to Avernus, where he consulted his father Anchises, and Odysseus's earlier consultation of Teiresias; it also shows the relevance of these myths to a common form of initiation rite in which the novice suffers a mock-death, receives mystical instruction from a pretending ghost, and is then reborn into a new clan, or secret society. Plutarch remarks that the Trophoniads – the mystagogues in the dark den – belong to the pre-Olympian age of Cronus, and correctly couples them with the Idaean Dactyls who performed the Samothracian Mysteries.

7. Black poplar was sacred to the Death-goddess at Pagae, and Persephone had a black poplar grove in the Far West (Pausanias: x. 30. 3 and see 170. *l*).

8. Amphilochus and Mopsus had killed each other, but their ghosts agreed to found a joint oracle (see 169. *e*).

# 52

## THE ALPHABET

THE Three Fates or, some say, Io the sister of Phoroneus, invented the five vowels of the first alphabet, and the consonants B and T; Palamedes, son of Nauplius, invented the remaining eleven consonants; and Hermes reduced these sounds to characters, using wedge shapes because cranes fly in wedge formation, and carried the system from Greece to Egypt. This was the Pelasgian alphabet, which Cadmus later brought back to Boeotia, and which Evander of Arcadia, a Pelasgian, introduced into Italy, where his mother Carmenta formed the familiar fifteen characters of the Latin alphabet.

*b.* Other consonants have since been added to the Greek alphabet by Simonides of Samos, and Epicharmus of Sicily; and two vowels, long O and short E, by the priests of Apollo, so that his sacred lyre now has one vowel for each of its seven strings.

*c.* Alpha was the first of the eighteen letters, because *alphe* means honour, and *alphainein* is to invent, and because the Alpheius is the most notable of rivers; moreover, Cadmus, though he changed the order of the letters, kept alpha in this place, because *aleph*, in the Phoenician tongue, means an ox, and because Boeotia is the land of oxen.[1]

1. Hyginus: *Fabula* 277; Isidore of Seville: *Origins* viii. 2. 84; Philostratus: *Heroica* x. 3; Pliny: *Natural History* vii. 57; Scholiast on Homer's *Iliad* xix. 593; Plutarch: *Symposiacs* ix. 3.

★

*1.* The Greek alphabet was a simplification of the Cretan hieroglyphs. Scholars are now generally agreed that the first written alphabet developed in Egypt during the eighteenth century B.C. under Cretan influence; which corresponds with Aristides's tradition, reported by Pliny, that an Egyptian called Menos ('moon') invented it 'fifteen years before the reign of Phoroneus, King of Argos'.

*2.* There is evidence, however, that before the introduction of the modified Phoenician alphabet into Greece an alphabet had existed there as a religious secret held by the priestesses of the Moon – Io, or the Three Fates: that it was closely linked with the calendar, and that its letters were represented not by written characters, but by twigs cut from different trees typical of the year's sequent months.

*3.* The ancient Irish alphabet, like that used by the Gallic druids of whom Caesar wrote, might not at first be written down, and all its letters were named after trees. It was called the *Beth-luis-nion* ('birch-rowan-ash') after its first three consonants; and its canon, which suggests a Phrygian provenience, corresponded with the Pelasgian and the Latin alphabets, namely thirteen consonants and five vowels. The original order was, A, B, L, N, O, F, S, H, U, D, T, C, E, M, G, Ng or Gn, R, I, which is likely also to have been the order used by Hermes. Irish ollaves made it into a deaf-and-dumb language, using finger-joints to represent the different letters, or one of verbal cyphers. Each consonant represented a twenty-eight-day month of a series of thirteen, beginning two days after the winter solstice; namely:

| | | | |
|---|---|---|---|
| 1 | Dec. 24 | B | birch, or wild olive |
| 2 | Jan. 21 | L | rowan |
| 3 | Feb. 18 | N | ash |
| 4 | March 18 | F | alder, or cornel |

| 5 | April 15 | S | willow; SS (Z), blackthorn |
| 6 | May 13 | H | hawthorn, or wild pear |
| 7 | June 10 | D | oak, or terebinth |
| 8 | July 8 | T | holly, or prickly oak |
| 9 | Aug. 5 | C | nut; CC (Q), apple, sorb or quince |
| 10 | Sept. 2 | M | vine |
| 11 | Sept. 30 | G | ivy |
| 12 | Oct. 28 | Ng or Gn | reed, or guelder rose |
| 13 | Nov. 25 | R | elder, or myrtle |

4. About 400 B.C., as the result of a religious revolution, the order was changed as follows to correspond with a new calendar system: B, L, F, S, N, H, D, T, C, Q, M, G, Ng, Z, R. This is the alphabet associated with Heracles Ogmius, or 'Ogma Sunface', as the earlier is with Phoroneus (see 132. 3).

5. Each vowel represented a quarterly station of the year: O (gorse) the Spring Equinox; U (heather) the Summer Solstice; E (poplar) the Autumn Equinox. A (fir, or palm) the birth-tree, and I (yew) the death-tree, shared the Winter Solstice between them. This order of trees is implicit in Greek and Latin myth and the sacral tradition of all Europe and, *mutatis mutandis*, Syria and Asia Minor. The goddess Carmenta (see 86. 2 and 132. 6) invented B and T as well as the vowels, because each of these calendar-consonants introduced one half of her year, as divided between the sacred king and his tanist.

6. Cranes were sacred to Hermes (see 17. 3 and 36. 2), protector of poets before Apollo usurped his power; and the earliest alphabetic characters were wedge-shaped. Palamedes ('ancient intelligence'), with his sacred crane (Martial: *Epigrams* xiii. 75) was the Carian counterpart of the Egyptian god Thoth, inventor of letters, with his crane-like ibis; and Hermes was Thoth's early Hellenic counterpart (see 162. 5). That Simonides and Epicharmus added new letters to the alphabet is history, not myth; though exactly why they did so remains doubtful. Two of the additions, *xi* and *psi*, were unnecessary, and the removal of the aspirate (H) and *digamma* (F) impoverished the canon.

7. It can be shown that the names of the letters preserved in the Irish *Beth-luis-nion*, which are traditionally reported to have come from Greece and reached Ireland by way of Spain (see 132. 5), formed an archaic Greek charm in honour of the Arcadian White Goddess Alphito who, by Classical times, had degenerated into a mere nursery bogey. The Cadmean order of letters, perpetuated in the familiar ABC, seems to be a deliberate mis-arrangement by Phoenician merchants; they used the secret alphabet for trade purposes but feared to offend the goddess by revealing its true order.

This complicated and important subject is discussed at length in *The White Goddess* (Chapters 1–15 and 21).

8. The vowels added by the priests of Apollo to his lyre were probably those mentioned by Demetrius, an Alexandrian philosopher of the first century B.C., when he writes in his dissertation *On Style*:

In Egypt the priests sing hymns to the Gods by uttering the seven vowels in succession, the sound of which produces as strong a musical impression on their hearers as if the flute and lyre were used . . . but perhaps I had better not enlarge on this theme.

This suggests that the vowels were used in therapeutic lyre music at Apollo's shrines.

# 53

## THE DACTYLS

SOME say that while Rhea was bearing Zeus, she pressed her fingers into the soil to ease her pangs and up sprang the Dactyls: five females from her left hand, and five males from her right. But it is generally held that they were living on Phrygian Mount Ida long before the birth of Zeus, and some say that the nymph Anchiale bore them in the Dictaean Cave near Oaxus. The male Dactyls were smiths and first discovered iron in near-by Mount Berecynthus; and their sisters, who settled in Samothrace, excited great wonder there by casting magic spells, and taught Orpheus the Goddess's mysteries: their names are a well-guarded secret.[1]

b. Others say that the males were the Curetes who protected Zeus's cradle in Crete, and that they afterwards came to Elis and raised a temple to propitiate Cronus. Their names were Heracles, Paeonius, Epimedes, Iasius, and Acesidas. Heracles, having brought wild-olive from the Hyperboreans to Olympia, set his younger brothers to run a race there, and thus the Olympic Games originated. It is also said that he crowned Paeonius, the victor, with a spray of wild-olive; and that, afterwards, they slept in beds made from its green leaves. But the truth is that wild-olive was not used for the victor's crown until the seventh Olympiad, when the Delphic Oracle had ordered Iphitus to substitute it for the apple-spray hitherto awarded as the prize of victory.[2]

c. Acmon, Damnameneus, and Celmis are titles of the three eldest

Dactyls; some say that Celmis was turned to iron as a punishment for insulting Rhea.[3]

1. Diodorus Siculus: v. 64; Sophocles: *The Deaf Satyrs*, quoted by Strabo: x. 3. 22; Apollonius Rhodius: 509 and 1130.
2. Pausanias: v. 7. 4; Phlegon of Tralles: *Fragmenta Historica Graeca* iii. 604.
3. Scholiast on Apollonius Rhodius: i. 1129; Ovid: *Metamorphoses* iv. 281.

*

1. The Dactyls personify the fingers, and Heracles's Olympic race is a childish fable illustrated by drumming one's fingers on a table, omitting the thumb – when the forefinger always wins the race. But Orphic secret lore was based on a calendar sequence of magical trees, each allotted a separate finger joint in the sign-language and a separate letter of the Orphic calendar-alphabet, which seems to have been Phrygian in origin (see 52. 3). Wild-olive belongs to the top-joint of the thumb, supposedly the seat of virility and therefore called Heracles. This Heracles was said to have had leaves growing from his body (Palaephatus: 37). The system is recalled in the popular Western finger-names: e.g. 'fool's finger', which corresponds with Epimedes, the middle finger, and the 'physic finger', which corresponds with Iasius, the fourth; and in the finger-names of palmistry: e.g. Saturn of Epimedes – Saturn having shown himself slow-witted in his struggle with Zeus; and Apollo, god of healing, for Iasius. The forefinger is given to Jupiter, or Zeus, who won the race. The little finger, Mercury or Hermes, is the magical one. Throughout primitive Europe, metallurgy was accompanied by incantations, and the smiths therefore claimed the fingers of the right hand as their Dactyls, leaving the left to the sorceresses.

2. The story of Acmon, Damnameneus, and Celmis, whose names refer to smithcraft, is another childish fable, illustrated by tapping the forefinger on the thumb, as a hammer on an anvil, and then slipping the tip of the middle finger between them, as though it were a piece of red-hot iron. Iron came to Crete through Phrygia from farther along the Southern Black Sea coast; and Celmis, being a personification of smelted iron, will have been obnoxious to the Great Goddess Rhea, patroness of smiths, whose religious decline began with the smelting of iron and the arrival of the iron-weaponed Dorians. She had recognized only gold, silver, copper, lead, and tin as terrestrial ores; though lumps of meteoric iron were highly prized because of their miraculous origin, and one may have fallen on Mount Berecynthus. An unworked lump was found in a neolithic deposit at Phaestus beside a squatting clay image of the goddess, sea-shells, and offering bowls. All early Egyptian iron is meteoric: it

contains a high proportion of nickel and is nearly rust-proof. Celmis's insult to Hera gave the middle finger its name: *digita impudica*.

3. The Olympic games originated in a foot race, run by girls, for the privilege of becoming the priestess of the Moon-goddess Hera (Pausanias: v. 16. 2); and since this event took place in the month Parthenios, 'of the maiden', it seems to have been annual. When Zeus married Hera – when, that is, a new form of sacred kingship had been introduced into Greece by the Achaeans (see 12. 7) – a second foot race was run by young men for the dangerous privilege of becoming the priestess's consort, Sun to her Moon, and thus King of Elis; just as Antaeus made his daughter's suitors race for her (Pindar: *Pythian Odes* ix), following the example of Icarius (see 160. *d*) and Danaus (see 60. *m*).

4. The Games were thereafter held every four years, instead of annually, the girls' foot race being run at a separate festival, either a fortnight before, or a fortnight after the Olympian Games proper; and the sacred kingship, conferred on the victor of the foot race at his marriage to the new priestess, is recalled in the divine honours that the victory continued to bestow in Classical times. Having been wreathed with Heracles's or Zeus's olive, saluted as 'King Heracles', and pelted with leaves like a Jack o' Green, he led the dance in a triumphal procession and ate sacrificial bull's flesh in the Council Hall.

5. The original prize, an apple, or an apple-spray, had been a promise of immortality when he was duly killed by his successor; for Plutarch (*Symposiac Questions* v. 2) mentions that though a foot race was the sole contest in the original Olympic Games, a single combat also took place, which ended only in the death of the vanquished. This combat is mythologically recorded in the story that the Olympic Games began with a wrestling match between Zeus and Cronus for the possession of Elis (Pausanias: v. 7), namely the midsummer combat between the king and his tanist; and the result was a foregone conclusion – the tanist came armed with a spear.

6. A scholiast on Pindar (*Olympian Odes* iii. 33), quoting Comarchus, shows that the Elian New Year was reckoned from the full moon nearest to the winter solstice, and that a second New Year began at midsummer. Presumably therefore the new Zeus-Heracles, that is to say, the winner of the foot race, killed the Old Year tanist, Cronus-Iphicles, at midwinter. Hence Heracles first instituted the Games and named the sepulchral Hill of Cronus 'at a season when the summit was wet with much snow' (Pindar: *Olympian Odes* x. 49).

7. In ancient times, Zeus-Heracles was pelted with oak-leaves and given the apple-spray at midsummer, just before being killed by his tanist; he had won the royal wild-olive branch at midwinter. The replacement of the apple by wild-olive, which is the tree that drives

away evil spirits, implied the abolition of this death-combat, and the
conversion of the single year, divided into two halves, into a Great Year.
This began at midwinter, when solar and lunar time coincided favourably for a Sun-and-Moon marriage, and was divided into two Olympiads
of four years apiece; the king and his tanist reigning successively or concurrently. Though by Classical times the solar chariot race – for which
the mythological authority is Pelops's contest with Oenomaus for Deidameia (see 109. 3) – had become the most important event in the Games,
it was still thought somehow unlucky to be pelted with leaves after a
victory in the foot race; and Pythagoras advised his friends to compete in
this event but not to win it. The victory-ox, eaten at the Council Hall,
was clearly a surrogate for the king, as at the Athenian Buphonia festival
(see 21. 13).

8. Olympia is not a Mycenaean site and the pre-Achaean myths are
therefore unlikely to have been borrowed from Crete; they seem to be
Pelasgian.


# 54

## THE TELCHINES

THE nine dog-headed, flipper-handed Telchines, Children of the Sea,
originated in Rhodes, where they founded the cities of Cameirus,
Ialysus, and Lindus; and migrating thence to Crete, became its first
inhabitants. Rhea entrusted the infant Poseidon to their care, and they
forged his trident but, long before this, had made for Cronus the
toothed sickle with which he castrated his father Uranus; and were,
moreover, the first to carve images of the gods.

b. Yet Zeus resolved to destroy them by a flood, because they had
been interfering with the weather, raising magic mists and blighting
crops by means of sulphur and Stygian water. Warned by Artemis,
they all fled overseas: some to Boeotia, where they built the temple
of Athene at Teumessus; some to Sicyon, some to Lycia, others to
Orchomenus, where they were the hounds that tore Actaeon to pieces.
But Zeus destroyed the Teumessian Telchines with a flood; Apollo,
disguised as a wolf, destroyed the Lycian ones, though they had tried
to placate him with a new temple; and they are no longer to be found
at Orchomenus. Rumour has it that some are still living in Sicyon.[1]

1. Eustathius on Homer, p. 771–2; Ovid: *Metamorphoses* vii. 365–7; Diodorus Siculus: iii. 55. 2–3; Strabo: xiv. 2. 7; Callimachus: *Hymn to Delos* 31; Servius on Virgil's *Aeneid* iv. 377.

*

1. That the nine Telchines were Children of the Sea, acted as the hounds of Artemis, created magic mists, and founded the cities named after the three Danaids, Cameira, Ialysa, and Linda (see 60. *d*) suggests that they were originally emanations of the Moon-goddess Danaë: each of her three persons in triad (see 60. *2*). 'Telchin' was derived by the Greek grammarians from *thelgein*, 'to enchant'. But, since women, dog and fish were likewise combined in pictures of Scylla the Tyrrhenian – who was also at home in Crete (see 91. *2*) – and in the figure-heads of Tyrrhenian ships, the word may be a variant of 'Tyrrhen' or 'Tyrsen'; *l* and *r* having been confused by the Libyans, and the next consonant being something between an aspirate and a sibilant. They were, it seems, worshipped by an early matriarchal people of Greece, Crete, Lydia, and the Aegean Islands, whom the invading patriarchal Hellenes persecuted; absorbed or forced to emigrate westward. Their origin may have been East African.

2. Magic mists were raised by willow spells. Styx water (see 31. *4*) was supposedly so holy that the least drop of it caused death, unless drunk from a cup made of a horse's hoof, which proves it sacred to the Mare-headed goddess of Arcadia. Alexander the Great is said to have been poisoned by Styx water (Pausanias: viii. 18. 2). The Telchines' magical use of it suggests that their devotees held near-by Mount Nonacris ('nine peaks'), at one time the chief religious centre of Greece; even the Olympic gods swore their most solemn oath by the Styx.

# 55

## THE EMPUSAE

THE filthy demons called Empusae, children of Hecate, are ass-haunched and wear brazen slippers – unless, as some declare, each has one ass's leg and one brazen leg. Their habit is to frighten travellers, but they may be routed by insulting words, at the sound of which they flee shrieking. Empusae disguise themselves in the forms of bitches, cows, or beautiful maidens and, in the latter shape, will lie with men by night, or at the time of midday sleep, sucking their vital forces until they die.[1]

1. Aristophanes: *Frogs* 288 ff.; *Parliament of Women* 1056 and 1094; *Papyri Magici Graeci* iv. 2334; Philostratus: *Life of Apollonius of Tyana* iv. 25; Suidas *sub* Empusae.

*

1. The Empusae ('forcers-in') are greedily seductive female demons, a concept probably brought to Greece from Palestine, where they went by the name of Lilim ('children of Lilith') and were thought to be ass-haunched, the ass symbolizing lechery and cruelty. Lilith ('scritch-owl') was a Canaanite Hecate, and the Jews made amulets to protect themselves against her as late as the Middle Ages. Hecate, the real ruler of Tartarus (see 31.*f*), wore a brazen sandal – the golden sandal was Aphrodite's – and her daughters, the Empusae, followed this example. They could change themselves into beautiful maidens or cows, as well as bitches, because the Bitch Hecate, being a member of the Moon-triad, was the same goddess as Aphrodite, or cow-eyed Hera.

# 56
## IO

Io, daughter of the River-god Inachus, was a priestess of Argive Hera. Zeus, over whom Iynx, daughter of Pan and Echo, had cast a spell, fell in love with Io, and when Hera charged him with infidelity and turned Iynx into a wryneck as a punishment, lied: 'I have never touched Io.' He then turned her into a white cow, which Hera claimed as hers and handed over for safe keeping to Argus Panoptes, ordering him: 'Tether this beast secretly to an olive-tree at Nemea.' But Zeus sent Hermes to fetch her back, and himself led the way to Nemea – or, some say, to Mycenae – dressed in woodpecker disguise. Hermes, though the cleverest of thieves, knew that he could not steal Io without being detected by one of Argus's hundred eyes; he therefore charmed him asleep by playing the flute, crushed him with a boulder, cut off his head, and released Io. Hera, having placed Argus's eyes in the tail of a peacock, as a constant reminder of his foul murder, set a gadfly to sting Io and chase her all over the world.

b. Io first went to Dodona, and presently reached the sea called the Ionian after her, but there turned back and travelled north to Mount Haemus and then, by way of the Danube's delta, coursed sun-wise around the Black Sea, crossing the Crimean Bosphorus, and following the River Hybristes to its source in the Caucasus, where Prometheus still languished on his rock. She regained Europe by way of Colchis, the land of the Chalybes, and the Thracian Bosphorus; then away she galloped through Asia Minor to Tarsus and Joppa, thence to Media, Bactria, and India and, passing south-westward through Arabia, across the Indian Bosphorus [the Straits of Bab-el-Mandeb], reached Ethiopia. Thence she travelled down from the sources of the Nile, where the pygmies make perpetual war with the cranes, and found rest at last in Egypt. There Zeus restored her to human form and, having married Telegonus, she gave birth to Epaphus – her son by Zeus, who had *touched* her to some purpose – and founded the worship of Isis, as she called Demeter. Epaphus, who was rumoured to be the divine bull Apis, reigned over Egypt, and had a daughter, Libya, the mother by Poseidon of Agenor and Belus.[1]

c. But some believe that Io bore Epaphus in a Euboean cave called Boösaule, and afterwards died there from the sting of the gadfly; and that, as a cow, she changed her colour from white to violet-red, and from violet-red to black.[2]

d. Others have a quite different story to tell. They say that Inachus, a son of Iapetus, ruled over Argos, and founded the city of Iopolis – for Io is the name by which the moon was once worshipped at Argos – and called his daughter Io in honour of the moon. Zeus Picus, King of the West, sent his servants to carry off Io, and outraged her as soon as she reached his palace. After bearing him a daughter named Libya, Io fled to Egypt, but found that Hermes, son of Zeus, was reigning there; so continued her flight to Mount Silpium in Syria, where she died of grief and shame. Inachus then sent Io's brothers and kinsfolk in search of her, warning them not to return empty-handed. With Triptolemus for their guide, they knocked on every door in Syria, crying: 'May the spirit of Io find rest!'; until at last they reached Mount Silpium, where a phantasmal cow addressed them with: 'Here am I, Io.' They decided that Io must have been buried on that spot, and therefore founded a second Iopolis, now called Antioch. In honour of Io, the Iopolitans knock at one another's door in the same way every year, using the same cry; and the Argives mourn annually for her.[3]

1. Callimachus: *On Birds, Fragment* 100; Apollodorus: ii. 1. 3; Hyginus: *Fabula* 145; Suidas *sub* Io; Lucian: *Dialogues of the Gods* 3; Moschus: *Idyll* ii. 59; Herodotus: i. 1 and ii. 41; Homer: *Iliad* iii. 6; Aeschylus: *Prometheus Bound* 705 ff. and *Suppliants* 547 ff.; Euripides: *Iphigeneia Among the Taurians* 382; Tzetzes: *On Lyco-phron* 835 ff.

2. Strabo: x. 1. 3; Stephanus of Byzantium *sub* Argura; Suidas *sub* Isis.

3. John Malalas: *Chronicles* ii. p. 28, ed. Dindorff.

\*

1. This myth consists of several strands. The Argives worshipped the moon as a cow, because the horned new moon was regarded as the source of all water, and therefore of cattle fodder. Her three colours: white for the new moon, red for the harvest moon, black for the moon when it waned, represented the three ages of the Moon-goddess – Maiden, Nymph, and Crone (see 90. *3*). Io changed her colour, as the moon changes, but for 'red' the mythographer substitutes 'violet' because *ion* is Greek for the violet flower. Woodpeckers were thought to be knocking for rain when they tapped on oak-trunks; and Io was the Moon as rain-bringer. The herdsmen needed rain most pressingly in late summer, when gadflies attacked their cattle and sent them frantic; in Africa, cattle-owning Negro tribes still hurry from pasture to pasture when attacked by them. Io's Argive priestesses seem to have performed an annual heifer-dance in which they pretended to be driven mad by gad-flies, while woodpecker-men, tapping on oak-doors and calling 'Io! Io!', invited the rain to fall and relieve their torments. This seems to be the origin of the myth of the Coan women who were turned into cows (see 137. *s*). Argive colonies founded in Euboea, the Bosphorus, the Black Sea, Syria, and Egypt, took their rain-making dance with them. The wryneck, the Moon-goddess's prime orgiastic bird, nests in willows, and was therefore concerned with water-magic (see 152. *2*).

2. The legend invented to account for the eastward spread of this ritual, as well as the similarity between the worship of Io in Greece, Isis in Egypt, Astarte in Syria, and Kali in India, has been grafted on two unrelated stories: that of the holy moon-cow wandering around the heavens, guarded by the stars – there is a cognate Irish legend of the 'Green Stripper' – and that of the Moon-priestesses whom the leaders of the invading Hellenes, each calling himself Zeus, violated to the dismay of the local population. Hera, as Zeus's wife, is then made to express jealousy of Io, though Io was another name for 'cow-eyed' Hera. Demeter's mourning for Persephone is recalled in the Argive festival of mourning for Io, since Io has been equated in the myth with Demeter.

Moreover, every three years Demeter's Mysteries were celebrated at
Celeae ('calling'), near Corinth, and said to have been founded by a
brother of Celeus ('woodpecker'), King of Eleusis. Hermes is called
the son of Zeus Picus ('woodpecker') – Aristophanes in his *Birds* (480)
accuses Zeus of stealing the woodpecker's sceptre – as Pan is said to have
been Hermes's son by the Nymph Dryope ('woodpecker'); and Faunus,
the Latin Pan, was the son of Picus ('woodpecker') whom Circe turned
into a woodpecker for spurning her love (Ovid: *Metamorphoses* xiv. 6).
Faunus's Cretan tomb bore the epitaph: 'Here lies the woodpecker who
was also Zeus' (Suidas *sub* Picos). All three are rain-making shepherd-
gods. Libya's name denotes rain, and the winter rains came to Greece
from the direction of Libya.

3. Zeus's fathering of Epaphus, who became the ancestor of Libya,
Agenor, Belus, Aegyptus, and Danaus, implies that the Zeus-worshipping
Achaeans claimed sovereignty over all the sea-peoples of the south-
eastern Mediterranean.

4. The myth of pygmies and cranes seems to concern the tall cattle-
breeding tribesmen who had broken into the upper Nile-valley from
Somaliland and driven the native pygmies southward. They were called
'cranes' because, then as now, they would stand for long periods on one
leg, holding the ankle of the other with the opposite hand, and leaning
on a spear.

# 57

## PHORONEUS

THE first man to found and people a market-town was Io's brother
Phoroneus, son of the River-god Inachus and the Nymph Melia; later
its name, Phoronicum, was changed to Argos. Phoroneus was also the
first to discover the use of fire, after Prometheus had stolen it. He
married the Nymph Cerdo, ruled the entire Peloponnese, and initiated
the worship of Hera. When he died, his sons Pelasgus, Iasus, and Agenor
divided the Peloponnese between them; but his son Car founded the
city of Megara.[1]

1. Hyginus: *Fabulae* 143 and 274; Apollodorus: ii. 1. 1; Pausanias:
i. 39. 4–6; ii. 15. 5 and iv. 40. 5.

\*

1. Phoroneus's name, which the Greeks read as 'bringer of a price' in
the sense that he invented markets, probably stands for Fearinus ('of the

dawn of the year', i.e. the Spring); variants are Bran, Barn, Bergn, Vron, Ephron, Gwern, Fearn, and Brennus. As the spirit of the alder-tree which presided over the fourth month in the sacred year (see 28. *1* and 5; 52. *3* and 170. *8*), during which the Spring Fire Festival was celebrated, he was described as a son of Inachus, because alders grow by rivers. His mother is the ash-nymph Melia, because the ash, the preceding tree of the same series, is said to 'court the flash' – lightning-struck trees were primitive man's first source of fire. Being an oracular hero, he was also associated with the crow (see 50. *1*). Phoroneus's discovery of the use of fire may be explained by the ancient smiths' and potters' preference for alder charcoal, which gives out more heat than any other. Cerdo ('gain' or 'art') is one of Demeter's titles; it was applied to her as weasel, or fox, both considered prophetic animals. 'Phoroneus' seems to have been a title of Cronus, with whom the crow and the alder are also associated (see 6. *2*), and therefore the Titan of the Seventh Day. The division of Phoroneus's kingdom between his sons Pelasgus, Iasus, and Agenor recalls that of Cronus's kingdom between Zeus, Poseidon, and Hades; but perhaps describes a pre-Achaean partition of the Peloponnese.

2. Car is Q're, or Carius, or the Great God Ker, who seems to have derived his title from his Moon-mother Artemis Caria, or Caryatis.

# 58

## EUROPE AND CADMUS

AGENOR, Libya's son by Poseidon and twin to Belus, left Egypt to settle in the Land of Canaan, where he married Telephassa, otherwise called Argiope, who bore him Cadmus, Phoenix, Cilix, Thasus, Phineus, and one daughter, Europe.[1]

*b*. Zeus, falling in love with Europe, sent Hermes to drive Agenor's cattle down to the seashore at Tyre, where she and her companions used to walk. He himself joined the herd, disguised as a snow-white bull with great dewlaps and small, gem-like horns, between which ran a single black streak. Europe was struck by his beauty and, on finding him gentle as a lamb, mastered her fear and began to play with him, putting flowers in his mouth and hanging garlands on his horns; in the end, she climbed upon his shoulders, and let him amble down with her to the edge of the sea. Suddenly he swam away, while she looked back in terror at the receding shore; one of her hands clung to his right horn, the other still held a flower-basket.[2]

*c.* Wading ashore near Cretan Gortyna, Zeus became an eagle and ravished Europe in a willow-thicket beside a spring; or, some say, under an evergreen plane-tree. She bore him three sons: Minos, Rhadamanthys, and Sarpedon.[3]

*d.* Agenor sent his sons in search of their sister, forbidding them to return without her. They set sail at once but, having no notion where the bull had gone, each steered a different course. Phoenix travelled westward, beyond Libya, to what is now Carthage, and there gave his name to the Punics; but, after Agenor's death, returned to Canaan, since renamed Phoenicia in his honour, and became the father of Adonis by Alphesiboea.[4] Cilix went to the Land of the Hypachaeans, which took his name, Cilicia;[5] and Phineus to Thynia, a peninsula separating the Sea of Marmara from the Black Sea, where he was later much distressed by harpies. Thasus and his followers, first making for Olympia, dedicated a bronze statue there to Tyrian Heracles, ten ells high, holding a club and a bow, but then set off to colonize the island of Thasos and work its rich gold mines. All this took place five generations before Heracles, son of Amphitryon, was born in Greece.[6]

*e.* Cadmus sailed with Telephassa to Rhodes, where he dedicated a brazen cauldron to Athene of Lindus, and built Poseidon's temple, leaving a herditary priesthood behind to care for it. They next touched at Thera, and built a similar temple, finally reaching the land of the Thracian Edonians, who received them hospitably. Here Telephassa died suddenly and, after her funeral, Cadmus and his companions proceeded on foot to the Delphic Oracle. When he asked where Europe might be found, the Pythoness advised him to give up his search and, instead, follow a cow and build a city wherever she should sink down for weariness.

*f.* Departing by the road that leads from Delphi to Phocis, Cadmus came upon some cowherds in the service of King Pelagon, who sold him a cow marked with a white full moon on each flank. This beast he drove eastward through Boeotia, never allowing her to pause until, at last, she sank down where the city of Thebes now stands, and here he erected an image of Athene, calling it by her Phoenician name of Onga.[7]

*g.* Cadmus, warning his companions that the cow must be sacrificed to Athene without delay, sent them to fetch lustral water from the

Spring of Ares, now called the Castalian Spring, but did not know that it was guarded by a great serpent. This serpent killed most of Cadmus's men, and he took vengeance by crushing its head with a rock. No sooner had he offered Athene the sacrifice, than she appeared, praising him for what he had done, and ordering him to sow the serpent's teeth in the soil. When he obeyed her, armed Sparti, or Sown Men, at once sprang up, clashing their weapons together. Cadmus tossed a stone among them and they began to brawl, each accusing the other of having thrown it, and fought so fiercely that, at last, only five survived: Echion, Udaeus, Chthonius, Hyperenor, and Pelorus, who unanimously offered Cadmus their services. But Ares demanded vengeance for the death of the serpent, and Cadmus was sentenced by a divine court to become his bondman for a Great Year.[8]

1. Apollodorus: iii. 1. 1; Hyginus: *Fabulae* 178 and 19; Pausanias: v. 25. 7; Apollonius Rhodius: ii. 178.
2. Ovid: *Metamorphoses* ii. 836 ff.; Moschus: *Idylls* ii. 37–62.
3. The Coins of Gortyna; Theophrastus: *History of Plants* i. 9. 5; Hyginus: *Fabula* 178.
4. Hyginus: *loc. cit.*; Apollodorus: iii. 1. 1 and 14. 4.
5. Herodotus: vii. 91.
6. Pausanias: v. 25. 7; Herodotus: iv. 47 and ii. 44.
7. Pausanias: ix. 12. 1–2.
8. Hyginus: *Fabula* 178; Apollodorus: iii. 4. 1–2.

\*

1. There are numerous confusing variations of the genealogy given above: for instance, Thasus is alternatively described as the son of Poseidon, Cilix (Apollodorus: iii. 1. 1), or Tityus (Pindar: *Pythian Odes* iv. 46). Agenor is the Phoenician hero Chnas, who appears in *Genesis* as 'Canaan'; many Canaanite customs point to an East African provenience, and the Canaanites may have originally come to Lower Egypt from Uganda. The dispersal of Agenor's sons seems to record the westward flight of Canaanite tribes early in the second millennium B.C., under pressure from Aryan and Semitic invaders.

2. The story of Inachus's sons and their search for Io the moon-cow (see 56. *d*) has influenced that of Agenor's sons and their search for Europe. Phoenix is a masculine form of Phoenissa ('the red, or bloody one'), a title given to the moon as goddess of Death-in-Life. Europe means 'broad-face', a synonym for the full moon, and a title of the Moon-goddesses Demeter at Lebadia and Astarte at Sidon. If, however, the word is not *eur-ope* but *eu-rope* (on the analogy of *euboea*), it may also

mean 'good for willows' – that is, 'well-watered'. The willow rules the fifth month of the sacred year (see 52. *3*), and is associated with witchcraft (see 28. *5*) and with fertility rites throughout Europe, especially on May Eve, which falls in this month. Libya, Telephassa, Argiope, and Alphesiboea are all, similarly, titles of the Moon-goddess.

*3*. Zeus's rape of Europe, which records an early Hellenic occupation of Crete, has been deduced from pre-Hellenic pictures of the Moon-priestess triumphantly riding on the Sun-bull, her victim; the scene survives in eight moulded plaques of blue glass, found in the Mycenaean city of Midea. This seems to have been part of the fertility ritual during which Europe's May-garland was carried in procession (Athenaeus: p. 678 a–b). Zeus's seduction of Europe in eagle-disguise recalls his seduction of Hera in cuckoo-disguise (see 12. *a*); since (according to Hesychius) Hella bore the title 'Europia'. Europe's Cretan and Corinthian name was Hellotis, which suggests Helice ('willow'); Helle (see 43. *1* and 70. *8*) and Helen are the same divine character. Callimachus in his *Epithalamion for Helen* mentions that the plane-tree was also sacred to Helen. Its sanctity lay in its five-pointed leaves, representing the hand of the goddess (see 53. *a*), and its annual sloughing of bark; but Apollo borrowed it (see 160. *10*), as the God Esmun did Tanit's (Neith's) open-hand emblem (see 21. *3*).

*4*. It is possible that the story of Europe also commemorates a raid on Phoenicia by Hellenes from Crete. John Malalas will hardly have invented the 'Evil Evening' at Tyre when he writes: 'Taurus ("bull"), King of Crete, assaulted Tyre after a sea-battle during the absence of Agenor and his sons. They took the city that same evening and carried off many captives, Europe among them; this event is still recalled in the annual "Evil Evening" observed at Tyre' (*Chronicles* ii. p. 30, ed. Dindorff). Herodotus (1. 2) agrees with Malalas (see 160. *1*).

*5*. Tyrian Heracles, whom Theseus worshipped at Olympia, was the god Melkarth; and a small tribe, speaking a Semitic language, seems to have moved up from the Syrian plains to Cadmeia in Caria – Cadmus is a Semitic word meaning 'eastern' – whence they crossed over to Boeotia towards the end of the second millennium, seized Thebes, and became masters of the country. The myth of the Sown Men and Cadmus's bondage to Ares suggest that the invading Cadmeans secured their hold on Boeotia by successfully intervening in a civil war among the Pelasgian tribes who claimed to be autochthonous; and that they accepted the local rule of an eight-year reign for the sacred king. Cadmus killed the serpent in the same sense as Apollo killed the Python at Delphi (see 21. *12*). The names of the Sown Men – Echion ('viper'); Udaeus ('of the earth'); Chthonius ('of the soil'); Hyperenor ('man who comes up') and Pelorus ('serpent') – are characteristic of oracular heroes. But 'Pelorus' suggests that all Pelasgians, not merely the Thebans, claimed to be born in this way; their common feast being the Peloria (see 1. 2). Jason's crop of dragon's teeth was probably sown at Iolcus or Corinth, not Colchis (see 152. 3).

6. Troy and Antioch were also said to have been founded on sites selected by sacred cows (see 158. h and 56. d). But it is less likely that this practice was literally carried out, than that the cow was turned loose in a restricted part of a selected site and the temple of the Moon-goddess founded where she lay down. A cow's strategic and commercial sensibilities are not highly developed.

# 59

## CADMUS AND HARMONIA

WHEN Cadmus had served eight years in bondage to Ares, to expiate the murder of the Castalian serpent, Athene secured him the land of Boeotia. With the help of his Sown Men, he built the Theban acropolis, named 'The Cadmea' in his own honour and, after being initiated into the mysteries which Zeus had taught Iasion, married Harmonia, the daughter of Aphrodite and Ares; some say that Athene had given her to him when he visited Samothrace.[1]

b. This was the first mortal wedding ever attended by the Olympians. Twelve golden thrones were set up for them in Cadmus's house, which stood on the site of the present Theban market place; and they all brought gifts. Aphrodite presented Harmonia with the famous golden necklace made by Hephaestus – originally it had been Zeus's love-gift to Cadmus's sister Europe – which conferred irresistible beauty on its wearer.[2] Athene gave her a golden robe, which similarly conferred divine dignity on its wearer, also a set of flutes; and Hermes a lyre. Cadmus's own present to Harmonia was another rich robe; and Electra, Iasion's mother, taught her the rites of the Great Goddess; while Demeter assured her a prosperous barley harvest by lying with Iasion in a thrice-ploughed field during the celebrations. The Thebans still show the place where the Muses played the flute and sang on this occasion, and where Apollo performed on the lyre.[3]

c. In his old age, to placate Ares, who had not yet wholly forgiven him for killing the serpent, Cadmus resigned the Theban throne in favour of his grandson Pentheus, whom his daughter Agave had borne to Echion the Sown Man, and lived quietly in the city. But when Pentheus was done to death by his mother, Dionysus foretold that Cadmus and Harmonia, riding in a chariot drawn by heifers, would rule over barbarian hordes. These same barbarians, he said, would sack many Greek cities until, at last, they plundered a temple of Apollo, whereupon they would suffer just punishment; but Ares would rescue Cadmus and Harmonia, after turning them into serpents, and they would live happily for all time in the Islands of the Blessed.[4]

d. Cadmus and Harmonia therefore emigrated to the land of the Encheleans who, when attacked by the Illyrians, chose them as their rulers, in accordance with Dionysus's advice. Agave was now married to Lycotherses, King of Illyria, at whose court she had taken refuge after her murder of Pentheus; but on hearing that her parents commanded the Enchelean forces, she murdered Lycotherses too, and gave the kingdom to Cadmus.[5]

e. In their old age, when the prophecy had been wholly fulfilled, Cadmus and Harmonia duly became blue-spotted black serpents, and were sent by Zeus to the Islands of the Blessed. But some say that Ares changed them into lions. Their bodies were buried in Illyria, where Cadmus had built the city of Buthoë. He was succeeded by Illyrius, the son of his old age.[6]

1. Pausanias: ix. 5. 1; Diodorus Siculus: v. 48; Apollodorus: iii. 4. 2.
2. Diodorus Siculus: v. 49 and iv. 65. 5; Pindar: *Pythian Odes* iii. 94; Pausanias: ix. 12. 3; Pherecydes, quoted by Apollodorus: iii. 4. 2.
3. Diodorus Siculus: v. 49; Pausanias: ix. 12. 3
4. Hyginus: *Fabula* 6; Apollodorus: iii. 4. 2; Euripides: *Bacchae* 43 and 1350 ff.
5. Hyginus: *Fabulae* 184 and 240.
6. Ovid: *Metamorphoses* iv. 562–602; Apollodorus: iii. 5. 4; Ptolemy Hephaestionos; i; Apollonius Rhodius: iv. 517.

\*

1. Cadmus's marriage to Harmonia, in the presence of the Twelve Olympian deities, is paralleled by Peleus's marriage to Thetis (see 81. *l*), and seems to record a general Hellenic recognition of the Cadmeian conquerors of Thebes, after they had been sponsored by the Athenians and decently initiated into the Samothracian Mysteries. His founding of Buthoë constitutes a claim by the Illyrians to rank as Greeks, and therefore to take part in the Olympic Games. Cadmus will have had an oracle in Illyria, if he was pictured there as a serpent; and the lions, into which he

and Harmonia are also said to have been transformed, were perhaps twin heraldic supporters of the Great Goddess's aniconic image – as on the famous Lion Gate at Mycenae. The mythographer suggests that he was allowed to emigrate with a colony at the close of his reign, instead of being put to death (see 117. 5).

# 60

## BELUS AND THE DANAIDS

KING BELUS, who ruled at Chemmis in the Thebaid, was the son of Libya by Poseidon, and twin-brother of Agenor. His wife Anchinoë, daughter of Nilus, bore him the twins Aegyptus and Danaus, and a third son, Cepheus.[1]

b. Aegyptus was given Arabia as his kingdom; but also subdued the country of the Melampodes, and named it Egypt after himself. Fifty sons were born to him of various mothers: Libyans, Arabians, Phoenicians, and the like. Danaus, sent to rule Libya, had fifty daughters, called the Danaids, also born of various mothers: Naiads, Hamadryads, Egyptian princesses of Elephantis and Memphis, Ethiopians, and the like.

c. On Belus's death, the twins quarrelled over their inheritance, and as a conciliatory gesture Aegyptus proposed a mass-marriage between the fifty princes and the fifty princesses. Danaus, suspecting a plot, would not consent and, when an oracle confirmed his fears that Aegyptus had it in his mind to kill all the Danaids, prepared to flee from Libya.[2]

d. With Athene's assistance, he built a ship for himself and his daughters – the first two-prowed vessel that ever took to sea – and they sailed towards Greece together, by way of Rhodes. There Danaus dedicated an image to Athene in a temple raised for her by the Danaids, three of whom died during their stay in the island; the cities of Lindus, Ialysus, and Cameirus are called after them.[3]

e. From Rhodes they sailed to the Peloponnese and landed near Lerna, where Danaus announced that he was divinely chosen to become King of Argos. Though the Argive King, Gelanor, naturally laughed at this claim, his subjects assembled that evening to discuss it. Gelanor would doubtless have kept the throne, despite Danaus's declaration that Athene was supporting him, had not the Argives postponed their decision until dawn, when a wolf came boldly down from the hills, attacked a herd of cattle grazing near the city walls, and killed the leading bull. This they read as an omen that Danaus would take the throne by violence if he were opposed, and therefore persuaded Gelanor to resign it peacefully.

*f.* Danaus, convinced that the wolf had been Apollo in disguise, dedicated the famous shrine to Wolfish Apollo at Argos, and became so powerful a ruler that all the Pelasgians of Greece called themselves Danaans. He also built the citadel of Argos, and his daughters brought the Mysteries of Demeter, called Thesmophoria, from Egypt and taught these to the Pelasgian women. But, since the Dorian invasion, the Thesmophoria are no longer performed in the Peloponnese, except by the Arcadians.[4]

*g.* Danaus had found Argolis suffering from a prolonged drought, since Poseidon, vexed by Inachus's decision that the land was Hera's, had dried up all the rivers and streams. He sent his daughters in search of water, with orders to placate Poseidon by any means they knew. One of them, by name Amymone, while chasing a deer in the forest, happened to disturb a sleeping satyr. He sprang up and tried to ravish her; but Poseidon, whom she invoked, hurled his trident at the satyr. The fleeing satyr dodged, the trident stuck quivering in a rock, and Poseidon himself lay with Amymone, who was glad that she could carry out her father's instructions so pleasantly. On learning her errand, Poseidon pointed to his trident and told her to pull it from the rock. When she did so, three streams of water jetted up from the three tine-holes. This spring, now named Amymone, is the source of the river Lerna, which never fails, even at the height of summer.[5]

*h.* At Amymone the monstrous Hydra was born to Echidne under a plane-tree. It lived in the near-by Lernaean Lake, to which murderers come for purification – hence the proverb: 'A Lerna of evils.'[6]

*i.* Aegyptus now sent his sons to Argos, forbidding them to return until they had punished Danaus and his whole family. On their arrival, they begged Danaus to reverse his former decision and let them marry his daughters – intending, however, to murder them on the wedding night. When he still refused, they laid siege to Argos. Now, there are no springs on the Argive citadel, and though the Danaids afterwards invented the art of sinking wells, and supplied the city with several of

these, including four sacred ones, it was waterless at the time in question. Seeing that thirst would soon force him to capitulate, Danaus
promised to do what the sons of Aegyptus asked, as soon as they raised
the siege.[7]

*j.* A mass-marriage was arranged, and Danaus paired off the couples:
his choice being made in some cases because the bride and bridegroom
had mothers of equal rank, or because their names were similar – thus
Cleite, Sthenele, and Chrysippe married Cleitus, Sthenelus, and Chrysippus – but in most cases he drew lots from a helmet.[8]

*k.* During the wedding-feast Danaus secretly doled out sharp pins
which his daughters were to conceal in their hair; and at midnight each
stabbed her husband through the heart. There was only one survivor;
on Artemis's advice, Hypermnestra saved the life of Lynceus, because
he had spared her maidenhead; and helped him in his flight to the city
of Lyncea, sixty furlongs away. Hypermnestra begged him to light a
beacon as a signal that he had reached safety, undertaking to answer it
with another beacon from the citadel; and the Argives still light annual
beacon-fires in commemoration of this pact. At dawn, Danaus learned
of Hypermnestra's disobedience, and she was tried for her life; but
acquitted by the Argive judges. She therefore raised an image to Victorious Aphrodite in the shrine of Wolfish Apollo, and also dedicated
a sanctuary to Persuasive Artemis.[9]

*l.* The murdered men's heads were buried at Lerna, and their bodies
given full funeral honours below the walls of Argos; but, although
Athene and Hermes purified the Danaids in the Lernaean Lake with
Zeus's permission, the Judges of the Dead have condemned them to
the endless task of carrying water in jars perforated like sieves.[10]

*m.* Lynceus and Hypermnestra were reunited, and Danaus, deciding
to marry off the other daughters as fast as he could before noon on the
day of their purification, called for suitors. He proposed a marriage
race starting from the street now called Apheta: the winner to have
first choice of a wife, and the others the next choices, in their order of
finishing the race. Since he could not find enough men who would
risk their lives by marrying murderesses, only a few ran; but when the
wedding night passed without disaster to the new bridegrooms, more
suitors appeared, and another race was run on the following day. All
descendants of these marriages rank as Danaans; and the Argives still
celebrate the race in their so-called Hymenaean Contest. Lynceus later
killed Danaus, and reigned in his stead. He would willingly have killed

his sisters-in-law at the same time, to avenge his murdered brothers, had the Argives permitted this.[11]

*n*. Meanwhile, Aegyptus had come to Greece, but when he learned of his sons' fate, fled to Aroe, where he died, and was buried at Patrae, in a sanctuary of Serapis.[12]

*o*. Amymone's son by Poseidon, Nauplius, a famous navigator, discovered the art of steering by the Great Bear, and founded the city of Nauplius, where he settled the Egyptian crew that had sailed with his grandfather. He was the ancestor of Nauplius the Wrecker, who used to lure hostile ships to their death by lighting false beacons.[13]

1. Herodotus: ii. 91; Euripides, quoted by Apollodorus: ii. 1. 4.
2. Apollodorus: ii. 1. 5; Hyginus: *Fabula* 168; Eustathius on Homer, p. 37.
3. Hyginus: *loc. cit.*; Apollodorus: ii. 1. 4; Herodotus: ii. 234; Diodorus Siculus: v. 58. 1; Strabo: xiv. 2. 8.
4. Pausanias: ii. 38. 4 and 19. 3; Euripides, quoted by Strabo: viii. 6. 9; Strabo: *loc. cit.*; Herodotus: ii. 171; Plutarch: *On the Malice of Herodotus* 13.
5. Hyginus: *Fabula* 169; Apollodorus: ii. 1. 4.
6. Pausanias: ii. 37. 1 and 4; Strabo: viii. 6. 8.
7. Hyginus: *Fabula* 168; Apollodorus: ii. 1. 5; Strabo: viii. 6. 9.
8. Apollodorus: *loc. cit.*; Hyginus: *Fabula* 170.
9. Apollodorus: *loc. cit.*; Pausanias: ii. 25. 4; 19. 6 and 21. 1.
10. Apollodorus: *loc. cit.*; Lucian: *Marine Dialogues* vi; Hyginus: *Fabula* 168; Ovid: *Heroides* xiv; Horace: *Odes* iii. 11. 30.
11. Pindar: *Pythian Odes* ix. 117 ff.; Pausanias: iii. 12. 2; Hyginus: *Fabula* 170; Servius on Virgil's *Aeneid* x. 497.
12. Pausanias: vii. 21. 6.
13. Apollonius Rhodius: i. 136–8; Theon on Aratus's *Phenomena* 27; Pausanias: iv. 35. 2.

\*

1. This myth records the early arrival in Greece of Helladic colonists from Palestine, by way of Rhodes, and their introduction of agriculture into the Peloponnese. It is claimed that they included emigrants from Libya and Ethiopia, which seems probable (see 6. *1* and 8. *2*). Belus is the Baal of the Old Testament, and the Bel of the Apocrypha; he had taken his name from the Sumerian Moon-goddess Belili, whom he ousted.

2. The three Danaids, also known as the Telchines, or 'enchanters', who named the three chief cities of Rhodes, were the Triple Moon-goddess Danaë (see 54. *1* and 73. *4*). The names Linda, Cameira, and Ialysa seem to be worn-down forms of *linodeousa* ('binder with linen

thread'), *catamerizousa* ('sharer out'), and *ialemistria* ('wailing woman') –
they are, in fact, the familiar Three Fates, or Moerae, otherwise known as
Clotho, Lachesis, and Atropos (see 10. 1) because they exercised these
very functions. The classical theory of the linen-thread was that the
goddess tied the human being to the end of a carefully measured thread,
which she paid out yearly, until the time came for her to cut it and thereby
relinquish his soul to death. But originally she bound the wailing infant
with a linen swaddling band on which his clan and family marks were
embroidered and thus assigned him his destined place in society.

3. Danaë's Sumerian name was Dam-kina. The Hebrews called her
Dinah (*Genesis* xxxiv), also masculinized as Dan. Fifty Moon-priestesses
were the regular complement of a college, and their duty was to keep the
land watered by rain-making charms, irrigation, and well-digging;
hence the Danaids' name has been connected with the Greek word *dānos*,
'parched', and with *danos*, 'a gift', the first *a* of which is sometimes long,
sometimes short. The twinship of Agenor and Belus, like that of Danaus
and Aegyptus, points to a regal system at Argos, in which each co-king
married a Chief-priestess and reigned for fifty lunar months, or half a
Great Year. Chief-priestesses were chosen by a foot race (the origin of the
Olympic Games), run at the end of the fifty months, or of forty-nine in
alternate years (see 53. 4). And the Near Year foot race at Olympia (see
53. 3), Sparta (see 160. d), Jerusalem (Hooke: *Origin of Early Semitic Ritual*,
1935, p. 53), and Babylon (Langdon: *Epic of Creation*, lines 57 and 58),
was run for the sacred kingship, as at Argos. A Sun-king must be swift.

4. The Hydra (see 34. 3 and 60. h), destroyed by Heracles, seems to
have personified this college of water-providing priestesses (see 124. 2–4),
and the myth of the Danaids apparently records two Hellenic attempts to
seize their sanctuary, the first of which failed signally. After the second,
successful attempt, the Hellenic leader married the Chief-priestess, and
distributed the water-priestesses as wives among his chieftains. 'The
street called Apheta' will have been the starting-point in the girls' race
for the office of Chief-priestess; but also used in the men's foot race for
the sacred kingship (see 53. 3 and 160. d). Lynceus, a royal title in Messene
too (see 74. 1), means 'of the lynx' – the caracal, a sort of lion, famous for
its sharp sight.

5. 'Aegyptus' and 'Danaus' seem to have been early titles of Theban
co-kings; and since it was a widespread custom to bury the sacred king's
head at the approaches of a city, and thus protect it against invasion
(see 146. 2), the supposed heads of Aegyptus's sons buried at Lerna were
probably those of successive sacred kings. The Egyptians were called
Melampodes ('black feet') because they paddled about in the black Nile
mud during the sowing season.

6. A later, monogamous, society represented the Danaids with their

leaking water-pots as undergoing eternal punishment for matricide. But in the icon from which this story derived, they were performing a necessary charm: sprinkling water on the ground to produce rain showers by sympathetic magic (see 41. 5 and 68. 1). It seems that the sieve, or leaking pot, remained a distinguishing mark of the wise woman many centuries after the abolition of the Danaid colleges: Philostratus writes (*Life of Apollonius of Tyana* vi. 11) of 'women with sieves in their hands who go about pretending to heal cattle for simple cowherds.'

7. Hypermnestra's and Lynceus's beacon-fires will have been those lighted at the Argive Spring Festival to celebrate the triumph of the Sun. It may be that at Argos the sacred king was put to death with a long needle thrust through his heart: a comparatively merciful end.

8. The Thesmophoria ('due offerings') were agricultural orgies celebrated at Athens (see 48. *b*), in the course of which the severed genitals of the sacred king, or his surrogate, were carried in a basket; these were replaced in more civilized times by phallus-shaped loaves and live serpents. Apollo Lycius may mean 'Apollo of the Light', rather than 'Wolfish Apollo', but the two concepts were connected by the wolves' habit of howling at the full moon.

# 61

## LAMIA

BELUS had a beautiful daughter, Lamia, who ruled in Libya, and on whom Zeus, in acknowledgement of her favours, bestowed the singular power of plucking out and replacing her eyes at will. She bore him several children, but all of them except Scylla were killed by Hera in a fit of jealousy. Lamia took her revenge by destroying the children of others, and behaved so cruelly that her face turned into a nightmareish mask.

*b.* Later, she joined the company of the Empusae, lying with young men and sucking their blood while they slept.[1]

1. Diodorus Siculus: xx. 41; Suidas *sub* Lamia; Plutarch: *On Curiosity* 2; Scholiast on Aristophanes's *Peace* 757; Strabo: i. 11. 8; Eustathius on Homer p. 1714; Aristotle: *Ethics* vii. 5.

\*

1. Lamia was the Libyan Neith, the Love-and-Battle goddess, also named Anatha and Athene (see 8. *1* and 25. *2*), whose worship the

Achaeans suppressed; like Alphito of Arcadia, she ended as a nursery bogey (see 52. 7). Her name, Lamia, seems to be akin to *lamyros* ('gluttonous'), from *laimos* ('gullet') – thus, of a woman: 'lecherous' – and her ugly face is the prophylactic Gorgon mask worn by her priestesses during their Mysteries (see 33. 3), of which infanticide was an integral part. Lamia's removable eyes are perhaps deduced from a picture of the goddess about to bestow mystic sight on a hero by proffering him an eye (see 73. 8). The Empusae were incubae (see 55. 1).

# 62

## LEDA

SOME say that when Zeus fell in love with Nemesis, she fled from him into the water and became a fish; he pursued her as a beaver [?], ploughing up the waves. She leaped ashore, and transformed herself into this wild beast or that, but could not shake Zeus off, because he borrowed the form of even fiercer and swifter beasts. At last she took to the air as a wild goose; he became a swan, and trod her triumphantly at Rhamnus in Attica. Nemesis shook her feathers resignedly, and came to Sparta, where Leda, wife of King Tyndareus, presently found a hyacinth-coloured egg lying in a marsh, which she brought home and hid in a chest: from it Helen of Troy was hatched.[1] But some say that this egg dropped from the moon, like the egg that, in ancient times, plunged into the river Euphrates and, being towed ashore by fishes and hatched by doves, broke open to reveal the Syrian Goddess of Love.[2]

*b.* Others say that Zeus, pretending to be a swan pursued by an eagle, took refuge in Nemesis's bosom, where he ravished her and that, in due process of time, she laid an egg, which Hermes threw between Leda's thighs, as she sat on a stool with her legs apart. Thus Leda gave birth to Helen, and Zeus placed the images of Swan and Eagle in the Heavens, to commemorate this ruse.[3]

*c.* The most usual account, however, is that it was Leda herself with whom Zeus companied in the form of a swan beside the river Eurotas; that she laid an egg from which were hatched Helen, Castor, and Polydeuces; and that she was consequently deified as the goddess

Nemesis.[4] Now, Leda's husband Tyndareus had also lain with her the same night and, though some hold that all these three were Zeus's children – and Clytaemnestra too, who had been hatched, with Helen, from a second egg – others record that Helen alone was a daughter of Zeus, and that Castor and Polydeuces were Tyndareus's sons;[5] others again, that Castor and Clytaemnestra were children of Tyndareus, while Helen and Polydeuces were children of Zeus.[6]

1. Athenaeus, quoting Homer's *Cypria* p. 334b; Apollodorus: iii. 10. 7; Sappho: *Fragment* 105; Pausanias: i. 33. 7; Eratosthenes: *Catasterismoi* 25.
2. Athenaeus: 57 f.; Plutarch: *Symposiacs* ii. 3. 3; Hyginus: *Fabula* 197.
3. Hyginus: *Poetic Astronomy* ii. 8.
4. Lactantius: i. 21; Hyginus: *Fabula* 77; First Vatican Mythographer: 78 and 204.
5. Homer: *Odyssey* xi. 299; *Iliad* iii. 426; Euripides: *Helena* 254, 1497 and 1680.
6. Pindar: *Nemean Odes* x. 80; Apollodorus: iii. 10. 6–7.

\*

1. Nemesis was the Moon-goddess as Nymph (see 32. 2) and, in the earliest form of the love-chase myth, she pursued the sacred king through his seasonal changes of hare, fish, bee, and mouse – or hare, fish, bird, and grain of wheat – and finally devoured him. With the victory of the patriarchal system, the chase was reversed: the goddess now fled from Zeus, as in the English ballad of the Coal-black Smith (see 89. 2). She had changed into an otter or beaver to pursue the fish, and Castor's name ('beaver') is clearly a survival of this myth, whereas that of Polydeuces ('much sweet wine') records the character of the festivities during which the chase took place.

2. *Lada* is said to be the Lycian (i.e. Cretan) word for 'woman', and Leda was the goddess Latona, or Leto, or Lat, who bore Apollo and Artemis at Delos (see 14. 2). The hyacinth-coloured egg recalls the blood-red Easter egg of the Druids, called the *glain*, for which they searched every year by the seashore; in Celtic myth it was laid by the goddess as sea-serpent. The story of its being thrown between Leda's thighs may have been deduced from a picture of the goddess seated on the birth-stool, with Apollo's head protruding from her womb.

3. Helen[a] and Helle, or Selene, are local variants of the Moon-goddess (see 43. 1; 70. 8; and 159. 1), whose identity with Lucian's Syrian goddess is emphasized by Hyginus. But Hyginus's account is confused: it was the goddess herself who laid the world-egg after coupling with the serpent

Ophion, and who hatched it on the waters, adopting the form of a dove. She herself rose from the Void (see 1. *a*). Helen had two temples near Sparta: one at Therapnae, built on a Mycenaean site; another at Dendra, connected with a tree cult, as her Rhodian shrine also was (see 88. *10*). Pollux (x. 191) mentions a Spartan festival called the Helenephoria, closely resembling Athene's Thesmophoria at Athens (see 48. *b*), during which certain unmentionable objects were carried in a special basket called a *helene*; such a basket Helen herself carries in reliefs showing her accompanied by the Dioscuri. The objects may have been phallic emblems; she was an orgiastic goddess.

4. Zeus tricked Nemesis, the goddess of the Peloponnesian swan cult, by appealing to her pity, exactly as he had tricked Hera of the Cretan cuckoo cult (see 12. *a*). This myth refers, it seems, to the arrival at Cretan or Pelasgian cities of Hellenic warriors who, to begin with, paid homage to the Great Goddess and provided her priestesses with obedient consorts, but eventually wrested the supreme sovereignty from her.

# 63

## IXION

IXION, a son of Phlegyas, the Lapith king, agreed to marry Dia, daughter of Eioneus, promising rich bridal gifts and inviting Eioneus to a banquet; but had laid a pitfall in front of the palace, with a great charcoal fire underneath, into which the unsuspecting Eioneus fell and was burned.

*b.* Though the lesser gods thought this a heinous deed, and refused to purify Ixion, Zeus, having behaved equally ill himself when in love, not only purified him but brought him to eat at his table.

*c.* Ixion was ungrateful, and planned to seduce Hera who, he guessed, would be glad of a chance to revenge herself on Zeus for his frequent unfaithfulness. Zeus, however, reading Ixion's intentions, shaped a cloud into a false Hera with whom Ixion, being too far gone in drink to notice the deception, duly took his pleasure. He was surprised in the act by Zeus, who ordered Hermes to scourge him mercilessly until he repeated the words: 'Benefactors deserve honour', and then bind him to a fiery wheel which rolled without cease through the sky.

*d.* The false Hera, afterwards called Nephele, bore Ixion the outcast child Centaurus who, when he grew to manhood, is said to have sired horse-centaurs on Magnesian mares, of whom the most celebrated was the learned Cheiron.[1]

1. Scholiast on Apollonius Rhodius: iii. 62; Hyginus: *Fabulae* 33 and 62; Pindar: *Pythian Odes* ii. 33–89, with scholiast; Lucian: *Dialogues of the Gods* 6; Scholiast on Euripides's *Phoenician Women* 1185.

\*

1. Ixion's name, formed from *ischys* ('strength') and *io* ('moon') (see 52. 2), also suggests *ixias* ('mistletoe'). As an oak-king with mistletoe genitals (see 50. 2), representing the thunder-god, he ritually married the rain-making Moon-goddess; and was then scourged, so that his blood and sperm would fructify the earth (see 116. 4), beheaded with an axe, emasculated, spread-eagled to a tree, and roasted; after which his kinsmen ate him sacramentally. *Eion* is the Homeric epithet for a river; but Dia's father is called Deioneus, meaning 'ravager', as well as Eioneus.

2. The Moon-goddess of the oak-cult was known as Dia ('of the sky'), a title of the Dodonan Oak-goddess (see 51. 1) and therefore of Zeus's wife Hera. That old-fashioned kings called themselves Zeus (see 45. 2; 68. 1; and 156. 4) and married Dia of the Rain Clouds, naturally displeased the Olympian priests, who misinterpreted the ritual picture of the spread-eagled Lapith king as recording his punishment for impiety, and invented the anecdote of the cloud. On an Etruscan mirror, Ixion is shown spread-eagled to a fire-wheel, with mushroom tinder at his feet; elsewhere, he is bound in the same 'fivefold bond' with which the Irish hero Curoi tied Cuchulain – bent backwards into a hoop (Philostratus: *Life of Apollonius of Tyana* vii. 12), with his ankles, wrists, and neck tied together, like Osiris in the *Book of the Dead*. This attitude recalls the burning wheels rolled downhill at European midsummer festivities, as a sign that the sun has reached its zenith and must now decline again until the winter solstice. Ixion's pitfall is unmetaphorical: surrogate victims were needed for the sacred king, such as prisoners taken in battle or, failing these, travellers caught in traps. The myth seems to record a treaty made by Zeus's Hellenes with the Lapiths, Phlegyans, and Centaurs, which was broken by the ritual murder of Hellenic travellers and the seizure of their womenfolk; the Hellenes demanded, and were given, an official apology.

3. Horses were sacred to the moon, and hobby-horse dances, designed to make rain fall, have apparently given rise to the legend that the Centaurs were half horse, half man. The earliest Greek representation of Centaurs – two men joined at the waist to horses' bodies – is found on a Mycenaean gem from the Heraeum at Argos; they face each other and

are dancing. A similar pair appear on a Cretan bead-seal; but, since there was no native horse cult in Crete, the motif has evidently been imported from the mainland. In archaic art, the satyrs were also pictured as hobby-horse men, but later goats. Centaurus will have been an oracular hero with a serpent's tail, and the story of Boreas's mating with mares is therefore attached to him (see 48. *e*).

# 64

## ENDYMION

ENDYMION was the handsome son of Zeus and the Nymph Calyce, an Aeolian by race though Carian by origin, and ousted Clymenus from the kingdom of Elis. His wife, known by many different names, such as Iphianassa, Hyperippe, Chromia, and Neis, bore him four sons; he also fathered fifty daughters on Selene, who had fallen desperately in love with him.[1]

*b.* Endymion was lying asleep in a cave on Carian Mount Latmus one still night when Selene first saw him, lay down by his side, and gently kissed his closed eyes. Afterwards, some say, he returned to the same cave and fell into a dreamless sleep. This sleep, from which he has never yet awakened, came upon him either at his own request, because he hated the approach of old age; or because Zeus suspected him of an intrigue with Hera; or because Selene found that she preferred gently kissing him to being the object of his too fertile passion. In any case, he has never grown a day older, and preserves the bloom of youth on his cheeks. But others say that he lies buried at Olympia, where his four sons ran a race for the vacant throne, which Epeius won.[2]

*c.* One of his defeated sons, Aetolus, later competed in a chariot-race at the funeral games of Azan, son of Arcas, the first ever celebrated in Greece. Since the spectators were unaware that they should keep off the course, Aetolus's chariot accidentally ran over Apis, son of Phoroneus, and fatally injured him. Salmoneus, who was present, banished Aetolus across the Gulf of Corinth, where he killed Dorus and his brothers and conquered the land now called Aetolia after him.[3]

1. Apollodorus: i. 7. 5–6; Pausanias: v. 8. 1 and 1. 2.
2. Apollodorus: i. 7. 6; Scholiast on Theocritus's *Idylls* iii. 49; Cicero; *Tuscan Debates* i. 38; Pausanias: v. 1. 3.

3. Pausanias: viii. 4. 2–3 and v. 1. 6; Apollodorus: i. 7. 6; Strabo: viii. 3. 33.

*

1. This myth records how an Aeolian chief invaded Elis, and accepted the consequences of marrying the Pelasgian Moon-goddess Hera's representative – the names of Endymion's wives are all moon-titles – head of a college of fifty water-priestesses (see 60. 3). When his reign ended he was duly sacrificed and awarded a hero shrine at Olympia. Pisa, the city to which Olympia belonged, is said to have meant in the Lydian (or Cretan) language 'private resting-place': namely, of the Moon (Servius on Virgil x. 179).

2. The name Endymion, from *enduein* (Latin: *inducere*), refers to the Moon's seduction of the king, as though she were one of the Empusae (see 55. *a*); but the ancients explain it as referring to *somnum ei inductum*, 'the sleep put upon him'.

3. Aetolus, like Pelops, will have driven his chariot around the Olympian stadium in impersonation of the sun (see 69. 1); and his accidental killing of Apis, which is made to account for the Elean colonization of Aetolia, seems to be deduced from a picture of the annual chariot crash, in which the king's surrogate died (see 71. 1 and 109. 4). But the foot race won by Epeius ('successor') was the earlier event (see 53. 3). The existence of an Endymion sanctuary on Mount Latmus in Caria suggests that an Aeolian colony from Elis settled there. His ritual marriage with Hera, like Ixion's, will have offended the priests of Zeus (see 63. 2).

4. Apis is the noun formed from *apios*, a Homeric adjective usually meaning 'far off' but, when applied to the Peloponnese (Aeschylus: *Suppliants* 262), 'of the pear-tree' (see 74. 6).

# 65

## PYGMALION AND GALATEA

PYGMALION, son of Belus, fell in love with Aphrodite and, because she would not lie with him, made an ivory image of her and laid it in his bed, praying to her for pity. Entering into this image, Aphrodite brought it to life as Galatea, who bore him Paphus and Metharme. Paphus, Pygmalion's successor, was the father of Cinyras, who founded the Cyprian city of Paphos and built a famous temple to Aphrodite there.[1]

1. Apollodorus: iii. 14. 3; Ovid: *Metamorphoses* x. 243 ff.; Arnobius: *Against the Nations* vi. 22.

*

1. Pygmalion, married to Aphrodite's priestess at Paphos, seems to have kept the goddess's white cult-image (cf. 1 *Samuel* xix. 13) in his bed as a means of retaining the Cyprian throne. If Pygmalion was, in fact, succeeded by a son whom this priestess bore him, he will have been the first king to impose the patrilinear system on the Cypriots. But it is more likely that, like his grandson Cinyras (see 18. 5), he refused to give up the goddess's image at the end of his eight-year reign; and that he prolonged this by marriage with another of Aphrodite's priestesses – technically his daughter, since she was heiress to the throne – who is called Metharme ('change'), to mark the innovation.

# 66

## AEACUS

THE River-god Asopus – whom some call the son of Oceanus and Tethys; some, of Poseidon and Pero; others, of Zeus and Eurynome – married Metope, daughter of the river Ladon, by whom he had two sons and either twelve or twenty daughters.[1]

b. Several of these had been carried off and ravished on various occasions by Zeus, Poseidon, or Apollo, and when the youngest, Aegina, twin sister of Thebe, one of Zeus's victims, also disappeared, Asopus set out in search of her. At Corinth he learned that Zeus was once again the culprit, went vengefully in pursuit, and found him embracing Aegina in a wood. Zeus, who was unarmed, fled ignominiously through the thickets and, when out of sight, transformed himself into a rock until Asopus had gone by; whereupon he stole back to Olympus and from the safety of its ramparts pelted him with thunderbolts. Asopus still moves slowly from the wounds he then received, and lumps of burned coal are often fetched from his river bed.[2]

c. Having thus disposed of Aegina's father, Zeus conveyed her secretly to the island then called Oenone, or Oenopia, where he lay with her in the form of an eagle, or of a flame, and cupids hovered over their couch, administering the gifts of love.[3] In course of time Hera discovered that Aegina had borne Zeus a son named Aeacus, and angrily resolved to destroy every inhabitant of Oenone, where he was now king. She introduced a serpent into one of its streams, which befouled the water and hatched out thousands of eggs; so that swarms of serpents went wriggling over the fields into all the other streams and rivers. Thick darkness and a drowsy heat spread across the island, which Aeacus had renamed Aegina, and the pestilential South Wind blew for no less than four months. Crops and pastures dried up, and famine ensued; but the islanders were chiefly plagued with thirst and, when their wine was exhausted, would crawl to the nearest stream, where they died as they drank its poisonous water.

*d.* Appeals to Zeus were in vain: the emaciated suppliants and their sacrificial beasts fell dead before his very altars, until hardly a single warm-blooded creature remained alive.[4]

*e.* One day, Aeacus's prayers were answered with thunder and lightning. Encouraged by this favourable omen, he begged Zeus to replenish the empty land, giving him as many subjects as there were ants carrying grains of corn up a near-by oak. The tree, sprung from a Dodonian acorn, was sacred to Zeus; at Aeacus's prayer, therefore, it trembled, and a rustling came from its widespread boughs, not caused by any wind. Aeacus, though terrified, did not flee, but repeatedly kissed the tree-trunk and the earth beneath it. That night, in a dream, he saw a shower of ants falling to the ground from the sacred oak, and springing up as men. When he awoke, he dismissed this as deceitful fantasy; but suddenly his son Telamon called him outside to watch a host of men approaching, and he recognized their faces from his dream. The plague of serpents had vanished, and rain was falling in a steady stream.

*f.* Aeacus, with grateful thanks to Zeus, divided the deserted city and lands among his new people, whom he called Myrmidons, that is 'ants', and whose descendants still display an ant-like thrift, patience, and tenacity. Later, these Myrmidons followed Peleus into exile from Aegina, and fought beside Achilles and Patroclus at Troy.[5]

*g.* But some say that Achilles's allies, the Myrmidons, were so named in honour of King Myrmidon, whose daughter Eurymedusa was seduced by Zeus in the form of an ant – which is why ants are sacred in Thessaly. And others tell of a nymph named Myrmex who, when her companion Athene invented the plough, boasted that she had made the discovery herself, and was turned into an ant as a punishment.[6]

*h*. Aeacus, who married Endeis of Megara, was widely renowned for his piety, and held in such honour that men longed to feast their eyes upon him. All the noblest heroes of Sparta and Athens clamoured to fight under his command, though he had made Aegina the most difficult of the Aegean islands to approach, surrounding it with sunken rocks and dangerous reefs, as a protection against pirates.[7] When all Greece was afflicted with a drought caused by Pelops's murder of the Arcadian king Stymphalus or, some say, by the Athenians' murder of Androgeus, the Delphic Oracle advised the Greeks: 'Ask Aeacus to pray for your delivery!' Thereupon every city sent a herald to Aeacus, who ascended Mount Panhellenius, the highest peak in his island, robed as a priest of Zeus. There he sacrificed to the gods, and prayed for an end to the drought. His prayer was answered by a loud thunder clap, clouds obscured the sky, and furious showers of rain soaked the whole land of Greece. He then dedicated a sanctuary to Zeus on Pan-hellenius, and a cloud settling on the mountain summit has ever since been an unfailing portent of rain.[8]

*i*. Apollo and Poseidon took Aeacus with them when they built the walls of Troy, knowing that unless a mortal joined in this work, the city would be impregnable and its inhabitants capable of defying the gods. Scarcely had they finished their task when three grey-eyed serpents tried to scale the walls. Two chose the part just completed by the gods, but tumbled down and died; the third, with a cry, rushed at Aeacus's part and forced his way in. Apollo then prophesied that Troy would fall more than once, and that Aeacus's sons would be among its captors, both in the first and fourth generations; as indeed came to pass in the persons of Telamon and Ajax.[9]

*j*. Aeacus, Minos, and Rhadamanthys were the three of Zeus's sons whom he would have most liked to spare the burden of old age. The Fates, however, would not permit this, and Zeus, by graciously accepting their ban, provided the other Olympians with a good example.[10]

*k*. When Aeacus died, he became one of the three Judges in Tartarus, where he gives laws to the shades, and is even called upon to arbitrate quarrels that may arise between the gods. Some add that he keeps the keys of Tartarus, imposes a toll and checks the ghosts brought down by Hermes against Atropos's invoice.[11]

1. Apollodorus: iii. 12. 6; Diodorus Siculus: iv. 72.

2. Diodorus Siculus: *loc. cit.*; Pindar: *Isthmian Odes* viii. 17 ff.; Callimachus: *Hymn to Delos* 78; Apollodorus: *loc. cit.*; Lactantius
   on Statius's *Thebaid* vii. 215.

3. Apollodorus: iii. 12. 6; Pindar: *loc. cit.*; Scholiast on Homer's
   *Iliad* i. 7; Pindar: *Nemean Odes* viii. 6; Ovid: *Metamorphoses* vi.
   113.

4. Hyginus: *Fabula* 52; Ovid: *Metamorphoses* vii. 520 ff.

5. Ovid: *Metamorphoses* vii. 614 ff.; Hyginus: *loc cit.*; Apollodorus:
   *loc. cit.*; Pausanias: ii. 29. 2; Strabo: viii. 6. 19 and ix. 5. 9.

6. Servius on Virgil's *Aeneid* ii. 7 and iv. 402; Clement of Alexandria: *Address to the Gentiles* ii. 39. 6.

7. Apollodorus: iii. 12. 6; Pindar: *Nemean Odes* viii. 8 ff.; Pausanias:
   ii. 29. 5.

8. Diodorus Siculus: iv. 61. 1; Clement of Alexandria: *Stromateis*
   vi. 3. 28; Pausanias: ii. 30. 4; Theophrastus: *Weather Signs* i. 24.

9. Pindar: *Olympian Odes* viii. 30 ff., with scholiast.

10. Ovid: *Metamorphoses* ix. 426 ff.

11. *Ibid.*: xiii. 25; Pindar: *Isthmian Odes* viii. 24; Apollodorus: iii. 12.
    6; Lucian: *Dialogues of the Dead* xx. 1; *Charon* 2; and *Voyage
    Below* iv.

*

1. Asopus's daughters ravished by Apollo and Poseidon will have been
colleges of Moon-priestesses in the Asopus valley of the North-eastern
Peloponnese, whose fertile lands were seized by the Aeolians. Aegina's
rape seems to record a subsequent Achaean conquest of Phlius, a city at
the headwaters of the Asopus; and an unsuccessful appeal made by their
neighbours for military aid from Corinth. Eurynome and Tethys (see
1. *a* and *d*), the names of Asopus's mother, were ancient titles of the
Moon-goddess, and 'Pero' points to *pera*, a leather bag (see 36. 1), and
thus to Athene's goat-skin aegis – as 'Aegina' also does.

2. The Aeacus myth concerns the conquest of Aegina by Phthiotian
Myrmidons, whose tribal emblem was an ant. Previously, the island
was, it seems, held by goat-cult Pelasgians, and their hostility towards the
invaders is recorded in Hera's poisoning of the streams. According to
Strabo, who always looked for reasonable explanations of myths, but
seldom looked far enough, the soil of Aegina was covered by a layer of
stones, and the Aeginetans called themselves Myrmidons because, like
ants, they had to excavate before they could till their fields, and because
they were troglodytes (Strabo: viii. 6. 16). But the Thessalian legend of
Myrmex is a simple myth of origin: the Phthiotian Myrmidons claimed
to be autochthonous, as ants are, and showed such loyalty to the laws of
their priestess, the Queen Ant, that Zeus's Hellenic representative who
married her had to become an honorary ant himself. If Myrmex was, in

fact, a title of the Mother-goddess of Northern Greece, she might well claim to have invented the plough, because agriculture had been established by immigrants from Asia Minor before the Hellenes reached Athens.

3. The Phthiotian colonists of Aegina later merged their myths with those of Achaean invaders from Phlius on the river Asopus; and, since these Phlians had retained their allegiance to the oak-oracle of Dodona (see 51. *a*), the ants are described as falling from a tree, instead of emerging from the ground.

4. In the original myth, Aeacus will have induced the rain-storm not by an appeal to Zeus, but by some such magic as Salmoneus used (see 68. *1*). His law-giving in Tartarus, like that of Minos and Rhadamanthys, suggests that an Aeginetan legal code was adopted in other parts of Greece. It probably applied to commercial, rather than criminal law, judging from the general acceptance, in Classical times, of the Aeginetan talent as the standard weight of precious metal. It was of Cretan origin and turned the scales at 100 lb. *avoirdupois*.

# 67

## SISYPHUS

Sisyphus, son of Aeolus, married Atlas's daughter Merope, the Pleiad, who bore him Glaucus, Ornytion, and Sinon, and owned a fine herd of cattle on the Isthmus of Corinth.[1]

*b*. Near him lived Autolycus, son of Chione, whose twin-brother Philammon was begotten by Apollo, though Autolycus himself claimed Hermes as his father.[2]

*c*. Now, Autolycus was a past master in theft, Hermes having given him the power of metamorphosing whatever beasts he stole, from horned to unhorned, or from black to white, and contrariwise. Thus, although Sisyphus noticed that his own herds grew steadily smaller, while those of Autolycus increased, he was unable at first to convict him of theft; and therefore, one day, engraved the inside of all his cattle's hooves with the monogram SS or, some say, with the words 'Stolen by Autolycus'. That night Autolycus helped himself as usual, and at dawn hoof-prints along the road provided Sisyphus with sufficient evidence to summon neighbours in witness of the theft. He visited Autolycus's stable, recognized his stolen beasts by their marked hooves and, leaving his witnesses to remonstrate with the thief, hurried around the house, entered by the portal, and while the argument was in progress outside seduced Autolycus's daughter Anticleia, wife to Laertes the Argive. She bore him Odysseus, the manner of whose conception is enough to account for the cunning he habitually showed, and for his nickname 'Hypsipylon'.[3]

d. Sisyphus founded Ephyra, afterwards known as Corinth, and peopled it with men sprung from mushrooms, unless it be true that Medea gave him the kingdom as a present. His contemporaries knew him as the worst knave on earth, granting only that he promoted Corinthian commerce and navigation.[4]

e. When, on the death of Aeolus, Salmoneus usurped the Thessalian throne, Sisyphus, who was the rightful heir, consulted the Delphic Oracle and was told: 'Sire children on your niece; they will avenge you!' He therefore seduced Tyro, Salmoneus's daughter, who, happening to discover that his motive was not love for her, but hatred of her father, killed the two sons she had borne him. Sisyphus entered then the market place of Larissa [? produced the dead bodies, falsely accused Salmoneus of incest and murder] and had him expelled from Thessaly.[5]

f. After Zeus's abduction of Aegina, her father the River-god Asopus came to Corinth in search of her. Sisyphus knew well what had happened to Aegina but would not reveal anything unless Asopus undertook to supply the citadel of Corinth with a perennial spring. Asopus accordingly made the spring Peirene rise behind Aphrodite's temple, where there are now images of the goddess, armed; of the Sun; and of Eros the Archer. Then Sisyphus told him all he knew.[6]

g. Zeus, who had narrowly escaped Asopus's vengeance, ordered his brother Hades to fetch Sisyphus down to Tartarus and punish him everlastingly for his betrayal of divine secrets. Yet Sisyphus would not be daunted: he cunningly put Hades himself in handcuffs by persuading him to demonstrate their use, and then quickly locking them. Thus Hades was kept a prisoner in Sisyphus's house for some days – an impossible situation, because nobody could die, even men who had been beheaded or cut in pieces; until at last Ares, whose interests were threatened, came hurrying up, set him free, and delivered Sisyphus into his clutches.

h. Sisyphus, however, kept another trick in reserve. Before descending to Tartarus, he instructed his wife Merope not to bury him; and, on reaching the Palace of Hades went straight to Persephone, and told

her that, as an unburied person, he had no right to be there but should
have been left on the far side of the river Styx. 'Let me return to the
upper world,' he pleaded, 'arrange for my burial, and avenge the
neglect shown me. My presence here is most irregular. I will be back
within three days.' Persephone was deceived and granted his request;
but as soon as Sisyphus found himself once again under the light of the
sun, he repudiated his promise to Persephone. Finally, Hermes was
called upon to hale him back by force.[7]

*i*. It may have been because he had injured Salmoneus, or because he
had betrayed Zeus's secret, or because he had always lived by robbery
and often murdered unsuspecting travellers – some say that it was
Theseus who put an end to Sisyphus's career, though this is not generally mentioned among Theseus's feats – at any rate, Sisyphus was given
an exemplary punishment.[8] The Judges of the Dead showed him a huge
block of stone – identical in size with that into which Zeus had turned
himself when fleeing from Asopus – and ordered him to roll it up the
brow of a hill and topple it down the farther slope. He has never yet
succeeded in doing so. As soon as he has almost reached the summit, he
is forced back by the weight of the shameless stone, which bounces to
the very bottom once more; where he wearily retrieves it and must
begin all over again, though sweat bathes his limbs, and a cloud of dust
rises above his head.[9]

*j*. Merope, ashamed to find herself the only Pleiad with a husband in
the Underworld – and a criminal too – deserted her six starry sisters in
the night sky and has never been seen since. And as the whereabouts of
Neleus's tomb on the Corinthian Isthmus was a secret which Sisyphus
refused to divulge even to Nestor, so the Corinthians are now equally
reticent when asked for the whereabouts of Sisyphus's own burial
place.[10]

1. Apollodorus: i. 9. 3; Pausanias: ii. 4. 3; Servius on Virgil's
   *Aeneid* ii. 79.
2. Hyginus: *Fabula* 200.
3. Polyaenus: vi. 52; Hyginus: *Fabula* 201; Suidas *sub* Sisyphus;
   Sophocles: *Ajax* 190; Scholiast on Sophocles's *Philoctetes* 417.
4. Apollodorus: i. 9. 3; Ovid: *Metamorphoses* vii. 393; Eumelus,
   quoted by Pausanias: ii. 3. 8; Homer: *Iliad* vi. 153; Scholiast on
   Aristophanes's *Acarnanians* 390; Scholiast on Sophocles's *Ajax*
   190; Tzetzes: *On Lycophron* 980; Ovid: *Heroides* xii. 203; Horace:
   *Satires* ii. 17. 12.

5. Hyginus: *Fabula* 60.
6. Pausanias: ii. 5. 1.
7. Theognis: 712 ff.; Eustathius on Homer's *Iliad* pp. 487, 631, and 1702.
8. Servius on Virgil's *Aeneid* vi. 616; Scholiast on Statius's *Thebaid* ii. 380; Hyginus: *Fabula* 38.
9. Scholiast on Homer's *Iliad* i. 180; Pausanias: x. 31. 3; Ovid: *Metamorphoses* iv. 459; Homer: *Odyssey* xi. 593–600.
10. Ovid: *Fasti* i. 175–6; Eumelus, quoted by Pausanias: ii. 2. 2.

*

1. 'Sisyphus', though the Greeks understood it to mean 'very wise', is spelt *Sesephus* by Hesychius, and is thought to be a Greek variant of Tesup, the Hittite Sun-god, identical with Atabyrius the Sun-god of Rhodes (see 42. 4 and 93. 1), whose sacred animal was a bull. Bronze statuettes and reliefs of this bull, dating from the fourteenth century B.C., have been found, marked with a sceptre and two disks on the flank, and with a trefoil on the haunch. Raids on the Sun-god's marked cattle are a commonplace in Greek myth: Odysseus's companions made them (see 170. *u*), so also did Alcyoneus, and his contemporary, Heracles (see 132. *d* and *w*). But Autolycus's use of magic in his theft from Sisyphus recalls the story of Jacob and Laban (*Genesis* xxix and xxx). Jacob, like Autolycus, had the gift of turning cattle to whatever colour he wanted, and thus diminished Laban's flocks. The cultural connexion between Corinth and Canaan, which is shown in the myths of Nisus (see 91. 1), Oedipus (see 105. 1 and 7), Alcathous (see 110. 2), and Melicertes (see 70. 2), may be Hittite. Alcyoneus also came from Corinth.

2. Sisyphus's 'shameless stone' was originally a sun-disk, and the hill up which he rolled it is the vault of Heaven; this made a familiar enough icon. The existence of a Corinthian Sun cult is well established: Helius and Aphrodite are said to have held the acropolis in succession, and shared a temple there (Pausanias: ii. 4. 7). Moreover, Sisyphus is invariably placed next to Ixion in Tartarus, and Ixion's fire-wheel is a symbol of the sun. This explains why the people of Ephyra sprang from mushrooms, mushrooms were the ritual tinder of Ixion's fire-wheel (see 63. 2), and the Sun-god demanded human burnt sacrifices to inaugurate his year. Anticleia's seduction has been deduced perhaps from a picture showing Helius's marriage to Aphrodite; and the mythographer's hostility towards Sisyphus voices Hellenic disgust at the strategic planting of non-Hellenic settlements on the narrow isthmus separating the Peloponnese from Attica. His outwitting of Hades probably refers to a sacred king's refusal to abdicate at the end of his reign (see 170. 1). To judge from the sun-bull's markings, he contrived to rule for two Great Years, represented by the sceptre and the sun-disks, and obtained the Triple-goddess's

assent, represented by the trefoil. Hypsipylon, Odysseus's nickname, is the masculine form of Hypsipyle: a title, probably, of the Moon-goddess (see 106. 3).

3. Sisyphus and Neleus were probably buried at strategic points on the Isthmus as a charm against invasion (see 101. 3 and 146. 2). A lacuna occurs in Hyginus's account of Sisyphus's revenge on Salmoneus; I have supplied a passage (para. e, above) which makes sense of the story.

4. Peirene, the spring on the citadel of Corinth where Bellerophon took Pegasus to drink (see 75. c), had no efflux and never failed (Pausanias: ii. 5. 1; Strabo: vii. 6. 21). Peirene was also the name of a fountain outside the city gate, on the way from the market-place to Lechaeum, where Peirene ('of the osiers') – whom the mythographers describe as the daughter of Achelous, or of Oebalus (Pausanias: loc. cit.); or of Asopus and Metope (Diodorus Siculus: iv. 72) – was said to have been turned into a spring when she wept for her son Cenchrias ('spotted serpent'), whom Artemis had unwittingly killed. 'Corinthian bronze' took its characteristic colour from being plunged red-hot into this spring (Pausanias: ii. 3. 3).

5. One of the seven Pleiads disappeared in early Classical times, and her absence had to be explained (see 41. 6).

6. A question remains: was the double-S really the monogram of Sisyphus? The icon illustrating the myth probably showed him examining the tracks of the stolen sheep and cattle which, since they 'parted the hoof', were formalized as CƆ. This sign stood for SS in the earliest Greek script, and could also be read as the conjoined halves of the lunar month and all that these implied – waxing and waning, increase and decline, blessing and cursing. Animals which 'parted the hoof' were self-dedicated to the Moon – they are the sacrifices ordained at the New Moon Festivals in Leviticus – and the SS will therefore have referred to Selene the Moon, alias Aphrodite, rather than to Sisyphus, who as Sun-king merely held her sacred herd in trust (see 42. 1). The figure CƆ, representing the full moon (as distinguished from O, representing the simple sun-disk) was marked on each flank of the sacred cow which directed Cadmus to the site of Thebes (see 58. f).


# 68

## SALMONEUS AND TYRO


SALMONEUS, a son, or grandson, of Aeolus and Enarete, reigned for a time in Thessaly before leading an Aeolian colony to the eastern confines of Elis, where he built the city of Salmonia near the source of the river Enipeus, a tributary of the Alpheius.[1] Salmoneus was hated by his subjects, and went so far in his royal insolence as to transfer Zeus's sacrifices to his own altars, and announce that he was Zeus. He even drove through the streets of Salmonia, dragging brazen cauldrons, bound with hide, behind his chariot to simulate Zeus's thunder, and hurling oaken torches into the air; some of these, as they fell, scorched his unfortunate subjects, who were expected to mistake them for lightning. One fine day Zeus punished Salmoneus by hurling a real thunderbolt, which not only destroyed him, chariot and all, but burned down the entire city.[2]

*b.* Alcidice, Salmoneus's wife, had died many years before, in giving birth to a beautiful daughter named Tyro. Tyro was under the charge of her stepmother Sidero, and treated with great cruelty as the cause of the family's expulsion from Thessaly; having killed the two sons she bore to her evil uncle Sisyphus. She now fell in love with the river Enipeus, and haunted its banks day after day, weeping for loneliness. But the River-god, although amused and even flattered by her passion, would not show her the least encouragement.

*c.* Poseidon decided to take advantage of this ridiculous situation. Disguising himself as the River-god, he invited Tyro to join him at the confluence of the Enipeus and the Alpheius; and there threw her into a magic sleep, while a dark wave rose up like a mountain and curled its crest to screen his knavery. When Tyro awoke, and found herself ravished, she was aghast at the deception; but Poseidon laughed as he told her to be off home and keep quiet about what had happened. Her reward, he said, would be fine twins, sons of a better father than a mere river-god.[3]

*d.* Tyro contrived to keep her secret until she bore the promised twins, but then, unable to face Sidero's anger, exposed them on a mountain. A passing horse-herd took them home with him, but not before his brood-mare had kicked the elder in the face. The horse-herd's wife reared the boys, giving the bruised one to the mare for suckling and calling him Pelias; the other, whom she called Neleus, took his savage nature from the bitch which served as his foster-mother. But some say that the twins were found floating down the Enipeus in a wooden ark. As soon as Pelias and Neleus discovered their mother's name and learned how unkindly she had been treated, they set out to avenge her. Sidero took refuge in the temple of Hera; but Pelias struck her down as she clung to the horns of the altar. This was the first of many insults that he offered the goddess.[4]

*e.* Tyro later married her uncle Cretheus, founder of Iolcus, to whom she bore Aeson, father of Jason the Argonaut; he also adopted Pelias and Neleus as his sons.[5]

*f.* After Cretheus's death, the twins came to blows: Pelias seized the throne of Iolcus, exiled Neleus, and kept Aeson a prisoner in the palace. Neleus led Cretheus's grandsons Melampus and Bias with a mixed company of Achaeans, Phthiotians, and Aeolians to the land of Messene, where he drove the Lelegans out of Pylus, and raised the city to such a height of fame that he is now acclaimed as its founder. He married Chloris; but all their twelve children, except Nestor, were eventually killed by Heracles.[6]

1. Apollodorus: i. 7. 3; Hyginus: *Poetic Astronomy* ii. 20; Strabo: viii. 3. 32.
2. Diodorus Siculus: iv. 68. 1; Apollodorus: i. 9. 7; Hyginus: *Fabula* 61.
3. Apollodorus: i. 9. 8; Homer: *Odyssey* xi. 235 ff.; Lucian: *Marine Dialogues* 13.
4. Apollodorus: *loc. cit.*; Eustathius on Homer's *Odyssey* xi. 253; Sophocles: *Tyro*, quoted by Aristotle: *Poetics* xvi. 1454.
5. Pausanias: iv. 2. 3; Apollodorus: i. 9. 11; Hyginus: *Fabula* 12.
6. Hesiod: *Theogony* 996; Scholiast on Euripides's *Alcestis* 255; Diodorus Siculus: iv. 68. 6; Pausanias: iv. 2. 3; 36. 1 and x. 29. 3; Homer: *Iliad* xi. 682.

*

1. Antigonus of Carystus (*Account of Marvellous Things* 15) records that a rain-bringing bronze wagon was kept at Crannon: which in time of drought the people drove over rough ground to shake it and make it clang – and also (as Crannonian coins show) to splash about the water from the jars which it contained. Rain always came, acccording to Antigonus. Thus Salmoneus's charm for inducing thunderstorms will have been common religious practice: like rattling pebbles in a dry gourd, tapping on oak doors, rolling stones about in a chest, dancing, beating shields, or swinging bull-roarers. He was pictured as a criminal only when the impersonation of Zeus had been forbidden by the Achaean central authority (see 45. 2). To judge from the Danaids' sieves (see 60. 6), and the Argive cow dance (see 56. 1), rain-making was originally a female prerogative – as it remains among certain primitive African tribes, such as the Hereros and the Damaras – but passed into the sacred king's hands when the Queen permitted him to act as her deputy (see 136. 4).

2. Tyro was the Goddess-mother of the Tyrians and Tyrrhenians, or Tyrsenians, and perhaps also of the Tirynthians; hers is probably a pre-Hellenic name, but supplied Greek with the word *tyrsis* ('walled city'), and so with the concept of 'tyranny'. Her ill-treatment by Sidero recalls that of Antiope by Dirce, a myth which it closely resembles (see 76. *a*); and may originally have recorded an oppression of the Tyrians by their neighbours, the Sidonians. River water was held to impregnate brides who bathed in it – bathing was also a purifying ritual after menstruation, or child-birth – and it is likely that Tyro's Enipeus, like the Scamander (see 137. *3*), was invoked to take away virginity. The anecdote of Tyro's seduction by Poseidon purports to explain why Salmoneus's descendants were sometimes called 'Sons of Enipeus', which was their original home, and sometimes 'Sons of Poseidon', because of their naval fame. Her previous seduction by Sisyphus suggests that the Corinthian Sun cult had been planted at Salmonia; Antiope was also connected by marriage with Sisyphus (see 76. *b*).

3. Tyro's ark, in which she sent the twins floating down the Enipeus, will have been of alder-wood, like that in which Rhea Silvia sent Romulus and Remus floating down the Tiber. The quarrel of Pelias and Neleus, with that of Eteocles and Polyneices, Acrisius and Proetus, Atreus and Thyestes, and similar pairs of kings, seems to record the breakdown of the system by which king and tanist ruled alternately for forty-nine or fifty months in the same kingdom (see 69. *1*; 73. *a* and 106. *b*).

4. The horns of the altar to which Sidero clung were those habitually fixed to the cult-image of the Cow-goddess Hera, Astarte, Io, Isis, or Hathor; and Pelias seems to have been an Achaean conqueror who forcibly reorganized the Aeolian Goddess cult of Southern Thessaly. In Palestine horned altars; like that to which Joab clung (1 *Kings* ii. 28, etc.), survived the dethronement of the Moon-cow and her golden Calf.

# 69

## ALCESTIS

ALCESTIS, the most beautiful of Pelias's daughters, was asked in marriage by many kings and princes. Not wishing to endanger his political position by refusing any of them, and yet clearly unable to satisfy more than one, Pelias let it be known that he would marry Alcestis to the man who could yoke a wild boar and a lion to his chariot and drive them around the race-course. At this, Admetus King of Pherae summoned

Apollo, whom Zeus had bound to him for one year as a herdsman, and asked: 'Have I treated you with the respect due to your godhead?' 'You have indeed,' Apollo assented, 'and I have shown my gratitude by making all your ewes drop twins.' 'As a final favour, then,' pleaded Admetus, 'pray help me to win Alcestis, by enabling me to fulfil Pelias's conditions.' 'I shall be pleased to do so,' replied Apollo. Heracles lent him a hand with the taming of the wild beasts and presently Admetus was driving his chariot around the race-course at Iolcus, drawn by this savage team.[1]

b. It is not known why Admetus omitted the customary sacrifice to Artemis before marrying Alcestis, but the goddess was quick enough to punish him. When, flushed with wine, anointed with essences and garlanded with flowers, he entered the bridal chamber that night, he recoiled in horror. No lovely naked bride awaited him on the marriage couch, but a tangled knot of hissing serpents. Admetus ran shouting for Apollo, who kindly intervened with Artemis on his behalf. The neglected sacrifice having been offered at once, all was well, Apollo even obtaining Artemis's promise that, when the day of Admetus's death came, he should be spared on condition that a member of his family died voluntarily for love of him.

c. This fatal day came sooner than Admetus expected. Hermes flew into the palace one morning and summoned him to Tartarus. General consternation prevailed; but Apollo gained a little time for Admetus by making the Three Fates drunk, and thus delayed the fatal scission of his life's thread. Admetus ran in haste to his old parents, clasped their knees, and begged each of them in turn to surrender him the butt-end of existence. Both roundly refused, saying that they still derived much enjoyment from life, and that he should be content with his appointed lot, like everyone else.

d. Then, for love of Admetus, Alcestis took poison and her ghost descended to Tartarus; but Persephone considered it an evil thing that a wife should die instead of a husband. 'Back with you to the upper air!' she cried.[2]

e. Some tell the tale differently. They say that Hades came in person to fetch Admetus and that, when he fled, Alcestis volunteered to take his place; but Heracles arrived unexpectedly with a new wild-olive club, and rescued her.[3]

1. Hyginus: *Fabula* 50; Apollodorus: iii. 10. 4; Callimachus: *Hymn*

to Apollo 47–54; Scholiast on Euripides's *Alcestis* 2; Fulgentius: i. 27.

2. Apollodorus: i. 9. 15.

3. Euripides: *Alcestis*.

*

1. The yoking of a lion and a wild boar to the same chariot is the theme of a Theban myth (see 106. *a*), where the original meaning has been equally obscured. Lion and boar were the animal symbols given to the first and second halves of the Sacred Year, respectively – they constantly occur, in opposition, on Etruscan vases – and the oracle seems to have proposed a peaceful settlement of the traditional rivalry between the sacred king and his tanist. This was that the kingdom should be divided in halves, and that they should reign concurrently, as Proetus and Acrisius eventually did at Argos (see 73. *a*), rather than keep it entire, and rule alternately – as Polyneices and Eteocles did at Thebes (see 106. *b*). A circuit of the race-course in a chariot was a proof of royalty (see 64. *3*).

2. Artemis was hostile to monogamic marriage because she belonged to the pre-Hellenic cult in which women mated promiscuously outside their own clans; so the Hellenes propitiated her with wedding sacrifices, carrying torches of the chaste hawthorn in her honour. The patriarchal practice of suttee, attested here and in the myths of Evadne (see 106. *l*) and Polyxena (see 168. *k*), grew from the Indo-European custom which forbade widows to remarry; once this ban was relaxed, suttee became less attractive (see 74. *a*).

3. In the first version of this myth, Persephone refused Alcestis's sacrifice – Persephone represents the matriarchal point of view. In the second version, Heracles forbade it, and was chosen as the instrument of Zeus's will, that is to say of patriarchal ethics, on the ground that he once harrowed Hell and rescued Theseus (see 103. *d*). Wild-olive served in Greece to expel evil influences (see 119. *2*); as the birch did in Italy and northern Europe (see 52. *3*).

# 70

## ATHAMAS

ATHAMAS the Aeolian, brother of Sisyphus and Salmoneus, ruled over Boeotia. At Hera's command, he married Nephele, a phantom whom Zeus created in her likeness when he wished to deceive Ixion the

Lapith, and who was now wandering disconsolately about the halls of
Olympus. She bore Athamas two sons: Phrixus and Leucon, and a
daughter, Helle. But Athamas resented the disdain in which Nephele
held him and, falling in love with Ino, daughter of Cadmus, brought
her secretly to his palace at the foot of Mount Laphystium, where he
begot Learchus and Melicertes on her.

*b*. Learning about her rival from the palace servants, Nephele returned in a fury to Olympus, complaining to Hera that she had been
insulted. Hera took her part, and vowed: 'My eternal vengeance shall
fall upon Athamas and his House!'

*c*. Nephele thereupon went back to Mount Laphystium, where she
publicly reported Hera's vow, and demanded that Athamas should die.
But the men of Boeotia, who feared Athamas more than Hera, would
not listen to Nephele; and the women of Boeotia were devoted to Ino,
who now persuaded them to parch the seed-corn, without their husbands' knowledge, so that the harvest would fail. Ino foresaw that
when the grain was due to sprout, but no blade appeared, Athamas
would send to ask the Delphic Oracle what was amiss. She had already
bribed Athamas's messengers to bring back a false reply: namely, that
the land would regain its fertility only if Nephele's son Phrixus were
sacrificed to Zeus on Mount Laphystium.

*d*. This Phrixus was a handsome young man, with whom his aunt
Biadice, Cretheus's wife, had fallen in love, and whom, when he
rebuffed her advances, she accused of trying to ravish her. The men of
Boeotia, believing Biadice's story, applauded Apollo's wise choice of
a sin-offering and demanded that Phrixus should die; whereupon
Athamas, loudly weeping, led Phrixus to the mountain top. He was
on the point of cutting his throat when Heracles, who happened to
be in the neighbourhood, came running up and wrested the sacrificial
flint from his hand. 'My father Zeus,' Heracles exclaimed, 'loathes
human sacrifices!' Nevertheless, Phrixus would have perished despite
this plea, had not a winged golden ram, supplied by Hermes at Hera's
order – or, some say, by Zeus himself – suddenly flown down to the
rescue from Olympus.

'Climb on my back!' cried the ram, and Phrixus obeyed.

'Take me too!' pleaded Helle. 'Do not leave me to the mercy of my
father.'

*e*. So Phrixus pulled her up behind him, and the ram flew eastwards,
making for the land of Colchis, where Helius stables his horses. Before

long, Helle felt giddy and lost her hold; she fell into the straits between Europe and Asia, now called the Hellespont in her honour; but Phrixus reached Colchis safely, and there sacrificed the ram to Zeus the Deliverer. Its golden fleece became famous a generation later when the Argonauts came in search of it.

*f.* Overawed by the miracle of Mount Laphystium, Athamas's messengers confessed that they had been bribed by Ino to bring back a false reply from Delphi; and presently all her wiles, and Biadice's, came to light. Nephele thereupon again demanded that Athamas should die, and the sacrificial fillet, which Phrixus had worn, was placed on his head; only Heracles's renewed intervention saved him from death.

*g.* But Hera was incensed with Athamas and drove him mad, not only on Nephele's account, but because he had connived at Ino's harbouring of the infant Dionysus, Zeus's bastard by her sister Semele, who was living in the palace disguised as a girl. Seizing his bow, Athamas suddenly yelled: 'Look, a white stag! Stand back while I shoot!' So saying, he transfixed Learchus with an arrow, and proceeded to tear his still-quivering body into pieces.

*h.* Ino snatched up Melicertes, her younger son, and fled; but would hardly have escaped Athamas's vengeance, had not the infant Dionysus temporarily blinded him, so that he began to flog a she-goat in mistake for her. Ino ran to the Molurian Rock, where she leaped into the sea and was drowned – this rock afterwards became a place of ill repute, because the savage Sciron used to hurl strangers from it. But Zeus, remembering Ino's kindness to Dionysus, would not send her ghost down to Tartarus and deified her instead as the Goddess Leucothea. He also deified her son Melicertes as the God Palaemon, and sent him to the Isthmus of Corinth riding on dolphin-back; the Isthmian Games, founded in his honour by Sisyphus, are still celebrated there every fourth year.

*i.* Athamas, now banished from Boeotia, and childless because his remaining son, Leucon, had sickened and died, enquired from the Delphic Oracle where he should settle, and was told: 'Wherever wild beasts entertain you to dinner.' Wandering aimlessly northward, without food or drink, he came on a wolf-pack devouring a flock of sheep in a desolate Thessalian plain. The wolves fled at his approach, and he and his starving companions ate what mutton had been left. Then he recalled the oracle and, having adopted Haliartus and Conorea, his Corinthian grand-nephews, founded a city which he called Alos, from

his wanderings, or from his serving-maid Alos; and the country was
called Athamania; afterwards he married Themisto and raised a new
family.[1]

*j.* Others tell the tale differently. Omitting Athamas's marriage to
Nephele, they say that one day, after the birth of Learchus and Melicertes, his wife Ino went out hunting and did not return. Bloodstains on
a torn tunic convinced him that she had been killed by wild beasts; but
the truth was that a sudden Bacchic frenzy had seized her when she
was attacked by a lynx. She had strangled it, flayed it with her teeth and
nails, and gone off, dressed only in the pelt, for a prolonged revel on
Mount Parna ;us. After an interval of mourning, Athamas married
Themisto who, a year later, bore him twin sons. Then, to his dismay,
he learned that Ino was still alive. He sent for her at once, installed her
in the palace nursery, and told Themisto: 'We have a likely-looking
nurse-maid, a captive taken in the recent raid on Mount Cithaeron.'
Themisto, whom her maids soon undeceived, visited the nursery, pretending not to know who Ino was. She told her: 'Pray, nurse, get
ready a set of white woollen garments for my two sons, and a set of
mourning garments for those of my unfortunate predecessor Ino. They
are to be worn tomorrow.'

*k.* The following day, Themisto ordered her guards to break into
the royal nursery and kill the twins who were dressed in mourning, but
spare the other two. Ino, however, guessing what was in Themisto's
mind, had provided white garments for her own sons, and mourning
garments for her rival's. Thus Themisto's twins were murdered, and
the news sent Athamas mad; he shot Learchus dead, mistaking him for
a stag, but Ino escaped with Melicertes, sprang into the sea, and became
immortal.

*l.* Others, again, say that Phrixus and Helle were Nephele's children
by Ixion. One day, as they wandered in a wood, their mother came
upon them in a Bacchic frenzy, leading a golden ram by the horns.
'Look,' she babbled, 'here is a son of your cousin Theophane. She had
too many suitors, so Poseidon changed her into a ewe and himself into
a ram, and tupped her on the Island of Crumissa.'

'What happened to the suitors, mother?' asked little Helle.

'They became wolves,' Ino answered, 'and howl for Theophane all
night long. Now ask me no more questions, but climb on this ram's
back, both of you, and ride away to the kingdom of Colchis, where
Helius's son Aeëtes reigns. As soon as you arrive, sacrifice it to Ares.'

*m*. Phrixus carried out his mother's strange instructions, and hung up the golden fleece in a temple of Ares at Colchis, where it was guarded by a dragon; and, many years later his son Presbon, or Cytisorus, coming to Orchomenus from Colchis, rescued Athamas as he was being sacrificed for a sin-offering.[2]

1. Pausanias: i. 44. 11; ix. 34. 4–5 and 23. 3; Apollodorus: i. 7. 3 and iii. 4. 3; Hyginus: *Fabulae* 2 and 4; *Poetic Astronomy* ii. 20; Fragments of Sophocles's *Athamas*; Nonnus: *Dionysiaca* x. 1 ff.; Scholiast on Homer's *Iliad* vii. 86; Eustathius on the same; Ovid: *Metamorphoses* iv. 480–541; *Etymologicum Magnum* 70. 8; Stephanus of Byzantium *sub* Athamania.
2. Hyginus: *Fabulae* 1, 3, 5 and 88; Fragments of Euripides's *Ino*; Herodotus: vii. 197; Pausanias: ix. 34. 5.

*

1. Athamas's name is connected in the myth with Athamania, the city which he is said to have founded in the Thessalian wilderness; but seems formed, rather, from *Ath* ('high'), and *amaein* ('to reap') – meaning 'the king dedicated to the Reaper on High', namely the Goddess of the Harvest Moon. The conflict between his rival wives Ino and Nephele was probably one between early Ionian settlers in Boeotia, who had adopted the worship of the Corn-goddess Ino, and the pastoral Aeolian invaders. An attempt to make over the agricultural rites of the Ionian goddess Ino to the Aeolian thunder-god and his wife Nephele, the rain-cloud, seems to have been foiled by the priestesses' parching of the seed-corn.

2. The myth of Athamas and Phrixus records the annual mountain sacrifice of the king, or of the king's surrogate – first a boy dressed in a ram's fleece, and later a ram – during the New Year rain-inducing festival which shepherds celebrated at the Spring Equinox. Zeus's ram-sacrifice on the summit of Mount Pelion, not far from Laphystium, took place in April when, according to the Zodiac, the Ram was in the ascendant; the chief men of the district used to struggle up, wearing white sheep-skins (Dicearchus: ii. 8), and the rite still survives there today in the mock-sacrifice and resurrection of an old man who wears a black sheep's mask (see 148. *10*). The mourning garments, ordered for the children sentenced to death, suggest that a black fleece was worn by the victim, and white ones by the priest and the spectators. Biadice's love for Phrixus recalls Potiphar's wife's love for Joseph, a companion myth from Canaan: much the same story is also told of Anteia and Bellerophon (see 75. *a*), Cretheis and Peleus (see 81. *g*), Phaedra and Hippolytus (see 101. *a–g*), Phylonome and Tenes (see 161. *g*).

3. That Nephele ('cloud') was Hera's gift to Athamas and created

in her own image, suggests that in the original version Athamas the
Aeolian king himself represented the thunder-god, like his predecessor
Ixion (see 63. *1*), and his brother Salmoneus (see 68. *1*); and that, when he
married Themisto (who, in Euripides's version of the myth, is Ino's
rival), she took the part of the thunder-god's wife.

4. Ino was Leucothea, 'the White Goddess', and proved her identity
with the Triple Muse by revelling on Mount Parnassus. Her name ('she
who makes sinewy') suggests ithyphallic orgies, and the sturdy growth
of corn; boys will have been bloodily sacrificed to her before every
winter sowing. Zeus is himself credited with having defied Ino in gratitude for her kindness to Dionysus, and Athamas bears an agricultural
name in her honour; in other words, the Ionian farmers settled their
religious differences with the Aeolian shepherds to their own advantage.

5. The myth, however, is a medley of early cult elements. The sacramental Zagreus cult, which became that of Dionysus the Kid (see 30. *3*),
is suggested when Athamas takes Ino for a she-goat; the sacramental
Actaeon cult is suggested when he takes Learchus for a stag, shoots him,
and tears him in pieces (see 22. *1*). Ino's younger son Melicertes is the
Canaanite Heracles Melkarth ('protector of the city'), *alias* Moloch who,
as the new-born solar king, comes riding on dolphin-back towards the
isthmus; and whose death, at the close of his four years' reign, was celebrated at the Isthmian Funeral Games. Infants were sacrificed to Melicertes on the Island of Tenedos, and probably also at Corinth (see 156.2),
as they were to Moloch at Jerusalem (*Leviticus* xviii. 21 and 1 *Kings* xi. 7).

6. Only when Zeus became god of the clear sky and usurped the
goddess's solar attributes did the fleece become golden – thus the First
Vatican Mythographer says that it was 'the fleece in which Zeus ascended
the sky' – but while he was inducer of the thunderstorm it had been
purple-black (Simonides: *Fragment* 21).

7. In one version of the myth (Hippias: *Fragment* 12), Ino is called
Gorgopis ('grim-faced'), a title of Athene's; and savage Sciron who
hurled travellers over the cliff, took his name from the white parasol –
more properly a paralune – carried in Athene's processions. The Molurian Rock was evidently the cliff from which the sacred king, or his
surrogates, were thrown into the sea in honour of the Moon-goddess
Athene, or Ino, the parasol being apparently used to break the fall (see
89. *6*; 92. *3*; 96. *3* and 98. *7*).

8. Helle's drowning parallels Ino's. Both are Moon-goddesses, and the
myth is ambivalent: it represents the nightly setting of the Moon and, at
the same time, the abandonment of Helle's lunar cult in favour of Zeus's
solar one. Both are equally Sea-goddesses: Helle gave her name to the
junction of two seas, Ino-Leucothea appeared to Odysseus in the guise of
a seamew and rescued him from drowning (see 170. *y*).

9. Athamas's tribe is more likely to have migrated from Boeotian Mount Laphystium and Athamania to Thessalian Mount Laphystius and Athamania, than contrariwise; he had a strong connexion with Corinth, the kingdom of his brother Sisyphus, and is said to have founded the city of Acraephia to the east of Lake Copais, where there was a 'Field of Athamas' (Stephanus of Byzantium *sub* Acraephia; Pausanias: ix. 24. 1). Several of his sons are also credited with the foundation of Boeotian cities. He is indeed plausibly described as a son of Minyas, and King of Orchomenus, which would have given him power over the Copaic Plain and Mount Laphystium (Scholiast on Apollonius Rhodius: i. 230; Hellanicus on Apollonius Rhodius: iii. 265) and allied him with Corinth against the intervening states of Athens and Thebes. The probable reason for the Athamanians' northward wanderings into Thessaly was the disastrous war fought between Orchomenus and Thebes, recorded in the Heracles cycle (see 121. *d*). Nephele's ragings on the mountain recall the daughters of Minyas who are said to have been overtaken by a Bacchic frenzy on Mount Laphystium (Scholiast on Lycophron's *Alexandra* 1237): the alleged origin of the Agrionia festival at Orchomenus.

# 71

## THE MARES OF GLAUCUS

GLAUCUS, son of Sisyphus and Merope, and father of Bellerophon, lived at Potniae near Thebes where, scorning the power of Aphrodite, he refused to let his mares breed. He hoped by this means to make them more spirited than other contestants in the chariot races which were his chief interest. But Aphrodite was vexed; and complained to Zeus that he had gone so far as to feed the mares on human flesh. When Zeus permitted her to take what action she pleased against Glaucus, she led the mares out by night to drink from a well sacred to herself, and graze on a herb called hippomanes which grew at its lip. This she did just before Jason celebrated the funeral games of Pelias on the seashore at Iolcus; and no sooner had Glaucus yoked the mares to his chariot pole than they bolted, overthrew the chariot, dragged him along the ground entangled in the reins, for the whole length of the stadium, and then ate him alive.[1] But some say that this took place at Potniae, not Iolcus; and others, that Glaucus leaped into the sea in grief for Melicertes son of Athamas; or that Glaucus was the name given to Melicertes after his death.[2]

*b.* Glaucus's ghost, called the Taraxippus, or Horse-scarer, still haunts the Isthmus of Corinth, where his father Sisyphus first taught him the charioteer's art, and delights in scaring the horses at the Isthmian Games, thus causing many deaths. Another horse-scarer is the ghost of Myrtilus whom Pelops killed. He haunts the stadium at Olympia, where charioteers offer him sacrifices in the hope of avoiding destruction.[3]

1. Homer: *Iliad* vi. 154; Apollodorus: ii. 3. 1; Pausanias: vi. 20. 9; Hyginus: *Fabulae* 250 and 273; Ovid: *Ibis* 557; Scholiast on Euripides's *Orestes* 318 and *Phoenician Women* 1131; Aelian: *Nature of Animals* xv. 25.
2. Strabo: ix. 2. 24; Athenaeus: vii. pp. 296–7.
3. Pausanias: vi. 20. 8.

*

*1.* The myths of Lycurgus (see 27. *e*) and Diomedes (see 130. *b*) suggest that the pre-Hellenic sacred king was torn in pieces at the close of his reign by women disguised as mares. In Hellenic times, this ritual was altered to death by being dragged at the tail of a four-horse chariot, as in the myths of Hippolytus (see 101. *g*), Laius (see 105. *d*), Oenomaus (see 109. *j*), Abderus (see 130. *1*), Hector (see 163. *4*), and others. At the Babylonian New Year festivities, when the Sun-god Marduk, incarnate in the King, was believed to be in Hell fighting the sea-monster Tiamat (see 73. 7), a chariot drawn by four masterless horses was let loose in the streets, to symbolize the chaotic state of the world during the demise of the crown; presumably with a puppet charioteer entangled in the reins. If the Babylonian ritual was of common origin with the Greek, a boy *interrex* will have succeeded to the King's throne and bed during his demise of a single day and, at dawn next morning, been dragged at the chariot's tail – as in the myths of Phaëthon (see 42. 2) and Hippolytus (see 101. *g*). The King was then reinstalled on his throne.

*2.* The myth of Glaucus is unusual: he is not only involved in a chariot-wreck, but eaten by the mares. That he despised Aphrodite and would not let his mares breed, suggests a patriarchal attempt to suppress Theban erotic festivities in honour of the Potniae, 'powerful ones', namely the Moon triad.

*3.* The Taraxippus seems to have been an archaic royal statue, marking the first turn of the race-course; horses new to the stadium were distracted by it at the moment when their charioteer was trying to cut in and take the inner berth; but this was also the place where the chariot-crash was staged for the old king, or his *interrex*, by the removal of his linchpins (see 109. *j*).

*4.* Glaucus ('grey-green') is likely to have been in one sense the Minoan representative who visited the Isthmus (see 90. *7*) with the annual edicts; and in another Melicertes (Melkarth 'guardian of the city'), a Phoenician title of the King of Corinth, who theoretically arrived every year, new-born, on dolphin-back (see 70. *5* and 87. *2*), and was flung into the sea when his reign ended (see 96. *3*).

# 72

## MELAMPUS

MELAMPUS the Minyan, Cretheus's grandson, who lived at Pylus in Messene, was the first mortal to be granted prophetic powers, the first to practise as a physician, the first to build temples to Dionysus in Greece, and the first to temper wine with water.[1]

*b.* His brother Bias, to whom he was deeply attached, fell in love with their cousin Pero; but so many suitors came for her hand that she was promised by her father Neleus to the man who could drive off King Phylacus's cattle from Phylace. Phylacus prized these cattle above everything in the world, except his only son Iphiclus, and guarded them in person with the help of an unsleeping and unapproachable dog.

*c.* Now, Melampus could understand the language of birds, his ears having been licked clean by a grateful brood of young serpents: he had rescued these from death at the hands of his attendants and piously buried their parents' dead bodies. Moreover, Apollo, whom he met one day by the banks of the river Alpheius, had taught him to prophesy from the entrails of sacrificial victims.[2] It thus came to his knowledge that whoever tried to steal the cattle would be made a present of them, though only after being imprisoned for exactly one year. Since Bias was in despair, Melampus decided to visit Phylacus's byre by dead of night; but as soon as he laid his hand on a cow, the dog bit his leg, and Phylacus, springing up from the straw, led him away to prison. This was, of course, no more than Melampus expected.

*d.* On the evening before his year of imprisonment ended Melampus heard two woodworms talking at the end of a beam which was socketed into the wall above his head. One asked with a sigh of fatigue: 'How many days yet of gnawing, brother?'

The other worm, his mouth full of wood-dust, replied: 'We are making good progress. The beam will collapse tomorrow at dawn, if we waste no time in idle conversation.'

Melampus at once shouted: 'Phylacus, Phylacus, pray transfer me to another cell!' Phylacus, though laughing at Melampus's reasons for this request, did not deny him. When the beam duly collapsed and killed one of the women who was helping to carry out the bed, Phylacus was astounded at Melampus's prescience. 'I will grant you both your freedom and the cattle,' he said, 'if only you would cure my son Iphiclus of impotency.'

*e.* Melampus agreed. He began the task by sacrificing two bulls to Apollo, and after he had burned the thigh-bones with the fat, left their carcasses lying by the altar. Presently two vultures flew down, and one remarked to the other: 'It must be several years since we were last here – that time when Phylacus was gelding rams and we collected our perquisites.'

'I well remember it,' said the other vulture. 'Iphiclus, who was then still a child, saw his father coming towards him with a blood-stained knife, and took fright. He apparently feared to be gelded himself, because he screamed at the top of his voice. Phylacus drove the knife into the sacred pear-tree over there, for safe-keeping, while he ran to comfort Iphiclus. That fright accounts for the impotency. Look, Phylacus forgot to recover the knife! There it still is, sticking in the tree, but bark has grown over its blade, and only the end of its handle shows.'

'In that case,' remarked the first vulture, 'the remedy for Iphiclus's impotency would be to draw out the knife, scrape off the rust left by the ram's blood and administer it to him, mixed in water, every day for ten days.'

'I concur,' said the other vulture. 'But who, less intelligent than ourselves, would have the sense to prescribe such a medicine?'

*f.* Thus Melampus was able to cure Iphiclus, who soon begot a son named Podarces; and, having claimed first the cattle and then Pero, he presented her, still a virgin, to his grateful brother Bias.[3]

*g.* Now, Proetus, son of Abas, joint-king of Argolis with Acrisius, had married Stheneboea, who bore him three daughters named Lysippe, Iphinoë, and Iphianassa – but some call the two younger ones Hipponoë and Cyrianassa. Whether it was because they had offended Dionysus, or because they had offended Hera by their over-indulgence in love-affairs, or by stealing gold from her image at Tiryns, their father's capital, all three were divinely afflicted by madness and went raging on the mountains, like cows stung by the gadfly, behaving in a most disorderly fashion and assaulting travellers.[4]

*h.* Melampus, when he heard the news, came to Tiryns and offered to cure them, on condition that Proetus paid him with a third share of his kingdom.

'The price is far too high,' said Proetus brusquely; and Melampus retired.

The madness then spread to the Argive women, a great many of whom killed their children, deserted their homes, and went raving off to join Proetus's three daughters, so that no roads were safe, and sheep and cattle suffered heavy losses because the wild women tore them in pieces and devoured them raw. At this Proetus sent hastily for Melampus, to say that he accepted his terms.

'No, no.' said Melampus, 'as the disease has increased, so has my fee! Give me one third of your kingdom, and another third to my brother Bias, and I undertake to save you from this calamity. If you refuse, there will not be one Argive woman left in her home.'

When Proetus agreed, Melampus advised him: 'Vow twenty red oxen to Helius – I will tell you what to say – and all will be well.'

*i.* Proetus accordingly vowed the oxen to Helius, on condition that his daughters and their followers were cured; and Helius, who sees everything, at once promised Artemis the names of certain kings who had omitted their sacrifices to her, on condition that she persuaded Hera to remove the curse from the Argive women. Now, Artemis had recently hunted the Nymph Callisto to death for Hera's sake, so found no difficulty in carrying out her side of the bargain. This is the way that business is done in Heaven as on earth: hand washes hand.

*j.* Then Melampus, helped by Bias and a chosen company of sturdy young men, drove the disorderly crowd of women down from the mountains to Sicyon, where their madness left them, and then purified them by immersion in a holy well. Not finding Proetus's daughters among this rabble, Melampus and Bias went off again and chased all three of them to Lusi in Arcadia, where they took refuge in a cave overlooking the river Styx. There Lysippe and Iphianassa regained their sanity and were purified; but Iphinoë had died on the way.

*k.* Melampus then married Lysippe, Bias (whose wife Pero had recently died) married Iphianassa, and Proetus rewarded them both

according to his promise. But some say that Proetus's true name was
Anaxagoras.[5]

1. Apollodorus: ii. 2. 2; Athenaeus: ii. p. 45.
2. Apollodorus: i. 9. 11.
3. Homer *Odyssey* xi. 281–97, with scholiasts; Apollodorus: i. 9. 12.
4. Hesiod: *Catalogue of Women*; Apollodorus: ii. 4. 1; Diodorus
   Siculus: iv. 68; Servius on Virgil's *Eclogues* vi. 48.
5. Apollodorus: ii. 2. 1–2; Bacchylides: *Epinicia* x. 40–112; Herodotus: ix. 34; Diodorus Siculus: iv. 68; Pausanias: ii. 18. 4; iv. 36.
   3; v. 5. 5 and viii. 18. 3; Scholiast on Pindar's *Nemean Odes* ix. 13.

*

1. It was a common claim of wizards that their ears had been licked by
serpents, which were held to be incarnate spirits of oracular heroes ('The
Language of Animals' by J. R. Frazer, *Archaeological Review* i, 1888),
and that they were thus enabled to understand the language of birds and
insects (see 105. *g* and 158. *p*). Apollo's priests appear to have been more
than usually astute in claiming prophesy by this means.

2. Iphiclus's disability is factual rather than mythical: the rust of the
gelding-knife would be an appropriate psychological cure for impotence
caused by a sudden fright, and in accordance with the principles of sympathetic magic. Apollodorus describes the tree into which the knife was
thrust as an oak, but it is more likely to have been the wild pear-tree
sacred to the White Goddess of the Peloponnese (see 74. *6*), which fruits
in May, the month of enforced chastity; Phylacus had insulted the goddess by wounding her tree. The wizard's claim to have been told of
the treatment by vultures – important birds in augury (see 119. *i*) –
would strengthen the belief in its efficacy. Pero's name has been interpreted as meaning 'maimed or deficient', a reference to Iphiclus's disability, which is the main point of the story, rather than as meaning
'leather bag', a reference to her control of the winds (see 36. *1*).

3. It appears that 'Melampus', a leader of Aeolians from Pylus, seized
part of Argolis from the Canaanite settlers who called themselves Sons
of Abas (the Semitic word for 'father'), namely the god Melkarth (see
70. *5*), and instituted a double kingdom. His winning of the cattle from
Phylacus ('guardian'), who has an unsleeping dog, recalls Heracles's
Tenth Labour, and the myth is similarly based on the Hellenic custom of
buying a bride with the proceeds of a cattle raid (see 132. *1*).

4. 'Proetus' seems to be another name for Ophion, the Demiurge
(see 1. *a*). The mother of his daughters was Stheneboea, the Moon-goddess as cow – namely Io, who was maddened in much the same way (see
56. *a*) – and their names are titles of the same goddess in her destructive
capacity as Lamia (see 61. *1*), and as Hippolyte, whose wild mares tore

the sacred king to pieces at the end of his reign (see 71. a). But the orgy for which the Moon-priestesses dressed as mares should be distinguished from the rain-making gadfly dance for which they dressed as heifers (see 56. 1); and from the autumn goat-cult revel, when they tore children and animals to pieces under the toxic influence of mead, wine, or ivy-beer (see 27. 2). The Aeolians' capture of the goddess's shrine at Lusi, recorded here in mythic form, will have put an end to the wild-mare orgies; Demeter's rape by Poseidon (see 16. 5) records the same event. Libations poured to the Serpent-goddess in an Arcadian shrine between Sicyon and Lusi may account for the story of Iphinoë's death.

5. The official recognition at Delphi, Corinth, Sparta, and Athens of Dionysus's ecstatic wine cult, given many centuries later, was aimed at the discouragement of all earlier, more primitive, rites; and seems to have put an end to cannibalism and ritual murder, except in the wilder parts of Greece. At Patrae in Achaea, for instance, Artemis Tridaria ('threefold assigner of lots') had required the annual sacrifice of boys and girls, their heads wreathed with ivy and corn, at her harvest orgies. This custom, said to atone for the desecration of the sanctuary by two lovers, Melanippus and Comaetho priestess of Artemis, was ended by the arrival of a chest containing an image of Dionysus, brought by Eurypylus (see 160. x) from Troy (Pausanias: vii. 19. 1–3).

6. Melampodes ('black feet'), is a common Classical name for the Egyptians (see 60. 5); and these stories of how Melampus understood what birds or insects were saying are likely to be of African, not Aeolian, origin.


# 73

## PERSEUS

ABAS, King of Argolis and grandson of Danaus, was so renowned a warrior that, after he died, rebels against the royal House could be put to flight merely by displaying his shield. He married Aglaia, to whose twin sons, Proetus and Acrisius, he bequeathed his kingdom, bidding them rule alternately. Their quarrel, which began in the womb, became more bitter than ever when Proetus lay with Acrisius's daughter Danaë, and barely escaped alive.[1] Since Acrisius now refused to give up the throne at the end of his term, Proetus fled to the court of Iobates, King of Lycia, whose daughter Stheneboea, or Anteia, he married;

returning presently at the head of a Lycian army to support his claims to the succession. A bloody battle was fought, but since neither side gained the advantage, Proetus and Acrisius reluctantly agreed to divide the kingdom between them. Acrisius's share was to be Argos and its environs; Proetus's was to be Tiryns, the Heraeum (now part of Mycenae), Midea, and the coast of Argolis.[2]

b. Seven gigantic Cyclopes, called Gasterocheires, because they earned their living as masons, accompanied Proetus from Lycia, and fortified Tiryns with massive walls, using blocks of stone so large that a mule team could not have stirred the least of them.[3]

c. Acrisius, who was married to Aganippe, had no sons, but only this one daughter Danaë whom Proteus had seduced; and, when he asked an oracle how to procure a male heir, was told: 'You will have no sons, and your grandson must kill you.' To forestall this fate, Acrisius imprisoned Danaë in a dungeon with brazen doors, guarded by savage dogs; but, despite these precautions, Zeus came upon her in a shower of gold, and she bore him a son named Perseus. When Acrisius learned of Danaë's condition, he would not believe that Zeus was the father, and suspected his brother Proetus of having renewed his intimacy with her; but, not daring to kill his own daughter, locked her and the infant Perseus in a wooden ark, which he cast into the sea. This ark was washed towards the island of Seriphos, where a fisherman named Dictys netted it, hauled it ashore, broke it open and found both Danaë and Perseus still alive. He took them at once to his brother, King Polydectes, who reared Perseus in his own house.[4]

d. Some years passed and Perseus, grown to manhood, defended Danaë against Polydectes who, with his subjects' support, had tried to force marriage upon her. Polydectes then assembled his friends and, pretending that he was about to sue for the hand of Hippodameia, daughter of Pelops, asked them to contribute one horse apiece as his love-gift. 'Seriphos is only a small island,' he said, 'but I do not wish to cut a poor figure beside the wealthy suitors from the mainland. Will you be able to help me, noble Perseus?'

'Alas,' answered Perseus, 'I possess no horse, nor any gold to buy one. But if you intend to marry Hippodameia, and not my mother, I will contrive to win whatever gift you name.' He added rashly: 'Even the Gorgon Medusa's head, if need be.'

e. 'That would indeed please me more than any horse in the world,' replied Polydectes at once.[5] Now, the Gorgon Medusa had serpents for hair, huge teeth, protruding tongue, and altogether so ugly a face that all who gazed at it were petrified with fright.

*f.* Athene overheard the conversation at Seriphos and, being a sworn enemy of Medusa's, for whose frightful appearance she had herself been responsible, accompanied Perseus on his adventure. First she led him to the city of Deicterion in Samos, where images of all the three Gorgons are displayed, thus enabling him to distinguish Medusa from her immortal sisters Stheno and Euryale; then she warned him never to look at Medusa directly, but only at her reflection, and presented him with a brightly-polished shield.

*g.* Hermes also helped Perseus, giving him an adamantine sickle with which to cut off Medusa's head. But Perseus still needed a pair of winged sandals, a magic wallet to contain the decapitated head, and the dark helmet of invisibility which belonged to Hades. All these things were in the care of the Stygian Nymphs, from whom Perseus had to fetch them; but their whereabouts were known only to the Gorgons' sisters, the three swan-like Graeae, who had a single eye and tooth among the three of them. Perseus accordingly sought out the Graeae on their thrones at the foot of Mount Atlas. Creeping up behind them, he snatched the eye and tooth, as they were being passed from one sister to another, and would not return either until he had been told where the Stygian Nymphs lived.[6]

*h.* Perseus then collected the sandals, wallet, and helmet from the nymphs, and flew westwards to the Land of the Hyperboreans, where he found the Gorgons asleep, among rain-worn shapes of men and wild beasts pertrified by Medusa. He fixed his eyes on the reflection in the shield, Athene guided his hand, and he cut off Medusa's head with one stroke of the sickle; whereupon, to his surprise, the winged horse Pegasus, and the warrior Chrysaor grasping a golden falchion, sprang fully-grown from her dead body. Perseus was unaware that these had been begotten on Medusa by Poseidon in one of Athene's temples, but decided not to antagonize them further. Hurriedly thrusting the head into his wallet, he took flight; and though Stheno and Euryale, awakened by their new nephews, rose to pursue him, the helmet made Perseus invisible, and he escaped safely southward.[7]

*i.* At sunset, Perseus alighted near the palace of the Titan Atlas to whom, as a punishment for his inhospitality, he showed the Gorgon's head and thus transformed him into a mountain; and on the following day turned eastward and flew across the Libyan desert, Hermes helping him to carry the weighty head. By the way he dropped the Graeae's eye and tooth into Lake Triton; and some drops of Gorgon blood fell on the desert sand, where they bred a swarm of venomous serpents, one of which later killed Mopsus the Argonaut.[8]

*j*. Perseus paused for refreshment at Chemmis in Egypt, where he is still worshipped, and then flew on. As he rounded the coast of Philistia to the north, he caught sight of a naked woman chained to a sea-cliff, and instantly fell in love with her. This was Andromeda, daughter of Cepheus, the Ethiopian King of Joppa, and Cassiopeia.[9] Cassiopeia had boasted that both she and her daughter were more beautiful than the Nereids, who complained of this insult to their protector Poseidon. Poseidon sent a flood and a female sea-monster to devastate Philistia; and when Cepheus consulted the Oracle of Ammon, he was told that his only hope of deliverance lay in sacrificing Andromeda to the monster. His subjects had therefore obliged him to chain her to a rock, naked except for certain jewels, and leave her to be devoured.

*k*. As Perseus flew towards Andromeda, he saw Cepheus and Cassiopeia watching anxiously from the shore near by, and alighted beside them for a hurried consultation. On condition that, if he rescued her, she should be his wife and return to Greece with him, Perseus took to the air again, grasped his sickle and, diving murderously from above, beheaded the approaching monster, which was deceived by his shadow on the sea. He had drawn the Gorgon's head from the wallet, lest the monster might look up, and now laid it face downwards on a bed of leaves and sea-weed (which instantly turned to coral), while he cleansed his hands of blood, raised three altars and sacrificed a calf, a cow, and a bull to Hermes, Athene, and Zeus respectively.[10]

*l*. Cepheus and Cassiopeia grudgingly welcomed him as their son-in-law and, on Andromeda's insistence, the wedding took place at once; but the festivities were rudely interrupted when Agenor, King Belus's twin brother, entered at the head of an armed party, claiming Andromeda for himself. He was doubtless summoned by Cassiopeia, since she and Cepheus at once broke faith with Perseus, pleading that the promise of Andromeda's hand had been forced from them by circumstances, and that Agenor's claim was the prior one.

'Perseus must die!' cried Cassiopeia fiercely.

*m*. In the ensuing fight, Perseus struck down many of his opponents but, being greatly outnumbered, was forced to snatch the Gorgon's head from its bed of coral and turn the remaining two hundred of them to stone.[11]

*n*. Poseidon set the images of Cepheus and Cassiopeia among the stars – the latter, as a punishment for her treachery, is tied in a market-basket which, at some seasons of the year, turns upside-down, so that she looks ridiculous. But Athene afterwards placed Andromeda's image in a more honourable constellation, because she had insisted on marrying Perseus, despite her parents' ill faith. The marks left by her chains are still pointed out on a cliff near Joppa; and the monster's petrified bones were exhibited in the city itself until Marcus Aemilius Scaurus had them taken to Rome during his aedileship.[12]

*o*. Perseus returned hurriedly to Seriphos, taking Andromeda with him, and found that Danaë and Dictys, threatened by the violence of Polydectes who, of course, never intended to marry Hippodameia, had taken refuge in a temple. He therefore went straight to the palace where Polydectes was banqueting with his companions, and announced that he had brought the promised love-gift. Greeted by a storm of insults, he displayed the Gorgon's head, averting his own gaze as he did so, and turned them all to stone; the circle of boulders is still shown in Seriphos. He then gave the head to Athene, who fixed it on her aegis; and Hermes returned the sandals, wallet, and helmet to the guardianship of the Stygian nymphs.[13]

*p*. After raising Dictys to the throne of Seriphos, Perseus set sail for Argos, accompanied by his mother, his wife, and a party of Cyclopes. Acrisius, hearing of their approach, fled to Pelasgian Larissa; but Perseus happened to be invited there for the funeral games which King Teutamides was holding in honour of his dead father, and competed in the fivefold contest. When it came to the discus-throw, his discus, carried out of its path by the wind and the will of the Gods, struck Acrisius's foot and killed him.[14]

*q*. Greatly grieved, Perseus buried his grandfather in the temple of Athene which crowns the local acropolis and then, being ashamed to reign in Argos, went to Tiryns, where Proetus had been succeeded by his son Megapenthes, and arranged to exchange kingdoms with him. So Megapenthes moved to Argos, while Perseus reigned in Tiryns and presently won back the other two parts of Proetus's original kingdom.

*r*. Perseus fortified Midea, and founded Mycenae, so called because, when he was thirsty, a mushroom [*mycos*] sprang up, and provided him with a stream of water. The Cyclopes built the walls of both cities.[15]

*

s. Others give a very different account of the matter. They say that Polydectes succeeded in marrying Danaë, and reared Perseus in the temple of Athene. Some years later, Acrisius heard of their survival and sailed to Seriphos, resolving this time to kill Perseus with his own hand. Polydectes intervened and made each of them solemnly swear never to attempt the other's life. However, a storm arose and, while Acrisius's ship was still hauled up on the beach, weather-bound, Polydectes died. During his funeral games, Perseus threw a discus which accidentally struck Acrisius on the head and killed him. Perseus then sailed to Argos and claimed the throne, but found that Proetus had usurped it, and therefore turned him into stone; thus he now reigned over the whole of Argolis, until Megapenthes avenged his father's death by murdering him.[16]

t. As for the Gorgon Medusa, they say that she was a beautiful daughter of Phorcys, who had offended Athene, and led the Libyans of Lake Tritonis in battle. Perseus, coming from Argos with an army, was helped by Athene to assassinate Medusa. He cut off her head by night, and buried it under a mound of earth in the market place at Argos. This mound lies close to the grave of Perseus's daughter Gorgophone, notorious as the first widow ever to remarry.[17]

1. Servius on Virgil's *Aeneid* iii. 286; Scholiast on Euripides's *Orestes* 965; Apollodorus: ii. 2. 1 and 4. 7.
2. Homer: *Iliad* vi. 160; Apollodorus: ii. 2. 1; Pausanias: ii. 16. 2.
3. Pausanias: ii. 25. 7; Strabo: viii. 6. 11.
4. Hyginus: *Fabula* 63; Apollodorus: ii. 4. 1; Horace: *Odes* iii. 16. 1.
5. Apollodorus: ii. 4. 2.
6. Apollodorus: *loc. cit.*; Hyginus: *Poetic Astronomy* ii. 12.
7. Pindar: *Pythian Odes* x. 31; Ovid: *Metamorphoses* iv. 780; Apollodorus: ii. 4. 3.
8. Euripides: *Electra* 459–63; Hyginus: *Poetic Astronomy* ii. 12; Apollonius Rhodius: iv. 1513 ff.
9. Herodotus: ii. 91; Tzetzes: *On Lycophron* 836; Strabo: i. 2. 35; Pliny: *Natural History* vi. 35.
10 Apollodorus: ii. 4. 3; Hyginus: *Fabula* 64; Ovid: *Metamorphoses* iv. 740 ff.
11. Hyginus: *loc. cit.*; Ovid: *Metamorphoses* v. 1–235; Apollodorus: *loc. cit.*

12. Hyginus: *Poetic Astronomy* ii. 9–10 and 12; Josephus: *Jewish Wars* iii. 9. 2; Pliny: *Natural History* ix. 4.
13. Strabo: x. 5. 10; Apollodorus: ii. 4. 3.
14. Scholiast on Euripides's *Orestes* 953; Apollodorus: ii. 4. 4.
15. Clement of Alexandria: *Address to the Greeks* iii. 45; Apollodorus: ii. 4. 4–5.
16. Ovid: *Metamorphoses* v. 236–41; Hyginus: *Fabulae* 63 and 244.
17. Pausanias: ii. 21. 6–8.

\*

1. The myth of Acrisius and Proetus records the foundation of an Argive double-kingdom: instead of the king's dying every midsummer, and being succeeded by his tanist for the rest of the year, each reigned in turn for forty-nine or fifty months – namely half a Great Year (see 106. 1). This kingdom was later, it seems, divided in halves, with co-kings ruling concurrently for an entire Great Year. The earlier theory, that the bright spirit of the Waxing Year, and his tanist twin, the dark spirit of the Waning Year, stand in endless rivalry pervades Celtic and Palestinian myth, as well as the Greek and Latin.

2. Two such pairs of twins occur in *Genesis*: Esau and Jacob (*Genesis* xxiv. 24–6), Pharez (see 159. 4) and Zarah (*Genesis* xxxviii. 27–30), both of whom quarrel for precedence in the womb, like Acrisius and Proetus. In the simpler Palestinian myth of Mot and Aleyn, the twins quarrel about a woman, as do Acrisius and Proetus; and as their counterparts do in Celtic myth – for instance, Gwyn and Gwythur, in the *Mabinogion*, duel every May Eve until the end of the world for the hand of Creiddylad, daughter of Llyr (Cordelia, daughter of King Lear). This woman is, in each case, a Moon-priestess, marriage to whom confers kingship.

3. The building of Argos and Tiryns by the seven Gasterocheires ('bellies with hands'), and the death of Acrisius, are apparently deduced from a picture of a walled city: seven sun-disks, each with three limbs but no head (see 23. 2), are placed above it, and the sacred king is being killed by an eighth sun-disk, with wings, which strikes his sacred heel. This would mean that seven yearly surrogates die for the king, who is then himself sacrificed at the priestess's orders; his successor, Perseus, stands by.

4. The myth of Danaë, Perseus, and the ark seems related to that of Isis, Osiris, Set, and the Child Horus. In the earliest version, Proetus is Perseus's father, the Argive Osiris; Danaë is his sister-wife, Isis; Perseus, the Child Horus; and Acrisius, the jealous Set who killed his twin Osiris and was taken vengeance on by Horus. The ark is the acacia-wood boat in which Isis and Horus searched the Delta for Osiris's body. A similar story occurs in one version of the Semele myth (see 27. 6), and in that of Rhoeo (see 160. 7). But Danaë, imprisoned in the brazen dungeon, where she bears a child, is the subject of a familiar New Year icon (see 43.2); Zeus's impregnation of Danaë with a shower of gold must refer to

the ritual marriage of the Sun and the Moon, from which the New Year king was born. It can also be read as pastoral allegory: 'water is gold' for the Greek shepherd, and Zeus sends thunder-showers on the earth – Danaë. The name 'Deicterion' means that the Gorgon's head was shown there to Perseus.

5. Dynastic disputes at Argos were complicated by the existence of an Argive colony in Caria – as appears both in this myth and in that of Bellerophon (see 75. *b*); when Cnossus fell about 1400 B.C., the Carian navy was, for a while, one of the strongest in the Mediterranean. The myths of Perseus and Bellerophon are closely related. Perseus killed the monstrous Medusa with the help of winged sandals; Bellerophon used a winged horse, born from the decapitated body of Medusa, to kill the monstrous Chimaera. Both feats record the usurpation by Hellenic invaders of the Moon-goddess's powers, and are unified in an archaic Boeotian vase-painting of a Gorgon-headed mare. This mare is the Moon-goddess, whose calendar-symbol was the Chimaera (see 75. *2*); and the Gorgon-head is a prophylactic mask, worn by her priestesses to scare away the uninitiated (see 33. *3*), which the Hellenes stripped from them.

6. In the second and simpler version of the myth, Perseus fights a Libyan queen, decapitates her, and buries her head in the market place of Argos. This must record an Argive conquest of Libya, the suppression there of the matriarchal system, and the violation of the goddess Neith's mysteries (see 8. *1*). The burial of the head in the market place suggests that sacred relics were locked in a chest there, with a prophylactic mask placed above them, to discourage municipal diggers from disturbing the magic. Perhaps the relics were a pair of little pigs, like those said in the *Mabinogion* to have been buried by King Lud in a stone chest at Carfax, Oxford, as a protective charm for the whole Kingdom of Britain; though pigs, in that context, may be a euphemism for children.

7. Andromeda's story has probably been deduced from a Palestinian icon of the Sun-god Marduk, or his predecessor Bel, mounted on his white horse and killing the sea-monster Tiamat. This myth also formed part of Hebrew mythology: Isaiah mentions that Jehovah (Marduk) hacked Rahab in pieces with a sword (*Isaiah* li. 9); and according to *Job* x. 13 and xxvi. 12, Rahab was the Sea. In the same icon, the jewelled, naked Andromeda, standing chained to a rock, is Aphrodite, or Ishtar, or Astarte, the lecherous Sea-goddess, 'ruler of men'. But she is not waiting to be rescued; Marduk has bound her there himself, after killing her emanation, Tiamat the sea-serpent, to prevent further mischief. In the Babylonian Creation Epic, it was she who sent the Flood. Astarte, as Sea-goddess, had temples all along the Palestinian coast, and at Troy she was Hesione, 'Queen of Asia', whom Heracles is said to have rescued from another sea-monster (see 137. *2*).

8. A Greek colony planted at Chemmis apparently towards the end of the second millennium B.C., identified Perseus with the god Chem, whose hieroglyph was a winged bird and a solar disk; and Herodotus emphasizes the connexion between Danaë, Perseus's mother, and the Libyan invasion of Argos by the Danaans. The myth of Perseus and the mushroom is perhaps told to account for an icon showing a hero studying a mushroom. Fire, mistaken for water, is spouting from it under a blazing sun. Here is tinder for his fire-wheel (see 63. 2).

9. The second, simpler version of the myth suggests that Perseus's visit to the Graeae, his acquisition of the eye, tooth, wallet, sickle, and helmet of darkness, and his pursuit by the other Gorgons after the decapitation of Medusa are extraneous to his quarrel with Acrisius. In the *White Goddess* (Chapter 13), I postulate that these fairy-tale elements are misreadings of a wholly different icon: which show Hermes, wearing his familiar winged sandals and helmet, being given a magic eye by the Three Fates (see 61. 1). This eye symbolizes the gift of perception: Hermes is enabled to master the tree-alphabet, which they have invented. They also give him a divinatory tooth, like the one used by Fionn in the Irish legend; a sickle, to cut alphabetic twigs from the grove; a crane-skin bag, in which to stow these safely; and a Gorgon-mask, to scare away the curious. Hermes is flying through the sky to Tartessus, where the Gorgons had a sacred grove (see 132. 3), escorted, not pursued, by a triad of goddesses wearing Gorgon-masks. On the earth below, the goddess is shown again, holding up a mirror which reflects a Gorgon's face, to emphasize the secrecy of his lesson (see 52. 7). Hermes's association with the Graeae, the Stygian Nymphs, and the helmet of invisibility proves that he is the subject of this picture; the confusion between him and Perseus may have arisen because Hermes, as the messenger of Death, had also earned the title of *Pterseus*, 'the destroyer'.

# 74

## THE RIVAL TWINS

WHEN the male line of Polycaon's House had died out after five generations, the Messenians invited Perieres, the son of Aeolus, to be their king, and he married Perseus's daughter Gorgophone. She survived him and was the first widow to remarry, her new husband being Oebalus the Spartan.[1] Hitherto it had been customary for women to commit suicide on the death of their husbands: as did Meleager's

daughter Polydora, whose husband Protesilaus was the first to leap
ashore when the Greek fleet reached the coast of Troy; Marpessa;
Cleopatra; and Evadne, daughter of Phylacus, who threw herself on
the funeral pyre when her husband perished at Thebes.[2]

b. Aphareus and Leucippus were Gorgophone's sons by Perieres,
whereas Tyndareus and Icarius were her sons by Oebalus.[3] Tyndareus
succeeded his father on the throne of Sparta, Icarius acting as his co-
king; but Hippocoön and his twelve sons expelled both of them –
though some, indeed, say that Icarius (later to become Odysseus's
father-in-law) took Hippocoön's side. Taking refuge with King Thestius in Aetolia, Tyndareus married his daughter Leda, who bore him
Castor and Clytaemnestra, at the same time bearing Helen and Polydeuces to Zeus.[4] Later, having adopted Polydeuces, Tyndareus regained the Spartan throne, and was one of those whom Asclepius
raised from the dead. His tomb is still shown at Sparta.[5]

c. Meanwhile, his half-brother Aphareus had succeeded Perieres on
the throne of Messene, where Leucippus – from whom, the Messenians
say, the city of Leuctra took its name – acted as his co-king and enjoyed
the lesser powers. Aphareus took to wife his half-sister Arene, who bore
him Idas and Lynceus; though Idas was, in truth, Poseidon's son.[6] Now,
Leucippus's daughters, the Leucippides, namely Phoebe, a priestess of
Athene, and Hilaeira, a priestess of Artemis, were betrothed to their
cousins, Idas and Lynceus; but Castor and Polydeuces, who are commonly known as the Dioscuri, carried them off, and had sons by them;
which occasioned a bitter rivalry between the two sets of twins.[7]

d. The Dioscuri, who were never separated from one another in any
adventure, became the pride of Sparta. Castor was famous as a soldier
and tamer of horses, Polydeuces as the best boxer of his day; both won
prizes at the Olympic Games. Their cousins and rivals were no less
devoted to each other; Idas had greater strength than Lynceus, but
Lynceus had such sharp eyes that he could see in the dark or divine
the whereabouts of buried treasure.[8]

e. Now, Evenus, a son of Ares, had married Alcippe, by whom he
became the father of Marpessa. In an attempt to keep her a virgin, he
invited each of her suitors in turn to run a chariot race with him; the
victor would win Marpessa, the vanquished would forfeit his head.
Soon many heads were nailed to the walls of Evenus's house and
Apollo, falling in love with Marpessa, expressed his disgust of so barbarous a custom; and said that he would soon end it by challenging

Evenus to a race. But Idas had also set his heart on Marpessa, and begged a winged chariot from his father Poseidon.[9] Before Apollo could act, he had driven to Aetolia, and carried Marpessa away from the midst of a band of dancers. Evenus gave chase, but could not overtake Idas, and felt such mortification that, after killing his horses, he drowned himself in the river Lycormas, ever since called the Evenus.[10]

*f*. When Idas reached Messene, Apollo tried to take Marpessa from him. They fought a duel, but Zeus parted them, and ruled that Marpessa herself should decide whom she preferred to marry. Fearing that Apollo would cast her off when she grew old, as he had done with many another of his loves, she chose Idas for her husband.[11]

*g*. Idas and Lynceus were among the Calydonian hunters, and sailed in the *Argo* to Colchis. One day, after the death of Aphareus, they and the Dioscuri patched up their quarrel sufficiently to join forces in a cattle-raid on Arcadia. The raid proved successful, and Idas was chosen by lot to divide the booty among the four of them. He therefore quartered a cow, and ruled that half the spoil should go to the man who ate his share first, the remainder to the next quickest. Almost before the others had settled themselves to begin the contest, Idas bolted his own share and then helped Lynceus to bolt his; soon down went the last gobbet, and he and Lynceus drove the cattle away towards Messene. The Dioscuri remained, until Polydeuces, the slower of the two, had finished eating; whereupon they marched against Messene, and protested to the citizens that Lynceus had forfeited his share by accepting help from Idas, and that Idas had forfeited his by not waiting until all the contestants were ready. Idas and Lynceus happened to be away on Mount Taygetus, sacrificing to Poseidon; so the Dioscuri seized the disputed cattle, and other plunder as well, and then hid inside a hollow oak to await their rivals' return. But Lynceus had caught sight of them from the summit of Taygetus; and Idas, hurrying down the mountain slope, hurled his spear at the tree and transfixed Castor. When Polydeuces rushed out to avenge his brother, Idas tore the carved headstone from Aphareus's tomb, and threw it at him. Although badly crushed, Polydeuces contrived to kill Lynceus with his spear; and at this point Zeus intervened on behalf of his son, striking Idas dead with a thunderbolt.[12]

*h*. But the Messenians say that Castor killed Lynceus, and that Idas, distracted by grief, broke off the fight and began to bury him. Castor then approached and insolently demolished the monument which Idas had just raised, denying that Lynceus was worthy of it. 'Your brother put up no better fight than a woman would have done!' he cried tauntingly. Idas turned, and plunged his sword into Castor's belly; but Polydeuces took instant vengeance on him.[13]

*i.* Others say that it was Lynceus who mortally wounded Castor in a battle fought at Aphidna; others again, that Castor was killed when Idas and Lynceus attacked Sparta; and still others, that both Dioscuri survived the fight, Castor being killed later by Meleager and Polyneices.[14]

*j.* It is generally agreed, at least, that Polydeuces was the last survivor of the two sets of twins and that, after setting up a trophy beside the Spartan race-course to celebrate his victory over Lynceus, he prayed to Zeus: 'Father, let me not outlive my dear brother!' Since, however, it was fated that only one of Leda's sons should die, and since Castor's father Tyndareus had been a mortal, Polydeuces, as the son of Zeus, was duly carried up to Heaven. Yet he refused immortality unless Castor might share it, and Zeus therefore allowed them both to spend their days alternately in the upper air, and under the earth at Therapne. In further reward of their brotherly love, he set their images among the stars as the Twins.[15]

*k.* After the Dioscuri had been deified, Tyndareus summoned Menelaus to Sparta, where he resigned the kingdom to him; and since the House of Aphareus was now also left without an heir, Nestor succeeded to the throne of all Messenia, except for the part ruled over by the sons of Asclepius.[16]

*l.* The Spartans still show the house where the Dioscuri lived. It was afterwards owned by one Phormio, whom they visited one night, pretending to be strangers from Cyrene. They asked him for lodging, and begged leave to sleep in their old room. Phormio replied that they were welcome to any other part of the house but that, regrettably, his daughter was now occupying the room of which they spoke. Next morning, the girl and all her possessions had vanished, and the room was empty, except for images of the Dioscuri and some herb-benjamin laid upon a table.[17]

*m.* Poseidon made Castor and Polydeuces the saviours of ship-wrecked sailors, and granted them power to send favourable winds; in response to a sacrifice of white lambs offered on the prow of any ship, they will come hastening through the sky, followed by a train of sparrows.[18]

*n.* The Dioscuri fought with the Spartan fleet at Aegospotamoi, and the victors afterwards hung up two golden stars in their honour at Delphi; but these fell down and disappeared shortly before the fatal battles of Leuctra.[19]

*o.* During the second Messenian War, a couple of Messenians aroused the Dioscuri's anger by impersonating them. It happened that the Spartan army was celebrating a feast of the demi-gods, when twin spearmen rode into the camp at full gallop, dressed in white tunics, purple cloaks, and egg-shell caps. The Spartans fell down to worship them, and the pretended Dioscuri, two Messenian youths named Gonippus and Panormus, killed many of them. After the battle of the Boar's Grave, therefore, the Dioscuri sat on a wild pear-tree, and spirited away the shield belonging to the victorious Messenian commander Aristomenes, which prevented him from pressing on the Spartan retreat, and thus saved many lives; again, when Aristomenes attempted to assault Sparta by night, the phantoms of the Dioscuri and of their sister Helen turned him back. Later, Castor and Polydeuces forgave the Messenians, who sacrificed to them when Epaminondas founded the new city of Messene.[20]

*p.* They preside at the Spartan Games, and because they invented the war-dance and war-like music are the patrons of all bards who sing of ancient battles. In Hilaeira and Phoebe's sanctuary at Sparta, the two priestesses are still called Leucippides, and the egg from which Leda's twins were hatched is suspended from the roof.[21] The Spartans represent the Dioscuri by two parallel wooden beams, joined by two transverse ones. Their co-kings always take these into battle and when, for the first time, a Spartan army was led by one king alone, it was decreed that one beam should also remain at Sparta. According to those who have seen the Dioscuri, the only noticeable difference between them is that Polydeuces's face bears the scars of boxing. They dress alike: each has his half egg-shell surmounted by a star, each his spear and white horse. Some say that Poseidon gave them their horses; others, that Polydeuces's Thessalian charger was a gift from Hermes.[22]

1. Pausanias: iv. 2. 2 and iii. 1. 4; Apollodorus: i. 9. 5.
2. *Cypria*, quoted by Pausanias: iv. 2. 5; Pausanias: iii. 1. 4.
3. Apollodorus: i. 9. 5; Pausanias: *loc. cit.*
4. Pausanias: *loc. cit.*; Apollodorus: iii. 10. 5–7.
5. Panyasis, quoted by Apollodorus: iii. 10. 3; Pausanias: iii. 17. 4.
6. Pausanias: iii. 26. 3 and iv. 2. 3; Apollodorus: iii. 10. 3.

7. Apollodorus: iii. 11. 2; Hyginus: *Fabula* 80.
8. Apollodorus: *loc. cit.* and iii. 10. 3; Homer: *Odyssey* xi. 300; Pausanias: iv. 2. 4; Hyginus: *Fabula* 14; Palaephatus: *Incredible Stories* x.
9. Hyginus: *Fabula* 242; Apollodorus: i. 7. 8; Plutarch: *Parallel Stories* 40; Scholiast and Eustathius on Homer's *Iliad* ix. 557.
10. Plutarch: *loc. cit.*; Apollodorus: *loc. cit.*
11. Apollodorus: i. 7. 9.
12. Apollodorus: i. 8. 2; i. 9. 16 and iii. 11. 2; Theocritus: *Idylls* xxii. 137 ff.; Pindar: *Nemean Odes* x. 55 ff.
13. Hyginus: *Fabula* 80.
14. Ovid: *Fasti* v. 699 ff.; Hyginus: *Poetic Astronomy* ii. 22; Theocritus: *loc. cit.*; Scholiast on Homer's *Odyssey* xi. 300.
15. Pausanias: iii. 14. 7; Apollodorus: iii. 11. 2; Pindar: *Nemean Odes* x. 55 ff.; Lucian: *Dialogues of the Gods* 26; Hyginus: *loc. cit.*
16. Apollodorus: *loc. cit.*; Pausanias: iv. 3. 1.
17. Pausanias: iii. 16. 3.
18. Hyginus: *Poetic Astronomy* ii. 22; Euripides: *Helen* 1503; *Homeric Hymn to the Dioscuri* 7 ff.
19. Cicero: *On Divination* i. 34. 75 and ii. 32. 68.
20. Pausanias: iv. 27. 1; iv. 16. 2 and v. 27. 3.
21. Pindar: *Nemean Odes* x. 49; Cicero: *On Oratory* ii. 8. 86; Theocritus: *Idylls* xxii. 215–20; Pausanias: iii. 16. 1–2.
22. Plutarch: *On Brotherly Love* i; Herodotus: v. 75; Lucian: *Dialogues of the Gods* 26; Hyginus: *Poetic Astronomy* ii. 22; Ptolemy Hephaestionos: viii. quoted by Photius: p. 409.

*

1. In order to allow the sacred king precedence over his tanist, he was usually described as the son of a god, by a mother on whom her husband subsequently fathered a mortal twin. Thus Heracles is Zeus's son by Alcmene, but his twin Iphicles is the son of her husband Amphitryon: a similar story is told about the Dioscuri of Laconia, and about their rivals, Idas and Lynceus of Messenia. The perfect harmony existing between the twins themselves marks a new stage in the development of kingship, when the tanist acts as vizier and chief-of-staff (see 94. 1), being nominally less powerful than the sacred king. Castor therefore, not Polydeuces, is the authority on war – he even instructs Heracles in military arts, thus identifying himself with Iphicles – and Lynceus, not Idas, is gifted with acute vision. But until the double-kingdom system had been evolved, the tanist was not regarded as immortal, nor granted the same posthumous status as his twin.

2. The Spartans were frequently at war with the Messenians and, in Classical times, had sufficient military power, and influence over the Delphic Oracle, to impose their twin heroes on the rest of Greece, as

enjoying greater favour with Father Zeus than any other pair; and the Spartan kingdom did indeed outlast all its rivals. Had this not been so, the constellation of the Twins might have commemorated Heracles and Iphicles, or Idas and Lynceus, or Acrisius and Proetus – instead of merely Castor and Polydeuces, who were not even the only heroes privileged to ride white horses: every hero worthy of a hero-feast was a horseman. It is these sunset feasts, at which a whole ox was eaten by the hero's descendants, that account for the gluttony attributed to Lepreus (see 138. *h*) and Heracles (see 143. *a*); and here to Idas, Lynceus and their rivals.

3. Marriage to the Leucippides enroyalled the Spartan co-kings. They were described as priestesses of Athene and Artemis, and given moonnames, being, in fact, the Moon-goddess's representatives; thus, in vasepaintings, the chariot of Selene is frequently attended by the Dioscuri. As the Spirit of the Waxing Year, the sacred king would naturally mate with Artemis, a Moon-goddess of spring and summer; and his tanist, as Spirit of the Waning Year, with Athene, who had become a Moongoddess of autumn and winter. The mythographer is suggesting that the Spartans defeated the Messenians, and that their leaders forcibly married the heiresses of Arene, a principal city of Messenia, where the Mareheaded Mother was worshipped; thus establishing a claim to the surrounding region.

4. Similarly with Marpessa: apparently the Messenians made a raid on the Aetolians in the Evenus valley, where the Sow-mother was worshipped, and carried off the heiress, Marpessa ('snatcher' or 'gobbler'). They were opposed by the Spartans, worshippers of Apollo, who grudged them their success; the dispute was then referred to the central authority at Mycenae, which supported the Messenians. But Evenus's chariot-race with Idas recalls the Pelops-Oenomaus (see 109. *j*) and the Heracles-Cycnus (see 143. *e–g*) myths. In each case the skulls of the king's rivals are mentioned. The icon from which all these stories are deduced must have shown the old king heading for his destined chariot crash (see 71. *1*) after having offered seven annual surrogates to the goddess (see 42. *2*). His horses are sacrificed as a preliminary to the installation of the new king (see 29. *1* and 81. *4*). The drowning of Evenus is probably misread: it shows Idas being purified before marriage and then riding off triumphantly in the Queen's chàriot. Yet these Pelasgian marriage rites have been combined in the story with the Hellenic custom of marriage by capture. The fatal cattle-raid may record a historical incident: a quarrel between the Messenians and Spartans about the sharing of spoil in a joint expedition against Arcadia (see 17. *1*).

5. Castor and Polydeuces's visit to Phormio's house is disingenuously described: the author is relating another trick played on the stupid Spartans by an impersonation of their national heroes. Cyrene, where the

Dioscuri were worshipped, supplied herb-benjamin, a kind of asafoetida, the strong smell and taste of which made it valued as a condiment. The two Cyrenian merchants were obviously what they professed themselves to be, and when they went off with Phormio's daughter, left their wares behind in payment: Phormio decided to call it a miracle.

6. Wild pear-trees were sacred to the Moon because of their white blossom, and the most ancient image of the Death-goddess Hera, in the Heraeum at Mycenae, was made of pear-wood. Plutarch (*Greek Questions* 51) and Aelian (*Varia Historia* iii. 39) mention the pear as a fruit peculiarly venerated at Argos and Tiryns; hence the Peloponnese was called Apia, 'of the pear-tree' (see 64. 4). Athene, also a Death-goddess, had the surname Oncë ('pear-tree') at her pear-sanctuary in Boeotia. The Dioscuri chose this tree for their perch in order to show that they were genuine heroes; moreover, the pear-tree forms fruit towards the end of May (see 72. 2), when the sun is in the house of the Twins; and when the sailing season begins in the Eastern Mediterranean. Sparrows that follow the Dioscuri, when they appear in answer to sailors' prayers, belong to the Sea-goddess Aphrodite; Xuthus ('sparrow'), the father of Aeolus (see 43. 1), was an ancestor of the Dioscuri, who worshipped her.

7. In the *Homeric Hymn to the Dioscuri* (7 ff.), it is not made clear whether Castor and Polydeuces are followed by sparrows or whether they come darting on 'sparrowy wings' through the upper air, to help distressed sailors; but on Etruscan mirrors they are sometimes pictured as winged. Their symbol at Sparta, the *docana*, represented the two supporting pillars of a shrine; another symbol consisted of two amphoras, each entwined by a serpent – the serpents being the incarnate Dioscuri who came to eat food placed in the amphoras.

8. Gorgophone defied the Indo-European convention of suttee by marrying again (see 69. 2; 74. *a* and 106. *l*).


# 75

## BELLEROPHON

BELLEROPHON, son of Glaucus and grandson of Sisyphus, left Corinth under a cloud, having first killed one Bellerus – which earned him his nickname Bellerophontes, shortened to Bellerophon – and then his own brother, whose name is usually given as Deliades.[1] He fled as a suppliant to Proetus, King of Tiryns; but (so ill luck would have it) Anteia, Proetus's wife whom some call Stheneboea, fell in love with him at sight. When he rejected her advances, she accused him of having tried to seduce her, and Proetus, who believed the story, grew incensed. Yet he dared not risk the Furies' vengeance by the direct murder of a suppliant, and therefore sent him to Anteia's father Iobates, King of Lycia, carrying a sealed letter, which read: 'Pray remove the bearer from this world; he has tried to violate my wife, your daughter.'

*b.* Iobates, equally loth to ill-treat a royal guest, asked Bellerophon to do him the service of destroying the Chimaera, a fire-breathing she-monster with lion's head, goat's body, and serpent's tail. 'She is', he explained, 'a daughter of Echidne, whom my enemy, the King of Caria, has made a household pet.' Before setting about this task, Bellerophon consulted the seer Polyeidus, and was advised to catch and tame the winged horse Pegasus, beloved by the Muses of Mount Helicon, for whom he had created the well Hippocrene by stamping his moon-shaped hoof.[2]

*c.* Pegasus was absent from Helicon, but Bellerophon found him drinking at Peirene, on the Acropolis of Corinth, another of his wells; and threw over his head a golden bridle, Athene's timely present. But some say that Athene gave Pegasus already bridled to Bellerophon; and others, that Poseidon, who was really Bellerophon's father, did so. Be that as it may, Bellerophon overcame the Chimaera by flying above her on Pegasus's back, riddling her with arrows, and then thrusting between her jaws a lump of lead which he had fixed to the point of his spear. The Chimaera's fiery breath melted the lead, which trickled down her throat, searing her vitals.[3]

*d.* Iobates, however, far from rewarding Bellerophon for this daring feat, sent him at once against the warlike Solymians and their allies, the Amazons; both of whom he conquered by soaring above them, well out of bowshot, and dropping large boulders on their heads. Next, in the Lycian Plain of Xanthus, he beat off a band of Carian pirates led by one Cheimarrhus, a fiery and boastful warrior, who sailed in a ship adorned with a lion figurehead and a serpent stern. When Iobates showed no gratitude even then but, on the contrary, sent the palace guards to ambush him on his return, Bellerophon dismounted and prayed that, while he advanced on foot, Poseidon would flood the Xanthian Plain behind him. Poseidon heard his prayer, and sent great waves rolling slowly forward as Bellerophon approached Iobates's palace; and, because no man could persuade him to retire, the Xanthian women hoisted their skirts to the waist and came rushing towards him full butt, offering themselves to him one and all, if only he would relent. Bellerophon's modesty was such that he turned tail and ran; and the waves retreated with him.

e. Convinced now that Proetus must have been mistaken about the attempt on Anteia's virtue, Iobates produced the letter, and demanded an exact account of the affair. On learning the truth, he implored Bellerophon's forgiveness, gave him his daughter Philonoë in marriage, and made him heir to the Lycian throne. He also praised the Xanthian women for their resourcefulness and ordered that, in future, all Xanthians should reckon descent from the mother, not the father.

f. Bellerophon, at the height of his fortune, presumptuously undertook a flight to Olympus, as though he were an immortal; but Zeus sent a gadfly, which stung Pegasus under the tail, making him rear and fling Bellerophon ingloriously to earth. Pegasus completed the flight to Olympus, where Zeus now uses him as a pack-beast for thunderbolts; and Bellerophon, who had fallen into a thorn-bush, wandered about the earth, lame, blind, lonely and accursed, always avoiding the paths of men, until death overtook him.[4]

1. Apollodorus: i. 9. 3; Homer: *Iliad* vi. 155.
2. Homer: *Iliad* vi. 160; Eustathius *on the same text*; Apollodorus: ii. 3. 1; Antoninus Liberalis: 9; Homer: *Iliad* xvi. 328 ff.
3. Hesiod *Theogony* 319 ff.; Apollodorus: ii. 3. 2; Pindar: *Olympian Odes* xiii. 63 ff.; Pausanias: ii. 4. 1; Hyginus: *Fabula* 157; Scholiast on Homer's *Iliad* vi. 155; Tzetzes: *On Lycophron* 17.
4. Pindar: *Olympian Odes* xiii. 87–90; *Isthmian Odes* vii. 44; Apollodorus: *loc. cit.*; Plutarch: *On the Virtues of Women* 9; Homer: *Iliad* vi. 155–203 and xvi. 328; Ovid: *Metamorphoses* ix. 646; Tzetzes: *On Lycophron* 838.

*

1. Anteia's attempted seduction of Bellerophon has several Greek parallels (see 70. 2), besides a Palestinian parallel in the story of Joseph and Potiphar's wife, and an Egyptian parallel in *The Tale of the Two Brothers*. The provenience of the myth is uncertain.

2. Echnide's daughter, the Chimaera, who is depicted on a Hittite building at Carchemish, was a symbol of the Great Goddess's tripartite Sacred Year – lion for spring, goat for summer, serpent for winter. A damaged glass plaque found at Dendra near Mycenae shows a hero tussling with a lion, from the back of which emerges what appears to be a goat's head; the tail is long and serpentine. Since the plaque dates from a period when the goddess was still supreme, this icon – paralleled in an

Etruscan fresco at Tarquinia, though the hero here is mounted, like Bellerophon – must be read as a king's coronation combat against men in beast disguise (see 81. 2 and 123. 1) who represent the different seasons of the year. After the Achaean religious revolution which subordinated the goddess Hera to Zeus, the icon became ambivalent: it could also be read as recording the suppression by Hellenic invaders, of the ancient Carian calendar.

3. Bellerophon's taming of Pegasus, the Moon-horse used in rain-making, with a bridle provided by Athene, suggests that the candidate for the sacred kingship was charged by the Triple Muse ('mountain goddess'), or her representative, with the capture of a wild horse; thus Heracles later rode Arion ('moon-creature on high') when he took possession of Elis (see 138. g). To judge from primitive Danish and Irish practice, the flesh of this horse was sacramentally eaten by the king after his symbolic rebirth from the Mare-headed Mountain-goddess. But this part of the myth is equally ambivalent: it can also be read as recording the seizure by Hellenic invaders of the Mountain-goddess's shrines at Ascra on Mount Helicon, and Corinth. A similar event is recorded in Poseidon's violation of the Mare-headed Arcadian Demeter (see 16. f), on whom he begot this same Moon-horse Arion; and of Medusa, on whom he begot Pegasus (see 73. h); which explains Poseidon's intrusion into the story of Bellerophon. How Zeus humbled Bellerophon is a moral anecdote told to discourage revolt against the Olympian faith; Bellerophon, the dart-bearer, flying across the sky, is the same character as his grandfather Sisyphus, or Tesup (see 67. 1), a solar hero whose cult was replaced by that of solar Zeus; he is therefore given a similarly luckless end, which recalls that of Helius's son Phaëthon (see 42. 2).

4. Bellerophon's enemies, the Solymians, were Children of Salma. Since all cities and capes beginning with the syllable *salm* have an easterly situation, she was probably the Goddess of the Spring Equinox; but she soon became masculinized as the Sun-god Solyma, or Selin, Solomon, or Ab-Salom, who gave his name to Jerusalem. The Amazons were the Moon-goddess's fighting priestesses (see 100. 1).

5. Bellerophon's retreat from the Xanthian women may have been deduced from an icon which showed the Wild Women maddened with *hippomanes* – either a herb, or the slimy vaginal issue of a mare in heat, or the black membrane cut from the forehead of a new-born foal – closing in on the sacred king by the seashore at the end of his reign. Their skirts were hoisted, as in the erotic worship of Egyptian Apis (Diodorus Siculus: i. 85), so that when they dismembered him, his spurting blood would quicken their wombs. Since Xanthus ('yellow') is the name of one of Achilles's horses, and of one belonging to Hector, and of one given to Peleus by Poseidon, these women perhaps wore ritual horse-masks

with moon-yellow manes, like those of palominos; for wild mares had eaten Bellerophon's father Glaucus by the seashore of Corinth (see 71. 1). Yet this reformed myth retains a primitive element: the approach of naked women from the chieftain's own clan, with whom intercourse was forbidden, would force him to retreat and hide his face, and in Irish legend this same ruse was employed against Cuchulain, when his fury could not otherwise be checked. The account of the Xanthian matrilineal reckoning of descent has been turned inside out: it was the Hellenes who, on the contrary, managed to enforce patrilineal reckoning on all Carians, except the conservative Xanthians.

6. Cheimarrhus's name is derived from *chimaros*, or *chimaera* ('goat'); both his fiery nature and his ship with the lion figurehead and serpent stern have been introduced into Bellerophon's story by some euhemerist to explain away the fire-breathing Chimaera. Mount Chimaera ('goat-mountain') was also the name of an active volcano near Phaselis in Lycia (Pliny: *Natural History* ii. 106 and v. 27), which accounts for the fiery breath.

# 76

## ANTIOPE

SOME say that when Zeus seduced Antiope, daughter of Nycteus the Theban, she fled to the King of Sicyon, who agreed to marry her, and thus occasioned a war in which Nycteus was killed. Antiope's uncle Lycus presently defeated the Sicyonians in a bloody battle and brought her back, a widow, to Thebes. After giving birth in a wayside thicket to the twins Amphion and Zethus, whom Lycus at once exposed on Mount Cithaeron, she was cruelly ill-treated for many years by her aunt Dirce. At last, she contrived to escape from the prison in which she was immured, and fled to the hut where Amphion and Zethus, whom a passing cattleman had rescued, were now living. But they mistook Antiope for a runaway slave, and refused to shelter her. Dirce then came rushing up in a Bacchic frenzy, seized hold of Antiope, and dragged her away.

'My lads,' cried the cattleman, 'you had better beware of the Furies!'

'Why the Furies?' they asked.

'Because you have refused to protect your mother, who is now being carried off for execution by that savage aunt of hers.'

The twins at once went in pursuit, rescued Antiope, and tied Dirce by the hair to the horns of a wild bull, which made short work of her.[1]

*b.* Others say that the river Asopus was Antiope's father, and that one night the King of Sicyon impersonated Lycus, to whom she was married, and seduced her. Lycus divorced Antiope in consequence and married Dirce, thus leaving Zeus free to court the lonely Antiope, and get her with child. Dirce, suspecting that this was Lycus's doing, confined Antiope in a dark dungeon; from which, however, she was freed by Zeus just in time to bring forth Amphion and Zethus on Mount Cithaeron. The twins grew up among the cattlemen with whom Antiope had taken refuge and, when they were old enough to understand how unkindly their mother had been treated, she persuaded them to avenge her. They met Dirce roaming the slopes of Mount Cithaeron in a Bacchic frenzy, tied her by the hair to the horns of a wild bull and, when she was dead, flung her body on the ground; where a spring welled up, afterwards called the Dircaean Stream. But Dionysus avenged this murder of his votary: he sent Antiope raging madly all over Greece until at last Phocus, a grandson of Sisyphus, cured and married her in Phocis.

*c.* Amphion and Zethus visited Thebes, where they expelled King Laius and built the lower city, Cadmus having already built the upper. Now Zethus had often taunted Amphion for his devotion to the lyre given him by Hermes. 'It distracts you', he would say, 'from useful work.' Yet when they became masons, Amphion's stones moved to the sound of his lyre and gently slid into place, while Zethus was obliged to use main force, lagging far behind his brother. The twins ruled jointly in Thebes, where Zethus married Thebe, after whom the city – previously known as Cadmeia – is now named; and Amphion married Niobe. But all her children except two were shot dead by Apollo and Artemis, whose mother Leto she had insulted. Amphion was himself killed by Apollo for trying to take vengeance on the Delphic priests, and further punished in Tartarus.[2] Amphion and Zethus are buried in one grave at Thebes, which is guarded carefully when the sun is in Taurus; for then the people of Phocian Tithorea try to steal earth from the mound and place it on the grave of Phocus and Antiope. An oracle once said that this act would increase the fertility of all Phocis at the expense of Thebes.[3]

1. Hyginus: *Fabula* 8; Apollodorus: iii. 5. 5; Pausanias: ii. 6. 2; Euripides: *Antiope*, Fragments; Apollonius Rhodius: iv. 1090, with scholiast.

2. Homer: *Odyssey* xi. 260; Hyginus: *Fabula* 7; Pausanias: vi. 20. 8; ix. 5. 3 and 17. 4; Horace: *Epistles* i. 18. 41; Apollonius Rhodius: i. 735–41.
3. Pausanias: ix. 17. 3.

\*

1. These two versions of the Dirce myth show how free the mythographers felt to make their narrative fit the main elements of a literary tradition which, in this case, seems to have been deduced from a series of sacred icons. Antiope, emerging joyfully out of her dungeon and followed by the scowling Dirce, recalls Core's annual reappearance in Hecate's company (see 24. *k*). She is called Antiope ('confronting') in this context, because her face is upturned to the sky, not bent towards the Underworld, and 'Daughter of Night' – Nycteis, not Nycteus – because she emerges from the darkness. The 'raging on the mountain' by Dirce and Antiope has been misinterpreted as a Bacchic orgy; theirs was clearly an erotic gadfly dance, for which they behaved like Moon-heifers in heat (see 56. *1*). Dirce's name ('double') stands for the horned moon, and the icon from which the myth is taken will have shown her not being tied to the bull in punishment, but ritually marrying the bull-king (see 88. *7*). A secondary meaning may be concealed in *dirce*: namely 'cleft', that is, 'in an erotic condition'. The Dircaean spring, like Hippocrene, will have been moon-shaped. Antiope's sons are the familiar royal twins borne by the Moon-goddess: her sacred king and his tanist.

2. Amphion's three-stringed lyre, with which he raised the walls of Lower Thebes – since Hermes was his employer, it can have had only three strings – was constructed to celebrate the Triple-goddess, who reigned in the air, on earth, and in the Underworld, and will have been played during the building to safeguard the city's foundations, gates, and towers. The name 'Amphion' ('native of two lands') records his citizenship of Sicyon and Thebes.

# 77

## NIOBE

NIOBE, sister of Pelops, had married Amphion King of Thebes and borne him seven sons and seven daughters, of whom she was so inordinately proud that, one day, she disparaged Leto herself for having only two children: Apollo and Artemis. Mante, the prophetic daughter of Teiresias, overhearing this rash remark, advised the Theban women

to placate Leto and her children at once: burning frankincense and
wreathing their hair with laurel branches. When the scent of incense
was already floating in the air, Niobe appeared, followed by a throng of
attendants and dressed in a splendid Phrygian robe, her long hair
flowing loose. She interrupted the sacrifice and furiously asked why
Leto, a woman of obscure parentage, with a mannish daughter and a
womanish son, should be preferred to her, Niobe, grandchild of Zeus
and Atlas, the dread of the Phrygians, and a queen of Cadmus's royal
house? Though fate or ill-luck might carry off two or three of her
children, would she not still remain the richer?

b. Abandoning the sacrifice, the terrified Theban women tried to
placate Leto with murmured prayers, but it was too late. She had
already sent Apollo and Artemis, armed with bows, to punish Niobe's
presumption. Apollo found the boys hunting on Mount Cithaeron and
shot them down one by one, sparing only Amyclas, who had wisely
offered a propitiatory prayer to Leto. Artemis found the girls spinning
in the palace and, with a quiverful of arrows, despatched all of them,
except Meliboëa, who had followed Amyclas's example. These two survivors hastened to build Leto a temple, though Meliboëa had turned so
pale with fear that she was still nicknamed Chloris when she married
Neleus some years later. But some say that none of Niobe's children
survived, and that her husband Amphion was also killed by Apollo.

c. For nine days and nine nights Niobe bewailed her dead, and found
no one to bury them, because Zeus, taking Leto's part, had turned all
the Thebans into stone. On the tenth day, the Olympians themselves
deigned to conduct the funeral. Niobe fled overseas to Mount Sipylus,
the home of her father Tantalus, where Zeus, moved by pity, turned
her into a statue which can still be seen weeping copiously in the early
summer.[1]

d. All men mourned for Amphion, deploring the extinction of his
race, but none mourned for Niobe, except her equally proud brother
Pelops.[2]

1. Hyginus: *Fabulae* 9 and 10; Apollodorus: iii. 5. 6; Homer: *Iliad*
xxiv. 612 ff.; Ovid: *Metamorphoses* vi. 146–312; Pausanias: v. 16.
3; viii. 2. 5 and i. 21. 5; Sophocles: *Electra* 150–52.
2. Ovid: *Metamorphoses* vi. 401–4.

*

1. The number of Niobe's children is given by Homer as twelve and
(according to various scholiasts) by Hesiod as twenty, by Herodotus as

four, and by Sappho as eighteen; but the account followed by Euripides and Apollodorus, which makes the best sense, is that she had seven sons and seven daughters. Since Niobe, in the Theban version of the myth, was a grand-daughter of the Titan Atlas, and, in the Argive version, was daughter or mother of Phoroneus (see 57. a), also described as a Titan (Apollodorus: ii. 1. 1 and Scholiast on Euripides's Orestes 932), and of Pelasgus; and could claim to be the first mortal woman violated by Zeus (Diodorus Siculus: iv. 9. 14; Apollodorus: loc. cit.; Pausanias: ii. 22. 6), the myth may concern the defeat of the seven Titans and Titanesses by the Olympians. If so, it records the supersession of the calendar system prevailing in Pelasgian Greece, Palestine, Syria, and North-western Europe; which was based on a month divided into four weeks of seven days, each ruled by one of the seven planetary bodies (see 1. 3 and 43. 4). Amphion and his twelve children, in Homer's version of the myth (Iliad xxiv. 603–17), perhaps stand for the thirteen months of this calendar. Mount Sipylus may have been the last home in Asia Minor of the Titan cult, as Thebes was in Greece. The statue of Niobe is a crag of roughly human shape, which seems to weep when the sun's arrows strike its winter cap of snow, and the likeness is reinforced by a Hittite Goddess-mother carved in rock on the same mountain and dating from perhaps the late fifteenth century B.C. 'Niobe' probably means snowy – the b representing the v in the Latin nivis, or the ph in the Greek nipha. One of her daughters is called Chiade by Hyginus: a word which makes no sense in Greek, unless it be a worn-down form of chionos niphades, 'snow flakes'.

2. Parthenius (Love Stories 33) gives a different account of Niobe's punishment: by Leto's contrivance, Niobe's father fell incestuously in love with her and, when she repulsed him, burned her children to death; her husband was then mangled by a wild boar, and she threw herself from a rock. This story, confirmed by the scholiast on Euripides's Phoenician Women (159), is influenced by the myths of Cinyras, Smyrna and Adonis (see 18. h), and by the custom of burning children to the god Moloch (see 70. 5 and 156. 2).

# 78

## CAENIS AND CAENEUS

POSEIDON once lay with the Nymph Caenis, daughter of Elatus the Magnesian or, some say, of Coronus the Lapith, and asked her to name a love-gift.

'Transform me', she said, 'into an invulnerable fighter. I am weary of being a woman.'

Poseidon obligingly changed her sex, and she became Caeneus, waging war with such success that the Lapiths soon elected her their king; and she even begot a son, Coronus, whom Heracles killed many years later while fighting for Aegimius the Dorian. Exalted by this new condition, Caeneus set up a spear in the middle of the market-place, where the people congregated, and made them sacrifice to it as if to a god, and honour no other deity whatsoever.

b. Zeus, hearing of Caeneus's presumption, instigated the Centaurs to an act of murder. During the wedding of Peirithous they made a sudden attack on her, but she had no difficulty in killing five or six of them, without incurring the slightest wound, because their weapons rebounded harmlessly from her charmed skin. However, the remaining Centaurs beat her on the head with fir logs, until they had driven her under the earth, and then piled a mound of logs above. So Caeneus smothered and died. Presently out flew a sandy-winged bird, which the seer Mopsus, who was present, recognized as her soul; and when they came to bury her, the corpse was again a woman's.[1]

1. Apollodorus: i. 9. 16; ii. 7. 7 and *Epitome* i. 22; Apollonius Rhodius: i. 57–64, with scholiast; Hyginus: *Fabula* 14; *Oxyrhynchus Papyri* xiii. p. 133 ff.; Servius on Virgil's *Aeneid* vi. 448; Ovid: *Metamorphoses* xii. 458–531; Scholiast on Homer's *Iliad* i. 264.

\*

1. This myth has three distinct strands. First, a custom which still prevails in Albania, of girls joining a war-band and dressing in men's clothes, so that when they are killed in battle the enemy is surprised to discover their sex. Second, a refusal of the Lapiths to accept Hellenic overlordship; the spear set up for worship is likely to have been a maypole in honour of the New Moon-goddess Caenis, or Elate ('fir-tree'), to whom the fir was sacred. The Lapiths were then defeated by the Aeolians of Iolcus who, with the help of their allies the Centaurs, subjected them to their god Poseidon, but did not interfere with tribal law. Only, as at Argos, the clan chieftainess will have been obliged to assume an artificial beard to assert her right to act as magistrate and commander: thus Caenis became Caeneus, and Elate became Elatus. A similar change of sex is still announced by the Queen of the South, a joint ruler of the Lozi Kingdom in the Zambesi basin, when she enters the council chamber: 'I am transformed to a man!' – but this is because one of her ancestresses usurped a patriarchal throne. Third, the ritual recorded on a black-figured oil jar (see 9. 1), in

which naked men, armed with mallets, beat an effigy of Mother Earth on the head, apparently to release Core, the Spirit of the New Year: 'Caenis' means 'new'.

2. The variety of sandy-winged bird released from the effigy will depend on the season at which the rite was performed. If spring, it may have been a cuckoo (see 12. *1*).

# 79

## ERIGONE

ALTHOUGH Oeneus was the first mortal to be given a vine plant by Dionysus, Icarius anticipated him in the making of wine. He offered a sample from his trial jarful to a party of shepherds in the Marathonian woods beneath Mount Pentelicus, who, failing to mix it with water, as Oenopion later advised, grew so drunk that they saw everything double, believed themselves bewitched, and killed Icarius. His hound Maera watched while they buried him under a pine-tree and, afterwards, led his daughter Erigone to the grave by catching at her robe, and then dug up the corpse. In despair, Erigone hanged herself from the pine, praying that the daughters of Athens should suffer the same fate as hers while Icarius remained unavenged. Only the gods heard her, and the shepherds fled overseas, but many Athenian maidens were found hanging from the pine one after another, until the Delphic Oracle explained that it was Erigone who demanded their lives. The guilty shepherds were sought out at once and hanged, and the present Vintage Festival instituted, during which libations are poured to Icarius and Erigone, while girls swing on ropes from the branches of the tree, their feet resting on small platforms; this is how swings were invented. Masks are also hung from the branches, which twist around with the wind.

*b*. The image of Maera the hound was set in the sky, and became the Lesser Dog-star; some, therefore, identify Icarius with Boötes and Erigone with the constellation of the Virgin.[1]

1. Scholiast on Homer's *Iliad* xxii. 29; Nonnus: *Dionysiaca* xlvii. 34–245; Hyginus: *Fabula* 130 and *Poetic Astronomy* ii. 4; Apollodorus: i. 8. 1 and iii. 14. 7; Athenaeus: xiv. 10; Festus *sub* Oscil-

lantes; Statius: *Thebaid* xi. 644–7; Servius on Virgil's *Georgics* ii. 388–9.

*

*1.* Maera was the name given to Priam's wife Hecabe, or Hecuba, after her transformation into a dog (see 168. *1*), and since Hecuba was really the three-headed Death-goddess Hecate (see 31. *7*), the libations poured to Erigone and Icarius were probably meant for her. The valley in which this ceremony took place is now called 'Dionysus'. Erigone's pine will have been the tree under which Attis the Phrygian was castrated and bled to death (Ovid: *Fasti* iv. 221 ff.; Servius on Virgil's *Aeneid* ix. 116), and the explanation of the myth seems to be that when the Lesser Dog-star was in the ascendant, the shepherds of Marathon sacrificed one of their number as an annual victim to the goddess called Erigone.

*2.* Icarius means 'from the Icarian Sea', i.e. from the Cyclades, whence the Attis cult came to Attica. Later, the Dionysus cult was superimposed on it; and the story of the Athenian girls' suicide may have been told to account for the masks of Dionysus, hung from a pine-tree in the middle of a vineyard, which turned with the wind and were supposed to fructify the vines wherever they looked. Dionysus was usually portrayed as a long-haired, effeminate youth, and his masks would have suggested hanged women. But it is likely that dolls representing the fertility goddess Ariadne or Helen were previously hung from fruit-trees (see 88. *10* and 98. *5*). The girls' swinging at the vintage festival will have been magical in its original intention: perhaps the semi-circular flight of the swing represented the rising and setting of the new moon. This custom may have been brought to Attica from Crete, since a terracotta group found at Hagia Triada shows a girl swinging between two pillars, on each of which a bird is perched.

*3.* The name Erigone is explained by the mythographer as 'child of strife', because of the trouble she occasioned; but its obvious meaning is 'plentiful offspring', a reference to the plentiful crop induced by the dolls.

80

## THE CALYDONIAN BOAR

OENEUS, King of Calydon in Aetolia, married Althaea. She first bore him Toxeus, whom Oeneus killed with his own hands for rudely leaping over the fosse which had been dug in defence of the city; and then Meleager, said to have been, in reality, her son by Ares. When

Meleager was seven days old, the Fates came to Althaea's bedroom and announced that he could live only so long as a certain brand on the hearth remained unburned. She at once snatched the brand from the fire, extinguishing it with a pitcherful of water, and then hid it in a chest.

*b.* Meleager grew up to be a bold and invulnerable fighter, and the best javelin-thrower in Greece, as he proved at Acastus's funeral games. He might still be alive but for an indiscretion committed by Oeneus who, one summer, forgot to include Artemis in his yearly sacrifices to the twelve gods of Olympus. Artemis, when informed of this neglect by Helius, sent a huge boar to kill Oeneus's cattle and labourers, and to ravage his crops; but Oeneus despatched heralds, inviting all the bravest fighters of Greece to hunt the boar, and promising that whoever killed it should have its pelt and tusks.

*c.* Many answered the call, among them Castor and Polydeuces from Sparta; Idas and Lynceus from Messene; Theseus from Athens and Peirithous from Larissa; Jason from Iolcus and Admetus from Pherae; Nestor from Pylus; Peleus and Eurytion from Phthia; Iphicles from Thebes; Amphiaraus from Argos; Telamon from Salamis; Caeneus from Magnesia; and finally Ancaeus and Cepheus from Arcadia, followed by their compatriot, the chaste, swift-footed Atalanta, only daughter of Iasus and Clymene.[1] Iasus had wished for a male heir and Atalanta's birth disappointed him so cruelly that he exposed her on the Parthenian Hill near Calydon, where she was suckled by a bear which Artemis sent to her aid. Atalanta grew to womanhood among a clan of hunters who found and reared her, but remained a virgin, and always carried arms. On one occasion she came fainting for thirst to Cyphanta and there, calling on Artemis, and striking a rock with the point of her spear, made a spring of water gush out. But she was not yet reconciled to her father.[2]

*d.* Oeneus entertained the huntsmen royally for nine days; and though Ancaeus and Cepheus at first refused to hunt in company with a woman, Meleager declared, on Oeneus's behalf, that unless they withdrew their objection he would cancel the chase altogether. The truth was that Meleager had married Idas's daughter Cleopatra, but now felt a sudden love for Atalanta and wished to ingratiate himself with her. His uncles, Althaea's brothers, took an immediate dislike to the girl, convinced that her presence could lead only to mischief, because he kept sighing deeply and exclaiming: 'Ah, how happy the man whom she marries!' Thus the chase began under bad auspices; Artemis herself had seen to this.

*e*. Amphiaraus and Atalanta were armed with bows and arrows; others with boar-spears, javelins, or axes, each being so anxious to win the pelt for himself that hunt discipline was neglected. At Meleager's suggestion, the company advanced in a half-moon, at some paces' interval, through the forest where the boar had its lair.

*f*. The first blood shed was human. When Atalanta posted herself on the extreme right flank at some distance from her fellow-hunters, two Centaurs, Hylaeus and Rhaecus, who had joined the chase, decided to ravish her, each in turn assisting the other. But as soon as they ran towards her, she shot them both down and went to hunt at Meleager's side.

*g*. Presently the boar was flushed from a water-course overgrown with willows. It came bounding out, killed two of the hunters, hamstrung another, and drove young Nestor, who afterwards fought at Troy, up a tree. Jason and several others flung ill-aimed javelins at the boar, Iphicles alone contriving to graze its shoulder. Then Telamon and Peleus went in boldly with boar-spears; but Telamon tripped over a tree root and, while Peleus was pulling him to his feet, the boar saw them and charged. Atalanta let fly a timely arrow, which sank in behind the ear, and sent it scurrying off. Ancaeus sneered: 'That is no way to hunt! Watch me!' He swung his battle-axe at the boar as it charged, but was not quick enough; the next instant he lay castrated and disembowelled. In his excitement, Peleus killed Eurytion with a javelin aimed at the boar, which Amphiaraus had succeeded in blinding with an arrow. Next, it rushed at Theseus, whose javelin flew wide; but Meleager also flung and transfixed its right flank, and then, as the boar whirled around in pain, trying to dislodge the missile, drove his hunting-spear deep under its left shoulder-blade to the heart.

The boar fell dead at last.

At once, Meleager flayed it, and presented the pelt to Atalanta, saying: 'You drew first blood, and had we left the beast alone, it would soon have succumbed to your arrow.'

*h*. His uncles were deeply offended. The eldest, Plexippus, argued that Meleager had won the pelt himself and that, on his refusal, it should have gone to the most honourable person present – namely himself, as Oeneus's brother-in-law. Plexippus's younger brother supported him with the contention that Iphicles, not Atalanta, had drawn first blood. Meleager, in a lover's rage, killed them both.

*i.* Althaea, as she watched the dead bodies being carried home, set a curse upon Meleager; which prevented him from defending Calydon when his two surviving uncles declared war on the city and killed many of its defenders. At last his wife Cleopatra persuaded him to take up arms, and he killed both these uncles, despite their support by Apollo; whereupon the Furies instructed Althaea to take the unburned brand from the chest and cast it on the fire. Meleager felt a sudden scorching of his inwards, and the enemy overcame him with ease. Althaea and Cleopatra hanged themselves, and Artemis turned all but two of Meleager's shrieking sisters into guinea-hens, which she brought to her island of Leros, the home of evil-livers.[3]

*j.* Delighted by Atalanta's success, Iasus recognized her at last as his daughter; but when she arrived at the palace his first words were: 'My child, prepare to take a husband!' – a disagreeable announcement, since the Delphic Oracle had warned her against marriage. She answered: 'Father, I consent on one condition. Any suitor for my hand must either beat me in a foot race, or else let me kill him.' 'So be it,' said Iasus.

*k.* Many unfortunate princes lost their lives in consequence, because she was the swiftest mortal alive; but Melanion, a son of Amphidamas the Arcadian, invoked Aphrodite's assistance. She gave him three golden apples, saying: 'Delay Atalanta by letting these fall, one after the other, in the course of the race.' The stratagem was successful. Atalanta stopped to pick up each apple in turn and reached the winning-post just behind Melanion.

*l.* The marriage took place, but the Oracle's warning was justified because, one day, as they passed by a precinct of Zeus, Melanion persuaded Atalanta to come inside and lie with him there. Vexed that his precinct had been defiled, Zeus changed them both into lions; for lions do not mate with lions, but only with leopards, and they were thus prevented from ever again enjoying each other. This was Aphrodite's punishment first for Atalanta's obstinacy in remaining a virgin, and then for her lack of gratitude in the matter of the golden apples.[4] But some say that before this Atalanta had been untrue to Melanion and borne Meleager a child called Parthenopaeus, whom she exposed on the same hill where the she-bear had suckled her. He too survived and afterwards defeated Idas in Ionia and marched with the Seven Champions against Thebes. According to others, Ares, not Meleager, was Parthenopaeus's father;[5] Atalanta's husband was not Melanion but Hippomenes; and she was the daughter of Schoeneus, who ruled

Boeotian Onchestus. It is added that she and he profaned a sanctuary not of Zeus but of Cybele, who turned them into lions and yoked them to her chariot.[6]

1. Aelian: *Varia Historia* xiii. 1; Callimachus: *Hymn to Artemis* 216.
2. Apollodorus: iii. 9. 2.
3. Homer: *Iliad* ix. 527–600; Apollodorus: i. 8. 2–3; Hyginus: *Fabulae* 171, 174, and 273; Ovid: *Metamorphoses* viii. 270–545; Diodorus Siculus: iv. 48; Pausanias: iv. 2. 5; viii. 4. 7; and x. 31. 2; Callimachus: *Hymn to Artemis* 220–24; Antoninus Liberalis: 2; Athenaeus: xiv. 71.
4. Apollodorus: iii. 9. 2; Hyginus: *Fabula* 185; Servius on Virgil's *Aeneid* iii. 113; First Vatican Mythographer: 39.
5. Hyginus: *Fabulae* 70, 99, and 270; First Vatican Mythographer: 174.
6. Apollodorus: iii. 9. 2, quoting Euripides's *Meleager*; Ovid: *Metamorphoses* x. 565 ff.; Tzetzes: *Chiliades* xiii. 453; Lactantius on Statius's *Thebaid* vi. 563; Hyginus: *Fabula* 185.

\*

1. Greek physicians credited the marshmallow (*althaia*, from *althainein*, 'to cure') with healing virtue and, being the first spring flower from which bees suck honey, it had much the same mythic importance as ivy-blossom, the last. The Calydonian hunt is heroic saga, based perhaps on a famous boar hunt, and on an Aetolian clan feud occasioned by it. But the sacred king's death at the onset of a boar – whose curved tusks dedicated it to the moon – is ancient myth (see 18. *3*), and explains the introduction into the theory of heroes from several different Greek states who had suffered this fate. The boar was peculiarly the emblem of Calydon (see 106. *c*), and sacred to Ares, Meleager's reputed father.

2. Toxeus's leap over the fosse is paralleled by Remus's leap over Romulus's wall; it suggests the widespread custom of sacrificing a royal prince at the foundation of a city (1 *Kings* xvi. 34). Meleager's brand recalls several Celtic myths: a hero's death taking place when some external object – a fruit, a tree, or an animal – is destroyed.

3. Artemis was worshipped as a *meleagris*, or guinea-hen, in the island of Leros, and on the Athenian Acropolis; the cult is of East African origin, to judge from this particular variety of guinea-fowl – which had a blue wattle, as opposed to the red-wattled Italian bird introduced from Numidia – and its queer cluckings were taken to be sounds of mourning. Devotees of neither Artemis nor Isis might eat guinea-fowl. The Lerians' reputation for evil-living may have been due to their religious conservatism, like the Cretan's reputation for lying (see 45. *2*).

4. She-bears were sacred to Artemis (see 22. *4*), and Atalanta's race

against Melanion is probably deduced from an icon wich showed the doomed king, with the golden apples in his hand (see 32. *1* and 53. *5*), being chased to death by the goddess. A companion icon will have shown an image of Artemis supported by two lions, as on the gate at Mycenae, and on several Mycenaean and Cretan seals. The second version of the myth seems to be the older, if only because Schoeneus, Atalanta's father, stands for Schoenis, a title of Aphrodite's; and because Zeus does not figure in it.

5. Why the lovers were punished – here the mythographers mistakenly refer to Pliny, though Pliny says, on the contrary, that lions vigorously punish lionesses for mating with leopards (*Natural History* viii. 17) – is a problem of greater interest than Sir James Frazer in his notes on Apollodorus allows. It seems to record an old exogamic ruling, according to which members of the same totem clan could not marry one another, nor could lion clansmen marry into the leopard clan, which belonged to the same sub-phratry; as the lamb and goat clans could not intermarry at Athens (see 97. *3*).

6. Oeneus was not the only Hellenic king who withheld a sacrifice from Artemis (see 69. *b* and 72. *i*). Her demands were much more severe than those of other Olympian deities, and even in Classical times included holocausts of living animals. These Oeneus will hardly have denied her; but the Arcadian and Boeotian practice was to sacrifice the king himself, or a surrogate, as the Actaeon stag (see 22. *1*); and Oeneus may well have refused to be torn in pieces.

# 81

## TELAMON AND PELEUS

THE mother of Aeacus's two elder sons, namely Telamon and Peleus, was Endeis, Sciron's daughter. Phocus, the youngest, was a son of the Nereid Psamathe, who had turned herself into a seal while unsuccessfully trying to escape from Aeacus's embraces. They all lived together in the island of Aegina.[1]

*b.* Phocus was Aeacus's favourite, and his excellence at athletic games drove Telamon and Peleus wild with jealousy. For the sake of peace, therefore, he led a party of Aeginetan emigrants to Phocis – where another Phocus, a son of Ornytion the Corinthian, had already colonized the neighbourhood of Tithorea and Delphi – and in the course of time his sons extended the state of Phocis to its present limits.

One day Aeacus sent for Phocus, perhaps intending to bequeath him the island kingdom; but, encouraged by their mother, Telamon and Peleus plotted to kill him on his return. They challenged Phocus to a fivefold athletic contest, and whether it was Telamon who felled him, as if accidentally, by throwing a stone discus at his head, and Peleus who then despatched him with an axe, or whether it was the other way about, has been much disputed ever since. In either case, Telamon and Peleus were equally guilty of fratricide, and together hid the body in a wood, where Aeacus found it. Phocus lies buried close to the Aeaceum.[2]

*c.* Telamon took refuge in the island of Salamis, where Cychreus was king, and sent back a messenger, denying any part in the murder. Aeacus, in reply, forbade him ever again to set foot in Aegina, though permitting him to plead his case from the sea. Rather than stand and shout on the rocking deck of his ship anchored behind the breakers, Telamon sailed one night into what is now called the Secret Harbour, and sent masons ashore to build a mole, which would serve him as rostrum; they finished this task before dawn, and it is still to be seen. Aeacus, however, rejected his eloquent plea that Phocus's death was accidental, and Telamon returned to Salamis, where he married the king's daughter Glauce, and succeeded to Cychreus's throne.[3]

*d.* This Cychreus, a son of Poseidon and Salamis, daughter of the river Asopus, had been chosen King of Salamis when he killed a serpent to end its widespread ravages. But he kept a young serpent of the same breed which behaved in the same destructive way until expelled by Eurylochus, a companion of Odysseus; Demeter then welcomed it at Eleusis as one of her attendants. But some explain that Cychreus himself, called 'Serpent' because of his cruelty, was banished by Eurylochus and took refuge at Eleusis, where he was appointed to a minor office in Demeter's sanctuary. He became, at all events, one of the guardian heroes of Salamis, the Serpent Isle; there he was buried, his face turned to the west, and appeared in serpent form among the Greek ships at the famous victory of Salamis. Sacrifices were offered at his tomb, and when the Athenians disputed the possession of the island with the Megarians, Solon the famous law-giver sailed across by night and propitiated him.[4]

*e.* On the death of his wife Glauce, Telamon married Periboea of Athens, a grand-daughter of Pelops, who bore him Great Ajax; and later the captive Hesione, daughter of Laomedon, who bore him the equally well-known Teucer.[5]

*f*. Peleus fled to the court of Actor, King of Phthia, by whose adopted son Eurytion he was purified. Actor then gave him his daughter Polymela in marriage, and a third part of the kingdom. One day Eurytion, who ruled over another third part, took Peleus to hunt the Calydonian boar, but Peleus speared him accidentally and fled to Iolcus, where he was once more purified, this time by Acastus, son of Pelias.[6]

*g*. Acastus's wife, Cretheis, tried to seduce Peleus and, when he rebuffed her advances, lyingly told Polymela: 'He intends to desert you and marry my daughter Sterope.' Polymela believed Cretheis's mischievous tale, and hanged herself. Not content with the harm she had done, Cretheis went weeping to Acastus, and accused Peleus of having attempted her virtue.

*h*. Loth to kill the man whom he had purified, Acastus challenged him to a hunting contest on Mount Pelion. Now, in reward for his chastity, the gods had given Peleus a magic sword, forged by Daedalus, which had the property of making its owner victorious in battle and equally successful in the chase. Thus he soon piled up a great heap of stags, bears, and boars; but when he went off to kill even more, Acastus's companions claimed the prey as their master's and jeered at his want of skill. 'Let the dead beasts decide this matter with their own mouths!' cried Peleus, who had cut out their tongues, and now produced them from a bag to prove that he had easily won the contest.[7]

*i*. After a festive supper, in the course of which he outdid all others as a trencherman, Peleus fell fast asleep. Acastus then robbed him of his magic sword, hid it under a pile of cow-dung, and stole away with his followers. Peleus awoke to find himself deserted, disarmed, and surrounded by wild Centaurs, who were on the point of murdering him; however, their king Cheiron not only intervened to save his life, but divined where the sword lay hidden and restored it to him.[8]

*j*. Meanwhile, on the advice of Themis, Zeus chose Peleus to be the husband of the Nereid Thetis, whom he would have married himself, had he not been discouraged by the Fates' prophecy that any son born to Thetis would become far more powerful than his father. He was also vexed that Thetis had rejected his advances, for her foster-mother Hera's sake, and therefore vowed that she should never marry an immortal. Hera, however, gratefully decided to match her with the noblest of mortals, and summoned all Olympians to the wedding when the moon should next be full, at the same time sending her messenger

Iris to King Cheiron's cave with an order for Peleus to make ready.⁹

*k.* Now, Cheiron foresaw that Thetis, being immortal, would at first resent the marriage; and, acting on his instructions, Peleus concealed himself behind a bush of parti-coloured myrtle-berries on the shores of a Thessalian islet, where Thetis often came, riding naked on a harnessed dolphin, to enjoy her midday sleep in the cave which this bush half screened. No sooner had she entered the cave and fallen asleep than Peleus seized hold of her. The struggle was silent and fierce. Thetis turned successively into fire, water, a lion, and a serpent;¹⁰ but Peleus had been warned what to expect, and clung to her resolutely, even when she became an enormous slippery cuttle-fish and squirted ink at him – a change which accounts for the name of Cape Sepias, the near-by promontory, now sacred to the Nereids. Though burned, drenched, mauled, stung, and covered with sticky sepia ink, Peleus would not let her go and, in the end, she yielded and they lay locked in a passionate embrace.¹¹

*l.* Their wedding was celebrated outside Cheiron's cave on Mount Pelion. The Olympians attended, seated on twelve thrones. Hera herself raised the bridal torch, and Zeus, now reconciled to his defeat, gave Thetis away. The Fates and the Muses sang; Ganymedes poured nectar; and the fifty Nereids performed a spiral dance on the white sands. Crowds of Centaurs attended the ceremony, wearing chaplets of grass, brandishing darts of fir, and prophesying good fortune.¹²

*m.* Cheiron gave Peleus a spear; Athene had polished its shaft, which was cut from an ash on the summit of Pelion; and Hephaestus had forged its blade. The Gods' joint gift was a magnificent suit of golden armour, to which Poseidon added the two immortal horses Balius and Xanthus – by the West Wind out of the Harpy Podarge.¹³

*n.* But the goddess Eris, who had not been invited, was determined to put the divine guests at loggerheads, and while Hera, Athene, and Aphrodite were chatting amicably together, arm in arm, she rolled a golden apple at their feet. Peleus picked it up, and stood embarrassed by its inscription: 'To the Fairest!', not knowing which of the three might be intended. This apple was the protocatarctical cause of the Trojan War.¹⁴

*o.* Some describe Peleus's wife Thetis as Cheiron's daughter, and a mere mortal; and say that Cheiron, wishing to honour Peleus, spread the rumour that he had married the goddess, her mistress.¹⁵

*p.* Meanwhile Peleus, whose fortunes the kindly Cheiron had restored, and who now also acquired large herds of cattle as a dowry, sent some of these to Phthia as an indemnity for his accidental killing of Eurytion; but, when the payment was refused by the Phthians, left them to roam at will about the countryside. This proved to have been a fortunate decision, because a fierce wolf which Psamathe had sent after them, to avenge the death of her son Phocus, so glutted its hunger on these masterless cattle that it could hardly crawl. When Peleus and Thetis came face to face with the wolf, it made as if to spring at Peleus's throat, but Thetis glowered balefully, with protruded tongue and turned it into a stone, which is still pointed out on the road between Locris and Phocis.[16]

*q.* Later, Peleus returned to Iolcus, where Zeus supplied him with an army of ants transformed into warriors; and thus he became known as King of the Myrmidons. He captured the city single-handed, killed first Acastus, then the cowering Cretheis; and led his Myrmidons into the city between the pieces of her dismembered body.[17]

*r.* Thetis successively burned away the mortal parts of her six sons by Peleus, in order to make them immortal like herself, and sent each of them in turn up to Olympus. But Peleus contrived to snatch the seventh from her when she had already made all his body, except the ankle-bone, immortal by laying it on the fire and afterwards rubbing it with ambrosia; the half-charred ankle-bone had escaped this final treatment. Enraged by his interference, Thetis said farewell to Peleus, and returned to her home in the sea, naming her son 'Achilles', because he had as yet placed *no lips* to her breast. Peleus provided Achilles with a new ankle-bone, taken from the skeleton of the swift giant Damysus, but this was fated to prove his undoing.[18]

*s.* Too old to fight at Troy himself, Peleus later gave Achilles the golden armour, the ashen spear, and the two horses which had been his wedding presents. He was eventually expelled from Phthia by Acastus's sons, who no longer feared him when they heard of Achilles's death; but Thetis instructed him to visit the cave by the myrtle-bush, where he had first mastered her, and wait there until she took him away to live with her for ever in the depths of the sea. Peleus went to the cave, and eagerly watched the passing ships, hoping that one of them might be bringing his grandson Neoptolemus back from Troy.[19]

*t.* Neoptolemus, meanwhile, was refitting his shattered fleet in Molossia and, when he heard of Peleus's banishment, disguised himself as a Trojan captive and took ship for Iolcus, there contriving to kill

Acastus's sons and seize the city. But Peleus, growing impatient, had chartered a vessel for a voyage to Molossia; rough weather drove her to the island of Icos, near Euboea, where he died and was buried, thus forfeiting the immortality which Thetis had promised him.[20]

1. Apollodorus: iii. 12. 6; Pindar: *Nemean Odes* v. 13.
2. Plutarch: *Parallel Stories* 25; Pausanias: x. 1. 1 and ii. 29. 7; Apollodorus: *loc. cit.*; *The Alcmaeonis*, quoted by scholiast on Euripides's *Andromache* 687; Tzetzes: *On Lycophron* 175; Diodorus Siculus: iv. 72.
3. Apollodorus: iii. 12. 7; Pausanias: ii. 29. 7; Diodorus Siculus: *loc. cit.*
4. Apollodorus: *loc. cit.*; Hesiod, quoted by Strabo: ix. 1. 9; Stephanus of Byzantium *sub* Kychreios Pagos; Eustathius on Dionysius's *Description of the Earth* 507; Plutarch: *Solon* 9; Lycophron: *Cassandra* 110; Pausanias: i. 36. 1.
5. Apollodorus: *loc. cit.*
6. *Ibid.*: iii. 13. 1–2; Diodorus Siculus: *loc. cit.*; Tzetzes: *On Lycophron* 175; Eustathius on Homer's *Iliad* ii. 648.
7. Pindar: *Nemean Odes* v. 26 ff. and iv. 59; Scholiast on Pindar's *Nemean Odes* iv. 54 and 59; Zenobius: *Proverbs* v. 20; Apollodorus: *loc. cit.*
8. Apollodorus: iii. 13. 3; Hesiod, quoted by Scholiast on Pindar's *Nemean Odes* iv. 59.
9. Apollonius Rhodius: iv. 790 ff.; Pindar: *Isthmian Odes* viii. 41ff.
10. Ovid: *Metamorphoses* xi. 221 ff.; Sophocles: *Troilus*, quoted by scholiast on Pindar's *Nemean Odes* iii. 35; Apollodorus: iii. 13. 5; Pindar: *Nemean Odes* iv. 62; Pausanias: v. 18. 1.
11. Tzetzes: *On Lycophron* 175 and 178; Scholiast on Apollonius Rhodius i. 582; Herodotus: vii. 191; Philostratus: *Heroica* xix. 1.
12. Euripides: *Iphigeneia in Aulis* 703 ff. and 1036 ff.; Apollonius Rhodius: iv. 790; Catullus: xliv. 305 ff.
13. Apollodorus: iii. 13. 5; Homer: *Iliad* xvi. 144; xviii. 84 and xvi. 149; *Cypria* quoted by scholiast on Homer's *Iliad* xvi. 140.
14. Hyginus: *Fabula* 92; Fulgentius: iii. 7.
15. Apollonius Rhodius: i. 558; Scholiast on Apollonius Rhodius iv. 816.
16. Antoninus Liberalis: *Transformations* 38; Tzetzes: *On Lycophron* 175 and 901.
17. Tzetzes: *On Lycophron* 175; Homer: *Iliad* xxiv. 536; Pindar: *Nemean Odes* iii. 34; Apollodorus: iii. 13. 7; Scholiast on Apollonius Rhodius: i. 224.
18. Ptolemy Hephaestionos: iv, quoted by Photius: p. 487; Apollodorus: iii. 13. 6; Lycophron: *Cassandra* 178 ff.; Scholiast on Homer's *Iliad* xvi. 37.
19. Homer: *Iliad* xviii. 434 and xvi. 149; Euripides: *Trojan Women* 1128, with scholiast; *Andromache* 1253 ff.

20. Dictys Cretensis: vi. 7–9; Stephanus of Byzantium *sub* Icos; *Palatine Anthology* vii. 2. 9 ff.

*

1. The myth of Aeacus, Psamathe ('sandy shore'), and Phocus ('seal') occurs in the folklore of almost every European country. Usually the hero sees a flock of seals swimming towards a deserted shore under a full moon, and then stepping out of their skins to reveal themselves as young women. He hides behind a rock, while they dance naked on the sand, then seizes one of the seal skins, thus winning power over its owner, whom he gets with child. Eventually they quarrel; she regains her skin and swims away. The dance of the fifty Nereids at Thetis's wedding, and her return to the sea after the birth of Achilles, appear to be fragments of the same myth – the origin of which seems to have been a ritual dance of fifty seal-priestesses, dedicated to the Moon, which formed a proem to the Chief-priestess's choice of a sacred king. Here the scene is set in Aegina but, to judge from the story of Peleus's struggle near Cape Sepias, a similar ritual was performed in Magnesia by a college of cuttle-fish priestesses – the cuttle-fish appears prominently in Cretan works of art, including the standard weight from the Royal Treasury at Cnossus, and also on megalithic monuments at Carnac and elsewhere in Brittany. It has eight tentacles, as the sacred anemone of Pelion has eight petals: eight being the number of fertility in Mediterranean myth. Peleus ('muddy') may have become the sacred king's title after he had been anointed with sepia, since he is described as the son of Endeis, 'the entangler', a synonym for the cuttle-fish.

2. Acastus's hunting party, the subsequent banquet, and the loss of Peleus's magic sword seem to be mistakenly deduced from an icon which showed the preliminaries to a coronation ceremony: coronation implying marriage to the tribal heiress. The scene apparently included the king's ritual combat with men dressed as beasts, and the drawing of a regal sword from a cleft rock (misinterpreted by the mythographer as a heap of cow dung) – as in the myths of Theseus (see 95. *e*) and King Arthur of Lyonesse. But the ashen spear cut by Cheiron from Mount Pelion is an earlier symbol of sovereignty than the sword.

3. Thetis's transformations suggest a display of the goddess's seasonal powers presented in a sequence of dances (see 9. *d* and 32. *b*). The myrtle behind which Peleus first met her, emblemized the last month of his predecessor's reign (see 52. *3* and 109. *4*); and therefore served as their rendezvous when his own reign ended.

This myth seems to record a treaty-marriage, attended by representatives of twelve confederate tribes or clans, between a Phthian prince and the Moon-priestess of Iolcus in Thessaly.

4. It may well be that the author of the old English *Seege or Battayle of Troy* drew on a lost Classical source when he made Peleus 'half man, half horse': that is to say, Peleus was adopted into an Aeacid horse-cult clan. Such an adoption will have implied a sacrificial horse-feast (see 75. 3): which explains the wedding gift of Balius and Xanthus without a chariot for them to draw. The Centaurs of Magnesia and the Thessalians of Iolcus seem to have been bound by an exogamic alliance: hence the statement by the scholiast on Apollonius Rhodius that Peleus's wife was, in reality, Cheiron's daughter.

5. Peleus's embarrassment when he looked at the apple thrown down by Eris suggests a picture of the Moon-goddess, in triad, presenting the apple of immortality to the sacred king (see 32. 4; 53. 5; and 159. 3). Acastus's murder, and Peleus's march into the city between the dismembered pieces of Cretheis's body, may be a misinterpretation of an icon which showed a new king about to ride through the streets of his capital after having ritually hacked his predecessor in pieces with an axe.

6. The frequent murders, accidental or intentional, which caused princes to leave home and be purified by foreign kings, whose daughters they then married, are an invention of later mythographers. There is no reason to suppose that Peleus left Aegina, or Phthia, under a cloud; at a time when kingship went by matrilineal succession, candidates for the throne always came from abroad, and the new king was reborn into the royal house after ritually murdering his predecessor. He then changed his name and tribe, which was expected to throw the vengeful ghost of the murdered man off his scent. Similarly, Telamon of Aegina went to Salamis, was chosen as the new king, killed the old king – who became an oracular hero – and married the chief-priestess of an owl college. It was found convenient, in more civilized times, when much the same ritual was used to purify ordinary criminals, to forget that kingship implied murder, and to suggest that Peleus, Telamon, and the rest had been involved in crimes or scandals unconnected with their accession to the throne. The scandal is frequently a false accusation of having attempted a queen's virtue (see 75. *a* and 101. *e*). Cychreus's connexion with the Eleusinian Mysteries and Telamon's marriage to an Athenian princess became important when, in 620 B.C., Athens and Megara disputed the possession of Salamis. The Spartans judged the case, and the Athenian ambassadors successfully based their claim on Telamon's connexion with Attica (Plutarch: *Solon* 8 and 9).

7. Phocus's death by the discus, like that of Acrisius (see 72. *p*), seems to be a misinterpretation of an icon which showed the end of the seal-king's reign – the flying discus being a sun-disk; as the myth makes plain, the sacrificial weapon was an axe. Several heroes besides Achilles were

killed by a heel wound, and not only in Greek but in Egyptian, Celtic, Lydian, Indian, and Norse mythology (see 90. *8* and 92. *10*).

*8*. The burning of Thetis's sons was common practice: the yearly sacrifice of boy surrogates for the sacred king (see 24. *10* and 156. *2*). At the close of the eighth year the king himself died (see 91. *4* and 109. *3*). A parallel in the Indian *Mahabharata* is the drowning by the Ganges-goddess of her seven sons by the God Krishna. He saves the last, Bhishma; then she deserts him. Actor's division of his kingdom into three parts is paralleled in the myth of Proetus (see 72. *h*): the sacred king, instead of letting himself be sacrificed when his reign was due to end, retained one part of his kingdom, and bequeathed the remainder to his successors. Subsequent kings insisted on a lifetime tenure of sovereignty.

*9*. Peleus's death at Cos suggests that his name was a royal title there as well as at Phthia, Iolcus, and Salamis. He became king of the Myrmidons because the Phthians worshipped their goddess as Myrmex ('ant' – see 66. *2*). Antoninus Liberalis's story of Thetis and the wolf seems to have been deduced from an icon which showed a priestess of Wolfish Aphrodite (Pausanias: ii. 31. *6*) wearing a Gorgon mask as she sacrifices cattle.

# 82

## ARISTAEUS

HYPSEUS, a high-king of the Lapiths, whom the Naiad Creusa bore to the River-god Peneius, married Chlidanope, another Naiad, and had by her a daughter, Cyrene. Cyrene despised spinning, weaving, and similar household tasks; instead, she would hunt wild beasts on Mount Pelion all day and half the night, explaining that her father's flocks and herds needed protection. Apollo once watched her wrestling with a powerful lion; he summoned King Cheiron the Centaur to witness the combat (from which Cyrene, as usual, emerged triumphant), asking her name, and whether she would make him a suitable bride. Cheiron laughed. He was aware that Apollo not only knew her name, but had already made up his mind to carry her off, either when he saw her guarding Hypseus's flocks by the river Peneius, or when she received two hunting dogs from his hands as a prize for winning the foot race at Pelias's funeral games.[1]

*b*. Cheiron further prophesied that Apollo would convey Cyrene overseas to the richest garden of Zeus, and make her the queen of a great city, having first gathered an island people about a hill rising from a plain. Welcomed by Libya to a golden palace, she would win a queendom equally beneficent to hunters and farmers, and there bear him a son. Hermes would act as man-midwife and carry the child, called Aristeus, or Aristaeus, to the enthroned Hours and Mother Earth, bidding them feed him on nectar and ambrosia. When Aristaeus grew to manhood, he would win the titles of 'Immortal Zeus', 'Pure Apollo', and 'Guardian of the Flocks'.[2]

c. Apollo duly took Cyrene away in his golden chariot, to the site of what is now the city of Cyrene; Aphrodite was waiting to greet their arrival, and bedded them without delay in Libya's golden chamber. That evening Apollo promised Cyrene a long life in which to indulge her passion for hunting and reign to over a fertile country. He then left her to the care of certain Myrtle-nymphs, children of Hermes, on the near by-hills, where she bore Aristaeus and, after a second visit from Apollo, Idmon the seer. But she also lay with Ares one night, and bore him the Thracian Diomedes, owner of the man-eating mares.[3]

d. The Myrtle-nymphs, nicknaming Aristaeus 'Agreus' and 'Nomius', taught him how to curdle milk for cheese, build bee-hives, and make the oleaster yield the cultivated olive. These useful arts he passed on to others, who gratefully paid him divine honours. From Libya he sailed to Boeotia, after which Apollo led him to Cheiron's cave for instruction in certain Mysteries.

e. When Aristaeus had grown to manhood, the Muses married him to Autonoë, by whom he became the father of the ill-fated Actaeon, and of Macris, nurse to Dionysus. They also taught him the art of healing and prophecy, and set him to watch over their sheep which grazed across the Athamantian Plain of Phthia, and about Mount Othrys, and in the valley of the river Apidanus. It was here that Aristaeus perfected the art of hunting, taught him by Cyrene.[4]

f. One day he went to consult the Delphic Oracle, and was told to visit the island of Ceos, where he would be greatly honoured. Setting sail at once, Aristaeus found that the scorching Dog-star had caused a plague among the islanders, in vengeance of Icarius whose secret murderers were sheltering among them. Aristaeus summoned the people, raised a great altar in the mountains, and offered sacrifices on it to Zeus, at the same time propitiating the Dog-star by putting the murderers to death. Zeus was gratified and ordered the Etesian Winds, in future, to cool all Greece and its adjacent islands for forty days from the Dog-star's rising. Thus the plague ceased, and the Ceans not only showered

Aristaeus with gratitude, but still continue to propitiate the Dog-star every year before its appearance.[5]

*g.* He then visited Arcadia and, later, settled at Tempe. But there all his bees died and, greatly distressed, he went to a deep pool in the river Peneius where he knew that Cyrene would be staying with her Naiad sisters. His aunt, Arethusa, heard an imploring voice through the water, put out her head, recognized Aristaeus, and invited him down to the wonderful palace of the Naiads. These washed him with water drawn from a perpetual spring and, after a sacrificial feast, he was advised by Cyrene: 'Bind my cousin Proteus, and force him to explain why your bees sickened.'

*h.* Proteus was taking his midday rest in a cave on the island of Pharos, sheltering from the heat of the Dog-star, and Aristaeus, having overcome him, despite his changes, learned that the bees' sickness was his punishment for having caused Eurydice's death; and it was true that, when he had made love to her on the river-bank near Tempe, she had fled from him and been bitten by a serpent.

*i.* Aristaeus now returned to the Naiads' palace, where Cyrene instructed him to raise four altars in the woods to the Dryads, Eurydice's companions, and sacrifice four young bulls and four heifers; then to pour a libation of blood, leaving the carcasses where they lay; and finally to return in the morning, nine days later, bringing poppies of forgetfulness, a fatted calf, and a black ewe to propitiate the ghost of Orpheus, who had now joined Eurydice below. Aristaeus obeyed and, on the ninth morning, a swarm of bees rose from the rotting carcasses, and settled on a tree. He captured the swarm, which he put into a hive; and the Arcadians now honour him as Zeus for having taught them this method of raising new swarms of bees.[6]

*j.* Later, distressed by the death of his son Actaeon, which roused in him a hatred of Boeotia, he sailed with his followers to Libya, where he asked Cyrene for a fleet in which to emigrate. She gladly complied, and soon he was at sea again, making north-westward. Enchanted by the savage beauty of Sardinia, his first landfall, he began to cultivate it and, having begotten two sons there, was presently joined by Daedalus; but is said to have founded no city there.[7]

*k.* Aristaeus visited other distant lands, and spent some years in Sicily, where he received divine honours, especially from the olive-growers. Finally he went to Thrace, and supplemented his education by taking part in the Mysteries of Dionysus. After living for a while near Mount Haemus, and founding the city of Aristaeum, he disappeared without trace, and is now worshipped as a god both by the Thracian barbarians and by civilized Greeks.[8]

1. Pindar: *Pythian Odes* ix. 5 ff.; Apollonius Rhodius: ii. 500 ff.; Callimachus: *Hymn to Artemis* 206.
2. Pindar: *loc. cit.*
3. Diodorus Siculus: iv. 81; Pindar: *loc. cit.*; Apollonius Rhodius: *loc. cit.*; Hyginus: *Fabula* 14; Apollodorus: ii. 5. 8.
4. Diodorus Siculus: *loc cit.*; Apollodorus: iii. 4. 4; Apollonius Rhodius: iv. 1131 and ii. 500 ff.; Pindar: *loc. cit.*
5. Apollonius Rhodius: ii. 500 ff.; Diodorus Siculus: iv. 82; Hyginus: *Poetic Astronomy* ii. 4.
6. Virgil: *Georgics* iv. 317–558; Pindar, quoted by Servius on Virgil's *Georgics* i. 14.
7. Servius: *loc. cit.*
8. Diodorus Siculus: *loc cit.*; Pausanias: x. 17. 3.

*

1. Aristaeus's origins have been embroidered upon by Pindar, to flatter a descendant of Battus who, in 691 B.C., led a colony from Thera to Libya, where he founded Cyrene, and was the first king of a long dynasty. The Cyreneans claimed their ancestor Aristaeus – according to Justin (xiii. 7), Battus ('tongue-tied') was only his nickname – as the son of Apollo, because Apollo had been worshipped in Thera; and the port of Cyrene was consequently called Apollonia. But Cyrene was a mythological figure long before Battus's time. Her association with the Centaurs shows that she was goddess of a Magnesian horse cult imported to Thera; for Cheiron's name also appears in early Theran rock inscriptions. The myth of Idmon's birth from Cyrene and Ares refers to this earlier goddess.

2. Myrtle is originally a death-tree (see 109. 4), and the Myrtle-nymphs were therefore prophetesses capable of instructing young Aristaeus; but it became symbolic of colonization, because emigrants took myrtle-boughs with them to demonstrate that they had ended an epoch.

3. Aristaeus was a cult-title of Arcadian and Cean Zeus; and elsewhere of Apollo and Hermes. According to Servius (on Virgil's *Georgics* i. 14) Hesiod called Aristaeus 'a pastoral Apollo'. At Tanagra in Boeotia (Pausanias: ix. 22. 1) Hermes was known as 'Ram-bearer', and fish were sacred to him at Pharae in Achaea (Pausanias: vii. 22. 2). Thus a tomb-painting at Cyrene shows 'Aristaeus' surrounded by sheep and fish and carrying a ram. His wanderings are offered in explanation of the cult-title Aristaeus, which occurs in Sicily, Sardinia, Ceos, Boeotia, Thessaly, Macedonia, and Arcadia. The Dog-star is the Egyptian god Thoth, identified with Hermes, who was known as Aristaeus by the Ceans.

4. His raising of bees from the carcasses of cattle has been mistold by

Virgil. They will have swarmed, rather, from the lion which Cyrene killed, or which was killed in her honour. This myth, like that of Samson's bees which swarmed from a lion's carcass, seems to be deduced from a primitive icon showing a naked woman tussling amorously with a lion, while a bee hovers above the carcass of another lion. The naked woman is the Lion-goddess Cyrene, or Hepatu the Hittite, or Anatha of Syria, or Hera the Lion-goddess of Mycenae, and her partner is the sacred king, who is due to die under the midsummer sign of Leo, emblemized by a knife in the Egyptian Zodiac. Like Theseus or Heracles, he wears a lion mask and skin, and is animated by the spirit of the dead lion, his predecessor, which appears as a bee (see 90. 3). This is spring-time, when bees first swarm, but afterwards, as the Midsummer Bee-goddess, she will sting him to death, and emasculate him (see 18. 3). The lion which the sacred king himself killed – as did both Heracles and his friend Phylius (see 153. e–f) in the Peloponnese; or Cyzicus on Mount Dindymum in the Sea of Marmara (see 149. h); or Samson in Philistia (Judges xiv. 6); or David at Bethlehem (1 Samuel xvii. 34) – was one of the beasts which challenged him to a ritual combat at his coronation.

5. Virgil's account of Aristaeus's visit to the river Peneius illustrates the irresponsible use of myth: Proteus, who lived at Pharos off the Nile Delta, has been dragged into the story by the heels – there was a famous Oracle of Apollo at Tempe, which Aristaeus, his son, would naturally have consulted; Arethusa, a Peloponnesian stream, had no business in the Peneius; and Aristaeus is shown different chambers in the Naiads' palace where the sources of the Tiber, the Po, the Anio, the Phasis, and other widely separated rivers are kept – a mythologically absurd conception.

6. Exports of oil to Sicily will have been more profitable to the Cretans than that of olive-grafts; but once Hellenic colonies had been founded on the southern coast in late Mycenaean times, olive-culture was established there. The Aristaeus who visited Sicily may be identified with Zeus Morius, who was responsible for distributing grafts of the sacred olive-trees descended from the one planted by Athene on the Athenian Acropolis (see 16. c). He may also have introduced the science of bee-keeping which came to Athens from Minoan Crete, where professional bee-keepers had a bee and a glove as their trade device, and used terracotta hives. The Greek word for bee-bread, cerinthos, is Cretan; and so must all the related words be, such as cērion, 'honey-bomb', cērinos, 'waxen', and cēraphis, 'bee-moth' – a kind of locust. Cer, in fact, whose name (also spelt Car or Q're) came generally to mean 'fate', 'doom', or 'destiny' – multiplied into ceres, 'spites, plagues, or unseen ills' – must have been the Cretan Bee-goddess, a goddess of Death in Life. Thus the Sphinx-goddess of Thebes is called by Aeschylus (Seven Against Thebes 777) 'the man-snatching Cer'.

# MIDAS

MIDAS, son of the Great Goddess of Ida, by a satyr whose name is not remembered, was a pleasure-loving King of Macedonian Bromium, where he ruled over the Brigians (also called Moschians) and planted his celebrated rose gardens.[1] In his infancy, a procession of ants was observed carrying grains of wheat up the side of his cradle and placing them between his lips as he slept – a prodigy which the soothsayers read as an omen of the great wealth that would accrue to him; and when he grew older, Orpheus tutored him.[2]

b. One day, the debauched old satyr Silenus, Dionysus's former pedagogue, happened to straggle from the main body of the riotous Dionysian army as it marched out of Thrace into Boeotia, and was found sleeping off his drunken fit in the rose gardens. The gardeners bound him with garlands of flowers and led him before Midas, to whom he told wonderful tales of an immense continent lying beyond the Oceans stream – altogether separate from the conjoined mass of Europe, Asia, or Africa – where splendid cities abound, peopled by gigantic, happy, and long-lived inhabitants, and enjoying a remarkable legal system. A great expedition – at least ten million strong – once set out thence across the Ocean in ships to visit the Hyperboreans; but on learning that theirs was the best land that the old world had to offer, retired in disgust. Among other wonders, Silenus mentioned a frightful whirlpool beyond which no traveller may pass. Two streams flow close by, and trees growing on the banks of the first bear fruit that causes those who eat it to weep and groan and pine away. But fruit growing by the other stream renews the youth even of the very aged: in fact, after passing backwards through middle age, young manhood, and adolescence, they become children again, then infants – and finally disappear! Midas, enchanted by Silenus's fictions, entertained him for five days and nights, and then ordered a guide to escort him to Dionysus's headquarters.[3]

c. Dionysus, who had been anxious on Silenus's account, sent to ask how Midas wished to be rewarded. He replied without hesitation: 'Pray grant that all I touch be turned into gold.' However, not only stones, flowers, and the furnishings of his house turned to gold but, when he sat down to table, so did the food he ate and the water he drank. Midas soon begged to be released from his wish, because he was fast dying of hunger and thirst; whereupon Dionysus, highly entertained, told him to visit the source of the river Pactolus, near Mount Tmolus, and there wash himself. He obeyed, and was at once freed from the golden touch, but the sands of the river Pactolus are bright with gold to this day.[4]

d. Midas, having thus entered Asia with his train of Brigians, was adopted by the childless Phrygian King Gordius. While only a poor peasant, Gordius had been surprised one day to see a royal eagle perch on the pole of his ox-cart. Since it seemed prepared to settle there all day, he drove the team towards Phrygian Telmissus, now a part of Galatia, where there was a reliable oracle; but at the gate of the city he met a young prophetess who, when she saw the eagle still perched on the pole, insisted on his offering immediate sacrifices to Zeus the King. 'Let me come with you, peasant,' she said, 'to make sure that you choose the correct victims.' 'By all means,' replied Gordius. 'You appear to be a wise and considerate young woman. Are you prepared to marry me?' 'As soon as the sacrifices have been offered,' she answered.

e. Meanwhile, the King of Phrygia had died suddenly, without issue, and an oracle announced: 'Phrygians, your new king is approaching with his bride, seated in an ox-cart!'

When the ox-cart entered the market place of Telmissus, the eagle at once attracted popular attention, and Gordius was unanimously acclaimed king. In gratitude, he dedicated the cart to Zeus, together with its yoke, which he had knotted to the pole in a peculiar manner. An oracle then declared that whoever discovered how to untie the knot would become the lord of all Asia. Yoke and pole were consequently laid up in the Acropolis at Gordium, a city which Gordius had founded, where the priests of Zeus guarded them jealously for centuries – until Alexander the Macedonian petulantly cut the knot with his sword.[5]

f. After Gordius's death, Midas succeeded to the throne, promoted the worship of Dionysus, and founded the city of Ancyra. The Brigians who had come with him became known as Phrygians, and the kings of Phrygia are alternately named Midas and Gordius to this day; so that the first Midas is now mistakenly described as a son of Gordius.[6]

g. Midas attended the famous musical contest between Apollo and Marsyas, umpired by the River-god Tmolus. Tmolus awarded the prize to Apollo who, when Midas dissented from the verdict, punished him with a pair of ass's ears. For a long time, Midas managed to conceal these under a Phrygian cap; but his barber, made aware of the deformity, found it impossible to keep the shameful secret close, as Midas had enjoined him to do on pain of death. He therefore dug a hole in the river-bank and, first making sure that nobody was about, whispered into it: 'King Midas has ass's ears!' Then he filled up the hole, and went away, at peace with himself until a reed sprouted from the bank and whispered the secret to all who passed. When Midas learned that his disgrace had become public knowledge, he condemned the barber to death, drank bull's blood, and perished miserably.[7]

1. Hyginus: *Fabula* 274; Philostratus: *Life of Apollonius of Tyana* vi. 27; Herodotus: i. 14 and viii. 138.
2. Cicero: *On Divination* i. 36; Valerius Maximus: i. 6. 3; Ovid: *Metamorphoses* xi. 92–3.
3. Aelian: *Varia Historia* iii. 18.
4. Plutarch: *Minos* 5; Ovid: *Metamorphoses* xi. 90 ff.; Hyginus: *Fabula* 191; Virgil; *Eclogues* vi. 13 ff.
5. Arrian: *Anabasis of Alexander* ii. 3.
6. Justin: xi. 7; Pausanias: i. 4. 5; Aelian: *Varia Historia* iv. 17.
7. Ovid: *Metamorphoses* xi. 146 ff.; Persius: *Satires* i. 121; Strabo: i. 3. 21.

\*

1. Midas has been plausibly identified with Mita, King of the Moschians ('calf-men'), or Mushki, a people of Pontic origin who, in the middle of the second millennium B.C., occupied the western part of Thrace, afterwards known as Macedonia; they crossed the Hellespont about the year 1200 B.C., broke the power of the Hittites in Asia Minor, and captured Pteria, their capital. 'Moschians' refers perhaps to a cult of the bull-calf as the spirit of the sacred year. Midas's rose gardens and the account of his birth suggest an orgiastic cult of Aphrodite, to whom the rose was sacred. The story of the golden touch has been invented to account for the riches of the Mita dynasty, and for the presence of gold in the Pactolus river; and it is often said that the ass's ears were suggested by Midas's representation as a satyr, with hideously lengthened ears, in Athenian comic drama.

2. But since asses were sacred to his benefactor Dionysus, who set a pair of them among the stars (Hyginus: *Poetic Astronomy* ii. 23), it is likely that the original Midas gloried in his ass disguise. A pair of ass's ears at the tip of a reed sceptre was the token of royalty carried by all Egyptian dynastic gods, in memory of the time when ass-eared Set (see 35. 4) ruled their pantheon. Set had greatly declined in power until his temporary

revival by the Hyksos kings of the early second millennium B.C.; but because the Hittites formed part of the great horde of northern conquerors led by the Hyksos, ass-eared Midas may well have claimed sovereignty over the Hittite Empire in Set's name. In pre-dynastic times, Set had ruled the second half of the year, and annually murdered his brother Osiris, the spirit of the first half, whose emblem was a bull: they were, in fact, the familiar rival twins perpetually contending for the favours of their sister, the Moon-goddess Isis.

3. It is likely that the icon from which the story of Midas's barber derives showed the death of the ass-king. His sun-ray hair, the seat of royal power, is shorn off, like Samson's (see 91. *1*); his decapitated head is buried in a hole to guard the city of Ancyra from invasion. The reed is an ambivalent symbol: as the 'tree' of the twelfth month (see 52. *3*), it gives him an oracular warning of imminent death; it also enroyals his successor. Because of the great magical potency of bull's blood, only priestesses of the Earth-mother could drink it without harm (see 51. *4* and 155. *a*), and being the blood of Osiris, it would be peculiarly poisonous to an ass-king.

4. The secret of the Gordian knot seems to have been a religious one, probably the ineffable name of Dionysus, a knot-cypher tied in the rawhide thong. Gordium was the key to Asia (Asia Minor) because its citadel commanded the only practicable trade route from Troy to Antioch; and the local priestess or priest will have communicated the secret to the King of Phrygia alone, as the High-priest alone was entrusted with the ineffable name of Jehovah at Jerusalem. Alexander's brutal cutting of the knot, when he marshalled his army at Gordium for the invasion of Greater Asia, ended an ancient dispensation by placing the power of the sword above that of religious mystery. Gordius (from *gruzein*, 'to grunt' or 'grumble') was perhaps so named from the muttering at his oracular shrine.

5. Why the story of the Atlantic Continent should have been attributed to the drunken Silenus may be divined from three incidents reported by Plutarch (*Life of Solon* 25–9). The first is that Solon travelled extensively in Asia Minor and Egypt; the second, that he believed the story of Atlantis (see 39. *b*) and turned it into an epic poem; the third, that he quarrelled with Thespis the dramatist who, in his plays about Dionysus, put ludicrous speeches, apparently full of topical allusions, into the mouths of satyrs. Solon asked: 'Are you not alarmed, Thespis, to tell so many lies to so large an audience?' When Thespis answered: 'What does it matter when the whole play is a joke?', Solon struck the ground violently with his staff: 'Encourage such jokes in our theatre, and they will soon creep into our contracts and treaties!' Aelian, who quotes Theopompus as his authority, seems to have had access at second or third

hand to a comedy by Thespis, or his pupil Pratinas, ridiculing Solon for
the Utopian lies told in the epic poem, and presenting him as Silenus,
wandering footloose about Egypt and Asia Minor (see 27. *b*). Silenus and
Solon are not dissimilar names and as Silenus was tutor to Dionysus, so
Solon was tutor to Peisistratus who – perhaps on his advice – founded
the Dionysian rites at Athens (see 27. 5).

6. It is possible that Solon during his travels had picked up scraps of
Atlantian lore which he incorporated in his epic, and which lent themselves to theatrical parody: such as the Gaelic legend of a Land of Youth
beyond the Ocean – where Niamh of the Golden Hair took Oisin, and
whence he returned centuries later on a visit to Ireland. Oisin, it will be
recalled, was disgusted with the degeneracy of his own people compared
with Niamh's, and bitterly regretted having come back. The unnavigable
whirlpool is the famous one, assumed by ancient physicists, where the
Ocean spills over the edge of the world into nothingness. Solon seems
also to have heard geographers discussing the possible existence of an
Atlantic Continent: Erathosthenes, Mela, Cicero, and Strabo speculated
on it and Seneca foretold its discovery in the second act of his *Medea* – a
passage which is said to have made a deep impression on the young
Columbus.

# 84

## CLEOBIS AND BITON

CLEOBIS and Biton, two young Argives, were the sons of Hera's
priestess at Argos. When the time came for her to perform the rites of
the goddess, and the white oxen which were to draw her sacred chariot
had not yet arrived from the pasture, Cleobis and Biton, harnessing
themselves to the chariot, dragged it to the temple, a distance of nearly
five miles. Pleased with their filial devotion, the priestess prayed that
the goddess would grant them the best gift she could bestow on mortals; and when she had performed her rites, they went to sleep in the
temple, never to wake again.[1]

*b*. A similar gift was granted to Agamedes and Trophonius, sons of
Erginus. These twins had built a stone threshold upon foundations laid
by Apollo himself for his temple at Delphi. His oracle told them: 'Live
merrily and indulge yourselves in every pleasure for six days; on the
seventh, your heart's desire shall be granted.' On the seventh day both

were found dead in their beds. Hence it is said: 'Those whom the gods love die young.[2]

*c.* Trophonius was later awarded an oracle of his own at Lebadeia in Boeotia.[3]

1. Herodotus: i. 31; Pausanias: ii. 20. 2.
2. Pindar, quoted by Plutarch: *Consolation to Apollonius* 14; *Homeric Hymn to Apollo* 294–99; Menander: *Fragments of Greek Comedy* iv. 105, ed. Meinecke.
3. Herodotus: i. 46; Euripides: *Ion* 300.

\*

1. The myth of Cleobis and Biton apparently refers to the human sacrifices offered when a new temple was dedicated to the Moon-goddess: at Argos, twin brothers were chosen as surrogates for the co-kings, and harnessed to a moon-chariot in place of the white bulls, the usual sacrifice. They will have been buried under the temple threshold to keep away hostile influences (see 169. *h*); perhaps this was why the twins Castor and Polydeuces (see 62. *c*) were sometimes called Oebalides, which may mean 'sons of the temple threshold' rather than 'of the speckled sheep-skin'. The priests of Apollo evidently adopted this practice at Delphi, although they denied the Moon-goddess, to whom the sacrifice should have been made, any foothold in the temple.

2. The seventh day, which was sacred to the Titan Cronus (and to Cronian Jehovah at Jerusalem) had 'repose' as its planetary function; but 'repose' signified death in the goddess's honour – hence the hero-oracle awarded to Trophonius (see 51. *1*).

# 85

## NARCISSUS

NARCISSUS was a Thespian, the son of the blue Nymph Leiriope, whom the River-god Cephisus had once encircled with the windings of his streams, and ravished. The seer Teiresias told Leiriope, the first person ever to consult him: 'Narcissus will live to a ripe old age, provided that he never knows himself.' Anyone might excusably have fallen in love with Narcissus, even as a child, and when he reached the age of sixteen, his path was strewn with heartlessly rejected lovers of both sexes; for he had a stubborn pride in his own beauty.

*b.* Among these lovers was the nymph Echo, who could no longer use her voice, except in foolish repetition of another's shout: a punishment for having kept Hera entertained with long stories while Zeus's concubines, the mountain nymphs, evaded her jealous eye and made good their escape. One day when Narcissus went out to net stags, Echo stealthily followed him through the pathless forest, longing to address him, but unable to speak first. At last Narcissus, finding that he had strayed from his companions, shouted: 'Is anyone here?'

'Here!' Echo answered, which surprised Narcissus, since no one was in sight.

'Come!'

'Come!'

'Why do you avoid me?'

'Why do you avoid me?'

'Let us come together here!'

'Let us come together here!' repeated Echo, and joyfully rushed from her hiding place to embrace Narcissus. Yet he shook her off roughly, and ran away. 'I will die before you ever lie with me!' he cried.

'Lie with me!' Echo pleaded.

But Narcissus had gone, and she spent the rest of her life in lonely glens, pining away for love and mortification, until only her voice remained.[1]

*c.* One day, Narcissus sent a sword to Ameinius, his most insistent suitor, after whom the river Ameinius is named; it is a tributary of the river Helisson, which flows into the Alpheius. Ameinius killed himself on Narcissus's threshold, calling on the gods to avenge his death.

*d.* Artemis heard the plea, and made Narcissus fall in love, though denying him love's consummation. At Donacon in Thespia he came upon a spring, clear as silver, and never yet disturbed by cattle, birds, wild beasts, or even by branches dropping off the trees that shaded it; and as he cast himself down, exhausted, on the grassy verge to slake his thirst, he fell in love with his reflection. At first he tried to embrace and kiss the beautiful boy who confronted him, but presently recognized himself, and lay gazing enraptured into the pool, hour after hour. How could he endure both to possess and yet not to possess? Grief was destroying him, yet he rejoiced in his torments; knowing at least that his other self would remain true to him, whatever happened.

*e.* Echo, although she had not forgiven Narcissus, grieved with him;

she sympathetically echoed 'Alas! Alas!' as he plunged a dagger in his
breast, and also the final 'Ah, youth, beloved in vain, farewell!' as he
expired. His blood soaked the earth, and up sprang the white narcissus
flower with its red corollary, from which an unguent balm is now dis-
tilled at Chaeronea. This is recommended for affections of the ears
(though apt to give headaches), and as a vulnerary, and for the cure of
frost-bite.[2]

1. Ovid: *Metamorphoses* iii. 341–401.
2. Pausanias: viii. 29. 4 and ix. 31. 6; Ovid: *Metamorphoses* 402–510;
   Conon: *Narrations* 24; Pliny: *Natural History* xxi. 75.

\*

*1.* The 'narcissus' used in the ancient wreath of Demeter and Persephone (Sophocles: *Oedipus at Colonus* 682–4), and also called *leirion* was
the three-petalled blue fleur-de-lys or iris: sacred to the Triple-goddess,
and worn as a chaplet when the Three Solemn Ones (see 115. *c*), or
Erinnyes, were being placated. It flowers in late autumn, shortly before
the 'poet's narcissus', which is perhaps why Leiriope has been described
as Narcissus's mother. This fanciful moral tale – incidentally accounting
for the medicinal properties of narcissus-oil, a well-known *narc*otic, as
the first syllable of 'Narcissus' implies – may be deduced from an icon
which showed the despairing Alcmaeon (see 107. *e*), or Orestes (see
114. *a*), lying crowned with lilies, beside a pool in which he has vainly
tried to purify himself after murdering his mother; the Erinnyes having
refused to be placated. Echo, in this icon, would represent the mocking
ghost of his mother, and Ameinius his murdered father.

*2.* But *-issus*, like *-inthus*, is a Cretan termination, and both Narcissus
and Hyacinthus seem to have been names for the Cretan springflower-
hero whose death the goddess bewails on the gold ring from the Mycenaean Acropolis; elsewhere he is called Antheus (see 159. *4*), a surname of
Dionysus. Moreover, the lily was the royal emblem of the Cnossian king.
In a painted relief found among the Palace ruins, he walks, sceptre in hand,
through a lily-meadow, wearing a crown and necklace of fleur-de-lys.

# 86

## PHYLLIS AND CARYA

PHYLLIS, a Thracian princess, was in love with Acamas a son of
Theseus, who had gone to fight at Troy. When Troy fell, and the

Athenian fleet returned, Phyllis paid frequent visits to the shore, hoping to sight his ship; but this had been delayed by a leak, and she died of grief after her ninth fruitless visit, at a place called Enneodos. She was metamorphosed by Athene into an almond-tree, and Acamas, arriving on the following day, embraced only her rough bark. In response to his caresses the branches burst into flower instead of leaf, which has been a peculiarity of almond-trees ever since. Every year, the Athenians dance in her honour, and in his.[1]

*b*. And Carya, daughter of a Laconian king, was beloved of Dionysus, but died suddenly at Caryae, and was metamorphosed by him into a walnut-tree. Artemis brought the news to the Laconians, who thereupon built a temple to Artemis Caryatis, from which Caryatids – female statues used as columns – take their name. At Caryae too, the Laconian women dance annually in the goddess's honour, having been instructed by the Dioscuri.[2]

1. Lucian: *On the Dance* 40; Hyginus: *Fabula* 59; Servius on Virgil's *Eclogues* v. 10; First Vatican Mythographer 159.
2. Pausanias: iii. 10. 8 and iv. 16. 5; Servius on Virgil's *Eclogues* viii. 29.

\*

*1*. Both these myths are told to account for the festal use of almond or walnut, in honour of Car, or Carya (see 57. 2), otherwise known as Metis (see 1. *d* and 9. *d*), the Titaness of Wisdom; and are apparently deduced from an icon which showed a young poet worshipping a nut-tree in the goddess's presence, while nine young women performed a round dance. Enneodos, which occurs also in the legend of the Thracian Phyllis who drove Demophon mad (see 169. *i*), means 'nine journeys', and the number nine was connected with nuts by the Irish bards, and nuts with poetic inspiration; and in their tree-alphabet (see 52. 3) the letter *coll* ('C'), meaning 'hazel', also expressed the number nine. According to the Irish *Dinnschenchas*, the fountain of inspiration in the river Boyne was overhung by the nine hazels of poetic art, and inhabited by spotted fish which sang. Another Caryae ('walnut-trees') in Arcadia, stood close to a stream reported by Pausanias to contain the same peculiar kind of fish (Pausanias: vii. 14. 1–3 and 21. 1; Athenaeus: viii. p. 331).

*2*. The goddess Car, who gave her name to Caria, became the Italian divinatory goddess Carmenta, 'Car the Wise' (see 52. 5; 82. 6; 95. 5 and 132. *o*), and the Caryatids are her nut-nymphs – as the Meliae are ash-nymphs; the Mēliae, apple-nymphs; and the Dryads, oak-nymphs. Pliny has preserved the tradition that Car invented augury (*Natural History*

viii. 57). Phyllis ('leafy') may be a humble Greek version of the Palestinian and Mesopotamian Great Goddess Belili; in the Demophon myth
she is associated with Rhea (see 169. j).

# 87

## ARION

ARION of Lesbos, a son of Poseidon and the Nymph Oneaea, was a
master of the lyre, and invented the dithyramb in Dionysus's honour.
One day his patron Periander, tyrant of Corinth, reluctantly gave him
permission to visit Taenarus in Sicily, where he had been invited to
compete in a musical festival. Arion won the prize, and his admirers
showered on him so many rich gifts that these excited the greed of the
sailors engaged to bring him back to Corinth.

'We much regret, Arion, that you will have to die,' remarked the
captain of the ship.

'What crime have I committed?' asked Arion.

'You are too rich,' replied the captain.

'Spare my life, and I will give you all my prizes,' Arion pleaded.

'You would only retract your promise on reaching Corinth,' said
the captain, 'and so would I, in your place. A forced gift is no gift.'

'Very well,' cried Arion resignedly. 'But pray allow me to sing a
last song.'

When the captain gave his permission, Arion, dressed in his finest
robe, mounted on the prow, where he invoked the gods with impas-
sioned strains, and then leaped overboard. The ship sailed on.

b. However, his song had attracted a school of music-loving dolphins, one of which took Arion on his back, and that evening he overtook the ship and reached the port of Corinth several days before it cast
anchor there. Periander was overjoyed at his miraculous escape, and
the dolphin, loth to part from Arion, insisted on accompanying him to
court, where it soon succumbed to a life of luxury. Arion gave it a
splendid funeral.

When the ship docked, Periander sent for the captain and crew,
whom he asked with pretended anxiety for news of Arion.

'He has been delayed at Taenarus,' the captain answered, 'by the lavish hospitality of the inhabitants.'

Periander made them all swear at the dolphin's tomb that this was the truth, and then suddenly confronted them with Arion. Unable to deny their guilt, they were executed on the spot. Apollo later set the images of Arion and his lyre among the stars.[1]

*c.* Nor was Arion the first man to have been saved by a dolphin. A dolphin rescued Enalus when he leaped overboard to join his sweetheart Phineis who, in accordance with an oracle, had been chosen by lot and thrown into the sea to appease Amphitrite – for this was the expedition which the sons of Penthilus were leading to Lesbos as the island's first colonists – and the dolphin's mate rescued Phineis. Another dolphin saved Phalanthus from drowning in the Crisaean Sea on his way to Italy. Likewise Icadius, the Cretan brother of Iapys, when shipwrecked on a voyage to Italy, was guided by a dolphin to Delphi and gave the place its name; for the dolphin was Apollo in disguise.[2]

1. Herodotus: i. 24; Scholiast on Pindar's *Olympian Odes* xiii. 25; Hyginus: *Fabula* 194; Pausanias: iii. 25. 5.
2. Plutarch: *Banquet of the Seven Wise Men* 20; Pausanias: x. 13. 5; Servius on Virgil's *Aeneid* iii. 332.

\*

1. Both Arion and Periander are historical characters of the seventh century B.C., and a fragment of Arion's *Hymn to Poseidon* survives. The story is perhaps based partly on a tradition that Arion's songs attracted a school of dolphins and thus dissuaded some sailors from murdering him for his money – dolphins and seals are notoriously susceptible to music – partly on a misinterpretation of a statue which showed the god Palaemon, lyre in hand, arriving at Corinth on dolphin-back (see 70. 5). Mythic colour is lent to the story by making Arion a son of Poseidon, as was his namesake, the wild horse Arion (see 16. *f*), and by giving his name to the Lyre constellation. Pausanias, a level-headed and truthful writer, doubts Herodotus's hearsay story about Arion; but reports that he has seen with his own eyes the dolphin at Poroselene, which was mauled by fishermen, but had its wounds dressed by a boy, coming in answer to the boy's call and gratefully allowing him to ride on its back (iii. 25. 5). This suggests that the ritual advent of the New Year Child was dramatically presented at Corinth with the aid of a tame dolphin trained by the Sun-priests.

2. The myth of Enalus and Phineis is probably deduced from an icon which showed Amphitrite and Triton riding on dolphins. Enalus is also associated by Plutarch with an octopus cult, and his name recalls that of

Oedipus the Corinthian New Year Child (see 105. 1), whose counterpart he will have been at Mytilene, as Phalanthus was in Italy. Taras, a son of Poseidon by Minos's daughter Satyraea ('of the satyrs'), was the dolphin-riding New Year Child of Tarentum, which he is said to have founded, and where he had a hero shrine (Pausanias: x. 10. 4 and 13. 5; Strabo: vi. 3. 2); Phalanthus, the founder of Dorian Tarentum in 708 B.C., took over the dolphin cult from the Cretanized Sicels whom he found there.

3. Icadius's name, which means 'twentieth', is connected perhaps with the date of the month on which his advent was celebrated.

# 88

## MINOS AND HIS BROTHERS

WHEN Zeus left Europe, after having fathered Minos, Rhadamanthys, and Sarpedon on her in Crete, she married Asterius, the reigning king, whose father Tectamus son of Dorus had brought a mixed colony of Aeolian and Pelasgian settlers to the island and there married a daughter of Cretheus the Aeolian.[1]

b. This marriage proving childless, Asterius adopted Minos, Rhadamanthys, and Sarpedon, and made them his heirs. But when the brothers grew to manhood, they quarrelled for the love of a beautiful boy named Miletus, begotten by Apollo on the Nymph Areia, whom some call Deione, and others, Theia.[2] Miletus having decided that he liked Sarpedon best, was driven from Crete by Minos, and sailed with a large fleet to Caria in Asia Minor, where he founded the city and kingdom of Miletus. For the previous two generations, this country, then called Anactoria, had been ruled by the giant Anax, a son of Uranus and Mother Earth, and by his equally gigantic son Asterius. The skeleton of Asterius, whom Miletus killed and afterwards buried on an islet lying off Lade, has lately been disinterred; it is at least ten cubits long. Some, however, say that Minos suspected Miletus of plotting to overthrow him and seize the kingdom; but that he feared Apollo, and therefore refrained from doing more than warn Miletus, who fled to Caria of his own accord.[3] Others say that the boy who occasioned the quarrel was not Miletus but one Atymnius, a son of Zeus and Cassiopeia, or of Phoenix.[4]

c. After Asterius's death, Minos claimed the Cretan throne and, in proof of his right to reign, boasted that the gods would answer whatever prayer he offered them. First dedicating an altar to Poseidon, and making all preparations for a sacrifice, he then prayed that a bull might emerge from the sea. At once, a dazzlingly white bull swam ashore, but Minos was so struck by its beauty that he sent it to join his own herds, and slaughtered another instead. Minos's claim to the throne was accepted by every Cretan, except Sarpedon who, still grieving for Miletus, declared that it had been Asterius's intention to divide the kingdom equally between his three heirs; and, indeed, Minos himself had already divided the island into three parts, and chosen a capital for each.[5]

*d.* Expelled from Crete by Minos, Sarpedon fled to Cilicia in Asia Minor, where he allied himself with Cilix against the Milyans, conquered them, and became their king. Zeus granted him the privilege of living for three generations; and when he finally died, the Milyan kingdom was called Lycia, after his successor Lycus, who had taken refuge with him upon being banished from Athens by Aegeus.[6]

*e.* Meanwhile, Minos had married Pasiphaë, a daughter of Helius and the nymph Crete, otherwise known as Perseis. But Poseidon, to avenge the affront offered him by Minos, made Pasiphaë fall in love with the white bull which had been withheld from sacrifice. She confided her unnatural passion to Daedalus, the famous Athenian craftsman, who now lived in exile at Cnossus, delighting Minos and his family with the animated wooden dolls he carved for them. Daedalus promised to help her, and built a hollow wooden cow, which he upholstered with a cow's hide, set on wheels concealed in its hooves, and pushed into the meadow near Gortys, where Poseidon's bull was grazing under the oaks among Minos's cows. Then, having shown Pasiphaë how to open the folding doors in the cow's back, and slip inside with her legs thrust down into its hindquarters, he discreetly retired. Soon the white bull ambled up and mounted the cow, so that Pasiphaë had all her desire, and later gave birth to the Minotaur, a monster with a bull's head and a human body.[7]

*f.* But some say that Minos, having annually sacrificed to Poseidon the best bull in his possession, withheld his gift one year, and sacrificed merely the next best; hence Poseidon's wrath; others say that it was Zeus whom he offended; others again, that Pasiphaë had failed for several years to propitiate Aphrodite, who now punished her with this monstrous lust. Afterwards, the bull grew savage and devastated the whole of Crete, until Heracles captured and brought it to Greece where it was eventually killed by Theseus.[8]

*g*. Minos consulted an oracle to know how he might best avoid scandal and conceal Pasiphaë's disgrace. The response was: 'Instruct Daedalus to build you a retreat at Cnossus!' This Daedalus did, and Minos spent the remainder of his life in the inextricable maze called the Labyrinth, at the very heart of which he concealed Pasiphaë and the Minotaur.[9]

*h*. Rhadamanthys, wiser than Sarpedon, remained in Crete; he lived at peace with Minos, and was awarded a third part of Asterius's dominions. Renowned as a just and upright law-giver, inexorable in his punishment of evildoers, he legislated both for the Cretans and for the islanders of Asia Minor, many of whom voluntarily adopted his judicial code. Every ninth year, he would visit Zeus's cave and bring back a new set of laws, a custom afterwards followed by his brother Minos.[10] But some deny that Rhadamanthys was Minos's brother, and call him a son of Hephaestus; as others deny that Minos was Zeus's son, making him the son of Lycastus and the nymph of Ida. He bequeathed land in Crete to his son Gortys, after whom the Cretan city is named, although the Tegeans insist that Gortys was an Arcadian, the son of Tegeates.[11] Rhadamanthys also bequeathed land in Asia Minor to his son Erythrus; and the island of Chios to Oenopion, the son of Ariadne, whom Dionysus first taught how to make wine; and Lemnos to Thoas, another of Ariadne's sons: and Cournos to Enyues; and Peparethos to Staphylus; and Maroneia to Euanthes; and Paros to Alcaeus; and Delos to Anius; and Andros to Andrus.[12]

*i*. Rhadamanthys eventually fled to Boeotia because he had killed a kinsman, and lived there in exile at Ocaleae, where he married Alcmene, Heracles's mother, after the death of Amphitryon. His tomb, and that of Alcmene, are shown at Haliartus, close to a plantation of the tough canes brought from Crete, from which javelins and flutes are cut. But some say that Alcmene was married to Rhadamanthys in the Elysian Fields, after her death.[13] For Zeus had appointed him one of the three Judges of the Dead; his colleagues were Minos and Aeacus, and he resided in the Elysian Fields.[14]

1. Diodorus Siculus: iv. 60 and v. 80.
2. Diodorus Siculus: iv. 60; Apollodorus: iii. 1. 2; Ovid: *Metamorphoses* ix. 442; Antoninus Liberalis: *Transformations* 30.
3. Pausanias: vii. 2. 3 and i. 35. 5; Ovid: *Metamorphoses* ix. 436 ff.

4. Apollodorus: *loc. cit.*; Scholiast on Apollonius Rhodius: ii. 178.

5. Strabo: x. 4. 8.

6. Apollodorus: *loc. cit.*; Herodotus: i. 173.

7. Diodorus Siculus: *loc. cit.*; Pausanias: vii. 4. 5; Virgil: *Eclogues* vi. 5 ff.; Apollodorus: *loc. cit.* and iii. 1. 3–4.

8. Diodorus Siculus: iv. 77. 2 and 13. 4; First Vatican Mythographer: 47; Hyginus: *Fabula* 40 [*but the text is corrupt*].

9. Ovid: *Metamorphoses* viii. 155 ff.; Apollodorus: iii. 1. 4.

10. Diodorus Siculus: iv. 60 and v. 79; Apollodorus: iii. 1. 2; Strabo; *loc. cit.*

11. Cinaethon, quoted by Pausanias: viii. 53. 2; Diodorus Siculus: iv. 60; Pausanias: viii. 53. 2.

12. Scholiast on Apollonius Rhodius: iii. 997; Diodorus Siculus: v. 79. 1–2.

13. Tzetzes: *On Lycophron* 50; Apollodorus: ii. 4. 11; Plutarch: *Lysander* 28; Strabo: ix. 11. 30; Pherecydes, quoted by Antoninus Liberalis: *Transformations* 33.

14. Diodorus Siculus: v. 79; Homer: *Odyssey* iv. 564.

*

1. Sir Arthur Evans's classification of successive periods of pre-Classical Cretan Culture as Minoan I, II, and III suggests that the ruler of Crete was already called Minos in the early third millennium B.C.; but this is misleading. Minos seems to have been the royal title of an Hellenic dynasty which ruled Crete early in the second millennium, each king ritually marrying the Moon-priestess of Cnossus and taking his title of 'Moon-being' from her. Minos is anachronistically made the successor of Asterius the grandson of Dorus, whereas the Dorians did not invade Crete until the close of the second millennium. It is more likely that the Aeolians and Pelasgians (perhaps including 'Ionians from Attica') brought in by Tectamus ('craftsman') – a name which identifies him with Daedalus, and with Hephaestus, Rhadamanthys's alleged father – were Minos's original companions; and that Asterius ('starry') is a masculinization of Asterië, the goddess as Queen of Heaven and creatrix of the planetary powers (see 1. *d*). *Crete* itself is a Greek word, a form of *crateia*, 'strong, or ruling, goddess' – hence Creteus, and Cretheus. Messrs M. Ventris and J. Chadwick's recent researches into the hitherto undeciphered Linear Script B, examples of which have been found at Pylus, Thebes, and Mycenae, as well as among the ruins of the Cnossian palace sacked in 1400 B.C., show that the official language at Cnossus in the middle of the second millennium was an early form of Aeolic Greek. The script seems to have been originally invented for use with a non-Aryan language and adapted to Greek with some difficulty. (Whether inscriptions in Linear Script A are written in Greek or Cretan has not yet been established.) A great number of names from Greek mythology occur in both Cretan and

mainland tablets, among them: Achilles, Idomeneus, Theseus, Cretheus, Nestor, Ephialtes, Xuthus, Ajax, Glaucus, and Aeolus – which suggests that many of these myths date back beyond the Fall of Troy.

2. Since Miletus is a masculine name, the familiar myth of two brothers who quarrel for the favours of a woman was given a homosexual turn. The truth seems to be that, during a period of disorder following the Achaean sack of Cnossus in about 1400 B.C., numerous Greek-speaking Cretan aristocrats of Aeolo-Pelasgian or Ionian stock, for whom the Moon-goddess was the supreme deity, migrated with their native dependants to Asia Minor, especially to Caria, Lycia, and Lydia; for, disregarding the tradition of Sarpedon's dynasty in Lycia, Herodotus records that the Lycians of his time still reckoned by matrilinear descent (Herodotus: i. 173; Strabo: xii. 8. 5), like the Carians (see 75. 5). *Miletos* may be a native Cretan word, or a transliteration of *milteios*, 'the colour of red ochre, or red lead'; and therefore a synonym for Erythrus, or Phoenix, both of which mean 'red'. Cretan complexions were redder than Hellenic ones, and the Lycians and Carians came of partly Cretan stock; as did the Puresati (Philistines), whose name also means 'red men' (see 38. 3).

3. The gigantic rulers of Anactoria recall the Anakim of *Genesis*, giants (*Joshua* xiv. 13) ousted by Caleb from the oracular shrine which had once belonged to Ephron the son of Heth (Tethys?). Ephron gave his name to Hebron (*Genesis* xxiii. 16), and may be identified with Phoroneus. These Anakim seem to have come from Greece, as members of the Sea-people's confederation which caused the Egyptians so much trouble in the fourteenth century B.C. Lade, the burial place of Anax's son Asterius, was probably so called in honour of the goddess Lat, Leto, or Latona (see 14. 2), and that this Asterius bears the same name as Minos's father suggests that the Milesians brought it with them from the Cretan Miletus (see 25. 6). According to a plausible tradition in the Irish *Book of Invasions*, the Irish Milesians originated in Crete, fled to Syria by way of Asia Minor, and thence sailed west in the thirteenth century B.C. to Gaetulia in North Africa, and finally reached Ireland by way of Brigantium (Compostela, in North-western Spain).

4. Miletus's claim to be Apollo's son suggests that the Milesian kings were given solar attributes, like those of Corinth (see 67. 2).

5. The triumph of Minos, son of Zeus, over his brothers refers to the Dorian's eventual mastery of Crete, but it was Poseidon to whom Minos sacrificed the bull, which again suggests that the earlier holders of the title 'Minos' were Aeolians. Crete had for centuries been a very rich country and, in the late eighth century B.C., was shared between the Achaeans, Dorians, Pelasgians, Cydonians (Aeolians), and in the far west of the island, 'true Cretans' (*Odyssey* xix. 171–5). Diodorus Siculus tries to distinguish Minos son of Zeus from his grandson, Minos son of

Lycastus; but two or three Minos dynasties may have successively reigned in Cnossus.

6. Sarpedon's name ('rejoicing in a wooden ark') suggests that he brought with him to Lycia (see 162. *n*) the ritual of the Sun-hero who, at New Year, makes his annual reappearance as a child floating in an ark – like Moses, Perseus (see 73. *c*), Anius (see 160. *t*), and others. A Cretan connexion with the Perseus myth is provided by Pasiphaë's mother Perseis. Zeus's concession to Sarpedon, that he should live for three generations, means perhaps that instead of the usual eight years – a Great Year – which was the length of Minos's reign, he was allowed to keep his throne until the nineteenth year, when a closer synchronization of solar and lunar time occurred than at the end of eight; and thus broke into the third Great Year (see 67. *2*).

7. Since 'Pasiphaë', according to Pausanias (iii. 26. 1), is a title of the Moon; and 'Itone', her other name, a title of Athene as rain-maker (Pausanias: ix. 34. 1), the myth of Pasiphaë and the bull points to a ritual marriage under an oak between the Moon-priestess, wearing cow's horns, and the Minos-king, wearing a bull's mask (see 76. *1*). According to Hesychius (*sub* Carten), 'Gortys' stands for *Carten*, the Cretan word for a ˙ cow; and the marriage seems to have been understood as one between Sun and Moon, since there was a herd of cattle sacred to the Sun in Gortys (Servius on Virgil's *Eclogues* vi. 60). Daedalus's discreet retirement from the meadow suggests that this was not consummated publicly in the Pictish or Moesynoechian style. Many later Greeks disliked the Pasiphaë myth, and preferred to believe that she had an affair not with a bull, but with a man called Taurus (Plutarch: *Theseus* 19; Palaephatus: *On Incredible Stories* ii). White bulls, which were peculiarly sacred to the Moon (see 84. *1*), figured in the annual sacrifice on the Alban mount at Rome, in the cult of Thracian Dionysus, in the mistletoe-and-oak ritual of the Gallic Druids (see 50. *2*) and, according to the *Book of the Dun Cow*, in the divinatory rites which preceded an ancient Irish coronation.

8. Minos's palace at Cnossus was a complex of rooms, ante-rooms, halls, and corridors in which a country visitor might easily lose his way. Sir Arthur Evans suggests that this was the Labyrinth, so called from the *labrys*, or double-headed axe; a familiar emblem of Cretan sovereignty – shaped like a waxing and a waning moon joined together back to back, and symbolizing the creative as well as the destructive power of the goddess. But the maze at Cnossus had a separate existence from the palace; it was a true maze, in the Hampton Court sense, and seems to have been marked out in mosaic on a pavement as a ritual dancing pattern – a pattern which occurs in places as far apart as Wales and North-eastern Russia, for use in the Easter maze-dance. This dance was performed in Italy (Pliny: *Natural History* xxxvi. 85), and in Troy (Scholiast on Euripides's

*Andromache* 1139), and seems to have been introduced into Britain, towards the end of the third millennium B.C., by neolithic immigrants from North Africa. Homer describes the Cnossus maze (*Iliad* xviii. 592):

> Daedalus in Cnossus once contrived
> A dancing-floor for fair-haired Ariadne

and Lucian refers to popular dances in Crete connected with Ariadne and the Labyrinth (*On the Dance* 49).

9. The cult of Rhadamanthys may have been brought from Boeotia to Crete, and not contrariwise. Haliartus, where he had a hero-shrine, was apparently sacred to the 'White Goddess of Bread', namely Demeter; for *Halia*, 'of the sea', was a title of the Moon as Leucothea, 'the White Goddess' (Diodorus Siculus: v. 55), and *artos* means 'bread'. Alcmene ('strong in wrath') is another Moon-title. Though said to be a Cretan word, Rhadamanthys may stand for *Rhabdomantis*, 'divining with a wand', a name taken from the reed-bed at Haliartus, where his spirit stirred the tops oracularly (see 83. 3). If so, the tradition of his having legislated for all Crete and the islands of Asia Minor will mean that a similar oracle in Crete was consulted at the beginning of each new reign, and that its pronouncements carried authority wherever Cretan weights, measures, and trading conventions were accepted. He is called a son of Zeus, rather than of Hephaestus, doubtless because the Rhadamanthine oracles came from the Dictaean Cave, sacred to Zeus (see 7. *b*).

10. At Petsofa in Crete a hoard of human heads and limbs, of clay, have been found, each with a hole through which a string could be passed. If once fixed to wooden trunks they may have formed part of Daedalus's jointed dolls, and represented the Fertility-goddess. Their use was perhaps to hang from a fruit-tree, with their limbs moving about in the wind, to ensure good crops. Such a doll is shown hanging from a fruit-tree in the famous gold ring from the Acropolis Treasure at Mycenae. Tree worship is the subject of several Minoan works of art, and Ariadne, the Cretan goddess, is said to have hanged herself (*Contest of Homer and Hesiod* 14), as the Attic Erigone did (see 79. *a*). Artemis the Hanged One, who had a sanctuary at Condyleia in Arcadia (Pausanias: viii. 23. 6), and Helen of the Trees, who had a sanctuary at Rhodes and is said to have been hanged by Polyxo (Pausanias: iii. 19. 10), may be variants of the same goddess.

# 89

## THE LOVES OF MINOS

MINOS lay with the nymph Paria, whose sons colonized Paros and were later killed by Heracles; also with Androgeneia, the mother of the lesser Asterius,[1] as well as many others; but especially he pursued Britomartis of Gortyna, a daughter of Leto. She invented hunting-nets and was a close companion to Artemis, whose hounds she kept on a leash.[2]

*b.* Britomartis hid from Minos under thick-leaved oak-saplings in the water meadows, and then for nine months he pursued her over craggy mountains and level plains until, in desperation, she threw herself into the sea, and was hauled to safety by fishermen. Artemis deified Britomartis under the name of Dictynna; but on Aegina she is worshipped as Aphaea, because she vanished; at Sparta as Artemis, surnamed 'the Lady of the Lake'; and on Cephallonia as Laphria; the Samians, however, use her true name in their invocations.[3]

*c.* Minos's many infidelities so enraged Pasiphaë that she put a spell upon him: whenever he lay with another woman he discharged, not seeds, but a swarm of noxious serpents, scorpions, and millepedes, which preyed on her vitals.[4] One day, Procris, daughter of the Athenian King Erechtheus, whom her husband Cephalus had deserted, visited Crete. Cephalus was provoked to this by Eos, who fell in love with him. When he politely refused her advances, on the ground that he could not deceive Procris, with whom he had exchanged vows of perpetual faithfulness, Eos protested that Procris, whom she knew better than he did, would readily forswear herself for gold. Since Cephalus indignantly denied this, Eos metamorphosed him into the likeness of one Pteleon, and advised him to tempt Procris to his bed by offering her a golden crown. He did so, and, finding that Procris was easily seduced, felt no compunction about lying with Eos, of whom she was painfully jealous.

*d.* Eos bore Cephalus a son named Phaëthon; but Aphrodite stole him while still a child, to be the night-watchman of her most sacred shrines; and the Cretans call him Adymnus, by which they mean the morning and the evening star.[5]

*e.* Meanwhile, Procris could not bear to stay in Athens, her desertion being the subject of general gossip, and therefore came to Crete, where Minos found her no more difficult to seduce than had the supposed Pteleon. He bribed her with a hound that never failed to catch his quarry, and a dart that never missed its mark, both of which had been given him by Artemis.[6] Procris, being an ardent huntress, gladly accepted these, but insisted that Minos should take a prophylactic draught – a decoction of magical roots invented by the witch Circe –

to prevent him from filling her with reptiles and insects. This draught had the desired effect, but Procris feared that Pasiphaë might bewitch her, and therefore returned hurriedly to Athens, disguised as a handsome boy, having first changed her name to Pterelas. She never saw Minos again.

*f.* Cephalus, whom she now joined on a hunting expedition, did not recognize her and coveted Laelaps, her hound, and the unerring dart so much that he offered to buy them, naming a huge sum of silver. But Procris refused to part with either, except for love, and when he agreed to take her to his bed, tearfully revealed herself as his wife. Thus they were reconciled at last, and Cephalus enjoyed great sport with the dog and the dart. But Artemis was vexed that her valuable gifts should thus be bandied from hand to hand by these mercenary adulterers, and plotted revenge. She put it into Procris's head to suspect that Cephalus was still visiting Eos when he rose two hours after midnight and went off to hunt.

*g.* One night Procris, wearing a dark tunic, crept out after him in the half light. Presently he heard a rustle in a thicket behind him, Laelaps growled and stiffened, Cephalus let fly with the unerring dart and transfixed Procris. In due course the Areiopagus sentenced him to perpetual banishment for murder.[7]

*h.* Cephalus retired to Thebes, where King Amphitryon, the supposed father of Heracles, borrowed Laelaps to hunt the Teumessian vixen which was ravaging Cadmeia. This vixen, divinely fated never to be caught, could be appeased only by the monthly sacrifice of a child. But, since Laelaps was divinely fated to catch whatever he pursued, doubt arose in Heaven as to how this contradiction should be resolved: in the end, Zeus angrily settled it by turning both Laelaps and the vixen into stone.[8]

*i.* Cephalus next assisted Amphitryon in a successful war against the Teleboans and Taphians. Before it began, Amphitryon made all his allies swear by Athene and Ares not to hide any of the spoils; only one, Panopeus, broke this oath and was punished by begetting a coward, the notorious Epeius.[9] The Teleboan king was Pterelaus, on whose head Poseidon, his grandfather, had planted a golden lock of immortality. His daughter Comaetho fell in love with Amphitryon and, wishing to gain his affections, plucked out the golden lock, so that Pterelaus died and Amphitryon swiftly conquered the Teleboans with the help of Cephalus; but he sentenced Comaetho to death for parricide.

*j*. Cephalus's share of the Teleboan dominions was the island of Cephallenia, which still bears his name. He never pardoned Minos for having seduced Procris and given her the fatal dart; nor yet could he acquit himself of responsibility. After all, he had been the first to forswear himself, because Procris's affair with the supposed Pteleon could not be reckoned as a breach of faith; 'No, no,' he grieved, 'I should never have bedded with Eos!' Though purified of his guilt, he was haunted by Procris's ghost and, fearing to bring misfortune on his companions, went one day to Cape Leucas, where he had built a temple to Apollo of the White Rock, and plunged into the sea from the cliff top. As he fell he called aloud on the name of Pterelas; for it was under this name that Procris had been most dear to him.[10]

1. Apollodorus: ii. 5. 9 and iii. 1. 2; Nonnus: *Dionysiaca* xiii. 222 and xl. 284.
2. Solinus: xi. 8; Callimachus: *Hymn to Artemis* 189; Euripides: *Iphigeneia Among the Taurians* 126; Diodorus Siculus: v. 76; Aristophanes: *Frogs* 1359.
3. Pausanias: ii. 30.3 and iii. 14. 2; Antoninus Liberalis: *Transformations* 40; Herodotus: iii. 59.
4. Antoninus Liberalis: *Transformations* 41.
5. Hesiod: *Theogony* 986; Solinus: xi. 9; Nonnus: *Dionysiaca* xi. 131 and xii. 217.
6. Apollodorus: ii. 4. 7; Ovid: *Metamorphoses* vii. 771; Hyginus: *Fabula* 189.
7. Apollodorus: *loc. cit.* and iii. 15. 1; Antoninus Liberalis: *loc. cit.*; Hyginus: *Fabulae* 125 and 189; Scholiast on Callimachus's *Hymn to Artemis* 209.
8. Pausanias: i. 37. 6 and ix. 19. 1.
9. Tzetzes: *On Lycophron* 933.
10. Apollodorus: ii. 4. 7; Strabo: x. 2. 9 and 14.

*

1. Minos's seduction of nymphs in the style of Zeus doubtless records the Cnossian king's ritual marriage to Moon-priestesses of various city states in his empire.

2. The Moon-goddess was called Britomartis in Eastern Crete. Hence the Greeks identified her with Artemis (Diodorus Siculus: v. 76; Euripides: *Hippolytus* 145 and *Iphigeneia Among the Taurians* 127; Hesychius *sub* Britomartis), and with Hecate (Euripides: *Hippolytus* 141, with scholiast). In Western Crete she was Dictynna, as Virgil knew: 'They called the Moon Dictynna after your name' (Virgil: *Ciris* 305). Dictynna is connected in the myth with *dictyon*, which means a net, of the sort used for hunting or fishing; and *Dicte* is apparently a worn-down form of

*dictynnaeon* – 'Dictynna's place'. After the introduction of the patriarchal system a murderous chase of the sacred king by the goddess armed with a net was converted into a love chase of the goddess by the sacred king (see 9. *1* and 32. *b*). Both chases occur frequently in European folklore (see 62. *1*). Minos's pursuit of Britomartis, which is paralleled in Philistia by Moxus's, or Mopsus's, chase of Derceto, begins when the oaks are in full leaf – probably in the Dog Days, which was when Set pursued Isis and the Child Horus in the water meadows of the Nile Delta – and ends nine months later, on May Eve. Zeus's seduction of Europe was also a May Eve event (see 58. *3*).

3. To judge from the ritual of the Celtic North, where the goddess is called Goda ('the Good') – Neanthes translates the syllable *brito* as 'good' (*Greek Historical Fragments* iii, ed. Müller) – she originally rode on a goat, naked except for a net, with an apple in one hand, and accompanied by a hare and a raven, to her annual love-feast. The carved *miserere* seat in Coventry Cathedral, where she was thus portrayed, recorded the pre-Christian May Eve ceremonies at Southam and Coventry, from which the legend of Lady Godiva has been piously evolved. In Celtic Germany, Scandinavia, and probably England too, Goda had ritual connexion with the goat, or with a man dressed in goat-skins – the sacred king who later became the Devil of the witch cult. Her apple is a token of the king's approaching death; the hare symbolizes the chase, during which she turns herself into a greyhound; her net will catch him when he becomes a fish; the raven will give oracles from his tomb.

4. It seems that, in Crete, the goat-cult preceded the bull-cult, and that Pasiphaë originally married a goat-king. Laphria ('she who wins booty'), Dictynna's title in Aegina, was also a title of the goat-goddess Athene, who is said to have been assaulted by the goatish Pallas, whose skin she flayed and converted into her aegis (see 9. *a*). 'Laphria' suggests that the goddess was the pursuer, not the pursued. Inscriptions from Aegina show that the great temple of Artemis belonged to Artemis Aphaea ('not dark', to distinguish her from Hecate); in the myth, Aphaea is taken to mean *aphanes*, 'disappearing'.

5. The story of Minos and Procris has passed from myth into anecdote, and from anecdote into street-corner romance, recalling some of the tales in the *Golden Ass*. Being linked with Minos's war against Athens, and the eventual downfall of Cnossus, it records, perhaps, the Cretan king's demand for a ritual marriage with the High-priestess of Athens, which the Athenians resented. Pteleon ('elm-grove'), the name of Procris's seducer, may refer to the vine-cult which spread from Crete in the time of Minos (see 88. *h*), since vines were trained on elms; but it may also be derived from *ptelos*, 'wild boar'. In that case, Cephalus and Pteleon will have originally been the sacred king and his tanist, disguised

as a wild boar (see 18. 7). Pasiphaë's witchcrafts are characteristics of an angry Moon-goddess; and Procris counters them with the witchcrafts of Circe, another title of the same goddess.

6. Cephalus's leap from the white rock at Cape Leucas rightly reminds Strabo (x. 2. 9) that the Leucadians used every year to fling a man, provided with wings to break his fall, and even with live birds corded to his body, over the cliff into the sea. The victim, a *pharmacos*, or scapegoat, whose removal freed the island from guilt, seems also to have carried a white sunshade as a parachute (see 70. 7). Boats were waiting to pick him up if he survived, and convey him to some other island (see 96. 3).

7. The myth of Comaetho and Pterelaus refers to the cutting of the solar king's hair before his death (see 83. 3; 91. 1 and 95. 5); but the name Pterelaus suggests that the winged *pharmacos* flung to his death was originally the king. The syllable *elāos*, or *elaios*, stands for the wild olive which, like the birch in Italy and North-western Europe, was used for the expulsion of evil spirits (see 52. 3); and in the Rhodian dialect *elaios* meant simply *pharmacos*. But the fates of Pterelaus and Cephalus are mythically linked by Procris's adoption of the name Pterelas, and this suggests that she was really the priestess of Athene, who launched the feathered Cephalus to his death.

8. The fox was the emblem of Messene (Apollodorus: ii. 8. 5 – see 49. 2 and 146. 6); probably because the Aeolians worshipped the Moon-goddess as a vixen; and the myth of the Teumessian vixen may record Aeolian raids on Cadmeia in search of child sacrifices, to which Zeus-worshipping Achaeans put an end.

9. Phaëthon and Adymnus (from *a-dyomenos*, 'he who does not set') are both allegorical names for the planet Venus. But Phaëthon, son of Eos and Cephalus, has been confused by Nonnus with Phaëthon, son of Helius, who drove the sun-chariot and was drowned (see 42. *d*); and with Atymnius (from *atos* and *hymnos*, 'insatiate of heroic praise'), a sun-hero worshipped by the Milesians (see 88. *b*).

10. Epeius, who built the wooden horse (see 167. *a*), appears in early legends as an outstandingly courageous warrior; but his name was ironically applied to boasters, until it became synonymous with cowardice (Hesychius *sub* Epeius).

# 90

## THE CHILDREN OF PASIPHAË

AMONG Pasiphaë's children by Minos were Acacallis, Ariadne, Androgeus, Catreus, Glaucus, and Phaedra.[1] She also bore Cydon to Hermes, and Libyan Ammon to Zeus.[2]

*b.* Ariadne, beloved first by Theseus, and then by Dionysus, bore many famous children. Catreus, who succeeded Minos on the throne, was killed in Rhodes by his own son. Phaedra married Theseus and won notoriety for her unfortunate love-affair with Hippolytus, her stepson. Acacallis was Apollo's first love; when he and his sister Artemis came for purification to Tarrha, from Aegialae on the mainland, he found Acacallis at the house of Carmanor, a maternal relative, and seduced her. Minos was vexed, and banished Acacallis to Libya where, some say, she became the mother of Garamas, though others claim that he was the first man ever to be born.[3]

*c.* Glaucus, while still a child, was playing ball one day in the palace at Cnossus or, perhaps, chasing a mouse, when he suddenly disappeared. Minos and Pasiphaë searched high and low but, being unable to find him, had recourse to the Delphic Oracle. They were informed that whoever could give the best simile for a recent portentous birth in Crete would find what was lost. Minos made enquiries and learned that a heifer-calf had been born among his herds which changed its colour thrice a day – from white to red, and from red to black. He summoned his soothsayers to the palace, but none could think of a simile until Polyeidus the Argive, a descendant of Melampus, said: 'This calf resembles nothing so much as a ripening blackberry [or mulberry].' Minos at once commanded him to go in search of Glaucus.[4]

*d.* Polyeidus wandered through the labyrinthine palace, until he came upon an owl sitting at the entrance to a cellar, frightening away a swarm of bees, and took this for an omen. Below in the cellar he found a great jar used for the storing of honey, and Glaucus drowned in it, head downwards. Minos, when this discovery was reported to him, consulted with the Curetes, and followed their advice by telling Polyeidus: 'Now that you have found my son's body, you must restore him to life!' Polyeidus protested that, not being Asclepius, he was incapable of raising the dead. 'Ah, I know better,' replied Minos. 'You will be locked in a tomb with Glaucus's body and a sword, and there you will remain until my orders have been obeyed!'

*e.* When Polyeidus grew accustomed to the darkness of the tomb he saw a serpent approaching the boy's corpse and, seizing his sword, killed it. Presently another serpent, gliding up, and finding that its mate was dead, retired, but came back shortly with a magic herb in its mouth, which it laid on the dead body. Slowly the serpent came to life again.

*f*. Polyeidus was astounded, but had the presence of mind to apply the same herb to the body of Glaucus, and with the same happy result. He and Glaucus then shouted loudly for help, until a passer-by heard them and ran to summon Minos, who was overjoyed when he opened the tomb and found his son alive. He loaded Polyeidus with gifts, but would not let him return to Argos until he had taught Glaucus the art of divination. Polyeidus unwillingly obeyed, and when he was about to sail home, told Glaucus: 'Boy, spit into my open mouth!' Glaucus did so, and immediately forgot all that he had learned.[5]

*g*. Later, Glaucus led an expedition westward, and demanded a kingdom from the Italians; but they despised him for failing to be so great a man as his father; however, he introduced the Cretan military girdle and shield into Italy, and thus earned the name Labicus, which means 'girdled'.[6]

*h*. Androgeus visited Athens, and won every contest in the All-Athenian Games. But King Aegeus knew of his friendship for the fifty rebellious sons of Pallas and fearing that he might persuade his father Minos to support these in an open revolt, conspired with the Megareans to have him ambushed at Oenoë on the way to Thebes, where he was about to compete in certain funeral games. Androgeus defended himself with courage, and a fierce battle ensued in which he was killed.[7]

*i*. News of Androgeus's death reached Minos while he was sacrificing to the Graces on the island of Paros. He threw down the garlands and commanded the flute-players to cease, but completed the ceremony; to this day they sacrifice to the Graces of Paros without either music or flowers.[8]

*j*. Glaucus son of Minos has sometimes been confused with Anthedonian Glaucus, son of Anthedon, or of Poseidon, who once observed the restorative property of a certain grass, sown by Cronus in the Golden Age, when a dead fish (or, some say, a hare) was laid upon it and came to life again. He tasted the herb and, becoming immortal, leaped into the sea, where he is now a marine god, famous for his amorous adventures. His underwater home lies off the coast of Delos, and every year he visits all the ports and islands of Greece, issuing oracles much prized by sailors and fishermen – Apollo himself is described as Glaucus's pupil.[9]

1. Pausanias: viii. 53. 2; Diodorus Siculus: iv. 60; Apollodorus: iii. 1. 2.
2. Pausanias: *loc. cit.*; Plutarch: *Agis* 9.

3. Plutarch: *Theseus* 20; Apollodorus: iii. 2. 1–2; Euripides: *Hippolytus*; Pausanias: ii. 7. 7; Apollonius Rhodius: iv. 1493 ff.
4. Hyginus: *Fabula* 136; Apollodorus: iii. 3. 1; Pausanias: i. 43. 5.
5. Apollodorus: *loc. cit.*; Hyginus: *loc. cit.*
6. Servius on Virgil's *Aeneid* vii. 796.
7. Diodorus Siculus: iv. 60. 4; Apollodorus: iii. 15. 7; Servius on Virgil's *Aeneid* vi. 14; Hyginus: *Fabula* 41.
8. Apollodorus: iii. 15. 7.
9. Athenaeus: vii. 48; Tzetzes: *On Lycophron* 754; Ovid: *Metamorphoses* xiii. 924 ff.; Pausanias: ix. 22. 6; Servius on Virgil's *Georgics* i. 437.

*

1. Pasiphaë as the Moon (see 51. *h*) has been credited with numerous sons: Cydon, the eponymous hero of Cydon near Tegea, and of the Cydonian colony on Crete; Glaucus, a Corinthian sea-hero (see 71. 4); Androgeus, in whose honour annual games were celebrated at Ceramicus, and whom the Athenians worshipped as 'Eurygyes' ('broad-circling'), to show that he was a spirit of the solar year (Hesychius *sub* Androgeus); Ammon, the oracular hero of the Ammon Oasis, later equated with Zeus; and Catreus, whose name seems to be a masculine form of Catarrhoa, the Moon as rain-maker. Her daughters Ariadne and Phaedra are reproductions of herself; Ariadne, though read as *ariagne*, 'most pure', appears to be a Sumerian name, *Ar-ri-an-de*, 'high fruitful mother of the barley', and Phaedra occurs in South Palestinian inscriptions as *Pdri*.

2. The myth of Acacallis ('unwalled') apparently records the capture, by invading Hellenes from Aegialae, of the West Cretan city of Tarrha which, like other Cretan cities, was unwalled (see 98. 1); and the flight of the leading inhabitants to Libya, where they became the rulers of the unwarlike Garamantians.

3. White, red, and black, the colours of Minos's heifer, were also those of Io the Moon-cow (see 56. 1); those of Augeias's sacred bulls (see 127.1); and on a Caeretan vase (*Monumenti Inediti* vi–vii. p. 77) those of the Minos bull which carried off Europe. Moreover, clay or plaster tripods sacred to the Cretan goddess found at Ninou Khani, and a similar tripod found at Mycenae, were painted in white, red, and black and according to Ctesias's *Indica*, these were the colours of the unicorn's horn – the unicorn, as a calendar symbol represented the Moon-goddess's dominion over the five seasons of the Osirian year, each of which contributed part of an animal to its composition. That Glaucus was chasing a mouse may point to a conflict between the Athenian worshippers of Athene, who had an owl (*glaux*) for her familiar, and the worshippers of Apollo Smintheus ('Mouse Apollo'); or the original story may have been that Minos gave him a mouse coated with honey to swallow – a desperate remedy prescribed for sick children in the ancient Eastern Mediterranean. His

manner of death may also refer to the use of honey as an embalming fluid – many jar-burials of children occur in Cretan houses – and the owl was a bird of death. The bees are perhaps explained by a misreading of certain cut gems (Weiseler: *Denkmale der Alten Kunst* ii. 252), which showed Hermes summoning the dead from burial jars, while their souls hovered above in the form of bees (see 39. *8* and 82. *4*).

4. Polyeidus is both the shape-shifting Zagreus (see 30. *a*) and the demi-god Asclepius, whose regenerative herb seems to have been mistletoe (see 50. *2*), or its Eastern-European counterpart, the loranthus. The Babylonian legend of Gilgamesh provides a parallel to the serpent's revivification. His herb of eternal life is stolen from him by a serpent, which thereupon casts its slough and grows young again; Gilgamesh, unable to recover the herb, resigns himself to death. It is described as resembling buckthorn: a plant which the Greeks took as a purge before performing their Mysteries.

5. Glaucus's spitting into the open mouth of Polyeidus recalls a similar action of Apollo when Cassandra failed to pay him for the gift of prophecy; in Cassandra's case, however, the result was not that she lost the gift, but that no one believed her (see 158. *q*).

6. The goddesses to whom Minos sacrificed without the customary flutes or flowers, when he heard that his son had died, were the Pariae, or Ancient Ones (see 89. *a*), presumably the Three Fates, euphemistically called the 'Graces'. Myth has here broken down into street-corner anecdote. Androgeus's death is a device used to account for the Cretan quarrel with Athens (see 98. *c*), based, perhaps, on some irrelevant tradition of a murder done at Oenoë.

7. Anthedonian Glaucus's oracular gifts, his name, and his love-affairs, one of which was with Scylla (see 170. *t*), suggest that he was a personification of Cretan sea-power. Both Minos (who received his oracles from Zeus) and Poseidon, patron of the Cretan confederacy (see 39. *7*), had enjoyed Scylla (see 91. *2*); and Anthedon ('rejoicing in flowers') was apparently a title of the Cretan Springflower hero incarnate in every Late Minoan king (see 85. *2*). The King of Cnossus seems to have been connected by sacred marriages with all member states of his confederacy (see 89. *1*); hence Glaucus's amatory reputation. It is probable that a representative from Cnossus made an annual progress around the Cretan overseas dependencies in the style of Talos (see 92. *7*), giving out the latest oracular edicts. Delos was a Cretan island and perhaps a distribution centre for oracles brought from the Dictaean Cave at Cnossus. But this Glaucus also resembles Proteus, the oracular sea-god of Cretan Pharos (see 169. *6*), and Melicertes the sea-god of Corinth, identified with another Glaucus (see 71. *4*). Cronus's grass of the Golden Age may have been the magical *herbe d'or* of the Druids.

8. A version of the Glaucus myth is quoted from the Lydian historian Xanthus by Pliny (*Natural History* xxv. 14) and Nonnus (*Dionysiaca* xxv. 451–551), and commemorated on a series of coins from Sardis. When the hero Tylon, or Tylus ('knot' or 'phallus'), was fatally bitten in the heel by a poisonous serpent (see 117. *1*), his sister Moera ('fate') appealed to the giant Damasen (subduer'), who avenged him. Another serpent then fetched 'the flower of Zeus' from the woods, and laid it on the lips of its dead mate, which came to life again; Moera followed this example and similarly restored Tylus.

# 91

## SCYLLA AND NISUS

MINOS was the first king to control the Mediterranean Sea, which he cleared of pirates, and in Crete ruled over ninety cities. When the Athenians had murdered his son Androgeus, he decided to take vengeance on them, and sailed around the Aegean collecting ships and armed levies. Some islanders agreed to help him, some refused. Siphnos was yielded to him by the Princess Arne, whom he bribed with gold; but the gods changed her into a jackdaw which loves gold and all things that glitter. He made an alliance with the people of Anaphe, but was rebuffed by King Aeacus of Aegina and departed, swearing revenge; Aeacus then answered an appeal from Cephalus to join the Athenians against Minos.[1]

*b.* Meanwhile, Minos was harrying the Isthmus of Corinth. He laid siege to Nisa, ruled by Nisus the Egyptian, who had a daughter named Scylla. A tower stood in the city, built by Apollo [and Poseidon?], and at its foot lay a musical stone which, if pebbles were dropped upon it from above, rang like a lyre – because Apollo had once rested his lyre there while he was working as a mason. Scylla used to spend much time at the top of the tower, playing tunes on the stone with a lapful of pebbles; and here she climbed daily when the war began, to watch the fighting.

*c.* The siege of Nisa was protracted, and Scylla soon came to know the name of every Cretan warrior. Struck by the beauty of Minos, and by his magnificent clothes and white charger, she fell perversely in love with him. Some say that Aphrodite willed it so; others blame Hera.[2]

*d.* One night Scylla crept into her father's chamber, and cut off the famous bright lock on which his life and throne depended; then, taking from him the keys of the city gate, she opened it, and stole out. She made straight for Minos's tent, and offered him the lock of hair in exchange for his love. 'It is a bargain!' cried Minos; and that same night, having entered the city and sacked it, he duly lay with Scylla; but would not take her to Crete, because he loathed the crime of parricide. Scylla, however, swam after his ship, and clung to the stern until her father Nisus's soul in the form of a sea-eagle swooped down upon her with talons and hooked beak. The terrified Scylla let go and was drowned; her soul flew off as a ciris-bird, which is well known for its purple breast and red legs.[3] But some say that Minos gave orders for Scylla to be drowned; and others that her soul became the fish ciris, not the bird of that name.[4]

*e.* Nisa was afterwards called Megara, in honour of Megareus, a son of Oenope by Hippomenes; he had been Nisus's ally and married his daughter Iphinoë, and is said to have succeeded him on the throne.[5]

*f.* This war dragged on until Minos, finding that he could not subdue Athens, prayed Zeus to avenge Androgeus's death; and the whole of Greece was consequently afflicted with earthquakes and famine. The kings of the various city states assembled at Delphi to consult the Oracle, and were instructed to make Aeacus offer up prayers on their behalf. When this had been done, the earthquakes everywhere ceased, except in Attica.

*g.* The Athenians thereupon sought to redeem themselves from the curse by sacrificing to Persephone the daughters of Hyacinthus, namely Antheis, Aegleis, Lyctaea, and Orthaea, on the grave of the Cyclops Geraestus. These girls had come to Athens from Sparta. Yet the earthquakes continued and, when the Athenians again consulted the Delphic Oracle, they were told to give Minos whatever satisfaction he might ask; which proved to be a tribute of seven youths and seven maidens, sent every nine years to Crete as a prey for the Minotaur.[6]

*h.* Minos then returned to Cnossus, where he sacrificed a hecatomb of bulls in gratitude for his success; but his end came in the ninth year.[7]

1. Strabo: x. 4. 8 and 15; Ovid: *Metamorphoses* vii. 480–viii. 6.
2. Hyginus: *Fabula* 198; Virgil: *Ciris*.
3. Apollodorus: iii. 15. 8; Hyginus: *loc. cit.*; Ovid: *Metamorphoses* viii. 6–151; Virgil: *loc. cit.*; Pausanias: ii. 34. 7.

4. Apollodorus: *loc. cit.*; Pausanias: *loc. cit.*
5. Pausanias: i. 39. 4–5.
6. Diodorus Siculus: iv. 61.
7. Ovid: *Metamorphoses* viii. 152 ff.; Homer: *Odyssey* xix. 178.

*

1. The historical setting of the Scylla myth is apparently a dispute between the Athenians and their Cretan overlords not long before the sack of Cnossus in 1400 B.C. The myth itself, almost exactly repeated in the Taphian story of Pterelaus and Comaetho, recalls those of Samson and Delilah in Philistia; Curoi, Blathnat, and Cuchulain in Ireland; Llew Llaw, Blodeuwedd, and Gronw in Wales: all variations on a single pattern. It concerns the rivalry between the sacred king and his tanist for the favour of the Moon-goddess who, at midsummer, cuts off the king's hair and betrays him. The king's strength resides in his hair, because he represents the Sun; and his long yellow locks are compared to its rays. Delilah shears Samson's hair before calling in the Philistines; Blathnat ties Curoi's to a bed-post before summoning her lover Cuchulain to kill him; Blodeuwedd ties Llew Llaw's to a tree before summoning her lover Gronw. Llew Llaw's soul takes the form of an eagle, and Blodeuwedd ('fair flower aspect'), a woman magically made of nine different flowers, is metamorphosed into an owl – as Scylla perhaps also was in the original Greek legend. A collation of these five myths shows that Scylla-Co-maetho-Blodeuwedd-Blathnat-Delilah is the Moon-goddess in her spring and summer aspect as Aphrodite Comaetho ('bright-haired'); in the autumn she turns into an owl, or a *ciris*, and becomes the Death-goddess Athene – who had many bird-epiphanies, including the owl (see 97. *4*) – or Hera, or Hecate. Her name Scylla indicates that the king was torn to pieces after his head had been shaven. As in the myth of Llew Llaw, the punishment subsequently inflicted on the traitress is a late moral addition.

2. Ovid (*Art of Love* i. 331) identifies this Scylla with a namesake whom Aphrodite turned into a dog-monster because Poseidon had seduced her (see 16. *2*), and says that she harboured wild dogs in her womb and loins as a punishment for cutting off Nisus's lock. Ovid is rarely mistaken in his mythology, and he may here be recording a legend that Pasiphaë's curse upon Minos made him fill Scylla's womb with puppies, rather than with serpents, scorpions, and millepedes. Pasiphaë and Amphritrite are the same Moon-and-Sea-goddess, and Minos, as the ruler of the Mediter-ranean, became identified with Poseidon.

3. The sacrifice of the daughters of Hyacinthus on Geraestus's tomb may refer to the 'gardens of Adonis' planted in honour of the doomed king – being cut flowers, they withered in a few hours. But Geraestus was a pre-Achaean Cyclops (see 3. *b*), and according to the *Etymologicum*

*Magnum* (*sub* Geraestides), his daughters nursed the infant Zeus at Gortyna; moreover, Geraestion was a city in Arcadia where Rhea swaddled Zeus. The Hyacinthides, then, were probably the nurses, not the daughters, of Hyacinthus: priestesses of Artemis who, at Cnidus, bore the title 'Hyacinthotrophos' ('nurse of Hyacinthus'), and identifiable with the Geraestides, since the annually dying Cretan Zeus (see 7. *1*) was indistinguishable from Hyacinthus. Perhaps, therefore, the myth concerns four dolls hung from a blossoming fruit-tree, to face the cardinal points of the compass, in a fructifying ceremony of the 'Hanged Artemis' (see 79. *2* and 88. *10*).

4. The seven Athenian youths dedicated to the Minotaur were probably surrogates sacrificed annually in place of the Cnossian king. It will have been found convenient to use foreign victims, rather than native Cretans; as happened with the Canaanite ritual of Crucifixion for which, in the end, captives and criminals sufficed as Tammuz's surrogates. 'Every ninth year' means 'at the end of every Great Year of one hundred lunations'. After seven boys had been sacrificed for the sacred king, he himself died (see 81. *8*). The seven Athenian maidens were not sacrificed; perhaps they became attendants on the Moon-priestess, and performed acrobatic feats at bull-fights, such as are shown in Cretan works of art: a dangerous but not necessarily fatal sport.

5. A set of musical stones may have existed at Megara on the model of a xylophone; it would not have been difficult to construct. But perhaps there is a recollection here of Memmon's singing statue in Egypt: hollow, with an orifice at the back of the open mouth, through which the hot air forced itself at dawn when the sun warmed the stone (see 164. *2*).

# 92

## DAEDALUS AND TALOS

THE parentage of Daedalus is disputed. His mother is named Alcippe by some; by others, Merope; by still others, Iphinoë; and all give him a different father, though it is generally agreed that he belonged to the royal house of Athens, which claimed descent from Erechtheus. He was a wonderful smith, having been instructed in his art by Athene herself.[1]

*b*. One of his apprentices, Talos the son of his sister Polycaste, or Perdix, had already surpassed him in craftsmanship while only twelve years old. Talos happened one day to pick up the jawbone of a serpent or, some say, a fish's spine; and, finding that he could use it to cut a stick in half, copied it in iron and thereby invented the saw. This, and other inventions of his – such as the potter's wheel, and the compass for marking out circles – secured him a great reputation at Athens, and Daedalus, who himself claimed to have forged the first saw, soon grew unbearably jealous.[2] Leading Talos up to the roof of Athene's temple on the Acropolis, he pointed out certain distant sights, and suddenly toppled him over the edge. Yet, for all his jealousy, he would have done Talos no harm had he not suspected him of incestuous relations with his mother Polycaste. Daedalus then hurried down to the foot of the Acropolis, and thrust Talos's corpse into a bag, proposing to bury it secretly. When challenged by passers-by, he explained that he had piously taken up a dead serpent, as the law required – which was not altogether untrue, Talos being an Erechtheid – but there were bloodstains on the bag, and his crime did not escape detection, whereupon the Areiopagus banished him for murder. According to another account he fled before the trial could take place.[3]

c. Now, the soul of Talos – whom some call Calus, Circinus, or Tantalus – flew off in the form of a partridge, but his body was buried where it had fallen. Polycaste hanged herself when she heard of his death, and the Athenians built a sanctuary in her honour beside the Acropolis.[4]

d. Daedalus took refuge in one of the Attic demes, whose people are named Daedalids after him; and then in Cretan Cnossus, where King Minos delighted to welcome so skilled a craftsman. He lived there for some time, at peace and in high favour, until Minos, learning that he had helped Pasiphaë to couple with Poseidon's white bull, locked him up for a while in the Labyrinth, together with his son Icarus, whose mother, Naucrate, was one of Minos's slaves; but Pasiphaë freed them both.[5]

e. It was not easy, however, to escape from Crete, since Minos kept all his ships under military guard, and now offered a large reward for his apprehension. But Daedalus made a pair of wings for himself, and another for Icarus, the quill feathers of which were threaded together, but the smaller ones held in place by wax. Having tied on Icarus's pair for him, he said with tears in his eyes: 'My son, be warned! Neither soar too high, lest the sun melt the wax; nor swoop too low, lest the feathers be wetted by the sea.' Then he slipped his arms into his own

pair of wings and they flew off. 'Follow me closely,' he cried, 'do not
set your own course!'

As they sped away from the island in a north-easterly direction, flap-
ping their wings, the fishermen, shepherds, and ploughmen who gazed
upwards mistook them for gods.

*f.* They had left Naxos, Delos, and Paros behind them on the left
hand, and were leaving Lebynthos and Calymne behind on the right,
when Icarus disobeyed his father's instructions and began soaring
towards the sun, rejoiced by the lift of his great sweeping wings.
Presently, when Daedalus looked over his shoulder, he could no longer
see Icarus; but scattered feathers floated on the waves below. The heat
of the sun had melted the wax, and Icarus had fallen into the sea and
drowned. Daedalus circled around, until the corpse rose to the surface,
and then carried it to the near-by island now called Icaria, where he
buried it. A partridge sat perched on a holm-oak and watched him,
chattering for delight – the soul of his sister Polycaste, at last avenged.
This island has now given its name to the surrounding sea.[6]

*g.* But some, disbelieving the story, say that Daedalus fled from
Crete in a boat provided by Pasiphaë; and that, on their way to Sicily,
they were about to disembark at a small island, when Icarus fell into
the sea and drowned. They add that it was Heracles who buried
Icarus; in gratitude for which, Daedalus made so lifelike a statue of him
at Pisa that Heracles mistook it for a rival and felled it with a stone.
Others say that Daedalus invented sails, not wings, as a means of outstripping Minos's galleys; and that Icarus, steering carelessly, was
drowned when their boat capsized.[7]

*h.* Daedalus flew westward until, alighting at Cumae near Naples,
he dedicated his wings to Apollo there, and built him a golden-roofed
temple. Afterwards, he visited Camicus in Sicily, where he was hospitably received by King Cocalus, and lived among the Sicilians, enjoying great fame and erecting many fine buildings.[8]

*i.* Meanwhile, Minos had raised a considerable fleet, and set out in
search of Daedalus. He brought with him a Triton shell, and wherever
he went promised to reward anyone who could pass a linen thread
through it: a problem which, he knew, Daedalus alone would be able
to solve. Arrived at Camicus, he offered the shell to Cocalus, who
undertook to have it threaded; and, sure enough, Daedalus found out
how to do this. Fastening a gossamer thread to an ant, he bored a hole
at the point of the shell and lured the ant up the spirals by smearing

honey on the edges of the hole. Then he tied the linen thread to the other end of the gossamer and drew that through as well. Cocalus returned the threaded shell, claiming the reward, and Minos, assured that he had at last found Daedalus's hiding-place, demanded his surrender. But Cocalus's daughters were loth to lose Daedalus, who made them such beautiful toys, and with his help they concocted a plot. Daedalus led a pipe through the roof of the bathroom, down which they poured boiling water or, some say, pitch upon Minos, while he luxuriated in a warm bath. Cocalus, who may well have been implicated in the plot, returned the corpse to the Cretans, saying that Minos had stumbled over a rug and fallen into a cauldron of boiling water.[9]

*j*. Minos's followers buried him with great pomp, and Zeus made him a judge of the dead in Tartarus, with his brother Rhadamanthys and his enemy Aeacus as colleagues. Since Minos's tomb occupied the centre of Aphrodite's temple at Camicus, he was honoured there for many generations by great crowds of Sicilians who came to worship Aphrodite. In the end, his bones were returned to Crete by Theron, the tyrant of Acragas.

*k*. After Minos's death the Cretans fell into complete disorder, because their main fleet was burned by the Sicilians. Of the crews who were forced to remain overseas, some built the city of Minoa, close to the beach where they had landed; others, the city of Hyria in Messapia; still others, marching into the centre of Sicily, fortified a hill which became the city of Enguos, so called from a spring which flows *close by*. There they built a temple of the Mothers, whom they continued to honour greatly, as in their native Crete.[10]

*l*. But Daedalus left Sicily to join Iolaus, the nephew and charioteer of Tirynthian Heracles, who led a body of Athenians and Thespians to Sardinia. Many of his works survive to this day in Sardinia; they are called Daedaleia.[11]

*m*. Now, Talos was also the name of Minos's bull-headed bronze servant, given him by Zeus to guard Crete. Some say that he was a survivor of the brazen race who sprang from the ash-trees; others, that he was forged by Hephaestus in Sardinia, and that he had a single vein which ran from his neck down to his ankles, where it was stoppered by a bronze pin. It was his task to run thrice daily around the island of Crete and throw rocks at any foreign ship; and also to go thrice yearly, at a more leisurely pace, through the villages of Crete, displaying Minos's laws inscribed on brazen tablets. When the Sardinians tried to

invade the island, Talos made himself red-hot in a fire and destroyed
them all with his burning embrace, grinning fiercely; hence the expression 'a Sardonic grin'. In the end, Medea killed Talos by pulling out the
pin and letting his life-blood escape; though some say that Poeas the
Argonaut wounded him in the ankle with a poisoned arrow.[12]

1. Apollodorus: iii. 15. 8; Plutarch: *Theseus* 19; Pherecydes, quoted
   by Scholiast on Sophocles's *Oedipus at Colonus* 472; Hyginus:
   *Fabula* 39.
2. Apollodorus: *loc. cit.*; Ovid: *Metamorphoses* viii. 236–59; Hyginus:
   *Fabula* 274; Pliny: *Natural History* vii. 57.
3. Fulgentius: *Myths* iii. 2; First Vatican Mythographer: 232; Second
   Vatican Mythographer: 130; Diodorus Siculus: iv. 76. 6; Hyginus: *Fabula* 39; Pausanias: vii. 4. 5.
4. Pausanias: i. 21. 6; Servius on Virgil's *Aeneid* vi. 14; Hellanicus,
   quoted by Scholiast on Euripides's *Orestes* 1650; Ovid: *loc. cit.*;
   Suidas and Photius *sub* Sanctuary of Perdix.
5. Diodorus Siculus: *loc. cit.*; Apollodorus: *Epitome* i. 12.
6. Isidore of Seville: *Origins* xiv. 6; Hyginus: *Fabula* 40; Ovid:
   *Metamorphoses* viii. 182–235.
7. Diodorus Siculus: iv. 77; Apollodorus: ii. 6. 3; Pausanias: ix.
   11. 2–3.
8. Virgil: *Aeneid* vi. 14 ff.; Pausanias: vii. 4. 5; Diodorus Siculus:
   iv. 78.
9. Pausanias: *loc. cit.*; Apollodorus: *Epitome* i. 14–15; Zenobius:
   *Proverbs* iv. 92; Diodorus Siculus: iv. 79.
10. Diodorus Siculus: *loc. cit.*; Herodotus: vii. 170.
11. Pausanias: vii. 2. 2; Diodorus Siculus: iv. 30.
12. Suidas *sub* Risus Sardonicus; Apollonius Rhodius: *Argonautica*
   1639 ff.; Apollodorus: i. 9. 26; Plato: *Minos* 320c.

\*

1. Hephaestus is sometimes described as Hera's son by Talos (see 12. *c*),
and Talos as Daedalus's young nephew; but Daedalus was a junior member of the House of Erechtheus, which was founded long after the birth
of Hephaestus. Such chronological discrepancies are the rule in mythology. Daedalus ('bright' or 'cunningly wrought'), Talos ('sufferer'),
and Hephaestus ('he who shines by day'), are shown by the similarity of
their attributes to be merely different titles of the same mythical character; Icarus (from *io-carios*, 'dedicated to the Moon-goddess Car') may
be yet another of his titles. For Hephaestus the smith-god married
Aphrodite, to whom the partridge was sacred; the sister of Daedalus the
smith was called Perdix ('partridge'); the soul of Talos the smith flew
off as a partridge; a partridge appeared at the burial of Daedalus's son
Icarus. Besides, Hephaestus was flung from Olympus; Talos was flung

from the Acropolis. Hephaestus hobbled when he walked; one of Talos's names was Tantalus ('hobbling, or lurching'); a cock-partridge hobbles in his love-dance, holding one heel ready to strike at rivals. Moreover, the Latin god Vulcan hobbled. His cult had been introduced from Crete, where he was called Velchanus and had a cock for his emblem, because the cock crows at dawn and was therefore appropriate to a Sun-hero. But the cock did not reach Crete until the sixth century B.C., and is likely to have displaced the partridge as Velchanus's bird.

2. It seems that in the spring an erotic partridge dance was performed in honour of the Moon-goddess, and that the male dancers hobbled and wore wings. In Palestine this ceremony, called the *Pesach* ('the hobbling') was, according to Jerome, still performed at Beth-Hoglah ('the Shrine of the Hobbler'), where the devotees danced in a spiral. Beth-Hoglah is identified with 'the threshing-floor of Atad', on which mourning was made for the lame King Jacob, whose name may mean *Jah Aceb* ('the heel-god'). Jeremiah warns the Jews not to take part in these orgiastic Canaanite rites, quoting: 'The partridge gathereth young that she hath not brought forth.' Anaphe, an island to the north of Crete, with which Minos made a treaty (see 91. *a*), was famous in antiquity as a resting-place for migrant partridges.

3. The myth of Daedalus and Talos, like its variant, the myth of Daedalus and Icarus, seems to combine the ritual of burning the solar king's surrogate, who had put on eagle's wings (see 29. *1*), in the spring bonfire – when the Palestinian New Year began – with the rituals of flinging the partridge-winged *pharmacos*, a similar surrogate, over a cliff into the sea (see 96. *3*), and of pricking the king in the heel with a poisoned arrow (see *10 below*). But the fisherman's and peasant's admiration of the flying Daedalus is probably borrowed from an icon of the winged Perseus or Marduk (see 73. *7*).

4. In one sense the labyrinth from which Daedalus and Icarus escaped was the mosaic floor with the maze pattern, which they had to follow in the ritual partridge dance (see 98. *2*); but Daedalus's escape to Sicily, Cumae, and Sardinia refers perhaps to the flight of the native bronze-workers from Crete as the result of successive Hellenic invasions. The ruse of the Triton shell, and Minos's burial in a shrine of Aphrodite to whom this shell was sacred (see 11. *3*), suggest that Minos was also, in this context, regarded as Hephaestus, the Sea-goddess's lover. His death in a bath is an incident that has apparently become detached from the myth of Nisus and Scylla (see 91. *b–d*); Nisus's Celtic counterpart, Llew Llaw, was killed in a bath by a trick; and so was another sacred King, Agamemnon of Mycenae (see 112. *1*).

5. The name Naucrate ('sea-power') records the historical conse-quences of Minos's defeat in Sicily – the passing of sea-power from

Cretan into Greek hands. That she was one of Minos's slaves suggests a palace revolution of Hellenic mercenaries at Cnossus.

6. If Polycaste, the other name of Talos's mother Perdix, means *polycassitere*, 'much tin', it belongs to the myth of the bronze man, Talos's namesake. Cretan supremacy depended largely on plentiful supplies of tin, to mix with Cyprian copper; according to Professor Christopher Hawkes, the nearest source was the island of Majorca.

7. Talos is said by Hesychius to be a name for the Sun; originally, therefore, Talos will have coursed only once a day around Crete. Perhaps, however, the harbours of Crete were guarded against pirates by three watches which sent out patrols. And since Talos the Sun was also called Taurus ('the bull' – Bekker: *Anecdotae* i. 344. 10 ff.; Apollodorus: i. 9. 26), his thrice-yearly visit to the villages was probably a royal progress of the Sun-king, wearing his ritual bull-mask – the Cretan year being divided into three seasons (see 75. 2). Talos's red-hot embrace may record the human burnt sacrifices offered to Moloch, *alias* Melkarth, who was worshipped at Corinth as Melicertes (see 70. 5), and probably also known in Crete. Since this Talos came from Sardinia, where Daedalus was said to have fled when pursued by Minos, and was at the same time Zeus's present to Minos, the mythographers have simplified the story by giving Hephaestus, rather than Daedalus, credit for its construction; Hephaestus and Daedalus being the same character. The *sardonicus risus*, or *rictus*, a twisting of the facial muscles, symptomatic of lock-jaw, was perhaps so called because the stag-man of early Sardinian bronzes wears the same mirthless, gaping grin.

8. Talos's single vein belongs to the mystery of early bronze casting by the *cire-perdue* method. First, the smith made a beeswax image which he coated with a layer of clay, and laid in an oven. As soon as the clay had been well baked he pierced the spot between heel and ankle, so that the hot wax ran out and left a mould, into which molten bronze could be poured. When he had filled this, and the metal inside had cooled, he broke the clay, leaving a bronze image of the same shape as the original wax one. The Cretans brought the *cire-perdue* method to Sardinia, together with the Daedalus cult. Since Daedalus learned his craft from Athene, who was known as Medea at Corinth, the story of Talos's death may have been a misreading of an icon which showed Athene demonstrating the *cire-perdue* method. The tradition that melted wax caused Icarus's death seems to belong, rather, to the myth of his cousin Talos; because Talos the bronze man is closely connected with his namesake, the worker in bronze and the reputed inventor of compasses.

9. Compasses are part of the bronze-worker's mystery, essential for the accurate drawing of concentric circles when bowls, helmets, or masks have to be beaten out. Hence Talos was known as Circinus, 'the circular',

a title which referred both to the course of the sun and to the use of the compass (see 3. 2). His invention of the saw has been rightly emphasized: the Cretans had minute double-toothed turning-saws for fine work, which they used with marvellous dexterity. Talos is the son of an ash-tree nymph, because ash-charcoal yields a very high heat for smelting. This myth sheds light also on Prometheus's creation of man from clay; in Hebrew legend Prometheus's part was played by the Archangel Michael, who worked under the eye of Jehovah.

10. Poeas's shooting of Talos recalls Paris's shooting of Achilles, also in the heel, and the deaths of the Centaurs Pholus and Cheiron (see 126. 3). These myths are closely related. Pholus and Cheiron died from Heracles's poisoned arrows. Poeas was the father of Philoctetes and, when Heracles had been poisoned by another Centaur, ordered him to kindle the pyre; as a result, Philoctetes obtained the same arrows (see 145. f), one of which poisoned him (see 161. l). Paris then borrowed Thessalian Apollo's deadly arrows to kill Achilles, Cheiron's foster-son (see 164. j); and finally, when Philoctetes avenged Achilles by shooting Paris, he used another from Heracles's quiver (see 166. e). The Thessalian sacred king was, it seems, killed by an arrow smeared with viper venom, which the tanist drove between his heel and ankle.

11. In Celtic myth the labyrinth came to mean the royal tomb (White Goddess p. 105); and that it also did so among the early Greeks is suggested by its definition in the Etymologicum Magnum as 'a mountain cave', and by Eustathius (On Homer's Odyssey xi. p. 1688) as 'a subterranean cave'. Lars Porsena the Etruscan made a labyrinth for his own tomb (Varro, quoted by Pliny: Natural History xxxvi. 91-3), and there were labyrinths in the 'Cyclopean', i.e. pre-Hellenic, caves near Nauplia (Strabo: viii. 6. 2); on Samos (Pliny: Natural History xxxiv. 83); and on Lemnos (Pliny: Natural History xxxvi. 90). To escape from the labyrinth, therefore, is to be reincarnate.

12. Although Daedalus ranks as an Athenian, because of the Attic deme named in his honour, the Daedalic crafts were introduced into Attica from Crete, not contrariwise. The toys that he made for the daughters of Cocalus are likely to have been dolls with movable limbs, like those which pleased Pasiphaë and her daughter Ariadne (see 88. e), and which seem to have been used in the Attic tree cult of Erigone. At any rate, Polycaste, Daedalus's sister, hanged herself, as did two Erigones and Ariadne herself (see 79. 2 and 88. 10).

13. The Messapians of Hyria, later Uria, now Oria, were known in Classical times for their Cretan customs – kiss-curl, flower-embroidered robes, double-axe, and so on; and pottery found there can be dated to 1400 B.C., which bears out the story.

# 93

## CATREUS AND ALTHAEMENES

CATREUS, Minos's eldest surviving son, had three daughters: Aerope, Clymene, and Apemosyne; and a son, Althaemenes. When an oracle predicted that Catreus would be killed by one of his own children, Althaemenes and the swift-footed Apemosyne piously left Crete, with a large following, in the hope of escaping the curse. They landed on the island of Rhodes, and founded the city of Cretinia, naming it in honour of their native island.¹ Althaemenes afterwards settled at Cameirus, where he was held in great honour by the inhabitants, and raised an altar to Zeus on the near-by Mount Atabyrius, from the summit of which, on clear days, he could gain a distant view of his beloved Crete. Around this altar he set brazen bulls, which roared aloud whenever danger threatened Rhodes.²

b. One day Hermes fell in love with Apemosyne, who rejected his advances and fled from him. That evening he surprised her near a spring. Again she turned to flee, but he had spread slippery hides on the one path of escape, so that she fell flat on her face and he succeeded in ravishing her. When Apemosyne returned to the palace, and ruefully told Althaemenes of this misadventure, he cried out 'Liar and harlot!' and kicked her to death.

c. Meanwhile Catreus, mistrusting Aerope and Clymene, the other two, banished them from Crete, of which he was now king. Aerope, after having been seduced by Thyestes the Pelopid, married Pleisthenes and became by him the mother of Agamemnon and Menelaus; and Clymene married Nauplius, the celebrated navigator. At last, in lonely old age and, so far as he knew, without an heir to his throne, Catreus went in search of Althaemenes, whom he loved dearly. Landing one night on Rhodes, he and his companions were mistaken for pirates, and attacked by the Cameiran cowherds. Catreus tried to explain who he was and why he had come, but the barking of dogs drowned his voice. Althaemenes rushed from the palace to beat off the supposed raid and, not recognizing his father, killed him with a spear. When he learned that the oracle had been fulfilled after all, despite his long, self-imposed exile, he prayed to be swallowed up by the earth. A chasm accordingly opened, and he disappeared, but is paid heroic honours to this day.³

1. Apollodorus: iii. 2. 1.
2. Diodorus Siculus: v. 78; Apollodorus: *loc. cit.*; Strabo: xiv. 2. 2; Scholiast on Pindar's *Olympian Odes* vii. 159.
3. Apollodorus: iii. 2. 1–2; Diodorus Siculus: *loc. cit.*

\*

1. This artificial myth, which records a Mycenaeo-Minoan occupation of Rhodes in the fifteenth century B.C., is intended also to account for libations poured down a chasm to a Rhodian hero, as well as for erotic sports in the course of which women danced on the newly-flayed hides of sacrificial beasts. The termination *byrios*, or *buriash*, occurs in the royal title of the Third Babylonian Dynasty, founded in 1750 B.C.; and the deity of Atabyrius in Crete, like that of Atabyrium (Mount Tabor) in Palestine, famous for its golden calf worship, was the Hittite Tesup, a cattle-owning Sun-god (see 67. 1). Rhodes first belonged to the Sumerian Moon-goddess Dam-Kina, or Danaë (see 60. 3), but passed into the possession of Tesup (see 42. 4); and, on the breakdown of the Hittite Empire, was colonized by Greek-speaking Cretans who retained the bull-cult, but made Atabyrius a son of Proteus ('first man') and Eurynome the Creatrix (see 1. *a*). In Dorian times Zeus Atabyrius usurped Tesup's Rhodian cult. The roar of bulls will have been produced by the whirling of *rhomboi*, or bull-roarers (see 30. 1), used to frighten away evil spirits.

2. Apemosyne's death at Cameira may refer to a brutal repression, by the Hittite rather than the Cretan invaders, of a college of Oracular priestesses at Cameirus. The three daughters of Catreus, like the Danaids, are the familiar Moon-triad: Apemosyne being the third person, Cameira's counterpart. Catreus accidentally murdered by Althaemenes, like Laius accidently murdered by his son Oedipus (see 105. *d*), and Odysseus by his son Telegonus (see 170. *k*), will have been a predecessor in the sacred kingship rather than a father; but the story has been mistold — the son, not the father, should land from the sea and hurl the sting-ray spear.

# 94

## THE SONS OF PANDION

WHEN Erechtheus, King of Athens, was killed by Poseidon, his sons Cecrops, Pandorus, Metion, and Orneus quarrelled over the succession; and Xuthus, by whose verdict Cecrops, the eldest, became king, had to leave Attica in haste.[1]

*b*. Cecrops, whom Metion and Orneus threatened to kill, fled first to Megara and then to Euboea, where Pandorus joined him and founded a colony. The throne of Athens fell to Cecrops's son Pandion, whose mother was Metiadusa, daughter of Eupalamus.² But he did not long enjoy his power, for though Metion died, his sons by Alcippe, of Iphinoë, proved to be as jealous as himself. These sons were named Daedalus, whom some, however, call his grandson; Eupalamus, whom others call his father; and Sicyon. Sicyon is also variously called the son of Erechtheus, Pelops, or Marathon, these genealogies being in great confusion.³

*c*. When the sons of Metion expelled Pandion from Athens he fled to the court of Pylas, Pylus, or Pylon, a Lelegian king of Megara,⁴ whose daughter Pylia he married. Later, Pylas killed his uncle Bias and, leaving Pandion to rule Megara, took refuge in Messenia, where he founded the city of Pylus. Driven thence by Neleus and the Pelasgians of Iolcus, he entered Elis, and there founded a second Pylus. Pylia bore Pandion four sons at Megara: Aegeus, Pallas, Nisus, and Lycus, though Aegeus's jealous brothers spread the rumour that he was the bastard son of one Scyrius.⁵ Pandion never returned to Athens. He enjoys a hero shrine in Megara, where his tomb is still shown on the Bluff of Athene the Diver-bird, in proof that this territory once belonged to Athens; it was disguised as this bird that Athene hid his father Cecrops under her wings, and carried him in safety to Megara.⁶

*d*. After Pandion's death his sons marched against Athens, drove out the sons of Metion, and divided Attica into four parts, as their father had instructed them to do. Aegeus, being the eldest, was awarded the sovereignty of Athens, while his brothers drew lots for the remainder of the kingdom: Nisus won Megara and the surrounding country as far west as Corinth; Lycus won Euboea; and Pallas Southern Attica, where he bred a rugged race of giants.⁷

*e*. Pylas's son Sciron, who married one of Pandion's daughters, disputed Nisus's claim to Megara, and Aeacus, called in to judge the dispute, awarded the kingship to Nisus and his descendants, but the command of its armies to Sciron. In those days Megara was called Nisa, and Nisus also gave his name to the port of Nisaea, which he founded. When Minos killed Nisus he was buried in Athens, where his tomb is still shown behind the Lyceum. The Megareans, however, who do not admit that their city was ever captured by the Cretans, claim that Megareus married Nisus's daughter Iphinoë and succeeded him.⁸

*f*. Aegeus, like Cecrops and Pandion, found his life constantly threatened by the plots of his kinsmen, among them Lycus, whom he is said to have exiled from Euboea. Lycus took refuge with Sarpedon, and gave his name to Lycia, after first visiting Aphareus at Arene, and initiating the royal household into the Mysteries the Great Goddesses Demeter and Persephone, and also into those of Atthis, at the ancient Messenian capital of Andania. This Atthis, who gave Attica its name, was one of the three daughters of Cranaus, the autochthonous king of Athens reigning at the time of the Deucalonian Flood. The oak-coppice at Andania, where Lycus purified the initiates, still bears his name.⁹ He had been granted the power of prophecy, and it was his oracle which later declared that if the Messenians kept a certain secret thing safely they would one day recover their partrimony, but if not, they would forfeit it for ever. Lycus was referring to an account of the Mysteries of the Great Goddess engraved on a sheet of tin, which the Messenians thereupon buried in a brazen urn between a yew and a myrtle, on the summit of Mount Ithone; Epaminondas the Theban eventually disinterred it when he restored the Messenians to their former glory.¹⁰

*g*. The Athenian Lyceum is also named in honour of Lycus; from the very earliest times it has been sacred to Apollo who there first received the surname 'Lycaean', and expelled wolves from Athens by the smell of his sacrifices.¹¹

1. Apollodorus: iii. 15. 1 and 5; Plutarch: *Theseus* 32; Pausanias: vii. 1. 2.
2. *Ibid.*: i. 5. 3; Eustathius on Homer p. 281; Apollodorus: iii. 15. 5.
3. Pherecydes, quoted by Scholiast on Sophocles's *Oedipus at Colonus* 472; Apollodorus: iii. 15. 8; Diodorus Siculus: iv. 76. 1; Pausanias: ii. 6. 3.
4. Apollodorus: iii. 15. 5; Pausanias: iv. 36. 1 and i. 29. 5.
5. Apollodorus: *loc. cit.*; Pausanias: iv. 36. 1.
6. Pausanias: i. 41. 6; i. 5. 3; and i. 39. 4; Hesychius *sub* Aethyia.
7. Apollodorus: iii. 15. 6; Sophocles, quoted by Strabo: i. 6; Pausanias: i. 5. 4 and i. 39. 4.
8. Pausanias: i. 39. 4–5 and 19. 5; Strabo: ix. 1. 6.
9. Herodotus: i. 173; Pausanias: i. 2. 5 and iv. 1. 4–5.
10. Pausanias: x. 12. 5; iv. 20. 2 and 26. 6.
11. *Ibid.*: i. 19. 4; Scholiast on Demosthenes: xxiv. 114.

*

*1*. Mythical genealogies such as these were quoted whenever the sovereignty of states or hereditary privileges came into dispute. The division of Megara between the sacred king, who performed necessary sacrifices, and his tanist, who commanded the army, is paralleled at Sparta (see 74. *1*). Aegeus's name records the goat cult in Athens (see 8. *1*), and Lycus's the wolf cult; any Athenian who killed a wolf was obliged to bury it by public subscription (Scholiast on Apollonius Rhodius: ii. 124). The diver-bird was sacred to Athene as protectress of ships and, since the Bluff of Athene overhung the sea, this may have been another of the cliffs from which her priestess launched the feathered *pharmacos* (see 70. 7; 89. *6*; etc.). Atthis (*actes thea*, 'goddess of the rugged coast') seems to have been a title of the Attic Triple-goddess; her sisters were named Cranaë ('stony') and Cranaechme ('rocky point – Apollodorus: iii. 14. *5*); and, since Procne and Philomela, when turned into birds, were jointly called Atthis (Martial: i. 54. 9 and v. 67. 2), she is likely to have been connected with the same cliff-top ritual. Atthis, as Athene, has several other bird epiphanies in Homer (see 97. *4*). The Mysteries of the Great Goddesses, which concerned resurrection, had been buried between yew and myrtle because these stood, respectively, for the last vowel and the last consonant of the tree alphabet (see 52. *3*), and were sacred to the Death-goddess.

# 95
## THE BIRTH OF THESEUS

AEGEUS'S first wife was Melite, daughter of Hoples: and his second, Chalciope, daughter of Rhexenor; but neither bore him any children. Ascribing this, and the misfortunes of his sisters Procne and Philomela, to Aphrodite's anger, he introduced her worship into Athens, and then went to consult the Delphic Oracle. The Oracle warned him not to untie the mouth of his bulging wine-skin until he reached the highest point of Athens, lest he die one day of grief, a response which Aegeus could not interpret.[1]

*b*. On his way home he called at Corinth; and here Medea made him swear a solemn oath that he would shelter her from all enemies if she ever sought refuge at Athens, and undertook in return to procure him a son by magic. Next, he visited Troezen, where his old comrades Pittheus and Troezen, sons of Pelops, had recently come from Pisa to share a kingdom with King Aetius. Aetius was the successor of his father Anthas, son of Poseidon and Alcyone who, having founded the cities Anthaea and Hyperea, had lately sailed off to found Halicarnassus in Caria. But Aetius seems to have enjoyed little power, because Pittheus, after Troezen's death, united Anthaea and Hyperea into a single city, which he dedicated jointly to Athene and Poseidon, calling it Troezen.[2]

*c*. Pittheus was the most learned man of his age, and one of his moral apothegms, on friendship, is often quoted: 'Blast not the hope that friendship hath conceived; but fill its measure high!' He founded a sanctuary of Oracular Apollo at Troezen, which is the oldest surviving shrine in Greece; and also dedicated an altar to the Triple-goddess Themis. Three white marble thrones, now placed above his tomb behind the temple of Artemis the Saviour, used to serve him and two others as judgement seats. He also taught the art of oratory in the Muses' sanctuary at Troezen – which was founded by Hephaestus's son Ardalus, the reputed inventor of the flute – and a treatise on rhetoric by his hand is extant.[3]

*d*. Now, while Pittheus was still living at Pisa, Bellerophon had asked to marry his daughter Aethra, but had been sent away to Caria in disgrace before the marriage could be celebrated; though still contracted to Bellerophon, she had little hope of his return. Pittheus, therefore, grieving at her enforced virginity, and influenced by the spell which Medea was casting on all of them from afar, made Aegeus drunk, and sent him to bed with Aethra. Later in the same night, Poseidon also enjoyed her. For, in obedience to a dream sent by Athene, she left the drunken Aegeus, and waded across to the island of Sphaeria, which lies close to the mainland of Troezen, carrying libations to pour at the tomb of Sphaerus, Pelops's charioteer. There, with Athene's connivance, Poseidon overpowered her, and Aethra subsequently changed the name of the island from Sphaeria to Hiera, and founded on it a temple of Apaturian Athene, establishing a rule that every Troezenian girl should henceforth dedicate her girdle to the goddess before marriage. Poseidon, however, generously conceded to Aegeus the paternity of any child born to Aethra in the course of the next four months.[4]

*e*. Aegeus, when he awoke and found himself in Aethra's bed, told her that if a son were born to them he must not be exposed or sent away, but secretly reared in Troezen. Then he sailed back to Athens, to celebrate the All-Athenian Festival, after hiding his sword and his sandals under a hollow rock, known as the Altar of Strong Zeus, which stood on the road from Troezen to Hermium. If, when the boy grew up, he could move this rock and recover the tokens, he was to be sent with them to Athens. Meanwhile, Aethra must keep silence, lest Aegeus's nephews, the fifty children of Pallas, plotted against her life. The sword was an heirloom from Cecrops.[5]

*f*. At a place now called Genethlium, on the way from the city to the harbour of Troezen, Aethra gave birth to a boy. Some say that she at once named him Theseus, because the tokens had been *deposited* for him; others, that he afterwards won this name at Athens. He was brought up in Troezen, where his guardian Pittheus discreetly spread the rumour that Poseidon had been his father; and one Connidas, to whom the Athenians still sacrifice a ram on the day before the Thesean Feasts, acted as his pedagogue. But some say that Theseus grew up at Marathon.[6]

*g*. One day Heracles, dining at Troezen with Pittheus, removed his lion-skin and threw it over a stool. When the palace children came in, they screamed and fled, all except seven-year-old Theseus, who ran to snatch an axe from the woodpile, and returned boldly, prepared to attack a real lion.[7]

*h*. At the age of sixteen years he visited Delphi, and offered his first manly hair-clippings to Apollo. He shaved, however, only the fore-part of his head, like the Arabians and Mysians, or like the war-like Abantes of Euboea, who thereby deny their enemies any advantage in close combat. This kind of tonsure, and the precinct where he per-formed the ceremony, are both still called Thesean. He was now a strong, intelligent and prudent youth; and Aethra, leading him to the rock underneath which Aegeus had hidden the sword and sandals, told him the story of his birth. He had no difficulty in moving the rock, since called the 'Rock of Theseus', and recovered the tokens. Yet, despite Pittheus's warnings and his mother's entreaties, he would not visit Athens by the safe sea route, but insisted on travelling overland; impelled by a desire to emulate the feats of his cousin-german Heracles, whom he greatly admired.[8]

1. Scholiast on Euripides's *Medea* 668; Apollodorus: iii. 15. 6; Pausanias: i. 14. 6.
2. Euripides: *Medea* 660 ff.; Strabo: viii. 6. 14; Plutarch: *Theseus* 2.
3. Plutarch: *loc. cit.*; Pausanias: ii. 31. 3–4 and 8–9.
4. Pausanias: ii. 31. 12 and 33. 1; Apollodorus: iii. 15. 7; Plutarch: *Theseus* 3; Hyginus: *Fabula* 37.
5. Plutarch: *loc. cit.*; Apollodorus: *loc. cit.*; Pausanias: ii. 32. 7.

6. Pausanias: ii. 32. 8; Plutarch: *Theseus* 4 and 6; Lactantius on
   Statius's *Thebaid* xii. 194.
7. Pausanias: i. 27. 8.
8. Homer: *Iliad* ii. 542; Pausanias: *loc. cit.* and ii. 32. 7; Plutarch:
   *Theseus* 5 and 7.

*

*1.* Pittheus is a masculine form of Pitthea. The names of the towns
which he united to form Troezen suggests a matriarchal calendar-triad
(see 75. 2), consisting of Anthea ('flowery'), the Goddess of Spring;
Hyperea ('being overhead'), the Goddess of Summer, when the sun is at
its zenith; and Pitthea ('pine-goddess'), worshipped in autumn when
Attis-Adonis (see 79. 1) was sacrificed on his pine. They may be identified
with the Triple-goddess Themis, to whom Pittheus raised an altar since
the name Troezen is apparently a worn-down form of *trion hezomenon*,
'[the city] of the three sitters', which refers to the three white thrones
which served 'Pittheus and two others' as seats of justice.

*2.* Theseus must originally have had a twin, since his mother lay with
both a god and a mortal on the same night; the myths of Idas and Lynceus
Castor and Polydeuces (see 74. 1), Heracles and Iphicles (see 118. 3), make
this certain. Moreover, he wore the lion-skin, like Heracles, and will
therefore have been the sacred king, not the tanist. But when, after the
Persian Wars, Theseus became the chief national hero of Athens, his
paternity at least had to be Athenian, because his mother came from
Troezen. The mythographers then decided to have it both ways: he was
an Athenian, the son of Aegeus, a mortal; but whenever he needed to
claim Poseidon as his father, he could do so (see 98. *j* and 101. *f*). In either
case, his mother remained a Troezenian; Athens had important interests
there. He was also allowed a honorary twin, Peirithous who, being
mortal, could not escape from Tartarus – as Heracles, Polydeuces, and
Theseus himself did (see 74. *j*; 103. *d*; and 134. *d*). No efforts were spared
to connect Theseus with Heracles, but the Athenians never grew powerful enough to make him into an Olympian god.

*3.* There seem, however, to have been at least three mythological
characters called Theseus: one from Troezen, one from Marathon in
Attica, and the third from Lapith territory. These were not unified into a
single character until the sixth century B.C., when (as Professor George
Thomson suggests) the Butads, a Lapith clan who had become leading
aristocrats at Athens and even usurped the native Pelasgian priesthood of
Erechtheus, put forward the Athenian Theseus as a rival to Dorian
Heracles (see 47. 4). Again, Pittheus was clearly both an Elean and a
Troezenian title – also borne by the eponymous hero of an Attic deme
belonging to the Cecropian tribe.

*4.* Aethra's visit to Sphaeria suggests that the ancient custom of self-prostitution by unmarried girls survived in Athene's temple for some time after the patriarchal system had been introduced. It can hardly have been brought from Crete, since Troezen is not a Mycenaean site; but was perhaps a Canaanite importation, as at Corinth.

5. Sandals and sword are ancient symbols of royalty; the drawing of a sword from a rock seems to have formed part of the Bronze Age coronation ritual (see 81. 2). Odin, Galahad, and Arthur were all in turn required to perform a similar feat; and an immense sword, lion-hilted and plunged into a rock, figures in the sacred marriage scene carved at Hattasus (see 145. 5). Since Aegeus's rock is called both the Altar of Strong Zeus and the Rock of Theseus, it may be assumed that 'Zeus' and 'Theseus' were alternative titles of the sacred king, who was crowned upon it; but the goddess armed him. The 'Apollo' to whom Theseus dedicated his hair will have been Karu ('son of the goddess Car' – see 82. 6 and 86. 2), otherwise known as Car, or Q're, or Carys, the solar king whose locks were annually shorn before his death (see 83. 3), like those of Tyrian Samson and Megarean Nisus (see 91. 1). At a feast called the Comyria ('hair trimming'), young men sacrificed their forelocks in yearly mourning for him, and were afterwards known as Curetes (see 7. 4). This custom, probably of Libyan origin (Herodotus: iv. 194), had spread to Asia Minor and Greece; an injunction against it occurs in *Leviticus* xxi. 5. But, by Plutarch's time, Apollo was worshipped as the immortal Sun-god and, in proof of this, kept his own hair rigorously unshorn.

6. Aetius's division of Troezenia between Troezen, Pittheus, and himself, recalls the arrangement made by Proetus with Melampus and Bias (see 72. h). The Pittheus who taught rhetoric and whose treatise survived until Classical times must have been a late historical character.

# 96

## THE LABOURS OF THESEUS

THESEUS set out to free the bandit-ridden coast road which led from Troezen to Athens. He would pick no quarrels but take vengeance on all who dared molest him, making the punishment fit the crime, as was Heracles's way.[1] At Epidaurus, Periphetes the cripple waylaid him. Periphetes, whom some call Poseidon's son, and others the son of Hephaestus and Anticleia, owned a huge brazen club, with which he used to kill wayfarers; hence his nickname Corunetes, or 'cudgel-man'.

Theseus wrenched the club from his hands and battered him to death. Delighted with its size and weight, he proudly carried it about ever afterwards; and though he himself had been able to parry its murderous swing, in his hands it never failed to kill.[2]

b. At the narrowest point of the Isthmus, where both the Corinthian and Saronic Gulfs are visible, lived Sinis, the son of Pemon; or, some say, of Polypemon and Sylea, daughter of Corinthus, who claimed to be Poseidon's bastard.[3] He had been nicknamed Pityocamptes, or 'pine-bender', because he was strong enough to bend down the tops of pine-trees until they touched the earth, and would often ask innocent passers-by to help him with this task, but then suddenly release his hold. As the tree sprang upright again, they were hurled high into the air, and killed by the fall. Or he would bend down the tops of two neighbouring trees until they met, and tie one of his victim's arms to each, so that he was torn asunder when the trees were released.[4]

c. Theseus wrestled with Sinis, overpowered him, and served him as he had served others. At this, a beautiful girl ran to hide herself in a thicket of rushes and wild asparagus. He followed her and, after a long search, found her invoking the plants, promising never to burn or destroy them if they hid her safely. When Theseus swore not to do her any violence, she consented to emerge, and proved to be Sinis's daughter Perigune. Perigune fell in love with Theseus at sight, forgiving the murder of her hateful father and, in due course, bore him a son, Melanippus. Afterwards he gave her in marriage to Deioneus the Oechalian. Melanippus's son Ioxus emigrated to Caria, where he became the ancestor of the Ioxids, who burn neither rushes nor wild asparagus, but venerate both.[5]

d. Some, however, say that Theseus killed Sinis many years later, and rededicated the Isthmian Games to him, although they had been founded by Sisyphus in honour of Melicertes, the son of Ino.[6]

e. Next, at Crommyum, he hunted and destroyed a fierce and monstrous wild sow, which had killed so many Crommyonians that they no longer dared plough their fields. This beast, named after the crone who bred it, was said to be the child of Typhon and Echidne.[7]

f. Following the coast road, Theseus came to the precipitous cliffs rising sheer from the sea, which had become a stronghold of the bandit Sciron; some call him a Corinthian, the son of Pelops, or of Poseidon; others, the son of Henioche and Canethus.[8] Sciron used to seat himself upon a rock and force passing travellers to wash his feet: when they stooped to the task he would kick them over the cliff into the sea, where a giant turtle swam about, waiting to devour them. (Turtles closely resemble tortoises, except that they are larger, and have flippers instead of feet.) Theseus, refusing to wash Sciron's feet, lifted him from the rock and flung him into the sea.[9]

g. The Megareans, however, say that the only Sciron with whom Theseus came in conflict was an honest and generous prince of Megara, the father of Endeis, who married Aeacus and bore him Peleus and Telamon; they add, that Theseus killed Sciron after the capture of Eleusis, many years later, and celebrated the Isthmian Games in his honour under the patronage of Poseidon.[10]

h. The cliffs of Sciron rise close to the Molurian Rocks, and over them runs Sciron's footpath, made by him when he commanded the armies of Megara. A violent north-westerly breeze which blows seaward across these heights is called Sciron by the Athenians.[11]

i. Now, sciron means 'parasol'; and the month of Scirophorion is so called because at the Women's Festival of Demeter and Core, on the twelfth day of Scirophorion, the priest of Erechtheus carries a white parasol, and a priestess of Athene Sciras carries another in solemn procession from the Acropolis – for on that occasion the goddess's image is daubed with sciras, a sort of gypsum, to commemorate the white image which Theseus made of her after he had destroyed the Minotaur.[12]

j. Continuing his journey to Athens, Theseus met Cercyon the Arcadian, whom some call the son of Branchus and the nymph Argiope; others, the son of Hephaestus, or Poseidon.[13] He would challenge passers-by to wrestle with him and then crush them to death in his powerful embrace; but Theseus lifted him up by the knees and, to the delight of Demeter, who witnessed the struggle, dashed him headlong to the ground. Cercyon's death was instantaneous. Theseus did not trust to strength so much as to skill, for he had invented the art of wrestling, the principles of which were not hitherto understood. The Wrestling-ground of Cercyon is still shown near Eleusis, on the road to Megara, close to the grave of his daughter Alope, whom Theseus is said to have ravished.[14]

k. On reaching Attic Corydallus, Theseus slew Sinis's father Polypemon, surnamed Procrustes, who lived beside the road and had two beds in his house, one small the other large. Offering a night's lodging to travellers, he would lay the short men on the large bed, and rack

them out to fit it; but the tall men on the small bed, sawing off as much
of their legs as projected beyond it. Some say, however, that he used
only one bed, and lengthened or shortened his lodgers according to its
measure. In either case, Theseus served him as he had served others.[15]

1. Diodorus Siculus: iv. 59; Plutarch: *Theseus* 7 and 11.
2. Hyginus: *Fabula* 38; Apollodorus: iii. 16. 1; Pausanias: ii. 1. 4;
   Plutarch: *Theseus* 8.
3. Pausanias: *loc. cit.*; Ovid: *Ibis* 507 ff.; Apollodorus: iii. 16. 2;
   Scholiast on Euripides's *Hippolytus* 977.
4. Ovid: *Metamorphoses* vii. 433 ff.; Apollodorus: *loc. cit.*; Hyginus:
   *loc. cit.*; Diodorus Siculus: iv. 59; Pausanias: *loc. cit.*
5. Plutarch: *Theseus* 8 and 29.
6. *Parian Marble* 35 ff.; Plutarch: *Theseus* 25.
7. Plutarch: *Theseus* 9; Diodorus Siculus: iv. 59; Ovid: *Metamorphoses* vii. 433 ff.; Apollodorus: *Epitome* i. 1; Hyginus: *Fabula* 38.
8. Strabo: ix. 1. 4; Apollodorus: *Epitome* i. 2; Plutarch: *Theseus* 25.
9. Scholiast on Statius's *Thebaid* i. 339; Pausanias: i. 44. 12; Apollodorus: *Epitome* i. 2–3.
10. Plutarch: *Theseus* 10 and 25.
11. Pausanias: i. 44. 10–12; Strabo: ix. 1. 4.
12. Scholiast on Aristophanes's *Parliament of Women* 18; Aristo-
    phanes: *Wasps* 925; *Etymologicum Magnum*: *sub* Scirophorion.
13. Plutarch: *Theseus* 11; Apollodorus: *Epitome* i. 3; Hyginus: *Fabula*
    38; Aulus Gellius: xiii. 21.
14. Ovid: *Ibis* 407 ff.; Apollodorus: *loc. cit.*; Pausanias: i. 39. 3;
    Plutarch: *Theseus* 11 and 29.
15. Diodorus Siculus: iv. 59; Apollodorus: *Epitome* i. 4; Pausanias:
    i. 38. 5; Hyginus: *Fabula* 38; Plutarch: *Theseus* 11.

*

1. The killing of Periphetes has been invented to account for Theseus's
brass-bound club, like the one carried by Heracles (see 120. 5). Periphetes
is described as a cripple because he was the son of Daedalus the smith, and
smiths were often ritually lamed (see 92. 1).

2. Since the North Wind, which bent the pines, was held to fertilize
women, animals, and plants, 'Pityocamptes' is described as the father of
Perigune, a cornfield-goddess (see 48. 1). Her descendants' attachment to
wild asparagus and rushes suggests that the sacred baskets carried in the
Thesmophoria Festival were woven from these, and therefore tabooed
for ordinary use. The Crommyonian Sow, *alias* Phaea, is the white Sow-
Demeter (see 24. 7 and 74. 4), whose cult was early suppressed in the
Peloponnese. That Theseus went out of his way to kill a mere sow
troubled the mythographers: Hyginus and Ovid, indeed, make her a
boar, and Plutarch describes her as a woman bandit whose disgusting

behaviour earned her the nickname of 'sow'. But she appears in early Welsh myth as the Old White Sow, Hen Wen, tended by the swineherd magician Coll ap Collfrewr, who introduced wheat and bees into Britain; and Demeter's swineherd magician Eubuleus was remembered in the Thesmophoria Festival at Eleusis, when live pigs were flung down a chasm in his honour. Their rotting remains later served to fertilize the seed-corn (Scholiast on Lucian's *Dialogues Between Whores* ii. 1).

3. The stories of Sciron and Cercyon are apparently based on a series of icons which illustrated the ceremony of hurling a sacred king as a *pharmacos* from the White Rock. The first hero who had met his death here was Melicertes (see 70. *h*), namely Heracles Melkarth of Tyre who seems to have been stripped of his royal trappings – club, lion-skin, and buskins – and then provided with wings, live birds, and a parasol to break his fall (see 89. *6*; 92. *3*; and 98. *7*). This is to suggest that Sciron, shown making ready to kick a traveller into the sea, is the *pharmacos* being prepared for his ordeal at the Scirophoria, which was celebrated in the last month of the year, namely at midsummer; and that a second scene, explained as Theseus's wrestling with Cercyon, shows him being lifted off his feet by his successor (as in the terracotta of the Royal Colonnade at Athens – Pausanias: i. 3. 1), while the priestess of the goddess looks on delightedly. This is a common mythological situation: Heracles, for instance, wrestled for a kingdom with Antaeus in Libya (see 133. *h*), and with Eryx in Sicily (see 132. *q*); Odysseus with Philomeleides on Tenedos see 161. *f*). A third scene, taken for Theseus's revenge on Sciron, shows the *pharmacos* hurtling through the air, parasol in hand. In a fourth, he has reached the sea, and his parasol is floating on the waves – the supposed turtle, waiting to devour him, was surely the parasol, since there is no record of an Attic turtle cult. The Second Vatican Mythographer (127) makes Daedalus, not Theseus, kill Sciron, probably because of Daedalus's mythic connexion with the *pharmacos* ritual of the partridge king (see 92. *3*).

4. All these feats of Theseus's seem to be interrelated. Grammarians associate the white parasol with a gypsum image of Athene. This recalls the white *pharmacos* dolls, called 'Argives' ('white men'), thrown into running water once a year at the May purification of temples (see 132. *p*); also the white cakes shaped like pigs, and made of flour mixed with gypsum (Pliny: *Natural History* xvii. 29. 2), which were used in the Thesmophoria to replace the pig remains recovered from Eubuleus's chasm – 'in order not to defraud his sacred serpents', explains the scholiast on Lucian's *Dialogues Between Whores*. The Scirophoria Festival formed part of the Thesmophoria. *Thes* has the same meaning in *Thesmophoria* as in *Theseus*: namely 'tokens deposited' – in the baskets woven of wild asparagus and rush which Perigune sanctified. They were phallic tokens

and the festival was an erotic one: this is justified by Theseus's seduction
of Perigune, and also by Hermes's seduction of Herse (see 25. d). The
priest of Erechtheus carried a parasol, because he was the president of the
serpent cult, and the sacred functions of the ancient kings rested with him
after the monarchy had been abolished: as they rested at Rome with the
Priest of Zeus.

5. Cercyon's name connects him with the pig cult. So does his parentage: Branchus refers to the grunting of pigs, and Argiope is a synonym
for Phaea. It will have been Poseidon's son Theseus who ravished Alope:
that is to say, suppressed the worship of the Megarean Moon-goddess as
Vixen (see 49. 2).

6. Sinis and Sciron are both described as the hero in whose honour the
Isthmian Games were rededicated; Sinis's nickname was Pityocamptes;
and Sciron, like Pityocamptes, was a north-westerly wind. But since the
Isthmian Games had originally been founded in memory of Heracles
Melkarth, the destruction of Pityocamptes seems to record the suppression of the Boreas cult in Athens – which was, however, revived after
the Persian Wars (see 48. 4). In that case, the Isthmian Games are analogous to the Pythian Games, founded in memory of Python, who was both
the fertilizing North Wind and the ghost of the sacred king killed by his
rival Apollo. Moreover, 'Procrustes', according to Ovid and the scholiast
on Euripides's *Hippolytus* (977), was only another nickname for Sinis-
Pityocamptes; and Procrustes seems to be a fictional character, invented
to account for a familiar icon: the hair of the old king – Samson, Pterelaus (see 89. 7), Nisus (see 91. 1), Curoi, Llew Llaw, or whatever he may
have been called – is tied to the bedpost by his treacherous bride, while
his rival advances, axe in hand, to destroy him. 'Theseus' and his Hellenes
abolished the custom of throwing the old king over the Molurian Rock,
and rededicated the Games to Poseidon at Ino's expense, Ino being one of
Athene's earlier titles.

# 97

## THESEUS AND MEDEA

ARRIVED in Attica, Theseus was met beside the River Cephissus by the
sons of Phytalus, who purified him from the blood he had spilled, but
especially from that of Sinis, a maternal kinsman of his. The altar
of Gracious Zeus, where this ceremony was performed, still stands by
the riverside. Afterwards, the Phytalids welcomed Theseus as their
guest, which was the first true hospitality he had received since leaving

Troezen. Dressed in a long garment that reached to his feet and with his hair neatly plaited, he entered Athens on the eighth day of the month Cronius, now called Hecatomboeon. As he passed the nearly-completed temple of Apollo the Dolphin, a group of masons working on the roof mistook him for a girl, and impertinently asked why he was allowed to wander about unescorted. Disdaining to reply, Theseus unyoked the oxen from the masons' cart and tossed one of them into the air, high above the temple roof.[1]

*b.* Now while Theseus was growing up in Troezen, Aegeus had kept his promise to Medea. He gave her shelter in Athens when she fled from Corinth in the celebrated chariot drawn by winged serpents, and married her, rightly confident that her spells would enable him to beget an heir; for he did not yet know that Aethra had borne him Theseus.[2]

*c.* Medea, however, recognised Theseus as soon as he arrived in the city, and grew jealous on behalf of Medus, her son by Aegeus, who was generally expected to succeed him on the Athenian throne. She therefore persuaded Aegeus that Theseus came as a spy or an assassin, and had him invited to a feast at the Dolphin Temple; Aegeus, who used the temple as his residence, was then to offer him a cup of wine already prepared by her. This cup contained wolfsbane, a poison which she had brought from Bithynian Acherusia, where it first sprang from the deadly foam scattered by Cerberus when Heracles dragged him out of Tartarus; because wolfsbane flourishes on bare rocks, the peasants call it 'aconite'.[3]

*d.* Some say that when the roast beef was served in the Dolphin Temple, Theseus ostentatiously drew his sword, as if to carve, and thus attracted his father's attention; but others, that he had unsuspectingly raised the cup to his lips before Aegeus noticed the Erechtheid serpents carved on the ivory sword-hilt and dashed the poison to the floor. The spot where the cup fell is still shown, barred off from the rest of the temple.

*e.* Then followed the greatest rejoicing that Athens had ever known. Aegeus embraced Theseus, summoned a public assembly, and acknowledged him as his son. He lighted fires on every altar and heaped the gods' images with gifts; hecatombs of garlanded oxen were sacrificed and, throughout the palace and the city, nobles and commoners feasted together, and sang of Theseus's glorious deeds that already outnumbered the years of his life.[4]

*f.* Theseus then went in vengeful pursuit of Medea, who eluded him by casting a magic cloud about herself; and presently left Athens with young Medus, and an escort which Aegeus generously provided. But some say that she fled with Polyxenus, her son by Jason.[5]

*g.* Pallas and his fifty sons, who even before this had declared that Aegeus was not a true Erechtheid and thus had no right to the throne, broke into open revolt when this footloose stranger threatened to baulk their hopes of ever ruling Athens. They divided their forces: Pallas with twenty-five of his sons and numerous retainers marched against the city from the direction of Sphettus, while the other twenty-five lay in ambush at Gargettus. But Theseus, informed of their plans by a herald named Leos, of the Agnian clan, sprang the ambush and destroyed the entire force. Pallas thereupon disbanded his command, and sued for peace. The Pallantids have never forgotten Leos's treachery, and still will not intermarry with the Agnians nor allow any herald to begin a proclamation with the words '*Akouete leoi!*' ('Hearken, ye people!'), because of the resemblance which *leoi* bears to the name of Leos.[6]

*h.* This Leos must be distinguished from the other Leos, Orpheus's son, and ancestor of the Athenian Leontids. Once, in a time of famine and plague, Leos obeyed the Delphic Oracle by sacrificing his daughters Theope, Praxithea, and Eubule to save the city. The Athenians set up the Leocorium in their honour.[7]

1. Pausanias: i. 37. 3 and 19. 1; Plutarch: *Theseus* 12.
2. Euripides: *Medea* 660 ff.; Apollodorus: i. 9. 28.
3. Plutarch: *Theseus* 12; Apollodorus: *Epitome* i. 6; Ovid: *Metamorphoses* vii. 402 ff.
4. Plutarch: *loc. cit.*; Ovid: *loc. cit.*
5. Ovid: *loc. cit.*; Apollodorus: *loc. cit.*; Diodorus Siculus: iv. 55. 6; Hellanicus, quoted by Pausanias: ii. 3. 7.
6. Plutarch: *Theseus* 13.
7. Pausanias: i. 5. 2; Suidas *sub* Leos; Aristides: *Panathenian Oration*; Jerome: *Against Jovinianus* p. 185, ed. Mart; Suidas *sub* Leocorium; Aelian: *Varia Historia* xii. 28.

\*

1. This artificial romance with its theatrical *dénouement* in the poisoning scene recalls that of Ion (see 44. *a*); and the incident of the ox tossed into the air seems merely a crude imitation of Heracles's feats. The masons' question is anachronistic, because in the heroic age young women

went about unescorted; neither could Theseus have been mistaken for a girl if he had already dedicated his hair to Apollo and become one of the Curetes. Yet the story's weaknesses suggest that it has been deduced from an ancient icon which, since the men on the temple roof were recognizably masons, will have shown a sacrifice performed on the day when the temple was completed (see 84. *1*). It is likely that the figure, taken for Theseus, who unyokes the sacrificial white ox from a cart, is a priestess; and that, because of its dolphin decorations, the temple has been misread as Apollo's, though the dolphin was originally an emblem of the Moon-goddess. The beast has not been tossed into the air. It is the deity in whose honour the sacrifice is being offered: either a white moon-cow, the goddess herself, or the white bull of Poseidon (see 88. *c*), who shared a shrine on the Acropolis with Athene and to whom, as Sea-god, dolphins were sacred; Apollo's priests, Plutarch not the least, were always zealous to enhance his power and authority at the expense of other deities. A companion icon, from which the story of the poisoned cup will have been deduced – aconite was a well-known paralysant – probably showed a priest or priestess pouring a libation to the ghosts of the men sacrificed when the foundations were laid, while Persephone and Cerberus stand by. Plutarch describes Aegeus as living in the Dolphin Temple rather than a private house; and this is correct since, as sacred king, he had apartments in the Queen's palace (see 25. *7*).

2. Medea's expulsion first from Corinth, and then from Athens, refers to the Hellenic suppression of the Earth-goddess's cult – her serpent chariot shows her to be a Corinthian Demeter (see 24. *m*). Theseus's defeat of the Pallantids similarly refers to the suppression of the original Athene cult (see 9. *1* and 16. *3*), with its college of fifty priestesses – *pallas* can mean either 'youth' or 'maiden'. Still another version of the same story is the sacrifice of Leos's three daughters, who are really the goddess in triad. The Maiden is Theope ('divine face'), the New Moon; the Nymph is Praxithea ('active goddess'), the Queen-bee. Cecrops's mother bore the same name in Euboea (Apollodorus: iii. 15. *1* and *5*); the Crone is Eubule ('good counsel'), the oracular goddess, whom Eubuleus the swineherd served at Eleusis.

3. That Pallantids and Agnians refrained from inter-marriage may have been a relic of exogamy, with its complex system of group-marriage between phratries, each phratry or sub-phratry consisting of several totem clans: if so, Pallantids and Agnians will have belonged to the same sub-phratry, marriage being permitted only between members of different ones (see 80. *5*). The Pallantid clan probably had a goat for its totem, as the Agnians had a lamb, the Leontids a lion, and the Erechtheids a serpent. Many other totem clans are hinted at in Attic mythology: among them, crow, nightingale, hoopoe, wolf, bear, and owl.

4. To judge from the Theseus and Heracles myths, both Athene's chief priestess at Athens, and Hera's at Argos, belonged to a lion clan, into which they adopted sacred kings; and a gold ring found at Tiryns shows four lion-men offering libation vessels to a seated goddess, who must be Hera, since a cuckoo perches behind her throne (see 12. 4). Despite the absence of lions in Crete, they figured there too as the Goddess's beasts. Athene was not associated with the cuckoo but had several other bird epiphanies, which may be totemistic by origin. In Homer she appears as a sea-eagle (Odyssey iii. 371) and a swallow (ibid. xxii. 239); in company with Apollo, as a vulture (Iliad vii. 58); and in company with Hera, as a dove (ibid v. 778). In a small Athenian vase of 500 B.C. she is shown as a lark; and Athene the diver-bird, or gannet, had a shrine near Megara (Pausanias: i. 5. 3. and 41. 6 – see 94. c). But the wise owl was her principal epiphany. The owl clan preserved their ritual until late Classical times: initiates in owl-disguise would perform a ceremony of catching their totem bird (Aelian: Varia Historia xv. 28; Pollux: iv. 103; Athenaeus: 391a–b and 629f).

5. Plutarch's story of Akouete leoi is plausible enough: it often happened in primitive religions that words were banned because they sounded like the name of a person, object, or animal, which could not be safely mentioned; especially words suggesting the names of dead kinsmen, even if they had come to a natural end.

6. The Pallantids' denial that Aegeus and Theseus were true Erechtheids may reflect a sixth-century protest at Athens against the usurpation of the immigrant Butadae (who refurbished the Theseus legend) of the native Erechtheid priesthood (see 95. 3).

# 98

## THESEUS IN CRETE

It is a matter of dispute whether Medea persuaded Aegeus to send Theseus against Poseidon's ferocious white bull, or whether it was after her expulsion from Athens that he undertook the destruction of this fire-breathing monster, hoping thereby to ingratiate himself further with the Athenians. Brought by Heracles from Crete, let loose on the plain of Argos, and driven thence across the Isthmus to Marathon, the bull had killed men by the hundred between the cities of Probalinthus and Tricorynthus, including (some say) Minos's son Androgeus. Yet Theseus boldly seized those murderous horns and dragged the bull in triumph through the streets of Athens, and up the steep slope of the Acropolis, where he sacrificed it to Athene, or to Apollo.[1]

*b.* As he approached Marathon, Theseus had been hospitably entertained by a needy old spinster named Hecale, or Hecalene, who vowed a ram to Zeus if he came back safely. But she died before his return, and he instituted the Hecalesian Rites, to honour her and Zeus Hecaleius, which are still performed today. Because Theseus was no more than a boy at this time, Hecale had caressed him with childish endearments, and is therefore commonly called by the diminutive Hecalene, rather than Hecale.[2]

*c.* In requital for the death of Androgeus, Minos gave orders that the Athenians should send seven youths and seven maidens every ninth year – namely at the close of every Great Year – to the Cretan Labyrinth, where the Minotaur waited to devour them. This Minotaur, whose name was Asterius, or Asterion, was the bull-headed monster which Pasiphaë had borne to the white bull.[3] Soon after Theseus's arrival at Athens the tribute fell due for the third time, and he so deeply pitied those parents whose children were liable to be chosen by lot, that he offered himself as one of the victims, despite Aegeus's earnest attempts at dissuasion. But some say that the lot had fallen on him. According to others, King Minos came in person with a large fleet to choose the victims; his eye lighted on Theseus who, though a native of Troezen, not Athens, volunteered to come on the understanding that if he conquered the Minotaur with his bare hands the tribute would be remitted.[4]

*d.* On the two previous occasions, the ship which conveyed the fourteen victims had carried black sails, but Theseus was confident that the gods were on his side, and Aegeus therefore gave him a white sail to hoist on return, in signal of success; though some say that it was a red sail, dyed in juice of the kerm-oak berry.[5]

*e.* When the lots had been cast at the Law Courts, Theseus led his companions to the Dolphin Temple where, on their behalf, he offered Apollo a branch of consecrated olive, bound with white wool. The fourteen mothers brought provisions for the voyage, and told their children fables and heroic tales to hearten them. Theseus, however, replaced two of the maiden victims with a pair of effeminate youths, possessed of unusual courage and presence of mind. These he commanded to take warm baths, avoid the rays of the sun, perfume their hair and bodies with unguent oils, and practise how to talk, gesture, and walk like women. He was thus able to deceive Minos by passing them off as maidens.[6]

*f.* Phaeax, the ancestor of the Phaeacians, among whom Odysseus fell, stood as pilot at the prow of the thirty-oared ship in which they sailed, because no Athenian as yet knew anything about navigation. Some say that the helmsman was Phereclus; but those who name him Nausitheus are likely to be right, since Theseus on his return raised monuments to Nausitheus and Phaeax at Phalerum, the port of departure; and the local Pilots' Festival is held in their joint honour.[7]

*g.* The Delphic Oracle had advised Theseus to take Aphrodite for his guide and companion on the voyage. He therefore sacrificed to her on the strand; and lo! the victim, a she-goat, became a he-goat in its death-throes. This prodigy won Aphrodite her title of Epitragia.[8]

*h.* Theseus sailed on the sixth day of Munychion [April]. Every year on this date the Athenians still send virgins to the Dolphin Temple in propitiation of Apollo, because Theseus had omitted to do so before taking his leave. The god's displeasure was shown in a storm, which forced him to take shelter at Delphi and there offer belated sacrifices.[9]

*i.* When the ship reached Crete some days afterwards, Minos rode down to the harbour to count the victims. Falling in love with one of the Athenian maidens – whether it was Periboea (who became the mother of Ajax) or Eriboea, or Phereboea, is not agreed, for these three bore confusingly similar names – he would have ravished her then and there, had Theseus not protested that it was his duty as Poseidon's son to defend virgins against outrage by tyrants. Minos, laughing lewdly, replied that Poseidon had never been known to show delicate respect for any virgins who took his fancy.[10]

'Ha!' he cried, 'prove yourself a son of Poseidon, by retrieving this bauble for me!' So saying, he flung his golden signet ring into the sea.

'First prove that you are a son of Zeus!' retorted Theseus.

*j.* This Minos did. His prayer: 'Father Zeus, hear me!' was at once answered by lightning and a clap of thunder. Without more ado, Theseus dived into the sea, where a large school of dolphins escorted him honourably down to the palace of the Nereids. Some say that Thetis the Nereid then gave him the jewelled crown, her wedding gift from Aphrodite, which Ariadne afterwards wore; others, that Amphitrite the Sea-goddess did so herself, and that she sent the Nereids swimming in every direction to find the golden ring. At all events, when Theseus emerged from the sea, he was carrying both the ring and the crown, as Micon has recorded in his painting on the third wall of Theseus's sanctuary.[11]

*k.* Aphrodite had indeed accompanied Theseus: for not only did both Periboea and Phereboea invite the chivalrous Theseus to their couches, and were not spurned, but Minos's own daughter Ariadne fell in love with him at first sight. 'I will help you to kill my half-brother, the Minotaur,' she secretly promised him, 'if I may return to Athens with you as your wife.' This offer Theseus gladly accepted, and swore to marry her. Now, before Daedalus left Crete, he had given Ariadne a magic ball of thread, and instructed her how to enter and leave the Labyrinth. She must open the entrance door and tie the loose end of the thread to the lintel; the ball would then roll along, diminishing as it went and making, with devious turns and twists, for the innermost recess where the Minotaur was lodged. This ball Ariadne gave to Theseus, and instructed him to follow it until he reached the sleeping monster, whom he must seize by the hair and sacrifice to Poseidon. He could then find his way back by rolling up the thread into a ball again.[12]

*l.* That same night Theseus did as he was told; but whether he killed the Minotaur with a sword given him by Ariadne, or with his bare hands, or with his celebrated club, is much disputed. A sculptured frieze at Amyclae shows the Minotaur bound and led in triumph by Theseus to Athens; but this is not the generally accepted story.[13]

*m.* When Theseus emerged from the labyrinth, spotted with blood, Ariadne embraced him passionately, and guided the whole Athenian party to the harbour. For, in the meantime, the two effeminate-looking youths had killed the guards of the women's quarters, and released the maiden victims. They all stole aboard their ship, where Nausitheus and Phaeax were expecting them, and rowed hastily away. But although Theseus had first stove in the hulls of several Cretan ships, to prevent pursuit, the alarm sounded and he was forced to fight a sea-battle in the harbour, before escaping, fortunately without loss, under cover of darkness.[14]

*n.* Some days later, after disembarking on the island then named Dia, but now known as Naxos, Theseus left Ariadne asleep on the shore, and sailed away. Why he did so must remain a mystery. Some say that he deserted her in favour of a new mistress, Aegle, daughter of Panopeus; others that, while wind-bound on Dia, he reflected on the scandal which Ariadne's arrival at Athens would cause.[15] Others, again that Dionysus, appearing to Theseus in a dream, threateningly de-

manded Ariadne for himself, and that, when Theseus awoke to see
Dionysus's fleet bearing down on Dia, he weighed anchor in sudden
terror; Dionysus having cast a spell which made him forget his promise
to Ariadne and even her very existence.[16]

*o*. Whatever the truth of the matter may be, Dionysus's priests at
Athens affirm that when Ariadne found herself alone on the deserted
shore, she broke into bitter laments, remembering how she had
trembled while Theseus set out to kill her monstrous half-brother;
how she had offered silent vows for his success; and how, through love
of him, she had deserted her parents and motherland. She now invoked
the whole universe for vengeance, and Father Zeus nodded assent. Then,
gently and sweetly, Dionysus with his merry train of satyrs and
maenads came to Ariadne's rescue. He married her without delay,
setting Thetis's crown upon her head, and she bore him many children.[17] Of these only Thoas and Oenopion are sometimes called
Theseus's sons. The crown, which Dionysus later set among the stars
as the Corona Borealis, was made by Hephaestus of fiery gold and red
Indian gems, set in the shape of roses.[18]

*p*. The Cretans, however, refuse to admit that the Minotaur ever
existed, or that Theseus won Ariadne by clandestine means. They
describe the Labyrinth as merely a well-guarded prison, where the
Athenian youths and maidens were kept in readiness for Androgeus's
funeral games. Some were sacrificed at his tomb; others presented to
the prizewinners as slaves. It happened that Minos's cruel and arrogant
general Taurus had carried all before him, year after year: winning
every event in which he competed, much to the disgust of his rivals. He
had also forfeited Minos's confidence because he was rumoured to be
carrying on an adulterous affair with Pasiphaë, connived at by Daedalus, and one of her twin sons bore a close resemblance to him. Minos,
therefore, gladly granted Theseus's request for the privilege of wrestling against Taurus. In ancient Crete, women as well as men attended
the games, and Ariadne fell in love with Theseus when, three times in
succession, she saw him toss the former champion over his head and
pin his shoulders to the ground. The sight afforded Minos almost equal
satisfaction: he awarded Theseus the prize, accepted him as his son-in-
law, and remitted the cruel tribute.[19]

*q*. A traditional Bottiaean song confirms this tradition that not all
the victims were put to death. It records that the Cretans sent an offering of their first-born to Delphi, for the most part children of Cretan-

ized Athenian slaves. The Delphians, however, could not support these on the resources of their small city, and therefore packed them off to found a colony at Iapygia in Italy. Later, they settled at Bottiaea in Thrace, and the nostalgic cry raised by the Bottiaean maidens: 'O let us return to Athens!', is a constant reminder of their origin.[20]

*r*. An altogether different account is given by the Cypriots and others. They say that Minos and Theseus agreed on oath that no ship – except the *Argo*, commanded by Jason, who had a commission to clear the sea of pirates – might sail in Greek waters with a crew larger than five. When Daedalus fled from Crete to Athens, Minos broke this pact by pursuing him with warships, and thus earned the anger of Poseidon, who had witnessed the oath, and now raised a storm which drove him to his death in Sicily. Minos's son Deucalion, inheriting the quarrel, threatened that unless the Athenians surrendered Daedalus, he would put to death all the hostages given him by Theseus at the conclusion of the pact. Theseus replied that Daedalus was his blood-relation, and enquired mildly whether some compromise could not be reached. He exchanged several letters on the subject with Deucalion, but meanwhile secretly built warships: some at Thymoetidae, a port off the beaten track, and others at Troezen, where Pittheus had a naval yard about which the Cretans knew nothing. Within a month or two his flotilla set sail, guided by Daedalus and other fugitives from Crete; and the Cretans mistook the approaching ships for part of Minos's lost fleet and gave them a resounding welcome. Theseus therefore seized the harbour without opposition, and made straight for Cnossus, where he cut down Deucalion's guards, and killed Deucalion himself in an inner chamber of the palace. The Cretan throne then passed to Ariadne, with whom Theseus generously came to terms; she surrendered the Athenian hostages, and a treaty of perpetual friendship was concluded between the two nations, sealed by a union of the crowns – in effect, she married Theseus.[21]

*s*. After long feasting they sailed together for Athens, but were driven to Cyprus by a storm. There Ariadne, already with child by Theseus, and fearing that she might miscarry from sea-sickness, asked to be put ashore at Amathus. This was done, but hardly had Theseus regained his ship when a violent wind forced the whole fleet out to sea again. The women of Amathus treated Ariadne kindly, comforting her with letters which, they pretended, had just arrived from Theseus, who was repairing his ship on the shores of a neighbouring island; and when she died in childbed, gave her a lavish funeral. Ariadne's tomb is still shown at Amathus, in a grove sacred to her as Aridela. Theseus, on his eventual return from the Syrian coast, was deeply grieved to learn that she had died, and endowed her cult with a large sum of money. The Cypriots still celebrate Ariadne's festival on the second day of September, when a youth lies down in her grove and imitates a travailing woman; and worship two small statues of her, one in silver, the other in brass, which Theseus left them. They say that Dionysus, so far from marrying Ariadne, was indignant that she and Theseus had profaned his Naxian grotto, and complained to Artemis, who killed her in childbed with merciless shafts; but some say that she hanged herself for fear of Artemis.[22]

*t.* To resume the history of Theseus: from Naxos he sailed to Delos, and there sacrificed to Apollo, celebrating athletic games in his honour. It was then that he introduced the novel custom of crowning the victor with palm-leaves, and placing a palm-stem in his right hand. He also prudently dedicated to the god a small wooden image of Aphrodite, the work of Daedalus, which Ariadne had brought from Crete and left aboard his ship – it might have been the subject of cynical comment by the Athenians. This image, still displayed at Delos, rests on a square base instead of feet, and is perpetually garlanded.[23]

*u.* A horned altar stands beside the round lake of Delos. Apollo himself built it, when he was only four years of age, with the closely compacted horns of countless she-goats killed by Artemis on Mount Cynthus – his first architectural feat. The foundations of the altar, and its enclosing walls, are also made entirely of horns; all taken from the same side of the victims – but whether from the left, or from the right, is disputed.[24] What makes the work rank among the seven marvels of the world is that neither mortar nor any other colligative has been used. It was around this altar – or, according to another version, around an altar of Aphrodite, on which the Daedalic image had been set – that Theseus and his companions danced the Crane, which consists of labyrinthine evolutions, trod with measured steps to the accompaniment of harps. The Delians still perform this dance, which Theseus introduced from Cnossus; Daedalus had built Ariadne a dancing floor there, marked with a maze pattern in white marble relief, copied from the Egyptian Labyrinth. When Theseus and his companions performed the Crane at Cnossus, this was the first occasion on which men and women danced together. Old-fashioned people, especially sailors, keep up much the same dance in many different cities of Greece and Asia Minor; so do children in the Italian countryside, and it is the foundation of the Troy Games.[25]

*v*. Ariadne was soon revenged on Theseus. Whether in grief for her loss, or in joy at the sight of the Attic coast, from which he had been kept by prolonged winds, he forgot his promise to hoist the white sail.[26] Aegeus, who stood watching for him on the Acropolis, where the Temple of the Wingless Victory now stands, sighted the black sail, swooned, and fell headlong to his death into the valley below. But some say that he deliberately cast himself into the sea, which was thenceforth named the Aegean.[27]

*w*. Theseus was not informed of this sorrowful accident until he had completed the sacrifices vowed to the gods for his safe return; he then buried Aegeus, and honoured him with a hero-shrine. On the eighth day of Pyanepsion [October], the date of the return from Crete, loyal Athenians flock down to the seashore, with cooking-pots in which they stew different kinds of beans – to remind their children how Theseus, having been obliged to place his crew on very short rations, cooked all his remaining provisions in one pot as soon as he landed, and filled their empty bellies at last. At this same festival a thanksgiving is sung for the end of hunger, and an olive-branch, wreathed in white wool and hung with the season's fruits, is carried to commemorate the one which Theseus dedicated before setting out. Since this was harvest time, Theseus also instituted the Festival of Grape Boughs, either in gratitude to Athene and Dionysus, both of whom appeared to him on Naxos, or in honour of Dionysus and Ariadne. The two bough-bearers represent the youths whom Theseus had taken to Crete disguised as maidens, and who walked beside him in the triumphal procession after his return. Fourteen women carry provisions and take part in this sacrifice; they represent the mothers of the rescued victims, and their task is to tell fables and ancient myths, as these mothers also did before the ship sailed.[28]

*x*. Theseus dedicated a temple to Saviour Artemis in the market place at Troezen; and his fellow-citizens honoured him with a sanctuary while he was still alive. Such families as had been liable to the Cretan tribute undertook to supply the needful sacrifices; and Theseus awarded his priesthood to the Phytalids, in gratitude for their hospitality. The vessel in which he sailed to Crete has made an annual voyage to Delos and back ever since; but has been so frequently overhauled and refitted that philosophers cite it as a stock instance, when discussing the problem of continuous identity.[29]

1. Apollodorus: *Epitome* i. 5; Servius on Virgil's *Aeneid* viii. 294; First Vatican Mythographer: 47; Pausanias: i. 27. 9; Plutarch: *Theseus* 14; Hesychius *sub* Bolynthos.

2. Plutarch: *loc. cit.*; Callimachus: *Fragment* 40, ed. Bentley; Ovid: *Remedies of Love* 747.

3. Diodorus Siculus: iv. 61; Hyginus: *Fabula* 41; Apollodorus: iii. 1. 4; Pausanias. ii. 31. 1.

4. Plutarch: *Theseus* 17; Apollodorus: *Epitome* i. 7; Scholiast on Homer's *Iliad* xviii. 590; Diodorus Siculus: *loc cit.*; Hellanicus, quoted by Plutarch: *Theseus* 19.

5. Plutarch: *loc. cit.*; Simonides, quoted by Plutarch: *loc. cit.*

6. Plutarch: *Theseus* 18; Demon's *History*, quoted by Plutarch: *Theseus* 23.

7. Philochorus, quoted by Plutarch: *Theseus* 17; Simonides, quoted by Plutarch: *loc. cit.*; Pausanias: i. 1. 2.

8. Plutarch: *Theseus* 18.

9. Plutrach: *loc cit.*; Scholiast on Aristophanes's *Knights* 725.

10. Pausanias: i. 42. 1; Hyginus: *Poetic Astronomy* ii. 5; Plutarch: *Theseus* 29.

11. Pausanias: i. 17. 3; Hyginus: *loc. cit.*

12. Plutarch: *Theseus* 29; Apollodorus: *Epitome* i. 8.

13. Scholiast on Homer's *Odyssey* xi. 322, quoted by Pherecydes; Homer: *Iliad* xviii. 590; Eustathius on Homer's *Odyssey* xi. 320; Apollodorus: *Epitome* i. 9; Ovid: *Heroides* iv. 115; Pausanias: iii. 18. 7.

14. Pausanias: ii. 31. 1; Pherecydes, quoted by Plutarch: *Theseus* 19; Demon, quoted by Plutarch: *loc cit.*

15. Scholiast on Theocritus's *Idylls* ii. 45; Diodorus Siculus: iv. 61. 5; Catullus: lxiv. 50 ff.; Plutarch: *Theseus* 29; Hyginus: *Fabula* 43.

16. Pausanias: x. 29. 2; Diodorus Siculus. v. 51. 4; Scholiast on Theocritus: *loc.cit.*

17. Pausanias: i. 20. 2; Catullus: lxiv. 50 ff.; Hyginus: *Poetic Astronomy* ii. 5.

18. Plutarch: *Theseus* 20; Bacchylides: xvi. 116.

19. Plutarch: *Romulus and Theseus Compared*; Philochorus, quoted by Plutarch: *Theseus* 15; Servius on Virgil's *Aeneid* vi. 14; Philochorus, quoted by Plutarch: *Theseus* 19.

20. Aristotle: *Constitution of the Bottiaeans*, quoted by Plutarch: *Theseus* 16; Plutarch: *Greek Questions* 35.

21. Cleidemus, quoted by Plutarch: *Theseus* 19.

22. Hesychius *sub* Aridela; Paeonius, quoted by Plutarch: *Theseus* 21; *Contest of Homer and Hesiod* 14.

23. Plutarch: *loc. cit.*; Pausanias: viii. 48. 2 and ix. 40. 2; Callimachus: *Hymn to Delos* 312.

24. Callimachus: *Hymn to Apollo* 60 ff.; Plutarch: *loc. cit.* and *Which Animals Are the Craftier?* 35.

25. Plutarch: *Theseus* 21; Callimachus: *Hymn to Delos* 312 ff.; Homer: *Iliad* xviii. 591–2; Pausanias: ix. 40. 2; Pliny: *Natural History* xxxvi. 19; Scholiast on Homer's *Iliad* xviii. 590; Eustathius on Homer's *Iliad* p. 1166; Virgil: *Aeneid* v. 588 ff.

26. Catullus: lxiv. 50 ff.; Apollodorus: *Epitome* i. 10; Plutarch: *Theseus* 22.

27. Catullus: *loc. cit.*; Pausanias: i. 22. 4–5; Plutarch: *loc. cit.* and *Romulus and Theseus Compared*; Hyginus: *Fabula* 43.

28. Pausanias: i. 22. 5; Plutarch: *Theseus* 22 and 23; Proclus: *Chrestomathy*, quoted by Photius: 989.

29. Pausanias: iii. 31. 1; Plutarch: *loc cit.*

\*

1. Greece was Cretanized towards the close of the eighteenth century B.C., probably by an Hellenic aristocracy which had seized power in Crete a generation or two earlier and there initiated a new culture. The straightforward account of Theseus's raid on Cnossus, quoted by Plutarch from Cleidemus, makes reasonable sense. It describes a revolt by the Athenians against a Cretan overlord who had taken hostages for their good behaviour; the secret building of a flotilla; the sack of the unwalled city of Cnossus during the absence of the main Cretan fleet in Sicily; and a subsequent peace treaty ratified by the Athenian king's marriage with Ariadne, the Cretan heiress. These events, which point to about the year 1400 B.C., are paralleled by the mythical account: a tribute of youths and maidens is demanded from Athens in requital for the murder of a Cretan prince. Theseus, by craftily killing the Bull of Minos, or defeating Minos's leading commander in a wrestling match, relieves Athens of this tribute; marries Ariadne, the royal heiress; and makes peace with Minos himself.

2. Theseus's killing of the bull-headed Asterius, called the Minotaur, or 'Bull of Minos'; his wrestling match with Taurus ('bull'); and his capture of the Cretan bull, are all versions of the same event. *Bolynthos*, which gave its name to Attic Probalinthus, was the Cretan name for 'wild bull'. 'Minos' was the title of a Cnossian dynasty, which had a sky-bull for its emblem – 'Asterius' could mean 'of the sun' or 'of the sky' – and it was in bull-form that the king seems to have coupled ritually with the Chief-priestess as Moon-cow (see 88. 7). One element in the formation of the Labyrinth myth may have been that the palace at Cnossus – the house of the *labrys*, or double-axe – was a complex of rooms and corridors, and that the Athenian raiders had difficulty in finding and killing the king when they captured it. But this is not all. An open space in front of the palace was occupied by a dance floor with a maze pattern

used to guide performers of an erotic spring dance (see 92. 4). The origin of this pattern, now also called a labyrinth, seems to have been the traditional brushwood maze used to decoy partridges towards one of their own cocks, caged in a central enclosure, which uttered food-calls, love-calls, and challenges; and the spring dancers will have imitated the ecstatic hobbling love-dance of the cock-partridges (see 92. 2), whose fate was to be knocked on the head by the hunter (*Ecclesiasticus* xi. 30).

3. An Etruscan wine-jar from Tragliatella (see 104. 4), showing two mounted heroes, explains the religious theory of the partridge-dance. The leader carries a shield with a partridge device and a death-demon perches behind him; the other hero carries a lance, and a shield with a duck device. To their rear is a maze of a pattern found not only on certain Cnossian coins, but in the British turf-cut mazes trodden by school-children at Easter until the nineteenth century. Love-jealousy lured the king to his death, the iconographer is explaining, like a partridge in the brushwood maze, and he was succeeded by his tanist. Only the exceptional hero – a Daedalus, or a Theseus – returned alive; and in this context the recent discovery near Bosinney in Cornwall of a Cretan maze cut on a rock-face is of great importance. The ravine where the maze was first noticed by Dr Renton Green is one of the last haunts of the Cornish chough; and this bird houses the soul of King Arthur – who harrowed Hell, and with whom Bosinney is closely associated in legend. A maze dance seems to have been brought to Britain from the eastern Mediterranean by neolithic agriculturists of the third millennium B.C., since rough stone mazes, similar to the British turf-cut ones, occur in the 'Beaker B' area of Scandinavia and North-eastern Russia; and ecclesiastic mazes, once used for penitential purposes, are found in South-eastern Europe. English turf-mazes are usually known as 'Troy-town', and so are the Welsh: *Caer-droia*. The Romans probably named them after their own Troy Game, a labyrinthine dance performed by young aristocrats in honour of Augustus's ancestor Aeneas the Trojan; though, according to Pliny, it was also danced by children in the Italian countryside.

4. At Cnossus the sky-bull cult succeeded the partridge cult, and the circling of the dancers came to represent the annual courses of the heavenly bodies. If, therefore, seven youths and maidens took part, they may have represented the seven Titans and Titanesses of the sun, moon, and five planets (see 1. 3 and 43. 4); although no definite evidence of the Titan cult has been found in Cretan works of art. It appears that the ancient Crane Dance of Delos – cranes, too, perform a love dance – was similarly adapted to a maze pattern. In some mazes the dancers held a cord, which helped them to keep their proper distance and execute the pattern fault-lessly; and this may have given rise to the story of the ball of twine (A. B. Cook: *Journal of Hellenic Studies* xiv. 101 ff., 1949); at Athens, as on

Mount Sipylus, the rope dance was called *cordax* (Aristophanes: *Clouds* 540). The spectacle in the Cretan bull ring consisted of an acrobatic display by young men and girls who in turn seized the horns of the charging bull and turned back-somersaults between them over his shoulders. This was evidently a religious rite: perhaps here also the performers represented planets. It cannot have been nearly so dangerous a sport as most writers on the subject suggest, to judge from the rarity of casualties among *banderilleros* in the Spanish bull ring; and a Cretan fresco shows that a companion was at hand to catch the somersaulter as he or she came to earth.

5. 'Ariadne', which the Greeks understood as 'Ariagne' ('very holy'), will have been a title of the Moon-goddess honoured in the dance, and in the bull ring: 'the high, fruitful Barley-mother', also called Aridela, 'the very manifest one'. The carrying of fruit-laden boughs in Ariadne's honour, and Dionysus's, and her suicide by hanging, 'because she feared Artemis', suggests that Ariadne-dolls were attached to these boughs (see 79. 2). A bell-shaped Boeotian goddess-doll hung in the Louvre, her legs dangling, is Ariadne, or Erigone, or Hanged Artemis; and bronze dolls with detachable limbs have been found in Daedalus's Sardinia. Ariadne's crown made by Hephaestus in the form of a rose-wreath is not a fancy; delicate gold wreaths with gemmed flowers were found in the Mochlos hoard.

6. Theseus's marriage to the Moon-priestess made him lord of Cnossus, and on one Cnossian coin a new moon is set in the centre of a maze. Matrilinear custom, however, deprived an heiress of all claims to her lands if she accompanied a husband overseas; and this explains why Theseus did not bring Ariadne back to Athens, or any farther than Dia, a Cretan island within sight of Cnossus. Cretan Dionysus, represented as a bull – Minos, in fact – was Ariadne's rightful husband; and wine, a Cretan manufacture, will have been served at her orgies. This might account for Dionysus's indignation, reported by Homer, that she and the intruder Theseus had lain together.

7. Many ancient Athenian customs of the Mycenaean period are explained by Plutarch and others in terms of Theseus's visit to Crete: for instance, the ritual prostitution of girls, and ritual sodomy (characteristic of Anatha's worship at Jerusalem (see 61. 1), and the Syrian Goddess's at Hierapolis), which survived vestigially among the Athenians in the propitiation of Apollo with a gift of maidens, and in the carrying of harvest branches by two male inverts. The fruit-laden bough recalls the *lulab* carried at the Jerusalem New Year Feast of Tabernacles, also celebrated in the early autumn. Tabernacles was a vintage festival, and corresponded with the Athenian Oschophoria, or 'carrying of grape clusters'; the principal interest of which lay in a foot race (Proclus: *Chrestomathia* 28).

Originally, the winner became the new sacred king, as at Olympia, and received a fivefold mixture of 'oil, wine, honey, chopped cheese, and meal' – the divine nectar and ambrosia of the gods. Plutarch associates Theseus, the new king, with this festival, by saying that he arrived accidentally while it was in progress, and exculpates him from any part in the death of his predecessor Aegeus. But the new king really wrestled against the old king and flung him, as a *pharmacos*, from the White Rock into the sea (see 96. 3). In the illustrative icon which the mythographer has evidently misread, Theseus's black-sailed ship must have been a boat standing by to rescue the *pharmacos*; it has dark sails, because Mediterranean fishermen usually tan their nets and canvas to prevent the salt water from rotting them. The kerm-berry, or cochineal, provided a scarlet dye to stain the sacred king's face, and was therefore associated with royalty. 'Hecalene', the needy old spinster, is probably a worn-down form of 'Hecate Selene', 'the far-shooting moon', which means Artemis.

8. Bean-eating by men seems to have been prohibited in pre-Hellenic times – the Pythagoreans continued to abstain from beans, on the ground that their ancestors' souls could well be resident in them and that, if a man (as opposed to a woman) ate a bean, he might be robbing an ancestor of his or her chance to be reborn. The popular bean-feast therefore suggests a deliberate Hellenic flouting of the goddess who imposed the taboo; so does Theseus's gift of a male priesthood to the Phytalids ('growers'), the feminine form of whose name is a reminder that fig-culture, like bean-planting, was at first a mystery confined to women (see 24. 13).

9. The Cypriots worshipped Ariadne as the 'Birth-goddess of Amathus', a title belonging to Aphrodite. Her autumn festival celebrated the birth of the New Year; and the young man who sympathetically imitated her pangs will have been her royal lover, Dionysus. This custom, known as *couvade*, is found in many parts of Europe, including some districts of East Anglia.

10. Apollo's horn temple on Delos has recently been excavated. The altar and its foundations are gone, and bull has succeeded goat as the ritual animal in the stone decorations – if it indeed ever was a goat; a Minoan seal shows the goddess standing on an altar made entirely of bulls' horns.

11. Micon's allegorical mural of Thetis presenting a crown and ring to Theseus, while Minos glowers in anger on the shore, will have depicted the passing of the thalassocracy from Cretan to Athenian hands. But it may be that Minos had symbolically married the Sea-goddess by throwing a ring into the sea, as the Doges of Venice did in the middle ages.

12. 'Oenopion and Thoas are sometimes called Theseus's sons' because these were the heroes of Chios and Lemnos (see 88. h), subject allies of the Athenians.

## THE FEDERALIZATION OF ATTICA

WHEN Theseus succeeded his father Aegeus on the throne of Athens, he reinforced his sovereignty by executing nearly all his opponents, except Pallas and the remainder of his fifty sons. Some years later he killed these too as a precautionary measure and, when charged with murder in the Court of Apollo the Dolphin, offered the unprecedented plea of 'justifiable homicide', which secured his acquittal. He was purified of their blood at Troezen, where his son Hippolytus now reigned as king, and spent a whole year there. On his return, he suspected a half-brother, also named Pallas, of disaffection, and banished him at once; Pallas then founded Pallantium in Arcadia, though some say that Pallas son of Lycaon had done so shortly after the Deucalionian Flood.[1]

b. Theseus proved to be a law-abiding ruler, and initiated the policy of federalization, which was the basis of Athens' later well-being. Hitherto, Attica had been divided into twelve communities, each managing its own affairs without consulting the Athenian king, except in time of emergency. The Eleusinians had even declared war on Erechtheus, and other internecine quarrels abounded. If these communities were to relinquish their independence, Theseus must approach each clan and family in turn; which he did. He found the yeomen and serfs ready to obey him, and persuaded most of the large landowners to agree with his scheme by promising to abolish the monarchy and substitute democracy for it, though remaining commander-in-chief and supreme judge. Those who remained unconvinced by the arguments he used respected his strength at least.[2]

c. Theseus was thus empowered to dissolve all local governments, after summoning their delegates to Athens, where he provided these with a common Council Hall and Law Court, both of which stand to this day. But he forbore to interfere with the laws of private property. Next, he united the suburbs with the city proper which, until then, had consisted of the Acropolis and its immediate Southern dependencies, including the ancient Temples of Olympian Zeus, Pythian Apollo, Mother Earth, Dionysus of the Marshes, and the Aqueduct of Nine Springs. The Athenians still call the Acropolis 'the City'.

*d.* He named the sixteenth day of Hecatomboeon [July] 'Federation Day', and made it a public festival in honour of Athene, when a bloodless sacrifice is also offered to Peace.[3] By renaming the Athenian Games celebrated on this day 'All-Athenian', he opened it to the whole of Attica; and also introduced the worship of Federal Aphrodite and of Persuasion. Then, resigning the throne, as he had promised, he gave Attica its new constitution, and under the best auspices: for the Delphic Oracle prophesied that Athens would now ride the stormy seas as safely as a pig's bladder.[4]

*e.* To enlarge the city still further, Theseus invited all worthy strangers to become his fellow-citizens. His heralds, who went throughout Greece, used a formula which is still employed, namely: 'Come hither, all ye people!' Great crowds thereupon flocked into Athens, and he divided the population of Attica into three classes: the Eupatrids, or 'those who deserved well of their fatherland'; the Georges, or 'farmers'; and the Demiurges, or 'artificers'. The Eupatrids took charge of religious affairs, supplied magistrates, interpreted the laws, embodying the highest dignity of all; the Georges tilled the soil and were the backbone of the state; the Demiurges, by far the most numerous class, furnished such various artificers as soothsayers, surgeons, heralds, carpenters, sculptors, and confectioners.[5] Thus Theseus became the first king to found a commonwealth, which is why Homer, in the *Catalogue of Ships*, styles only the Athenians a sovereign people – and his constitution remained in force until the tyrants seized power. Some, however, deny the truth of this tradition: they say that Theseus continued to reign as before and that, after the death of King Menestheus, who led the Athenians against Troy, his dynasty persisted for three generations.[6]

*f.* Theseus, the first Athenian king to mint money, stamped his coins with the image of a bull. It is not known whether this represented Poseidon's bull, or Minos's general Taurus; or whether he was merely encouraging agriculture; but this coinage caused the standard of value to be quoted in terms of 'ten oxen', or 'one hundred oxen', for a considerable time. In emulation of Heracles, who had appointed his father Zeus patron of the Olympic Games, Theseus now appointed his father Poseidon patron of the Isthmian Games. Hitherto the god thus honoured had been Melicertes son of Ino, and the games, which were held at night, had been mysteries rather than a public spectacle. Next, Theseus made good the Athenian claim to the sovereignty of Megara and then, having summoned Peloponnesian delegates to the Isthmus, prevailed upon them to settle a long-standing frontier dispute with their Ionian neighbours. At a place agreed by both parties, he raised the celebrated column marked on its eastern side: 'This is not the Peloponnese, but Ionia!', and on the western: 'This is not Ionia, but the Peloponnese!' He also won Corinthian assent to the Athenians' taking the place of honour at the Isthmian Games; it consisted of as much ground as was covered by the mainsail of the ship that had brought them.[7]

1. Hyginus: *Fabula* 244; Apollodorus: *Epitome* i. 11; Servius on Virgil's *Aeneid* viii. 54; Euripides: *Hippolytus* 34–7; Pausanias: i. 22. 2; i. 28. 10 and viii. 3. 1.

2. Diodorus Siculus: iv. 61; Thucydides: ii. 15; Plutarch: *Theseus* 24.

3. Thucydides: *loc. cit.*; Plutarch: *loc. cit.*; Scholiast on Aristophanes's *Peace* 962.

4. Pausanias: viii. 2.1 and i. 22. 3; Plutarch: *loc cit.*

5. Plutarch: *Theseus* 25; Homer: *Odyssey* 383 ff. and xix. 135; Plato: *Symposium* 188d and *Republic* 529e; Herodotus: vii. 31.

6. Plutarch: *loc. cit.*; Homer: *Iliad* ii. 552 ff.; Pausanias: i. 3. 2.

7. Strabo: ix. 1. 6.

\*

1. The mythical element of the Theseus story has here been submerged in what purports to be Athenian constitutional history; but the Federalization of Attica is dated several hundred years too early; and Theseus's democratic reforms are fifth-century propaganda, probably invented by Cleisthenes. Legal reforms made during the late Jewish monarchy were similarly attributed to Moses by the editors of the Pentateuch.

2. Oxen provided the standard of value in ancient Greece, Italy, and Ireland, as they still do among backward pastoral tribes of East Africa, and the Athenians struck no coins until nearly five hundred years after the Trojan War. But it is true that Cretan copper ingots of a fixed weight were officially stamped with a bull's head, or a recumbent calf (Sir Arthur Evans: *Minoan Weights and Mediums of Currency* p. 335); and the Butadae of Athens, who seem to have been largely responsible for the development of the Theseus myth, may have had this tradition in mind when they coined money stamped with the ox-head, their clan-device.

3. The division of Attica into twelve communities is paralleled by a similar arrangement in the Nile Delta and in Etruria, and by the distribution of conquered Canaanite territory among the twelve tribes of Israel; the number may in each case have been chosen to allow for a monthly progress of the monarch from tribe to tribe. Greeks of the heroic age did

not distinguish between murder and manslaughter; in either case a blood-price had to be paid to the victim's clan, and the killer then changed his name and left the city for ever. Thus Telamon and Peleus continued to be highly regarded by the gods after their treacherous murder of Phocus (see 81. *b*); and Medea killed Apsyrtus without antagonizing her new Corinthian subjects (see 153. *a* and 156. *a*). At Athens, however, in the Classical period, wilful murder (*phonos*) carried the death penalty: man-slaughter (*akousia*), that of banishment; and the clan was bound by law to prosecute. *Phonos hekousios* (justifiable homicide) and *phonos akousios* (excusable homicide) were later refinements, which Draco probably introduced in the seventh century B.C.; the latter alone demanded expia-tion by ritual cleansing. The mythographers have not understood that Theseus evaded permanent exile for the murder of the Pallantids only by exterminating the entire clan, as David did with the 'House of Saul'. A year's absence at Troezen sufficed to rid the city of the pollution caused by the murder.

# 100

## THESEUS AND THE AMAZONS

SOME say that Theseus took part in Heracles's successful expedition against the Amazons, and received as his share of the booty their queen Antiope, also called Melanippe; but that this was not so unhappy a fate for her as many thought, because she had betrayed the city of Themis-cyra on the river Thermodon to him, in proof of the passion he had already kindled in her heart.[1]

*b*. Others say that Theseus visited their country some years later, in the company of Peirithous and his comrades; and that the Amazons, delighted at the arrival of so many handsome warriors, offered them no violence. Antiope came to greet Theseus with gifts, but she had hardly climbed aboard his ship, before he weighed anchor and abducted her. Others again say that he stayed for some time in Amazonia, and entertained Antiope as his guest. They add that among his companions were three Athenian brothers, Euneus, Thoas, and Soloön, the last of whom fell in love with Antiope but, not daring to approach her directly, asked Euneus to plead his cause. Antiope rejected these advances, though continuing to treat Soloön no less civilly than before, and it was not until he had thrown himself into the river Thermodon and drowned, that Theseus realized what had been afoot, and became much distressed. Remembering a warning given him by the Delphic Oracle that, if he should ever find himself greatly afflicted in a strange country, he must found a city and leave behind some of his companions to govern it, he built Pythopolis, in honour of Pythian Apollo, and named the near-by river Soloön. There he left Euneus, Thoas, and one Hermus, an Athenian noble, whose former residence in Pythopolis is now mistakenly called 'Hermes's House'. He then sailed away with Antiope.[2]

*c.* Antiope's sister Oreithyia, mistaken by some for Hippolyte whose girdle Heracles won, swore vengeance on Theseus. She concluded an alliance with the Scythians, and led a large force of Amazons across the ice of the Cimmerian Bosphorus, then crossed the Danube and passed through Thrace, Thessaly, and Boeotia. At Athens she encamped on the Areiopagus and there sacrificed to Ares; an event from which, some say, the hill won its name; but first she ordered a detachment to invade Laconia and discourage the Peloponnesians from reinforcing Theseus by way of the Isthmus.[3]

*d.* The Athenian forces were already marshalled, but neither side cared to begin hostilities. At last, on the advice of an oracle, Theseus sacrificed to Phobus, son of Ares, and offered battle on the seventh day of Boedromion, the date on which the Boedromia is now celebrated at Athens; though some say the festival had already been founded in honour of the victory which Xuthus won over Eumolpus in the reign of Erechtheus. The Amazons' battle-front stretched between what is now called the Amazonium and the Pnyx Hill near Chrysa. Theseus's right wing moved down from the Museum and fell upon their left wing, but was routed and forced to retire as far as the Temple of the Furies. This incident is recalled by a stone raised to the local commander Chalcodon, in a street lined with the tombs of those who fell, and called after him. The Athenian left wing, however, charged from the Palladium, Mount Ardettus and the Lyceum, and drove the Amazon right wing back to their camp, inflicting heavy casualties.[4]

*e.* Some say that the Amazons offered peace terms only after four months of hard fighting; the armistice, sworn near the sanctuary of Theseus, is still commemorated in the Amazonian sacrifice on the eve of his festival. But others say that Antiope, now Theseus's wife, fought heroically at his side, until shot dead by one Molpadia, whom Theseus then killed; that Oreithyia with a few followers escaped to Megara, where she died of grief and despair; and that the remaining Amazons, driven from Attica by the victorious Theseus, settled in Scythia.[5]

*f.* This, at any rate, was the first time that the Athenians repulsed foreign invaders. Some of the Amazons left wounded on the field of battle were sent to Chalcis to be cured. Antiope and Molpadia are buried near the temple of Mother Earth, and an earthen pillar marks Antiope's grave. Others lie in the Amazonium. Those Amazons who fell while crossing Thessaly lie buried between Scotussaea and Cynoscephalae; a few more, near Chaeronaea by the river Haemon. In the Pyrrhichan region of Laconia, shrines mark the place where the Amazons halted their advance and dedicated two wooden images to Artemis and Apollo; and at Troezen a temple of Ares commemorates Theseus's victory over this detachment when it attempted to force the Isthmus on its return.[6]

*g.* According to one account, the Amazons entered Thrace by way of Phrygia, not Scythia, and founded the sanctuary of Ephesian Artemis as they marched along the coast. According to another, they had taken refuge in this sanctuary on two earlier occasions: namely in their flight from Dionysus, and after Heracles's defeat of Queen Hippolyte; and its true founders were Cresus and Ephesus.[7]

*h.* The truth about Antiope seems to be that she survived the battle, and that Theseus was eventually compelled to kill her, as the Delphic Oracle had foretold, when he entered into an alliance with King Deucalion the Cretan, and married his sister Phaedra. The jealous Antiope, who was not his legal wife, interrupted the wedding festivities by bursting in, fully armed, and threatening to massacre the guests. Theseus and his companions hastily closed the doors, and despatched her in a grim combat, though she had borne him Hippolytus, also called Demophoön, and never lain with another man.[8]

1. Apollodorus: *Epitome* i. 16; Hegias of Troezen, quoted by Pausanias: i. 2. 1.
2. Pindar, quoted by Pausanias: i. 2. 1; Pherecydes and Bion, quoted by Plutarch: *Theseus* 26; Menecrates, quoted by Plutarch: *loc cit*.
3. Justin: ii. 4; Hellanicus, quoted by Plutarch: *Theseus* 26–7; Diodorus Siculus: iv. 28; Apollodorus: *Epitome* i. 16; Aeschylus: *Eumenides* 680 ff.
4. Plutarch: *Theseus* 27; *Etymologicum Magnum: sub* Boedromia; Euripides: *Ion* 59; Cleidemus, quoted by Plutarch: *loc. cit.*

5. Cleidemus, quoted by Plutarch: *loc. cit.*; Plutarch: *loc. cit.*; Pausanias: i. 41. 7; Diodorus Siculus: iv. 28.
6. Plutarch: *loc cit.*; Pausanias: i. 2. 1; i. 41. 7; iii. 25. 2 and ii. 32. 8.
7. Pindar, quoted by Pausanias: vii. 2. 4.
8. Hyginus: *Fabula* 241; Apollodorus: *Epitome* i. 17; Diodorus Siculus: iv. 62; Ovid: *Heroides* 121 ff.; Pausanias: i. 22. 2; Pindar, quoted by Plutarch: *Theseus* 28.

*

1. 'Amazons', usually derived from *a* and *mazon*, 'without breasts', because they were believed to sear away one breast in order to shoot better (but this notion is fantastic), seems to be an Armenian word, meaning 'moon-women'. Since the priestesses of the Moon-goddess on the South-eastern shores of the Black Sea bore arms, as they also did in the Libyan Gulf of Sirte (see 8. *1*), it appears that the accounts of them which travellers brought back confused the interpretation of certain ancient Athenian icons depicting women warriors, and gave rise to the Attic fable of an Amazonian invasion from the river Thermodon. These icons, which were extant in Classical times on the footstool of Zeus's throne at Olympia (Pausanias: v. 11. 2), at Athens on the central wall of the Painted Colonnade (Pausanias: i. 15. 2), on Athene's shield, in the sanctuary of Theseus, and elsewhere (Pausanias: i. 17. 1), represented either the fight between the pre-Hellenic priestesses of Athene for the office of High-priestess or a Hellenic invasion of Attica and the resistance offered by them. There will also have been armed priestesses at Ephesus – a Minoan colony, as the name of the founder Cresus ('Cretan') suggests – and in all cities where Amazons' graves were shown. Oreithyia, or Hippolyte, is supposed to have gone several hundred miles out of her way through Scythia; probably because the Cimmerian Bosphorus – the Crimea – was the seat of Artemis's savage Taurian cult, where the priestess despatched male victims (see 116. *2*).

2. Antiope's interruption of Phaedra's wedding may have been deduced from an icon which showed the Hellenic conqueror about to violate the High-priestess, after he had killed her companions. Antiope was not Theseus's legal wife, because she belonged to a society which resisted monogamy (see 131. *k*). The names Melanippe and Hippolytus associate the Amazons with the pre-Hellenic horse cult (see 43. *2*). Soloön's name ('egg-shaped weight') may be derived from a weight-tossing event in the funeral games celebrated at the Greek colony of Pythopolis, so called after the oracular serpent of its heroic founder; there seems to have been a practice here of throwing human victims into the river Thermodon. The Boedromia ('running for help') was a festival of Artemis, about which little is known: perhaps armed priestesses took part in it, as in the Argive festival of the Hybristica (see 160. *5*).

## PHAEDRA AND HIPPOLYTUS

AFTER marrying Phaedra, Theseus sent his bastard son Hippolytus to Pittheus, who adopted him as heir to the throne of Troezen. Thus Hippolytus had no cause to dispute the right of his legitimate brothers Acamas and Demophoön, Phaedra's sons, to reign over Athens.[1]

b. Hippolytus, who had inherited his mother Antiope's exclusive devotion to chaste Artemis, raised a new temple to the goddess at Troezen, not far from the theatre. Thereupon Aphrodite, determined to punish him for what she took as an insult to herself, saw to it that when he attended the Eleusinian Mysteries, Phaedra should fall passionately in love with him. He came dressed in white linen, his hair garlanded, and though his features wore a harsh expression, she thought them admirably severe.[2]

c. Since at that time Theseus was away in Thessaly with Peirithous, or it may have been in Tartarus, Phaedra followed Hippolytus to Troezen. There she built the Temple of Peeping Aphrodite to overlook the gymnasium, and would daily watch unobserved while he kept himself fit by running, leaping, and wrestling, stark naked. An ancient myrtle-tree stands in the Temple enclosure; Phaedra would jab at its leaves, in frustrated passion, with a jewelled hair-pin, and they are still much perforated. When, later, Hippolytus attended the All-Athenian Festival and lodged in Theseus's palace, she used the Temple of Aprodite on the Acropolis for the same purpose.[3]

d. Phaedra disclosed her incestuous desire to no one, but ate little, slept badly, and grew so weak that her old nurse guessed the truth at last, and officiously implored her to send Hippolytus a letter. This Phaedra did: confessing her love, and saying that she was now converted by it to the cult of Artemis, whose two wooden images, brought from Crete, she had just rededicated to the goddess. Would he not come hunting one day? 'We women of the Cretan Royal House,' she wrote, 'are doubtless fated to be dishonoured in love: witness my grandmother Europe, my mother Pasiphaë, and lastly my own sister Ariadne! Ah, wretched Ariadne, deserted by your father, the faithless Theseus, who has since murdered your own royal mother – why have the Furies not punished you for showing such unfilial indifference to her fate? – and must one day murder me! I count on you to revenge yourself on him by paying homage to Aphrodite in my company. Could we not go away and live together, for awhile at least, and make a hunting expedition the excuse? Meanwhile, none can suspect our true feelings for each other. Already we are lodged under the same roof, and our affection will be regarded as innocent, and even praiseworthy.'4

*e.* Hippolytus burned this letter in horror, and came to Phaedra's chamber, loud with reproaches; but she tore her clothes, threw open the chamber doors, and cried out: 'Help, help! I am ravished!' Then she hanged herself from the lintel, and left a note accusing him of monstrous crimes.5

*f.* Theseus, on receiving the note, cursed Hippolytus, and gave orders that he must quit Athens at once, never to return. Later he remembered the three wishes granted him by his father Poseidon, and prayed earnestly that Hippolytus might die that very day. 'Father.' he pleaded, 'send a beast across Hippolytus's path, as he makes for Troezen!'6

*g.* Hippolytus had set out from Athens at full speed. As he drove along the narrow part of the Isthmus a huge wave, which overtopped even the Molurian Rock, rolled roaring shoreward; and from its crest sprang a great dog-seal (or, some say, a white bull), bellowing and spouting water. Hippolytus's four horses swerved towards the cliff, mad with terror, but being an expert charioteer he restrained them from plunging over the edge. The beast then galloped menacingly behind the chariot, and he failed to keep his team on a straight course. Not far from the sanctuary of Saronian Artemis, a wild olive is still shown, called the Twisted Rhachos – the Troezenian term for a barren olive-tree is *rhachos* – and it was on a branch of this tree that a loop of Hippolytus's reins caught. His chariot was flung sideways against a pile of rocks and broken into pieces. Hippolytus, entangled in the reins, and thrown first against the tree-trunk, and then against the rocks, was dragged to death by his horses, while the pursuer vanished.7

*h.* Some, however, relate improbably that Artemis then told Theseus the truth, and rapt him in the twinkling of an eye to Troezen, where he arrived just in time to be reconciled to his dying son; and that she revenged herself on Aphrodite by procuring Adonis's death. For certain, though, she commanded the Troezenians to pay Hippolytus divine honours, and all Troezenian brides henceforth to cut off a lock of their hair, and dedicate it to him. It was Diomedes who dedicated the ancient temple and image of Hippolytus at Troezen, and who first offered him his annual sacrifice. Both Phaedra's and Hippolytus's tombs, the latter a mound of earth, are shown in the enclosure of this temple, near the myrtle-tree with the pricked leaves.

*i.* The Troezenians themselves deny that Hippolytus was dragged to death by horses, or even that he lies buried in his temple; nor will they reveal the whereabouts of his real tomb. Yet they declare that the gods set him among the stars as the Charioteer.[8]

*j.* The Athenians raised a barrow in Hippolytus's memory close to the Temple of Themis, because his death had been brought about by curses. Some say that Theseus, accused of his murder, was found guilty, ostracized, and banished to Scyros, where he ended his life in shame and grief. But his downfall is more generally believed to have been caused by an attempted rape of Persephone.[9]

*k.* Hippolytus's ghost descended to Tartarus, and Artemis, in high indignation, begged Asclepius to revive his corpse. Asclepius opened the doors of his ivory medicine cabinet and took out the herb with which Cretan Glaucus had been revived. With it he thrice touched Hippolytus's breast, repeating certain charms, and at the third touch the dead man raised his head from the ground. But Hades and the Three Fates, scandalized by this breach of privilege, persuaded Zeus to kill Asclepius with a thunderbolt.

*l.* The Latins relate that Artemis then wrapped Hippolytus in a thick cloud, disguised him as an aged man, and changed his features. After hesitating between Crete and Delos as suitable places of concealment, she brought him to her sacred grove at Italian Aricia.[10] There, with her consent, he married the nymph Egeria, and he still lives beside the lake among dark oak-woods, surrounded by sheer precipices. Lest he should be reminded of his death, Artemis changed his name to Virbius, which means *vir bis*, or 'twice a man'; and no horses are allowed in the vicinity. The priesthood of Arician Artemis is open only to runaway slaves.[11] In her grove grows an ancient oak-tree, the branches of which may not be broken, but if a slave dares do so then the priest, who has himself killed his predecessor and therefore lives in hourly fear of death, must fight him, sword against sword, for the priesthood. The Aricians say that Theseus begged Hippolytus to remain with him at Athens, but he refused.

*m.* A tablet in Asclepius's Epidaurian sanctuary records that Hippolytus dedicated twenty horses to him, in gratitude for having been revived.[12]

1. Apollodorus: *Epitome* i. 18; Pausanias: i. 22. 2; Ovid: *Heroides* iv. 67 ff.
2. Pausanias: ii. 31. 6; Ovid: *loc. cit.*
3. Ovid: *loc. cit.*; Seneca: *Hippolytus* 835 ff.; Pausanias: ii. 32. 3 and i. 22. 2; Euripides: *Hippolytus* 1 ff.; Diodorus Siculus: iv. 62.
4. Ovid: *loc. cit.*; Pausanias: i. 18. 5.
5. Apollodorus: *Epitome* i. 18; Diodorus Siculus: iv. 62; Hyginus: *Fabula* 47.
6. Plutarch: *Parallel Stories* 34; Servius on Virgil's *Aeneid* vi. 445.
7. Pausanias: ii. 32. 8; Euripides: *Hippolytus* 1193 ff.; Ovid: *Metamorphoses* xv. 506 ff.; Plutarch: *loc. cit.*; Diodorus Siculus: iv. 62.
8. Euripides: *Hippolytus* 1282 ff. and 1423 ff.; Pausanias: ii. 32. 1–2.
9. Pausanias: i. 22. 1; Philostatus: *Life of Apollonius of Tyana* vii. 42; Diodorus Siculus: iv. 62.
10. Ovid: *Metamorphoses* xv. 532 ff. and *Fasti* vi. 745.
11. Virgil: *Aeneid* vii. 775; Ovid: *Fasti* v. 312 and *Metamorphoses* xv. 545; Strabo: iii. 263 ff.; Pausanias: ii. 27. 4.
12. Servius on Virgil's *Aeneid* vi. 136; Strabo: v. 3. 12; Suetonius: *Caligula* 35; Pausanias: *loc cit.*

\*

*1.* The incident of Phaedra's incestuous love for Hippolytus, like that of Potiphar's wife and her adulterous love for Joseph (see 75. *1*), is borrowed either from the Egyptian *Tale of the Two Brothers*, or from a common Canaanite source. Its sequel has been based upon the familiar icon showing the chariot crash at the end of a sacred king's reign (see 71. *1*). If, as in ancient Ireland, a prophetic roaring of the November sea warned the king that his hour was at hand, this warning will have been pictured as a bull, or seal, poised open-mouthed on the creast of a wave. Hippolytus's reins must have caught in the myrtle, rather than in the sinister-looking olive later associated with the crash: the myrtle, in fact, which grew close to his hero shrine, and was famous for its perforated leaves. Myrtle symbolized the last month of the king's reign: as appears in the story of Oenomaus's chariot crash (see 109. *j*); whereas wild olive symbolized the first month of his successor's reign. *Vir bis* is a false derivation of Virbius, which seems to represent the Greek *hierobios*, 'holy life' – the *h* often becoming *v*: as in *Hestia* and *Vesta*, or *Hesperos* and *Vesper*. In the *Golden Bough* Sir James Frazer has shown that the branch which the priest guarded so jealously was mistletoe; and it is likely that Glaucus son of Minos (see 90. *c*), who has been confused with Glaucus son of Sisyphus (see 71. *a*), was revived by mistletoe. Though the pre-Hellenic mistletoe and oak cult had been suppressed in Greece (see 50. *2*), a refugee priesthood from the Isthmus may well have brought it to

Aricia. Egeria's name shows that she was a death-goddess, living in a grove of black poplars (see 51. 7 and 170. *l*).

2. Hippolytus's perquisite of the bride's lock must be a patriarchal innovation, designed perhaps to deprive women of the magical power resident in their hair, as Mohammedan women are shaved on marriage.

3. The concealment of Hippolytus's tomb is paralleled in the stories of Sisyphus and Neleus (see 67. *3*), which suggests that he was buried at some strategic point of the Isthmus.


# IO2

## LAPITHS AND CENTAURS

SOME say that Peirithous the Lapith was the son of Ixion and Dia, daughter of Eioneus; others, that he was the son of Zeus who, disguised as a stallion, coursed around Dia before seducing her.[1]

*b*. Almost incredible reports of Theseus's strength and valour had reached Peirithous, who ruled over the Magnetes, at the mouth of the river Peneus; and one day he resolved to test them by raiding Attica and driving away a herd of cattle that were grazing at Marathon. When Theseus at once went in pursuit, Peirithous boldly turned about to face him; but each was filled with such admiration for the other's nobility of appearance that the cattle were forgotten, and they swore an oath of everlasting friendship.[2]

*c*. Peirithous married Hippodameia, or Deidameia, daughter of Butes – or, some say, of Adrastus – and invited all the Olympians to his wedding, except Ares and Eris; he remembered the mischief which Eris had caused at the marriage of Peleus and Thetis. Since more feasters came to Peirithous's palace than it could contain, his cousins the Centaurs, together with Nestor, Caeneus, and other Thessalian princes, were seated at tables in a vast, tree-shaded cave near by.

*d*. The Centaurs, however, were unused to wine and, when they smelled its fragrance, pushed away the sour milk which was set before them, and ran to fill their silver horns from the wine-skins. In their ignorance they swilled the strong liquor unmixed with water, becoming so drunk that when the bride was escorted into the cavern to greet them, Eurytus, or Eurytion, leaped from his stool, overturned the table, and dragged her away by the hair. At once the other Centaurs followed his disgraceful example, lecherously straddling the nearest women and boys.[3]

*e*. Peirithous and his paranymph Theseus sprang to Hippodameia's rescue, cut off Eurytion's ears and nose and, with the help of the Lapiths, threw him out of the cavern. The ensuring fight, in the course of which Caeneus the Lapith was killed, lasted until nightfall; and thus began the long feud between the Centaurs and their Lapith neighbours, engineered by Ares and Eris in revenge for the slight offered them.[4]

*f*. On this occasion the Centaurs suffered a serious reverse, and Theseus drove them from their ancient hunting grounds on Mount Pelion to the land of the Aethices near Mount Pindus. But it was not an easy task to subdue the Centaurs, who had already disputed Ixion's kingdom with Peirithous, and who now, rallying their forces, invaded Lapith territory. They surprised and slaughtered the main Lapith army, and when the survivors fled to Pholoë in Elis, the vengeful Centaurs expelled them and converted Pholoë into a bandit stronghold of their own. Finally the Lapiths settled in Malea.

*g*. It was during Theseus's campaign against the Centaurs that he met Heracles again for the first time since his childhood; and presently initiated him into the Mysteries of Demeter at Eleusis.[5]

1. Diodorus Siculus: iv. 70; Eustathius on Homer p. 101.
2. Strabo: *Fragment* 14; *Vatican Epitome*; Plutarch: *Theseus* 30.
3. Apollodorus: *Epitome* i. 21; Diodorus Siculus: iv. 70; Hyginus: *Fabula* 33; Servius on Virgil's *Aeneid* vii. 304.
4. Pindar: *Fragment* 166f, quoted by Athenaeus: xi. 476b; Apollodorus: *loc. cit.*; Ovid: *Metamorphoses* xii. 210 ff.; Homer *Odyssey* xxi. 295; Pausanias: v. 10. 2.
5. Plutarch: *loc. cit.*; Homer: *Iliad* ii. 470 ff.; Diodorus Siculus: *loc. cit.*; Herodotus, quoted by Plutarch: *loc. cit.*

\*

1. Both Lapiths and Centaurs claimed descent from Ixion, an oak-hero, and had a horse cult in common (see 63. *a* and *d*). They were primitive mountain tribes in Northern Greece, of whose ancient rivalry the Hellenes took advantage by allying themselves first with one, and then with the other (see 35. 2; 78. 1; and 81. 3). *Centaur* and *Lapith* may be Italic words: *centuria*, 'war-band of one hundred', and *lapicidae*, 'flint-chippers'. (The usual Classical etymology is, respectively, from *cent-tauroi*, 'those who spear bulls', and *lapizein*, 'to swagger'.) These mountaineers seem to have had erotic orgies, and thus won a reputation for

promiscuity among the monogamous Hellenes; members of this neolithic race survived in the Arcadian mountains, and on Mount Pindus,
until Classical times, and vestiges of their pre-Hellenic language are to be
found in modern Albania.

2. It is, however, unlikely that the battle between Lapiths and Centaurs
– depicted on the gable of Zeus's temple at Olympia (Pausanias: v. 10. 2);
at Athens in the sanctuary of Theseus (Pausanias: i. 17. 2); and on Athene's
aegis (Pausanias: i. 28. 2) – recorded a mere struggle between frontier
tribes. Being connected with a royal wedding feast, divinely patronized,
at which Theseus in his lion-skin assisted, it will have depicted a ritual
event of intimate concern to all Hellenes. Lion-skinned Heracles also
fought the Centaurs on a similarly festive occasion (see 126. 2). Homer
calls them 'shaggy wild beasts', and since they are not differentiated from
satyrs in early Greek vase-paintings, the icon probably shows a newly-
installed king – it does not matter who – battling with dancers disguised
as animals: an event which A. C. Hocart in his *Kingship* proves to have
been an integral part of the ancient coronation ceremony. Eurytion is
playing the classical part of interloper (see 142. 5).

3. Whether Ixion or Zeus was Peirithous's father depended on Ixion's
right to style himself Zeus. The myth of his parentage has evidently been
deduced from an icon which showed a priestess of Thetis – Dia, daughter
of Eioneus, 'the divine daughter of the seashore' – halter in hand, encouraging the candidate for kingship to master the wild horse (see 75. 3).
Hippodameia's name ('horse-tamer') refers to the same icon. Zeus, disguised as stallion, 'coursed around' Dia, because that is the meaning of
the name Peirithous; and Ixion, as the Sun-god, spread-eagled to his
wheel, coursed around the heavens (see 63. 2).

# 103

## THESEUS IN TARTARUS

AFTER Hippodameia's death Peirithous persuaded Theseus, whose
wife Phaedra had recently hanged herself, to visit Sparta in his company
and carry away Helen, a sister of Castor and Polydeuces, the Dioscuri,
with whom they were both ambitious to be connected by marriage.
Where the sanctuary of Serapis now stands at Athens, they swore to
stand by each other in this perilous enterprise; to draw lots for Helen
when they had won her; and then to carry off another of Zeus's
daughters for the loser, whatever the danger might be.[1]

*b*. This decided, they led an army into Lacedaemon; then, riding ahead of the main body, seized Helen while she was offering a sacrifice in the Temple of Upright Artemis at Sparta, and galloped away with her. They soon outdistanced their pursuers, shaking them off at Tegea where, as had been agreed, lots were drawn for Helen; and Theseus proved the winner.[2] He foresaw, however, that the Athenians would by no means approve of his having thus picked a quarrel with the redoubtable Dioscuri, and therefore sent Helen, who was not yet nubile – being a twelve-year-old child or, some say, even younger – to the Attic village of Aphidnae, where he charged his friend Aphidnus to guard her with the greatest attention and secrecy. Aethra, Theseus's mother, accompanied Helen and cared well for her. Some try to exculpate Theseus by recording that it was Idas and Lynceus who stole Helen, and then entrusted her to the protection of Theseus, in revenge for the Dioscuri's abduction of the Leucippides. Others record that Helen's father Tyndareus himself entrusted her to Theseus, on learning that his nephew Enarephorus, son of Hippocoön, was planning to abduct her.[3]

*c*. Some years passed and, when Helen was old enough for Theseus to marry her, Peirithous reminded him of their pact. Together they consulted an oracle of Zeus, whom they had called upon to witness their oath, and his ironical response was: 'Why not visit Tartarus and demand Persephone, the wife of Hades, as a bride for Peirithous? She is the noblest of my daughters.' Theseus was outraged when Peirithous, who took this suggestion seriously, held him to his oath; but he dared not refuse to go, and presently they descended, sword in hand, to Tartarus. Avoiding the ferry-passage across Lethe, they chose the back way, the entrance to which is in a cavern of Laconian Taenarus, and were soon knocking at the gates of Hades's palace. Hades listened calmly to their impudent request and, feigning hospitality, invited them to be seated. Unsuspectingly they took the settee he offered, which proved to be the Chair of Forgetfulness and at once became part of their flesh, so that they could not rise again without self-mutilation. Coiled serpents hissed all about them, and they were well lashed by the Furies and mauled by Cerberus's teeth, while Hades looked on, smiling grimly.[4]

*d*. Thus they remained in torment for four full years, until Heracles, coming at Eurystheus's command to fetch up Cerberus, recognized them as they mutely stretched out their hands, pleading for his help. Persephone received Heracles like a brother, graciously permitting him to release the evil-doers and take them back to the upper air, if he could.⁵ Heracles thereupon grasped Theseus by both hands and heaved with gigantic strength until, with a rending noise, he was torn free; but a great part of his flesh remained sticking to the rock, which is why Theseus's Athenian descendants are all so absurdly small-buttocked. Next, he seized hold of Peirithous's hands, but the earth quaked warningly, and he desisted; Peirithous had, after all, been the leading spirit in this blasphemous enterprise.⁶

*e.* According to some accounts, however, Heracles released Peirithous as well as Theseus; while, according to others, he released neither, but left Theseus chained for ever to a fiery chair, and Peirithous reclining beside Ixion on a golden couch – before their famished gaze rise magnificent banquets which the Eldest of the Furies constantly snatches away. It has even been said that Theseus and Peirithous never raided Tartarus at all, but only a Thesprotian or Molossian city named Cichyrus, whose king Aidoneus, finding that Peirithous intended to carry off his wife, threw him to a pack of hounds, and confined Theseus in a dungeon, from which Heracles eventually rescued him.⁷

1. Diodorus Siculus: iv. 63; Pindar, quoted by Pausanias: i. 18. 5; Pausanias: i. 41. 5.
2. Diodorus Siculus: *loc. cit.*; Hyginus: *Fabula* 79; Plutarch: *Theseus* 31.
3. Apollodorus: *Epitome* i. 24; Tzetzes: *On Lycophron* 143; Eustathius on Homer's *Iliad* p. 215; Plutarch: *loc. cit.*
4. Hyginus: *Fabula* 79; Diodorus Siculus: *loc. cit.*; Horace: *Odes* iv. 7. 27; Panyasis, quoted by Pausanias: x. 29. 4; Apollodorus: *Epitome* i. 24.
5. Seneca: *Hippolytus* 835 ff.; Apollodorus: ii. 5. 12; Diodorus Siculus iv.: 26; Euripides: *Madness of Heracles* 619; Hyginus: *loc. cit.*
6. Apollodorus: *loc. cit.*; Suidas *sub* Lispoi; Scholiast on Aristophanes's *Knights* 1368.
7. Diodorus Siculus: iv. 63; Virgil: *Aeneid* vi. 601–19; Aelian: *Varia Historia* iv. 5; Plutarch: *Theseus* 31.

\*

1. Leading heroes in several mythologies are said to have harrowed Hell: Theseus, Heracles (see 134. *c*), Dionysus (see 170. *m*), and Orpheus (see 28. *c*) in Greece; Bel and Marduk in Babylonia (see 71. *1*); Aeneas in Italy; Cuchulain in Ireland; Arthur, Gwydion, and Amathaon in Britain; Ogier le Danois in Brittany. The origin of the myth seems to be a tem-

porary death which the sacred king pretended to undergo at the close of his normal reign, while a boy *interrex* took his place for a single day, thus circumventing the law which forbade him to extend his term beyond the thirteen months of a solar year (see 7. *1*; 41. *1*; 123. *4*, etc.).

2. Bel and his successor Marduk, spent their period of demise in battle with the marine monster Tiamat, an embodiment of the Sea-goddess Ishtar who sent the Deluge (see 73. *7*); like ancient Irish kings, who are reported to have gone out to do battle with the Atlantic breakers, they seem to have ceremonially drowned. An Etruscan vase shows the moribund king, whose name is given as Jason (see 148. *4*), in the jaws of a sea-monster: an icon from which the moral anecdote of Jonah and the Whale has apparently been deduced, Jonah being Marduk.

3. Athenian mythographers have succeeded in disguising the bitter rivalry between Theseus and his acting-twin Peirithous (see 95. *2*) for the favours of the Goddess of Death-in-Life – who appears in the myth as both Helen (see 62. *3*) and Persephone – by presenting them as a devoted royal pair who, like Castor and Polydeuces, made an amatory raid on a neighbouring city (see 74. *c*), and one of whom was excused death because he could claim divine birth. Idas and Lynceus, a similar pair of twins, have been introduced into the story to emphasize this point. But Peirithous's name, 'he who turns about', suggests that he was a sacred king in his own right, and on vase-paintings from Lower Italy he is shown ascending to the upper air and saying farewell to Theseus, who remains beside the Goddess of Justice, as though Theseus were merely his tanist.

4. Helen's abduction during a sacrifice recalls that of Oreithyia by Boreas (see 48. *a*), and may have been deduced from the same icon showing erotic orgies at the Athenian Thesmophoria. It is possible, of course, that a shrine of the Attic goddess Helen at Aphidnae contained an image or other cult object stolen by the Athenians from her Laconian counterpart – if the visit to Tartarus is a doublet of the story, they may have made a sea-raid on Taenarus – and that this was subsequently recovered by the Spartans.

5. The four years of Theseus's stay in Tartarus are the usual period during which a sacred king made room for his tanist; a new sacred king, Theseus *redivivus*, would then be installed. An attempt was made by the Athenians to raise their national hero to the status of an Olympian god, like Dionysus and Heracles, by asserting that he had escaped from death; but their Peloponnesian enemies successfully opposed this claim. Some insisted that he had never escaped, but was punished eternally for his insolence, like Ixion and Sisyphus. Others rationalized the story by saying that he raided Cichyrus, not Tartarus; and took the trouble to explain that Peirithous had not been mauled by Cerberus, but by Molos-

sian hounds, the largest and fiercest breed in Greece. The most generous
concession made to Athenian myth was that Theseus, released on bail
after a humiliating session in the Chair of Forgetfulness (see 37. 2), had
apologetically transferred most of his temples and sanctuaries to Heracles
the Rescuer, whose labours and sufferings he aped.

6. Yet Theseus was a hero of some importance, and must be given the
credit of having harrowed Hell, in the sense that he penetrated to the
centre of the Cretan maze, where Death was waiting, and came safely
out again. Had the Athenians been as strong on land as they were at sea,
he would doubtless have become an Olympian or, at least, a national
demi-god. The central source of this hostility towards Theseus is probably Delphi, where Apollo's Oracles was notoriously subservient to the
Spartans in their struggle against Athens.

# 104

## THE DEATH OF THESEUS

DURING Theseus's absence in Tartarus the Dioscuri assembled an
army of Laconians and Arcadians, marched against Athens, and demanded the return of Helen. When the Athenians denied that they
were sheltering her, or had the least notion where she might be, the
Dioscuri proceeded to ravage Attica, until the inhabitants of Deceleia,
who disapproved of Theseus's conduct, guided them to Aphidnae,
where they found and rescued their sister. The Dioscuri then razed
Aphidnae to the ground; but the Deceleians are still immune from all
Spartan taxes and entitled to seats of honour at Spartan festivals – their
lands alone were spared in the Peloponnesian War, when the invading
Spartans laid Attica waste.[1]

b. Others say that the revealer of Helen's hiding-place was one
Academus, or Echedemus, an Arcadian, who had come to Attica on
Theseus's invitation. The Spartans certainly treated him with great
honour while he was alive and, in their later invasions, spared his small
estate on the river Cephissus, six stadia distant from Athens. This is
now called the Academia: a beautiful, well-watered garden, where
philosophers meet and express their irreligious views on the nature of
the gods.[2]

c. Marathus led the Arcadian contingent of the Dioscuri's army and,
in obedience to an oracle, offered himself for sacrifice at the head of

his men. Some say that it was he, not Marathon the father of Sicyon and Corinthus, who gave his name to the city of Marathon.³

*d*. Now, Peteos son of Orneus and grandson of Erechtheus had been banished by Aegeus, and the Dioscuri, to spite Theseus, brought back his son Menestheus from exile, and made him regent of Athens. This Menestheus was the first demagogue. During Theseus's absence in Tartarus he ingratiated himself with the people by reminding the nobles of the power which they had forfeited through Federalization, and by telling the poor that they were being robbed of country and religion, and had become subject to an adventurer of obscure origin – who, however, had now vacated the throne and was rumoured dead.⁴

*e*. When Aphidnae fell, and Athens was in danger, Menestheus persuaded the people to welcome the Dioscuri into the city as their benefactors and deliverers. They did indeed behave most correctly, and asked only to be admitted to the Eleusinian Mysteries, as Heracles had been. This request was granted, and the Dioscuri became honorary citizens of Athens. Aphidnus was their adoptive father, as Pylius had been Heracles's on a similar occasion. Divine honours were thereafter paid them at the rising of their constellation, in gratitude for the clemency which they had shown to the common people; and they cheerfully brought Helen back to Sparta, with Theseus's mother Aethra and a sister of Peirithous as her bond-woman. Some say that they found Helen still a virgin; others, that Theseus had got her with child and that at Argos, on the way home, she gave birth to a girl, Iphigeneia, and dedicated a sanctuary to Artemis in gratitude for her safe delivery.⁵

*f*. Theseus, who returned from Tartarus soon afterwards, at once raised an altar to Heracles the Saviour, and reconsecrated to him all but four of his own temples and groves. However, he had been greatly weakened by his tortures, and found Athens so sadly corrupted by faction and sedition that he was no longer able to maintain order.⁶ First smuggling his children out of the city to Euboea, where Elpenor son of Chalcodon sheltered them – but some say that they had fled there before his return – and then solemnly cursing the people of Athens from Mount Gargettus, he sailed for Crete, where Deucalion had promised to shelter him.

*g*. A storm blew the ship off her course, and his first landfall was the island of Scyros, near Euboea, where King Lycomedes, though a close friend of Menestheus, received him with all the splendour due to his fame and lineage. Theseus, who had inherited an estate on Scyros, asked permission to settle there. But Lycomedes had long regarded this estate as his own and, under the pretence of showing Theseus its boundaries, inveigled him to the top of a high cliff, pushed him over, and then gave out that he had fallen accidentally while taking a drunken, post-prandial stroll.[7]

*h.* Menestheus, now left in undisturbed possession of the throne, was among Helen's suitors, and led the Athenian forces to Troy, where he won great fame as a strategist but was killed in battle. The sons of Theseus succeeded him.[8]

*i.* Theseus is said to have forcibly abducted Anaxo of Troezen; and to have lain with Iope, daughter of Tirynthian Iphicles. His love-affairs caused the Athenians such frequent embarrassment that they were slow to appreciate his true worth even for several generations after he had died. At the Battle of Marathon, however, his spirit rose from the earth to hearten them, bearing down fully armed upon the Persians; and when victory had been secured, the Delphic Oracle gave orders that his bones should be brought home. The people of Athens had suffered from the Scyrians' contumely for many years, and the Oracle announced that this would continue so long as they retained the bones.[9] But to recover them was a difficult task, because the Scyrians were no less surly than fierce and, when Cimon captured the island, would not reveal the whereabouts of Theseus's grave. However, Cimon observed a she-eagle on a hill-top, tearing up the soil with her talons. Acclaiming this as a sign from Heaven, he seized a mattock, hastened to the hole made by the eagle, and began to enlarge it. Almost at once the mattock struck a stone coffin, inside which he found a tall skeleton, armed with a bronze lance and a sword; it could only be that of Theseus. The skeleton was reverently brought to Athens, and re-interred amid great ceremony in Theseus's sanctuary near the Gymnasium.[10]

*j.* Theseus was a skilled lyre-player and has now become joint-patron with Heracles and Hermes of every gymnasium and wrestling school in Greece. His resemblance to Heracles is proverbial. He took part in the Calydonian Hunt; avenged the champions who fell at Thebes; and only failed to be one of the Argonauts through being detained in Tartarus when they sailed for Colchis. The first war between the Peloponnesians and the Athenians was caused by his abduction of Helen, and the second by his refusal to surrender Heracles's sons to King Eurystheus.[11]

*k*. Ill-treated slaves and labourers, whose ancestors looked to him for protection against their oppressors, now seek refuge in his sanctuary, where sacrifices are offered to him on the eighth day of every month. This day may have been chosen because he first arrived at Athens from Troezen on the eighth of Hecatomboeon, and returned from Crete on the eighth day of Pyanepsion. Or perhaps because he was a son of Poseidon: for Poseidon's feasts are also observed on that day of the month, since eight, being the first cube of an even number, represents Poseidon's unshakeable power.[12]

1. Apollodorus: *Epitome* i. 23; Hereas, quoted by Plutarch: *Theseus* 32; Herodotus: ix. 73.
2. Dicaearchus, quoted by Plutarch: *loc. cit.*; Diogenes Laertius: iii. 1. 9; Plutarch: *Cimon* 13.
3. Dicaearchus, quoted by Plutarch: *Theseus* 32; Pausanias: ii. 1. 1.
4. Pausanias: x. 35. 5; Apollodorus: *Epitome* i. 23; Plutarch: *loc. cit.*
5. Plutarch: *Theseus* 33; Hyginus: *Fabula* 79; Pausanias: ii. 22. 7.
6. Aelian: *Varia Historia* iv. 5; Philochorus, quoted by Plutarch: *Theseus* 35; Plutarch: *loc. cit.*
7. Pausanias: i. 17. 6; Plutarch: *loc. cit.*
8. Plutarch: *loc. cit.*; Apollodorus: iii. 10. 8.
9. Plutarch: *Theseus* 29 and 36; Pausanias: i. 15. 4; and iii. 3. 6.
10. Pausanias: i. 17. 6; Plutarch: *loc. cit.*
11. Pausanias: v. 19. 1; iv. 32. 1 and i. 32. 5; Plutarch: *Theseus* 29 and 36; Apollonius Rhodius: i. 101.
12. Plutarch: *Theseus* 36.

\*

*1*. Menestheus the Erechtheid, who is praised in *Iliad* ii. 552 ff. for his outstanding military skill, and reigned at Athens during Theseus's four years' absence in Tartarus, seems to have been his mortal twin and co-king, the Athenian counterpart of Peirithous the Lapith. Here he appears as a prototype of the Athenian demagogues who, throughout the Peloponnesian War, favoured peace with Sparta at any price; but the mythographer, while deploring his tactics, is careful not to offend the Dioscuri, to whom Athenian sailors prayed for succour when overtaken by storms.

*2*. The theme of the feathered *pharmacos* reappears in the names of Menestheus's father and grandfather, and in the death of Theseus himself. This took place on the island of Scyros ('stony'), also spelled *Sciros*; which suggests that, in the icon from which the story has been deduced, the word *scir* (an abbreviated form of Scirophoria, explaining why the king is being flung from a cliff) has been mistaken for the name of the island. If so, Lycomedes will have been the victim; his was a common

Athenian name. Originally, it seems, sacrifices were offered to the Moon-goddess on the eighth day of each lunation, when she entered her second phase, this being the right time of the month for planting; but when Poseidon married her, and appropriated her cult, the month became a solar period, no longer linked with the moon.

3. The mythic importance of Marathus ('fennel') lay in the use made of fennel stalks for carrying the new sacred fire from a central hearth to private ones (see 39. g), after their annual extinction (see 149. 3).

4. Before closing the story of Theseus, let me here add a further note to the Tragliatella vase (see 98. 3), which shows the sacred king and his tanist escaping from a maze. I have now seen the picture on the other side of this vase, which is of extraordinary interest as the prologue to this escape: a sunwise procession on foot led by the unarmed sacred king. Seven men escort him, each armed with three javelins and a shield with a boar device, the spear-armed tanist bringing up the rear. These seven men evidently represent the seven months ruled by the tanist, which fall between the apple harvest and Easter – the boar being his household badge (see 18. 7). The scene takes place on the day of the king's ritual death, and the Moon-queen (Pasiphaë – see 88. 7) has come to meet him: a terrible robed figure with one arm threateningly akimbo. With the outstretched other arm she is offering him an apple, which is his passport to Paradise; and the three spears that each man carries spell death. Yet the king is being guided by a small female figure robed like the other – we may call her the princess Ariadne (see 98. k), who helped Theseus to escape from the death-maze at Cnossos. And he is boldly displaying, as a counter-charm to the apple, an Easter-egg, the egg of resurrection. Easter was the season when the Troy-town dances were performed in the turf-cut mazes of Britain, and Etruria too. An Etruscan sacred egg of polished black trachite, found at Perugia, with an arrow in relief running around it, is this same holy egg.

## OEDIPUS

LAIUS, son of Labdacus, married Iocaste, and ruled over Thebes. Grieved by his prolonged childlessness, he secretly consulted the Delphic Oracle, which informed him that this seeming misfortune was a blessing, because any child born to Iocaste would become his murderer. He therefore put Iocaste away, though without offering any reason for his decision, which caused her such vexation that, having made him drunk, she inveigled him into her arms again as soon as night fell. When, nine months later, Iocaste was brought to bed of a son, Laius snatched him from the nurse's arms, pierced his feet with a nail and, binding them together, exposed him on Mount Cithaeron.

b. Yet the Fates had ruled that this boy should reach a green old age. A Corinthian shepherd found him, named him Oedipus because his feet were deformed by the nail-wound, and brought him to Corinth, where King Polybus was reigning at the time.[1]

c. According to another version of the story, Laius did not expose Oedipus on the mountain, but locked him in a chest, which was lowered into the sea from a ship. This chest drifted ashore at Sicyon, where Periboea, Polybus's queen, happened to be on the beach, supervising her royal laundry-women. She picked up Oedipus, retired to a thicket and pretended to have been overcome by the pangs of labour. Since the laundry-women were too busy to notice what she was about, she deceived them all into thinking that he had only just been born. But Periboea told the truth to Polybus who, also being childless, was pleased to rear Oedipus as his own son.

One day, taunted by a Corinthian youth with not in the least resembling his supposed parents, Oedipus went to ask the Delphic Oracle what future lay in store for him. 'Away from the shrine, wretch!' the Pythoness cried in disgust. 'You will kill your father and marry your mother!'

d. Since Oedipus loved Polybus and Periboea, and shrank from bringing disaster upon them, he at once decided against returning to Corinth. But in the narrow defile between Delphi and Daulis he happened to meet Laius, who ordered him roughly to step off the road and make way for his betters; Laius, it should be explained, was in a chariot and Oedipus on foot. Oedipus retorted that he acknowledged no betters except the gods and his own parents.

'So much the worse for you!' cried Laius, and ordered his charioteer Polyphontes to drive on.

One of the wheels bruised Oedipus's foot and, transported by rage, he killed Polyphontes with his spear. Then, flinging Laius on the road entangled in the reins, and whipping up the team, he made them drag him to death. It was left to the king of Plataeae to bury both corpses.[2]

*e.* Laius had been on his way to ask the Oracle how he might rid Thebes of the Sphinx. This monster was a daughter of Typhon and Echidne or, some say, of the dog Orthrus and the Chimaera, and had flown to Thebes from the uttermost part of Ethiopia. She was easily recognized by her woman's head, lion's body, serpent's tail, and eagle's wings.[3] Hera had recently sent the Sphinx to punish Thebes for Laius's abduction of the boy Chrysippus from Pisa and, settling on Mount Phicium, close to the city, she now asked every Theban wayfarer a riddle taught her by the Three Muses: 'What being, with only one voice, has sometimes two feet, sometimes three, sometimes four, and is weakest when it has the most?' Those who could not solve the riddle she throttled and devoured on the spot, among which unfortunates was Iocaste's nephew Haemon, whom the Sphinx made *haimon*, or 'bloody', indeed.

Oedipus, approaching Thebes fresh from the murder of Laius, guessed the answer. 'Man,' he replied, 'because he crawls on all fours as an infant, stands firmly on his two feet in his youth, and leans upon a staff in his old age.' The mortified Sphinx leaped from Mount Phicium and dashed herself to pieces in the valley below. At this the grateful Thebans acclaimed Oedipus king, and he married Iocaste, unaware that she was his mother.

*f.* Plague then descended upon Thebes, and the Delphic Oracle, when consulted once more, replied: 'Expel the murderer of Laius!' Oedipus, not knowing whom he had met in the defile, pronounced a curse on Laius's murderer and sentenced him to exile.

*g.* Blind Teiresias, the most renowned seer in Greece at this time, now demanded an audience with Oedipus. Some say that Athene, who had blinded him for having inadvertently seen her bathing, was moved by his mother's plea and, taking the serpent Erichthonius from her aegis, gave the order: 'Cleanse Teiresias's ears with your tongue that he may understand the language of prophetic birds.'

*h.* Others say that once, on Mount Cyllene, Teiresias had seen two serpents in the act of coupling. When both attacked him, he struck at them with his staff, killing the female. Immediately he was turned into a woman, and became a celebrated harlot; but seven years later he happened to see the same sight again at the same spot, and this time regained his manhood by killing the male serpent. Still others say that when Aphrodite and the three Charites, Pasithea, Cale, and Eurphosyne, disputed as to which of the four was most beautiful, Teiresias awarded Cale the prize; whereupon Aphrodite turned him into an old woman. But Cale took him with her to Crete and presented him with a lovely head of hair. Some days later Hera began reproaching Zeus for his numerous infidelities. He defended them by arguing that, at any rate, when he did share her couch, she had the more enjoyable time by far. 'Women, of course, derive infinitely greater pleasure from the sexual act than men,' he blustered.

'What nonsense!' cried Hera. 'The exact contrary is the case, and well you know it.'

Teiresias, summoned to settle the dispute from his personal experience, answered:

> 'If the parts of love-pleasure be counted as ten,
> Thrice three go to women, one only to men.'

Hera was so exasperated by Zeus's triumphant grin that she blinded Teiresias; but Zeus compensated him with inward sight, and a life extended to seven generations.[4]

*i.* Teiresias now appeared at Oedipus's court, leaning on the cornelwood staff given him by Athene, and revealed to Oedipus the will of the gods: that the plague would cease only if a Sown Man died for the sake of the city. Iocaste's father Menoeceus, one of those who had risen out of the earth when Cadmus sowed the serpent's teeth, at once leaped from the walls, and all Thebes praised his civic devotion.

Teiresias then announced further: 'Menoeceus did well, and the plague will now cease. Yet the gods had another of the Sown Men in mind, one of the third generation: for he has killed his father and married his mother. Know, Queen Iocaste, that it is your husband Oedipus!'

*j.* At first, none would believe Teiresias, but his words were soon confirmed by a letter from Periboea at Corinth. She wrote that the sudden death of King Polybus now allowed her to reveal the circumstances of Oedipus's adoption; and this she did in damning detail. Iocaste then hanged herself for shame and grief, while Oedipus blinded himself with a pin taken from her garments.[5]

k. Some say that, although tormented by the Erinnyes, who accused him of having brought about his mother's death, Oedipus continued to reign over Thebes for a while, until he fell gloriously in battle.[6] According to others, however, Iocaste's brother Creon expelled him, but not before he had cursed Eteocles and Polyneices – who were at once his sons and his brothers – when they insolently sent him the inferior portion of the sacrificial beast, namely haunch instead of royal shoulder. They therefore watched dry-eyed as he left the city which he had delivered from the Sphinx's power. After wandering for many years through country after country, guided by his faithful daughter Antigone, Oedipus finally came to Colonus in Attica, where the Erinnyes, who have a grove there, hounded him to death, and Theseus buried his body in the precinct of the Solemn Ones at Athens, lamenting by Antigone's side.[7]

1. Apollodorus: iii. 5. 7.
2. Hyginus: *Fabula* 66; Scholiast on Euripides's *Phoenician Women* 13 and 26; Apollodorus: *loc. cit.*; Pausanias: x. 5. 2.
3. Apollodorus: iii. 5. 8; Hesiod: *Theogony* 326; Sophocles: *Oedipus the Tyrant* 391; Scholiast on Aristophanes's *Frogs* 1287.
4. Apollodorus: iii. 6. 7; Hyginus: *Fabula* 75; Ovid: *Metamorphoses* iii. 320; Pindar: *Nemean Odes* i. 91; Tzetzes: *On Lycophron* 682; Sosostratus, quoted by Eustathius: p. 1665.
5. Apollodorus: iii. 5. 8; Sophocles: *Oedipus the Tyrant* 447, 713, 731, 774, 1285, etc.
6. Homer: *Odyssey* xi. 270 and *Iliad* xxiii. 679.
7. Sophocles: *Oedipus at Colonus* 166 and scholiast on 1375; Euripides: *Phoenician Women, Proem*; Apollodorus: iii. 5. 9; Hyginus: *Fabula* 67; Pausanias: i. 20. 7.

*

1. The story of Laius, Iocaste, and Oedipus has been deduced from a set of sacred icons by a deliberate perversion of their meaning. A myth which would explain Labdacus's name ('help with torches') has been lost; but it may refer to the torchlight arrival of a Divine Child, carried by cattlemen or shepherds at the New Year ceremony, and acclaimed as a son of the goddess Brimo ('raging'). This *eleusis*, or advent, was the most important incident in the Eleusinian Mysteries, and perhaps also in the Isthmian (see 70. 5), which would explain the myth of Oedipus's

arrival at the court of Corinth. Shepherds fostered or paid homage to many other legendary or semi-legendary infant princes, such as Hippothous (see 49. *a*), Pelias (see 68. *d*), Amphion (see 76. *a*), Aegisthus (see 111. *i*), Moses, Romulus, and Cyrus, who were all either exposed on a mountain or else consigned to the waves in an ark, or both. Moses was found by Pharaoh's daughter when she went down to the water with her women. It is possible that *Oedipus*, 'swollen foot', was originally *Oedipais*, 'son of the swelling sea', which is the meaning of the name given to the corresponding Welsh hero, Dylan; and that the piercing of Oedipus's feet with a nail belongs to the end, not to the beginning, of his story, as in the myth of Talus (see 92. *m* and 154. *h*).

2. Laius's murder is a record of the solar king's ritual death at the hands of his successor: thrown from a chariot and dragged by the horses (see 71. *1*). His abduction of Chrysippus probably refers to the sacrifice of a surrogate (see 29. *1*) when the first year of his reign ended.

3. The anecdote of the Sphinx has evidently been deduced from an icon showing the winged Moon-goddess of Thebes, whose composite body represents the two parts of the Theban year – lion for the waxing part, serpent for the waning part – and to whom the new king offers his devotions before marrying her priestess, the Queen. It seems also that the riddle which the Sphinx learned from the Muses has been invented to explain a picture of an infant, a warrior, and an old man, all worshipping the Triple-goddess: each pays his respects to a different person of the triad. But the Sphinx, overcome by Oedipus, killed herself, and so did her priestess Iocaste. Was Oedipus a thirteenth-century invader of Thebes, who suppressed the old Minoan cult of the goddess and reformed the calendar? Under the old system, the new king, though a foreigner, had theoretically been a son of the old king whom he killed and whose widow he married; a custom that the patriarchal invaders misrepresented as parricide and incest. The Freudian theory that the 'Oedipus complex' is an instinct common to all men was suggested by this perverted anecdote; and while Plutarch records (*On Isis and Osiris* 32) that the hippopotamus 'murdered his sire and forced his dam', he would never have suggested that every man has a hippopotamus complex.

4. Though Theban patriots, loth to admit that Oedipus was a foreigner who took their city by storm, preferred to make him the lost heir to the kingdom, the truth is revealed by the death of Menoeceus, a member of the pre-Hellenic race that celebrated the Peloria festival in memory of Ophion the Demiurge, from whose teeth they claimed to have sprung. He leaped to his death in the desperate hope of placating the goddess, like Mettus Curtius, when a chasm opened in the Roman Forum (Livy: vii. 6); and the same sacrifice was offered during the War of the 'Seven Against Thebes' (see 106. *j*). However, he died in vain;

otherwise the Sphinx, and her chief priestess, would not have been obliged to commit suicide. The story of Iocaste's death by hanging is probably an error; Helen of the Olive-trees, like Erigone and Ariadne of the vine cult, was said to have died in this way – perhaps to account for figurines of the Moon-goddess which dangled from the boughs of orchard trees, as a fertility charm (see 79. *2*; 88. *10* and 98. *5*). Similar figurines were used at Thebes; and when Iocaste committed suicide, she doubtless leaped from a rock, as the Sphinx did.

5. The occurrence of 'Teiresias', a common title for soothsayers, throughout Greek legendary history suggested that Teiresias had been granted a remarkably long life by Zeus. To see snakes coupling is still considered unlucky in Southern India; the theory being that the witness will be punished with the 'female disease' (as Herodotus calls it), namely homosexuality; here the Greek fabulist has taken the tale a stage further in order to raise a laugh against women. Cornel, a divinatory tree sacred to Cronus (see 52. *3* and 170. *5*), symbolized the fourth month, that of the Spring Equinox; Rome was founded at this season, on the spot where Romulus's cornel-wood javelin struck the ground. Hesiod turned the traditional two Charites into three (see 13. *3*), calling them Euphrosyne, Aglaia, and Thalia (*Theogony* 945). Sosostratus's account of the beauty contest makes poor sense, because *Pasithea Cale Euphrosyne*, 'the Goddess of Joy who is beautiful to all', seems to have been Aphrodite's own title. He may have borrowed it from the Judgement of Paris (see 159. *i* and *3*).

6. Two incompatible accounts of Oedipus's end survive. According to Homer, he died gloriously in battle. According to Apollodorus and Hyginus, he was banished by Iocaste's brother, a member of the Cadmean royal house, and wandered as a blind beggar through the cities of Greece until he came to Colonus in Attica, where the Furies hounded him to death. Oedipus's remorseful self-blinding has been interpreted by psychologists to mean castration; but though the blindness of Achilles's tutor Phoenix (see 160. *l*) was said by Greek grammarians to be a euphemism for impotence, primitive myth is always downright, and the castration of Uranus and Attis continued to be recorded unblushingly in Classical textbooks. Oedipus's blinding, therefore, reads like a theatrical invention, rather than original myth. Furies were personifications of conscience, but conscience in a very limited sense: aroused only by the breach of a maternal taboo.

7. According to the non-Homeric story, Oedipus's defiance of the City-goddess was punished by exile, and he eventually died a victim of his own superstitious fears. It is probable that his innovations were repudiated by a body of Theban conservatives; and, certainly, his sons' and brothers' unwillingness to award him the shoulder of the sacrificial victim

amounted to a denial of his divine authority. The shoulder-blade was the priestly perquisite at Jerusalem (*Leviticus* vii. 32 and xi. 21, etc.) and Tantalus set one before the goddess Demeter at a famous banquet of the gods (see 108. *c*). Among the Akan, the right shoulder still goes to the ruler.

Did Oedipus, like Sisyphus, try to substitute patrilineal for matrilineal laws of succession, but get banished by his subjects? It seems probable. Theseus of Athens, another patriarchal revolutionary from the Isthmus, who destroyed the ancient Athenian clan of Pallantids (see 99. *a*), is associated by the Athenian dramatists with Oedipus's burial, and was likewise banished at the close of his reign (see 104. *f*).

8. Teiresias here figures dramatically as the prophet of Oedipus's final disgrace, but the story, as it survives, seems to have been turned inside-out. It may once have run something like this:

> Oedipus of Corinth conquered Thebes and became king by marrying Iocaste, a priestess of Hera. Afterwards he announced that the kingdom should henceforth be bequeathed from father to son in the male line, which is a Corinthian custom, instead of remaining the gift of Hera the Throttler. Oedipus confessed that he felt himself disgraced as having let chariot horses drag to death Laius, who was accounted his father, and as having married Iocaste, who had enroyalled him by a ceremony of rebirth. But when he tried to change these customs, Iocaste committed suicide in protest, and Thebes was visited by a plague. Upon the advice of an oracle, the Thebans then withheld from Oedipus the sacred shoulder-blade, and banished him. He died in a fruitless attempt to regain his throne by warfare.

# 106

## THE SEVEN AGAINST THEBES

So many princes visited Argos in the hope of marrying either Aegeia, or Deipyla, the daughters of King Adrastus, that, fearing to make powerful enemies if he singled out any two of them as his sons-in-law, he consulted the Delphic Oracle. Apollo's response was: 'Yoke to a two-wheeled chariot the boar and lion which fight in your palace.'

*b.* Among the less fortunate of these suitors were Polyneices and Tydeus. Polyneices and his twin Eteocles had been elected co-kings of Thebes after the banishment of Oedipus, their father. They agreed to reign for alternate years, but Eteocles, to whom the first term fell, would not relinquish his throne at the end of the year, pleading the evil disposition shown by Polyneices, and banished him from the city. Tydeus, son of Oeneus of Calydon, had killed his brother Melanippus when out hunting; though he claimed that this was an accident, it had been prophesied that Melanippus would kill him, and the Calydonians therefore suspected him of having tried to forestall his fate, and he was also banished.

*c.* Now, the emblem of Thebes is a lion, and the emblem of Calydon, a boar; and the two fugitive suitors displayed these devices on their shields. That night, in Adrastus's palace, they began to dispute about the riches and glories of their respective cities, and murder might have been done, had not Adrastus parted and reconciled them. Then, mindful to the prophecy, he married Aegeia to Polyneices, and Deipyla to Tydeus, with a promise to restore both princes to their kingdoms; but said that he would first march against Thebes, which lay nearer.[1]

*d.* Adrastus mustered his Argive chieftains: Capaneus, Hippomedon, his brother-in-law Amphiaraus the seer, and his Arcadian ally Parthenopaeus, son of Meleager and Atalanta, bidding them arm themselves and set out eastward. Of these champions, only one was reluctant to obey: namely Amphiaraus who, foreseeing that all except Adrastus would die fighting against Thebes, at first refused to go.

*e.* It happened that Adrastus had formerly quarrelled with Amphiaraus about Argive affairs of state, and the two angry men might have killed each other, but for Adrastus's sister Eriphyle, who was married to Amphiaraus. Snatching her distaff, she flung herself between them, knocked up their swords, and made them swear always to abide by her verdict in any future dispute. Apprised of this oath, Tydeus called Polyneices and said: 'Eriphyle fears that she is losing her looks; now, if you were to offer her the magic necklace which was Aphrodite's wedding gift to your ancestress Harmonia, Cadmus's wife, she would soon settle the dispute between Amphiaraus and Adrastus by compelling him to come with us.'

*f.* This was discreetly done, and the expedition set out, led by the seven champions: Polyneices, Tydeus, and the five Argives.[2] But some say that Polyneices did not count as one of the seven, and add the name of Eteoclus the Argive, a son of Iphis.[3]

*g.* Their march took them through Nemea, where Lycurgus was king. When they asked leave to water their troops in his country, Lycurgus consented, and his bond-woman Hypsipyle guided them to the nearest spring. Hypsipyle was a Lemnian princess, but when the women of Lemnos had sworn to murder all their men in revenge for an injury done them, she saved the life of her father Thoas: they therefore sold her into slavery, and here she was, acting as nursemaid to Lycurgus's son Opheltes. She set the boy down for a moment while she guided the Argive army to the drinking pool, whereupon a serpent writhed around his limbs and bit him to death. Adrastus and his men returned from the spring too late to do more than kill the serpent and bury the boy.

*h*. When Amphiaraus warned them that this was an ominous sign, they instituted the Nemean Games in the boy's honour, calling him Archemorus, which means 'the beginner of doom'; and each of the champions had the satisfaction of winning one of the seven events. The judges at the Nemean Games, which are celebrated every four years, have ever since worn dark robes in mourning for Opheltes, and the victor's wreath is plaited of luckless parsley.[4]

*i*. Arrived at Cithaeron, Adrastus sent Tydeus as his herald to the Thebans, with a demand that Eteocles should resign the throne in favour of Polyneices. When this was refused, Tydeus challenged their chieftains to single combat, one after another, and emerged victorious from every encounter; soon, no more Thebans dared come forward. The Argives then approached the city walls, and each of the champions took up his station facing one of the seven gates.

*j*. Teiresias the seer, whom Eteocles consulted, prophesied that the Thebans would be victorious only if a prince of the royal house freely offered himself as a sacrifice to Ares; whereupon Menoeceus, the son of Creon, killed himself before the gates, much as his namesake and uncle had leaped headlong from the walls on a previous occasion. Teiresias's prophecy was fulfilled: the Thebans were, indeed, defeated in a skirmish and withdrew into the city; but no sooner had Capaneus set a scaling-ladder against the wall and begun to mount it, than Zeus struck him dead with a thunderbolt. At this, the Thebans took courage, made a furious sally, killing three more of the seven champions; and one of their number, who happened to be named Melanippus, wounded Tydeus in the belly. Athene cherished an affection for Tydeus and, pitying him as he lay half-dead, hastened to beg an infallible elixir from her father Zeus, which would have soon set him upon his feet again. But Amphiaraus hated Tydeus for having forced the Argives to march and, being sharp-witted, ran at Melanippus and cut off his head. 'Here is revenge!' he cried, handing the head to Tydeus. 'Split open the skull and gulp his brains!' Tydeus did so, and Athene, arriving at that moment with the elixir, spilt it on the ground and retired in disgust.

*k.* Only Polyneices, Amphiaraus, and Adrastus now remained of the seven champions; and Polyneices, to save further slaughter, offered to decide the succession of the throne by single combat with Eteocles. Eteocles accepted the challenge and, in the course of a bitter struggle, each mortally wounded the other. Creon, their uncle, then took command of the Theban army and routed the dismayed Argives. Amphiaraus fled in his chariot along the banks of the river Ismenus, and was on the point of being thrust between the shoulders by a Theban pursuer, when Zeus cleft the earth with a thunderbolt and he vanished from sight, chariot and all, and now reigns alive among the dead. Baton, his charioteer, went with him.⁵

*l.* Seeing that the day was lost, Adrastus mounted his winged horse Arion and escaped; but when, later, he heard that Creon would not permit his dead enemies to be buried, visited Athens as a suppliant and persuaded Theseus to march against Thebes and punish Creon's impiety. Theseus took the city in a surprise attack, imprisoned Creon, and gave the dead champions' corpses to their kinsfolk, who heaped a great pyre for them. But Evadne, Capaneus's wife, seeing that her husband had been heroized by Zeus's thunderbolt, would not be parted from him. Since custom demanded that a lightning-struck man should be buried apart from the rest, and his grave fenced off, she flung herself on the general pyre, and was consumed alive.⁶

*m.* Now, before Theseus's arrival at Thebes, Antigone, sister of Eteocles and Polyneices, had disobeyed Creon's orders by secretly building a pyre and laying Polyneices's corpse upon it. Looking out of his palace window, Creon noticed a distant glow which seemed to proceed from a burning pyre and, going to investigate, surprised Antigone in her act of disobedience. He summoned his son Haemon, to whom Antigone had been affianced, and ordered him to bury her alive in Polyneices's tomb. Haemon feigned readiness to do as he was told but, instead, married Antigone secretly, and sent her away to live among his shepherds. She bore him a son who, many years later, came to Thebes, and took part in certain funeral games; but Creon, who was still King of Thebes, guessed his identity by the serpent mark on his body, borne by all descendants of Cadmus, and sentenced him to death. Heracles interceded for his life, but Creon proved obdurate; whereupon Haemon killed both Antigone and himself.⁷

1. Hyginus: *Fabula* 69; Euripides: *Phoenician Women* 408 ff., with scholiast on 409; *Suppliants* 132 ff.; Apollodorus: iii. 6. 1.

2. Aeschylus: *Seven Against Thebes* 375 ff.; Homer: *Odyssey* xi. 326 ff. and xv. 247; Sophocles: *Electra* 836 ff. and Fragments of *Eriphyle*; Hyginus: *Fabula* 73; Pausanias: v. 17. 7 ff. and ix. 41. 2; Diodorus Siculus: iv. 65. 5 ff.; Apollodorus: iii. 6. 2–3.

3. Aeschylus: *Seven Against Thebes* 458 ff.; Sophocles: *Oedipus at Colonus* 1316; Pausanias: x. 10. 3.

4. Apollodorus: i. 9. 17 and iii. 6. 4; Hyginus: *Fabulae* 74 and 273; Scholiast on the *Argument* of Pindar's *Nemean Odes*.

5. Aeschylus: *Seven Against Thebes* 375 ff.; Euripides: *Phoenician Women* 105 ff. and 1090 ff.; Diodorus Siculus: iv. 65. 7–9; Apollodorus: iii. 6. 8; Hyginus: *Fabulae* 69 and 70; Scholiast on Pindar's *Nemean Odes* x. 7; Pausanias: ix. 18. 1; Ovid: *Ibis* 427 ff. and 515 ff.

6. Hyginus: *Fabulae* 273; Apollodorus: *loc. cit.*; Euripides: *The Suppliants*; Plutarch: *Theseus* 29; Isocrates: *Panegyric* 54–8; Pausanias: i. 39. 2.

7. Sophocles: *Antigone, passim*; Hyginus: *Fabula* 72; Fragments of Euripides's *Antigone*; Aeschylus: *Seven Against Thebes* 1005 ff.; Apollodorus: iii. 7. 1.

\*

1. Apollo's lion-and-boar oracle will have originally conveyed the wisdom of forming double kingdoms; in order to prevent political strife between the sacred king and his tanist, such as brought about the fall of Thebes (see 69. *1*). But the emblem of Thebes was a lion, because of the lion-bodied Sphinx, its former goddess; and the emblem of Calydon was a boar, probably because Ares, who had a shrine there, liked to adopt this disguise (see 18. *j*). The oracle has therefore been applied to a different situation. Shields with animal devices were regularly used in early Classical times (see 98. *3* and 160. *n*).

2. The mythographers often made play with the syllable *eri* in a name, pretending that it meant *eris*, 'strife', rather than 'plentiful'. Hence the myths of Erichthonius (see 25. *1*) and Erigone (see 79. *3*). Eriphyle originally meant 'many leaves', rather than 'tribal strife'. Hesiod (*Works and Days* 161 ff.) says that Zeus wiped out two generations of heroes, the first at Thebes in the war for Oedipus's sheep, the second at Troy in the war occasioned by fair-haired Helen. 'Oedipus's sheep' is not explained; but Hesiod must be referring to this war between Eteocles and Polyneices, in which the Argives supported an unsuccessful candidate for the throne of Thebes. The cause of a similar dispute between brothers was the golden fleece, for which Atreus and Thyestes contended (see 111. *c–d*); its possession set the owner on the throne of Mycenae. Also, Zeus had golden-fleeced rams on Mount Laphystium, which seem to have been the royal

insignia of neighbouring Orchomenus and which caused much bloodshed (see 70. 6).

3. Hypsipyle ('high gate') was probably a title of the Moon-goddess's, whose course describes a high arch across the sky; and the Nemean Games, like the Olympian, will have been celebrated at the end of the sacred king's term, when he had reigned his fifty lunar months as the Chief-priestess's husband. The myth preserves the tradition that boys were sacrificed annually to the goddess, as surrogates for the king; though the word *Opheltes*, which means simply 'benefactor', has here been given a forced sense: 'wound about by a serpent', as though it were derived from *ophis*, 'serpent' and *eilein*, 'to press together'. Neither does *Archemorus* mean 'the beginning of doom', but rather 'original olive stock', which refers to cuttings from Athene's sacred olive (see 16. *c*), presumably those used in the Games as crowns for the victors of the various events. After the disasters of the Persian War, the use of olive was discontinued at the Nemean Games in favour of parsley, a token of mourning (scholiast on Pindar's *Argument to the Nemean Games*). Parsley was unlucky, perhaps because of its notoriety as an abortificient – the English proverb has it: 'parsley grows rank in cuckolds' gardens.' It grew rank in the death-island of Ogygia (see 170. *w*).

4. Tydeus's gulping of Melanippus's brains is reported as a moral anecdote. This old-established means of improving one's fighting skill, introduced by the Hellenes and still practised by the Scythians in Classical times (Herodotus: iv. 64), had come to be regarded as barbarous. But the icon from which the mythographers deduced their story probably showed Athene pouring a libation to Melanippus's ghost, in approval of Tydeus's action. The lost epic of the *Seven Against Thebes* must have closely resembled the Indian *Mahabharata*, which glorifies the Maryannu soldier-caste: the same theme of kinsman pitted against kinsman occurs, the conduct of the fighters is nobler and more tragic than in the *Iliad*, the gods play no mischievous part, suttee is honoured, and Bhishma, like Tydeus, drinks his enemy's blood (see 81. 8).

5. Amphiaraus's end provides yet another example of the sacred king's death in a chariot crash (see 71. *a*; 101. *g*; 105. *d*; 109. *j*, etc.). The descent of Baton ('blackberry') to Tartarus in his company seems to be told to account for the widespread European taboo on the eating of blackberries, which is associated with death.

6. Evadne's self-immolation recalls the myth of Alcestis (see 69. *d*). Relics of a royal cremation found in a bee-hive tomb at Dendra near Mycenae suggest that, in this particular instance, the king and queen were buried at the same time; and A. W. Persson believes that the queen died voluntarily. But they may both have been murdered, or died of the same illness, and no similar Mycenaean burial is reported elsewhere.

Suttee, in fact, which seems to have been a Hellenic practice, soon went out of fashion (see 74. *8*). Lightning was an evidence of Zeus's presence, and since 'holy' and 'unclean' mean much the same in primitive religion – the tabooed animals in *Leviticus* were unclean because they were holy – the grave of a man struck by lightning was fenced off, like that of a calf that has died of anthrax on a modern farm, and he was given heroic rites. The graveyard near Eleusis where the champions are said by Pausanias to have been eventually interred, has now been identified and opened by Professor Mylonas. He found one double burial surrounded by a stone circle, and five single burials; the skeletons, as was customary in the thirteenth century B.C., to which the vase fragments are attributable, showed no signs of cremation. Early grave-robbers had evidently removed the bronze weapons and other metallic objects, originally buried with the bodies; and it may have been their finding of two skeletons in the stone circle, and the anomaly of the circle itself, which suggested to the people of Eleusis that this was the grave of Capaneus, struck by lightning, and of his faithful wife Evadne.

7. The myth of Antiope, Haemon, and the shepherds seems to have been deduced from the same icon as those of Arne (see 43. *d*) and Alope (see 49. *a*). We are denied the expected end of the story: that he killed his grandfather Creon with a discus (see 73. *p*).

# 107

## THE EPIGONI

THE sons of the seven champions who had fallen at Thebes swore to avenge their fathers. They are known as the Epigoni. The Delphic Oracle promised them victory if Alcmaeon, son of Amphiaraus, took command. But he felt no desire to attack Thebes, and hotly disputed the propriety of the campaign with his brother Amphilochus. When they could not agree whether to make war or no, the decision was referred to their mother Eriphyle. Recognizing the situation as a familiar one, Thersander, the son of Polyneices, followed his father's example: he bribed Eriphyle with the magic robe which Athene had given his ancestress Harmonia at the same time as Aphrodite had given her the magic necklace. Eriphyle decided for war, and Alcmaeon reluctantly assumed command.

*b*. In a battle fought before the walls of Thebes, the Epigoni lost Aegialeus, son of Adrastus, and Teiresias the seer then warned the

Thebans that their city would be sacked. The walls, he announced, were fated to stand only so long as one of the original seven champions remained alive, and Adrastus, now the sole survivor, would die of grief when he heard of Aegialeus's death. Consequently, the Thebans' wisest course was to flee that very night. Teiresias added that whether they took his advice or no made no odds to him; he was destined to die as soon as Thebes fell into Argive hands. Under cover of darkness, therefore, the Thebans escaped northward with their wives, children, weapons, and a few belongings, and when they had travelled far enough, called a halt and founded the city of Hestiaea. At dawn, Teiresias, who went with them, paused to drink at the spring of Tilphussa, and suddenly expired.

*c.* That same day, which was the very day on which Adrastus heard of Aegialeus's death and died of grief, the Argives, finding Thebes evacuated, broke in, razed the walls, and collected the booty. They sent the best of it to Apollo at Delphi, including Teiresias's daughter Manto, or Daphne, who had stayed behind; and she became his Pythoness.[1]

*d.* Nor was this the end of the matter. Thersander happened to boast in Alcmaeon's hearing that most of the credit for the Argive victory was due to himself: he had bribed Eriphyle, just as his father Polyneices did before him, to give the order to march. Alcmaeon thus learned for the first time that Eriphyle's vanity had caused his father's death, and might well have caused his own. He consulted the Delphic Oracle, and Apollo replied that she deserved death. Alcmaeon mistook this for a dispensation to matricide and, on his return, he duly killed Eriphyle, some say with the aid of his brother Amphilochus. But Eriphyle, as she lay dying, cursed Alcmaeon, and cried out: 'Lands of Greece and Asia, and of all the world: deny shelter to my murderers!' The avenging Erinnyes thereupon pursued him and drove him mad.

*e.* Alcmaeon fled first to Thesprotia, where he was refused entry, and then to Psophis, where King Phegeus purified him for Apollo's sake. Phegeus married him to his daughter Arsinoë, to whom Alcmaeon gave the necklace and the robe which he had brought in his baggage. But the Erinnyes, disregarding this purification, continued to plague him, and the land of Psophis grew barren on his account. The Delphic Oracle then advised Alcmaeon to approach the River-god Achelous, by whom he was once more purified; he married Achelous's daughter Callirrhoë, and settled on land recently formed by the silt of the river, which had not been included in Eriphyle's ban. There he lived at peace for a while.

*f.* A year later, Callirrhoë, fearing that she might lose her beauty, refused Alcmaeon admittance to her couch unless he gave her the celebrated robe and necklace. For love of Callirrhoë, he dared revisit Psophis, where he deceived Phegeus: making no mention of his marriage to Callirrhoë, he invented a prediction of the Delphic Oracle, to the effect that he would never be rid of the Erinnyes until he had dedicated both robe and necklace to Apollo's shrine. Phegeus thereupon made Arsinoë surrender them, which she was glad to do, believing that Alcmaeon would return to her as soon as the Erinnyes left him; for they were hard on his track again. But one of Alcmaeon's servants blabbed the truth about Callirrhoë, and Phegeus grew so angry that he ordered his sons to ambush and kill Alcmaeon when he left the palace. Arsinoë witnessed the murder from a window and, unaware of Alcmaeon's double-dealing, loudly upbraided her father and brothers for having violated guest-right and made her a widow. Phegeus begged her to be silent and listen while he justified himself; but Arsinoë stopped her ears and wished violent death upon him and her brothers before the next new moon. In retaliation, Phegeus locked her in a chest and presented her as a slave to the King of Nemea; at the same time telling his sons: 'Take this robe and this necklace to Delphic Apollo. He will see to it that they cause no further mischief.'

*g.* Phegeus's sons obeyed him; but, meanwhile, Callirrhoë, informed of what had happened at Psophis, prayed that her infant sons by Alcmaeon might become full-grown men in a day, and avenge his murder. Zeus heard her plea, and they shot up into manhood, took arms, and went to Nemea where, they knew, the sons of Phegeus had broken their return journey from Delphi in the hope of persuading Arsinoë to retract her curse. They tried to tell her the truth about Alcmaeon, but she would not listen to them either; and Callirrhoë's sons not only surprised and killed them but, hastening towards Psophis, killed Phegeus too, before the next moon appeared in the sky. Since no king or river-god in Greece would consent to purify them of their crimes, they travelled westward to Epirus, and colonized Acarnania, which was named after the elder of the two, Acarnan.

*h.* The robe and necklace were shown at Delphi until the Sacred War [fourth century B.C.], when the Phocian bandit Phayllos carried them off, and it is not known whether the amber necklace set in gold which the people of Amathus claim to be Eriphyle's is genuine or false.[2]

*i*. And some say that Teiresias had two daughters, Daphne and Manto. Daphne remained a virgin and became a Sibyl, but Alcmaeon begot Amphilochus and Tisiphone on Manto before sending her to Apollo at Delphi; he entrusted both children to King Creon of Corinth. Years later, Creon's wife, jealous of Tisiphone's extraordinary beauty, sold her as a slave; and Alcmaeon, not knowing who she was, bought her as his serving-girl but fortunately abstained from incest. As for Manto: Apollo sent her to Colophon in Ionia, where she married Rhacius, King of Caria; their son was Mopsus, the famous soothsayer.[3]

1. Diodorus Siculus: iv. 66; Pausanias: ix. 5. 13 ff., ix. 8. 6, and ix. 9. 4 ff.; Hyginus: *Fabula* 70; Fragments of Aeschylus's and Sophocles's *Epigoni*.
2. Apollodorus: iii. 7. 5–7; Athenaeus: vi. 22; Ovid: *Metamorphoses* ix. 413 ff.; Pausanias: viii. 24. 8–10 and ix. 41. 2; Parthenius: *Narrations* 25.
3. Apollodorus: iii. 7. 7, quoting Euripides's *Alcmaeon;* Pausanias: vii. 3. 1 and ix. 33. 1; Diodorus Siculus: iv. 66.

\*

1. This is a popular minstrel tale, containing few mythic elements, which could be told either in Thebes or Argos without causing offence; which would be of interest to the people of Psophis, Nemea, and the Achelous valley; which purposed to account for the founding of Hestiaea, and the colonization of Acarnania; and which had a strong moral flavour. It taught the instability of women's judgement, the folly of men in humouring their vanity or greed, the wisdom of listening to seers who are beyond suspicion, the danger of misinterpreting oracles, and the inescapable curse that fell on any son who killed his mother, even in placation of his murdered father's ghost (see 114. *a*).

2. Eriphyle's continuous power to decide between war and peace is the most interesting feature of the story. The true meaning of her name, 'very leafy', suggests that she was an Argive priestess of Hera in charge of a tree-oracle, like that of Dodona (see 51. *1*). If so, this tree is likely to have been a pear, sacred to Hera (see 74. *6*). Both the 'War of the Seven Against Thebes', which Hesiod calls the 'War of Oedipus's Sheep', and its sequel here recounted, seem to have preceded the Argonautic expedition and the Trojan War, and may be tentatively referred to the fourteenth century B.C.

# 108

## TANTALUS

THE parentage and origin of Tantalus are disputed. His mother was Pluto, a daughter of Cronus and Rhea or, some say, of Oceanus and Tethys;[1] and his father either Zeus, or Tmolus, the oak-chapleted deity of Mount Tmolus who, with his wife Omphale, ruled over the kingdom of Lydia and had judged the contest between Pan and Apollo.[2] Some, however, call Tantalus a king of Argos, or of Corinth; and others say that he went northward from Sipylus in Lydia to reign in Paphlagonia; whence, after he had incurred the wrath of the gods, he was expelled by Ilus the Phrygian, whose young brother Ganymedes he had abducted and seduced.[3]

b. By his wife Euryanassa, daughter of the River-god Pactolus; or by Eurythemista, daughter of the River-god Xanthus; or by Clytia, daughter of Amphidamantes; or by the Pleiad Dione, Tantalus became the father of Pelops, Niobe, and Broteas.[4] Yet some call Pelops a bastard, or the son of Atlas and the nymph Linos.[5]

c. Tantalus was the intimate friend of Zeus, who admitted him to Olympian banquets of nectar and ambrosia until, good fortune turning his head, he betrayed Zeus's secrets and stole the divine food to share among his mortal friends. Before this crime could be discovered, he committed a worse. Having called the Olympians to a banquet on Mount Sipylus, or it may have been at Corinth, Tantalus found that the food in his larder was insufficient for the company and, either to test Zeus's omniscience, or merely to demonstrate his good will, cut up his son Pelops, and added the pieces to the stew prepared for them, as the sons of Lycaon had done with their brother Nyctimus when they entertained Zeus in Arcadia.[6] None of the gods failed to notice what was on their trenchers, or to recoil in horror, except Demeter who, being dazed by her loss of Persephone, ate the flesh from the left shoulder.[7]

d. For these two crimes Tantalus was punished with the ruin of his kingdom and, after his death by Zeus's own hand, with eternal torment in the company of Ixion, Sisyphus, Tityus, the Danaids, and others. Now he hangs, perennially consumed by thirst and hunger, from the bough of a fruit-tree which leans over a marshy lake. Its waves lap against his waist, and sometimes reach his chin, yet whenever he bends down to drink, they slip away, and nothing remains but the black mud at his feet; or, if he ever succeeds in scooping up a handful of water, it slips through his fingers before he can do more than wet his cracked lips, leaving him thirstier than ever. The tree is laden with pears, shining apples, sweet figs, ripe olives and pomegranates, which dangle against his shoulders; but whenever he reaches for the luscious fruit, a gust of wind whirls them out of his reach.[8]

*e*. Moreover, an enormous stone, a crag from Mount Sipylus, overhangs the tree and eternally threatens to crush Tantalus's skull.[9] This is his punishment for a third crime: namely theft, aggravated by perjury. One day, while Zeus was still an infant in Crete, being suckled by the she-goat Amaltheia, Hephaestus had made Rhea a golden mastiff to watch over him; which subsequently became the guardian of his temple at Dicte. But Pandareus son of Merops, a native of Lydian or, it may have been Cretan, Miletus – if, indeed, it was not Ephesus – dared to steal the mastiff, and brought it to Tantalus for safe keeping on Mount Sipylus. After the hue and cry had died down, Pandareus asked Tantalus to return it to him, but Tantalus swore by Zeus that he had neither seen nor heard of a golden dog. This oath coming to Zeus's ears, Hermes was given orders to investigate the matter; and although Tantalus continued to perjure himself, Hermes recovered the dog by force or by stratagem, and Zeus crushed Tantalus under a crag of Mount Sipylus. The spot is still shown near the Tantalid Lake, a haunt of white swan-eagles. Afterwards, Pandareus and his wife Harmothoë fled to Athens, and thence to Sicily, where they perished miserably.[10]

*f*. According to others, however, it was Tantalus who stole the golden mastiff, and Pandareus to whom he entrusted it and who, on denying that he had ever received it was destroyed, together with his wife, by the angry gods, or turned into stone. But Pandareus's orphaned daughters Merope and Cleothera, whom some call Cameiro and Clytië, were reared by Aphrodite on curds, honey, and sweet wine. Hera endowed them with beauty and more than human wisdom; Artemis made them grow tall and strong; Athene instructed them in every known handicraft. It is difficult to understand why these goddesses showed such solicitude, or chose Aphrodite to soften Zeus's heart towards these orphans and arrange good marriages for them – unless, of course, they had themselves encouraged Pandareus to commit the theft. Zeus must have suspected something, because while Aphrodite was closeted with him on Olympus, the Harpies snatched away the three girls, with his consent, and handed them over to the Erinnyes, who made them suffer vicariously for their father's sins.[11]

*g*. This Pandareus was also the father of Aëdon, the wife of Zethus, to whom she bore Itylus. Aëdon was racked with envy of her sister Niobe, who rejoiced in the love of six sons and six daughters and, when trying to murder Sipylus, the eldest of them, she killed Itylus by mistake; whereupon Zeus transformed her into the Nightingale who, in early summer, nightly laments her murdered child.[12]

*h*. After punishing Tantalus, Zeus was pleased to revive Pelops; and therefore ordered Hermes to collect his limbs and boil them again in the same cauldron, on which he laid a spell. The Fate Clotho then re-articulated them; Demeter gave him a solid ivory shoulder in place of the one she had picked clean; and Rhea breathed life into him; while Goat-Pan danced for joy.[13]

*i*. Pelops emerged from the magic cauldron clothed in such radiant beauty that Poseidon fell in love with him on the spot, and carried him off to Olympus in a chariot drawn by golden horses. There he appointed him his cup-bearer and bed-fellow; as Zeus later appointed Ganymedes, and fed him on ambrosia. Pelops first noticed that his left shoulder was of ivory when he bared his breast in mourning for his sister Niobe. All true descendants of Pelops are marked in this way and, after his death, the ivory shoulder-blade was laid up at Pisa.[14]

*j*. Pelops's mother Euryanassa, meanwhile, made the most diligent search for him, not knowing about his ascension to Olympus; she learned from the scullions that he had been boiled and served to the gods, who seemed to have eaten every last shred of his flesh. This version of the story became current throughout Lydia; many still credit it and deny that the Pelops whom Tantalus boiled in the cauldron was the same Pelops who succeeded him.[15]

*k*. Tantalus's ugly son Broteas carved the oldest image of the Mother of the Gods, which still stands on the Coddinian Crag, to the north of Mount Sipylus. He was a famous hunter, but refused to honour Artemis, who drove him mad; crying aloud that no flame could burn him, he threw himself upon a lighted pyre and let the flames consume him. But some say that he committed suicide because everyone hated his ugliness. Broteas's son and heir was named Tantalus, after his grandfather.[16]

1.  Pausanias: ii. 22. 4; Scholiast on Pindar's *Olympian Odes* iii. 41; Hesiod: *Theogony* 355, with scholiast.
2.  Pausanias: *loc. cit.*; Scholiast on Euripides's *Orestes* 5; Pliny: *Natural History* v. 30; Ovid: *Metamorphoses* ii. 156; Apollodorus: ii. 6. 3.
3.  Hyginus: *Fabula* 124; Servius on Virgil's *Aeneid* vi. 603; Diodorus Siculus: iv. 74; Tzetzes: *On Lycophron* 355.
4.  Plutarch: *Parallel Stories* 33; Tzetzes: *On Lycophron* 52; Pherecydes, quoted by scholiast on Euripides's *Orestes* 11; Hyginus: *Fabula* 83; Pausanias: 111. 22. 4.
5.  Lactantius: *Stories from Ovid's Metamorphoses* vi. 6; Servius on Virgil's *Aeneid* viii. 130.
6.  Hyginus: *Fabula* 82; Pindar: *Olympian Odes* i. 38 and 60; Servius on Virgil's *Aeneid* vi. 603 ff.; Lactantius: *loc. cit.*; Servius on Virgil's *Georgics* iii. 7; Tzetzes: *On Lycophron* 152.
7.  Hyginus: *Fabula* 83; Tzetzes: *loc. cit.*; Ovid: *Metamorphoses* vi. 406.
8.  Diodorus Siculus: iv. 74; Plato: *Cratylus* 28; Lucian: *Dialogues of the Dead* 17; Homer: *Odyssey* xi. 582–92; Ovid: *Metamorphoses* iv. 456; Pindar: *Olympian Odes* i. 60; Apollodorus: *Epitome* ii. 1; Hyginus: *Fabula* 82.
9.  Pausanias: x. 31. 4; Archilochus, quoted by Plutarch: *Political Precepts* 6; Euripides: *Orestes* 7.
10. Antoninus Liberalis: *Transformations* 36 and 11; Eustathius and Scholiast on Homer's *Odyssey* xix. 518; Pausanias: x. 30. 1 and vii. 7. 3.
11. Pausanias: x. 30. 1; Scholiast on Homer: *loc. cit.*; Homer: *Odyssey* xx. 66 ff.; Antoninus Liberalis: *Transformations* 36.
12. Homer: *Odyssey* xix. 518 ff.; Apollodorus: iii. 5. 6; Pherecydes: *Fragment* p. 138, ed. Sturz.
13. Servius on Virgil's *Aeneid* vi. 603; Pindar: *Olympian Odes* i. 26; Hyginus: *Fabula* 83; Scholiast on Aristides: p. 216, ed. Frommel.
14. Apollodorus: *Epitome* ii. 3; Pindar: *Olympian Odes* i. 37 ff.; Lucian: *Charidemus* 7; Ovid: *Metamorphoses* vi. 406; Tzetzes: *On Lycophron* 152; Pausanias: v. 13. 3.
15. Pindar: *loc. cit.*; Euripides: *Iphigeneia Among the Taurians* 387.
16. Pausanias: iii. 22. 4; Apollodorus: *Epitome* ii. 2; Ovid: *Ibis* 517, with scholiast.

\*

1. According to Strabo (xii. 8. 21), Tantalus, Pelops, and Niobe were Phrygians; and he quotes Demetrius of Scepsis, and also Callisthenes (xiv. 5. 28), as saying that the family derived their wealth from the mines of Phrygia and Mount Sipylus. Moreover, in Aeschylus's *Niobe* (cited by Strabo: xii. 8. 21) the Tantalids are said to have had 'an altar of Zeus, their paternal god, on Mount Ida'; and Sipylus is located 'in the Idaean land'. Democles, whom Strabo quoted at second hand, rationalizes the

Tantalus myth, saying that his reign was marked by violent earthquakes in Lydia and Ionia, as far as the Troad: entire villages disappeared, Mount Sipylus was overturned, marshes were converted into lakes, and Troy was submerged (Strabo: i. 3. 17). According to Pausanias, also, a city on Mount Sipylus disappeared into a chasm, which subsequently filled with water and became Lake Saloë, or Tantalis. The ruins of the city could be seen on the lake bottom until this was silted up by a mountain stream (Pausanias: vii. 24. 7). Pliny agrees that Tantalis was destroyed by an earthquake (*Natural History* ii. 93), but records that three successive cities were built on its site before this was finally flooded (*Natural History* v. 31).

2. Strabo's historical view, however, even if archaeologically plausible, does not account for Tantalus's connexion with Argos, Corinth, and Cretan Miletus. The rock poised over him in Tartarus, always about to fall, identifies him with Sisyphus of Corinth, whose similarly perpetual punishment was deduced from an icon which showed the Sun-Titan laboriously pushing the sun-disk up the slope of Heaven to its zenith (see 67. 2). The scholiast on Pindar was dimly aware of this identification, but explained Tantalus's punishment rationalistically, by recording that: 'some understand the stone to represent the sun, and Tantalus, a physicist, to be paying the penalty for having proved that the sun is a mass of white-hot metal' (scholiast on Pindar's *Olympian Odes* i. 97). Confusingly, this icon of the Sun-Titan has been combined with another: that of a man peering in agony through an interlace of fruit-bearing boughs, and up to his chin in water – a punishment which the rhetoricians used as an allegory of the fate meted out to the rich and greedy (Servius on Virgil's *Aeneid* vi. 603; Fulgentius: *Mythological Compendium* ii. 18). The apples, pears, figs, and such-like, dangling on Tantalus's shoulders are called by Fulgentius 'Dead Sea fruit', of which Tertullian writes that 'as soon as touched with the finger, the apple turns into ashes.'

3. To make sense of this scene, it must be remembered that Tantalus's father Tmolus is described as having been wreathed with oak, and that his son Pelops, one of whose grandsons was also called Tantalus (see 112. *c*), enjoyed hero-rites at Olympia, in which 'Zeus's forester' took part. Since, as is now generally agreed, the criminals in Tartarus were gods or heroes of the pre-Olympian epoch, Tantalus will have represented the annual Sacred King, dressed in fruit-hung branches, like those carried at the Oschophoria (see 98. *w*), who was flung into a river as a *pharmacos* – a custom surviving in the Green George ritual of the Balkan countryside, described by Frazer. The verb *tantalize*, derived from this myth, has prevented scholars from realizing that Tantalus's agony is caused not by thirst, but by fear of drowning or of subsequent immolation on a pyre, which was the fate of his ugly son Broteas.

4. Plato (*Cratylus* 28) may be right when he derives *Tantalus* from

*talantatos*, 'most wretched', formed from the same root, *tla*, 'suffering', or 'enduring', which yields the names of Atlas and Telamon, both oak heroes. But *talanteuein* means 'to weigh out money', and may be a reference to his riches; and *talanteuesthai* can mean 'to lurch from side to side', which is the gait of the sacred king with the lame thigh (see 23. *1*). It seems, then, that Tantalus is both a Sun-Titan and a woodland king, whose worship was brought from Greece to Asia Minor by way of Crete – Pandareus is described as a Cretan – in the mid-second millennium B.C., and reimported into Greece towards its close, when the collapse of the Hittite Empire forced wealthy Greek-speaking colonists of Asia Minor to abandon their cities.

5. When the mythographers recorded that Tantalus was a frequent guest on Olympus, they were admitting that his cult had once been dominant in the Peloponnese; and, although the banquets to which the gods invited Tantalus are carefully distinguished from the one to which he invited them, in every case the main dish will have been the same umble soup which the cannibalistic Arcadian shepherds of the oak cult prepared for Wolfish Zeus (see 38. *b*). It is perhaps no coincidence that, in Normandy, the Green George victim is called 'Green Wolf', and was formerly thrown alive into the midsummer bonfire. The eating of Pelops, however, is not directly connected with the wolf cult. Pelops's position as Poseidon's minion, his name, 'muddy face', and the legend of his ivory shoulder, point rather to a porpoise cult on the Isthmus (see 8. *3* and 70. *5*) – 'dolphin' in Greek includes the porpoise – and suggests that the Palladium, said to have been made from his bones (see 159. *3* and 166. *h*), was a cult object of porpoise ivory. This would explain why, according to the scholiast on Pindar's *Olympian Odes* i. 37, Thetis the Sea-goddess, and not Demeter, ate Pelops's shoulder. But the ancient seated statue of Mare-headed Demeter at Phigalia held a dove in one hand, a dolphin (or porpoise) in the other; and, as Pausanias directly says: 'Why the image was thus made is plain to anyone of ordinary intelligence who has studied mythology' (viii. 43. 3). He means that she presided over the horse cult, the oak cult, and the porpoise cult.

6. This ancient myth distressed the later mythographers. Not content with exculpating Demeter from the charge of deliberate man-eating, and indignantly denying that all the gods ate what was set before them, to the last morsel, they invented an over-rationalistic explanation of the myth. Tantalus, they wrote, was a priest who revealed Zeus's secrets to the uninitiated. Whereupon the gods unfrocked him, and afflicted his son with a loathsome disease; but the surgeons cut him about and patched him up with bone-graftings, leaving scars which made him look as if he had been hacked in pieces and joined together again (Tzetzes: *On Lycophron 152*).

7. Pandareus's theft of the golden mastiff should be read as a sequel to Heracles's theft of Cerberus, which suggests the Achaeans' defiance of the death curse, symbolized by a dog, in their seizure of a cult object sacred to the Earth-goddess Rhea (Tantalus's grandmother), and conferring sovereignty on its possessor. The Olympian goddesses were clearly abetting Pandareus's theft, and the dog, though Rhea's property, was guarding the sanctuary of the annually dying Cretan Zeus; thus the myth points not to an original Achaean violation of Rhea's shrine, but to a temporary recovery of the cult object by the goddess's devotees.

8. The nature of the stolen cult object is uncertain. It may have been a golden lamb, the symbol of Pelopid sovereignty; or the cuckoo-tipped sceptre which Zeus is known to have stolen from Hera; or the porpoise-ivory Palladium; or the aegis bag with its secret contents. It is unlikely to have been a golden dog, since the dog was not the cult object, but its guardian; unless this is a version of the Welsh myth of Amathaon ap Don who stole a dog from Arawn ('eloquence') King of Annwm ('Tartarus') and was by its means enabled to guess the secret name of the god Bran (*White Goddess* pp. 30 and 48–53).

9. The three daughters of Pandareus, one of whom, Cameiro, bears the same name as the youngest of the three Rhodian Fates (see 60. *2*), are the Triple-goddess, here humiliated by Zeus for her devotees' rebellion. Tantalus's loyalty to the goddess is shown in the stories of his son Broteas, who carved her image on Mount Sipylus, and of his daughter Niobe, priestess of the White Goddess, who defied the Olympians and whose bird was the white swan-eagle of Lake Tantalis. Omphale, the name of Tantalus's mother, suggests a prophetic navel-shrine like that at Delphi.

10. The annual *pharmacos* was chosen for his extreme ugliness, which accounts for Broteas. It is recorded that in Asia Minor, the *pharmacos* was first beaten on the genitals with squill (see 26. *3*) to the sound of Lydian flutes – Tantalus (Pausanias: ix. 5. 4) and his father Tmolus (Ovid: *Metamorphoses* ii. 156) are both associated in legend with Lydian flutes – then burned on a pyre of forest wood; his ashes were afterwards thrown into the sea (Tzetzes: *History* xxiii. 726–56, quoting Hipponax – sixth century B.C.). In Europe, the order seems to have been reversed: the Green George *pharmacos* was first ducked, then beaten, and finally burned.

# 109
## PELOPS AND OENOMAUS

PELOPS inherited the Paphlagonian throne from his father Tantalus, and for a while resided at Enete, on the shores of the Black Sea, whence he also ruled over the Lydians and Phrygians. But he was expelled from Paphlagonia by the barbarians, and retired to Lydian Mount Sipylus, his ancestral seat. When Ilus, King of Troy, would not let him live in peace even there, but ordered him to move on, Pelops brought his fabulous treasures across the Aegean Sea. He was resolved to make a new home for himself and his great horde of followers,[1] but first to sue for the hand of Hippodameia, daughter of King Oenomaus, the Arcadian, who ruled over Pisa and Elis.[2]

*b.* Some say that Oenomaus had been begotten by Ares on Harpina, daughter of the River-god Asopus; or on the Pleiad Asterië; or on Asterope; or on Eurythoë, daughter of Danaus; while others call him the son of Alxion; or of Hyperochus.[3]

*c.* By his wife Sterope, or Euarete, daughter of Acrisius, Oenomaus became the father of Leucippus, Hippodamus, and Dysponteus, founder of Dyspontium; and of one daughter, Hippodameia.[4] Oenomaus was famous for his love of horses, and forbade his subjects under the penalty of a curse ever to mate mares with asses. To this day, if the Eleans need mules, they must take their mares abroad to mate and foal.[5]

*d.* Whether he had been warned by an oracle that his son-in-law would kill him, or whether he had himself fallen in love with Hippodameia, is disputed; but Oenomaus devised a new way to prevent her from ever getting married. He challenged each of Hippodameia's suitors in turn to a chariot race, and laid out a long course from Pisa, which lies beside the river Alpheius, opposite Olympia, to Poseidon's altar on the Isthmus of Corinth. Some say that the chariots were drawn by four horses;[6] others say, by two. Oenomaus insisted that Hippodameia must ride beside each suitor, thus distracting his attention from the team – but allowed him a start of half an hour or so, while he himself sacrificed a ram on the altar of Warlike Zeus at Olympia. Both chariots would then race towards the Isthmus and the suitor, if overtaken, must die; but should he win the race, Hippodameia would be his, and Oenomaus must die.[7] Since, however, the wind-begotten mares, Psylla and Harpinna, which Pelops's father Ares had given him, were immeasurably the best in Greece, being swifter even than the North Wind;[8] and since his chariot, skilfully driven by Myrtilus, was especially designed for racing, he had never yet failed to overtake his rival and transfix him with his spear, another gift from Ares.[9]

*e.* In this manner Oenomaus disposed of twelve or, some say, thirteen princes, whose heads and limbs he nailed above the gates of his palace, while their trunks were flung barbarously in a heap on the ground. When he killed Marmax, the first suitor, he also butchered his mares, Parthenia and Eripha, and buried them beside the river Parthenia, where their tomb is still shown. Some say that the second suitor, Alcathous, was buried near the Horse-scarer in the hippodrome at Olympia, and that it is his spiteful ghost which baulks the charioteers.[10]

*f*. Myrtilus, Oenomaus's charioteer, was the son of Hermes by Theobule, or Cleobule; or by the Danaid Phaethusa; but others say that he was the son of Zeus and Clymene. He too had fallen in love with Hippodameia, but dared not enter the contest.[11] Meanwhile, the Olympians had decided to intervene and put an end to the slaughter, because Oenomaus was boasting that he would one day build a temple of skulls: as Evenus, Diomedes, and Antaeus had done.[12] When therefore Pelops, landing in Elis, begged his lover Poseidon, whom he invoked with a sacrifice on the seashore, either to give him the swiftest chariot in the world for his courtship of Hippodameia, or to stay the rush of Oenomaus's brazen spear, Poseidon was delighted to be of assistance. Pelops soon found himself the owner of a winged golden chariot, which could race over the sea without wetting the axles, and was drawn by a team of tireless, winged, immortal horses.[13]

*g*. Having visited Mount Sipylus and dedicated to Temnian Aphrodite an image made of green myrtle-wood, Pelops tested his chariot by driving it across the Aegean Sea. Almost before he had time to glance about him, he had reached Lesbos, where his charioteer Cillus, or Cellas, or Cillas, died because of the swiftness of the flight. Pelops spent the night on Lesbos and, in a dream, saw Cillus's ghost lamenting his fate, and pleading for heroic honours. At dawn, he burned his body, heaped a barrow over the ashes, and founded the sanctuary of Cillaean Apollo close by. Then he set out again, driving the chariot himself.[14]

*h*. On coming to Pisa, Pelops was alarmed to see the row of heads nailed above the palace gates, and began to regret his ambition. He therefore promised Myrtilus, if he betrayed his master, half the kingdom and the privilege of spending the bridal night with Hippodameia when she had been won.[15]

*i*. Before entering the race – the scene is carved on the front gable of Zeus's temple at Olympia – Pelops sacrificed to Cydonian Athene. Some say that Cillus's ghost appeared and undertook to help him; others, that Sphaerus was his charioteer; but it is more generally believed that he drove his own team, Hippodameia standing beside him.[16]

*j*. Meanwhile, Hippodameia had fallen in love with Pelops and, far from hindering his progress, had herself offered to reward Myrtilus generously, if her father's course could by some means be checked. Myrtilus therefore removed the lynch-pins from the axles of Oenomaus's chariot, and replaced them with others made of wax. As the chariots reached the neck of the Isthmus and Oenomaus, in hot pursuit, was poising his spear, about to transfix Pelops's back, the wheels of his chariot flew off, he fell entangled in the wreckage and was dragged to death. His ghost still haunts the Horse-scarer at Olympia.[17] There are some, however, who say that the swiftness of Poseidon's winged chariot and horses easily enabled Pelops to out-distance Oenomaus, and reach the Isthmus first; whereupon Oenomaus either killed himself in despair, or was killed by Pelops at the winning-post. According to others, the contest took place in the Hippodrome at Olympia, and Amphion gave Pelops a magic object which he buried by the Horse-scarer, so that Oenomaus's team bolted and wrecked his chariot. But all agree that Oenomaus, before he died, laid a curse on Myrtilus, praying that he might perish at the hands of Pelops.[18]

*k*. Pelops, Hippodameia, and Myrtilus then set out for an evening drive across the sea. 'Alas!' cried Hippodameia, 'I have drunk nothing all day; thirst parches me.' The sun was setting and Pelops called a halt at the desert island of Helene, which lies not far from the island of Euboea, and went up the strand in search of water. When he returned with his helmet filled, Hippodameia ran weeping towards him and complained that Myrtilus had tried to ravish her. Pelops sternly rebuked Myrtilus, and struck him in the face, but he protested indignantly: 'This is the bridal night, on which you swore that I should enjoy Hippodameia. Will you break your oath?' Pelops made no reply, but took the reins from Myrtilus and drove on.[19] As they approached Cape Geraestus – the southernmost promontory of Euboea, now crowned with a remarkable temple of Poseidon – Pelops dealt Myrtilus a sudden kick, which sent him flying head-long into the sea; and Myrtilus, as he sank, laid a curse on Pelops and all his house.[20]

*l*. Hermes set Myrtilus's image among the stars as the constellation of the Charioteer; but his corpse was washed ashore on the coast of Euboea and buried in Arcadian Pheneus, behind the temple of Hermes; once a year nocturnal sacrifices are offered him there as a hero. The Myrtoan Sea, which stretches from Euboea, past Helene, to the Aegean, is generally believed to take its name from Myrtilus rather than, as the Euboeans insist, from the nymph Myrto.[21]

*m.* Pelops drove on, until he reached the western stream of Oceanus, where he was cleansed of blood guilt by Hephaestus; afterwards he came back to Pisa, and succeeded to the throne of Oenomaus. He soon subjugated nearly the whole of what was then known as Apia, or Pelasgiotis, and renamed it the Peloponnese, meaning 'the island of Pelops', after himself. His courage, wisdom, wealth, and numerous children, earned him the envy and veneration of all Greece.[22]

*n.* From King Epeius, Pelops took Olympia, and added it to his kingdom of Pisa; but being unable to defeat King Stymphalus of Arcadia by force of arms, he invited him to a friendly debate, cut him in pieces, and scattered his limbs far and wide; a crime which caused a famine throughout Greece. But his celebration of the Olympian Games in honour of Zeus, about a generation after that of Endymion, was more splendid than any before.

*o.* To atone for the murder of Myrtilus, who was Hermes's son, Pelops built the first temple of Hermes in the Peloponnese; he also tried to appease Myrtilus's ghost by building a cenotaph for him in the hippodrome at Olympia, and paying him heroic honours. Some say that neither Oenomaus, nor the spiteful Alcathous, nor the magic object which Pelops buried, is the true Horse-scarer: it is the ghost of Myrtilus.[23]

*p.* Over the tomb of Hippodameia's unsuccessful suitors, on the farther side of the river Alpheius, Pelops raised a tall barrow, paying them heroic honours too; and about a furlong away stands the sanctuary of Artemis Cordax, so called because Pelops's followers there celebrated his victories by dancing the Rope Dance, which they had brought from Lydia.[24]

*q.* Pelops's sanctuary, where his bones are preserved in a brazen chest, was dedicated by Tirynthian Heracles, his grandson, when he came to celebrate the Olympian Games; and the Elean magistrates still offer Pelops the annual sacrifice of a black ram, roasted on a fire of white poplar-wood. Those who partake of this victim are forbidden to enter Zeus's temple until they have bathed, and the neck is the traditional perquisite of his forester. The sanctuary is thronged with visitors every year, when young men scourge themselves at Pelops's altar, offering him a libation of their blood. His chariot is shown on the roof of the Anactorium in Phliasia; the Sicyonians keep his gold-hilted sword in their treasury at Olympia; and his spear-shaped sceptre, at Chaeronea, is perhaps the only genuine work of Hephaestus still extant. Zeus sent it to Pelops by the hand of Hermes, and Pelops bequeathed it to King Atreus.[25]

*r.* Pelops is also styled 'Cronian One', or 'Horse-beater'; and the Achaeans claim him as their ancestor.[26]

1. Apollonius Rhodius: *Argonautica* ii. 358 and 790; Sophocles: *Ajax* 1292; Pausanias: ii. 22. 4 and vi. 22. 1; Pindar: *Olympian Odes* i. 24.

2. Servius on Virgil's *Georgics* iii. 7; Lucian: *Charidemus* 19; Apollodorus: *Epitome* ii. 4.

3. Diodorus Siculus: iv. 73; Hyginus: *Fabula* 250; *Poetic Astronomy* ii. 21; Scholiast on Apollonius Rhodius: i. 752; Pausanias: v. 1. 5; Tzetzes: *On Lycophron* 149.

4. Hyginus: *Poetic Astronomy* ii. 21; *Fabula* 84; Pausanias: viii. 20. 2 and vi. 22. 2; Lactantius on Statius's *Thebaid* vi. 336; Diodorus Siculus: *loc. cit.*

5. Plutarch: *Greek Questions* 52; Pausanias: v. 5. 2 and 9. 2.

6. Apollodorus: *Epitome* ii. 4; Lucian: *Charidemus* 19; Pausanias: v. 10. 2, v. 17. 4 and vi. 21. 6; Diodorus Siculus: iv. 73.

7. Apollodorus: *Epitome* ii. 5; Lucian: *loc. cit.*; Pausanias: v. 14. 5; Diodorus Siculus: *loc. cit.*

8. Servius on Virgil's *Georgics* iii. 7; Tzetzes: *On Lycophron* 166; Lucian: *loc. cit.*; Hyginus: Fabula 84; Apollodorus: *loc. cit.*

9. Pausanias: viii. 14. 7; Apollonius Rhodius: i. 756; Apollodorus: *loc. cit.*

10. Apollodorus: *loc. cit.*; Pindar: *Olympian Odes* i. 79 ff.; Ovid: *Ibis* 365; Hyginus: *Fabula* 84; Pausanias: vi. 21. 6–7 and 20. 8.

11. Hyginus: *Fabula* 224; Tzetzes: *On Lycophron* 156 and 162; Scholiast on Apollonius Rhodius: i. 752; Scholiast on Euripides's *Orestes* 1002; Pausanias: viii. 14. 7.

12. Lucian: *Charidemus* 19; Tzetzes: *On Lycophron* 159.

13. Pindar: *Olympian Odes* i. 65 ff. and i. 79; Apollodorus: *Epitome* ii. 3; Pausanias: v. 17. 4.

14. Pausanias: v. 13. 4 and 10. 2; Theon: *On Aratus* p. 21; Scholiast on Homer's *Iliad* i. 38.

15. Hyginus: *Fabula* 84; Scholiast on Horace's *Odes* i. 1; Pausanias: viii. 14. 7.

16. Pausanias: vi. 21. 5 and v. 10. 2; Scholiast on Homer's *Iliad: loc. cit.*; Apollonius Rhodius: i. 753.

17. Apollodorus: *Epitome* ii. 7; Tzetzes: *On Lycophron* 156; Apollonius Rhodius: i. 752 ff.; Pausanias: vi. 20. 8.

18. Pindar: *Olympic Odes* i. 87; Lucian: *Charidemus* 19; Diodorus Siculus: iv. 73; Apollodorus: *loc. cit.*

19. Apollodorus: *Epitome* ii. 8; Scholiast on Homer's *Iliad* ii. 104; Pausanias: viii. 14. 8; Hyginus: *Fabula* 84.

20. Strabo: x. 1. 7; Sophocles: *Electra* 508 ff.; Apollodorus: *loc. cit.*;
    Pausanias: viii. 14. 7.

21. Hyginus: *Poetic Astronomy* ii. 13; Pausanias: *loc. cit.* and viii. 14.
    8; Apollodorus: *loc. cit.*

22. Apollodorus: *Epitome* ii. 9; Diodorus Siculus: iv. 73; Thucy-
    dides: i. 9; Plutarch: *Theseus* 3.

23. Pausanias: v. 1. 5; v. 8. 1 and vi. 20. 8; Apollodorus: iii. 12. 6.

24. Pausanias: vi. 21. 7 and 22. 1.

25. Pausanias: v. 13. 1–2; vi. 22. 1; ii. 14. 3; vi. 19. 3 and ix. 41. 1;
    Apollodorus: ii. 7. 2; Pindar: *Olympian Odes* i. 90 ff.; Scholiast
    on Pindar's *Olympian Odes* i. 146; Homer: *Iliad* ii. 100 ff.

26. Pindar: *Olympian Odes* iii. 23; Homer: *Iliad* ii. 104; Pausanias:
    v. 25. 5.

*

**1.** According to Pausanias and Apollodorus, Tantalus never left Asia
Minor; but other mythographers refer to him and to Pelops as native
kings of Greece. This suggests that their names were dynastic titles taken
by early Greek colonists to Asia Minor, where they were attested by hero-
shrines; and brought back by emigrants before the Achaean invasion of
the Peloponnese in the thirteenth century B.C. It is known from Hittite
inscriptions that Hellenic kings reigned in Pamphylia and Lesbos as early
as the fourteenth century B.C. Pelopo-Tantalids seem to have ousted the
Cretanized dynasty of 'Oenomaus' from the Peloponnesian High Kingship.

**2.** The horse, which had been a sacred animal in Pelasgian Greece long
before the cult of the Sun-chariot, was a native European pony dedicated
to the Moon, not the Sun (see 75. *3*). The larger Trans-Caspian horse
came to Egypt with the Hyksos invaders in 1850 B.C. – horse chariotry
displaced ass chariotry in the Egyptian armed forces about the year 1500
B.C. – and had reached Crete before Cnossus fell a century later. Oenomaus's religious ban on mules should perhaps be associated with the death
of Cillus: in Greece, as at Rome, the ass cult was suppressed (see 83. *2*)
when the sun-chariot became the symbol of royalty. Much the same
religious reformation took place at Jerusalem (2 *Kings* xxiii. 11), where
a tradition survived in Josephus's time of an earlier ass cult (Josephus:
*Against Apion* ii. 7 and 10). Helius of the Sun-chariot, an Achaean deity,
was then identified in different cities with solar Zeus or solar Poseidon,
but the ass became the beast of Cronus, whom Zeus and Poseidon had
dethroned, or of Pan, Silenus, and other old-fashioned Pelasgian god-
lings. There was also a solar Apollo; since his hatred of asses is mentioned
by Pindar, it will have been Cillaean Apollo to whom hecatombs of

asses were offered by the Hyperboreans (Pindar: *Pythian Odes* x. 30 ff.).

3. Oenomaus, who represented Zeus as the incarnate Sun, is therefore called a son of Asterië, who ruled Heaven (see 88. *1*), rather than a similarly named Pleiad; and Queen Hippodameia, by marriage to whom he was enroyalled, represented Hera as the incarnate Moon. Descent remained matrilinear in the Peloponnese, which assured the goodwill of the conservative peasantry. Nor might the King's reign be prolonged beyond a Great Year of one hundred months, in the last of which the solar and lunar calendars coincided; he was then fated to be destroyed by horses. As a further concession to the older cult at Pisa, where Zeus's representative had been killed by his tanist each mid-summer (see 53. *5*), Oenomaus agreed to die a mock death at seven successive mid-winters, on each occasion appointing a surrogate to take his place for twenty-four hours and ride in the sun-chariot beside the Queen. At the close of this day, the surrogate was killed in a chariot crash, and the King stepped out from the tomb where he had been lurking (see 41. *1* and 123. *4*), to resume his reign. This explains the myth of Oenomaus and the suitors, another version of which appears in that of Evenus (see 74. *e*). The mythographers must be mistaken when they mention 'twelve or thirteen' suitors. These numbers properly refer to the lunations – alternately twelve and thirteen – of a solar year, not to the surrogates; thus in the chariot race at Olympia twelve circuits of the stadium were made in honour of the Moon-goddess. Pelops is a type of lucky eighth prince (see 81. *8*) spared the chariot crash and able to despatch the old king with his own sceptre-spear.

4. This annual chariot crash was staged in the Hippodrome. The surrogate could guide his horses – which seem, from the myth of Glaucus (see 71. *a*), to have been maddened by drugs – down the straight without coming to grief, but where the course bent around a white marble statue, called the Marmaranax ('marble king'), or the Horse-scarer, the outer wheel flew off for want of a lynch-pin, the chariot collapsed, and the horses dragged the surrogate to death. Myrtle was the death-tree, that of the thirteenth month, at the close of which the chariot crash took place (see 101. *1*); hence Myrtilus is said to have removed the metal lynch-pins, and replaced them with wax ones – the melting of wax also caused the death of Icarus, the Sun-king's surrogate – and laid a curse upon the House of Pelops.

5. In the second half of the myth, Myrtilus has been confused with the surrogate. As *interrex*, the surrogate was entitled to ride beside the Queen in the sun-chariot, and to sleep with her during the single night of his reign; but, at dawn on the following day, the old King destroyed him and, metaphorically, rode on in his sun-chariot to the extreme west, where he was purified in the Ocean stream. Myrtilus's fall from the

chariot into the sea is a telescoping of myths: a few miles to the east of the Hippodrome, where the Isthmian Games took place (see 71. *b*), the surrogate 'Melicertes', in whose honour they had been founded, was flung over a cliff (see 96. *3*) and an identical ceremony was probably performed at Geraestus, where Myrtilus died. Horse-scarers are also reported from Thebes and Iolcus (see 71. *b*), which suggests that there, too, chariot crashes were staged in the hippodromes. But since the Olympian Hippodrome, sacred to solar Zeus, and the Isthmian Hippodrome, sacred to solar Poseidon, were both associated with the legend of Pelops, the mythographers have presented the contest as a cross-country race between them. Lesbos enters the story perhaps because 'Oenomaus' was a Lesbian dynastic title.

6. Amphion's entry into this myth, though a Theban, is explained by his being also a native of Sicyon on the Isthmus (see 76. *a*). 'Myrto' will have been a title of the Sea-goddess as destroyer, the first syllable standing for 'sea', as in Myrtea, 'sea-goddess'; Myrtoessa, a longer form of Myrto, was one of Aphrodite's titles. Thus Myrtilus may originally mean 'phallus of the sea': *myr-tylos*.

7. Pelops hacks Stymphalus in pieces, as he himself is said to have been treated by Tantalus; this more ancient form of the royal sacrifice has been rightly reported from Arcadia. The Pelopids appear indeed to have patronized several local cults, beside that of the Sun-chariot: namely the Arcadian shepherd cult of oak and ram, attested by Pelops's connexion with Tantalus and his sacrifice of a black ram at Olympia; the partridge cult of Crete, Troy, and Palestine, attested by the *cordax* dance; the Titan cult, attested by Pelops's title of 'Cronian'; the porpoise cult (see 108. *5*); and the cult of the ass-god, in so far as Cillus's ghost assisted him in the race.

8. The butchering of Marmax's mares may refer to Oenomaus's coronation ceremony (see 81. *4*), which involved mare-sacrifice. A 'Cydonian apple', or quince, will have been in the hand of the Death-goddess Athene, to whom Pelops sacrificed, as his safe-conduct to the Elysian Fields (see 32. *1*; 53. *5* and 133. *4*); and the white poplar, used in his heroic rites at Olympia, symbolized the hope of reincarnation (see 31. *5* and 134. *f*) after he had been hacked in pieces – because those who went to Elysium were granted the prerogative of rebirth (see 31. *c*). A close parallel to the bloodshed at Pelops's Olympic altar is the scourging of young Spartans who were bound to the image of Upright Artemis (see 116. *4*). Pelops was, in fact, the victim, and suffered in honour of the goddess Hippodameia (see 110. *3*).

# IIO

## THE CHILDREN OF PELOPS

IN gratitude to Hera for facilitating her marriage with Pelops, Hippo-dameia summoned sixteen matrons, one from every city of Elis, to help her institute the Heraean Games. Every fourth year, ever since, the Sixteen Matrons, their successors, have woven a robe for Hera and celebrated the Games; which consist of a single race between virgins of different ages, the competitors being handicapped according to their years, with the youngest placed in front. They run clad in tunics of less than knee length, their right breasts bared, their hair flying free. Chloris, Niobe's only surviving daughter, was the first victrix in these games; the course of which has been fixed at five-sixths of the Olympic circuit. The prize is an olive wreath, and a share of the cow sacrificed to Hera; a victrix may also dedicate a statue of herself in her own name.[1]

b. The Sixteen Matrons once acted as peace-makers between the Pisans and the Eleans. Now they also organize two groups of dancers, one in honour of Hippodameia, the other in honour of Physcoa, the Elean. Physcoa bore Narcaeus to Dionysus, a renowned warrior who founded the sanctuary of Athene Narcaea and was the first Elean to worship Dionysus. Since some of the sixteen cities no longer exist, the Sixteen Matrons are now supplied by the eight Elean tribes, a pair from each. Like the umpires, they purify themselves, before the Games begin, with the blood of a suitable pig and with water drawn from the Pierian Spring which one passes on the road between Olympia and Elis.[2]

c. The following are said to have been children of Pelops and Hippo-dameia: Pittheus of Troezen; Atreus and Thyestes; Alcathous, not the one killed by Oenomaus; the Argonaut Hippalcus, Hippalcmus, or Hippalcimus; Copreus the herald; Sciron the bandit; Epidaurus the Argive, sometimes called the son of Apollo;[3] Pleisthenes; Dias; Cybo-surus; Corinthius; Hippasus; Cleon; Argeius; Aelinus; Astydameia, whom some call the mother of Amphitryon; Lysidice, whose daughter Hippothoë was carried off by Poseidon to the Echinadian Islands, and there bore Taphius; Eurydice, whom some call the mother of Alcmene; Nicippe; Antibia;[4] and lastly Archippe, mother of Eurystheus and Alcyone.[5]

*d.* The Megarians, in an attempt to obliterate the memory of how Minos captured their city, and to suggest that King Nisus was peaceably succeeded by his son-in-law Megareus, and he in turn by his son-in-law, Alcathous, son of Pelops, say that Megareus had two sons, the elder of whom, Timalcus, was killed at Aphidnae during the invasion of Attica by the Dioscuri; and that, when the younger, Euippus, was killed by the lion of Cithaeron, Megareus promised his daughter Euaechme, and his throne, to whoever avenged Euippus. Forthwith, Alcathous killed the lion and, becoming king of Megara, built a temple there to Apollo the Hunter and Artemis the Huntress. The truth is, however, that Alcathous came from Elis to Megara immediately after the death of Nisus and the sack of the city; that Megareus never reigned in Megara; and that Alcathous sacrificed to Apollo and Poseidon as 'Previous Builders', and then rebuilt the city wall on new foundations, the course of the old wall having been obliterated by the Cretans.[6]

*e.* Alcathous was the father of Ischepolis; of Callipolis; of Iphinoë, who died a virgin, and at whose tomb, between the Council Hall and the shrine of Alcathous, Megarian brides pour libations – much as the Delian brides dedicate their hair to Hecaerge and Opis; also of Automedusa, who bore Iolaus to Iphicles; and of Periboea, who married Telamon, and whose son Ajax succeeded Alcathous as King of Megara. Alcathous's elder son, Ischepolis, perished in the Calydonian Hunt; and Callipolis, the first Megarian to hear the sorrowful news, rushed up to the Acropolis, where Alcathous was offering burnt sacrifices to Apollo, and flung the faggots from the altar in token of mourning. Unaware of what had happened, Alcathous raged at his impiety and struck him dead with a faggot.[7]

*f.* Ischepolis and Euippus are buried in the Law Courts; Megareus on the right side of the ascent to the second Megarian Acropolis. Alcathous's hero-shrine is now the public Record Office; and that of Timalcus, the Council Hall.[8]

*g.* Chrysippus also passed as a son of Pelops and Hippodameia; but was, in fact, a bastard, whom Pelops had begotten on the nymph Astyoche,[9] a Danaid. Now it happened that Laius, when banished from Thebes, was hospitably received by Pelops at Pisa, but fell in love with Chrysippus, to whom he taught the charioteer's art; and, as soon as the sentence of banishment was annulled, carried the boy off in his chariot, from the Nemean Games, and brought him to Thebes as his catamite.[10] Some say that Chrysippus killed himself for shame; others, that Hippodameia, to prevent Pelops from appointing Chrysippus his successor over the heads of her own sons, came to Thebes, where she tried to persuade Atreus and Thyestes to kill the boy by throwing him down a well. When both refused to murder their father's guest, Hippodameia, at dead of night, stole into Laius's chamber and, finding him asleep, took down his sword from the wall and plunged it into his bedfellow's belly. Laius was at once accused of the murder, but Chrysippus had seen Hippodameia as she fled, and accused her with his last breath.[11]

*h*. Meanwhile, Pelops marched against Thebes to recover Chrysippus but, finding that Laius was already imprisoned by Atreus and Thyestes, nobly pardoned him, recognizing that only an overwhelming love had prompted this breach of hospitality. Some say that Laius, not Thamyris, or Minos, was the first pederast; which is why the Thebans, far from condemning the practice, maintain a regiment, called the Sacred Band, composed entirely of boys and their lovers.[12]

*i*. Hippodameia fled to Argolis, and there killed herself; but later, in accordance with an oracle, her bones were brought back to Olympia, where women enter her walled sanctuary once a year to offer her sacrifices. At one of the turns of the Hippodrome stands Hippodameia's bronze statue, holding a ribbon with which to decorate Pelops for his victory.[13]

1. Pausanias: v. 16. 2–3.
2. Pausanias: v. 16. 3–5.
3. Apollodorus: iii. 12. 7; ii. 5. 1 and ii. 26. 3; *Epitome* ii. 10 and i. 1; Hyginus: *Fabulae* 84 and 14; Scholiast on Pindar's *Olympian Odes* i. 144.
4. Scholiast on Euripides's *Orestes* 5; Apollodorus: ii. 4. 5; Plutarch: *Theseus* 6; Diodorus Siculus: iv. 9. 1; Scholiast on Homer's *Iliad* xix. 119.
5. Tzetzes: *Chiliades* ii. 172 and 192; Scholiast on Thucydides: i. 9; Apollodorus: *loc. cit.*
6. Pausanias: i. 43. 4; i. 41. 4–5 and i. 42. 2.
7. Pausanias: i. 42. 2 and 7 and i. 43. 4; Apollodorus: ii. 4. 11.
8. Pausanias: i. 43. 2 and 4; i. 42. 1 and 3.
9. Scholiast on Pindar's *Olympian Odes* i. 144; Hyginus: *Fabula* 85; Plutarch: *Parallel Stories* 33.
10. Apollodorus: iii. 5. 5; Hyginus: *Fabulae* 85 and 271; Athenaeus: xiii. 79.
11. Scholiast on Euripides's *Phoenician Women* 1760; Plutarch: *Parallel Stories* 33; Hyginus: *Fabula* 85; Scholiast on Euripides's *Orestes* 813.
12. Hyginus: *loc. cit.*; Plutarch: *loc. cit.*; Aelian: *Varia Historia* xiii. 5.

13. Hyginus: *loc. cit.*; Pausanias: vi. 20. 4 and 10.

*

1. The Heraean Games took place on the day before the Olympic Games. They consisted of a girls' foot race, originally for the office of High-priestess to Hera (see 60. *4*), and the victrix, who wore the olive as a symbol of peace and fertility, became one with the goddess by partaking of her sacred cow. The Sixteen Matrons may once have taken turns to officiate as the High-priestess's assistant during the sixteen seasons of the four-year Olympiad – each wheel of the royal chariot represented the solar year, and had four spokes, like a fire-wheel or swastika. 'Narcaeus' is clearly a back-formation from Athene Narcaea ('benumbing'), a death-goddess. The matrons who organized the Heraean Games, which had once involved human sacrifice, propitiated the goddess with pig's blood, and then washed themselves in running water. Hippodameia's many children attest the strength of the confederation presided over by the Pelopid dynasty – all their names are associated with the Peloponnese or the Isthmus.

2. Alcathous's murder of his son Callipolis at the altar of Apollo has probably been deduced from an icon which showed him offering his son as a burnt sacrifice to the 'previous builder', the city-god Melicertes, or Moloch, when he refounded Megara – as a king of Moab also did (*Joshua* vi. 26). Moreover, like Samson and David, he had killed a lion in ritual combat. Corinthian mythology has many close affinities with Palestinian (see 67. *1*).

3. The myth of Chrysippus survives in degenerate form only. That he was a beautiful Pisan boy who drove a chariot, was carried off like Ganymedes, or Pelops himself (though not, indeed, to Olympus), and killed by Hippodameia, suggests that, originally, he was one of the royal surrogates who died in the chariot crash; but his myth has become confused with a justification of Theban pederasty, and with the legend of a dispute about the Nemean Games between Thebes and Pisa. Hippodameia, 'horse-tamer', was a title of the Moon-goddess, whose mare-headed statue at Phigalia held a Pelopid porpoise in her hand; four of Pelops's sons and daughters bear horse-names.

# III

## ATREUS AND THYESTES

SOME say that Atreus, who fled from Elis after the death of Chrysippus, in which he may have been more deeply implicated than Pelops knew, took refuge in Mycenae. There fortune favoured him. His nephew Eurystheus, who was just about to march against the sons of Heracles, appointed him regent in his absence; and, when presently news came of Eurystheus's defeat and death, the Mycenaean notables chose Atreus as their king, because he seemed a likely warrior to protect them against the Heraclids and had already won the affection of the commons. Thus the royal house of Pelops became more famous even than that of Perseus.[1]

*b*. But others say, with greater authority, that Eurystheus's father, Sthenelus, having banished Amphitryon, and seized the throne of Mycenae, sent for Atreus and Thyestes, his brother-in-law, and installed them at near-by Midea. A few years later, when Sthenelus and Eurytheus were both dead, an oracle advised the Mycenaeans to choose a prince of the Pelopid house to rule over them. They thereupon summoned Atreus and Thyestes from Midea and debated which of these two (who were fated to be always at odds) should be crowned king.[2]

*c*. Now, Atreus had once vowed to sacrifice the finest of his flocks to Artemis; and Hermes, anxious to avenge the death of Myrtilus on the Pelopids, consulted his old friend Goat-Pan, who made a horned lamb with a golden fleece appear among the Acarnanian flock which Pelops had left to his sons Atreus and Thyestes. He foresaw that Atreus would claim it as his own and, from his reluctance to give Artemis the honours due to her, would become involved in fratricidal war with Thyestes. Some, however, say that it was Artemis herself who sent the lamb, to try him.[3] Atreus kept his vow, in part at least, by sacrificing the lamb's flesh; but he stuffed and mounted the fleece and locked it in a chest. He grew so proud of his life-like treasure that he could not refrain from boasting about it in the market place, and the jealous Thyestes, for whom Atreus's newly-married wife Aerope had conceived a passion, agreed to be her lover if she gave him the lamb [which, he said, had been stolen by Atreus's shepherds from his own half of the flock]. For Artemis had laid a curse upon it, and this was her doing.[4]

*d*. In a debate at the Council Hall, Atreus claimed the throne of Mycenae by right of primogeniture, and also as possessor of the lamb. Thyestes asked him: 'Do you then publicly declare that its owner should be king?' 'I do,' Atreus replied. 'And I concur,' said Thyestes, smiling grimly. A herald then summoned the people of Mycenae to acclaim their new king; the temples were hung with gold, and their doors thrown open; fires blazed on every altar throughout the city;

and songs were sung in praise of the horned lamb with the golden fleece. But Thyestes unexpectedly rose to upbraid Atreus as a vainglorious boaster, and led the magistrates to his home, where he displayed the lamb, justified his claim to its ownership, and was pronounced the rightful king of Mycenae.[5]

*e.* Zeus, however, favoured Atreus, and sent Hermes to him, saying: 'Call Thyestes, and ask him whether, if the sun goes backward on the dial, he will resign his claim to the throne in your favour?' Atreus did as he was told, and Thyestes agreed to abdicate should such a portent occur. Thereupon Zeus, aided by Eris, reversed the laws of Nature, which hitherto had been immutable. Helius, already in mid-career, wrested his chariot about and turned his horses' heads towards the dawn. The seven Pleiades, and all the other stars, retraced their courses in sympathy; and that evening, for the first and last time, the sun set in the east. Thyestes's deceit and greed being thus plainly attested, Atreus succeeded to the throne of Mycenae, and banished him.[6]

When, later, Atreus discovered that Thyestes had committed adultery with Aerope, he could hardly contain his rage. Nevertheless, for a while he feigned forgiveness.[7]

*f.* Now, this Aerope, whom some call Europe, was a Cretan, the daughter of King Catreus. One day, she had been surprised by Catreus while entertaining a lover in the palace, and was on the point of being thrown to the fishes when, countermanding his sentence at the plea of Nauplius, he sold her, and his other daughter Clymene as well, whom he suspected of plotting against his life, as slaves to Nauplius for a nominal price; only stipulating that neither of them should ever return to Crete. Nauplius then married Clymene, who bore him Oeax and Palamedes the inventor.[8] But Atreus, whose wife Cleola had died after giving birth to a weakly son, Pleisthenes – this was Artemis's revenge on him for his failure to keep the vow – married Aerope, and begot on her Agamemnon, Menelaus, and Anaxibia. Pleisthenes had also died: the cut-throats whom Atreus sent to murder his namesake, Thyestes's bastard son by Aerope, murdered him in error – Thyestes saw to that.[9]

*g.* Atreus now sent a herald to lure Thyestes back to Mycenae, with the offer of an amnesty and a half-share in the kingdom; but, as soon as Thyestes accepted this, slaughtered Aglaus, Orchomenus, and Callileon, Thyestes's three sons by one of the Naiads, on the very altar of Zeus where they had taken refuge; and then sought out and killed the infant Pleisthenes the Second, and Tantalus the Second, his twin. He hacked them all limb from limb, and set chosen morsels of their flesh, boiled in a cauldron, before Thyestes, to welcome him on his return. When Thyestes had eaten heartily, Atreus sent in their bloody heads and feet and hands, laid out on another dish, to show him what was now inside his belly. Thyestes fell back, vomiting, and laid an ineluctable curse upon the seed of Atreus.[10]

*h*. Exiled once more, Thyestes fled first to King Thesprotus at Sicyon, where his own daughter Pelopia, or Pelopeia, was a priestess. For, desiring revenge at whatever cost, he had consulted the Delphic Oracle and been advised to beget a son on his own daughter.[11] Thyestes found Pelopia sacrificing by night to Athene Colocasia and, being loth to profane the rites, concealed himself in a near-by grove. Presently Pelopia, who was leading the solemn dance, slipped in a pool of blood that had flowed from the throat of a black ewe, the victim, and stained her tunic. She ran at once to the temple fish-pond, removed her tunic, and was washing out the stain, when Thyestes sprang from the grove and ravished her. Pelopia did not recognize him, because he was wearing a mask, but contrived to steal his sword and carry it back to the temple, where she hid it under the pedestal of Athene's image; and Thyestes, finding the scabbard empty and fearing detection, escaped to Lydia, the land of his fathers.[12]

*i*. Meanwhile, fearing the consequences of his crime, Atreus consulted the Delphic Oracle, and was told: 'Recall Thyestes from Sicyon!' He reached Sicyon too late to meet Thyestes and, falling in love with Pelopia, whom he assumed to be King Thesprotus's daughter, asked leave to make her his third wife; having by this time executed Aerope. Eager for an alliance with so powerful a king, and wishing at the same time to do Pelopia a service, Thesprotus did not undeceive Atreus, and the wedding took place at once. In due course she bore the son begotten on her by Thyestes, whom she exposed on a mountain; but goatherds rescued him and gave him to a she-goat for suckling – hence his name, Aegisthus, or 'goat-strength'. Atreus believed that Thyestes had fled from Sicyon at news of his approach; that the child was his own; and that Pelopia had been affected by the temporary madness which sometimes overtakes women after childbirth. He therefore recovered Aegisthus from the goatherds and reared him as his heir.

*j*. A succession of bad harvests then plagued Mycenae, and Atreus sent Agamemnon and Menelaus to Delphi for news of Thyestes, whom they met by chance on his return from a further visit to the Oracle. They haled him back to Mycenae, where Atreus, having thrown him into prison, ordered Aegisthus, then seven years of age, to kill him as he slept.

*k.* Thyestes awoke suddenly to find Aegisthus standing over him, sword in hand; he quickly rolled sideways and escaped death. Then he rose, disarmed the boy with a shrewd kick at his wrist, and sprang to recover the sword. But it was his own, lost years before in Sicyon! He seized Aegisthus by the shoulder and cried: 'Tell me instantly how this came into your possession?' Aegisthus stammered: 'Alas, my mother Pelopia gave it me.' 'I will spare your life, boy,' said Thyestes, 'if you carry out the three orders I now give you.' 'I am your servant in all things,' wept Aegisthus, who had expected no mercy. 'My first order is to bring your mother here,' Thyestes told him.

*l.* Aegisthus thereupon brought Pelopia to the dungeon and, recognizing Thyestes, she wept on his neck, called him her dearest father, and commiserated with his sufferings. 'How did you come by this sword, daughter?' Thyestes asked. 'I took it from the scabbard of an unknown stranger who ravished me one night at Sicyon,' she replied. 'It is mine,' said Thyestes. Pelopia, stricken with horror, seized the sword, and plunged it into her breast. Aegisthus stood aghast, not understanding what had been said. 'Now take this sword to Atreus,' was Thyestes's second order, 'and tell him that you have carried out your commission. Then return!' Dumbly Aegisthus took the bloody thing to Atreus, who went joyfully down to the seashore, where he offered a sacrifice of thanksgiving to Zeus, convinced that he was rid of Thyestes at last.

*m.* When Aegisthus returned to the dungeon, Thyestes revealed himself as his father, and issued his third order: 'Kill Atreus, my son Aegisthus, and this time do not falter!' Aegisthus did as he was told, and Thyestes reigned once more in Mycenae.[13]

*n.* Another golden-fleeced horned lamb then appeared among Thyestes's flocks and grew to be a ram and, afterwards, every new Pelopid king was thus divinely confirmed in possession of his golden sceptre; these rams grazed at ease in a paddock enclosed by unscaleable walls. But some say that the token of royalty was not a living creature, but a silver bowl, on the bottom of which a golden lamb had been inlaid; and others, that it cannot have been Aegisthus who killed Atreus, because he was only an infant in swaddling clothes when

Agamemnon drove his father Thyestes from Mycenae, wresting the sceptre from him.[14]

*o*. Thyestes lies buried beside the road that leads from Mycenae to Argos, near the shrine of Perseus. Above his tomb stands the stone figures of a ram. The tomb of Atreus, and his underground treasury, are still shown among the ruins of Mycenae.[15]

*p*. Thyestes was not the last hero to find his own child served up to him on a dish. This happened some years later to Clymenus, the Arcadian son of Schoenus, who conceived an incestuous passion for Harpalyce, his daughter by Epicaste. Having debauched Harpalyce, he married her to Alastor, but afterwards took her away again. Harpalyce, to revenge herself, murdered the son she bore him – who was also her brother – cooked the corpse and laid it before Clymenus. She was transformed into a bird of prey, and Clymenus hanged himself.[16]

1. Scholiast on Euripides's *Orestes* 813; Thucydides: i. 9.
2. Apollodorus: ii. 4. 6 and *Epitome* ii. 11; Euripides: *Orestes* 12.
3. Apollodorus: *Epitome* ii. 10; Euripides: *Orestes* 995 ff., with scholiast; Seneca: *Electra* 699 ff.; Scholiast on Euripides's *Orestes* 812, 990, and 998; Tzetzes: *Chiliades* i. 433 ff.; Pherecydes, quoted by scholiast on Euripides's *Orestes* 997.
4. Apollodorus: *Epitome* ii. 11; Scholiast on Euripides's *Orestes* 812; Scholiast on Homer's *Iliad* ii. 106.
5. Tzetzes: *Chiliades* i. 426; Apollodorus: *loc. cit.*; Scholiast on Homer's *Iliad* ii. 106; Euripides: *Electra* 706 ff.
6. Apollodorus: *Epitome* ii. 12; Scholiast on Homer: *loc. cit.*; Euripides: *Orestes* 1001; Ovid: *Art of Love* 327 ff.; Scholiast on Euripides's *Orestes* 812.
7. Hyginus: *Fabula* 86; Apollodorus: *Epitome* ii. 13.
8. Lactantius on Statius's *Thebaid* vi. 306; Apollodorus: iii. 2. 2 and *Epitome* ii. 10; Sophocles: *Ajax* 1295 ff.; Scholiast on Euripides's *Orestes* 432.
9. Hyginus: *Fabulae* 97 and 86; Euripides: *Helen* 392; Homer: *Iliad* ii. 131, etc.
10. Tzetzes: *Chiliades* i. 18 ff.; Apollodorus: *Epitome* ii. 13; Hyginus: *Fabulae* 88, 246, and 258; Scholiast on Horace's *Art of Poetry*; Aeschylus: *Agamemnon* 1590 ff.
11. Apollodorus: *Epitome* ii. 13–14; Hyginus: *Fabulae* 87–8; Servius on Virgil's *Aeneid* ii. 262.
12. Athenaeus: iii. 1; Hyginus: *loc. cit.*; Fragments of Sophocles's *Thyestes*; Apollodorus: *Epitome* ii. 14.
13. Hyginus: *loc. cit.*; Apollodorus: *loc. cit.*
14. Seneca: *Thyestes* 224 ff.; Cicero: *On the Nature of the Gods* iii. 26 and 68; Herodotus of Heracleia, quoted by Athenaeus: 231 c;

Eustathius on Homer's *Iliad* pp. 268 and 1319; Aeschylus: *Aga-memnon* 1603 ff.
15. Pausanias: ii. 16. 5 and ii. 18. 2–3.
16. Parthenius: *Erotica*; Hyginus: *Fabulae* 242, 246, and 255.

*

*1*. The Atreus-Thyestes myth, which survives only in highly theatrical versions, seems to be based on the rivalry between Argive co-kings for supreme power, as in the myth of Acrisius and Proetus (see 73. *a*). It is a good deal older than the story of Heracles's Sons (see 146. *k*) – the Dorian invasion of the Peloponnese, about the year 1050 B.C. – with which Thucydides associates it. Atreus's golden lamb, withheld from sacrifice, recalls Poseidon's white bull, similarly withheld by Minos (see 88. *c*); but is of the same breed as the golden-fleeced rams sacred to Zeus on Mount Laphystium, and to Poseidon on the island of Crumissa (see 70. *l*). To possess this fleece was a token of royalty, because the king used it in an annual rain-making ceremony (see 70. *2* and *6*). The lamb is metaphorically golden: in Greece 'water is gold', and the fleece magically produced rain. This metaphor may, however, have been reinforced by the use of fleeces to collect gold dust from the rivers of Asia Minor; and the occasional appearance, in the Eastern Mediterranean, of lambs with gilded teeth, supposedly descendants of those that the youthful Zeus tended on Mount Ida. (In the eighteenth century, Lady Mary Wortley Montagu investigated this persistent anomaly, but could not discover its origin.) It may also be that the Argive royal sceptre was topped by a golden ram. Apollodorus is vague about the legal background of the dispute, but Thyestes's claim was probably the same as that made by Maeve for the disputed bull in the fratricidal Irish *War of the Bulls*: that the lamb had been stolen from his own flocks at birth.

*2*. Euripides has introduced Eris at a wrong point in the story: she will have provoked the quarrel between the brothers, rather than helped Zeus to reverse the course of the sun – a phenomenon which she was not empowered to produce. Classical grammarians and philosophers have explained this incident in various ingenious ways which anticipate the attempts made by twentieth-century Protestants to account scientifically for the retrograde movement of the Sun's shadow on 'the dial of Ahaz' (2 *Kings* xx. 1–11). Lucian and Polybius write that when Atreus and Thyestes quarrelled over the succession, the Argives were already habitual star-gazers and agreed that the best astronomer should be elected king. In the ensuing contest, Thyestes pointed out that the sun always rose in the Ram at the Spring Festival – hence the story of the golden lamb – but the soothsayer Atreus did better: he proved that the sun and the earth travel in different directions, and that what appear to be sunsets are, in fact, settings of the earth. Whereupon the Argives made him king (Lucian: *On Astrology* 12; Polybius, quoted by Strabo: i. 2. 15). Hyginus and Servius both agree that Atreus was an astronomer, but make him the first to predict an eclipse of the sun mathematically; and say that, when the calculation proved correct, his jealous brother Thyestes left the city in chagrin (Hyginus: *Fabula* 258; Servius on Virgil's *Aeneid* i. 572). Socrates took the myth more literally: regarding it as evidence of his theory that the universe winds and unwinds itself in alternate cycles of vast duration, the reversal of motion at the close of each cycle being accompanied by great destruction of animal life (Plato: *The Statesman* 12–14).

3. To understand the story, however, one must think not allegorically nor philosophically, but mythologically; namely in terms of the archaic conflict between the sacred king and his tanist. The king reigned until the summer solstice, when the sun reached its most northerly point and stood still; then the tanist killed him and took his place, while the sun daily retreated southward towards the winter solstice. This mutual hatred, sharpened by sexual jealousy, because the tanist married his rival's widow, was renewed between Argive co-kings, whose combined reigns extended for a Great Year; and they quarrelled over Aerope, as Acrisius and Proetus had done over Danaë. The myth of Hezekiah, who was on the point of death when, as a sign of Jehovah's favour, the prophet Isaiah added ten years to his reign by turning back the sun ten degrees on the dial of Ahaz (2 *Kings* xx. 8–11 and *Isaiah* xxxviii. 7–8), suggests a Hebrew, or perhaps a Philistine, tradition of how the king, after the calendar reform caused by adoption of the metonic cycle, was allowed to prolong his reign to the nineteenth year, instead of dying in the ninth. Atreus, at Mycenae, may have been granted a similar dispensation.

4. The cannibalistic feast in honour of Zeus, which appears in the myth of Tantalus (see 108. *c*), has here been confused with the annual sacrifice of child surrogates, and with Cronus's vomiting up of his children by Rhea (see 7. *d*). Thyestes's rape of Pelopia recalls the myth of Cinyras and Smyrna (see 17. *h*), and is best explained as the king's attempt to prolong his reign beyond the customary limit by marriage with his step-daughter, the heiress. Aerope's rescue from the Cretan fishes identifies her with Dictynna-Britomartis, whom her grandfather Minos had chased into the sea (see 89. *b*). Aegisthus, suckled by a she-goat, is the familiar New Year child of the Mysteries (see 24. *6*; 44. *1*; 76, *a*; 105. *1*, etc.).

5. The story of Clymenus and Harpalyce – there was another Thracian character of the same name, a sort of Atalanta – combines the myth of Cinyras and Smyrna (see 18. *h*) with that of Tereus and Procne (see 46. *a*). Unless this is an artificial composition for the theatre, as Clymenus's unmythical suicide by hanging suggests, he will have tried to regain a

title to the throne when his reign ended, by marrying the heiress, technically his daughter, to an *interrex* and then killing him and taking her himself. Alastor means 'avenger', but this vengeance does not appear in the myth; perhaps the original version made Alastor the victim of the human sacrifice.

# 112

## AGAMEMNON AND CLYTAEMNESTRA

SOME say that Agamemnon and Menelaus were of an age to arrest Thyestes at Delphi; others, that when Aegisthus killed Atreus, they were still infants, whom their nurse had the presence of mind to rescue. Snatching them up, one under each arm, she fled with them to Polypheides, the twenty-fourth king of Sicyon, at whose instance they were subsequently entrusted to Oeneus the Aetolian. It is agreed, however, that after they had spent some years at Oeneus's court, King Tyndareus of Sparta restored their fortunes. Marching against Mycenae, he exacted an oath from Thyestes, who had taken refuge at the altar of Hera, that he would bequeath the sceptre to Agamemnon, as Atreus's heir, and go into exile, never to return. Thyestes thereupon departed to Cythera, while Aegisthus, fearing Agamemnon's vengeance, fled to King Cylarabes, son of King Sthenelus the Argive.[1]

*b*. It is said that Zeus gave power to the House of Aeacus, wisdom to the House of Amythaon, but wealth to the House of Atreus. Wealthy indeed it was: the kings of Mycenae, Corinth, Cleonae, Orneiae, Arathyrea, Sicyon, Hyperesia, Gonoessa, Pellene, Aegium, Aegialus, and Helice, all paid tribute to Agamemnon, both on land and sea.[2]

*c*. Agamemnon first made war against Tantalus, King of Pisa, the son of his ugly uncle Broteas, killed him in battle and forcibly married his widow Clytaemnestra, whom Leda had borne to King Tyndareus of Sparta. The Dioscuri, Clytaemnestra's brothers, thereupon marched on Mycenae; but Agamemnon had already gone as a suppliant to his benefactor Tyndareus, who forgave him and let him keep Clytaemnestra. After the death of the Dioscuri, Menelaus married their sister Helen, and Tyndareus abdicated in his favour.[3]

*d*. Clytaemnestra bore Agamemnon one son, Orestes, and three daughters: Electra, or Laodice; Iphigeneia, or Iphianassa; and Chrysothemis; though some say that Iphigeneia was Clytaemnestra's niece, the daughter of Theseus and Helen, whom she took pity upon and adopted.[4]

*e.* When Paris, the son of King Priam of Troy, abducted Helen and thus provoked the Trojan War, both Agamemnon and Menelaus were absent from home for ten years; but Aegisthus did not join their expedition, preferring to stay behind at Argos and seek revenge on the House of Atreus.[5]

*f.* Now, Nauplius, the husband of Clymene, having failed to obtain requital from Agamemnon and the other Greek leaders for the stoning of his son Palamedes, had sailed away from Troy and coasted around Attica and the Peloponnese, inciting the lonely wives of his enemies to adultery. Aegisthus, therefore, when he heard that Clytaemnestra was among those most eager to be convinced by Nauplius, planned not only to become her lover, but to kill Agamemnon, with her assistance, as soon as the Trojan War ended.[6]

*g.* Hermes, sent to Aegisthus by Omniscient Zeus, warned him to abandon this project, on the ground that when Orestes had grown to manhood, he would be bound to avenge his father. For all his eloquence, however, Hermes failed to deter Aegisthus, who went to Mycenae with rich gifts in his hands, but hatred in his heart. At first, Clytaemnestra rejected his advances, because Agamemnon, apprised of Nauplius's visit to Mycenae, had instructed his court bard to keep close watch on her and report to him, in writing, the least sign of infidelity. But Aegisthus seized the old minstrel and marooned him without food on a lonely island, where birds of prey were soon picking his bones. Clytaemnestra then yielded to Aegisthus's embraces, and he celebrated his unhoped-for success with burnt offerings to Aphrodite, and gifts of tapestries and gold to Artemis, who was nursing a grudge against the House of Atreus.[7]

*h.* Clytaemnestra had small cause to love Agamemnon: after killing her former husband Tantalus, and the new-born child at her breast, he had married her by force, and then gone away to a war which promised never to end; he had also sanctioned the sacrifice of Iphigeneia at Aulis – and, this she found even harder to bear – was said to be bringing back Priam's daughter Cassandra, the prophetess, as his wife in all but name. It is true that Cassandra had borne Agamemnon twin sons: Teledamus and Pelops, but he does not seem to have intended any insult to Clytaemnestra. Her informant had been Nauplius's surviving son Oeax who, in vengeance for his brother's death, was maliciously provoking her to do murder.⁸

_i._ Clytaemnestra therefore conspired with Aegisthus to kill both Agamemnon and Cassandra. Fearing, however, that they might arrive unexpectedly, she wrote Agamemnon a letter asking him to light a beacon on Mount Ida when Troy fell; and herself arranged for a chain of fires to relay his signal to Argolis by way of Cape Hermaeum on Lemnos, and the mountains of Athos, Macistus, Messapius, Cithaeron, Aegiplanctus, and Arachne. A watchman was also stationed on the roof of the palace at Mycenae: a faithful servant of Agamemnon's, who spent one whole year, crouched on his elbows like a dog, gazing towards Mount Arachne and filled with gloomy forebodings. At last, one dark night, he saw the distant beacon blaze and ran to wake Clytaemnestra. She celebrated the news with sacrifices of thanksgiving; though, indeed, she would now have liked the siege of Troy to last for ever. Aegisthus thereupon posted one of his own men in a watch-tower near the sea, promising him two gold talents for the first news of Agamemnon's landing.

_j._ Hera had rescued Agamemnon from the fierce storm which destroyed many of the returning Greek ships and drove Menelaus to Egypt; and, at last, a fair wind carried him to Nauplia. No sooner had he disembarked, than he bent down to kiss the soil, weeping for joy. Meanwhile the watchman hurried to Mycenae to collect his fee, and Aegisthus chose twenty of the boldest warriors, posted them in ambush inside the palace, ordered a great banquet and then, mounting his chariot, rode down to welcome Agamemnon.⁹

_k._ Clytaemnestra greeted her travel-worn husband with every appearance of delight, unrolled a purple carpet for him, and led him to the bath-house, where slave-girls had prepared a warm bath; but Cassandra remained outside the palace, caught in a prophetic trance, refusing to enter, and crying that she smelt blood, and that the curse of Thyestes was heavy upon the dining-hall. When Agamemnon had washed himself and set one foot out of the bath, eager to partake of the rich banquet now already set on the tables, Clytaemnestra came forward, as if to wrap a towel about him, but instead threw over his head a garment of net, woven by herself, without either neck or sleeve-holes. Entangled in this, like a fish, Agamemnon perished at the hands of Aegisthus, who struck him twice with a two-edged sword.¹⁰ He fell back, into the silver-sided bath, where Clytaemnestra avenged her wrongs by beheading him with an axe.[11] She then ran out to kill Cassandra with the same weapon, not troubling first to close her husband's eyelids or mouth; but wiped off on his hair the blood which had splashed her, to signify that he had brought about his own death.[12]

*l.* A fierce battle was now raging in the palace, between Agamemnon's bodyguard and Aegisthus's supporters. Warriors were slain like swine for a rich man's feast, or lay wounded and groaning beside the laden boards in a welter of blood; but Aegisthus won the day. Outside, Cassandra's head rolled to the ground, and Aegisthus also had the satisfaction of killing her twin sons by Agamemnon; yet he failed to do away with another of Agamemnon's bastards, by name Halesus, or Haliscus. Halesus contrived to make his escape and, after long wandering in exile, founded the Italian city of Falerii, and taught its inhabitants the Mysteries of Hera, which are still celebrated there in the Argive manner.[13]

*m.* This massacre took place on the thirteenth day of the month Gamelion [January] and, unafraid of divine retribution, Clytaemnestra decreed the thirteenth day a monthly festival, celebrating it with dancing and offerings of sheep to her guardian deities. Some applaud her resolution; but others hold that she brought eternal disgrace upon all women, even virtuous ones. Aegisthus, too, gave thanks to the goddess who had assisted him.[14]

*n.* The Spartans claim that Agamemnon is buried at Amyclae, now no more than a small village, where are shown the tomb and statue of Clytaemnestra, also the sanctuary and statue of Cassandra; the inhabitants even believe that he was killed there. But the truth is that Agamemnon's tomb stands among the ruins of Mycenae, close to those of his charioteer, of his comrades murdered with him by Aegisthus, and of Cassandra's twins.[15]

*o.* Menelaus was later informed of the crime by Proteus, the prophet of Pharos and, having offered hecatombs to his brother's ghost, built a cenotaph in his honour beside the River of Egypt. Returning to Sparta, eight years later, he raised a temple to Zeus Agamemnon; there are other such temples at Lapersae in Attica and at Clazomene in Ionia, although Agamemnon never reigned in either of these places.[16]

1. Hyginus: *Fabula* 88; Eusebius: *Chronicles* i. 175–6, ed. Schoene; Homer: *Iliad* ii. 107–8 and *Odyssey* iii. 263; Aeschylus: *Agamemnon* 529; Pausanias: ii. 18. 4; Tzetzes: *Chiliades* i. 433 ff.
2. Hesiod, quoted by Suidas *sub* Alce; Homer: *Iliad* 108 and 569–80.

3. Apollodorus: iii. 10. 6 and *Epitome* ii. 16; Euripides: *Iphigeneia in Aulis* 1148 ff.

4. Apollodorus: *loc. cit.*; Homer: *Iliad* ix. 145; Duris, quoted by Tzetzes: *On Lycophron* 183.

5. Homer: *Odyssey* iii. 263.

6. Apollodorus: *Epitome* vi. 8–9.

7. Homer: *Odyssey* i. 35 ff. and iii. 263–75.

8. Euripides: *Iphigeneia in Aulis* 1148 ff.; Sophocles: *Electra* 531; Pausanias: iii. 16. 5 and ii. 16. 5; Hyginus: *Fabula* 117.

9. Hyginus: *loc. cit.*; Aeschylus: *Agamemnon* i. ff. and 282 ff.; Euripides: *Electra* 1076 ff.; Homer: *Odyssey* iv. 524–37; Pausanias: ii. 16. 5.

10. Aeschylus: *Agamemnon* 1220 – 1391 ff., 1521 ff. and *Eumenides* 631–5; Euripides: *Electra* 157 and *Orestes* 26; Tzetzes: *On Lycophron* 1375; Servius on Virgil's *Aeneid* xi. 267; Triclinius on Sophocles's *Electra* 195; Homer: *Odyssey* iii. 193 ff. and 303–5; xi. 529–37.

11. Sophocles: *Electra* 99; Aeschylus: *Agamemnon* 1372 ff. and 1535.

12. Aeschylus: *loc. cit.*; Sophocles: *Electra* 445–6.

13. Homer: *Odyssey* xi. 400 and 442; Pausanias: ii. 16. 5; Virgil: *Aeneid* vii. 723; Servius on Virgil's *Aeneid* vii. 695; Ovid: *Art of Love* iii. 13. 31.

14. Sophocles: *Electra* 278–81; Homer: *Odyssey* iii. 263; xi. 405 and vi. 512 ff.

15. Pausanias: ii. 16. 5 and iii. 19. 5; Pindar: *Pythian Odes* i. 32; Homer: *Iliad* iv. 228.

16. Homer: *Odyssey* iv. 512 ff. and 581 ff.; Tzetzes: *On Lycophron* 112–114 and 1369; Pausanias: vii. 5. 5.

\*

1. The myth of Agamemnon, Aegisthus, Clytaemnestra, and Orestes has survived in so stylized a dramatic form that its origins are almost obliterated. In tragedy of this sort, the clue is usually provided by the manner of the king's death: whether he is flung over a cliff like Theseus, burned alive like Heracles, wrecked in a chariot like Oenomaus, devoured by wild horses like Diomedes, drowned in a pool like Tantalus, or killed by lightning like Capaneus. Agamemnon dies in a peculiar manner: with a net thrown over his head, with one foot still in the bath, but the other on the floor, and in the bath-house annexe – that is to say, 'neither clothed nor unclothed, neither in water nor on dry land, neither in his palace nor outside' – a situation recalling the midsummer death, in the *Mabinogion*, of the sacred king Llew Llaw, at the hands of his treacherous wife Blodeuwedd and her lover Gronw. A similar story told by Saxo Grammaticus in his late twelfth-century *History of Denmark* suggests that

Clytaemnestra may also have given Agamemnon an apple to eat, and killed him as he set it to his lips: so that he was 'neither fasting, nor feasting' (*White Goddess*, pp. 308 and 401). Basically, then, this is the familiar myth of the sacred king who dies at midsummer, the goddess who betrays him, the tanist who succeeds him, the son who avenges him. Clytaemnestra's axe was the Cretan symbol of sovereignty, and the myth has affinities with the murder of Minos, which also took place in a bath. Aegisthus's mountain beacons, one of which Aeschylus records to have been built of heather (see 18. *3*), are the bonfires of the midsummer sacrifice. The goddess in whose honour Agamemnon was sacrificed appears in triad as his 'daughters': Electra ('amber'), Iphigeneia ('mothering a strong race'), and Chrysothemis ('golden order').

*2.* This ancient story has been combined with the legend of a dispute between rival dynasties in the Peloponnese. Clytaemnestra was a Spartan royal heiress; and the Spartan's claim, that their ancestor Tyndareus raised Agamemnon to the throne of Mycenae, suggests that they were victorious in a war against the Mycenaeans for the possession of Amyclae, where Agamemnon and Clytaemnestra were both honoured.

*3.* 'Zeus Agamemnon', 'very resolute Zeus', will have been a divine title borne not only by the Mycenaean kings, but by those of Lapersae and Clazomene; and, presumably, also by the kings of a Danaan or Achaean settlement beside the River of Egypt – not to be confused with the Nile. The River of Egypt is mentioned in *Joshua* xv. 4 as marking the boundary between Palestine and Egypt; farther up the coast, at Ascalon and near Tyre, there were other Danaan or Achaean settlements (see 69. *f.*).

*4.* The thirteenth day, also observed as a festal day in Rome, where it was called the Ides, had corresponded with the full moon at a time when the calendar month was a simple lunation. It seems that the sacrifice of the king always took place at the full moon. According to the legend, the Greek fleet, returning late in the year from Troy, ran into winter storms; Agamemnon therefore died in January, not in June.

# 113

## THE VENGEANCE OF ORESTES

ORESTES was reared by his loving grand-parents Tyndareus and Leda and, as a boy, accompanied Clytaemnestra and Iphigeneia to Aulis.[1] But some say that Clytaemnestra sent him to Phocis, shortly before

Agamemnon's return; and others that on the evening of the murder, Orestes, then ten years of age, was rescued by his noble-hearted nurse Arsinoë, or Laodameia, or Geilissa who, having sent her own son to bed in the royal nursery, let Aegisthus kill him in Orestes's place.[2] Others again say that his sister Electra, aided by her father's ancient tutor, wrapped him in a robe embroidered with wild beasts, which she herself had woven, and smuggled him out of the city.[3]

*b.* After hiding for a while among the shepherds of the river Tanus, which divides Argolis from Laconia, the tutor made his way with Orestes to the court of Strophius, a firm ally of the House of Atreus, who ruled over Crisa, at the foot of Mount Parnassus.[4] This Strophius had married Agamemnon's sister Astyochea, or Anaxibia, or Cyndragora. At Crisa, Orestes found an adventurous playmate, namely Strophius's son Pylades, who was somewhat younger than himself, and their friendship was destined to become proverbial.[5] From the old tutor he learned with grief that Agamemnon's body had been flung out of the house and hastily buried by Clytaemnestra, without either libations or myrtle-boughs; and that the people of Mycenae had been forbidden to attend the funeral.[6]

*c.* Aegisthus reigned at Mycenae for seven years, riding in Agamemnon's chariot, sitting on his throne, wielding his sceptre, wearing his robes, sleeping in his bed, and squandering his riches. Yet despite all these trappings of kingship, he was little more than a slave to Clytaemnestra, the true ruler of Mycenae.[7] When drunk, he would leap on Agamemnon's tomb and pelt the head-stone with rocks, crying: 'Come, Orestes, come and defend your own!' The truth was, however, that he lived in abject fear of vengeance, even while surrounded by a trusty foreign bodyguard, never passed a single night in sound sleep, and had offered a handsome reward in gold for Orestes's assassination.[8]

*d.* Electra had been betrothed to her cousin Castor of Sparta, before his death and demi-deification. Though the leading princes of Greece now contended for her hand, Aegisthus feared that she might bear a son to avenge Agamemnon, and therefore announced that no suitor could be accepted. He would gladly have destroyed Electra, who showed him implacable hatred, lest she lay secretly with one of the Palace officers and bare him a bastard; but Clytaemnestra, feeling no qualms about her part in Agamemnon's murder, and scrupulous not to incur the displeasure of the gods, forbade him to do so. She allowed him, however, to marry Electra to a Mycenaean peasant who, being afraid of Orestes and also chaste by nature, never consummated their unequal union.⁹

*e*. Thus, neglected by Clytaemnestra, who had now borne Aegisthus three children, by name Erigone, Aletes, and the second Helen, Electra lived in disgraceful poverty, and was kept under constant close supervision. In the end it was decided that, unless she would accept her fate, as her sister Chrysothemis had done, and refrain from publicly calling Aegisthus and Clytaemnestra 'murderous adulterers', she would be banished to some distant city and there confined in a dungeon where the light of the sun never penetrated. Yet Electra despised Chrysothemis for her subservience and disloyalty to their dead father and secretly sent frequent reminders to Orestes of the vengeance required from him.¹⁰

*f*. Orestes, now grown to manhood, visited the Delphic Oracle, to inquire whether or not he should destroy his father's murderers. Apollo's answer, authorized by Zeus, was that if he neglected to avenge Agamemnon he would become an outcast from society, debarred from entering any shrine or temple, and afflicted with a leprosy that ate into his flesh, making it sprout white mould.¹¹ He was recommended to pour libations beside Agamemnon's tomb, lay a ringlet of his hair upon it and, unaided by any company of spearmen, craftily exact the due punishment from the murderers. At the same time the Pythoness observed that the Erinnyes would not readily forgive a matricide, and therefore, on behalf of Apollo, she gave Orestes a bow of horn, with which to repel their attacks, should they become insupportable. After fulfilling his orders, he must come again to Delphi, where Apollo would protect him.¹²

*g*. In the eighth year – or, according to some, after a passage of twenty years – Orestes secretly returned to Mycenae, by way of Athens, determined to destroy both Aegisthus and his own mother.¹³

One morning, with Pylades at his side, he visited Agamemnon's tomb and there, cutting off a lock of his hair, he invoked Infernal Hermes, patron of fatherhood. When a group of slave-women approached, dirty and dishevelled for the purposes of mourning, he took shelter in a near-by thicket to watch them. Now, on the previous night, Clytaemnestra had dreamed that she gave birth to a serpent, which she wrapped in swaddling clothes and suckled. Suddenly she screamed in her sleep, and alarmed the whole Palace by crying that the serpent had drawn blood from her breast, as well as milk. The opinion of the sooth-

sayers whom she consulted was that she had incurred the anger of the
dead; and these mourning slave-women consequently came on her
behalf to pour libations upon Agamemnon's tomb, in the hope of
appeasing his ghost. Electra, who was one of the party, poured the
libations in her own name, not her mother's; offered prayers to
Agamemnon for vengeance, instead of pardon; and bade Hermes
summon Mother Earth and the gods of the Underworld to hear her
plea. Noticing a ringlet of fair hair upon the tomb, she decided that it
could belong only to Orestes: both because it closely resembled her
own in colour and texture, and because no one else would have dared
to make such an offering.[14]

*h.* Torn between hope and doubt, she was measuring her feet against
Orestes's foot-prints in the clay beside the tomb, and finding a family
resemblance, when he emerged from his hiding place, showed her that
the ringlet was his own, and produced the robe in which he had escaped
from Mycenae.

Electra welcomed him with delight, and together they invoked their
ancestor, Father Zeus, whom they reminded that Agamemnon had
always paid him great honour and that, were the House of Atreus to
die out, no one would be left in Mycenae to offer him the customary
hecatombs: for Aegisthus worshipped other deities.[15]

*i.* When the slave-women told Orestes of Clytaemnestra's dream,
he recognized the serpent as himself, and declared that he would indeed
play the cunning serpent and draw blood from her false body. Then he
instructed Electra to enter the Palace and tell Clytaemnestra nothing
about their meeting; he and Pylades would follow, after an interval,
and beg hospitality at the gate, as strangers and suppliants, pretending
to be Phocians and using the Parnassian dialect. If the porter refused
them admittance, Aegisthus's inhospitality would outrage the city; if
he granted it, they would not fail to take vengeance.

Presently Orestes knocked at the Palace gate, and asked for the master
or mistress of the house. Clytaemnestra herself came out, but did not
recognize Orestes. He pretended to be an Aeolian from Daulis, bearing
sad news from one Strophius, whom he had met by chance on the road
to Argos: namely, that her son Orestes was dead, and that his ashes were
being kept in a brazen urn. Strophius wished to know whether he
should send these back to Mycenae, or bury them at Crisa.[16]

*j.* Clytaemnestra at once welcomed Orestes inside and, concealing
her joy from the servants, sent his old nurse, Geilissa, to fetch Aegisthus

from a near-by temple. But Geilissa saw through Orestes's disguise and, altering the message, told Aegisthus to rejoice because he could now safely come alone and weaponless to greet the bearers of glad tidings: his enemy was dead.[17]

Unsuspectingly, Aegisthus entered the Palace where, to create a further distraction, Pylades had just arrived, carrying a brazen urn. He told Clytaemnestra that it held Orestes's ashes, which Strophius had now decided to send to Mycenae. This seeming confirmation of the first message put Aegisthus completely off his guard; thus Orestes had no difficulty in drawing his sword and cutting him down. Clytaemnestra then recognized her son, and tried to soften his heart by baring her breast, and appealing to his filial duty; Orestes, however, beheaded her with a single stroke of the same sword, and she fell beside the body of her paramour. Standing over the corpses, he addressed the Palace servants, holding aloft the still blood-stained net in which Agamemnon had died, eloquently exculpating himself for the murder of Clytaemnestra by this reminder of her treachery, and adding that Aegisthus had suffered the sentence prescribed by law for adulterers.[18]

*k.* Not content with killing Aegisthus and Clytaemnestra, Orestes next disposed of the second Helen, their daughter; and Pylades beat off the sons of Nauplius, who had come to Aegisthus's rescue.[19]

*l.* Some say, however, that these events took place in Argos, on the third day of Hera's Festival, when the virgins' procession was about to begin. Aegisthus had prepared a banquet for the Nymphs near the horse-meadows, before sacrificing a bull to Hera, and was gathering myrtle-boughs to wreathe his head. It is added that Electra, meeting Orestes by Agamemnon's tomb, would not believe at first that he was her long-lost brother, despite the similarity of their hair, and the robe he showed her. Finally, a scar on his forehead convinced her; because once, when they were children together, chasing a deer, he had slipped and fallen, cutting his head upon a sharp rock.

*m.* Obeying her whispered instructions, Orestes went at once to the altar where the bull had now been slaughtered and, as Aegisthus bent to inspect its entrails, struck off his head with the sacrificial axe. Meanwhile, Electra, to whom he presented the head, enticed Clytaemnestra from the palace by pretending that, ten days before, she had borne a son to her peasant husband; and when Clytaemnestra, anxious to inspect her first grand-child, visited the cottage, Orestes was waiting behind the door and killed her without mercy.[20]

*n*. Others, though agreeing that the murder took place at Argos, say that Clytaemnestra sent Chrysothemis to Agamemnon's tomb with the libations, having dreamed that Agamemnon, restored to life, snatched his sceptre from Aegisthus's hands and planted it so firmly in the ground that it budded and put forth branches, which overshadowed the entire land of Mycenae. According to this account, the news which deceived Aegisthus and Clytaemnestra was that Orestes had been accidentally killed while competing in the chariot race at the Pythian Games; and that Orestes showed Electra neither a ringlet nor an embroidered robe, nor a scar, in proof of his identity, but Agamemnon's own seal, which was carved from a piece of Pelops's ivory shoulder.[21]

*o*. Still others, denying that Orestes killed Clytaemnestra with his own hands, say that he committed her for trial by the judges, who condemned her to death, and that his one fault, if it may be called a fault, was that he did not intercede on her behalf.[22]

1. Euripides: *Orestes* 462 and *Iphigeneia in Aulis* 622.

2. Aeschylus: *Agamemnon* 877 ff. and *Libation-bearers* 732; Euripides: *Electra* 14 ff.; Pindar: *Pythian Odes* xi. 17, with scholiast.

3. Apollodorus: *Epitome* vi. 24; Euripides: *loc. cit.* and 542 ff.; Aeschylus: *Libation-bearers* 232.

4. Euripides: *Electra* 409–12; Sophocles: *Electra* 11 ff.; Pindar: *Pythian Odes* xi. 34–6.

5. Hyginus: *Fabula* 117; Scholiast on Euripides's *Orestes* 33, 764, and 1235; Euripides: *Iphigeneia Among the Taurians* 921; Apollodorus: *Epitome* vi. 24; Ovid: *Pontic Epistles* iii. 2. 95–8.

6. Euripides: *Electra* 289 and 323–5; Aeschylus: *Libation-bearers* 431.

7. Homer: *Odyssey* iii. 305; Euripides: *Electra* 320 ff. and 931 ff.; Sophocles: *Electra* 267 ff. and 651.

8. Euripides: *Electra* 33, 320 ff. and 617 ff.; Hyginus: *Fabula* 119.

9. Euripides: *Electra* 19 ff., 253 ff., and 312 ff.

10. Hyginus: *Fabula* 122; Ptolemy Hephaestionos: iv, quoted by Photius p. 479; Euripides: *Electra* 60–4; Aeschylus: *Libation-bearers* 130 ff.; Sophocles: *Electra* 341 ff., 379 ff. and 516 ff.

11. Apollodorus: *Epitome* vi. 24; Aeschylus: *Eumenides* 622 and *Libation-bearers* 269 ff.

12. Sophocles: *Electra* 36–7 and 51–2; Euripides: *Orestes* 268–70; Aeschylus: *Libation-bearers* 1038.

13. Homer: *Odyssey* iii. 306 ff.; *Hypothesis* of Sophocles's *Electra*; Apollodorus: *Epitome* vi. 25.

14. Aeschylus: *Libation-bearers*.

15. Aeschylus: *ibid.*

16. Aeschylus: *ibid.*

17. Aeschylus: *ibid*.
18. Hyginus: *Fabula* 119; Aeschylus: *Eumenides* 592 and *Libation-bearers* 973 ff.
19. Ptolemy Hephaestionos: iv, quoted by Photius p. 479; Pausanias: i. 22. 6.
20. Euripides: *Electra*.
21. Sophocles: *Electra* 326 and 417 ff.; 47–50 and 1223, with scholiast.
22. Servius on Virgil's *Aeneid* xi. 268.

1. This is a crucial myth with numerous variants. Olympianism had been formed as a religion of compromise between the pre-Hellenic matriarchal principle and the Hellenic patriarchal principle; the divine family consisting, at first, of six gods and six goddesses. An uneasy balance of power was kept until Athene was reborn from Zeus's head, and Dionysus, reborn from his thigh, took Hestia's seat at the divine Council (see 27. *k*); thereafter male preponderance in any divine debate was assured – a situation reflected on earth – and the goddesses' ancient prerogatives could now be successfully challenged.

2. Matrilinear inheritance was one of the axioms taken over from the pre-Hellenic religion. Since every king must necessarily be a foreigner, who ruled by virtue of his marriage to an heiress, royal princes learned to regard their mother as the main support of the kingdom, and matricide as an unthinkable crime. They were brought up on myths of the earlier religion, according to which the sacred king had always been betrayed by his goddess-wife, killed by his tanist, and avenged by his son; they knew that the son never punished his adulterous mother, who had acted with the full authority of the goddess whom she served.

3. The antiquity of the Orestes myth is evident from his friendship for Pylades, to whom he stands in exactly the same relation as Theseus to Peirithous. In the archaic version, he was doubtless a Phocian prince who ritually killed Aegisthus at the close of the eighth year of his reign, and became the new king by marriage to Chrysothemis, Clytaemnestra's daughter.

4. Other tell-tale traces of the archaic version persist in Aeschylus, Sophocles, and Euripides. Aegisthus is killed during the festival of the Death-goddess Hera, while cutting myrtle-boughs; and despatched, like the Minos bull, with a sacrificial axe. Geilissa's rescue of Orestes ('mountaineer') in a robe 'embroidered with wild beasts', and the tutor's stay among the shepherds of Tanus, together recall the familiar tale of a royal prince who is wrapped in a robe, left 'on a mountain' to the mercy of wild beasts, and cared for by shepherds – the robe being eventually recognized, as in the Hippothous myth (see 49. *a*). Geilissa's substitution of her own

son for the royal victim refers, perhaps, to a stage in religious history when the king's annual child-surrogate was no longer a member of the royal clan.

5. How far, then, can the main features of the story, as given by the Attic dramatists, be accepted? Though it is improbable that the Erinnyes have been wantonly introduced into the myth – which, like that of Alcmaeon and Eriphyle (see 107. *d*), seems to have been a moral warning against the least disobedience, injury, or insult that a son might offer his mother – yet it is equally improbable that Orestes killed Clytaemnestra. Had he done so, Homer would certainly have mentioned the fact, and refrained from calling him 'god-like'; he records only that Orestes killed Aegisthus, whose funeral feast he celebrated jointly with that of his hateful mother (*Odyssey* iii. 306 ff.). The *Parian Chronicle*, similarly, makes no mention of matricide in Orestes's indictment. It is probable therefore that Servius has preserved the true account: how Orestes, having killed Aegisthus, merely handed over Clytaemnestra to popular justice – a course significantly recommended by Tyndareus in Euripides's *Orestes* (496 ff.). Yet to offend a mother by a refusal to champion her cause, however wickedly she had behaved, sufficed under the old dispensation to set the Erinnyes on his track.

6. It seems, then, that this myth, which was of wide currency, had placed the mother of a household in so strong a position, when any family dispute arose, that the priesthood of Apollo and of Zeus-born Athene (a traitress to the old religion) decided to suppress it. They did so by making Orestes not merely commit Clytaemnestra to trial, but kill her himself, and then secure an acquittal in the most venerable court of Greece: with Zeus's support, and the personal intervention of Apollo, who had similarly encouraged Alcmaeon to murder his treacherous mother Eriphyle. It was the priests' intention, once and for all, to invalidate the religious axiom that motherhood is more divine than fatherhood.

7. In the revision patrilocal marriage and patrilinear descent are taken for granted, and the Erinnyes are successfully defied. Electra, whose name, 'amber', suggests the paternal cult of Hyperborean Apollo, is favourably contrasted with Chrysothemis, whose name is a reminder that the ancient concept of matriarchal law was still golden in most parts of Greece, and whose 'subservience' to her mother had hitherto been regarded as pious and noble. Electra is 'all for the father', like the Zeus-born Athene. Moreover, the Erinnyes had always acted for the mother only; and Aeschylus is forcing language when he speaks of Erinnyes charged with avenging paternal blood (*Libation-bearers* 283–4). Apollo's threat of leprosy if Orestes did not kill his mother, was a most daring one: to inflict, or heal, leprosy had long been the sole prerogative of the White Goddess Leprea, or Alphito (*White Goddess*, Chapter 24). In the sequel,

not all the Erinnyes accept Apollo's Delphic ruling, and Euripedes appeases his female audience by allowing the Dioscuri to suggest that Apollo's injunctions had been most unwise (*Electra* 1246).

8. The wide variations in the recognition scene, and in the plot by which Orestes contrives to kill Aegisthus and Clytaemnestra, are of interest only as proving that the Classical dramatists were not bound by tradition. Theirs was a new version of an ancient myth; and both Sophocles and Euripides tried to improve on Aeschylus, who first formulated it, by making the action more plausible.

# 114

## THE TRIAL OF ORESTES

THE Mycenaeans who had supported Orestes in his unheard-of action would not allow the bodies of Clytaemnestra and Aegisthus to lie within their city, but buried them at some distance beyond the walls.[1] That night, Orestes and Pylades stood guard at Clytaemnestra's tomb, lest anyone should dare rob it; but, during their vigil, the serpent-haired, dog-headed, bat-winged Erinnyes appeared, swinging their scourges. Driven to distraction by these fierce attacks, against which Apollo's bow of horn was of little avail, Orestes fell prostrate on a couch, where he lay for six days, his head wrapped in a cloak – refusing either to eat or to wash.

b. Old Tyndareus now arrived from Sparta, and brought a charge of matricide against Orestes, summoning the Mycenaean chieftains to judge his case. He decreed that, pending the trial, none should speak either to Orestes or Electra, and that both should be denied shelter, fire, and water. Thus Orestes was prevented even from washing his blood-stained hands. The streets of Mycenae were lined with citizens in arms; and Oeax, son of Nauplius, delighted in this opportunity to persecute Agamemnon's children.[2]

c. Meanwhile, Menelaus, laden with treasure, landed at Nauplia, where a fisherman told him that Aegisthus and Clytaemnestra had been murdered. He sent Helen ahead to confirm the news at Mycenae; but by night, lest the kinsmen of those who had perished at Troy should stone her. Helen, feeling ashamed to mourn in public for her sister Clytaemnestra, since she herself had caused even more bloodshed by her infidelities, asked Electra, who was now nursing the afflicted Orestes: 'Pray, niece, take offerings of my hair and lay them on Clytaemnestra's tomb, after pouring libations to her ghost.' Electra, when she saw that Helen had been prevented by vanity from cutting off more than the very tips of her hair, refused to do so. 'Send your daughter Hermione instead,' was her curt advice. Helen thereupon summoned Hermione from the palace. She had been only a nine-year-old child when her mother eloped with Paris, and Menelaus had committed her to Clytaemnestra's charge at the outbreak of the Trojan War; yet she recognized Helen at once and dutifully went off to do as she was told.[3]

*d.* Menelaus then entered the palace, where he was greeted by his foster-father Tyndareus, clad in deep mourning, and warned not to set foot on Spartan soil until he had punished his criminal nephew and niece. Tyndareus held that Orestes should have contented himself with allowing his fellow-citizens to banish Clytaemnestra. If they had demanded her death he should have interceded on her behalf. As matters now stood, they must be persuaded, willy-nilly, that not only Orestes, but Electra who had spurred him on, should be stoned to death as matricides.

*e.* Fearing to offend Tyndareus, Menelaus secured the desired verdict. But at the eloquent plea of Orestes himself, who was present in court and had the support of Pylades (now disowned by Strophius for his part in the murder), the judges commuted the sentence to one of suicide. Pylades then led Orestes away, nobly refusing to desert either him or Electra, to whom he was betrothed; and proposed that, since all three must die, they should first punish Menelaus's cowardice and disloyalty by killing Helen, the originator of every misfortune that had befallen them. While, therefore, Electra waited outside the walls to execute her own design – that of intercepting Hermione on her return from Clytaemnestra's tomb and holding her as a hostage for Menelaus's good behaviour – Orestes and Pylades entered the palace, with swords hidden beneath their cloaks, and took refuge at the central altar, as though they were suppliants. Helen, who sat near by, spinning wool for a purple robe to lay as a gift on Clytaemnestra's tomb, was deceived by their lamentations, and approached to welcome them. Whereupon both drew their swords and, while Pylades chased away Helen's Phrygian slaves, Orestes attempted to murder her. But Apollo, at Zeus's command, rapt her in a cloud to Olympus, where she became an immortal; joining her brothers, the Dioscuri, as a guardian of sailors in distress.[4]

*f.* Meanwhile, Electra had secured Hermione, led her into the palace, and barred the gates. Menelaus, seeing that death threatened his daughter, ordered an immediate rescue. His men burst open the gates, and Orestes was just about to set the palace alight, kill Hermione, and die himself either by sword or fire, when Apollo providentially appeared, wrenched the torch from his hand, and drove back Menelaus's warriors. In the awed hush caused by his presence, Apollo commanded Menelaus to take another wife, betroth Hermione to Orestes, and return to rule over Sparta; Clytaemnestra's murder need no longer concern him, now that the gods had intervened.[5]

*g.* With wool-wreathed laurel-branch and chaplet, to show that he was under Apollo's protection, Orestes then set out for Delphi, still pursued by the Erinnyes. The Pythian Priestess was terrified to see him crouched as a suppliant on the marble navel-stone – stained by the blood from his unwashed hands – and the hideous troop of black Erinnyes sleeping beside him. Apollo, however, reassured her by promising to act as advocate for Orestes, whom he ordered to face his ordeal with courage. After a period of exile, he must make his way to Athens, and there embrace the ancient image of Athene who, as the Dioscuri had already prophesied, would shield him with her Gorgonfaced aegis, and annul the curse.[6] While the Erinnyes were still fast asleep, Orestes escaped under the guidance of Hermes; but Clytaemnestra's ghost soon entered the precinct, taking them to task, and reminding them that they had often received libations of wine and grim midnight banquets from her hand. They therefore set off in renewed pursuit, scornful of Apollo's angry threats to shoot them down.[7]

*h.* Orestes's exile lasted for one year – the period which must elapse before a homicide may again move among his fellow-citizens. He wandered far, over land and sea, pursued by the tireless Erinnyes and constantly purified both with the blood of pigs and with running water; yet these rites never served to keep his tormentors at bay for more than an hour or two, and he soon lost his wits. To begin with, Hermes escorted him to Troezen, where he was lodged in what is now called the Booth of Orestes, which faces the Sanctuary of Apollo; and presently nine Troezenians purified him at the Sacred Rock, close to the Temple of Wolfish Artemis; using water from the Spring of Hippocrene, and the blood of sacrificial victims. An ancient laurel-tree marks the place where the victims were afterwards buried; and the descendants of these nine men still dine annually at the Booth on a set day.[8]

*i*. Opposite the island of Cranaë, three furlongs from Gythium, stands an unwrought stone, named the stone of Zeus the Reliever, upon which Orestes sat and was temporarily relieved of his madness. He is said to have also been purified in seven streams near Italian Rhegium, where he built a temple; in three tributaries of the Thracian Hebrus; and in the Orontes, which flows past Antioch.[9]

*j*. Seven furlongs down the high road from Megalopolis to Messene, on the left, is shown a sanctuary of the Mad Goddesses, a title of the Erinnyes, who inflicted a raging fit of madness on Orestes; also a small mound, surmounted by a stone finger and called the Finger Tomb. This marks the place where, in desperation, he bit off a finger to placate these black goddesses, and some of them, at least, changed their hue to white, so that his sanity was restored. He then shaved his head at a near-by sanctuary called Acë, and made a sin-offering to the black goddesses, also a thank-offering to the white. It is now customary to sacrifice to the latter conjointly with the Graces.[10]

*k*. Next, Orestes went to live among the Azanes and Arcadians of the Parrhasian Plain which, with the neighbouring city formerly called Oresthasium after its founder Orestheus, son of Lycaon, changed its name to Oresteium. Some, however, say that Oresteium was formerly called Azania, and that he went to live there only after a visit to Athens. Others, again, say that he spent his exile in Epirus, where he founded the city of Orestic Argos and gave his name to the Orestae Paroraei, Epirots who inhabit the rugged foothills of the Illyrian mountains.[11]

*l*. When a year had passed, Orestes visited Athens, which was then governed by his kinsman Pandion; or, some say, by Demophoön. He went at once to Athene's temple on the Acropolis, sat down, and embraced her image. The Black Erinnyes soon arrived, out of breath, having lost track of him while he crossed the Isthmus. Though at his first arrival none wished to receive him, as being hated by the gods, presently some were emboldened to invite him into their houses, where he sat at a separate table and drank from a separate wine cup.[12]

*m*. The Erinnyes, who had already begun to accuse him to the Athenians, were soon joined by Tyndareus with his grand-daughter Erigone, daughter of Aegisthus and Clytaemnestra; also, some say, by Clytaemnestra's cousin Perilaus, son of Icarius. But Athene, having heard Orestes's supplication from Scamander, her newly-acquired Trojan territory, hurried to Athens and, swearing-in the noblest citizens as judges, summoned the Areopagus to try what was then only the second case of homicide to come before it.[13]

*n.* In due course the trial took place, Apollo appearing as counsel for the defence, and the eldest of the Erinnyes as public prosecutrix. In an elaborate speech, Apollo denied the importance of motherhood, asserting that a woman was no more than the inert furrow in which the husbandman cast his seed; and that Orestes had been abundantly justified in his act, the father being the one parent worthy of the name. When the voting proved equal, Athene confessed herself wholly on the father's side, and gave her casting vote in favour of Orestes. Thus honourably acquitted, he returned in joy to Argolis, swearing to be a faithful ally of Athens so long as he lived. The Erinnyes, however, loudly lamented this subversal of the ancient law by upstart gods; and Erigone hanged herself for mortification.[14]

*o.* Of Helen's end three other contradictory accounts survive. The first: that in fulfilment of Proteus's prophecy, she returned to Sparta and there lived with Menelaus in peace, comfort, and prosperity, until they went hand in hand to the Elysian Fields. The second: that she visited the Taurians with him, whereupon Iphigeneia sacrificed them both to Artemis. The third: that Polyxo, widow of the Rhodian King Tlepolemus, avenged his death by sending some of her serving women, disguised as Erinnyes, to hang Helen.[15]

1. Pausanias: ii. 16. 5.
2. Euripides: *Orestes*.
3. Homer: *Odyssey* iii. 306 ff.; Apollodorus: *Epitome* iii. 3; Euripides: *ibid*.
4. Euripides: *ibid*.
5. Euripides: *ibid*.
6. Hyginus: *Fabula* 120; Aeschylus: *Libation-bearers* 1034 ff. and *Eumenides* 34 ff., 64 ff., and 166–7; Euripides: *Electra* 1254–7.
7. Aeschylus: *Eumenides* 94 ff., 106–9, and 179 ff.
8. Asclepiades, quoted by Scholiast on Euripides's *Orestes* 1645. Aeschylus: *Eumenides* 235 ff. and 445 ff.; Pausanias: ii. 31. 7 and 11.
9. Pausanias: iii. 22. 1; Varro, quoted by Probus on Virgil's *Eclogues* i. 4, ed. Keil; Lampridius: *Life of Heliogabulus* vii. p. 809; Libanius: xi. 366d.
10. Pausanias: viii. 34. 1–2.
11. Euripides: *Orestes* 1645–7 and *Electra* 1254 ff.; Pausanias: viii. 3. 1; Stephanus of Byzantium *sub* Azania; Strabo: vii. 7. 8.

12. Scholiast on Aristophanes's *Knights* 95; *Acharnanians* 960; *Parian Chronicle* 40 ff.; Tzetzes: *On Lycophron* 1374; Aeschylus: *Eumenides* 235 ff.; Euripides: *Iphigeneia Among the Taurians* 947 ff.

13. Apollodorus: *Epitome* vi. 25; Pausanias: viii. 34. 2; Aeschylus: *Eumenides* 397, 470 ff., and 681 ff.

14. Euripides: *Iphigeneia Among the Taurians* 961 ff.; Aeschylus: *Eumenides* 574 ff., 734 ff., and 778 ff.; *Etymologicum Magnum* p. 42: *sub* Aiōra.

15. Homer: *Odyssey* iv. 561; Ptolemy Hephaestionos: iv.; Pausanias: iii. 19. 10.

*

1. The tradition that Clytaemnestra's Erinnyes drove Orestes mad cannot be dismissed as an invention of the Attic dramatists; it was too early established, not only in Greece, but in Greater Greece. Yet, just as Oedipus's crime, for which the Erinnyes hounded him to death, was not that he killed his mother, but that he inadvertently caused her suicide (see 105. *k*), so Orestes's murder seems also to have been in the second degree only: he had failed in filial duty by not opposing the Mycenaeans' death sentence. The court was easily enough swayed, as Menelaus and Tyndareus soon demonstrated when they secured a death sentence against Orestes.

2. Erinnyes were personified pangs of conscience, such as are still capable, in pagan Melanesia, of killing a man who has rashly or inadvertently broken a taboo. He will either go mad and leap from a coconut palm, or wrap his head in a cloak, like Orestes, and refuse to eat or drink until he dies of starvation; even if nobody else is informed of his guilt. Paul would have suffered a similar fate at Damascus but for the timely arrival of Ananias (*Acts* ix. 9 ff.). The common Greek method of purging ordinary blood guilt was for the homicide to sacrifice a pig and, while the ghost of the victim greedily drank its blood, to wash in running water, shave his head in order to change his appearance, and go into exile for one year, thus throwing the vengeful ghost off the scent. Until he had been purified in this manner, his neighbours shunned him as unlucky, and would not allow him to enter their homes or share their food, for fear of themselves becoming involved in his troubles; and he might still have to reckon with the victim's family, should the ghost demand vengeance from them. A mother's blood, however, carried with it so powerful a curse, that common means of purification would not serve: and, short of suicide, the most extreme means was to bite off a finger. This self-mutilation seems to have been at least partially successful in Orestes's case; thus also Heracles, to placate the aggrieved Hera, will have bitten off the finger which he is said to have lost while tussling with the Nemean Lion

(see 123. *e*). In some regions of the South Seas a finger-joint is always lopped off at the death of a close relative, even when he or she has died a natural death. In the *Eumenides* (397 ff.) Aeschylus is apparently disguising a tradition that Orestes fled to the Troad and lived, untroubled by the Erinnyes, under Athene's protection on silt land wrested from the Scamander and therefore free from the curse (see 107. *e*). Why else should the Troad be mentioned?

3. Wine instead of blood libations, and offerings of small hair-snippings instead of the whole crop, were Classical amendments on this ritual of appeasement, the significance of which was forgotten; as the present-day custom of wearing black is no longer consciously connected with the ancient habit of deceiving ghosts by altering one's normal appearance.

4. Euripides's imaginative account of what happened when Helen and Menelaus returned to Mycenae contains no mythical element, except for Helen's dramatic apotheosis; and Helen as the Moon-goddess had been a patroness of sailors long before the Heavenly Twins were recognized as a constellation. Like Aeschylus, Euripides was writing religious propaganda: Orestes's absolution records the final triumph of patriarchy, and is staged at Athens, where Athene – formerly the Libyan goddess Neith, or Palestinian Anatha, a supreme matriarch, but now reborn from Zeus's head and acknowledging, as Aeschylus insists, no divine mother – connives at matricide even in the first degree. The Athenian dramatists knew that this revolutionary theme could not be accepted elsewhere in Greece: hence Euripides makes Tyndareus, as Sparta's representative, declare passionately that Orestes must die; and the Dioscuri venture to condemn Apollo for having prompted the crime.

5. Orestes's name, 'mountaineer', has connected him with a wild, mountainous district in Arcadia which no King of Mycenae is likely to have visited.

6. These alternative versions of Helen's death are given for different reasons. The first purports to explain the cult of Helen and Menelaus at Therapne; the second is a theatrical variation on the story of Orestes's visit to the Taurians (see 116. *a–g*); the third accounts for the Rhodian cult of Helena Dendritis, 'Helen of the Tree', who is the same character as Ariadne and the other Erigone (see 79. *2* and 88. *10*). This Erigone was also hanged.

# 115

## THE PACIFICATION OF THE ERINNYES

IN gratitude for his acquittal, Orestes dedicated an altar to Warlike Athene; but the Erinnyes threatened, if the judgement were not reversed, to let fall a drop of their own hearts' blood which would bring barrenness upon the soil, blight the crops, and destroy all the offspring of Athens. Athene nevertheless soothed their anger by flattery: acknowledging them to be far wiser than herself, she suggested that they should take up residence in a grotto at Athens, where they would gather such throngs of worshippers as they could never hope to find elsewhere. Hearth-altars proper to Underworld deities should be theirs, as well as sober sacrifices, torchlight libations, first-fruits offered after the consummation of marriage or the birth of children, and even seats in the Erechtheum. If they accepted this invitation she would decree that no house where worship was withheld from them might prosper; but they, in return, must undertake to invoke fair winds for her ships, fertility for her land, and fruitful marriages for her people – also rooting out the impious, so that she might see fit to grant Athens victory in war. The Erinnyes, after a short deliberation, graciously agreed to these proposals.

*b*. With expressions of gratitude, good wishes, and charms against withering winds, drought, blight, and sedition, the Erinnyes – henceforth addressed as the Solemn Ones – bade farewell to Athene, and were conducted by her people in a torchlight procession of youths, matrons, and crones (dressed in purple, and carrying the ancient image of Athene) to the entrance of a deep grotto at the south-eastern angle of the Areopagus. Appropriate sacrifices were there offered to them, and they descended into the grotto, which is now both an oracular shrine and, like the Sanctuary of Theseus, a place of refuge for suppliants.[1]

*c*. Yet only three of the Erinnyes had accepted Athene's generous offer; the remainder continued to pursue Orestes; and some people go so far as to deny that the Solemn Ones were ever Erinnyes. The name 'Eumenides' was first given to the Erinnyes by Orestes, in the following year, after his daring adventure in the Tauric Chersonese, when he finally succeeded in appeasing their fury at Carneia with the holocaust of a black sheep. They are called Eumenides also at Colonus, where none may enter their ancient grove; and at Achaean Cerynea where, towards the end of his life, Orestes dedicated a new sanctuary to them.[2]

*d*. In the grotto of the Solemn Ones at Athens – which is closed only to the second-fated, that is to say, to men who have been prematurely mourned for dead – their three images wear no more terrible an aspect than do those of the Underworld gods standing beside them, namely Hades, Hermes, and Mother Earth. Here those who have been acquitted of murder by the Areopagus sacrifice a black victim; numerous other offerings are brought to the Solemn Ones in accordance with Athene's promise; and one of the three nights set aside every month by the Areopagus for the hearing of murder trials is assigned to each of them.[3]

*e.* The rites of the Solemn Ones are silently performed; hence their priesthood is hereditary in the clan of the Hesychids, who offer the preliminary sacrifice of a ram to their ancestor Hesychus at his heroshrine outside the Nine Gates.[4]

*f.* A hearth-altar has also been provided for the Solemn Ones at Phlya, a small Attic township; and a grove of evergreen oaks is sacred to them near Titane, on the farther bank of the river Asopus. At their Phlyan festival, celebrated yearly, pregnant sheep are sacrificed, libations of honey-water poured, and flowers worn instead of the usual myrtle wreaths. Similar rites are performed at the altar of the Fates, which stands in the oak-grove, unprotected from the weather.[5]

1. Pausanias: i. 28. 5–6; Porphyry: *Concerning the Caves of the Nymphs* 3; Euripides: *Electra* 1272; Aristophanes: *Knights* 1312; Aeschylus: *Eumenides* 778–1047.
2. Euripides: *Iphigeneia Among the Taurians* 968 ff.; Philemon the Comedian, quoted by scholiast on Sophocles's *Oedipus at Colonus* 42; *Hypothesis* of Aeschylus's *Eumenides*; Pausanias: vii. 25. 4; Sophocles: *Oedipus at Colonus* 37 and 42–3.
3. Hesychius *sub* Deuteropotmoi; Polemon, quoted by scholiast on Sophocles: *loc. cit.* and 89; Pausanias: i. 28. 6; Scholiast on Aeschines's *Against Timarchus* 1. 188c; Lucian: *On the Hall* 18; Aeschylus: *Eumenides* 705.
4. Hesychius *sub* Hesychidae.
5. Pausanias: i. 31. 2 and ii. 11. 4.

\*

*1.* The 'hearts' blood' of the Erinnyes, with which Attica was threatened, seems to be a euphemism for menstrual blood. An immemorial charm used by witches who wish to curse a house, field, or byre is to run naked around it, counter-sunwise, nine times, while in a menstrual condition. This curse is considered most dangerous to crops, cattle, and children during an eclipse of the moon; and altogether unavoidable if the witch is a virgin menstruating for the first time.

*2.* Philemon the Comedian did right to question the Athenian identification of the Erinnyes with the Solemn Ones. According to the most respected authorities, there were only three Erinnyes: Tisiphone, Alecto, and Megaera (see 31. *g*), who lived permanently in Erebus, not at Athens. They had gods' heads, bats' wings, and serpents for hair; yet, as Pausanias points out, the Solemn Ones were portrayed as august matrons. Athene's offer, in fact, was not what Aeschylus has recorded; but an ultimatum from the priesthood of Zeus-born Athene to the priestesses of the Solemn Ones – the ancient Triple-goddess of Athens – that, unless they accepted the new view of fatherhood as superior to motherhood, and consented to share their grotto with such male underworld deities as Hades and Hermes, they would forfeit all worship whatsoever, and with it their traditional perquisites of first-fruits.

3. Second-fated men were debarred from entering the grotto of the Underworld goddesses, who might be expected to take offence that their dedicated subjects still wandered at large in the upper world. A similar embarrassment is felt in India when men recover from a death-like trance on their way to the burning ghat: in the last century, according to Rudyard Kipling, they used to be denied official existence and smuggled away to a prison colony of the dead. The evergreen oak, also called the kerm-oak, because it provides the kerm-berries (cochineal insects) from which the Greeks extracted scarlet dye, was the tree of the tanist who killed the sacred king, and therefore appropriate for a grove of the Solemn Ones. Sacrifices of pregnant sheep, honey, and flowers would encourage these to spare the remainder of the flock during the lambing season, favour the bees, and enrich the pasture.

4. The Erinnyes' continued pursuit of Orestes, despite the intervention of Athene and Apollo, suggests that, in the original myth, he went to Athens and Phocis for purification, but without success; as, in the myth of Eriphyle, Alcmaeon went unsuccessfully to Psophis and Thesprotia. Since Orestes is not reported to have found peace on the reclaimed silt of any river (see 107. *e*) – unless perhaps of the Scamander (see 114. 2)– he will have met his death in the Tauric Chersonese, or at Brauron (see 116. *1*).

# 116

## IPHIGENEIA AMONG THE TAURIANS

STILL pursued by such of the Erinnyes as had turned deaf ears to Athene's eloquent speeches, Orestes went in despair to Delphi, where he threw himself on the temple floor and threatened to take his own life unless Apollo saved him from their scourgings. In reply, the Pythian priestess ordered him to sail up the Bosphorus and northward across the Black Sea; his woes would end only when he had seized an ancient wooden image of Artemis from her temple in the Tauric Chersonese, and brought it to Athens or (some say) to Argolis.[1]

*b*. Now, the king of the Taurians was the fleet-footed Thoas, a son of Dionysus and Ariadne, and father of Hypsipyle; and his people, so called because Osiris once yoked bulls (*tauroi*) and ploughed their land, came of Scythian stock.[2] They still live by rapine, as in Thoas's days; and whenever one of their warriors takes a prisoner, he beheads him, carries the head home, and there impales it on a tall stake above the chimney, so that his household may live under the dead man's protection. Moreover, every sailor who has been shipwrecked, or driven into their port by rough weather, is publicly sacrificed to Taurian Artemis. When they have performed certain preparatory rites, they fell him with a club and nail his severed head to a cross; after which the body is either buried, or tossed into the sea from the precipice crowned by Artemis's temple. But any princely stranger who falls into their hands is killed with a sword by the goddess's virgin-priestess; and she throws his corpse into the sacred fire, welling up from Tartarus, which burns in the divine precinct. Some, however, say that the priestess, though supervising the rites, and performing the preliminary lustration and hair-cropping of the victim, does not herself kill him. The ancient image of the goddess, which Orestes was ordered to seize, had fallen here from Heaven. This temple is supported by vast columns, and approached by forty steps; its altar of white marble is permanently stained with blood.[3]

*c*. Taurian Artemis has several Greek titles: among them are Artemis Tauropolus, or Tauropole; Artemis Dictynna; Artemis Orthia; Thoantea; Hecate; and to the Latins she is Trivia.[4]

*d*. Now, Iphigeneia had been rescued from sacrifice at Aulis by Artemis, wrapped in a cloud, and wafted to the Tauric Chersonese, where she was at once appointed Chief Priestess and granted the sole right of handling the sacred image. The Taurians thereafter addressed her as Artemis, or Hecate, or Orsiloche. Iphigeneia loathed human sacrifice, but piously obeyed the goddess.[5]

*e*. Orestes and Pylades knew nothing of all this; they still believed that Iphigeneia had died under the sacrificial knife at Aulis. Nevertheless, they hastened to the land of the Taurians in a fifty-oared ship which, on arrival, they left at anchor, guarded by their oarsmen, while they hid in a sea-cave. It was their intention to approach the temple at nightfall, but they were surprised beforehand by some credulous herdsmen who, assuming them to be the Dioscuri, or some other pair of immortals, fell down and adored them. At this juncture Orestes went mad once more, bellowing like a calf and howling like a dog; he mistook a herd of calves for Erinnyes, and rushed from the cave, sword in hand, to slaughter them. The disillusioned herdsmen thereupon overpowered the two friends who, at Thoas's orders, were marched off to the temple for immediate sacrifice.[6]

*f.* During the preliminary rites Orestes conversed in Greek with Iphigeneia; soon they joyfully discovered each other's identity, and on learning the nature of his mission, she began to lift down the image for him to carry away. Thoas, however, suddenly appeared, impatient at the slow progress of the sacrifice, and the resourceful Iphigeneia pretended to be soothing the image. She explained to Thoas that the goddess had averted her gaze from the victims whom he had sent, because one was a matricide, and the other was abetting him: both were quite unfit for sacrifice. She must take them, together with the image, which their presence had polluted, to be cleansed in the sea, and offer the goddess a torchlight sacrifice of young lambs. Meanwhile, Thoas was to purify the temple with a torch, cover his head when the strangers emerged, and order everyone to remain at home and thus avoid pollution.

*g.* Thoas, wholly deceived, stood for a time lost in admiration of such sagacity, and then began to purify the temple. Presently Iphigeneia, Orestes, and Pylades conveyed the image down to the shore by torchlight but, instead of bathing it in the sea, hastily carried it aboard their ship. The Taurian temple-servants, who had come with them, now suspected treachery and showed fight. They were subdued in a hard struggle, after which Orestes's oarsmen rowed the ship away. A sudden gale, however, sprang up, driving her back towards the rocky shore, and all would have perished, had not Poseidon calmed the sea at Athene's request; with a favouring breeze, they made the Island of Sminthos.[7]

*h.* This was the home of Chryses, the priest of Apollo, and his grandson of the same name, whose mother Chryseis now proposed to surrender the fugitives to Thoas. For, although some hold that Athene had visited Thoas, who was manning a fleet to sail in pursuit, and cajoled him so successfully that he even consented to repatriate Iphi-

geneia's Greek slave-women, it is certain that he came to Sminthos
with murderous intentions. Then Chryses the Elder, learning the
identity of his guests, revealed to Chryses the Younger that he was not,
as Chryseis had always pretended, Apollo's son, but Agamemnon's,
and therefore half-brother to Orestes and Iphegeneia. At this, Chryses
and Orestes rushed shoulder to shoulder against Thoas, whom they
succeeded in killing; and Orestes, taking up the image, sailed safely
home to Mycenae, where the Erinnyes at last abandoned their chase.[8]

*i.* But some say that a storm drove Orestes to Rhodes where, in
accordance with the Helian Oracle, he set up the image upon a city
wall. Others say that, since Attica was the land to which he had been
instructed to bring it, by Apollo's orders, Athene visited him on
Sminthos and specified the frontier city of Brauron as its destination:
it must be housed there in a temple of Artemis Tauropolus, and placated with blood drawn from a man's throat. She designated Iphigeneia
as the priestess of this temple, in which she was destined to end her days
peacefully; the perquisites would include the clothes of rich women
who had died in childbed. According to this account, the ship finally
made port at Brauron, where Iphigeneia deposited the image and then,
while the temple was being built, went with Orestes to Delphi; she met
Electra in the shrine and brought her back to Athens for marriage to
Pylades.[9]

*j.* What is claimed to be the authentic wooden image of Tauric
Artemis may still be seen at Brauron. Some, however, say that it is only
a replica, the original having been captured by Xerxes in the course of
his ill-fated expedition against Greece, and taken to Susa; afterwards,
they add, it was presented by King Seleucus of Syria to the Laodicaeans,
who worship it to this day. Others, again, loth to allow credit to
Xerxes, say that Orestes himself, on his homeward voyage from the
Tauric Chersonese, was driven by a storm to the region now named
Seleuceia, where he left the image; and that the natives renamed Mount
Melantius, where the madness finally left him, Mount Amanon, that is
'not mad', in his memory. But the Lydians, who have a sanctuary of
Artemis Anaeitis, also claim to possess the image; and so do the people
of Cappadocian Comana, whose city is said to take its name from the
mourning tresses (*comai*) which Orestes deposited there, when he
brought the rites of Artemis Tauropolus into Cappadocia.[10]

*k.* Others, again, say that Orestes concealed the image in a bundle of
faggots, and took it to Italian Aricia, where he himself died and was

buried, his bones being later transferred to Rome; and that the image
was sent from Aricia to Sparta, because the cruelty of its rites displeased
the Romans; and there placed in the Sanctuary of Upright Artemis.[11]

*l.* But the Spartans claim that the image has been theirs since long
before the foundation of Rome, Orestes having brought it with him
when he became their king, and hidden it in a willow thicket. For centuries, they say, its whereabouts were forgotten; until, one day, Astra-
bacus and Alopecus, two princes of the royal house, entering the
thicket by chance, were driven mad at the sight of the grim image,
which was kept upright by the willow-branches wreathed around it –
hence its names, Orthia and Lygodesma.

*m.* No sooner was the image brought to Sparta, than an ominous
quarrel arose between rival devotees of Artemis, who were sacrificing
together at her altar: many of them were killed in the sanctuary itself,
the remainder died of plague shortly afterwards. When an oracle
advised the Spartans to propitiate the image by drenching the altar
with human blood, they cast lots for a victim and sacrificed him; and
this ceremony was repeated yearly until King Lycurgus, who abhorred
human sacrifice, forbade it, and instead ordered boys to be flogged at
the altar until it reeked with blood.[12] Spartan boys now compete once
a year as to who can endure the most blows. Artemis's priestess stands
by, carrying the image which, although small and light, acquired such
relish for blood in the days when human sacrifices were offered to it by
the Taurians that, even now, if the floggers lay on gently, because the
boy is of noble birth, or exceptionally handsome, it grows almost too
heavy for her to hold, and she chides the floggers: 'Harder, harder!
You are weighing me down!'[13]

*n.* Little credence should be given to the tale that Helen and Menelaus went in search of Orestes and, arriving among the Taurians shortly
after he did, were both sacrificed to the goddess by Iphigeneia.[14]

1. Apollodorus: *Epitome* vi. 26; Euripides: *Iphigeneia Among the
   Taurians* 77 and 970 ff.; Hyginus: *Fabula* 120.
2. Euripides: *Iphigeneia Among the Taurians* 32; Scholiast on Apollonius Rhodius: iii. 997; Eustathius: *On Dionysus* 306; Apollodorus: *Epitome* vi. 26.
3. Herodotus: iv. 103; Ovid: *Pontic Epistles* iii. 2. 45 ff.; Apollodorus: *Epitome* vi. 26; Euripides: *Iphigeneia Among the Taurians*
   40 ff. and 88 ff.
4. Diodorus Siculus: iv. 44. 7; Sophocles: *Ajax* 172; Pausanias: i. 23.
   9; Servius on Virgil's *Aeneid* ii. 116; Valerius Flaccus: viii. 208;

Ovid: *Ibis* 384 and *Pontic Epistles* iii. 2. 71; *Orphic Argonautica* 1065.

5. Euripides: *Iphigeneia Among the Taurians* 784 and 1045; Ovid: *Pontic Epistles* iii. 2. 45 ff.; Herodotus: iv. 103; Hesiod: *Catalogue of Women*, quoted by Pausanias: i. 43. 1; Ammianus Marcellinus: xxii. 8. 34.

6. Hyginus: *Fabula* 120; Apollodorus: *Epitome* vi. 27.

7. Ovid: *Pontic Epistles loc. cit.*; Hyginus: *loc. cit.*; Euripides: *Iphigeneia Among the Taurians* 1037 ff.

8. Hyginus: *Fabulae* 120 and 121; Euripides: *Iphigeneia Among the Taurians* 1435 ff.; Hyginus: *Fabula* 121.

9. Apollodorus: *Epitome* vi. 27; Euripides: *Iphigeneia Among the Taurians* 89–91 and 1446 ff.; Pausanias: i. 33. 1; Tzetzes: *On Lycophron* 1374.

10. Pausanias: i. 23. 9, iii. 16. 6 and viii. 46. 2; Tzetzes: *loc. cit.*; Strabo: xii. 2. 3.

11. Servius on Virgil's *Aeneid* ii. 116 and vi. 136; Hyginus: *Fabula* 261.

12. Pausanias: iii. 16. 6–7.

13. Hyginus: *Fabula* 261; Servius on Virgil's *Aeneid* ii. 116; Pausanias: *loc. cit.*

14. Ptolemy Hephaestionos: iv, quoted by Photius: p. 479.

*

1. The mythographers' anxiety to conceal certain barbarous traditions appears plainly in this story and its variants. Among the suppressed elements are Artemis's vengeance on Agamemnon for the murder of Iphigeneia, and Oeax's vengeance, also on Agamemnon, for the murder of his brother Palamedes. Originally, the myth seems to have run somewhat as follows: Agamemnon was prevailed upon, by his fellow-chieftains, to execute his daughter Iphigeneia as a wtch when the Greek expedition against Troy lay windbound at Aulis. Artemis, whom Iphigeneia had served as priestess, made Agamemnon pay for this insult to her: she helped Aegisthus to supplant and murder him on his return. At her inspiration also, Oeax offered to take Orestes on a voyage to the land reclaimed from the river Scamander and thus help him to escape the Erinnyes; for Athene would protect him there (see 115. 4). Instead, Oeax put in at Brauron, where Orestes was acclaimed as the annual *pharmacos*, a scapegoat for the guilt of the people, and had his throat slit by Artemis's virgin-priestess. Oeax, in fact, told Electra the truth when they met at Delphi: that Orestes had been sacrificed by Iphigeneia, which seems to have been a title of Artemis (see 117. *1*).

2. Patriarchal Greeks of a later era will have disliked this myth – a version of which, making Menelaus, not Orestes, the object of Artemis's

vengeance, has been preserved by Photius. They exculpated Agamemnon of murder, and Artemis of opposing the will of Zeus, by saying that she doubtless rescued Iphigeneia, and carried her away to be a sacrificial priestess – not at Brauron, but among the savage Taurians, for whose actions they disclaimed responsibility. And that she certainly did not kill Orestes (or, for the matter of that, any Greek victim) but, on the contrary, helped him to take the Tauric image to Greece at Apollo's orders.

3. This face-saving story, influenced by the myth of Jason's expedition to the Black Sea – in Servius's version, Orestes steals the image from Colchis, not the Tauric Chersonese – explained the tradition of human throat-slitting at Brauron, now modified to the extraction of a drop of blood from a slight cut, and similar sacrifices at Mycenae, Aricia, Rhodes, and Comana. 'Tauropolus' suggests the Cretan bull sacrifice, which survived in the Athenian Buphonia (Pausanias: i. 28. 11); the original victim is likely to have been the sacred king.

4. The Spartan fertility rites, also said to have once involved human sacrifice, were held in honour of Upright Artemis. To judge from primitive practice elsewhere in the Mediterranean, the victim was bound with willow-thongs, full of lunar magic, to the image – a sacred treestump, perhaps of pear-wood (see 74. 6), and flogged until the lashes induced an erotic reaction and he ejaculated, fertilizing the land with semen and blood. Alopecus's name, and the well-known legend of the youth who allowed his vitals to be gnawed by a fox rather than cry out, suggest that the Vixen-goddess of Teumessus was also worshipped at Sparta (see 49. 2 and 89. 8).

5. Meteorites were often paid divine honours, and so were small ritual objects of doubtful origin which could be explained as having similarly fallen from heaven – such as the carefully worked neolithic spearheads, identified with Zeus's thunderbolts by the later Greeks (as flint arrows are called 'elf shots' in the English countryside), or the bronze pestle hidden in the head-dress worn by the image of Ephesian Artemis. The images themselves, such as the Brauronian Artemis and the olive-wood Athene in the Erechtheum, were then likewise said to have fallen from heaven, through a hole in the roof (see 158. k). It is possible that the image at Brauron contained an ancient sacrificial knife of obsidian – a volcanic glass from the island of Melos – with which the victims' throats were slit.

6. Osiris's ploughing of the Tauric Chersonese (the Crimea), seems forced; but Herodotus insists on a close link between Colchis and Egypt (ii. 104), and Colchis has here been confused with the land of the Taurians. Osiris, like Triptolemus, is said to have introduced agriculture into many foreign lands (see 24. m).

## THE REIGN OF ORESTES

AEGISTHUS's son Aletes now usurped the kingdom of Mycenae, believing the malicious rumour [? spread by Oeax] that Orestes and Pylades had been sacrificed on the altar of Tauric Artemis. But Electra, doubting its truth, went to consult the Delphic Oracle. Iphigeneia had just arrived at Delphi, and [? Oeax] pointed her out to Electra as Orestes's murderess. Revengefully she seized a firebrand from the altar and, not recognizing Iphigeneia after the lapse of years, was about to blind her with it, when Orestes himself entered and explained all. The reunited children of Agamemnon then went joyfully back to Mycenae, where Orestes ended the feud between the House of Atreus and the House of Thyestes, by killing Aletes; whose sister Erigone, it is said, would also have perished by his hand, had not Artemis snatched her away to Attica. But afterwards Orestes relented towards her.[1]

b. Some say that Iphigeneia died either at Brauron, or at Megara, where she now has a sanctuary; others, that Artemis immortalized her as the Younger Hecate. Electra, married to Pylades, bore him Medon and Strophius the Second; she lies buried at Mycenae. Orestes married his cousin Hermione – having been present at the sacrificial murder of Achilles's son Neoptolemus, to whom she was betrothed.[2] By her he became the father of Tisamenus, his heir and successor; and by Erigone his second wife, of Penthilus.[3]

c. When Menelaus died, the Spartans invited Orestes to become their king, preferring him, as a grandson of Tyndareus, to Nicostratus and Megapenthes, begotten by Menelaus on a slave-girl. Orestes who, with the help of troops furnished by his Phocian allies, had already added a large part of Arcadia to his Mycenaean domains, now made himself master of Argos as well; for King Cylarabes, grandson of Capaneus, left no issue. He also subdued Achaea but, in obedience to the Delphic Oracle, finally emigrated from Mycenae to Arcadia where, at the age of seventy, he died of a snake bite at Oresteium, or Orestia, the town which he had founded during his exile.[4]

d. Orestes was buried at Tegea, but in the reign of Anaxandrides, co-king with Aristo, and the only Laconian who ever had two wives and occupied two houses at the same time, the Spartans, in despair because they had hitherto lost every battle fought with the Tegeans, sent to Delphi for advice, and were instructed to possess themselves of Orestes's bones. Since the whereabouts of these were unknown, they sent Lichas, one of Sparta's benefactors, to ask for further enlightenment. He was given the following response in hexameters:

> *Level and smooth the plain of Arcadian Tegea. Go thou*
> *Where two winds are ever, by strong necessity, blowing;*
> *Where stroke rings upon stroke, where evil lies upon evil;*
> *There all-teeming earth doth enclose the prince whom thou seekest.*
> *Bring thou him to thy house, and thus be Tegea's master!*

Because of a temporary truce between the two states, Lichas had no difficulty in visiting Tegea; where he came upon a smith forging a sword of iron, instead of bronze, and gazed open-mouthed at the novel sight. 'Does this work surprise you?' cried the jovial smith. 'Well, I have something here to surprise you even more! It is a coffin, seven cubits long, containing a corpse of the same length, which I found beneath the smithy floor while I was digging yonder well.'

*e.* Lichas guessed that the winds mentioned in the verses must be those raised by the smith's bellows; the strokes those of his hammer; and the evil lying upon evil, his hammer-head beating out the iron sword – for the Iron Age brought in cruel days. He at once returned with the news to Sparta, where the judges, at his own suggestion, pretended to condemn him for a crime of violence; then, fleeing to Tegea as if from execution, he persuaded the smith to hide him in the smithy. At midnight, he stole the bones out of the coffin and hurried back to Sparta, where he re-interred them near the sanctuary of the Fates; the tomb is still shown. Spartan armies have ever since been consistently victorious over the Tegeans.⁵

*f.* Pelops's spear-sceptre, which his grandson Orestes also wielded, was discovered in Phocis about this time: lying buried with a hoard of gold on the frontier between Chaeronea and Phanoteus, where it had probably been hidden by Electra. When an inquest was held on this treasure-trove, the Phanotians were content with the gold; but the Chaeroneans took the sceptre, and now worship it as their supreme deity. Each priest of the spear, appointed for one year, keeps it in his own house, offering daily victims to its divinity, beside tables lavishly spread with every kind of food.⁶

*g.* Yet some deny that Orestes died in Arcadia. They say that after his term of exile there, he was ordered by an oracle to visit Lesbos and

Tenedos and found colonies, with settlers gathered from various cities, including Amyclae. He did so, calling his new people Aeolians because Aeolis was their nearest common ancestor, but died soon after building a city in Lesbos. This migration took place, they say, four generations before the Ionian. Others, however, declare that Orestes's son Penthilus, not Orestes himself, conquered Lesbos; that his grandson Gras, aided by the Spartans, occupied the country between Ionia and Mysia, now called Aeolis; and that another grandson, Archelaus, took Aeolian settlers to the present city of Cyzicene, near Dascylium, on the southern shores of the Sea of Marmara.[7]

*h*. Tisamenus meanwhile succeeded to his father's dominions, but was driven from the capital cities of Sparta, Mycenae, and Argos by the sons of Heracles, and took refuge with his army in Achaea. His son Cometes emigrated to Asia.[8]

1. Hyginus: *Fabula* 122.
2. Euripides: *Iphigeneia Among the Taurians* 1464 and 915; Pausanias: i. 43. 1 and x. 24. 4–5; Hellanicus, quoted by Pausanias: ii. 16. 5; Hyginus: *Fabula* 123; Strabo: ix. 3. 9.
3. Apollodorus: *Epitome* vi. 28; Cinaethon, quoted by Pausanias: ii. 18. 5; Tzetzes: *On Lycophron* 1374.
4. Pausanias: ii. 18. 5 and viii. 5. 1–3; Asclepiades, quoted by scholiast on Euripides's *Orestes* 1647; Apollodorus: *loc. cit.*; Tzetzes: *loc. cit.*
5. Pausanias: iii. 3. 7; iii. 11. 8; iii. 3. 5–7 and viii. 54. 3; Herodotus: i. 67–8.
6. Pausanias: ix. 40. 6.
7. Pindar: *Nemean Odes* xi. 33–5; Hellanicus, quoted by Tzetzes: *On Lycophron* 1374; Pausanias: iii. 2. 1; Strabo: xiii. 1. 3.
8. Pausanias: ii. 8. 6–7 and vii. 6. 21.

*

*1*. Iphigeneia seems to have been a title of the earlier Artemis, who was not merely maiden, but also nymph – 'Iphigeneia' means 'mothering a strong race' – and 'crone', namely the Solemn Ones or Triple Hecate. Orestes is said to have reigned in so many places that his name must also be regarded as a title. His death by snake bite at Arcadian Oresteia links him with other primitive kings: such as Apesantus son of Acrisius (see 123. *e*), identifiable with Opheltes of Nemea (see 106. *g*); Munitus son of Athamas (see 168. *e*); Mopsus the Lapith (see 154. *f*), bitten by a Libyan snake; and Egyptian Ra, an aspect of Osiris, also bitten by a Libyan snake. These bites are always in the heel; in some cases, among them those of Cheiron and Pholus the Centaurs, Talus the Cretan, Achilles the Myr-

midon, and Philoctetes the Euboean, the venom seems to have been conveyed on an arrow-point (see 92. *10*). The Arcadian Orestes was, in fact,
a Pelasgian with Libyan connexions.

2. Artemis's rescue of Erigone from Orestes's vengeance is one more
incident in the feud between the House of Thyestes, assisted by Artemis,
and the House of Atreus, assisted by Zeus. Tisamenus's name ('avenging
strength') suggests that the feud was bequeathed to the succeeding
generation: because, according to one of Apollodorus's accounts (*Epitome* vi. 28), he was Erigone's son, not Hermione's. Throughout the
story of this feud it must be remembered that the Artemis who here
measures her strength with Zeus is the earlier matriarchal Artemis, rather
than Apollo's loving twin, the maiden huntress; the mythographers
have done their best to obscure Apollo's active participation, on Zeus's
side, in this divine quarrel.

3. Giants' bones, usually identified with those of a tribal ancestor, were
regarded as a magical means of protecting a city; thus the Athenians, by
oracular inspiration, recovered what they claimed to be Theseus's bones
from Scyros and brought them back to Athens (see 104. *i*). These may
well have been unusually large, because a race of giants – of which the
Hamitic Watusi who live in Equatorial Africa are an offshoot – flour-
ished in neolithic Europe, and their seven-foot skeletons have occasionally been found even in Britain. The Anakim of Palestine and Caria (see
88. *3*) belonged to this race. However, if Orestes was an Achaean of the
Trojan War period, the Athenians could not have found and measured
his skeleton, since the Homeric nobles practised cremation, not inhuma-
tion in the neolithic style.

4. 'Evil lying upon evil' is usually interpreted as the iron sword that
was being forged on an iron anvil; but stone anvils were the rule until a
comparatively late epoch, and the hammer-head as it rests upon the
sword is the more likely explanation – though, indeed, iron hammers
were also rare until Roman times. Iron was too holy and infrequent a
metal for common use by the Mycenaeans – not being extracted from
ore, but collected in the form of divinely-sent meteorites – and when
eventually iron weapons were imported into Greece from Tibarene on
the Black Sea, the smelting process and manufacture remained secret for
some time. Blacksmiths continued to be called 'bronze workers' even in
the Hellenistic period. But as soon as anyone might possess an iron
weapon or tool, the age of myth came to an end; if only because iron was
not included among the five metals sacred to the goddess and linked with
her calendar rites: namely, silver, gold, copper, tin, and lead (see 53. *2*).

5. Pelops's spear-sceptre, token of sovereignty, evidently belonged to
the ruling priestess; thus, according to Euripides, the spear with which
Oenomaus was killed – presumably the same instrument – was hidden

in Iphigeneia's bedroom; Clytaemnestra then claims to possess it (Sophocles: *Electra* 651); and Electra is said by Pausanias to have brought it to Phocis. The Greeks of Asia Minor were pleased to think that Orestes had founded the first Aeolian colony there: his name being one of their royal titles. They may have been relying on a tradition that concerned a new stage in the history of kingship: when the king's reign came to an end, he was now spared death and allowed to sacrifice a surrogate – an act of homicide that would account for Orestes's second exile – after which he might lead a colony overseas. The mythographers who explained that the Spartans preferred Orestes to Menelaus's sons because these were born of a slave-woman, did not realize that descent was still matrilinear. Orestes, as a Mycenaean, could reign by marriage to the Spartan heiress Hermione; her brothers must seek kingdoms elsewhere. In Argolis a princess could have free-born children by a slave; and there was nothing to prevent Electra's peasant husband at Mycenae from raising claimants for the throne.

6. The psalmist's tradition that 'the days of a man are three score and ten,' is founded not on observation, but on religious theory: seven was the number of holiness, and ten of perfection. Orestes similarly attained seventy years.

7. Anaxandrides's breach of the monogamic tradition may have been due to dynastic necessity; perhaps Aristo, his co-king, died too soon before the end of his reign to warrant a new coronation and, since he had ruled by virtue of his marriage to an heiress, Anaxandrides substituted for him both as king and husband.

8. Hittite records show that there was already an Achaean kingdom in Lesbos during the late fourteenth century B.C.


# 118

## THE BIRTH OF HERACLES

ELECTRYON, son of Perseus, High King of Mycenae and husband of Anaxo, marched vengefully against the Taphians and Teleboans. They had joined in a successful raid on his cattle, planned by one Pterelaus, a claimant to the Mycenaean throne; which had resulted in the death of Electryon's eight sons. While he was away, his nephew King Amphitryon of Troezen acted as regent. 'Rule well, and when I return victorious, you shall marry my daughter Alcmene,' Electryon cried in farewell. Amphitryon, informed by the King of Elis that the stolen cattle were now in his possession, paid the large ransom demanded, and recalled Electryon to identify them. Electryon, by no means pleased to learn that Amphitryon expected him to repay this ransom, asked harshly what right had the Eleans to sell stolen property, and why did Amphitryon condone in a fraud? Disdaining to reply, Amphitryon vented his annoyance by throwing a club at one of the cows which had strayed from the herd; it struck her horns, rebounded, and killed Electryon. Thereupon Amphitryon was banished from Argolis by his uncle Sthenelus; who seized Mycenae and Tiryns and entrusted the remainder of the country, with Midea for its capital, to Atreus and Thyestes, the sons of Pelops.[1]

*b*. Amphitryon, accompanied by Alcmene, fled to Thebes, where King Creon purified him and gave his sister Perimede in marriage to Electryon's only surviving son, Licymnius, a bastard borne by a Phrygian woman named Midea.[2] But the pious Alcmene would not lie with Amphitryon until he had avenged the death of her eight brothers. Creon therefore gave him permission to raise a Boeotian army for this purpose, on condition that he freed Thebes of the Teumessian vixen; which he did by borrowing the celebrated hound Laelaps from Cephalus the Athenian. Then, aided by Athenian, Phocian, Argive, and Locrian contingents, Amphitryon overcame the Teleboans and Taphians, and bestowed their islands on his allies, among them his uncle Heleius.

*c*. Meanwhile, Zeus, taking advantage of Amphitryon's absence, impersonated him and, assuring Alcmene that her brothers were now avenged – since Amphitryon had indeed gained the required victory that very morning – lay with her all one night, to which he gave the length of three.[3] For Hermes, at Zeus's command, had ordered Helius to quench the solar fires, have the Hours unyoke his team, and spend the following day at home; because the procreation of so great a champion as Zeus had in mind could not be accomplished in haste. Helius obeyed, grumbling about the good old times, when day was day, and night was night; and when Cronus, the then Almighty God, did not leave his lawful wife and go off to Thebes on love adventures. Hermes next ordered the Moon to go slowly, and Sleep to make mankind so drowsy that no one would notice what was happening.[4] Alcmene, wholly deceived, listened delightedly to Zeus's account of the crushing defeat inflicted on Pterelaus at Oechalia, and sported innocently with her supposed husband for the whole thirty-six hours. On the next day, when Amphitryon returned, eloquent of victory and of his passion for her, Alcmene did not welcome him to the marriage couch so rapturously as he had hoped. 'We never slept a wink last night,' she complained. 'And surely you do not expect me to listen twice to the story of your exploits?' Amphitryon, unable to understand these remarks, consulted the seer Teiresias, who told him that he had been cuckolded by Zeus; and thereafter he never dared sleep with Alcmene again, for fear of incurring divine jealousy.[5]

*d.* Nine months later, on Olympus, Zeus happened to boast that he had fathered a son, now at the point of birth, who would be called Heracles, which means 'Glory of Hera', and rule the noble House of Perseus. Hera thereupon made him promise that any prince born before nightfall to the House of Perseus should be High King. When Zeus swore an unbreakable oath to this effect, Hera went at once to Mycenae, where she hastened the pangs of Nicippe, wife of King Sthenelus. She then hurried to Thebes, and squatted cross-legged at Alcmene's door, with her clothing tied into knots, and her fingers locked together; by which means she delayed the birth of Heracles, until Eurystheus, son of Sthenelus, a seven-months child, already lay in his cradle. When Heracles appeared, one hour too late, he was found to have a twin named Iphicles, Amphitryon's son and the younger by a night. But some say that Heracles, not Iphicles, was the younger by a night; and others, that the twins were begotten on the same night, and born together, and that Father Zeus divinely illumined the birth chamber. At first, Heracles was called Alcaeus, or Palaemon.[6]

*e.* When Hera returned to Olympus, and calmly boasted of her success in keeping Eileithyia, goddess of childbirth, from Alcmene's door, Zeus fell into a towering rage; seizing his eldest daughter Ate, who had blinded him to Hera's deceit, he took a mighty oath that she should never visit Olympus again. Whirled around his head by her golden hair, Ate was sent hurtling down to earth. Though Zeus could not go back on his word and allow Heracles to rule the House of Perseus, he persuaded Hera to agree that, after performing whatever twelve labours Eurystheus might set him, his son should become a god.[7]

*f.* Now, unlike Zeus's former human loves, from Niobe onwards, Alcmene had been selected not so much for his pleasure – though she surpassed all other women of her day in beauty, stateliness, and wisdom – as with a view to begetting a son powerful enough to protect both gods and men against destruction. Alcmene, sixteenth in descent from the same Niobe, was the last mortal woman with whom Zeus lay, for he saw no prospect of begetting a hero to equal Heracles by any other; and he honoured Alcmene so highly that, instead of roughly violating her, he took pains to disguise himself as Amphitryon and woo her with affectionate words and caresses. He knew Alcmene to be incorruptible and when, at dawn, he presented her with a Carchesian goblet, she accepted it without question as spoil won in the victory: Telebus's legacy from his father Poseidon.[8]

*g*. Some say that Hera did not herself hinder Alcmene's travail, but sent witches to do so, and that Historis, daughter of Teiresias, deceived them by raising a cry of joy from the birth chamber – which is still shown at Thebes – so that they went away and allowed the child to be born. According to others, it was Eileithyia who hindered the travail on Hera's behalf, and a faithful handmaiden of Alcmene's, the yellow-haired Galanthis, or Galen, who left the birth chamber to announce, untruly, that Alcmene had been delivered. When Eileithyia sprang up in surprise, unclasping her fingers and uncrossing her knees, Heracles was born, and Galanthis laughed at the successful deception – which provoked Eileithyia to seize her by the hair and turn her into a weasel. Galanthis continued to frequent Alcmene's house, but was punished by Hera for having lied: she was condemned in perpetuity to bring forth her young through the mouth. When the Thebans pay Heracles' divine honours, they still offer preliminary sacrifices to Galanthis, who is also called Galinthias and described as Proetus's daughter; saying that she was Heracles's nurse and that he built her a sanctuary.[9]

*h*. This Theban account is derided by the Athenians. They hold that Galanthis was a harlot, turned weasel by Hecate in punishment for practising unnatural lust, who when Hera unduly prolonged Alcmene's labour, happened to run past and frighten her into delivery.[10]

*i*. Heracles's birthday is celebrated on the fourth day of every month; but some hold that he was born as the Sun entered the Tenth Sign; others that the Great Bear, swinging westward at midnight over Orion – which it does as the Sun quits the Twelfth Sign – looked down on him in his tenth month.[11]

1. Apollodorus: ii. 4. 5–6; Tzetzes: *On Lycophron* 932; Hesiod: *Shield of Heracles* 11 ff.
2. Apollodorus: *loc. cit.*
3. Hesiod: *Shield of Heracles* 1–56; Apollodorus: ii. 4. 7–8; Hyginus: *Fabula* 28; Tzetzes: *On Lycophron* 33 and 932; Pindar: *Isthmian Odes* vii. 5.

4. Lucian: *Dialogues of the Gods* x.
5. Hesiod: *Shield of Heracles* 1–56; Apollodorus: ii. 4. 7–8; Hyginus: *Fabula* 29; Tzetzes: *On Lycophron* 33 and 932; Pindar: *Isthmian Odes* vii. 5.
6. Hesiod: *Shield of Heracles* i. 35, 56, and 80; Homer: *Iliad* xix. 95; Apollodorus: ii. 4–5; Theocritus, quoted by scholiast on Pindar's *Nemean Odes* i. 36; Plautus: *Amphitryo* 1096; Diodorus Siculus: iv. 10; Tzetzes: *On Lycophron* 662.
7. Homer: *Iliad* xix. 119 ff. and 91; Diodorus Siculus: iv. 9 and 14.
8. Hesiod: *Shield of Heracles* 4 ff. and 26 ff.; Pherecydes, quoted by Athenaeus: xi. 7; Athenaeus: xi. 99; Plautus: *Amphitryo* 256 ff.
9. Pausanias: ix. 11. 1–2; Ovid: *Metamorphoses* ix. 285 ff.; Aelian: *Nature of Animals* xii. 5; Antoninus Liberalis: *Transformations* 29.
10. Aelian: *Nature of Animals* xv. 11; Antoninus Liberalis: *loc. cit.*
11. Philochorus: *Fragment* 177; Ovid: *Metamorphoses* ix. 285 ff.; Theocritus: *Idylls* xxiv. 11–12.

*

1. Alcmene ('strong in wrath') will have originally been a Mycenaean title of Hera, whose divine sovereignty Heracles ('glory of Hera') protected against the encroachments of her Achaean enemy Perseus ('destroyer'). The Achaeans eventually triumphed, and their descendants claimed Heracles as a member of the usurping House of Perseus. Hera's detestation of Heracles is likely to be a later invention; he was worshipped by the Dorians who overran Elis and there humbled the power of Hera.

2. Diodorus Siculus (iii. 73) writes of three heroes named Heracles: an Egyptian; a Cretan Dactyl; and the son of Alcmene. Cicero raises this number to six (*On the Nature of the Gods* iii. 16); Varro to forty-four (Servius on Virgil's *Aeneid* viii. 564). Herodotus (ii. 42) says that when he asked for Heracles's original home, the Egyptians referred him to Phoenicia. According to Diodorus Siculus (i. 17 and 24; iii. 73), the Egyptian Heracles, called Som, or Chon, lived ten thousand years before the Trojan War, and his Greek namesake inherited his exploits. The story of Heracles is, indeed, a peg on which a great number of related, unrelated, and contradictory myths have been hung. In the main, however, he represents the typical sacred king of early Hellenic Greece, consort of a tribal nymph, the Moon-goddess incarnate; his twin Iphicles acted as his tanist. This Moon-goddess has scores of names: Hera, Athene, Auge, Iole, Hebe, and so forth. On an early Roman bronze mirror Jupiter is shown celebrating a sacred marriage between 'Hercele' and 'Juno'; moreover, at Roman weddings the knot in the bride's girdle consecrated to Juno was called the 'Herculean knot', and the bridegroom had to untie it (Festus: 63). The Romans derived this tradition from the Etruscans, whose Juno was named 'Unial'. It may be assumed that the central

story of Heracles was an early variant of the Babylonian Gilgamesh epic – which reached Greece by way of Phoenicia. Gilgamesh has Enkidu for his beloved comrade, Heracles has Iolaus. Gilgamesh is undone by his love for the goddess Ishtar, Heracles by his love for Deianeira. Both are of divine parentage. Both harrow Hell. Both kill lions and overcome divine bulls; and when sailing to the Western Isle Heracles, like Gilgamesh, uses his garment for a sail (see 132. *c*). Heracles finds the magic herb of immortality (see 35. *b*) as Gilgamesh does, and is similarly connected with the progress of the sun around the Zodiac.

3. Zeus is made to impersonate Amphitryon because when the sacred king underwent a rebirth at his coronation, he became titularly a son of Zeus, and disclaimed his mortal parentage (see 74. *1*). Yet custom required the mortal tanist – rather than the divinely born king, the elder of the twins – to lead military expeditions; and the reversal of this rule in Heracles's case suggests that he was once the tanist, and Iphicles the sacred king. Theocritus certainly makes Heracles the younger of the twins, and Herodotus (ii. 43), who calls him a son of Amphitryon, surnames him 'Alcides' – after his grandfather Alcaeus, not 'Cronides' after his grandfather Cronus. Moreover, when Iphicles married Creon's youngest daughter, Heracles married an elder one; although in matrilinear society the youngest was commonly the heiress, as appears in all European folktales. According to Hesiod's *Shield of Heracles* (89 ff.), Iphicles humbled himself shamefully before Eurystheus; but the circumstances, which might throw light on this change of roles between the twins, are not explained. No such comradeship as existed between Castor and Polydeuces, or Idas and Lynceus, is recorded between Heracles and Iphicles. Heracles usurps his twin's functions and prerogatives, leaving him an ineffective and spiritless shadow who soon fades away, unmourned. Perhaps at Tiryns, the tanist usurped all the royal power, as sometimes happens in Asiatic states where a religious king rules jointly with a war-king, or Shogun.

4. Hera's method of delaying childbirth is still used by Nigerian witches; the more enlightened now reinforce the charm by concealing imported padlocks beneath their clothes.

5. The observation that weasels, if disturbed, carry their young from place to place in their mouths, like cats, gave rise to the legend of their viviparous birth. Apuleius's account of the horrid performance of Thessalian witches disguised as weasels, Hecate's attendants, and Pausanias's mention of human sacrifices offered to the Teumessian Vixen (see 89. *h*), recall Cerdo ('weasel' or 'vixen'), wife of Phoroneus, who is said to have introduced Hera's worship into the Peloponnese (see 57. *a*). The Theban cult of Galinthias is a relic of primitive Hera-worship, and when the witches delayed Heracles's birth they will have been disguised as

weasels. This myth is more than usually confused; though it appears that Zeus's Olympianism was resented by conservative religious opinion in Thebes and Argolis, and that the witches made a concerted attack on the House of Perseus.

6. To judge from Ovid's remark about the Tenth Sign, and from the story of the Erymanthian Boar, which presents Heracles as the Child Horus, he shared a midwinter birthday with Zeus, Apollo, and other calendar gods. The Theban year began at midwinter. If, as Theocritus says, Heracles was ten months old at the close of the twelfth, then Alcmene bore him at the spring equinox, when the Italians, Babylonians, and others, celebrated New Year. No wonder that Zeus is said to have illumined the birth chamber. The fourth day of the month will have been dedicated to Heracles because every fourth year was his, as founder of the Olympic Games.

# 119

## THE YOUTH OF HERACLES

ALCMENE, fearing Hera's jealousy, exposed her newly-born child in a field outside the walls of Thebes; and here, at Zeus's instigation, Athene took Hera for a casual stroll. 'Look, my dear! What a wonderfully robust child!' said Athene, pretending surprise as she stopped to pick him up. 'His mother must have been out of her mind to abandon him in a stony field! Come, you have milk. Give the poor little creature suck!' Thoughtlessly Hera took him and bared her breast, at which Heracles drew with such force that she flung him down in pain, and a spurt of milk flew across the sky and became the Milky Way. 'The young monster!' Hera cried. But Heracles was now immortal, and Athene returned him to Alcmene with a smile, telling her to guard and rear him well. The Thebans still show the place where this trick was played on Hera; it is called 'The Plain of Heracles'.[1]

b. Some, however, say that Hermes carried the infant Heracles to Olympus; that Zeus himself laid him at Hera's breast while she slept; and that the Milky Way was formed when she awoke and pushed him away, or when he greedily sucked more milk than his mouth would hold, and coughed it up. At all events, Hera was Heracles's foster-mother, if only for a short while; and the Thebans therefore style him her son, and say that he had been Alcaeus before she gave him suck, but was renamed in her honour.[2]

*c.* One evening, when Heracles had reached the age of eight or ten months or, as others say, one year, and was still unweaned, Alcmene having washed and suckled her twins, laid them to rest under a lamb-fleece coverlet, on the broad brazen shield which Amphitryon had won from Pterelaus. At midnight, Hera sent two prodigious azure-scaled serpents to Amphitryon's house, with strict orders to destroy Heracles. The gates opened as they approached; they glided through, and over the marble floors to the nursery – their eyes shooting flames, and poison dripping from their fangs.[3]

*d.* The twins awoke, to see the serpents writhed above them, with darting, forked tongues; for Zeus again divinely illumined the chamber. Iphicles screamed, kicked off the coverlet and, in an attempt to escape, rolled from the shield to the floor. His frightened cries, and the strange light shining under the nursery door, roused Alcmene. 'Up with you, Amphitryon!' she cried. Without waiting to put on his sandals, Amphitryon leaped from the cedar-wood bed, seized his sword which hung close by on the wall, and drew it from its polished sheath. At that moment the light in the nursery went out. Shouting to his drowsy slaves for lamps and torches, Amphitryon rushed in; and Heracles, who had not uttered so much as a whimper, proudly displayed the serpents, which he was in the act of strangling, one in either hand. As they died, he laughed, bounced joyfully up and down, and threw them at Amphitryon's feet.

*e.* While Alcmene comforted the terror-stricken Iphicles, Amphitryon spread the coverlet over Heracles again, and returned to bed. At dawn, when the cock had crowed three times, Alcmene summoned the aged Teiresias and told him of the prodigy. Teiresias, after foretelling Heracles's future glories, advised her to strew a broad hearth with dry faggots of gorse, thorn and brambles, and burn the serpents upon them at midnight. In the morning, a maid-servant must collect their ashes, take them to the rock where the Sphinx had perched, scatter them to the winds, and run away without looking back. On her return, the palace must be purged with fumes of sulphur and salted spring water; and its roof crowned with wild olive. Finally, a boar must be sacrificed at Zeus's high altar. All this Alcmene did. But some hold that the serpents were harmless, and placed in the cradle by Amphitryon himself; he had wished to discover which of the twins was his son, and now he knew well.[4]

*f.* When Heracles ceased to be a child, Amphitryon taught him how to drive a chariot, and how to turn corners without grazing the goal. Castor gave him fencing lessons, instructed him in weapon drill, in cavalry and infantry tactics, and in the rudiments of strategy. One of Hermes's sons became his boxing teacher – it was either Autolycus, or else Harpalycus, who had so grim a look when fighting that none dared face him. Eurytus taught him archery; or it may have been the Scythian Teutarus, one of Amphitryon's herdsmen, or even Apollo.[5] But Heracles surpassed all archers ever born, even his companion Alcon, father of Phalerus the Argonaut, who could shoot through a succession of rings set on the helmets of soldiers standing in file, and could cleave arrows held up on the points of swords or lances. Once, when Alcon's son was attacked by a serpent, which wound its coils about him, Alcon shot with such skill as to wound it mortally without hurting the boy.[6]

*g.* Eumolpus taught Heracles how to sing and play the lyre; while Linus, son of the River-god Ismenius, introduced him to the study of literature. Once, when Eumolpus was absent, Linus gave the lyre lessons as well; but Heracles, refusing to change the principles in which he had been grounded by Eumolpus, and being beaten for his stubbornness, killed Linus with a blow of the lyre.[7] At his trial for murder, Heracles quoted a law of Rhadamanthys, which justified forcible resistance to an aggressor, and thus secured his own acquittal. Nevertheless Amphitryon, fearing that the boy might commit further crimes of violence, sent him away to a cattle ranch, where he remained until his eighteenth year, outstripping his contemporaries in height, strength, and courage. Here he was chosen to be a laurel-bearer of Ismenian Apollo; and the Thebans still preserve the tripod which Amphitryon dedicated for him on this occasion. It is not known who taught Heracles astronomy and philosophy, yet he was learned in both these subjects.[8]

*h.* His height is usually given as four cubits. Since, however, he stepped out the Olympian stadium, making it six hundred feet long, and since later Greek stadia are also nominally six hundred feet long, but considerably shorter than the Olympic, the sage Pythagoras decided that the length of Heracles's stride, and consequently his stature, must have been in the same ratio to the stride and stature of other men, as the length of the Olympic stadium is to that of other stadia. This calculation made him four cubits and one foot high – yet some hold that he was not above average stature.[9]

*i.* Heracles's eyes flashed fire, and he had an unerring aim, both with javelin and arrow. He ate sparingly at noon; for supper his favourite food was roast meat and Doric barley-cakes, of which he ate sufficient (if that is credible) to have made a hired labourer grunt 'enough!' His tunic was short-skirted and neat; and he preferred a night under the stars to one spent indoors.[10] A profound knowledge of augury led him especially to welcome the appearance of vultures, whenever he was about to undertake a new Labour. 'Vultures', he would say, 'are the most righteous of birds: they do not attack even the smallest living creature.'[11]

*j.* Heracles claimed never to have picked a quarrel, but always to have given aggressors the same treatment as they intended for him. One Termerus used to kill travellers by challenging them to a butting match; Heracles's skull proved the stronger, and he crushed Termerus's head as though it had been an egg. Heracles was, however, naturally courteous, and the first mortal who freely yielded the enemy their dead for burial.[12]

1. Diodorus Siculus: iv. 9; Tzetzes: *On Lycophron* 1327; Pausanias: ix. 25. 2.
2. Eratosthenes: *Catasterismoi* 44; Hyginus: *Poetic Astronomy* ii. 43; Ptolemy Hephaestionos, quoted by Photius p. 477; Diodorus Siculus: iv. 10.
3. Apollodorus: ii. 4. 8; Theocritus: *Idylls* xxiv; Scholiast on Pindar's *Nemean Odes* i. 43.
4. Servius on Virgil's *Aeneid* viii. 288; Theocritus: *loc. cit.*; Pindar: *Nemean Odes* i. 35 ff.; Pherecydes, quoted by Apollodorus: ii. 4. 8.
5. Theocritus: *loc. cit.*; Apollodorus: ii. 4. 9; Tzetzes: *On Lycophron* 56; Diodorus Siculus: iv. 14.
6. Servius on Virgil's *Eclogues* v. 11; Valerius Flaccus: i. 399 ff.; Apollonius Rhodius: i. 97; Hyginus: *Fabula* 14.
7. Pausanias: ix. 29. 3; Theocritus: *loc. cit.*; Apollodorus: ii. 4. 9; Diodorus Siculus: iii. 67.
8. Apollodorus: *loc. cit.*; Diodorus Siculus: iv. 10; Pausanias: ix. 10. 4; Scholiast on Apollonius Rhodius: i. 865; Servius on Virgil's *Aeneid* i. 745.
9. Apollodorus: ii. 4. 9; Plutarch, quoted by Aulus Gellius: i. 1; Herodotus, quoted by Tzetzes: *On Lycophron* 662; Pindar: *Isthmian Odes* iv. 53.
10. Apollodorus: *loc. cit.*; Theocritus: *Idyll* xxiv; Plutarch: *Roman Questions* 28.
11. Plutarch: *Roman Questions* 93.

12. Plutarch: *Theseus* 11 and 29.

\*

1. According to another account, the Milky Way was formed when Rhea forcibly weaned Zeus (see 7. *b*). Hera's suckling of Heracles is a myth apparently based on the sacred king's ritual rebirth from the queen-mother (see 145. *3*).

2. An ancient icon on which the post-Homeric story of the strangled serpents is based, will have shown Heracles caressing them while they cleansed his ears with their tongues, as happened to Melampus (see 72. *c*), Teiresias (see 105. *g*), Cassandra (see 158. *p*), and probably the sons of Laocoön (see 167. *3*). Without this kindly attention he would have been unable to understand the language of vultures; and Hera, had she really wanted to kill Heracles, would have sent a Harpy to carry him off. The icon has been misread by Pindar, or his informant, as an allegory of the New Year Solar Child, who destroys the power of Winter, symbolized by the serpents. Alcmene's sacrifice of a boar to Zeus is the ancient midwinter one, surviving in the Christmas boar's head of Old England. Wild olive in Greece, like birch in Italy and North-western Europe, was the New Year tree, symbol of inception, and used as a besom to expel evil spirits (see 53. *7*); Heracles had a wild-olive tree for his club, and brought a sapling to Olympia from the land of the Hyperboreans (see 138. *j*). What Teiresias told Alcmene to light was the Candlemas bonfire, still lighted on 2 February in many parts of Europe: its object being to burn away the old scrub and encourage young shoots to grow.

3. The cake-eating Dorian Heracles, as opposed to his cultured Aeolian and Achaean predecessors, was a simple cattle-king, endowed with the limited virtues of his condition, but making no pretensions to music, philosophy, or astronomy. In Classical times, the mythographers, remembering the principle of *mens sana in corpore sano*, forced a higher education upon him, and interpreted his murder of Linus as a protest against tyranny, rather than against effeminacy. Yet he remained an embodiment of physical, not mental, health; except among the Celts (see 132. *3*), who honoured him as the patron of letters and all the bardic arts. They followed the tradition that Heracles, the Idaean Dactyl whom they called Ogmius, represented the first consonant of the Hyperborean tree-alphabet, Birch or Wild Olive (see 52. *3* and 125. *1*), and that 'on a switch of birch was cut the first message ever sent, namely Birch seven times repeated' (*White Goddess* p. 121).

4. Alcon's feat of shooting the serpent suggests an archery trial like that described in the fifteenth-century *Malleus Maleficarum*: when the candidate for initiation into the archers' guild was required to shoot at an object placed on his own son's cap – either an apple or a silver penny. The

brothers of Laodemeia, competing for the sacred kingship (see 163. *n*), were asked to shoot through a ring placed on a child's breast; but this myth must be misreported, since child-murder was not their object. It seems that the original task of a candidate for kingship had been to shoot through the coil of a golden serpent, symbolizing immortality, set on a head-dress worn by a royal child; and that in some tribes this custom was changed to the cleaving of an apple, and in others to the shooting between the recurved blades of a double axe, or through the crest-ring of a helmet; but later, as marksmanship improved, through either a row of helmet-rings, the test set Alcon; or a row of axe-blades, the test set Odysseus (see 171. *h*). Robin Hood's merry men, like the German archers, shot at silver pennies, because these were marked with a cross; the archer-guilds being defiantly anti-Christian.

5. Greek and Roman archers drew the bow-string back to the chest, as children shoot, and their effective range was so short that the javelin remained the chief missile weapon of the Roman armies until the sixth century A.D., when Belisarius armed his cataphracts with heavy bows, and taught them to draw the string back to the ear, in Scythian fashion. Heracles's accurate marksmanship is therefore accounted for by the legend that his tutor was Teutarus the Scythian – the name is apparently formed from *teutaein*, 'to practise assiduously', which the ordinary Greek archer does not seem to have done. It may be because of the Scythians' outstanding skill with the bow that they were described as Heracles's descendants: and he was said to have bequeathed a bow to Scythes, the only one of his sons who could bend it as he did (see 132. *v*).

# 120

## THE DAUGHTERS OF THESPIUS

IN his eighteenth year, Heracles left the cattle ranch and set out to destroy the lion of Cithaeron, which was havocking the herds of Amphitryon and his neighbour, King Thespius, also called Thestius, the Athenian Erechtheid. The lion had another lair on Mount Helicon, at the foot of which stands the city of Thespiae. Helicon has always been a gay mountain: the Thespians celebrate an ancient festival on its summit in honour of the Muses, and play amorous games at its foot around the statue of Eros, their patron.[1]

*b*. King Thespius had fifty daughters by his wife Megamede, daughter of Arneus, as gay as any in Thespiae. Fearing that they might make unsuitable matches, he determined that every one of them should have a child by Heracles, who was now engaged all day in hunting the lion; for Heracles lodged at Thespiae for fifty nights running. 'You may have my eldest daughter Procris as your bed-fellow,' Thespius told him hospitably. But each night another of his daughters visited Heracles, until he had laid with every one. Some say, however, that he enjoyed them all in a single night, except one, who declined his embraces and remained a virgin until her death, serving as his priestess in the shrine at Thespiae: for to this day the Thespian priestess is required to be chaste. But he had begotten fifty-one sons on her sisters: Procris, the eldest, bearing him the twins Antileon and Hippeus; and the youngest sister, another pair.[2]

*c.* Having at last tracked down the lion, and dispatched it with an untrimmed club cut from a wild-olive tree which he uprooted on Helicon, Heracles dressed himself in its pelt and wore the gaping jaws for a helmet. Some, however, say that he wore the pelt of the Nemean Lion; or of yet another beast, which he killed at Teumessus near Thebes; and that it was Alcathous who accounted for the lion of Cithaeron.[3]

1. Apollodorus: ii. 4. 8–9; Pausanias: ix. 26. 4; 27. 1 and 31. 1; Scholiast on Theocritus's *Idyll* xiii. 6.
2. Apollodorus: ii. 4. 10 and 7. 8; Pausanias: ix. 27. 5; Diodorus Siculus: iv. 29; Scholiast on Hesiod's *Theogony* 56.
3. Theocritus: *Idyll* xxv; Apollodorus: ii. 4. 10; Diodorus Siculus: iv. 11; Lactantius on Statius's *Thebaid* i. 355–485; Pausanias: i. 41. 4.

\*

1. Thespius's fifty daughters – like the fifty Danaids, Pallantids, and Nereids, or the fifty maidens with whom the Celtic god Bran (Phoroneus) lay in a single night – must have been a college of priestesses serving the Moon-goddess, to whom the lion-pelted sacred king had access once a year during their erotic orgies around the stone phallus called Eros ('erotic desire'). Their number corresponded with the lunations which fell between one Olympic Festival and the next. 'Thesius' is perhaps a masculinization of *thea hestia*, 'the goddess Hestia'; but Thespius ('divinely sounding') is not an impossible name, the Chief-priestess having an oracular function.

2. Hyginus (*Fabula* 162) mentions only twelve Thespiads, perhaps because this was the number of Latin Vestals who guarded the phallic Palladium and who seem to have celebrated a similar annual orgy on the Alban Hill, under the early Roman monarchy.

3. Both the youngest and the eldest of Thespius's daughters bore Heracles twins: namely, a sacred king and his tanist. The mythographers are confused here, trying to reconcile the earlier tradition that Heracles married the youngest daughter – matrilineal ultimogeniture – with the patrilineal rights of primogeniture. Heracles, in Classical legend, is a patrilineal figure; with the doubtful exception of Macaria (see 146. *b*), he begets no daughters at all. His virgin-priestess at Thespiae, like Apollo's Pythoness at Delphi, theoretically became his bride when the prophetic power overcame her, and could therefore be enjoyed by no mortal husband.

4. Pausanias, dissatisfied with the myth, writes that Heracles could neither have disgraced his host by this wholesale seduction of the Thespiads, nor dedicated a temple to himself – as though he were a god – so early in his career; and consequently refuses to identify the King of Thespiae with the Thespiads' father.

The killing of a lion was one of the marriage tasks imposed on the candidate for kingship (see 123. *1*).

5. Heracles cut his club from the wild-olive, the tree of the first month, traditionally used for the expulsion of evil spirits (see 52. *3*; 89. *7*; 119. *2*, etc.).

# 121

## ERGINUS

SOME years before these events, during Poseidon's festival at Onchestus, a trifling incident vexed the Thebans, whereupon Menoeceus's charioteer flung a stone which mortally wounded the Minyan King Clymenus. Clymenus was carried back, dying, to Orchomenus where, with his last breath, he charged his sons to avenge him. The eldest of these, Erginus, whose mother was the Boeotian princess Budeia, or Buzyge, mustered an army, marched against the Thebans, and utterly defeated them. By the terms of a treaty then confirmed with oaths, the Thebans would pay Erginus an annual tribute of one hundred cattle for twenty years in requital for Clymenus's death.[1]

*b*. Heracles, on his return from Helicon, fell in with the Minyan heralds as they went to collect the Theban tribute. When he inquired their business, they replied scornfully that they had come once more to remind the Thebans of Erginus's clemency in not lopping off the ears, nose, and hands of every man in the city. 'Does Erginus indeed hanker for such tribute?' Heracles asked angrily. Then he maimed the heralds in the very manner that they had described, and sent them back to Orchomenus, with their bloody extremities tied on cords about their necks.[2]

*c.* When Erginus instructed King Creon at Thebes to surrender the author of this outrage, he was willing enough to obey, because the Minyans had disarmed Thebes; nor could he hope for the friendly intervention of any neighbour, in so bad a cause. Yet Heracles persuaded his youthful comrades to strike a blow for freedom. Making a round of the city temples, he tore down all the shields, helmets, breastplates, greaves, swords, and spears, which had been dedicated there as spoils; and Athene, greatly admiring such resolution, girded these on him and on his friends. Thus Heracles armed every Theban of fighting age, taught them the use of their weapons, and himself assumed command. An oracle promised him victory if the noblest-born person in Thebes would take his own life. All eyes turned expectantly towards Antipoenus, a descendant of the Sown Men; but, when he grudged dying for the common good, his daughters Androcleia and Alcis gladly did so in his stead, and were afterwards honoured as heroines in the Temple of Famous Artemis.[3]

*d.* Presently, the Minyans marched against Thebes, but Heracles ambushed them in a narrow pass, killing Erginus and the greater number of his captains. This victory, won almost single-handed, he exploited by making a sudden descent on Orchomenus, where he battered down the gates, sacked the palace, and compelled the Minyans to pay a double tribute to Thebes. Heracles had also blocked up the two large tunnels built by the Minyans of old, through which the river Cephissus emptied into the sea; thus flooding the rich cornlands of the Copaic Plain.[4] His object was to immobilize the cavalry of the Minyans, their most formidable arm, and carry war into the hills, where he could meet them on equal terms; but, being a friend of all mankind, he later unblocked these tunnels. The shrine of Heracles the Horsebinder at Thebes commemorates an incident in this campaign: Heracles came by night into the Minyan camp and, after stealing the chariot horses, which he bound to trees a long way off, put the sleeping men to the sword. Unfortunately, Amphitryon, his foster-father, was killed in the fighting.[5]

*e.* On his return to Thebes, Heracles dedicated an altar to Zeus the

Preserver; a stone lion to Famous Artemis; and two stone images to Athene the Girder-on-of-Arms. Since the gods had not punished Heracles for his ill-treatment of Erginus's heralds, the Thebans dared to honour him with a statue, called Heracles the Nose-docker.[6]

*f.* According to another account, Erginus survived the Minyan defeat and was one of the Argonauts who brought back the Golden Fleece from Colchis. After many years spent in recovering his former prosperity, he found himself rich indeed, but old and childless. An oracle advising him to put a new shoe on the battered plough coulter, he married a young wife, who bore him Trophonius and Agamedes, the renowned architects, and Azeus too.[7]

1. Apollodorus: ii. 4. 11; Pausanias: ix. 37. 1–2; Eustathius on Homer p. 1076; Scholiast on Apollonius Rhodius: i. 185.
2. Diodorus Siculus: iv. 10.
3. Diodorus Siculus: *loc. cit.*; Apollodorus: ii. 4. 11; Pausanias: ix. 17. 1.
4. Euripides: *Heracles* 220; Diodorus Siculus: *loc. cit.*; Pausanias: ix. 38. 5; Strabo: ix. 11. 40.
5. Polyaenus: i. 3. 5; Diodorus Siculus: iv. 18. 7; Pausanias: ix. 26. 1; Apollodorus: ii. 4. 11.
6. Euripides: *Heracles* 48–59; Pausanias: ix. 17. 1–2 and 25. 4.
7. Pausanias: ix. 37. 2–3 and 25. 4; Eustathius on Homer p. 272.

\*

1. Heracles's treatment of the Minyan heralds is so vile – a herald's person being universally held sacrosanct, with whatever insolence he might behave – that he must here represent the Dorian conquerors of 1050 B.C., who disregarded all civilized conventions.

2. According to Strabo (ix. 2. 18), certain natural limestone channels which drained the waters of the Cephissus were sometimes blocked and at other times freed by earthquakes; but eventually the whole Copaic Plain became a marsh, despite the two huge tunnels which had been cut by the Bronze Age Minyans – Minoanized Pelasgians – to make the natural channels more effective. Sir James Frazer, who visited the Plain about fifty years ago, found that three of the channels had been artificially blocked with stones in ancient times, perhaps by the Thebans who destroyed Orchomenus in 368 B.C., put all the male inhabitants to the sword, and sold the women into slavery (Pausanias: ix. 15. 3). Recently a British company has drained the marshland and restored the plain to agriculture.

3. When the city of Thebes was in danger (see 105. *i* and 106. *j*), the Theban Oracle frequently demanded a royal *pharmacos*; but only in a fully patriarchal society would Androcleia and Alcis have leaped to death.

Their names, like those of Erechtheus's daughters, said to have been sacrificed in the same way (see 47. d), seem to be titles of Demeter and Persephone, who demanded male sacrifices. It looks as if two priestesses 'paid the penalty instead of' the sacred king – thereafter renamed Antipoenus – who refused to follow Menoeceus's example. In this sense the Sphinx leaped from the cliff and dashed herself to pieces (see 105. 6).

4. 'Heracles the Horse-binder' may refer to his capture of Diomedes's wild mares, and all that this feat implied (see 130. 1).

5. Athene Girder-on-of-Arms was the earlier Athene, who distributed arms to her chosen sons; in Celtic and German myths, the giving of arms is a matriarchal prerogative, properly exercised at a sacred marriage (see 95. 5).

# 122

## THE MADNESS OF HERACLES

HERACLES'S defeat of the Minyans made him the most famous of heroes; and his reward was to marry King Creon's eldest daughter Megara, or Megera, and be appointed protector of the city; while Iphicles married the youngest daughter. Some say that Heracles had two sons by Megara; others that he had three, four, or even eight. They are known as the Alcaids.[1]

b. Heracles next vanquished Pyraechmus, King of the Euboeans, an ally of the Minyans, when he marched against Thebes; and created terror throughout Greece by ordering his body to be torn in two by colts and exposed unburied beside the river Heracleius, at a place called the Colts of Pyraechmus, which gives out a neighing echo whenever horses drink there.[2]

c. Hera, vexed by Heracles's excesses, drove him mad. He first attacked his beloved nephew Iolaus, Iphicles's eldest son, who managed to escape his wild lunges; and then, mistaking six of his own children for enemies, shot them down, and flung their bodies into a fire, together with two other sons of Iphicles, by whose side they were performing martial exercises. The Thebans celebrate an annual festival in honour of these eight mail-clad victims. On the first day, sacrifices are offered and fires burn all night; on the second, funeral games are held and the winner is crowned with white myrtle. The celebrants grieve in memory of the brilliant futures that had been planned for Heracles's sons. One was to have ruled Argos, occupying Eurystheus's palace, and Heracles had thrown his lion pelt over his shoulders; another was to have been king of Thebes, and in his right hand Heracles had set the mace of defence, Daedalus's deceitful gift; a third was promised Oechalia, which Heracles afterwards laid waste; and the choicest brides had been chosen for them all – alliances with Athens, Thebes, and Sparta. So dearly did Heracles love these sons that many deny now his guilt, preferring to believe that they were treacherously slain by his guests: by Lycus, perhaps, or as Socrates has suggested, by Augeias.[3]

*d.* When Heracles recovered his sanity, he shut himself up in a dark chamber for some days, avoiding all human intercourse and then, after purification by King Thespius, went to Delphi, to inquire what he should do. The Pythoness, addressing him for the first time as Heracles, rather than Palaemon, advised him to reside at Tiryns; to serve Eurystheus for twelve years; and to perform whatever Labours might be set him, in payment for which he would be rewarded with immortality. At this, Heracles fell into deep despair, loathing to serve a man whom he knew to be far inferior to himself, yet afraid to oppose his father Zeus. Many friends came to solace him in his distress; and, finally, when the passage of time had somewhat alleviated his pain, he placed himself at Eurystheus's disposal.[4]

*e.* Some, however, hold that it was not until his return from Tartarus that Heracles went mad and killed the children; that he killed Megara too; and that the Pythoness then told him: 'You shall no longer be called Palaemon! Phoebus Apollo names you Heracles, since from Hera you shall have undying fame among men!' – as though he had done Hera a great service. Others say that Heracles was Eurystheus's lover, and performed the Twelve Labours for his gratification; others again, that he undertook to perform them only if Eurystheus would annul the sentence of banishment passed on Amphitryon.[5]

*f.* It has been said that when Heracles set forth on his Labours, Hermes gave him a sword, Apollo a bow and smooth-shafted arrows, feathered with eagle feathers; Hephaestus a golden breast-plate; and Athene a robe. Or that Athene gave him the breast-plate, but Hephaestus bronze greaves and an adamantine helmet. Athene and Hephaestus, it is added, vied with one another throughout in benefiting Heracles: she gave him enjoyment of peaceful pleasures; he, protection from the dangers of war. The gift of Poseidon was a team of horses; that of Zeus a magnificent and unbreakable shield. Many were the stories worked on this shield in enamel, ivory, electrum, gold, and lapis lazuli; moreover, twelve serpents' heads carved about the boss clashed their jaws whenever Heracles went into battle, and terrified his opponents.[6] The truth, however, is that Heracles scorned armour and, after his first Labour, seldom carried even a spear, relying rather on his club, bow and arrows. He had little use for the bronze-tipped club which Hephaestus gave him, preferring to cut his own from wild-olive: first on Helicon, next at Nemea. This second club he later replaced with a third, also cut from wild-olive, by the shores of the Saronic Sea: the club which, on his visit to Troezen, he leaned against the image of Hermes. It struck root, sprouted, and is now a stately tree.[7]

*g.* His nephew Iolaus shared in the Labours as his charioteer, or shield-bearer.[8]

1. Scholiast on Pindar's *Isthmian Odes* iv. 114 and 61; Apollodorus: ii. 4. 11; Diodorus Siculus: iv. 10; Hyginus: *Fabula* 31; Tzetzes: *On Lycophron* 38.
2. Plutarch: *Parallel Stories* 7.
3. Diodorus Siculus: iv. 11; Apollodorus: ii. 4. 12; Pindar: *loc. cit.*; Euripides: *Heracles* 462 ff.; Lysimachus, quoted by scholiast on Pindar's *Isthmian Odes* iv. 114.
4. Diodorus Siculus: iv. 10–11; Apollodorus: *loc. cit.*
5. Euripides: *Heracles* 1 ff. and 1000 ff.; Tzetzes: *On Lycophron* 38 and 662–3; Diotimus: *Heraclea*, quoted by Athenaeus xiii. 8.
6. Apollodorus: ii. 4. 11; Hesiod: *Shield of Heracles* 122 ff., 141 ff., 161 ff., and 318–19; Pausanias: v. 8. 1.
7. Euripides: *Heracles* 159 ff.; Apollonius Rhodius: i. 1196; Diodorus Siculus: iv. 14; Theocritus: *Idyll* xxv; Apollodorus: ii. 4. 11; Pausanias: ii. 31. 13.
8. Plutarch: *On Love* 17; Pausanias: v. 8. 1 and 17. 4; Euripides: *Children of Heracles* 216.

*

1. Madness was the Classical Greek excuse for child-sacrifice (see 27. *e* and 70. *g*); the truth being that the sacred king's boy-surrogates (see 42. *2*; 81. *8*; and 156. *2*) were burned alive after he had lain hidden for twenty-four hours in a tomb, shamming death, and then reappeared to claim the throne once more.

2. The death of Pyraechmus, torn in two by wild horses, is a familiar one (see 71. *1*). Heracles's title Palaemon identifies him with Melicertes of Corinth, who was deified under that name; Melicertes is Melkarth, the Lord of the City, the Tyrian Heracles. The eight Alcaids seem to have

been members of a sword-dancing team whose performance, like that of the eight morris-dancers in the English Christmas Play, ended in the victim's resurrection. Myrtle was the tree of the thirteenth twenty-eight-day month, and symbolized departure; wild-olive, the tree of the first month, symbolized inception (see 119. *2*). Electryon's eight sons (see 118. *a*), may have formed a similar team at Mycenae.

3. Heracles's homosexual relations with Hylas, Iolaus, and Eurystheus, and the accounts of his luxurious armour, are meant to justify Theban military custom. In the original myth, he will have loved Eurystheus's daughter, not Eurystheus himself. His twelve Labours, Servius points out, were eventually equated with the Twelve Signs of the Zodiac; although Homer and Hesiod do not say that there were twelve of them, nor does the sequence of Labours correspond with that of the Signs. Like the Celtic God of the Year, celebrated in the Irish *Song of Amergin*, the Pelasgian Heracles seems to have made a progress through a thirteen-month year. In Irish and Welsh myth the successive emblems were: stag, or bull; flood; wind; dewdrop; hawk; flower; bonfire; spear; salmon; hill; boar; breaker; sea-serpent. But Gilgamesh's adventures in the Babylonian Gilgamesh epic are related to the signs of the Zodiac, and the Tyrian Heracles had much in common with him. Despite Homer and Hesiod, the scenes pictured on ancient shields seem not to have been dazzling works of art, but rough pictograms, indicative of the owner's origin and rank, scratched on the spiral band which plated each shield.

4. The occasion on which the twelve Olympians heaped gifts on Heracles was doubtless his sacred marriage, and they will have all been presented to him by his priestess-bride – Athene, Auge, Iole, or whatever her name happened to be – either directly, or by the hands of attendants (see 81. *l*). Here Heracles was being armed for his Labours, that is to say, for his ritual combats and magical feats.

# 123

## THE FIRST LABOUR: THE NEMEAN LION

THE First Labour which Eurystheus imposed on Heracles, when he came to reside at Tiryns, was to kill and flay the Nemaen, or Cleonaean lion, an enormous beast with a pelt proof against iron, bronze, and stone.[1]

*b.* Although some call this lion the offspring of Typhon, or of the Chimaera and the Dog Orthrus, others say that Selene bore it with a fearful shudder and dropped it to earth on Mount Tretus near Nemea, beside a two-mouthed cave; and that, in punishment for an unfulfilled sacrifice, she set it to prey upon her own people, the chief sufferers being the Bambinaeans.[2]

*c.* Still others say that, at Hera's desire, Selene created the lion from sea foam enclosed in a large ark; and that Iris, binding it with her girdle, carried it to the Nemean mountains. These were named after a daughter of Asopus, or of Zeus and Selene; and the lion's cave is still shown about two miles from the city of Nemea.[3]

*d.* Arriving at Cleonae, between Corinth and Argos, Heracles lodged in the house of a day-labourer, or shepherd, named Molorchus, whose son the lion had killed. When Molorchus was about to offer a ram in propitiation of Hera, Heracles restrained him. 'Wait thirty days,' he said. 'If I return safely, sacrifice to Saviour Zeus; if I do not, sacrifice to me as a hero!'

*e.* Heracles reached Nemea at midday, but since the lion had depopulated the neighbourhood, he found no one to direct him; nor were any tracks to be seen. Having first searched Mount Apesas – so called after Apesantus, a shepherd whom the lion had killed; though some say that Apesantus was a son of Acrisius, who died of a snake-bite in his heel – Heracles visited Mount Tretus, and presently descried the lion coming back to its lair, bespattered with blood from the day's slaughter.[4] He shot a flight of arrows at it, but they rebounded harmlessly from the thick pelt, and the lion licked its chops, yawning. Next, he used his sword, which bent as though made of lead; finally he heaved up his club and dealt the lion such a blow on the muzzle that it entered its double-mouthed cave, shaking its head – not for pain, however, but because of the singing in its ears. Heracles, with a rueful glance at his shattered club, then netted one entrance of the cave, and went in by the other. Aware now that the monster was proof against all weapons, he began to wrestle with it. The lion bit off one of his fingers; but, holding its head in chancery, Heracles squeezed hard until it choked to death.[5]

*f.* Carrying the carcass on his shoulders, Heracles returned to Cleonae, where he arrived on the thirtieth day, and found Molorchus on the point of offering him a heroic sacrifice; instead, they sacrificed together to Saviour Zeus. When this had been done, Heracles cut himself a new club and, after making several alterations in the Nemean Games hitherto celebrated in honour of Opheltes, and rededicating them to Zeus, took the lion's carcass to Mycenae. Eurystheus, amazed and terrified, forbade him ever again to enter the city; in future he was to display the fruits of his Labours outside the gates.[6]

g. For a while, Heracles was at a loss how to flay the lion, until, by divine inspiration, he thought of employing its own razor-sharp claws, and soon could wear the invulnerable pelt as armour, and the head as a helmet. Meanwhile, Eurystheus ordered his smiths to forge him a brazen urn, which he buried beneath the earth. Henceforth, whenever the approach of Heracles was signalled, he took refuge in it and sent his orders by a herald – a son of Pelops, named Copreus, whom he had purified for murder.[7]

h. The honours received by Heracles from the city of Nemea in recognition of this feat, he later ceded to his devoted allies of Cleonae, who fought at his side in the Elean War, and fell to the number of three hundred and sixty. As for Molorchus, he founded the near-by city of Molorchia, and planted the Nemean Wood, where the Nemean Games are now held.[8]

i. Heracles was not the only man to strangle a lion in those days. The same feat was accomplished by his friend Phylius as the first of three love-tasks imposed on him by Cycnus, a son of Apollo by Hyria. Phylius had also to catch alive several monstrous man-eating birds, not unlike vultures, and after wrestling with a fierce bull, lead it to the altar of Zeus. When all three tasks had been accomplished, Cycnus further demanded an ox which Phylius had won as a prize at certain funeral games. Heracles advised Phylius to refuse this and press for a settlement of his claim with Cycnus who, in desperation, leaped into a lake; thereafter called the Cycnean lake. His mother Hyria followed him to his death, and both were transformed into swans.[9]

1. Apollodorus: ii. 5. 1; Valerius Flaccus: i. 34; Diodorus Siculus: iv. 11.

2. Apollodorus: *loc. cit.*; Hesiod: *Theogony* 326 ff.; Epimenides: *Fragment* 5, quoted by Aelian: *Nature of Animals* xii. 7; Plutarch: *On the Face Appearing in the Orb of the Moon* 24; Servius on Virgil's *Aeneid* viii. 295; Hyginus: *Fabula* 30; Theocritus: *Idyll* xxv. 200 ff.

3. Demodocus: *History of Heracles* i, quoted by Plutarch: *On Rivers* 18; Pausanias: ii. 15. 2–3; Scholiast on the *Hypothesis* of Pindar's *Nemean Odes*.

4. Strabo: viii. 6. 19; Apollodorus: ii. 5. 1; Servius on Virgil's *Georgics* iii. 19; Lactantius on Statius's *Thebaid* iv. 161; Plutarch: *loc. cit.*; Theocritus: *Idyll* xxv. 211 ff.

5. Bacchylides: xiii. 53; Theocritus: *loc. cit.*; Ptolemy Hephaes-

tionos: ii., quoted by Photius p. 474; Apollodorus: *loc. cit.*; Diodorus Siculus: iv. 11; Euripides: *Heracles* 153.

6. Apollodorus: *loc. cit.* and ii. 4. 11; Scholiast on the *Hypothesis* of
Pindar's *Nemean Odes*.

7. Theocritus: *Idyll* xxv. 272 ff.; Diodorus Siculus: iv. 11; Euripides:
*Heracles* 359 ff.; Apollodorus: *loc. cit.*

8. Aelian: *Varia Historia* iv. 5; Stephanus of Byzantium *sub* Molorchia; Virgil: *Georgics* iii. 19; Servius: *ad loc.*

9. Antoninus Liberalis: *Transformations* 12; Ovid: *Metamorphoses*
vii. 371 ff.

\*

1. The sacred king's ritual combat with wild beasts formed a regular
part of the coronation ritual in Greece, Asia Minor, Babylonia, and
Syria; each beast representing one season of the year. Their number
varied with the calendar: in a three-seasoned year, they consisted, like the
Chimaera, of lion, goat, and serpent (see 75. *2*) – hence the statement that
the lion of Cithaeron was the Chimaera's child by Orthrus the Dog-star
(see 34. *3*); or of bull, lion, and serpent, which were Dionysus's seasonal
changes (see 27. *4*), according to Euripides's *Bacchae*; or of lion, horse, and
dog, like Hecate's heads (see 31. *7*). But in a four-seasoned year, they will
have been bull, ram, lion, and serpent, like the heads of Phanes (see 2. *b*)
described in *Orphic Fragment* 63; or bull, lion, eagle, and seraph, as in
Ezekiel's vision (*Ezekiel* i); or, more simply, bull, lion, scorpion, and
water-snake, the four Signs of the Zodiac which fell at the equinoxes
and solstices. These last four appear, from the First, Fourth, Seventh, and
Eleventh Labours, to be the beasts which Heracles fought; though the
boar has displaced the scorpion – the scorpion being retained only in the
story of Orion, another Heracles, who was offered a princess in marriage
if he killed certain wild beasts (see 41. *a–d*). The same situation recurs in
the story of Cycnus and Phylius – with its unusual substitution of vultures
for the serpent – though Ovid and Antoninus Liberalis have given it a
homosexual twist. Theoretically, by taming these beasts, the king obtained dominion over the seasons of the year ruled by them. At Thebes,
Heracles's native city, the Sphinx-goddess ruled a two-seasoned year;
she was a winged lioness with a serpent's tail (see 105. *3*); hence, he
wore a lion pelt and mask, rather than a bull mask like Minos (see
98. *2*). The lion was shown with the other calendar beasts in the new-
moon ark, an icon which, it seems, gave rise both to the story of Noah
and the Flood, and to that of Dionysus and the pirates (see 27. *5*); hence
Selene ('the Moon') is said to have created it.

2. Photius denies that Heracles lost his finger in fighting the lion;
Ptolemy Hephaestionos says (*Nova Historia* ii), that he was poisoned by a

sting-ray (see 171. 3). But it is more probable that he bit it off to placate the ghosts of his children – as Orestes did when pursued by his mother's Erinnyes. Another two-mouthed cave is mentioned incidentally in *Odyssey* xiii. 103 ff., as one near which Odysseus first slept on his return to Ithaca at the head of the Bay of Phorcys. Its northern entrance was for men, the southern for gods; and it contained two-handled jars used as hives, stone basins, and plentiful spring-water. There were also stone looms – stalactites? – on which the Naiads wove purple garments. If Porphyry (*On the Cave of the Nymphs*) was right in making this a cave where rites of death and divine rebirth were practised, the basins served for blood and the springs for lustration. The jars would then be burial urns over which souls hovered like bees (see 90. 3), and the Naiads (daughters of the Death-god Phorcys, or Orcus) would be Fates weaving garments with royal clan-marks for the reborn to wear (see 10. 1). The Nemean Lion's cave is two-mouthed because this First Labour initiated Heracles's passage towards his ritual death, after which he becomes immortal and marries the goddess Hebe.

3. The death of three hundred and sixty Cleonaeans suggests a calendar mystery – this being the number of days in the sacred Egyptian year, exclusive of the five set apart in honour of Osiris, Isis, Nephthys, Set, and Horus. Heracles's modifications of the Nemean Games may have involved a change in the local calendar.

4. If the King of Mycenae, like Orion's enemy Oenopion of Hyria (see 41. c), took refuge in a bronze urn underground and emerged only after the danger had passed, he will have made an annual pretence at dying, while his surrogate reigned for a day, and then reappeared. Heracles's children were among such surrogates (see 122. 1).

5. Apesantus was one of several early heroes bitten in the heel by a viper (see 177. 1). He may be identified with Opheltes (see 106. g) of Nemea, though what part of Opheltes's body the serpent bit is not related.

# 124

## THE SECOND LABOUR: THE LERNAEAN HYDRA

THE Second Labour ordered by Eurystheus was the destruction of the Lernaean Hydra, a monster born to Typhon and Echidne, and reared by Hera as a menace to Heracles.[1]

b. Lerna stands beside the sea, some five miles from the city of Argos. To the west rises Mount Pontinus, with its sacred grove of plane-trees stretching down to the sea. In this grove, bounded on one flank by the river Pontinus – beside which Danaus dedicated a shrine to Athene – and on the other by the river Amymone, stand images of Demeter, Dionysus the Saviour, and Prosymne, one of Hera's nurses; and, on the shore, a stone image of Aphrodite, dedicated by the Danaids. Every year, secret nocturnal rites are held at Lerna in honour of Dionysus, who descended to Tartarus at this point when he went to fetch Semele; and, not far off, the Mysteries of Lernaean Demeter are celebrated in an enclosure which marks the place where Hades and Persephone also descended to Tartarus.[2]

*c.* This fertile and holy district was once terrorized by the Hydra, which had its lair beneath a plane-tree at the sevenfold source of the river Amymone and haunted the unfathomable Lernaean swamp near by – the Emperor Nero recently tried to sound it, and failed – the grave of many an incautious traveller.[3] The Hydra had a prodigious dog-like body, and eight or nine snaky heads, one of them immortal; but some credit it with fifty, or one hundred, or even ten thousand heads. At all events, it was so venomous that its very breath, or the smell of its tracks, could destroy life.[4]

*d.* Athene had pondered how Heracles might best kill this monster and, when he reached Lerna, driven there in his chariot by Iolaus, she pointed out the Hydra's lair to him. On her advice, he forced the Hydra to emerge by pelting it with burning arrows, and then held his breath while he caught hold of it. But the monster twined around his feet, in an endeavour to trip him up. In vain did he batter at its heads with his club: no sooner was one crushed, than two or three more grew in its place.[5]

*e.* An enormous crab scuttered from the swamp to aid the Hydra, and nipped Heracles's foot; furiously crushing its shell, he shouted to Iolaus for assistance. Iolaus set one corner of the grove alight and then, to prevent the Hydra from sprouting new heads, seared their roots with blazing branches; thus the flow of blood was checked.[6]

*f.* Now using a sword, or a golden falchion, Heracles severed the immortal head, part of which was of gold, and buried it, still hissing, under a heavy rock beside the road to Elaeus. The carcass he disembowelled, and dipped his arrows in the gall. Henceforth, the least wound from one of them was invariably fatal.

*g.* In reward for the crab's services, Hera set its image among the twelve signs of the Zodiac; and Eurystheus would not count this

Labour as duly accomplished, because Iolaus had supplied the fire-brands.[7]

1. Hesiod: *Theogony* 313 ff.
2. Pausanias: ii. 37. 1–3 and 5; ii. 36. 6–8.
3. Pausanias: ii. 37. 4; Apollodorus: ii. 5. 2; Strabo: viii. 6. 8.
4. Euripides: *Heracles* 419–20; Zenobius: *Proverbs* vi. 26; Apollodorus: *loc. cit.*; Simonides, quoted by scholiast on Hesiod's *Theogony* p. 257, ed. Heinsius; Diodorus Siculus: iv. 11; Hyginus: *Fabula* 30.
5. Hesiod: *Theogony* 313 ff.; Apollodorus: *loc. cit.*; Hyginus: *loc. cit.*; Servius on Virgil's *Aeneid* vi. 287.
6. Apollodorus: *loc. cit.*; Hyginus: *loc. cit.* and *Poetic Astronomy* ii. 23; Diodorus Siculus: iv. 11.
7. Euripides: *Ion* 192; Hesiod: *Theogony* 313 ff.; Apollodorus: *loc. cit.*; Alexander Myndius, quoted by Photius p. 475.

\*

1. The Lernaean Hydra puzzled the Classical mythographers. Pausanias held that it might well have been a huge and venomous water-snake; but that 'Pisander had first called it many-headed, wishing to make it seem more terrifying and, at the same time, add to the dignity of his own verses' (Pausanias: ii. 37. 4). According to the euhemeristic Servius (on Virgil's *Aeneid* vi. 287), the Hydra was a source of underground rivers which used to burst out and inundate the land: if one of its numerous channels were blocked, the water broke through elsewhere, therefore Heracles first used fire to dry the ground, and then closed the channels.

2. In the earliest version of this myth, Heracles, as the aspirant for kingship, is likely to have wrestled in turn with a bull, a lion, a boar, or scorpion, and then dived into a lake to win gold from the water-monster living in its depth. Jason was set much the same tasks, and the helpful part played by Medea is here given to Athene – as Heracles's bride-to-be. Though the Hydra recalls the sea-serpent which Perseus killed with a golden falchion, or new-moon sickle, it was a fresh-water monster, like most of those mentioned by Irish and Welsh mythographers – *piastres* or *avancs* (see 148. 5) – and like the one recorded in the Homeric epithet for Lacedaemon, namely *cetoessa*, 'of the water-monster', doubtless haunting some deep pool of the Eurotas (see 125. 3). The dog-like body is a reminiscence of the sea-monster Scylla (see 16. 2), and of a seven-headed monster (on a late Babylonian cylinder-seal) which the hero Gilgamesh kills. Astrologers have brought the crab into the story so as to make Heracles's Twelve Labours correspond with the Signs of the Zodiac; but it should properly have figured in his struggle with the Nemean lion, the next Sign.

3. This ritual myth has become attached to that of the Danaids, who

were the ancient water-priestesses of Lerna. The number of heads given the Hydra varies intelligibly: as a college of priestesses it had fifty heads; as the sacred cuttle-fish, a disguise adopted by Thetis – who also had a college of fifty priestesses (see 81. *1*) – it had eight snaky arms ending in heads, and one head on its trunk, together making nine in honour of the Moon-goddess; one hundred heads suggest the *centuriae*, or war bands, which raided Argos from Lerna; and ten thousand is a typical embellishment by Euripides, who had little conscience as a mythographer. On Greek coins, the Hydra usually has seven heads: doubtless a reference to the seven outlets of the river Amymone.

4. Heracles's destruction of the Hydra seems to record a historical event: the attempted suppression of the Lernaean fertility rites. But new priestesses always appeared in the plane-tree grove – the plane-tree suggests Cretan religious influence, as does the cuttle-fish – until the Achaeans, or perhaps the Dorians, burned it down. Originally, it is clear, Demeter formed a triad with Hecate as Crone, here called Prosymne, 'addressed with hymns', and Persephone the Maiden; but Dionysus's Semele (see 27. *k*) ousted Persephone. There was a separate cult of Aphrodite – Thetis by the seaside.

# 125

## THE THIRD LABOUR: THE CERYNEIAN HIND

HERACLES's Third Labour was to capture the Ceryneian Hind, and bring her alive from Oenoe to Mycenae. The swift, dappled creature had brazen hooves and golden horns like a stag, so that some call her a stag.[1] She was sacred to Artemis who, when only a child, saw five hinds, larger than bulls, grazing on the banks of the dark-pebbled Thessalian river Anaurus at the foot of the Parrhasian Mountains; the sun twinkled on their horns. Running in pursuit, she caught four of them, one after the other, with her own hands, and harnessed them to her chariot; the fifth fled across the river Celadon to the Ceryneian Hill – as Hera intended, already having Heracles's Labours in mind. According to another account, this hind was a masterless monster which used to ravage the fields, and which Heracles, after a severe struggle, sacrificed to Artemis on the summit of Mount Artemisium.[2]

b. Loth either to kill or wound the hind, Heracles performed this Labour without exerting the least force. He hunted her tirelessly for one whole year, his chase taking him as far as Istria and the Land of the

Hyperboreans. When, exhausted at last, she took refuge on Mount Artemisium, and thence descended to the river Ladon, Heracles let fly and pinned her forelegs together with an arrow, which passed between bone and sinew, drawing no blood. He then caught her, laid her across his shoulders, and hastened through Arcadia to Mycenae. Some, however, say that he used nets; or followed the hind's track until he found her asleep underneath a tree. Artemis came to meet Heracles, rebuking him for having ill-used her holy beast, but he pleaded necessity, and put the blame on Eurystheus. Her anger was thus appeased, and she let him carry the hind alive to Mycenae.[3]

*c.* Another version of the story is that this hind was one which Taygete the Pleiad, Alcyone's sister, had dedicated to Artemis in gratitude for being temporarily disguised as a hind and thus enabled to elude Zeus's embraces. Nevertheless, Zeus could not long be deceived, and begot Lacedaemon on her; whereupon she hanged herself on the summit of Mount Amyclaeus, thereafter called Mount Taygetus.[4] Taygete's niece and namesake married Lacedaemon and bore him Himerus, whom Aphrodite caused to deflower his sister Cleodice unwittingly, on a night of promiscuous revel. Next day, learning what he had done, Himerus leaped into the river, now sometimes known by his name, and was seen no more; but oftener it is called the Eurotas, because Lacedaemon's predecessor, King Eurotas, having suffered an ignominious defeat at the hands of the Athenians – he would not wait for the full moon before giving battle – drowned himself in its waters. Eurotas, son of Myles, the inventor of water mills, was Amyclas's father, and grandfather both of Hyacinthus and of Eurydice, who married Acrisius.[5]

1. Apollodorus: ii. 5. 3; Diodorus Siculus: iv. 13; Euripides: *Heracles* 375 ff.; Virgil: *Aeneid* vi. 802; Hyginus: *Fabula* 30.
2. Apollodorus: *loc. cit.*; Callimachus: *Hymn to Delos* 103 and *Hymn to Artemis* 100 ff.; Euripides: *loc. cit.*; Pausanias: ii. 25. 3.
3. Apollodorus: *loc. cit.*; Diodorus Siculus: iv. 13; Pindar: *Olympian Odes* iii. 26–7; Hyginus: *Fabula* 30.
4. Pindar: *Olympian Odes* iii. 29 ff.; Apollodorus: ii. 10. 1; Plutarch: *On Rivers* 17.
5. Pausanias: iii. 1. 2–3 and 20.2; Plutarch: *loc. cit.*; Apollodorus: iii. 10. 3.

*

*1.* This Third Labour is of a different order from most of the others. Historically it may record the Achaean capture of a shrine where Artemis was worshipped as Elaphios ('hind-like'); her four chariot-stags represent the years of the Olympiad, and at the close of each a victim dressed in deer-skins was hunted to death (see 22. 1). Elaphios, at any rate, is said to have been Artemis's nurse, which means Artemis herself (Pausanias: vi. 22. 11). Mythically, however, the Labour seems to concern Heracles the Dactyl (see 52. 3), identified by the Gauls with Ogmius (Lucian: *Heracles* i), who invented the Ogham alphabet and all bardic lore (see 132. 3). The chase of the hind, or roe, symbolized the pursuit of Wisdom, and she is found, according to the Irish mystical tradition, harboured under a wild-apple tree (*White Goddess* p. 217). This would explain why Heracles is not said by anyone, except the ill-informed Euripides, to have done the roe any harm: instead he pursued her indefatigably without cease, for an entire year, to the Land of the Hyperboreans, experts in these very mysteries. According to Pollux, Heracles was called Melon ('of apples'), because apples were offered to him, presumably in recognition of his wisdom; but such wisdom came only with death, and his pursuit of the hind, like his visit to the Garden of the Hesperides, was really a journey to the Celtic Paradise. Zeus had similarly chased Taygete, who was a daughter of Atlas and therefore a non-Hellenic character.

2. In Europe, only reindeer does have horns, and reports of these may have come down from the Baltic by the Amber Route; reindeer, unlike other deer, can of course be harnessed.

3. The drowning of Taygete's son Himerus, and of her father-in-law Eurotas, suggests that early kings of Sparta were habitually sacrificed to the Eurotas water-monster, by being thrown, wrapped in branches, into a deep pool. So, it seems, was Tantalus (see 108. 3), another son of Taygete (Hyginus: *Fabula* 82). Lacedaemon means 'lake demon' (see 124. 2), and Laconia is the domain of Lacone ('lady of the lake'), whose image was rescued from the Dorian invaders by one Preugenes and brought to Patrae in Achaea (Pausanias: vii. 20. 4). The story behind Taygete's metamorphosis seems to be that the Achaean conquerors of Sparta called themselves Zeus, and their wives Hera. When Hera came to be worshipped as a cow, the Lelegian cult of Artemis the Hind was suppressed. A ritual marriage between Zeus as bull and Hera as cow may have been celebrated, as in Crete (see 90. 7).

4. Nights of promiscuous revel were held in various Greek states (see 44. a), and during the Alban Holiday at Rome: a concession to archaic sexual customs which preceded monogamy.

# THE FOURTH LABOUR: THE ERYMANTHIAN BOAR

THE Fourth Labour imposed on Heracles was to capture alive the Erymanthian Boar: a fierce, enormous beast which haunted the cypress-covered slopes of Mount Erymanthus, and the thickets of Arcadian Mount Lampeia; and ravaged the country around Psophis.[1] Mount Erymanthus takes its name from a son of Apollo, whom Aphrodite blinded because he had seen her bathing; Apollo in revenge turned himself into a boar and killed her lover Adonis. Yet the mountain is sacred to Artemis.[2]

b. Heracles, passing through Pholoë on his way to Erymanthus – where he killed one Saurus, a cruel bandit – was entertained by the Centaur Pholus, whom one of the ash-nymphs bore to Silenus. Pholus set roast meat before Heracles, but himself preferred the raw, and dared not open the Centaurs' communal wine jar until Heracles reminded him that it was the very jar which, four generations earlier, Dionysus had left in the cave against this very occasion.[3] The Centaurs grew angry when they smelt the strong wine. Armed with great rocks, up-rooted fir-trees, firebrands, and butchers' axes, they made a rush at Pholus's cave. While Pholus hid in terror, Heracles boldly repelled Ancius and Agrius, his first two assailants, with a volley of firebrands.[4] Nephele, the Centaurs' cloudy grandmother, then poured down a smart shower of rain, which loosened Heracles's bow-string and made the ground slippery. However, he showed himself worthy of his former achievements, and killed several Centaurs, among them Oreus and Hylaeus. The rest fled as far as Malea, where they took refuge with Cheiron, their king, who had been driven from Mount Pelion by the Lapiths.[5]

c. A parting arrow from Heracles's bow passed through Elatus's arm, and stuck quivering in Cheiron's knee. Distressed at the accident to his old friend, Heracles drew out the arrow and though Cheiron himself supplied the vulneraries for dressing the wound, they were of no avail and he retired howling in agony to his cave; yet could not die, because he was immortal. Prometheus later offered to accept immortality in his stead, and Zeus approved this arrangement; but some say that Cheiron chose death not so much because of the pain he suffered as because he had grown weary of his long life.[6]

*d*. The Centaurs now fled in various directions: some with Eurytion to Pholoë; some with Nessus to the river Evenus; some to Mount Malea; others to Sicily, where the Sirens destroyed them. Poseidon received the remainder at Eleusis, and hid them in a mountain. Among those whom Heracles later killed was Homadus the Arcadian, who had tried to rape Eurystheus's sister Alcyone; by thus nobly avenging an insult offered to an enemy, Heracles won great fame.[7]

*e*. Pholus, in the meantime, while burying his dead kinsmen, drew out one of Heracles's arrows and examined it. 'How can so robust a creature have succumbed to a mere scratch?' he wondered. But the arrow slipped from his fingers and, piercing his foot, killed him there and then. Heracles broke off the pursuit and returned to Pholoë, where he buried Pholus with unusual honours at the foot of the mountain which has taken his name. It was on this occasion that the river Anigrus acquired the foul smell which now clings to it from its very source on Mount Lapithus: because a Centaur named Pylenor, whom Heracles had winged with an arrow, fled and washed his wound there. Some, however, hold that Melampus had caused the stench some years before, by throwing into the Anigrus the foul objects used for purifying the daughters of Proetus.[8]

*f*. Heracles now set off to chase the boar by the river Erymanthus. To take so savage a beast alive was a task of unusual difficulty; but he dislodged it from a thicket with loud halloos, drove it into a deep snow drift, and sprang upon its back. He bound it with chains, and carried it alive on his shoulders to Mycenae; but when he heard that the Argonauts were gathering for their voyage to Colchis, dropped the boar outside the market place and, instead of waiting for further orders from Eurystheus, who was hiding in his bronze jar, went off with Hylas to join the expedition. It is not known who dispatched the captured boar, but its tusks are preserved in the temple of Apollo at Cumae.[9]

*g*. According to some accounts, Cheiron was accidentally wounded by an arrow that pierced his left foot, while he and Pholus and the young Achilles were entertaining Heracles on Mount Pelion. After nine days, Zeus set Cheiron's image among the stars as the Centaur. But others hold that the Centaur is Pholus, who was honoured by Zeus in this way because he excelled all men in the art of prophesying from entrails. The Bowman in the Zodiac is likewise a Centaur: one Crotus, who lived on Mount Helicon, greatly beloved by his foster-sisters, the Muses.[10]

1. Ovid: *Heroides* ix. 87; Apollonius Rhodius: i. 127; Apollodorus: ii. 5. 4; Diodorus Siculus: iv. 12.

2. Ptolemy Hephaestionos: i. 306; Homer: *Odyssey* vi. 105.

3. Pausanias: vi. 21. 5; Apollodorus: *loc. cit.*; Diodorus Siculus: *loc. cit.*

4. Tzetzes: *On Lycophron* 670; Diodorus Siculus: *loc. cit.*; Apollodorus: *loc. cit.*

5. Pausanias: iii. 18. 9; Virgil: *Aeneid* viii. 293–4; Diodorus Siculus: *loc. cit.*; Apollodorus: *loc. cit.*

6. Apollodorus: *loc. cit.*; Lucian: *Dialogues of the Dead* 26.

7. Tzetzes: *On Lycophron* 670; Apollodorus: *loc. cit.*; Diodorus Siculus: *loc. cit.*

8. Apollodorus: *loc. cit.*; Diodorus Siculus: *loc. cit.*; Pausanias: v. 5. 6.

9. Apollodorus: *loc. cit.*; Pausanias: viii. 24. 2; Diodorus Siculus: *loc. cit.*; Apollonius Rhodius: i. 122 ff.

10. Theocritus: *Idyll* vii; Ovid: *Fasti* v. 380 ff.; Hyginus: *Poetic Astronomy* ii. 38 and 27; *Fabula* 224.

*

*1.* Boars were sacred to the Moon because of their crescent-shaped tusks, and it seems that the tanist who killed and emasculated his twin, the sacred king, wore boar-disguise when he did so (see 18. *7* and 151. *2*). The snowdrift in which the Erymanthian Boar was overcome indicates that this Labour took place at midwinter. Here Heracles is the Child Horus and avenges the death of his father Osiris on his uncle Set who comes disguised as a boar; the Egyptian taboo on boar's flesh was lifted only at midwinter. The boar's head Yuletide ceremony has its origin in this same triumph of the new sacred king over his rival. Adonis is murdered to avenge the death of Erymanthus, the previous year's tanist, whose name, 'divining by lots', suggests that he was chosen by lot to kill the sacred king. Mount Erymanthus being sacred to Artemis, not Aphrodite, Artemis must have been the goddess who took her bath, and the sacred king, not his tanist, must have seen her doing so (see 22. *i*).

*2.* It is probable that Heracles's battle with the Centaurs, like the similar battle at Peirithous's wedding (see 102. *2*), originally represented the ritual combat between a newly installed king and opponents in beast-disguise. His traditional weapons were arrows, one of which, to establish his sovereignty, he shot to each of the four quarters of the sky, and a fifth straight up into the air. Frontier wars between the Hellenes and the pre-Hellenic mountaineers of Northern Greece are also perhaps recorded in this myth.

*3.* Poisoned arrows dropped upon, or shot into, a knee or foot, caused the death not only of Pholus and Cheiron, but also of Achilles, Cheiron's pupil (see 92. *10* and 164. *j*): all of them Magnesian sacred kings, whose souls the Sirens naturally received. The presence of Centaurs at Malea derives from a local tradition that Pholus's father Silenus was born there (Pausanias: iii. 25. 2); Centaurs were often represented as half goat, rather than half horse. Their presence at Eleusis, where Poseidon hid them in a mountain, suggests that when the initiate into the Mysteries celebrated a sacred marriage with the goddess, hobby-horse dancers took part in the proceedings.

# 127

## THE FIFTH LABOUR: THE STABLES OF AUGEIAS

HERACLES's Fifth Labour was to cleanse King Augeias's filthy cattle yard in one day. Eurystheus gleefully pictured Heracles's disgust at having to load the dung into baskets and carry these away on his shoulders. Augeias, King of Elis, was the son of Helius, or Eleius, by Naupiadame, a daughter of Amphidamas; or, some say, by Iphiboë. Others call him the son of Poseidon. In flocks and herds he was the wealthiest man on earth: for, by a divine dispensation, his were immune against disease and inimitably fertile, nor did they ever miscarry. Although in almost every case they produced female offspring, he nevertheless had three hundred white-legged black bulls and two hundred red stud-bulls; besides twelve outstanding silvery-white bulls, sacred to his father Helius. These twelve defended his herds against marauding wild beasts from the wooded hills.[1]

b. Now, the dung in Augeias's cattle yard and sheepfolds had not been cleared away for many years, and though its noisome stench did not affect the beasts themselves, it spread a pestilence across the whole Peloponnese. Moreover, the valley pastures were so deep in dung that they could no longer be ploughed for grain.[2]

c. Heracles hailed Augeias from afar, and undertook to cleanse the yard before nightfall in return for a tithe of the cattle. Augeias laughed incredulously, and called Phyleus, his eldest son, to witness Heracles's offer. 'Swear to accomplish the task before nightfall', Phyleus demanded. The oath which Heracles now took by his father's name was the first and last one he ever swore. Augeias likewise took an oath to keep his side of the bargain. At this point, Phaethon, the leader of the twelve white bulls, charged at Heracles, mistaking him for a lion; whereupon he seized the bull's left horn, forced its neck downwards, and floored it by main strength.[3]

d. On the advice of Menedemus the Elean, and aided by Iolaus, Heracles first breached the wall of the yard in two places, and next diverted the neighbouring rivers Alpheus and Peneius, or Menius, so that their streams rushed through the yard, swept it clean and then went on to cleanse the sheepfolds and the valley pastures. Thus Heracles accomplished this Labour in one day, restoring the land to health, and not soiling so much as his little finger. But Augeias, on being informed by Copreus that Heracles had already been under orders from Eurystheus to cleanse the cattle yards, refused to pay the reward and even dared deny that he and Heracles had struck a bargain.

e. Heracles suggested that the case be submitted to arbitration; yet when the judges were seated, and Phyleus, subpoenaed by Heracles, testified to the truth, Augeias sprang up in a rage and banished them both from Elis, asserting that he had been tricked by Heracles, since the River-gods, not he, had done the work. To make matters even worse, Eurystheus refused to count this Labour as one of the ten, because Heracles had been in Augeias's hire.

f. Phyleus then went to Dulichium; and Heracles to the court of Dexamenus, King of Olenus, whose daughter Mnesimache he later rescued from the Centaur Eurytion.[4]

1. Apollodorus: ii. 5. 5 and 7. 2; Diodorus Siculus: iv. 13; Pausanias: v. 1. 7; Tzetzes: *On Lycophron* 41; Hyginus: *Fabula* 14.
2. Apollodorus: ii. 5. 5; Servius on Virgil's *Aeneid* viii. 300; Diodorus Siculus: *loc. cit.*; Pausanias: *loc. cit.*
3. Pausanias: *loc. cit.*; Apollodorus: *loc. cit.*; Plutarch: *Roman Questions* 28; Theocritus: *Idyll* xxv. 115 ff.
4. Ptolemy Hephaestionos: v, quoted by Photius p. 486; Hyginus: *Fabula* 30; Pausanias: *loc. cit.*; Apollodorus: *loc. cit.*; Diodorus Siculus: *loc. cit.*; Servius: *loc. cit.*; Callimachus: *Hymn to Delos* 102.

\*

*1.* This confused myth seems to be founded on the legend that Heracles, like Jason, was ordered to tame two bulls, yoke them, clean an overgrown hill, then plough, sow, and reap it in a single day – the usual tasks set a candidate for kingship (see 152. 3). Here, the hill had to be cleared not of trees and stones, as in the Celtic versions of the myth, but of dung – probably because the name of Eurystheus's herald, who delivered the order, was Copreus ('dung man'). Sir James Frazer, commenting on Pausanias (v. 10. 9), quotes a Norse tale, 'The Mastermaid', in which a prince who wishes to win a giant's daughter must first clean three stables. For each pitch-fork of dung which he tosses out, ten return. The princess then advises him to turn the pitchfork upside-down and use the handle. He does so, and the stable is soon cleansed. Frazer suggests that, in the original version, Athene may have given Heracles the same advice; more likely, however, the Norse tale is a variant of this Labour. Augeias's cattle are irrelevant to the story, except to account for the great mass of dung to be removed. Cattle manure, as the myth shows, was not valued by Greek farmers. Hesiod, in his *Works and Days*, does not mention it; and H. Mitchell (*Economics of Ancient Greece*) shows that the grazing of cattle on fallow land is prohibited in several ancient leases. Odysseus's dog Argus did, indeed, lie on a midden used for dunging the estate (*Odyssey* xvii. 299), but wherever the *Odyssey* may have been written – and it certainly was not on the Greek mainland – the references to agriculture and arboriculture suggest a survival of Cretan practice. According to some mythographers, Augeias was the son of Eleius, which means no more than 'King of Elis'; according to others, a son of Poseidon, which suggests that he was an Aeolian. But Eleius has here been confused with Helius, the Corinthian Sun-god; and Augeias is therefore credited with a herd of sacred cattle, like that owned by Sisyphus (see 67. 1). The number of heads in such herds was 350, representing twelve complete lunations less the sacred five-day holiday of the Egyptian year (see 42. 1); that they were lunar cattle was proved by their red, white, and black colours (see 90. 3); and the white bulls represent these twelve lunations. Such sacred cattle were often stolen – as by Heracles himself in his Tenth Labour – and the sequel to his quarrel with Augeias was that he won these twelve bulls as well.

2. The Fifth Labour, which properly concerns only ploughing, sowing, and reaping tasks has, in fact, been confused with two others: the Tenth, namely the lifting of Geryon's cattle; and the Seventh, namely the capture of Poseidon's white Cretan bull – which was not, however, used for ploughing. In the cult of Poseidon – who is also described as Augeias's father – young men wrestled with bulls, and Heracles's struggle against Phaethon, like Theseus's against the Minotaur, is best understood as a coronation rite: by magical contact with the bull's horn, he became capable of fertilizing the land, and earned the title of Potidan, or Poseidon, given to the Moon-goddess's chosen lover. Similarly, in a love-contest Heracles fought the river Achelous, represented as a bull-headed man, and broke off his cornucopia (see 141. d). The deflection of the Alpheius suggests that the icon from which this incident is deduced showed

Heracles twisting the Cretan Bull around by the horns, beside the banks of a river, where numerous cattle were grazing. This bull was mistaken for a river-god, and the scene read as meaning that he had deflected the river in order to cleanse the fields for ploughing.

# 128

## THE SIXTH LABOUR: THE STYMPHALIAN BIRDS

HERACLES's Sixth Labour was to remove the countless brazen-beaked, brazen-clawed, brazen-winged, man-eating birds, sacred to Ares which, frightened by the wolves of Wolves' Ravine on the Orchomenan Road, had flocked to the Stymphalian Marsh.[1] Here they bred and waded beside the river of the same name, occasionally taking to the air in great flocks, to kill men and beasts by discharging a shower of brazen feathers and at the same time muting a poisonous excrement, which blighted the crops.

b. On arrival at the marsh, which lay surrounded by dense woods, Heracles found himself unable to drive away the birds with his arrows; they were too numerous. Moreover, the marsh seemed neither solid enough to support a man walking, nor liquid enough for the use of a boat. As Heracles paused irresolutely on the bank, Athene gave him a pair of brazen castanets, made by Hephaestus; or it may have been a rattle. Standing on a spur of Mount Cyllene, which overlooks the marsh, Heracles clacked the castanets, or shook the rattle, raising such a din that the birds soared up in one great flock, mad with terror. He shot down scores of them as they flew off to the Isle of Ares in the Black Sea, where they were afterwards found by the Argonauts; some say that Heracles was with the Argonauts at the time, and killed many more of the birds.[2]

c. Stymphalian birds are the size of cranes, and closely resemble ibises, except that their beaks can pierce a metal breast-plate, and are not hooked. They also breed in the Arabian Desert, and there cause more trouble even than lions or leopards by flying at travellers' breasts and transfixing them. Arabian hunters have learned to wear protective cuirasses of plaited bark, which entangle those deadly beaks and enable them to seize and wring the necks of their assailants. It may be that a flock of these birds migrated from Arabia to Stymphalus, and gave their name to the whole breed.[3]

d. According to some accounts, the so-called Stymphalian Birds were women: daughters of Stymphalus and Ornis, whom Heracles killed because they refused him hospitality. At Stymphalus, in the ancient temple of Stymphalian Artemis, images of these birds are hung from the roof, and behind the building stand statues of maidens with birds' legs. Here also Temenus, a son of Pelasgus, founded three shrines in Hera's honour: in the first she was worshipped as Child, because Temenus had reared her; in the second as Bride, because she had married Zeus; in the third as Widow, because she had repudiated Zeus and retired to Stymphalus.[4]

1. Pausanias: viii. 22. 4–6; Apollodorus: ii. 5. 6.
2. Apollonius Rhodius: ii. 1052 ff.; Pausanias: loc. cit.; Servius on Virgil's Aeneid viii. 300; Apollonius Rhodius: ii. 1037 and 1053, with scholiast; Diodorus Siculus: iv. 13; Apollodorus: loc. cit.; Hyginus: Fabula 30.
3. Pausanias: viii. 22. 4.
4. Mnaseas, quoted by scholiast on Apollonius Rhodius: ii. 1054; Pausanias: viii. 22. 2. and 5.

*

1. Though Athene continues to help Heracles, this Labour does not belong to the marriage-task sequence but glorifies him as the healer who expels fever demons, identified with marsh-birds. The helmeted birds shown on Stymphalian coins are spoon-bills, cousins to the cranes which appear in English medieval carvings as sucking the breath of sick men. They are, in fact, bird-legged Sirens, personifications of fever; and castanets, or rattles, were used in ancient times (and still are among primitive peoples) to drive away fever demons. Artemis was the goddess who had power to inflict or cure fever with her 'merciful shafts'.

2. The Stymphalian marsh used to increase in size considerably whenever the underground channel which carried away its waters became blocked, as happened in Pausanias's time (viii. 22. 6); and Iphicratus, when besieging the city, would have blocked it deliberately, had not a sign from heaven prevented him (Strabo: viii. 8. 5). It may well be that in one version of the story Heracles drained the marsh by freeing the channel; as he had previously drained the Plain of Tempe (Diodorus Siculus: iv. 18).

3. The myth, however, seems to have a historical, as well as a ritual, meaning. Apparently a college of Arcadian priestesses, who worshipped the Triple-goddess as Maiden, Bride, and Crone, took refuge at Stym-

phalus, after having been driven from Wolves' Ravine by invaders who worshipped Wolfish Zeus; and Mnaseas has plausibly explained the expulsion, or massacre, of the Stymphalian Birds as the suppression of this witch-college by Heracles – that is to say, by a tribe of Achaeans. The name Stymphalus suggests erotic practices.

4. Pausanias's 'strong-beaked Arabian birds' may have been sun-stroke demons, kept at bay by bark spine-protectors, and confused with the powerfully beaked ostriches, which the Arabs still hunt.

*Leuc-erodes*, 'white heron', is the Greek name for spoon-bill; an ancestor of Herod the Great is said to have been a temple slave to Tyrian Heracles (Africanus, quoted by Eusebius: *Ecclesiastical History* i. 6. 7), which accounts for the family name. The spoon-bill is closely related to the ibis, another marsh-bird, sacred to the god Thoth, inventor of writing; and Tyrian Heracles, like his Celtic counterpart, was a protector of learning, which made Tyre famous (*Ezekiel* xxviii. 12). In Hebrew tradition, his priest Hiram of Tyre exchanged riddles with Solomon.

# 129
## THE SEVENTH LABOUR: THE CRETAN BULL

EURYSTHEUS ordered Heracles, as his Seventh Labour, to capture the Cretan Bull; but it is much disputed whether this was the bull sent by Zeus, which ferried Europe across to Crete, or the one, withheld by Minos from sacrifice to Poseidon, which sired the Minotaur on Pasiphaë. At this time it was ravaging Crete, especially the region watered by the river Tethris, rooting up crops and levelling orchard walls.[1]

b. When Heracles sailed to Crete, Minos offered him every assistance in his power, but he preferred to capture the bull single-handed, though it belched scorching flames. After a long struggle, he brought the monster across to Mycenae, where Eurystheus, dedicating it to Hera, set it free. Hera however, loathing a gift which redounded to Heracles's glory, drove the bull first to Sparta, and then back through Arcadia and across the Isthmus to Attic Marathon, whence Theseus later dragged it to Athens as a sacrifice to Athene.[2]

c. Nevertheless, many still deny the identity of the Cretan and Marathonian bulls.[3]

1. Apollodorus: ii. 5. 7; Diodorus Siculus: iv. 13; Pausanias: i. 27. 9; First Vatican Mythographer: 47.

2. Diodorus Siculus: *loc. cit.*; Servius on Virgil's *Aeneid* viii. 294; Apollodorus: *loc. cit.*; First Vatican Mythographer: *loc. cit.*
3. Theon: *On Aratus* p. 24.

*

*1.* The combat with a bull, or a man in bull's disguise – one of the ritual tasks imposed on the candidate for kingship (see 123. *1*) – also appears in the story of Theseus and the Minotaur (see 98. *2*), and of Jason and the fire-breathing bulls of Aeëtes (see 152. *3*). When the immortality implicit in the sacred kingship was eventually offered to every initiate of the Dionysian Mysteries, the capture of a bull and its dedication to Dionysus Plusodotes ('giver of wealth') became a common rite both in Arcadia (Pautanias: viii. 19. 2) and Lydia (Strabo: xiv. 1. 44), where Dionysus held the title of Zeus. His principal theophany was as a bull, but he also appeared in the form of a lion and a serpent (see 27. *4*). Contact with the bull's horn (see 127. *2*) enabled the sacred king to fertilize the land in the name of the Moon-goddess by making rain – the magical explanation being that a bull's bellow portended thunderstorms, which *rhombi*, or bull-roarers, were accordingly swung to induce. Torches were also flung to simulate lightning (see 68. *a*) and came to suggest the bull's fiery breath.

*2.* Dionysus is called Plutodotes ('wealth-giver') because of his cornucopia, torn from a bull, which was primarily a water charm (see 142. *b*); he developed from Cretan Zagreus, and among Zagreus's changes are lion, a horned serpent, a bull, and 'Cronus making rain' (see 30. *3*).

130

THE EIGHTH LABOUR: THE MARES<br>OF DIOMEDES

EURYSTHEUS ordered Heracles, as his Eighth Labour, to capture the four savage mares of Thracian King Diomedes – it is disputed whether he was the son of Ares and Cyrene, or born of an incestuous relationship between Asterië and her father Atlas – who ruled the warlike Bistones, and whose stables, at the now vanished city of Tirida, were the terror of Thrace. Diomedes kept the mares tethered with iron chains to bronze mangers, and fed them on the flesh of his unsuspecting guests. One version of the story makes them stallions, not mares, and names them Podargus, Lampon, Xanthus, and Deinus.[1]

*b.* With a number of volunteers, Heracles set sail for Thrace, visiting his friend King Admetus of Pherae on the way. Arrived at Tirida, he overpowered Diomedes's grooms and drove the mares down to the sea, where he left them on a knoll in charge of his minion Abderus, and then turned to repel the Bistones as they rushed in pursuit. His party being outnumbered, he overcame them by ingeniously cutting a channel which caused the sea to flood the low-lying plain; when they turned to run, he pursued them, stunned Diomedes with his club, dragged his body around the lake that had now formed, and set it before his own mares, which tore at the still living flesh. Their hunger being now fully assuaged – for, while Heracles was away, they had also devoured Abderus – he mastered them without much trouble.[2]

c. According to another account Abderus, though a native of Opus in Locris, was employed by Diomedes. Some call him the son of Hermes; and others the son of Heracles's friend, Opian Menoetius, and thus brother to Patroclus who fell at Troy. After founding the city of Abdera beside Abderus's tomb, Heracles took Diomedes's chariot and harnessed the mares to it, though hitherto they had never known bit or bridle. He drove them speedily back across the mountains until he reached Mycenae, where Eurystheus dedicated them to Hera and set them free on Mount Olympus.[3] They were eventually destroyed by wild beasts; yet it is claimed that their descendants survived until the Trojan War and even until the time of Alexander the Great. The ruins of Diomedes's palace are shown at Cartera Come, and at Abdera athletic games are still celebrated in honour of Abderus – they include all the usual contests, except chariot-racing; which accounts for the story that Abderus was killed when the man-eating mares wrecked a chariot to which he had harnessed them.[4]

1. Apollodorus: ii. 5. 8; Hyginus: *Fabulae* 250 and 30; Pliny: *Natural History* iv. 18; Diodorus Siculus: iv. 15.
2. Apollodorus: *loc. cit.*; Euripides: *Alcestis* 483; Strabo: *Fragments* 44 and 47; Diodorus Siculus: *loc. cit.*
3. Hyginus: *Fabula* 30; Apollodorus: *loc. cit.*; Diodorus Siculus: iv. 39; Homer: *Iliad* xi. 608; Euripides: *Heracles* 380 ff.
4. Apollodorus: *loc. cit.*; Servius on Virgil's *Aeneid* i. 756; Diodorus Siculus: iv. 15; Strabo: *Fragment* 44; Philostratus: *Imagines* ii. 25; Hyginus: *Fabula* 250.

\*

1. The bridling of a wild horse, intended for a sacrificial horse feast (see 75. 3), seems to have been a coronation rite in some regions of Greece.

Heracles's mastery of Arion (see 138. *g*) – a feat also performed by Oncus and Adrastus (Pausanias: viii. 25. 5) – is paralleled by Bellerophon's capture of Pegasus. This ritual myth has here been combined with a legend of how Heracles, perhaps representing the Teans who seized Abdera from the Thracians (Herodotus: i. 168), annulled the custom by which wild women in horse-masks used to chase and eat the sacred king at the end of his reign (see 27. *d*); instead he was killed in an organized chariot crash (see 71. *1*; 101. *g* and 109. *j*). The omission of chariot-racing from the funeral games at Abdera points to a ban on this revised sacrifice. Podargus is called after Podarge the Harpy, mother of Xanthus, an immortal horse given by Poseidon to Peleus as a wedding present (see 81. *m*); Lampus recalls Lampon, one of Eos's team (see 40. *a*). Diodorus's statement that these mares were let loose on Olympus may mean that the cannibalistic horse cult survived there until Hellenistic times.

2. Canals, tunnels, or natural underground conduits were often described as the work of Heracles (see 127. *d*; 138. *d* and 142. *3*).

# 131

## THE NINTH LABOUR: HIPPOLYTE'S GIRDLE

HERACLES's Ninth Labour was to fetch for Eurystheus's daughter Admete the golden girdle of Ares worn by the Amazonian queen Hippolyte. Taking one ship or, some say, nine, and a company of volunteers, among whom were Iolaus, Telamon of Aegina, Peleus of Iolcus and, according to some accounts, Theseus of Athens, Heracles set sail for the river Thermodon.[1]

*b.* The Amazons were children of Ares by the Naiad Harmonia, born in the glens of Phrygian Acmonia; but some call their mother Aphrodite, or Otrere, daughter of Ares.[2] At first they lived beside the river Amazon, now named after Tanais, a son of the Amazon Lysippe, who offended Aphrodite by his scorn of marriage and his devotion to war. In revenge, Aphrodite caused Tanais to fall in love with his mother; but, rather than yield to an incestuous passion, he flung himself into the river and drowned. To escape the reproaches of his ghost, Lysippe then led her daughters around the Black Sea coast, to a plain by the river Thermodon, which rises in the lofty Amazonian mountains. There they formed three tribes, each of which founded a city.[3]

*c.* Then as now, the Amazons reckoned descent only through the mother, and Lysippe had laid it down that the men must perform all household tasks, while the women fought and governed. The arms and legs of infant boys were therefore broken to incapacitate them for war or travel. These unnatural women, whom the Scythians call Oeorpata, showed no regard for justice or decency, but were famous warriors, being the first to employ cavalry.⁴ They carried brazen bows and short shields shaped like a half moon; their helmets, clothes, and girdles were made from the skins of wild beasts.⁵ Lysippe, before she fell in battle, built the great city of Themiscyra, and defeated every tribe as far as the river Tanais. With the spoils of her campaigns she raised temples to Ares, and others to Artemis Tauropolus whose worship she established. Her descendants extended the Amazonian empire westward across the river Tanais, to Thrace; and again, on the southern coast, westward across the Thermodon to Phrygia. Three famous Amazonian queens, Marpesia, Lampado, and Hippo, seized a great part of Asia Minor and Syria, and founded the cities of Ephesus, Smyrna, Cyrene, and Myrine. Other Amazonian foundations are Thiba and Sinope.⁶

*d.* At Ephesus, they set up an image of Artemis under a beech-tree, where Hippo offered sacrifices; after which her followers performed first a shield dance, and then a round dance, with rattling quivers, beating the ground in unison, to the accompaniment of pipes – for Athene had not yet invented the flute. The temple of Ephesian Artemis, later built around this image and unrivalled in magnificence even by that of Delphic Apollo, is included among the seven wonders of the world; two streams, both called Selenus, and flowing in opposite directions, surround it. It was on this expedition that the Amazons captured Troy, Priam being then still a child. But while detachments of the Amazonian army went home laden with vast quantities of spoil, the rest, staying to consolidate their power in Asia Minor, were driven out by an alliance of barbarian tribes, and lost their queen Marpesia.⁷

*e.* By the time that Heracles came to visit the Amazons, they had all returned to the river Thermodon, and their three cities were ruled by Hippolyte, Antiope, and Melanippe. On his way, he put in at the island of Paros, famous for its marble, which King Rhadamanthys had bequeathed to one Alcaeus, a son of Androgeus; but four of Minos's sons, Eurymedon, Chryses, Nephalion, and Philolaus, had also settled there. When a couple of Heracles's crew, landing to fetch water, were murdered by Minos's sons, he indignantly killed all four of them, and pressed the Parians so hard that they sent envoys offering, in requital for the dead sailors, any two men whom he might choose to be his slaves. Satisfied by this proposal, Heracles raised the siege and chose King Alcaeus and his brother Sthenelus, whom he took aboard his ship. Next, he sailed through the Hellespont and Bosphorus to Mariandyne in Mysia, where he was entertained by King Lycus the Paphlagonian, son of Dascylus and grandson of Tantalus.[8] In return, he supported Lycus in a war with the Bebrycans, killing many, including their king Mygdon, brother of Amycus, and recovered much Paphlagonian land from the Bebrycans; this he restored to Lycus, who renamed it Heracleia in his honour. Later, Heracleia was colonized by Megarians and Tanagrans on the advice of the Pythoness at Delphi, who told them to plant a colony beside the Black Sea, in a region dedicated to Heracles.[9]

*f.* Arrived at the mouth of the river Thermodon, Heracles cast anchor in the harbour of Themiscyra, where Hippolyte paid him a visit and, attracted by his muscular body, offered him Ares's girdle as a love gift. But Hera had meanwhile gone about, disguised in Amazon dress, spreading a rumour that these strangers planned to abduct Hippolyte; whereupon the incensed warrior-women mounted their horses and charged down on the ship. Heracles, suspecting treachery, killed Hippolyte offhand, removed her girdle, seized her axe and other weapons, and prepared to defend himself. He killed each of the Amazon leaders in turn, putting their army to flight after great slaughter.[10]

*g.* Some, however, say that Melanippe was ambushed, and ransomed by Hippolyte at the price of the girdle; or contrariwise. Or that Theseus captured Hippolyte, and presented her girdle to Heracles who, in return, allowed him to make Antiope his slave. Or that Hippolyte refused to give Heracles the girdle and that they fought a pitched battle; she was thrown off her horse, and he stood over her, club in hand, offering quarter, but she chose to die rather than yield. It is even said that the girdle belonged to a daughter of Briareus the Hundred-handed One.[11]

*h.* On his return from Themiscyra, Heracles came again to Mariandyne, and competed in the funeral games of King Lycus's brother Priolas, who had been killed by the Mysians, and for whom dirges are still sung. Heracles boxed against the Mariandynian champion Titias, knocked out all his teeth and killed him with a blow to the temple. In proof of his regret for this accident, he subdued the Mysians and the Phrygians on Dascylus's behalf; but he also subdued the Bithynians, as far as the mouth of the river Rhebas and the summit of Mount Colone, and claimed their kingdom for himself. Pelops's Paphlagonians voluntarily surrendered to him. However, no sooner had Heracles departed, than the Bebrycans, under Amycus, son of Poseidon, once more robbed Lycus of his land, extending their frontier to the river Hypius.[12]

*i.* Sailing thence to Troy, Heracles rescued Hesione from a sea-monster; and continued his voyage to Thracian Aenus, where he was entertained by Poltys; and, just as he was putting to sea again, shot and killed on the Aenian beach Poltys's insolent brother Sarpedon, a son of Poseidon. Next, he subjugated the Thracians who had settled in Thasos, and bestowed the island on the sons of Androgeus, whom he had carried off from Paros; and at Torone was challenged to a wrestling match by Polygonus and Telegonus, sons of Proteus, both of whom he killed.[13]

*j.* Returning to Mycenae at last, Heracles handed the girdle to Eurystheus, who gave it to Admete. As for the other spoil taken from the Amazons: he presented their rich robes to the Temple of Apollo at Delphi, and Hippolyte's axe to Queen Omphale, who included it among the sacred regalia of the Lydian kings. Eventually it was taken to a Carian temple of Labradian Zeus, and placed in the hand of his divine image.[14]

*k.* Amazons are still to be found in Albania, near Colchis, having been driven there from Themiscyra at the same time as their neighbours, the Gargarensians. When they reached the safety of the Albanian mountains, the two peoples separated: the Amazons settling at the foot of the Caucasian Mountains, around the river Mermodas, and the Gargarensians immediately to the north. On an appointed day every spring, parties of young Amazons and young Gargarensians meet at the summit of the mountain which separates their territories and, after performing a joint sacrifice, spend two months together, enjoying promiscuous intercourse under the cover of night. As soon as an Amazon finds herself pregnant, she returns home. Whatever girl-children are born become Amazons, and the boys are sent to the Gargarensians who, because they have no means of ascertaining their paternity, distribute them by lot among their huts.[15] In recent times, the Amazon queen Minythyia set out from her Albanian court to meet Alexander the Great in tiger-haunted Hyrcania; and there enjoyed his company for thirteen days, hoping to have offspring by him – but died childless soon afterwards.[16]

*l.* These Amazons of the Black Sea must be distinguished from Dionysus's Libyan allies who once inhabited Hespera, an island in Lake Tritonis which was so rich in fruit-bearing trees, sheep and goats, that they found no need to grow corn. After capturing all the cities in the island, except holy Mene, the home of the Ethiopian fish-eaters (who mine emeralds, rubies, topazes, and sard) they defeated the neighbouring Libyans and nomads, and founded the great city of Chersonesus, so called because it was built on a peninsula.[17] From this base they attacked the Atlantians, the most civilized nation west of the Nile, whose capital is on the Atlantic island of Cerne. Myrine, the Amazonian queen, raised a force of thirty thousand cavalry and three thousand infantry. All of them carried bows with which, when retreating, they used to shoot accurately at their pursuers, and were armoured with the skins of the almost unbelievably large Libyan serpents.

*m.* Invading the land of the Atlantians, Myrine defeated them decisively and, crossing over to Cerne, captured the city; she then put every man to the sword, enslaved the women and children, and razed the city walls. When the remaining Atlantians agreed to surrender, she treated them fairly, made friends with them and, in compensation for their loss of Cerne, built the new city of Myrine, where she settled the captives and all others desirous of living there. Since the Atlantians now offered to pay her divine honours, Myrine protected them against the neighbouring tribe of Gorgons, of whom she killed a great many in a pitched battle, besides taking no less than three thousand prisoners.[18] That night, however, while the Amazons were holding a victory banquet, the prisoners stole their swords and, at a signal, the main body of Gorgons who had rallied and hidden in an oak-wood, poured down from all sides to massacre Myrine's followers.

*n.* Myrine contrived to escape – her dead lie buried under three huge mounds, still called the Mounds of the Amazons – and, after traversing most of Libya, entered Egypt with a new army, befriended King Horus, the son of Isis, and passed on to the invasion of Arabia. Some hold that it was these Libyan Amazons, not those from the Black Sea, who conquered Asia Minor; and that Myrine, after selecting the most suitable sites in her new empire, founded a number of coastal cities, including Myrine, Cyme, Pitane, Priene, and others farther inland. She also subdued several of the Aegean Islands, notably Lesbos, where she built the city of Mitylene, named after a sister who had shared in the campaign. While Myrine was still engaged in conquering the islands, a storm

overtook her fleet; but the Mother of the Gods bore every ship safely
to Samothrace, then uninhabited, which Myrine consecrated to her,
founding altars and offering splendid sacrifices.

*o.* Myrine then crossed over to the Thracian mainland, where King
Mopsus and his ally, the Scythian Sipylus, worsted her in fair fight, and
she was killed. The Amazon army never recovered from this setback:
defeated by the Thracians in frequent engagements, its remnants finally
retired to Libya.[19]

1. Scholiast on Pindar's *Nemean Odes* iii. 64; Apollodorus: ii. 5. 9;
   Justin: ii. 4; Pindar: *Nemean Odes* iii. 38 and *Fragment* 172; Philochorus, quoted by Plutarch: *Theseus* 26.
2. Apollonius Rhodius: ii. 990–2; Cicero: *In Defence of Flaccus* 15;
   Scholiast on Homer's *Iliad* i. 189; Hyginus: *Fabula* 30; Scholiast
   on Apollonius Rhodius: ii. 1033.
3. Servius on Virgil's *Aeneid* xi. 659; Plutarch: *On Rivers* 14; Apollonius Rhodius: ii. 976–1000.
4. Arrian: *Fragment* 58; Diodorus Siculus: ii. 451; Herodotus: iv.
   100; Apollonius Rhodius: ii. 987–9; Lysias, quoted by Tzetzes:
   *On Lycophron* 1332.
5. Pindar: *Nemean Odes* iii. 38; Servius on Virgil's *Aeneid* i. 494;
   Strabo: xi. 5. 1.
6. Diodorus Siculus: ii. 45–6; Strabo: xi. 5. 4; Justin: ii. 4; Hecataeus:
   *Fragment* 352.
7. Callimachus: *Hymn to Artemis* 237 ff.; Hyginus: *Fabulae* 223 and
   225; Pliny: *Natural History* v. 31; Homer: *Iliad* iii. 189; Tzetzes:
   *On Lycophron* 69; Justin: ii. 4.
8. Diodorus Siculus: v. 79; Herodotus: vii. 72; Scholiast on Apollonius Rhodius: ii. 754.
9. Strabo: xii. 3. 4; Apollodorus: ii. 5. 9; Pausanias: v. 26. 6; Justin:
   xvi. 3.
10. Diodorus Siculus: iv. 16; Apollodorus: *loc. cit.*; Plutarch: *Greek
    Questions* 45.
11. Apollonius Rhodius: ii. 966–9, Diodorus Siculus: *loc. cit.*; Tzetzes:
    *On Lycophron* 1329; Ibycus, quoted by scholiast on Apollonius
    Rhodius: *loc. cit.*
12. Apollonius Rhodius: ii. 776 ff.
13. Apollodorus: ii. 5. 9.
14. Apollodorus: *loc. cit.*; Tzetzes: *On Lycophron* 1327; Euripides:
    *Heracles* 418 and *Ion* 1145; Plutarch: *Greek Questions* 45.
15. Strabo: xi. 5. 1–2 and 4; Servius on Virgil's *Aeneid* xi. 659.
16. Justin: ii. 4; Cleitarchus, quoted by Strabo: xi. 5. 4.
17. Diodorus Siculus: iii. 52–3.
18. Diodorus Siculus: iii. 54.

19. Diodorus Siculus: iii. 55.

*

1. If Admete was the name of the princess for whose sake Heracles performed all these marriage tasks, the removal of her girdle in the wedding chamber must have marked the end of his Labours. But first Admete will have struggled with him, as Hippolyte did, and as Penthesileia struggled with Achilles (see 164. *a* and *2*), or Thetis with Peleus (see 81. *k*) – whose introduction into the story is thus explained. In that case, she will have gone through her usual transformations, which suggests that the cuttlefish-like Hydra was Admete – the gold-guarding serpent which he overcame being Ladon (see 133. *a*) – and that she may also have turned into a crab (see 124. *e*), a hind (see 125. *c*), a wild mare (see 16. *f*), and a cloud (see 126. *b*) before he contrived to win her maidenhead.

2. A tradition of armed priestesses still lingered at Ephesus and other cities in Asia Minor; but the Greek mythographers, having forgotten the former existence of similar colleges at Athens and other cities in Greece itself, sent Heracles in search of Hippolyte's girdle to the Black Sea, where matriarchal tribes were still active (see 100. *1*). A three-tribe system is the general rule in matriarchal society. That the girdle belonged to a daughter of Briareus ('strong'), one of the Hundred-handed Ones, points to an early setting of the marriage-test story in Northern Greece.

3. Admete is another name for Athene, who must have appeared in the icons standing by, under arms, watching Heracles's feats and helping him when in difficulties. Athene was Neith, the Love-and-Battle goddess of the Libyans (see 8. *1*); her counterpart in Asia Minor was the great Moon-goddess Marian, Myrine, Ay-Mari, Mariamne or Marienna, who gave her name to Mariandyne – 'Marian's Dune' – and to Myrine, the city of the gynocratic Lemnians (see 149. *1*); and whom the Trojans worshipped as 'Leaping Myrine' (Homer: *Iliad* ii. 814). 'Smyrna' is 'Myrine' again, preceded by the definite article. Marienna, the Sumerian form, means 'High fruitful Mother', and the Ephesian Artemis was a fertility-goddess.

4. Myrine is said to have been caught in a storm and saved by the Mother of the Gods – in whose honour she founded altars at Samothrace – because she was herself the Mother of the Gods, and her rites saved sailors from shipwreck (see 149. *2*). Much the same mother-goddess was anciently worshipped in Thrace, the region of the river Tanais (Don), Armenia, and throughout Asia Minor and Syria. Theseus's expedition to Amazonia, a myth modelled on that of Heracles, confuses the issue, and has tempted mythographers to invent the fictitious invasion of Athens by Amazons and Scythians combined (see 100. *c*).

5. That the Amazons set up an image under an Ephesian beech is a

mistake made by Callimachus who, being an Egyptian, was unaware that beeches did not grow so far south; it must have been a date-palm, symbol of fertility (see 14. 2), and a reminder of the goddess's Libyan origin, since her statue was hung with large golden dates, generally mistaken for breasts. Mopsus's defeat of the Amazons is the story of the Hittites' defeat by the Moschians about 1200 B.C.; the Hittites had originally been wholly patriarchal, but under the influence of the matriarchal societies of Asia Minor and Babylonia had accepted goddess-worship. At Hattusas, their capital, a sculptural relief of a battle-goddess has recently been discovered by Garstang; who regards the Ephesian Artemis cult as of Hittite origin. The victories over the Amazons secured by Heracles, Theseus, Dionysus, Mopsus, and others, record, in fact, setbacks to the matriarchal system in Greece, Asia Minor, Thrace, and Syria.

6. Stephanus of Byzantium (*sub* Paros) records the tradition that Paros was a Cretan colony. Heracles's expedition there refers to a Hellenic occupation of the island. His bestowal of Thasos on the sons of Androgeus is a reference to its capture by a force of Parians mentioned in Thucydides iv. 104: this took place towards the close of the eighth century B.C. Euboeans colonized Torone at about the same time, representing Torone ('shrill queen') as a daughter of Proteus (Stephanus of Byzantium *sub* Torone). Hippolyte's double axe (*labrys*) was not, however, placed in Labradean Zeus's hand instead of a thunderbolt; it was itself a thunderbolt, and Zeus carried it by permission of the Cretan goddess who ruled in Lydia.

7. The Gargarensians are the Gogarenians, whom Ezekiel calls Gog (*Ezekiel* xxxviii and xxxix).

8. In his account of Myrine, Diodorus Siculus quotes early Libyan traditions which had already acquired a fairy-tale lustre; it is established, however, that in the third millennium B.C. neolithic emigrants went out from Libya in all directions, probably expelled by an inundation of their fields (see 39. 3–6). The Nile Delta was largely populated by Libyans.

9. According to Apollonius Rhodius (i. 1126–9), Titias was 'one of the only three Idaean Dactyls ("fingers") who dispense doom'. He names another Dactyl 'Cyllenius'. I have shown (*White Goddess* p. 281) that in finger-magic Titias, the Dactyl, represented the middle finger; that Cyllenius, *alias* Heracles, was the thumb; and that Dascylus, the third Dactyl, was the index-finger, as his name implies (see 53. 1). These three raised, while the fourth and little finger are turned down, made the 'Phrygian blessing'. Originally given in Myrine's name, it is now used by Catholic priests in that of the Christian Trinity.

10. Tityus, whom Apollo killed (see 21. d), may be a doublet of Titias. Myrine's capture of the island of Cerne seems a late and unauthorized addition to the story. Cerne has been identified with Fedallah near Fez;

or with Santa Cruz near Cape Ghir, or (most plausibly) with Arguin, a little south of Cabo Blanco. It was discovered and colonized by the Carthaginian Hanno, who described it as lying as far from the Pillars of Heracles as these lay from Carthage, and it became the great emporium of West African trade.

*

*11.* So much for the mythical elements of the Ninth Labour. Yet Heracles's expedition to the Thermodon and his wars in Mysia and Phrygia must not be dismissed as wholly unhistorical. Like the voyage of the *Argo* (see 148. *10*), they record Greek trading ventures in the Black Sea perhaps as far back as the middle of the second millennium B.C.; and the intrusion of Minyans from Iolcus, Aeacans from Aegina, and Argives in these waters suggests that though Helen may have been beautiful, and may have eloped with Paris of Troy, it was not her face that launched a thousand ships, but mercantile interest. Achilles the son of Peleus, Ajax the son of Telamon, and Diomedes the Argive were among the Greek allies of Agamemnon who insisted that Priam should allow them the free passage through the Hellespont enjoyed by their fathers – unless he wished his city to be sacked as Laomedon's had been, and for the same reason (see 137. *1*). Hence the dubious Athenian claims to have been represented in Heracles's expedition by Theseus, in the voyage of the *Argo* by Phalerus, and at Troy by Menestheus, Demophon, and Acamas. These were intended to justify their eventual control of Black Sea trade which the destruction of Troy and the decline of Rhodes had allowed them to seize (see 159. *2*; 160. *2–3* and 162. *3*).

# 132

## THE TENTH LABOUR: THE CATTLE
OF GERYON

HERACLES's Tenth Labour was to fetch the famous cattle of Geryon from Erytheia, an island near the Ocean stream, without either demand or payment. Geryon, a son of Chrysaor and Callirrhoë, a daughter of the Titan Oceanus, was the King of Tartessus in Spain, and reputedly the strongest man alive.[1] He had been born with three heads, six hands, and three bodies joined together at the waist. Geryon's shambling red cattle, beasts of marvellous beauty, were guarded by the herdsman Eurytion, son of Ares, and by the two-headed watchdog Orthrus – formerly Atlas's property – born of Typhon and Echidne.[2]

*b.* During his passage through Europe, Heracles destroyed many wild beasts and, when at last he reached Tartessus, erected a pair of pillars facing each other across the straits, one in Europe, one in Africa. Some hold that the two continents were formerly joined together, and that he cut a channel between them, or thrust the cliffs apart; others say that, on the contrary, he narrowed the existing straits to discourage the entry of whales and other sea-monsters.[3]

*c.* Helius beamed down upon Heracles who, finding it impossible to work in such heat, strung his bow and let fly an arrow at the god. 'Enough of that!' cried Helius angrily. Heracles apologized for his ill-temper, and unstrung his bow at once. Not to be outdone in courtesy, Helius lent Heracles his golden goblet, shaped like a water-lily, in which he sailed to Erytheia; but the Titan Oceanus, to try him, made the goblet pitch violently upon the waves. Heracles again drew his bow, which frightened Oceanus into calming the sea. Another account is that Heracles sailed to Erytheia in a brazen urn, using his lion pelt as a sail.[4]

*d.* On his arrival, he ascended Mount Abas. The dog Orthrus rushed at him, barking, but Heracles's club struck him lifeless; and Eurytion, Geryon's herdsman, hurrying to Orthrus's aid, died in the same manner. Heracles then proceeded to drive away the cattle. Menoetes, who was pasturing the cattle of Hades near by – but Heracles had left these untouched – took the news to Geryon. Challenged to battle, Heracles ran to Geryon's flank and shot him sideways through all three bodies with a single arrow; but some say that he stood his ground and let loose a flight of three arrows. As Hera hastened to Geryon's assistance, Heracles wounded her with an arrow in the right breast, and she fled. Thus he won the cattle, without either demand or payment, and embarked in the golden goblet, which he then sailed across to Tartessus and gratefully returned to Helius. From Geryon's blood sprang a tree which, at the time of the Pleiades' rising, bears stoneless cherry-like fruit. Geryon did not, however, die without issue: his daughter Erytheia became by Hermes the mother of Norax, who led a colony to Sardinia, even before the time of Hyllus, and there founded Nora, the oldest city in the island.[5]

*e.* The whereabouts of Erytheia, also called Erythrea, or Erythria, is disputed. Though some describe it as an island beyond the Ocean stream, others place it off the coast of Lusitania.[6] Still others identify it with the island of Leon, or with an islet hard by, on which the earliest city of Gades was built, and where the pasture is so rich that the milk yields no whey but only curds, and the cattle must be cupped every fifty days, lest they choke for excess of blood. This islet, sacred to Hera, is called either Erytheia, or Aphrodisias. Leon, the island on which the present city of Gades stands, used to be called Cotinusa, from its olives, but the Phoenicians renamed it Gadira, or 'Fenced City'. On the western cape stands a temple of Cronus, and the city of Gades; on the eastern, a temple of Heracles, remarkable for a spring which ebbs at flood tide, and flows at ebb tide; and Geryon lies buried in the city, equally famed for a secret tree that takes diverse forms.[7]

*f.* According to another account, however, Geryon's cattle were not pastured in any island, but on the mountain slopes of the farther part of Spain, confronting the Ocean; and 'Geryon' was a title of the renowned King Chrysaor, who ruled over the whole land, and whose three strong and courageous sons helped him in the defence of his kingdom, each leading an army recruited from warlike races. To combat these, Heracles assembled a large expedition in Crete, the birthplace of his father Zeus. Before setting out, he was splendidly honoured by the Cretans and, in return, rid their island of bears, wolves, serpents, and other noxious creatures, from which it is still immune. First, he sailed to Libya, where he killed Antaeus, slaughtered the wild beasts that infested the desert, and gave the country unsurpassed fertility. Next, he visited Egypt, where he killed Busiris; then he marched westward, across North Africa, annihilating the Gorgons and the Libyan Amazons as he went, founded the city of Hecatompylus, now Capsa, in southern Numidia, and reached the Ocean near Gades. There he set up pillars on either side of the straits and, ferrying his army across to Spain, found that the sons of Chrysaor, with their three armies, were encamped at some distance from one another. He conquered and killed them, each in turn, and finally drove off Geryon's famous herds, leaving the government of Spain to the most worthy of the surviving inhabitants.[8]

*g.* The Pillars of Heracles are usually identified with Mount Calpe in Europe, and Abyle, or Abilyx in Africa. Others make them the islets near Gades, of which the larger is sacred to Hera. All Spaniards and Libyans, however, take the word 'Pillars' literally, and place them at Gades, where brazen columns are consecrated to Heracles, eight cubits high and inscribed with the cost of their building; here sailors offer sacrifices whenever they return safely from a voyage. According to the people of Gades themselves, the King of Tyre was ordered by an oracle to found a colony near the Pillars of Heracles, and sent out three successive parties of exploration. The first party, thinking that the oracle had referred to Abyle and Calpe, landed inside the straits, where the city of Exitani now stands; the second sailed about two hundred miles beyond the straits, to an island sacred to Heracles, opposite the Spanish city of Onoba; but both were discouraged by unfavourable omens when they offered sacrifices, and returned home. The third party reached Gades, where they raised a temple to Heracles on the eastern cape and successfully founded the city of Gades on the western.[9]

*h*. Some, however, deny that it was Heracles who set up these pillars, and assert that Abyle and Calpe were first named 'The Pillars of Cronus', and afterwards 'The Pillars of Briareus', a giant whose power extended thus far; but that, the memory of Briareus (also called Aegaeon) having faded, they were renamed in honour of Heracles – perhaps because the city of Tartessus, which stands only five miles from Calpe, was founded by him, and used to be known as Heracleia. Vast ancient walls and ship-sheds are still shown there.[10] But it must be remembered that the earliest Heracles had also been called Briareus. The number of Heracles's Pillars is usually given as two; but some speak of three, or four.[11] So-called Pillars of Heracles are also reported from the northern coast of Germany; from the Black Sea; from the western extremity of Gaul; and from India.[12]

*i*. A temple of Heracles stands on the Sacred Promontory in Lusitania, the most westerly point of the world. Visitants are forbidden to enter the precinct by night, the time when the gods take up their abode in it. Perhaps when Heracles set up his pillars to mark the utmost limits of legitimate seafaring, this was the site he chose.[13]

*j*. How he then drove the cattle to Mycenae is much disputed. Some say that he forced Abyle and Calpe into temporary union and went across the resultant bridge into Libya; but according to a more probable account he passed through the territory of what is now Abdera, a Phoenician settlement, and then through Spain, leaving behind some of his followers as colonists.[14] In the Pyrenees, he courted and buried the Bebrycan princess Pyrene, from whom this mountain range takes its name; the river Danube is said to have its source there, near a city also named in her honour. He then visited Gaul, where he abolished a barbarous native custom of killing strangers, and won so many hearts by his generous deeds that he was able to found a large city, to which he gave the name Alesia, or 'Wandering', in commemoration of his travels. The Gauls to this day honour Alesia as the hearth and mother-city of their whole land – it was unconquered until Caligula's reign – and claim descent from Heracles's union with a tall princess named Galata, who chose him as her lover and bred that warlike people.[15]

*k.* When Heracles was driving Geryon's cattle through Liguria, two sons of Poseidon named Ialebion and Dercynus tried to steal them from him, and were both killed. At one stage of his battle with hostile Ligurian forces, Heracles ran out of arrows, and knelt down, in tears, wounded and exhausted. The ground being of soft mould, he could find no stones to throw at the enemy – Ligys, the brother of Ialebion, was their leader – until Zeus, pitying his tears, overshadowed the earth with a cloud, from which a shower of stones hailed down; and with these he put the Ligurians to flight. Zeus set among the stars an image of Heracles fighting the Ligurians, known as the constellation Engonasis. Another memorial of this battle survives on earth: namely the broad, circular plain lying between Marseilles and the mouths of the river Rhône, about fifteen miles from the sea, called 'The Stony Plain', because it is strewn with stones the size of a man's fist; brine springs are also found there.[16]

*l.* In his passage over the Ligurian Alps, Heracles carved a road fit for his armies and baggage trains; he also broke up all robber bands that infested the pass, before entering what is now Cis-alpine Gaul and Etruria. Only after wandering down the whole coast of Italy, and crossing into Sicily, did it occur to him: 'I have taken the wrong road!' The Romans say that, on reaching the Albula – afterwards called the Tiber – he was welcomed by King Evander, an exile from Arcadia. At evening, he swam across, driving the cattle before him, and lay down to rest on a grassy bed.[17] In a deep cave near by, lived a vast hideous, three-headed shepherd named Cacus, a son of Hephaestus and Medusa, who was the dread and disgrace of the Aventine Forest, and puffed flames from each of his three mouths. Human skulls and arms hung nailed above the lintels of his cave, and the ground inside gleamed white with the bones of his victims. While Heracles slept, Cacus stole the two finest of his bulls; as well as four heifers, which he dragged backwards by their tails into his lair.[18]

*m.* At the first streak of dawn, Heracles awoke, and at once noticed that the cattle were missing. After searching for them in vain, he was about to drive the remainder onward, when one of the stolen heifers lowed hungrily. Heracles traced the sound to the cave, but found the

entrance barred by a rock which ten yoke of oxen could hardly have
moved; nevertheless, he heaved it aside as though it had been a pebble
and, undaunted by the smoky flames which Cacus was now belching,
grappled with him and battered his face to pulp.[19]

*n*. Aided by King Evander, Heracles then built an altar to Zeus, at
which he sacrificed one of the recovered bulls, and afterwards made
arrangements for his own worship. Yet the Romans tell this story in
order to glorify themselves; the truth being that it was not Heracles
who killed Cacus, and offered sacrifices to Zeus, but a gigantic herdsman named Garanus, or Recaranus, the ally of Heracles.[20]

*o*. King Evander ruled rather by personal ascendancy than by force:
he was particularly reverenced for the knowledge of letters which he
had imbibed from his prophetic mother, the Arcadian nymph Nicostrate, or Themis; she was a daughter of the river Ladon, and though
already married to Echenus, bore Evander to Hermes. Nicostrate persuaded Evander to murder his supposed father; and, when the Arcadians banished them both, went with him to Italy, accompanied by a
body of Pelasgians.[21] There, some sixty years before the Trojan War,
they founded the small city of Pallantium, on the hill beside the river
Tiber, later called Mount Palatine; the site having been Nicostrate's
choice; and soon there was no more powerful king than Evander in all
Italy. Nicostrate, now called Carmenta, adapted the thirteen-consonant
Pelasgian alphabet, which Cadmus had brought back from Egypt, to
form the fifteen-consonant Latin one. But some assert that it was
Heracles who taught Evander's people the use of letters, which is why
he shares an altar with the Muses.[22]

*p*. According to the Romans, Heracles freed King Evander from
the tribute owed to the Etruscans; killed King Faunus, whose custom
was to sacrifice strangers at the altar of his father Hermes; and begot
Latinus, the ancestor of the Latins, on Faunus's widow, or daughter.
But the Greeks hold that Latinus was a son of Circe by Odysseus.
Heracles, at all events, suppressed the annual Cronian sacrifice of two
men, who were flung into the river Tiber, and forced the Romans to
use puppets instead; even now, in the month of May, when the moon
is full, the chief Vestal Virgin, standing on the oaken-timbered Pons
Sublicius, throws whitewashed images of old men, plaited from bul-
rushes, and called 'Argives', into the yellow stream.[23] Heracles is also
believed to have founded Pompeii and Herculaneum; to have fought
giants on the Phlegraean Plain of Cumae; and to have built a causeway

one mile long across the Lucrine Gulf, now called the Heracleian Road, down which he drove Geryon's cattle.[24]

*q.* It is further said that he lay down to rest near the frontier of Rhegium and Epizephyrian Locris and, being much disturbed by cicadas, begged the gods to silence them. His prayer was immediately granted; and cicadas have never been heard since on the Rhegian side of the river Alece, although they sing lustily on the Locrian side. That day a bull broke away from the herd and, plunging into the sea, swam over to Sicily. Heracles, going in pursuit, found it concealed among the herds of Eryx, King of the Elymans, a son of Aphrodite by Butes.[25] Eryx, who was a wrestler and a boxer, challenged him to a fivefold contest. Heracles accepted the challenge, on condition that Eryx would stake his kingdom against the runaway bull, and won the first four events; finally, in the wrestling match, he lifted Eryx high into the air, dashed him to the ground and killed him – which taught the Sicilians that not everyone born of a goddess is necessarily immortal. In this manner, Heracles won Eryx's kingdom, which he left the inhabitants to enjoy until one of his own descendants should come to claim it.[26]

*r.* Some say that Eryx – whose wrestling-ground is still shown – had a daughter named Psophis, who bore Heracles two sons: Echephron and Promachus. Having been reared in Erymanthus, they renamed it Psophis after their mother; and there built a shrine to Erycinian Aphrodite, of which today only the ruins remain. The hero-shrines of Echephron and Promachus have long since lost their importance, and Psophis is usually regarded as a daughter of Xanthus, the grandson of Arcas.[27]

*s.* Continuing on his way through Sicily, Heracles came to the site where now stands the city of Syracuse; there he offered sacrifices, and instituted the annual festival beside the sacred chasm of Cyane, down which Hades snatched Core to the Underworld. To those who honoured Heracles in the Plain of Leontini, he left undying memorials of his visit. Close to the city of Agyrium, the hoof marks of his cattle were found imprinted on a stony road, as though in wax; and, regarding this as an intimation of his own immortality, Heracles accepted from the inhabitants those divine honours which he had hitherto consistently refused. Then, in acknowledgement of their favours, he dug a lake four furlongs in circumference outside the city walls, and established local sanctuaries of Iolaus and Geryon.[28]

*t.* Returning to Italy in search of another route to Greece, Heracles drove his cattle up the eastern coast, to the Lacinian Promontory, where the ruler, King Lacinius, was afterwards able to boast that he had put Heracles to flight; this he did merely by building a temple to Hera, at the sight of which Heracles departed in disgust. Six miles farther on, Heracles accidentally killed one Croton, buried him with every honour, and prophesied that, in time to come, a great city would rise, called by his name. This prophecy Heracles made good after his deification: he appeared in a dream to one of his descendants, the Argive Myscelus, threatening him with terrible punishments if he did not lead a party of colonists to Sicily and found the city; and when the Argives were about to condemn Myscelus to death for defying their embargo on emigration, he miraculously turned every black voting-pebble into a white one.[29]

*u*. Heracles then proposed to drive Geryon's cattle through Istria into Epirus, and thence to the Peloponnese by way of the Isthmus. At at the head of the Adriatic Gulf Hera sent a gadfly, which stampeded the cows, driving them across Thrace and into the Scythian desert. There Heracles pursued them, and one cold, stormy night drew the lion pelt about him and fell fast asleep on a rocky hillside. When he awoke, he found that his chariot-mares, which he had unharnessed and put out to graze, were likewise missing. He wandered far and wide in search of them until he reached the wooded district called Hylaea, where a strange being, half woman, half serpent, shouted at him from a cave. She had his mares, she said, but would give them back to him only if he became her lover. Heracles agreed, though with a certain reluctance, and kissed her thrice; whereupon the serpent-tailed woman embraced him passionately, and when, at last, he was free to go, asked him: 'What of the three sons whom I now carry in my womb? When they grow to manhood, shall I settle them here where I am mistress, or shall I send them to you?'

*v*. 'When they grow up, watch carefully!' Heracles replied. 'And if ever one of them bends this bow – thus, as I now bend it – and girds himself with this belt – thus, as I now gird myself – choose him as the ruler of your country.'

So saying, he gave her one of his two bows, and his girdle which had a golden goblet hanging from its clasp; then went on his way. She named her triplets Agathyrsus, Gelonus, and Scythes. The eldest two were unequal to the tasks that their father had set, and she drove them away; but Scythes succeeded in both and was allowed to remain, thus becoming the ancestor of all royal Scythian kings who, to this day, wear golden goblets on their girdles.[30] Others, however, say that it was Zeus, not Heracles, who lay with the serpent-tailed woman, and that, when his three sons by her were still ruling the land, there fell from the sky four golden implements: a plough, a yoke, a battle axe, and a cup. Agathyrsus first ran to recover them, but as he came close, the gold flamed up and burned his hands. Gelonus was similarly rejected. However, when Scythes, the youngest, approached, the fire died down at once; whereupon he carried home the four golden treasures and the elder brothers agreed to yield him the kingdom.[31]

*w*. Heracles, having recovered his mares and most of the strayed cattle, drove them back across the river Strymon, which he dammed with stones for the purpose, and encountered no further adventures until the giant herdsman Alcyoneus, having taken possession of the Corinthian Isthmus, hurled a rock at the army which once more followed Heracles, crushing no less than twelve chariots and double that number of horsemen. This was the same Alcyoneus who twice stole Helius's sacred cattle: from Erytheia, and from the citadel of Corinth. He now ran forward, picked up the rock again, and this time hurled it at Heracles, who bandied it back with his club and so killed the giant; the very rock is still shown on the Isthmus.[32]

1. Pausanias: iv. 36. 3; Apollodorus: ii. 5. 10; Servius on Virgil's *Aeneid* vi. 289; Hesiod: *Theogony* 981.

2. Hesiod: *Theogony* 287 ff.; Lucian: *Toxaris* 72; Apollodorus: *loc. cit.*; Livy: i. 7; Servius on Virgil's *Aeneid* viii. 300; Scholiast on Apollonius Rhodius: iv. 1399.

3. Apollodorus: ii. 5. 10; Diodorus Siculus: iv. 18; Pomponius Mela: i. 5. 3 and ii. 6. 6.

4. Apollodorus: *loc. cit.*; Pherecydes, quoted by Athenaeus: xi. 39; Servius on Virgil's *Aeneid* vii. 662 and viii. 300.

5. Apollodorus: *loc. cit.*; Hyginus: *Fabula* 30; Euripides: *Heracles* 423; Servius on Virgil's *Aeneid* vii. 662; Pausanias: x. 17. 4; Ptolemy Hephaestionos, quoted by Photius: p. 475; Pindar: *Fragment* 169.

6. Solinus: xxiii. 12; Pomponius Mela: iii. 47; Hesiod: *Theogony* 287 ff.; Pliny: *Natural History* iv. 36.

7. Pherecydes, quoted by Strabo: iii. 2. 11; Strabo: iii. 5. 3–4 and 7; Timaeus, quoted by Pliny: *loc. cit.*; Polybius, quoted by Strabo: iii. 5. 7; Pausanias: i. 35. 6.

8. Diodorus Siculus: iii. 55 and iv. 17–19.

9. Pliny: *Natural History* iii. *Proem*; Strabo: iii. 5. 5.

10. Eustathius on Dionysius's *Description of the Earth* 64 ff.; Scholiast on Pindar's *Nemean Odes* iii. 37; Aristotle, quoted by Aelian: *Varia Historia* v. 3; Pliny: *Natural History* iii. 3; Timotheus, quoted by Strabo: iii. 1. 7.

11. Erasmus: *Chiliades* i. 7; Zenobius: *Proverbs* v. 48; Aeschylus: *Prometheus Bound* 349 and 428; Hesychius *sub* stelas distomous.

12. Tacitus: *Germania* 34; Servius on Virgil's *Aeneid* xi. 262; Scymnius Chius: 188; Strabo: ii. 5. 6.

13. Strabo: iii. 1. 4; Pindar: *Nemean Odes* iii. 21 ff.

14. Avienus: *Ora Maritima* 326; Apollodorus: ii. 5. 10; Strabo: iii. 4. 3; Asclepiades of Myrtea, quoted by Strabo: *loc. cit.*

15. Silius Italicus: iii. 417; Herodotus: ii. 33; Diodorus Siculus: iv. 19 and 24.

16. Apollodorus: ii. 5. 10; Tzetzes: *Chiliades* ii. 340 ff. and *On Lycophron* 1312; Aeschylus: *Prometheus Unbound*, quoted by Hyginus: *Poetic Astronomy* ii. 6 and by Strabo: iv. 1. 7; Theon: *On Aratus* p. 12, ed. Morell.

17. Diodorus Siculus: iv. 21; Ovid: *Fasti* v. 545 ff.; Livy: i. 7.

18. Propertius: *Elegies* iv. 9. 10; Ovid: *Fasti* i. 545 ff.; Livy: *loc. cit.*; Virgil: *Aeneid* viii. 207–8.

19. Livy: *loc. cit.*; Virgil: *Aeneid* viii. 217 and 233 ff.; Ovid: *loc. cit.*

20. Plutarch: *Roman Questions* 18; Ovid: *loc. cit.*; Livy: *loc. cit.*; Verrius Flaccus, quoted by Servius on Virgil's *Aeneid* viii. 203; Aurelius Victor: *On the Origins of the Roman Race* 8.

21. Servius on Virgil's *Aeneid* viii. 51; 130 and 336; Livy: i. 7; Plutarch: *Roman Questions* 56; Pausanias: viii. 43. 2; Dionysius: *Roman Antiquities* i. 31.

22. Servius on Virgil's *Aeneid* viii. 130 and 336; Ovid: *Fasti* v. 94–5 and i. 542; Hyginus: *Fabula* 277; Juba, quoted by Plutarch: *Roman Questions* 59.

23. Plutarch: *Roman Questions* 18 and 32; Dercyllus: *Italian History* iii, quoted by Plutarch: *Parallel Stories* 38; Tzetzes: *On Lycophron* 1232; Justin: xliii. 1; Hesiod: *Theogony* 1013; Ovid: *Fasti* v. 621 ff.

24. Solinus: ii. 5; Dionysius: i. 44; Diodorus Siculus: iv. 21–2 and 24; Strabo: vi. 3. 5 and 4. 6.

25. Diodorus Siculus: iv. 22; Strabo: vi. 1. 19; Apollodorus: ii. 5. 10; Servius on Virgil's *Aeneid* i. 574.

26. Pausanias: iv. 36. 3; Diodorus Siculus: iv. 23; Apollodorus: *loc. cit.*; Tzetzes: *On Lycophron* 866; Servius on Virgil's *Aeneid* x. 551.

27. Tzetzes: *loc. cit.*; Pausanias: viii. 24. 1 and 3.

28. Diodorus Siculus: iv. 23–4 and v. 4.

29. Diodorus Siculus: iv. 24; Servius on Virgil's *Aeneid* iii. 552; Ovid: *Metamorphoses* xv. 12 ff.

30. Diodorus Siculus: iv. 25; Herodotus: iv. 8–10.

31. Diodorus Siculus: ii. 43; Herodotus: iv. 5.

32. Apollodorus: ii. 5. 10 and i. 6. 1; Pindar: *Nemean Odes* iv. 27 ff.
and *Isthmian Odes* vi. 32 ff.; Scholiast on Pindar's *Nemean Odes*
*loc. cit.* and *Isthmian Odes* vi. 32.

\*

1. The main theme of Heracles's Labours is his performance of certain
ritual feats before being accepted as consort to Admete, or Auge, or
Athene, or Hippolyte, or whatever the Queen's name was. This wild
Tenth Labour may originally have been relevant to the same theme, if it
records the patriarchal Hellenic custom by which the husband bought his
bride with the proceeds of a cattle raid. In Homeric Greece, women were
valued at so many cattle, and still are in parts of East and Central Africa.
But other irrelevant elements have become attached to the myth, including a visit to the Western Island of Death, and his successful return, laden
with spoil; the ancient Irish parallel is the story of Cuchulain who harrowed Hell – Dun Scaith, 'shadow city' – and brought back three cows
and a magic cauldron, despite storms which the gods of the dead sent
against him. The bronze urn in which Heracles sailed to Erytheia was an
appropriate vessel for a visit to the Island of Death, and has perhaps been
confused with the bronze cauldron. In the Eleventh Tablet of the Babylonian Gilgamesh Epic, Gilgamesh makes a similar journey to a sepulchral island across a sea of death, using his garment for a sail. This incident
calls attention to many points of resemblance between the Heracles and
Gilgamesh myths; the common source is probably Sumerian. Like Heracles, Gilgamesh kills a monstrous lion and wears its pelt (see 123. *e*); seizes
a sky-bull by the horns and overcomes it (see 129. *b*); discovers a secret
herb of invulnerability (see 135. *b*); takes the same journey as the Sun
(see 132. *d*); and visits a Garden of the Hesperides where, after killing a
dragon coiled about a sacred tree, he is rewarded with two sacred objects
from the Underworld (see 133. *e*). The relations of Gilgamesh and his
comrade Enkidu closely resemble those of Theseus, the Athenian Heracles,
and his comrade Peirithous who goes down to Tartarus and fails to
return (see 103. *c* and *d*); and Gilgamesh's adventure with the Scorpions
has been awarded to the Boeotian Orion (see 41. *3*).

2. Pre-Phoenician Greek colonies planted in Spain, Gaul, and Italy
under Heracles's protection have contributed to the myth; and, in the
geographical sense, the Pillars of Heracles – at which one band of settlers
arrived about the year 1100 B.C. – are Ceuta and Gibraltar.

3. In a mystical Celto-Iberian sense, however, the Pillars are alpha-
betical abstractions. 'Marwnad Ercwlf', an ancient Welsh poem in the
*Red Book of Hergest*, treats of the Celtic Heracles – whom the Irish called
'Ogma Sunface' and Lucian, 'Ogmius' (see 125. *1*) – and records how
Ercwlf raised 'four columns of equal height capped with red gold',

apparently the four columns of five letters each, which formed the twenty-lettered Bardic alphabet known as the Boibel-Loth (*White Goddess* pp. 133, 199, and 278). It seems that, about the year 400 B.C., this new alphabet, the Greek letter-names of which referred to Celestial Heracles's journey in the sun-goblet, his death on Mount Oeta, and his powers as city-founder and judge (*White Goddess* p. 136), displaced the Beth-Luis-Nion tree-alphabet, the letter-names of which referred to the murderous sacrifice of Cronus by the wild women (*White Goddess* p. 374). Since the Gorgons had a grove on Erytheia – 'Red Island', identified by Phere-cydes with the island of Gades – and since 'trees' in all Celtic languages means 'letters', I read 'the tree that takes diverse forms' as meaning the Beth-Luis-Nion alphabet, whose secret the Gorgons guarded in their sacred grove until Heracles 'annihilated' them. In this sense, Heracles's raid on Erytheia, where he killed Geryon and the dog Orthrus – the Dog-star Sirius – refers to the supersession of the Cronus-alphabet by the Heracles-alphabet.

4. Hesiod (*Theogony* 287) calls Geryon *tricephalon*, 'three-headed'; another reading of which is *tricarenon*, meaning the same thing. 'Tricare-non' recalls *Tarvos Trigaranus*, the Celtic god with two left hands, shown in the company of cranes and a bull on the Paris Altar, felling a willow-tree. *Geryon*, a meaningless word in Greek, seems to be a worn-down form of *Trigaranus*. Since alike in Greek and Irish tradition cranes are associated with alphabetical secrets (see 52. 6), and with poets, Geryon appears to be the Goddess's guardian of the earlier alphabet: in fact, Cronus accompanied by the Dactyls. At the sepulchral island of Erytheia, Cronus-Geryon, who was once a sun-hero of the Heracles-Briareus type, had become a god of the dead, with Orthrus as his Cerberus; and the Tenth Labour, therefore, has been confused with the Twelfth, Menoe-tes figuring in both. Though the 'stoneless cherry-like fruit' sprung from Geryon's blood may have been arbutus-berries, native to Spain, the story has been influenced by the sacredness to Cronus-Saturn of the early-fruiting cornel-cherry (*White Goddess* p. 171), which yields a red dye like the kerm-berry. Chrysaor's part in the story is important. His name means 'golden falchion', the weapon associated with the Cronus cult, and he was said to be the Gorgon Medusa's son (see 33. *b*; 73. *h* and 138. *j*).

5. Norax, Geryon's grandson by Erytheia and Hermes – Hermes is recorded to have brought the tree-alphabet from Greece to Egypt, and back again – seems to be a miswriting of *Norops*, the Greek word for 'Sun-face'. This genealogy has been turned inside-out by the Irish mythographers: they record that their own Geryon, whose three persons were known as Brian, Iuchar, and Iucharba – a form of Mitra, Varuna, and Indra – had Ogma for a grandfather, not a grandson, and that his son

was the Celt-Iberian Sun-god Lugh, Llew, or Lugos. They also insisted that the alphabet had come to them from Greece by way of Spain. Cronus's crow was sacred to Lugos, according to Plutarch who records (*On Rivers and Mountains* v) that 'Lugdunum' – Lyons, the fortress of Lugos – 'was so called because an auspice of crows suggested the choice of its site; *lug* meaning a crow in the Allobrigian dialect.'

6. Verrius Flaccus seems to have been misreported by Servius; he is more likely to have said that 'three-headed Garanus (Geryon), not Cacus, was the name of Heracles's victim, and Evander aided Heracles.' This would fit in with the account of how Evander's mother Carmenta suppressed the thirteen-consonant alphabet, Cronus's Beth-Luis-Nion, in favour of Heracles-Ogma's fifteen-consonant Boibel-Loth (*White Goddess* p. 272). King Juba, whom Plutarch quotes as saying that Heracles taught Evander's people the use of letters, was an honorary magistrate of Gades, and must have known a good deal of local alphabetic lore. In this Evander story, Heracles is plainly described as an enemy of the Cronus cult, since he abolishes human sacrifice. His circumambulation of Italy and Sicily has been invented to account for the many temples there raised to him; his fivefold contest with Eryx, to justify the sixth-century colonizing expeditions which Pentathlus of Cnidos, the Hera-clid, and Dorieus the Spartan, led to the Eryx region. The Heracles honoured at Agyrium, a Sicel city, may have been an ancestor who led the Sicels across the straits from Italy about the year 1050 B.C. (Thucydides: vi. 2. 5). He was also made to visit Scythia; the Greek colonists on the western and northern shores of the Black Sea incorporated a Scythian Heracles, an archer hero (see 119. 5), in the omniumgatherum Tenth Labour. His bride, the serpent-tailed woman, was an Earth-goddess, mother of the three principal Scythian tribes mentioned by Herodotus; in another version of the myth, represented by the English ballad of *The Laidley Worm*, when he has kissed her three times, she turns into 'the fairest woman you ever did see'.

7. The Alcyoneus anecdote seems to have become detached from the myth of the Giants' assault on Olympus and their defeat at Heracles's hands (see 35. *a–e*). But Alcyoneus's theft of Helius's cattle from Erytheia, and again from the citadel of Corinth, is an older version of Heracles's theft of Geryon's cattle; their owner being an active solar consort of the Moon-goddess, not a banished and enfeebled god of the Dead.

8. The arrow which Heracles shot at the noon-day sun will have been one discharged at the zenith during his coronation ceremony (see 126. 2 and 135. 1).

# THE ELEVENTH LABOUR: THE APPLES
## OF THE HESPERIDES

HERACLES had performed these Ten Labours in the space of eight
years and one month; but Eurystheus, discounting the Second and the
Fifth, set him two more. The Eleventh Labour was to fetch fruit from
the golden apple-tree, Mother Earth's wedding gift to Hera, with
which she had been so delighted that she planted it in her own divine
garden. This garden lay on the slopes of Mount Atlas, where the panting chariot-horses of the Sun complete their journey, and where Atlas's
sheep and cattle, one thousand herds of each, wander over their undisputed pastures. When Hera found, one day, that Atlas's daughters, the
Hesperides, to whom she had entrusted the tree, were pilfering the
apples, she set the ever-watchful dragon Ladon to coil around the tree
as its guardian.[1]

b. Some say that Ladon was the offspring of Typhon and Echidne;
others, that he was the youngest-born of Ceto and Phorcys; others
again, that he was a parthogenous son of Mother Earth. He had one
hundred heads, and spoke with divers tongues.[2]

c. It is equally disputed whether the Hesperides lived on Mount
Atlas in the Land of the Hyperboreans; or on Mount Atlas in Mauretania; or somewhere beyond the Ocean stream; or on two islands near
the promontory called the Western Horn, which lies close to the
Ethiopian Hesperiae, on the borders of Africa. Though the apples were
Hera's, Atlas took a gardener's pride in them and, when Themis
warned him: 'One day long hence, Titan, your tree shall be stripped of
its gold by a son of Zeus,' Atlas, who had not then been punished with
his terrible task of supporting the celestial globe upon his shoulders,
built solid walls around the orchard, and expelled all strangers from his
land; it may well have been he who set Ladon to guard the apples.[3]

d. Heracles, not knowing in what direction the Garden of the Hesperides lay, marched through Illyria to the river Po, the home of the
oracular sea-god Nereus. On the way he crossed the Echedorus, a small
Macedonian stream, where Cycnus, the son of Ares and Pyrene, challenged him to a duel. Ares acted as Cycnus's second, and marshalled the
combatants, but Zeus hurled a thunderbolt between them and they

broke off the fight. When at last Heracles came to the Po, the river-nymphs, daughters of Zeus and Themis, showed him Nereus asleep. He seized the hoary old sea-god and, clinging to him despite his many Protean changes, forced him to prophesy how the golden apples could be won. Some say, however, that Heracles went to Prometheus for this information.[4]

*e*. Nereus had advised Heracles not to pluck the apples himself, but to employ Atlas as his agent, meanwhile relieving him of his fantastic burden; therefore, on arriving at the Garden of the Hesperides, he asked Atlas to do him this favour. Atlas would have undertaken almost any task for the sake of an hour's respite, but he feared Ladon, whom Heracles thereupon killed with an arrow shot over the garden wall. Heracles now bent his back to receive the weight of the celestial globe, and Atlas walked away, returning presently with three apples plucked by his daughters. He found the sense of freedom delicious. 'I will take these apples to Eurystheus myself without fail,' he said, 'if you hold up the heavens for a few months longer.' Heracles pretended to agree but, having been warned by Nereus not to accept any such offer, begged Atlas to support the globe for only one moment more, while he put a pad on his head. Atlas, easily deceived, laid the apples on the ground and resumed his burden; whereupon Heracles picked them up and went away with an ironical farewell.

*f*. After some months Heracles brought the apples to Eurystheus, who handed them back to him; he then gave them to Athene, and she returned them to the nymphs, since it was unlawful that Hera's property should pass from their hands.[5] Feeling thirsty after this Labour, Heracles stamped his foot and made a stream of water gush out, which later saved the lives of the Argonauts when they were cast up high and dry on the Libyan desert. Meanwhile Hera, weeping for Ladon, set his image among the stars as the constellation of the Serpent.[6]

*g*. Heracles did not return to Mycenae by a direct route. He first traversed Libya, whose King Antaeus, son of Poseidon and Mother Earth, was in the habit of forcing strangers to wrestle with him until they were exhausted, whereupon he killed them; for not only was he a strong and skilful athlete, but whenever he touched the earth, his strength revived. He saved the skulls of his victims to roof a temple of Poseidon.[7] It is not known whether Heracles, who was determined to end this barbarous practice, challenged Antaeus, or was challenged by him. Antaeus, however, proved no easy victim, being a giant who lived in a cave beneath a towering cliff, where he feasted on the flesh of lions, and slept on the bare ground in order to conserve and increase his already colossal strength. Mother Earth, not yet sterile after her birth of the Giant, had conceived Antaeus in a Libyan cave, and found more reason to boast of him than even of her monstrous elder children, Typhon, Tityus, and Briareus. It would have gone ill with the Olympians if he had fought against them on the Plains of Phlegra.

*h.* In preparation for the wrestling match, both combatants cast off their lion pelts, but while Heracles rubbed himself with oil in the Olympian fashion, Antaeus poured hot sand over his limbs lest contact with the earth through the soles of his feet alone should prove insufficient. Heracles planned to preserve his strength and wear Antaeus down, but after tossing him full length on the ground, he was amazed to see the giant's muscles swell and a healthy flush suffuse his limbs as Mother Earth revived him. The combatants grappled again, and presently Antaeus flung himself down of his own accord, not waiting to be thrown; upon which, Heracles, realizing what he was at, lifted him high into the air, then cracked his ribs and, despite the hollow groans of Mother Earth, held him aloft until he died.[8]

*i.* Some say that this conflict took place at Lixus, a small Mauretanian city some fifty miles from Tangier, near the sea, where a hillock is shown as Antaeus's tomb. If a few basketsful of soil are taken from this hillock, the natives believe, rain will fall and continue to fall until they are replaced. It is also claimed that the Gardens of the Hesperides were the near-by island, on which stands an altar of Heracles; but, except for a few wild-olive trees, no trace of the orchard now remains. When Sertorius took Tangier, he opened the tomb to see whether Antaeus's skeleton were as large as tradition described it. To his astonishment, it measured sixty cubits, so he at once closed up the tomb and offered Antaeus heroic sacrifices. It is said locally either that Antaeus founded Tangier, formerly called Tingis; or that Sophax, whom Tinga, Antaeus's widow, bore to Heracles, reigned over that country, and gave his mother's name to the city. Sophax's son Diodorus subdued many African nations with a Greek army recruited from the Myeenaean colonists whom Heracles had settled there.[9] The Mauretanians are of eastern origin and, like the Pharusii, descended from certain Persians who accompanied Heracles to Africa; but some hold that they are descendants of those Canaanites whom Joshua the Israelite expelled from their country.[10]

*j*. Next, Heracles visited the Oracle at Ammon, where he asked for an interview with his father Zeus; but Zeus was loth to reveal himself and, when Heracles persisted, flayed a ram, put on the fleece, with the ram's head hiding his own, and issued certain instructions. Hence the Egyptians give their images of Zeus Ammon a ram's face. The Thebans sacrifice rams only once a year when, at the end of Zeus's festival, they slay a single ram and use its fleece to cover Zeus's image; after which the worshippers beat their breasts in mourning for the victim, and bury it in a sacred tomb.[11]

*k*. Heracles then struck south, and founded a hundred-gated city, named Thebes in honour of his birthplace; but some say that Osiris had already founded it. All this time, the King of Egypt was Antaeus's brother Busiris, a son of Poseidon by Lysianassa, the daughter of Epaphus or, as others say, by Anippe, a daughter of the river Nile.[12] Now, Busiris's kingdom had once been visited with drought and famine for eight or nine years, and he had sent for Greek augurs to give him advice. His nephew, a learned Cyprian seer, named Phrasius, Thrasius, or Thasius, son of Pygmalion, announced that the famine would cease if every year one stranger were sacrificed in honour of Zeus. Busiris began with Phrasius himself, and afterwards sacrificed other chance guests, until the arrival of Heracles, who let the priests hale him off to the altar. They bound his hair with a fillet, and Busiris, calling upon the gods, was about to raise the sacrificial axe, when Heracles burst his bonds and slew Busiris, Busiris's son Amphidamas, and all the priestly attendants.[13]

*l*. Next, Heracles traversed Asia and put in at Thermydrae, the harbour of Rhodian Lindus, where he unyoked one of the bullocks from a farmer's cart, sacrificed it, and feasted on its flesh, while the owner stood upon a certain mountain and cursed him from afar. Hence the Lindians still utter curses when they sacrifice to Heracles. Finally he reached the Caucasus Mountains, where Prometheus had been fettered for thirty years – or one thousand, or thirty thousand years – while every day a griffon-vulture, born of Typhon and Echidne, tore at his liver. Zeus had long repented of his punishment, because Prometheus had since sent him a kindly warning not to marry Thetis, lest he might beget one greater than himself; and now, when Heracles pleaded for Prometheus's pardon, granted this without demur.[14] Having once, however, condemned him to everlasting punishment, Zeus stipulated that, in order still to appear a prisoner, he must wear a ring made from

his chains and set with Caucasian stone – and this was the first ring ever
to contain a setting. But Prometheus's sufferings were destined to last
until some immortal should voluntarily go to Tartarus in his stead; so
Heracles reminded Zeus of Cheiron, who was longing to resign the
gift of immortality ever since he had suffered his incurable wound.
Thus no further impediment remained, and Heracles, invoking Hunter
Apollo, shot the griffon-vulture through the heart and set Prometheus
free.[15]

*m.* Mankind now began to wear rings in Prometheus's honour, and
also wreaths; because when released, Prometheus was ordered to
crown himself with a willow wreath, and Heracles, to keep him company, assumed one of wild-olive.[16]

*n.* Almighty Zeus set the arrow among the stars as the constellation
Sagitta; and to this day the inhabitants of the Caucasus Mountains
regard the griffon-vulture as the enemy of mankind. They burn out
its nests with flaming darts, and set snares for it to avenge Prometheus's
suffering.[17]

1. Apollodorus: ii. 5. 11; Euripides: *Heracles* 396; Pherecydes: *Mar-
    riage of Hera* ii, quoted by scholiast on Apollonius Rhodius: iv.
    1396; Eratosthenes: *Catasterismoi* iii; Hyginus: *Poetic Astronomy*
    ii. 3; Germanicus Caesar: *On Aratus's Phenomena*; *sub* Draco.
2. Apollodorus: ii. 5. 11; Hesiod: *Theogony* 333–5; Scholiast on
    Apollonius Rhodius: iv. 1396.
3. Apollodorus: *loc. cit.*; Scholiast on Virgil's *Aeneid* iv. 483; Hesiod:
    *Theogony* 215; Pliny: *Natural History* vi. 35–6; Ovid: *Metamor-
    phoses* iv. 637 ff.
4. Apollodorus: *loc. cit.*; Herodotus: vii. 124–7; Hyginus: *Poetic
    Astronomy* ii. 15.
5. Apollodorus: *loc. cit.*; Pherecydes, quoted by scholiast on Apollo-
    nius Rhodius: iv. 1396; Apollonius Rhodius: 1396–1484.
6. Hyginus: *Poetic Astronomy* ii. 3.
7. Apollodorus: *loc. cit.*; Hyginus: *Fabula* 31; Diodorus Siculus: iv. 17.
8. Diodorus Siculus: *loc. cit.*; Apollodorus: *loc. cit.*; Pindar: *Isthmian
    Odes* iv. 52–5; Lucan: iv. 589–655.
9. Pliny: *Natural History* v. 1; Strabo: xvii. 3. 2; Pomponius Mela:
    iii. 106; Plutarch: *Sertorius* 9.
10. Strabo: xvii. 3. 7; Pliny: *Natural History* v. 8; Procopius: *On the
    Vandal War* ii. 10.
11. Callisthenes, quoted by Strabo: xvii. 1. 43; Herodotus: ii. 42.
12. Diodorus Siculus: i. 15 and iv. 18; Ovid: *Ibis* 399; Apollodorus:
    ii. 5. 11; Agathon of Samos, quoted by Plutarch: *Parallel Stories* 38.
13. Philargyrius on Virgil's *Georgics* iii. 5; Apollodorus: *loc. cit.*;
    Hyginus: *Fabulae* 31 and 56; Ovid: *Art of Love* i. 649.

14. Apollodorus: *loc. cit.*; Hyginus: *Fabula* 54; Strabo: xi. 5. 5; Aeschylus, quoted by Hyginus: *Poetic Astronomy* ii. 15; Hesiod: *Theogony* 529 ff.

15. Servius on Virgil's *Eclogues* vi. 42; Hyginus: *loc. cit.*; Pliny: *Natural History* xxxiii. 4 and xxxvii. 1; Aeschylus: *Prometheus Bound* 1025 and *Prometheus Unbound, Fragment* 195, quoted by Plutarch: *On Love* 14; Apollodorus: *loc. cit.*

16. Athenaeus: xv. 11–13; Aeschylus: *Fragments* 202 and 235, quoted by Athenaeus p. 674d; Apollodorus: *loc. cit.*

17. Hyginus: *Poetic Astronomy* ii. 15; Philostratus: *Life of Apollonius of Tyana* ii. 3.

\*

1. The different locations of the Hesperides represent different views of what constituted the Farthest West. One account placed the scene of this Labour at Berenice, formerly called the city of the Hesperides (Pliny: *Natural History* v. 5), Eusperides (Herodotus: iv. 171), or Euesperites (Herodotus: iv. 198), but renamed after the wife of Ptolemy Euergetes. It was built on Pseudopenias (Strabo: xvii. 3. 20), the western promontory of the Gulf of Sirte. This city, washed by the river Lathon, or Lethon, had a sacred grove, known as the 'Gardens of the Hesperides'. Moreover, the Lathon flowed into a Hesperian Lake: and near by lay another, Lake Tritonis, enclosing a small island with a temple of Aphrodite (Strabo: *loc. cit.*; Pliny: *loc. cit.*), to whom the apple-tree was sometimes said to belong (Servius on Virgil's *Aeneid* iv. 485). Herodotus (*loc. cit.*) describes this as one of the few fertile parts of Libya; in the best years, the land brought forth one hundredfold.

2. Besides these geographical disputes, there were various rationalizations of the myth. One view was that the apples had really been beautiful sheep (*melon* means both 'sheep' and 'apple'), or sheep with a peculiar red fleece resembling gold, which were guarded by a shepherd named Dragon to whom Hesperus's daughters, the Hesperides, used to bring food. Heracles carried off the sheep (Servius on Virgil's *Aeneid: loc. cit.*; Diodorus Siculus: iv. 26) and killed (Servius: *loc. cit.*) or abducted, the shepherd (Palaephatus: 19). Palaephatus (*loc. cit.*) makes Hesperus a native of Carian Miletus, which was still famous for its sheep, and says that though Hesperus had long been dead at the time of Heracles's raid, his two daughters survived him.

3. Another view was that Heracles rescued the daughters of Atlas, who had been abducted from their family orchard by Egyptian priests; and Atlas, in gratitude, not only gave him the object of his Labour, but taught him astronomy into the bargain. For Atlas, the first astronomer, knew so much that he carried the celestial globe upon his shoulders, as it were; hence Heracles is said to have taken the globe from him (Diodorus

Siculus: iii. 60 and iv. 27). Heracles did indeed become Lord of the Zodiac, but the Titan astronomer whom he superseded was Coeus (*alias* Thoth), not Atlas (see 1.3).

4. The true explanation of this Labour is, however, to be found in ritual, rather than allegory. It will be shown (see 148. 5) that the candidate for the kingship had to overcome a serpent and take his gold; and this Heracles did both here and in his battle with the Hydra. But the gold which he took should not properly have been in the form of golden apples – those were given him at the close of his reign by the Triple-goddess, as his passport to Paradise. And, in this funerary context, the Serpent was not his enemy, but the form that his own oracular ghost would assume after he had been sacrificed. Ladon was hundred-headed and spoke with divers tongues because many oracular heroes could call themselves 'Heracles': that is to say, they had been representatives of Zeus, and dedicated to the service of Hera. The Garden of the three Hesperides – whose names identify them with the sunset (see 33. 7 and 39. 1) – is placed in the Far West because the sunset was a symbol of the sacred king's death. Heracles received the apples at the close of his reign, correctly recorded as a Great Year of one hundred lunations. He had taken over the burden of the sacred kingship from his predecessor, and with it the title 'Atlas', 'the long-suffering one'. It is likely that the burden was originally not the globe, but the sun-disk (see 67. 2).

5. Nereus's behaviour is modelled on that of Proteus (see 169. *a*), whom Menelaus consulted on Pharos (Homer: *Odyssey* iv. 581 ff.). Heracles is said to have ascended the Po, because it led to the Land of the Hyperboreans (see 125. *b*). We know that the straw-wrapped gifts from the Hyperboreans to Delos came by this route (Herodotus: iv. 33). But though their land was, in one sense, Britain – as the centre of the Boreas cult – it was Libya in another, and the Caucasus in another; and the Paradise lay either in the Far West, or at the back of the North Wind, the mysterious region to which the wild geese flew in summertime (see 161. 4). Heracles's wanderings illustrate this dubiety. If he was in search of the Libyan Paradise, he would have consulted Proteus King of Pharos (see 169. *a*); if of the Caucasian Paradise, Prometheus (which is, indeed, Apollodorus's version); if of the Northern, Nereus, who lived near the sources of the Po, and whose behaviour resembled that of Proteus.

6. Antaeus's bones were probably those of a stranded whale, about which a legend grew at Tangier: 'This must have been a giant – only Heracles could have killed him. Heracles, who put up those enormous pillars at Ceuta and Gibraltar!' A wrestling match between the candidate for kingship and local champions was a widely observed custom: the fight with Antaeus for the possession of the kingdom, like Theseus's fight with Sciron (see 96. 3), or Odysseus's with Philomeleides (see 161. *f*),

must be understood in this context. Praxiteles, the sculptor of the Parthenon, regarded the overthrow of Antaeus as a separate labour (Pausanias: iv. 11. 4).

7. An ancient religious association linked Dodona and Ammon; and the Zeus worshipped in each was originally a shepherd-king, annually sacrificed, as on Mounts Pelion and Laphystius. Heracles did right to visit his father Zeus when passing through Libya; Perseus had done so on his way to the East, and Alexander the Great followed suit centuries later.

8. The god Set had reddish hair, and the Busirians therefore needed victims with hair of that colour to offer Osiris, whom Set murdered; redheads were rare in Egypt, but common among the Hellenes (Diodorus Siculus: i. 88; Plutarch: On Isis and Osiris 30, 33 and 73). Heracles's killing of Busiris may record some punitive action taken by the Hellenes, whose nationals had been waylaid and killed; there is evidence for an early Hellenic colony at Chemmis.

9. Curses uttered during sacrifices to Heracles (see 143. a) recall the well-established custom of cursing and insulting the king from a near-by hill while he is being crowned, in order to ward off divine jealousy – Roman generals were similarly insulted at their triumphs while they impersonated Mars. But sowers also cursed the seed as they scattered it in the furrows.

10. The release of Prometheus seems to have been a moral fable invented by Aeschylus, not a genuine myth (see 39. h). His wearing of the willow-wreath – corroborated on an Etruscan mirror – suggests that he had been dedicated to the Moon-goddess Anatha, or Neith, or Athene (see 9. 1). Perhaps he was originally bound with willow thongs to the sacrificial altar of her autumn festival (see 116. 4).

11. According to one legend, Typhon killed Heracles in Libya, and Iolaus restored him to life by holding a quail to his nostrils (Eudoxus of Cnidus: Circuit of the Earth i, quoted by Athenaeus: ix. 11). But it was the Tyrian Heracles Melkarth, whom the god Esmun ('he whom we evoke'), or Asclepius, restored in this way; the meaning is that the year begins in March with the arrival of the quails from Sinai, and that quail-orgies were then celebrated in honour of the goddess (see 14. 3).

# 134

## THE TWELFTH LABOUR: THE CAPTURE
## OF CERBERUS

HERACLES'S last, and most difficult, Labour was to bring the dog Cerberus up from Tartarus. As a preliminary, he went to Eleusis where he asked to partake of the Mysteries and wear the myrtle wreath.[1] Nowadays, any Greek of good repute may be initiated at Eleusis, but since in Heracles's day Athenians alone were admitted, Theseus suggested that a certain Pylius should adopt him. This Pylius did, and when Heracles had been purified for his slaughter of the Centaurs, because no one with blood-stained hands could view the Mysteries, he was duly initiated by Orpheus's son Musaeus, Theseus acting as his sponsor.[2] However, Eumolpus, the founder of the Greater Mysteries, had decreed that no foreigners should be admitted, and therefore the Eleusinians, loth to refuse Heracles's request, yet doubtful whether his adoption by Pylius would qualify him as a true Athenian, established the Lesser Mysteries on his account; others say that Demeter herself honoured him by founding the Lesser Mysteries on this occasion.[3]

*b*. Every year, two sets of Eleusinian Mysteries are held: the Greater in honour of Demeter and Core, and the Lesser in honour of Core alone. These Lesser Mysteries, a preparation for the Greater, are a dramatic reminder of Dionysus's fate, performed by the Eleusinians at Agrae on the river Ilissus in the month Anthesterion. The principal rites are the sacrifice of a sow, which the initiates first wash in the river Cantharus, and their subsequent purification by a priest who bears the name Hydranus.[4] They must then wait at least one year until they may participate in the Greater Mysteries, which are held at Eleusis itself in the month Boedromion; and must also take an oath of secrecy, administered by the mystagogue, before being prepared for these. Meanwhile, they are refused admittance to the sanctuary of Demeter, and wait in the vestibule throughout the solemnities.[5]

*c*. Thus cleansed and prepared, Heracles descended to Tartarus from Laconian Taenarum; or, some say, from the Acherusian peninsula near Heracleia on the Black Sea, where marks of his descent are still shown at a great depth. He was guided by Athene and Hermes – for whenever, exhausted by his Labours, he cried out in despair to Zeus, Athene always came hastening down to comfort him.[6] Terrified by Heracles's scowl, Charon ferried him across the river Styx without demur; in punishment of which irregularity he was fettered by Hades for one entire year. As Heracles stepped ashore from the crazy boat, all the ghosts fled, except Meleager and the Gorgon Medusa. At sight of Medusa he drew his sword, but Hermes reassured him that she was only a phantom; and when he aimed an arrow at Meleager, who was wearing bright armour, Meleager laughed. 'You have nothing to fear from the dead,' he said, and they chatted amicably for awhile, Heracles offering in the end to marry Meleager's sister Deianeira.[6]

d. Near the gates of Tartarus, Heracles found his friends Theseus and Peirithous fastened to cruel chairs, and wrenched Theseus free, but was obliged to leave Peirithous behind; next, he rolled away the stone under which Demeter had imprisoned Ascalaphus; and then, wishing to gratify the ghosts with a gift of warm blood, slaughtered one of Hades's cattle. Their herdsman, Menoetes, or Menoetius, the son of Ceuthonymus, challenged him to a wrestling match, but was seized around the middle and had his ribs crushed. At this, Persephone, who came out from her palace and greeted Heracles like a brother, intervened and pleaded for Menoetes's life.[8]

e. When Heracles demanded Cerberus, Hades, standing by his wife's side, replied grimly: 'He is yours, if you can master him without using your club or your arrows.' Heracles found the dog chained to the gates of Acheron, and resolutely gripped him by the throat – from which rose three heads, each maned with serpents. The barbed tail flew up to strike, but Heracles, protected by the lion pelt, did not relax his grip until Cerberus choked and yielded.[9]

f. On his way back from Tartarus, Heracles wove himself a wreath from the tree which Hades had planted in the Elysian Fields as a memorial to his mistress, the beautiful nymph Leuce. The outer leaves of this wreath remained black, because that is the colour of the Underworld; but those next to Heracles's brow were bleached a silver-white by his glorious sweat. Hence the white poplar, or aspen, is sacred to him: its colour signifying that he has laboured in both worlds.[10]

g. With Athene's assistance, Heracles recrossed the river Styx in safety, and then half-dragged, half-carried Cerberus up the chasm near Troezen, through which Dionysus had conducted his mother Semele. In the temple of Saviour Artemis, built by Theseus over the mouth of this chasm, altars now stand sacred to the infernal deities. At Troezen, also, a fountain discovered by Heracles and called after him is shown in front of Hippolytus's former palace.[11]

h. According to another account, Heracles dragged Cerberus, bound with adamantine chains, up a subterrene path which leads to the gloomy cave of Acone, near Mariandyne on the Black Sea. As Cerberus resisted, averting his eyes from the sunlight, and barking furiously with all three mouths, his slaver flew across the green fields and gave birth to the poisonous plant aconite, also called hecateis, because Hecate was the

first to use it. Still another account is that Heracles came back to the
upper air through Taenarum, famous for its cave-like temple with an
image of Poseidon standing before it; but if a road ever led thence to
the Underworld, it has since been blocked up. Finally, some say that
he emerged from the precinct of Laphystian Zeus, on Mount Laphystius, where stands an image of Bright-eyed Heracles.[12]

*i.* Yet all agree at least that, when Heracles brought Cerberus to
Mycenae, Eurystheus, who was offering a sacrifice, handed him a
slave's portion, reserving the best cuts for his own kinsmen; and that
Heracles showed his just resentment by killing three of Eurystheus's
sons: Perimedes, Eurybius, and Eurypilus.[13]

*j.* Besides the aconite, Heracles also discovered the following simples:
the all-heal heracleon, or 'wild origanum'; the Siderian heracleon, with
its thin stem, red flower, and leaves like the coriander's, which grows
near lakes and rivers, and is an excellent remedy for all wounds inflicted by iron; and the hyoscyamos, or henbane, which causes vertigo
and insanity. The Nymphaean heracleon, which has a club-like root,
was named after a certain nymph deserted by Heracles, who died of
jealousy; it makes men impotent for the space of twelve days.[14]

1. Homer: *Odyssey* xi. 624; Apollodorus: ii. 5. 12.
2. Herodotus: viii. 65; Apollodorus: *loc. cit.*; Plutarch: *Theseus* 30
   and 33; Diodorus Siculus: iv. 25.
3. Tzetzes: *On Lycophron* 1328; Diodorus Siculus: iv. 14.
4. Scholiast on Aristophanes's *Plutus* 85 and *Peace* 368; Stephanus of
   Byzantium *sub* Agra; Plutarch: *Demetrius* 26 and *Phocion* 28;
   Aristophanes: *Acharnians* 703, with scholiast on 720; Varro: *On
   Gountry Matters* ii. 4; Hesychius *sub* Hydranus; Polyaenus:
   v. 17.
5. Plutarch: *Phocion* 28; Seneca: *Natural Questions* vii. 31.
6. Apollodorus: ii. 5. 12; Xenophon: *Anabasis* ci. 2. 2; Homer:
   *Odyssey* xi. 626 and *Iliad* viii. 362 ff.
7. Servius on Virgil's *Aeneid* vi. 392; Apollodorus: *loc. cit.*; Bacchylides: *Epincia* v. 71 ff. and 165 ff.
8. Apollodorus: *loc. cit.*; Tzetzes: *Chiliades*: ii. 396 ff.
9. Apollodorus: *loc. cit.*
10. Servius on Virgil's *Aeneid* viii. 276 and *Eclogues* vii. 61.
11. Homer: *Iliad* viii. 369; Apollodorus: *loc. cit.*; Pausanias: ii. 31. 12
    and ii. 32. 3.
12. Ovid: *Metamorphoses* vii. 409 ff.; Germanicus Caesar on Virgil's
    *Georgics* ii. 152; Pausanias: iii. 25. 4 and ix. 34. 4.

13. Anticlides, quoted by Athenaeus: iv. 14; Scholiast on Thucydides: i. 9.
14. Pliny: *Natural History* xxv. 12, 15, 27, and 37.

\*

1. This myth seems to have been deduced from an icon which showed Heracles descending to Tartarus, where Hecate the Goddess of the Dead welcomed him in the form of a three-headed monster – perhaps with one head for each of the seasons (see 31. *f* and 75. *2*) – and, as a natural sequel to her gift of the golden apples, led him away to the Elysian Fields. Cerberus, in fact, was here carrying off Heracles; not contrariwise. The familiar version is a logical result of his elevation to godhead: a hero must remain in the Underworld, but a god will escape and take his gáoler with him. Moreover, deification of a hero in a society which formerly worshipped only the Goddess implies that the king has defied immemorial custom and refused to die for her sake. Thus the possession of a golden dog was proof of the Achaean High King's sovereignty and escape from matriarchal tutelage (see 24. *4*). Menoetes's presence in Tartarus, and Heracles's theft of one of Hades's cattle, shows that the Tenth Labour is another version of the Twelfth: a harrowing of Hell (see 132. *1*). To judge from the corresponding Welsh myth, Menoetes's father, though purposely 'nameless', was the alder-god Bran, or Phoroneus, or Cronus; which agrees with the context of the Tenth Labour (*White Goddess* p. 48).

2. The Greater Eleusinian Mysteries were of Cretan origin, and held in Boedromion ('running for help') which, in Crete, was the first month of the year, roughly September, and so named, according to Plutarch (*Theseus* 27), to commemorate Theseus's defeat of the Amazons, which means his suppression of the matriarchal system. Originally, the Mysteries seem to have been the sacred king's preparation, at the autumnal equinox, for his approaching death at midwinter – hence the premonitory myrtle wreath (see 109. *4*) – in the form of a sacred drama, which advised him what to expect in the Underworld. After the abolition of royal male sacrifices, a feature of matriarchy, the Mysteries were open to all judged worthy of initiation; as in Egypt, where the *Book of the Dead* gave similar advice, any man of good repute could become an Osiris by being purified of all uncleanness and undergoing a mock death. In Eleusis, Osiris was identified with Dionysus. White poplar leaves were a Sumerian symbol of renascence and, in the tree-calendar, white poplar stood for the autumnal equinox (see 52. *3*).

3. The Lesser Mysteries, which became a preparation for the Greater, seem to have been an independent Pelasgian festival, also based on the hope of rebirth, but taking place early in February at Candlemas, when the trees first leaf – which is the meaning of 'Anthesterion'.

4. Now, since Dionysus was identified with Osiris, Semele must be Isis; and we know that Osiris did not rescue Isis from the Underworld, but she, him. Thus the icon at Troezen will have shown Semele restoring Dionysus to the upper air. The goddess who similarly guides Heracles is Isis again; and his rescue of Alcestis was probably deduced from the same icon – he is led, not leading. His emergence in the precinct of Mount Laphystius makes an interesting variant. No cavern exists on the summit, and the myth must refer to the death and resurrection of the sacred king which was celebrated there – a rite that helped to form the legend of the Golden Fleece (see 70. 2 and 148. 10).

5. Aconite, a poison and paralysant, was used by the Thessalian witches in the manufacture of their flying ointment: it numbed the feet and hands and gave them a sensation of being off the ground. But since it was also a febrifuge, Heracles, who drove the fever-birds from Stymphalus, became credited with its discovery.

6. The sequence of Heracles's feats varies considerably. Diodorus Siculus and Hyginus arrange the Twelve Labours in the same order as Apollodorus, except that they both place the Fourth before the Third, and the Sixth before the Fifth; and that Diodorus places the Twelfth before the Eleventh. Nearly all mythographers agree that the killing of the Nemean Lion was the First Labour, but in Hyginus's sequence of 'the Twelve Labours of Heracles set by Eurystheus' (*Fabula* 30), it is preceded by the strangling of the serpents. In one place, Diodorus Siculus associates the killing of Anaeus and Busiris with the Tenth Labour (iv. 17–18); in another, with the Eleventh (iv. 27). And while some writers make Heracles sail with the Argonauts in his youth (Silius Italicus: i. 512); others place this adventure after the Fourth Labour (Apollonius Rhodius: i. 122); and others after the Eighth (Diodorus Siculus: iv. 15). But some make him perform the Ninth (Valerius Flaccus: *Argonautica* v. 91) and Twelfth (*ibid*.: ii. 382) Labours, and break the horns of 'both bulls' (*ibid*.: i. 36) before he sailed with the Argonauts; and others deny that he sailed at all, on the ground that he was then serving as Queen Omphale's slave (Herodotus, quoted by Apollodorus: i. 9. 19).

7. According to *Lycophron* 1328, Heracles was initiated into the Eleusinian Mysteries before setting out on the Ninth Labour; but Philochorus (quoted by Plutarch: *Theseus* 26) says that Theseus had him initiated in the course of its performance (*ibid*.: 30), and was rescued by him from Tartarus during the Twelfth Labour (Apollodorus: ii. 5. 12). According to Pausanias (i. 27. 7), Theseus was only seven years old when Heracles came to Troezen, wearing the lion pelt; and cleared the Isthmus of malefactors on his way to Athens, at the time when Heracles was serving Omphale (Apollodorus: ii. 6. 3). Euripides believed that Heracles had fought with Ares's son Cycnus before setting out on the Eighth Labour

(*Alcestis* 501 ff.); Propertius (iv. 19. 41), that he had already visited Tartarus when he killed Cacus; and Ovid (*Fasti* v. 388), that Cheiron died accidentally when Heracles had almost completed his Labours, not during the Fourth.

8. Albricus (22) lists the following Twelve Labours in this order, with allegorical explanations: defeating the Centaurs at a wedding; killing the lion; rescuing Alcestis from Tartarus and chaining Cerberus; winning the apples of the Hesperides; destroying the Hydra; wrestling with Achelous; killing Cacus; winning the mares of Diomedes; defeating Antaeus; capturing the boar; lifting the cattle of Geryon; holding up the heavens.

9. Various Labours and bye-works of Heracles were represented on Apollo's throne at Amyclae (Pausanias: iii. 18. 7–9); and in the bronze shrine of Athene on the Spartan acropolis (Pausanias: iii. 17. 3). Praxiteles's gable sculptures on the Theban shrine of Heracles showed most of the Twelve Labours, but the Stymphalian Birds were missing, and the wrestling match with Antaeus replaced the cleansing of Augeias's stables. The evident desire of so many cities to be associated with Heracles's Labours suggests that much the same ritual marriage-task drama, as a preliminary to coronation, was performed over a wide area.

# 135

## THE MURDER OF IPHITUS

WHEN Heracles returned to Thebes after his Labours, he gave Megara, his wife, now thirty-three years old, in marriage to his nephew and charioteer Iolaus, who was only sixteen, remarking that his own union with her had been inauspicious.[1] He then looked about for a younger and more fortunate wife; and, hearing that his friend Eurytus, a son of Melanius, King of Oechalia, had offered to marry his daughter Iole to any archer who could outshoot him and his four sons, took the road there.[2] Eurytus had been given a fine bow and taught its use by Apollo himself, whom he now claimed to surpass in marksmanship, yet Heracles found no difficulty in winning the contest. The result displeased Eurytus excessively and, when he learned that Heracles had discarded Megara after murdering her children, he refused to give him Iole. Having drunk a great deal of wine to gain confidence, 'You could never compare with me and my sons as an archer,' he told Heracles, 'were it not that you unfairly use magic arrows, which cannot miss their mark. This contest is void, and I would not, in any case, entrust my beloved daughter to such a ruffian as yourself! Moreover, you are Eurystheus's slave and, like a slave, deserve only blows from a free man.' So saying, he drove Heracles out of the Palace. Heracles did not retaliate at once, as he might well have done; but swore to take vengeance.[3]

b. Three of Eurytus's sons, namely Didaeon, Clytius, and Toxeus, had supported their father in his dishonest pretensions. The eldest, however, whose name was Iphitus, declared that Iole should in all fairness have been given to Heracles; and when, soon afterwards, twelve strong-hooved brood-mares and twelve sturdy mule-foals disappeared from Euboea, he refused to believe that Heracles was the thief. As a matter of fact, they had been stolen by the well-known thief Autolycus, who magically changed their appearance and sold them to the unsuspecting Heracles as if they were his own.[4] Iphitus followed the tracks of the mares and foals and found that they led towards Tiryns, which made him suspect that Heracles was, after all, avenging the insult offered him by Eurytus. Coming suddenly face to face with Heracles, who had just returned from his rescue of Alcestis, he concealed his suspicions and merely asked for advice in the matter. Heracles did not recognize the beasts from Iphitus's description as those sold to him by Autolycus, and with his usual heartiness promised to search for them if Iphitus would consent to become his guest. Yet he now divined that he was suspected of theft, which galled his sensitive heart. After a grand banquet, he led Iphitus to the top of the highest tower in Tiryns. 'Look about you!' he demanded, 'and tell me whether your mares are grazing anywhere in sight.' 'I cannot see them', Iphitus admitted. 'Then you have falsely accused me in your heart of being a thief!' Heracles roared, distraught with anger, and hurled him to his death.[5]

c. Heracles presently went to Neleus, King of Pylus, and asked to be purified; but Neleus refused, because Eurytus was his ally. Nor would any of his sons, except the youngest, Nestor, consent to receive Heracles, who eventually persuaded Deiphobus, the son of Hippolytus, to purify him at Amyclae. However, he still suffered from evil dreams, and went to ask the Delphic Oracle how he might be rid of them.[6] The Pythoness Xenoclea refused to answer this question. 'You murdered your guest,' she said. 'I have no oracles for such as you!' 'Then I shall be obliged to institute an oracle of my own!' cried Heracles. With that, he plundered the shrine of its votive offerings and even pulled away the tripod on which Xenoclea sat. 'Heracles of Tiryns is a very different man from his Canopic namesake,' the Pythoness said severely as he carried the tripod from the shrine; she meant that the Egyptian Heracles had once come to Delphi and behaved with courtesy and reverence.[7]

*d.* Up rose the indignant Apollo, and fought Heracles until Zeus parted the combatants with a thunderbolt, making them clasp hands in friendship. Heracles restored the sacred tripod, and together they founded the city of Gythium, where images of Apollo, Heracles, and Dionysus now stand side by side in the market place. Xenoclea then gave Heracles the following oracle: 'To be rid of your affliction you must be sold into slavery for one whole year and the price you fetch must be offered to Iphitus's children.[8] Zeus is enraged that you have violated the laws of hospitality, whatever the provocation.' 'Whose slave am I to be?' asked Heracles humbly. 'Queen Omphale of Lydia will purchase you,' Xenoclea replied. 'I obey,' said Heracles, 'but one day I shall enslave the man who has brought this suffering upon me, and all his family too!'[9] Some, however, say that Heracles did not return the tripod and that, when one thousand years later, Apollo heard that it had been taken to the city of Pheneus, he punished the Pheneans by blocking the channel which Heracles had dug to carry off the heavy rains, and flooded their city.[10]

*e.* Another wholly different account of these events is current, according to which Lycus the Euboean, son of Poseidon and Dirce, attacked Thebes during a time of sedition, killed King Creon, and usurped the throne. Believing Copreus's report that Heracles had died, Lycus tried to seduce Megara and, when she resisted him, would have killed her and the children had Heracles not returned from Tartarus just in time to exact vengeance. Thereupon Hera, whose favourite Lycus was, drove Heracles mad: he killed Megara and his own sons, also his minion, the Aetolian Stichius.[11] The Thebans, who show the children's tomb, say that Heracles would have killed his foster-father Amphitryon as well, if Athene had not knocked him insensible with a huge stone; to which they point, saying: 'We nick-name it "The Chastener".' But Amphitryon had, in fact, died long before, in the Orchomenan campaign. The Athenians claim that Theseus, grateful to Heracles for his rescue from Tartarus, arrived at this juncture with an Athenian army, to help Heracles against Lycus. He stood aghast at the murder, yet promised Heracles every honour for the rest of his life, and after his death as well, and brought him to Athens, where Medea cured his madness with medicines. Sicalus then purified him once more.[12]

1. Plutarch: *On Love* 9; Apollodorus: ii. 6. 1; Pausanias: x. 29. 3.
2. Diodorus Siculus: iv. 31; Pausanias: iv. 33. 5; Sophocles: *Trachinian Women* 260 ff.
3. Hyginus: *Fabula* 14; Apollonius Rhodius: i. 88–9; Homer: *Odyssey* viii. 226–8; Apollodorus: *loc. cit.*; Diodorus Siculus: *loc. cit.*; Sophocles: *loc. cit.*
4. Hesiod, quoted by scholiast on Sophocles's *Trachinian Women* 266; Homer: *Odyssey* xxi. 15 ff.; Diodorus Siculus: *loc. cit.*; Apollodorus: ii. 6. 2; Scholiast on Homer's *Odyssey* xxi. 22.
5. Apollodorus: *loc. cit.*; Sophocles: *Trachinian Women* 271; Homer: *loc. cit.*, with scholiast quoting Pherecydes; Diodorus Siculus: *loc. cit.*
6. Apollodorus: *loc. cit.*; Diodorus Siculus: *loc. cit.*
7. Apollodorus: *loc. cit.*; Pausanias: x. 13. 4; Hyginus: *Fabula* 32.
8. Apollodorus: *loc. cit.*; Hyginus: *loc. cit.*; Pausanias: ii. 21. 7; Diodorus Siculus: *loc. cit.*
9. Sophocles: *Trachinian Women* 248 ff. and 275 ff.; Hyginus: *loc. cit.*; Servius on Virgil's *Aeneid* viii. 300.
10. Plutarch: *On the Slowness of Divine Vengeance* 12; Pausanias: viii. 14. 3.
11. Hyginus: *Fabula* 32; Euripides: *Heracles* 26 ff. and 553; Servius on Virgil's *Aeneid* viii. 300; Scholiast on Sophocles's *Trachinian Women* 355; Ptolemy Hephaestionos: vii, quoted by Photius p.490.
12. Euripides: *Heracles* 26 ff., 1163 ff., and 1322; Pausanias: ix. 11. 2; Diodorus Siculus: iv. 55; Menocrates, quoted by scholiast on Pindar's *Isthmian Odes* iv. 104 ff.

*

1. In matrilineal society, divorce of a royal wife implies abandonment of the kingdom which has been her marriage portion; and it seems likely that, once the ancient conventions were relaxed in Greece, a sacred king could escape death at the end of his reign by abandoning his kingdom and marrying the heiress of another. If this is so, Eurytus's objection to Heracles as a son-in-law will not have been that he had killed his children – the annual victims sacrificed while he reigned at Thebes – but that he had evaded his royal duty of dying. The winning of a bride by a feat of archery was an Indo-European custom: in the *Mahabharata*, Arjuna wins Draupadi thus, and in the *Ramayana*, Rama bends Shiva's powerful bow and wins Sita. Moreover, the shooting of one arrow towards each cardinal point of the compass, and one towards the zenith (see 126. *2* and 132. *8*), formed part of the royal marriage rites in India and Egypt. The mares may have figured sacrificially at the marriage of Heracles and Iole, when

he became King of Oechalia (see 81. *4*). Iphitus, at any rate, is the king's surrogate flung from the Theban walls at the end of every year, or at any other time in placation of some angry deity (see 105. *6*; 106. *j*; and 121. *3*).

2. Heracles's seizure of the Delphic tripod apparently records a Dorian capture of the shrine; as the thunderbolt thrown between Apollo and Heracles records a decision that Apollo should be allowed to keep his Oracle, rather than yield it to Heracles – provided that he served the Dorian interests as patron of the Dymanes, a tribe belonging to the Doric League. It was notorious that the Spartans, who were Dorians, controlled the Delphic Oracle in Classical times. Euripides omits the tripod incident in his *Heracles* because, in 421 B.C., the Athenians had been worsted by the Treaty of Nicias in their attempt to maintain the Phocians' sovereignty over Delphi; the Spartans insisted on making it a separate puppet state which they themselves controlled. In the middle of the fourth century, when the dispute broke out again, the Phocians seized Delphi and appropriated some of its treasures to raise forces in their own defence; but were badly beaten, and all their cities destroyed.

3. The Pythoness's reproach seems to mean that the Dorians, who had conquered the Peloponnese, called themselves 'Sons of Heracles', and did not show her the same respect as their Achaean, Aeolian, and Ionian predecessors, whose religious ties were with the agricultural Libyans of the Egyptian Delta, rather than with the Hellenic cattle-kings; Xenoclea's predecessor Herophile ('dear to Hera'), had been Zeus's daughter by Lamia and called 'Sibyl' by the Libyans over whom she ruled (Pausanias: x. 12. 1; Euripides: *Prologue* to *Lamia*). Cicero confirms this view when he denies that Alcmene's son (i.e. the pre-Dorian Heracles) was the one who fought Apollo for the tripod (*On the Nature of the Gods* iii). Attempts were later made, in the name of religious decency, to patch up the quarrel between Apollo the Phocian and Heracles the Dorian. Thus Plutarch, a Delphic priest, suggests (*Dialogue on the E at Delphi* 6) that Heracles became an expert diviner and logician, and 'seemed to have seized the tripod in friendly rivalry with Apollo.' When describing Apollo's vengeance on the people of Pheneus, he tactfully suppresses the fact that it was Heracles who had dug them the channel (see 138. *d*).

# 136

## OMPHALE

HERACLES was taken to Asia and offered for sale as a nameless slave by Hermes, patron of all important financial transactions, who afterwards handed the purchase money of three silver talents to Iphitus's orphans. Nevertheless, Eurytus stubbornly forbade his grandchildren to accept any monetary compensation, saying that only blood would pay for blood; and what happened to the silver, Hermes alone knows.[1] As the Pythoness had foretold, Heracles was bought by Omphale, Queen of Lydia, a woman with a good eye for a bargain; and he served her faithfully either for one year, or for three, ridding Asia Minor of the bandits who infested it.[2]

*b.* This Omphale, a daughter of Jordanes and, according to some authorities, the mother of Tantalus, had been bequeathed the kingdom by her unfortunate husband Tmolus, son of Ares and Theogone. While out hunting on Mount Carmanorium – so called in honour of Carmanor son of Dionysus and Alixirrhoë, who was killed there by a wild boar – he fell in love with a huntress named Arrhippe, a chaste attendant of Artemis. Arrhippe, deaf to Tmolus's threats and entreaties, fled to her mistress's temple where, disregarding its sanctity, he ravished her on the goddess's own couch. She hanged herself from a beam, after invoking Artemis, who thereupon let loose a mad bull; Tmolus was tossed into the air, fell on pointed stakes and sharp stones and died in torment. Theoclymenus, his son by Omphale, buried him where he lay, renaming the mountain 'Tmolus'; a city of the same name, built upon its slopes, was destroyed by a great earthquake in the reign of the Emperor Tiberius.[3]

*c.* Among the many bye-works which Heracles performed during this servitude was his capture of the two Ephesian Cercopes, who had constantly robbed him of his sleep. They were twin brothers named either Passalus and Acmon; or Olus and Eurybatus; or Sillus and Triballus – sons of Oceanus by Theia, and the most accomplished cheats and liars known to mankind, who roamed the world, continually practising new deceptions. Theia had warned them to keep clear of Heracles and her words 'My little White-bottoms, you have yet to meet the great Black-bottom!' becoming proverbial, 'white-bottom' now means 'cowardly, base, or lascivious'.[4] They would buzz around Heracles's bed in the guise of bluebottles, until one night he grabbed them, forced them to resume their proper shape, and bore them off, dangling head-downwards from a pole which he carried over his shoulder. Now, Heracles's bottom, which the lion's pelt did not cover, had been burned as black as an old leather shield by exposure to the sun, and by the fiery breaths of Cacus and of the Cretan bull; and the Cer-

copes burst into a fit of immoderate laughter to find themselves suspended upside-down, staring at it. Their merriment surprised Heracles,
and when he learned its cause, he sat down upon a rock and laughed so
heartily himself that they persuaded him to release them. But though
we know of an Asian city named Cercopia, the haunts of the Cercopes
and a rock called 'Black Bottom' are shown at Thermopylae; this
incident therefore is likely to have taken place on another occasion.[5]

d. Some say that the Cercopes were eventually turned to stone for
trying to deceive Zeus; others, that he punished their fraudulence by
changing them into apes with long yellow hair, and sending them to
the Italian islands named Pithecusae.[6]

e. In a Lydian ravine lived one Syleus, who used to seize passing
strangers and force them to dig his vineyard; but Heracles tore up the
vines by their roots. Again, when Lydians from Itone began plundering
Omphale's country, Heracles recovered the spoil and razed their city.[7]
And at Celaenae lived Lityerses the farmer, a bastard son of King Minos,
who would offer hospitality to wayfarers but force them to compete
with him in reaping his harvest. If their strength flagged, he would
whip them and at evening, when he had won the contest, would behead
them and conceal their bodies in sheaves, chanting lugubriously as he
did so. Heracles visited Celaenae in order to rescue the shepherd Daphnis, a son of Hermes who, after searching throughout the world for
his beloved Pimplea, carried off by pirates, had at last found her among
the slave-girls of Lityerses. Daphnis was challenged to the reaping contest, but Heracles taking his place out-reaped Lityerses, whom he
decapitated with a sickle, throwing the trunk into the river Maeander.
Not only did Daphnis win back his Pimplea, but Heracles gave her
Lityerses's palace as a dowry. In honour of Lityerses, Phrygian reapers
still sing a harvest dirge closely resembling that raised in honour of
Maneros, son of the first Egyptian king, who also died in the harvest
field.[8]

f. Finally, beside the Lydian river Sagaris, Heracles shot dead a
gigantic serpent which was destroying men and crops; and the grateful
Omphale, having at last discovered his identity and parentage, released
him and sent him back to Tiryns, laden with gifts; while Zeus contrived
the constellation Ophiuchus to commemorate the victory. This river
Sagaris, by the way, was named after a son of Myndon and Alexirrhoë
who, driven mad by the Mother of the Gods for slighting her Mysteries
and insulting her eunuch priests, drowned himself in its waters.[9]

*g.* Omphale had bought Heracles as a lover rather than a fighter. He fathered on her three sons, namely Lamus; Agelaus, ancestor of a famous King Croesus who tried to immolate himself on a pyre when the Persians captured Sardis; and Laomedon.[10] Some add a fourth, Tyrrhenus, or Tyrsenus, who invented the trumpet and led Lydian emigrants to Eturia, where they took the name Tyrrhenians; but it is more probable that Tyrrhenus was the son of King Atys, and a remote descendant of Heracles and Omphale.[11] By one of Omphale's women, named Malis, Heracles was already the father of Cleodaeus, or Cleolaus; and of Alcaeus, founder of the Lydian dynasty which King Croesus ousted from the throne of Sardis.[12]

*h.* Reports reached Greece that Heracles had discarded his lion pelt and his aspen wreath, and instead wore jewelled necklaces, golden bracelets, a woman's turban, a purple shawl, and a Maeonian girdle. There he sat – the story went – surrounded by wanton Ionian girls, teasing wool from the polished wool-basket, or spinning the thread; trembling, as he did so, when his mistress scolded him. She would strike him with her golden slipper if ever his clumsy fingers crushed the spindle, and make him recount his past achievements for her amusement; yet apparently he felt no shame. Hence painters show Heracles wearing a yellow petticoat, and letting himself be combed and manicured by Omphale's maids, while she dresses up in his lion pelt, and wields his club and bow.[13]

*i.* What, however, had happened was no more than this. One day, when Heracles and Omphale were visiting the vineyards of Tmolus, she in a purple, gold-embroidered gown, with perfumed locks, he gallantly holding a golden parasol over her head, Pan caught sight of them from a high hill. Falling in love with Omphale, he bade farewell to the mountain-goddesses, crying: 'Henceforth she alone shall be my love!' Omphale and Heracles reached their destination, a secluded grotto, where it amused them to exchange clothes. She dressed him in a net-work girdle, absurdly small for his waist, and her purple gown. Though she unlaced this to the fullest extent, he split the sleeves; and the ties of her sandals were far too short to meet across his instep.

*j.* After dinner, they went to sleep on separate couches, having vowed a dawn sacrifice to Dionysus, who requires marital purity from his devotees on such occasions. At midnight, Pan crept into the grotto and, fumbling about in the darkness, found what he thought was Omphale's couch, because the sleeper was clad in silk. With trembling hands he untucked the bed-clothes from the bottom, and wormed his way in; but Heracles, waking and drawing up one foot, kicked him across the grotto. Hearing a loud crash and a howl, Omphale sprang up and called for lights, and when these came she and Heracles laughed until they cried to see Pan sprawling in a corner, nursing his bruises. Since that day, Pan has abhorred clothes, and summons his officials naked to his rites; it was he who revenged himself on Heracles by spreading the rumour that his whimsical exchange of garments with Omphale was habitual and perverse.[14]

1. Apollodorus: ii. 6. 3; Diodorus Siculus: iv. 31; Pherecydes, quoted by scholiast on Homer's *Odyssey* xxi. 22.

2. Sophocles: *Trachinian Women* 253; Apollodorus: ii. 6. 2; Diodorus Siculus: *loc. cit.*

3. Apollodorus: ii. 6. 3; Plutarch: *On Rivers* 7; Tacitus: *Annals* ii. 47.

4. Apollodorus: *loc. cit.*; Suidas *sub* Cercopes; Scholiast on Lucian's *Alexander* 4; Tzetzes: *On Lycophron* 91.

5. W. H. Roscher: *Lexikon der griechischen und römischen Mytologie* ii. 1166 ff.; K. O. Müller: *Dorians* i. 464; Ptolemy Claudius: v. 2; Herodotus: vii. 216.

6. Suidas *sub* Cercopes; Harpocration *sub* Cercopes, quoting Xenagoras; Eustathius on Homer's *Odyssey* xix. 247; Ovid: *Metamorphoses* xiv. 88 ff.

7. Tzetzes: *Chiliades* ii. 432 ff.; Diodorus Siculus: iv. 31; Dionysius: *Description of the Earth* 465; Stephanus of Byzantium *sub* Itone.

8. Scholiast on Theocritus's *Idylls* x. 41; Athenaeus: x. 615 and xiv. 619; Eustathius on Homer 1164; Hesychius, Photius, and Suidas *sub* Lityerses; Pollux: iv. 54.

9. Hyginus: *Poetic Astronomy* ii. 14; Plutarch: *On Rivers* 12.

10. Diodorus Siculus: iv. 31; Bacchylides: iii. 24–62; Apollodorus: ii. 6. 3; Palaephatus: 45.

11. Pausanias: ii. 21. 3; Herodotus: i. 94; Strabo: v. 2. 2; Dionysius of Halicarnassus: i. 28.

12. Hellanicus: *Fragment* 102, ed. Didot; Diodorus Siculus: *loc. cit.*; Eusebius: *Preparation for the Gospel* ii. 35; Herodotus: i. 7.

13. Ovid: *Heroides* ix. 54 ff.; Lucian: *Dialogues of the Gods* 13; Plutarch: *On Whether an Aged Man Ought to Meddle in State Affairs* 4.

14. Ovid: *Fasti* ii. 305.

\*

1. Carmanor will have been a title of Adonis (see 18. 7), also killed by a boar. Tmolus's desecration of the temple of Artemis cannot be dated; neither can the order that Heracles should compensate Eurytus for his son's murder. Both events, however, seem to be historical in origin. It is

likely that Omphale stands for the Pythoness, guardian of the Delphic *omphalus*, who awarded the compensation, making Heracles a temple-slave until it should be paid, and that, 'Omphale' being also the name of a Lydian queen, the scene of his servitude was changed by the mytho-graphers, to suit another set of traditions.

2. The Cercopes, as their various pairs of names show, were *ceres*, or Spites, coming in the shape of delusive and mischievous dreams, and could be foiled by an appeal to Heracles who, alone, had power over the Nightmare (see 35. *3–4*). Though represented at first as simple ghosts, like Cecrops (whose name is another form of *cercops*), in later works of art they figure as *cercopithecoi*, 'apes', perhaps because of Heracles's association with Gibraltar, one of his Pillars, from which Carthaginian merchants brought them as pets for rich Greek and Roman ladies. No apes seem to have frequented Ischia and Procida, two islands to the north of the Bay of Naples, which the Greeks called Pithecusae; their name really refers to the *pithoi*, or jars, manufactured there (Pliny: *Natural History* iii. 6. 12).

3. The vine-dressers' custom of seizing and killing a stranger at the vintage season, in honour of the Vine-spirit, was widespread in Syria and Asia Minor; and a similar harvest sacrifice took place both there and in Europe. Sir James Frazer has discussed this subject exhaustively in his *Golden Bough*. Heracles is here credited with the abolition of human sacrifice: a social reform on which the Greeks prided themselves, even when their wars grew more and more savage and destructive.

4. Classical writers made Heracles's servitude to Omphale an allegory of how easily a strong man becomes enslaved by a lecherous and ambi-tious woman; and that they regarded the navel as the seat of female passion sufficiently explains Omphale's name in this sense. But the fable refers, rather, to an early stage in the development of the sacred kingship from matriarchy to patriarchy, when the king, as the Queen's consort, was privileged to deputize for her in ceremonies and sacrifices – but only if he wore her robes. Reveillout has shown that this was the system at Lagash in early Sumerian times, and in several Cretan works of art men are shown wearing female garments for sacrificial purposes – not only the spotted trouser-skirt, as on the Hagia Triada sarcophagus, but even, as on a palace-fresco at Cnossus, the flounced skirt. Heracles's slavery is explained by West African matriarchal native customs: in Loango, Daura, and the Abrons, as Briffault has pointed out, the king is of servile birth and without power; in Agonna, Latuka, Ubemba, and elsewhere, there is only a queen, who does not marry but takes servile lovers. Moreover, a similar system survived until Classical times among the ancient Locrian nobility who had the privilege of sending priestesses to Trojan Athene (see 158. *8*); they were forced to emigrate in 683 B.C. from

Central Greece to Epizephyrian Locri, on the toe of Italy, 'because of the scandal caused by their noblewomen's indiscriminate love affairs with slaves' (see 18. 8). These Locrians, who were of non-Hellenic origin and made a virtue of pre-nuptial promiscuity in the Cretan, Carian, or Amorite style (Clearchus: 6), insisted on strictly matrilinear succession (Dionysius: *Description of the Earth* 365–7; Polybius: xii. 6b). The same customs must have been general in pre-Hellenic Greece and Italy, but it is only at Bagnara, near the ruins of Epizephyrian Locri, that the matriarchal tradition is recalled today. The Bagnarotte wear long, pleated skirts, and set off barefoot on their commercial rounds which last for several days, leaving the men to mind the children; they can carry as much as two *quintals* on their heads. The men take holidays in the spring swordfish season, when they show their skill with the harpoon; and in the summer, when they go to the hills and burn charcoal. Although the official patron of Bagnera is St Nicholas, no Bagnarotte will acknowledge his existence; and their parish priest complains that they pay far more attention to the Virgin than even to the Son – the Virgin having succeeded Core, the Maid, for whose splendid temple Locri was famous in Classical times.

# 137

## HESIONE

AFTER serving as a slave to Queen Omphale, Heracles returned to Tiryns, his sanity now fully restored, and at once planned an expedition against Troy.[1] His reasons were as follows. He and Telamon, either on their way back from the country of the Amazons, or when they landed with the Argonauts at Sigeium, had been astonished to find Laomedon's daughter Hesione, stark naked except for her jewels, chained to a rock on the Trojan shore.[2] It appeared that Poseidon had sent a sea-monster to punish Laomedon for having failed to pay him and Apollo their stipulated fee when they built the city walls and tended his flocks. Some say that he should have sacrificed to them all the cattle born in his kingdom that year; others, that he had promised them only a low wage as day-labourers, but even so cheated them of more than thirty Trojan drachmae. In revenge, Apollo sent a plague, and Poseidon ordered this monster to prey on the plainsfolk and ruin their fields by spewing sea water over them. According to another account, Laomedon fulfilled his obligations to Apollo, but not to Poseidon, who therefore sent the plague as well as the monster.[3]

b. Laomedon visited the Oracle of Zeus Ammon, and was advised by him to expose Hesione on the seashore for the monster to devour. Yet he obstinately refused to do so unless the Trojan nobles would first let him sacrifice their own daughters. In despair, they consulted Apollo who, being no less angry than Poseidon, gave them little satisfaction. Most parents at once sent their children abroad for safety, but Laomedon tried to force a certain Phoenodamas, who had kept his three daughters at home, to expose one of them; upon which Phoenodamas harangued the assembly, pleading that Laomedon was alone responsible for their present distress, and should be made to suffer for it by sacrificing his daughter. In the end, it was decided to cast lots, and the lot fell upon Hesione, who was accordingly bound to the rock, where Heracles found her.[4]

c. Heracles now broke her bonds, went up to the city, and offered to destroy the monster in return for the two matchless, immortal, snow-white horses, or mares, which could run over water and standing corn like the wind, and which Zeus had given Laomedon as compensation for the rape of Ganymedes. Laomedon readily agreed to the bargain.[5]

d. With Athene's help, the Trojans then built Heracles a high wall which served to protect him from the monster as it poked its head out of the sea and advanced across the plain. On reaching the wall, it opened its great jaws and Heracles leaped fully-armed down its throat. He spent three days in the monster's belly, and emerged victorious, although the struggle had cost him every hair on his head.[6]

e. What happened next is much disputed. Some say that Laomedon gave Hesione to Heracles as his bride – at the same time persuading him to leave her, and the mares, at Troy, while he went off with the Argonauts – but that, after the Fleece had been won, his cupidity got the better of him, and he refused to let Heracles have either Hesione or the mares. Others say that he had made this refusal a month or two previously, when Heracles came to Troy in search of Hylas.[7]

f. The most circumstantial version, however, is that Laomedon cheated Heracles by substituting mortal horses for the immortal ones; whereupon Heracles threatened to make war on Troy, and put to sea in a rage. First he visited the island of Paros, where he raised an altar to Zeus and Apollo; and then the Isthmus of Corinth, where he prophesied Laomedon's doom; finally he recruited soldiers in his own city of Tiryns.[8]

*g*. Laomedon, in the meantime, had killed Phoenodamas and sold his three daughters to Sicilian merchants come to buy victims for the wild-beast shows; but in Sicily they were rescued by Aphrodite, and the eldest, Aegesta, lay with the river Crimissus, who took the form of a dog – and bore him a son, Aegestes, called Acestes by the Latins.[9] This Aegestes, aided by Anchises's bastard son Elymus, whom he brought from Troy, founded the cities of Aegesta, later called Segesta; Entella, which he named after his wife; Eryx; and Asca. Aegesta is said to have eventually returned to Troy and there married one Capys, by whom she became the mother of Anchises.[10]

*h*. It is disputed whether Heracles embarked for Troy with eighteen long ships of fifty oars each; or with only six small craft and scanty forces.[11] But among his allies were Iolaus; Telamon son of Aeacus; Peleus; the Argive Oicles; and the Boeotian Deimachus.[12]

*i*. Heracles had found Telamon at Salamis feasting with his friends. He was at once offered the golden wine-bowl and invited to pour the first libation to Zeus; having done so, he stretched out his hands to heaven and prayed: 'O Father, send Telamon a fine son, with a skin as tough as this lion pelt, and courage to match!' For he saw that Periboea, Telamon's wife, was on the point of giving birth. Zeus sent down his eagle in answer, and Heracles assured Telamon that the prayer would be granted; and, indeed, as soon as the feast was over, Peribeoa gave birth to Great Ajax, around whom Heracles threw the lion pelt, thus making him invulnerable, except in his neck and arm-pit, where the quiver had interposed.[13]

*j*. On disembarking near Troy, Heracles left Oicles to guard the ships, while he himself led the other champions in an assault on the city. Laomedon, taken by surprise, had no time to marshal his army, but supplied the common folk with swords and torches and hurried them down to burn the fleet. Oicles resisted him to the death, fighting a noble rear-guard action, while his comrades launched the ships and escaped. Laomedon then hurried back to the city and, after a skirmish with Heracles's straggling forces, managed to re-enter and bar the gates behind him.

*k*. Having no patience for a long siege, Heracles ordered an immediate assault. The first to breach the wall and enter was Telamon, who chose the western curtain built by his father Aeacus as the weakest spot, but Heracles came hard at his heels, mad with jealousy. Telamon, suddenly aware that Heracles's drawn sword was intended for his own vitals, had the presence of mind to stoop and collect some large stones dislodged from the wall. 'What are you at?' roared Heracles. 'Building an altar to Heracles the Victor, Heracles the Averter of Ills!' answered the resourceful Telamon. 'I leave the sack of Troy to you.'[14] Heracles thanked him briefly, and raced on. He then shot down Laomedon and all his sons, except Podarces, who alone had maintained that Heracles should be given the immortal mares; and sacked the city. After glutting his vengeance, he rewarded Telamon with the hand of Hesione, whom he gave permission to ransom any one of her fellow captives. She chose Podarces. 'Very well,' said Heracles. 'But first he must be sold as a slave.' So Podarces was put up for sale, and Hesione redeemed him with the golden veil which bound her head: hence Podarces won the name of Priam, which means 'redeemed'. But some say that he was a mere infant at the time.[15]

*l.* Having burned Troy and left its highways desolate, Heracles set Priam on the throne, and put to sea. Hesione accompanied Telamon to Salamis, where she bore him Teucer; whether in wedlock or in bastardy is not agreed.[16] Later she deserted Telamon, escaped to Asia Minor, and swam across to Miletus, where King Arion found her hidden in a wood. There she bore Telamon a second son, Trambelus, whom Arion reared as his own, and appointed king of Telamon's Asiatic kinsmen the Lelegians or, some say, of the Lesbians. When, in the course of the Trojan War, Achilles raided Miletus, he killed Trambelus, learning too late that he was Telamon's son, which caused him great grief.[17]

*m.* Some say that Oicles did not fall at Troy, but was still alive when the Erinnyes drove his grandson Alcmaeon mad. His tomb is shown in Arcadia, near the Megalopolitan precinct of Boreas.[18]

*n.* Heracles now sailed from the Troad, taking with him Glaucia, a daughter of the river Scamander. During the siege, she had been Deimachus's mistress, and when he fell in battle, had applied to Heracles for protection. Heracles led her aboard his ship, overjoyed that the stock of so gallant a friend should survive: for Glaucia was pregnant, and later gave birth to a son named Scamander.[19]

*o.* Now, while Sleep lulled Zeus into drowsiness, Hera summoned Boreas to raise a storm, which drove Heracles off his course to the island of Cos. Zeus awoke in a rage and threatened to cast Sleep down from the upper air into the gulf of Erebus; but she fled as a suppliant to Night, whom even Zeus dared not displease. In his frustration he began tossing the gods about Olympus. Some say that it was on this occasion that he chained Hera by her wrists to the rafters, tying anvils to her ankles; and hurled Hephaestus down to earth. Having thus vented his ill-temper to the full, he rescued Heracles from Cos and led him back to Argos, where his adventures are variously described.[20]

*p.* Some say that the Coans mistook him for a pirate and tried to prevent his approach by pelting his ship with stones. But he forced a landing, took the city of Astypalaea in a night assault, and killed the king, Eurypylus, a son of Poseidon and Astypalaea. He was himself wounded by Chalcodon, but rescued by Zeus when on the point of being despatched.[21] Others say that he attacked Cos because he had fallen in love with Chalciope, Eurypylus's daughter.[22]

*q.* According to still another account, five of Heracles's six ships foundered in the storm. The surviving one ran aground at Laceta on the island of Cos, he and his shipmates saving only their weapons from the wreck. As they stood wringing the sea water out of their clothes, a flock of sheep passed by, and Heracles asked the Meropian shepherd, one Antagoras, for the gift of a ram; whereupon Antagoras, who was of powerful build, challenged Heracles to wrestle with him, offering the ram as a prize. Heracles accepted the challenge but, when the two champions came to grips, Antagoras's Meropian friends ran to his assistance, and the Greeks did the same for Heracles, so that a general rough-and-tumble ensued. Exhausted by the storm and by the number of his enemies, Heracles broke off the fight and fled to the house of a stout Thracian matron, in whose clothes he disguised himself, thus contriving to escape.

*r.* Later in the day, refreshed by food and sleep, he fought the Meropians again and worsted them; after which he was purified of their blood and, still dressed in women's clothes, married Chalciope, by whom he became the father of Thessalus.[23] Annual Sacrifices are now offered to Heracles on the field where this battle was fought; and Coan bridegrooms wear women's clothes when they welcome their brides home – as the priest of Heracles at Antimacheia also does before he begins a sacrifice.[24]

*s.* The women of Astypalaea were offended at Heracles, and abused him, whereupon Hera honoured them with horns like cows; but some say that this was a punishment inflicted on them by Aphrodite for daring to extol their beauty above hers.[25]

t. Having laid waste Cos, and all but annihilated the Meropians, Heracles was guided by Athene to Phlegra, where he helped the gods to win their battle against the giants.[26] Thence he came to Boeotia where, at his insistence, Scamander was elected king. Scamander renamed the river Inachus after himself, and a near-by stream after his mother Glaucia; he also named the spring Acidusa after his wife, by whom he had three daughters, still honoured locally under the name of 'Máidens'.[27]

1. Apollodorus: ii. 4. 6.
2. Apollodorus: ii. 5. 9; Hyginus: *Fabula* 89; Diodorus Siculus: iv. 42; Tzetzes: *On Lycophron* 34.
3. Apollodorus: *loc. cit.*; Hyginus: *loc. cit.*; Lucian: *On Sacrifices* 4; Tzetzes: *loc. cit.*; Diodorus Siculus: *loc. cit.*; Servius on Virgil's *Aeneid* iii. 3.
4. Servius on Virgil's *Aeneid* v. 30 and i. 554; Tzetzes: *On Lycophron* 472; Hyginus: *Fabula* 89.
5. Diodorus Siculus: iv. 42; Tzetzes: *On Lycophron* 34; Valerius Flaccus: ii. 487; Hyginus: *loc. cit.*; Apollodorus: ii. 5. 9; Hellanicus, quoted by scholiast on Homer's *Iliad* xx. 146.
6. Homer: *Iliad* xx. 145–8; Tzetzes: *loc. cit.*; Hellanicus: *loc. cit.*
7. Diodorus Siculus: iv. 42 and 49; Servius on Virgil's *Aeneid* i. 623.
8. Apollodorus: ii. 5. 9; Hellanicus: *loc. cit.*; Pindar: *Fragment* 140a, ed. Schroeder, and *Isthmian Odes* vi. 26 ff.
9. Tzetzes: *On Lycophron* 472 and 953; Servius on Virgil's *Aeneid* i. 554 and v. 30.
10. Tzetzes: *On Lycophron* 472, 953, and 965; Servius on Virgil's *Aeneid* i. 554; v. 30 and 73.
11. Diodorus Siculus: iv. 32; Apollodorus: ii. 6. 4; Homer: *Iliad* v. 638 ff.
12. Scholiast on Pindar's *Nemean Odes* iii. 61 and *Isthmian Odes* i. 21–3; Apollodorus: *loc. cit.* and i. 8. 2; Homer: *Odyssey* xv. 243; Plutarch: *Greek Questions* 41.
13. Apollodorus: iii. 12. 7; Pindar: *Isthmian Odes* vi. 35 ff.; Tzetzes: *On Lycophron* 455; Scholiast on Sophocles's *Ajax* 833; Scholiast On Homer's *Iliad* xxiii. 821.
14. Apollodorus: ii. 6. 4; Hellanicus, quoted by Tzetzes: *On Lycophron* 469.
15. Diodorus Siculus: iv. 32; Tzetzes: *On Lycophron* 337; Apollodorus: *loc. cit.*; Hyginus: *Fabula* 89; Homer: *Iliad* v. 638 ff.
16. Apollodorus: iii. 12. 7; Servius on Virgil's *Aeneid* iii. 3; Homer: *Iliad* viii. 283 ff., and scholiast on 284.
17. Tzetzes: *On Lycophron* 467; Athenaeus: ii. 43; Parthenius: *Love Stories* 26.

18. Apollodorus: iii. 7. 5; Pausanias: viii. 36. 4.
19. Plutarch: *Greek Questions* 41.
20. Homer: *Iliad* xiv. 250 ff. and xv. 18 ff.; Apollodorus: i. 3. 5 and ii. 7. 1.
21. Apollodorus: ii. 7. 1.
22. Scholiast on Pindar's *Nemean Odes* iv. 40.
23. Apollodorus: ii. 7. 8; Homer: *Iliad* ii. 678–9.
24. Plutarch: *Greek Questions* 58.
25. Ovid: *Metamorphoses* vii. 363–4; Lactantius: *Stories of Ovid's Metamorphoses* vii. 10.
26. Apollodorus: ii. 7. 1; Pindar: *Isthmian Odes* vi. 31 ff.
27. Plutarch: *Greek Questions* 41.

*

1. This legend concerns the sack of the fifth, or pre-Homeric, city of Troy: probably by Minyans, that is to say Aeolian Greeks, supported by Lelegians, when a timely earthquake overthrew its massive walls (see 158. *8*). From the legend of the Golden Fleece we gather that Laomedon had opposed Lelegian as well as Minyan mercantile ventures in the Black Sea (see 148. *10*), and that the only way to bring him to reason was to destroy his city, which commanded the Hellespont and the Scamander plain where the East-West fair was annually held. The Ninth Labour refers to Black Sea enterprises of the same sort (see 131. *11*). Heracles's task was assisted by an earthquake, dated about 1260 B.C.

2. Heracles's rescue of Hesione, paralleled by Perseus's rescue of Andromeda (see 73. *7*), is clearly derived from an icon common in Syria and Asia Minor: Marduk's conquest of the Sea-monster Tiamat, an emanation of the goddess Ishtar, whose power he annulled by chaining her to a rock. Heracles is swallowed by Tiamat, and disappears for three days before fighting his way out. So also, according to a Hebrew moral tale apparently based on the same icon, Jonah spent three days in the Whale's belly; and so Marduk's representative, the King of Babylon, spent a period in demise every year, during which he was supposedly fighting Tiamat (see 71. *1*; 73. *7* and 103. *1*). Marduk's or Perseus's white solar horse here becomes the reward for Hesione's rescue. Heracles's loss of hair emphasizes his solar character: a shearing of the sacred king's locks when the year came to an end, typified the reduction of his magical strength, as in the story of Samson (see 91. *1*). When he reappeared, he had no more hair than an infant. Hesione's ransom of Podarces may represent the Queen-mother of Seha's (Scamander?) intervention with the Hittite King Mursilis on behalf of her scapegrace son Manapadattas.

3. Phoenodamas's three daughters represent the Moon-goddess in triad, ruling the three-cornered island of Sicily. The dog was sacred to her

as Artemis, Aphrodite, and Hecate. Greek-speaking Sicilians were addicted to the Homeric epics, like the Romans, and equally anxious to claim Trojan ancestry on however insecure grounds. Scamander's three daughters represent the same goddess in Boeotia. Glaucia's bearing of a child to Scamander was not unusual. According to the pseudo-Aeschines (*Dialogues* 10. 3), Trojan brides used to bathe in the river, and cry: 'Scamander, take my virginity!'; which points to an archaic period when it was thought that river water would quicken their wombs (see 68. *2*).

4. To what Hellenic conquest of the Helladic island of Cos Heracles's visit refers is uncertain, but the subsequent wearing of women's dress by the bridegroom, when he welcomed his bride home, seems to be a concession to the former matrilocal custom by which she welcomed him to her house, not contrariwise (see 160. *3*). A cow-dance will have been performed on Cos, similar to the Argive rite honouring the Moon-goddess Io (see 56. *1*). At Antimacheia, the sacred king was still at the primitive stage of being the Queen's deputy, and obliged therefore to wear female dress (see 18. *8* and 136. *4*).

5. Laomedon's mares were of the same breed as those sired at Troy by Boreas (see 29. *e*).

6. The Inachus was an Argive river; Plutarch seems to be the sole authority for a Boeotian Inachus, or Scamander.

# 138

## THE CONQUEST OF ELIS

N o t long after his return, Heracles collected a force of Tirynthians and Arcadians and, joined by volunteers from the noblest Greek families, marched against Augeias, King of Elis, whom he owed a grudge on account of the Fifth Labour.[1] Augeias, however, foreseeing this attack, had prepared to resist it by appointing as his generals Eurytus and Cteatus, the sons of his brother Actor and Molione, or Moline, a daughter of Molus; and by giving a share in the Elean government to the valiant Amarynceus, who is usually described as a son of the Thessalian immigrant Pyttius.[2]

*b.* The sons of Actor are called Moliones, or Molionides, after their mother, to distinguish them from those of the other Actor, who married Aegina. They were twins, born from a silver egg, and surpassed all their contemporaries in strength; but, unlike the Dioscuri, had been joined together at the waist from birth.[3] The Moliones married the twin daughters of Dexamenus the Centaur and, one generation later, their sons reigned in Elis jointly with Augeias's grandson and Amarynceus's son. Each of these four commanded ten ships in the expedition to Troy. Actor already possessed a share of the kingdom through his mother Hyrmine, a daughter of Neleus, whose name he gave to the now vanished city of Hyrmine.[4]

c. Heracles did not cover himself with glory in this Elean War. He fell sick, and when the Moliones routed his army, which was encamped in the heart of Elis, the Corinthians intervened by proclaiming the Isthmian Truce. Among those wounded by the Moliones was Heracles's twin brother Iphicles; his friends carried him fainting to Pheneus in Arcadia, where he eventually died and became a hero. Three hundred and sixty Cleonensians also died bravely, fighting at Heracles's side; to them he ceded the honours awarded him by the Nemeans after he had killed the lion.[5] He now retired to Olenus, the home of his friend Dexamenus, father-in-law of the Moliones, whose youngest daughter Deianeira he deflowered, after promising to marry her. When Heracles had passed on, the Centaur Eurytion asked for her hand, which Dexamenus feared to refuse him; but on the wedding day Heracles reappeared without warning, shot down Eurytion and his brothers, and took Deianeira away with him. Some say, however, that Heracles's bride was named Mnesimache, or Hippolyte; on the ground that Deianeira is more usually described as the daughter of Oeneus. Dexamenus had been born at Bura, famous for its dice-oracle of Heracles.[6]

d. When Heracles returned to Tiryns, Eurystheus accused him of designs on the high kingship in which he had himself been confirmed by Zeus, and banished him from Argolis. With his mother Alcmene, and his nephew Iolaus, Heracles then rejoined Iphicles at Pheneus, where he took Laonome, daughter of Guneus, as his mistress. Through the middle of the Pheneatian Plain, he dug a channel for the river Aroanius, some fifty furlongs long and as much as thirty feet deep; but the river soon deserted this channel, which has caved in here and there, and returned to its former course. He also dug deep chasms at the foot of the Phenean Mountains to carry off flood water; these have served their purpose well, except that on one occasion, after a cloud-burst, the Aroanius rose and inundated the ancient city of Pheneus – the highwater marks of this flood are still shown on the mountainside.[7]

e. Afterwards, hearing that the Eleans were sending a procession to honour Poseidon at the Third Isthmian Festival, and that the Moliones would witness the games and take part in the sacrifices, Heracles ambushed them from a roadside thicket below Cleonae, and shot both dead; and killed their cousin, the other Eurytus, as well, a son of King Augeias.[8]

*f.* Molione soon learned who had murdered her sons, and made the Eleans demand satisfaction from Eurystheus, on the ground that Heracles was a native of Tiryns. When Eurystheus disclaimed responsibility for the misdeeds of Heracles, whom he had banished, Molione asked the Corinthians to exclude all Argives from the Isthmian Games until satisfaction had been given for the murder. This they declined to do, whereupon Molione laid a curse on every Elean who might take part in the festival. Her curse is still respected: no Elean athlete will ever enter for the Isthmian Games.[9]

*g.* Heracles now borrowed the black-maned horse Arion from Oncus, mastered him, raised a new army in Argos, Thebes, and Arcadia, and sacked the city of Elis. Some say that he killed Augeias and his sons, restored Phyleus, the rightful king, and set him on the Elean throne; others, that he spared Augeias's life at least. When Heracles decided to repeople Elis by ordering the widows of the dead Eleans to lie with his soldiers, the widows offered a common prayer to Athene that they might conceive at the first embrace. This prayer was heard and, in gratitude, they founded a sanctuary of Athene the Mother. So widespread was the joy at this fortunate event that the place where they had met their new husbands, and the stream flowing by it, was called *Bady*, which is the Elean word for 'sweet'. Heracles then gave the horse Arion to Adrastus, saying that, after all, he preferred to fight on foot.[10]

*h.* About this time, Heracles won his title of Buphagus, or 'Ox-eater'. It happened as follows. Lepreus, the son of Caucon and Astydameia, who founded the city of Lepreus in Arcadia (the district derived its name from the leprosy which had attacked the earliest settlers), had foolishly advised King Augeias to fetter Heracles when he asked to be paid for having cleansed the cattle-yards. Hearing that Heracles was on his way to the city, Astydameia persuaded Lepreus to receive him courteously and plead for forgiveness. This Heracles granted, but challenged Lepreus to a triple contest: of throwing the discus, drinking bucket after bucket of water, and eating an ox. Then, though Heracles won the discus-throw and the drinking-match, Lepreus ate the ox in less time than he. Flushed with success, he challenged Heracles to a duel, and was at once clubbed to death; his tomb is shown at Phigalia. The Lepreans, who worship Demeter and Zeus of the White Poplar, have always been subjects of Elis; and if one of them ever wins a prize at Olympia, the herald proclaims him an Elean from Lepreus. King Augeias is still honoured as a hero by the Eleans, and it was only during the reign of Lycurgus the Spartan that they were persuaded to forget their enmity of Heracles and sacrifice to him also; by which means they averted a pestilence.[11]

*i*. After the conquest of Elis, Heracles assembled his army at Pisa, and used the spoil to establish the famous four-yearly Olympic Festival and Games in honour of his father Zeus, which some claim was only the eighth athletic contest ever held.[12] Having measured a precinct for Zeus, and fenced off the Sacred Grove, he stepped out the stadium, named a neighbouring hillock 'The Hill of Cronus', and raised six altars to the Olympian gods: one for every pair of them. In sacrificing to Zeus, he burnt the victims' thighs upon a fire of white poplar wood cut from trees growing by the Thesprotian river Acheron; he also founded a sacrificial hearth in honour of his great-grandfather Pelops, and assigned him a shrine. Being much plagued by flies on this occasion, he offered a second sacrifice to Zeus the Averter of Flies: who sent them buzzing across the river Alpheius. The Eleans still sacrifice to this Zeus, when they expel the flies from Olympia.[13]

*j*. Now, at the first full moon after the summer solstice all was ready for the Festival, except that the valley lacked trees to shade it from the sun. Heracles therefore returned to the Land of the Hyperboreans, where he had admired the wild olives growing at the source of the Danube, and persuaded Apollo's priests to give him one for planting in Zeus's precinct. Returning to Olympia, he ordained that the Aetolian umpire should crown the victors with its leaves: which were to be their only reward, because he himself had performed his Labours without payment from Eurystheus. This tree, called 'The Olive of the Fair Crown', still grows in the Sacred Grove behind Zeus's temple. The branches for the wreaths are lopped with a golden sickle by a nobly-born boy, both of whose parents must be alive.[14]

*k*. Some say that Heracles won all the events by default, because none dared compete against him; but the truth is that every one was hotly disputed. No other entrants could, however, be found for the wrestling match, until Zeus, in disguise, condescended to enter the ring.

The match was drawn, Zeus revealed himself to his son Heracles, all the spectators cheered, and the full moon shone as bright as day.[15]

*l*. But the more ancient legend is that the Olympic Games were founded by Heracles the Dactyl, and that it was he who brought the wild olive from the land of the Hyperboreans. Charms and amulets in honour of Heracles the Dactyl are much used by sorceresses, who have little regard for Heracles son of Alcmene. Zeus's altar, which stands at an equal distance between the shrine of Pelops and the sanctuary of Hera, but in front of both, is said to have been built by this earlier Heracles, like the altar at Pergamus, from the ashes of the thigh-bones he sacrificed to Zeus. Once a year, on the nineteenth day of the Elean month Elaphius, soothsayers fetch the ashes from the Council Hall, and after moistening them with water from the river Alpheius – no other will serve – apply a fresh coat of this plaster to the altar.[16]

*m*. This is not, however, to deny that Heracles the son of Alcmene refounded the Games: for an ancient walled gymnasium is shown at Elis, where athletes train. Tall plane-trees grow between the running-tracks, and the enclosure is called Xystus because Heracles exercised himself there by *scraping* up thistles. But Clymenus the Cretan, son of Cardis a descendant of the Dactyl, had celebrated the Festival, only fifty years after the Deucalionian Flood; and subsequently Endymion had done the same, and Pelops, and Amythaon son of Cretheus, also Pelias and Neleus, and some say Augeias.[17]

*n*. The Olympic Festival is held at an interval alternately of forty-nine and fifty months, according to the calendar, and now lasts for five days: from the eleventh to the fifteenth of the month in which it happens to fall. Heralds proclaim an absolute armistice throughout Greece for the whole of this month, and no athlete is permitted to attend who has been guilty of any felony or offence against the gods. Originally, the Festival was managed by the Pisans; but, after the final return of the Heraclids, their Aetolian allies settled in Elis and were charged with the task.[18]

*o*. On the northern side of the Hill of Cronus, a serpent called Sosipolis is housed in Eileithyia's shrine; a white-veiled virgin-priestess feeds it with honey-cakes and water. This custom commemorates a miracle which drove away the Arcadians when they fought against the holy land of Elis: an unknown woman came to the Elean generals with a suckling child and gave it to them as their champion. They believed her, and when she sat the child down between the two armies, it changed into a serpent; the Arcadians fled, pursued by the Eleans, and suffered fearful losses. Eileithyia's shrine marks the place where the serpent disappeared into the Hill of Cronus. On the summit, sacrifices are offered to Cronus at the spring equinox in the month of Elaphius, by priestesses known as 'Queens'.[19]

1. Apollodorus: ii. 7. 2; Pindar: *Olympian Odes* x. 31–3.
2. Pausanias: v. 1. 8 and v. 2. 2; Eustathius on Homer's *Iliad* ix. 834 and xxiii. 1442.
3. Homer: *Iliad* xi. 709; Apollodorus: *loc. cit.*; Ibycus, quoted by Athenaeus: ii. 50; Porphyry: *Questions Relevant to Homer's Iliad* 265; Plutarch: *On Brotherly Love* i.
4. Pausanias: v. 1. 8 and v. 3. 4; Homer: *Iliad* ii. 615–24; Scholiast on Apollonius Rhodius i. 172.
5. Apollodorus: *loc. cit.*; Pindar: *Olympian Odes* x. 31–3; Pausanias: v. 2. 1 and viii. 14. 6; Aelian: *Varia Historia* iv. 5.
6. Hyginus: *Fabula* 33; Apollodorus: ii. 5. 5 and 7. 5; Diodorus Siculus: iv. 33; Pausanias: vii. 25. 5–6.
7. Diodorus Siculus: *loc. cit.*; Pausanias: viii. 14. 1–3.
8. Apollodorus: ii. 7. 2; Diodorus Siculus: *loc. cit.*; Pausanias: ii. 15. 1; Pindar: *Olympian Odes* x. 26 ff.
9. Pausanias: v. 2. 2–3.
10. Pausanias: viii. 25. 5 and v. 3. 1; Apollodorus: ii. 7. 2; Homeric scholiast, quoted by Meursius: *On Lycophron* 40; Servius on Virgil's *Aeneid* vii. 666.
11. Athenaeus: x. 412; Pausanias: v. 4. 1; 4. 4 and 5. 3–4.
12. Pindar: *Olympian Odes* x. 43 ff.; Tzetzes: *On Lycophron* 41; Hyginus: *Fabula* 273.
13. Pindar: *loc. cit.*; Apollodorus: *loc. cit.*; Pausanias: v. 13. 1 and 14. 2–3.
14. Pindar: *Olympian Odes* iii. 11 ff.; Diodorus Siculus: iv. 14; Pausanias: v. 15. 3.
15. Diodorus Siculus: *loc. cit.*; Pindar: *Olympian Odes* x. 60 ff.; Pausanias: v. 8. 1; Tzetzes: *On Lycophron* 41.
16. Pausanias: v. 7. 4 and 13. 5; Diodorus Siculus: v. 64.
17. Pausanias: vi. 23. 1 and v. 8. 1.
18. Scholiast on Pindar's *Olympian Odes* iii. 35 and v. 6; Demosthenes: *Against Aristocrates* pp. 631–2; Strabo: viii. 3. 33.
19. Pausanias: vi. 20. 1–3.

\*

1. This myth apparently records an unsuccessful Achaean invasion of the Western Peloponnese followed, at the close of the thirteenth century B.C., by a second, successful, invasion which has, however, been confused with the Dorian invasion of the eleventh century B.C. – Heracles having

also been a Dorian hero. The murder of Eurytion may be deduced from the same wedding-icon that showed the killing of Pholus. Heracles's digging of the Aroanian channel is paralleled by similar feats in Elis (see 121. *d*), Boeotia (see 142. *3*), and Thrace (see 130. *b*); and the honours paid to the three hundred and sixty Cleonensians probably refer to a calendar mystery, since three hundred and sixty are the number of days in the Egyptian year, exclusive of the five sacred to Osiris, Horus, Set, Isis, and Nephthys.

2. The leprosy associated with Lepreus was *vitiligo*, a skin disease caused by foul food, which the Moon-goddess of the white poplar could cure (*White Goddess*, p. 432); true leprosy did not reach Europe until the first century B.C.

3. Heracles's title of Buphagus originally referred to the eating of an ox by his worshippers.

4. Sosopolis must have been the ghost of Cronus after whom the hillock was called, and whose head was buried on its northern slopes, to protect the stadium which lay behind it, near the junction of the Cladeus and Alpheius. His British counterpart Bran similarly guarded Tower Hill, commanding London (see 146. 2). The spring equinox, when fawns are dropped, occurs during the alder-month of the tree-calendar, also called Elaphius ('of the fawn'), and peculiarly sacred to Cronus-Bran (*White Goddess*, pp. 168–72 and 206–7). This suggests that, originally, the Elean New Year began at the spring solstice, as in parts of Italy, when the King of the old year, wearing horns like Actaeon (see 22. *1*), was put to death by the wild women, or 'Queens'; Heracles the Dactyl belongs to this cult (see 53. *b*). The Pelopians seem to have changed the calendar when they arrived with their solar chariot and porpoise, making the funeral games celebrate the midsummer murder and supersession of Zeus, the sacred king, by his tanist – as the king revenged himself on the tanist at midwinter. In Classical times, therefore, the Elean New Year was celebrated in the summer. The mention of Pelops suggests that the king was sacrificially eaten and the ashes of his bones mixed with water to plaster the Goddess's altar. He was called the Green Zeus, or Achilles (see 164. *5*), as well as Heracles. 

5. Wild olive, used in Greece to expel old-year demons and spites, who took the form of flies, was introduced from Libya, where the cult of the North Wind originated (see 48. *1* and 133. *5*), rather than the North. At Olympia, it will have been mistletoe (or Ioranthus), not wild-olive, which the boy lopped with a golden sickle (see 7. *1* and 50. *2*); wild-olive figured in the Hyperborean tree-calendar (see 119. *3*). The girls' foot-race for the position of priestess to Hera was the earliest event; but when the single year of the king's reign was prolonged to a Great Year of nominally a hundred months – to permit a more exact synchronization

of solar and lunar time – the king reigned for one half of this period, his tanist for the other. Later, both ruled concurrently under the title of Moliones, and were no less closely united than the kings of Sparta (see 74. *1*). It may be that a case of Siamese twins had occurred in Greece to reinforce the metaphor. But Augeias's division of Elis, reported by Homer, shows that at a still later stage, the sacred king retained a third part of his kingdom when he was due to retire; as Proetus did at Argos. Amarynceus's share was evidently gained by conquest.

6. Molione is perhaps a title of the Elean Moon-goddess, the patroness of the Games, meaning 'Queen of the Moly'; the *moly* being a herb which elsewhere defied moon-magic (see 170. *5*). She was also known as Agamede ('very cunning'); and this is the name of Augeias's sorceress daughter, who 'knew all the drugs that grow on earth' (Homer: *Iliad* xi. 739–41). In Classical Greece, 'Athene the Mother' was a strange and indecent concept and had to be explained away (see 25. *2* and 141. *1*), but the Elean tradition suggests that erotic orgies had been celebrated in her honour beside the river Bady.

7. The mastery of Arion, it seems, formed part of the coronation rite at Arcadian Oncus (see 130. *1*).


# 139

## THE CAPTURE OF PYLUS

HERACLES next sacked and burned the city of Pylus, because the Pylians had gone to the aid of Elis. He killed all Neleus's sons, except the youngest, Nestor, who was away at Gerania, but Neleus himself escaped with his life.[1]

b. Athene, champion of justice, fought for Heracles; and Pylus was defended by Hera, Poseidon, Hades, and Ares. While Athene engaged Ares, Heracles made for Poseidon, club against trident, and forced him to give way. Next, he ran to assist Athene, spear in hand, and his third lunge pierced Ares's shield, dashing him headlong to the ground; then, with a powerful thrust at Ares's thigh, he drove deep into the divine flesh. Ares fled in anguish to Olympus, where Apollo spread soothing unguents on the wound and healed it within the hour; so he renewed the fight, until one of Heracles's arrows pierced his shoulder, and forced him off the field for good. Meanwhile, Heracles had also wounded Hera in the right breast with a three-barbed arrow.[2]

c. Neleus's eldest son, Periclymenus the Argonaut, was gifted by

Poseidon with boundless strength and the power of assuming whatever shape he pleased, whether of bird, beast, or tree. On this occasion he turned himself first into a lion, then into a serpent and after a while, to escape scrutiny, perched on the yoke-boss of Heracles's horses in the form of an ant, or fly, or bee.[3] Heracles, nudged by Athene, recognized Periclymenus and reached for his club, whereupon Periclymenus became an eagle, and tried to peck out his eyes, but a sudden arrow from Heracles's bow pierced him underneath his wing. He tumbled to earth, and the arrow was driven through his neck by the fall, killing him. Some say, however, that he flew away in safety; and that Heracles had attacked Poseidon on an earlier occasion, after the murder of Iphitus, when Neleus refused to purify him; and that the fight with Hades took place at the other Pylus, in Elis, when Heracles was challenged for carrying off Cerberus without permission.[4]

d. Heracles gave the city of Messene to Nestor, in trust for his own descendants, remembering that Nestor had taken no part in robbing him of Geryon's cattle; and soon came to love him more even than Hylas and Iolaus. It was Nestor who first swore an oath by Heracles.[5]

e. The Eleans, though they themselves rebuilt Pylus, took advantage of the Pylians' weakness to oppress them in petty ways. Neleus kept his patience until one day, having sent a chariot and a prize-winning team of four horses to contest for a tripod in the Olympic Games, he learned that Augeias had appropriated them and sent the charioteer home on foot. At this, he ordered Nestor to make a retaliatory raid on the Elean Plain; and Nestor managed to drive away fifty herds of cattle, fifty flocks of sheep, fifty droves of swine, fifty flocks of goats, and one hundred and fifty chestnut mares, many with foal, beating off the Eleans who opposed him and blooding his spear in this, his first fight. Neleus's heralds then convoked all in Pylus who were owed a debt by the Eleans, and when he had divided the booty among the claimants, keeping back the lion's share for Nestor, sacrificed lavishly to the gods. Three days later, the Eleans advanced on Pylus in full array – among them the two orphaned sons of the Moliones, who had inherited their title – and crossed the Plain from Thryoessa. But Athene came by night to warn and marshal the Pylians; and when battle had been joined, Nestor, who was on foot, struck down Amarynceus, the Elean commander and, seizing his chariot, rushed like a black tempest through the Elean ranks, capturing fifty other chariots and killing a hundred men. The Moliones would also have fallen to his busy spear, had not Poseidon wrapped them in an impenetrable mist and spirited them away. The Eleans, hotly pursued by Nestor's army, fled as far as the Olenian Rock, where Athene called a halt.[6]

f. A truce being then agreed upon, Amarynceus was buried at Buprasium, and awarded funeral games, in which numerous Pylians took part. The Moliones won the chariot race by crowding Nestor at the turn, but he is said to have won all the other events: the boxing and the wrestling match, the foot-race and the javelin-throw. Of these feats, it is only right to add, Nestor himself, in garrulous old age, was the principal witness; since by the grace of Apollo, who granted him the years of which his maternal uncles had been deprived, he lived for three centuries, and no contemporary survived to gainsay him.[7]

1. Pausanias: ii. 2. 2; iii. 26. 6 and v. 3. 1; Apollodorus: ii. 7. 3, Diodorus Siculus: iv. 68.
2. Pausanias: vi. 25. 3; Scholiast on Homer's *Iliad* xi. 689; Hesiod: *Shield of Heracles* 359 ff.; Pindar: *Olympian Odes* x. 30–1; Homer: *Iliad* v. 392 ff.; Tzetzes: *On Lycophron* 39.
3. Apollonius Rhodius: i. 156–60; Eustathius on Homer's *Odyssey* xi. 285; Scholiast on Homer's *Iliad* ii. 336 and xi. 286.
4. Apollodorus: i. 9. 9; Hersiod, quoted by scholiast on Apollonius Rhodius i. 156; Ovid: *Metamorphoses* xii. 548 ff.; Hyginus: *Fabula* 10; Scholiast on Pindar's *Olympian Odes* ix. 30 ff.
5. Pausanias: ii. 18. 6; Philostratus: *Heroica* 2.
6. Pausanias: vi. 22. 3; Homer: *Iliad* xi. 671 and 761.
7. Homer: *Iliad* xxiii. 630–42; Hyginus: *Fabula* 10.

*

1. The capture of Pylus seems to be another incident in the thirteenth-century Achaean invasion of the Peloponnese. Hera, Poseidon, Hades, and Ares, the elder deities, are aiding Elis; the younger ones, Athene reborn from Zeus's head, and Heracles as Zeus's son, oppose them. Heracles's defeat of Periclymenus, the shape-shifter, may mark the suppression of a New Year child-sacrifice; and Periclymenus's power to take the shape of any tree refers, apparently, to the succession of thirteen months through which the *interrex* passed in his ritual ballet, each month having an emblematic tree, from wild-olive to myrtle (see 52. 3 and 169. 6). The wounding of Hades presents Heracles as the champion destined to cheat the grave and become immortal (see 145. h); moreover, according to Homer (*Iliad* v. 319 ff.), he wounded Hades 'at Pylus, among the corpses' – which could equally mean: 'at the gate, among the dead'; the gate being that of the Underworld, perhaps in the Far North (see 170. 4). If so, Hades is a substitute for Cronus, whom Heracles defeated

in the sepulchral island of Erytheia (see 132. d), and the encounter is a doublet of the Twelfth Labour, when he harrowed Hell. Heracles's Pylian allies, significantly aided by Athene, are described by Homer (*Iliad* xi. 617 and 761) as Achaeans, though Neleus's dynasty was, in fact, Aeolian.

2. Heracles's wounding of Hera in the right breast with a three-barbed arrow seems to allegorize the Dorian invasion of the Western Peloponnese when the three tribes, who called themselves Sons of Heracles, humbled the power of the Elean Goddess (see 146. 1).

# 140

## THE SONS OF HIPPOCOÖN

HERACLES decided to attack Sparta and punish the sons of Hippocoön. They had not only refused to purify him after the death of Iphitus, and fought against him under Neleus's command, but also murdered his friend, Oeonus. It happened that Oeonus son of Licymnius, who had accompanied Heracles to Sparta, was strolling about the city when, just outside Hippocoön's palace, a huge Molossian hound ran at him; in self-defence, he threw a stone which struck it on the muzzle. Out darted the sons of Hippocoön and beat him with cudgels. Heracles ran to Oeonus's rescue from the other end of the street, but arrived too late. Oeonus was cudgelled to death, and Heracles, wounded in the hollow of his hand and in the thigh, fled to the shrine of Eleusinian Demeter, near Mount Taygetus; where Asclepius hid him and healed his wounds.[1]

b. Having mustered a small army, Heracles now marched to Tegea in Arcadia and there begged Cepheus the son of Aleus to join him with his twenty sons. At first, Cepheus refused, fearing for the safety of Tegea if he left home. But Heracles, whom Athene had given a lock of the Gorgon's hair in a brazen jar, presented it to Cepheus's daughter Aerope: should the city be attacked, he said, she was to display the lock thrice from its walls, turning her back to the enemy, who would immediately flee. As events proved, however, Aerope had no need of the charm.[2]

c. Thus Cepheus joined the expedition against Sparta, in which, by ill fortune, he and seventeen of his sons fell. Some say that Iphicles was also killed, but this is likely to have been the Aetolian Argonaut of that name, not Amphitryon's son. Heracles's army suffered few other casualties, whereas the Spartans lost Hippocoön and all his twelve sons, with numerous other men of high rank; and their city was taken by storm. Heracles then restored Tyndareus, leaving him the kingdom in trust for his own descendants.[3]

d. Since Hera, inexplicably, had not thwarted him in this campaign, Heracles built her a shrine at Sparta, and sacrificed goats, having no other victims at his disposal. The Spartans are thus the only Greeks who surname Hera 'Goat-eating', and offer goats to her. Heracles also raised a temple to Athene of the Just Deserts; and, on the road to Therapne, a shrine to Cotylaean Asclepius which commemorates the wound in the hollow of his hand. A shrine at Tegea, called 'The Common Hearth of the Arcadians', is remarkable for its statue of Heracles with the wound in his thigh.[4]

1. Apollodorus: ii. 7. 3; Pausanias: iii. 15. 3; iii. 19. 7; iii. 20. 5 and viii. 53. 3.
2. Apollodorus: *loc. cit.*; Pausanias: viii. 47. 4.
3. Apollodorus: *loc. cit.* and iii. 10. 5; Diodorus Siculus: iv. 33.
4. Pausanias: iii. 15. 7, iii. 19. 7 and viii. 53. 3.

*

1. Here the Heracles myth is lost in saga; and pseudo-myth is introduced to explain such anomalies as Goat-eating Hera, Hollow-of-the-Hand Asclepius, Heracles of the Wounded Thigh, and Tegea's long immunity from capture. But Hera's wild women had once eaten Zagreus, Zeus, and Dionysus in wild-goat form; Asclepius's statue probably held medicines in the hollow of the hand; the wound in Heracles's thigh will have been made by a boar (see 157. e); and the Tegeans may have displayed a Gorgon's head on their gates as a prophylactic charm. To assault a city thus protected was, as it were, to violate the maiden-goddess Athene: a superstition also fostered by the Athenians.

2. Whenever Heracles leaves an Achaean, Aetolian, Sicilian, or Pelasgian city in trust for his descendants, this is an attempted justification of its later seizure by the Dorians (see 132. q and 6; 143. d; and 146. e).

# 141

## AUGE

ALEUS, king of Tegea, the son of Apheidas, married Neaera, a daughter of Pereus, who bore him Auge, Cepheus, Lycurgus, and Aphidamas. An ancient shrine of Athene Alea, founded at Tegea by Aleus, still contains a sacred couch of the goddess.[1]

*b*. When, on a visit to Delphi, Aleus was warned by the Oracle that Neaera's two brothers would die by the hand of her daughter's son, he hurried home and appointed Auge a priestess of Athene, threatening to kill her if she were unchaste. Whether Heracles came to Tegea on his way to fight King Augeias, or on his return from Sparta, is disputed; at all events, Aleus entertained him hospitably in Athene's temple. There, flushed with wine, Heracles violated the virgin-priestess beside a fountain which is still shown to the north of the shrine; since, however, Auge made no outcry, it is often suggested that she came there by assignation.[2]

*c*. Heracles continued on his way, and at Stymphalus begot Eures on Parthenope, the daughter of Stymphalus; but meanwhile pestilence and famine came upon Tegea, and Aleus, informed by the Pythoness that a crime had been committed in Athene's sacred precinct, visited it and found Auge far gone with child. Though she wept and declared that Heracles had violated her in a fit of drunkenness, Aleus would not believe this. He dragged her to the Tegean market place, where she fell upon her knees at the site of the present temple of Eileithyia, famed for its image of 'Auge on her Knees'.[3] Ashamed to kill his daughter in public, Aleus engaged King Nauplius to drown her. Nauplius accordingly set out with Auge for Nauplia; but on Mount Parthenius she was overtaken by labour-pangs, and made some excuse to turn aside into a wood. There she gave birth to a son and, hiding him in a thicket, returned to where Nauplius was patiently waiting for her by the roadside. However, having no intention of drowning a princess when he could dispose of her at a high price in the slave-market, he sold Auge to some Carian merchants who had just arrived at Nauplia and who, in turn, sold her to Teuthras, king of Mysian Teuthrania.[4]

*d*. Auge's son was suckled by a doe on Mount Parthenius (where he now has a sacred precinct) and some cattle-men found him, named him Telephus, and took him to their master, King Corythus. At the same time, by a coincidence, Corythus's shepherds discovered Atalanta's infant son, whom she had borne to Meleager, exposed on the same hillside: they named him Parthenopaeus, which is 'son of a pierced maidenhead', because Atalanta was pretending to be still a virgin.[5]

*e*. When Telephus grew to manhood, he approached the Delphic Oracle for news of his parents. He was told: 'Sail and seek King

Teuthras the Mysian'. In Mysia he found Auge, now married to Teuthras, from whom he learned that she was his mother and Heracles his father; and this he could well believe, for no woman had ever borne Heracles a son so like himself. Teuthras thereupon gave Telephus his daughter Argiope in marriage, and appointed him heir to the kingdom.

*f*. Others say that Telephus, after having killed Hippothous and Nereus, his maternal uncles, went silent and speechless to Mysia in search of his mother. 'The silence of Telephus' became proverbial; but Parthenopaeus came with him as spokesman.[7] It happened that the renowned Argonaut Idas, son of Aphareus, was about to seize the Mysian throne, and Teuthras in desperation promised to resign it to Telephus and give him his adopted daughter in marriage, if only Idas were driven away. Thereupon Telephus, with Parthenopaeus's help, routed Idas in a single battle. Now, Teuthras's adopted daughter happened to be Auge, who did not recognize Telephus, nor did he know that she was his mother. Faithful to Heracles's memory, she took a sword into her bedroom on the wedding night, and would have killed Telephus when he entered, had not the gods sent a large serpent between them. Auge threw down the sword in alarm and confessed her murderous intentions. She then apostrophized Heracles; and Telephus, who had been on the point of matricide, was inspired to cry out: 'O mother, mother!' They fell weeping into each other's arms, and the next day, returned with Teuthras's blessing to their native land. Auge's tomb is shown at Pergamus beside the river Caicus. The Pergamenians claim to be Arcadian emigrants who crossed to Asia with Telephus, and offer him heroic sacrifices.[8]

*g*. Others say that Telephus married Astyoche, or Laodice, a daughter of Trojan Priam. Others, again, that Heracles had lain with Auge at Troy when he went there to fetch Laomedon's immortal horses. Still others, that Aleus locked Auge and her infant in an ark, which he committed to the waves; and that, under Athene's watchful care, the chest drifted towards Asia Minor and was cast ashore at the mouth of the river Caicus, where King Teuthras married Auge and adopted Telephus.[9]

*h*. This Teuthras, hunting on Mount Teuthras, once pursued a monstrous boar, which fled to the temple of Orthosian Artemis. He was about to force his way in, when the boar cried out: 'Spare me, my lord! I am the Goddess's nursling!' Teuthras paid no attention, and killed it, thereby offending Artemis so deeply that she restored the boar

to life, punished Teuthras with leprous scabs and sent him raving away
to the mountain peaks. However, his mother, Leucippe, hastened to the
forest, taking with her the seer Polyeidus, and appeased Artemis with
bountiful sacrifices. Teuthras was cured of his leprous scabs by means
of the stone Antipathes, which is still found in quantities on the summit
of Mount Teuthras; whereupon Leucippe built an altar to Orthosian
Artemis, and had a man-headed mechanical boar made, entirely from
gold, which when pursued, takes refuge in the temple, and utters the
words 'Spare me!'[10]

*i.* While Heracles was in Arcadia he visited Mount Ostracina, where
he seduced Phialo, a daughter of the hero Alcimedon. When she bore a
son named Aechmagoras, Alcimedon turned them both out of his cave
to die of hunger on the mountain. Aechmagoras cried piteously, and a
well-intentioned jay flew off to find Heracles, mimicking the sound,
and thus drew him to the tree where Phialo sat, gagged and bound by
her cruel father. Heracles rescued them, and the child grew to manhood.
The neighbouring spring has been called Cissa, after the jay, ever since.[11]

1. Apollodorus: iii. 9. 1; Pausanias: viii. 4. 5–6 and 47. 2.
2. Alcidamas: *Odysseus* 14–16; Diodorus Siculus: iv. 33; Apollodorus: ii. 7. 4; Pausanias: viii. 4. 6 and 47. 3.
3. Diodorus Siculus: *loc. cit.*; Apollodorus: ii. 7. 8; Pausanias: viii.
   48. 5.
4. Callimachus: *Hymn to Delos* 70; Diodorus Siculus: *loc. cit.*; Apollodorus: i. 7. 4 and iii. 9. 1.
5. Pausanias: viii. 54. 5; Apollodorus: iii. 9. 1; Diodorus Siculus: iv.
   33; Hyginus: *Fabula* 99.
6. Pausanias: x. 28. 4; Alcidamas: *Odysseus* 14–16; Apollodorus: *loc.
   cit.*; Diodorus Siculus: *loc. cit.*
7. Hyginus: *Fabula* 244; Aristotle: *Poetics* 24. 1460a; Alexis, quoted
   by Athenaeus: x. 18. 421d; Amphis, quoted by Athenaeus: vi. 5.
   224d.
8. Pausanias: i. 4. 6; v. 13. 2 and viii. 4. 6.
9. Hyginus: *Fabula* 101; Dictys Cretensis: ii. 5; Hesiod: *Oxyrhynchus
   Papyrus* 1359, *Fragment* 1; Hecataeus, quoted by Pausanias: viii. 4.
   6; Euripides, quoted by Strabo: xiii. 1. 69.
10. Plutarch: *On Rivers* 21.
11. Pausanias: viii. 12. 2.

*

1. Athene's couch at Tegea, and Heracles's alleged violation of her
priestess Auge, identify this Athene with Neith, or Anatha, an orgiastic
Moon-goddess, whose priestess performed an annual marriage with the
sacred king to ensure good crops. Relics of this custom were found in

Heracles's temple at Rome, where his bride was called Acca – counterpart of the Peloponnesian White Goddess Acco – and at Jerusalem where, before the religious reforms of the Exile, a sacred marriage seems to have been celebrated every September between the High-priest, a representative of Jehovah, and the goddess Anatha. Professor Raphael Patai summarizes the evidence for the Jerusalem marriage in his *Man and Temple* (pp. 88–94, London, 1947). The divine children supposedly born of such unions became the Corn-spirits of the coming year; thus Athene Alea was a corn-goddess, patroness of corn-mills. The numerous sons whom Heracles fathered on nymphs witness to the prevalence of this religious theory. He is credited with only one anomalous daughter, Macaria ('blessed').

The Auge myth has been told to account for an Arcadian emigration to Mysia, probably under pressure from the Achaeans; also for Tegean festivities in honour of the New Year god as fawn which, to judge from the Hesiod fragment, had their counterpart in the Troad.

2. That Auge and her child drifted in an ark to the river Caicus – a scene illustrated on the altar of Pergamus, and on Pergamene coins – means merely that the cult of Auge and Telephus had been imported into Mysia by Tegean colonists, and that Auge, as the Moon-goddess, was supposed to ride in her crescent boat to the New Year celebrations. Athene's subsequent change from orgiastic bride to chaste warrior-maiden has confused the story: in some versions Teuthras becomes Auge's bridegroom, but in others he piously adopts her. Hyginus's version is based on some late and artificial drama.

3. The myth of the golden boar refers partly to the curative properties of the *antipathes* stone on Mount Teuthras; partly, perhaps, to a Mysian custom of avenging the death of Adonis, who had been killed by Apollo in the form of a boar. It looks as if Adonis's representative, a man wearing a boar's hide with golden tusks, was now spared if he could take refuge from his pursuers in the sanctuary of Apollo's sister Artemis. The kings of Tegea, Auge's birthplace, were, it seems, habitually killed by boars (see 140. 1 and 157. e).

4. Phialo's adventure with the jay is an anecdotal fancy, supposed to account for the name of the spring, which may originally have been sacred to a jay totem-clan.

# 142

## DEIANEIRA

AFTER spending four years in Pheneus, Heracles decided to leave the Peloponnese. At the head of a large Arcadian force, he sailed across to

Calydon in Aetolia, where he took up his residence. Having now no legitimate sons, and no wife, he courted Deianeira, the supposed daughter of Oeneus, thus keeping his promise to the ghost of her brother Meleager. But Deianeira was really the daughter of the god Dionysus, by Oeneus's wife Althaea, as had become apparent when Meleager died and Artemis turned his lamenting sisters into guinea-fowl; for Dionysus then persuaded Artemis to let Deianeira and her sister Gorge retain their human shapes.[1]

*b.* Many suitors came to Oeneus's palace in Pleuron, demanding the hand of lovely Deianeira, who drove a chariot and practised the art of war; but all abandoned their claims when they found themselves in rivalry with Heracles and the River-god Achelous. It is common knowledge that immortal Achelous appears in three forms: as a bull, as a speckled serpent, and as a bull-headed man. Streams of water flow continually from his shaggy beard, and Deianeira would rather have died than marry him.[2]

*c.* Heracles, when summoned by Oeneus to plead his suit, boasted that if he married Deianeira, she would not only have Zeus for a father-in-law, but enjoy the reflected glory of his own Twelve Labours.

Achelous (now in bull-headed form) scoffed at this, remarking that he was a well-known personage, the father of all Greek waters, not a footloose stranger like Heracles, and that the Oracle of Dodona had instructed all visitants to offer him sacrifices. Then he taunted Heracles: 'Either you are not Zeus's son, or your mother is an adulteress!'

Heracles scowled. 'I am better at fighting than debating,' he said, 'and I will not hear my mother insulted!'

*d.* Achelous cast aside his green garment, and wrestled with Heracles until he was thrown on his back, whereupon he deftly turned into a speckled serpent and wriggled away.

'I strangled serpents in my cradle!' laughed Heracles, stooping to grip his throat. Next, Achelous became a bull and charged; Heracles nimbly stepped aside and, catching hold of both his horns, hurled him to the ground with such force that the right horn snapped clean off. Achelous retired, miserably ashamed, and hid his injury under a chaplet of willow-branches.[3] Some say that Heracles returned the broken horn to Achelous in exchange for the horn of Goat Amaltheia; and some, that it was changed into Amaltheia's by the Naiads, and that Heracles presented it to Oeneus as a bridal gift.[4] Others say that in the course of his Twelfth Labour, he took the horn down to Tartarus, filled by the

Hesperides with golden fruit and now called the Cornucopia, as a gift for Plutus, Tyche's assistant.[5]

*e.* After marrying Deianeira, Heracles marched with the Calydonians against the Thesprotian city of Ephyra – later Cichyrus – where he overcame and killed King Phyleus. Among the captives was Phyleus's daughter Astyoche, by whom Heracles became the father of Tlepolemus; though some say that Tlepolemus's mother was Astydameia, daughter of Amyntor, whom Heracles abducted from Elean Ephyra, a city famous for its poisons.[6]

*f.* On the advice of an Oracle, Heracles now sent word to his friend Thespius: 'Keep seven of your sons in Thespiae, send three to Thebes, and order the remaining forty to colonize the island of Sardinia!' Thespius obeyed. Descendants of those who went to Thebes are still honoured there; and descendants of those who stayed behind in Thespiae, the so-called Demuchi, governed the city until recent times. The forces led to Sardinia by Iolaus included Thespian and Athenian contingents, this being the first Greek colonial expedition in which the kings came of different stock from the common people. Having defeated the Sardinians in battle, Iolaus divided the island into provinces, planted olive-trees, and made it so fertile that the Carthaginians have since been prepared to undergo immense troubles and danger for its possession. He founded the city of Olbia, and encouraged the Athenians to found that of Ogryle. With the consent of the sons of Thespius, who regarded Iolaus as their second father, he called the colonists after himself, Iolarians; and they still sacrifice to Father Iolaus, just as the Persians do to Father Cyrus. It has been said that Iolaus eventually returned to Greece, by way of Sicily, where some of his followers settled and awarded him hero rites; but according to the Thebans, who should know, none of the colonists ever came back.[7]

*g.* At a feast three years later, Heracles grew enraged with a young kinsman of Oeneus, variously named Eunomus, Eurynomus, Ennomus, Archias, or Chaerias, the son of Architeles, who was told to pour water on Heracles's hands, and clumsily splashed his legs. Heracles boxed the boy's ears harder than he intended, and killed him. Though forgiven by Architeles for this accident, Heracles decided to pay the due penalty of exile, and went away with Deianeira, and their son Hyllus, to Trachis, the home of Amphitryon's nephew Ceyx.[8]

*h.* A similar accident had occurred at Phlius, a city which lies to the east of Arcadia, when Heracles returned from the Garden of the Hesperides. Disliking the drink set before him, he struck Cyathus, the cup-bearer, with one finger only, but killed him none the less. A chapel to Cyathus's memory has been built against Apollo's Phlian temple.[9]

*i.* Some say that Heracles wrestled against Achelous before the murder of Iphitus, which was the cause of his removal to Trachis; others, that he went there when first exiled from Tiryns.[10] At all events, he came with Deianeira to the river Evenus, then in full flood, where the Centaur Nessus, claiming that he was the gods' authorized ferry-man and chosen because of his righteousness, offered, for a small fee, to carry Deianeira dry-shod across the water while Heracles swam. He agreed, paid Nessus the fare, threw his club and bow over the river, and plunged in. Nessus, however, instead of keeping to his bargain, gal-loped off in the opposite direction with Deianeira in his arms; then threw her to the ground and tried to violate her. She screamed for help, and Heracles, quickly recovering his bow, took careful aim and pierced Nessus through the breast from half a mile away.

*j.* Wrenching out the arrow, Nessus told Deianeira: 'If you mix the seed which I have spilt on the ground with blood from my wound, add olive oil, and secretly anoint Heracles's shirt with the mixture, you will never again have cause to complain of his unfaithfulness.' Deianeira hurriedly collected the ingredients in a jar, which she sealed and kept by her without saying a word to Heracles on the subject.[11]

*k.* Another version of the story is that Nessus offered Deianeira wool soaked in his own blood, and told her to weave it into a shirt for Heracles. A third version is that he gave her his own blood-stained shirt as a love-charm, and then fled to a neighbouring tribe of Locrians, where he died of the wound; but his body rotted unburied, at the foot of Mount Taphiassus, tainting the country with its noisome smell – hence these Locrians are called Ozolian. The spring beside which he died still smells foetid and contains clots of blood.[12]

*l.* By Deianeira, Heracles had already become the father of Hyllus, Ctesippus, Glenus, and Hodites; also of Macaria, his only daughter.[13]

1. Diodorus Siculus: iv. 34; Apollodorus: i. 8. 1 and ii. 7. 5; Bacchy-lides: *Epinicia* v. 165 ff.; Antoninus Liberalis: *Transformations* 2.

2. Ovid: *Metamorphoses* ix. 1–100; Apollodorus: i. 8. 1; Sophocles: *Trachinian Women* 1 ff.

3. Ovid: *loc. cit.*; Ephorus, quoted by Macrobius: v. 18; Tzetzes: *On Lycophron* 50.

4. Apollodorus: *loc. cit.* and ii. 7. 5; Ovid: *loc. cit.*; Diodorus Siculus: iv. 35; Strabo: x. 2. 19.

5. Hyginus: *Fabula* 31; Lactantius on Statius's *Thebaid* iv. 106.

6. Strabo: vii. 7. 5 and 11; Apollodorus: ii. 7. 6; Diodorus Siculus: iv. 36; Pindar: *Olympian Odes* vii. 23 ff., with scholiast; Homer: *Iliad* ii. 658–60 and *Odyssey* i. 259–61.

7. Apollodorus: *loc. cit.*; Diodorus Siculus: iv. 29–30; Pausanias: vii. 2. 2; x. 17. 4 and ix. 23. 1.

8. Diodorus Siculus: iv. 36; Apollodorus: *loc. cit.*; Tzetzes: *On Lycophron* 50; Eustathius on Homer's *Iliad* p. 1900; Scholiast on Sophocles's *Trachinian Women* 39.

9. Pausanias: ii. 13. 8.

10. Sophocles: *Trachinian Women* 1–40; Pausanias: i. 32. 5.

11. Apollodorus: ii. 7. 6; Sophocles: *Trachinian Women* 555–61; Ovid: *Metamorphoses* ix. 101 ff.; Diodorus Siculus: iv. 46.

12. Scholiast on Horace's *Epodes* iii; Ovid: *loc. cit.*; Pausanias: x. 38. 1; Strabo: ix. 4. 8.

13. Apollodorus: ii. 7. 8; Diodorus Siculus: iv. 37; Pausanias: i. 32. 5.

*

*1.* The story of Meleager's sisters is told to account for a guinea-fowl cult of Artemis on Leros (see 80.*3*).

*2.* Deianeira's love of war reveals her as a representative of the pre-Olympian Battle-goddess Athene, with whose sacred marriages in different localities this part of the Heracles legend is chiefly concerned (see 141. *1*).

*3.* Heracles's contest with Achelous, like that of Theseus with the Minotaur, should be read as part of the royal marriage ritual. Bull and Serpent stood for the waxing and the waning year – 'the bull who is the serpent's father, and the serpent whose son is the bull' – over both of which the sacred king won domination. A bull's horn, regarded from earliest times as the seat of fertility, enroyalled the candidate for kingship who laid hold of it when he wrestled either with an actual bull, or with a bull-masked opponent. The Babylonian hero Enkidu, Gilgamesh's mortal twin, and devotee of the Queen of Heaven, seized the Bull of Heaven by the horns and killed it with his sword; and the winning of a cornucopia was a marriage-task imposed on the Welsh hero Peredur in the *Mabinogion* (see 148. 5). In Crete, the bull cult had succeeded that of the wild-goat, whose horn was equally potent. But it seems that the icon which showed this ritual contest was interpreted by the Greeks as illustrating Heracles's struggle with the River Achelous: namely the dyking and draining of the Paracheloitis, a tract of land, formed of the silt brought down by the Achelous, which had slowly been joining the Echinadian Isles to the mainland; and the consequent recovery of a large area of farmland. Heracles was often credited with engineering feats such as these (Strabo: x. 2. 19; Diodorus Siculus: iv. 35). The sacrifice ordered by the Dodonian Oracle will hardly have been to the river Achelous; more likely it was prescribed for Achelois, the Moon-goddess 'who drives away pain'.

4. Eunomus and Cyathus will have been boy-victims: surrogates for the sacred king at the close of his reign.

5. Nessus's attempted rape of Deianeira recalls the disorderly scenes at the wedding of Peirithous, when Theseus (the Athenian Heracles) intervened to save Hippodameia from assault by the Centaur Eurytion (see 102. *d*). Since the Centaurs were originally depicted as goat-men, the icon on which the incident is based probably showed the Queen riding on the goat-king's back, as she did at the May Eve celebrations of Northern Europe, before her sacred marriage; Eurytion is the 'interloper', a stock-character made familiar by the comedies of Aristophanes, who still appears at Northern Greek marriage festivities. The earliest mythical example of the interloper is the same Enkidu: he interrupted Gilgamesh's sacred marriage with the Goddess of Erech, and challenged him to battle. Another interloper is Agenor, who tried to take Andromeda from Perseus at his wedding feast (see 73. *l*).

6. The first settlers in Sardinia, neolithic Libyans, managed to survive in the mountainous parts; subsequent immigrants – Cretans, Greeks, Carthaginians, Romans, and Jews – attempted to hold the coastal districts, but malaria always defeated them. Only during the last few years has the mortality been checked by spraying the pools where the malarial mosquito breeds.

7. 'Ozolian' ('smelly'), a nickname given to the Locrians settled near Phocis, to distinguish them from their Opuntian and Epizephyrian kinsfolk, probably referred to their habit of wearing undressed goat-skins which had a foetid smell in damp weather. The Locrians themselves preferred to derive it from *ozoi*, 'vine shoots' (Pausanias: x. 38. 1), because of the first vinestock planted in their country (see 38. 7).

# 143

## HERACLES IN TRACHIS

STILL accompanied by his Arcadian allies, Heracles came to Trachis where he settled down for awhile, under the protection of Ceyx. On his way, he had passed through the country of the Dryopians, which is overshadowed by Mount Parnassus, and found their king Theiodamas, the son of Dryops, ploughing with a yoke of oxen.¹ Being hungry and also eager for a pretext to make war on the Dryopians – who, as everyone knew, had no right to the country – Heracles demanded one of the oxen; and, when Theiodamas refused, killed him. After slaughtering the ox, and feasting on its flesh, he bore off Theiodamas's infant son Hylas, whose mother was the nymph Menodice, Orion's daughter.² But some call Hylas's father Ceyx, or Euphemus, or Theiomenes; and insist that Theiodamas was the Rhodian ploughman who cursed from afar while Heracles sacrificed one of his oxen.³

*b.* It seems that Phylas, Theiodamas's successor, violated Apollo's temple at Delphi. Outraged on Apollo's behalf, Heracles killed Phylas and carried off his daughter Meda; she bore him Antiochus, founder of the Athenian deme which bears his name.⁴ He then expelled the Dryopians from their city on Mount Parnassus, and gave it to the Malians who had helped in its conquest. The leading Dryopians he took to Delphi and dedicated them at the shrine as slaves; but, Apollo having no use for them, they were sent away to the Peloponnese, where they sought the favour of Eurystheus the High King. Under his orders, and with the assistance of other fugitive compatriots, they built three cities, Asine, Hermione, and Eion. Of the remaining Dryopians, some fled to Euboea, others to Cyprus and to the island of Cynthos. But only the men of Asine still pride themselves on being Dryopians; they have built a shrine to their ancestor Dryops, with an ancient image, and celebrate mysteries in his honour every second year.⁵

*c.* Dryops was Apollo's son by Dia, a daughter of King Lycaon, for fear of whom she hid the infant in a hollow oak; hence his name. Some say that Dryops himself brought his people from the Thessalian river Spercheius to Asine, and that he was a son of Spercheius by the nymph Polydora.⁶

*d.* A boundary dispute had arisen between the Dorians of Hestiaeotis, ruled by King Aegimius, and the Lapiths of Mount Olympus, former allies of the Dryopians, whose king was Coronus, a son of Caeneus. The Dorians, greatly outnumbered by the Lapiths, fled to Heracles and appealed for help, offering him in return a third share of their kingdom; whereupon Heracles and his Arcadian allies defeated the Lapiths, slew Coronus and most of his subjects, and forced them to quit the disputed land. Some of them settled at Corinth. Aegimius then held Heracles's third share in trust for his descendants.⁷

*e.* Heracles now came to Itonus, a city of Phthiotis, where the ancient temple of Athene stands. Here he met Cycnus, a son of Ares and Pelopia, who was constantly offering valuable prizes to guests who dared fight a chariot duel with him. The ever-victorious Cycnus would cut off their heads and use the skulls to decorate the temple of his father Ares. This, by the way, was not the Cycnus whom Ares had begotten on Pyrene and transformed into a swan when he died.[8]

*f.* Apollo, growing vexed with Cycnus, because he waylaid and carried off herds of cattle which were being sent for sacrifice to Delphi, incited Heracles to accept Cycnus's challenge. It was agreed that Heracles should be supported by his charioteer Iolaus, and Cycnus by his father Ares. Heracles, though this was not his usual style of fighting, put on the polished bronze greaves which Hephaestus had made for him, the curiously wrought golden breast-plate given him by Athene, and a pair of iron shoulder-guards. Armed with bow and arrows, spear, helmet, and a stout shield which Zeus had ordered Hephaestus to supply, he lightly mounted his chariot.

*g.* Athene, descending from Olympus, now warned Heracles that, although empowered by Zeus to kill and despoil Cycnus, he must do no more than defend himself against Ares and, even if victorious, not deprive him of either his horses or his splendid armour. She then mounted beside Heracles and Iolaus, shaking her aegis, and Mother Earth groaned as the chariot whirled forward. Cycnus drove to meet them at full speed, and both he and Heracles were thrown to the ground by the shock of their encounter, spear against shield. Yet they sprang to their feet and, after a short combat, Heracles thrust Cycnus through the neck. He then boldly faced Ares, who hurled a spear at him; and Athene, with an angry frown, turned it aside. Ares ran at Heracles sword in hand, only to be wounded in the thigh for his pains, and Heracles would have dealt him a further blow as he lay on the ground, had not Zeus parted the combatants with a thunderbolt. Heracles and Iolaus then despoiled Cycnus's corpse and resumed their interrupted journey; while Athene led the fainting Ares back to Olympus. Cycnus was buried by Ceyx in the valley of the Anaurus but, at Apollo's command, the swollen river washed away his headstone.[9]

*h.* Some, however, say that Cycnus lived at Amphanae, and that Heracles transfixed him with an arrow beside the river Peneius, or at Pegasae.[10]

*i.* Passing through Pelasgiotis, Heracles now came to Ormenium, a

small city at the foot of Mount Pelion, where King Amyntor refused
to give him his daughter Astydameia. 'You are married already,' he
said, 'and have betrayed far too many princesses for me to trust you
with another.' Heracles attacked the city and, after killing Amyntor, carried off Astydameia, who bore him Ctesippus or, some say,
Tlepolemus.[11]

1. Diodorus Siculus: iv. 36; Probus, on Virgil's *Georgics* iii. 6;
   Scholiast on Apollonius Rhodius: i. 131.
2. Apollodorus: ii. 7. 7; Apollonius Rhodius: i. 1212 ff.; Hyginus:
   *Fabula* 14.
3. Nicander, quoted by Antoninus Liberalis: 26; Hellanicus, quoted
   by scholiast on Apollonius Rhodius: i. 131 and 1207; Philostratus: *Imagines* ii. 24.
4. Diodorus Siculus: iv. 37; Pausanias: i. 5. 2.
5. Diodorus Siculus: *loc. cit.*; Herodotus: viii. 46; Pausanias: iv. 34.
   6 and viii. 34. 6.
6. Tzetzes: *On Lycophron* 480; Aristotle, quoted by Strabo: viii. 6.
   13; Antoninus Liberalis: *Transformations* 32.
7. Apollodorus: ii. 7. 7; Diodorus Siculus: iv. 37.
8. Euripides: *Heracles* 389–93; Pausanias: i. 27. 7; Scholiast on Pindar's *Olympian Odes* ii. 82 and x. 15; Eustathius on Homer's
   *Iliad* p. 254.
9. Hesiod: *Shield of Heracles* 57–138 and 318–480; Hyginus: *Fabula*
   31; Apollodorus: ii. 7. 7; Diodorus Siculus: iv. 37; Euripides:
   *loc. cit.*
10. Pausanias: i. 27. 7; Hesiod: *Shield of Heracles* 318–480.
11. Diodorus Siculus: iv. 37; Strabo: ix. 5. 18; Apollodorus: iii. 13.
    8 and ii. 7. 7–8; Pindar: *Olympian Odes* vii. 23 ff., with scholiast.

\*

1. Heracles's sacrifice of a plough ox, Theiodamas's cursing, and the
appearance of the infant Hylas from a furrow, are all parts of the pre-
Hellenic sowing ritual. Ox blood propitiates the Earth-goddess, curses
avert divine anger from the sprouting seeds, the child represents the
coming crop – namely Plutus, whom Demeter bore to Iasius after they
had embraced in the thrice-ploughed field (see 24. *a*). Theiodamas is
the spirit of the old year, now destroyed. The annual mourning for the
doomed tree-spirit Hylas (see 150. *d–e*) has here been confused with
mourning for the doomed corn-spirit.
2. Heracles's expulsion of the Dryopians from Parnassus with Dorian
assistance, and the Dryopian emigration to Southern Greece, are likely
to have taken place in the twelfth century B.C., before the Dorian invasion

of the Peloponnese (see 146. 1). His combat with Cycnus recalls Pelops's race with Oenomaus (see 109. d–j), another son of Ares, and equally notorious as a head-hunter. In both cases one of the chariots contained a woman: namely Oenomaus's daughter Hippodameia (the subject of his contention with Pelops) and Athene, who is, apparently, the same character – namely the new king's destined bride. Cycnus, like Spartan Polydeuces, is a king of the swan cult whose soul flies off to the far northern otherworld (see 161. 4).

3. Aegimius's name – if it means 'acting the part of a goat' – suggests that he performed a May Eve goat-marriage with the tribal queen, and that in his war against the Lapiths of Northern Thessaly his Dorians fought beside the Centaurs, the Lapiths' hereditary enemies who, like the Satyrs, are depicted in early works of art as goat-men (see 142. 5).

4. Cypselus the tyrant of Corinth, famous for his carved chest, claimed descent from the Lapith royal house of Caeneus (see 78. 1).

# 144

## IOLE

AT Trachis Heracles mustered an army of Arcadians, Melians, and Epicnemidian Locrians, and marched against Oechalia to revenge himself on King Eurytus, who refused to surrender the princess Iole, fairly won in an archery contest; but he told his allies no more than that Eurytus had been unjustly exacting tribute from the Euboeans. He stormed the city, riddled Eurytus and his son with arrows and, after burying certain of his comrades who had fallen in the battle, namely Ceyx's son Hippasus, and Argeius and Melas, sons of Licymnius, pillaged Oechalia and took Iole captive.[1] Rather than yield to Heracles, Iole had allowed him to murder her entire family before her very eyes, and then leaped from the city wall; yet she survived, because her skirts were billowed out by the wind and broke the fall. Now Heracles sent her, with other Oechalian women, to Deianeira at Trachis, while he visited the Euboean headland of Cenaeum.[2] It should be noted here that when taking leave of Deianeira, Heracles had divulged a prophecy: at the end of fifteen months, he was fated either to die, or to spend the remainder of his life in perfect tranquillity. The news had been conveyed to him by the twin doves of the ancient oak oracle at Dodona.[3]

*b.* It is disputed which of several towns named Oechalia was sacked on this occasion: whether the Messenian; the Thessalian; the Euboean; the Trachinian; or the Aetolian.[4] Messenian Oechalia is the most likely of these, since Eurytus's father Melaneus, King of the Dryopians – a skilled archer, and hence called a son of Apollo – came to Messenia in the reign of Perieres, son of Aeolus, who gave him Oechalia as his home. Oechalia was called after Melaneus's wife. Here, in a sacred cypress-grove, heroic sacrifices to Eurytus, whose bones are preserved in a brazen urn, initiate the Great Goddess's Mysteries. Others identify Oechalia with Andania, a mile from the cypress-grove, where these Mysteries were formerly held. Eurytus was one of the heroes whom the Messenians invited to dwell among them when Epaminondas restored their Peloponnesian patrimony.[5]

1. Athenaeus: xi. 461; Apollodorus: ii. 7. 7.
2. Nicias of Mallus, quoted by Plutarch: *Parallel Stories* 13; Hyginus: *Fabula* 35; Sophocles: *Trachinian Women* 283 ff.; Apollodorus: *loc. cit.*
3. Sophocles: *Trachinian Women* 44–5.
4. Homer: *Iliad* ii. 596 and 730; *Odyssey* xxi. 13–14; Servius on Virgil's Aeneid viii. 291; Strabo: ix. 5. 17 and x. 1. 10.
5. Antoninus Liberalis: *Transformations* 4; Pausanias: iv. 2. 2; 3. 6; 33. 5–6 and 27. 4; Strabo: x. 1. 18.

\*

*1.* Eurytus had refused to yield Iole on the ground that Heracles was a slave (see 135. *a*). Though Iole's suicidal leap makes a plausible story – Mycenaean skirts were bell-shaped, and my father once saw a mid-Victorian suicide saved by her vast crinoline – it has most likely been deduced from a Mycenaean picture of the goddess hovering above an army as it assaulted her city. The name Oechalia, 'house of flour', shows that the goddess in whose honour the mysteries were performed was Demeter.

# 145

## THE APOTHEOSIS OF HERACLES

Having consecrated marble altars and a sacred grove to his father Zeus on the Cenaean headland, Heracles prepared a thanksgiving sacrifice for the capture of Oechalia. He had already sent Lichas back to ask Deianeira for a fine shirt and a cloak of the sort which he regularly wore on such occasions.[1]

*b.* Deianeira, comfortably installed at Trachis, was by now resigned to Heracles's habit of taking mistresses; and, when she recognized Iole as the latest of these, felt pity rather than resentment for the fatal beauty which had been Oechalia's ruin. Yet was it not intolerable that Heracles expected Iole and herself to live together under the same roof? Since she was no longer young, Deianeira decided to use Nessus's supposed love-charm as a means of holding her husband's affection. Having woven him a new sacrificial shirt against his safe return, she covertly unsealed the jar, soaked a piece of wool in the mixture, and rubbed the shirt with it. When Lichas arrived she locked the shirt in a chest which she gave to him, saying: 'On no account expose the shirt to light or heat until Heracles is about to wear it at the sacrifice.' Lichas had already driven off at full speed in his chariot when Deianeira, glancing at the piece of wool which she had thrown down into the sunlit courtyard, was horrified to see it burning away like saw-dust, while red foam bubbled up from the flag-stones. Realizing that Nessus had deceived her, she sent a courier post-haste to recall Lichas and, cursing her folly, swore that if Heracles died she would not survive him.[2]

*c.* The courier arrived too late at the Cenaean headland. Heracles had by now put on the shirt and sacrificed twelve immaculate bulls as the first-fruits of his spoils: in all, he had brought to the altar a mixed herd of one hundred cattle. He was pouring wine from a bowl on the altars and throwing frankincense on the flames when he let out a sudden yell as if he had been bitten by a serpent. The heat had melted the Hydra's poison in Nessus's blood, which coursed all over Heracles's limbs, corroding his flesh. Soon the pain was beyond endurance and, bellowing in anguish, he overturned the altars. He tried to rip off the shirt, but it clung to him so fast that his flesh came away with it, laying bare the bones. His blood hissed and bubbled like spring water when red-hot metal is being tempered. He plunged headlong into the nearest stream, but the poison burned only the fiercer; these waters have been scalding hot ever since and are called Thermopylae, or 'hot passage'.[3]

*d.* Ranging over the mountain, tearing up trees as he went, Heracles came upon the terrified Lichas crouched in the hollow of a rock, his knees clasped with his hands. In vain did Lichas try to exculpate himself:

Heracles seized him, whirled him thrice about his head and flung him
into the Euboean Sea. There he was transformed: he became a rock of
human appearance, projecting a short distance above the waves, which
sailors still call Lichas and on which they are afraid to tread, believing
it to be sentient. The army, watching from afar, raised a great shout of
lamentation, but none dared approach until, writhing in agony, Heracles summoned Hyllus, and asked to be carried away to die in solitude.
Hyllus conveyed him to the foot of Mount Oeta in Trachis (a region
famous for its white hellebore), the Delphic Oracle having already
pointed this out to Licymnius and Iolaus as the destined scene of their
friend's death.[4]

*e.* Aghast at the news, Deianeira hanged herself or, some say, stabbed
herself with a sword in their marriage bed. Heracles's one thought had
been to punish her before he died, but when Hyllus assured him that
she was innocent, as her suicide proved, he sighed forgivingly and
expressed a wish that Alcmene and all his sons should assemble to hear
his last words. Alcmene, however, was at Tiryns with some of his
children, and most of the others had settled at Thebes. Thus he could
reveal Zeus's prophecy, now fulfilled, only to Hyllus: 'No man alive
may ever kill Heracles; a dead enemy shall be his downfall.' Hyllus then
asked for instructions, and was told: 'Swear by the head of Zeus that
you will convey me to the highest peak of this mountain, and there
burn me, without lamentation, on a pyre of oak-branches and trunks
of the male wild-olive. Likewise swear to marry Iole as soon as you
come of age.' Though scandalized by these requests, Hyllus promised
to observe them.[5]

*f.* When all had been prepared, Iolaus and his companions retired a
short distance, while Heracles mounted the pyre and gave orders for
its kindling. But none dared obey, until a passing Aeolian shepherd
named Poeas ordered Philoctetes, his son by Demonassa, to do as
Heracles asked. In gratitude, Heracles bequeathed his quiver, bow, and
arrows to Philoctetes and, when the flames began to lick at the pyre,
spread his lion-pelt over the platform at the summit and lay down, with
his club for pillow, looking as blissful as a garlanded guest surrounded
by wine-cups. Thunderbolts then fell from the sky and at once reduced
the pyre to ashes.[6]

*g.* In Olympus, Zeus congratulated himself that his favourite son
had behaved so nobly. 'Heracles's immortal part', he announced, 'is
safe from death, and I shall soon welcome him to this blessed region.

But if anyone here grieves at his deification, so richly merited, that god or goddess must nevertheless approve it willy-nilly!'

All the Olympians assented, and Hera decided to swallow the insult, which was clearly aimed at her, because she had already arranged to punish Philoctetes, for his kindly act, by the bite of a Lemnian viper.

*h*. The thunderbolts had consumed Heracles's mortal part. He no longer bore any resemblance to Alcmene but, like a snake that has cast its slough, appeared in all the majesty of his divine father. A cloud received him from his companions' sight as, amid peals of thunder, Zeus bore him up to heaven in his four-horse chariot; where Athene took him by the hand and solemnly introduced him to her fellow deities.[7]

*i*. Now, Zeus had destined Heracles as one of the Twelve Olympians, yet was loth to expel any of the existing company of gods in order to make room for him. He therefore persuaded Hera to adopt Heracles by a ceremony of rebirth: namely, going to bed, pretending to be in labour, and then producing him from beneath her skirts – which is the adoption ritual still in use among many barbarian tribes. Henceforth, Hera regarded Heracles as her son and loved him next only to Zeus. All the immortals welcomed his arrival; and Hera married him to her pretty daughter Hebe, who bore him Alexiares and Anicetus. And, indeed, Heracles had earned Hera's true gratitude in the revolt of the Giants by killing Pronomus, when he tried to violate her.[8]

*j*. Heracles became the porter of heaven, and never tires of standing at the Olympian gates, towards nightfall, waiting for Artemis's return from the chase. He greets her merrily, and hauls the heaps of prey out of her chariot, frowning and wagging a finger in disapproval if he finds only harmless goats and hares. 'Shoot wild boars,' he says, 'that trample down crops and gash orchard-trees; shoot man-killing bulls, and lions, and wolves! But what harm have goats and hares done us?' Then he flays the carcasses, and voraciously eats any titbits that take his fancy.[9] Yet while the immortal Heracles banquets at the divine table, his mortal phantom stalks about Tartarus, among the twittering dead; bow drawn, arrow fitted to the string. Across his shoulder is slung a golden baldric, terrifyingly wrought with lions, bears, wild boars, and scenes of battle and slaughter.[10]

*k*. When Iolaus and his companions returned to Trachis, Menoetius, the son of Actor, sacrificed a ram, a bull, and a boar to Heracels, and instituted his hero-worship at Locrian Opus; the Thebans soon followed suit; but the Athenians, led by the people of Marathon, were the first to worship him as a god, and all mankind now follows their glorious example.[11] Heracles's son Phaestus found that the Sicyonians were offering his father hero-rites, but himself insisted on sacrificing to him as a god. To this day, therefore, the people of Sicyon, after killing a lamb and burning its thighs on the altar to Heracles the god, devote part of its flesh to Heracles the hero. At Oeta, he is worshipped under the name of Cornopion because he scared away the locusts which were about to settle on the city; but the Ionians of Erythrae worship him as Heracles Ipoctonus, because he destroyed the *ipes*, which are worms that attack vines in almost every other region.

*l*. A Tyrian image of Heracles, now in his shrine at Erythrae, is said to represent Heracles the Dactyl. It was found floating on a raft in the Ionian Sea off Cape Mesate, exactly half way between the harbour of Erythrae and the island of Chios. The Erythraeans on one side and the Chians on the other, strained every nerve to tow the raft to their own shore – but without success. At last an Erythraean fisherman named Phormio, who had lost his sight, dreamed that the women of Erythrae must plait a rope from their shorn tresses; with this, the men would be able to tow the raft home. The women of a Thracian clan that had settled in Erythrae complied, and the raft was towed ashore; and only their descendants are now permitted to enter the shrine where the rope is laid up. Phormio recovered his sight, and kept it until he died.[12]

1. Sophocles: *Trachinian Women* 298 and 752–4; Apollodorus: ii. 7. 7; Diodorus Siculus: iv. 38.

2. Sophocles: *Trachinian Women* 460–751; Hyginus: *Fabula* 36.

3. Sophocles: *Trachinian Women* 756 ff.; Nonnus – Westermann's *Mythographi Graeci: Appendix Narrationum* xxviii. 8; Tzetzes: *On Lycophron* 50–51.

4. Ovid: *Metamorphoses* ix. 155 ff.; Hyginus: *Fabula* 36; Sophocles: *Trachinian Women* 783 ff.; Apollodorus: ii. 7. 7; Pliny: *Natural History* xxv. 21; Diodorus Siculus: iv. 38.

5. Apollodorus: *loc. cit.;* Sophocles: *Trachinian Women* 912 to end.

6. Diodorus Siculus: *loc. cit.*; Hyginus: *Fabula* 102; Ovid: *Metamorphoses* ix. 299 ff.

7. Ovid: *Metamorphoses* ix. 241–73; Apollodorus: *loc. cit.*; Hyginus: *loc. cit.*; Pausanias: iii. 18. 7.

8. Diodorus Siculus: iv. 39; Hesiod on Onomacritus: *Fragment*, ed. Evelyn-White pp. 615–16, Loeb; Pindar: *Isthmian Odes* iv. 59 and

*Nemean Odes* x. 18; Apollodorus: *loc. cit.*; Sotas of Byzantium, quoted by Tzetzes: *On Lycophron* 1349–50.
9. Callimachus: *Hymn to Artemis* 145 ff.
10. Homer: *Odyssey* xi. 601 ff.
11. Diodorus Siculus: iv. 39; Pausanias: i. 15. 4.
12. Pausanias: ii. 10. 1; ix. 27. 5 and vii. 5. 3; Strabo: xiii. 1. 64.

\*

*1*. Before sacrificing and thus immortalizing the sacred king – as Calypso promised to immortalize Odysseus (see 170. *w*) – the Queen will have stripped him of his clothes and regalia. What floggings and mutilations he suffered until he was laid on the pyre for immortalization is not suggested here, but the icons from which the account seems to be deduced probably showed him bleeding and in agony, as he struggled into the white linen shirt which consecrated him to the Death-goddess.

*2*. A tradition that Heracles died on the Cenaean headland has been reconciled with another that had him die on Mount Oeta, where early inscriptions and statuettes show that the sacred king continued to be burned in effigy for centuries after he ceased to be burned in the flesh. Oak is the correct wood for the midsummer bonfire; wild-olive is the wood of the New Year, when the king began his reign by expelling the spirits of the old year. Poeas, or Philoctetes, who lighted the pyre, is the king's tanist and successor; he inherits his arms and bed – Iole's marriage to Hyllus must be read in this light – and dies by snake-bite at the end of the year.

*3*. Formerly, Heracles's soul had gone to the Western Paradise of the Hesperides; or to the silver castle, the Corona Borealis, at the back of the North Wind – a legend which Pindar has uncomprehendingly included in a brief account of the Third Labour (see 125. *k*). His admission to the Olympian Heaven – where, however, he never secured a seat among the twelve, as Dionysus did (see 27. *5*) – is a late conception. It may be based on the misreading of the same sacred icon which accounts for the marriage of Peleus and Thetis (see 81. *1–5*), for the so-called rape of Ganymedes (see 29. *1*), and for the arming of Heracles (see 123. *1*). This icon will have shown Athene, or Hebe, the youthful queen and bride, introducing the king to twelve witnesses of the sacred marriage, each representing a clan of a religious confederacy or a month of the sacred year; he has been ritually reborn either from a mare, or (as here) from a woman. Heracles figures as a heavenly porter because he died at midsummer – the year being likened to an oaken door which turned on a hinge, opened to its widest extent at the midsummer solstice, then gradually closed, as the days began to shorten (*White Goddess* pp. 175–7). What kept him from becoming a full Olympian seems to have been the authority of Homer: the *Odyssey* had recorded the presence of his shade in Tartarus.

4. If the Erythraean statue of Heracles was of Tyrian provenience, the rope in the temple will have been woven not of women's hair but of hair shorn from the sacred king before his death at the winter solstice – as Delilah shore that of Samson, a Tyrian sun-hero. A similar sun-hero had been sacrificed by the Thracian women who adopted his cult (see 28. 2). The statue was probably towed on a raft to avoid the hallowing of a merchant vessel and its consequent withdrawal from trade. 'Ipoctonus' may have been a local variant of Heracles's more usual title Ophioctonus, 'serpent-killing'. His renovation by death 'like a snake that casts its slough', was a figure borrowed from the Egyptian *Book of the Dead*; snakes were held to put off old age by casting their slough, 'slough' and 'old age' both being *geros* in Greek (see 160. 11). He rides to Heaven in a four-horse chariot as a solar hero and patron of the Olympic Games; each horse representing one of the four years between the Games, or one season of a year divided by equinoxes and solstices. A square image of the sun, worshipped as Heracles the Saviour, stood in the Great Goddess's precinct at Megalopolis (Pausanias: viii. 31. 4); it was probably an ancient altar, like several square blocks found in the palace at Cnossus, and another found in the West Court of the palace at Phaestus.

5. Hebe, Heracles's bride, may not, perhaps, be the goddess as Youth, but a deity mentioned in the 48th and 49th *Orphic Hymns* as Hipta the Earth-mother, to whom Dionysus was delivered for safe-keeping. Proclus says (*Against Timaeus* ii. 124c) that she carried him on her head in a winnowing basket. Hipta is associated with Zeus Sabazius (see 27. 3) in two early inscriptions from Maeonia, then inhabited by a Lydo-Phrygian tribe; and Professor Kretschmer has identified her with the Mitannian goddess Hepa, Hepit, or Hebe, mentioned in the texts from Boghaz-Keui and apparently brought to Maeonia from Thrace. If Heracles married this Hebe, the myth concerns the Heracles who did great deeds in Phrygia (see 131. h), Mysia (see 131. e), and Lydia (see 136. a–f); he can be identified with Zeus Sabazius. Hipta was well known throughout the Middle East. A rock-carving at Hattusas in Lycaonia (see 13. 2) shows her mounted on a lion, about to celebrate a sacred marriage with the Hittite Storm-god. She is there called Hepatu, said to be a Hurrian word, and Professor B. Hrozný (*Civilization of the Hittites and Subareans*, ch. xv) equates her with Hawwa, 'the Mother of All Living', who appears in *Genesis* ii as Eve. Hrozný mentions the Canaanite prince of Jerusalem Abdihepa; and Adam, who married Eve, was a tutelary hero of Jerusalem (Jerome: *Commentary on Ephesians* v. 15).

## THE CHILDREN OF HERACLES

ALCMENE, the mother of Heracles, had gone to Tiryns, taking some of his sons with her; others were still at Thebes and Trachis. Eurystheus now decided to expel them all from Greece, before they could reach manhood and depose him. He therefore sent a message to Ceyx, demanding the extradition not only of the Heraclids, but also of Iolaus, the whole house of Licymnius, and Heracles's Arcadian allies. Too weak to oppose Eurystheus, they left Trachis in a body – Ceyx pleading that he was powerless to help them – and visited most of the great Greek cities as suppliants, begging for hospitality. The Athenians under Theseus alone dared defy Eurystheus: their innate sense of justice prevailed when they saw the Heraclids seated at the Altar of Mercy.[1]

b. Theseus settled the Heraclids and their companions at Tricorythus – a city of the Attic tetrapolis – and would not surrender them to Eurystheus, which was the cause of the first war between Athens and the Peloponnese. For, when all the Heraclids had grown to manhood, Eurystheus assembled an army and marched against Athens; Iolaus, Theseus, and Hyllus being appointed to command the combined Athenians and Heraclids. But some say that Theseus had now been succeeded by his son Demophon. Since an oracle announced that the Athenians must be defeated unless one of Heracles's children would die for the common good, Macaria, Heracles's only daughter, killed herself at Marathon, and thus gave her name to the Macarian spring.[2]

c. The Athenians, whose protection of the Heraclids is even today a source of civic pride, then defeated Eurystheus in a pitched battle and killed his sons Alexander, Iphimedon, Eurybius, Mentor, and Perimedes, besides many of his allies. Eurystheus fled in his chariot, pursued by Hyllus, who overtook him at the Scironian Rocks and there cut off his head, from which Alcmene gouged the eyes with weaving-pins; his tomb is shown near by.[3] But some say that he was captured by Iolaus at the Scironian Rocks, and taken to Alcmene, who ordered his execution. The Athenians interceded for him, though in vain, and before the sentence was carried out, Eurystheus shed tears of gratitude and declared that he would reveal himself, even in death, as their firm friend, and a sworn enemy to the Heraclids. 'Theseus,' he cried, 'you need not pour libations or blood on my tomb: even without such offerings I undertake to drive all enemies from the land of Attica!' Then he was executed and buried in front of Athene's sanctuary at Pellene, midway between Athens and Marathon. A very different account is that the Athenians assisted Eurystheus in a battle which he fought against the Heraclids at Marathon; and that Iolaus, having cut off his head beside the Macarian spring, close to the chariot road, buried it at Tricorythus, and sent the trunk to Gargettus for burial.[4]

d. Meanwhile, Hyllus and the Heraclids who had settled by the Electrian Gate at Thebes invaded the Peloponnese, capturing all its cities in a sudden onset; but when, next year, a plague broke out and an oracle announced: 'The Heraclids have returned before the due time!' Hyllus withdrew to Marathon. Obeying his father's last wish, he had married Iole and been adopted by Aegimius the Dorian; he now went to ask the Delphic Oracle when 'the due time' would come, and was warned to 'wait for the third crop'. Taking this to mean three years, he rested until these had passed and then marched again. On the Isthmus he was met by Atreus, who had meanwhile succeeded to the Mycenaean throne and rode at the head of an Achaean army.[5]

e. To avoid needless slaughter Hyllus challenged any opponent of rank to single combat. 'If I win,' he said, 'let the throne and kingdom be mine. If I lose, we sons of Heracles will not return along this road for another fifty years.' Echemus, King of Tegea, accepted the challenge, and the duel took place on the Corintho–Megarid frontier. Hyllus fell, and was buried in the city of Megara; whereupon the Heraclids honoured his undertaking and once more retired to Tricorythus, and thence to Doris, where they claimed from Aegimius that share of the kingdom which their father had entrusted to him. Only Licymnius and his sons, and Heracles's son Tlepolemus, who was invited to settle at Argos, remained in the Peloponnese. Delphic Apollo, whose seemingly unsound advice had earned him many reproaches, explained that by the 'third crop' he meant the third generation.[6]

f. Alcmene went back to Thebes and, when she died there at a great age, Zeus ordered Hermes to plunder the coffin which the Heraclids were carrying to the grave; and this he did, adroitly substituting a stone for the body, which he carried off to the Islands of the Blessed. There, revived and rejuvenated, Alcmene became the wife of Rhadamanthys. Meanwhile, finding the coffin too heavy for their shoulder, the Heraclids opened it, and discovered the fraud. They set up the stone in a sacred grove at Thebes, where Alcmene is now worshipped as a goddess. But some say that she married Rhadamanthys at Ocaleae, before her death; and others, that she died in Megara, where her tomb is still shown, on a journey from Argos to Thebes – they add, that when a dispute arose among the Heraclids, some wishing to convey her corpse back to Argos, others to continue the journey, the Delphic Oracle advised them to bury her in Megara. Another so-called tomb of Alcmene is shown at Haliartus.[7]

*g*. The Thebans awarded Iolaus a hero-shrine, close to Amphitryon's, where lovers plight their troths for Heracles's sake; although it is generally admitted that Iolaus died in Sardinia.[8]

*h*. At Argos, Tlepolemus accidentally killed his beloved grand-uncle Licymnius. He was chastising a servant with an olive-wood club when Licymnius, now old and blind, stumbled between them and caught a blow on his skull. Threatened with death by the other Heraclids, Tlepolemus built a fleet, gathered a large number of companions and, on Apollo's advice, fled to Rhodes, where he settled after long wandering and many hardships.[9] In those days Rhodes was inhabited by Greek settlers under Triops, a son of Phorbas, with whose consent Tlepolemus divided the island into three parts and is said to have founded the cities of Lindus, Ialysus, and Cameirus. His people were favoured and enriched by Zeus. Later, Tlepolemus sailed to Troy with a fleet of nine Rhodian ships.[10]

*i*. Heracles begot another Hyllus on the water-nymph Melite, daughter of the River-god Aegaeus, in the land of the Phaeacians. He had gone there after the murder of his children, in the hope of being purified by King Nausithous and by Macris, the nurse of Dionysus. This was the Hyllus who emigrated to the Cronian Sea with a number of Phaecian settlers, and gave his name to the Hyllaeans.[11]

*j*. The latest-born of all the Heraclids is said to have been the Thasian athelte Theagenes, whose mother was visited one night in the temple of Heracles by someone whom she took for his priest, her husband Timosthenes, but who proved to be the god himself.[12]

*k*. The Heraclids eventually reconquered the Peloponnese in the fourth generation under Temenus, Cresphontes, and the twins Procles and Eurysthenes, after killing the High King Tisamenes of Mycenae, a son of Orestes. They would have succeeded earlier, had not one of their princes murdered Carnus, an Acarnanian poet, as he came towards them chanting prophetic verses; mistaking him for a magician sent against them by Tisamenes. In punishment of this sacrilege the Heraclid fleet was sunk and famine caused their army to disband. The Delphic Oracle now advised them 'to banish the slayer for ten years and take Triops as a guide in his place.' They were about to fetch Triops son of Phorbas from Rhodes, when Temenus noticed an Aetolian chieftain named Oxylus, who had just expiated some murder or other with a year's exile in Elis, riding by on a one-eyed horse. Now, Triops means 'three-eyed', and Temenus therefore engaged him as guide and, landing on the coast of Elis with his Heraclid kinsmen, soon conquered the whole Peloponnese, and divided it by lot. The lot marked with a toad meant Argos and went to Temenus; that marked with a serpent meant Sparta and went to the twins Procles and Eurysthenes; that marked with a fox meant Messene and went to Cresphontes.[13]

1. Sophocles: *Trachinian Women* 1151–5; Hecataeus, quoted by Longinus: *De Sublimitate* 27; Diodorus Siculus: iv. 57; Apollodorus: ii. 8. 1 and iii. 7. 1; Pausanias: i. 32. 5.

2. Diodorus Siculus: *loc. cit.*; Apollodorus: ii. 8. 1; Pausanias: *loc. cit*; Pherecydes, quoted by Antoninus Liberalis: *Transformations* 33; Zenobius: *Proverbs* ii. 61.

3. Lysias: ii. 11–16; Isocratas: *Panegyric* 15–16; Apollodorus: ii. 8. 1 Diodorus Siculus: *loc. cit.*; Pausanias: i. 44. 14.

4. Euripides: *Children of Heracles* 843 ff., 928 ff. and 1026 ff.; Strabo: viii. 6. 19.

5. Pherecydes, quoted by Antoninus Liberalis: *Transformations* 33; Strabo: ix. 40. 10.

6. Pausanias: i. 44. 14 and 41. 3; Diodorus Siculus: iv. 58; Apollodorus: ii. 81. 2.

7. Diodorus Siculus: *loc. cit.*; Apollodorus: ii. 4. 11 and iii. 1. 2; Pausanias: i. 41. 1; Plutarch: *Lysander* 28.

8. Pindar: *Pythian Odes* ix. 79 ff.; Plutarch: *On Love* 17; Pausanias: ix. 23. 1.

9. Homer: *Iliad* ii. 653–70; Apollodorus: ii. 8. 2; Pindar: *Olympian Odes* vii. 27 ff.

10. Diodorus Siculus: iv. 58; Homer: *loc. cit.*; Apollodorus: *Epitome* iii. 13.

11. Apollonius Rhodius: iv. 538 ff.

12. Pausanias: vi. 11. 12.

13. Apollodorus: ii 8. 2–5; Pausanias: ii. 18. 7, iii. 13. 4, v. 3. 5–7 and viii. 5. 6; Strabo: viii. 3. 33; Herodotus: vi. 52.

\*

1. The disastrous invasion of the Mycenaean Peloponnese by uncultured patriarchal mountaineers from Central Greece which, according to

Pausanias (iv. 3. 3) and Thucydides (i. 12. 3), took place about 1100 B.C., was called the Dorian because its leaders came from the small state of Doris. Three tribes composed this Dorian League: the Hylleids, who worshipped Heracles; the Dymanes ('enterers'), who worshipped Apollo; and the Pamphylloi ('men from every tribe'), who worshipped Demeter. After overrunning Southern Thessaly, the Dorians seem to have allied themselves with the Athenians before they ventured to attack the Peloponnese. The first attempt failed, though Mycenae was burned about 1100 B.C., but a century later they conquered the eastern and southern regions, having by now destroyed the entire ancient culture of Argolis. This invasion, which caused emigrations from Argolis to Rhodes, from Attica to the Ionian coast of Asia Minor, and apparently also from Thebes to Sardinia, brought the Dark Ages into Greece.

2. Strategic burial of a hero's head is commonplace in myth: thus, according to the *Mabinogion*, Bran's head was buried on Tower Hill to guard London from invasion by way of the Thames: and according to Ambrose (*Epistle* vii. 2), Adam's head was buried at Golgotha, to protect Jerusalem from the north. Moreover, Euripides (*Rhesus* 413–15) makes Hector declare that the ghosts even of strangers could serve as Troy's guardian spirits (see 28. 6). Both Tricorythus and Gargettus lie at narrow defiles commanding the approaches to Attica. Iolaus's pursuit of Eurystheus past the Scironian Rocks seems to have been borrowed from the same icon that suggested the myth of Hippolytus (see 101. g).

3. The land of the Phaeacians (see 170. γ) was Corcyra, or Drepane, now Corfu, off which lay the sacred islet of Macris (see 154. a); the Cronian Sea was the Gulf of Finland, whence amber seems to have been fetched by Corcyrian enterprise – Corcyra is associated with the Argonaut amber-expedition to the head of the Adriatic (see 148. 9).

4. Triops, the Greek colonist of Rhodes, is a masculinization of the ancient Triple-goddess Danaë, or Damkina, after whose three persons Lindus, Ialysus, and Cameirus were named. According to other accounts, these cities were founded by the Telchines (see 54. a), or by Danaus (see 60. d).

5. Alcmene being merely a title of Hera's, there was nothing remarkable in the dedication of a temple to her.

6. Polygnotus, in his famous painting at Delphi, showed Menelaus with a serpent badge on his shield (Pausanias: x. 26. 3) – presumably the water-serpent of Sparta (see 125. 3). A fox helped the Messenian hero Aristomenes to escape from a pit into which the Spartans had thrown him (Pausanias: iv. 18. 6); and the goddess as vixen was well known in Greece (see 49. 2 and 89. 8). The toad seems to have become the Argive emblem, not only because it had a reputation of being dangerous to handle, and of causing a hush of awe among all who saw it (Pliny:

*Natural History* xxxii. 18), but because Argos was first called Phoronicum (see 57. *a*); in the syllabary which preceded the alphabet at Argos, the radicals PHRN could be expressed by a toad, *phryne*.

# 147

## LINUS

THE child Linus of Argos must be distinguished from Linus, the son of Ismenius, whom Heracles killed with a lyre. According to the Argives, Psamathe, the daughter of Crotopus, bore the child Linus to Apollo and, fearing her father's wrath, exposed him on a mountain. He was found and reared by shepherds, but afterwards torn in pieces by Crotopus's mastiffs. Since Psamathe could not disguise her grief, Crotopus soon guessed that she was Linus's mother, and condemned her to death. Apollo punished the city of Argos for this double crime by sending a sort of Harpy named Poene, who snatched young children from their parents until one Coroebus took it upon himself to destroy her. A plague then descended on the city and, when it showed no sign of abating, the Argives consulted the Delphic Oracle, which advised them to propitiate Psamathe and Linus. Accordingly they offered sacrifices to their ghosts, the women and maidens chanting dirges, still called *linoi*; and since Linus had been reared among lambs, named the festival *arnis*, and the month in which it was held *arneios*. The plague still raging, at last Coroebus went to Delphi and confessed to Poene's murder. The Pythoness would not let him return to Argos, but said: 'Carry my tripod hence, and build a temple to Apollo wherever it falls from your hands!' This happened to him on Mount Geraneia, where he founded first the temple and then the city of Tripodisci, and took up residence there. His tomb is shown in the market place at Megara; surmounted by a group of statuary, which depicts Poene's murder – the most ancient sculptures of that kind still surviving in Greece.[1] This second Linus is sometimes called Oetolinus, and harpists mourn him at banquets.[2]

*b.* A third Linus likewise lies buried at Argos: he was the poet whom some describe as a son of Oeagrus and the Muse Calliope – thus making him Orpheus's brother. Others call him the son of Apollo and the Muse

Urania, or Arethusa, a daughter of Poseidon; or of Hermes and Urania; others, again, of Amphimarus, Poseidon's son, and Urania; still others, of Magnes and the Muse Clio.[3] Linus was the greatest musician who ever appeared among mankind, and jealous Apollo killed him. He had composed ballads in honour of Dionysus and other ancient heroes, afterwards recording them in Pelasgian letters; also an epic of the Creation. Linus, in fact, invented rhythm and melody, was universally wise, and taught both Thamyris and Orpheus.[4]

*c.* The lament for Linus spread all over the world and is the theme, for instance, of the Egyptian *Song of Maneros*. On Mount Helicon, as one approached the Muses' grove, Linus's portrait is carved in the wall of a small grotto, where annual sacrifices to him precede those offered to the Muses. It is claimed that he lies buried at Thebes, and that Philip, father of Alexander the Great, after defeating the Greeks at Chaeronea, removed his bones to Macedonia, in accordance with a dream; but afterwards dreamed again, and sent them back.[5]

1. Pausanias: i. 43. 7 and ii. 19. 7; Conon: *Narrations* 19; Athenaeus: iii. 99.
2. Sappho, quoted by Pausanias: ix. 29. 3; Homer: *Iliad* xviii. 569–70; Hesiod, quoted by Diogenes Laertius: viii. 1. 25.
3. Apollodorus: i. 3. 2; Hyginus: *Fabula* 161; *Contest of Homer and Hesiod* 314; Diogenes Laertius: *Prooemium* 3; Pausanias: ix. 29. 3; Tzetzes: *On Lycophron* 831.
4. Diodorus Siculus: iii. 67; Diogenes Laertius: *loc. cit.*; Hesiod, quoted by Clement of Alexandria: *Stromateis* i. p. 121.
5. Pausanias: *loc. cit.*

\*

*1.* Pausanias connects the myth of the Child Linus with that of Maneros, the Egyptian Corn-spirit, for whom dirges were chanted at harvest time; but Linus seems to have been the spirit of the flax-plant (*linos*), sown in spring and harvested in summer. He had Psamathe for mother because, according to Pliny (*Natural History* xix. 2), 'they sowed flax in *sandy* soil.' His grandfather, and murderer, was Crotopus because – again according to Pliny – the yellowing flax-stalks, after having been plucked out by the roots, and hung up in the open air, were bruised with the 'pounding feet' of tow-mallets. And Apollo, whose priests wore linen, and who was patron of all Greek music, fathered him. Linus's destruction by dogs evidently refers to the maceration of the flax-stems with iron hatchets, a process which Pliny describes in the same passage. Frazer suggests, although without supporting evidence, that Linus is a

Greek mishearing of the Phoenician *ai lanu*, 'woe upon us'. Oetolinus means 'doomed Linus'.

2. The myth has, however, been reduced to the familiar pattern of the child exposed for fear of a jealous grandfather and reared by shepherds; which suggests that the linen industry in Argolis died out, owing to the Dorian invasion or Egyptian underselling, or both, and was replaced by a woollen industry; yet the annual dirges for the child Linus continued to be chanted. The flax industry is likely to have been established by the Cretans who civilized Argolis; the Greek word for flax-rope is *merinthos*, and all *-inthos* words are of Cretan origin.

3. Coroebus, when he killed Poene ('punishment'), probably forbade child sacrifices at the Linus festival, and substituted lambs, renaming the month 'Lamb Month'; he has been identified with an Elean of the same name who won the foot-race at the First Olympiad (776 B.C.). Tripodiscus seems to have no connexion with tripods, but to be derived from *tripodizein*, 'to fetter thrice'.

4. Since the flax-harvest was the occasion of plaintive dirges and rhythmic pounding, and since at midsummer – to judge from the Swiss and Suabian examples quoted in Frazer's *Golden Bough* – young people leaped around a bonfire to make the flax grow high, another mystical Linus was presumed: one who attained manhood and became a famous musician, the inventor of rhythm and melody. This Linus had a Muse mother, and for his father Arcadian Hermes, or Thracian Oeagrius, or Magnes, the eponymous ancestor of the Magnesians; he was, in fact, not a Hellene, but guardian of the pre-Hellenic Pelasgian culture, which included the tree-calendar and Creation lore. Apollo, who tolerated no rivals in music – as he had shown in the case of Marsyas (see 21. *f*) – is said to have killed him off-hand; but this was an incorrect account, since Apollo adopted, rather than murdered, Linus. Later, his death was more appropriately laid at the door of Heracles, patron of the uncivilized Dorian invaders (see 146. 1).

5. Linus is called Orpheus's brother because of a similarity in their fate (see 28. 2). In the Austrian Alps (I am informed by Margarita Schön-Wels) men are not admitted to the flax-harvest, or to the process of drying, beating, and macerating, or to the spinning-rooms. The ruling spirit is the *Harpatsch*: a terrifying hag, whose hands and face are rubbed with soot. Any man who meets her accidentally, is embraced, forced to dance, sexually assaulted, and smeared with soot. Moreover, the women who beat the flax, called *Bechlerinnen*, chase and surround any stranger who blunders into their midst. They make him lie down, step over him, tie his hands and feet, wrap him in tow, scour his face and hands with prickly flax-waste, rub him against the rough bark of a felled tree, and finally roll him downhill. Near Feldkirch, they only make the trespasser

lie down and step over him; but elsewhere they open his trouser-flies and stuff them with flax-waste, which is so painful that he has to escape barelegged. Near Salzburg, the Bechlerinnen untrouser the trespasser themselves, and threaten to castrate him; after his flight, they purify the place by burning twigs and clashing sickles together.

6. Little is known of what goes on in the spinning-rooms, the women being so secretive; except that they chant a dirge called the *Flachses Qual* ('Flax's Torment'), or *Leinen Klage* ('Linen Lament'). It seems likely, then, that at the flax-harvest women used to catch, sexually assault, and dismember a man who represented the flax-spirit; but since this was also the fate of Orpheus, who protested against human sacrifice and sexual orgies (see 28. *d*), Linus has been described as his brother. The *Harpatsch* is familiar: she is the carline-wife of the corn harvest, representative of the Earth-goddess. Sickles are clashed solely in honour of the moon; they are not used in the flax harvest. Linus is credited with the invention of music because these dirges are put into the mouth of the Flax-spirit himself, and because some lyre-strings were made from flaxen thread.

# 148

## THE ARGONAUTS ASSEMBLE

AFTER the death of King Cretheus the Aeolian, Pelias, son of Poseidon, already an old man, seized the Iolcan throne from his half-brother Aeson, the rightful heir. An oracle presently warning him that he would be killed by a descendant of Aeolus, Pelias put to death every prominent Aeolian he dared lay hands upon, except Aeson, whom he spared for his mother Tyro's sake, but kept a prisoner in the palace; forcing him to renounce his inheritance.

*b*. Now, Aeson had married Polymele, also known as Amphinome, Perimede, Alcimede, Polymede, Polypheme, Scarphe, or Arne, who bore him one son, by name Diomedes.[1] Pelias would have destroyed the child without mercy, had not Polymele summoned her kinswomen to weep over him, as though he were still-born, and then smuggled him out of the city to Mount Pelion; where Cheiron the Centaur reared him, as he did before, or afterwards, with Asclepius, Achilles, Aeneas, and other famous heroes.[2]

*c*. A second oracle warned Pelias to beware a one-sandalled man and when, one day on the seashore, a group of his princely allies joined him in a solemn sacrifice to Poseidon, his eye fell upon a tall, long-haired Magnesian youth, dressed in a close-fitting leather tunic and a leopard-skin. He was armed with two broad-bladed spears, and wore only one sandal.[3]

d. The other sandal he had lost in the muddy river Anaurus – which some miscall the Evenus, or Enipeus – by the contrivance of a crone who, standing on the farther bank, begged passers-by to carry her across. None took pity on her, until this young stranger courteously offered her his broad back; but he found himself staggering under the weight, since she was none other than the goddess Hera in disguise. For Pelias had vexed Hera by withholding her customary sacrifices, and she was determined to punish him for this neglect.[4]

e. When, therefore, Pelias asked the stranger roughly: 'Who are you, and what is your father's name?', he replied that Cheiron, his foster-father, called him Jason, though he had formerly been known as Diomedes, son of Aeson.

Pelias glared at him balefully. 'What would you do,' he inquired suddenly, 'if an oracle announced that one of your fellow-citizens were destined to kill you?'

'I should send him to fetch the golden ram's fleece from Colchis,' Jason replied, not knowing that Hera had placed those words in his mouth. 'And, pray, whom have I the honour of addressing?'

f. When Pelias revealed his identity, Jason was unabashed. He boldly claimed the throne usurped by Pelias, though not the flocks and herds which had gone with it; and since he was strongly supported by his uncle Pheres, king of Pherae, and Amathaon, king of Pylus, who had come to take part in the sacrifice, Pelias feared to deny him his birth-right. 'But first,' he insisted, 'I require you to free our beloved country from a curse!'

g. Jason then learned that Pelias was being haunted by the ghost of Phrixus, who had fled from Orchomenus a generation before, riding on the back of a divine ram, to avoid being sacrificed. He took refuge in Colchis where, on his death, he was denied proper burial; and, according to the Delphic Oracle, the land of Iolcus, where many of Jason's Minyan relatives were settled, would never prosper unless his ghost were brought home in a ship, together with the golden ram's fleece. The fleece now hung from a tree in the grove of Colchian Ares, guarded night and day by an unsleeping dragon. Once this pious feat had been accomplished, Pelias declared, he would gladly resign the kingship, which was becoming burdensome for a man of his advanced years.[5]

*h*. Jason could not deny Pelias this service, and therefore sent heralds to every court of Greece, calling for volunteers who would sail with him. He also prevailed upon Argus the Thespian to build him a fifty-oared ship; and this was done at Pagasae, with seasoned timber from Mount Pelion; after which Athene herself fitted an oracular beam into the *Argo*'s prow, cut from her father Zeus's oak at Dodona.[6]

*i*. Many different muster-rolls of the Argonauts – as Jason's companions are called – have been compiled at various times; but the following names are those given by the most trustworthy authorities:

Acastus, son of King Pelias
Actor, son of Deion the Phocian
Admetus, prince of Pherae
Amphiaraus, the Argive seer
Great Ancaeus of Tegea, son of Poseidon
Little Ancaeus, the Lelegian of Samos
Argus the Thespian, builder of the *Argo*
Ascalaphus the Orchomenan, son of Ares
Asterius, son of Cometes, a Pelopian
Atalanta of Calydon, the virgin huntress
Augeias, son of King Phorbas of Elis
Butes of Athens, the bee-master
Caeneus the Lapith, who had once been a woman
Calais, the winged son of Boreas
Canthus the Euboean
Castor, the Spartan wrestler, one of the Dioscuri
Cepheus, son of Aleus the Arcadian
Coronus the Lapith, of Gyrton in Thessaly
Echion, son of Hermes, the herald
Erginus of Miletus
Euphemus of Taenarum, the swimmer
Euryalus, son of Mecisteus, one of the Epigoni
Eurydamas the Dolopian, from Lake Xynias
Heracles of Tiryns, the strongest man who ever lived, now a god
Hylas the Dryopian, squire to Heracles
Idas, son of Aphareus of Messene
Idmon the Argive, Apollo's son
Iphicles, son of Thestius the Aetolian

Iphitus, brother of King Eurystheus of Mycenae
Jason, the captain of the expedition
Laertes, son of Acrisius the Argive
Lynceus, the look-out man, brother to Idas
Melampus of Pylus, son of Poseidon
Meleager of Calydon
Mopsus the Lapith
Nauplius the Argive, son of Poseidon, a noted navigator
Oïleus the Locrian, father of Ajax
Orpheus, the Thracian poet
Palaemon, son of Hephaestus, an Aetolian
Peleus the Myrmidon
Peneleos, son of Hippalcimus, the Boeotian
Periclymenus of Pylus, the shape-shifting son of Poseidon
Phalerus, the Athenian archer
Phanus, the Cretan son of Dionysus
Poeas, son of Thaumacus the Magnesian
Polydeuces, the Spartan boxer, one of the Dioscuri
Polyphemus, son of Elatus, the Arcadian
Staphylus, brother of Phanus
Tiphys, the helmsman, of Boeotian Siphae
Zetes, brother of Calais

– and never before or since was so gallant a ship's company gathered together.[7]

*j*. The Argonauts are often known as Minyans, because they brought back the ghost of Phrixus, grandson of Minyas, and the fleece of his ram; and because many of them, including Jason himself, sprang from the blood of Minyas's daughters. This Minyas, a son of Chryses, had migrated from Thessaly to Orchomenus in Boeotia, where he founded a kingdom, and was the first king ever to build a treasury.[8]

1. Scholiast on Homer's *Odyssey* xii. 70; Diodorus Siculus: iv. 50. 1; Apollonius Rhodius: i. 232; Apollodorus: i. 9. 16; Scholiast on Apollonius Rhodius: i. 45; Tzetzes: *On Lycophron* 872.
2. Pindar: *Pythian Odes* iv. 198 ff. and *Nemean Odes* iii. 94 ff.; Homer: *Iliad* xvi. 143.
3. Apollonius Rhodius: i. 7; Apollodorus: *loc. cit.*; Pindar: *Pythian Odes* iv. 128 ff.
4. Apollonius Rhodius: i. 8–17; Apollodorus: *loc. cit.*; Pindar: *loc. cit.*; Hyginus: *Fabula* 13; Valerius Flaccus: i. 84.

5. Apollodorus: *loc. cit.*; Pindar: *loc. cit.*; Diodorus Siculus: iv. 40; Scholiast on Homer's *Odyssey* xii. 70; Hesiod: *Theogony* 992 ff.

6. Pindar: *loc. cit.*; Valerius Flaccus: i. 39; Apollodorus: *loc. cit.*

7. Apollodorus: *loc. cit.*; Pindar: *loc. cit.*; Hyginus: *Fabulae* 12 and 14–23; Apollonius Rhodius: i. 20; Diodorus Siculus: iv. 40–9; Tzetzes: *On Lycophron* 175; Ovid: *Metamorphoses* vii. 1 ff.; Valerius Flaccus: *Argonautica* i. *passim*.

8. Apollonius Rhodius: i. 229; Pausanias: ix. 36. 3.

*

1. In Homer's day, a ballad cycle about the *Argo*'s voyage to the land of Aeëtes ('mighty') was 'on everyone's lips' (*Odyssey* xii. 40), and he places the Planctae – through which she had passed even before Odysseus did – near the Islands of the Sirens, and not far from Scylla and Charybdis. All these perils occur in the fuller accounts of the *Argo*'s return from Colchis.

2. According to Hesiod, Jason, son of Aeson, after accomplishing many grievous tasks imposed by Pelias, married Aeëtes's daughter who came with him to Iolcus, where 'she was subject to him' and bore his son Medeius, whom Cheiron educated. But Hesiod seems to have been misinformed: in heroic times no princess was brought to her husband's home – he came to hers (see 137. *4* and 160. *3*). Thus Jason either married Aeëtes's daughter and settled at his court, or else he married Pelias's daughter and settled at Iolcus. Eumelus (eighth century) reports that, when Corinthus died without issue, Medea successfully claimed the vacant throne of Corinth, being a daughter of Aeëtes who, not content with his heritage, had emigrated thence to Colchis; and that Jason, her husband, thereupon became king.

3. Neither Colchis, nor its capital of Aea, are mentioned in these early accounts, which describe Aeëtes as the son of Helius, and the brother of Aeaean Circe. Nor must it be supposed that the story known to Homer had much in common with the one told by Apollodorus and Apollonius Rhodius; the course, even, of the *Argo*'s outward voyage, let alone her homeward one, was not yet fixed by Herodotus's time – for Pindar, in his *Fourth Pythian Ode* (462 B.C.), had presented a version very different from his.

4. The myth of Pelias and Diomedes – Jason's original name – seems to have been about a prince exposed on a mountain, reared by horseherds, and set seemingly impossible tasks by the king of a neighbouring city, not necessarily a usurper: such as the yoking of fire-breathing bulls, and the winning of a treasure guarded by a sea-monster – Jason, half-dead in the sea-monster's maw, is the subject of Etruscan works of art. His reward will have been to marry the royal heiress. Similar myths are

common in Celtic mythology – witness the labours imposed upon Kilhwych, the *Mabinogion* hero, when he wished to marry the sorceress Olwen – and apparently refer to ritual tests of a king's courage before his coronation.

5. It is indeed from the *Tale of Kilhwych and Olwen*, and from the similar *Tale of Peredur Son of Evrawc*, also in the *Mabinogion*, that the most plausible guesses can be made at the nature of Diomedes's tasks. Kilhwych, falling in love with Olwen, was ordered by her father to yoke a yellow and a brindled bull, to clear a hill of thorns and scrub, sow this with corn, and then harvest the grain in a single day (see 127. *1* and 152. *3*); also to win a horn of plenty, and a magic Irish cauldron. Peredur, falling in love with an unknown maiden, had to kill a water-monster, called the *Avanc*, in a lake near the Mound of Mourning – Aeaea means 'mourning'. On condition that he swore faith with her, she gave him a magic stone, which enabled him to defeat the Avanc, and win 'all the gold a man might desire'. The maiden proved to be the Empress of Cristinobyl, a sorceress, who lived in great style 'towards India'; and Peredur remained her lover for fourteen years. Since the only other Welsh hero to defeat an *Avanc* was Hu Gadarn the Mighty, ancestor of the Cymry, who by yoking two bulls to the monster, dragged it out of the Conwy River (*Welsh Triads* iii. 97), it seems likely that Jason also hauled his monster from the water, with the help of his fire-breathing team.

6. The Irish cauldron fetched by Kilhwych was apparently the one mentioned in the *Tale of Peredur*: a cauldron of regeneration, like that subsequently used by Medea – a giant had found it at the bottom of an Irish lake. Diomedes may have been required to fetch a similar one for Pelias. The scene of his labours will have been some ungeographical country 'towards the rising sun'. No cornucopia is mentioned in the Argonaut legend, but Medea, for no clear reason, rejuvenates the nymph Macris and her sisters, formerly the nurses of Dionysus, when she meets them on Drepane, or Corcyra. Since Dionysus had much in common with the infant Zeus, whose nurse, the goat Amaltheia, provided the original cornucopia (see 7. *b*), Medea may have helped Diomedes to win another cornucopia from the nymphs by lending them her services. Heracles's Labours (like those of Theseus and Orion) are best understood as marriage tasks and included 'the breaking of the horns of both bulls' (the Cretan and the Acheloan – see 134. *6*).

7. This marriage-task myth, one version of which seems to have been current at Iolcus, with Pelias as villain, and another at Corinth, with Corinthus as villain, evidently became linked to the semi-historical legend of a Minyan sea expedition sent out from Iolcus by the Orchomenans. Orchomenus belonged to the ancient amphictyony, or league, of Calaureia (Strabo: viii. 6. 14), presided over by the Aeolian god Poseidon

which included six seaside states of Argos and Attica; it was the only inland city of the seven and strategically placed between the Gulf of Corinth and the Thessalian Gulf. Its people, like Hesiod's Boeotians, may have been farmers in the winter and sailors in the summer.

*8.* The supposed object of the expedition was to recover a sacred fleece, which had been carried away 'to the land of Aeëtes' by King Phrixus, a grandson of Minyas, when about to be sacrificed on Mount Laphystium (see 70. *d*), and to escort Phrixus's ghost home to Orchomenus. Its leader will have been a Minyan – which Diomedes son of Aeson was not – perhaps Cytisorus (Herodotus: vii. 197), son of Phrixus, whom Apollonius Rhodius brings prominently into the story (see 151. *f* and 152. *b*), and who won the surname Jason ('healer') at Orchomenus when he checked the drought and plague caused by Phrixus's escape. Nevertheless, Diomedes was a Minyan on his mother's side; and descent is likely to have been matrilinear both at Orchomenus and Pelasgian Iolcus.

*9.* In this Minyan legend, the land of Aeëtes cannot have lain at the other end of the Black Sea; all the early evidence points to the head of the Adriatic. The Argonauts are believed to have navigated the river Po, near the mouth of which, across the Gulf, lay Circe's Island of Aeaea, now called Lussin; and to have been trapped by Aeëtes's Colchians at the mouth of the Ister – not the Danube but, as Diodorus Siculus suggests, the small river Istrus, which gives Istria its name. Medea then killed her brother Apsyrtus, who was buried in the neighbouring Apsyrtides; and when she and Jason took refuge with Alcinous, King of Drepane (Corcyra), a few days' sail to the southward, the Colchians, cheated of their vengeance, feared to incur Aeëtes's anger by returning empty-handed and therefore built the city of Pola on the Istrian mainland. Moreover, Siren-land, the Clashing Rocks, Scylla and Charybdis, all lie close to Sicily, past which the *Argo* was then blown by the violent north-easter.

'Colchis' may, in fact, be an error for 'Colicaria' on the Lower Po, not far from Mantua, apparently a station on the Amber Route; since Helius's daughters, who wept amber tears, are brought into the story as soon as the *Argo* enters the Po (see 42. *d*). Amber was sacred to the Sun, and Electra ('amber'), the island at which the *Argo* is said to have touched, will hardly have been Samothrace, as the scholiasts believe; but 'the land of Aeëtes', a trading post at the terminus of the Amber Route – perhaps Corinthian, because Aeëtes had brought his Sun cult from Corinth, but perhaps Pelasgian, because according to Dionysius's *Description of the Earth* (i. 18) a Pelasgian colony, originating from Dodona, once maintained a powerful fleet at one of the mouths of the Po.

*10.* To the ungeographical myth of Diomedes, now combined with the legend of a Minyan voyage to the land of Aeëtes, a third element was added: the tradition of an early piratical raid along the southern coast of the Black Sea, made at the orders of another Minyan king. The sixth city of Troy, by its command of the Hellespont, enjoyed a monopoly of the Black Sea trade, which this raid will have been planned to challenge (see 137. *1*). Now, the Minyans' supposed objective on their Adriatic voyage was not a golden, but, according to Simonides (quoted by scholiast on Apollonius Rhodius: iv. 77) a purple, fleece which the First Vatican Mythographer describes as that 'in which Zeus used to ascend to Heaven'. In other words, it was a black fleece worn in a royal rain-making rite, like the one still performed every May Day on the summit of Mount Pelion: where an old man in a black sheepskin mask is killed and brought to life again by his companions, who are dressed in white fleeces (*Annals of the British School at Athens* xvi. 244–9, 1909–16). According to Dicearchus (ii. 8), this rite was performed in Classical times under the auspices of Zeus Actaeus, or Acraeus ('of the summit'). Originally the man in the black sheepskin mask will have been the king, Zeus's representative, who was sacrificed at the close of his reign. The use of the same ceremony on Mount Pelion as on Mount Laphystium will account for the combining of the two Iolcan traditions, namely the myth of Diomedes and the legend of the Black Sea raid, with the tradition of a Minyan voyage to undo the mischief caused by Phrixus.

11. Yet the Minyans' commission will hardly have been to bring back the lost Laphystian fleece, which was easily replaced: they are far more likely to have gone in search of amber, with which to propitiate the injured deity, the Mountain-goddess. It should be remembered that the Minyans held 'Sandy Pylus' on the western coast of the Peloponnese – captured from the Lelegians by Neleus with the help of Iolcan Pelasgians (see 94. *c*) – and that, according to Aristotle (*Mirabilia* 82), the Pylians brought amber from the mouth of the Po. On the site of this Pylus (now the village of Kakovatos) huge quantities of amber have recently been unearthed.

12. On the easterly voyage this fleece became 'golden', because Diomedes's feat of winning the sea-monster treasure had to be included; and because, as Strabo points out, the Argonauts who broke into the Black Sea went in search of alluvial gold from the Colchian Phasis (now the Rion), collected by the natives in fleeces laid on the river bed. Nor was it only the confusion of Colchis with Colicaria, of Aea ('earth') with Aeaea ('wailing'), and of the Pelionian black fleece with the Laphystian, that made these different traditions coalesce. The dawn palace of Aeëtes's father Helius lay in Colchis (see 42. *a*), the most easterly country known to Homer; and *Jasonica*, shrines of Heracles the Healer, were reported from the Eastern Gulf of the Black Sea, where the Aeolians had established trading posts. According to some authorities, Heracles led the

Black Sea expedition. Moreover, since Homer had mentioned Jason only as the father of Euneus, who provided the Greeks with wine during the siege of Troy (see 162. *i*), and since Lemnos lay east of Thessaly, the *Argo* was also thought to have headed east. The Wandering, or Clashing, Rocks, which Homer placed in Sicilian waters, have thus been transferred to the Bosphorus.

*13.* Every city needed a representative Argonaut to justify its trading rights in the Black Sea, and travelling minstrels were willing enough to introduce another name or two into this composite ballad cycle. Several nominal rolls of Argonauts therefore survive, all irreconcilable, but for the most part based on the theory that they used a fifty-oared vessel – not, indeed, an impossibility in Mycenaean times; Tzetzes alone gives a hundred names. Yet not even the most hardened sceptic seems to have doubted that the legend was in the main historical, or that the voyage took place before the Trojan War, sometime in the thirteenth century B.C.

*14.* Jason's single sandal proved him to be a fighting man. Aetolian warriors were famous for their habit of campaigning with only the left foot shod (Macrobius: v. 18–21; Scholiast on Pindar's *Pythian Odes* iv. 133), a device also adopted during the Peloponnesian War by the Plataeans, to gain better purchase in the mud (Thucydides: iii. 22). Why the foot on the shield side, rather than the weapon side, remained shod, may have been because it was advanced in a hand-to-hand struggle, and could be used for kicking an opponent in the groin. Thus the left was the hostile foot, and never set on the threshold of a friend's house; the tradition survives in modern Europe, where soldiers invariably march off to war with the left foot foremost.

*15.* Hera's quarrel with Pelias, over the withholding of her sacrifice, suggests tension between a Poseidon-worshipping Achaean dynasty at Iolcus and the goddess-worshipping Aeolo-Magnesians, their subjects.

# 149

## THE LEMNIAN WOMEN AND KING CYZICUS

HERACLES, after capturing the Erymanthian Boar, appeared suddenly at Pagasae, and was invited by a unanimous vote to captain the *Argo*; but generously agreed to serve under Jason who, though a novice, had planned and proclaimed the expedition. Accordingly, when the ship had been launched, and lots drawn for the benches, two oarsmen to each bench, it was Jason who sacrificed a yoke of oxen to Apollo of Embarkations. As the smoke of his sacrifice rose propitiously to heaven in dark, swirling columns, the Argonauts sat down to their farewell banquet, at which Orpheus with his lyre appeased certain drunken brawls. Sailing thence by the first light of dawn, they shaped a course for Lemnos.[1]

*b*. About a year before this, the Lemnian men had quarrelled with their wives, complaining that they stank, and made concubines of Thracian girls captured on raids. In revenge, the Lemnian women murdered them all without pity, old and young alike, except King Thoas, whose life his daughter Hypsipyle secretly spared, setting him adrift in an oarless boat. Now, when the *Argo* hove in sight and the Lemnian women mistook her for an enemy ship from Thrace, they donned their dead husbands' armour and ran boldly shoreward, to repel the threatened attack. The eloquent Echion, however, landing staff in hand as Jason's herald, soon set their minds at rest; and Hysipyle called a council at which she proposed to send a gift of food and wine to the Argonauts, but not to admit them into her city of Myrine, for fear of being charged with the massacre. Polyxo, Hypsipyle's aged nurse, then rose to plead that, without men, the Lemnian race must presently become extinct. 'The wisest course', she said, 'would be to offer yourselves in love to those well-born adventurers, and thus not only place our island under strong protection, but breed a new and stalwart stock.'

*c*. This disinterested advice was loudly acclaimed, and the Argonauts were welcomed to Myrine. Hypsipyle did not, of course, tell Jason the whole truth but, stammering and blushing, explained that after much ill-treatment at the hands of their husbands, her companions had risen in arms and forced them to emigrate. The vacant throne of Lemnos, she said, was now his for the asking. Jason, although gratefully accepting her offer, declared that before settling in fertile Lemnos he must complete his quest of the Golden Fleece. Nevertheless, Hypsipyle soon persuaded the Argonauts to postpone their departure; for each adventurer was surrounded by numerous young women, all itching to bed with him.[2] Hypsipyle claimed Jason for herself, and royally she entertained him; it was then that he begot Euneus, and his twin Nebrophonus, whom some call Deiphilus, or Thoas the Younger. Euneus eventually became king of Lemnos and supplied the Greeks with wine during the Trojan War.

*d*. Many children were begotten on this occasion by the other Argonauts too and, had it not been for Heracles, who was guarding the *Argo* and at last strode angrily into Myrine, beating upon the house doors with his club and summoning his comrades back to duty, it is unlikely that the golden fleece would ever have left Colchis. He soon forced them down to the shore; and that same night they sailed for Samothrace, where they were duly initiated into the mysteries of Persephone and her servants, the Cabeiri, who save sailors from shipwreck.[3]

*e.* Afterwards, when the Lemnian women discovered that Hypsipyle, in breach of her oath, had spared Thoas – he was cast ashore on the island of Sicinos, and later reigned over the Taurians – they sold her into slavery to King Lycurgus of Nemea. But some say that Thracian pirates raided Myrine and captured her. On attaining manhood, Euneus purified the island of blood guilt, and the rites he used are still repeated at the annual festival of the Cabeiri: for the space of nine days, all Lemnian hearth-fires are extinguished, and offerings made to the dead, after which new fire is brought by ship from Apollo's altar at Delos.[4]

*f.* The Argonauts sailed on, leaving Imbros to starboard and, since it was well known that King Laomedon of Troy guarded the entrance to the Hellespont and let no Greek ship enter, they slipped through the Straits by night, hugging the Thracian coast, and reached the Sea of Marmara in safety. Approaching Dolionian territory, they landed at the neck of a rugged peninsula, named Arcton, which is crowned by Mount Dindymum. Here they were welcomed by King Cyzicus, the son of Aeneus, Heracles's former ally, who had just married Cleite of Phrygian Percote and warmly invited them to share his wedding banquet. While the revelry was still in progress, the *Argo*'s guards were attacked with rocks and clubs by certain six-handed Earth-born giants from the interior of the peninsula, but beat them off.

*g.* Afterwards, the Argonauts dedicated their anchor-stone to Athene, in whose temple it is shown to this day, and, taking aboard a heavier one, rowed away with cordial farewells, shaping a course for the Bosphorus. But a north-easterly wind suddenly whirled down upon them, and soon they were making so little way that Tiphys decided to about ship, and ran back to the lee of the peninsula. He was driven off his course; and the Argonauts, beaching their ship at random in the pitch-dark, were at once assailed by well-armed warriors. Only when they had overcome these in a fierce battle, killing some and putting the remainder to flight, did Jason discover that he had made the eastern shore of Arcton, and that noble King Cyzicus, who had mistaken the Argonauts for pirates, lay dead at his feet. Cleite, driven mad by the news, hanged herself; and the nymphs of the grove wept so pite-ously that their tears formed the fountain which now bears her name.

*h.* The Argonauts held funeral games in Cyzicus's honour, but remained weather-bound for many days more. At last a halcyon flut-tered above Jason's head, and perched twittering on the prow of the *Argo*; whereupon Mopsus, who understood the language of birds, ex-plained that all would be well if they placated the goddess Rhea. She had exacted Cyzicus's death in requital for that of her sacred lion's, killed by him on Mount Dindymum, and was now vexed with the Argonauts for having caused such carnage among her six-armed Earth-born brothers. They therefore raised an image to the goddess, carved by Argus from an ancient vine-stock, and danced in full armour on the mountain top. Rhea acknowledged their devotion: she made a spring – now called the Spring of Jason – gush from the neighbouring rocks. A fair breeze then arose, and they continued the voyage. The Dolionians, however, prolonged their mourning to a full month, lighting no fires, and subsisting on uncooked foods, a custom which is still observed during the annual Cyzican Games.[5]

1. Apollonius Rhodius: i. 317 ff.
2. Apollonius Rhodius: i. 1–607; Herodotus: vi. 138; Apollodorus: i. 9. 17; *Argonautica Orphica* 473 ff.; Valerius Flaccus: *Argonautica* ii. 77; Hyginus: *Fabula* 15.
3. Homer: *Iliad* vii. 468, with scholiast; Statius: *Thebaid* vi. 34; Apollonius Rhodius: *loc. cit.*; Apollodorus: *loc. cit.*; Valerius Flaccus: *loc. cit.*; Hyginus: *loc. cit.*; *Fragments of Sophocles* ii. 51 ff., ed. Pearson.
4. Apollodorus: iii. 6. 4; Hyginus: *loc. cit.*; Philostratus: *Heroica* xx. 24.
5. First Vatican Mythographer: 49; Apollonius Rhodius: i. 922 ff. and 935–1077; *Argonautica Orphica* 486 ff.; Valerius Flaccus: *Argonautica* ii. 634; Hyginus: *Fabula* 16.

*

*1.* Jason is made to call at Lemnos because, according to Homer, Euneus, who reigned there during the Trojan War, was his son; and because Euphemus, another Argonaut, begot Leucophanes ('white ap-pearance') on a Lemnian woman (Tzetzes: *On Lycophron* 886; Scholiast on Pindar's *Pythian Odes* iv. 455), thus becoming the ancestor of a long-lived Cyrenean dynasty. The Lemnian massacre suggests that the islanders retained the gynocratic form of society, supported by armed priestesses, which was noted among certain Libyan tribes in Herodotus's time (see

8. *1*), and that visiting Hellenes could understand this anomaly only in terms of a female revolution. Myrine was the name of their goddess (see **131. 3**). Perhaps the Lemnian women were said to have stunk because they worked in woad – used by their Thracian neighbours for tattooing – which has so nauseous and lingering a smell that Norfolk woad-making families have always been obliged to intermarry.

*2.* Samothrace was a centre of the Helladic religion, and initiates into its Moon-goddess Mysteries – the secret of which has been well kept – were entitled to wear a purple amulet (Apollonius Rhodius: i. 197; Diodorus Siculus: v. 49), valued as a protection against dangers of all kinds, but especially shipwreck. Philip of Macedon and his wife Olympias became initiates (Aristophanes: *Peace* 277, with scholiast); Germanicus Caesar was prevented from taking part in the Mysteries only by an omen and died soon after (Tacitus: *Annals* ii. 54). Certain ancient bronze vessels laid up in Samothrace were said to have been dedicated by the Argonauts.

*3.* Rhea's brothers, the six-armed Earth-born of Bear Island, are perhaps deduced from pictures of shaggy men, wearing bear-skins with the paws extended. The account of Cyzicus's death is circumstantial enough to suggest a genuine tradition of the Black Sea raid, though one as little connected with the annual extinction of fires at Cyzicus, as was the supposed Lemnian massacre with a similar ceremony at Myrine, during the nine-day festival of the Cabeiri. At the close of the year, when the sacred king was sacrificed, fires were habitually extinguished in many kingdoms, to be renewed afterwards as one of the rites in the new king's installation.

*4.* The killing of Rhea's lion probably refers to the suppression of her worship at Cyzicus in favour of Olympianism.

*5.* Halcyons were messengers of the Sea-goddess Alcyone ('the queen who wards off [storms]' – see **45. 1–2**).

# 150

## HYLAS, AMYCUS AND PHINEUS

A T Heracles's challenge the Argonauts now engaged in a contest to see who could row the longest. After many laborious hours, relieved only by Orpheus's lyre, Jason, the Dioscuri, and Heracles alone held out; their comrades having each in turn confessed themselves beaten. Castor's strength began to ebb, and Polydeuces, who could not otherwise induce him to desist, shipped his own oar. Jason and Heracles, however, continued to urge the *Argo* forward, seated on opposite sides of the ship, until presently, as they reached the mouth of the river Chius in Mysia, Jason fainted. Almost at once Heracles's oar snapped. He glared about him, in anger and disgust; and his weary companions, thrusting their oars through the oar-holes again, beached the *Argo* by the river-side.

*b*. While they prepared the evening meal, Heracles went in search of a tree which would serve to make him a new oar. He uprooted an enormous fir, but when he dragged it back for trimming beside the camp fire, found that his squire Hylas had set out, an hour or two previously, to fetch water from the near-by pool of Pegae, and not yet returned; Polyphemus was away, searching for him. Hylas had been Heracles's minion and darling ever since the death of his father, Theiodamas, king of the Dryopians, whom Heracles had killed when refused the gift of a plough-ox.

Crying 'Hylas! Hylas!', Heracles plunged frantically into the woods and soon met Polyphemus, who reported: 'Alas, I heard Hylas shouting for help; and ran towards his voice. But when I reached Pegae I found no signs of a struggle either with wild beasts or with other enemies. There was only his water-pitcher lying abandoned by the pool side.' Heracles and Polyphemus continued their search all night, and forced every Mysian whom they met to join in it, but to no avail; the fact being that Dryope and her sister-nymphs of Pegae had fallen in love with Hylas, and enticed him to come and live with them in an underwater grotto.

*c*. At dawn, a favourable breeze sprang up and, since neither Heracles nor Polyphemus appeared, though everyone shouted their names until the hillsides echoed, Jason gave orders for the voyage to be resumed. This decision was loudly contested and, as the *Argo* drew farther away from the shore, several of the Argonauts accused him of having marooned Heracles to avenge his defeat at rowing. They even tried to make Tiphys turn the ship about; but Calais and Zetes interposed, which is why Heracles later killed them in the island of Tenos, where he set a tottering logan-stone upon their tomb.

*d*. After threatening to lay Mysia waste unless the inhabitants continued their search for Hylas, dead or alive, and then leading a successful raid on Troy, Heracles resumed his Labours; but Polyphemus settled near Pegae and built the city of Crius, where he reigned until the

Chalybians killed him in battle.[1] For Heracles's sake, the Mysians still sacrifice once a year to Hylas at Prusa, near Pegae; their priest thrice calls his name aloud, and the devotees pretend to search for him in the woods.[2]

*e*. Hylas, indeed, suffered the same fate as Bormus, or Borimus, son of Upius, a Mariandynian youth of extraordinary beauty who once, at harvest time, went to a well to fetch water for the reapers. He too was drawn into the well by the nymphs and never seen again. The country people of Bithynia celebrate his memory every year at harvest time with plaintive songs to the accompaniment of flutes.[3]

*f*. Some therefore deride the story of Hylas, saying that he was really Bormus, and that Heracles had been abandoned at Magnesian Aphetae, close to Pagasae, when he went ashore to draw water, soon after the voyage began; the oracular beam of the *Argo* having announced that he would be too heavy for her to carry. Others, on the contrary, say that he not only reached Colchis, but commanded the expedition throughout.[4]

*g*. Next, the *Argo* touched at the island of Bebrycos, also in the Sea of Marmara, ruled by the arrogant King Amycus, a son of Poseidon. This Amycus fancied himself as a boxer, and used to challenge strangers to a match, which invariably proved their undoing; but if they declined, he flung them without ceremony over a cliff into the sea. He now approached the Argonauts, and refused them food or water unless one of their champions would meet him in the ring. Polydeuces, who had won the boxing contest at the Olympic Games, stepped forward willingly, and drew on the raw-hide gloves which Amycus offered him.

*h*. Amycus and Polydeuces went at it, hammer and tongs, in a flowery dell, not far from the beach. Amycus's gloves were studded with brazen spikes, and the muscles on his shaggy arms stood out like boulders covered with seaweed. He was by far the heavier man, and the younger by several years; but Polydeuces, fighting cautiously at first, and avoiding his bull-like rushes, soon discovered the weak points in his defence and, before long, had him spitting blood from a swollen mouth. After a prolonged bout, in which neither showed the least sign of flagging, Polydeuces broke through Amycus's guard, flattened his nose with a straight left-handed punch, and dealt further merciless punishment on either side of it, using hooks and jolts. In pain and desperation, Amycus grasped Polydeuces's left fist and tugged at it with his left hand, while he brought up a powerful right swing; but Polydeuces threw himself in the direction of the tug. The swing went wide, and he countered with a stunning right-handed hook to the ear, followed by so irresistible an upper cut that it broke the bones of Amycus's temple and killed him instantly.

*i.* When they saw their king lying dead, the Bebrycans sprang to arms, but Polydeuces's cheering companions routed them easily and sacked the royal palace. To placate Poseidon, Amycus's father, Jason then offered a holocaust of twenty red bulls, which were found among the spoils.[5]

*j.* The Argonauts put to sea again on the next day, and came to Salmydessus in Eastern Thrace, where Phineus, the son of Agenor, reigned. He had been blinded by the gods for prophesying the future too accurately, and was also plagued by a pair of Harpies; loathsome, winged, female creatures who, at every meal, flew into the palace and snatched victuals from his table, befouling the rest, so that it stank and was inedible. One Harpy was called Aellopus, and the other Ocypete.[6] When Jason asked Phineus for advice on how to win the golden fleece, he was told: 'First rid me of the Harpies!' Phineus's servants spread the Argonauts a banquet, upon which the Harpies immediately descended, playing their usual tricks. Calais and Zetes, however, the winged sons of Boreas, arose sword in hand, and chased them into the air and far across the sea. Some say that they caught up with the Harpies at the Strophades islands, but spared their lives when they turned back and implored mercy; for Iris, Hera's messenger, intervened, promising that they would return to their cave in Cretan Dicte and never again molest Phineus. Others say that Ocypete made terms at these islands, but that Aellopus flew on, only to be drowned in the Peloponnesian river Tigris, now called Harpys after her.

*k.* Phineus instructed Jason how to navigate the Bosphorus, and gave him a detailed account of what weather, hospitality, and fortune to expect on his way to Colchis, a country first colonized by the Egyptians, which lies at the easternmost end of the Black Sea, under the shadow of the Caucasus Mountains. He added: 'And once you have reached Colchis, trust in Aphrodite!'[7]

*l.* Now, Phineus had married first Cleopatra, sister to Calais and Zetes and then, on her death, Idaea, a Scythian princess. Idaea was jealous of Cleopatra's two sons, and suborned false witnesses to accuse them of all manner of wickedness. Calais and Zetes, however, detecting the conspiracy, freed their nephews from prison, where they were being daily flogged by Scythian guards, and Phineus not only restored them to favour, but sent Idaea back to her father.[8]

*m.* And some say that Phineus was blinded by the gods after the Argonauts' visit, because he had given them prophetic advice.[9]

1. Apollonius Rhodius: i. 1207 ff.; Theocritus: *Idylls* xiii; *Argonautica Orphica* 646 ff.; Valerius Flaccus: *Argonautica* iii. 521 ff.; Hyginus: *Fabula* 14; Apollodorus: i. 9. 19.

2. Theocritus: *Idylls* xiii. 73 ff.; Strabo: xii. 4. 3; Antoninus Liberalis: *Transformations* 26.

3. Athenaeus: xiv. 620; Aeschylus: *Persian Women* 941; Scholiast on Dionysius's *Description of the Earth* 791; Pollux: iv. 54.

4. Herodotus: i. 193; Apollodorus: i. 9. 19; Theocritus: *Idylls* xiii. 73 ff.

5. Apollodorus: i. 9. 20; Apollonius Rhodius: ii. 1 ff.; Theocritus: *Idylls* xxii. 27 ff.; *Argonautica Orphica* 661 ff.; Valerius Flaccus: *Argonautica* iv. 99 ff.; Hyginus: *Fabula* 17; Lactantius on Statius's *Thebaid* iii. 353.

6. Apollodorus: i. 9. 21; Hesiod: *Theogony* 265–9.

7. Herodotus: ii. 147; Apollodorus: *loc. cit.*; Apollonius Rhodius ii. 176 ff.; Valerius Flaccus: *Argonautica* iv. 22 ff.; Hyginus: *Fabula* 19; First Vatican Mythographer: 27; Servius on Virgil's *Aeneid* iii. 209.

8. Diodorus Siculus: iv. 44.

9. Apollodorus: *loc. cit.*

\*

1. In the legend of the Iolcans' easterly voyage to the Black Sea – though not in that of the Minyans' westerly voyage to Istria – Heracles may have led the expedition. The story of Hylas's disappearance was invented to explain the Mysian rites, still practised at Prusa, near Pegae, in Roman times, of mourning for Adonis of the Woods. Hylas's fate at the hands of Dryope and her nymphs will have been that of Leucippus (see 21. *6*), Actaeon (see 22. *i*), Orpheus (see 28. *d*), or any other sacred kings of the oak cult: namely, to be dismembered and eaten by wild women, who then purified themselves in a spring and announced that he had unaccountably vanished. 'Dryope' means 'woodpecker' (literally: 'oakface'), a bird whose tapping on the oak-trunk suggested the search for Hylas, a Dryopian by birth, and was held to portend wet weather (see 56. *1*); the main object of this sacrifice being to bring on the autumn rains. Heracles, as the new king, will have pretended to join in the search for his predecessor. Bormus, or Borimus, is possibly a variant of Brimos's son Brimus (see 24. *6*).

2. The story of Amycus may be derived from an icon which showed the funeral games celebrated after the old king had been flung over a cliff (see 96. *3* and *6*). Boxing, a Cretan sport, mentioned in the *Iliad* and *Odyssey*, seems to have been clean enough until the civic rivalry of the Olympic Games introduced professionalism. Roman amphitheatre pugilists used spiked gloves and knuckledusters, not the traditional rawhide thongs; Theocritus, in his expert account of the Polydeuces-Amycus fight, is lamenting the lost glories of the ring.

Harpies were originally personifications of the Cretan Death-goddess as a whirlwind (Homer: *Odyssey* i. 241 and xx. 66 and 77) but, in this context, appear to have been sacred birds, kites or sea-eagles, for which the Thracians regularly set out food. Diodorus Siculus, when describing the Argonauts' visit to Phineus's court, studiously avoids any mention of the Harpies – for fear perhaps of incurring their wrath – yet contrives to hint that blind Phineus's second wife, a Scythian, tricked him by pretending that Harpies were snatching away his food, and befouling what they left, whereas his own servants were doing this at her orders. Phineus was slowly starving to death when Calais and Zetes – the brothers of his first wife – detected her guilt and released their nephews from the prison into which she had persuaded Phineus to cast them.

3. The Strophades ('turning') islands were so called because ships could expect the wind to turn as they approached.

4. Logan-stones, enormous boulders so carefully balanced that they will rock from side to side at the least impulse, are funerary monuments, apparently set up by avenue-building emigrants from Libya, towards the end of the third millennium. A few are still working in Cornwall and Devon, others have been displaced by the concerted efforts of idle soldiers or tourists. The dedication of a Tenian logan-stone to Calais and Zetes, the winged sons of Boreas, suggests that spirits of heroes were invoked to rock the boulder in the form of winds, and thus crush a live victim laid underneath.

# 151

## FROM THE SYMPLEGADES TO COLCHIS

PHINEUS had warned the Argonauts of the terrifying rocks, called Symplegades, or Planctae, or Cyaneae which, perpetually shrouded in sea mist, guarded the entrance to the Bosphorus. When a ship attempted to pass between them, they drove together and crushed her; but, at

Phineus's advice, Euphemus let loose a dove or, some say, a heron, to fly ahead of the *Argo*. As soon as the rocks had nipped off her tail feathers, and recoiled again, the Argonauts rowed through with all speed, aided by Athene and by Orpheus's lyre, and lost only their stern ornament. Thereafter, in accordance with a prophecy, the rocks remained rooted, one on either side of the straits, and though the force of the current made the ship all but unmanageable, the Argonauts pulled at their oars until they bent like bows, and gained the Black Sea without disaster.[1]

*b*. Coasting along the southern shore, they presently touched at the islet of Thynias, where Apollo deigned to appear before them in a blaze of divine glory. Orpheus at once raised an altar and sacrificed a wild goat to him as Apollo of the Dawn. At his instance, the Argonauts now swore never to desert one another in time of danger, an oath commemorated in the Temple of Harmonia since built on this island.

*c*. Thence they sailed to the city of Mariandyne – famous for the near-by chasm up which Heracles dragged the dog Cerberus from the Underworld – and were warmly welcomed by King Lycus. News that his enemy, King Amycus, was dead had already reached Lycus by runner, and he gratefully offered the Argonauts his son Dascylus to guide them on their journey along the coast. The following day, as they were about to embark, Idmon the seer was attacked by a ferocious boar lurking in the reed-beds of the river Lycus, which gashed his thigh deeply with its great tusks. Idas sprang to Idmon's assistance and, when the boar charged again, impaled it on his spear; however, Idmon bled to death despite their care, and the Argonauts mourned him for three days. Then Tiphys sickened and died, and his comrades were plunged in grief as they raised a barrow over his ashes, beside the one that they had raised for Idmon. Great Ancaeus first, and after him Erginus, Nauplius and Euphemus, all offered to take Tiphys's place as navigator; but Ancaeus was chosen, and served them well.[2]

*d*. From Mariandyne they continued eastward under sail for many days, until they reached Sinope in Paphlagonia, a city named after the river Asopus's daughter, to whom Zeus, falling in love with her, had promised whatever gift she wished. Sinope craftily chose virginity, made her home here, and spent the remainder of her life in happy solitude. At Sinope, Jason found recruits to fill three of the vacant seats on his benches: namely the brothers Deileon, Autolycus, and Phlogius, of Tricca, who had accompanied Heracles on his expedition to the

Amazons but, being parted from him by accident, were now stranded in this outlandish region.

*e.* The *Argo* then sailed past the country of the Amazons; and that of the iron-working Chalybians, who neither till the soil, nor tend flocks, but live wholly on the gains of their forges; and the country of the Tibarenians, where it is the custom for husbands to groan, as if in child-bed, while their wives are in labour; and the country of the Moesy-noechians, who live in wooden castles, couple promiscuously, and carry immensely long spears and white shields in the shape of ivy-leaves.[3]

*f.* Near the islet of Ares, great flocks of birds flew over the *Argo*, dropping brazen plumes, one of which wounded Oileus in the shoulder. At this, the Argonauts, recalling Phineus's injunctions, donned their helmets and shouted at the top of their voices; half of them rowing, while the remainder protected them with shields, against which they clashed their swords. Phineus had also counselled them to land on the islet, and this they now did, driving away myriads of birds, until not one was left. That night they praised his wisdom, when a huge storm arose and four Aeolians clinging to a baulk of timber were cast ashore, close to their camp; these castaways proved to be Cytisorus, Argeus, Phrontis, and Melanion, sons of Phrixus by Chalciope, daughter to King Aeëtes of Colchis, and thus closely related to many of those present. They had been shipwrecked on a journey to Greece, where they were intending to claim the Orchomenan kingdom of their grand-father Athamas. Jason greeted them warmly, and all together offered sober sacrifices on a black stone in the temple of Ares, where its foun-dress, the Amazon Antiope, had once sacrificed horses. When Jason explained that his mission was to bring back the soul of Phrixus to Greece, and also recover the fleece of the golden ram on which he had ridden, Cytisorus and his brothers found themselves in a quandary: though owing devotion to their father's memory, they feared to offend their grandfather by demanding the fleece. However, what choice had they but to make common cause with these cousins who had saved their lives?[4]

*g.* The *Argo* then coasted past the island of Philyra, where Cronus once lay with Philyra, daughter of Oceanus, and was surprised by Rhea in the act; whereupon he had turned himself into a stallion, and gall-oped off, leaving Philyra to bear her child, half man, half horse – which proved to be Cheiron the learned Centaur. Loathing the monster she now had to suckle, Philyra prayed to become other than she was; and was metamorphosed into a linden-tree. But some say that this took place in Thessaly, or Thrace; not on the island of Philyra.[5]

*h.* Soon the Caucasus Range towered above the Argonauts, and they entered the mouth of the broad Phasis river, which waters Colchis. First pouring a libation of wine mixed with honey to the gods of the land, Jason concealed the *Argo* in a sheltered backwater, where he called a council of war.[6]

1. Apollonius Rhodius: ii. 329; *Argonautica Orphica* 688; Homer: *Odyssey* xii. 61; Herodotus: iv. 85; Pliny: *Natural History* vi. 32; Valerius Flaccus: iv. 561 ff.; Apollodorus: i. 9. 22.
2. Apollonius Rhodius: ii. 851–98; *Argonautica Orphica* 729 ff.; Tzetzes: *On Lycophron* 890; Valerius Flaccus: v. 13 ff.; Hyginus: *Fabulae* 14 and 18; Apollodorus: i. 9. 23.
3. Apollonius Rhodius: ii. 946–1028; Valerius Flaccus: v. 108; *Argonautica Orphica* 738–46; Xenophon: *Anabasis* v. 4. 1–32 and 5. 1–3.
4. Apollonius Rhodius: ii. 1030–1230.
5. Apollonius Rhodius: ii. 1231–41; Hyginus: *Fabula* 138; Philargurius on Virgil's *Georgics* iii. 93; Valerius Flaccus: v. 153; *Argonautica Orphica* 747.
6. Apollonius Rhodius: ii. 1030–1285; *Argonautica Orphica* 747–55; Valerius Flaccus: v. 153–83.

\*

1. The Clashing, Wandering, or Blue Rocks, shrouded in sea mist, seem to have been ice-floes from the Russian rivers adrift in the Black Sea; reports of these were combined with discouraging accounts of the Bosphorus, down which the current, swollen by the thawing of the great Russian rivers, often runs at five knots. Other Wandering Islands in the Baltic Sea seem to have been known to the amber-merchants (see 170. 4).

2. Cenotaphs later raised by Greek colonists to honour the heroes Idmon and Tiphys may account for the story of their deaths during the voyage. Idmon is said to have been killed by a boar, like Cretan Zeus, Ancaeus, and Adonis – all early sacred kings (see 18. 7). The name Idmon ('knowing') suggests that his was an oracular shrine and, indeed, Apollonius Rhodius describes him as a seer.

3. Mariandyne is named after Ma-ri-enna (Sumerian for 'high fruitful mother of heaven'), *alias* Myrine, Ay-mari, of Mariamne, a well-known goddess of the Eastern Mediterranean. *Chalybs* was the Greek for 'iron', and 'Chalybians' seems to have been another name for the Tibarenians, the first iron workers of antiquity. In *Genesis* x. 2, their land is called Tubal (*Tubal* = *Tibar*), and Tubal Cain stands for the Tibarenians who

had come down from Armenia into Canaan with the Hyksos hordes. Modified forms of the *couvade* practised by the Tibarenians survive in many parts of Europe. The customs of the Moesynoechians, described by Xenophon – whose *Anabasis* Apollonius Rhodius had studied – are remarkably similar to those of the Scottish Picts and the Irish Sidhe, tribes which came to Britain in the early Bronze Age from the Black Sea region.

4. Jason's encounter with the birds on the islet of Ares, now Puga Islet, near the Kessab river, suggests that the *Argo* arrived there at the beginning of May; she will have navigated the Bosphorus before the current grew too powerful to stem, and reached Puga at the time of the great spring migration of birds from the Sinai peninsula. It appears that a number of exhausted birds, having flown across the mountains of Asia Minor, on their way to the Volga, found their usual sanctuary of Puga islet overcrowded and alighted on the *Argo*, frightening the superstitious crew nearly out of their wits. According to Nicoll's *Birds of Egypt*, these migrants include 'kestrels, larks, harriers, ducks and waders', but since the islet was dedicated to Ares, they are credited by the mythographers with brazen feathers and hostile intentions. Heracles's expulsion of the Stymphalian birds to an island in the Eastern Black Sea is likely to have been deduced from the Argonauts' adventure, rather than contrariwise as is usually supposed.

5. Cheiron's fame as a doctor, scholar, and prophet won him the title Son of Philyra ('linden'); he is also called a descendant of Ixion (see 63. *d*). Linden flowers were much used in Classical times as a restorative, and still are; moreover, the bast, or inner bark, of the linden provided handy writing tablets, and when torn into strips was used in divination (Herodotus: iv. 67; Aelian: *Varia Historia* xiv. 12). But Philyra island will have derived its name from a clump of linden-trees which grew there, rather than from any historical ties with Thessaly or Thrace. None of these coastal islands is more than a hundred yards long.

6. Colchis is now known as Georgia, and the Phasis river as the Rion.


## 152

### THE SEIZURE OF THE FLEECE

In Olympus, Hera and Athene were anxiously debating how their favourite, Jason, might win the golden fleece. At last they decided to approach Aphrodite, who undertook that her naughty little son Eros would make Medea, King Aeëtes's daughter, conceive a sudden passion for him. Aphrodite found Eros rolling dice with Ganymedes, but cheating at every throw, and begged him to let fly one of his arrows at Medea's heart. The payment she offered was a golden ball enamelled with blue rings, formerly the infant Zeus's plaything; when tossed into the air, it left a track like a falling star. Eros eagerly accepted this bribe, and Aphrodite promised her fellow-goddesses to keep Medea's passion glowing by means of a novel charm: a live wryneck, spread-eagled to a firewheel.

*b.* Meanwhile, at the council of war held in the backwater, Jason proposed going with Phrixus's sons to the near-by city of Colchian Aea, where Aeëtes ruled, and demanding the fleece as a favour; only if this were denied would they resort to guile or force. All welcomed his suggestion, and Augeias, Aeëtes's half-brother, joined the party. They approached Aea by way of Circe's riverside cemetery, where male corpses wrapped in untanned ox-hides were exposed on the tops of willow-trees for birds to eat – the Colchians bury only female corpses. Aea shone splendidly down on them from a hill, sacred to Helius, Aeëtes's father, who stabled his white horses there. Hephaestus had built the royal palace in gratitude for Helius's rescue of him when overwhelmed by the Giants during their assault on Olympus.

*c.* King Aeëtes's first wife, the Caucasian nymph Asterodeia, mother of Chalciope, Phrixus's widow, and of Medea, Hecate's witch-priestess, was dead some years before this; and his second wife, Eidyia, had now borne him a son, Apsyrtus.

*d.* As Jason and his companions approached the palace, they were met first by Chalciope, who was surprised to see Cytisorus and her other three sons returning so soon and, when she heard their story, showered thanks on Jason for his rescue of them. Next came Aeëtes, accompanied by Eidyia and showing great displeasure – for Laomedon had undertaken to prevent all Greeks from entering the Black Sea – and asked Aegeus, his favourite grandson, to explain the intrusion. Aegeus replied that Jason, to whom he and his brothers owed their lives, had come to fetch away the golden fleece in accordance with an oracle. Seeing that Aeëtes's face wore a look of fury, he added at once: 'In return for which favour, these noble Greeks will gladly subject the Sauromatians to your Majesty's rule.' Aeëtes gave a contemptuous laugh, then ordered Jason – and Augeias, whom he would not deign to acknowledge as his brother – to return whence they came, before he had their tongues cut out and their hands lopped off.

*e.* At this point, the princess Medea emerged from the palace, and when Jason answered gently and courteously, Aeëtes, somewhat ashamed of himself, undertook to yield the fleece, though on what seemed impossible terms. Jason must yoke two fire-breathing brazen-footed bulls, creations of Hephaestus; plough the Field of Ares to the extent of four ploughgates; and then sow it with the serpent's teeth given him by Athene, a few left over from Cadmus's sowing at Thebes. Jason stood stupefied, wondering how to perform these unheard-of feats, but Eros aimed one of his arrows at Medea, and drove it into her heart, up to the feathers.

*f.* Chalciope, visiting Medea's bedroom that evening, to enlist her help on behalf of Cytisorus and his brothers, found that she had fallen head over heels in love with Jason. When Chalcipoe offered herself as a go-between, Medea eagerly undertook to help him yoke the fire-breathing bulls and win the fleece; making it her sole condition that she should sail back in the *Argo* as his wife.

*g.* Jason was summoned, and swore by all the gods of Olympus to keep faith with Medea for ever. She offered him a flask of lotion, blood-red juice of the two-stalked, saffron-coloured Caucasian crocus, which would protect him against the bulls' fiery breath; this potent flower first sprang from the blood of the tortured Prometheus. Jason gratefully accepted the flask and, after a libation of honey, unstoppered it and bathed his body, spear and shield in the contents. He was thus able to subdue the bulls and harness them to a plough with an adamantine yoke. All day he ploughed, and at nightfall sowed the teeth, from which armed men immediately sprouted. He provoked these to fight one against another, as Cadmus had done on a similar occasion, by throwing a stone quoit into their midst; then dispatched the wounded survivors.

*h.* King Aeëtes, however, had no intention of parting with the fleece, and shamelessly repudiated his bargain. He threatened to burn the *Argo*, which was now moored off Aea, and massacre her crew; but Medea, in whom he had unwisely confided, led Jason and a party of Argonauts to the precinct of Ares, some six miles away. There the fleece hung, guarded by a loathsome and immortal dragon of a thousand coils, larger than the *Argo* herself, and born from the blood of the monster Typhon, destroyed by Zeus. She soothed the hissing dragon with incantations and then, using freshly-cut sprigs of juniper, sprinkled soporific drops on his eyelids. Jason stealthily unfastened the fleece from the oak-tree, and together they hurried down to the beach where the *Argo* lay.

*i*. An alarm had already been raised by the priests of Ares, and in a running fight, the Colchians wounded Iphitus, Meleager, Argus, Atalanta, and Jason. Yet all of them contrived to scramble aboard the waiting *Argo*, which was rowed off in great haste, pursued by Aeëtes's galleys. Iphitus alone succumbed to his wounds; Medea soon healed the others with vulneraries of her own invention.[1]

*j*. Now, the Sauromatians whom Jason had undertaken to conquer were descendants of three shiploads of Amazons captured by Heracles during his Ninth Labour; they broke their fetters and killed the sailors set as guards over them, but knowing nothing of seamanship, drifted across to the Cimmerian Bosphorus, where they landed at Cremni in the country of the free Scythians. There they captured a herd of wild horses, mounted them and began to ravage the land. Presently the Scythians, discovering from some corpses which fell into their hands that the invaders were women, sent out a band of young men to offer the Amazons love rather than battle. This did not prove difficult, but the Amazons consented to marry them only if they would move to the eastern bank of the river Tanais; where their descendants, the Sauromatians, still live and preserve certain Amazon customs, such as that every girl must have killed a man in battle before she can find a husband.[2]

1. Apollodorus: i. 9. 23; Apollonius Rhodius: ii. 1260–iv. 246; Diodorus Siculus: iv. 48. 1–5; Valerius Flaccus: v. 177–viii. 139; Hyginus: *Fabula* 22; Pindar: *Pythian Odes* iv. 221 ff.; Ovid: *Metamorphoses* vii. 1. 138–9; Plutarch: *On Rivers* v. 4; *Argonautica Orphica* 755–1012.
2. Herodotus: iv. 110–17.

\*

1. This part of the legend embodies the primitive myth of the tasks imposed on Diomedes by the king whose daughter he wished to marry.

2. Aphrodite's love charm, carefully described by Theocritus (*Idylls* ii. 17), was used throughout Greece, including Socrates's circle (Xenophon: *Memorabilia* iii. 11. 17). Because the wryneck builds in willows, hisses like a snake and lays white eggs, it has always been sacred to the moon; Io ('moon') sent it as her messenger to amorous Zeus (see 56. *a*). One of its popular names in Europe is 'cuckoo's mate', and the cuckoo appears in the story of how Zeus courted the Moon-goddess Hera (see

12. *a*). Fire-kindling by friction was sympathetic magic to cause love – as the English word *punk* means both tinder and a harlot. Eros with torch and arrows is post-Homeric but, by the time of Apollonius Rhodius, his naughty behaviour and Aphrodite's despair had become a literary joke (see 18. *a*) which Apuleius took one stage further in *Cupid and Psyche*.

3. The Colchian custom of wrapping corpses in hides and exposing them on the tops of willow-trees recalls the Parsee custom of leaving them on platforms for the vultures to eat, in order not to defile the sacred principle of fire, the Sun's holy gift, by the act of cremation. Apollonius Rhodius mentions it, apparently to emphasize Pelias's concern for Phrixus's ghost: being a Greek, he could not consider it an adequate funeral rite. Aeëtes's fire-breathing bulls, again, recall those brazen ones in which prisoners were roasted alive by Phalaris of Agrigentum – a Rhodian colony – presumably in honour of their god Helius, whose symbol was a brazen bull (Pindar: *Pythian Odes* i. 185, with scholiast); but the sown men with whom Jason contended are inappropriate to the story. Though it was reasonable for Cadmus, a Canaanite stranger, to fight the Pelasgian autochthons when he invaded Boeotia (see 58. *g*), Jason as a native-born candidate for the kingship will rather have been set Kilhwych's task of ploughing, sowing, and reaping a harvest in one day (see 148. 5) – a ritual act easily mimed at midsummer – then wrestled with a bull and fought the customary mock battle against men in beast-disguise. His winning of the golden fleece is paralleled by Heracles's winning of the golden apples, which another unsleeping dragon guarded (see 133. *a*). At least four of Heracles's Labours seem to have been imposed on him as a candidate for the kingship (see 123. *1*; 124. *2*; 127. *1* and 129. *1*).

4. Jason and Heracles are, in fact, the same character so far as the marriage-task myth is concerned; and the First and Seventh Labours survive vestigially here in the killing of the Mariandynian Boar and the Cyzican Lion, with both of which Jason should have been credited. 'Jason' was, of course, a title of Heracles.

5. Medea's Colchian crocus is the poisonous *colchicum*, or meadow-saffron, used by the ancients as the most reliable specific against gout, as it still remains. Its dangerous reputation contributed to Medea's.

6. The Sauromatians were the mounted Scythian bowmen of the steppes (see 132. 6); no wonder Aeëtes laughed at the notion that Jason and his heavily armed infantry could subdue them.

## THE MURDER OF APSYRTUS

MANY different accounts survive of the *Argo*'s return to Thessaly, though it is generally agreed that, following Phineus's advice, the Argonauts sailed counter-sunwise around the Black Sea. Some say that when Aeëtes overtook them, near the mouth of the Danube, Medea killed her young half-brother Apsyrtus, whom she had brought aboard, and cut him into pieces, which she consigned one by one to the swift current. This cruel stratagem delayed the pursuit, because obliging Aeëtes to retrieve each piece in turn for subsequent burial at Tomi.[1] The true name of Medea's half-brother is said to have been Aegialeus; for 'Apsyrtus', meaning 'swept down', merely records what happened to his mangled limbs after he had died.[2] Others place the crime at Aea itself, and say that Jason also killed Aeëtes.[3]

b. The most circumstantial and coherent account, however, is that Apsyrtus, sent by Aeëtes in pursuit of Jason, trapped the *Argo* at the mouth of the Danube, where the Argonauts agreed to set Medea ashore on a near-by island sacred to Artemis, leaving her in charge of a priestess for a few days; meanwhile a king of the Brygians would judge the case and decide whether she was to return home or follow Jason to Greece, and in whose possession the fleece should remain. But Medea sent a private message to Apsyrtus, pretending that she had been forcibly abducted, and begging him to rescue her. That night, when he visited the island and thereby broke the truce, Jason followed, lay in wait and struck him down from behind. He then cut off Apsyrtus's extremities, and thrice licked up some of the fallen blood, which he spat out again each time, to prevent the ghost from pursuing him. As soon as Medea was once more aboard the *Argo*, the Argonauts attacked the leaderless Colchians, scattered their flotilla, and escaped.[4]

c. Some would have it that, after Apsyrtus's murder, the *Argo* turned back and sailed up the Phasis into the Caspian Sea, and thence into the Indian Ocean, regaining the Mediterranean by way of Lake Tritonis.[5] Others, that she sailed up the Danube and Save, and then down the Po, which joins the Save, into the Adriatic Sea;[6] but was pursued by storms and driven around the whole coast of Italy, until she reached Circe's island of Aeaea. Others again, that she sailed up the Danube, and then reached Circe's island by way of the Po and the eddying pools where it is joined by the mighty Rhône.[7]

*d.* Still others hold that the Argonauts rowed up the Don until they reached its source; then dragged the *Argo* to the headwaters of another river which runs north into the Gulf of Finland. Or that from the Danube they dragged her to the source of the river Elbe and, borne on its waters, reached Jutland. And that they then shaped a westerly course towards the Ocean, passing by Britain and Ireland, and reached Circe's island after sailing between the Pillars of Heracles and along the coasts of Spain and Gaul.[8]

*e.* These are not, however, feasible routes. The truth is that the *Argo* returned by the Bosphorus, the way she had come, and passed through the Hellespont in safety, because the Trojans could no longer oppose her passage. For Heracles, on his return from Mysia, had collected a fleet of six ships [supplied by the Dolionians and their Percotean allies] and, sailing up the river Scamander under cover of darkness, surprised and destroyed the Trojan fleet. He then battered his way into Troy with his club, and demanded from King Laomedon the man-eating mares of King Diomedes, which he had left in his charge some years previously. When Laomedon denied any knowledge of these, Heracles killed him and all his sons, except the infant Podarces, or Priam, whom he appointed king in his stead.[9]

*f.* Jason and Medea were no longer aboard the *Argo*. Her oracular beam had spoken once more, refusing to carry either of them until they had been purified of murder, and from the mouth of the Danbue they had set out overland for Aeaea, the island home of Medea's aunt Circe. This was not the Campanian Aeaea where Circe later went to live, but her former Istrian seat; and Medea led Jason there by the route down which the straw-wrapped gifts of the Hyperboreans are yearly brought to Delos. Circe, to whom they came as suppliants, grudgingly purified them with the blood of a young sow.[10]

*g.* Now, their Colchian pursuers had been warned not to come back without Medea and the fleece and, guessing that she had gone to Circe for purification, followed the *Argo* across the Aegean Sea, around the Peloponnese, and up the Illyrian coast, rightly concluding that Medea and Jason had arranged to be fetched from Aeaea.[11]

*h.* Some, however, say that Apsyrtus was still commanding the Colchian flotilla at this time, and that Medea trapped and murdered him in one of the Illyrian islands now called the Apsyrtides.[12]

1. Apollodorus: i. 9. 24; Pherecydes, quoted by scholiast on Apollonius Rhodius: iv. 223 and 228; Ovid: *Tristia* iii. 9; Stephanus of Byzantium *sub* Tomeus.
2. Cicero: *On the Nature of the Gods* iii. 19; Justin: xlii. 3; Diodorus Siculus: iv. 45.
3. Sophocles, quoted by scholiast on Apollonius Rhodius: iv. 228; Euripides: *Medea* 1334; Diodorus Siculus: iv. 48.
4. Apollonius Rhodius: iv. 212–502.
5. Pindar: *Pythian Odes* iv. 250 ff.; Mimnermus, quoted by Strabo: i. 2. 40.
6. Apollodorus: i. 9. 24; Diodorus Siculus: iv. 56. 7–8.
7. Apollonius Rhodius: iv. 608–560.
8. Timaeus, quoted by Diodorus Siculus: iv. 56. 3; *Argonautica Orphica* 1030–1204.
9. Diodorus Siculus: iv. 48; Homer: *Odyssey* xii. 69 ff. and *Iliad* v. 638 ff.
10. Apollodorus: *loc. cit.*; Herodotus: iv. 33; Apollonius Rhodius: iv. 659–717.
11. Hyginus: *Fabula* 23; Apollodorus: *loc. cit.*
12. Strabo: vii. 5. 5.

\*

*1.* The combination of the westerly with the easterly voyage passed muster until Greek geographical knowledge increased and it became impossible to reconcile the principal elements in the story: namely, the winning of the fleece from the Phasis, and the purification of Medea and Jason by Circe, who lived either in Istria or off the western coast of Italy. Yet, since no historian could afford to offend his public by rejecting the voyage as fabulous, the Argonauts were supposed, at first, to have returned from the Black Sea by way of the Danube, the Save, and the Adriatic; then, when explorers found that the Save does not enter the Adriatic, a junction was presumed between the Danube and the Po, down which the *Argo* could have sailed; and when, later, the Danube proved to be navigable only up to the Iron Gates, and not to join the Po, she was held to have passed up the Phasis into the Caspian Sea, and thus into the Indian Ocean (where another Colchis stretched along the Malabar coast – Ptolemy Hephaestionos: viii. 1. 10), and back by way of the 'Ocean Stream' and Lake Tritonis.

*2.* The feasibility of this third route, too, being presently denied, mythographers suggested that the *Argo* had sailed up the Don, presumed to have its source in the Gulf of Finland, from which she could circumnavigate Europe, and return to Greece through the Straits of Gibraltar. Or somehow to have reached the Elbe by way of the Danube and a long *portage*, then sailed down to its mouth and so home, coasting past Ireland

and Spain. Diodorus Siculus, who had the sense to see that the *Argo* could have returned only through the Bosphorus, as she came, discussed this problem most realistically, and made the illuminating point that the Ister (now the Danube) was often confused with the Istrus, a trifling stream which entered the Adriatic near Trieste. Indeed, even in the time of Augustus, the geographer Pomponius Mela could report (ii. 3. 13 and 4. 4) that the western branch of the Danube 'flows into the Adriatic with a turbulence and violence equal to that of the Po'. The seizure of the fleece, the Colchians' pursuit, and the death of Apsyrtus, will all have originally taken place in the northern Adriatic. Ovid preferred to believe that Apsyrtus had been murdered at the mouth of the Danube and buried at Tomi: because that was his own destined death-place.

3. Aeaea (see 170. *i–l* and 5) is said to have belonged to Chryses, father of Minyas, and great-grandfather of Phrixus; and *Chryses* means 'golden'. It may well have been his spirit, rather than that of Phrixus, which the Minyans were ordered to appease when they fetched the fleece. According to Strabo, Phrixus enjoyed a hero-shrine in Moschia on the Black Sea, 'where a ram is never sacrificed'; this will, however, have been a late foundation, prompted by the fame of the *Argo*'s voyage – thus the Romans also built temples to Greek heroes and heroines fictitiously introduced into their national history.

4. The name 'Apsyrtus', which commemorates the sweeping of his remains downstream, was perhaps a local title of Orpheus after his dismemberment by the Maenads (see 28. *d*).

5. Valerius Flaccus and Diodorus Siculus both record that Heracles sacked Troy on the outward, not the homeward, voyage; but this seems to be a mistake.

# 154

## THE *ARGO* RETURNS TO GREECE

ARRIVED at Corcyra, which was then named Drepane, the Colchians found the *Argo* beached opposite the islet of Macris; her crew were joyfully celebrating the successful outcome of their expedition. The Colchian leader now visited King Alcinous and Queen Arete, demanding on Aeëtes's behalf the surrender of Medea and the fleece. Arete, to whom Medea had appealed for protection, kept Alcinous awake that night by complaining of the ill-treatment to which fathers too often subject their errant daughters: for instance, of Nycteus's cruelty to

Antiope, and of Acrisius's to Danaë. 'Even now,' she said, 'that poor princess Metope languishes in an Epeirot dungeon, at the orders of her ogreish father, King Echetus! She has been blinded with brazen spikes, and set to grind iron barley-corns in a heavy quern: "When they are flour, I will restore your sight," he taunts the poor girl. Aeëtes is capable of treating this charming Medea with equal barbarity, if you give him the chance.'[1]

*b.* Arete finally prevailed upon Alcinous to tell her what judgement he would deliver next morning, namely: 'If Medea is still a virgin, she shall return to Colchis; if not, she is at liberty to stay with Jason.' Leaving him sound asleep, Arete sent her herald to warn Jason what he must expect; and he married Medea without delay in the Cave of Macris, the daughter of Aristaeus and sometime Dionysus's nurse. The Argonauts celebrated the wedding with a sumptuous banquet and spread the golden fleece over the bridal couch. Judgement was duly delivered in the morning, Jason claimed Medea as his wife, and the Colchians could neither implement Aeëtes's orders nor, for fear of his wrath, return home. Some therefore settled in Corcyra, and others occupied those Illyrian islands, not far from Circe's Aeaea, which are now called the Apsyrtides; and afterwards built the city of Pola on the Istrian mainland.[2]

*c.* When, a year or two later, Aeëtes heard of these happenings, he nearly died of rage and sent a herald to Greece demanding the person of Medea and requital for the injuries done him; but was informed that no requital had yet been made for Io's abduction by men of Aeëtes's race (though the truth was that she fled because a gadfly pursued her) and none should therefore be given for the voluntary departure of Medea.[3]

*d.* Jason now needed only to double Cape Malea, and return with the fleece to Iolcus. He cruised in safety past the Islands of the Sirens, where the ravishing strains of these bird-women were countered by the even lovelier strains of Orpheus's lyre. Butes alone sprang overboard in an attempt to swim ashore, but Aphrodite rescued him; she took him to Mount Eryx by way of Lilybaeum, and there made him her lover. Some say that the Sirens, who had already lost their wings as a result of an unsuccessful singing contest with the Muses, sponsored by Hera, committed suicide because of their failure to outcharm Orpheus; yet they were still on their island when Odysseus came by a generation later.[4]

*e.* The Argonauts then sailed in fine weather along the coast of

Eastern Sicily, where they watched the matchless white herds of Helius grazing on the shore, but refrained from stealing any of them.⁵ Suddenly they were struck by a frightful North Wind which, in nine days' time, drove them to the uttermost parts of Libya; there, an enormous wave swept the *Argo* over the perilous rocks which line the coast and retreated, leaving her high and dry a mile or more inland. A lifeless desert stretched as far as the eye could see, and the Argonauts had already prepared themselves for death, when the Triple-goddess Libya, clad in goat skins, appeared to Jason in a dream and gave him reassurance. At this, they took heart, and [setting the *Argo* on rollers] moved her by the force of their shoulders to the salt Lake Tritonis, which lay several miles off, a task that occupied twelve days. All would have died of thirst, but for a spring which Heracles, on his way to fetch the golden apples of the Hesperides, had recently caused to gush from the ground.⁶

*f.* Canthus was now killed by Caphaurus, a Garamantian shepherd whose flocks he was driving off, but his comrades avenged him.⁷ And hardly had the two corpses been buried than Mopsus trod upon a Libyan serpent which bit him in the heel; a thick mist spread over his eyes, his hair fell out, and he died in agony. The Argonauts, after giving him a hero's burial, once more began to despair, being unable to find any outlet to the Lake.⁸

*g.* Jason, however, before he embarked on this voyage, had consulted the Pythoness at Delphi who gave him two massive brazen tripods, with one of which Orpheus now advised him to propitiate the deities of the land. When he did so, the god Triton appeared and took up the tripod without so much as a word of thanks, but Euphemus barred his way and asked him politely: 'Pray, my lord, will you kindly direct us to the Mediterranean Sea?' For answer, Triton merely pointed towards the Tacapae river but, as an afterthought, handed him a clod of earth, which gave his descendants sovereignty over Libya to this day. Euphemus acknowledged the gift with the sacrifice of a sheep, and Triton consented to draw the *Argo* along by her keel, until once more she entered the Mediterranean Sea, predicting, as he went, that when the descendant of a certain Argonaut should seize and carry off the brazen tripod from his temple, a hundred Greek cities would rise around Lake Tritonis. The Libyan troglodytes, overhearing these words, at once hid the tripod in the sand; and the prophecy has not yet been fulfilled.⁹

*h.* Heading northward, the Argonauts reached Crete, where they were prevented from landing by Talos the bronze sentinel, a creation of Hephaestus, who pelted the *Argo* with rocks, as was his custom. Medea called sweetly to this monster, promising to make him immortal if he drank a certain magic potion; but it was a sleeping draught and, while he slept, she removed the bronze nail which stoppered the single vein running from his neck to his ankles. Out rushed the divine ichor, a colourless liquid serving him for blood, and he died. Some, however, say that, bewitched by Medea's eyes, Talos staggered about, grazed his heel against a rock, and bled to death. Others, that Poeas shot him in the heel with an arrow.[10]

*i.* On the following night, the *Argo* was caught in a storm from the south, but Jason invoked Apollo, who sent a flash of light, revealing to starboard the island of Anaphe, one of the Sporades, where Ancaeus managed to beach the ship. In gratitude, Jason raised an altar to Apollo; and Medea's twelve Phaeacian bond-maidens, given her by Queen Arete, laughed merrily when, for lack of a victim, he and his comrades poured water libations upon the burning brands of the sacrifice. The Argonauts taunted them in reply, and tussled amorously with them – a custom which survives to this day at the Autumn Festival of Anaphe.

*j.* Sailing to Aegina, they held a contest: as to who could first draw a pitcher of water and carry it back to the ship; a race still run by the Aeginetans. From Aegina it was a simple voyage to Iolcus, such as scores of ships make every year, and they made it in fair weather without danger.[11]

*k.* Some minstrels arrange these events in a different order: they say that the Argonauts repopulated Lemnos on the homeward journey, not as they were sailing for Colchis;[12] others, that their visit to Libya took place before the voyage to Aea began, when Jason went in the *Argo* to consult the Delphic Oracle and was driven off his course by a sudden storm.[13] Others again hold that they cruised down the western coast of Italy and named a harbour in the island of Elba, where they landed, 'Argous' after the *Argo*, and that when they scraped off their sweat on the beach, it turned into pebbles of variegated forms. Further, that they founded the temple of Argive Hera at Leucania; that, like Odysseus, they sailed between Scylla and Charybdis; and that Thetis with her Nereids guided them past the flame-spouting Planctae, or Wandering Rocks, which are now firmly anchored to the sea-bed.[14]

*l.* Still others maintain that Jason and his companions explored the country about Colchian Aea, advancing as far as Media; that one of

them, Armenus, a Thessalian from Lake Boebe, settled in Armenia,
and gave his name to the entire country. This view they justify by
pointing out that the heroic monuments in honour of Jason, which
Armenus erected at the Caspian Gates, are much revered by the barbarians; and that the Armenians still wear the ancient Thessalian dress.[15]

1. Apollonius Rhodius: iv. 1090–95; Homer: *Odyssey* xviii. 83 and
   xxi. 307, with scholiast.
2. Strabo: i. 2. 39 and vii. 5. 5; Apollonius Rhodius: iv. 511 –21;
   Hyginus: *Fabula* 23; Apollodorus: i. 9. 25; Callimachus, quoted
   by Strabo: i. 2. 39.
3. Herodotus: i. 1.
4. Pausanias: ix. 34. 2; Strabo: vi. 1. 1; *Argonautica Orphica* 1284;
   Homer: *Odyssey* xii. 1–200.
5. Apollonius Rhodius: iv. 922–79; *Argonautica Orphica* 1270–97;
   Hyginus: *Fabula* 14.
6. Apollonius Rhodius: iv. 1228–1460.
7. Hyginus: *loc. cit.*; Apollonius Rhodius: iv. 1461–95; Valerius
   Flaccus: vi. 317 and vii. 422.
8. Tzetzes: *On Lycophron* 881; Apollonius Rhodius: iv. 1518–36.
9. Pindar: *Pythian Odes* iv. 17–39 and 255–61; Apollonius Rhodius:
   iv. 1537–1628; Diodorus Siculus: iv. 56. 6; *Argonautica Orphica*
   1335–6; Herodotus: iv. 179.
10. Apollodorus: i. 9. 26; Apollonius Rhodius: iv. 1639–93; *Argo-
    nautica Orphica* 1337–40; Lucian: *On the Dance* 49; Sophocles,
    quoted by scholiast on Apollonius Rhodius: iv. 1638.
11. Apollonius Rhodius: iv. 1765–72; Apollodorus: *loc. cit.*; *Argo-
    nautica Orphica* 1344–8.
12. Pindar: *Pythian Odes* iv. 252.
13. Herodotus: iii. 127.
14. Strabo: v. 2. 6 and vi. 1. 1; Apollodorus: i. 9. 24; Apollonius
    Rhodius: iv. 922 ff.
15. Strabo: xi. 14. 12 and 13. 10.

*

1. The myth of Metope, given in full neither by Homer nor by
Apollonius Rhodius, recalls those of Arne (see 43. 2) and Antiope (see
76. *b*). She has, it seems, been deduced from an icon showing the Fate-
goddess seated in a tomb; her quern being the world-mill around which,
according to Varro's *Treatise on Rustic Affairs*, the celestial system turns,
and which appears both in the Norse *Edda*, worked by the giantesses
Fenja and Menja, and in *Judges*, worked by the blinded Tyrian Sun-hero
Samson. Demeter, goddess of corn-mills, was an underground deity.

2. Herodotus's account of Aeëtes's embassy to Greece makes little
sense, unless he held that the Argive princess Io did not flee to Colchis in

a fit of madness, disguised as a heifer, and eventually become deified by the Egyptians as Isis (see 56. *b*), but was taken in a raid by the Colchians (whom he describes as relics of Pharaoh Sesostris's army that invaded Asia) and sold into Egypt.

3. The three Sirens – Homer makes them only two – were singing daughters of Earth, who beguiled sailors to the meadows of their island, where the bones of former victims lay mouldering in heaps (*Odyssey* xii. 39 ff. and 184 ff.). They were pictured as bird-women, and have much in common with the Birds of Rhiannon in Welsh myth, who mourned for Bran and other heroes; Rhiannon was a mare-headed Demeter. Siren-land is best understood as the sepulchral island which receives the dead king's ghost, like Arthur's Avalon (see 31. *2*); the Sirens were both the priestesses who mourned for him, and the birds that haunted the island – servants of the Death-goddess. As such, they belonged to a pre-Olympian cult – which is why they are said to have been worsted in a contest with Zeus's daughters, the Muses. Their home is variously given as the Siren-usian Islands off Paestum; Capri; and 'close to Sicilian Cape Pelorus' (Strabo: i. 2. 12). Pairs of Sirens were still carved on tombs in the time of Euripides (*Helen* 167), and their name is usually derived from *seirazein*, 'to bind with a cord'; but if, as is more likely, it comes from the other *seirazein* which means 'to dry up', the two Sirens will have represented twin aspects of the goddess at midsummer when the Greek pastures dry up: Ante-vorta and Post-vorta – she who looks prophetically forward to the new king's reign and she who mourns the old (see 170. *7*). The mermaid type of Siren is post-Classical.

4. Helius's herd consisted of three hundred and fifty head, the gift of his mother, the Moon-goddess (see 42. *1* and 170. *10*). Several colonies from Corinth and Rhodes, where his sky-bull was worshipped, had been planted in Sicily. Odysseus knew Helius as 'Hyperion' (see 170. *u*).

5. Lake Tritonis, once an enormous inland sea that had overwhelmed the lands of the neolithic Atlantians, has been slowly shrinking ever since, and though still of respectable size in Classical times – the geographer Scylax reckoned it at some nine hundred square miles – is now reduced to a line of salt marshes (see 39. *6*). Neith, the skin-clad Triple-goddess of Libya, anticipated Athene with her aegis (see 8. *1*).

6. Mopsus, whose death by snake-bite in the heel was a common one (see 106. *g*; 117. *c* and 168. *e*) appears also in the myth of Derceto (see 89. *2*), the Philistine Dictynna. Another Mopsus, Teiresias's grandson, survived the Trojan War (see 169. *c*).

7. Caphaurus is an odd name for a Libyan – *caphaura* being the Arabic for 'camphor', which does not grow in Libya – but the mythographers had a poor sense of geography.

8. Talos the bronze man is a composite character: partly sky-bull,

partly sacred king with a vulnerable heel, partly a demonstration of the *cire-perdue* method of bronze casting (see 92. *8*).

9. The water-sacrifice at Anaphe recalls that offered by the Jews on the Day of Willows, the climax of their festival of Tabernacles, when water was brought up in solemn procession from the Pool of Siloam; the Aeginetan water-race will have been part of a similar ceremony. Tabernacles began as an autumn fertility feast and, according to the Talmud, the Pharisees found it difficult to curb the traditional 'lightheadedness' of the women.

10. 'Pebbles of variegated form', iron crystals, are still found on the shores of Elba.

11. Thetis guided the *Argo* through the Planctae at the entrance to the Straits of Messina, as Athene guided her through the Planctae at the entrance to the Bosphorus. Odysseus avoided them by choosing the passage between Scylla and Charybdis (see 170. *t*). The western Planctae are the volcanic Lipari Islands.

12. Armenia, meaning Ar-Minni, 'the high land of Minni' – Minni is summoned by Jeremiah (li. 27) to war against Babylon – has no historical connexion with Armenus of Lake Boebe. But *Minni* is apparently the Minyas whom Josephus mentions (*Antiquities* i. 1. 6) when describing Noah's Flood: and the name of the Thessalian Minyas, ancestor of the Minyans, offered a plausible link between Armenia and Thessaly.

# 155

## THE DEATH OF PELIAS

ONE autumn evening, the Argonauts regained the well-remembered beach of Pagasae, but found no one there to greet them. Indeed, it was rumoured in Thessaly that all were dead; Pelias had therefore been emboldened to kill Jason's parents, Aeson and Polymele, and an infant son, Promachus, born to them since the departure of the *Argo*. Aeson, however, asked permission to take his own life and, his plea being granted, drank bull's blood and thus expired; whereupon Polymele killed herself with a dagger or, some say, a rope, after cursing Pelias, who mercilessly dashed out Promachus's brains on the palace floor.[1]

*b*. Jason, hearing this doleful story from a solitary boatman, forbade him to spread the news of the *Argo*'s homecoming, and summoned a council of war. All his comrades were of the opinion that Pelias deserved death, but when Jason demanded an immediate assault on Iolcus, Acastus remarked that he could hardly be expected to oppose his father; and the others thought it wiser to disperse, each to his own home and there, if necessary, raise contingents for a war on Jason's behalf. Iolcus, indeed, seemed too strongly garrisoned to be stormed by a company so small as theirs.

*c.* Medea, however, spoke up and undertook to reduce the city singlehanded. She instructed the Argonauts to conceal their ship, and themselves, on some wooded and secluded beach within sight of Iolcus. When they saw a torch waved from the palace roof, this would mean that Pelias was dead, the gates open, and the city theirs for the taking.

*d.* During her visit to Anaphe, Medea had found a hollow image of Artemis and brought it aboard the *Argo*. She now dressed her twelve Phaeacian bond-maidens in strange disguises and led them, each in turn carrying the image, towards Iolcus. On reaching the city gates Medea, who had given herself the appearance of a wrinkled crone, ordered the sentinels to let her pass. She cried in a shrill voice that the goddess Artemis had come from the foggy land of the Hyperboreans, in a chariot drawn by flying serpents, to bring good fortune to Iolcus. The startled sentinels dared not disobey, and Medea with her bond-maidens, raging through the streets like maenads, roused the inhabitants to a religious frenzy.

*e.* Awakened from sleep, Pelias inquired in terror what the goddess required of him. Medea answered that Artemis was about to acknowledge his piety by rejuvenating him, and thus allowing him to beget heirs in place of the unfilial Acastus, who had lately died in a shipwreck off the Libyan coast. Pelias doubted this promise, until Medea, by removing the illusion of old age that she had cast about herself, turned young again before his very eyes. 'Such is the power of Artemis!' she cried. He then watched while she cut a bleary-eyed old ram into thirteen pieces and boiled them in a cauldron. Using Colchian spells, which he mistook for Hyperborean ones, and solemnly conjuring Artemis to assist her, Medea then pretended to rejuvenate the dead ram – for a frisky lamb was hidden, with other magical gear, inside the goddess's hollow image. Pelias, now wholly deceived, consented to lie on a couch, where Medea soon charmed him to sleep. She then commanded his daughters, Alcestis, Evadne, and Amphinome, to cut him up, just as they had seen her do with the ram, and boil the pieces in the same cauldron.

*f.* Alcestis piously refused to shed her father's blood in however good a cause; but Medea, by giving further proof of her magic powers, persuaded Evadne and Amphinome to wield their knives with resolution. When the deed was done, she led them up to the roof, each carrying a torch, and explained that they must invoke the Moon while the cauldron was coming to a boil. From their ambush, the Argonauts saw the distant gleam of torches and, welcoming the signal, rushed into Iolcus, where they met with no opposition.

*g.* Jason, however, fearing Acastus's vengeance, resigned the kingdom to him, neither did he dispute the sentence of banishment passed on him by the Iolcan Council: for he hoped to sit upon a richer throne elsewhere.[2]

*h.* Some deny that Aeson was forced to take his own life, and declare that, on the contrary, Medea, after first draining the effete blood from his body, restored his youth by a magic elixir, as she had also restored Macris and her sister-nymphs on Corcyra; and presented him, stalwart and vigorous, to Pelias at the palace gates. Having thus persuaded Pelias to undergo the same treatment, she deceived him by omitting the appropriate spells, so that he died miserably.[3]

*i.* At Pelias's funeral games, celebrated the following day, Euphemus won the two-horse chariot race; Polydeuces, the boxing contest; Meleager, the javelin throw; Peleus, the wrestling match; Zetes, the shorter foot race, and his brother Calais (or, some say, Iphiclus) the longer one; and Heracles, now returned from his visit to the Hesperides, the all-in fighting. But during the four-horse chariot race, which Heracles's charioteer Iolaus won, Glaucus, son of Sisyphus, was devoured by his horses which the goddess Aphrodite had maddened with hippomanes.[4]

*j.* As for Pelias's daughters: Alcestis married Admetus of Pherae, to whom she had long been affianced; Evadne and Amphinome were banished by Acastus to Mantinea in Arcadia where, after purification, they succeeded in making honourable marriages.[5]

1. Diodorus Siculus: iv. 50. 1; Apollodorus: i. 9. 16 and 27; Valerius Flaccus: i. 777 ff.
2. Apollodorus: i. 9. 27; Diodorus Siculus: iv. 51. 1–53. 1; Pausanias: viii. 11. 2; Plautus: *Pseudolus* iii. 868 ff.; Cicero: *On Old Age* xxiii. 83; Ovid: *Metamorphoses* vii. 297–349; Hyginus: *Fabula* 24.

3. *Hypothesis* to Euripides's *Medea*; Scholiast on Euripides's *Knights* 1321; Ovid: *Metamorphoses* vii. 251–94.
4. Pausanias: v. 17. 9; Hyginus: *Fabula* 278.
5. Diodorus Siculus: iv. 53. 2; Hyginus: *Fabula* 24; Pausanias: viii. 11. 2.

*

1. The Cretans and Mycenaeans used bull's blood, plentifully diluted with water, as a magic to fertilize crops and trees; only the priestess of Mother Earth could drink it pure without being poisoned (see 51. 4).

2. Classical mythographers find it hard to decide how far Medea was an illusionist or cheat, and how far her magic was genuine. Cauldrons of regeneration are common in Celtic myth (see 148. 5–6); hence Medea pretends to be a Hyperborean, that may mean a British, goddess. The underlying religious theory seems to have been that at midsummer the sacred king, wearing a black ram's mask, was slaughtered on a mountain top and his pieces stewed into a soup, for the priestesses to eat; his spirit would then pass into one of them, to be born again as a child in the next lambing season. Phrixus's avoidance of this fate had been the original cause of the Argonauts' expedition (see 70. 2 and 148. g).

3. Medea's serpent-drawn chariot – serpents are underworld creatures – had wings because she was both earth-goddess and moon-goddess. She appears in triad here as Persephone-Demeter-Hecate: the three daughters of Pelias dismembering their father. The theory that the Sun-king marries the Moon-queen, who then graciously invites him to mount her chariot (see 24. *m*), changed as the patriarchal system hardened: by Classical times, the serpent-chariot was Helius's undisputed property, and in the later myth of Medea and Theseus (see 154. *d*) he lent it to his grand-daughter Medea only because she stood in peril of death (see 156. *d*). The Indian Earth-goddess of the *Ramayana* also rides in a serpent-chariot.

4. Callimachus seems to credit the huntress Cyrene with winning the foot race at Pelias's funeral games (see 82. *a*).

# 156
## MEDEA AT EPHYRA

JASON first visited Boeotian Orchomenus, where he hung up the golden fleece in the temple of Laphystian Zeus; next, he beached the *Argo* on the Isthmus of Corinth, and there dedicated her to Poseidon.

*b*. Now, Medea was the only surviving child of Aeëtes, the rightful king of Corinth, who when he emigrated to Colchis had left behind as his regent a certain Bunus. The throne having fallen vacant, by the death without issue of the usurper Corinthus, son of Marathon (who styled himself 'Son of Zeus'), Medea claimed it, and the Corinthians accepted Jason as their king. But, after reigning for ten prosperous and happy years, he came to suspect that Medea had secured his succession by poisoning Corinthus; and proposed to divorce her in favour of Glauce the Theban, daughter of King Creon.

*c*. Medea, while not denying her crime, held Jason to the oath which he had sworn at Aea in the name of all the gods, and when he protested that a forced oath was invalid, pointed out that he also owed the throne of Corinth to her. He answered: 'True, but the Corinthians have learned to have more respect for me than for you.' Since he continued obdurate Medea, feigning submission, sent Glauce a wedding gift by the hands of the royal princes – for she had borne Jason seven sons and seven daughters – namely, a golden crown and a long white robe. No sooner had Glauce put them on, than unquenchable flames shot up, and consumed not only her – although she plunged headlong into the palace fountain – but King Creon, a crowd of other distinguished Theban guests, and everyone else assembled in the palace, except Jason; who escaped by leaping from an upper window.

*d*. At this point Zeus, greatly admiring Medea's spirit, fell in love with her, but she repulsed all his advances. Hera was grateful: 'I will make your children immortal,' said she, 'if you lay them on the sacrificial altar in my temple.' Medea did so; and then fled in a chariot drawn by winged serpents, a loan from her grandfather Helius, after bequeathing the kingdom to Sisyphus.[1]

*e*. The name of only one of Medea's daughters by Jason is remembered: Eriopis. Her eldest son, Medeius, or Polyxenus, who was being educated by Cheiron on Mount Pelion, afterwards ruled the country of Media; but Medeius's father is sometimes called Aegeus.[2] The other sons were Mermerus, Pheres, or Thessalus, Alcimedes, Tisander, and Argus; all of whom the Corinthians, enraged by the murder of Glauce and Creon, seized and stoned to death. For this crime they have ever since made expiation: seven girls and seven boys, wearing black garments and with their heads shaven, spend a whole year in the temple of Hera on the Heights, where the murder was committed.[3] By order of the Delphic Oracle, the dead children's corpses were buried in the

Temple, their souls, however, became immortal, as Hera had promised. There are those who charge Jason with condoning this murder, but explain that he was vexed beyond endurance by Medea's ambition on behalf of his children.[4]

f. Others again, misled by the dramatist Euripides, whom the Corinthians bribed with fifteen talents of silver to absolve them of guilt, pretend that Medea killed two of her own children;[5] and that the remainder perished in the palace which she had set on fire – except Thessalus, who escaped and later reigned over Iolcus, giving his name to all Thessaly; and Pheres, whose son Mermerus inherited Medea's skill as a poisoner.[6]

1. Eumelus: *Fragments* 2–4; Diodorus Siculus: iv. 54; Apollodorus: i. 9. 16; Ovid: *Metamorphoses* vii. 391–401; Ptolemy Hephaestionos ii.; Apuleius: *Golden Ass* i. 10; Tzetzes: *On Lycophron* 175; Euripides: *Medea*.

2. Hesiod: *Theogony* 981 ff.; Pausanias: ii. 3. 7 and iii. 3. 7; Hyginus: *Fabulae* 24 and 27.

3. Apollodorus: i. 9. 28; Pausanias: ii. 3. 6; Aelian: *Varia Historia* v. 21; Scholiast on Euripides's *Medea* 9 and 264; Philostratus: *Heroica* xx. 24.

4. Diodorus Siculus: v. 55; Scholiast on Euripides's *Medea* 1387.

5. Scholiast on Euripides: *loc. cit.*; Hyginus: *Fabula* 25; Euripides: *Medea* 1271; Servius on Virgil's *Eclogue* viii. 47.

6. Diodorus Siculus: iv. 54; Homer: *Odyssey* i. 260, with scholiast.

\*

1. The number of Medea's children recalls that of the Titans and Titanesses (see 1. 3 and 43. 4), but the fourteen boys and girls who were annually confined in Hera's Temple may have stood for the odd and even days of the first half of the sacred month.

2. Glauce's death was perhaps deduced from an icon showing the annual holocaust in the Temple of Hera, like that described by Lucian at Hierapolis (*On the Syrian Goddess* 49). But Glauce will have been the diademed priestess who directed the conflagration, not its victim; and the well, her ritual bath. Lucian explains that the Syrian goddess was, on the whole, Hera; though she also had some attributes of Athene and the other goddesses (*ibid.* 32). Here Eriopis ('large-eyed') points to cow-eyed Hera, and Glauce ('owl') to owl-eyed Athene. In Lucian's time, domestic animals were hung from the branches of trees piled in the temple court of Hierapolis, and burned alive; but the death of Medea's fourteen children, and the expiation made for them suggest that human victims were originally offered. Melicertes, the Cretan god who presided

over the Isthmian Games at Corinth (see 70. *h* and 96. *6*), was Melkarth, 'protector of the city', the Phoenician Heracles, in whose name children were certainly burned alive at Jerusalem (*Leviticus* xviii. 21 and xx. 2; 1 *Kings* xi. 7; 2 *Kings* xxiii. 10; *Jeremiah* xxxii. 35). Fire, being a sacred element, immortalized the victims, as it did Heracles himself when he ascended his pyre on Mount Oeta, lay down and was consumed (see 145. *f*).

3. Whether Medea, Jason, or the Corinthians sacrificed the children became an important question only later, when Medea had ceased to be identified with Ino, Melicertes's mother, and human sacrifice denoted barbarism. Since any drama which won a prize at the Athenian festival in honour of Dionysus at once acquired religious authority, it is very probable that the Corinthians recompensed Euripides well for his generous manipulation of the now discreditable myth.

4. Zeus's love for Medea, like Hera's for Jason (Homer: *Odyssey* xii. 72; Apollonius Rhodius: iii. 66), suggests that 'Zeus' and 'Hera' were titles of the Corinthian king and queen (see 43. *2* and 68. *1*). Corinthus, though the son of Marathon, was also styled 'son of Zeus', and Marathon's father Epopeus ('he who sees all') had the same wife as Zeus (Pausanias: ii. 1. 1; Asius: *Fragment* 1).

# 157

## MEDEA IN EXILE

MEDEA fled first to Heracles at Thebes, where he had promised to shelter her should Jason ever prove unfaithful, and cured him of the madness that had made him kill his children; nevertheless, the Thebans would not permit her to take up residence among them because Creon, whom she had murdered, was their King. So she went to Athens, and King Aegeus was glad to marry her. Next, banished from Athens for her attempted poisoning of Theseus, she sailed to Italy and taught the Marrubians the art of snake-charming; they still worship her as the goddess Angitia.[1] After a brief visit to Thessaly, where she unsuccessfully competed with Thetis in a beauty contest judged by Idomeneus the Cretan, she married an Asian king whose name has not survived but who is said to have been Medeius's true father.

b. Hearing, finally, that Aeëtes's Colchian throne had been usurped by her uncle Perses, Medea went to Colchis with Medeius, who killed

Perses, set Aeëtes on his throne again, and enlarged the kingdom of Colchis to include Media. Some pretend that she was by that time reconciled to Jason, and took him with her to Colchis; but the history of Medea has, of course, been embellished and distorted by the extravagant fancies of many tragic dramatists.[2] The truth is that Jason, having forfeited the favour of the gods, whose names he had taken in vain when he broke faith with Medea, wandered homeless from city to city, hated of men. In old age he came once more to Corinth, and sat down in the shadow of the *Argo*, remembering his past glories, and grieving for the disasters that had overwhelmed him. He was about to hang himself from the prow, when it suddenly toppled forward and killed him. Poseidon then placed the image of the *Argo*'s stern, which was innocent of homicide, among the stars.[3]

*c*. Medea never died, but became an immortal and reigned in the Elysian Fields where some say that she, rather than Helen, married Achilles.[4]

*d*. As for Athamas, whose failure to sacrifice Phrixus had been the cause of the Argonauts' expedition, he was on the point of being himself sacrificed at Orchomenus, as the sin-offering demanded by the Oracle of Laphystian Zeus, when his grandson Cytisorus returned from Aeaea and rescued him. This vexed Zeus, who decreed that, henceforth, the eldest son of the Athamantids must avoid the Council Hall in perpetuity, on pain of death; a decree which has been observed ever since.[5]

*e*. The homecomings of the Argonauts yield many tales; but that of Great Ancaeus, the helmsman, is the most instructive. Having survived so many hardships and perils, he returned to his palace at Tegea, where a seer had once warned him that he would never taste the wine of a vineyard which he had planted some years previously. On the day of his arrival, Ancaeus was informed that his steward had harvested the first grapes, and that the wine awaited him. He therefore filled a wine-cup, set it to his lips and, calling the seer, reproached him for prophesying falsely. The seer answered: 'Sire, there is many a slip 'twixt the cup and the lip!', and at that instant Ancaeus's servants ran up, shouting: 'My lord, a wild boar! It is ravaging your vineyard!' He set down the untasted cup, grasped his boar-spear, and hurried out; but the boar lay concealed behind a bush and, charging, killed him.[6]

1. Diodorus Siculus: iv. 54; Apollodorus: i. 9. 28; Plutarch: *Theseus* 12; Servius on Virgil's *Aeneid* vii. 750.

2. Ptolemy Hephaestionos: v.; Diodorus Siculus: iv. 55–66. 2; Hyginus: *Fabula* 26; Justin: xlii. 2; Tacitus: *Annals* vi. 34.
3. Diodorus Siculus: iv. 55; Scholiast on the *Hypothesis* of Euripides's *Medea*; Hyginus: *Poetic Astronomy* xxxvi.
4. Scholiast on Euripides's *Medea* 10; and on Apollonius Rhodius: iv. 814.
5. Herodotus: vii. 197.
6. Scholiast on Apollonius Rhodius: i. 185.

\*

1. An Attic cult of Demeter as Earth-goddess has given rise to the story of Medea's stay at Athens (see 97. *b*). Similar cults account for her visits to Thebes, Thessaly, and Asia Minor; but the Marrubians may have emigrated to Italy from Libya, where the Psyllians were adept in the art of snake-charming (Pliny: *Natural History* vii. 2). Medea's reign in the Elysian fields is understandable: as the goddess who presided over the cauldron of regeneration, she could offer heroes the chance of another life on earth (see 31. *c*). Helen ('moon') will have been one of her titles (see 159. 1).

2. In the heroic age, it seems, the king of Orchomenus, when his reign ended, was led for sacrifice to the top of Mount Laphystium. This king was also a priest of Laphystian Zeus, an office hereditary in the matrilinear Minyan clan; and at the time of the Persian Wars, according to Herodotus, the clan chief was still expected to attend the Council Hall when summoned for sacrifice. No one, however, forced him to obey this summons, and he seems from Herodotus's account to have been represented by a surrogate except on occasions of national disaster, such as a plague or drought, when he would feel obliged to attend in person.

The deaths of Jason and Ancaeus are moral tales, emphasizing the dangers of excessive fame, prosperity, or pride. But Ancaeus dies royally in his own city, from the gash of a boar's tusk (see 18. 7); whereas Jason, like Bellerophon (see 75. *f*) and Oedipus (see 105. *k*), wanders from city to city, hated of men, and is eventually killed by accident. In the Isthmus where Jason had reigned, the custom was for the royal *pharmacos* to be thrown over the cliff, but rescued from the sea by a waiting boat and banished to the life of an anonymous beggar, taking his ill-luck with him (see 89. 6 and 98. 7).

3. Sir Isaac Newton was the first, so far as I know, to point out the connexion between the Zodiac and the *Argo*'s voyage; and the legend may well have been influenced at Alexandria by the Zodiacal Signs: the Ram of Phrixus, the Bulls of Aeëtes, the Dioscuri as the Heavenly Twins, Rhea's Lion, the Scales of Alcinous, the Water-carriers of Aegina, Heracles as Bowman, Medea as Virgin, and the Goat, symbol of

lechery, to record the love-making on Lemnos. When the Egyptian
Zodiacal Signs are used, the missing elements appear: Serpent for
Scorpion; and Scarab, symbol of regeneration, for Crab.

# 158

## THE FOUNDATION OF TROY

ONE story told about the foundation of Troy is that, in time of famine,
a third of the Cretan people, commanded by Prince Scamander, set out
to found a colony. On reaching Phrygia, they pitched their camp
beside the sea, not far from the city of Hamaxitus,[1] below a high
mountain which they named Ida in honour of Zeus's Cretan home.
Now, Apollo had advised them to settle wherever they should be
attacked by earth-born enemies under cover of darkness; and that same
night a horde of famished field mice invaded the tents and nibbled at
bow-strings, leather shield-straps, and all other edible parts of the
Cretans' war-gear. Scamander accordingly called a halt, dedicated a
temple to Sminthian Apollo (around which the city of Sminthium
soon grew) and married the nymph Idaea, who bore him a son, Teucer.
With Apollo's help, the Cretans defeated their new neighbours, the
Bebrycians, but in the course of the fighting Scamander had leaped into
the river Xanthus, which thereupon took his name. Teucer, after whom
the settlers were called Teucrians, succeeded him. Yet some say that
Teucer himself led the Cretan immigrants, and was welcomed to
Phrygia by Dardanus, who gave him his daughter in marriage and
called his own subjects Teucrians.[2]

*b*. The Athenians tell a wholly different story. They deny that the
Teucrians came from Crete, and record that a certain Teucer, belong-
ing to the deme of Troes, emigrated from Athens to Phrygia; and that
Dardanus, Zeus's son by the Pleiad Electra, and a native of Arcadian
Pheneus, was welcomed to Phrygia by this Teucer, not contrariwise.
In support of this tradition it is urged that Erichthonius appears in the
genealogy both of the Athenian and the Teucrian royal houses.[3] Dar-
danus, the Athenians go on to say, married Chryse, the daughter of
Pallas, who bore him two sons, Idaeus and Deimas. These reigned for
a while over the Arcadian kingdom founded by Atlas, but were parted

by the calamities of the Deucalionian Flood. Deimas remained in Arcadia, but Idaeus went with his father Dardanus to Samothrace, which they colonized together, the island being thereafter called Dardania. Chryse had brought Dardanus as her dowry the sacred images of the Great Deities whose priestess she was, and he now introduced their cult into Samothrace, though keeping their true names a secret. Dardanus also founded a college of Salian priests to perform the necessary rites; which were the same as those performed by the Cretan Curetes.[4]

c. Grief at the death of his brother Iasion drove Dardanus across the sea to the Troad. He arrived alone, paddling a raft made of an inflated skin which he had ballasted with four stones. Teucer received him hospitably and, on condition that he helped to subdue certain neighbouring tribes, gave him a share of the kingdom and married him to the princess Bateia. Some say that this Bateia was Teucer's aunt; others, that she was his daughter.[5]

d. Dardanus proposed to found a city on the small hill of Ate, which rises from the plain where Troy, or Ilium, now stands; but when an oracle of Phrygian Apollo warned him that misfortune would always attend its inhabitants, he chose a site on the lower slopes of Mount Ida, and named his city Dardania.[6] After Teucer's death, Dardanus succeeded to the remainder of the kingdom, giving it his own name, and extended his rule over many Asiatic nations; he also sent out colonies to Thrace and beyond.[7]

e. Meanwhile, Dardanus's youngest son Idaeus had followed him to the Troad, bringing the sacred images; which enabled Dardanus to teach his people the Samothracian Mysteries. An oracle then assured him that the city which he was about to found would remain invincible only so long as his wife's dowry continued under Athene's protection.[8] His tomb is still shown in that part of Troy which was called Dardania before it merged with the villages of Ilium and Tros into a single city. Idaeus settled on the Idaean Mountains which, some say, are called after him; and there instituted the worship and Mysteries of the Phrygian Mother of the Gods.[9]

f. According to the Latin tradition, Iasion's father was the Tyrrhenian prince Corythus; and his twin, Dardanus, the son of Zeus by Corythus's wife Electra. Both emigrated from Etruria, after dividing these sacred images between them: Iasion went to Samothrace, and Dardanus to the Troad. While battling with the Bebrycians, who tried to throw the Tyrrhenians back into the sea, Dardanus lost his helmet and, although his troops were in retreat, led them back to recover it. This time he was victorious, and founded a city named Corythus on the battle-field: as much in memory of his helmet (*corys*), as of his father.[10]

*g*. Idaeus had two elder brothers, Erichthonius and Ilus, or Zacyn-thus; and a daughter, Idaea, who became Phineus's second wife. When Erichthonius succeeded to the kingdom of Dardanus, he married Asty-oche, the daughter of Simoeis, who bore him Tros.[11] Erichthonius, described also as a king of Crete, was the most prosperous of men, owner of the three thousand mares with which Boreas fell in love. Tros succeeded his father Erichthonius, and not only Troy but the whole Troad took his name. By his wife Callirrhoë, a daughter of Scamander, he became the father of Cleopatra the Younger, Ilus the Younger, Assaracus, and Ganymedes.[12]

*h*. Meanwhile, Ilus the brother of Erichthonius had gone to Phrygia where, entering for the games which he found in progress, he was vic-torious in the wrestling match and won fifty youths and fifty maidens as his prize. The Phrygian king (whose name is now forgotten) also gave him a dappled cow, and advised him to found a city wherever she should first lie down. Ilus followed her; she lay down on reaching the hill of Ate; and there he built the city of Ilium though, because of the warning oracle delivered to his father Dardanus, he raised no fortifica-tions. Some, however, say that it was one of Ilus's own Mysian cows which he followed, and that his instructions came from Apollo. But others hold that Ilium was founded by Locrian immigrants, and that they gave the name of their mountain Phriconis to the Trojan moun-tain of Cyme.[13]

*i*. When the circuit of the city boundaries had been marked out, Ilus prayed to Almighty Zeus for a sign, and next morning noticed a wooden object lying in front of his tent, half buried in the earth, and overgrown with weeds. This was the Palladium, a legless image three cubits high, made by Athene in memory of her dead Libyan playmate Pallas. Pallas, whose name Athene added to her own, held a spear aloft in the right hand, and a distaff and spindle in the left; around her breast was wrapped the aegis. Athene had first set up the image on Olympus, beside Zeus's throne, where it received great honour; but, when Ilus's great-grandmother, the Pleiad Electra, was violated by Zeus and de-filed it with her touch, Athene angrily cast her, with the image, down to earth.[14]

*j*. Apollo Smintheus now advised Ilus: 'Preserve the Goddess who fell from the skies, and you will preserve your city: for wherever she goes, she carries empire!' Accordingly he raised a temple on the citadel to house the image.[15]

*k*. Some say that the temple was already rising when the image descended from heaven as the goddess's gift. It dropped through a part of the roof which had not yet been completed, and was found standing exactly in its proper place.[16] Others say that Electra gave the Palladium to Dardanus, her son by Zeus, and that it was carried from Dardania to Ilium after his death.[17] Others, again, say that it fell from heaven at Athens, and that the Athenian Teucer brought it to the Troad. Still others believe that there were two Palladia, an Athenian and a Trojan, the latter carved from the bones of Pelops, just as the image of Zeus at Olympia was carved from Indian ivory; or, that there were many Palladia, all similarly cast from heaven, including the Samothracian images brought to the Troad by Idaeus.[18] The College of Vestals at Rome now guard what is reputed to be the genuine Palladium. No man may look at it with impunity. Once, while it was still in Trojan hands, Ilus rushed to its rescue at an alarm of fire, and was blinded for his pains; later, however, he contrived to placate Athene and regained his sight.[19]

*l*. Eurydice, daughter of Adrastus, bore to Ilus Laomedon, and Themiste who married the Phrygian Capys and, some say, became the mother of Anchises.[20] By Strymo, a daughter of Scamander and Leucippe, or Zeuxippe, or Thoösa, Laomedon had five sons: namely, Tithonus, Lampus, Clytius, Hicetaon, and Podarces; as well as three daughters: Hesione, Cilla, and Astyoche. He also begot bastard twins on the nymph-shepherdess Calybe. It was he who decided to build the famous walls of Troy and was lucky enough to secure the services of the gods Apollo and Poseidon, then under Zeus's displeasure for a revolt they made against him and forced to serve as day-labourers. Poseidon did the building, while Apollo played the lyre and fed Laomedon's flocks; and Aeacus the Lelegian lent Poseidon a hand. But Laomedon cheated the gods of their pay and earned their bitter resentment. This was the reason why he and all his sons – except Podarces, now renamed Priam – perished in Heracles's sack of Troy.[21]

*m*. Priam, to whom Heracles generously awarded the Trojan throne, surmised that the calamity which had befallen Troy was due to its luckless site, rather than to the anger of the gods. He therefore sent one of his nephews to ask the Pythoness at Delphi whether a curse still lay on the hill of Ate. But the priest of Apollo, Panthous the son of Othrias, was so beautiful that Priam's nephew, forgetting his commission, fell in love with him and carried him back to Troy. Though vexed, Priam had not the heart to punish his nephew. In compensation for the injury done he appointed Panthous priest of Apollo and, ashamed to consult the Pythoness again, rebuilt Troy on the same foundations. Priam's first wife was Arisbe, a daughter of Merops, the seer. When she had borne him Aesacus, he married her to Hyrtacus, by whom she became the mother of the Hyrtacides: Asius and Nisus.[22]

*n.* This Aesacus, who learned the art of interpreting dreams from his grandfather Merops, is famous for the great love he showed Asterope, a daughter of the river Cebren: when she died, he tried repeatedly to kill himself by leaping from a sea-cliff until, at last, the gods took pity on his plight. They turned Aesacus into a diving bird, thus allowing him to indulge his obsession with greater decency.[23]

*o.* Hecabe, Priam's second wife – whom the Latins call Hecuba – was a daughter of Dymas and the nymph Eunoë; or, some say, of Cisseus and Telecleia; or of the river Sangarius and Metope; or of Glaucippe, the daughter of Xanthus.[24] She bore Priam nineteen of his fifty sons, the remainder being the children of concubines; all fifty occupied adjacent bed-chambers of polished stone. Priam's twelve daughters slept with their husbands on the farther side of the same courtyard.[25] Hecabe's eldest son was Hector, whom some call the son of Apollo; next, she bore Paris; then Creusa, Laodice, and Polyxena; then Deiphobus, Helenus, Cassandra, Pammon, Polites, Antiphus, Hipponous, and Polydorus. But Troilus was certainly begotten on her by Apollo.[26]

*p.* Among Hecabe's younger children were the twins Cassandra and Helenus. At their birthday feast, celebrated in the sanctuary of Thymbraean Apollo, they grew tired of play and fell asleep in a corner, while their forgetful parents, who had drunk too much wine, staggered home without them. When Hecabe returned to the temple, she found the sacred serpents licking the children's ears, and screamed for terror. The serpents at once disappeared into a pile of laurel boughs, but from that hour both Cassandra and Helenus possessed the gift of prophecy.[27]

*q.* Another account of the matter is that one day Cassandra fell asleep in the temple, Apollo appeared and promised to teach her the art of prophecy if she would lie with him. Cassandra, after accepting his gift, went back on the bargain; but Apollo begged her to give him one kiss and, as she did so, spat into her mouth, thus ensuring that none would ever believe what she prophesied.[28]

r. When, after several years of prudent government, Priam had restored Troy to its former wealth and power, he summoned a Council to discuss the case of his sister Hesione, whom Telamon the Aeacid had taken away to Greece. Though he himself was in favour of force, the Council recommended that persuasion should first be tried. His brother-in-law Antenor and his cousin Anchises therefore went to Greece and delivered the Trojan demands to the assembled Greeks at Telamon's court; but were scornfully sent about their business. This incident was a main cause of the Trojan War,[29] the gloomy end of which Cassandra was now already predicting. To avoid scandal, Priam locked her up in a pyramidal building on the citadel; the wardress who cared for her had orders to keep him informed of all her prophetic utterances.[30]

1. Strabo: xiii. 1. 48.
2. Servius on Virgil's *Aeneid* iii. 108; Strabo: *loc. cit.*; Tzetzes: *On Lycophron* 1302.
3. Apollodorus: iii. 12. 1; Servius on Virgil's *Aeneid* iii. 167; Strabo: *loc. cit.*
4. Dionysius of Halicarnassus: *Roman Antiquities* i. 61 and ii. 70–1; Eustathius on Homer's *Iliad* p. 1204; Conon: *Narrations* 21; Servius on Virgil's *Aeneid* viii. 285.
5. Apollodorus: iii. 12. 1; Lycophron: 72 ff, with Tzetzes's comments; Scholiast on Homer's *Iliad* xx. 215; Servius on Virgil's *Aeneid* iii. 167; Tzetzes: *On Lycophron* 29.
6. Tzetzes: *loc. cit.*; Diodorus Siculus: v. 48; Strabo: *Fragment* 50; Homer: *Iliad* xx. 215 ff.
7. Apollodorus: *loc. cit.*; Servius: *loc. cit.*; Diodorus Siculus: *loc. cit.*
8. Strabo: *loc. cit.*; Dionysius of Halicarnassus: i. 61; Eustathius on Homer's *Iliad* p. 1204; Conon: *Narrations* 21; Servius on Virgil's *Aeneid* ii. 166.
9. Tzetzes: *On Lycophron* 72; Dionysius of Halicarnassus: *loc. cit.*
10. Servius: *loc. cit.*; vii. 207 and iii. 15.
11. Apollodorus: iii. 12 2 and iii. 15. 3; Dionysius of Halicarnassus: i. 50. 3.
12. Homer: *Iliad* xx. 220 ff.; Dionysius of Halicarnassus: i. 62; Apollodorus: iii. 12. 2.
13. Apollodorus: iii. 12. 3; Tzetzes: *On Lycophron* 29: Lesses of Lampsacus, quoted by Tzetzes: *loc. cit.*; Pindar: *Olympian Odes* viii. 30 ff., with scholiast; Strabo: xiii. 1. 3 and 3. 3.
14. Ovid: *Fasti* vi. 420 ff.; Apollodorus: *loc. cit.*

15. Ovid: *loc cit.*; Apollodorus: *loc. cit.*
16. Dictys Cretensis: v. 5.
17. Scholiast on Euripides's *Phoenician Women* 1136; Dionysius of Halicarnassus: i. 61; Servius on Virgil's *Aeneid* ii. 166.
18. Clement of Alexandria: *Protrepticon* iv. 47; Servius: *loc. cit.*; Pherecydes, quoted by Tzetzes: *On Lycophron* 355; *Etymologicum Magnum*: *sub* Palladium pp. 649–50.
19. Dercyllus: *Foundations of Cities* i, quoted by Plutarch: *Parallel Stories* 17.
20. Apollodorus: iii. 12. 2 and 3.
21. Apollodorus: ii. 59; ii. 6. 4 and iii. 12. 3; Scholiast on Homer's *Iliad* iii. 250; Homer: *Iliad* vi. 23–6; xxi. 446 and vii. 542; Horace: *Odes* iii. 3. 21; Pindar: *Olympic Odes* viii. 41, with scholiast; Diodorus Siculus: iv. 32.
22. Servius on Virgil's *Aeneid* ii. 319; Apollodorus: iii. 12. 5; Homer: *Iliad* ii. 831 and 837; Virgil: *Aeneid* ix. 176–7.
23. Servius on Virgil's *Aeneid* v. 128; Apollodorus: *loc. cit.*; Ovid: *Metamorphoses* xi. 755–95.
24. Perecydes, quoted by scholiast on Homer's *Iliad* xvi. 718; and on Euripides's *Hecabe* 32; Athenion, quoted by scholiast on Homer: *loc. cit.*; Apollodorus: *loc. cit.*
25. Homer: *Iliad* xxiv. 495–7 and vi. 242–50.
26. Stesichorus, quoted by Tzetzes: *On Lycophron* 266; Apollodorus: *loc. cit.*
27. Anticlides, quoted by scholiast on Homer's *Iliad* vii. 44.
28. Hyginus: *Fabula* 93; Apollodorus: iii. 12. 5; Servius on Virgil's *Aeneid* ii. 247.
29. Benoit: *Roman de Troie* 385 and 3187 ff.; *The Seege or Batayle of Troye* 349 ff. and 385; Tzetzes: *On Lycophron* 340; Dares: 5; Servius on Virgil's *Aeneid* iii. 80.
30. Aeschylus: *Agamemnon* 1210; Tzetzes: *Hypothesis of Lycophron's Alexandra*; *On Lycophron* 29 and 350.

\*

*1.* The situation of Troy on a well-watered plain at the entrance to the Hellespont, though establishing it as the main centre of Bronze Age trade between East and West, provoked frequent attacks from all quarters. Greek, Cretan, and Phrygian claims to have founded the city were not irreconcilable, since by Classical times it had been destroyed and rebuilt often enough: there were ten Troys in all, the seventh being the Homeric city. The Troy with which Homer is concerned seems to have been peopled by a federation of three tribes – Trojans, Ilians, and Dardanians – a usual arrangement in the Bronze Age.

*2.* 'Sminthian Apollo' points to Crete, *Sminthos* being the Cretan word for 'mouse', a sacred animal not only at Cnossus (see 90. *3*), but in

Philistia (1 *Samuel* vi. 4) and Phocis (Pausanias: x. 12. 5); and Erichthonius, the fertilizing North Wind, was worshipped alike by the Pelasgians of Athens and the Thracians (see 48. 3). But the Athenian claim to
have founded Troy may be dismissed as political propaganda. The white
mice kept in Apollo's temples were prophylactic both against plague and
against sudden invasions of mice such as Aelian (*History of Animals* xii. 5.
and 41) and Aristotle (*History of Animals* vi. 370) mention. Dardanus
may have been a Tyrrhenian from Lydia (see 136. g) or Samothrace; but
Servius errs in recording that he came from Etruria, where the Tyrrhenians settled long after the Trojan War. 'Zacinthus', a Cretan word,
figuring in the Trojan royal pedigree, was the name of an island belonging
to Odysseus's kingdom; and this suggests that he claimed hereditary
rights at Troy.

3. The Palladium, which the Vestal Virgins guarded at Rome, as the
luck of the city, held immense importance for Italian mythographers;
they claimed that it had been rescued from Troy by Aeneas (Pausanias:
ii. 23. 5) and brought to Italy. It was perhaps made of porpoise-ivory
(see 108. 5). 'Palladium' means a stone or other cult-object around which
the girls of a particular clan danced, as at Thespiae (see 120. a), or young
men leaped, *pallas* being used indiscriminately for both sexes. The Roman
College of Salii was a society of leaping priests. When such cult-objects
became identified with tribal prosperity and were carefully guarded
against theft or mutilation, *palladia* was read as meaning *palta*, 'or things
hurled from heaven'. *Palta* might not be hidden from the sky; thus the
sacred thunder-stone of Terminus at Rome stood under a hole in the roof
of Juppiter's temple – which accounts for the similar opening at Troy.

4. Worship of meteorites was easily extended to ancient monoliths,
the funerary origin of which had been forgotten; then from monolith to
stone image, and from stone image to wooden or ivory image is a short
step. But the falling of a shield from heaven – Mars's *ancile* (Ovid: *Fasti*
iii. 259–73) is the best-known instance – needs more explanation. At
first, meteorites, as the only genuine *palta*, were taken to be the origin of
lightning, which splits forest trees. Next, neolithic stone axes, such as the
one recently found in the Mycenaean sanctuary of Asine, and early
Bronze Age celts or pestles, such as Cybele's pestle at Ephesus (*Acts* xix.
35), were mistaken for thunderbolts. But the shield was also a thunder
instrument. Pre-Hellenic rain-makers summoned storms by whirling
bull-roarers to imitate the sound of rising wind and, for thunder, beat on
huge, tightly-stretched ox-hide shields, with double-headed drum-sticks
like those carried by the Salian priests in the Anagni relief. The only way
to keep a bull-roarer sounding continuously is to whirl it in a figure-of-
eight, as boys do with toy windmills, and since torches, used to imitate
lightning, were, it seems, whirled in the same pattern, the rain-making

shield was cut to form a figure-of-eight, and the double drum-stick beat
continuously on both sides. This is why surviving Cretan icons show the
Thunder-spirit descending as a figure-of-eight shield; and why therefore
ancient shields were eventually worshipped as *palta*. A painted limestone
tablet from the Acropolis at Mycenae proves, by the colour of the flesh,
that the Thunder-spirit was a goddess, rather than a god; on a gold ring
found near by, the sex of the descending shield is not indicated.

5. Cassandra and the serpents recall the myth of Melampus (see 122. *c*),
and Apollo's spitting into her mouth that of Glaucus (see 90. *f*). Her
prison was probably a bee-hive tomb from which she uttered prophecies
in the name of the hero who lay buried there (see 43. *2* and 154. *1*).

6. Aesacus, the name of Priam's prophetic son, meant the myrtle-
branch which was passed around at Greek banquets as a challenge to sing
or compose. Myrtle being a death-tree (see 101. *1* and 109. *4*), such poems
may originally have been prophecies made at a hero-feast. The diving
bird was sacred to Athene in Attica and associated with the drowning of
the royal *pharmacos* (see 94. *1*). Scamander's leaping into the river Xanthus
must refer to a similar Trojan custom of drowning the old king (see
108. *3*); his ghost supposedly impregnated girls when they came there to
bathe (see 137. *3*). Tantalus, who appears to have suffered the same fate,
married Xanthus's daughter (see 108. *b*).

7. Priam had fifty sons, nineteen of whom were legitimate; this suggests that at Troy the length of the king's reign was governed by the
nineteen-year metonic cycle, not the cycle of one hundred lunations
shared between king and tanist, as in Crete (see 138. *5*) and Arcadia (see
38. *2*). His twelve daughters were perhaps guardians of the months.

8. The importance of Aeacus's share in building the walls of Troy
should not be overlooked: Apollo had prophesied that his descendants
should be present at its capture both in the first and the fourth generation
(see 66. *i*), and only the part built by Aeacus could be breached (Pindar:
*Pythian Odes* viii. 39–46). Andromache reminded Hector that this part
was the curtain on the west side of the wall 'near the fig tree', where the
city might be most easily assailed (Homer: *Iliad* vi. 431–9), and 'where
the most valiant men who follow the two Ajax's have thrice attempted
to force an entry – whether some soothsayer has revealed the secret to
them, or whether their own spirit urges them on.' Dörpfeld's excava-
tions of Troy proved that the wall was, unaccountably, weakest at this
point; but the Ajax's or 'Aeacans' needed no soothsayer to inform them
of this if, as Polybius suggests, 'Aeacus' came from Little Ajax's city of
Opuntian Locris. Locris, which seems to have provided the Ilian element
in Homeric Troy, and enjoyed the privilege of nominating Trojan
priestesses (see 168. *2*), was a pre-Hellenic Lelegian district with matrilinear and even matriarchal institutions (see 136. *4*); another tribe of

Lelegians, perhaps of Locrian descent, lived at Pedasus in the Troad. One of their princesses, Laothoë, came to Troy and had a child by Priam (Homer: *Iliad* xxi. 86). It seems to have been the Locrian priestesses' readiness to smuggle away the Palladium to safety in Locris that facilitated the Greeks' capture of the city (see 168. *4*).

9. Since one Teucer was Scamander's son, and another was Aeacus's grandson and son of Priam's sister Hesione (see 137. *2*), the Teucrian element at Troy may be identified with the Lelegian, or Aeacan, or Ilian; the other two elements being the Lydian, or Dardanian, or Tyrrhenian; and the Trojan, or Phrygian.

# 159

## PARIS AND HELEN

WHEN Helen, Leda's beautiful daughter, grew to womanhood at Sparta in the palace of her foster-father Tyndareus, all the princes of Greece came with rich gifts as her suitors, or sent their kinsmen to represent them. Diomedes, fresh from his victory at Thebes, was there with Ajax, Teucer, Philoctetes, Idomeneus, Patroclus, Menestheus, and many others. Odysseus came too, but empty-handed, because he had not the least chance of success – for, even though the Dioscuri, Helen's brothers, wanted her to marry Menestheus of Athens, she would, Odysseus knew, be given to Prince Menelaus, the richest of the Achaeans, represented by Tyndareus's powerful son-in-law Agamemnon.[1]

*b.* Tyndareus sent no suitor away, but would, on the other hand, accept none of the proffered gifts; fearing that his partiality for any one prince might set the others quarrelling. Odysseus asked him one day: 'If I tell you how to avoid a quarrel will you, in return, help me to marry Icarius's daughter Penelope?' 'It is a bargain,' cried Tyndareus. 'Then,' continued Odysseus, 'my advice to you is: insist that all Helen's suitors swear to defend her chosen husband against whoever resents his good fortune.' Tyndareus agreed that this was a prudent course. After sacrificing a horse, and jointing it, he made the suitors stand on its bloody pieces, and repeat the oath which Odysseus had formulated; the joints were then buried at a place still called 'The Horse's Tomb'.

*c.* It is not known whether Tyndareus himself chose Helen's husband, or whether she declared her own preference by crowning him with a wreath.[2] At all events, she married Menelaus, who became King of Sparta after the death of Tyndareus and the deification of the Dioscuri. Yet their marriage was doomed to failure: years before, while sacrificing to the gods, Tyndareus had stupidly overlooked Aphrodite, who took her revenge by swearing to make all three of his daughters – Clytaemnestra, Timandra, and Helen – notorious for their adulteries.[3]

d. Menelaus had one daughter by Helen, whom she named Hermione; their sons were Aethiolas, Maraphius – from whom the Persian family of the Maraphions claim descent – and Pleisthenes. An Aetolian slave-girl named Pieris later bore Menelaus twin bastards: Nicostratus and Megapenthes.[4]

e. Why, it is asked, had Zeus and Themis planned the Trojan War? Was it to make Helen famous for having embroiled Europe and Asia? Or to exalt the race of the demi-gods, and at the same time to thin out the populous tribes that were oppressing the surface of Mother Earth? Their reason must remain obscure, but the decision had already been taken when Eris threw down a golden apple inscribed 'For the Fairest' at the wedding of Peleus and Thetis. Almighty Zeus refused to decide the ensuing dispute between Hera, Athene, and Aphrodite, and let Hermes lead the goddesses to Mount Ida, where Priam's lost son Paris would act as arbiter.[5]

f. Now, just before the birth of Paris, Hecabe had dreamed that she brought forth a faggot from which wriggled countless fiery serpents. She awoke screaming that the city of Troy and the forests of Mount Ida were ablaze. Priam at once consulted his son Aesacus, the seer, who announced: 'The child about to be born will be the ruin of our country! I beg you to do away with him.'[6]

g. A few days later, Aesacus made a further announcement: 'The royal Trojan who brings forth a child today must be destroyed, and so must her offspring!' Priam thereupon killed his sister Cilla, and her infant son Munippus, born that morning from a secret union with Thymoetes, and buried them in the sacred precinct of Tros. But Hecabe was delivered of a son before nightfall, and Priam spared both their lives, although Herophile, priestess of Apollo, and other seers, urged Hecabe at least to kill the child. She could not bring herself to do so; and in the end Priam was prevailed upon to send for his chief herdsman, one Agelaus, and entrust him with the task. Agelaus, being too soft-hearted to use a rope or a sword, exposed the infant on Mount Ida, where he was suckled by a she-bear. Returning after five days, Agelaus was amazed at the portent, and brought the waif home in a wallet – hence the name 'Paris' – to rear with his own new-born son;[7] and took a dog's tongue to Priam as evidence that his command had been obeyed. But some say that Hecabe bribed Agelaus to spare Paris and keep the secret from Priam.[8]

*h*. Paris's noble birth was soon disclosed by his outstanding beauty, intelligence, and strength: when little more than a child, he routed a band of cattle-thieves and recovered the cows they had stolen, thus winning the surname Alexander.[9] Though ranking no higher than a slave at this time, Paris became the chosen lover of Oenone, daughter of the river Oeneus, a fountain-nymph. She had been taught the art of prophecy by Rhea, and that of medicine by Apollo while he was acting as Laomedon's herdsman. Paris and Oenone used to herd their flocks and hunt together; he carved her name in the bark of beech-trees and poplars.[10] His chief amusement was setting Agelaus's bulls to fight one another; he would crown the victor with flowers, and the loser with straw. When one bull began to win consistently, Paris pitted it against the champions of his neighbours' herds, all of which were defeated. At last he offered to set a golden crown upon the horns of any bull that could overcome his own; so, for a jest, Ares turned himself into a bull, and won the prize. Paris's unhesitating award of this crown to Ares surprised and pleased the gods as they watched from Olympus; which is why Zeus chose him to arbitrate between the three goddesses.[11]

*i*. He was herding his cattle on Mount Gargarus, the highest peak of Ida, when Hermes, accompanied by Hera, Athene, and Aphrodite, delivered the golden apple and Zeus's message: 'Paris, since you are as handsome as you are wise in affairs of the heart, Zeus commands you to judge which of these goddesses is the fairest.'

Paris accepted the apple doubtfully. 'How can a simple cattle-man like myself become an arbiter of divine beauty?' he cried. 'I shall divide this apple between all three.'

'No, no, you cannot disobey Almighty Zeus!' Hermes replied hurriedly. 'Nor am I authorized to give you advice. Use your native intelligence!'

'So be it,' sighed Paris. 'But first I beg the losers not to be vexed with me. I am only a human being, liable to make the stupidest mistakes.'

The goddesses all agreed to abide by his decision.

'Will it be enough to judge them as they are?' Paris asked Hermes, 'or should they be naked?'

'The rules of the contest are for you to decide,' Hermes answered with a discreet smile.

'In that case, will they kindly disrobe?'

Hermes told the goddesses to do so, and politely turned his back.

*j.* Aphrodite was soon ready, but Athene insisted that she should remove the famous magic girdle, which gave her an unfair advantage by making everyone fall in love with the wearer. 'Very well,' said Aphrodite spitefully. 'I will, on condition that you remove your helmet – you look hideous without it.'

'Now, if you please, I must judge you one at a time,' announced Paris, 'to avoid distractive arguments. Come here, Divine Hera! Will you other two goddesses be good enough to leave us for a while?'

'Examine me conscientiously,' said Hera, turning slowly around, and displaying her magnificent figure, 'and remember that if you judge me the fairest, I will make you lord of all Asia, and the richest man alive.'[12]

'I am not to be bribed, my Lady. . . . Very well, thank you. Now I have seen all that I need to see. Come, Divine Athene!'

*k.* 'Here I am,' said Athene, striding purposefully forward. 'Listen, Paris, if you have enough common sense to award me the prize, I will make you victorious in all your battles, as well as the handsomest and wisest man in the world.'

'I am a humble herdsman, not a soldier,' said Paris. 'You can see for yourself that peace reigns throughout Lydia and Phrygia, and that King Priam's sovereignty is uncontested. But I promise to consider fairly your claim to the apple. Now you are at liberty to put on your clothes and helmet again. Is Aphrodite ready?'

*l.* Aphrodite sidled up to him, and Paris blushed because she came so close that they were almost touching.

'Look carefully, please, pass nothing over. . . . By the way, as soon as I saw you, I said to myself: "Upon my word, there goes the handsomest young man in Phrygia! Why does he waste himself here in the wilderness herding stupid cattle?" Well, why do you, Paris? Why not move into a city and lead a civilized life? What have you to lose by marrying someone like Helen of Sparta, who is as beautiful as I am, and no less passionate? I am convinced that, once you two have met, she will abandon her home, her family, everything, to become your mistress. Surely you have heard of Helen?'

'Never until now, my Lady. I should be most grateful if you would describe her.'

*m*. 'Helen is of fair and delicate complexion, having been hatched from a swan's egg. She can claim Zeus for a father, loves hunting and wrestling, caused one war while she was still a child – and, when she came of age, all the princes of Greece were her suitors. At present she is married to Menelaus, brother of the High King Agamemnon; but that makes no odds – you can have her if you like.'

'How is that possible, if she is already married?'

'Heavens! How innocent you are! Have you never heard that it is my divine duty to arrange affairs of this sort? I suggest now that you tour Greece with my son Eros as your guide. Once you reach Sparta, he and I will see that Helen falls head over heels in love with you.'

'Would you swear to that?' Paris asked excitedly.

Aphrodite uttered a solemn oath, and Paris, without a second thought, awarded her the golden apple.

By this judgement he incurred the smothered hatred of both Hera and Athene, who went off arm-in-arm to plot the destruction of Troy; while Aphrodite, with a naughty smile, stood wondering how best to keep her promise.[13]

*n*. Soon afterwards, Priam sent his servants to fetch a bull from Agelaus's herd. It was to be a prize at the funeral games now annually celebrated in honour of his dead son. When the servants chose the champion bull, Paris was seized by a sudden desire to attend the games, and ran after them. Agelaus tried to restrain him: 'You have your own private bull fights, what more do you want?' But Paris persisted and in the end, Agelaus accompanied him to Troy.

*o*. It was a Trojan custom that, at the close of the sixth lap of the chariot race, those who had entered for the boxing match should begin fighting in front of the throne. Paris decided to compete and, despite Agelaus's entreaties, sprang into the arena and won the crown, by sheer courage rather than by skill. He also came home first in the foot-race, which so exasperated Priam's sons that they challenged him to another; thus he won his third crown. Ashamed at this public defeat, they decided to kill him and set an armed guard at every exit of the stadium, while Hector and Deiphobus attacked him with their swords.

Paris leaped for the protection of Zeus's altar, and Agelaus ran towards Priam, crying: 'Your Majesty, this youth is your long-lost son!' Priam at once summoned Hecabe who, when Agelaus displayed a rattle which had been found in Paris's hands, confirmed his identity. He was taken triumphantly to the palace, where Priam celebrated his return with a huge banquet and sacrifices to the gods. Yet, as soon as the priests of Apollo heard the news, they announced that Paris must be put to death immediately, else Troy would perish. This was reported to Priam, who answered: 'Better that Troy should fall, than that my wonderful son should die!'[14]

*p*. Paris's married brothers presently urged him to take a wife; but he told them that he trusted Aphrodite to choose one for him, and used to offer her prayers every day. When another Council was called to discuss the rescue of Hesione, peaceful overtures having failed, Paris volunteered to lead the expedition, if Priam would provide him with a large, well-manned fleet. He cunningly added that, should he fail to bring Hesione back, he might perhaps carry off a Greek princess of equal rank to hold in ransom for her. His heart was, of course, secretly set on going to Sparta to fetch back Helen.[15]

*q*. That very day, Menelaus arrived unexpectedly at Troy and inquired for the tombs of Lycus and Chimaerus, Prometheus's sons by Celaeno the Atlantid: he explained that the remedy which the Delphic Oracle had prescribed him for a plague now ravaging Sparta was to offer them heroic sacrifices. Paris entertained Menelaus and begged, as a favour, to be purified by him at Sparta, since he had accidentally killed Antenor's young son Antheus with a toy sword. When Menelaus agreed, Paris, on Aphrodite's advice, commissioned Phereclus, the son of Tecton, to build the fleet which Priam had promised him; the figurehead of his flag-ship was to be an Aphrodite holding a miniature Eros. Paris's cousin Aeneas, Anchises's son, agreed to accompany him.[16] Cassandra, her hair streaming loose, foretold the conflagration that the voyage would cause, and Helenus concurred; but Priam took no notice of either of his prophetic children. Even Oenone failed to dissuade Paris from the fatal journey, although he wept when kissing her good-bye. 'Come back to me if ever you are wounded,' she said, 'because I alone can heal you.'[17]

*r*. The fleet put out to sea, Aphrodite sent a favouring breeze, and Paris soon reached Sparta, where Menelaus feasted him for nine days. At the banquet, Paris presented Helen with the gifts that he had brought from Troy; and his shameless glances, loud sighs and bold signals caused her considerable embarrassment. Picking up her goblet he would set his lips to that part of the rim from which she had drunk; and once she found the words 'I love you, Helen!' traced in wine on the table top. She grew terrified that Menelaus might suspect her of encouraging Paris's passion; but, being an unobservant man, he cheerfully sailed off to Crete, where he had to attend the obsequies of his grandfather Catreus, leaving her to entertain the guests and rule the kingdom during his absence.[18]

*s.* Helen eloped with Paris that very night, and gave herself to him in love at the first port of call, which was the island of Cranaë. On the mainland, opposite Cranaë, stands a shrine of Aphrodite the Uniter, founded by Paris to celebrate this occasion.[19] Some record untruthfully that Helen rejected his advances, and that he carried her off by force while she was out hunting; or by a sudden raid on the city of Sparta; or by disguising himself, with Aphrodite's aid, as Menelaus. She abandoned her daughter Hermione, then nine years of age, but took away her son Pleisthenes, the greater part of the palace treasures, and gold to the value of three talents stolen from Apollo's temple; as well as five serving women, among whom were the two former queens, Aethra the mother of Theseus, and Theisadië, Peirithous's sister.[20]

*t.* As they steered towards Troy, a great storm sent by Hera forced Paris to touch at Cyprus. Thence he sailed to Sidon, and was entertained by the king whom, being now instructed in the ways of the Greek world, he treacherously murdered and robbed in his own banqueting hall. While the rich booty was being embarked, a company of Sidonians attacked him; these he beat off, after a bloody fight and the loss of two ships, and came safely away. Fearing pursuit by Menelaus, Paris delayed for several months in Phoenicia, Cyprus, and Egypt; but, reaching Troy at last, he celebrated his wedding with Helen.[21] The Trojans welcomed her, entranced by such divine beauty; and one day, finding a stone on the Trojan citadel, which dripped blood when rubbed against another, she recognized this as a powerful aphrodisiac and used it to keep Paris's passion ablaze. What was more, all Troy, not Paris only, fell in love with her; and Priam took an oath never to let her go.[22]

*u.* An altogether different account of the matter is that Hermes stole Helen at Zeus's command, and entrusted her to King Proteus of Egypt; meanwhile, a phantom Helen, fashioned from clouds by Hera (or, some say, by Proteus) was sent to Troy at Paris's side: with the sole purpose of provoking strife.[23]

*v.* Egyptian priests record, no less improbably, that the Trojan fleet was blown off its course, and that Paris landed at the Salt Pans in the Canopic mouth of the Nile. There stands Heracles's temple, a sanctuary for runaway slaves who, on arrival, dedicate themselves to the god and receive certain sacred marks on their bodies. Paris's servants fled here and, after securing the priests' protection, accused him of having abducted Helen. The Canopic warden took cognizance of the matter and reported it to King Proteus at Memphis, who had Paris arrested and brought before him, together with Helen and the stolen treasure. After a close interrogation, Proteus banished Paris but detained Helen and the treasure in Egypt, until Menelaus should come to recover them. In Memphis stands a temple of Aphrodite the Stranger, said to have been dedicated by Helen herself.

Helen bore Paris three sons, Bunomus, Aganus, and Idaeus, all of them killed at Troy while still infants by the collapse of a roof; and one daughter, also called Helen.[24] Paris had an elder son by Oenone, named Corythus, whom, in jealousy of Helen, she sent to guide the avenging Greeks to Troy.[25]

1. Apollodorus: iii. 10. 8; Hyginus: *Fabula* 81; Ovid: *Heroides* xvii. 104; Hesiod: *The Catalogues of Women*, Fragment 68, pp. 192 ff., ed. Evelyn-White.
2. Hesiod: *loc. cit.*; Apollodorus: iii. 10. 9; Pausanias: iii. 20. 9; Hyginus: *Fabula* 78.
3. Stesichorus, quoted by scholiast on Euripides's *Orestes* 249; Hyginus: *loc. cit.*; Apollodorus: iii. 11. 2.
4. Homer: *Odyssey* iv. 12–14; Scholiast on Homer's *Iliad* iii. 175; *Cypria*, quoted by scholiast on Euripides's *Andromache* 898; Pausanias: ii. 18. 5.
5. *Cypria*, quoted by Proclus: *Chrestomathy* 1; Apollodorus: *Epitome* iii. 1–2; *Cypria*, quoted by scholiast on Homer's *Iliad* i. 5.
6. Apollodorus: iii. 12. 5; Hyginus: *Fabula* 91; Tzetzes: *On Lycophron* 86; Pindar: *Fragment of Paean* 8, pp. 544–6, ed. Sandys.
7. Tzetzes: *On Lycophron* 224 and 314; Servius on Virgil's *Aeneid* ii. 32; Pausanias: x. 12. 3; Scholiast on Euripides's *Andromache* 294; and on *Iphigeneia in Aulis* 1285; Apollodorus: *loc. cit.*; Hyginus: *Fabula* 91; Konrad von Würzburg: *Der trojanische Krieg* 442 ff. and 546 ff.
8. Dictys Cretensis: iii. Rawlinson: *Excidium Troiae*.
9. Apollodorus: *loc. cit.*; Ovid: *Heroides* xvi. 51–2 and 359–6c.
10. Ovid: *Heroides* v. 12–30 and 139; Tzetzes: *On Lycophron* 57; Apollodorus: iii. 12. 6.

11. *Trojanska Priča* p. 159; Rawlinson: *Excidium Troiae*.
12. Ovid: *Heroides* xvi. 71–3 and v. 35–6; Lucian: *Dialogues of the Gods* 20; Hyginus: *Fabula* 92.
13. Hyginus: *loc. cit.*; Ovid: *Heroides* xvi. 149–52; Lucian: *loc. cit.*
14. Rawlinson: *Excidium Troiae*; Hyginus: *Fabula* 91; Servius on Virgil's *Aeneid* v. 370; Ovid: *Heroides* xvi. 92 and 361–2.
15. Dares: 4–8; Rawlinson: *loc. cit.*
16. Tzetzes: *On Lycophron* 132; *Cypria*, quoted by Proclus: *Chrestomathy* 1; Homer: *Iliad* v. 59 ff.; Apollodorus: *Epitome* iii. 2; Ovid: *Heroides* xvi. 115–16.
17. *Cypria*, quoted by Proclus: *loc. cit.*; Ovid: *Heorides* xvi. 119 ff. and 45 ff.; Apollodorus: iii. 12. 6.
18. Ovid: *Heroides* xvi. 21–3; xvii. 74 ff.; 83 and 155 ff.; Apollodorus: *Epitome* iii. 3; *Cypria*, quoted by Proclus: *loc. cit.*
19. Ovid: *Heroides* xvi. 259–62; *Cypria*, quoted by Proclus: *loc. cit.*; Pausanias: iii. 22. 2; Apollodorus: *loc. cit.*; Homer: *Iliad* iii. 445.
20. Servius on Virgil's *Aeneid* i. 655; Eustathius on Homer, p. 1946; Apollodorus: *loc. cit.*; *Cypria*, quoted by Proclus: *loc. cit.*; Dares: 10; Tzetzes: *On Lycophron* 132 ff.; Hyginus: *Fabula* 92.
21. Homer: *Odyssey* iv. 227–30; Proclus: *Chrestomathy* 1; Dictys Cretensis: i. 5; Apollodorus: *Epitome* iii. 4; Tzetzes: *On Lycophron* 132 ff.
22. Servius on Virgil's *Aeneid* ii. 33.
23. Apollodorus: *Epitome* iii. 5; Euripides: *Electra* 128 and *Helen* 31 ff.; Servius on Virgil's *Aeneid* i. 655 and ii. 595; Stesichorus, quoted by Tzetzes: *On Lycophron* 113.
24. Herodotus: ii. 112–15; Dictys Cretensis: v. 5; Tzetzes: *On Lycophron* 851; Ptolemy Hephaestionos: iv.
25. Conon: *Narrations* 22; Tzetzes: *On Lycophron* 57 ff.

*

1. Stesichorus, the sixth-century Sicilian poet, is credited with the story that Helen never went to Troy and that the war was fought for 'only a phantom'. After writing a poem which presented her in a most unfavourable light, he went blind, and afterwards learned that he lay under her posthumous displeasure (see 164. *m*). Hence his palinode beginning: 'This tale is true, thou didst not go aboard The well-benched ships, nor reach the towers of Troy,' a public declamation of which restored his sight (Plato: *Phaedrus* 44; Pausanias: iii. 19. 11). And, indeed, it is not clear in what sense Paris, or Theseus before him, had abducted Helen. 'Helen' was the name of the Spartan Moon-goddess, marriage to whom, after a horse-sacrifice (see 81. *4*), made Menelaus king; yet Paris did not usurp the throne. It is of course possible that the Trojans raided Sparta, carrying off the heiress and the palace treasures in retaliation for a Greek

sack of Troy, which Hesione's story implies. Yet though Theseus's Helen was, perhaps, flesh and blood (see 103. *4*), the Trojan Helen is far more likely to have been 'only a phantom', as Stesichorus claimed.

2. This is to suggest that the *mnēstēres tēs Helenēs*, 'suitors of Helen', were really *mnēstēres tou hellēspontou*, 'those who were mindful of the Hellespont', and that the solemn oath which these kings took on the bloody joints of the horse sacred to Poseidon, the chief patron of the expedition, was to support the rights of any member of the confederacy to navigate the Hellespont, despite the Trojans and their Asiatic allies (see 148. *10*; 160. *1* and 162. *3*). After all, the Hellespont bore the name of their own goddess Helle. The Helen story comes, in fact, from the Ugarit epic *Keret*, in which Keret's lawful wife Huray is abducted to Udm.

3. Paris's birth follows the mythical pattern of Aeolus (see 43. *c*), Pelias (see 68. *d*), Oedipus (see 105. *a*), Jason (see 148. *b*), and the rest; he is the familiar New Year child, with Agelaus's son for twin. His defeat of the fifty sons of Priam in a foot-race is no less familiar (see 53. *3* and 60. *m*). 'Oenone' seems to have been a title of the princess whom he won on this occasion (see 53. *3*; 60. *4*; 98. *7* and 160. *d*).

He did not, in fact, award the apple to the fairest of the three goddesses. This tale is mistakenly deduced from the icon which showed Heracles being given an apple-bough by the Hesperides (see 133. *4*) – the naked Nymph-goddess in triad – Adanus of Hebron being immortalized by the Canaanite Mother of All Living, or the victor of the foot-race at Olympia receiving his prize (see 53. *7*); as is proved by the presence of Hermes, Conductor of Souls, his guide to the Elysian Fields.

4. During the fourteenth century B.C., Egypt and Phoenicia suffered from frequent raids by the Keftiu, or 'peoples of the sea', in which the Trojans seem to have taken a leading part. Among the tribes that gained a foothold in Palestine were the Girgashites (*Genesis* x. 16), namely Teucrians from Gergis, or Gergithium, in the Troad (Homer: *Iliad* viii. 304; Herodotus: v. 122 and vii. 43; Livy: xxxviii. 39). Priam and Anchises figure in the Old Testament as Piram and Achish (*Joshua* x. 3 and 1 *Samuel* xxvii. 2); and Pharez, an ancestor of the racially mixed tribe of Judah, who fought with his twin inside their mother's womb (*Genesis* xxxviii. 29), seems to be Paris. Helen's 'bleeding stone', found on the Trojan citadel, is explained by the execution there of Priam's nephew Munippus: Paris remained the queen's consort at the price of annual child sacrifice. Antheus ('flowery'), is a similar victim: his name, a title of the Spring Dionysus (see 85. *2*), was given to other unfortunate princes, cut down in the flower of their lives; among them the son of Poseidon, killed and flayed by Cleomenes (Philostephanus: *Fragment* 8); and Antheus of Halicarnassus, drowned in a well by Cleobis (Parthenius: *Narrations* 14).

5. Cilla, whose name means 'the divinatory dice made from ass's

bone' (Hesychius *sub* Cillae) must be Athene, the goddess of the Trojan citadel, who invented this art of prognostication (see 17. *3*) and presided over the death of Munippus.

# 160

## THE FIRST GATHERING AT AULIS

WHEN Paris decided to make Helen his wife, he did not expect to pay for his outrage of Menelaus's hospitality. Had the Cretans been called to account when, in the name of Zeus, they stole Europe from the Phoenicians? Had the Argonauts been asked to pay for their abduction of Medea from Colchis? Or the Athenians for their abduction of Cretan Ariadne? Or the Thracians for that of Athenian Oreithyia?[1] This case, however, proved to be different. Hera sent Iris flying to Crete with news of the elopement; and Menelaus hurried to Mycenae, where he begged his brother Agamemnon to raise levies at once and lead an army against Troy.

*b.* Agamemnon consented to take this course only if the envoys whom he now sent to Troy, demanding Helen's return and compensation for the injury done to Menelaus, came back empty-handed. When Priam denied all knowledge of the matter – Paris being still in Southern waters – and asked what satisfaction his own envoys had been offered for the rape of Hesione, heralds were sent by Menelaus to every prince who had taken his oath on the bloody joints of the horse, reminding him that Paris's act was an affront to the whole of Greece. Unless the crime were punished in an exemplary fashion, nobody could henceforth be sure of his wife's safety. Menelaus now fetched old Nestor from Pylus, and together they travelled over the Greek mainland, summoning the leaders of the expedition.[2]

*c.* Next, accompanied by Menelaus and Palamedes, the son of Nauplius, Agamemnon visited Ithaca, where he had the greatest difficulty in persuading Odysseus to join the expedition. This Odysseus, though he passed as the son of Laertes, had been secretly begotten by Sisyphus on Anticleia, daughter of the famous thief Autolycus. Just after the birth, Autolycus came to Ithaca and on the first night of his stay, when supper ended, took the infant on his knee. 'Name him, father,' said Anticleia. Autolycus answered: 'In the course of my life I have antagonized many princes, and I shall therefore name this grandson Odysseus, meaning The Angry One, because he will be the victim of my enmities. Yet if he ever comes to Mount Parnassus to reproach me, I shall give him a share of my possessions, and assuage his anger.' As soon as Odysseus came of age, he duly visited Autolycus but, while out hunting with his uncles, was gashed in the thigh by a boar, and carried the scar to his grave. However, Autolycus looked after him well enough, and he returned to Ithaca laden with the promised gifts.[3]

*d.* Odysseus married Penelope, daughter of Icarius and the Naiad Periboea; some say, at the request of Icarius's brother Tyndareus, who arranged for him to win a suitors' race down the Spartan street called 'Apheta'. Penelope, formerly named Arnaea, or Arnacia, had been flung into the sea by Nauplius at her father's order; but a flock of purple-striped ducks buoyed her up, fed her, and towed her ashore. Impressed by this prodigy, Icarius and Periboea relented, and Arnaea won the new name of Penelope, which means 'duck'.[4]

*e.* After marrying Penelope to Odysseus, Icarius begged him to remain at Sparta and, when he refused, followed the chariot in which the bridal pair were driving away, entreating her to stay behind. Odysseus, who had hitherto kept his patience, turned and told Penelope: 'Either come to Ithaca of your own free will; or, if you prefer your father, stay here without me!' Penelope's only reply was to draw down her veil. Icarius, realizing that Odysseus was within his rights, let her go, and raised an image to Modesty, which is still shown some four miles from the city of Sparta, at the place where this incident happened.[5]

*f.* Now, Odysseus had been warned by an oracle: 'If you go to Troy, you will not return until the twentieth year, and then alone and destitute.' He therefore feigned madness, and Agamemnon, Menelaus, and Palamedes found him wearing a peasant's felt cap shaped like a half-egg, ploughing with an ass and an ox yoked together, and flinging salt over his shoulder as he went. When he pretended not to recognize his distinguished guests, Palamedes snatched the infant Telemachus from Penelope's arms and set him on the ground before the advancing team. Odysseus hastily reined them in to avoid killing his only son and, his sanity having thus been established, was obliged to join the expedition.[6]

*g.* Menelaus and Odysseus then travelled with Agamemnon's herald

Talthybius to Cyprus, where King Cinyras, another of Helen's former suitors, handed them a breastplate as a gift for Agamemnon, and swore to contribute fifty ships. He kept his promise, but sent only one real ship and forty-nine small earthenware ones, with dolls for crews, which the captain launched as he approached the coast of Greece. Invoked by Agamemnon to avenge this fraud, Apollo is said to have killed Cinyras, whereupon his fifty daughters leapt into the sea and became halcyons; the truth is, however, that Cinyras killed himself when he discovered that he had committed incest with his daughter Smyrne.[7]

*h*. Calchas the priest of Apollo, a Trojan renegade, had foretold that Troy could not be taken without the aid of young Achilles, the seventh son of Peleus. Achilles's mother Thetis had destroyed his other brothers by burning away their mortal parts, and he would have perished in the same way, had not Peleus snatched him from the fire, replacing his charred ankle-bone with one borrowed from the disinterred skeleton of the giant Damysus. But some say that Thetis dipped him in the river Styx, so that only the heel by which she held him was not immortalized.[8]

*i*. When Thetis deserted Peleus, he took the child to Cheiron the Centaur, who reared him on Mount Pelion, feeding him on the umbles of lions and wild boars, and the marrow of bears, to give him courage; or, according to another account, on honey-comb, and fawns' marrow to make him run swiftly. Cheiron instructed him in the arts of riding, hunting, pipe-playing, and healing; the Muse Calliope, also, taught him how to sing at banquets. When only six years of age he killed his first boar, and thenceforth was constantly dragging the panting bodies of boars and lions back to Cheiron's cave. Athene and Artemis gazed in wonder at this golden-haired child, who was so swift of foot that he could overtake and kill stags without the help of hounds.[9]

*j*. Now, Thetis knew that her son would never return from Troy if he joined the expedition, since he was fated either to gain glory there and die early, or to live a long but inglorious life at home. She disguised him as a girl, and entrusted him to Lycomedes, king of Scyros, in whose palace he lived under the name of Cercysera, Aissa, or Pyrrha; and had an intrigue with Lycomedes's daughter Deidameia, by whom he became the father of Pyrrhus, later called Neoptolemus. But some say that Neoptolemus was the son of Achilles and Iphigeneia.[10]

*k*. Odysseus, Nestor, and Ajax were sent to fetch Achilles from Scyros, where he was rumoured to be hidden. Lycomedes let them search the palace, and they might never have detected Achilles, had not Odysseus laid a pile of gifts – for the most part jewels, girdles, embroidered dresses and such – in the hall, and asked the court-ladies to take their choice. Then Odysseus ordered a sudden trumpet-blast and clash of arms to sound outside the palace and, sure enough, one of the girls stripped herself to the waist and seized the shield and spear which he had included among the gifts. It was Achilles, who now promised to lead his Myrmidons to Troy.[11]

*l*. Some authorities disdain this as a fanciful tale and say that Nestor and Odysseus came on a recruiting tour to Phthia, where they were entertained by Peleus, who readily allowed Achilles, now fifteen years of age, to go off under the tutorship of Phoenix, the son of Amyntor and Cleobule; and that Thetis gave him a beautiful inlaid chest, packed with tunics, wind-proof cloaks, and thick rugs for the journey.[12] This Phoenix had been accused by Phthia, his father's concubine, of having violated her. Amyntor blinded Phoenix, at the same time setting a curse of childlessness on him; and whether the accusation was true or false, childless he remained. However, he fled to Phthia, where Peleus not only persuaded Cheiron to restore his sight, but appointed him king of the neighbouring Dolopians. Phoenix then volunteered to become the guardian of Achilles who, in return, became deeply attached to him. Some, therefore, hold that Phoenix's blindness was not true loss of sight, but metaphorical of impotence – a curse which Peleus lifted by making him a second father to Achilles.[13]

*m*. Achilles had an inseparable companion: his cousin Patroclus, who was older than he, though neither so strong, nor so swift, nor so well-born. The name of Patroclus's father is sometimes given as Menoetius of Opus, and sometimes as Aeacus; and his mother is variously called Sthenele, daughter of Acastus; Periopis, daughter of Pheres; Polymele, daughter of Peleus; or Philomele, daughter of Actor.[14] He had fled to Peleus's court after killing Amphidamas's son Cleiteonymus, or Aeanes, in a quarrel over a game of dice.[15]

*n*. When the Greek fleet was already drawn up at Aulis, a protected beach in the Euboean straits, Cretan envoys came to announce that their King Idomeneus, son of Deucalion, would bring a hundred ships to Troy, if Agamemnon agreed to share the supreme command with him; and this condition was accepted. Idomeneus, a former suitor of Helen's, and famous for his good looks, brought as his lieutenant Meriones, son of Molus, reputedly one of Minos's bastards. He bore the figure of a cock on his shield, because he was descended from Helius, and wore a helmet garnished with boars' tusks.[16] Thus the expedition became a Creto-Hellene enterprise. The Hellenic land forces were commanded by Agamemnon, with Odysseus, Palamedes and Diomedes as his lieutenants; and the Hellenic fleet by Achilles, with the support of Great Ajax and Phoenix.[17]

*o*. Of all his counsellors, Agamemnon set most store by Nestor King of Pylus, whose wisdom was unrivalled, and whose eloquence sweeter than honey. He ruled over three generations of men, but remained, despite his great age, a bold fighter, and the one commander who surpassed the Athenian king Menestheus in cavalry and infantry tactics. His sound judgement was shared by Odysseus, and these two always advised the same course for the successful conduct of the war.[18]

*p*. Great Ajax, son of Telamon and Periboea, came from Salamis. He was second only to Achilles in courage, strength, and beauty, and stood head and shoulders taller than his nearest rival, carrying a shield of proof made from seven bulls' hides. His body was invulnerable, except in the armpit, and some say, at the neck, because of the charm Heracles had laid upon him.[19] As he went aboard his vessel, Telamon gave him this parting advice: 'Set your mind on conquest, but always with the help of the gods.' Ajax boasted: 'With the help of the gods, any coward or fool can win glory; I trust to do so even without them!' By this boast, and others like it, he incurred divine anger. On one occasion, when Athene came to urge him on in battle, he shouted back: 'Be off, Goddess, and encourage my fellow-Greeks: for, where I am, no enemy will ever break through!'[20] Ajax's half-brother Teucer, a bastard son of Telamon and Hesione, and the best archer in Greece, used to fight from behind Ajax's shield, returning to its shelter as a child runs to his mother.[21]

*q*. Little Ajax the Locrian, son of Oïleus and Eriopis, though small, outdid all the Greeks in spear-throwing and, next to Achilles, ran the swiftest. He was the third member of Great Ajax's team of fighters, and could easily be recognized by his linen corslet and the tame serpent, longer than a man, which followed him everywhere like a dog.[22] His half-brother Medon, a bastard son of Oïleus and the nymph Rhene, came from Phylace, where he had been banished for having slain Eriopis's brother.[23]

*r*. Diomedes, the son of Tydeus and Deipyle, came from Argos, accompanied by two fellow-Epigoni, namely Sthenelus, son of Capaneus, and Euryalus the Argonaut, son of Mecisteus. He had been deeply in love with Helen, and took her abduction by Paris as a personal affront.[24]

*s.* Tlepolemus the Argive, a son of Heracles, brought nine ships from Rhodes.[25]

*t.* Before leaving Aulis, the Greek fleet received supplies of corn, wine, and other provisions from Anius, king of Delos, whom Apollo had secretly begotten on Rhoeo, daughter of Staphylus and Chryso-themis. Rhoeo was locked in a chest and set adrift by her father when he found her with child; but, being washed ashore on the coast of Euboea, gave birth to a boy whom she named Anius, because of the *trouble* she had suffered on his account; and Apollo made him his own prophetic priest-king at Delos. Some say, however, that Rhoeo's chest drifted directly to Delos.[26]

*u.* By his wife Dorippe, Anius was the father of three daughters: Elais, Spermo, and Oeno, who are called the Winegrowers; and of a son, Andron, king of Andros, to whom Apollo taught the art of augury. Being himself a priest of Apollo, Anius dedicated the Wine-growers to Dionysus, wishing his family to be under the protection of more than one god. In return, Dionysus granted that whatever Elais touched, after invoking his help, should be turned into oil; whatever Spermo touched, into corn; and whatever Oeno touched, into wine.[27] Thus Anius found it easy enough to provision the Greek fleet. Yet Agamemnon was not satisfied: he sent Menelaus and Odysseus to Delos, where they asked Anius whether they might take the Winegrowers on the expedition. Anius refused this request, telling Menelaus that it was the will of the gods that Troy should be taken only in the tenth year. 'Why not all remain here on Delos for the intervening period?' he suggested hospitably. 'My daughters will keep you supplied with food and drink until the tenth year, and they shall then accompany you to Troy, if necessary.' But, because Agamemnon had strictly ordered: 'Bring them to me, whether Anius consents or not!', Odysseus bound the Winegrowers, and forced them to embark in his vessel.[28] When they escaped, two of them fleeing to Euboea and the other to Andros, Agamemnon sent ships in pursuit, and threatened war if they were not given up. All three surrendered, but called upon Dionysus, who turned them into doves; and to this day doves are closely protected on Delos.[29]

*v.* At Aulis, while Agamemnon was sacrificing to Zeus and Apollo, a blue serpent with blood-red markings on its back darted from beneath the altar, and made straight for a fine plane-tree which grew near by. On the highest branch lay a sparrow's nest, containing eight young birds and their mother: the serpent devoured them all and then, still coiled around the branch, was turned to stone by Zeus. Calchas explained this portent as strengthening Anius's prophecy: nine years must pass before Troy could be taken, but taken it would be. Zeus further heartened them all with a flash of lightning on their right, as the fleet set sail.[30]

*w*. Some say that the Greeks left Aulis a month after Agamemnon had persuaded Odysseus to join them, and Calchas piloted them to Troy by his second-sight. Others, that Oenone sent her son Corythus to guide them.[31] But, according to a third, more generally accepted account, they had no pilot, and sailed in error to Mysia, where they disembarked and began to ravage the country, mistaking it for the Troad. King Telephus drove them back to their ships and killed the brave Thersander, son of Theban Polyneices, who alone had stood his ground. Then up ran Achilles and Patroclus, at sight of whom Telephus turned and fled along the banks of the river Caicus. Now, the Greeks had sacrificed to Dionysus at Aulis, whereas the Mysians had neglected him; as a punishment, therefore, Telephus was tripped up by a vine that sprang unexpectedly from the soil, and Achilles wounded him in the thigh with the famous spear which only he could wield, Cheiron's gift to his father Peleus.[32]

*x*. Thersander was buried at Mysian Elaea, where he now has a hero-shrine; the command of his Boeotians passed first to Peneleos and next, when he was killed by Telephus's son Eurypylus, to Thersander's son Tisamenus, who had not been of age at the time of his father's death. But some pretend that Thersander survived, and was one of those who hid in the Wooden Horse.[33]

*y*. Having bathed their wounded in the hot Ionian springs near Smyrna, called 'The Baths of Agamemnon', the Greeks put to sea once more but, their ships being scattered by a violent storm which Hera had raised, each captain steered for his own country. It was on this occasion that Achilles landed at Scyros, and formally married Deidameia.[34] Some believe that Troy fell twenty years after the abduction of Helen: that the Greeks made this false start in the second year; and that eight years elapsed before they embarked again. But it is far more probable that their council of war at Spartan Hellenium was held in the same year as their retirement from Mysia; they were still, it is said, in great perplexity because they had no competent pilot to steer them to Troy.[35]

*z*. Meanwhile, Telephus's wound still festered, and Apollo announced that it could be healed only by its cause. So he visited Agamemnon at Mycenae, clad in rags like a suppliant, and on Clytaemnestra's advice snatched the infant Orestes from his cradle. 'I will kill your son,' he cried, 'unless you cure me!' But Agamemnon, having been warned by an oracle that the Greeks could not take Troy without Telephus's advice, gladly undertook to aid him, if he would guide the fleet to Troy. When Telephus agreed, Achilles, at Agamemnon's request, scraped some rust off his spear into the wound and thus healed it; with the further help of the herb *achilleos*, a vulnerary which he had himself discovered.[36] Telephus later refused to join the expedition, on the ground that his wife, Laodice, also called Hiera, or Astyoche, was Priam's daughter; but he showed the Greeks what course to shape, and Calchas confirmed the accuracy of his advice by divination.[37]

1. Herodotus: i. 1–4; Ovid: *Heroides* xvi. 341–50.
2. Herodotus: i. 3; *Cypria*, quoted by Proclus: *Chrestomathy* 1; Apollodorus: *Epitome* iii. 6.
3. Hyginus: *Fabula* 95; Homer: *Odyssey* xxiv. 115–19 and xix. 399–466; Apollodorus: *Epitome* iii. 12; Servius on Virgil's *Aeneid* vi. 529.
4. Apollodorus: iii. 10. 6 and 9; Pausanias: iii. 12. 2; Tzetzes: *On Lycophron* 792; Didymus, quoted by Eustathius on Homer, p. 1422.
5. Pausanias: iii. 20. 2.
6. Hyginus: *loc. cit.*; Servius on Virgil's *Aeneid* ii. 81; Tzetzes: *On Lycophron* 818; Apollodorus: *Epitome* iii. 7.
7. Apollodorus: *Epitome* iii. 9; Eustathius on Homer's *Iliad* xi. 20; Nonnus: *Dionysiaca* xiii. 451; Hyginus: *Fabula* 242.
8. Apollodorus: iii. 13. 8; Ptolemy Hephaestionos: vi.; Lycophron: *Alexandra* 178 ff., with scholiast; Scholiast on Homer's *Iliad* xvi. 37; Scholiast on Aristophanes's *Clouds* 1068; Scholiast on Apollonius Rhodius: iv. 816.
9. Servius on Virgil's *Aeneid* vi. 57; Fulgentius: *Mythologicon* iii. 7; Apollodorus: iii. 13. 6; Philostratus: *Heroica* xx. 2 and xix. 2; *Argonautica Orphica* 392 ff.; Statius: *Achilleid* i. 269 ff.; Homer: *Iliad* xi. 831–2; Pindar: *Nemean Odes* iii. 43 ff.
10. Apollodorus: iii. 13. 8; Homer: *Iliad* ix. 410 ff.; Ptolemy Hephaestionos: i; Tzetzes: *On Lycophron* 183.
11. Apollodorus: *loc. cit.*; Scholiast on Homer's *Iliad* xix. 332; Ovid: *Metamorphoses* xiii. 162 ff.; Hyginus: *Fabula* 96.

12. Homer: *Iliad* ix. 769 ff.; 438 ff. and xvi. 298.
13. Apollodorus: *loc. cit.*; Tzetzes: *On Lycophron* 421; Homer: *Iliad* ix. 447 ff. and 485.
14. Homer: *Iliad* xi. 786–7; Pindar: *Olympian Odes* ix. 69–70; Hesiod, quoted by Eustathius on Homer's *Iliad* i. 337; Apollodorus: *loc. cit.*; Hyginus: *Fabula* 97; Scholiast on Apollonius Rhodius: iv. 816.
15. Apollodorus: *loc. cit.*; Strabo: ix. 4. 2.
16. Apollodorus: iii. 3. 1; Philostratus: *Heroica* 7; Diodorus Siculus: v. 79; Hyginus: *Fabula* 81; Pausanias: v. 23. 5; Homer: *Iliad* x. 61 ff.
17. Dictys Cretensis: i. 16; Apollodorus: *Epitome* iii. 6.
18. Homer: *Iliad* ii. 21 and i. 247–52; iv. 310 ff.; ii. 553–5; *Odyssey* iii. 244 and 126–9.
19. Homer: *Iliad* xvii. 279–80 and iii. 226–7; Sophocles: *Ajax* 576 and 833, with scholiast; Scholiast on Homer's *Iliad* xxiii. 821; Tzetzes: *On Lycophron* 455 ff.
20. Sophocles: *Ajax* 762–77.
21. Homer: *Iliad* viii. 266–72.
22. Homer: *Iliad* xiii. 697; ii. 527–30; xiv. 520 and xiii. 701 ff.; Hyginus: *Fabula* 97; Philostratus: *Heroica* viii. 1.
23. Homer: *Iliad* ii. 728 and xiii. 694–7.
24. Apollodorus: i. 8. 5; Hyginus: *loc. cit.*; Homer: *Iliad* ii. 564–6.
25. Homer: *Iliad* ii. 653–4; Hyginus: *loc. cit.*
26. Dictys Cretensis: i. 23; Servius on Virgil's *Aeneid* iii. 80; Diodorus Siculus: v. 62; Tzetzes: *On Lycophron* 570.
27. Tzetzes: *loc. cit.*; Apollodorus: *Epitome* iii. 10; Ovid: *Metamorphoses* xiii. 650 ff.; Servius: *loc. cit.*
28. Stesichorus, quoted by scholiast on Homer's *Odyssey* vi. 164; Tzetzes: *On Lycophron* 583; Servius: *loc. cit.*; Pherecydes, quoted by Tzetzes: *On Lycophron* 570.
29. Ovid: *Metamorphoses* 643–74; Servius: *loc. cit.*
30. Apollodorus: *Epitome* iii. 15; Homer: *Iliad* ii. 303–53; Ovid: *Metamorphoses* xii. 13–23.
31. Homer: *Odyssey* xxiv. 118–19 and *Iliad* i. 71; Tzetzes: *On Lycophron* 57 ff.
32. Apollodorus: *Epitome* iii. 17; Pindar: *Olympian Odes* ix. 70 ff.; Tzetzes: *On Lycophron* 206 and 209; Scholiast on Homer's *Iliad*, i. 59; Homer: *Iliad* xvi. 140–4.
33. Pausanias: ix. 5. 7–8; Virgil: *Aeneid* ii. 261.
34. Philostratus: *Heroica* iii. 35; Apollodorus: *Epitome* iii. 18; *Cypria* quoted by Proclus: *Chrestomathy* 1.
35. Homer: *Iliad* xxiv. 765; Apollodorus: *loc. cit.*; Pausanias: iii. 12. 5.
36. Apollodorus: *Epitome* iii. 19–20; Hyginus: *Fabula* 101; Pliny: *Natural History* xxv. 19.
37. Hyginus: *loc. cit.*; Philostratus: *Heroica* ii. 18; Scholiast on Homer's *Odyssey* i. 520; Apollodorus: *Epitome* iii. 20.

*

1. After the fall of Cnossus, about the year 1400 B.C., a contest for sea-power arose between the peoples of the Eastern Mediterranean. This is reflected in Herodotus's account, which John Malalas supports (see 58. 4), of the raids preceding Helen's abduction, and in Apollodorus's record of how Paris raided Sidon (see 159. *t*), and Agamemnon's people, Mysia. A Trojan confederacy offered the chief obstacle to Greek mercantile ambitions, until the High King of Mycenae gathered his allies, including the Greek overlords of Crete, for a concerted attack on Troy. The naval war, as opposed to the siege of Troy, may well have lasted for nine or ten years.

2. Among Agamemnon's independent allies were the islanders of Ithaca, Same, Dulichium, and Zacynthus led by Odysseus; the Southern Thessalians led by Achilles; and their Aeacan cousins from Locris and Salamis, led by the two Ajaxes. These chieftains proved an awkward team to handle and Agamemnon could keep them from each other's throats only by intrigue, with the loyal support of his Peloponnesian henchmen Menelaus of Sparta, Diomedes of Argos, and Nestor of Pylus. Ajax's rejection of the Olympian gods and his affront to the Zeus-born Athene have been misrepresented as evidence of atheism; they record, rather, his religious conservatism. The Aeacids were of Lelegian stock and worshipped the pre-Hellenic goddess (see 158. *8* and 168. *2*).

3. The Thebans and Athenians seem to have kept out of the war; though Athenian forces are mentioned in the *Catalogue of Ships*, they play no memorable part before Troy. But the presence of King Menestheus has been emphasized to justify later Athenian expansion along the Black Sea coast (see 162. *3*). Odysseus is a key-figure in Greek mythology. Despite his birth from a daughter of the Corinthian Sun-god and his old-fashioned foot-race winning of Penelope, he breaks the ancient matrilocal rule by insisting that Penelope shall come to his kingdom, rather than he to hers (see 137. *4*). Also, like his father Sisyphus (see 67. *2*), and Cretan Cinyras (see 18. *5*), he refuses to die at the end of his proper term – which is the central allegory of the *Odyssey* (see 170. *1* and 171. *3*). Odysseus, moreover, is the first mythical character credited with an irrelevant physical peculiarity: legs short in proportion to his body, so that he 'looks nobler sitting than standing.' The scarred thigh, however, should be read as a sign that he escaped the death incumbent on boar-cult kings (see 18. *3* and 151. *2*).

4. Odysseus's pretended madness, though consistent with his novel reluctance to act as behoved a king, seems to be misreported. What he did was to demonstrate prophetically the uselessness of the war to which he had been summoned. Wearing a conical hat which marked the mystagogue or seer, he ploughed a field up and down. Ox and ass stood for Zeus and Cronus, or summer and winter; and each furrow, sown with salt, for a wasted year. Palamedes, who also had prophetic powers (see 52.

6), then seized Telemachus and halted the plough, doubtless at the tenth furrow, by setting him in front of the team: he thereby showed that the *decisive battle*, which is the meaning of 'Telemachus', would take place then.

5. Achilles, a more conservative character, hides among women, as befits a solar hero (*White Goddess* p. 212), and takes arms in the fourth month, when the Sun has passed the equinox and so from the tutelage of his mother, Night. Cretan boys were called *scotioi*, 'children of darkness' (see 27. 2), while confined to the women's quarters, not having yet been given arms and liberty by the priestess-mother (see 121. 5). In the *Mabinogion*, Odysseus's ruse for arming Achilles is used by Gwydion (the god Odin, or Woden) on a similar occasion: wishing to release Llew Llaw Gyffes, another solar hero, from the power of his mother Arianrhod, he creates a noise of battle outside the castle and frightens her into giving Llew Llaw sword and shield. The Welsh is probably the elder version of the myth, which the Argives dramatized on the first day of the fourth month by a fight between boys dressed in girls' clothes and women dressed in men's – the festival being called the Hybristica ('shameful behaviour'). Its historical excuse was that, early in the fifth century, the poetess Telesilla, with a company of women, had contrived to hold Argos against King Cleomenes of Sparta, after the total defeat of the Argive army (Plutarch: *On the Virtues of Women* 4). Since Patroclus bears an inappropriately patriarchal name ('glory to the father'), he may have once been Phoenix ('blood red'), Achilles's twin and tanist under the matrilinear system.

6. All the Greek leaders before Troy are sacred kings. Little Ajax's tame serpent cannot have accompanied him into battle: he did not have one until he became an oracular hero. Idomeneus's boar's tusk helmet, attested by finds in Crete and Mycenaean Greece, was originally perhaps worn by the tanist (see 18. 7); his cock, sacred to the sun, and representing Zeus Velchanos, must be a late addition to Homer because the domestic hen did not reach Greece until the sixth century B.C. The original device is likely to have been a cock partridge (see 92. 1). These cumbrous shields consisted of bull's hides sewn together, the extremities being rounded off, and the waist nipped, in figure-of-eight shape, for ritual use. They covered the entire body from chin to ankle. Achilles ('lipless') seems to have been a common title of oracular heroes, since there were Achilles cults at Scyros, Phthia, and Elis (Pausanias: vi. 23. 3).

7. Rhoeo, daughter of Staphylus and Chrysothemis ('Pomegranate, daughter of Bunch of Grapes and Golden Order') came to Delos in a chest and is the familiar fertility-goddess with her new-moon boat. She also appears in triad as her grand-daughters the Winegrowers, whose names mean 'olive oil', 'grain' and 'wine'. Their mother is Dorippe, or 'gift mare', which suggests that Rhoeo was the mare-headed Demeter

(see 16. 5). Her cult survives vestigially today in the three-cupped *kernos*, a vessel used by Greek Orthodox priests to hold the gifts of oil, grain, and wine brought to church for sanctification. A *kernos* of the same type has been found in an early Minoan tomb at Koumasa; and the Winegrowers, being great-grandchildren of Ariadne, must have come to Delos from Crete (see 27. 8).

8. The Greeks' difficulty in finding their way to Troy is contradicted by the ease with which Menelaus had sailed there; perhaps in the original legend Trojan Aphrodite cast a spell which fogged their memory, as she afterwards dispersed the fleets on the return voyage (see 169. 2).

9. Achilles's treatment of the spear wound, based on the ancient homoeopathic principle that 'like cures like', recalls Melampus's use of rust from a gelding-knife to restore Iphiclus (see 72. e).

10. Maenads, in vase-paintings, sometimes have their limbs tattooed with a woof-and-warp pattern formalized as a ladder. If their faces were once similarly tattooed as a camouflage for woodland revelling, this might explain the name Penelope ('with a web over her face'), as a title of the orgiastic mountain-goddess; alternatively, she may have worn a net in her orgies, like Dictynna and the British goddess Goda (see 89. 2 and 3). Pan's alleged birth from Penelope, after she had slept promiscuously with all her suitors in Odysseus's absence (see 161. l), records a tradition of pre-Hellenic sexual orgies; the penelope duck, like the swan, was probably a totem-bird of Sparta (see 62. 3–4).

11. No commentator has hitherto troubled to explain precisely why Calchas's nest of birds should have been set on a plane-tree and devoured by a serpent; but the fact is that serpents cast their slough each year and renew themselves, and so do plane-trees – which makes them both symbols of regeneration. Calchas therefore knew that the birds which were devoured stood for years, not months. Though later appropriated by Apollo, the plane was the Goddess's sacred tree in Crete and Sparta (see 58. 3), because its leaf resembled a green hand with the fingers stretched out to bless – a gesture frequently found in her archaic statuettes. The blue spots on the serpent showed that it was sent by Zeus, who wore a blue nimbus as god of the sky. Cinyras's toy ships perhaps reflect a Cyprian custom borrowed from Egypt, of burying terracotta ships beside dead princes for their voyage to the Otherworld.

12. The fifty daughters of Cinyras's who turned into halcyons will have been a college of Aphrodite's priestesses. One of her titles was 'Alcyone', 'the queen who wards off [storms]', and the halcyons, or kingfishers, which were sacred to her, portended calms (see 45. 2).

## THE SECOND GATHERING AT AULIS

CALCHAS, the brother of Leucippe and Theonoë, had learned the art of prophecy from his father Thestor. One day, Theonoë was walking on the seashore near Troy, when Carian pirates bore her off, and she became mistress to King Icarus. Thestor at once set out in pursuit, but was shipwrecked on the Carian coast and imprisoned by Icarus. Several years later, Leucippe, who had been a mere child when these sad events took place, went to Delphi for news of her father and sister. Advised by the Pythoness to disguise herself as a priest of Apollo and go to Caria in search of them, Leucippe obediently shaved her head and visited the court of King Icarus; but Theonoë, not seeing through the disguise, fell in love with her, and told one of the guards: 'Bring that young priest to my bedroom!' Leucippe, failing to recognize Theonoë, and fearing to be put to death as an imposter, rebuffed her; whereupon Theonoë, since she could not ask the palace servants to commit sacrilege by killing a priest, gave orders that one of the foreign prisoners must do so, and sent a sword for his use.

b. Now, the prisoner chosen was Thestor, who went to the bedroom in which Leucippe had been locked, displayed his sword, and despairingly told her his story. 'I will not kill you, sir,' he said, 'because I too worship Apollo, and prefer to kill myself! But let me first reveal my name: I am Thestor, son of Idmon the Agonaut, a Trojan priest.' He was about to plunge the sword into his own breast, when Leucippe snatched it away. 'Father, father!' she exclaimed, 'I am Leucippe, your daughter! Do not turn this weapon against yourself; use it to kill King Icarus's abominable concubine. Come, follow me!' They hurried to Theonoë's embroidery-chamber. 'Ah, lustful one,' cried Leucippe, bursting in and dragging Thestor after her. 'Prepare to die by the hand of my father, Thestor son of Idmon!' Then it was Theonoë's turn to exclaim: 'Father, father!'; and when the three had wept tears of joy, and given thanks to Apollo, King Icarus generously sent them all home, laden with gifts.[1]

c. Now Priam, after rejecting Agamemnon's demand for the return of Helen, sent Thestor's son Calchas, a priest of Apollo, to consult the Delphic Pythoness. Having foretold the fall of Troy and the total ruin of Priam's house, she ordered Calchas to join the Greeks and prevent them from raising the siege until they were victorious. Calchas then swore an oath of friendship with Achilles, who lodged him in his own house, and presently brought him to Agamemnon.[2]

*d.* When the Greek fleet assembled for the second time at Aulis, but was windbound there for many days, Calchas prophesied that they would be unable to sail unless Agamemnon sacrificed the most beautiful of his daughters to Artemis. Why Artemis should have been vexed is disputed. Some say that, on shooting a stag at long range, Agamemnon had boasted: 'Artemis herself could not have done better!'; or had killed her sacred goat; or had vowed to offer her the most beautiful creature born that year in his kingdom, which happened to be Iphigeneia; or that his father Atreus had withheld a golden lamb which was her due.[3] At any rate, Agamemnon refused to do as he was expected, saying that Clytaemnestra would never let Iphigeneia go. But when the Greeks swore: 'We shall transfer our allegiance to Palamedes if he continues obdurate,' and when Odysseus, feigning anger, prepared to sail home, Menelaus came forward as peace-maker. He suggested that Odysseus and Talthybius should fetch Iphigeneia to Aulis, on the pretext of marrying her to Achilles as a reward for his daring feats in Mysia. To this ruse Agamemnon agreed, and though he at once sent a secret message, warning Clytaemnestra not to believe Odysseus, Menelaus intercepted this, and she was tricked into bringing Iphigeneia to Aulis.[4]

*e.* When Achilles found that his name had been misused, he undertook to protect Iphigeneia from injury; but she nobly consented to die for the glory of Greece, and offered her neck to the sacrificial axe without a word of complaint. Some say that, in the nick of time, Artemis carried her off to the land of the Taurians, substituting a hind at the altar; or a she-bear; or an old woman. Others, that a peal of thunder was heard and that, at Artemis's order and Clytaemnestra's plea, Achilles intervened, saved Iphigeneia, and sent her to Scythia; or that he married her, and that she, not Deidameia, bore him Neoptolemus.[5]

*f.* But whether Iphigeneia died or was spared, the north-easterly gale dropped, and the fleet set sail at last. They first touched at Lesbos, where Odysseus entered the ring against King Philomeleides, who always compelled his guests to wrestle with him; and, amid the loud cheers of every Greek present, threw him ignominiously. Next, they landed on Tenedos, which is visible from Troy, and was then ruled by

Tenes who, though reputedly the son of Cycnus and Procleia, daughter of Laomedon, could call Apollo his father.

*g*. This Cycnus, a son of Poseidon and Calyce, or Harpale, ruled Colonae. He had been born in secret, and exposed on the seashore, but was found by some fishermen who saw a swan flying down to comfort him.[6] After the death of Procleia, he married Phylonome, daughter of Tragasus: she fell in love with her step-son Tenes, failed to seduce him, and vengefully accused him of having tried to violate her. She called the flautist Molpus as a witness; and Cycnus, believing them, locked Tenes and his sister Hemithea in a chest and set them adrift on the sea. They were washed ashore on the island of Tenedos, hitherto called Leucophrys, which means 'white brow'.[7] Later, when Cycnus learned the truth, he had Molpus stoned to death, buried Phylonome alive and, hearing that Tenes survived and was living on Tenedos, hastened there to admit his error. But Tenes, in an unforgiving mood, cut the cables of Cycnus's ship with an axe: hence the proverbial expression for an angry refusal – 'He cut him with an axe from Tenedos.' Finally, however, Tenes softened, and Cycnus settled near him on Tenedos.[8]

*h*. Now, Thetis had warned Achilles that if ever he killed a son of Apollo, he must himself die by Apollo's hand; and a servant named Mnemon accompanied him for the sole purpose of reminding him of this. But Achilles, when he saw Tenes hurling a huge rock from a cliff at the Greek ships, swam ashore, and thoughtlessly thrust him through the heart. The Greeks then landed and ravaged Tenedos; and realizing too late what he had done, Achilles put Mnemon to death because he had failed to remind him of Thetis's words. He buried Tenes where his shrine now stands: no flautist may enter there, nor may Achilles's name be mentioned.[9] Achilles also killed Cycnus with a blow on the head, his only vulnerable part; and pursued Hemithea, who fled from him like a hind, but would have been overtaken and violated, had not the earth swallowed her up. It was in Tenedos, too, that Achilles first quarrelled with Agamemnon, whom he accused of having invited him to join the expedition only as an afterthought.[10]

*i*. Palamedes offered a hecatomb to Apollo Smintheus in gratitude for the Tenedan victory but, as he did so, a water-snake approached the altar and bit Philoctetes, the famous archer, in the foot. Neither unguents nor fomentations availed, and the wound grew so noisome, and Philoctetes's groans so loud, that the army could no longer tolerate his company. Agamemnon therefore ordered Odysseus to put him ashore in a deserted district of Lemnos, where he sustained life for several years by shooting birds; and Medon assumed the command of his troops.[11]

*j.* According to another account, the accident happened on Chryse, an islet off Lemnos, which has since vanished beneath the sea. There either the nymph Chryse fell in love with Philoctetes and, when he rejected her advances, provoked a viper to bite him while he was clearing away the earth from a buried altar of Athene Chryse; or else a serpent that guarded Athene's temple bit him when he came too close.[12]

*k.* According to a third account, Philoctetes was bitten in Lemnos itself by a serpent which Hera sent as a punishment for his having dared to kindle Heracles's funeral pyre. He was, at the time, raptly gazing at the altar raised to Athene by Jason, and planning to raise another to Heracles.[13]

*l.* A fourth account is that Philoctetes was bitten while admiring Troilus's tomb in the temple of Thymbraean Apollo.[14] A fifth, that he was wounded by one of Heracles's envenomed arrows. Heracles, it is said, had made him swear never to divulge the whereabouts of his buried ashes; but when the Greeks learned that Troy could not be sacked without the use of Heracles's arrows, they went in search of Philoctetes. Though at first denying all knowledge of Heracles, he ended by telling them exactly what had happened on Mount Oeta; so they eagerly asked him where they might find the grave. This question he refused to answer, but they became so insistent that he went to the place, and there wordlessly stamped on the ground. Later, as he passed the grave on his way to the Trojan War, one of Heracles's arrows leaped from the quiver and pierced his foot: a warning that one must not reveal divine secrets even by a sign or hint.[15]

1. Hyginus: *Fabula* 190.
2. Benoit: *Le Roman de Troie*.
3. Ptolemy Hephaestionos: vi, quoted by Photius p. 483; Euripides: *Iphigeneia Among the Taurians*; Apollodorus: *Epitome* iii. 21.
4. Ptolemy Hephaestionos: *loc. cit.*; Euripides: *loc. cit.*; Apollodorus: *Epitome* iii. 22; Dictys Cretensis: i. 20.
5. Euripides: *Iphigeneia in Aulis*; Sophocles: *Electra* 574; Apollodorus: *loc. cit.*; Dictys Cretensis: i. 19; Tzetzes: *On Lycophron* 183.
6. Homer: *Odyssey* iv. 342–4; Apollodorus: *Epitome* iii. 23–4; Pausanias: x. 14. 2; Hyginus: *Fabula* 157; Scholiast on Pindar's *Olympian Odes* ii. 147; Tzetzes: *On Lycophron* 232–3.
7. Apollodorus: *Epitome* iii. 24; Pausanias: *loc. cit.*; Tzetzes: *loc. cit.*
8. Apollodorus: *Epitome* iii. 25; Pausanias: x. 14. 2; Tzetzes: *loc. cit.*

9. Tzetzes: *loc. cit.*; Plutarch: *Greek Questions* 28.
10. Tzetzes: *loc. cit.*; Apollodorus: *Epitome* iii. 31; *Cypria*, quoted by Proclus: *Chrestomathy* 1.
11. Dictys Cretensis: ii. 14; *Cypria*, quoted by Proclus: *loc. cit.*; Apollodorus: *Epitome* iii. 27; Homer: *Iliad* ii. 727.
12. Pausanias: viii. 33. 2; Tzetzes: *On Lycophron* 911; Sophocles: *Philoctetes* 1327; Philostratus: *Imagines* 17; Eustathius on Homer p. 330.
13. Hyginus: *Fabula* 102; Scholiast on Sophocles's *Philoctetes*, verses 2, 193 and 266.
14. Philostratus: *loc. cit.*
15. Servius on Virgil's *Aeneid* iii. 402.

*

1. The lost play from which Hyginus has taken the story of Thestor and his daughters shows the Greek dramatists at their most theatrical; it has no mythological value.

2. A version of the 'Jephthah's daughter' myth (see 169. 5) seems to have been confused with Agamemnon's sacrifice of a priestess at Aulis, on a charge of raising contrary winds by witchcraft; Sir Francis Drake once hanged one of his sailors, a spy in Cecil's pay, on the same charge. Agamemnon's high-handed action, it seems, offended conservative opinion at home, women being traditionally exempt from sacrifice. The Taurians, to whom Iphigeneia was said to have been sent by Artemis, lived in the Crimea and worshipped Artemis as a man-slayer; Agamemnon's son Orestes fell into their clutches (see 116. *e*).

3. Odysseus's wrestling match with King Philomeleides, whose name means 'dear to the apple-nymphs', is probably taken from a familiar icon, showing the ritual contest in which the old king is defeated by the new and given an apple-bough (see 53. *b*).

4. Achilles killed a second Cycnus (see 162. *f*); Heracles killed a third (see 143. *g*), and was prevented by Zeus from killing a fourth (see 133. *d*). The name implied that swans conveyed these royal souls to the Northern Paradise. When Apollo appears in ancient works of art riding on swan-back, or in a chariot drawn by swans (Overbeck: *Griechische Kunstmythologie*) on a visit to the Hyperboreans, this is a polite way of depicting his representative's annual death at midsummer. Singing swans then fly north to their breeding grounds in the Arctic circle, and utter two trumpet-like notes as they go; which is why Pausanias (i. 30. 3) says that swans are versed in the Muses' craft. 'Swans sing before they die': the sacred king's soul departs to the sound of music.

5. Philoctetes's wound has been associated with many different localities because the icon from which his story derives was widely current. He is the sacred king of Tenedos, Lemnos, Euboea, or any other

Halladic state, receiving the prick of an envenomed arrow in his foot (see 126. 3; 154. *h*; 164. *j* and 166. *e*) beside the goddess's altar.

6. Heracles was not the only sacred king whose grave remained a secret; this seems to have been common practice on the Isthmus of Corinth (see 67. *j*), and among the primitive Hebrews (*Deuteronomy* xxxiv. 6).

7. Tenes hurling rocks may be a misinterpretation of the familiar icon which shows a sun-hero pushing the sun-boulder up to the zenith (see 67. 2), since Talos, a Cretan sun-hero, also hurled rocks at approaching ships (see 154. *h*). The ships in this icon would merely indicate that Crete, or Tenedos, was a naval power.

# 162

## NINE YEARS OF WAR

A T what point the Greeks sent Priam envoys to demand the return of Helen and of Menelaus's property is disputed. Some say, soon after the expedition had landed in the Troad; others, before the ships assembled at Aulis; but it is commonly held that the embassy, consisting of Menelaus, Odysseus, and Palamedes, went ahead from Tenedos.[1] The Trojans, however, being determined to keep Helen, would have murdered them all had not Antenor, in whose house they were lodging, forbidden the shameful deed.[2]

b. Vexed by this obduracy, the Greeks sailed from Tenedos and beached their ships within sight of Troy. The Trojans at once flocked down to the sea and tried to repel the invaders with showers of stones. Then, while all the others hesitated – even Achilles, whom Thetis had warned that the first to land would be the first to die – Protesilaus leaped ashore, killed a number of Trojans, and was struck dead by Hector; or it may have been Euphorbus; or Aeneas's friend Achates.[3]

c. This Protesilaus, an uncle of Philoctetes, and son of that Iphiclus whom Melampus cured of impotence, had been called Iolaus, but was renamed from the circumstance of his death.[4] He lies buried in the Thracian Chersonese, near the city of Elaeus, where he is now given divine honours. Tall elm-trees, planted by nymphs, stand within his precinct and overshadow the tomb. The boughs which face Troy across the sea burst early into leaf, but presently go bare; while those on the other side are still green in winter-time. When the elms grow so high that the walls of Troy can be clearly discerned by a man posted in their upper branches, they wither; saplings, however, spring again from the roots.⁵

*d.* Protesilaus's wife Laodameia, daughter of Acastus (whom some call Polydora daughter of Meleager) missed him so sadly that as soon as he sailed for Troy she made a brazen, or wax, statue of him and laid it in her bed. But this was poor comfort, and when news came of his death, she begged the gods to take pity and let him revisit her, if only for three hours. Almighty Zeus granted Laodameia's request, and Hermes brought up Protesilaus's ghost from Tartarus to animate the statue. Speaking with its mouth, Protesilaus then adjured her not to delay in following him, and the three hours had no sooner ended than she stabbed herself to death in his embrace.⁶ Others say that Laodameia's father Acastus forced her to remarry, but that she spent her nights with Protesilaus's statue until one day a servant, bringing apples for a dawn sacrifice, looked through a crack in the bedroom-door and saw her embracing what he took to be a lover. He ran and told Acastus who, bursting into the room, discovered the truth. Rather than that she should torture herself by fruitless longing, Acastus ordered the statue to be burned; but Laodameia threw herself into the flames and perished with it.⁷

*e.* According to another tradition, Protesilaus survived the Trojan War and set sail for home. He took back, as his prisoner, Priam's sister Aethylla. On the way he landed at the Macedonian peninsula of Pellene but, while he went ashore in search of water, Aethylla persuaded the other captive women to burn the ships; and Protesilaus, thus obliged to remain on Pellene, founded the city of Scione. This, however, is an error: Aethylla, with Astyoche and her fellow-captives, set fire to the vessels beside the Italian river Navaethus, which means 'burning of ships'; and Protesilaus did not figure among their captors.⁸

*f.* Achilles was the second Greek to land on the Trojan shore, closely followed by his Myrmidons, and killed Cycnus son of Poseidon with a well-flung stone. Thereupon the Trojans broke and fled back to their city, while the remainder of the Greeks disembarked and pressed murderously on the rout. According to another account, Achilles, mindful of Protesilaus's fate, was the very last to land, and then took such a prodigious leap from his ship that a spring gushed out where his feet struck the shore. In the ensuing battle, it is said, Cycnus, who was invulnerable, killed Greeks by the hundred; but Achilles, after trying sword and spear against him in vain, battered furiously at his face with the hilt of his sword, forced him backwards until he tripped over a stone, then knelt on his breast and strangled him with the straps of his helmet; however, Poseidon turned his spirit into a swan, which flew away. The Greeks then laid siege to Troy and drew up their ships behind a stockade.⁹

*g*. Now, the city was fated not to fall if Troilus could attain the age of twenty. Some say that Achilles fell in love with him as they fought together, and 'I will kill you,' he said, 'unless you yield to my caresses!' Troilus fled and took sanctuary in the temple of Thymbraean Apollo; but Achilles cared nothing for the god's wrath and since Troilus remained coy, beheaded him at the altar, the very place where he himself later perished.¹⁰ Others say that Achilles speared Troilus while he was exercising his horses in the temple precinct; or that he lured him out by offering a gift of doves, and that Troilus died with crushed ribs and livid face, in such bear-like fashion did Achilles make love. Others, again, say that Troilus sallied vengefully from Troy after the death of Memnon and encountered Achilles, who killed him – or else he was taken prisoner and then publicly slaughtered in cold blood at Achilles's orders – and that, being then middle-aged, with a swarthy complexion and a flowing beard, he can hardly have excited Achilles's passion. But whatever the manner of his death, Achilles caused it, and the Trojans mourned for him as grievously as for Hector.¹¹

*h*. Troilus is said to have loved Briseis, Calchas's beautiful daughter, who had been left behind in Troy by her father and, since she had played no part in his defection, continued to be treated there with courtesy. Calchas, knowing that Troy must fall, persuaded Agamemnon to ask Priam for her on his behalf, lest she should be made a prisoner of war. Priam generously gave his assent and several of his sons escorted Briseis to the Greek camp. Although she had sworn undying fidelity to Troilus, Briseis soon transferred her affections to Diomedes the Argive, who fell passionately in love with her and did his best to kill Troilus whenever he appeared on the battlefield.¹²

*i*. On a night expedition, Achilles captured Lycaon, surprising him in his father Priam's orchard, where he was cutting fig-tree shoots for use as chariot-rails. Patroclus took Lycaon to Lemnos, and sold him to Jason's son, King Euneus, who supplied the Greek forces with wine; the price being a silver Phoenician mixing-bowl. But Eëtion of Imbros ransomed him, and he returned to Troy, only to perish at the hand of Achilles twelve days later.[13]

*j*. Achilles now set out with a band of volunteers to ravage the Trojan countryside. On Mount Ida he cut off Aeneas the Dardanian from his cattle, chased him down the wooded slopes and, after killing the cattlemen and Priam's son Mestor, captured the herd and sacked the city of Lyrnessus, where Aeneas had taken refuge. Mynes and Epistrophus, sons of King Evenus, died in the fighting; but Zeus helped Aeneas to escape. Mynes's wife, another Briseis, daughter of Briseus, was made captive, and her father hanged himself.[14]

*k*. Though Aeneas had connived at Paris's abduction of Helen, he remained neutral for the first few years of the war; being born of the goddess Aphrodite by Anchises, the grandson of Tros, he resented the disdain shown him by his cousin Priam.[15] Yet Achilles's provocative raid obliged the Dardanians to join forces with the Trojans at last. Aeneas proved a skilled fighter and even Achilles did not disparage him: for if Hector was the hand of the Trojans, Aeneas was their soul. His divine mother frequently helped him in battle; and once, when Diomedes had broken his hip with the cast of a stone, rescued him from death; and when Diomedes had wounded her too, with a spear-thrust in the wrist, Apollo carried Aeneas off the field for Leto and Artemis to cure. On another occasion his life was saved by Poseidon who, though hostile to the Trojans, respected the decrees of fate and knew that the royal line of Aeneas must eventually rule Troy.[16]

*l*. Many cities allied to Troy were now taken by Achilles: Lesbos, Phocaea, Colophon, Smyrna, Clazomenae, Cyme, Aegialus, Tenos, Adramyttium, Dide, Endium, Linnaeum, Colone, Lyrnessus, Antandrus, and several others, including Hypoplacian Thebes, where another Eëtion, father of Hector's wife Andromache, and his comrade Podes, ruled over the Cilicians. Achilles killed Eëtion, and seven of his sons besides, but did not despoil his corpse: he burned it fully armoured and around the barrow which he heaped, mountain-nymphs planted a grove of elm-trees.[17] The captives included Astynome, or Chryseis, daughter of Chryses, priest of Apollo in the island of Sminthos. Some call Astynome Eëtion's wife; others say that Chryses had sent her to Lyrnessus for protection, or to attend a festival of Artemis. When the spoils were distributed, she fell to Agamemnon, as did Briseis to Achilles. From Hypoplacian Thebes, Achilles also brought away the swift horse Pedasus, whom he yoked to his immortal team.[18]

*m*. Great Ajax sailed to the Thracian Chersonese, where he captured Lycaon's blood-brother Polydorus – their mother was Laothoë – and in Teuthrania killed King Teuthras, and carried off great spoils, among them the princess Tecmessa, whom he made his concubine.[19]

*n*. As the tenth year of the war approached, the Greeks refrained from raiding the coast of Asia Minor, and concentrated their forces before Troy. The Trojans marshalled their allies against them – Dardanians, led by Aeneas and the two sons of Antenor; Thracian Ciconians; Paeonians; Paphlagonians; Mysians; Phrygians; Maeonians; Carians; Lycians; and so forth. Sarpedon, whom Bellerophon's daughter Laodemeia had borne to Zeus, led the Lycians. This is his story. When Laodameia's brother Isander and Hippolochus were contending for the kingdom, it was proposed that whichever of them might shoot an arrow through a gold ring hung upon a child's breast should be king. Each hotly demanded the other's child as the victim, but Laodameia prevented them from murdering each other by offering to tie the ring around the neck of her own son, Sarpedon. Astounded at such noble unselfishness, they both agreed to resign their claims to the kingdom in favour of Sarpedon; with whom Glaucus, the son of Hippolochus, was now reigning as co-king.[20]

*o*. Agamemnon had sent Odysseus on a foraging expedition to Thrace, and when he came back empty-handed, Palamedes son of Nauplius upbraided him for his sloth and cowardice. 'It was not my fault,' cried Odysseus, 'that no corn could be found. If Agamemnon had sent you in my stead, you would have had no greater success.' Thus challenged Palamedes set sail at once and presently reappeared with a ship-load of grain.[21]

*p*. After days of tortuous thought, Odysseus at last hit upon a plan by which he might be revenged on Palamedes; for his honour was wounded. He sent word to Agamemnon: 'The gods have warned me in a dream that treachery is afoot: the camp must be moved for a day and a night.' When Agamemnon gave immediate orders to have this done, Odysseus secretly buried a sackful of gold at the place where Palamedes's tent had been pitched. He then forced a Phrygian prisoner to write a letter, as if from Priam to Palamedes, which read: 'The gold that I have sent is the price you asked for betraying the Greek camp.' Having then ordered the prisoner to hand Palamedes this letter, Odysseus had him killed just outside the camp, before he could deliver it. Next day, when the army returned to the old site, someone found the prisoner's corpse and took the letter to Agamemnon. Palamedes was court-martialled and, when he hotly denied having received gold from Priam or anyone else, Odysseus suggested that his tent should be searched. The gold was discovered, and the whole army stoned Palamedes to death as a traitor.[22]

q. Some say that Agamemnon, Odysseus, and Diomedes were all implicated in this plot, and that they jointly dictated the false letter to the Phrygian and afterwards bribed a servant to hide it with the gold under Palamedes's bed. When Palamedes was led off to the place of stoning he cried aloud: 'Truth, I mourn for you, who have predeceased me!'[23]

r. Others, again, say that Odysseus and Diomedes, pretending to have discovered a treasure in a deep well, let Palamedes down into it by a rope, and then tumbled large stones on his head; or that they drowned him on a fishing excursion. Still others say that Paris killed him with an arrow. It is not even agreed whether his death took place at Trojan Colonae, at Geraestus, or on Tenedos; but he has a heroshrine near Lesbian Methymna.[24]

s. Palamedes had deserved the gratitude of his comrades by the invention of dice, with which they whiled away their time before Troy; and the first set of which he dedicated in the temple of Tyche at Argos. But all envied him his superior wisdom, because he had also invented lighthouses, scales, measures, the discus, the alphabet, and the art of posting sentinels.[25]

t. When Nauplius heard of the murder, he sailed to Troy and claimed satisfaction; yet this was denied him by Agamemnon, who had been Odysseus's accomplice and enjoyed the confidence of all the Greek leaders. So Nauplius returned to Greece with his surviving son Oeax, and brought false news to the wives of Palamedes's murderers, saying to each: 'Your husband is bringing back a Trojan concubine as his new queen.' Some of these unhappy wives thereupon killed themselves. Others committed adultery: as did Agamemnon's wife Clytaemnestra, with Aegisthus; Diomedes's wife Aegialeia, with Cometes son of Sthenelus; and Idomeneus's wife Meda, with one Leucus.[26]

1. *Cypria*, quoted by Proclus: *Chrestomathy* 1; Tzetzes: *Antehomerica* 154 ff.; Scholiast on Homer's *Iliad* iii. 206.
2. Dictys Cretensis: i. 4; Apollodorus: *Epitome* iii. 28–9; Homer: *Iliad* iii. 207.
3. Apollodorus: *Epitome* iii. 29–30; Hyginus: *Fabula* 103; Eustathius on Homer pp. 325 and 326.

4. Hyginus: *loc. cit.*; Eustathius on Homer p. 245.

5. Pausanias: i. 34. 2; Tzetzes: *On Lycophron* 532–3; Philostratus: *Heroica* iii. 1; Quintus Smyrnaeus: *Posthomerica* vii. 408 ff.; Pliny: *Natural History* xvi. 88.

6. Hyginus: *Fabulae* 103 and 104; *Cypria*, quoted by Pausanias: iv. 2. 5; Ovid: *Heroides* xiii. 152; Eustathius on Homer p. 325; Apollodorus: *Epitome* iii. 30; Servius on Virgil's *Aeneid* vi. 447.

7. Eustathius on Homer, *loc. cit.*; Hyginus: *Fabula* 104.

8. Conon: *Narrations* 13; Apollodorus: *Epitome*, quoted by Tzetzes: *On Lycophron* 941; Strabo: vi. 1. 12.

9. Apollodorus: *Epitome* iii. 31; Tzetzes: *On Lycophron* 245; Ovid: *Metamorphoses* xii. 70–145.

10. First Vatican Mythographer: 210; Tzetzes: *On Lycophron* 307.

11. Eustathius on Homer's *Iliad* xxiv. 251, p. 1348; Servius on Virgil's *Aeneid* i. 478; Dictys Cretensis: iv. 9; Tzetzes: *loc. cit.*

12. Benoit: *Le Roman de Troie.*

13. Apollodorus: *Epitome* iii. 32; Homer: *Iliad* xxi. 34 ff. and 85–6; xxiii. 740–7 and vii. 467–8.

14. Apollodorus: *Epitome* iii. 32; Homer: *Iliad* ii. 690–3; xx. 89 ff. and 188 ff.; Eustathius on Homer's *Iliad* iii. 58; Scholiast on Homer's *Iliad* i. 184; *Cypria*, quoted by Proclus: *Chrestomathy* i; Dictys Cretensis: ii. 17.

15. Hyginus: *Fabula* 115; Homer: *Iliad* xiii. 460 ff. and xx. 181 ff.; Hesiod: *Theogony* 1007.

16. Homer: *Iliad* v. 305 ff.; xx. 178 ff. and 585 ff.; Philostratus: *Heroica* 13.

17. Homer: *Iliad* ix. 328–9; vi. 395–7; xvii. 575–7 and vi. 413–28; Apollodorus: *Epitome* iii. 33.

18. Dictys Cretensis: ii. 17; Homer: *Iliad* i. 366 ff. and xvi. 149–54; Eustathius on Homer pp. 77, 118 and 119.

19. Dictys Cretensis: ii. 18; Sophocles: *Ajax* 210; Horace: *Odes* ii. 4. 5.

20. Heracleides Ponticus: *Homeric Allegories* pp. 424–5; Homer: *Iliad* vi. 196 ff.; Apollodorus: *Epitome* iii. 34–5; Eustathius on Homer p. 894.

21. *Cypria*, quoted by Proclus: *loc. cit.*; Servius on Virgil's *Aeneid* ii. 81.

22. Apollodorus: *Epitome* iii. 8; Hyginus: *Fabula* 105.

23. Scholiast on Euripides's *Orestes* 432; Philostratus: *Heroica* 10.

24. Dictys Cretensis: ii. 15; *Cypria*, quoted by Pausanias: x. 31. 1; Tzetzes: *On Lycophron* 384 ff. and 1097; Dares: 28.

25. Pausanias: x. 31. 1 and ii. 20. 3; Philostratus: *loc. cit.*; Scholiast on Euripides's *Orestes* 432; Servius on Virgil's *Aeneid* ii. 81; Tzetzes: *On Lycophron* 384.

26. Apollodorus: *Epitome* vi. 8–9; Tzetzes: *On Lycophron* 384 ff.; Eustathius on Homer p. 24; Dictys Cretensis: vi. 2.

*

1. The *Iliad* deals in sequence only with the tenth year of the siege, and each mythographer has arranged the events of the preceding years in a different order. According to Apollodorus (*Epitome* iii. 32–3), Achilles kills Troilus; captures Lycaon; raids Aeneas's cattle; and takes many cities. According to the *Cypria* (quoted by Proclus: *Chrestomathy* i), the Greeks, failing to take Troy by assault, lay waste the country and cities round about; Aphrodite and Thetis contrive a meeting between Achilles and Helen; the Greeks decide to go home but are restrained by Achilles, who then drives off Aeneas's cattle, sacks many cities, and kills Troilus; Patroclus sells Lycaon on Lemnos; the spoils are divided; Palamedes is stoned to death.

2. According to Tzetzes (*On Lycophron* 307), Troilus outlives Memnon and Hector. Similarly, according to Dares the Phrygian, Troilus succeeds Hector as commander of the Trojan forces (Dares: 30), until one of his chariot horses is wounded and Achilles, driving up, runs him through; Achilles tries to drag away the body, but is wounded by Memnon, whom he kills; the Trojans take refuge within the city and Priam gives both Troilus and Memnon a magnificent funeral (Dares: 33).

3. The Trojan War is historical, and whatever the immediate cause may have been, it was a trade war. Troy controlled the valuable Black Sea trade in gold, silver, iron, cinnabar, ship's timber, linen, hemp, dried fish, oil, and Chinese jade. When once Troy had fallen, the Greeks were able to plant colonies all along the eastern trade route, which grew as rich as those of Asia Minor and Sicily. In the end, Athens, as the leading maritime power, profited most from the Black Sea trade, especially from its cheap grain; and it was the loss of a fleet guarding the entrance to the Hellespont that ruined her at Aegospotami in 405 B.C., and ended the long Peloponnesian Wars. Perhaps, therefore, the constant negotiations between Agamemnon and Priam did not concern the return of Helen so much as the restoration of the Greek rights to enter the Hellespont.

4. It is probable that the Greeks prepared for their final assault by a series of raids on the coasts of Thrace and Asia Minor, to cripple the naval power of the Trojan alliance; and that they maintained a camp at the mouth of the Scamander to prevent Mediterranean trade from reaching Troy, or the annual East-West Fair from being celebrated on the Plain. But the *Iliad* makes it clear that Troy was not besieged in the sense that her lines of communication with the interior were cut, and though, while Achilles was about, the Trojans did not venture by day through the Dardanian Gate, the one which led inland (*Iliad* v. 789); and the Greek laundresses feared to wash their clothes at the spring a bow's shot from the walls (*Iliad* xxii. 256); yet supplies and reinforcements entered freely, and the Trojans held Sestos and Abydos, which kept them in close

touch with Thrace. That the Greeks boasted so loudly of a raid on the cattle of Mount Ida, and another on Priam's fig-orchard, suggests that they seldom went far inland. The fig-shoots used for the rail of Lycaon's chariot were apparently designed to place it under the protection of Aphrodite. In the pre-Trojan-War tablets found at Cnossus, a number of 'red-painted Cydonian chariots' are mentioned, 'with joinery work complete', but only the wood of the rails is specified: it is always fig. Yet fig was not nearly so suitable a wood for the purpose as many others available to the Cretans and Trojans.

5. Agamemnon had engaged in a war of attrition, the success of which Hector confesses (*Iliad* xvii. 225 and xviii. 287-92) when he speaks of the drain on Trojan resources caused by the drying up of trade, and the need to subsidize allies. The Paphlagonians, Thracians, and Mysians were producers, not merchants, and ready to have direct dealings with the Greeks. Only the mercantile Lycians, who imported goods from the South-east, seem to have been much concerned about the fate of Troy, which secured their northern trade routes; indeed, when Troy fell, the trade of Asia Minor was monopolized by Agamemnon's allies the Rhodians, and the Lycians were ruined.

6. The coldblooded treatment of women, suppliants, and allies serves as a reminder that the *Iliad* is not Bronze Age myth. With the fall of Cnossus (see 39. 7 and 89. 1) and the consequent disappearance of the *pax Cretensis*, imposed by the Cretan Sea-goddess upon all countries within her sphere of influence, a new Iron Age morality emerges: that of the conquering tyrant, a petty Zeus, who acknowledges no divine restraint. Iphigeneia's sacrifice, Odysseus's hateful revenge on Palamedes, the selling of Lycaon for a silver cup, Achilles's shameless pursuit of Troilus and the forced concubinage of Briseis and Chryseis are typical of barbarous saga. It is proper that Palamedes should have been the innocent victim of an unholy alliance between Agamemnon, Odysseus, and Diomedes, since he represents the Cretan culture planted in Argolis – the inventions with which he is credited being all of Cretan origin. His murder in a well may have been suggested by 'Truth, I mourn you, who have predeceased me!' and by the familiar connexion of truth with wells. *Palamedes* means 'ancient wisdom' and, like Hephaestus, his Lemnian counterpart, he was an oracular hero. His inventions reveal him at Thoth or Hermes (see 17. *g*). Dice have the some history as cards: they were oracular instruments before being used for games of chance (see 17. *3*).

7. The elm-tree, which does not form part of the tree-calendar (see 53. *3*), is mainly associated with the Dionysus cult, since the Greeks trained vines on elm-saplings; but elms were planted by nymphs around the tombs of Protesilaus and Eëtion, presumably because the leaves and bark served as vulneraries (Pliny: *Natural History* xxiv. 33), and promised

to be even more efficacious if taken from the graves of princes who had succumbed to many wounds.

8. Laodameia's perverse attachment to Protesilaus's statue may have been deduced from a sacred-wedding icon: in some Hittite marriage-seals, the procumbent king is carved so stiffly that he looks like a statue. The apple brought by a servant, and Acastus's sudden entry, suggest that the scene represented a queen's betrayal of a king to her lover the tanist, who cuts the fatal apple containing his soul – as in the Irish legend of Cuchulain, Dechtire, and Curoi.

Briseis (accusative case: *Briseida*) became confused with Chryses, or Chryseis, daughter of Chryses, who had borne a bastard to Agamemnon (see 116. *h*); and the medieval Latin legend of Criseis (accusative case: *Criseida*) developed vigorously until Henrysoun's *Testament of Cresseid* and Shakespeare's *Troilus and Cressida*.

9. Teuthrania may have been so called after the *teuthis*, or octopus, sacred to the Cretan Goddess (see 81. *1*), whose chief priestess was Tecmessa ('she who ordains').

Though the Sarpedon myth is confused, its elements are all familiar. Apparently the kingdom of Lycia, founded by another Sarpedon, uncle of another Glaucus – Greek-speaking Cretans of Aeolian or Pelasgian stock, who were driven overseas by the Achaeans – was a double one, with matrilinear succession, the title of the Moon-priestess being Laodemeia ('tamer of the people'). Its sacred king seems to have been ritually 'born from a mare' (see 81. *4* and 167. *2*) – hence his name, Hippolochus – and Isander ('impartial man') acted as his tanist. Sarpedon's name ('rejoicing in a wooden ark') refers apparently to the annual arrival of the New Year Child in a boat. Here the Child is the *interrex*, to whom Hippolochus resigns his kingship for a single day; he must then be suffocated in honey, like Cretan Glaucus (see 71. *d*), or killed in a chariot crash, like the Isthmian Glaucus (see 90. *1*), or transfixed with an arrow by the revived Hippolochus, like Learchus son of Athamas (see 70. *5*).

10. To shoot an apple poised upon the head, or at a penny set in the cap, of one's own son was a test of marksmanship prescribed to medieval archers, whose guild (as appears in the *Malleus Maleficarum* and in the *Little Geste of Robin Hood*) belonged to the pagan witch cult both in England and Celtic Germany. In England this test was, it seems, designed to choose a 'gudeman' for Maid Marian, by marriage to whom he became Robin Hood, Lord of the Greenwood. Since the northern witch cult had much in common with neolithic religion of the Aegean, it may be that the Lycians did not place the ring on a boy's breast, but on his head, and that it represented a golden serpent (see 119. *4*); or that it was the ring of an axe which he held in his hand, like those through which Odysseus shot when he recovered Penelope from the suitors (see 171.

*h*). The mythographer has perhaps confused the shooting test demanded of a new candidate for the kingship with the sacrifice of an *interrex*.

*11*. Aethylla means 'kindling timber', and the annual burning of a boat may have originated the Scione legend.

Protesilaus ('first of the people') must have been so common a royal title that several cities claimed his tomb.

# 163

## THE WRATH OF ACHILLES

WINTER now drew on, and since this has never been a battle season among civilized nations, the Greeks spent it enlarging their camp and practising archery. Sometimes they came across Trojan notables in the temple of Thymbraean Apollo, which was neutral territory; and once, while Hecabe happened to be sacrificing there, Achilles arrived on the same errand and fell desperately in love with her daughter Polyxena. He made no declaration at the time but, returning to his hut in torment, sent the kindly Automedon to ask Hector on what terms he might marry Polyxena. Hector replied: 'She shall be his on the day that he betrays the Greek camp to my father Priam.' Achilles seemed willing enough to accept Hector's conditions, but drew back sullenly when informed that if he failed to betray the camp, he must swear instead to murder his cousin Great Ajax and the sons of Athenian Pleisthenes.[1]

*b*. Spring came and fighting was resumed. In the first engagement of the season Achilles sought out Hector, but the watchful Helenus pierced his hand with an arrow shot from an ivory bow, Apollo's love gift, and forced him to give ground. Zeus himself guided the arrow-head; and as he did so decided to relieve the Trojans, whom the raids and the consequent desertion of certain Asiatic allies had greatly discouraged, by plaguing the Greeks and detaching Achilles from his fellow-chieftains.[2] When, therefore, Chryses came to ransom Chryseis, Zeus persuaded Agamemnon to drive him away with opprobrious words; and Apollo, invoked by Chryses, posted himself vengefully near the ships, shooting deadly arrows among the Greeks day after day. Hundreds perished, though (as it happened) no kings or princes suffered, and on the tenth day Calchas made known the presence of

the god. At his instance, Agamemnon grudgingly sent Chryseis back
to her father, with propitiatory gifts, but recouped his loss by seizing
Briseis from Achilles, to whom she had been allotted; whereupon
Achilles, in a rage, announced that he would take no further part in the
War; and his mother Thetis indignantly approached Zeus, who promised her satisfaction on his behalf. But some say that Achilles kept out
of the fighting in order to show his goodwill towards Priam as Polyxena's father.[3]

*c.* When the Trojans became aware that Achilles and his Myrmidons
had withdrawn from the field, they took heart and made a vigorous
sortie. Agamemnon, in alarm, granted them a truce, during which
Paris and Menelaus were to fight a duel for the possession of Helen and
the stolen treasure. The duel, however, proved indecisive, because
when Aphrodite saw that Paris was getting the worst of it, she wrapped
him in a magic mist and carried him back to Troy. Hera then sent
Athene down to break the truce by making Pandarus son of Lycaon
shoot an arrow at Menelaus, which she did; at the same time she
inspired Diomedes to kill Pandarus and wound Aeneas and his mother
Aphrodite. Glaucus son of Hippolochus now opposed Diomedes, but
both recalled the close friendship that had bound their fathers, and
courteously exchanged arms.[4]

*d.* Hector challenged Achilles to single combat; and when Achilles
sent back word that he had retired from the war, the Greeks chose
Great Ajax as his substitute. These two champions fought without
pause until nightfall, when heralds parted them and each gaspingly
praised the other's skill and courage. Ajax gave Hector the brilliant
purple baldric by which he was later dragged to his death; and Hector
gave Ajax the silver-studded sword with which he was later to commit
suicide.[5]

*e.* An armistice being agreed upon, the Greeks raised a long barrow
over their dead, and crowned it with a wall beyond which they dug a
deep, palisaded trench. But they had omitted to appease the deities
who supported the Trojans and, when fighting was resumed, were
driven across the trench and behind the wall. That night the Trojans
encamped close to the Greek ships.[6]

*f.* In despair, Agamemnon sent Phoenix, Ajax, Odysseus and two
heralds to placate Achilles, offering him countless gifts and the return
of Briseis (they were to swear that she was still a virgin) if only he
would fight again. It should be explained that Chryses had meanwhile

brought back his daughter, who protested that she had been very well treated by Agamemnon and wished to remain with him; she was pregnant at the time and later gave birth to Chryses the Second, a child of doubtful paternity. Achilles greeted the deputation with a pleasant smile, but refused their offers, and announced that he must sail home next morning.[7]

*g.* That same night about the third watch when the moon was high, Odysseus and Diomedes, encouraged by a lucky auspice from Athene – a heron on their right hand – decided to raid the Trojan lines. They happened to stumble over Dolon, son of Eumelus, who had been sent out on patrol by the enemy and, after forcibly extracting information from him, cut his throat. Odysseus then hid Dolon's ferret-skin cap, wolf-skin cloak, bow and spear in a tamarisk bush and hurried with Diomedes to the right flank of the Trojan line where, they now knew, Rhesus the Thracian was encamped. He is variously described as the son of the Muse Euterpe, or Calliope, by Eioneus, or Ares, or Strymon. Having stealthily assassinated Rhesus and twelve of his companions in their sleep, they drove off his magnificent horses, white as snow and swifter than the wind, and recovered the spoils from the tamarisk bush on their way back.[8] The capture of Rhesus's horses was of the highest importance, since an oracle had foretold that Troy would become impregnable once they had eaten Trojan fodder and drunken from the river Scamander, and this they had not yet done. When the surviving Thracians awoke, to find King Rhesus dead and his horses gone, they fled in despair; the Greeks killed nearly every one of them.[9]

*h.* On the following day, however, after a fierce struggle, in which Agamemnon, Diomedes, Odysseus, Euryplus, and Machaon the surgeon were all wounded, the Greeks took to flight and Hector breached their wall.[10] Encouraged by Apollo, he pushed on towards the ships and, despite assistance lent by Poseidon to the two Ajaxes and Idomeneus, broke through the Greek line. At this point Hera, who hated the Trojans, borrowed Aphrodite's girdle and persuaded Zeus to come and sleep with her; a ruse which allowed Poseidon to turn the battle in the Greeks' favour. But Zeus, soon discovering that he had been duped, revived Hector (nearly killed by Ajax with a huge stone), ordered Poseidon off the field, and restored the Trojans' courage. Forward they went again: Medon killing Periphetes son of Copreus, and many other champions.[11]

*i.* Even Great Ajax was forced to yield ground; and Achilles, when

he saw flames swirling from the stern of Protesilaus's ship, set on fire by
the Trojans, so far forgot his grudge as to marshal the Myrmidons and
hurry them to Patroclus's assistance. Patroclus had flung a spear into the
mass of Trojans gathered around Protesilaus's ship and transfixed
Puraechmes, king of the Paeonians. At this the Trojans, mistaking him
for Achilles, fled; and Patroclus extinguished the fire, saving the bows
of the ship at least, and cut down Sarpedon. Though Glaucus tried to
rally his Lycians and so protect Sarpedon's body from despoilment,
Zeus let Patroclus chase the whole Trojan army towards the city;
Hector being the first to retire, wounded severely by Ajax.

*j.* The Greeks stripped Sarpedon of his armour, but at Zeus's orders
Apollo rescued the body, which he prepared for burial, whereupon
Sleep and Death bore it away to Lycia. Patroclus meanwhile pressed on
the rout, and would have taken Troy single-handed, had not Apollo
hastily mounted the wall, and thrice thrust him back with a shield as he
attempted to scale it. Fighting continued until nightfall, when Apollo,
wrapped in a thick mist, came up behind Patroclus and buffeted him
smartly between the shoulderblades. Patroclus's eyes started from his
head; his helmet flew off; his spear was shattered into splinters; his
shield fell to the ground; and Apollo grimly unlaced his corslet.
Euphorbus son of Panthous, observing Patroclus's plight, wounded
him without fear of retaliation, and as he staggered away, Hector, who
had returned to the battle, despatched him with a single blow.[12]

*k.* Up ran Menelaus and killed Euphorbus – who is said, by the way,
to have been reincarnate centuries later in the philosopher Pythagoras –
and strutted off to his hut with the spoils; leaving Hector to strip
Patroclus of his borrowed armour. Menelaus and Great Ajax then
reappeared and together defended Patroclus's body until dusk, when
they contrived to carry it back to the ships. But Achilles, on hearing the
news, rolled in the dust, and yielded to an ecstasy of grief.[13]

*l.* Thetis entered her son's hut carrying a new suit of armour, which
included a pair of valuable tin greaves, hurriedly forged by Hephaestus.
Achilles put the suit on, made peace with Agamemnon (who delivered
Briseis to him inviolate, swearing that he had taken her in anger, not
lust) and set out to avenge Patroclus.[14] None could stand against his
wrath. The Trojans broke and fled to the Scamander, where he split
them into two bodies, driving one across the plain towards the city,
and penning the other in a bend of the river. Furiously, the River-god
rushed at him, but Hephaestus took Achilles's part and dried up the

waters with a scorching flame. The Trojan survivors regained the city, like a herd of frightened deer.¹⁵

*m.* When Achilles at last met Hector and engaged him in single combat, both sides drew back and stood watching amazed. Hector turned and began to run around the city walls. He hoped by this manoeuvre to weary Achilles, who had long been inactive and should therefore have been short of breath. But he was mistaken. Achilles chased him thrice around the walls, and whenever he made for the shelter of a gate, counting on the help of his brothers, always headed him off. Finally Hector halted and stood his ground, but Achilles ran him through the breast, and refused his dying plea that his body might be ransomed for burial. After possessing himself of the armour, Achilles slit the flesh behind the tendons of Hector's heels. He then passed leather thongs through the slits, secured them to his chariot and, whipping up Balius, Xanthus, and Pedasus, dragged the body towards the ships at an easy canter. Hector's head, its black locks streaming on either side, churned up a cloud of dust behind him. But some say that Achilles dragged the corpse three times around the city walls, by the baldric which Ajax had given him.¹⁶

*n.* Achilles now buried Patroclus. Five Greek princes were sent to Mount Ida in search of timber for the funeral pyre, upon which Achilles sacrificed not only horses, and two of Patroclus's own pack of nine hounds, but twelve noble Trojan captives, several sons of Priam among them, by cutting their throats. He even threatened to throw Hector's corpse to the remaining hounds; Aphrodite, however, restrained him. At Patroclus's funeral games Diomedes won the chariot race, and Epeius, despite his cowardice, the boxing-match; Ajax and Odysseus tied in the wrestling match.¹⁷

*o.* Still consumed by grief, Achilles rose every day at dawn to drag Hector's body three times around Patroclus's tomb. Yet Apollo protected it from corruption and laceration and, eventually, at the command of Zeus, Hermes led Priam to the Greek camp under cover of night, and persuaded Achilles to accept a ransom.¹⁸ On this occasion Priam showed great magnanimity towards Achilles whom he had found asleep in his hut and might easily have murdered. The ransom agreed upon was Hector's weight in gold. Accordingly, the Greeks set up a pair of scales outside the city walls, laid the corpse on one pan, and invited the Trojans to heap gold in the other. When Priam's treasury had been ransacked of ingots and jewels, and Hector's huge bulk still depressed the pan, Polyxena, watching from the wall, threw down her bracelets to supply the missing weight. Overcome by admiration, Achilles told Priam: 'I will cheerfully barter Hector against Polyxena. Keep your gold; marry her to me; and if you then restore Helen to Menelaus, I undertake to make peace between your people and ours.' Priam, for the moment, was content to ransom Hector at the agreed price in gold; but promised to give Polyxena to Achilles freely if he persuaded the Greeks to depart without Helen. Achilles replied that he would do what he could, and Priam then took away the corpse for burial. So great an uproar arose at Hector's funeral – the Trojans lamenting, the Greeks trying to drown their dirges with boos and cat-calls – that birds flying overhead fell down stunned by the noise.[19]

*p.* At the command of an oracle, Hector's bones were eventually taken to Boeotian Thebes, where his grave is still shown beside the fountain of Oedipus. Some quote the Oracle as follows:

'Hearken, ye men of Thebes, who dwell in the city of Cadmus,
  Should you desire your land to be prosperous, wealthy and blame-
    less,
  Carry the bones of Hector, Priam's son, to your city.
  Asia holds them now; there Zeus will attend to his worship.'

Others say that when a plague ravaged Greece, Apollo ordered the reburial of Hector's bones in a famous Greek city which had taken no part in the Trojan War.[20]

*q.* A wholly different tradition makes Hector a son of Apollo, whom Penthesileia the Amazon killed.[21]

1. Dictys Cretensis: iii. 1–3.
2. Ptolemy Hephaestionos: vi.; Dictys Cretensis: iii. 6; *Cypria*, quoted by Proclus: *Chrestomathy* 1.
3. Homer: *Iliad* i; Dictys Cretensis: ii. 30; First Vatican Mythographer: 211.
4. Homer: *Iliad* iii.; iv. 1–129; v. 1–417 and vi. 119–236.
5. Athenaeus: i. 8; Rawlinson: *Excidum Troiae*; Homer: *Iliad* vii. 66–132; Hyginus: *Fabula* 112.
6. Homer: *Iliad* vii. 436–50 and viii.
7. Dictys Cretensis: ii. 47; Hyginus: *Fabula* 121; Homer: *Iliad* ix.
8. Servius on Virgil's *Aeneid* i. 473; Apollodorus: i. 3. 4; Homer: *Iliad* x.
9. Servius: *loc. cit.*; Dictys Cretensis: ii. 45–6.
10. Homer: *Iliad* xi and xii.
11. Homer: *Iliad* xii–xiv.

12. Dictys Cretensis: ii. 43; Homer: *Iliad* xvi.
13. Hyginus: *Fabula* 112; Philostratus: *Life of Apollonius of Tyana* i. 1 and *Heroica* 19. 4; Pausanias: ii. 17. 3; Homer: *Iliad* xvii.
14. Dictys Cretensis: ii. 48–52; Homer: *Iliad* xviii–xix.
15. Homer: *Iliad* xxi.
16. Homer: *Iliad* xxii.
17. Hyginus: *loc. cit.*; Virgil: *Aeneid* i. 487; Dictys Cretensis: iii. 12–14; Homer: *Iliad* xxiii.
18. Homer: *Iliad* xxiv.
19. Servius on Virgil's *Aeneid* i. 491; Rawlinson: *Excidium Troiae*; Dares: 27; Dictys Cretensis: iii. 16 and 27.
20. Pausanias: ix. 18. 4; Tzetzes: *On Lycophron* 1194.
21. Stesichorus, quoted by Tzetzes: *On Lycophron* 266; Ptolemy Hephaestionos: vi., quoted by Photius p. 487.

*

*1.* According to Proclus (*Chrestomathy* xcix. 19–20), *Homerus* means 'blind' rather than 'hostage', which is the usual translation; minstrelsy was a natural vocation for the blind, since blindness and inspiration often went together (see 105. *h*). The identity of the original Homer has been debated for some two thousand five hundred years. In the earliest tradition he is plausibly called an Ionian from Chios. A clan of Homeridae, or 'Sons of the Blind Man', who recited the traditional Homeric poems and eventually became a guild (Scholiast on Pindar's *Nemean Odes* ii. 1), had their headquarters at Delos, the centre of the Ionian world, where Homer himself was said to have recited (*Homeric Hymn* iii. 165–73). Parts of the *Iliad* date from the tenth century B.C.; the subject matter is three centuries older. By the sixth century unauthorized recitals of the *Iliad* were slowly corrupting the text; Peisistratus, tyrant of Athens, therefore ordered an official recension, which he entrusted to four leading scholars. They seem to have done the task well but, since Homer had come to be regarded as a prime authority in disputes between cities, Peisistratus's enemies accused him of interpolating verses for political ends (Strabo: ix. 1. 10).

*2.* The twenty-four books of the *Iliad* have grown out of a poem called 'The Wrath of Achilles' – which could perhaps have been recited in a single night, and which dealt with the quarrel between Achilles and Agamemnon over the possession of a captured princess. It is unlikely that the text of the central events has been radically edited since the first *Iliad* of about 750 B.C. Yet the quarrels are so unedifying, and all the Greek leaders behave so murderously, deceitfully, and shamelessly, while the Trojans by contrast behave so well, that it is obvious on whose side the author's sympathy lay. As a legatee of the Minoan court bards he found his spiritual home among the departed glories of Cnossus and Mycenae, not beside the camp fires of the barbarous invaders from the North.

Homer faithfully describes the lives of his new overlords, who have usurped ancient religious titles by marrying tribal heiresses and, though calling them godlike, wise, and noble, holds them in deep disgust. They live by the sword and perish by the sword, disdaining love, friendship, faith, or the arts of peace. They care so little for the divine names by which they swear that he dares jest in their presence about the greedy, sly, quarrelsome, lecherous, cowardly Olympians who have turned the world upside down. One would dismiss him as an irreligious wretch, were he not clearly a secret worshipper of the Great Goddess of Asia (whom the Greeks had humiliated in this war); and did not glints of his warm and honourable nature appear whenever he is describing family life in Priam's palace. Homer has drawn on the Babylonian *Gilgamesh* epic for the Achilles story; with Achilles as Gilgamesh, Thetis as Ninsun, Patroclus as Enkidu.

3. Achilles's hysterical behaviour when he heard that Patroclus was dead must have shocked Homer, but he has clothed the barbarities of the funeral in mock-heroic language, confident that his overlords will not recognize the sharpness of the satire – Homer may be said, in a sense, to have anticipated Goya, whose caricature-portraits of the Spanish royal family were so splendidly painted that they could be accepted by the victims as honest likenesses. But the point of the *Iliad* as satire has been somewhat blunted by the Homeridae's need to placate their divine hosts at Delos; Apollo and Artemis must support the Trojans and display dignity and discretion, in contrast at least with the vicious deities of the Hellenic camp. One result of the *Iliad's* acceptance by Greek city authorities as a national epic was that no one ever again took the Olympian religion seriously, and Greek morals always remained barbarous – except in places where Cretan mystery cults survived and the mystagogues required a good-conduct certificate from their initiates. The Great Goddess, though now officially subordinate to Zeus, continued to exert a strong spiritual influence at Eleusis, Corinth and Samothrace, until the suppression of her mysteries by early Byzantine emperors. Lucian, who loved his Homer and succeeded him as the prime satirist of the Olympians, also worshipped the Goddess, to whom he had sacrificed his first hair-clippings at Hierapolis.

4. Hector's bones were said to have been brought to Thebes from Troy, yet 'Hector' was a title of the Theban sacred king before the Trojan War took place; and he suffered the same fate when his reign ended – which was to be dragged in the wreck of a circling chariot, like Glaucus (see 71. *a*), Hippolytus (see 101. *g*), Oenomaus (see 109. *g*), and Abderus (see 130. *b*). Since 'Achilles' was also a title rather than a name, the combat may have been borrowed from the lost Theban saga of 'Oedipus's Sheep', in which co-kings fought for the throne (see 106. 2).

# 164

## THE DEATH OF ACHILLES

THE Amazon Queen Penthesileia, daughter of Otrere and Ares, had sought refuge in Troy from the Erinnyes of her sister Hippolyte (also called Glauce, or Melanippe), whom she had accidentally shot, either while out hunting or, according to the Athenians, in the fight which followed Theseus's wedding with Phaedra. Purified by Priam, she greatly distinguished herself in battle, accounting for many Greeks, among them (it is said) Machaon, though the commoner account makes him fall by the hand of Eurypylus, son of Telephus.[1] She drove Achilles from the field on several occasions – some even claim that she killed him and that Zeus, at the plea of Thetis, restored him to life but at last he ran her through, fell in love with her dead body, and committed necrophily upon it there and then.[2] When he later called for volunteers to bury Penthesileia, Thersites, a son of Aetolian Agrius, and the ugliest Greek at Troy, who had gouged out her eyes with his spear as she lay dying, jeeringly accused Achilles of filthy and unnatural lust. Achilles turned and struck Thersites so hard that he broke every tooth in his head and sent his ghost scurrying down to Tartarus.[3]

b. This caused high indignation among the Greeks, and Diomedes, who was a cousin of Thersites and wished to show his disdain for Achilles, dragged Penthesileia's body along by the foot and threw it into the Scamander; whence, however, it was rescued and buried on the bank with great honour – some say by Achilles; others, by the Trojans. Achilles then set sail for Lesbos, where he sacrificed to Apollo, Artemis, and Leto; and Odysseus, a sworn enemy to Thersites, purified him of the murder. The dying Penthesileia, supported by Achilles, is carved on the throne of Zeus at Olympia.[4] Her nurse, the Amazon Clete, hearing that she had fled to Troy after the death of Hippolyte, set out to search for her, but was driven by contrary winds to Italy, where she settled and founded the city of Clete.[5]

c. Priam had by now persuaded his half-brother, Tithonus of Assyria, to send his son Memnon the Ethiopian to Troy; the bribe he offered was a golden vine.[6] A so-called palace of Memnon is shown in Ethiopia, although when Tithonus emigrated to Assyria and founded Susa, Memnon, then only a child, had gone with him. Susa is now commonly known as the City of Memnon; and its inhabitants as Cissians, after Memnon's mother Cissia. His palace on the Acropolis was standing until the time of the Persians.[7]

*d.* Tithonus governed the province of Persia for the Assyrian king Teutamus, Priam's overlord, who put Memnon in command of a thousand Ethiopians, a thousand Susians, and two hundred chariots. The Phrygians still show the rough, straight road, with camp-sites every fifteen miles or so, by which Memnon, after he had subjugated all the intervening nations, marched to Troy. He was black as ebony, but the handsomest man alive, and like Achilles wore armour forged by Hephaestus.[8] Some say that he led a large army of Ethiopians and Indians to Troy by way of Armenia, and that another expedition sailed from Phoenicia at his orders under a Sidonian named Phalas. Landing on Rhodes, the inhabitants of which favoured the Greek cause, Phalas was asked in public: 'Are you not ashamed, sir, to assist Paris the Trojan and other declared enemies of your native city?' The Phoenician sailors, who now heard for the first time where they were bound, stoned Phalas to death as a traitor and settled in Ialysus and Cameirus, after dividing among themselves the treasure and munitions of war which Phalas had brought with him.[9]

*e.* Meanwhile, at Troy, Memnon killed several leading Greeks, including Antilochus, son of Nestor, when he came to his father's rescue: for Paris had shot one of Nestor's chariot horses and terror made its team-mate unmanageable.[10] This Antilochus had been exposed as a child on Mount Ida by his mother Anaxibia, or Eurydice, and there suckled by a bitch. Though too young to sail from Aulis at the beginning of the war, he followed some years later and begged Achilles to soothe Nestor's anger at his unexpected arrival. Achilles, delighted with Antilochus's warlike spirit, undertook to mediate between them and, at his desire, Nestor introduced him to Agamemnon.[11] Antilochus was one of the youngest, handsomest, swiftest and most courageous Greeks who fought at Troy and Nestor, having been warned by an oracle to protect him against an Ethiopian, appointed Chalion as his guardian; but in vain.[12] The bones of Antilochus were laid beside those of his friends, Achilles and Patroclus, whose ghosts he accompanied to the Asphodel Fields.[13]

*f.* That day, with the help of Memnon's Ethiopians, the Trojans nearly succeeded in burning the Greek ships, but darkness fell and they retired. After burying their dead, the Greeks chose Great Ajax to engage Memnon; and next morning the single combat had already begun, when Thetis sought out Achilles, who was absent from the camp, and broke the news of Antilochus's death. Achilles hastened back to take vengeance, and while Zeus, calling for a pair of scales, weighed his fate against that of Memnon,[14] he brushed Ajax aside and made the combat his own. The pan containing Memnon's fate sank in Jove's hand, Achilles dealt the death-blow, and presently black head and bright armour crowned the flaming pyre of Antilochus.[15]

*g*. Some, however, report that Memnon was ambushed by Thessalians; and that his Ethiopians, having burned his body, carried the ashes to Tithonus; and that they now lie buried on a hill overlooking the mouth of the river Aesepus, where a village bears his name.[16] Eos, who is described as Memnon's mother, implored Zeus to confer immortality upon him and some further honour as well. A number of phantom hen-birds, called Memnonides, were consequently formed from the embers and smoke of his pyre, and rising into the air, flew three times around it. At the fourth circuit they divided into two flocks, fought with claws and beaks, and fell down upon his ashes as a funeral sacrifice. Memnonides still fight and fall at his tomb when the Sun has run through all the signs of the Zodiac.[17]

*h*. According to another tradition, these birds are Memnon's girl companions, who lamented for him so excessively that the gods, in pity, metamorphosed them into birds. They make an annual visit to his tomb, where they weep and lacerate themselves until some of them fall dead. The Hellespontines say that when the Memnonides visit Memnon's grave beside the Hellespont, they use their wings to sprinkle it with water from the river Aesepus; and that Eos still weeps tears of dew for him every morning. Polygnotus has pictured Memnon facing his rival Sarpedon and dressed in a cloak embroidered with these birds. The gods are said to observe the anniversaries of both their deaths as days of mourning.[18]

*i*. Others believe that Memnon's bones were taken to Cyprian Paphus, and thence to Rhodes, where his sister Himera, or Hemera, came to fetch them away. The Phoenicians who had rebelled against Phalas allowed her to do so on condition that she did not press for the return of their stolen treasure. To this she agreed, and brought the urn to Phoenicia; she buried it there at Palliochis and then disappeared.[19] Others, again, say that Memnon's tomb is to be seen near Palton in Syria, beside the river Badas. His bronze sword hangs on the wall of

Asclepius's temple at Nicomedeia; and Egyptian Thebes is famous for a colossal black statue – a seated stone figure – which utters a sound like the breaking of a lyre-string every day at sunrise. All Greek-speaking people call it Memnon; not so the Egyptians.[20]

*j.* Achilles now routed the Trojans and pursued them towards the city, but his course, too, was run. Poseidon and Apollo, pledged to avenge the deaths of Cycnus and Troilus, and to punish certain insolent boasts that Achilles had uttered over Hector's corpse, took counsel together. Veiled with cloud and standing by the Scaean Gate, Apollo sought out Paris in the thick of battle, turned his bow and guided the fatal shaft. It struck the one vulnerable part of Achilles's body, the right heel, and he died in agony.[21] But some say that Apollo, assuming the likeness of Paris, himself shot Achilles; and that this was the account which Neoptolemus, Achilles's son, accepted. A fierce battle raged all day over the corpse. Great Ajax struck down Glaucus, despoiled him of his armour, sent it back to the camp and, despite a shower of darts, carried dead Achilles through the midst of the enemy, Odysseus bringing up the rear. A tempest sent by Zeus then put an end to the struggle.[22]

*k.* According to another tradition, Achilles was the victim of a plot. Priam had offered him Polyxena in marriage on condition that the siege of Troy was raised. Put Polyxena, who could not forgive Achilles for murdering her brother Troilus, made him disclose the vulnerability of his heel, since there is no secret that women cannot extract from men in proof of love. At her request he came, barefoot and unarmed, to ratify the agreement by sacrificing to Thymbraean Apollo; then, while Deiphobus clasped him to his breast in pretended friendship, Paris, hiding behind the god's image, pierced his heel with a poisoned arrow or, some say, a sword. Before dying, however, Achilles seized firebrands from the altar and laid about him vigorously, felling many Trojans and temple servants.[23] Meanwhile, Odysseus, Ajax, and Diomedes, suspecting Achilles of treachery, had followed him to the temple. Paris and Deiphobus rushed past them through the doorway, they entered, and Achilles, expiring in their arms, begged them, after Troy fell, to sacrifice Polyxena at his tomb. Ajax carried the body out of the shrine on his shoulders; the Trojans tried to capture it, but the Greeks drove them off and conveyed it to the ships. Some say, on the other hand, that the Trojans won the tussle and did not surrender Achilles's body until the ransom which Priam paid for Hector had been returned.[24]

*l.* The Greeks were dismayed by their loss. Poseidon, however, promised Thetis to bestow on Achilles an island in the Black Sea, where the coastal tribes would offer him divine sacrifices for all eternity. A company of Nereids came to Troy to mourn with her and stood desolately around his corpse, while the nine Muses chanted the dirge. Their mourning lasted seventeen days and nights, but though Agamemnon and his fellow-leaders shed many tears, none of the common soldiers greatly regretted the death of so notorious a traitor. On the eighteenth day, Achilles's body was burned upon a pyre and his ashes, mixed with those of Patroclus, were laid in a golden urn made by Hephaestus, Thetis's wedding gift from Dionysus; this was buried on the headland of Sigaeum, which dominates the Hellespont, and over it the Greeks raised a lofty cairn as a landmark.[25] In a neighbouring village called Achilleum stands a temple sacred to Achilles, and his statue wearing a woman's ear-ring.[26]

*m.* While the Achaeans were holding funeral games in his honour – Eumelus winning the chariot race, Diomedes the foot-race, Ajax the discus-throw, and Teucer the archery contest – Thetis snatched Achilles's soul from the pyre and conveyed it to Leuce, an island about twenty furlongs in circumference, wooded and full of beasts, both wild and tame, which lies opposite the mouths of the Danube, and is now sacred to him. Once, when a certain Crotonian named Leonymus, who had been severely wounded in the breast while fighting his neighbours, the Epizephyrian Locrians, visited Delphi to inquire how he might be cured, the Pythoness told him: 'Sail to Leuce. There Little Ajax, whose ghost your enemies invoked to fight for them, will appear and heal your wound.' He returned some months later, safe and well, reporting that he had seen Achilles, Patroclus, Antilochus, Great Ajax, and finally Little Ajax, who had healed him. Helen, now married to Achilles, had said: 'Pray, Leonymus, sail to Himera, and tell the libeller of Helen that the loss of his sight is due to her displeasure.' Sailors on the northward run from the Bosphorus to Olbia frequently hear Achilles chanting Homer's verses across the water, the sound being accompanied by the clatter of horses' hooves, shouts of warriors, and clash of arms.[27]

*n.* Achilles first lay with Helen, not long before his death, in a dream arranged by his mother Thetis. This experience afforded him such pleasure that he asked Helen to display herself to him in waking life on the wall of Troy. She did so, and he fell desperately in love. Since he was her fifth husband, they call him Pemptus, meaning 'fifth', in Crete; Theseus, Menelaus, Paris, and finally Deiphobus, having been his predecessors.[28]

*o.* But others hold that Achilles remains under the power of Hades, and complains bitterly of his lot as he strides about the Asphodel Meadows; others, again, that he married Medea and lives royally in the Elysian Fields, or the Islands of the Blessed.[29]

*p.* By order of an oracle, a cenotaph was set up for Achilles in the ancient gymnasium at Olympia; there, at the opening of the festival, as the sun is sinking, the Elean women honour him with funeral rites. The Thessalians, at the command of the Dodonian Oracle, also sacrifice annually to Achilles; and on the road which leads northwards from Sparta stands a sanctuary built for him by Prax, his great-grandson, which is closed to the general public; but the boys who are required to fight in a near-by plane-tree grove enter and sacrifice to him beforehand.[30]

1. Quintus Smyrnaeus: *Posthomerica* i. 18 ff.; Apollodorus: *Epitome* v. 1–2; Lesches: *Little Iliad*, quoted by Pausanias: iii. 26. 7.
2. Eustathius on Homer p. 1696; Apollodorus: *loc. cit.*; Rawlinson: *Excidium Troiae*.
3. Apollodorus: i. 8. 6; Homer: *Iliad* ii. 212 ff., with scholiast on 219; Tzetzes: *On Lycophron* 999.
4. Tzetzes: *loc. cit.*; Servius on Virgil's *Aeneid* i. 495; Tryphiodorus: 37; Arctinus of Miletus: *Aethiopis*, quoted by Proclus: *Chrestomathy* 2; Pausanias: x. 31. 1 and v. 11. 2.
5. Tzetzes: *On Lycophron* 995.
6. Servius on Virgil's *Aeneid* i. 493; Apollodorus: iii. 12. 4 and *Epitome* v. 3.
7. Diodorus Siculus: ii. 22; Pausanias: i. 42. 2; Herodotus: v. 54; Strabo: xv. 3. 2; Aeschylus, quoted by Strabo: *loc. cit.*
8. Diodorus Siculus: *loc. cit.*; Pausanias: x. 31. 2; Ovid: *Amores* i. 8. 3–4; Homer: *Odyssey* xi. 522; Arctinus, quoted by Proclus: *Chrestomathy* 2.
9. Dictys Cretensis: iv. 4.
10. Apollodorus: *Epitome* v. 3; Pindar: *Pythian Odes* vi. 28 ff.
11. Apollodorus: i. 9. 9. and iii. 10. 8; Homer: *Odyssey* iii. 452; Hyginus: *Fabula* 252; Philostratus: *Heroica* iii. 2.
12. Homer: *Odyssey* iii. 112; xxiv. 17 and *Iliad* xxxiii. 556; Eustathius on Homer p. 1697.
13. Homer: *Odyssey* xxiv. 16 and 78; Pausanias: iii. 19. 11.
14. Dictys Cretensis: iv. 5; Quintus Smyrnaeus: *Posthomerica* ii. 224 ff.; Philostratus: *Imagines* ii. 7; Aeschylus: *Psychostasia*, quoted by Plutarch: *How a Young Man Should Listen to Poetry* 2.

15. Dictys Cretensis: iv. 6; Philostratus: *Heroica* iii. 4.
16. Diodorus Siculus: ii. 22; Strabo: xiii. 1. 11.
17. Apollodorus: iii. 12. 4; Arctinus of Miletus: *Aethiopis*, quoted by Proclus: *Chrestomathy* 2; Ovid: *Metamorphoses* xiii. 578 ff.
18. Servius on Virgil's *Aeneid* i. 755 and 493; Pausanias: x. 31. 2; Scholiast on Aristophanes's *Clouds* 622.
19. Dictys Cretensis: vi. 10.
20. Simonides, quoted by Strabo: xv. 3. 2; Pausanias: iii. 3. 6 and i. 42. 2.
21. Arctinus of Miletus: *Aethiopis*, quoted by Proclus: *Chestomathy* 2; Ovid: *Metamorphoses* xii. 580 ff.; Hyginus: *Fabula* 107; Apollodorus: *Epitome* v. 3.
22. Hyginus: *loc. cit.*; Apollodorus: *Epitome* v. 4; Homer: *Odyssey* xxiv. 42.
23. Rawlinson: *Excidium Troiae*; Dares: 34; Dictys Cretensis: iv. 11; Servius on Virgil's *Aeneid* vi. 57; Second Vatican Mythographer: 205.
24. Dictys Cretensis: iv. 10–13; Servius on Virgil's *Aeneid* iii. 322; Tzetzes: *On Lycophron* 269.
25. Quintus Smyrnaeus: iii. 766–80; Apollodorus: *Epitome* v. 5; Dictys Cretensis: iv. 13–14; Tzetzes: *Posthomerica* 431–67; Homer: *Odyssey* xxiv. 43–84.
26. Strabo: xi. 2.6; Arctinus of Miletus: *Aethiopis*, quoted by Proclus: *Crestomathy* 2; Apollodorus: *loc. cit.*
27. Pausanias: iii. 19. 11; Philostratus: *Heroica* xx. 32–40.
28. Tzetzes: *On Lycophron* 143 and 174; Servius on Virgil's *Aeneid* i. 34.
29. Homer: *Odyssey* xi. 471–540; Ibycus, quoted by scholiast on Apollonius Rhodius: iv. 815; Apollodorus: *loc. cit.*
30. Philostratus: *Heroica* xix. 14; Pausanias: vi. 23. 2 and iii. 20. 8.

\*

1. Penthesileia was one of the Amazons defeated by Theseus and Heracles: that is to say, one of Athene's fighting priestesses, defeated by the Aeolian invaders of Greece (see 100. *1* and 131. *2*). The incident has been staged at Troy because Priam's confederacy is said to have comprised all the tribes of Asia Minor. Penthesileia does not appear in the *Iliad*, but Achilles's outrage of her corpse is characteristically Homeric, and since she is mentioned in so many other Classical texts, a passage about her may well have been suppressed by Peisistratus's editors. Dictys Cretensis (iv. 2–3) modernizes the story: he says that she rode up at the head of a large army and, finding Hector dead, would have gone away again, had not Paris bribed her to stay with gold and silver. Achilles speared

Penthesileia in their first encounter, and dragged her from the saddle by the hair. As she lay dying on the ground, the Greek soldiers cried: 'Throw this virago to the dogs as a punishment for exceeding the nature of womankind!' Though Achilles demanded an honourable funeral, Diomedes took the corpse by its feet and dragged it into the Scamander.

Old Nurses in Greek legend usually stand for the Goddess as Crone (see 24. 9); and Penthesileia's nurse Clete ('invoked') is no exception.

2. Cissia ('ivy') seems to be an early title of the variously named goddess who presided over the ivy and vine revels in Greece, Thrace, Asia Minor, and Syria (see 168. 3); Memnon's 'Cissians', however, are a variant of 'Susians' ('lily-men'), so called in honour of the Lily-goddess Susannah, or Astarte. Priam probably applied for help not to the Assyrians but to the Hittites, who may well have sent reinforcements by land, and also by sea, from Syria. 'Memnon' ('resolute'), a common title of Greek kings – intensified in 'Agamemnon' ('very resolute') – has here been confused with Mnemon, a title of Artaxerxes the Assyrian, and with Amenophis, the name of the Pharoah in whose honour the famous black singing statue was constructed at Thebes. The first rays of the sun warmed the hollow stone, making the air inside expand and rush through the narrow throat.

3. Achilles in his birth, youth, and death is mythologically acceptable as the ancient Pelasgian sacred king, destined to become the 'lipless' oracular hero. His mythic opponent bore various names, such as 'Hector' and 'Paris' and 'Apollo'. Here it is Memnon son of Cissia. Achilles's duel with Memnon, each supported by his mother, was carved on the Chest of Cypselus (Pausanias: v. 19. 1), and on the throne of Apollo at Amyclae (Pausanias: iii. 18. 7); besides figuring in a large group by the painter Lycius, which the inhabitants of Apollonia dedicated at Olympia (Pausanias: v. 22. 2). These two represent sacred king and tanist – Achilles, son of the Sea-goddess, bright Spirit of the Waxing Year: Memnon, son of the Ivy-goddess, dark Spirit of the Waning Year, to whom the golden vine is sacred. They kill each other alternately, at the winter and summer solstices; the king always succumbs to a heel-wound, his tanist is beheaded with a sword. Achilles, in this ancient sense, untainted by the scandalous behaviour of the Achaean and Dorian chieftains who usurped the name, was widely worshipped as a hero; and the non-Homeric story of his betrayal by Polyxena, who wormed from him the secret of his vulnerable heel, places him beside Llew Llaw, Cuchulain, Samson, and other Bronze Age heroes of honest repute. His struggle with Penthesileia is therefore likely to have been of the same sort as his father Peleus's struggle with Thetis (see 81. k). The recipient of Helen's message from Leuce – which is now a treeless Rumanian prison island – was the poet Stesichorus (see 31. 9 and 159. 1).

4. Because Memnon came from the East to help Priam, he was styled 'the son of Eos' ('dawn'); and because he needed a father, Eos's lover Tithonus seemed the natural choice (see 40. *c*). A fight at the winter solstice between girls in bird-disguise, which Ovid records, is a more likely explanation of the Memnonides than that they are fanciful embodiments of sparks flying up from a corpse on the pyre; the fight will originally have been for the high-priestess-ship, in Libyan style (see 8. *1*).

5. Achilles as the sacred king of Olympia was mourned after the summer solstice, when the Olympic funeral games were held in his honour; his tanist, locally called 'Cronus', was mourned after the winter solstice (see 138. *4*). In the British Isles these feasts fell on Lammas and St Stephen's Day respectively; but though the corpse of the golden-crested wren, the bird of Cronus, is still carried in procession through country districts on St Stephen's Day, the British Memnonides 'fell a-sighing and a-sobbing' only for the robin, not for his victim, the wren: the tanist, not the sacred king.

6. Achilles's hero-shrine in Crete must have been built by Pelasgian immigrants; but the plane is a Cretan tree. Since the plane-leaf represented Rhea's green hand, Achilles may have been called Pemptus ('fifth') to identify him with Acesidas, the fifth of her Dactyls, namely the oracular little finger, as Heracles was identified with the first, the virile thumb (see 53. *1*).

7. Priam's golden vine, his bribe to Tithonus for sending Memnon, seems to have been the one given Tros by Zeus in compensation for the rape of Ganymedes (see 29. *b*).

# 165

## THE MADNESS OF AJAX

WHEN Thetis decided to award the arms of Achilles to the most courageous Greek left alive before Troy, only Ajax and Odysseus, who had boldly defended the corpse together,[1] dared come forward to claim them. Some say that Agamemnon, from a dislike of the whole House of Aeacus, rejected Ajax's pretensions and divided the arms between Menelaus and Odysseus, whose goodwill he valued far more highly;[2] others, that he avoided the odium of a decision by referring the case to the assembled Greek leaders, who settled it by a secret ballot; or that he referred it to the Cretans and other allies; or that he forced his Trojan prisoners to declare which of the two claimants had done them most harm.³ But the truth is that, while Ajax and Odysseus were still competitively boasting of their achievements, Nestor advised Agamemnon to send spies by night to listen under the Trojan walls for the enemy's unbiased opinion on the matter. The spies overheard a party of young girls chattering together; and when one praised Ajax for bearing dead Achilles from the battlefield through a storm of missiles, another, at Athene's instigation, replied: 'Nonsense! Even a slave-woman will do as much, once someone has set a corpse on her shoulders; but thrust weapons into her hand, and she will be too frightened to use them. Odysseus, not Ajax, bore the brunt of our attack.'⁴

b. Agamemnon therefore awarded the arms to Odysseus. He and Menelaus would never, of course, have dared to insult Ajax in this manner had Achilles still been alive: for Achilles thought the world of his gallant cousin. It was Zeus himself who provoked the quarrel.⁵

c. In a dumb rage, Ajax planned to revenge himself on his fellow-Greeks that very night; Athene, however, struck him with madness and turned him loose, sword in hand, among the cattle and sheep which had been lifted from Trojan farms to form part of the common spoil. After immense slaughter, he chained the surviving beasts together, hauled them back to the camp, and there continued his butcher's work. Choosing two white-footed rams, he lopped off the head and tongue of one, which he mistook for Agamemnon, or Menelaus; and tied the other upright to a pillar, where he flogged it with a horse's halter, screaming abuse and calling it perfidious Odysseus.⁶

d. At last coming to his senses in utter despair, he summoned Eurysaces, his son by Tecmessa, and gave him the huge, sevenfold shield after which he had been named. 'The rest of my arms will be buried with me when I die,' he said. Ajax's half-brother Teucer, son of Priam's captive sister Hesione, happened to be away in Mysia, but Ajax left a message appointing him guardian of Eurysaces, who was to be taken home to his grandparents Telamon and Eriboea of Salamis. Then, with a word to Tecmessa that he would escape Athene's anger by bathing in a sea pool and finding some untrodden patch of ground where the sword might be securely buried, he set out, determined on death.

e. He fixed the sword – the very one which Hector had exchanged for the purple baldric – upright in the earth, and after calling on Zeus to tell Teucer where his corpse might be found; on Hermes, to conduct his soul to the Asphodel Fields; and on the Erinnyes, for vengeance, threw himself upon it. The sword, loathing its task, doubled back in the shape of a bow, and dawn had broken before he contrived to commit suicide by driving the point underneath his vulnerable arm-pit.[7]

f. Meanwhile Teucer, returning from Mysia, narrowly escaped murder by the Greeks, who were indignant at the slaughter of their livestock. Calchas, having been granted no prophetic warning of the suicide, took Teucer aside and advised him to confine Ajax to his hut, as one maddened by the wrath of Athene. Podaleirius son of Asclepius agreed; he was as expert a physician as his brother Machaon was a surgeon, and had been the first to diagnose Ajax's madness from his flashing eyes.[8] But Teucer merely shook his head, having already been informed by Zeus of his brother's death, and went sadly out with Tecmessa to find the corpse.

g. There Ajax lay in a pool of blood, and dismay overcame Teucer. How could he return to Salamis, and face his father Telamon? As he stood, tearing his hair, Menelaus strode up and forbade him to bury Ajax, who must be left for the greedy kites and pious vultures. Teucer sent him about his business, and leaving Eurysaces in suppliant's dress to display locks of his own, Teucer's, and Tecmessa's hair, and so guard Ajax's corpse – over which Tecmessa had spread her robe – he came raging before Agamemnon. Odysseus intervened in the ensuing dispute, and not only urged Agamemnon to permit the funeral rites, but offered to help Teucer carry them out. This service Teucer declined, while acknowledging Odysseus's courtesy. Finally Agamemnon, on Calchas's advice, allowed Ajax to be buried in a suicide's coffin at Cape Rhoeteum, rather than burned on a pyre as if he had fallen honourably in battle.[9]

h. Some hold that the cause of the quarrel between Ajax and Odysseus was the possession of Palladium, and that it took place after Troy had fallen.[10] Others deny that Ajax committed suicide, and say that, since he was proof against steel, the Trojans killed him with lumps of clay, having been advised to do so by an oracle. But this may have been another Ajax[11].

i. Afterwards, when Odysseus visited the Asphodel Fields, Ajax was the only ghost who stood aloof from him, rejecting his excuses that Zeus had been responsible for this unfortunate affair. Odysseus had by that time wisely presented the arms to Achilles's son Neoptolemus; though the Aeolians who later settled at Troy say that he lost them in a shipwreck as he sailed home, whereupon by Thetis's contrivance the waves deposited them beside Ajax's tomb at Rhoeteum. During the reign of the Emperor Hadrian, high seas washed open the tomb and his bones were seen to be of gigantic size, the knee-caps alone being as large as a discus used by boys practising for the pentathlon; at the Emperor's orders, they were at once reinterred.[12]

*j*. The Salaminians report that a new flower appeared in their island when Ajax died: white, tinged with red, smaller than a lily and, like the hyacinth, bearing letters which spell *Ai! Ai!* ('*woe, woe!*'). But it is generally believed that the new flower sprang from Ajax's blood where he fell, since the letters also stand for *Aias Aiacides* – 'Ajax the Aeacid'. In the Salaminian market place stands a temple of Ajax, with an ebony image; and not far from the harbour a boulder is shown on which Telamon sat gazing at the ship which bore his sons away to Aulis.[13]

*k*. Teucer eventually returned to Salamis, but Telamon accused him of fractricide in the second degree, since he had not pressed Ajax's claim to the disputed arms. Forbidden to land, he pleaded his case from the sea while the judges listened on the shore; Telamon himself had been forced to do the same by his own father Aeacus, when accused of murdering his brother Phocus. But as Telamon had been found guilty and banished, so also was Teucer, on the ground that he had brought back neither Ajax's bones, nor Tecmessa, nor Eurysaces; which proved neglect. He set sail for Cyprus, where with Apollo's favour and the permission of King Belus the Sidonian he founded the other Salamis.[14]

*l*. The Athenians honour Ajax as one of their eponymous heroes, and insist that Philaeus, the son of Eurysaces, became an Athenian citizen and surrendered the sovereignty of Salamis to them.[15]

1. Homer: *Odyssey* xi. 543 ff.; *Argument* of Sophocles's *Ajax*.
2. Hyginus: *Fabula* 107.
3. Pindar: *Nemean Odes* viii. 26 ff.; Ovid: *Metamorphoses* xii. 620 ff.; Apollodorus: *Epitome* v. 6; Scholiast on Homer's *Odyssey* xi. 547.
4. Lesches: *Little Iliad*, quoted by scholiast on Aristophanes's *Knights* 1056.
5. Homer: *Odyssey* xi. 559–60.
6. Sophocles: *Ajax*, with *Argument*; Zenobius: *Proverbs* i. 43.
7. Sophocles: *Ajax*; Aeschylus, quoted by scholiast on *Ajax* 833 and on *Iliad* xxiii. 821; Arctinus of Miletus: *Aethiopis*, quoted by scholiast on Pindar's *Isthmian Odes* iii. 53.
8. Arctinus: *Sack of Ilium*, quoted by Eustathius on Homer's *Iliad* xiii. 515.
9. Apollodorus: *Epitome* v. 7; Philostratus: *Heroica* xiii. 7.
10. Dictys Cretensis: v. 14–15.

11. *Argument* of Sophocles's *Ajax*.
12. Homer: *Odyssey* xi. 543 ff.; Pausanias: i. 35. 3; Philostratus: *Heroica* i. 2.
13. Pausanias: i. 35. 2–3; Ovid: *Metamorphoses* xiii. 382 ff.
14. Pausanias: i. 28. 12 and viii. 15. 3; Servius on Virgil's *Aeneid* i. 619; Pindar: *Nemean Odes* iv. 60; Aeschylus: *Persians* i. 35. 2 and 5. 2.
15. Herodotus: vi. 35; Pausanias: i. 35. 2; Plutarch: *Solon* xi.

\*

1. Here the mythological element is small. Ajax was perhaps shown on some Cyprian icon tying the ram to a pillar; not because he had gone mad, but because this was a form of sacrifice introduced into Cyprus from Crete (see 39. 2).

2. Homer's hyacinth is the blue larkspur – *hyacinthos grapta* – which has markings on the base of its petals resembling the early Greek letters *AI*; it had also been sacred to Cretan Hyacinthus (see 21. 8).

3. The bones of Ajax reinterred by Hadrian, like those of Theseus (see 104. *i*), probably belonged to some far more ancient hero. Peisistratus made use of Ajax's alleged connexion with Attica to claim sovereignty over the island of Salamis, previously held by Megara, and is said to have supported his claim by the insertion of forged verses (see 163. *1*) into the Homeric canon (*Iliad* ii. 458–559; Aristotle: *Rhetoric* i. 15; Plutarch: *Solon* 10). *Aia* is an old form of *gaia* ('earth'), and *aias* ('Ajax') will have meant 'countryman'.

4. To kill a man with lumps of clay, rather than swords, was a primitive means of avoiding blood guilt; and this other Ajax's murder must therefore have been the work of his kinsmen, not the Trojan enemy.

5. That Odysseus and Ajax quarrelled for the possession of the Palladium is historically important; but Sophocles has carelessly confused Great Ajax with Little Ajax (see 166. 2).

# 166

## THE ORACLES OF TROY

ACHILLES was dead, and the Greeks had begun to despair. Calchas now prophesied that Troy could not be taken except with the help of Heracles's bow and arrows. Odysseus and Diomedes were therefore deputed to sail for Lemnos and fetch them from Philoctetes, their present owner.[1]

*b.* Some say that King Actor's shepherd Phimachus, son of Dolophion, had sheltered Philoctetes and dressed his noisome wound for the past ten years. Others record that some of Philoctetes's Meliboean troops settled beside him in Lemnos, and that the Asclepiads had already cured him, with Lemnian earth, before the deputation arrived; or that Pylius, or Pelius, a son of Hephaestus, did so. Philoctetes is said to have then conquered certain small islands off the Trojan coast for King Eeneus, dispossessing the Carian population – a kindness which Euneus acknowledged by giving him the Lemnian district of Acesa.[2] Thus, it is explained, Odysseus and Diomedes had no need to tempt Philoctetes with offers of medical treatment; he came willingly enough, carrying his bow and arrows, to win the war for them and glory for himself. According to still another account, the deputation found him long dead of the wound and persuaded his heirs to let them borrow the bow.[3]

*c.* The truth is, however, that Philoctetes stayed in Lemnos, suffering painfully, until Odysseus tricked him into handing over the bow and arrows; but Diomedes (not, as some mistakenly say, Neoptolemus) declined to be implicated in the theft and advised Philoctetes to demand the return of his property. At this, the god Heracles intervened. 'Go with them to Troy, Philoctetes,' he said, 'and I will send an Asclepiad there to cure you; for Troy must fall a second time to my arrows. You shall be chosen from among the Greeks as the boldest fighter of all. You shall kill Paris, take part in the sack of Troy, and send home the spoils, reserving the noblest prize for your father Poeas. But remember: you cannot take Troy without Neoptolemus son of Achilles, nor can he do so without you!'[4]

*d.* Philoctetes obeyed, and on his arrival at the Greek camp was bathed with fresh water and put to sleep in Apollo's temple; as he slept, Machaon the surgeon cut away the decaying flesh from the wound, poured in wine, and applied healing herbs and the serpentine stone. But some say that Machaon's brother Podaleirius, the physician, took charge of the case.[5]

*e.* No sooner was Philoctetes about again, than he challenged Paris to a combat in archery. The first arrow he shot went wide, the second pierced Paris's bow-hand, the third blinded his right eye, and the fourth struck his ankle, wounding him mortally. Despite Menelaus's attempt to despatch Paris, he contrived to hobble from the field and take refuge in Troy. That night the Trojans carried him to Mount Ida, where he begged his former mistress, the nymph Oenone, to heal him; from an inveterate hatred of Helen, however, she cruelly shook her head and he was brought back to die. Presently Oenone relented, and ran to Troy with a basketful of healing drugs, but found him already dead. In a frenzy of grief she leaped from the walls, or hanged herself, or burned herself to death on his pyre – no one remembers which. Some excuse Oenone by saying that she would have healed Paris at once, had not her father prevented her; she was obliged to wait until he had left the house before bringing the simples, and then it proved too late.[6]

*f*. Helenus and Deiphobus now quarrelled for Helen's hand, and Priam supported Deiphobus's claim on the ground that he had shown the greater valour; but, though her marriage to Paris had been divinely arranged, Helen could not forget that she was still Queen of Sparta and wife to Menelaus. One night, a sentry caught her tying a rope to the battlements in an attempt to escape. She was led before Deiphobus, who married her by force – much to the disgust of the other Trojans. Helenus immediately left the city and went to live with Arisbe on the slopes of Mount Ida.[7]

*g*. Upon hearing from Calchas that Helenus alone knew the secret oracles which protected Troy, Agamemnon sent Odysseus to waylay and drag him to the Greek camp. Helenus happened to be staying as Chryses's guest in the temple of Thymbraean Apollo, when Odysseus came in search of him, and proved ready enough to disclose the oracles, on condition that he would be given a secure home in some distant land. He had deserted Troy, he explained, not because he feared death, but because neither he nor Aeneas could overlook Paris's sacrilegious murder of Achilles in this very temple, for which no amends had yet been made to Apollo.[8]

*h*. 'So be it. Hold nothing back, and I will guarantee your life and safety,' said Odysseus.

'The oracles are brief and clear,' Helenus answered. 'Troy falls this summer, if a certain bone of Pelops is brought to your camp; if Neoptolemus takes the field; and if Athene's Palladium is stolen from the citadel – because the walls cannot be breached while it remains there.'[9]

Agamemnon at once sent to Pisa for Pelops's shoulder-blade. Meanwhile, Odysseus, Phoenix, and Diomedes sailed to Scyros, where they persuaded Lycomedes to let Neoptolemus come to Troy – some say that he was then only twelve years old. The ghost of Achilles appeared before him on his arrival, and he forthwith distinguished himself both in council and in war, Odysseus gladly resigning Achilles's arms to him.[10]

*i.* Eurypylus son of Telephus now reinforced the Trojans with an army of Mysians, and Priam, who had offered his mother Astyoche a golden vine if he came, betrothed him to Cassandra. Eurypylus proved a resolute fighter, and killed Machaon the surgeon; which is why, in Asclepius's sanctuary at Pergamus, where every service begins with a hymn celebrating Telephus, the name of his son Eurypylus may not be spoken on any occasion. Machaeon's bones were taken back to Pylus by Nestor, and sick people are healed in the sanctuary at Geraneia; his garlanded bronze statue dominates the sacred place called 'The Rose'. Eurypylus himself was killed by Neoptolemus.[11]

*j.* Shortly before the fall of Troy, the dissensions between Priam's sons grew so fierce that he authorized Antenor to negotiate peace with Agamemnon. On his arrival at the Greek camp Antenor, out of hatred for Deiphobus, agreed to betray the Palladium and the city into Odysseus's hands; his price was the kingship and half of Priam's treasure. Aeneas, he told Agamemnon, could also be counted upon to help.[12]

*k.* Together they concocted a plan, in pursuance of which Odysseus asked Diomedes to flog him mercilessly; then, bloodstained, filthy, and dressed in rags, he gained admittance into Troy as a runaway slave. Helen alone saw through his disguise, but when she privately questioned him, was fobbed off with evasive answers. Nevertheless, he could not decline an invitation to her house, where she bathed, anointed and clothed him in fine robes; and his identity being thus established beyond question, swore a solemn oath that she would not betray him to the Trojans – so far she had confided only in Hecabe – if he revealed all the details of his plan to her. Helen explained that she was now kept a prisoner in Troy, and longed to go home. At this juncture, Hecabe entered. Odysseus at once threw himself at her feet, weeping for terror, and implored her not to denounce him. Surprisingly enough, she agreed. He then hurried back, guided by Hecabe, and reached his friends in safety with a harvest of information; claiming to have killed a number of Trojans who would not open the gates for him.[13]

*l.* Some say that Odysseus stole the Palladium on this occasion, single-handed. Others say that he and Diomedes, as favourites of Athene, were chosen to do so, and that they climbed up to the citadel by way of a narrow and muddy conduit, killed the sleeping guards, and together took possession of the image, which priestess Theano, Antenor's wife, willingly surrendered.[14] The common account, however, is that Diomedes scaled the wall by climbing upon Odysseus's shoulders, because the ladder was short, and entered Troy alone. When he reappeared, carrying the Palladium in his arms, the two of them set out for the camp, side by side, under a full moon; but Odysseus wanted all the glory. He dropped behind Diomedes, to whose shoulders the image was now strapped, and would have murdered him, had not the shadow of his sword caught Diomedes's eye, the moon being still low in the heavens. He spun about, drew his own sword and, disarming Odysseus, pinioned his hands and drove him back to the ships with repeated kicks and blows. Hence the phrase 'Diomedes's compulsion', often applied to those whose actions are coerced.[15]

*m.* The Romans pretend that Odysseus and Diomedes carried off a mere replica of the Palladium which was on public display, and that Aeneas, at the fall of Troy, rescued the authentic image, smuggled it out with the remainder of his sacred luggage, and brought it safe to Italy.[16]

1. Apollodorus: *Epitome* v. 8; Tzetzes: *On Lycophron* 911; Sophocles: *Philoctetes* i. ff.
2. Hyginus: *Fabula* 102; Eustathius on Homer p. 330; Ptolemy Hephaestionos: vi., quoted by Photius p.490; Philostratus: *Heroica* 5.
3. Ptolemy Hephaestionos: v., quoted by Photius p. 486; Pausanias: i. 22. 6.
4. Apollodorus: *loc. cit.*; Philostratus: *loc. cit.* and *Philoctetes* 915 ff. and 1409 ff.
5. Orpheus and Dionysius, quoted by Tzetzes: *On Lycophron* 911; Apollodorus: *loc. cit.*
6. Tzetzes: *On Lycophron* 61–2; 64 and 911; Lesches: *Little Iliad*; Apollodorus: iii. 12. 6.
7. Apollodorus: *Epitome* v.9; Tzetzes: *On Lycophron* 143 and 168; Euripides: *Trojan Women* 955–60; Servius on Virgil's *Aeneid* ii. 166.
8. Apollodorus: *Epitome* v. 9–10; Sophocles: *Philoctetes* 606; Orpheus, quoted by Tzetzes: *On Lycophron* 911; Dictys Cretensis: iv. 18.
9. Sophocles: *Philoctetes* 1337–42; Apollodorus: *loc. cit.*; Tzetzes: *loc. cit.*
10. Apollodorus: *Epitome* v. 11; Pausanias: v. 13. 3; Homer: *Odyssey* xi. 506 ff.; Philostratus: *Imagines* 2; Quintus Smyrnaeus: *Posthomerica* vi. 57–113 and vii. 169–430; Rawlinson: *Excidium Troiae*; Lesches: *loc. cit.*
11. Scholiast on Homer's *Odyssey* xi. 520; Dictys Cretensis: iv. 14;

*Little Iliad,* quoted by Pausanias: iii. 26. 7; Apollodorus: *Epitome* v. 12.

12. Dictys Cretensis: vi. 22 and v. 8.
13. Euripides: *Hecabe* 239–50; Homer: *Odyssey* iv. 242 ff.; Lesches: *loc. cit.*
14. Apollodorus: *Epitome* v. 13; Sophocles: *Fragment* 367; Servius on Virgil's *Aeneid* ii. 166; Scholiast on Homer's *Iliad* vi. 311; Suidas *sub* Palladium; Johannes Malalas: *Chronographica* v. p. 109, ed. Dindorf: Dictys Cretensis: v. 5 and 8.
15. Conon: *Narrations* 34; Servius: *loc. cit.*
16. Dionysius of Halicarnassus: i. 68 ff.; Ovid: *Fasti* vi. 434.

*

1. All this is idle romance, or drama, except for the stealing of the Palladium, Hecabe's mysterious refusal to betray Odysseus (see 168. 5), and the death of Paris from a wound in his ankle (see 92. 10; 126. 3 and 164. j). Pelops's shoulder-blade was probably of porpoise-ivory (see 109. 5). The account which makes Philoctetes succumb to poison – of Heracles's arrows dipped in the Hydra's blood – seems to be the earliest one (see 162. l).

2. Pausanias reports (v. 13. 3): 'When the Greeks returned from Troy, the ship that carried the shoulder-blade of Pelops was sunk off Euboea in a storm. Many years later an Eretrian fisherman named Damarmenus ("subduer of sails") drew up a bone in his net, which was of such astonishing size that he hid it in the sand while he went to ask the Delphic Oracle whose bone it was, and what ought to be done with it. Apollo had arranged that an Elean embassy should arrive that same day requiring a remedy for a plague. The Pythoness answered the Eleans: "Recover the shoulder-blade of Pelops." To Damarmenus she said: "Give your bone to those ambassadors." The Eleans rewarded him well, making the custodianship of the bone hereditary in his house. It was no longer to be seen when I visited Elis: doubtless age and the action of the sea-water in which it had lain so long had mouldered it away.'

# 167

## THE WOODEN HORSE

ATHENE now inspired Prylis, son of Hermes, to suggest that entry should be gained into Troy by means of a wooden horse; and Epeius, son of Panopeus, a Phocian from Parnassus, volunteered to build one under Athene's supervision. Afterwards, of course, Odysseus claimed all the credit for this stratagem.[1]

*b.* Epeius had brought thirty ships from the Cyclades to Troy. He held the office of water-bearer to the House of Atreus; as appears in the frieze of Apollo's temple at Carthea, and though a skilled boxer and a consummate craftsman, was born a coward, in divine punishment for his father's breach of faith – Panopeus had falsely sworn in Athene's name not to embezzle any part of the Taphian booty won by Amphitryon. Epeius's cowardice has since become proverbial.[2]

*c.* He built an enormous hollow horse of fir-planks, with a trap-door fitted into one flank, and large letters cut on the other which consecrated it to Athene: 'In thankful anticipation of a safe return to their homes, the Greeks dedicate this offering to the Goddess.'[3] Odysseus persuaded the bravest of the Greeks to climb fully armed up a rope-ladder and through the trap-door into the belly of the horse. Their number is variously given as twenty-three, thirty or more, fifty, and, absurdly enough, three thousand. Among them were Menelaus, Odysseus, Diomedes, Sthenelus, Acamas, Thoas, and Neoptolemus. Coaxed, threatened, and bribed, Epeius himself joined the party. He climbed up last, drew the ladder in after him and, since he alone knew how to work the trap-door, took his seat beside the lock.[4]

*d.* At nightfall, the remaining Greeks under Agamemnon followed Odysseus's instructions, which were to burn their camp, put out to sea, and wait off Tenedos and the Calydnian Islands until the following evening. Only Odysseus's first cousin Sinon, a grandson of Autolycus, stayed behind to light a signal beacon for their return.[5]

*e.* At break of day, Trojan scouts reported that the camp lay in ashes and that the Greeks had departed, leaving a huge horse on the seashore. Priam and several of his sons went out to view it and, as they stood staring in wonder, Thymoetes was the first to break the silence. 'Since this is a gift to Athene,' he said, 'I propose that we take it into Troy and haul it up to her citadel.' 'No, no!' cried Capys. 'Athene favoured the Greeks too long; we must either burn it at once or break it open to see what the belly contains.' But Priam declared: 'Thymoetes is right. We will fetch it in on rollers. Let nobody desecrate Athene's property.' The horse proved too broad to be squeezed through the gates. Even when the wall had been breached, it stuck four times. With enormous efforts the Trojans then hauled it up to the citadel; but at least took the precaution of repairing the breach behind them. Another heated argument followed when Cassandra announced that the horse contained armed men, and was supported in her view by the seer Laocoön, son of Antenor, whom some mistakenly call the brother of Anchises. Crying: 'You fools, never trust a Greek even if he brings you gifts!', he hurled his spear, which stuck quivering in the horse's flank and caused the weapons inside to clash together. Cheers and shouts arose: 'Burn it!' 'Hurl it over the walls!' But, 'Let it stay,' pleaded Priam's supporters.[6]

*f*. This argument was interrupted by the arrival of Sinon, whom a couple of Trojan soldiers were marching up in chains. Under interrogation, he said that Odysseus had long been trying to destroy him because he knew the secret of Palamedes's murder. The Greeks, he went on, were heartily sick of the war, and would have sailed home months before this, but that the uninterrupted bad weather prevented them. Apollo had advised them to placate the Winds with blood, as when they were delayed at Aulis. Whereupon,' Sinon continued, 'Odysseus dragged Calchas forward, and asked him to name the victim. Calchas would not give an immediate answer and went into retirement for ten days, at the end of which time, doubtless bribed by Odysseus, he entered the Council hut and pointed at me. All present welcomed this verdict, every man relieved at not being chosen as the scapegoat, and I was put in fetters; but a favourable wind sprang up, my companions hurriedly launched their vessels, and in the confusion I made my escape.'

*g*. Thus Priam was tricked into accepting Sinon as a suppliant, and had his fetters broken. 'Now tell us about this horse,' he said kindly. Sinon explained that the Greeks had forfeited Athene's support, on which they depended, when Odysseus and Diomedes stole the Palladium from her temple. No sooner had they brought it to their camp than the image was three times enveloped by flames, and its limbs sweated in proof of the goddess's wrath. Calchas thereupon advised Agamemnon to sail for home and assemble a fresh expedition in Greece, under better auspices, leaving the horse as a placatory gift to Athene. 'Why was it built so big?' asked Priam. Sinon, well coached by Odysseus, replied: 'To prevent you from bringing it into the city. Calchas foretells that if you despise this sacred image, Athene will ruin you; but once it enters Troy, you shall be empowered to marshal all the forces of Asia, invade Greece, and conquer Mycenae.'[7]

*h*. 'These are lies,' cried Laocoön, 'and sound as if they were invented by Odysseus. Do not believe him, Priam!' He added: 'Pray, my lord, give me leave to sacrifice a bull to Poseidon. When I come back I hope to see this wooden horse reduced to ashes.' It should be explained that the Trojans, having stoned their priest of Poseidon to death nine years before, had decided not to replace him until the war seemed to have ended. Now they chose Laocoön by lot to propitiate Poseidon. He was already the priest of Thymbraean Apollo, whom he had angered by marrying and begetting children, despite a vow of celibacy and, worse, by lying with his wife Antiope in sight of the god's image.[8]

*i*. Laocoön retired to select a victim and prepare the altar but, in warning of Troy's approaching doom, Apollo sent two great sea-serpents, named Porces and Chariboea, or Curissia, or Periboea, rushing towards Troy from Tenedos and the Calydnian Islands.[9]

They darted ashore and, coiling around the limbs of Laocoön's twin sons Antiphas and Thymbraeus, whom some call Melanthus, crushed them to death. Laocoön ran to their rescue, but he too died miserably. The serpents then glided up to the citadel and while one wound about Athene's feet, the other took refuge behind her aegis. Some, however, say that only one of Laocoön's sons was killed and that he died in the temple of Thymbraean Apollo, not beside Poseidon's altar; and others that Laocoön himself escaped death.[10]

*j*. This terrible portent served to convince the Trojans that Sinon had spoken the truth. Priam mistakenly assumed that Laocoön was being punished for hurling his spear at the horse, rather than for having insulted Apollo. He at once dedicated the horse to Athene and although Aeneas's followers retired in alarm to their huts on Mount Ida, nearly all Priam's Trojans began to celebrate the victory with banquets and merrymaking. The women gathered flowers from the river banks, garlanded the horse's mane, and spread a carpet of roses around its hooves.[11]

*k*. Meanwhile, inside the horse's belly, the Greeks had been trembling for terror, and Epeius wept silently, in an ecstasy of fear. Only Neoptolemus showed no emotion, even when the point of Laocoön's spear broke through the timbers close to his head. Time after time he nudged Odysseus to order the assault – for Odysseus was in command – and clutched his lance and sword-hilt menacingly. But Odysseus would not consent. In the evening Helen strolled from the palace and went around the horse three times, patting its flanks and, as if to amuse Deiphobus who was with her, teased the hidden Greeks by imitating the voice of each of their wives in turn. Menelaus and Diomedes, squatting in the middle of the horse next to Odysseus, were tempted to leap out when they heard themselves called by name; but he restrained them and, seeing that Antielus was on the point of answering, clapped a hand over his mouth and, some say, strangled him.[12]

*l.* That night, exhausted with feasting and revelry, the Trojans slept soundly, and not even the bark of a dog broke the stillness. But Helen lay awake, and a bright round light blazed above her chamber as a signal to the Greeks. At midnight, just before the full moon rose – the seventh of the year – Sinon crept from the city to kindle a beacon on Achilles's tomb, and Antenor waved a torch.[13]

Agamemnon answered these signals by lighting pine-wood chips in a cresset on the deck of his ship, which was now heaved-to a few bow-shots from the coast; and the whole fleet drove shoreward. Antenor, cautiously approaching the horse, reported in a low voice that all was well, and Odysseus ordered Epeius to unlock the trap-door.[14]

*m.* Echion, son of Portheus, leaping out first, fell and broke his neck; the rest descended by Epeius's rope-ladder. Some ran to open the gates for the landing party, others cut down drowsy sentries guarding the citadel and palace; but Menelaus could think only of Helen, and ran straight towards her house.[15]

1. Hyginus: *Fabula* 108; Tzetzes: *On Lycophron* 219 ff.; Apollodorus: *Epitome* v. 14.
2. Euripides: *Trojan Women* 10; Dictys Cretensis: i. 17; Stesichorus, quoted by Eustathius on Homer p. 1323; Athenaeus: x. p. 457; Homer: *Iliad* xxiii. 665; Tzetzes: *On Lycophron* 930; Hesychius *sub* Epeius.
3. Homer: *Odyssey* viii. 493; Apollodorus: *Epitome* v. 14–15.
4. Tzetzes: *loc. cit.* and *Posthomerica* 641–50; Quintus Smyrnaeus: *Posthomerica* xii. 314–35; Apollodorus: *Epitome* v. 14; *Little Iliad*, quoted by Apollodorus: *loc. cit.*; Hyginus: *loc. cit.*
5. Apollodorus: *Epitome* v. 14–15; Tzetzes: *On Lycophron* 344.
6. Virgil: *Aeneid* ii. 13–249; Lesches: *Little Iliad*; Tzetzes: *On Lycophron* 347; Apollodorus: *Epitome* v. 16–17; Hyginus: *Fabula* 135.
7. Virgil: *loc. cit.*
8. Euphorion, quoted by Servius on Virgil's *Aeneid* ii. 201; Hyginus: *loc. cit.*; Virgil: *loc. cit.*
9. Apollodorus: *Epitome* v. 18; Hyginus: *loc. cit.*; Tzetzes: *loc. cit.*; Lysimachus, quoted by Serv on Virgil's *Aeneid* ii. 211.

10. Thessandrus, quoted by Servius on Virgil's *Aeneid*: *loc. cit.*; Hyginus: *loc. cit.*; Quintus Smyrnaeus: *Posthomerica* xii. 444–97; Arctinus of Miletus: *Sack of Ilium*; Tzetzes: *loc. cit.*; Virgil: *loc. cit.*

11. Homer: *Odyssey* viii. 504 ff.; Apollodorus: *Epitome* v. 16–17; Arctinus of Miletus: *ibid.*; Lesches: *loc. cit.*; Tryphiodorus: *Sack of Troy* 316 ff. and 340–4.

12. Homer: *Odyssey* xi. 523–32 and iv. 271–89; Tryphiodorus: *Sack of Troy* 463–90.

13. Tryphiodorus: *Sack of Troy* 487–521; Servius on Virgil's *Aeneid* ii. 255; Lesches: *loc. cit.*, quoted by Tzetzes: *On Lycophron* 344; Apollodorus: *Epitome* v. 19.

14. Virgil: *Aeneid* ii. 256 ff.; Hyginus: *Fabula* 108; Apollodorus: *Epitome* v. 20; Tzetzes: *On Lycophron* 340.

15. Apollodorus: *loc. cit.*

\*

1. Classical commentators on Homer were dissatisfied with the story of the wooden horse. They suggested, variously, that the Greeks used a horse-like engine for breaking down the wall (Pausanias: i. 23. 10); that Antenor admitted the Greeks into Troy by a postern which had a horse painted on it; or that the sign of a horse was used to distinguish the Greeks from their enemies in the darkness and confusion; or that when Troy had been betrayed, the oracles forbade the plundering of any house marked with the sign of a horse – hence those of Antenor and others were spared; or that Troy fell as the result of a cavalry action; or that the Greeks, after burning their camp, concealed themselves behind Mount Hippius ('of the horse').

2. Troy is quite likely to have been stormed by means of a wheeled wooden tower, faced with wet horse hides as a protection against incendiary darts, and pushed towards the notoriously weak part of the defences – the western curtain which Aeacus had built (see 158. 8). But this would hardly account for the legend that the Trojan leaders were concealed in the horse's 'belly'. Perhaps the Homeridae invented this to explain a no longer intelligible icon showing a walled city, a queen, a solemn assembly, and the sacred king in the act of rebirth, head first, from a mare, which was the sacred animal both of the Trojans (see 48. 3) and of the Aeacids (see 81. 4). A wooden mare built of fir, the birth-tree (see 51. 5), may have been used in this ceremony, as a wooden cow facilitated the sacred marriage of Minos and Pasiphaë (see 88. e). Was the struggle between Odysseus and Antielus deduced perhaps from an icon that showed twins quarrelling in the womb (see 73. 2)?

3. The story of Laocoön's son, or sons, recalls that of the two serpents strangled by Heracles (see 119. 2). According to some versions, their death occurred in Apollo's shrine, and Laocoön himself, like Amphi-

tryon, escaped unharmed. The serpents will, in fact, have merely been
cleansing the boys' ears to give them prophetic powers. 'Antiphas' apparently means 'prophet' – 'one who speaks instead of' the god.

4. On the divine level this war was fought between Aphrodite, the
Trojan Sea-goddess, and the Greek Sea-god Poseidon (see 169. *1*) – hence
Priam's suppression of Poseidon's priesthood.

5. Sweating images have been a recurrent phenomenon ever since the
Fall of Troy; Roman gods later adopted this warning signal, and so did
the Catholic saints who took their places.

6. In early saga Epeius's reputation for courage was such that his name
became ironically applied to a braggart; and from braggart to coward is
only a short step (see 88. *10*).

# 168

## THE SACK OF TROY

ODYSSEUS, it seems, had promised Hecabe and Helen that all who
offered no resistance should be spared. Yet now the Greeks poured
silently through the moonlit streets, broke into the unguarded houses,
and cut the throats of the Trojans as they slept. Hecabe took refuge with
her daughters beneath an ancient laurel-tree at the altar raised to Zeus of
the Courtyard, where she restrained Priam from rushing into the thick
of the fight. 'Remain among us, my lord,' she pleaded, 'in this safe
place. You are too old and feeble for battle.' Priam, grumbling, did as
she asked until their son Polites ran by, closely pursued by the Greeks,
and fell transfixed before their eyes.[1] Cursing Neoptolemus, who had
delivered the death blow, Priam hurled an ineffectual spear at him;
whereupon he was hustled away from the altar steps, now red with
Polites's blood, and butchered at the threshold of his own palace. But
Neoptolemus, remembering his filial duty, dragged the body to Achilles's tomb on the Sigaean promontory, where he left it to rot, headless
and unburied.[2]

*b.* Meanwhile Odysseus and Menelaus had made for Deiphobus's
house, and there engaged in the bloodiest of all their combats, emerging
victorious only with Athene's aid. Which of the two killed Deiphobus
is disputed. Some even say that Helen herself plunged a dagger into his
back; and that this action, and the sight of her naked breasts, so weak-

ened the resolution of Menelaus, who had sworn 'She must die!', that he threw away his sword and led her in safety to the ships. Deiphobus's corpse was atrociously mangled, but Aeneas later raised a monument to him on Cape Rhoeteum.[3]

Odysseus saw Glaucus, one of Antenor's sons, fleeing down a street with a company of Greeks in hot pursuit. He intervened, and at the same time rescued Glaucus's brother Helicaon, who had been seriously wounded. Menelaus then hung a leopard's skin over the door of Antenor's house, as a sign that it should be spared.[4] Antenor, his wife Theano, and his four sons, were allowed to go free, taking all their goods with them; some days later they sailed away in Menelaus's ship, and settled first at Cyrene, next in Thrace, and finally at Henetica on the Adriatic.[5] Henetica was so called because Antenor took command of certain refugees from Paphlagonian Enete, whose King Pylaemenes had fallen at Troy, and led them in a successful war against the Euganei of the Northern Italian plain. The port and district where they disembarked was renamed 'New Troy', and they themselves are now known as Venetians. Antenor is also said to have founded the city of Padua.[6]

*c.* According to the Romans, the only other Trojan family spared by the Greeks was that of Aeneas who, like Antenor, had lately urged the surrender of Helen and the conclusion of a just peace; Agamemnon, seeing him lift the venerable Anchises upon his shoulders and carry him towards the Dardanian Gate without a sideways glance, gave orders that so pious a son should not be molested. Some, however, say that Aeneas was absent in Phrygia when the city fell.[7] Others, that he defended Troy to the last, then retired to the citadel of Pergamus and, after a second bold stand, sent his people forward under cover of darkness to Mount Ida, where he followed them as soon as he might with his family, his treasure, and the sacred images; and that, being offered honourable terms by the Greeks, he passed over into Thracian Pellene, and died either there or at Arcadian Orchomenus. But the Romans say that he wandered at last to Latium, founded the city of Lavinium and, falling in battle, was carried up to Heaven. All these are fables: the truth is that Neoptolemus led him away captive on board his ship, the most honourable prize won by any of the Greeks, and held him for ransom, which in due course the Dardanians paid.[8]

*d.* Helicaon's wife Laodice (whom some call the wife of Telephus) had lain with Acamas the Athenian, when he came to Troy in Diomedes's embassy ten years before, and secretly borne him a son named Munitus, whom Helen's slave-woman Aethra – mother to Theseus, and thus the infant's great-grandmother – had reared for her. At the fall of Troy, as Laodice stood in the sanctuary of Tros, beside the tombs of Cilla and Munippus, the earth gaped and swallowed her before the eyes of all.[9]

*e.* In the confusion, Aethra fled with Munitus to the Greek camp, where Acamas and Demophon recognized her as their long-lost grandmother, whom they had sworn either to rescue or to ransom. Demophon at once approached Agamemnon and demanded her repatriation, with that of her fellow-captive, the sister of Peirithous. Menestheus of Athens supported their plea, and since Helen had often shown her dislike of Aethra by setting a foot on her head and tugging at her hair, Agamemnon gave his assent; but obliged Demophon and Acamas to waive their claims to any other Trojan spoil. Unfortunately, when Acamas landed in Thrace on his homeward voyage, Munitus, who was accompanying him, died of a serpent's bite.[10]

*f.* No sooner had the massacre begun in Troy than Cassandra fled to the temple of Athene and clutched the wooden image which had replaced the stolen Palladium. There Little Ajax found her and tried to drag her away, but she embraced the image so tightly that he had to take it with him when he carried her off into concubinage; which was the common fate of all Trojan women. Agamemnon, however, claimed Cassandra as the particular award of his own valour, and Odysseus obligingly put it about that Ajax had violated Cassandra in the shrine; which was why the image kept its eyes upturned to Heaven, as if horror-stricken.[11] Thus Cassandra became Agamemnon's prize, while Ajax earned the hatred of the whole army; and, when the Greeks were about to sail, Calchas warned the Council that Athene must be placated for the insult offered to her priestess. To gratify Agamemnon, Odysseus then proposed the stoning of Ajax; but he escaped by taking sanctuary at Athene's altar, where he swore a solemn oath that Odysseus was lying as usual; nor did Cassandra herself support the charge of rape. Nevertheless, Calchas's prophecy could hardly be disregarded; Ajax therefore expressed sorrow for having forcibly removed the image, and offered to expiate his crime. This he was prevented from doing by death: the ship in which he sailed home to Greece being wrecked on the Gyraean Rocks. When he scrambled ashore, Poseidon split the rocks with his trident and drowned him; or, some say, Athene borrowed Zeus's thunderbolt and struck him dead. But Thetis buried his body on the island of Myconos; and his fellow-countrymen wore black for a whole year, and now annually launch a black-sailed ship, heaped with gifts, and burn it in his honour.[12]

*g*. Athene's wrath then fell on the land of Opuntian Locris, and the Delphic Oracle warned Ajax's former subjects that they would have no relief from famine and pestilence unless they sent two girls to Troy every year for a thousand years. Accordingly, the Hundred Houses of Locris have ever since shouldered this burden in proof of their nobility. They choose the girls by lot, and land them at dead of night on the Rhoetean headland, each time varying the season; with them go kinsmen who know the country and can smuggle them into the sanctuary of Athene. If the Trojans catch these girls, they are stoned to death, burned as a defilement to the land, and their ashes scattered on the sea; but once inside the shrine, they are safe. Their hair is then shorn, they are given the single garment of a slave, and spend their days in menial temple duties until relieved by another pair. It happened many years ago that when the Trarians captured Troy and killed a Locrian priestess in the temple itself, the Locrians decided that their long penance must be over and therefore sent no more girls; but, famine and pestilence supervening, they hastened to resume their ancient custom, the term of which is only now drawing to an end. These girls gain Athene's sanctuary by way of an underground passage, the secret entrance to which is at some distance from the walls, and which leads to the muddy culvert used by Odysseus and Diomedes when they stole the Palladium. The Trojans have no notion how the girls contrive to enter, and never know on what night the relief is due to arrive, so that they seldom catch them, and then only by accident.[13]

*h*. After the massacre, Agamemnon's people plundered and burned Troy, divided the spoils, razed the walls, and sacrificed holocausts to their gods. The Council had debated for a while what should be done with Hector's infant son Astyanax, otherwise called Scamandrius; and when Odysseus recommended the systematic extirpation of Priam's descendants, Calchas settled the boy's fate by prophesying that, if allowed to survive, he would avenge his parents and his city. Though all other princes shrank from infanticide, Odysseus willingly hurled Astyanax from the battlements.[14] But some say that Neoptolemus, to whom Hector's widow Andromache had fallen as a prize in the division of spoil, snatched Astyanax from her, in anticipation of the Council's decree, whirled him around his head by one foot and flung him upon the rocks far below.[15] And others say that Astyanax leaped to his death from the wall, while Odysseus was reciting Calchas's prophecy and invoking the gods to approve the cruel rite.[16]

*i.* The Council also debated Polyxena's fate. As he lay dying, Achilles had begged that she should be sacrificed upon his tomb, and more recently had appeared in dreams to Neoptolemus and other chieftains, threatening to keep the fleet windbound at Troy until they fulfilled his demand. A voice was also heard complaining from the tomb: 'It is unjust that none of the spoil has been awarded to me!' And a ghost appeared on the Rhoetean headland, clad in golden armour, crying: 'Whither away, Greeks? Would you leave my tomb unhonoured?'[17]

*j.* Calchas now declared that Polyxena must not be denied to Achilles, who loved her. Agamemnon disserted, arguing that enough blood was already shed, of old men and infants as well as of warriors, to glut Achilles's vengeance, and that dead men, however famous, enjoyed no rights over live women. But Demophon and Acamas, who had been defrauded of their fair share in the spoils, clamoured that Agamemnon was expressing this view only to please Polyxena's sister Cassandra and make her submit more readily to his embraces. They asked: 'Which deserves the greater respect, Achilles's sword or Cassandra's bed?' Feeling ran high and Odysseus, intervening, persuaded Agamemnon to give way.[18]

*k.* The Council then instructed Odysseus to fetch Polyxena, and invited Neoptolemus to officiate as priest. She was sacrificed on Achilles's tomb, in the sight of the whole army, who hastened to give her honourable burial; whereupon favouring winds sprang up at once.[19] But some say that the Greek fleet had already reached Thrace when the ghost of Achilles appeared, threatening them with contrary winds, and that Polyxena was sacrificed there.[20] Others record that she went of her own free will to Achilles's tomb, before Troy fell, and threw herself on the point of a sword, thus expiating the wrong she had done him.[21]

*l.* Though Achilles had killed Polydorus, Priam's son by Laothoë, the youngest and best-loved of his children, yet another prince of the same name survived. He was Priam's son by Hecabe and had been sent for safety to the Thracian Chersonese, where his aunt Iliona, wife of King Polymnestor, reared him. Iliona treated Polydorus as though he were a true brother to Deiphilus, whom she had borne to Polymnestor.

Agamemnon, pursuing Odysseus's policy of extirpation, now sent messengers to Polymnestor promising him Electra for a wife and a dowry of gold if he would do away with Polydorus. Polymnestor accepted the bribe, yet could not bring himself to harm a child whom he had sworn to protect, and instead killed his own son Deiphilus in the presence of the messengers, who went back deceived. Polydorus, not knowing the secret of his birth, but realizing that he was the cause of Iliona's estrangement from Polymnestor, went to Delphi and asked the Pythoness: 'What ails my parents?' She answered: 'Is it a small thing that your city is reduced to ashes, your father butchered and your mother enslaved, that you should come to me with such a question?' He returned to Thrace in great anxiety, but found nothing changed since his departure. 'Can Apollo have been mistaken?' he wondered. Iliona told him the truth and, indignant that Polymnestor should have murdered his only child for gold and the promise of another queen, he first blinded and then stabbed him.[22]

*m.* Others say that Polymnestor was threatened by the Greeks with relentless war unless he would give up Polydorus and that, when he yielded, they brought the boy to their camp and offered to exchange him for Helen. Since Priam declined to discuss the proposal, Agamemnon had Polydorus stoned to death beneath the walls of Troy, afterwards sending his body to Helen with the message: 'Show Priam this, and ask him whether he regrets his decision.' It was an act of wanton spite, because Priam had pledged his word never to surrender Helen while she remained under Aphrodite's protection, and was ready to ransom Polydorus with the rich city of Antandrus.[23]

*n.* Odysseus won Hecabe as his prize, and took her to the Thracian Chersonese, where she uttered such hideous invectives against him and the other Greeks, for their barbarity and breaches of faith, that they found no alternative but to put her to death. Her spirit took the shape of one of those fearful black bitches that follow Hecate, leaped into the sea and swam away towards the Hellespont; they called the place of her burial 'The Bitch's Tomb'.[24] Another version of the story is that after the sacrifice of Polyxena, Hecabe found the dead body of Polydorus washed up on the shore, her son-in-law Polymnestor having murdered him for the gold with which Priam was defraying the expenses of his education. She summoned Polymnestor, promising to let him into the secret of a treasure concealed among the ruins of Troy, and when he approached with his two sons, drew a dagger from her bosom, stabbed the boys to death and tore out Polymnestor's eyes; a display of ill-temper which Agamemnon pardoned because of her age and misfortunes. The Thracian nobles would have taken vengeance on Hecabe with darts and stones, but she transformed herself into a bitch named Maera, and ran around howling dismally, so that they retired in confusion.[25]

*o.* Some say that Antenor founded a new Trojan kingdom upon the ruins of the old one. Others, that Astyanax survived and became King of Troy after the departure of the Greeks; and that, when he was expelled by Antenor and his allies, Aeneas put him back on the throne – to which, however, Aeneas's son Ascanius eventually succeeded, as had been prophesied. Be that as it may, Troy has never since been more than a shadow of its former self.[26]

1. Apollodorus: *Epitome* v. 21; Euripides: *Hecabe* 23; Virgil: *Aeneid* ii. 506–57.

2. Lesches: *Little Iliad*, quoted by Pausanias: x. 27. 1; Virgil: *loc. cit.*; Apollodorus: *loc. cit.*; Euripides: *Trojan Women* 16–17.

3. Homer: *Odyssey* viii. 517–20; Apollodorus: *Epitome* v. 22; Hyginus: *Fabula* 240; Pausanias: v 18. 1; Lesches: *Little Iliad*, quoted by scholiast on Aristophanes's *Lysistrata* 155; Virgil: *Aeneid* vi. 494 ff.; Dictys Cretensis: v. 12.

4. Apollodorus: *Epitome* v. 21; Homer: *Iliad* iii. 123; Lesches: *Little Iliad*, quoted by Pausanias: x. 26. 3; Servius on Virgil's *Aeneid* i. 246; Sophocles: *Capture of Troy*, quoted by Strabo: xiii. 1. 53.

5. Pausanias: x. 27. 2; Pindar: *Pythian Odes* v. 82 ff.; Servius on Virgil's *Aeneid* i. 246; Strabo: xiii. 1. 53.

6. Livy: i. 1; Servius on Virgil's *Aeneid* i. 246.

7. Livy: *loc. cit.*; Apollodorus: *Epitome* v. 21; Dionysius of Halicarnassus: i. 48.

8. Dionysius of Halicarnassus: i. 48, 49, and 64; Aelian: *Varia Historia* iii. 22; Hyginus: *Fabula* 254; Strabo: xiii. 608; Pausanias: viii. 12. 5; Virgil: *Aeneid*, passim; Plutarch: *Romulus* 3; Livy: 1. 2; Lesches: *Little Iliad*, quoted by Tzetzes: *On Lycophron* 1268.

9. Hyginus: *Fabula* 101; Homer: *Iliad* iii. 123–4; Tzetzes: *On Lycophron* 495 ff. and 314; Apollodorus: *Epitome* v. 23.

10. Scholiast on Euripides's *Trojan Women* 31; Apollodorus: *Epitome* v. 22; Lesches: *Little Iliad*, quoted by Pausanias: x. 25. 3; Hyginus *Fabula* 243; Pausanias: v. 19. 1; Dio Chrysostom: *Orations* xi. i. p. 179, ed. Dindorff; Tzetzes: *On Lycophron* 495; Parthenius: *Love Stories* 16.

11. Arctinus of Miletus: *Sack of Ilium*; Virgil: *Aeneid* ii. 406; Apollodorus: *loc. cit.*; Scholiast on Homer's *Iliad* xiii. 66.

12. Tzetzes: *On Lycophron* 365; Apollodorus: *Epitome* v. 23; Pausanias: x. 31. 1; i. 15. 3 and x. 26. 1; Homer: *Odyssey* iv. 99.

13. Hyginus: *Fabula* 116; Scholiast on Homer's *Iliad* xiii. 66; Lycophron: 1141–73, with Tzetzes's *scholia*; Polybius: xii. 5; Plutarch: *On the Slowness of Divine Justice* xii; Strabo: xiii. 1. 40; Aelian: *Varia Historia, Fragment* 47; Aeneas Tacticus: xxxi. 24.

14. Homer: *Iliad* vi. 402; Apollodorus: *loc. cit.*; Euripides: *Trojan Women* 719 ff.; Hyginus: *Fabula* 109; Servius on Virgil's *Aeneid* ii. 457; Tryphiodorus: *Sack of Troy* 644–6.

15. Apollodorus: *loc. cit.*; Lesches: *Little Iliad*, quoted by Tzetzes: *On Lycophron* 1268; Pausanias: x. 25. 4.

16. Seneca: *Troades* 524 ff. and 1063 ff.

17. Servius on Virgil's *Aeneid* iii. 322; Tzetzes: *On Lycophron* 323; Quintus Smyrnaeus: *Posthomerica* xiv. 210–328; Euripides: *Hecabe* 107 ff.

18. Servius on Virgil's *Aeneid*: *loc. cit.*; Euripides: *loc. cit.*

19. Euripides: *Hecabe* 218 ff. and 521–82.

20. Ovid: *Metamorphoses* xiii. 439 ff.; Pausanias: x. 25. 4.

21. Philostratus: *Herioca* xix. 11.

22. Homer: *Iliad* xxii. 48 and xx. 407 ff.; Hyginus: *loc. cit.* and 240.

23. Dictys Cretensis: ii. 18, 22, and 27; Servius on Virgil's *Aeneid* iii. 6.

24. Apollodorus: *loc. cit.*; Hyginus: *Fabula* 111; Dictys Cretensis: v. 16; Tzetzes: *On Lycophron* 1176.

25. Euripides: *Hecabe*; Ovid: *Metamorphoses* xiii. 536 ff.

26. Dictys Cretensis: v. 17; Abas, quoted by Servius on Virgil's *Aeneid* ix. 264; Livy: i. 1.

\*

*1.* Odysseus's considerate treatment of such renegades as Antenor and Calchas is contrasted here with the treachery he showed to his honest comrades Palamedes, Great Ajax, Little Ajax, and Diomedes, and with his savage handling of Astyanax, Polydorus, and Polyxena; but because Julius Caesar and Augustus claimed descent from Aeneas – another traitor spared by Odysseus, and regarded at Rome as a model of piety – the satiric implications are lost on modern readers. It is a pity that the exact terms of Hecabe's invectives against Odysseus and his comrades in dishonour, which must have expressed Homer's true feelings, have not survived; but her conversion into the Cretan Hecate, Maera, or Scylla the sea-bitch (see 16. *2*; 91. *2*; and 170. *t*), suggests that he regarded the curses as valid – kingdoms founded on barbarity and ill-faith could never prosper. Maera was Scylla's emblem in heaven, the Lesser Dog-star, and when it rose, human sacrifices were offered at Marathon in Attica: the most famous victim being King Icarius (see 79. *1*), whose daughter

Odysseus had married and whose fate he will therefore have shared in the original myth (see 159. *b*).

2. The well-authenticated case of the Locrian girls is one of the strangest in Greek history, since Little Ajax's alleged violation of Cassandra was dismissed by reputable mythographers as an Odyssean lie, and it is clear that the Locrian girls gained entry into Troy as a matter of civic pride, not of penance. A genuine attempt was made by the Trojans to keep them out, if we can trust Aeneas Tacticus's account – he is discussing the danger of building cities with secret entrances – and that they were treated 'as a defilement of the land' if caught, and as slaves if they managed to gain entry, is consistent with this view. Little Ajax was the son of Locrian Oïleus; whose name, also borne by a Trojan warrior whom Agamemnon killed (*Iliad* xi. 9. 3), is an early form of 'Ilus'; and Priam's Ilium had, it seems, been partly colonized by Locrians, a pre-Hellenic tribe of Leleges (Aristotle: *Fragment* 560; Dionysius of Halicarnassus: i. 17; Strabo: xiii. 1. 3 and 3. 3). They gave the name of the Locrian mountain Phricones to what was hitherto called Cyme; and enjoyed a hereditary right to supply Athene with a quota of priestesses (see 158. 8). This right they continued to exercise long after the Trojan War – when the city had lost its political power and became merely a place of sentimental pilgrimage – much to the disgust of the Trojans, who regarded the girls as their natural enemies.

3. The curse, effective for a thousand years, ended about 264 B.C. – which would correspond with the Delian (and thus the Homeric) dating of the Trojan War, though Eratosthenes reckoned it a hundred years later. Odysseus's secret conduit has been discovered in the ruins of Troy and is described by Walter Leaf in his *Troy: A Study in Homeric Geography* (London, 1912, pp. 126–44). But why did Theano turn traitress and surrender the Palladium? Probably because being a Locrian – Theano was also the name of the famous poetess of Epizephyrian Locri – she either disagreed with Priam's anti-Locrian trade policy, or knew that Troy must fall and wanted the image removed to safety, rather than captured by Agamemnon. Homer makes her a daughter of Thracian Cisseus, and there was at least one Locrian colony in Thrace, namely Abdera (see 130. *c*). As a Locrian, however, Theano will have reckoned descent matrilineally (Polybius: xii. 5. 6); and was probably surnamed Cisseis, 'ivy-woman', in honour of Athene whose chief festival fell during the ivy-month (see 52. 3).

4. Sophocles, in the *Argument* to his *Ajax*, mentions a quarrel between Odysseus and Ajax over the Palladium after the fall of Troy; but this must have been Little Ajax, since Great Ajax had already killed himself. We may therefore suppose that Little Ajax, rather than Diomedes, led Odysseus up the conduit to fetch away the Palladium with the connivance of his compatriot Theano; that Odysseus accused Little Ajax of

laying violent hands on a non-Locrian priestess who clung to the image which Theano was helping him to remove; and that afterwards Ajax, while admitting his error, explained that he had been as gentle as possible in the circumstances. Such an event would have justified the Trojans of later centuries in trying to restrain the Locrian girls from exercising their rights as Trojan priestesses; in representing their continued arrival as a penance due for Ajax's crime, even though Athene had summarily punished him with a thunderbolt; and in treating them as menials. Odysseus may have insisted upon accompanying Little Ajax into the citadel, on the ground that Zacynthus, eponymous ancestor of his subjects the Zacynthians, figured in a list of early Trojan kings.

5. This, again, would explain Hecabe's failure to denounce Odysseus to the Trojans when he entered the city as a spy. She too is described as a 'daughter of Cisseus'; was she another Locrian from Thrace who connived at Ajax's removal of the Palladium? Hecabe had no cause to love Odysseus, and her reason for facilitating his escape can only have been to prevent him from denouncing her to the Trojans. Odysseus doubtless slipped out quietly by the culvert and not, as he boasted, by the gate 'after killing many Trojans'. Presumably he demanded old Hecabe as his share of the spoil because she had been a material witness of the Palladium incident and he wanted to stop her mouth. She seems, however, to have revealed everything before she died.

6. One of the principal causes of the Trojan War (see 158. r and 160. b) was Telamon's abduction of Priam's sister Hesione, the mother of Great Ajax and thus a kinswoman of Little Ajax; this points to long-standing friction between Priam and the Locrians of Greece. Patroclus, who caused the Trojans such heavy losses, was yet another Locrian, described as Abderus's brother.

The name Astyanax ('king of the city'), and the solemnity of the debate about his death, suggests that the icon on which the story is based represented the ritual sacrifice of a child at the dedication of a new city – an ancient custom in the Eastern Mediterranean (1 *Kings* xvi. 34).

7. Agamemnon's allies did not long enjoy the fruits of their triumph over Troy. Between 1100 and 1050 B.C., the Dorian invasion overwhelmed Mycenaean culture in the Peloponnese and the Dark Ages supervened; it was a century or two before the Ionians, forced by the Dorians to emigrate to Asia Minor, began their cultural renascence; which was based solidly on Homer.

8. Aeneas's wanderings belong to Roman, not Greek, mythology; and have therefore been omitted here.

## THE RETURNS

'LET us sail at once,' said Menelaus, 'while the breeze holds.' 'No, no,' replied Agamemnon, 'let us first sacrifice to Athene.' 'We Greeks owe Athene nothing!' Menelaus told him. 'She defended the Trojan citadel too long.' The brothers parted on ill terms and never saw each other again, for whereas Agamemnon, Diomedes, and Nestor enjoyed a prosperous homeward voyage, Menelaus was caught in a storm sent by Athene; and lost all but five vessels. These were blown to Crete, whence he crossed the sea to Egypt, and spent eight years in southern waters, unable to return. He visited Cyprus, Phoenicia, Ethiopia, and Libya, the princes of which received him hospitably and gave him many rich gifts. At last he came to Pharos, where the nymph Eidothea advised him to capture her prophetic father, Proteus the sea-god, who alone could tell him how to break the adverse spell and secure a southerly breeze.

Menelaus and three companions accordingly disguised themselves in stinking seal-skins and lay waiting on the shore, until they were joined at midday by hundreds of seals, Proteus's flock. Proteus himself then appeared and went to sleep among the seals: whereupon Menelaus and his party seized him, and though he turned successively into lion, serpent, panther, boar, running water, and leafy tree, held him fast and forced him to prophesy. He announced that Agamemnon had been murdered, and that Menelaus must visit Egypt once more and propitiate the gods with hecatombs. This he duly did, and no sooner had he raised a cenotaph to Agamemnon, beside the River of Egypt, than the winds blew fair at last. He arrived at Sparta, accompanied by Helen, on the very day that Orestes avenged Agamemnon's murder.[1]

*b.* A great many ships, though containing no leaders of note, were wrecked on the Euboean coast, because Nauplius had kindled a beacon on Mount Caphareus to lure his enemies to their death, as if guiding them into the shelter of the Pagasaean Gulf; but this crime became known to Zeus, and it was by a false beacon that Nauplius himself met his end many years later.[2]

*c.* Amphilochus, Calchas, Podaleirius and a few others travelled by land to Colophon, where Calchas died, as had been prophesied, on meeting a wiser seer than himself – none other than Mopsus, the son of Apollo and Teiresias's daughter Manto. A wild fig-tree covered with fruit grew at Colophon, and Calchas, wishing to abash Mopsus, challenged him as follows: 'Can you perhaps tell me, dear colleague, exactly how many figs will be harvested from that tree?' Mopsus, closing his eyes, as one who trusts to inner sight rather than vulgar computation, answered: 'Certainly: first ten thousand figs, then an Aeginetan bushel of figs, carefully weighed – yes, and a single fig left over.' Calchas laughed scornfully at the single fig, but when the tree had been stripped, Mopsus's intuition proved unerring. 'To descend from thousands to lesser quantities, dear colleague,' Mopsus now said, with an unpleasant smile, 'how many piglings, would you say, repose in the paunch of that pregnant sow; and how many of each sex will she farrow; and when?'

'Eight piglings, all male, and she will farrow them within nine days,' Calchas answered at random, hoping to be gone before his guess could be disproved. 'I am of a different opinion,' said Mopsus, again closing his eyes. 'My estimate is three piglings, only one of them a boar; and the time of their birth will be midday tomorrow, not a minute earlier or later.' Mopsus was right once more, and Calchas died of a broken heart. His comrades buried him at Nothium.[3]

d. The timorous Podaleirius, instead of asking his prophetic friends where he should settle, preferred to consult the Delphic Pythoness, who advised him irritably to go wherever he would suffer no harm, even if the skies were to fall. After much thought, he chose a place in Caria called Syrnos, ringed around with mountains; their summits would, he hoped, catch and support the blue firmament should Atlas ever let it slip from his shoulders. The Italians built Podaleirius a hero-shrine on Mount Drium in Daunia, at the summit of which the ghost of Calchas now maintains a dream oracle.[4]

e. A dispute arose between Mopsus and Amphilochus. They had jointly founded the city of Mallus in Cilicia, and when Amphilochus retired to his own city of Amphilochian Argos, Mopsus became sole sovereign. Amphilochus, dissatisfied with affairs at Argos, came back after twelve months to Mallus, expecting to resume his former powers, but Mopsus gruffly told him to begone. When the embarrassed Mallians suggested that this dispute should be decided by single combat, the rivals fought and each killed the other. The funeral pyres were so placed that Mopsus and Amphilochus could not exchange unseemly scowls during their cremation, yet the ghosts somehow became so tenderly linked in friendship that they set up a common oracle; which has now earned a higher reputation for truth even than Delphic Apollo's. All questions are written on wax tablets, and the responses given in dreams, at the remarkably low price of two coppers apiece.[5]

*f.* Neoptolemus sailed homeward as soon as he had offered sacrifices to the gods and to his father's ghost; and escaped the great tempest which caught Menelaus and Idomeneus, by taking the prophetic advice of his friend Helenus and running for Molossia. After killing King Phoenix and marrying his own mother to Helenus, who became king of the Molossians and founded a new capital city, Neoptolemus regained Ioclus at last.[6] There he succeeded to the kingdom of his grandfather Peleus, whom the sons of Acastus had expelled;[7] but on Helenus's advice did not stay to enjoy it. He burned his ships and marched inland to Lake Pambrotis in Epirus, near the Oracle of Dodona, where he was welcomed by a company of his distant kinsmen. They were bivouacking under blankets supported by spear-butts stuck into the ground. Neoptolemus remembered the words of Helenus: 'When you find a house with foundations of iron, wooden walls, and a woollen roof, halt, sacrifice to the gods, build a city!' Here he begot two more sons on Andromache, namely Pielus and Pergamus.

*g.* His end was inglorious. Going to Delphi, he demanded satisfaction for the death of his father Achilles whom Apollo, disguised as Paris, was said to have shot in his temple at Troy. When the Pythoness coldly denied him this, he plundered and burned the shrine. Next he went to Sparta, and claimed that Menelaus had betrothed Hermione to him before Troy; but that her grandfather Tyndareus had instead given her to Agamemnon's son Orestes. Orestes now being pursued by the Erinnyes, and under a divine curse, it was only just, he argued, that Hermione should become his wife. Despite Orestes's protests, the Spartans granted his plea, and the marriage took place at Sparta. Hermione, however, proving barren, Neoptolemus returned to Delphi and, entering the smoke-blackened sanctuary, which Apollo had decided to rebuild, asked why this should be.

*h.* He was ordered to offer placatory sacrifices to the god and, while doing so, met Orestes at the altar. Orestes would have killed him then and there, had not Apollo, foreseeing that Neoptolemus must die by another hand that very day, prevented it. Now, the flesh of the sacrifices offered to the god at Delphi has always been a perquisite of the temple servants; but Neoptolemus, in his ignorance, could not bear to see the fat carcasses of the oxen which he had slaughtered being hauled away before his eyes, and tried to prevent it by force. 'Let us be rid of this troublesome son of Achilles!' said the Pythoness shortly; whereupon one Machaereus, a Phocian, cut down Neoptolemus with his sacrificial knife.

'Bury him beneath the threshold of our new sanctuary,' she commanded. 'He was a famous warrior, and his ghost will guard it against all attacks. And if he has truly repented of his insult to Apollo, let him preside over processions and sacrifices in honour of heroes like himself.'

But some say that Orestes instigated the murder.[8]

*i*. Demophon the Athenian touched at Thrace on his return to Athens, and there Phyllis, a Bisaltian princess, fell in love with him. He married her and became king. When he tired of Thrace, and decided to resume his travels, Phyllis could do nothing to hold him. 'I must visit Athens and greet my mother, whom I last saw eleven years ago,' said Demophon. 'You should have thought of that before you accepted the throne,' Phyllis answered, in tears. 'It is not lawful to absent yourself for more than a few months at most.' Demophon swore by every god in Olympus that he would be back within the year; but Phyllis knew that he was lying. She accompanied him as far as the port called Enneodos, and there gave him a casket. 'This contains a charm,' Phyllis said. 'Open it only when you have abandoned all hope of returning to me.'

*j*. Demophon had no intention of going to Athens. He steered a south-easterly course for Cyprus, where he settled; and when the year was done, Phyllis cursed him in Mother Rhea's name, took poison, and died. At that very hour, curiosity prompted Demophon to open the casket, and the sight of its contents – who knows what they were? – made a lunatic of him. He leaped on his horse and galloped off in panic, belabouring its head with the flat of his sword until it stumbled and fell. The sword flew from his hand, stuck point upwards in the ground, and transfixed him as he was flung over the horse's head.

A story is told of another Thracian princess named Phyllis, who had fallen in love with Demophon's brother Acamas and, when storms delayed his return from Troy, died of sorrow and was metamorphosed into an almond-tree. These two princesses have often been confused.[9]

*k*. Diomedes, like Agamemnon and others, experienced Aphrodite's

bitter enmity. He was first wrecked on the Lycian coast, where King
Lycus would have sacrificed him to Ares, had not the princess Callirrhoë helped him to escape; and, on reaching Argos, found that his wife
Aegialeia had been persuaded by Nauplius to live in adultery with
Cometes or, some say, with Hippolytus. Retiring to Corinth, he learned
there that his grandfather Oeneus needed assistance against certain
rebels; so he sailed for Aetolia and set him firmly on his throne again.
But some say that Diomedes had been forced to leave Argos long before
the Trojan War, on his return from the Epigoni's successful Theban
campaign; and that Agamemnon had since assisted him to win back his
kingdom.[10] He spent the remainder of his life in Italian Daunia, where
he married Euippe, daughter of King Daunus; and built many famous
cities, including Brundisium, which may have been why Daunus
jealously murdered him when he was an old man, and buried him in
one of the islands now called the Diomedans. According to another
account, however, he suddenly disappeared by an act of divine magic,
and his comrades turned into gentle and virtuous birds, which still
nest on those islands. Diomedes's golden armour has been preserved
by the priests of Athene at Apulian Luceria, and he is worshipped as a
god in Venetia, and throughout Southern Italy.[11]

*l.* Nauplius had also persuaded Idomeneus's wife Meda to be faithless. She took one Leucus for her lover, but he soon drove her and
Idomeneus's daughter Cleisithyra from the palace and murdered them
both in the temple where they had taken sanctuary. Leucus then
seduced ten cities from allegiance to their rightful king, and usurped
the throne. Caught in a storm as he sailed for Crete, Idomeneus vowed
to dedicate to Poseidon the first person whom he met; and this happened to be his own son or, some say, another of his daughters. He was
on the point of fulfilling his vow when a pestilence visited the country
and interrupted the sacrifice. Leucus now had a good excuse for banish-
ing Idomeneus, who emigrated to the Sallentine region of Calabria,
and lived there until his death.[12]

*m.* Few of the other Greeks reached home again, and those who did
found only trouble awaiting them. Philoctetes was expelled by rebels
from his city of Meliboea in Thessaly, and fled to Southern Italy, where
he founded Petelia, and Crimissa near Croton, and sent some of his
followers to help Aegestes fortify Sicilian Aegesta. He dedicated his
famous bow at Crimissa, in the sanctuary of Distraught Apollo, and
when he died was buried beside the river Sybaris.[13]

*n.* Contrary winds forced Guneus to the Cynips river in Libya, and
he made his home there. Pheidippus with his Coans went first to Andros
and thence to Cyprus, where Agapenor had also settled. Menestheus
did not resume his reign at Athens, but accepted the vacant kingship of
Melos; some say, however, that he died at Troy. Elpenor's followers
were wrecked on the shores of Epirus, and occupied Apollonia; those
of Protesilaus, near Pellene in the Thracian Chersonese; and Tlepolemus's Rhodians, on one of the Iberian islands, whence a party of them
sailed westward again to Italy and were helped by Philoctetes in their
war against the barbarous Lucanians.[14] The tale of Odysseus's wanderings is now Homeric entertainment for twenty-four nights.

*o.* Only Nestor, who had always shown himself just, prudent,
generous, courteous, and respectful to the gods, returned safe and
sound to Pylus, where he enjoyed a happy old age, untroubled by wars,
and surrounded by bold, intelligent sons. For so Almighty Zeus
decreed.[15]

1. Apollodorus: *Epitome* vi. 1; Homer: *Odyssey* iii. 130 ff. and iv.
   77–592; Hagias, quoted by Proclus (*Greek Epic Fragments* p. 53.
   ed. Kinkel).
2. Apollodorus: ii. 1. 5 and *Epitome* vi. 11; Euripides: *Helen* 766 ff.
   and 1126 ff.; Hyginus: *Fabula* 116; Servius on Virgil's *Aeneid* xi.
   260.
3. Apollodorus: *Epitome* vi. 2–4; Strabo: xiv. 1. 27, quoting Hesiod,
   Sophocles, and Pherecydes; Tzetzes: *On Lycophron* 427 and 980.
4. Apollodorus: *Epitome* vi. 18; Pausanias: iii. 26. 7; Stephanus of
   Byzantium *sub* Syrna; Strabo: vi. 3. 9; Tzetzes: *On Lycophron*
   1047.
5. Apollodorus: iii. 7. 7 and *Epitome* vi. 19; Tzetzes: *On Lycophron*
   440–42; Strabo: xiv. 5. 16; Pausanias: i. 34. 3; Lucian: *Alexander*
   19; Plutarch: *Why the Oracles Are Silent* 45; Cicero: *On Divination*
   i. 40. 88; Dio Cassius: lxxii. 7.
6. Apollodorus: *Epitome* vi. 12 and 13; Hagias: *loc. cit.*; Servius on
   Virgil's *Aeneid* ii. 166; Scholiast on Homer's *Odyssey* iii. 188.
7. Dictys Cretensis: vi. 7–9.
8. Homer: *Odyssey* iv. 1–9; Apollodorus: *Epitome* vi. 13–14; Euripides: *Andromache* 891–1085 and *Orestes* 1649, with scholiast;
   Hyginus: *Fabula* 123; Eustathius on Homer's *Odyssey* iv. 3; Scholiast on Euripides's *Andromache* 32 and 51; Ovid: *Heroides* viii. 31 ff.;
   *Fragments of Sophocles* ii. 441 ff., ed. Pearson; Pausanias: x. 7. 1
   and x. 24. 4–5; Pindar: *Nemean Odes* vii. 50–70, with scholiast;
   Virgil: *Aeneid* iii. 330; Strabo: ix. 3. 9.
9. Apollodorus: *Epitome* v. 16; Tzetzes: *On Lycophron* 495; Lucian:

*On the Dance* 40; Hyginus: *Fabula* 59; Servius on Virgil's *Eclogues* v. 10.

10. Plutarch: *Parallel Stories* 23; Dictys Cretensis: vi. 2; Tzetzes: *On Lycophron* 609; Servius on Virgil's *Aeneid* viii. 9; Hyginus: *Fabula* 175; Apollodorus: i. 8. 6; Pausanias: iii 25. 2.

11. Pausanias: i. 11; Servius on Virgil's *Aeneid* viii. 9 and xi. 246; Tzetzes: *On Lycophron* 602 and 618; Strabo: vi. 3. 8–9; Scholiast on Pindar's *Nemean Odes* x. 12; Scylax: p. 6.

12. Apollodorus: *Epitome* vi. 10; Tzetzes: *On Lycophron* 384–6; Servius on Virgil's *Aeneid* iii. 121 and xi. 264; First Vatican Mythographer: 195; Second Vatican Mythographer: 210; Virgil: *Aeneid* 121 ff. and 400 ff.

13. Tzetzes: *On Lycophron* 911, quoting Apollodorus's *Epitome*; Homer: *Iliad* ii. 717 ff.; Strabo: vi. 1. 3; Aristotle: *Mirabilia* 107.

14. Tzetzes: *On Lycophron* 911; Pausanias: i. 17. 6.

15. Homer: *Odyssey* iv. 209; Pausanias: iv. 3. 4; Hyginus: *Fabula* 10.

\*

1. The mythographers make Aphrodite fight against the Greeks because, as Love-goddess, she had backed Paris's abduction of Helen. But she was also the Sea-goddess whom the Trojans invoked to destroy the commercial confederacy patronized by Poseidon – and the storms allegedly raised by Athene or Poseidon to deny the victors a safe return must first have been ascribed to her. This principle of vengeance enabled a great many cities in Italy, Libya, Cyprus, and elsewhere to claim foundation by heroes shipwrecked on their way back from Troy; rather than by refugees from the Dorian invasion of Greece.

2. To bury a young warrior under a temple threshold was common practice, and since Neoptolemus had burned the old shrine at Delphi, the Pythoness naturally chose him as her victim when the a new building was planted on its ruins. The previous guardians of the threshold had been Agamedes and Trophonius (see 84. *b*).

3. Rhea, who sanctified the mysterious object in Demophon's casket, was also called Pandora, and this myth may therefore be an earlier version of how Epimetheus's wife Pandora opened the box of spites (see 39. *j*): a warning to men who pry into women's mysteries, rather than contrariwise. 'Mopsus' was an eighth century B.C. royal title in Cilicia.

4. The birds into which Diomedes's followers were transformed are described as 'virtuous' evidently to distinguish them from their cruel bird-neighbours, the Sirens (see 154. *d* and *3*; 170. *7*).

5. A vow like Idomeneus's was made by Maeander ('searching for a man'), when he vowed to the Queen of Heaven the first person who should congratulate him on his storm of Pessinus; and this proved to be his son Archelaus ('ruler of the people'). Maeander killed him and then

remorsefully leaped into the river (Plutarch: *On Rivers* ix. 1). A more familiar version of the same myth is found in *Judges* xi. 30 ff., where Jephthah vows his daughter as a burnt offering to Jehovah if he is successful in war. These variants suggest that Idomeneus vowed a male sacrifice to Aphrodite, rather than to Poseidon; as Maeander did to the Queen of Heaven, and as Jephthah doubtless did to Anatha, who required such burnt offerings on her holy Judaean mountains. It looks, indeed, as if sacrifice of a royal prince in gratitude for a successful campaign was once common practice – Jonathan would have been slaughtered by his father, King Saul, after the victory near Michmash, had not the people protested – and that the interruption of Idomeneus's sacrifice, like Abraham's on Mount Moriah, or Athamas's on Mount Laphystium (see 70. *d*) was a warning that this custom no longer pleased Heaven. The substitution of a princess for a prince, as in the story of Jephthah, or in the First Vatican Mythographer's account of Idomeneus's vow, marks the anti-matriarchal reaction characteristic of heroic saga.

6. Menelaus's wanderings in the Southern Mediterranean refer to Achaean piracies and attempts at colonization. According to Xanthus, an early Lydian historian, the Phoenician city of Ascalon was founded by Ascalus ('untilled'), brother of Pelops, and therefore a collateral ancestor of Menelaus. Again, when Joshua conquered Canaan in the thirteenth century B.C., the men of Gibeon (*Agabon* in one Septuagint text, meaning *Astu Achaivon*, 'the city of the Achaeans') came as suppliants to Joshua in Greek fashion, pleading that they were not native Canaanites, but Hivites, i.e. Achaeans, from overseas. Joshua recognized their rights as foresters of the sacred groves and drawers of sacred water (*Joshua* ix). It seems from verse 9 that they reminded Joshua of the ancient maritime league of Keftiu presided over by Minos of Cnossus, to which the Achaeans and Abraham's people both once belonged. Abraham, who came into the Delta with the Hyksos kings, had married his sister Sarah to 'Pharaoh', meaning the Cnossian ruler of Pharos – then the chief trading depôt of the confederacy. But by the time of Menelaus, Cnossus lay in ruins, the confederates had turned pirates and been defeated by the Egyptians at the Battle of Piari (1229 B.C.) – 'I trapped them like wildfowl, they were dragged, hemmed in, laid low on the beach, their ships and goods were fallen into the sea' – and Pharos, no longer the largest port in the ancient world, became a mere breeding place for seals. A submarine disaster had overwhelmed its harbour works (see 39. *2*), and in early Classical times foreign trade passed through Naucratis, the Milesian *entrepôt* (see 25. *6*).

7. Menelaus's struggle with Proteus is a degenerate version of a familiar myth: the Seal-goddess Thetis has been masculinized into Proteus, and Menelaus, instead of waiting for the seal-skin to be discarded, and then

amorously grappling with the deity, as Peleus did (see 81. *1–3*), uses a seal-skin as a disguise, calls upon three men to help him, and requires no more from his captive than an oracular answer. Proteus rapidly transforms himself, as Thetis did with Peleus, or as Dionysus-Zagreus, who is associated with Pharos (see 27. *7*), did when threatened by the Titans. The Homeric list of his transformations is a muddled one: two or three seasonal sequences have been telescoped. Lion and boar are intelligible emblems of a two-season year (see 69. *1*); so are bull, lion, and water-serpent, of a three-season year (see 27. *4* and 123. *1*); the panther is sacred to Dionysus (see 27. *4*); and the 'leafy tree', paralleled in the story of Periclymenus, refers perhaps to the sacred trees of the months (see 53. *3* and 139. *1*). Proteus's changes make amusing fiction, but are wholly inappropriate to the oracular context, unless the real story is that after a reign of eight years, and the annual killing of an *interrex* in Cretan style, Menelaus became the oracular hero of a settlement founded beside the River of Egypt (see 112. *3*).

# 170

## ODYSSEUS'S WANDERINGS

ODYSSEUS, setting sail from Troy in the sure knowledge that he must wander for another ten years before he could hope to regain Ithaca, touched first at Ciconian Ismarus and took it by storm. In the pillage he spared only Maro, Apollo's priest, who gratefully presented him with several jars of sweet wine; but the Ciconians of the interior saw the pall of smoke spread high above the burned city, and charging down on the Greeks as they drank by the seashore, scattered them in all directions. When Odysseus had rallied and re-embarked his men with heavy losses, a fierce north-easterly gale drove him across the Aegean Sea towards Cythera.[1] On the fourth day, during a tempting lull, he tried to double Cape Malea and work up northward to Ithaca, but the wind rose again more violently than before. After nine days of danger and misery, the Libyan promontory where the Lotus-eaters live hove in sight. Now, the lotus is a stoneless, saffron-coloured fruit about the size of a bean, growing in sweet and wholesome clusters, though with the property of making those who have tasted it lose all memory of their own land; some travellers, however, describe it as a kind of apple from which a heavy cider is brewed. Odysseus landed to draw water, and sent out a patrol of three men, who ate the lotus offered them by the natives and so forgot their mission. After a while he went in search of them at the head of a rescue party, and though himself tempted to taste the lotus, refrained. He brought the deserters back by force, clapped them in irons, and sailed away without more ado.[2]

*b.* Next he came to a fertile, well-wooded island, inhabited only by countless wild goats, and shot some of these for food. There he beached the whole fleet, except a single ship in which he set out to explore the opposite coast. It proved to be the land of the fierce and barbarous Cyclopes, so called because of the large, round eye that glared from the centre of each forehead. They have lost the art of smithcraft known to their ancestors who worked for Zeus, and are now shepherds without laws, assemblies, ships, markets, or knowledge of agriculture; living sullenly apart from one another, in caverns hollowed from the rocky hills. Seeing the high, laurel-hung entrance of such a cavern, beyond a stock-yard walled with huge stones, Odysseus and his companions entered, unaware that the property belonged to a Cyclops named Polyphemus, a gigantic son of Poseidon and the nymph Thoösa, who loved to dine off human flesh. The Greeks made themselves at home by lighting a large fire; then slaughtered and roasted some kids that they found penned at the back of the cavern, helped themselves to cheese from baskets hung on the walls, and feasted cheerfully. Towards evening Polyphemus appeared. He drove his flock into the cavern and closed the entrance behind him with a slab of stone so huge that twenty teams of oxen could scarcely have stirred it; then, not observing that he had guests, sat down to milk his ewes and goats. Finally he glanced up from the pail and saw Odysseus and his comrades reclined around the hearth. He asked gruffly what business they had in his cavern. Odysseus replied: 'Gentle monster, we are Greeks on our way home after the sack of Troy; pray remember your duty to the gods and entertain us hospitably.' For answer Polyphemus snorted, seized two sailors by the feet, dashed out their brains on the floor, and devoured the carcasses raw, growling over the bones like any mountain lion.

*c.* Odysseus would have taken bloody vengeance before dawn, but dared not, because Polyphemus alone was strong enough to shift the stone from the entrance. He passed the night, head clasped between hands, elaborating a plan of escape, while Polyphemus snored dreadfully. For breakfast, the monster brained and killed another two sailors, after which he silently drove out his flock before him and closed the cavern with the same slab of stone; but Odysseus took a stake of green olive-wood, sharpened and hardened one end in the fire, then concealed it under a heap of dung. That evening the Cyclops returned and ate two more of the twelve sailors, whereupon Odysseus politely offered him an ivy-wood bowl of the heady wine given him by Maro in Ciconian Ismarus; fortunately, he had brought a full wine-skin ashore. Polyphemus drank greedily, called for a second bowlful, never in his life having tasted any drink stronger than buttermilk, and condescended to ask Odysseus his name. 'My name is Oudeis,' Odysseus replied, 'or that is what everyone calls me, for short.' Now, Oudeis means 'Nobody'. 'I will eat you last, friend Oudeis,' Polyphemus promised.

*d.* As soon as the Cyclops had fallen into a drunken sleep, the wine having been untempered with water, Odysseus and his remaining companions heated the stake in the embers of the fire, then drove it into the single eye and twisted it about, Odysseus bearing down heavily from above, as one drills a bolt hole in ship's timber. The eye hissed, and Polyphemus raised a horrible yell, which set all his neighbours hurrying from near and far to learn what was amiss.

'I am blinded and in frightful agony! It is the fault of Oudeis,' he bellowed.

'Poor wretch!' they replied. 'If, as you say, nobody is to blame, you must be in a delirious fever. Pray to our Father Poseidon for recovery, and stop making so much noise!'

They went off grumbling, and Polyphemus felt his way to the cavern mouth, removed the slab of stone and, groping expectantly with his hands, waited to catch the surviving Greeks as they tried to escape. But Odysseus took withies and tied each of his comrades in turn under the belly of a ram, the middle one of three, distributing the weight evenly. He himself chose an enormous tup, the leader of the flock, and prepared to curl up underneath it, gripping the fleece with his fingers and toes.

*e.* At dawn, Polyphemus let his flock out to pasture, gently stroking their backs to make sure that no one was astride of them. He lingered awhile talking sorrowfully to the beast under which Odysseus lay concealed, asking it: 'Why, dear ram, are you not to the fore, as usual? Do you pity me in my misfortune?' But at last he allowed it to pass.

*f.* Thus Odysseus contrived both to free his companions and to drive a flock of fat rams down to the ship. Quickly she was launched, and as the men seized their oars and began to row off, Odysseus could not refrain from shouting an ironical goodbye. For answer, Polyphemus hurled a large rock, which fell half a length ahead of the ship; its backwash nearly fetched her ashore again. Odysseus laughed, and cried: 'Should anyone ask who blinded you, answer that it was not Oudeis, but Odysseus of Ithaca!' The enraged Cyclops prayed aloud to Poseidon: 'Grant, father, that if my enemy Odysseus ever returns home, he may arrive late, in evil plight, from a foreign ship, having lost all his comrades; may he also find a heap of troubles massed on the threshold!' He hurled another, even larger, rock and this time it fell half a length astern of the ship; so that the wave which it raised carried her swiftly to the island where Odysseus's other followers were anxiously awaiting him. But Poseidon listened to Polyphemus, and promised the required vengeance.[3]

*g*. Odysseus now steered to the north, and presently reached the Isle of Aeolus, Warden of the Winds, who entertained him nobly for an entire month and, on the last day, handed him a bag of winds, explaining that while its neck was secured with silver wire, all would be well. He had not, he said, imprisoned the gentle West Wind, which would waft the fleet steadily over the Ionian Sea towards Ithaca, but Odysseus might release the others one by one, if for any reason he needed to alter his course. Smoke could already be descried rising from the chimneys of Odysseus's palace, when he fell asleep, overcome by exhaustion. His men, who had been watching for this moment, untied the bag, which promised to contain wine. At once the Winds roared homeward in a body, driving the ship before them; and Odysseus soon found himself on Aeolus's island again. With profuse apologies he asked for further help, but was told to begone and use oars this time; not a breath of West Wind should he be given. 'I cannot assist a man whom the gods oppose,' cried Aeolus, slamming the door in his face.[4]

*h*. After a seven days' voyage, Odysseus came to the land of the Laestrygones, ruled over by King Lamus, which is said by some to have lain in the north-western part of Sicily. Others place it near Formiae in Italy, where the noble House of Lamia claims descent from King Lamus; and this seems credible, because who would admit descent from cannibals, unless it were a matter of common tradition?[5] In the land of the Laestrygones, night and morning come so close together that shepherds leading home their flocks at sunset hail those who drive theirs out at dawn. Odysseus's captains boldly entered the harbour of Telepylus which, except for a narrow entrance, is ringed by abrupt cliffs, and beached their ships near a cart track that wound up a valley. Odysseus himself, being more cautious, made his ship fast to a rock outside the harbour, after sending three scouts inland to reconnoitre. They followed the track until they found a girl drawing water from a spring. She proved to be a daughter of Antiphates, a Laestrygonian chieftain, to whose house she led them. There, however, they were mercilessly set upon by a horde of savages who seized one of them and killed him for the pot; the other two ran off at full speed, but the savages, instead of pursuing them, made for the cliff tops and stove in the ships with a cascade of boulders before they could be launched. Then, descending to the beach, they massacred and devoured the crews at their leisure. Odysseus escaped by cutting the hawser of his ships with a sword, and calling on his comrades to row for dear life.[6]

*i*. He steered his sole remaining vessel due east and, after a long voyage, reached Aeaea, the Island of Dawn, ruled over by the goddess Circe, daughter of Helius and Perse, and thus sister to Aeëtes, the baleful king of Colchis. Circe was skilled in all enchantments, but had little love for human-kind. When lots were cast to decide who should stay to guard the ships and who should reconnoitre the island, Odysseus's mate Eurylochus was chosen to go ashore with twenty-two others. He found Aeaea rich in oaks and other forest trees, and at last came upon Circe's palace, built in a wide clearing towards the centre of the island. Wolves and lions prowled around but, instead of attacking Eurylochus and his party, stood upright on their hind legs and caressed them. One might have taken these beasts for human beings, and so indeed they were, though thus transformed by Circe's spells.

*j*. Circe sat in her hall, singing to her loom and, when Eurylochus's party raised a halloo, stepped out with a smile and invited them to dine at her table. All entered gladly, except Eurylochus himself who, suspecting a trap, stayed behind and peered anxiously in at the windows. The goddess set a mess of cheese, barley, honey, and wine before the hungry sailors; but it was drugged, and no sooner had they begun to eat than she struck their shoulders with her wand and transformed them into hogs. Grimly then she opened the wicket of a sty, scattered a few handfuls of acorns and cornel-cherries on the miry floor, and left them there to wallow.

*k*. Eurylochus came back, weeping, and reported this misfortune to

Odysseus, who seized his sword and went off, bent on rescue, though without any settled plan in his head. To his surprise he encountered the god Hermes, who greeted him politely and offered him a charm against Circe's magic: a scented white flower with a black root, called *moly*, which only the gods can recognize and cull. Odysseus accepted the gift gratefully and, continuing on his way, was in due course entertained by Circe. When he had eaten his drugged meal, she raised her wand and struck him on the shoulder. 'Go join your comrades in the sty,' she commanded. But having surreptitiously smelt the moly flower, he remained unenchanted, and leaped up, sword in hand. Circe fell weeping at his feet. 'Spare me,' she cried, 'and you shall share my couch and reign in Aeaea with me!' Well aware that witches have power to enervate and destroy their lovers, by secretly drawing off their blood in little bladders, Odysseus exacted a solemn oath from Circe not to plot any further mischief against him. This oath she swore by the blessed gods and, after giving him a deliciously warm bath, wine in golden cups, and a tasty supper served by a staid housekeeper, prepared to pass the night with him in a purple coverleted bed. Yet Odysseus would not respond to her amorous advances until she consented to free not only his comrades but all the other sailors enchanted by her. Once this was done, he gladly stayed in Aeaea until she had borne him three sons, Agrius, Latinus, and Telegonus.[7]

*l.* Odysseus longed to be on his way again, and Circe consented to let him go. But he must first visit Tartarus, and there seek out Teiresias the seer, who would prophesy the fate prepared for him in Ithaca, should he ever reach it, and afterwards. 'Run before the North Wind,' Circe said, 'until you come to the Ocean Stream and the Grove of Persephone, remarkable for its black poplars and aged willows. At the point where the rivers Phlegethon and Cocytus flow into the Acheron, dig a trench, and sacrifice a young ram and a black ewe – which I myself will provide – to Hades and Persephone. Let the blood enter the trench, and as you wait for Teiresias to arrive drive off all other ghosts with your sword. Allow him to drink as much as he pleases and then listen carefully to his advice.'

*m.* Odysseus forced his men aboard, unwilling though they were to sail from pleasant Aeaea to the land of Hades. Circe supplied a favourable breeze, which wafted them swiftly to the Ocean Stream and those lost frontiers of the world where the fog-bound Cimmerians, citizens of Perpetual Dusk, are denied all view of the Sun. When they sighted

Persephone's Grove, Odysseus landed, and did exactly as Circe had advised him. The first ghost to appear at the trench was that of Elpenor, one of his own crew who, only a few days previously, had drunken himself to sleep on the roof of Circe's palace, awoken in a daze, toppled over the edge, and killed himself. Odysseus, having left Aeaea so hurriedly that Elpenor's absence had escaped his notice until too late, now promised him decent burial. 'To think that you came here on foot quicker than I have come by ship!' he exclaimed. But he denied Elpenor the least sip of the blood, however piteously he might plead.

*n*. A mixed crowd of ghosts swarmed about the trench, men and women of all dates and every age, including Odysseus's mother Anticleia; but he would not let even her drink before Teiresias had done so. At last Teiresias appeared, lapped the blood gratefully, and warned Odysseus to keep his men under strict control once they had sighted Sicily, their next landfall, lest they be tempted to steal the cattle of the Sun-Titan Hyperion. He must expect great trouble in Ithaca, and though he could hope to avenge himself on the scoundrels who were devouring his substance there, his travels would not yet have finished. He must take an oar and carry it on his shoulder until he came to an inland region where no man salted his meat, and where the oar would be mistaken for a winnowing-bat. If he then sacrificed to Poseidon, he might regain Ithaca and enjoy a prosperous old age; but in the end death would come to him from the sea.

*o*. Having thanked Teiresias and promised him the blood of another black ewe on his return to Ithaca, Odysseus at last permitted his mother to quench her thirst. She gave him further news from home, but kept a discreet silence about her daughter-in-law's suitors. When she had said goodbye, the ghosts of numerous queens and princesses trooped up to lap the blood. Odysseus was delighted to meet such well-known personages as Antiope, Iocaste, Chloris, Pero, Leda, Iphimedeia, Phaedra, Procris, Ariadne, Maera, Clymene, and Eriphyle.

*p*. He next entertained a troop of former comrades: Agamemnon, who advised him to land on Ithaca in secret; Achilles, whom he cheered by reporting Neoptolemus's mighty feats; and Great Ajax, who had by no means yet forgiven him and strode sulkily away. Odysseus also saw Minos judging, Orion hunting, Tantalus and Sisyphus suffering, and Heracles – or rather his wraith, for Heracles himself banquets at ease among the immortal gods – who commiserated with him on his long labours.[8]

q. Odysseus sailed back safely to Aeaea, where he buried the body of Elpenor and planted his oar on the barrow as a memorial. Circe greeted him merrily. 'What hardihood to have visited the land of Hades!' she cried. 'One death is enough for most men; but now you will have had two!' She warned him that he must next pass the Island of the Sirens, whose beautiful voices enchanted all who sailed near. These children of Achelous or, some say, Phorcys, by either the Muse Terpsichore, or by Sterope, Porthaön's daughter, had girls' faces but birds' feet and feathers, and many different stories are told to account for this peculiarity: such as that they had been playing with Core when Hades abducted her, and that Demeter, vexed because they had not come to her aid, gave them wings, saying: 'Begone, and search for my daughter all over the world!' Or that Aphrodite turned them into birds because, for pride, they would not yield their maidenheads either to gods or men. They no longer had the power of flight, however, since the Muses had defeated them in a musical contest and pulled out their wing feathers to make themselves crowns. Now they sat and sang in a meadows among the heaped bones of sailors whom they had drawn to their death. 'Plug your men's ears with bees-wax,' advised Circe, 'and if you are eager to hear their music, have your crew bind you hand and foot to the mast, and make them swear not to let you escape, however harshly you may threaten them.' Circe warned Odysseus of other perils in store for him, when he came to say goodbye; and he sailed off, once more conveyed by a fair breeze.

r. As the ship approached Siren Land, Odysseus took Circe's advice, and the Sirens sang so sweetly, promising him foreknowledge of all future happenings on earth, that he shouted to his companions, threatening them with death if they would not release him; but, obeying his earlier orders, they only lashed him tighter to the mast. Thus the ship sailed by in safety, and the Sirens committed suicide for vexation.[9]

s. Some believe that there were only two Sirens; others, that there were three, namely Parthenope, Leucosia, and Ligeia; or Peisinoë, Aglaope, and Thelxepeia; or Aglaophonos, Thelxiope, and Molpe. Still others name four: Teles, Raidne, Thelxiope, and Molpe.[10]

t. Odysseus's next danger lay in passing between two cliffs, one of which harboured Scylla, and the other Charybdis, her fellow-monster. Charybdis, daughter of Mother Earth and Poseidon, was a voracious woman, who had been hurled by Zeus's thunderbolt into the sea and now, thrice daily, sucked in a huge volume of water and presently spewed it out again. Scylla, the once beautiful daughter of Hecate Crataeis by Phorcys, or Phorbas – or of Echidne by Typhon, Triton, or Tyrrhenius – had been changed into a dog-like monster with six fearful heads and twelve feet. This was done either by Circe when jealous of the sea-god Glaucus's love for her, or by Amphitrite, similarly jealous of Poseidon's love. She would seize sailors, crack their bones, and slowly swallow them. Almost the strangest thing about Scylla was her yelp: no louder than the whimper of a newly-born puppy. Trying to escape from Charybdis, Odysseus steered a trifle too near Scylla who, leaning over the gunwales, snatched six of his ablest sailors off the deck, one in each mouth, and whisked them away to the rocks, where she devoured them at leisure. They screamed and stretched out their hands to Odysseus, but he dared not attempt a rescue, and sailed on.[11]

*u*. Odysseus took this course in order to avoid the Wandering, or Clashing, Rocks, between which only the *Argo* had ever succeeded in passing; he was unaware that they were now rooted to the sea-bed. Soon he sighted Sicily, where Hyperion the Sun-Titan, whom some call Helius, had seven herds of splendid cattle at pasture, fifty to a herd, and large flocks of sturdy sheep as well. Odysseus made his men swear a solemn oath to be content with the provisions which Circe had supplied, and not steal a single cow. They then landed and beached the ship, but the South Wind blew for thirty days, food grew scarce, and though the sailors hunted or fished every day, they had little success. At last Eurylochus, desperate with hunger, drew his comrades aside and persuaded them to slaughter some of the cattle – in compensation for which, he hastened to add, they would build Hyperion a splendid temple on their return to Ithaca. They waited until Odysseus had fallen asleep, caught several cows, slaughtered them, sacrificed the thigh-bones and fat to the gods, and roasted enough good beef for a six days' feast.

*v*. Odysseus was horrified when he awoke to find what had happened; and so was Hyperion on hearing the story from Lampetia, his daughter and chief herdswoman. Hyperion complained to Zeus who, seeing that Odysseus's ship had been launched again, sent a sudden westerly storm to bring the mast crashing down on the helmsman's skull; and then flung a thunderbolt on deck. The ship foundered, and all aboard were drowned, except Odysseus. He contrived to lash the floating mast and keel together with the raw-hide back-stay, and clamber astride this makeshift vessel. But a southerly gale sprang up, and he found himself sucked towards Charybdis's whirlpool. Clutching at the bole of a wild fig-tree which grew from the cliff above, he hung on grimly until the mast and keel had been swallowed and regurgitated; then mounted them once more and paddled away with his hands. After nine days he drifted ashore on the island of Ogygia, where lived Calypso, the daughter of Thetis by Oceanus, or it may have been Nereus, or Atlas.[12]

*w*. Thickets of alder, black poplar, and cypress, with horned owls, falcons, and garrulous sea-crows roosting in their branches, sheltered Calypso's great cavern. A grape-vine twisted across the entrance. Parsley and irises grew thick in an adjoining meadow, which was fed by four clear streams. Here lovely Calypso welcomed Odysseus as he stumbled ashore, and offered him plentiful food, heady drink and a share of her soft bed. 'If you stay with me,' she pleaded, 'you shall enjoy immortality and ageless youth.' Some say that it was Calypso, not Circe, who bore him Latinus, besides the twins Nausithous and Nausinous.

*x*. Calypso detained Odysseus on Ogygia for seven years – or perhaps only for five – and tried to make him forget Ithaca; but he had soon tired of her embraces, and used to sit despondently on the shore, staring out to sea. At last, taking advantage of Poseidon's absence, Zeus sent Hermes to Calypso with an order for Odysseus's release. She had no option but to obey, and therefore told him to build a raft, which she would victual sufficiently: providing a sack of corn, skins of wine and water, and dried meat. Though Odysseus suspected a trap, Calypso swore by the Styx that she would not deceive him, and lent him axe, adze, augers, and all other necessary gear. He needed no urging, but improvised a raft from a score of tree-trunks lashed together; launched it on rollers; kissed Calypso goodbye, and set sail with a gentle breeze.

*y*. Poseidon had been visiting his blameless friends the Ethiopians, and as he drove home across the sea in his winged chariot, suddenly saw the raft. At once Odysseus was swept overboard by a huge wave, and the rich robes which he wore dragged him down to the sea-depths until his lungs seemed about to burst. Yet being a powerful swimmer, he managed to divest himself of the robes, regain the surface, and scramble back on the raft. The pitiful goddess Leucothea, formerly Ino, wife of Athamas, alighted beside him there, disguised as a seamew. In her beak she carried a veil, which she told Odysseus to wind around his middle before plunging into the sea again. This veil would save him, she promised. He hesitated to obey but, when another wave shattered the raft, wound the veil around him and swam off. Since Poseidon had now returned to his underwater palace near Euboea, Athene dared send a wind to flatten the waves in Odysseus's path, and two days later he was cast ashore, utterly exhausted, on the island of Drepane then occupied by the Phaeacians. He lay down in the shelter of a copse beside a stream, heaped dry leaves over himself, and fell fast asleep.[13]

z. Next morning the lovely Nausicaa, daughter of King Alcinous and Queen Arete, the royal pair who had once shown such kindness to Jason and Medea, came to wash her linen in the stream. When the work was done she played at ball with her women. Their ball happened to bounce into the water, a shout of dismay rang out, and Odysseus awoke in alarm. He had no clothes, but used a leafy olive-branch to conceal his nakedness and, creeping forward, addressed such honeyed words to Nausicaa that she discreetly took him under her protection and had him brought to the palace. There Alcinous heaped gifts on Odysseus and, after listening to his adventures, sent him off to Ithaca in a fine ship. His escort knew the island well. They cast anchor in the haven of Phorcys, but decided not to disturb his sound sleep, carried him ashore and laid him gently on the sand, stacking Alcinous's gifts beneath a tree not far off. Poseidon, however, was so vexed by the Phaeacians' kindness to Odysseus that he struck the ship with the flat of his hand as she sailed home, and turned her into stone, crew and all. Alcinous at once sacrificed twelve choice bulls to Poseidon, who was now threatening to deprive the city of its two harbours by dropping a great mountain between; and some say that he was as good as his word. 'This will teach us not to be hospitable in future!' Alcinous told Arete in bitter tones.[14]

1. Homer: *Odyssey* ix. 39–66.

2. Apollodorus: *Epitome* vii. 2–3; Homer: *Odyssey* ix. 82–104; Herodotus: iv. 177; Pliny: *Natural History* xiii. 32; Hyginus: *Fabula* 125.

3. Homer: *Odyssey* ix. 105–542; Hyginus: *loc. cit.*; Euripides: *Cyclops*; Apollodorus: *Epitome* vii. 4–9.

4. Homer: *Odyssey* x. 1–76; Hyginus: *loc. cit.*; Ovid: *Metamorphoses* xiv. 223–32.

5. Thucydides: i. 2; Pliny: *Natural History* iii. 5. 9 and 8. 14; Tzetzes: *On Lycophron* 662 and 956; Silius Italicus: vii. 410 and xiv. 126; Cicero: *Against Atticus* ii. 13; Horace: *Odes* iii. 17.

6. Homer: *Odyssey* x. 30–132; Hyginus: *loc. cit.*; Apollodorus: *Epitome* vii. 12; Ovid: *Metamorphoses* xiv. 233–44.

7. Homer: *Odyssey* x. 133–574 and xii. 1–2; Hyginus: *loc. cit.*; Ovid: *Metamorphoses* xiv. 246–404; Hesiod: *Theogony* 1011–14; Eustathius on Homer's *Odyssey* xvi. 118.

8. Homer: *Odyssey* xi; Hyginus: *loc. cit.*; Apollodorus: *Epitome* vii. 17.

9. Homer: *Odyssey* xii; Apollodorus: *Epitome* vii. 19; Apollonius Rhodius: iv. 898; Aelian: *On the Nature of Animals* xvii. 23; Ovid: *Metamorphoses* v. 552–62; Pausanias: ix. 34. 3; Hyginus: *Fabulae* 125 and 141; Sophocles: *Odysseus, Fragment* 861, ed. Pearson.

10. Plutarch: *Convivial Questions* ix. 14. 6; Scholiast on Homer's *Odyssey* xii. 39; Hyginus: *Fabulae loc. cit.* and *Preface*; Tzetzes: *On Lycophron* 712; Eustathius on Homer's *Odyssey* xii. 167.

11. Servius on Virgil's *Aeneid* iii. 420; Apollodorus: *Epitome* vii. 21; Homer: *Odyssey* xii. 73–126 and 222–59; Hyginus: *Fabulae* 125, 199 and *Preface*; Apollonius Rhodius: iv. 828, with scholiast; Eustathius on Homer p. 1714; Tzetzes: *On Lycophron* 45 and 650; Ovid: *Metamorphoses* xiii. 732 ff. and 906 ff.

12. Homer: *Odyssey* xii. 127–453; Apollodorus: i. 2. 7 and *Epitome* vii. 22–3; Hesiod: *Theogony* 359.

13. Homer: *Odyssey* v. 13–493 and vii. 243–66; Hyginus: *Fabula* 125; Hesiod: *Theogony* 1111 ff.; Scholiast on Apollonius Rhodius: iii. 200; Eustathius on Homer's *Odyssey* xvi. 118; Apollodorus: *Epitome* vii. 24.

14. Homer: *Odyssey* xiii. 1–187; Apollodorus: *Epitome* vii. 25; Hyginus: *loc. cit.*

\*

1. Apollodorus records (*Epitome* vii. 29) that 'some have taken the *Odyssey* to be an account of a voyage around Sicily.' Samuel Butler came independently to the same view and read Nausicaa as a self-portrait of the authoress – a young and talented Sicilian noblewoman of the Eryx district. In his *Authoress of the Odyssey*, he adduces the intimate knowledge here shown of domestic life at court, contrasted with the sketchy knowledge of seafaring or pastoral economy, and emphasizes the 'preponderance of female interest'. He points out that only a woman could have made Odysseus interview the famous women of the past before the famous men and, in his farewell speech to the Phaeacians, hope that 'they will continue to please their wives and children,' rather than the other way about (*Odyssey* xiii. 44–5); or made Helen pat the Wooden Horse and tease the men inside (see 167. *k*). It is difficult to disagree with Butler. The light, humorous, naïve, spirited touch of the *Odyssey* is almost certainly a woman's. But Nausicaa has combined, and localized in her native Sicily, two different legends, neither of them invented by herself: Odysseus's semi-historical return from Troy, and the allegorical adventures of

another hero – let us call him Ulysses – who, like Odysseus's grandfather Sisyphus (see 67. 2), would not die when his term of sovereignty ended. The Odysseus legend will have included the raid on Ismarus; the tempest which drove him far to the south-west; the return by way of Sicily and Italy; the shipwreck on Drepane (Corfu); and his eventual vengeance on the suitors. All, or nearly all, the other incidents belong to the Ulysses story. Lotus-land, the cavern of the Cyclops, the harbour of Telepylus, Aeaea, Persephone's Grove, Siren Land, Ogygia, Scylla and Charybdis, the Depths of the Sea, even the Bay of Phorcys – all are different metaphors for the death which he evaded. To these evasions may be added his execution of old Hecabe, otherwise known as Maera the Lesser Dog Star, to whom Icarius's successor should have been sacrificed (see 168. 1).

2. Both Scylax (*Periplus* 10) and Herodotus (iv. 77) knew the Lotuseaters as a nation living in Western Libya near the matriarchal Gindanes. Their staple was the palatable and nourishing *cordia myxa*, a sweet, sticky fruit growing in grape-like clusters which, pressed and mixed with grain (Pliny: *Natural History* xiii. 32; Theophrastus: *History of Plants* iv. 3. 1), once fed an army marching against Carthage. *Cordia myxa* has been confused with *rhamnus zizyphus*, a sort of crab-apple which yields a rough cider and has a stone instead of pips. The forgetfulness induced by lotuseating is sometimes explained as due to the potency of this drink; but lotus-eating is not the same as lotus-drinking. Since, therefore, the sacred king's tasting of an apple given him by the Belle Dame Sans Merci was tantamount to accepting death at her hands (see 33. 7 and 133. 4), the cautious Ulysses, well aware that pale kings and warriors languished in the Underworld because of an apple, will have refused to taste the *rhamnus*. In a Scottish witch-cult ballad, Thomas the Rhymer is warned not to touch the apples of Paradise shown him by the Queen of Elphame.

3. The cavern of the Cyclops is plainly a place of death, and Odysseus's party consisted of thirteen men: the number of months for which the primitive king reigned. One-eyed Polyphemus, who sometimes has a witch-mother, occurs in folk-tale throughout Europe, and can be traced back to the Caucasus; but the twelve companions figure only in the *Odyssey*. Whatever the meaning of the Caucasian tale may have been, A. B. Cook in his *Zeus* (pp. 302–23) shows that the Cyclops's eye was a Greek solar emblem. Yet when Odysseus blinded Polyphemus, to avoid being devoured like his companions, the Sun itself continued to shine. Only the eye of the god Baal, or Moloch, or Tesup, or Polyphemus ('famous'), who demanded human sacrifice, had been put out, and the king triumphantly drove off his stolen rams. Since the pastoral setting of the Caucasian tale was retained in the *Odyssey*, and its ogre had a single eye, he could be mistaken for one of the pre-Hellenic Cyclopes, famous metalworkers, whose culture had spread to Sicily, and who perhaps had an

eye tattooed in the centre of their foreheads as a clan mark (see 3. 2).

4. Telepylus, which means 'the far-off gate [of Hell]', lies in the extreme north of Europe, the Land of the Midnight Sun, where the incoming shepherd hails the outgoing shepherd. To this cold region, 'at the back of the North Wind', belong the Wandering, or Clashing, Rocks, namely ice-floes (see 151. 1), and also the Cimmerians, whose darkness at noon complemented their midnight sun in June. It was perhaps at Telepylus that Heracles fought Hades (see 139. 1); if so, the battle will have taken place during his visit to the Hyperboreans (see 125. 1). The Laestrygonians ('of a very harsh race') were perhaps Norwegian fiord-dwellers of whose barbarous behaviour the amber merchants were warned on their visits to Bornholm and the Southern Baltic coast.

5. Aeaea ('wailing') is a typical death island where the familiar Death-goddess sings as she spins. The Argonautic legend places it at the head of the Adriatic Gulf; it may well be Lussin near Pola (see 148. 9). Circe means 'falcon', and she had a cemetery in Colchis, planted with willows, sacred to Hecate. The men transformed into beasts suggest the doctrine of metempsychosis, but the pig is particularly sacred to the Death-goddess, and she feeds them on Cronus's cornel-cherries, the red food of the dead, so they are perhaps simply ghosts (see 24. 11 and 33. 7). What Hermes's moly was, the grammarians could not decide. Tzetzes (On Lycophron 679) says that the druggists call it 'wild rue'; but the description in the Odyssey suggests the wild cyclamen, which is difficult to find, besides being white-petalled, dark-bulbed and very sweet-scented. Late Classical writers attached the name 'moly' to a sort of garlic with a yellow flower which was believed to grow (as the onion, squill, and true garlic did) when the moon waned, rather than when it waxed, and hence to serve as a counter-charm against Hecate's moon magic. Marduk, the Babylonian hero, sniffed at a divine herb as an antidote to the noxious smell of the Sea-goddess Tiamat, but its species is not particularized in the epic (see 35. 5).

6. Persephone's black-poplar grove lay in the far-western Tartarus, and Odysseus did not 'descend' into it – like Heracles (see 134. c), Aeneas, and Dante – though Circe assumed that he had done so (see 31. a). Phlegethon, Cocytus, and Acheron belong properly to the Underground Hell. However, the authoress of the Odyssey had little geographical knowledge, and called upon West, South or North winds at random. Odysseus should have been taken by east winds to Ogygia and Persephone's Grove, and by south winds to Telepylus and Aeaea: yet she had some justification for making Odysseus steer due East to Aeaea, as the Land of Dawn, where the heroes Orion and Tithonus had met their deaths. The entrances of Mycenaean bee-hive tombs face east; and Circe, being Helius's daughter, had Eos ('dawn') for an aunt.

7. Sirens (see 154. 3) were carved on funeral monuments as death angels chanting dirges to lyre music, but also credited with erotic designs on the heroes whom they mourned; and, since the soul was believed to fly off in the form of a bird, were pictured, like the Harpies, as birds of prey waiting to catch and secure it. Though daughters of Phorcys, or Hell, and therefore first cousins of the Harpies, they did not live underground, or in caverns, but on a green sepulchral island resembling Aeaea or Ogygia; and proved particularly dangerous in windless weather at mid-day, the time of sunstroke and siesta-nightmares. Since they are also called daughters of Achelous, their island may originally have been one of the Echinades, at the mouth of the river Achelous (see 142. 3). The Sicilians placed them near Cape Pelorus (now Faro) in Sicily; the Latins, on the Sirenusian Islands near Naples, or on Capri (Strabo: i. 12 – see 154. *d* and 3).

8. 'Ogygia', the name of yet another sepulchral island, seems to be the same word as 'Oceanus', *Ogen* being an intermediate form; and Calypso ('hidden' or 'hider') is one more Death-goddess, as is shown by her cavern surrounded with alders – sacred to the Death-god Cronus, or Bran – in the branches of which perch his sea-crows, or choughs (see 98. 3), and her own horned owls and falcons. Parsley was an emblem of mourning (see 106. 3), and the iris a death flower (see 85. 1). She prom-ised Odysseus ageless youth, but he wanted life, not heroic immortality.

9. Scylla ('she who rends'), daughter of Phorcys, or Hecate, and Charybdis ('the sucker-down'), are titles of the destructive Sea-goddess. These names became attached to rocks and currents on either side of the Straits of Messina, but must be understood in a larger sense (see 16. 2 and 91. 2). Leucothea (see 70. 4) as a seamew was the Sea-goddess mourning over a shipwreck (see 45. 2). Since the Cretan Sea-goddess was also repre-sented as an octopus (see 81. 1), and Scylla dragged the sailors from Odysseus's ship, it may be that Cretans who traded with India knew of large tropical varieties, unknown in the Mediterranean, which are credited with this dangerous habit. The description of Scylla's yelp is of greater mythological importance than first appears: it identifies her with the white, red-eared death-hounds, the Spectral Pack, or Gabriel Ratches, of British legend, which pursue the souls of the damned. They were the ancient Egyptian hunting dogs, sacred to Anubis and still bred in the island of Iviza, which when in pursuit of their quarry make a 'questing' noise like the whimper of puppies or the music of the migrating barnacle-goose (see *White Goddess* p. 411).

10. Only two incidents falling between Odysseus's skirmish with the Ciconians and his arrival at Phaeacia seem not to concern the ninefold rejection of death: namely his visit to the Island of Aeolus, and the theft of Hyperion's cattle. But the winds under Aeolus's charge were spirits of

the dead (see 43. *5*); and Hyperion's cattle are the herd stolen by Heracles on his Tenth Labour – essentially a harrowing of Hell (see 132. *1*). That Odysseus claimed to have taken no part in the raid means little; neither did his maternal grandfather Autolycus (see 160. *c*) own up to his lifting of sun-cattle (see 67. *c*).

*11.* Odysseus, whose name, meaning 'angry', stands for the red-faced sacred king (see 27. *12*), is called 'Ulysses' or 'Ulixes' in Latin – a word probably formed from *oulos*, 'wound' and *ischea*, 'thigh' – in reference to the boar's-tusk wound which his old nurse recognized when he came back to Ithaca (see 160. *c* and 171. *g*). It was a common form of royal death to have one's thigh gored by a boar, yet Odysseus had somehow survived the wound (see 18. *7* and 151. *2*).

# 171

## ODYSSEUS'S HOMECOMING

WHEN Odysseus awoke he did not at first recognize his native island, over which Athene had cast a distortive glamour. Presently she came by, disguised as a shepherd boy, and listened to his long, lying tale of how he was a Cretan who, after killing Idomeneus's son, had fled northward in a Sidonian ship, and been put ashore here against his will. 'What island is this?' he asked. Athene laughed and caressed Odysseus's cheek: 'A wonderful liar you are, indeed!' she said. 'But for knowing the truth I might easily have been deceived. What surprises me, though, is that you did not penetrate my disguise. I am Athene; the Phaeacians landed you here at my instructions. I regret having taken so many years to fetch you home; but I did not dare offend my uncle Poseidon by supporting you too openly.' She helped him to stow away his Phaeacian cauldrons, tripods, purple cloaks and golden cups in the shelter of a cave, and then transformed him beyond recognition – withered his skin, thinned and whitened his red locks, clothed him in filthy rags, and directed him to the hut of Eumaeus, the faithful old palace-swineherd. Athene was just back from Sparta, where Telemachus had gone to ask Menelaus, recently returned from Egypt, whether he could supply any news of Odysseus.

Now, it should be explained that, presuming Odysseus's death, no less than one hundred and twelve insolent young princes of the islands which formed the kingdom – Dulichium, Same, Zacynthus, and Ithaca itself – were courting his wife Penelope, each hoping to marry her and take the throne; and had agreed among themselves to murder Telemachus on his return from Sparta.[1]

*b.* When they first asked Penelope to decide between them, she declared that Odysseus must certainly still be alive, because his eventual home-coming had been foretold by a reliable oracle; and later, being hard-pressed, promised a decision as soon as she completed the shroud which she must weave against the death of old Laertes, her father-in-law. But she took three years over the task, weaving by day and unravelling it by night, until at last the suitors detected the ruse. All this time they were disporting themselves in Odysseus's palace, drinking his wine, slaughtering his pigs, sheep, and cattle, and seducing his maid-servants.[2]

*c.* To Eumaeus, who received Odysseus kindly, he gave another false account of himself, though declaring on oath that Odysseus was alive and on the way home. Telemachus now landed unexpectedly, evading the suitors' plots to murder him, and came straight to Eumaeus's hut; Athene had sent him back in haste from Sparta. Odysseus, however, did not disclose his identity until Athene gave the word and magically restored him to his true appearance. A touching scene of recognition between father and son followed. But Eumaeus had not yet been taken into the secret, nor was Telemachus allowed to enlighten Penelope.

*d.* Once more disguised as a beggar, Odysseus went to spy upon the suitors. On the way he encountered his goat-herd Melantheus, who railed indecently at him and kicked him on the hip; yet Odysseus refrained from immediate vengeance. When he reached the palace court, he found old Argus, once a famous hunting hound, stretched on a dunghill, mangy, decrepit, and tormented by fleas. Argus wagged his raw stump of a tail and drooped his tattered ears in recognition of Odysseus, who covertly brushed away a tear as Argus expired.[3]

*e.* Eumaeus led Odysseus into the banqueting hall, where Telemachus, pretending not to know who he was, offered him hospitality. Athene then appeared, though inaudible and invisible to all but Odysseus, and suggested that he should make a round of the hall begging scraps from the suitors, and thus learn what sort of men they were. This he did, and found them no less niggardly than rapacious. The most shameless of the entire company, Antinous of Ithaca (to whom he told a wholly different tale of his adventures) angrily threw a footstool at him. Odysseus, nursing a bruised shoulder, appealed to the other suitors, who agreed that Antinous should have shown more courtesy; and Penelope, when her maids reported the incident, was scandalized. She sent for the supposed beggar, hoping to have news from him of her lost husband. Odysseus promised to visit the royal parlour that evening, and tell her whatever she wished to know.[4]

*f*. Meanwhile, a sturdy Ithacan beggar, nicknamed 'Irus' because, like the goddess Iris, he was at everyone's beck and call, tried to chase Odysseus from the porch. When he would not stir, Irus challenged him to a boxing match, and Antinous, laughing heartily, offered the winner a goat's haggis and a seat at the suitors' mess. Odysseus hoisted his rags, tucked them under the frayed belt which he was wearing, and squared up to Irus. The ruffian shrank away at sight of his bulging muscles, but was kept from precipitate flight by the taunts of the suitors; then Odysseus felled him with a single blow, taking care not to attract too much notice by making it a mortal one. The suitors applauded, sneered, quarrelled, settled to their afternoon's feasting, toasted Penelope, who now came to extract bridal gifts from them all (though with no intention of making a definite choice), and at nightfall dispersed to their various lodgings.[5]

*g*. Odysseus instructed Telemachus to take down the spears which hung on the walls of the banqueting hall and store them in the armoury, while he went to visit Penelope.

She did not know him, and he spun her a long, circumstantial yarn, describing a recent encounter with Odysseus; who had, he said, gone to consult Zeus's Oracle at Dodona, but should soon be back in Ithaca. Penelope listened attentively, and ordered Eurycleia, Odysseus's aged nurse, to give him a foot-bath. Eurycleia presently recognized the scar on his thigh, and cried out in joy and surprise; so he gripped her withered throat and hissed for silence. Penelope missed the incident; Athene had distracted her attention.[6]

*h*. On the following day, at another banquet, Agelaus of Same, one of the suitors, asked Telemachus whether he could not persuade his mother to make up her mind. Penelope thereupon announced that she was ready to accept any suitor who would emulate Odysseus's feat of shooting an arrow through twelve axe-rings; the axes to be set in a straight row with their butts planted in a trench. She showed them the bow which they must use: one given to Odysseus by Iphitus, twenty-five years ago, when he went to protest at Messene against the theft from Ithaca of three hundred sheep and their shepherds. It once belonged to Eurytus, the father of Iphitus, whom Apollo himself had instructed in archery, but whom Heracles outshot and killed. Some of the suitors now tried to string the powerful weapon, and were unable to bend it, even after softening the wood with tallow; it was therefore decided to postpone the trial until the next day. Telemachus, who came nearest to accomplishing the feat, laid down the bow again at a warning sign from Odysseus. Then Odysseus, despite protests and vulgar insults – in the course of which Telemachus was forced to order Penelope back to her room – seized the bow, strung it easily, and twanged the string melodiously for all to hear. Taking careful aim he shot an arrow through every one of the twelve axe-rings. Meanwhile Telemachus, who had hurriedly slipped out, re-entered with sword and spear, and Odysseus declared himself at last by shooting Antinous in the throat.

*i*. The suitors sprang up and rushed to the walls, only to find that the spears were no longer in their usual places. Eurymachus begged for mercy, and when Odysseus refused it, drew sword and lunged at him, whereupon an arrow transfixed his liver and he fell dying. A fierce fight ensued between the desperate suitors armed with swords, and Odysseus, unarmed except for the bow but posted before the main entrance to the hall. Telemachus ran back to the armoury, and brought shields, spears and helmets to arm his father and Eumaeus and Philoetius, the two faithful servants who were standing by him; for though Odysseus had shot down the suitors in heaps, his stock of arrows was nearly expended. Melantheus, stealing off by a side door to fetch weapons for the suitors, was caught and trussed up on his second visit to the armoury, before he had succeeded in arming more than a few of them. The slaughter then continued, and Athene in the guise of a swallow flew twittering around the hall until every one of the suitors and their supporters lay dead, except only Medon the herald, and Phemius the bard; these Odysseus spared, because they had not actively wronged him, and because their persons were sacrosanct. He now paused to ask Eurycleia, who had locked the palace women in their quarters, how many of these had remained true to his cause. She answered: 'Only twelve have disgraced themselves, my lord.' The guilty maid-servants were summoned and set to cleanse the hall of blood with sponges and water; when they had done, Odysseus hanged them in a row. They kicked a little, but soon all was over. Afterwards, Eumaeus and

Philoetius docked Melantheus of his extremities – nose, ears, hands, feet, and genitals, which were cast to the dogs.[7]

*j.* Odysseus, at last reunited with Penelope, and with his father Laertes, told them his various adventures, this time keeping to the truth. A force of Ithacan rebels approached, the kinsmen of Antinous and other dead suitors, and seeing that Odysseus was outnumbered, the aged Laertes joined vigorously in the fight, which was going well enough for them until Athene intervened and imposed a truce.[8] The rebels then brought a combined legal action against Odysseus, appointing as their judge Neoptolemus, King of the Epirot Islands. Odysseus agreed to accept his verdict, and Neoptolemus ruled that he should leave his kingdom and not return until ten years had passed, during which time the heirs of the suitors were ordered to compensate him for their depredations, with payments made to Telemachus, now king.[9]

*k.* Poseidon, however, still remained to be placated; and Odysseus set out on foot, as Teiresias had instructed, across the mountains of Epirus, carrying an oar over his shoulder. When he reached Thesprotis, the countryfolk cried: 'Stranger, why a winnowing-bat in Springtime?' He accordingly sacrificed a ram, bull, and boar to Poseidon, and was forgiven.[10] Since he could not return to Ithaca even yet, he married Callidice, Queen of the Thesprotians, and commanded her army in a war against the Brygians, under the leadership of Ares; but Apollo called for a truce. Nine years later, Polypoetes, Odysseus's son by Callidice, succeeded to the Thesprotian kingdom, and Odysseus went home to Ithaca, which Penelope was now ruling in the name of their young son Poliporthis; Telemachus had been banished to Cephallenia, because an oracle announced: 'Odysseus, your own son shall kill you!' At Ithaca, death came to Odysseus from the sea, as Teiresias had foretold. His son by Circe, Telegonus, sailing in search of him, raided Ithaca (which he mistook for Corcyra) and Odysseus sallied out to repel the attack. Telegonus killed him on the seashore, and the fatal weapon was a spear armed with the spine of a sting-ray. Having spent the required year in exile, Telegonus married Penelope. Telemachus then married Circe; thus both branches of the family became closely united.[11]

*l.* Some deny that Penelope remained faithful to Odysseus. They accuse her of companying with Amphinomus of Dulichium, or with all the suitors in turn, and say that the fruit of this union was the monstrous god Pan – at sight of whom Odysseus fled for shame to Aetolia,

after sending Penelope away in disgrace to her father Icarius at Mantinea, where her tomb is still shown. Others record that she bore Pan
to Hermes, and that Odysseus married an Aetolian princess, the daughter of King Thoas, begot on her his youngest son Leontophonus, and
died in prosperous old age.[12]

1. Homer: *Odyssey* xiii. 187 ff. and xvi. 245–53; Apollodorus:
   *Epitome* vii. 26–30.
2. Homer: *Odyssey* xix. 136–58 and xiv. 80–109; Hyginus: *Fabula*
   126; Apollodorus: *Epitome* vii. 31.
3. Homer: *Odyssey* xiv–xvi; Apollodorus: *Epitome* vii. 32.
4. Homer: *Odyssey* xvii; Apollodorus: *loc. cit.*
5. Homer: *Odyssey* xviii.
6. Homer: *Odyssey* xix.
7. Homer: *Odyssey* xx–xxii; Hyginus: *loc. cit.*; Apollodorus: *Epitome* vii. 33.
8. Homer: *Odyssey* xxii–xxiv.
9. Plutarch: *Greek Questions* 14.
10. Homer: *Odyssey* xi. 119–31; Apollodorus: *Epitome* vii. 34.
11. Apollodorus: *loc. cit.*; Eugammon of Cyrene, quoted by Proclus:
    *Epicorum Graecorum Fragmenta* 57 ff., ed. Kinkel; Hyginus: *Fabula*
    127; Pausanias: viii. 12. 6; Scholiast on *Odyssey* xi. 134; Eusta-
    thius on *Odyssey* xi. 133; Parthenius: *Love Stories* 3; Tzetzes: *On
    Lycophron* 794; Dictys Cretensis: vi. 4 ff.; Servius on Virgil's
    *Aeneid* ii. 44; *Fragments of Sophocles* ii. 105 ff., ed. Pearson.
12. Servius: *loc. cit.*; Pausanias: viii. 12. 5 ff.; Cicero: *On the Nature of
    the Gods* iii. 22. 56; Tzetzes: *On Lycophron* 772, quoting Duris the
    Samian.

*

1. Odysseus's assassination of the suitors belongs to the Ulysses allegory: one more instance of the sacred king's refusal to die at the close of
his reign. He intervenes, that is to say, in the archery contest held to
decide his successor (see 135. *1*), and destroys all the candidates. One
primitive archery test of the candidate for kingship seems to have consisted in shooting through a ring placed on a boy's head (see 162. *10*).

2. The *Odyssey* nowhere directly suggests that Penelope has been
unfaithful to her husband during his long absence, though in Book xviii.
281–3 she bewitches the suitors by her coquetry, extorts tribute from
them, and shows a decided preference for Amphinomus of Dulichium
(*Odyssey* xvi. 394–8). But Odysseus does not trust her well enough to
reveal himself until he has killed his rivals; and his mother Anticleia
shows that there is something to conceal when she says not one word to
him about the suitors (*Odyssey* xi. 180 ff.). The archaic account that makes
Penelope the mother of Pan by Hermes, or alternatively by all the suitors,

refers, it seems, to the Goddess Penelope and her primitive spring orgies, (see 26. 2). Her cuckolding of Odysseus and eventual return to Mantinea, another archaic story, are a reminder of his insolence in forcing her to come with him to Ithaca, against ancient matrilocal custom (see 160. e). But Nausicaa, the authoress, tells the story in her own way, white-washing Penelope. She accepts the patriarchal system into which she has been born, and prefers gentle irony to the bitter satire found in the Iliad. The goddess is now displaced by Almighty Zeus, kings are no longer sacrificed in her honour, and the age of myth has ended – very well! That need not greatly disturb Nausicaa, while she can still joke and play ball with her good-natured servant girls, pull the hair of those who displease her, listen to old Eurycleia's tales, and twist Father Alcinous around one finger.

3. So the Odyssey breaks off with Laertes, Odysseus, and Telemachus, a patriarchal male triad of heroes, supported by Zeus-born Athene and triumphing over their foes; while the serving wenches hang in a row for their lack of discretion, to show that Nausicaa disapproves of pre-marital promiscuity as cheapening the marriage-market.

The end has been preserved by other mythographers. Odysseus is banished to Thesprotia, and Telemachus to Cephallenia, whereas Penelope stays contentedly at the palace, ruling in the name of her son Poliporthis. Teiresias's prophecy remains, of course, to be fulfilled: Odysseus will not die comfortably of old age, like the respected and garrulous Nestor. Death must strike him down in the traditional style which he thought to abolish: the New Year Child riding on dolphin-back will run him through with a sting-ray spear. Much the same fate overtook Catreus of Rhodes: his son Althaemenes accidentally speared him on the beach (see 93. 2). Sting-ray spears, also used by the Polynesians, cause inflamed wounds, which the Greeks and Latins held to be incurable (Aelian: Nature of Animals i. 56); the sting-ray (trygon pastinaca) is common in the Mediterranean. Heracles is said to have been wounded by one (see 123. 2).

4. Telemachus's marriage to Circe, and Telegonus's to Penelope, are surprising at first sight. Sir James Frazer (Apollodorus ii. p. 303, Loeb) connects these apparently incestuous unions with the rule by which, in polygamous societies, a king inherited all his father's concubines, except his own mother (2 Samuel xvi. 21 ff.). But polygamy never became a Greek institution, and neither Telemachus, nor Telegonus, nor Oedipus, a New Year Child, 'born of the swelling wave', who killed his father and married the widowed Iocaste (see 105. e), nor Heracles's son Hyllus, who married his step-mother Iole (see 145. e), was polygamous. Each merely killed and succeeded the King of the Old Year in the ancient mythic style, and was thereafter called his son. This explains why Telemachus prepares to string the bow – which would have given him Penelope

as his wife – but Odysseus frowns at him, and he desists; it is a detail surviving from the Ulysses story, uncritically retained in the *Odyssey*.

5. Who knows whether Odysseus's red hair has any mythic significance (see 133. 8), or whether it is an irrelevant personal peculiarity, like his short legs, belonging to some adventurer in Sicily whom Nausicaa has portrayed as Odysseus? Autolycus, of course, named him 'the angry one' at birth (see 160. *c*), and red hair is traditionally associated with ill temper. But though masquerading as an epic, the *Odyssey* is the first Greek novel; and therefore wholly irresponsible where myths are concerned. I have suggested the possible circumstances of its composition in another novel: *Homer's Daughter*.*

*London and New York, 1955

# MAP OF THE GREEK WORLD

IERNE

BRITANNIA

BALTIC SEA

Elbe R.

ALEMANI

Rhine R.

Seine R.

GALLIA

Danube R.

Alesia   HELVETICA

Rhône R.

Po R.   ISTRIA

Stony   LIGURIA   Save R.
Plain

Pyrenaei Mt

ETRURIA   ADRIATIC

Massilia   ITALIA   Phlegraia

LATIUM   Melita Is.

Corsica   DAUNIA

HISPANIA   UMBRIA   SEA

LUSITANIA   Baleares   TYRRHENIAN   LUCANIA

Tartessus   Sardinia   SEA   LUCANIA

Sacred Pr   Onoba   IONIAN
Gades   SEA
Calpe Mt   Sicily   Syracusae
Tingis   Pillars of Hercules   SICILIAN
Abyle Mt   SEA

MAURETANIA   Lampedusa Is.   Melita Is.

NUMIDIA   LIBYAN

Faterii   Tibur   Hecatompylus   SEA
Roma
Aricia   Marsi   Tapacae   SYRTIS MINOR
Meninx Is.
Gabes R.
Cumae   Vesuvius Mt   Oea
Neapolis   Hyria   L. Tritonis   SYRTIS MAIOR
Pithecusae   Tarentum
Psylli
MESSAPIA   Nasamones

Petelia   Garama
Croton   Garamantes

Lipari Is.
Eryx   Locri   Miles
Mt   Agyrium
Segesta   Rhegium   0   500
Agrigentum   Enna   Aetna Mt
or Camicus   Scale of inset maps in miles
Pantellaria Is.   Syracusae   0   200

BLACK SEA

Salmydessus
Thynias Is.
Bathynias
Vistula R
Calpe
Mariandyni
SEA OF
MARMARA
Bebryces
Cyzicene
Dascylium
Prusa

Sinope
Enete

Amisus
Thermiscyra
Oenoë
Chalybes
Jasonium Pr.
Isle of Ares
Coniana
Tibareni
Mosynoeci
Trapezus

Gordium
Halys R.

Borysthenes R.
Tanais R.
Sarmatae

CASPIAN SEA

Beroë
Scythians
Leuce Is.
Istria
Tomi
CRIMEA
Taurians

Royal Scythians
Apsilaeans
Aea
Phasis R.

Ister R.
BLACK SEA
Phasis
COLCHIS
Haemus Mt
Acherusian Pr.
Lepte Pr.
Moschi
Gogarene

THRACIA
Bosphorus
CHALCEDON
PAPHLAGONIA
Thermodon R.
Araxes R.
Ararat Mt
ARMENIA
MEDIA

ILLYRIS
EPIRUS
Olympus Mt
Troy
DARDANIA
PHRYGIA
BITHYNIA
Halys R.
Scylax R.

GRECIA
Lesbos Is.
MYSIA
LYDIA
Euboea
Maeander R.
Celaenae
Lycus R.
Thymbrium
LYCAONIA
Comana
CAPPADOCIA

Tigris R.
ASSYRIA

Sicyon
Athens
Sparta
Peloponnesus
ICARIAN SEA
CARIA
PAMPHYLIA
LYCIA
CILICIA
Cydnus R.
Mallus
Amanus Mt
Casius Mt
Euphrates R.
Babylon

Crete
Telmissus
Rhodes
Cyprus
Paphos
Salamis
Amathus
Orontes R.
SYRIA

CYRENIC SEA
Byblus
Libanus Mt
Sidon
Tyre
PHOENICIA
Damascus
Atabyrium Mt

Cyrene
Alexandria
Pharos Is.
Canopus
Joppa
Ascalon
Gaza
Jerusalem

LIBYA
Naucratis
Pelusium
River of Egypt

Memphis
Heliopolis
Zeus Ammon
EGYPT
Nile R.
ARABIA

Chemmis
ARABIAN GULF
Thebes

MAP SHOWING SITES
MENTIONED IN THE TEXT

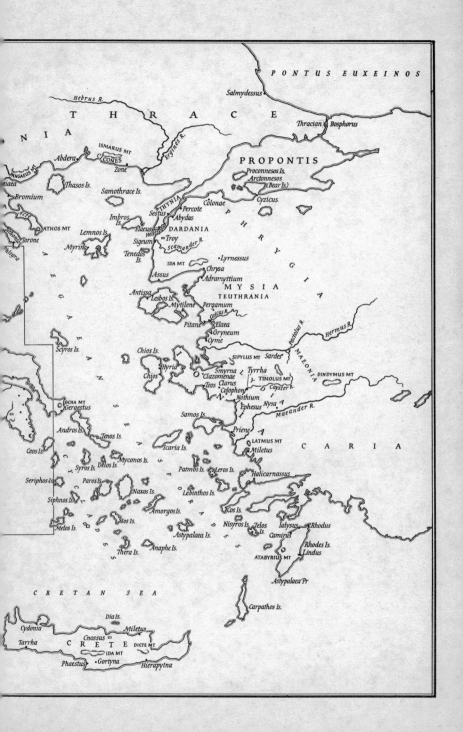

# INDEX

*Many of the meanings are doubtful. Names in italics refer to characters in non-Hellenic mythology. References are to paragraph numbers, not page numbers.*